Tarzan the Untamed

With the speed of the great apes, Tarzan rushed through the jungle toward his home and family. But he was already too late. The marauders had been there before him …

Tarzan the Terrible

Lieutenant Obergatz had fled in terror from the awful vengeance of Tarzan of the Apes. And with him, by force, he had taken Tarzan's beloved mate, Jane. Now the ape-man was following the faint spoor of their flight, into a region no man had ever penetrated …

Tarzan and the Golden Lion

Tarzan had been betrayed. Drugged and helpless, he was delivered into the hands of the dreadful priests of Opar, last bastion of ancient Atlantis. The High Priestess, La, had saved him once again but now she, in turn, was betrayed and threatened by her people. To save her, Tarzan fled with her into the legendary Valley of Diamonds …

Tarzan and the Ant Men

Tarzan finds himself in a strange country of stone-age savages and knee-high warriors who ride miniature African deer as though they were horses. But the Minunians are not so small that they cannot take the Ape Man captive, and put him to work in their underground quarries.

Tarzan, Lord of the Jungle

Cruel slave traders had invaded the jungle of Tarzan of the Apes. Now they were headed toward a fabled empire of riches which no outsider had ever seen, intent on looting. And toward the same legendary land was stumbling the lost James Blake, an American whom Tarzan had vowed to rescue …

Tarzan and the Lost Empire

Tarzan and a young German find a lost remnant of the Roman Empire hidden in the mountains of Africa …

Also by Edgar Rice Burroughs

Tarzan

1. Tarzan of the Apes (1912)
2. The Return of Tarzan (1913)
3. The Beasts of Tarzan (1914)
4. The Son of Tarzan (1914)
5. Tarzan and the Jewels of Opar (1916)
6. Jungle Tales of Tarzan (1916, 1917)
7. Tarzan the Untamed (1919, 1921)
8. Tarzan the Terrible (1921)
9. Tarzan and the Golden Lion (1922, 1923)
10. Tarzan and the Ant Men (1924)
11. Tarzan, Lord of the Jungle (1927, 1928)
12. Tarzan and the Lost Empire (1928)
13. Tarzan at the Earth's Core (1929)
14. Tarzan the Invincible (1930–31.)
15. Tarzan Triumphant (1931)
16. Tarzan and the City of Gold (1932)
17. Tarzan and the Lion Man (1933, 1934)
18. Tarzan and the Leopard Men (1935)
19. Tarzan's Quest (1935, 1936)
20. Tarzan the Magnificent (1936, 1937)
21. Tarzan and the Forbidden City (1938)
22. Tarzan and the Foreign Legion (1947)
23. Tarzan and the Madman (1964)
24. Tarzan and the Castaways (1965)
25. Tarzan and the Valley of Gold (1965) (authorized sequel by Fritz Leiber)

*Martian Tales**

1. A Princess of Mars (1917) (aka Under The Moons Of Mars, 1912)
2. The Gods of Mars (1918)
3. The Warlord of Mars (1919)
4. Thuvia, Maid of Mars (1920)
5. The Chessmen of Mars (1922)
6. The Master Mind of Mars (1927)
7. A Fighting Man of Mars (1930)
8. Swords of Mars (1934)
9. Synthetic Men of Mars (1938)
10. Llana of Gathol (1948)
11. John Carter of Mars (1941)

Pellucidar

1. At the Earth's Core (1914)
2. Pellucidar (1923)
3. Tanar of Pellucidar (1928)
4. Back to the Stone Age (1937)
5. Land of Terror (1944)
6. Savage Pellucidar (1963)

Venus

1. Pirates of Venus (1934)
2. Lost on Venus (1935)
3. Carson of Venus (1939)
4. Escape on Venus (1946)
5. The Wizard of Venus (1970)

The Land That Time Forgot

1. The Land That Time Forgot (1918)
2. The People That Time Forgot (1918)
3. Out of Time's Abyss (1918)

Other Science Fiction

The Moon Maid (1926) (aka The Moon Men)
Beyond the Farthest Star (1941)
The Lost Continent (1916)
The Monster Men (1929)
The Resurrection of Jimber-Jaw (1937)

The Mucker

1. The Mucker (1914)
2. The Return of the Mucker (1916)
3. The Oakdale Affair (1917)

Jungle Adventure Novels

The Man-Eater (1915)
The Cave Girl (1925)
The Eternal Lover (1925) (aka The Eternal Savage)
Jungle Girl (1932) (aka Land of the Hidden Men)
The Lad and the Lion (1938)

* Not available as SF Gateway eBooks

Tarzan the Untamed and Other Tales

SF GATEWAY OMNIBUS

Edgar Rice Burroughs

GOLLANCZ
LONDON

First published in Great Britain in 2014 by
Gollancz
An imprint of the Orion Publishing Group
Orion House, 5 Upper St Martin's Lane,
London WC2H 9EA

An Hachette UK Company

A CIP catalogue record for this book
is available from the British Library

ISBN 978 0 575 12917 7

1 3 5 7 9 10 8 6 4 2

Typeset by Jouve (UK), Milton Keynes

Printed and bound by CPI Group (UK) Ltd, Croydon, CR0 4YY

The Orion Publishing Group's policy is to use papers that are natural, renewable and recyclable products and made from wood grown in sustainable forests. The logging and manufacturing processes are expected to conform to the environmental regulations of the country of origin.

www.orionbooks.co.uk
www.gollancz.co.uk

CONTENTS

ENTER THE SF GATEWAY . . .

Towards the end of 2011, in conjunction with the celebration of fifty years of coherent, continuous science fiction and fantasy publishing, Gollancz launched the SF Gateway.

Over a decade after launching the landmark SF Masterworks series, we realised that the realities of commercial publishing are such that even the Masterworks could only ever scratch the surface of an author's career. Vast troves of classic SF and fantasy were almost certainly destined never again to see print. Until very recently, this meant that anyone interested in reading any of those books would have been confined to scouring second-hand bookshops. The advent of digital publishing changed that paradigm for ever.

Embracing the future even as we honour the past, Gollancz launched the SF Gateway with a view to utilising the technology that now exists to make available, for the first time, the entire backlists of an incredibly wide range of classic and modern SF and fantasy authors. Our plan, at its simplest, was – and still is! – to use this technology to build on the success of the SF and Fantasy Masterworks series and to go even further.

The SF Gateway was designed to be the new home of classic science fiction and fantasy – the most comprehensive electronic library of classic SFF titles ever assembled. The programme has been extremely well received and we've been very happy with the results. So happy, in fact, that we've decided to complete the circle and return a selection of our titles to print, in these omnibus editions.

We hope you enjoy this selection. And we hope that you'll want to explore more of the classic SF and fantasy we have available. These are wonderful books you're holding in your hand, but you'll find much, much more … through the SF Gateway.

www.sfgateway.com

INTRODUCTION

from The Encyclopedia of Science Fiction

Edgar Rice Burroughs (1875–1950) was a US writer whose early life was marked by numerous false starts and failures – at the time he began to write, at the age of 36, he was a pencil-sharpener salesman – but it would seem that the impulse to create the psychically charged Science-Fantasy dream-worlds that became his trademark territory was deep-set and powerful. Once he began to write, with a great rush of built-up energy, within two years he had initiated three of his four most important series. He never stopped.

Certainly the first of his published works has ever since its first appearance served as a successful escape from mid-life burdens and frustrations. *A Princess of Mars* (1917), which was originally published February-July 1912 *All-Story* as 'Under the Moons of Mars' as by Norman Bean, opens the long Barsoom sequence of novels set on Mars (Barsoom). (Many of Burroughs's novels appeared first in magazines; we are giving only first book publications here). The long array of Barsoom tales established that planet as a venue for dream-like and interminable Planetary Romance sagas in which sf and fantasy protocols mixed indiscriminately as an enabling pretext, a place where white women (in all but name) could bare their breasts, and white men were preternaturally strong, due to the manly intensity of their native Earth gravity. *The Gods of Mars* (1918) and *The Warlord of Mars* (1919) further recount the exploits of John Carter as he battles with various green, yellow and black breeds without the law, and wins the hand of the red-skinned (and oviparous) princess Dejah Thoris. Starring different central characters, the series continued in *Thuvia, Maid of Mars* (1920), *The Chessmen of Mars* (1922), *The Master Mind of Mars* (1928), *A Fighting Man of Mars* (1931), *Swords of Mars* (1936), *Synthetic Men of Mars* (1940), *Llana of Gathol* (1948) and *John Carter of Mars* (1964). 'John Carter and the Giant of Mars' (January 1941 *Amazing*), from the last volume, was originally written as a juvenile tale by Burroughs's son, John Coleman Burroughs. The standard of storytelling and invention is high in the Barsoom books, *Chessmen* and *Swords* being particularly fine; but it has always been difficult for some critics to accept the Planetary Romance as being, in any cognitive sense, good sf. Although Carter's adventures take place on another planet, he incontrovertibly travels there by magical means, and Barsoom itself is inconsistent and scientifically implausible. It is clear, however, that Burroughs's immense popularity has nothing to do with conventional sf virtues, for it depends on storylines and venues as malleable as dreams, exotic and dangerous and unending.

The long Tarzan saga came next (see below), occupying much of his time before the creation of his third major series. The Pellucidar novels based on the Hollow-Earth theory of John Cleves Symmes, began with *At the Earth's Core* (1922) and continued in *Pellucidar* (1923), *Tanar of Pellucidar* (1930), *Tarzan at the Earth's Core* (1930) – a notable 'overlap' volume – *Back to the Stone Age* (1937), *Land of Terror* (1944) and *Savage Pellucidar* (1963). Pellucidar is perhaps the best of Burroughs's locales – a world without time where Dinosaurs and beast-men roam circularly forever – and is a perfect setting for bloodthirsty romantic adventure. The first of the series was filmed disappointingly as At the Earth's Core (*1976*).

His fourth series, the Venus sequence – created much later in Burroughs's career – concerns the exploits of spaceman Carson Napier on Venus, and consists of *Pirates of Venus* (1934), *Lost on Venus* (1935), *Carson of Venus* (1939) and *Escape on Venus* (1946). These books are not as stirring and vivid as the Barsoom series. A posthumous story, 'The Wizard of Venus', was published in *Tales of Three Planets* (1964) and subsequently as the title story of a separate paperback, *The Wizard of Venus* (1970). Two of the stories from *Tales of Three Planets*, 'Beyond the Farthest Star' (January 1942 *Blue Book*) and the posthumous 'Tangor Returns' (in *Tales of Three Planets* 1964), form the opening of a fifth series which Burroughs abandoned. They are of particular sf interest because they are his only tales with an interstellar setting. The two stories were subsequently republished as a paperback entitled *Beyond the Farthest Star* (1965).

Of Burroughs's non-series tales, perhaps the finest is *The Land that Time Forgot* (1924; revised in three volumes under the original magazine titles: *The Land that Time Forgot* 1962, *The People that Time Forgot* 1962 and *Out of Time's Abyss* 1962), set in the lost world of Caspak near the South Pole, and cunningly presenting in literal form – for animals here metamorphose through evolutionary stages – the dictum that ontogeny recapitulates phylogeny. The book was loosely adapted into two films, *The Land That Time Forgot* (1975) and *The People That Time Forgot* (1977). Also of interest is *The Moon Maid* 1926), which describes a civilization in the hollow interior of the Moon and a future Invasion of the Earth.

Among Burroughs's other books, those which can be claimed as sf include: *The Eternal Lover* (1925), a prehistoric adventure involving Time Travel featuring a character, Barney Custer, who reappears in the Ruritanian *The Mad King* (1926); *The Monster Men* (1929), a reworking of the Frankenstein theme, which should not be confused with *The Man without a Soul* (1922), which is not fantasy or sf; *The Cave Girl* (1925), another prehistoric romance; *Jungle Girl* (1932), about a lost civilization in Cambodia; and *Beyond Thirty*

(1956), a story set in the twenty-second century after the collapse of European civilization.

It cannot be claimed that Burroughs's works aim at literary polish, or that their merits are intellectual. His lovers and his critics agree on this. Nevertheless, because their lack of realistic referents frees them from time, because their efficient narrative style helps to compensate for their prudery and racism, and because Burroughs had a genius for highly-energized literalizations of dream-worlds, they have endured. Tarzan is a figure with the iconic density of Sherlock Holmes or Dracula. His 'rediscovery' during the 1960s was an astonishing publishing phenomenon, with the majority of his books being reprinted regularly. He had never been forgotten, however. Burroughs has probably had more imitators than any other sf writer, ranging from Otis Adelbert Kline in the 1930s to Kenneth Bulmer (writing as Alan Burt Akers) in the 1970s, with homages from much later writers like Terry Bisson in *Voyage to the Red Planet* (1990) and Hitoshi Yoshioka in *Nangun Kihei Taii John Carter* ['Southern Cavalry Captain John Carter'] (2005). Serious sf writers who owe a debt to Burroughs include Leigh Brackett, Ray Bradbury, Michael Moorcock and, above all, Philip José Farmer, whose Lord Grandrith and Ancient Opar novels are among the most enjoyable of latter-day Burroughs-inflected romances. Burroughs was posthumously inducted into the Science Fiction Hall of Fame in 2003. It was clear he belonged there.

The massive Tarzan saga, which begins with *Tarzan of the Apes and Other Tales* (Gollancz centenary omnibus, 2012), is just as much sf (or non-sf) as the Barsoom series. Though clearly influenced by H Rider Haggard, Burroughs did not attempt to imitate one of that writer's prime virtues: Haggard's effort to embed his tales in a vision of history, even though (to modern eyes) his work seems almost dementedly dated, certainly in its imperialist assumptions about race. Allan Quatermain's Africa, even though it is romantically exaggerated, can distress modern readers; but Tarzan's Africa is a Never Never Land, and must accepted as being no more governed by the reality principle than Barsoom. *Tarzan of the Apes* (1914), the story of an English aristocrat's son raised in the jungle by 'great apes' (of a non-existent species) as a kind of feral child or Noble Savage, was immensely popular from the beginning, and Burroughs continued producing sequels to the end of his career. In most of them Tarzan has unashamedly fantastic adventures, some of which – discovering lost cities and live Dinosaurs, being reduced to 18 in (46 cm) in height, visiting the Earth's core – marvellously evoke the conventions of Pulp sf. Burroughs did not perhaps entirely grasp the iconic power of his aristocrat/barbarian lord in *Tarzan of the Apes* itself – which continues with *The Return of Tarzan* (1915), *The Beasts of Tarzan* (1916), *The Son of Tarzan* (1917) and *Tarzan and the Jewels of Opar* (1918), all relatively uninspired. *Jungle*

Tales of Tarzan (1919) gains creative fire through its clever reminders of Rudyard Kipling's two *Jungle Books* (1894, 1895); and in 'Tarzan's First Love' (September 1916 *Blue Book*) Burroughs invokes Apes-as-Human material otherwhere left tacit: which is to say Tarzan falls in love with an ape.

But perhaps the very best Tarzan books, the six tales assembled in this omnibus, came next: *Tarzan the Untamed* (1920), *Tarzan the Terrible* (1921), *Tarzan and the Golden Lion* (1923), *Tarzan and the Ant Men* (1924), *Tarzan, Lord of the Jungle* (1928) and *Tarzan and the Lost Empire* (1929). There is a smell of Eden in these volumes, a rough-hewed nostalgia for a world all the more lost after the catastrophe of World War One. The action is continuous; Tarzan himself grows in stature and savvy; every new story is a new discovery.

For a more detailed version of the above, see Edgar Rice Burroughs' author entry in *The Encyclopedia of Science Fiction*: http://sf-encyclopedia.com/entry/burroughs_edgar_rice

Some terms above are capitalised when they would not normally be so rendered; this indicates that the terms represent discrete entries in *The Encyclopedia of Science Fiction*.

TARZAN THE UNTAMED

1

Murder and Pillage

Hauptmann Fritz Schneider trudged wearily through the somber aisles of the dark forest. Sweat rolled down his bullet head and stood upon his heavy jowls and bull neck. His lieutenant marched beside him while Underlieutenant von Goss brought up the rear, following with a handful of askaris, the tired and all but exhausted porters whom the black soldiers, following the example of their white officer, encouraged with the sharp points of bayonets and the metal-shod butts of rifles.

There were no porters within reach of Hauptmann Schneider so he vented his Prussian spleen upon the askaris nearest at hand, yet with greater circumspection since these men bore loaded rifles – and the three white men were alone with them in the heart of Africa.

Ahead of the hauptmann marched half his company, behind him the other half – thus were the dangers of the savage jungle minimized for the German captain. At the forefront of the column staggered two naked savages fastened to each other by a neck chain. These were the native guides impressed into the service of Kultur and upon their poor, bruised bodies Kultur's brand was revealed in diverse cruel wounds and bruises.

Thus even in darkest Africa was the light of German civilization commencing to reflect itself upon the undeserving natives just as at the same period, the fall of 1914, it was shedding its glorious effulgence upon benighted Belgium.

It is true that the guides had led the party astray; but this is the way of most African guides. Nor did it matter that ignorance rather than evil intent had been the cause of their failure. It was enough for Hauptmann Fritz Schneider to know that he was lost in the African wilderness and that he had at hand human beings less powerful than he who could be made to suffer by torture. That he did not kill them outright was partially due to a faint hope that they might eventually prove the means of extricating him from his difficulties and partially that so long as they lived they might still be made to suffer.

The poor creatures, hoping that chance might lead them at last upon the right trail, insisted that they knew the way and so led on through a dismal forest along a winding game trail trodden deep by the feet of countless generations of the savage denizens of the jungle.

Here Tantor, the elephant, took his long way from dust wallow to water. Here Buto, the rhinoceros, blundered blindly in his solitary majesty, while by night the great cats paced silently upon their padded feet beneath the dense canopy of overreaching trees toward the broad plain beyond, where they found their best hunting.

It was at the edge of this plain which came suddenly and unexpectedly before the eyes of the guides that their sad hearts beat with renewed hope. Here the hauptmann drew a deep sigh of relief, for after days of hopeless wandering through almost impenetrable jungle the broad vista of waving grasses dotted here and there with open parklike woods and in the far distance the winding line of green shrubbery that denoted a river appeared to the European a veritable heaven.

The Hun smiled in his relief, passed a cheery word with his lieutenant, and then scanned the broad plain with his field glasses. Back and forth they swept across the rolling land until at last they came to rest upon a point near the center of the landscape and close to the green-fringed contours of the river.

'We are in luck,' said Schneider to his companions. 'Do you see it?'

The lieutenant, who was also gazing through his own glasses, finally brought them to rest upon the same spot that had held the attention of his superior.

'Yes,' he said, 'an English farm. It must be Greystoke's, for there is none other in this part of British East Africa. God is with us, Herr Captain.'

'We have come upon the English schweinhund long before he can have learned that his country is at war with ours,' replied Schneider. 'Let him be the first to feel the iron hand of Germany.'

'Let us hope that he is at home,' said the lieutenant, 'that we may take him with us when we report to Kraut at Nairobi. It will go well indeed with Herr Hauptmann Fritz Schneider if he brings in the famous Tarzan of the Apes as a prisoner of war.'

Schneider smiled and puffed out his chest. 'You are right, my friend,' he said, 'it will go well with both of us; but I shall have to travel far to catch General Kraut before he reaches Mombasa. These English pigs with their contemptible army will make good time to the Indian Ocean.'

It was in a better frame of mind that the small force set out across the open country toward the trim and well-kept farm buildings of John Clayton, Lord Greystoke; but disappointment was to be their lot since neither Tarzan of the Apes nor his son was at home.

Lady Jane, ignorant of the fact that a state of war existed between Great Britain and Germany, welcomed the officers most hospitably and gave orders through her trusted Waziri to prepare a feast for the black soldiers of the enemy.

Far to the east, Tarzan of the Apes was traveling rapidly from Nairobi toward the farm. At Nairobi he had received news of the World War that had already started, and, anticipating an immediate invasion of British East Africa by the

Germans, was hurrying homeward to fetch his wife to a place of greater security. With him were a score of his ebon warriors, but far too slow for the ape-man was the progress of these trained and hardened woodsmen.

When necessity demanded, Tarzan of the Apes sloughed the thin veneer of his civilization and with it the hampering apparel that was its badge. In a moment the polished English gentleman reverted to the naked ape-man.

His mate was in danger. For the time, that single thought dominated. He did not think of her as Lady Jane Greystoke, but rather as the she he had won by the might of his steel thews, and that he must hold and protect by virtue of the same offensive armament.

It was no member of the House of Lords who swung swiftly and grimly through the tangled forest or trod with untiring muscles the wide stretches of open plain – it was a great he-ape filled with a single purpose that excluded all thoughts of fatigue or danger.

Little Manu, the monkey, scolding and chattering in the upper terraces of the forest, saw him pass. Long had it been since he had thus beheld the great Tarmangani naked and alone hurtling through the jungle. Bearded and gray was Manu, the monkey, and to his dim old eyes came the fire of recollection of those days when Tarzan of the Apes had ruled supreme, Lord of the Jungle, over all the myriad life that trod the matted vegetation between the boles of the great trees, or flew or swung or climbed in the leafy fastness upward to the very apex of the loftiest terraces.

And Numa, the lion, lying up for the day close beside last night's successful kill, blinked his yellow-green eyes and twitched his tawny tail as he caught the scent spoor of his ancient enemy.

Nor was Tarzan senseless to the presence of Numa or Manu or any of the many jungle beasts he passed in his rapid flight toward the west. No particle had his shallow probing of English society dulled his marvelous sense faculties. His nose had picked out the presence of Numa, the lion, even before the majestic king of beasts was aware of his passing.

He had heard noisy little Manu, and even the soft rustling of the parting shrubbery where Sheeta passed before either of these alert animals sensed his presence.

But however keen the senses of the ape-man, however swift his progress through the wild country of his adoption, however mighty the muscles that bore him, he was still mortal. Time and space placed their inexorable limits upon him; nor was there another who realized this truth more keenly than Tarzan. He chafed and fretted that he could not travel with the swiftness of thought and that the long tedious miles stretching far ahead of him must require hours and hours of tireless effort upon his part before he would swing at last from the final bough of the fringing forest into the open plain and in sight of his goal.

Days it took, even though he lay up at night for but a few hours and left to chance the finding of meat directly on his trail. If Wappi, the antelope, or Horta, the boar, chanced in his way when he was hungry, he ate, pausing but long enough to make the kill and cut himself a steak.

Then at last the long journey drew to its close and he was passing through the last stretch of heavy forest that bounded his estate upon the east, and then this was traversed and he stood upon the plain's edge looking out across his broad lands toward his home.

At the first glance his eyes narrowed and his muscles tensed. Even at that distance he could see that something was amiss. A thin spiral of smoke arose at the right of the bungalow where the barns had stood, but there were no barns there now, and from the bungalow chimney from which smoke should have arisen, there arose nothing.

Once again Tarzan of the Apes was speeding onward, this time even more swiftly than before, for he was goaded now by a nameless fear, more product of intuition than of reason. Even as the beasts, Tarzan of the Apes seemed to possess a sixth sense. Long before he reached the bungalow, he had almost pictured the scene that finally broke upon his view.

Silent and deserted was the vine-covered cottage. Smoldering embers marked the site of his great barns. Gone were the thatched huts of his sturdy retainers, empty the fields, the pastures, and corrals. Here and there vultures rose and circled above the carcasses of men and beasts.

It was with a feeling as nearly akin to terror as he ever had experienced that the ape-man finally forced himself to enter his home. The first sight that met his eyes set the red haze of hate and bloodlust across his vision, for there, crucified against the wall of the living room, was Wasimbu, giant son of the faithful Muviro and for over a year the personal bodyguard of Lady Jane.

The overturned and shattered furniture of the room, the brown pools of dried blood upon the floor, and prints of bloody hands on walls and woodwork evidenced something of the frightfulness of the battle that had been waged within the narrow confines of the apartment. Across the baby grand piano lay the corpse of another black warrior, while before the door of Lady Jane's boudoir were the dead bodies of three more of the faithful Greystoke servants.

The door of this room was closed. With drooping shoulders and dull eyes Tarzan stood gazing dumbly at the insensate panel which hid from him what horrid secret he dared not even guess.

Slowly, with leaden feet, he moved toward the door. Gropingly his hand reached for the knob. Thus he stood for another long minute, and then with a sudden gesture he straightened his giant frame, threw back his mighty shoulders and, with fearless head held high, swung back the door and stepped across the threshold into the room which held for him the dearest memories and associations of his life. No change of expression crossed his grim and stern-set features as he strode across the room and stood beside the little couch and the inanimate form which lay face downward upon it; the still, silent thing that had pulsed with life and youth and love.

No tear dimmed the eye of the ape-man; but the God who made him alone could know the thoughts that passed through that still half-savage brain. For a long time he stood there just looking down upon the dead body, charred beyond recognition, and then he stooped and lifted it in his arms. As he turned the body over and saw how horribly death had been meted he plumbed, in that instant, the uttermost depths of grief and horror and hatred.

Nor did he require the evidence of the broken German rifle in the outer room, or the torn and bloodstained service cap upon the floor, to tell him who had been the perpetrators of this horrid and useless crime.

For a moment he had hoped against hope that the blackened corpse was not that of his mate, but when his eyes discovered and recognized the rings upon her fingers the last faint ray of hope forsook him.

In silence, in love, and in reverence he buried, in the little rose garden that had been Jane Clayton's pride and love, the poor, charred form and beside it the great black warriors who had given their lives so futilely in their mistress's protection.

At one side of the house Tarzan found other newly made graves and in these he sought final evidence of the identity of the real perpetrators of the atrocities that had been committed there in his absence.

Here he disinterred the bodies of a dozen German askaris and found upon their uniforms the insignia of the company and regiment to which they had belonged. This was enough for the ape-man. White officers had commanded these men, nor would it be a difficult task to discover who they were.

Returning to the rose garden, he stood among the Hun-trampled blooms and bushes above the grave of his dead – with bowed head he stood there in a last mute farewell. As the sun sank slowly behind the towering forests of the west, he turned slowly away upon the still-distinct trail of Hauptmann Fritz Schneider and his bloodstained company.

His was the suffering of the dumb brute – mute; but though voiceless no less poignant. At first his vast sorrow numbed his other faculties of thought – his brain was overwhelmed by the calamity to such an extent that it reacted to but a single objective suggestion: She is dead! She is dead! She is dead! Again and again this phrase beat monotonously upon his brain – a dull, throbbing pain, yet mechanically his feet followed the trail of her slayer while, subconsciously, his every sense was upon the alert for the ever-present perils of the jungle.

Gradually the labor of his great grief brought forth another emotion so real, so tangible, that it seemed a companion walking at his side. It was Hate – and it brought to him a measure of solace and of comfort, for it was a sublime hate that ennobled him as it has ennobled countless thousands since – hatred for Germany and Germans. It centered about the slayer of his mate, of course; but it included everything German, animate or inanimate. As the thought took firm hold upon him he paused and, raising his face to Goro, the moon, cursed with upraised hand the authors of the hideous crime that had been perpetrated in that once peaceful bungalow behind him; and he cursed their progenitors, their progeny, and all their kind the while he took silent oath to war upon them relentlessly until death overtook him.

There followed almost immediately a feeling of content, for, where before his future at best seemed but a void, now it was filled with possibilities the contemplation of which brought him, if not happiness, at least a surcease of absolute grief, for before him lay a great work that would occupy his time.

Stripped not only of all the outward symbols of civilization, Tarzan had also reverted morally and mentally to the status of the savage beast he had been reared. Never had his civilization been more than a veneer put on for the sake of her he loved because he thought it made her happier to see him thus. In reality he had always held the outward evidences of so-called culture in deep contempt. Civilization meant to Tarzan of the Apes a curtailment of freedom in all its aspects – freedom of action, freedom of thought, freedom of love, freedom of hate. Clothes he abhorred – uncomfortable, hideous, confining things that reminded him somehow of bonds securing him to the life he had seen the poor creatures of London and Paris living. Clothes were the emblems of that hypocrisy for which civilization stood – a pretense that the wearers were ashamed of what the clothes covered, of the human form made in the semblance of God. Tarzan knew how silly and pathetic the lower orders of animals appeared in the clothing of civilization, for he had seen several poor creatures thus appareled in various traveling shows in Europe, and he knew, too, how silly and pathetic man appears in them, since the only men he had seen in the first twenty years of his life had been, like himself, naked savages. The ape-man had a keen admiration for a well-muscled, well-proportioned body, whether lion, or antelope, or man, and it had ever been beyond him to understand how clothes could be considered more beautiful than a clear, firm, healthy skin, or coat and trousers more graceful than the gentle curves of rounded muscles playing beneath a flexible hide.

In civilization Tarzan had found greed and selfishness and cruelty far beyond that which he had known in his familiar, savage jungle, and though civilization had given him his mate and several friends whom he loved and admired, he never had come to accept it as you and I who have known little or nothing else; so it was with a sense of relief that he now definitely abandoned it and all that it stood for, and went forth into the jungle once again stripped to his loincloth and weapons.

The hunting knife of his father hung at his left hip, his bow and his quiver of arrows were slung across his shoulders, while around his chest over one shoulder and beneath the opposite arm was coiled the long grass rope without which Tarzan would have felt quite as naked as would you should you be suddenly thrust upon a busy highway clad only in a union suit. A heavy war spear which he sometimes carried in one hand and again slung by a thong about his neck so that it hung down his back completed his armament and his apparel. The diamond-studded locket with the pictures of his mother and father that he had worn always until he had given it as a token of his highest devotion to Jane Clayton before their marriage was missing. She always had worn it since; but it had not been upon her body when he found her slain in her boudoir, so that now his quest for vengeance included also a quest for the stolen trinket.

Toward midnight Tarzan commenced to feel the physical strain of his long hours of travel and to realize that even muscles such as his had their limitations. His pursuit of the murderers had not been characterized by excessive speed; but rather more in keeping with his mental attitude, which was marked by a dogged determination to require from the Germans more than an eye for an eye and more than a tooth for a tooth, the element of time entering but slightly into his calculations.

Inwardly as well as outwardly Tarzan had reverted to beast and in the lives of beasts, time, as a measurable aspect of duration, has no meaning. The beast is actively interested only in *now*, and as it is always *now* and always shall be, there is an eternity of time for the accomplishment of objects. The ape-man, naturally, had a slightly more comprehensive realization of the limitations of time; but, like the beasts, he moved with majestic deliberation when no emergency prompted him to swift action.

Having dedicated his life to vengeance, vengeance became his natural state and, therefore, no emergency, so he took his time in pursuit. That he had not rested earlier was due to the fact that he had felt no fatigue, his mind being occupied by thoughts of sorrow and revenge; but now he realized that he was tired, and so he sought a jungle giant that had harbored him upon more than a single other jungle night.

Dark clouds moving swiftly across the heavens now and again eclipsed the bright face of Goro, the moon, and forewarned the ape-man of impending storm. In the depth of the jungle the cloud shadows produced a thick blackness that might almost be felt – a blackness that to you and me might have proven terrifying with its accompaniment of rustling leaves and cracking twigs, and its even more suggestive intervals of utter silence in which the crudest of imaginations might have conjured crouching beasts of prey tensed for the fatal charge; but through it Tarzan passed unconcerned, yet always alert. Now he swung lightly to the lower terraces of the overarching trees when some subtle sense warned him that Numa lay upon a kill directly in his path, or again he sprang lightly to one side as Buto, the rhinoceros, lumbered toward him along the narrow, deep-worn trail, for the ape-man, ready to fight upon necessity's slightest pretext, avoided unnecessary quarrels.

When he swung himself at last into the tree he sought, the moon was obscured by a heavy cloud, and the treetops were waving wildly in a steadily increasing wind whose soughing drowned the lesser noises of the jungle. Upward went Tarzan toward a sturdy crotch across which he long since had laid and secured a little platform of branches. It was very dark now, darker even than it had been before, for almost the entire sky was overcast by thick, black clouds.

Presently the man-beast paused, his sensitive nostrils dilating as he sniffed the air about him. Then, with the swiftness and agility of a cat, he leaped far outward upon a swaying branch, sprang upward through the darkness, caught another, swung himself upon it and then to one still higher. What could have so suddenly transformed his matter-of-fact ascent of the giant bole to the swift and wary action of his detour among the branches? You or I could have seen nothing – not even the little platform that an instant before had been just above him and which now was immediately below – but as he swung above it we should have heard an ominous growl; and then as the moon was momentarily uncovered, we should have seen both the platform, dimly, and a dark mass that lay stretched upon it – a dark mass that presently, as our eyes became accustomed to the lesser darkness, would take the form of Sheeta, the panther.

In answer to the cat's growl, a low and equally ferocious growl rumbled upward from the ape-man's deep chest – a growl of warning that told the panther he was trespassing upon the other's lair, but Sheeta was in no mood to be dispossessed. With upturned, snarling face he glared at the brown-skinned Tarmangani above him. Very slowly the ape-man moved inward along the branch until he was directly above the panther. In the man's hand was the hunting knife of his long-dead father – the weapon that had first given him his real ascendency over the beasts of the jungle; but he hoped not to be forced to use it, knowing as he did that more jungle battles were settled by hideous growling than by actual combat, the law of bluff holding quite as good in the jungle as elsewhere – only in matters of love and food did the great beasts ordinarily close with fangs and talons.

Tarzan braced himself against the bole of the tree and leaned closer toward Sheeta.

'Stealer of balus!' he cried. The panther rose to a sitting position, his bared fangs but a few feet from the ape-man's taunting face. Tarzan growled hideously and struck at the cat's face with his knife. 'I am Tarzan of the Apes,' he roared. 'This is Tarzan's lair. Go, or I will kill you.' Though he spoke in the language of the great apes of the jungle, it is doubtful that Sheeta understood the words, though he knew well enough that the hairless ape wished to frighten him from his well-chosen station past which edible creatures might be expected to wander sometime during the watches of the night.

Like lightning the cat reared and struck a vicious blow at his tormentor with great, bared talons that might well have torn away the ape-man's face had the blow landed; but it did not land – Tarzan was even quicker than Sheeta. As the panther came to all fours again upon the little platform, Tarzan unslung his heavy spear and prodded at the snarling face, and as Sheeta warded off the blows, the two continued their horrid duet of bloodcurdling roars and growls.

Goaded to frenzy the cat presently determined to come up after this disturber of his peace; but when he essayed to leap to the branch that held Tarzan he found the sharp spear point always in his face, and each time as he dropped back he was prodded viciously in some tender part; but at length, rage having conquered his better judgment, he leaped up the rough bole to the very branch upon which Tarzan stood. Now the two faced each other upon even footing and Sheeta saw a quick revenge and a supper all in one. The hairless ape-thing with the tiny fangs and the puny talons would be helpless before him.

The heavy limb bent beneath the weight of the two beasts as Sheeta crept cautiously out upon it and Tarzan backed slowly away, growling. The wind had risen to the proportions of a gale so that even the greatest giants of the forest swayed, groaning, to its force and the branch upon which the two faced each other rose and fell like the deck of a storm-tossed ship. Goro was now entirely obscured, but vivid flashes of lightning lit up the jungle at brief intervals, revealing the grim tableau of primitive passion upon the swaying limb.

Tarzan backed away, drawing Sheeta farther from the stem of the tree and out upon the tapering branch, where his footing became ever more precarious. The cat, infuriated by the pain of spear wounds, was overstepping the bounds of caution. Already he had reached a point where he could do little more than maintain a secure footing, and it was this moment that Tarzan chose to charge. With a roar that mingled with the booming thunder from above he leaped toward the panther, who could only claw futilely with one huge paw while he clung to the branch with the other, but the ape-man did not come within that parabola of destruction. Instead he leaped above menacing claws and snapping fangs, turning in midair and alighting upon Sheeta's back, and at the instant of impact his knife struck deep into the tawny side. Then Sheeta, impelled by pain and hate and rage and the first law of Nature, went mad. Screaming and clawing he attempted to turn upon the ape-thing clinging to his back. For an instant he toppled upon the now wildly gyrating limb, clutched frantically to save himself, and then plunged downward into the darkness with Tarzan still clinging to him. Crashing through splintering branches the two fell. Not for an instant did the ape-man consider relinquishing his death-hold upon his adversary. He had entered the lists in mortal combat and true to the primitive instincts of the wild – the unwritten law of the jungle – one or both must die before the battle ended.

Sheeta, catlike, alighted upon four outsprawled feet, the weight of the ape-man crushing him to the earth, the long knife again imbedded in his side. Once the panther struggled to rise; but only to sink to earth again. Tarzan felt the giant muscles relax beneath him. Sheeta was dead. Rising, the ape-man placed a foot upon the body of his vanquished foe, raised his face toward the thundering heavens, and as the lightning flashed and the torrential rain broke upon him, screamed forth the wild victory cry of the bull ape.

Having accomplished his aim and driven the enemy from his lair, Tarzan gathered an armful of large fronds and climbed to his dripping couch. Laying a few of the fronds upon the poles he lay down and covered himself against the rain with the others, and despite the wailing of the wind and the crashing of the thunder, immediately fell asleep.

2

The Lion's Cave

The rain lasted for twenty-four hours and much of the time it fell in torrents so that when it ceased, the trail he had been following was entirely obliterated. Cold and uncomfortable – it was a savage Tarzan who threaded the mazes of the soggy jungle. Manu, the monkey, shivering and chattering in the dank trees, scolded and fled at his approach. Even the panthers and the lions let the growling Tarmangani pass unmolested.

When the sun shone again upon the second day and a wide, open plain let the full heat of Kudu flood the chilled, brown body, Tarzan's spirits rose; but it was still a sullen, surly brute that moved steadily onward into the south where he hoped again to pick up the trail of the Germans. He was now in German East Africa and it was his intention to skirt the mountains west of Kilimanjaro, whose rugged peaks he was quite willing to give a wide berth, and then swing eastward along the south side of the range to the railway that led to Tanga, for his experience among men suggested that it was toward this railroad that German troops would be likely to converge.

Two days later, from the southern slopes of Kilimanjaro, he heard the boom of cannon far away to the east. The afternoon had been dull and cloudy and now as he was passing through a narrow gorge a few great drops of rain began to splatter upon his naked shoulders. Tarzan shook his head and growled his disapproval; then he cast his eyes about for shelter, for he had had quite enough of the cold and drenching. He wanted to hasten on in the direction of the booming noise, for he knew that there would be Germans fighting against the English. For an instant his bosom swelled with pride at the thought that he was English and then he shook his head again viciously. 'No!' he muttered, 'Tarzan of the Apes is not English, for the English are men and Tarzan is Tarmangani'; but he could not hide even from his sorrow or from his sullen hatred of mankind in general that his heart warmed at the thought it was Englishmen who fought the Germans. His regret was that the English were human and not *great white apes* as he again considered himself.

'Tomorrow,' he thought, 'I will travel that way and find the Germans,' and then he set himself to the immediate task of discovering some shelter from the storm. Presently he espied the low and narrow entrance to what appeared to be a cave at the base of the cliffs which formed the northern side of the gorge. With drawn knife he approached the spot warily, for he knew that if it were a cave it was doubtless the lair of some other beast. Before the entrance lay many large fragments of rock of different sizes, similar to others scattered along the entire base of the cliff, and it was in Tarzan's mind that if he found the cave unoccupied he would barricade the door and insure himself a quiet and peaceful night's repose within the sheltered interior. Let the storm rage without – Tarzan would remain within until it ceased, comfortable and dry. A tiny rivulet of cold water trickled outward from the opening.

Close to the cave Tarzan kneeled and sniffed the ground. A low growl escaped him and his upper lip curved to expose his fighting fangs. 'Numa!' he muttered; but he did not stop. Numa might not be at home – he would investigate. The entrance was so low that the ape-man was compelled to drop to all fours before he could poke his head within the aperture; but first he looked, listened, and sniffed in each direction at his rear – he would not be taken by surprise from that quarter.

His first glance within the cave revealed a narrow tunnel with daylight at its farther end. The interior of the tunnel was not so dark but that the ape-man could readily see that it was untenanted at present. Advancing cautiously he crawled toward the opposite end imbued with a full realization of what it would mean if Numa should suddenly enter the tunnel in front of him; but

Numa did not appear and the ape-man emerged at length into the open and stood erect, finding himself in a rocky cleft whose precipitous walls rose almost sheer on every hand, the tunnel from the gorge passing through the cliff and forming a passageway from the outer world into a large pocket or gulch entirely enclosed by steep walls of rock. Except for the small passageway from the gorge, there was no other entrance to the gulch which was some hundred feet in length and about fifty in width and appeared to have been worn from the rocky cliff by the falling of water during long ages. A tiny stream from Kilimanjaro's eternal snowcap still trickled over the edge of the rocky wall at the upper end of the gulch, forming a little pool at the bottom of the cliff from which a small rivulet wound downward to the tunnel through which it passed to the gorge beyond. A single great tree flourished near the center of the gulch, while tufts of wiry grass were scattered here and there among the rocks of the gravelly floor.

The bones of many large animals lay about and among them were several human skulls. Tarzan raised his eyebrows. 'A man-eater,' he murmured, 'and from appearances he has held sway here for a long time. Tonight Tarzan will take the lair of the man-eater and Numa may roar and grumble upon the outside.'

The ape-man had advanced well into the gulch as he investigated his surroundings and now as he stood near the tree, satisfied that the tunnel would prove a dry and quiet retreat for the night, he turned to retrace his way to the outer end of the entrance that he might block it with boulders against Numa's return; but even with the thought there came something to his sensitive ears that froze him into statuesque immobility with eyes glued upon the tunnel's mouth. A moment later the head of a huge lion framed in a great black mane appeared in the opening. The yellow-green eyes glared, round and unblinking, straight at the trespassing Tarmangani, a low growl rumbled from the deep chest, and lips curled back to expose the mighty fangs.

'Brother of Dango!' shouted Tarzan, angered that Numa's return should have been so timed as to frustrate his plans for a comfortable night's repose. 'I am Tarzan of the Apes, Lord of the Jungle. Tonight I lair here – go!'

But Numa did not go. Instead he rumbled forth a menacing roar and took a few steps in Tarzan's direction. The ape-man picked up a rock and hurled it at the snarling face. One can never be sure of a lion. This one might turn tail and run at the first intimation of attack – Tarzan had bluffed many in his time – but not now. The missile struck Numa full upon the snout – a tender part of a cat's anatomy – and instead of causing him to flee it transformed him into an infuriated engine of wrath and destruction.

Up went his tail, stiff and erect, and with a series of frightful roars he bore down upon the Tarmangani at the speed of an express train. Not an instant too soon did Tarzan reach the tree and swing himself into its branches and there he squatted, hurling insults at the king of beasts while Numa paced a circle beneath him, growling and roaring in rage.

It was raining now in earnest, adding to the ape-man's discomfort and disappointment. He was very angry; but as only direct necessity had ever led him to close in mortal combat with a lion, knowing as he did that he had only luck and agility to pit against the frightful odds of muscle, weight, fangs, and talons, he did not now even consider descending and engaging in so unequal and useless a duel for the mere reward of a little added creature comfort. And so he sat perched in the tree while the rain fell steadily and the lion padded round and round beneath, casting a baleful eye upward after every few steps.

Tarzan scanned the precipitous walls for an avenue of escape. They would have baffled an ordinary man; but the ape-man, accustomed to climbing, saw several places where he might gain a foothold, precarious possibly; but enough to give him reasonable assurance of escape if Numa would but betake himself to the far end of the gulch for a moment. Numa, however, notwithstanding the rain, gave no evidence of quitting his post so that at last Tarzan really began to consider seriously if it might not be as well to take the chance of a battle with him rather than remain longer cold and wet and humiliated in the tree.

But even as he turned the matter over in his mind Numa turned suddenly and walked majestically toward the tunnel without even a backward glance. The instant that he disappeared, Tarzan dropped lightly to the ground upon the far side of the tree and was away at top speed for the cliff. The lion had no sooner entered the tunnel than he backed immediately out again and, pivoting like a flash, was off across the gulch in full charge after the flying ape-man; but Tarzan's lead was too great – if he could find finger-or foothold upon the sheer rock wall he would be safe; but should he slip from the wet rocks his doom was already sealed as he would fall directly into Numa's clutches where even the Great Tarmangani would be helpless.

With the agility of a cat Tarzan ran up the cliff for thirty feet before he paused, and there finding a secure foothold, he stopped and looked down upon Numa who was leaping upward in a wild and futile attempt to scale the rocky wall to his prey. Fifteen or twenty feet from the ground the lion would scramble only to fall backward again defeated. Tarzan eyed him for a moment and then commenced a slow and cautious ascent toward the summit. Several times he had difficulty in finding holds but at last he drew himself over the edge, rose, picked up a bit of loose rock, hurled it at Numa and strode away.

Finding an easy descent to the gorge, he was about to pursue his journey in the direction of the still-booming guns when a sudden thought caused him to halt and a half-smile to play about his lips. Turning, he trotted quickly back to the outer opening of Numa's tunnel. Close beside it he listened for a moment and then rapidly began to gather large rocks and pile them within the entrance. He had almost closed the aperture when the lion appeared upon the inside – a very ferocious and angry lion that pawed and clawed at the rocks and uttered mighty roars that caused the earth to tremble; but roars did not frighten Tarzan of the Apes. At Kala's shaggy breast he had closed his infant eyes in sleep upon countless nights in years gone by to the savage chorus of similar roars. Scarcely a day or night of his jungle life – and practically all his life had been spent in the jungle – had he not heard the roaring of hungry lions, or angry lions, or lovesick lions. Such sounds affected Tarzan as the tooting of an automobile horn may affect you – if you are in front of the automobile it warns you out of the way, if you are not in front of it you scarcely notice it. Figuratively Tarzan was not in front of the automobile – Numa could not reach him and Tarzan knew it, so he continued deliberately to choke the entrance until there was no possibility of Numa's getting out again. When he was quite through he made a grimace at the hidden lion beyond the barrier and resumed his way toward the east. 'A man-eater who will eat no more men,' he soliloquized.

That night Tarzan lay up under an overhanging shelf of rock. The next morning he resumed his journey, stopping only long enough to make a kill and satisfy his hunger. The other beasts of the wild eat and lie up; but Tarzan never let his belly interfere with his plans. In this lay one of the greatest differences between the ape-man and his fellows of the jungles and forests. The firing ahead rose and fell during the day. He had noticed that it was highest at dawn and immediately after dusk and that during the night it almost ceased. In the middle of the afternoon of the second day he came upon troops moving up toward the front. They appeared to be raiding parties, for they drove goats and cows along with them and there were native porters laden with grain and other foodstuffs. He saw that these natives were all secured by neck chains and he also saw that the troops were composed of native soldiers in German uniforms. The officers were white men. No one saw Tarzan, yet he was here and there about and among them for two hours. He inspected the insignia upon their uniforms and saw that they were not the same as that which he had taken from one of the dead soldiers at the bungalow and then he passed on ahead of them, unseen in the dense bush. He had come upon Germans and had not killed them; but it was because the killing of Germans at large was not yet the prime motive of his existence – now it was to discover the individual who slew his mate. After he had accounted for him he would take up the little matter of slaying *all* Germans who crossed his path, and he meant that many should cross it, for he would hunt them precisely as professional hunters hunt the man-eaters.

As he neared the front lines the troops became more numerous. There were motor trucks and ox teams and all the impedimenta of a small army and always there were wounded men walking or being carried toward the rear. He had crossed the railroad some distance back and judged that the wounded were being taken to it for transportation to a base hospital and possibly as far away as Tanga on the coast.

It was dusk when he reached a large camp hidden in the foothills of the Pare Mountains. As he was approaching from the rear he found it but lightly guarded and what sentinels there were, were not upon the alert, and so it was an easy thing for him to enter after darkness had fallen and prowl about listening at the backs of tents, searching for some clue to the slayer of his mate.

As he paused at the side of a tent before which sat a number of native soldiers he caught a few words spoken in native dialect that riveted his attention instantly: 'The Waziri fought like devils; but we are greater fighters and we killed them all. When we were through the captain came and killed the woman. He stayed outside and yelled in a very loud voice until all the men were killed. Underlieutenant von Goss is braver – he came in and stood beside the door shouting at us, also in a very loud voice, and bade us nail one of the Waziri who was wounded to the wall, and then he laughed loudly because the man suffered. We all laughed. It was very funny.'

Like a beast of prey, grim and terrible, Tarzan crouched in the shadows beside the tent. What thoughts passed through that savage mind? Who may say? No outward sign of passion was revealed by the expression of the handsome face; the cold, gray eyes denoted only intense watchfulness. Presently the soldier Tarzan had heard first rose and with a parting word turned away. He passed within ten feet of the ape-man and continued on toward the rear of the camp. Tarzan followed and in the shadows of a clump of bushes overtook his quarry. There was no sound as the man-beast sprang upon the back of his prey and bore it to the ground for steel fingers closed simultaneously upon the soldier's throat, effectually stifling any outcry. By the neck Tarzan dragged his victim well into the concealment of the bushes.

'Make no sound,' he cautioned in the man's own tribal dialect as he released his hold upon the other's throat.

The fellow gasped for breath, rolling frightened eyes upward to see what manner of creature it might be in whose power he was. In the darkness he saw only a naked brown body bending above him; but he still remembered the terrific strength of the mighty muscles that had closed upon his windpipe and dragged him into the bushes as though he had been but a little child. If any thought of resistance had crossed his mind he must have discarded it at once, as he made no move to escape.

'What is the name of the officer who killed the woman at the bungalow where you fought with the Waziri?' asked Tarzan.

'Hauptmann Schneider,' replied the black when he could again command his voice.

'Where is he?' demanded the ape-man.

'He is here. It may be that he is at headquarters. Many of the officers go there in the evening to receive orders.'

'Lead me there,' commanded Tarzan, 'and if I am discovered I will kill you immediately. Get up!'

The black rose and led the way by a roundabout route back through the camp. Several times they were forced to hide while soldiers passed; but at last they reached a great pile of baled hay from about the corner of which the black pointed out a two-story building in the distance.

'Headquarters,' he said. 'You can go no farther unseen. There are many soldiers about.'

Tarzan realized that he could not proceed farther in company with the black. He turned and looked at the fellow for a moment as though pondering what disposition to make of him.

'You helped to crucify Wasimbu, the Waziri,' he accused in a low yet nonetheless terrible tone.

The black trembled, his knees giving beneath him. 'He ordered us to do it,' he pleaded.

'Who ordered it done?' demanded Tarzan.

'Underlieutenant von Goss,' replied the soldier. 'He, too, is here.'

'I shall find him,' returned Tarzan, grimly. 'You helped to crucify Wasimbu, the Waziri, and, while he suffered, you laughed.'

The fellow reeled. It was as though in the accusation he read also his death sentence. With no other word Tarzan seized the man again by the neck. As before there was no outcry. The giant muscles tensed. The arms swung quickly upward and with them the body of the black soldier who had helped to crucify Wasimbu, the Waziri, described a circle in the air – once, twice, three times, and then it was flung aside and the ape-man turned in the direction of General Kraut's headquarters.

A single sentinel in the rear of the building barred the way. Tarzan crawled, belly to the ground, toward him, taking advantage of cover as only the jungle-bred beast of prey can do. When the sentinel's eyes were toward him, Tarzan hugged the ground, motionless as stone; when they were turned away, he moved swiftly forward. Presently he was within charging distance. He waited until the man had turned his back once more and then he rose and sped noiselessly down upon him. Again there was no sound as he carried the dead body with him toward the building.

The lower floor was lighted, the upper dark. Through the windows Tarzan saw a large front room and a smaller room in rear of it. In the former were many officers. Some moved about talking to one another, others sat at field tables writing. The windows were open and Tarzan could hear much of the conversation; but nothing that interested him. It was mostly about the German successes in Africa and conjectures as to when the German army in

Europe would reach Paris. Some said the Kaiser was doubtlessly already there, and there was a great deal of damning Belgium.

In the smaller back room a large, red-faced man sat behind a table. Some other officers were also sitting a little in rear of him, while two stood at attention before the general, who was questioning them. As he talked, the general toyed with an oil lamp that stood upon the table before him. Presently there came a knock upon the door and an aide entered the room. He saluted and reported: 'Fräulein Kircher has arrived, sir.'

'Bid her enter,' commanded the general, and then nodded to the two officers before him in sign of dismissal.

The Fräulein, entering, passed them at the door. The officers in the little room rose and saluted, the Fräulein acknowledging the courtesy with a bow and a slight smile. She was a very pretty girl. Even the rough, soiled riding habit and the caked dust upon her face could not conceal the fact, and she was young. She could not have been over nineteen.

She advanced to the table behind which the general stood and, taking a folded paper from an inside pocket of her coat, handed it to him.

'Be seated, Fräulein,' he said, and another officer brought her a chair. No one spoke while the general read the contents of the paper.

Tarzan appraised the various people in the room. He wondered if one might not be Hauptmann Schneider, for two of them were captains. The girl he judged to be of the intelligence department – a spy. Her beauty held no appeal for him – without a glimmer of compunction he could have wrung that fair, young neck. She was German and that was enough; but he had other and more important work before him. He wanted Hauptmann Schneider.

Finally the general looked up from the paper.

'Good,' he said to the girl, and then to one of his aides, 'Send for Major Schneider.'

Major Schneider! Tarzan felt the short hairs at the back of his neck rise. Already they had promoted the beast who had murdered his mate – doubtless they had promoted him for that very crime.

The aide left the room and the others fell into a general conversation from which it became apparent to Tarzan that the German East African forces greatly outnumbered the British and that the latter were suffering heavily. The ape-man stood so concealed in a clump of bushes that he could watch the interior of the room without being seen from within, while he was at the same time hidden from the view of anyone who might chance to pass along the post of the sentinel he had slain. Momentarily he was expecting a patrol or a relief to appear and discover that the sentinel was missing, when he knew an immediate and thorough search would be made.

Impatiently he awaited the coming of the man he sought and at last he was rewarded by the reappearance of the aide who had been dispatched to fetch him accompanied by an officer of medium size with fierce, upstanding mustaches. The newcomer strode to the table, halted and saluted, reporting. The general acknowledged the salute and turned toward the girl.

'Fräulein Kircher,' he said, 'allow me to present Major Schneider –'

Tarzan waited to hear no more. Placing a palm upon the sill of the window he vaulted into the room into the midst of an astounded company of the Kaiser's officers. With a stride he was at the table and with a sweep of his hand sent the lamp crashing into the fat belly of the general who, in his mad effort to escape cremation, fell over backward, chair and all, upon the floor. Two of the aides sprang for the ape-man who picked up the first and flung him in the face of the other. The girl had leaped from her chair and stood flattened against the wall. The other officers were calling aloud for the guard and for help. Tarzan's purpose centered upon but a single individual and him he never lost sight of. Freed from attack for an instant he seized Major Schneider, threw him over his shoulder and was out of the window so quickly that the astonished assemblage could scarce realize what had occurred.

A single glance showed him that the sentinel's post was still vacant and a moment later he and his burden were in the shadows of the hay dump. Major Schneider had made no outcry for the very excellent reason that his wind was shut off. Now Tarzan released his grasp enough to permit the man to breathe.

'If you make a sound you will be choked again,' he said.

Cautiously and after infinite patience Tarzan passed the final outpost. Forcing his captive to walk before him he pushed on toward the west until, late into the night, he recrossed the railway where he felt reasonably safe from discovery. The German had cursed and grumbled and threatened and asked questions; but his only reply was another prod from Tarzan's sharp war spear. The ape-man herded him along as he would have driven a hog, with the difference that he would have had more respect and therefore more consideration for a hog.

Until now Tarzan had given little thought to the details of revenge. Now he pondered what form the punishment should take. Of only one thing was he certain – it must end in death. Like all brave men and courageous beasts Tarzan had little natural inclination to torture – none, in fact; but this case was unique in his experience. An inherent sense of justice called for an eye for an eye and his recent oath demanded even more. Yes, the creature must suffer even as he had caused Jane Clayton to suffer. Tarzan could not hope to make the man suffer as he had suffered, since physical pain may never approach the exquisiteness of mental torture.

All through the long night the ape-man goaded on the exhausted and now terrified Hun. The awful silence of his captor wrought upon the German's nerves. If he would only speak! Again and again Schneider tried to force or coax a word from him; but always the result was the same – continued silence and a vicious and painful prod from the spear point. Schneider was bleeding and sore. He was so exhausted that he staggered at every step, and often he fell only to be prodded to his feet again by that terrifying and remorseless spear.

It was not until morning that Tarzan reached a decision and it came to him then like an inspiration from above. A slow smile touched his lips and he immediately sought a place to lie up and rest – he wished his prisoner to be fit now for what lay in store for him. Ahead was a stream which Tarzan had crossed the day before. He knew the ford for a drinking place and a likely spot to make an easy kill. Cautioning the German to utter silence with a gesture the two approached the stream quietly. Down the game trail Tarzan saw some deer about to leave the water. He shoved Schneider into the brush at one side and, squatting next to him, waited. The German watched the silent giant with puzzled, frightened eyes. In the new dawn he, for the first time, was able to obtain a good look at his captor, and, if he had been puzzled and frightened before, those sensations were nothing to what he experienced now.

Who and what could this almost naked, white savage be? He had heard him speak but once – when he had cautioned him to silence – and then in excellent German and the well-modulated tones of culture. He watched him now as the fascinated toad watches the snake that is about to devour it. He saw the graceful limbs and symmetrical body motionless as a marble statue as the creature crouched in the concealment of the leafy foliage. Not a muscle, not a nerve moved. He saw the deer coming slowly along the trail, downwind and unsuspecting. He saw a buck pass – an old buck – and then a young and plump one came opposite the giant in ambush, and Schneider's eyes went wide and a scream of terror almost broke from his lips as he saw the agile beast at his side spring straight for the throat of the young buck and heard from those human lips the hunting roar of a wild beast. Down went the buck and Tarzan and his captive had meat. The ape-man ate his raw, but he permitted the German to build a fire and cook his portion.

The two lay up until late in the afternoon and then took up the journey once again – a journey that was so frightful to Schneider because of his ignorance of its destination that he at times groveled at Tarzan's feet begging for an explanation and for mercy; but on and on in silence the ape-man went, prodding the failing Hun whenever the latter faltered.

It was noon of the third day before they reached their destination. After a steep climb and a short walk they halted at the edge of a precipitous cliff and Schneider looked down into a narrow gulch where a single tree grew beside a tiny rivulet and sparse grass broke from a rock-strewn soil. Tarzan motioned him over the edge; but the German drew back in terror. The ape-man seized him and pushed him roughly toward the brink. 'Descend,' he said. It was the second time he had spoken in three days and perhaps his very silence, ominous in itself, had done more to arouse terror in the breast of the Boche than even the spear point, ever ready as it always was.

Schneider looked fearfully over the edge; but was about to essay the attempt when Tarzan halted him. 'I am Lord Greystoke,' he said. 'It was my wife you murdered in the Waziri country. You will understand now why I came for you. Descend.'

The German fell upon his knees. 'I did not murder your wife,' he cried. 'Have mercy! I did not murder your wife. I do not know anything about –'

'Descend!' snapped Tarzan, raising the point of his spear. He knew that the man lied and was not surprised that he did. A man who would murder for no cause would lie for less. Schneider still hesitated and pled. The ape-man jabbed him with the spear and Schneider slid fearfully over the top and began the perilous descent. Tarzan accompanied and assisted him over the worst places until at last they were within a few feet of the bottom.

'Be quiet now,' cautioned the ape-man. He pointed at the entrance to what appeared to be a cave at the far end of the gulch. 'There is a hungry lion in there. If you can reach that tree before he discovers you, you will have several days longer in which to enjoy life and then – when you are too weak to cling longer to the branches of the tree Numa, the man-eater, will feed again for the last time.' He pushed Schneider from his foothold to the ground below. 'Now run,' he said.

The German, trembling in terror, started for the tree. He had almost reached it when a horrid roar broke from the mouth of the cave and almost simultaneously a gaunt, hunger-mad lion leaped into the daylight of the gulch. Schneider had but a few yards to cover, but the lion flew over the ground to circumvent him while Tarzan watched the race with a slight smile upon his lips.

Schneider won by a slender margin, and as Tarzan scaled the cliff to the summit, he heard behind him mingled with the roaring of the baffled cat, the gibbering of a human voice that was at the same time more bestial than the beast's.

Upon the brink of the cliff the ape-man turned and looked back into the gulch. High in the tree the German clung frantically to a branch across which his body lay. Beneath him was Numa – waiting.

The ape-man raised his face to Kudu, the sun, and from his mighty chest rose the savage victory cry of the bull ape.

3

In the German Lines

Tarzan was not yet fully revenged. There were many millions of Germans yet alive – enough to keep Tarzan pleasantly occupied the balance of his life, and yet not enough, should he kill them all, to recompense him for the great loss he had suffered – nor could the death of all those million Germans bring back his loved one.

While in the German camp in the Pare Mountains, which lie just east of the boundary line between German and British East Africa, Tarzan had overheard enough to suggest that the British were getting the worst of the fighting in Africa. At first he had given the matter but little thought, since, after the death of his wife, the one strong tie that had held him to civilization, he had renounced all mankind, considering himself no longer man, but ape.

After accounting for Schneider as satisfactorily as lay within his power he circled Kilimanjaro and hunted in the foothills to the north of that mightiest of mountains as he had discovered that in the neighborhood of the armies there was no hunting at all. Some pleasure he derived through conjuring mental pictures from time to time of the German he had left in the branches of the lone tree at the bottom of the high-walled gulch in which was penned the starving lion. He could imagine the man's mental anguish as he became weakened from hunger and maddened by thirst, knowing that sooner or later he must slip exhausted to the ground where waited the gaunt man-eater. Tarzan wondered if Schneider would have the courage to descend to the little rivulet for water should Numa leave the gulch and enter the cave, and then he pictured the mad race for the tree again when the lion charged out to seize his prey as he was certain to do, since the clumsy German could not descend to the rivulet without making at least some slight noise that would attract Numa's attention.

But even this pleasure palled, and more and more the ape-man found himself thinking of the English soldiers fighting against heavy odds and especially of the fact that it was Germans who were beating them. The thought made him lower his head and growl and it worried him not a little – a bit, perhaps, because he was finding it difficult to forget that he was an Englishman when he wanted only to be an ape. And at last the time came when he could no longer endure the thought of Germans killing Englishmen while he hunted in safety a bare march away.

His decision made, he set out in the direction of the German camp, no well-defined plan formulated; but with the general idea that once near the field of operations he might find an opportunity to harass the German command as he so well knew how to do. His way took him along the gorge close to the gulch in which he had left Schneider, and, yielding to a natural curiosity, he scaled the cliffs and made his way to the edge of the gulch. The tree was empty, nor was there sign of Numa, the lion. Picking up a rock he hurled it into the gulch, where it rolled to the very entrance to the cave. Instantly the lion appeared in the aperture; but such a different-looking lion from the great sleek brute that Tarzan had trapped there two weeks before. Now he was gaunt and emaciated, and when he walked he staggered.

'Where is the German?' shouted Tarzan. 'Was he good eating, or only a bag of bones when he slipped and fell from the tree?'

Numa growled. 'You look hungry, Numa,' continued the ape-man. 'You must have been very hungry to eat all the grass from your lair and even the bark from the tree as far up as you can reach. Would you like another German?' and smiling he turned away.

A few minutes later he came suddenly upon Bara, the deer, asleep beneath a tree, and as Tarzan was hungry he made a quick kill, and squatting beside his prey proceeded to eat his fill. As he was gnawing the last morsel from a bone his quick ears caught the padding of stealthy feet behind him, and turning he confronted Dango, the hyena, sneaking up on him. With a growl the ape-man picked up a fallen branch and hurled it at the skulking brute. 'Go away, eater of carrion!' he cried; but Dango was hungry and being large and powerful he only snarled and circled slowly about as though watching for an opportunity to charge. Tarzan of the Apes knew Dango even better than Dango knew himself. He knew that the brute, made savage by hunger, was mustering its courage for an attack, that it was probably accustomed to man and therefore more or less fearless of him and so he unslung his heavy spear and laid it ready at his side while he continued his meal, all the time keeping a watchful eye upon the hyena.

He felt no fear, for long familiarity with the dangers of his wild world had so accustomed him to them that he took whatever came as a part of each day's existence as you accept the homely though no less real dangers of the farm, the range, or the crowded metropolis. Being jungle bred he was ready to protect his kill from all comers within ordinary limitations of caution. Under favorable conditions Tarzan would face even Numa himself and, if forced to seek safety by flight, he could do so without any feeling of shame. There was no braver creature roamed those savage wilds and at the same time there was none more wise – the two factors that had permitted him to survive.

Dango might have charged sooner but for the savage growls of the ape-man – growls which, coming from human lips, raised a question and a fear in the hyena's heart. He had attacked women and children in the native fields and he had frightened their men about their fires at night; but he never had seen a man-thing who made this sound that reminded him more of Numa angry than of a man afraid.

When Tarzan had completed his repast he was about to rise and hurl a clean-picked bone at the beast before he went his way, leaving the remains of his kill to Dango; but a sudden thought stayed him and instead he picked up the carcass of the deer, threw it over his shoulder, and set off in the direction of the gulch. For a few yards Dango followed, growling, and then realizing that he was being robbed of even a taste of the luscious flesh he cast discretion to the winds and charged. Instantly, as though Nature had given him eyes in the back of his head, Tarzan sensed the impending danger and, dropping Bara to the ground, turned with raised spear. Far back went the brown, right hand and then forward, lightninglike, backed by the power of giant muscles and the weight of his brawn and bone. The spear, released at the right instant, drove straight for Dango, caught him in the neck where it joined the shoulders, and passed through the body.

When he had withdrawn the shaft from the hyena Tarzan shouldered both carcasses and continued on toward the gulch. Below lay Numa beneath the shade of the lone tree and at the ape-man's call he staggered slowly to his feet, yet weak as he was, he still growled savagely, even essaying a roar at the sight of his enemy. Tarzan let the two bodies slide over the rim of the cliff. 'Eat, Numa!' he cried. 'It may be that I shall need you again.' He saw the lion, quickened to new life at the sight of food, spring upon the body of the deer and then he left him rending and tearing the flesh as he bolted great pieces into his empty maw.

The following day Tarzan came within sight of the German lines. From a wooded spur of the hills he looked down upon the enemy's left flank and beyond to the British lines. His position gave him a bird's-eye view of the field of battle, and his keen eyesight picked out many details that would not have been apparent to a man whose every sense was not trained to the highest point of perfection as were the ape-man's. He noted machine-gun emplacements cunningly hidden from the view of the British and listening posts placed well out in No Man's Land.

As his interested gaze moved hither and thither from one point of interest to another he heard from a point upon the hillside below him, above the roar of cannon and the crack of rifle fire, a single rifle spit. Immediately his attention was centered upon the spot where he knew a sniper must be hid. Patiently he awaited the next shot that would tell him more surely the exact location of the rifleman, and when it came he moved down the steep hillside with the stealth and quietness of a panther. Apparently he took no cognizance of where he stepped, yet never a loose stone was disturbed nor a twig broken – it was as though his feet saw.

Presently, as he passed through a clump of bushes, he came to the edge of a low cliff and saw upon a ledge some fifteen feet below him a German soldier prone behind an embankment of loose rock and leafy boughs that hid him from the view of the British lines. The man must have been an excellent shot, for he was well back of the German lines, firing over the heads of his fellows. His high-powered rifle was equipped with telescope sights and he also carried binoculars which he was in the act of using as Tarzan discovered him, either to note the effect of his last shot or to discover a new target. Tarzan let his eye move quickly toward that part of the British line the German seemed to be scanning, his keen sight revealing many excellent targets for a rifle placed so high above the trenches.

The Hun, evidently satisfied with his observations, laid aside his binoculars and again took up his rifle, placed its butt in the hollow of his shoulder and took careful aim. At the same instant a brown body sprang outward from the cliff above him. There was no sound and it is doubtful that the German ever knew what manner of creature it was that alighted heavily upon his back, for at the instant of impact the sinewy fingers of the ape-man circled the hairy throat of the Boche. There was a moment of futile struggling followed by the sudden realization of dissolution – the sniper was dead.

Lying behind the rampart of rocks and boughs, Tarzan looked down upon the scene below. Near at hand were the trenches of the Germans. He could see officers and men moving about in them and almost in front of him a well-hidden machine gun was traversing No Man's Land in an oblique direction, striking the British at such an angle as to make it difficult for them to locate it.

Tarzan watched, toying idly with the rifle of the dead German. Presently he fell to examining the mechanism of the piece. He glanced again toward the German trenches and changed the adjustment of the sights, then he placed the rifle to his shoulder and took aim. Tarzan was an excellent shot. With his civilized friends he had hunted big game with the weapons of civilization and though he never had killed except for food or in self-defense he had amused himself firing at inanimate targets thrown into the air and had perfected himself in the use of firearms without realizing that he had done so. Now indeed would he hunt big game. A slow smile touched his lips as his finger closed gradually upon the trigger. The rifle spoke and a German machine gunner collapsed behind his weapon. In three minutes Tarzan picked off the crew of that gun. Then he spotted a German officer emerging from a dugout and the three men in the bay with him. Tarzan was careful to leave no one in the immediate vicinity to question how Germans could be shot in German trenches when they were entirely concealed from enemy view.

Again adjusting his sights he took a long-range shot at a distant machine-gun crew to his right. With calm deliberation he wiped them out to a man. Two guns were silenced. He saw men running through the trenches and he picked off several of them. By this time the Germans were aware that something was amiss – that an uncanny sniper had discovered a point of vantage from which this sector of the trenches was plainly visible to him. At first they sought to discover his location in No Man's Land; but when an officer looking over the parapet through a periscope was struck full in the back of the head with a rifle bullet which passed through his skull and fell to the bottom of the trench they realized that it was beyond the parados rather than the parapet that they should search.

One of the soldiers picked up the bullet that had killed his officer, and then it was that real excitement prevailed in that particular bay, for the bullet was obviously of German make. Hugging the parados, messengers carried the word in both directions and presently periscopes were leveled above the parados and keen eyes were searching out the traitor. It did not take them long to locate the position of the hidden sniper and then Tarzan saw a machine gun being trained upon him. Before it had gotten into action its crew lay dead about it; but there were other men to take their places, reluctantly perhaps; but driven on by their officers they were forced to it and at the same time two other machine guns were swung around toward the ape-man and put into operation.

Realizing that the game was about up Tarzan with a farewell shot laid aside the rifle and melted into the hills behind him. For many minutes he could hear the sputter of machine-gun fire concentrated upon the spot he had just quit and smiled as he contemplated the waste of German ammunition.

'They have paid heavily for Wasimbu, the Waziri, whom they crucified, and for his slain fellows,' he mused, 'but for Jane they can never pay – no, not if I killed them all.'

After dark that night he circled the flanks of both armies and passed through the British out-guards and into the British lines. No man saw him come. No man knew that he was there.

Headquarters of the Second Rhodesians occupied a sheltered position far enough back of the lines to be comparatively safe from enemy observation. Even lights were permitted, and Colonel Capell sat before a field table, on which was spread a military map, talking with several of his officers. A large tree spread above them, a lantern sputtered dimly upon the table, while a small fire burned upon the ground close at hand. The enemy had no planes and no other observers could have seen the lights from the German lines.

The officers were discussing the advantage in numbers possessed by the enemy and the inability of the British to more than hold their present position. They could not advance. Already they had sustained severe losses in every attack and had always been driven back by overwhelming numbers.

There were hidden machine guns, too, that bothered the colonel considerably. It was evidenced by the fact that he often reverted to them during the conversation.

'Something silenced them for a while this afternoon,' said one of the younger officers. 'I was observing at the time and I couldn't make out what the fuss was about; but they seemed to be having a devil of a time in a section of trench on their left. At one time I could have sworn they were attacked in the rear – I reported it to you at the time, sir, you'll recall – for the blighters were pepperin' away at the side of that bluff behind them. I could see the dirt fly. I don't know what it could have been.'

There was a slight rustling among the branches of the tree above them and simultaneously a lithe, brown body dropped in their midst. Hands moved quickly to the butts of pistols; but otherwise there was no movement among the officers. First they looked wonderingly at the almost naked white man standing there with the firelight playing upon rounded muscles, took in the primitive attire and the equally primitive armament and then all eyes turned toward the colonel.

'Who the devil are you, sir?' snapped that officer.

'Tarzan of the Apes,' replied the newcomer.

'Oh, Greystoke!' cried a major, and stepped forward with outstretched hand.

'Preswick,' acknowledged Tarzan as he took the proffered hand.

'I didn't recognize you at first,' apologized the major. 'The last time I saw you you were in London in evening dress. Quite a difference – 'pon my word, man, you'll have to admit it.'

Tarzan smiled and turned toward the colonel. 'I overheard your conversation,' he said. 'I have just come from behind the German lines. Possibly I can help you.'

The colonel looked questioningly toward Major Preswick who quickly rose to the occasion and presented the ape-man to his commanding officer and fellows. Briefly Tarzan told them what it was that brought him out alone in pursuit of the Germans.

'And now you have come to join us?' asked the colonel.

Tarzan shook his head. 'Not regularly,' he replied. 'I must fight in my own way; but I can help you. Whenever I wish I can enter the German lines.'

Capell smiled and shook his head. 'It's not so easy as you think,' he said; 'I've lost two good officers in the last week trying it – and they were experienced men; none better in the Intelligence Department.'

'Is it more difficult than entering the British lines?' asked Tarzan.

The colonel was about to reply when a new thought appeared to occur to him and he looked quizzically at the ape-man. 'Who brought you here?' he asked. 'Who passed you through our out-guards?'

'I have just come through the German lines and yours and passed through your camp,' he replied. 'Send word to ascertain if anyone saw me.'

'But who accompanied you?' insisted Capell.

'I came alone,' replied Tarzan, drawing himself to his full height. 'You men of civilization, when you come into the jungle, are as dead among the quick. Manu, the monkey, is a sage by comparison. I marvel that you exist at all – only your numbers, your weapons, and your power of reasoning save you. Had I a few hundred great apes with your reasoning power I could drive the Germans into the ocean as quickly as the remnant of them could reach the coast. Fortunate it is for you that the dumb brutes cannot combine. Could they, Africa would remain forever free of men. But come, can I help you? Would you like to know where several machine-gun emplacements are hidden?'

The colonel assured him that they would, and a moment later Tarzan had traced upon the map the location of three that had been bothering the English. 'There is a weak spot here,' he said, placing a finger upon the map. 'It is held by blacks; but the machine guns out in front are manned by whites. If – wait! I have a plan. You can fill that trench with your own men and enfilade the trenches to its right with their own machine guns.'

Colonel Capell smiled and shook his head. 'It sounds very easy,' he said.

'It *is* easy – for me,' replied the ape-man. 'I can empty that section of trench without a shot. I was raised in the jungle – I know the jungle folk – the Gomangani as well as the others. Look for me again on the second night,' and he turned to leave.

'Wait,' said the colonel. 'I will send an officer to pass you through the lines.'

Tarzan smiled and moved away. As he was leaving the little group about headquarters he passed a small figure wrapped in an officer's heavy overcoat. The collar was turned up and the visor of the military cap pulled well down over the eyes; but, as the ape-man passed, the light from the fire illuminated the features of the newcomer for an instant, revealing to Tarzan a vaguely familiar face. Some officer he had known in London, doubtless, he surmised, and went his way through the British camp and the British lines all unknown to the watchful sentinels of the out-guard.

Nearly all night he moved across Kilimanjaro's foothills, tracking by instinct an unknown way, for he guessed that what he sought would be found on some wooded slope higher up than he had come upon his other recent journeys in this, to him, little known country. Three hours before dawn his keen nostrils apprised him that somewhere in the vicinity he would find what he wanted, and so he climbed into a tall tree and settled himself for a few hours' sleep.

4
When the Lion Fed

Kudu, the sun, was well up in the heavens when Tarzan awoke. The ape-man stretched his giant limbs, ran his fingers through his thick hair, and swung lightly down to earth. Immediately he took up the trail he had come in search of, following it by scent down into a deep ravine. Cautiously he went now, for his nose told him that the quarry was close at hand, and presently from an overhanging bough he looked down upon Horta, the boar, and many of his kinsmen. Unslinging his bow and selecting an arrow, Tarzan fitted the shaft and, drawing it far back, took careful aim at the largest of the great pigs. In the ape-man's teeth were other arrows, and no sooner had the first one sped, than he had fitted and shot another bolt. Instantly the pigs were in turmoil, not knowing from whence the danger threatened. They stood stupidly at first and then commenced milling around until six of their number lay dead or dying about them; then with a chorus of grunts and squeals they started off at a wild run, disappearing quickly in the dense underbrush.

Tarzan then descended from the tree, dispatched those that were not already dead and proceeded to skin the carcasses. As he worked, rapidly and with great skill, he neither hummed nor whistled as does the average man of civilization. It was in numerous little ways such as these that he differed from other men, due, probably, to his early jungle training. The beasts of the jungle that he had been reared among were playful to maturity but seldom thereafter. His fellow-apes, especially the bulls, became fierce and surly as they grew older. Life was a serious matter during lean seasons – one had to fight to secure one's share of food then, and the habit once formed became lifelong. Hunting for food was the life labor of the jungle bred, and a life labor is a thing not to be approached with levity nor prosecuted lightly. So all work found Tarzan serious, though he still retained what the other beasts lost as they grew older – a sense of humor, which he gave play to when the mood suited him. It was a grim humor and sometimes ghastly; but it satisfied Tarzan.

Then, too, were one to sing and whistle while working on the ground, concentration would be impossible. Tarzan possessed the ability to concentrate each of his five senses upon its particular business. Now he worked at skinning the six pigs and his eyes and fingers worked as though there was naught else in all the world than these six carcasses; but his ears and his nose were as busily engaged elsewhere – the former ranging the forest all about and the latter assaying each passing zephyr. It was his nose that first discovered the approach of Sabor, the lioness, when the wind shifted for a moment.

As clearly as though he had seen her with his eyes, Tarzan knew that the lioness had caught the scent of the freshly killed pigs and immediately had moved downwind in their direction. He knew from the strength of the scent spoor and the rate of the wind about how far away she was and that she was approaching from behind him. He was finishing the last pig and he did not hurry. The five pelts lay close at hand – he had been careful to keep them thus together and near him – an ample tree waved its low branches above him.

He did not even turn his head for he knew she was not yet in sight; but he bent his ears just a bit more sharply for the first sound of her nearer approach. When the final skin had been removed he rose. Now he heard Sabor in the bushes to his rear, but not yet too close. Leisurely he gathered up the six pelts and one of the carcasses, and as the lioness appeared between the boles of two trees he swung upward into the branches above him. Here he hung the hides over a limb, seated himself comfortably upon another with his back against the bole of the tree, cut a hind-quarter from the carcass he had carried with him and proceeded to satisfy his hunger. Sabor slunk, growling, from the brush, cast a wary eye upward toward the ape-man and then fell upon the nearest carcass.

Tarzan looked down upon her and grinned, recalling an argument he had once had with a famous big-game hunter who had declared that the king of beasts ate only what he himself had killed. Tarzan knew better for he had seen Numa and Sabor stoop even to carrion.

Having filled his belly, the ape-man fell to work upon the hides – all large and strong. First he cut strips from them about half an inch wide. When he had sufficient number of these strips he sewed two of the hides together, afterward piercing holes every three or four inches around the edges. Running another strip through these holes gave him a large bag with a drawstring. In similar fashion he produced four other like bags, but smaller, from the four remaining hides and had several strips left over.

All this done he threw a large, juicy fruit at Sabor, cached the remainder of the pig in a crotch of the tree and swung off toward the southwest through the middle terraces of the forest, carrying his five bags with him. Straight he went to the rim of the gulch where he had imprisoned Numa, the lion. Very stealthily he approached the edge and peered over. Numa was not in sight. Tarzan sniffed and listened. He could hear nothing, yet he knew that Numa must be within the cave. He hoped that he slept – much depended upon Numa not discovering him.

Cautiously he lowered himself over the edge of the cliff, and with utter noiselessness commenced the descent toward the bottom of the gulch. He stopped often and turned his keen eyes and ears in the direction of the cave's mouth at the far end of the gulch, some hundred feet away. As he neared the foot of the cliff his danger increased greatly. If he could reach the bottom and cover half the distance to the tree that stood in the center of the gulch he would feel comparatively safe for then, even if Numa appeared, he felt that he could beat him either to the cliff or to the tree, but to scale the first thirty feet of the cliff rapidly enough to elude the leaping beast would require a running start of at least twenty feet as there were no very good hand-or footholds close to the bottom – he had had to run up the first twenty feet like a squirrel running up a tree that other time he had beaten an infuriated Numa to it. He had no desire to attempt it again unless the conditions were equally favorable at least, for he had escaped Numa's raking talons by only a matter of inches on the former occasion.

At last he stood upon the floor of the gulch. Silent as a disembodied spirit he advanced toward the tree. He was halfway there and no sign of Numa. He reached the scarred bole from which the famished lion had devoured the bark and even torn pieces of the wood itself and yet Numa had not appeared. As he drew himself up to the lower branches he commenced to wonder if Numa were in the cave after all. Could it be possible that he had forced the barrier of rocks with which Tarzan had plugged the other end of the passage where it opened into the outer world of freedom? Or was Numa dead? The ape-man doubted the verity of the latter suggestion as he had fed the lion the entire carcasses of a deer and a hyena only a few days since – he could not have starved in so short a time, while the little rivulet running across the gulch furnished him with water aplenty.

Tarzan started to descend and investigate the cavern when it occurred to him that it would save effort were he to lure Numa out instead. Acting upon the thought he uttered a low growl. Immediately he was rewarded by the sound of a movement within the cave and an instant later a wild-eyed, haggard lion rushed forth ready to face the devil himself were he edible. When Numa saw Tarzan, fat and sleek, perched in the tree he became suddenly the embodiment of frightful rage. His eyes and his nose told him that this was the creature responsible for his predicament and also that this creature was good to eat. Frantically the lion sought to scramble up the bole of the tree. Twice he leaped high enough to catch the lowest branches with his paws, but both times he fell backward to the earth. Each time he became more furious. His growls and roars were incessant and horrible and all the time Tarzan sat grinning down upon him, taunting him in jungle billingsgate for his inability to reach him and mentally exulting that always Numa was wasting his already waning strength.

Finally the ape-man rose and unslung his rope. He arranged the coils carefully in his left hand and the noose in his right, and then he took a position with each foot on one of two branches that lay in about the same horizontal plane and with his back pressed firmly against the stem of the tree. There he stood hurling insults at Numa until the beast was again goaded into leaping upward at him, and as Numa rose the noose dropped quickly over his head and about his neck. A quick movement of Tarzan's rope hand tightened the coil and when Numa slipped backward to the ground only his hind feet touched, for the ape-man held him swinging by the neck.

Moving slowly outward upon the two branches Tarzan swung Numa out so that he could not reach the bole of the tree with his raking talons, then he made the rope fast after drawing the lion clear of the ground, dropped his five pigskin sacks to earth and leaped down himself. Numa was striking frantically at the grass rope with his foreclaws. At any moment he might sever it and Tarzan must, therefore, work rapidly.

First he drew the larger bag over Numa's head and secured it about his neck with the drawstring, then he managed, after considerable effort, during which he barely escaped being tom to ribbons by the mighty talons, to hog-tie Numa – drawing his four legs together and securing them in that position with the strips trimmed from the pigskins.

By this time the lion's efforts had almost ceased – it was evident that he was being rapidly strangled and as that did not at all suit the purpose of the Tarmangani the latter swung again into the tree, unfastened the rope from above and lowered the lion to the ground where he immediately followed it and loosed the noose about Numa's neck. Then he drew his hunting knife and cut two round holes in the front of the head bag opposite the lion's eyes for the double purpose of permitting him to see and giving him sufficient air to breathe.

This done Tarzan busied himself fitting the other bags, one over each of Numa's formidably armed paws. Those on the hind feet he secured not only by tightening the drawstrings but also rigged garters that fastened tightly around the legs above the hocks. He secured the front-feet bags in place similarly above the great knees. Now, indeed, was Numa, the lion, reduced to the harmlessness of Bara, the deer.

By now Numa was showing signs of returning life. He gasped for breath and struggled; but the strips of pigskin that held his four legs together were numerous and tough. Tarzan watched and was sure that they would hold, yet Numa is mightily muscled and there was the chance, always, that he might struggle free of his bonds after which all would depend upon the efficacy of Tarzan's bags and drawstrings.

After Numa had again breathed normally and was able to roar out his protests and his rage, his struggles increased to titanic proportions for a short time; but as a lion's powers of endurance are in no way proportionate to his size and strength he soon tired and lay quietly. Amid renewed growling and another futile attempt to free himself, Numa was finally forced to submit to the further indignity of having a rope secured about his neck; but this time it was no noose that might tighten and strangle him; but a bowline knot, which does not tighten or slip under strain.

The other end of the rope Tarzan fastened to the stem of the tree, then he quickly cut the bonds securing Numa's legs and leaped aside as the beast sprang to his feet. For a moment the lion stood with legs far outspread, then he raised first one paw and then another, shaking them energetically in an effort to dislodge the strange footgear that Tarzan had fastened upon them. Finally he began to paw at the bag upon his head. The ape-man, standing with ready spear, watched Numa's efforts intently. Would the bags hold? He sincerely hoped so. Or would all his labor prove fruitless?

As the clinging things upon his feet and face resisted his every effort to dislodge them, Numa became frantic. He rolled upon the ground, fighting, biting, scratching, and roaring; he leaped to his feet and sprang into the air; he charged Tarzan, only to be brought to a sudden stop as the rope securing him to the tree tautened. Then Tarzan stepped in and rapped him smartly on the head with the shaft of his spear. Numa reared upon his hind feet and struck at the ape-man and in return received a cuff on one ear that sent him reeling sideways. When he returned to the attack he was again sent sprawling. After the fourth effort it appeared to dawn upon the king of beasts that he had met his master, his head and tail dropped and when Tarzan advanced upon him he backed away, though still growling.

Leaving Numa tied to the tree Tarzan entered the tunnel and removed the barricade from the opposite end, after which he returned to the gulch and strode straight for the tree. Numa lay in his path and as Tarzan approached growled menacingly. The ape-man cuffed him aside and unfastened the rope from the tree. Then ensued a half-hour of stubbornly fought battle while Tarzan endeavored to drive Numa through the tunnel ahead of him and Numa persistently refused to be driven. At last, however, by dint of the unrestricted use of his spear point, the ape-man succeeded in forcing the lion to move ahead of him and eventually guided him into the passageway. Once inside, the problem became simpler since Tarzan followed closely in the rear with his sharp spear point, an unremitting incentive to forward movement on the part of the lion. If Numa hesitated he was prodded. If he backed up the result was extremely painful and so, being a wise lion who was learning rapidly, he decided to keep on going and at the end of the tunnel, emerging into the outer world, he sensed freedom, raised his head and tail and started off at a run.

Tarzan, still on his hands and knees just inside the entrance, was taken unaware with the result that he was sprawled forward upon his face and dragged a hundred yards across the rocky ground before Numa was brought to a stand. It was a scratched and angry Tarzan who scrambled to his feet. At first he was tempted to chastise Numa; but, as the ape-man seldom permitted his temper to guide him in any direction not countenanced by reason, he quickly abandoned the idea.

Having taught Numa the rudiments of being driven, he now urged him forward and there commenced as strange a journey as the unrecorded history of the jungle contains. The balance of that day was eventful both for Tarzan and for Numa. From open rebellion at first the lion passed through stages of stubborn resistance and grudging obedience to final surrender. He was a very tired, hungry, and thirsty lion when night overtook them; but there was to be no food for him that day or the next – Tarzan did not dare risk removing the head bag, though he did cut another hole which permitted Numa to quench his thirst shortly after dark. Then he tied him to a tree, sought food for himself, and stretched out among the branches above his captive for a few hours' sleep.

Early the following morning they resumed their journey, winding over the low foothills south of Kilimanjaro, toward the east. The beasts of the jungle who saw them took one look and fled. The scent spoor of Numa, alone, might have been enough to have provoked flight in many of the lesser animals, but the sight of this strange apparition that smelled like a lion, but looked like nothing they ever had seen before, being led through the jungles by a giant Tarmangani was too much for even the more formidable denizens of the wild.

Sabor, the lioness, recognizing from a distance the scent of her lord and master intermingled with that of a Tarmangani and the hide of Horta, the boar, trotted through the aisles of the forest to investigate. Tarzan and Numa heard her coming, for she voiced a plaintive and questioning whine as the baffling mixture of odors aroused her curiosity and her fears, for lions, however terrible they may appear, are often timid animals and Sabor, being of the gentler sex, was, naturally, habitually inquisitive as well.

Tarzan unslung his spear for he knew that he might now easily have to fight to retain his prize. Numa halted and turned his outraged head in the direction of the coming she. He voiced a throaty growl that was almost a purr. Tarzan was upon the point of prodding him on again when Sabor broke into view, and behind her the ape-man saw that which gave him instant pause – four full-grown lions trailing the lioness.

To have goaded Numa then into active resistance might have brought the whole herd down upon him and so Tarzan waited to learn first what their attitude would be. He had no idea of relinquishing his lion without a battle; but knowing lions as he did, he knew that there was no assurance as to just what the newcomers would do.

The lioness was young and sleek, and the four males were in their prime – as handsome lions as he ever had seen. Three of the males were scantily maned but one, the foremost, carried a splendid, black mane that rippled in the breeze as he trotted majestically forward. The lioness halted a hundred feet from Tarzan, while the lions came on past her and stopped a few feet nearer. Their ears were upstanding and their eyes filled with curiosity. Tarzan could not even guess what they might do. The lion at his side faced them fully, standing silent now and watchful.

Suddenly the lioness gave vent to another little whine, at which Tarzan's lion voiced a terrific roar and leaped forward straight toward the beast of the black mane. The sight of this awesome creature with the strange face was too much for the lion toward which he leaped, dragging Tarzan after him, and with a growl the lion turned and fled, followed by his companions and the she.

Numa attempted to follow them; Tarzan held him in leash and when he turned upon him in rage, beat him unmercifully across the head with his spear. Shaking his head and growling, the lion at last moved off again in the direction they had been traveling; but it was an hour before he ceased to sulk. He was very hungry – half famished in fact – and consequently of an ugly temper, yet so thoroughly subdued by Tarzan's heroic methods of lion taming that he was presently pacing along at the ape-man's side like some huge St. Bernard.

It was dark when the two approached the British right, after a slight delay farther back because of a German patrol it had been necessary to elude. A short distance from the British line of out-guard sentinels Tarzan tied Numa to a tree and continued on alone. He evaded a sentinel, passed the out-guard and support, and by devious ways came again to Colonel Capell's headquarters, where he appeared before the officers gathered there as a disembodied spirit materializing out of thin air.

When they saw who it was that came thus unannounced they smiled and the colonel scratched his head in perplexity.

'Someone should be shot for this,' he said. 'I might just as well not establish an outpost if a man can filter through whenever he pleases.'

Tarzan smiled. 'Do not blame them,' he said, 'for I am not a man. I am Tarmangani. Any Mangani who wished to, could enter your camp almost at will; but if you have them for sentinels no one could enter without their knowledge.'

'What are the Mangani?' asked the colonel. 'Perhaps we might enlist a bunch of the beggars.'

Tarzan shook his head. 'They are the great apes,' he explained; 'my people; but you could not use them. They cannot concentrate long enough upon a single idea. If I told them of this they would be much interested for a short time – I might even hold the interest of a few long enough to get them here and explain their duties to them; but soon they would lose interest and when you needed them most they might be off in the forest searching for beetles instead of watching their posts. They have the minds of little children – that is why they remain what they are.'

'You call them Mangani and yourself Tarmangani – what is the difference?' asked Major Preswick.

'*Tar* means white,' replied Tarzan, 'and *Mangani*, great ape. My name – the name they gave me in the tribe of Kerchak – means White-skin. When I was a little balu my skin, I presume, looked very white indeed against the beautiful, black coat of Kala, my foster mother and so they called me Tarzan, the Tarmangani. They call you, too, Tarmangani,' he concluded, smiling.

Capell smiled. 'It is no reproach, Greystoke,' he said, 'and, by Jove, it would be a mark of distinction if a fellow could act the part. And now how about your plan? Do you still think you can empty the trench opposite our sector?'

'Is it still held by Gomangani?' asked Tarzan.

'What are Gomangani?' inquired the colonel. 'It is still held by native troops, if that is what you mean.'

'Yes,' replied the ape-man, 'the Gomangani are the great black apes – the Negroes.'

'What do you intend doing and what do you want us to do?' asked Capell.

Tarzan approached the table and placed a finger on the map. 'Here is a listening post,' he said; 'they have a machine gun in it. A tunnel connects it with this trench at this point.' His finger moved from place to place on the map as he talked. 'Give me a bomb and when you hear it burst in this listening post let your men start across No Man's Land slowly. Presently they will hear a commotion in the enemy trench; but they need not hurry, and, whatever they do, have them come quietly. You might also warn them that I may be in the trench and that I do not care to be shot or bayoneted.'

'And that is all?' queried Capell, after directing an officer to give Tarzan a hand grenade; 'You will empty the trench alone?'

'Not exactly alone,' replied Tarzan with a grim smile; 'but I shall empty it, and, by the way, your men may come in through the tunnel from the listening post if you prefer. In about half an hour, Colonel,' and he turned and left them.

As he passed through the camp there flashed suddenly upon the screen of recollection, conjured there by some reminder of his previous visit to headquarters, doubtless, the image of the officer he had passed as he quit the colonel that other time and simultaneously recognition of the face that had been revealed by the light from the fire. He shook his head dubiously. No, it could not be and yet the features of the young officer were identical with those of Fräulein Kircher, the German spy he had seen at German headquarters the night he took Major Schneider from under the nose of the Hun general and his staff.

Beyond the last line of sentinels Tarzan moved quickly in the direction of Numa, the lion. The beast was lying down as Tarzan approached, but he rose as the ape-man reached his side. A low whine escaped his muzzled lips. Tarzan smiled for he recognized in the new note almost a supplication – it was more like the whine of a hungry dog begging for food than the voice of the proud king of beasts.

'Soon you will kill – and feed,' he murmured in the vernacular of the great apes.

He unfastened the rope from about the tree and, with Numa close at his side, slunk into No Man's Land. There was little rifle fire and only an occasional shell vouched for the presence of artillery behind the opposing lines. As the shells from both sides were falling well back of the trenches, they constituted no menace to Tarzan; but the noise of them and that of the rifle fire had a marked effect upon Numa who crouched, trembling, close to the Tarmangani as though seeking protection.

Cautiously the two beasts moved forward toward the listening post of the Germans. In one hand Tarzan carried the bomb the English had given him, in the other was the coiled rope attached to the lion. At last Tarzan could see the position a few yards ahead. His keen eyes picked out the head and shoulders of the sentinel on watch. The ape-man grasped the bomb firmly in his right hand. He measured the distance with his eye and gathered his feet beneath him, then in a single motion he rose and threw the missile, immediately flattening himself prone upon the ground.

Five seconds later there was a terrific explosion in the center of the listening post. Numa gave a nervous start and attempted to break away; but Tarzan held him and, leaping to his feet, ran forward, dragging Numa after him. At the edge of the post he saw below him but slight evidence that the position had been occupied at all, for only a few shreds of tom flesh remained. About the only thing that had not been demolished was a machine gun which had been protected by sandbags.

There was not an instant to lose. Already a relief might be crawling through the communication tunnel, for it must have been evident to the sentinels in the Hun trenches that the listening post had been demolished. Numa hesitated to follow Tarzan into the excavation; but the ape-man, who was in no mood to temporize, jerked him roughly to the bottom. Before them lay the mouth of the tunnel that led back from No Man's Land to the German trenches. Tarzan pushed Numa forward until his head was almost in the aperture, then as though it were an afterthought, he turned quickly and, taking the machine gun from the parapet, placed it in the bottom of the hole close at hand, after which he turned again to Numa, and with his knife quickly cut the garters that held the bags upon his front paws. Before the lion could know that a part of his formidable armament was again released for action, Tarzan had cut the rope from his neck and the head bag from his face, and grabbing the lion from the rear had thrust him partially into the mouth of the tunnel.

Then Numa balked, only to feel the sharp prick of Tarzan's knife point in his hindquarters. Goading him on the ape-man finally succeeded in getting the lion sufficiently far into the tunnel so that there was no chance of his escaping other than by going forward or deliberately backing into the sharp blade at his rear. Then Tarzan cut the bags from the great hind feet, placed his shoulder and his knife point against Numa's seat, dug his toes into the loose earth that had been broken up by the explosion of the bomb, and shoved.

Inch by inch at first Numa advanced. He was growling now and presently he commenced to roar. Suddenly he leaped forward and Tarzan knew that he had caught the scent of meat ahead. Dragging the machine gun beside him the ape-man followed quickly after the lion whose roars he could plainly hear ahead mingled with the unmistakable screams of frightened men. Once again a grim smile touched the lips of this man-beast.

'They murdered my Waziri,' he muttered; 'they crucified Wasimbu, son of Muviro.'

When Tarzan reached the trench and emerged into it there was no one in sight in that particular bay, nor in the next, nor the next as he hurried forward in the direction of the German center; but in the fourth bay he saw a dozen men jammed in the angle of the traverse at the end while leaping upon them and rending with talons and fangs was Numa, a terrific incarnation of ferocity and ravenous hunger.

Whatever held the men at last gave way as they fought madly with one another in their efforts to escape this dread creature that from their infancy had filled them with terror, and again they were retreating. Some clambered over the parados and some even over the parapet, preferring the dangers of No Man's Land to this other soul-searing menace.

As the British advanced slowly toward the German trenches, they first met terrified blacks who ran into their arms only too willing to surrender. That pandemonium had broken loose in the Hun trench was apparent to the Rhodesians not only from the appearance of the deserters, but from the sounds of screaming, cursing men which came clearly to their ears; but there was one that baffled them for it resembled nothing more closely than the infuriated growling of an angry lion.

And when at last they reached the trench, those farthest on the left of the advancing Britishers heard a machine gun sputter suddenly before them and saw a huge lion leap over the German parados with the body of a screaming Hun soldier between his jaws and vanish into the shadows of the night, while squatting upon a traverse to their left was Tarzan of the Apes with a machine gun before him with which he was raking the length of the German trenches.

The foremost Rhodesians saw something else – they saw a huge German officer emerge from a dugout just in rear of the ape-man. They saw him snatch up a discarded rifle with bayonet fixed and creep up on the apparently unconscious Tarzan. They ran forward, shouting warnings; but above the pandemonium of the trenches and the machine gun their voices could not reach him. The German leaped upon the parapet behind him – the fat hands raised the rifle butt aloft for the cowardly downward thrust into the naked back and then, as moves Ara, the lightning, moved Tarzan of the Apes.

It was no man who leaped forward upon that Boche officer, striking aside the sharp bayonet as one might strike aside a straw in a baby's hand – it was a wild beast and the roar of a wild beast was upon those savage lips, for as that strange sense that Tarzan owned in common with the other jungle-bred creatures of his wild domain warned him of the presence behind him and he had whirled to meet the attack, his eyes had seen the corps and regimental insignia upon the other's blouse – it was the same as that worn by the murderers of his wife and his people, by the despoilers of his home and his happiness.

It was a wild beast whose teeth fastened upon the shoulder of the Hun – it was a wild beast whose talons sought that fat neck. And then the boys of the Second Rhodesian Regiment saw that which will live forever in their memories. They saw the giant ape-man pick the heavy German from the ground and shake him as a terrier might shake a rat – as Sabor, the lioness, sometimes shakes her prey. They saw the eyes of the Hun bulge in horror as he vainly struck with his futile hands against the massive chest and head of his assailant. They saw Tarzan suddenly spin the man about and placing a knee in the middle of his back and an arm about his neck bend his shoulders slowly backward. The German's knees gave and he sank upon them; but still that irresistible force bent him further and further. He screamed in agony for a moment – then something snapped and Tarzan cast him aside, a limp and lifeless thing.

The Rhodesians started forward, a cheer upon their lips – a cheer that never was uttered – a cheer that froze in their throats, for at that moment Tarzan placed a foot upon the carcass of his kill and, raising his face to the heavens, gave voice to the weird and terrifying victory cry of the bull ape.

Underlieutenant von Goss was dead.

Without a backward glance at the awestruck soldiers Tarzan leaped the trench and was gone.

5
The Golden Locket

The little British army in East Africa, after suffering severe reverses at the hands of a numerically much superior force, was at last coming into its own. The German offensive had been broken and the Huns were now slowly and doggedly retreating along the railway to Tanga. The break in the German lines had followed the clearing of a section of their left-flank trenches of native soldiers by Tarzan and Numa, the lion, upon that memorable night that the ape-man had loosed a famishing man-eater among the superstitious and terror-stricken blacks. The Second Rhodesian Regiment had immediately taken possession of the abandoned trench and from this position their flanking fire had raked contiguous sections of the German line, the diversion rendering possible a successful night attack on the part of the balance of the British forces.

Weeks had elapsed. The Germans were contesting stubbornly every mile of waterless, thorn-covered ground and clinging desperately to their positions along the railway. The officers of the Second Rhodesians had seen nothing more of Tarzan of the Apes since he had slain Underlieutenant von Goss and disappeared toward the very heart of the German position, and there were those among them who believed that he had been killed within the enemy lines.

'They may have killed him,' assented Colonel Capell, 'but I fancy they never captured the beggar alive.'

Nor had they, nor killed him either. Tarzan had spent those intervening weeks pleasantly and profitably. He had amassed a considerable fund of knowledge concerning the disposition and strength of German troops, their methods of warfare, and the various ways in which a lone Tarmangani might annoy an army and lower its morale.

At present he was prompted by a specific desire. There was a certain German spy whom he wished to capture alive and take back to the British. When he had made his first visit to German headquarters, he had seen a young woman deliver a paper to the German general, and later he had seen that same young woman within the British lines in the uniform of a British officer. The conclusions were obvious – she was a spy.

And so Tarzan haunted German headquarters upon many nights hoping to see her again or to pick up some clue as to her whereabouts, and at the same time he utilized many an artifice whereby he might bring terror to the hearts of the Germans. That he was successful was often demonstrated by the snatches of conversation he overheard as he prowled through the German camps. One night as he lay concealed in the bushes close beside a regimental headquarters he listened to the conversation of several Boche officers. One of the men reverted to the stories told by the native troops in connection with their rout by a lion several weeks before and the simultaneous appearance in their trenches of a naked, white giant whom they were perfectly assured was some demon of the jungle.

'The fellow must have been the same as he who leaped into the general's headquarters and carried off Schneider,' asserted one. 'I wonder how he happened to single out the poor major. They say the creature seemed interested in no one but Schneider. He had von Kelter in his grasp, and he might easily have taken the general himself; but he ignored them all except Schneider. Him he pursued about the room, seized and carried off into the night. Gott knows what his fate was.'

'Captain Fritz Schneider has some sort of theory,' said another. 'He told me only a week or two ago that he thinks he knows why his brother was taken – that it was a case of mistaken identity. He was not so sure about it until von Goss was killed, apparently by the same creature, the night the lion entered the trenches. Von Goss was attached to Schneider's company. One of Schneider's men was found with his neck wrung the same night that the major was carried off and Schneider thinks that this devil is after him and his command – that it came for him that night and got his brother by mistake. He says Kraut told him that in presenting the major to Fräulein Kircher the former's name was no sooner spoken than this wild man leaped through the window and made for him.'

Suddenly the little group became rigid – listening. 'What was that?' snapped one, eyeing the bushes from which a smothered snarl had issued as Tarzan of the Apes realized that through his mistake the perpetrator of the horrid crime at his bungalow still lived – that the murderer of his wife went yet unpunished.

For a long minute the officers stood with tensed nerves, every eye riveted upon the bushes from whence the ominous sound had issued. Each recalled recent mysterious disappearances from the heart of camps as well as from lonely out-guards. Each thought of the silent dead he had seen, slain almost within sight of their fellows by some unseen creature. They thought of the marks upon dead throats – made by talons or by giant fingers, they could not tell which – and those upon shoulders and jugulars where powerful teeth had fastened and they waited with drawn pistols.

Once the bushes moved almost imperceptibly and an instant later one of the officers, without warning, fired into them; but Tarzan of the Apes was not there. In the interval between the moving of the bushes and the firing of the shot he had melted into the night. Ten minutes later he was hovering on the outskirts of that part of camp where were bivouacked for the night the black soldiers of a native company commanded by one Hauptmann Fritz Schneider. The men were stretched upon the ground without tents; but there were tents pitched for the officers. Toward these Tarzan crept. It was slow and perilous work, as the Germans were now upon the alert for the uncanny foe that crept into their camps to take his toll by night, yet the ape-man passed their sentinels, eluded the vigilance of the interior guard, and crept at last to the rear of the officers' line.

Here he flattened himself against the ground close behind the nearest tent and listened. From within came the regular breathing of a sleeping man – one only. Tarzan was satisfied. With his knife he cut the tie strings of the rear flap and entered. He made no noise. The shadow of a falling leaf, floating gently to earth upon a still day, could have been no more soundless. He moved to the side of the sleeping man and bent low over him. He could not know, of course, whether it was Schneider or another, as he had never seen Schneider; but he meant to know and to know even more. Gently he shook the man by the shoulder. The fellow turned heavily and grunted in a thick guttural.

'Silence!' admonished the ape-man in a low whisper. 'Silence – I kill.'

The Hun opened his eyes. In the dim light he saw a giant figure bending over him. Now a mighty hand grasped his shoulder and another closed lightly about his throat.

'Make no outcry,' commanded Tarzan, 'but answer in a whisper my questions. What is your name?'

'Luberg,' replied the officer. He was trembling. The weird presence of this naked giant filled him with dread. He, too, recalled the men mysteriously murdered in the still watches of the night camps. 'What do you want?'

'Where is Hauptmann Fritz Schneider?' asked Tarzan. 'Which is his tent?'

'He is not here,' replied Luberg. 'He was sent to Wilhelmstal yesterday.'

'I shall not kill you – now,' said the ape-man. 'First I shall go and learn if you have lied to me and if you have your death shall be the more terrible. Do you know how Major Schneider died?'

Luberg shook his head negatively.

'I do,' continued Tarzan, 'and it was not a nice way to die – even for an accursed German. Turn over with your face down and cover your eyes. Do not move or make any sound.'

The man did as he was bid and the instant that his eyes were turned away, Tarzan slipped from the tent. An hour later he was outside the German camp and headed for the little hill town of Wilhelmstal, the summer seat of government of German East Africa.

Fräulein Bertha Kircher was lost. She was humiliated and angry – it was long before she would admit it, that she, who prided herself upon her woodcraft, was lost in this little patch of country between the Pangani and the Tanga railway. She knew that Wilhelmstal lay southeast of her about fifty miles; but, through a combination of untoward circumstances, she found herself unable to determine which was southeast.

In the first place she had set out from German headquarters on a well-marked road that was being traveled by troops and with every reason to believe that she would follow that road to Wilhelmstal. Later she had been warned from this road by word that a strong British patrol had come down the west bank of the Pangani, effected a crossing south of her, and was even then marching on the railway at Tonda.

After leaving the road she found herself in thick bush and as the sky was heavily overcast she presently had recourse to her compass and it was not until then that she discovered to her dismay that she did not have it with her. So sure was she of her woodcraft, however, that she continued on in the direction she thought west until she had covered sufficient distance to warrant her in feeling assured that, by now turning south, she could pass safely in rear of the British patrol.

Nor did she commence to feel any doubts until long after she had again turned toward the east well south, as she thought, of the patrol. It was late afternoon – she should long since have struck the road again south of Tonda; but she had found no road and now she began to feel real anxiety.

Her horse had traveled all day without food or water, night was approaching and with it a realization that she was hopelessly lost in a wild and trackless country notorious principally for its tsetse flies and savage beasts. It was maddening to know that she had absolutely no knowledge of the direction she was traveling – that she might be forging steadily farther from the railway, deeper into the gloomy and forbidding country toward the Pangani; yet it was impossible to stop – she must go on.

Bertha Kircher was no coward, whatever else she may have been; but as night began to close down around her she could not shut out from her mind entirely contemplation of the terrors of the long hours ahead before the rising sun should dissipate the Stygian gloom – the horrid jungle night – that lures forth all the prowling, preying creatures of destruction.

She found, just before dark, an open meadowlike break in the almost interminable bush. There was a small clump of trees near the center and here she decided to camp. The grass was high and thick, affording feed for her horse and a bed for herself, and there was more than enough dead wood lying about the trees to furnish a good fire well through the night. Removing the saddle and bridle from her mount she placed them at the foot of a tree and then picketed the animal close by. Then she busied herself collecting firewood and by the time darkness had fallen she had a good fire and enough wood to last until morning.

From her saddlebags she took cold food and from her canteen a swallow of water. She could not afford more than a small swallow for she could not know how long a time it might be before she should find more. It filled her with sorrow that her poor horse must go waterless, for even German spies may have hearts and this one was very young and very feminine.

It was now dark. There was neither moon nor stars and the light from her fire only accentuated the blackness beyond. She could see the grass about her and the boles of the trees which stood out in brilliant relief against the solid background of impenetrable night, and beyond the firelight there was nothing.

The jungle seemed ominously quiet. Far away in the distance she heard faintly the boom of big guns; but she could not locate their direction. She strained her ears until her nerves were on the point of breaking; but she could not tell from whence the sound came. And it meant so much to her to know, for the battle lines were north of her and if she could but locate the direction of the firing she would know which way to go in the morning.

In the morning! Would she live to see another morning? She squared her shoulders and shook herself together. Such thoughts must be banished – they would never do. Bravely she hummed an air as she arranged her saddle near the fire and pulled a quantity of long grass to make a comfortable seat over which she spread her saddle blanket. Then she unstrapped a heavy, military coat from the cantle of her saddle and donned it, for the air was already chill.

Seating herself where she could lean against the saddle she prepared to maintain a sleepless vigil throughout the night. For an hour the silence was broken only by the distant booming of the guns and the low noises of the feeding horse and then, from possibly a mile away, came the rumbling thunder of a lion's roar. The girl started and laid her hand upon the rifle at her side. A little shudder ran through her slight frame and she could feel the goose-flesh rise upon her body.

Again and again was the awful sound repeated and each time she was certain that it came nearer. She could locate the direction of this sound although she could not that of the guns, for the origin of the former was much closer. The lion was upwind and so could not have caught her scent as yet, though he might be approaching to investigate the light of the fire which could doubtless be seen for a considerable distance.

For another fear-filled hour the girl sat straining her eyes and ears out into the black void beyond her little island of light. During all that time the lion did not roar again; but there was constantly the sensation that it was creeping up on her. Again and again she would start and turn to peer into the blackness beyond the trees behind her as her overwrought nerves conjured the stealthy fall of padded feet. She held the rifle across her knees at the ready now and she was trembling from head to foot.

Suddenly her horse raised his head and snorted, and with a little cry of terror the girl sprang to her feet. The animal turned and trotted back toward her until the picket rope brought him to a stand, and then he wheeled about and with ears up-pricked gazed out into the night; but the girl could neither see nor hear aught.

Still another hour of terror passed during which the horse often raised his head to peer long and searchingly into the dark. The girl replenished the fire from time to time. She found herself becoming very sleepy. Her heavy lids persisted in drooping; but she dared not sleep. Fearful lest she might be overcome by the drowsiness that was stealing through her she rose and walked briskly to and fro, then she threw some more wood on the fire, walked over and stroked her horse's muzzle and returned to her seat.

Leaning against the saddle she tried to occupy her mind with plans for the morrow; but she must have dozed. With a start she awoke. It was broad daylight. The hideous night with its indescribable terrors was gone.

She could scarce believe the testimony of her senses. She had slept for hours, the fire was out and yet she and the horse were safe and alive, nor was there sign of savage beast about. And, best of all, the sun was shining, pointing the straight road to the east. Hastily she ate a few mouthfuls of her precious rations, which with a swallow of water constituted her breakfast. Then she saddled her horse and mounted. Already she felt that she was as good as safe in Wilhelmstal.

Possibly, however, she might have revised her conclusions could she have seen the two pairs of eyes watching her every move intently from different points in the bush.

Lighthearted and unsuspecting, the girl rode across the clearing toward the bush while directly before her two yellow-green eyes glared round and terrible, a tawny tail twitched nervously and great, padded paws gathered beneath a sleek barrel for a mighty spring. The horse was almost at the edge of the bush when Numa, the lion, launched himself through the air. He struck the animal's right shoulder at the instant that it reared, terrified, to wheel in flight. The force of the impact hurled the horse backward to the ground and so quickly that the girl had no opportunity to extricate herself; but fell to the earth with her mount, her left leg pinned beneath its body.

Horror-stricken, she saw the king of beasts open his mighty jaws and seize the screaming creature by the back of its neck. The great jaws closed, there was an instant's struggle as Numa shook his prey. She could hear the vertebrae crack as the mighty fangs crunched through them, and then the muscles of her faithful friend relaxed in death.

Numa crouched upon his kill. His terrifying eyes riveted themselves upon the girl's face – she could feel his hot breath upon her cheek and the odor of the fetid vapor nauseated her. For what seemed an eternity to the girl the two lay staring at each other and then the lion uttered a menacing growl.

Never before had Bertha Kircher been so terrified – never before had she had such cause for terror. At her hip was a pistol – a formidable weapon with which to face a man; but a puny thing indeed with which to menace the great beast before her. She knew that at best it could but enrage him and yet she meant to sell her life dearly, for she felt that she must die. No human succor could have availed her even had it been there to offer itself. For a moment she tore her gaze from the hypnotic fascination of that awful face and breathed a last prayer to her God. She did not ask for aid, for she felt that she was beyond even divine succor – she only asked that the end might come quickly and with as little pain as possible.

No one can prophesy what a lion will do in any given emergency. This one glared and growled at the girl for a moment and then fell to feeding upon the dead horse. Fräulein Kircher wondered for an instant and then attempted to draw her leg cautiously from beneath the body of her mount; but she could not budge it. She increased the force of her efforts and Numa looked up from his feeding to growl again. The girl desisted. She hoped that he might satisfy his hunger and then depart to lie up; but she could not believe that he would leave her there alive. Doubtless he would drag the remains of his kill into the bush for hiding and, as there could be no doubt that he considered her part of his prey, he would certainly come back for her, or possibly drag her in first and kill her.

Again Numa fell to feeding. The girl's nerves were at the breaking point. She wondered that she had not fainted under the strain of terror and shock. She recalled that she often had wished she might see a lion, close to, make a kill and feed upon it. God! how realistically her wish had been granted.

Again she bethought herself of her pistol. As she had fallen, the holster had slipped around so that the weapon now lay beneath her. Very slowly she reached for it; but in so doing she was forced to raise her body from the ground. Instantly the lion was aroused. With the swiftness of a cat he reached across the carcass of the horse and placed a heavy, taloned paw upon her breast, crushing her back to earth, and all the time he growled and snarled horribly. His face was a picture of frightful rage incarnate. For a moment neither moved and then from behind her the girl heard a human voice uttering bestial sounds.

Numa suddenly looked up from the girl's face at the thing beyond her. His growls increased to roars as he drew back, ripping the front of the girl's waist almost from her body with his long talons, exposing her white bosom, which through some miracle of chance the great claws did not touch.

Tarzan of the Apes had witnessed the entire encounter from the moment that Numa had leaped upon his prey. For some time before, he had been watching the girl, and after the lion attacked her he had at first been minded to let Numa have his way with her. What was she but a hated German and a spy besides? He had seen her at General Kraut's headquarters in conference with the German staff and again he had seen her within the British lines masquerading as a British officer. It was the latter thought that prompted him to interfere. Doubtless General Jan Smuts would be glad to meet and question her. She might be forced to divulge information of value to the British commander before Smuts had her shot.

Tarzan had recognized not only the girl, but the lion as well. All lions may look alike to you and me; but not so to their intimates of the jungle. Each has his individual characteristics of face and form and gait as well defined as those that differentiate members of the human family, and besides these the creatures of the jungle have a still more positive test – that of scent. Each of us, man or beast, has his own peculiar odor, and it is mostly by this that the beasts of the jungle, endowed with miraculous powers of scent, recognize individuals.

It is the final proof. You have seen it demonstrated a thousand times – a dog recognizes your voice and looks at you. He knows your face and figure. Good, there can be no doubt in his mind but that it is you; but is he satisfied? No, sir – he must come up and smell of you. All his other senses may be fallible, but not his sense of smell, and so he makes assurance positive by the final test.

Tarzan recognized Numa as he whom he had muzzled with the hide of Horta, the boar – as he whom he handled by a rope for two days and finally loosed in a German frontline trench, and he knew that Numa would recognize him – that he would remember the sharp spear that had goaded him into submission and obedience and Tarzan hoped that the lesson he had learned still remained with the lion.

Now he came forward calling to Numa in the language of the great apes – warning him away from the girl. It is open to question that Numa, the lion, understood him; but he did understand the menace of the heavy spear that the Tarmangani carried so readily in his brown, right hand, and so he drew back, growling, trying to decide in his little brain whether to charge or flee.

On came the ape-man with never a pause, straight for the lion. 'Go away, Numa,' he cried, 'or Tarzan will tie you up again and lead you through the jungle without food. See Arad, my spear! Do you recall how his point stuck into you and how with his haft I beat you over the head? Go, Numa! I am Tarzan of the Apes!'

Numa wrinkled the skin of his face into great folds, until his eyes almost disappeared and he growled and roared and snarled and growled again, and when the spear point came at last quite close to him he struck at it viciously with his armed paw; but he drew back. Tarzan stepped over the dead horse and the girl lying behind him gazed in wide-eyed astonishment at the handsome figure driving an angry lion deliberately from its kill.

When Numa had retreated a few yards, the ape-man called back to the girl in perfect German, 'Are you badly hurt?'

'I think not,' she replied, 'but I cannot extricate my foot from beneath my horse.'

'Try again,' commanded Tarzan. 'I do not know how long I can hold Numa thus.'

The girl struggled frantically; but at last she sank back upon an elbow.

'It is impossible,' she called to him.

He backed slowly until he was again beside the horse, when he reached down and grasped the cinch, which was still intact. Then with one hand he raised the carcass from the ground. The girl freed herself and rose to her feet.

'You can walk?' asked Tarzan.

'Yes,' she said, 'my leg is numb; but it does not seem to be injured.'

'Good,' commented the ape-man. 'Back slowly away behind me – make no sudden movements. I think he will not charge.'

With utmost deliberation the two backed toward the bush. Numa stood for a moment, growling, then he followed them, slowly. Tarzan wondered if he would come beyond his kill or if he would stop there. If he followed them beyond, then they could look for a charge, and if Numa charged it was very likely that he would get one of them. When the lion reached the carcass of the horse Tarzan stopped and so did Numa, as Tarzan had thought that he would and the ape-man waited to see what the lion would do next. He eyed them for a moment, snarled angrily and then looked down at the tempting meat. Presently he crouched upon his kill and resumed feeding.

The girl breathed a deep sigh of relief as she and the ape-man resumed their slow retreat with only an occasional glance from the lion, and when at last they reached the bush and had turned and entered it, she felt a sudden giddiness overwhelm her so that she staggered and would have fallen had Tarzan not caught her. It was only a moment before she regained control of herself.

'I could not help it,' she said, in half apology. 'I was so close to death – such a horrible death – it unnerved me for an instant; but I am all right now. How can I ever thank you? It was so wonderful – you did not seem to fear the frightful creature in the least; yet he was afraid of you. Who are you?'

'He knows me,' replied Tarzan, grimly – 'that is why he fears me.'

He was standing facing the girl now and for the first time he had a chance to look at her squarely and closely. She was very beautiful – that was undeniable; but Tarzan realized her beauty only in a subconscious way. It was superficial – it did not color her soul which must be black as sin. She was German – a German spy. He hated her and desired only to compass her destruction; but he would choose the manner so that it would work most grievously against the enemy cause.

He saw her naked breasts where Numa had torn her clothing from her and dangling there against the soft, white flesh he saw that which brought a sudden scowl of surprise and anger to his face – the diamond-studded, golden locket of his youth – the love token that had been stolen from the breast of his mate by Schneider, the Hun. The girl saw the scowl but did not interpret it correctly. Tarzan grasped her roughly by the arm.

'Where did you get this?' he demanded, as he tore the bauble from her.

The girl drew herself to her full height. 'Take your hand from me,' she demanded, but the ape-man paid no attention to her words, only seizing her more forcibly.

'Answer me!' he snapped. 'Where did you get this?'

'What is it to you?' she countered.

'It is mine,' he replied. 'Tell me who gave it to you or I will throw you back to Numa.'

'You would do that?' she asked.

'Why not?' he queried. 'You are a spy and spies must die if they are caught.'

'You were going to kill me, then?'

'I was going to take you to headquarters. They would dispose of you there; but Numa can do it quite as effectively. Which do you prefer?'

'Hauptmann Fritz Schneider gave it to me,' she said.

'Headquarters it will be then,' said Tarzan. 'Come!' The girl moved at his side through the bush and all the time her mind worked quickly. They were moving east, which suited her, and as long as they continued to move east she was glad to have the protection of the great, white savage. She speculated much upon the fact that her pistol still swung at her hip. The man must be mad not to take it from her.

'What makes you think I am a spy?' she asked after a long silence.

'I saw you at German headquarters,' he replied, 'and then again inside the British lines.'

She could not let him take her back to them. She must reach Wilhelmstal at once and she was determined to do so even if she must have recourse to her pistol. She cast a side glance at the tall figure. What a magnificent creature! But yet he was a brute who would kill her or have her killed if she did not slay him. And the locket! She must have that back – it must not fail to reach Wilhelmstal. Tarzan was now a foot or two ahead of her as the path was very narrow. Cautiously she drew her pistol. A single shot would suffice and he was so close that she could not miss. As she figured it all out her eyes rested on the brown skin with the graceful muscles rolling beneath it and the perfect limbs and head and the carriage that a proud king of old might have envied. A wave of revulsion for her contemplated act surged through her. No, she could not do it – yet, she must be free and she must regain possession of the locket. And then, almost blindly, she swung the weapon up and struck Tarzan heavily upon the back of the head with its butt. Like a felled ox he dropped in his tracks.

6

Vengeance and Mercy

It was an hour later that Sheeta, the panther, hunting, chanced to glance upward into the blue sky where his attention was attracted by Ska, the vulture, circling slowly above the bush a mile away and downwind. For a long minute the yellow eyes stared intently at the gruesome bird. They saw Ska dive and rise again to continue his ominous circling and in these movements their woodcraft read that which, while obvious to Sheets, would doubtless have meant nothing to you or me.

The hunting cat guessed that on the ground beneath Ska was some living thing of flesh – either a beast feeding upon its kill or a dying animal that Ska did not yet dare attack. In either event it might prove meat for Sheeta, and so the wary feline stalked by a circuitous route, upon soft, padded feet that gave forth no sound, until the circling *aasvogel* and his intended prey were upwind. Then, sniffing each vagrant zephyr, Sheeta, the panther, crept cautiously forward, nor had he advanced any considerable distance before his keen nostrils were rewarded with the scent of man – a Tarmangani.

Sheeta paused. He was not a hunter of men. He was young and in his prime; but always before he had avoided this hated presence. Of late he had become more accustomed to it with the passing of many soldiers through his ancient hunting ground, and as the soldiers had frightened away a great part of the game Sheeta had been wont to feed upon, the days had been lean, and Sheeta was hungry.

The circling Ska suggested that this Tarmangani might be helpless and upon the point of dying, else Ska would not have been interested in him, and so easy prey for Sheeta. With this thought in mind the cat resumed his stalking. Presently he pushed through the thick bush and his yellow-green eyes rested gloatingly upon the body of an almost naked Tarmangani lying facedown in a narrow game trail.

Numa, sated, rose from the carcass of Bertha Kircher's horse and seized the partially devoured body by the neck and dragged it into the bush; then he started east toward the lair where he had left his mate. Being uncomfortably full he was inclined to be sleepy and far from belligerent. He moved slowly and majestically with no effect at silence or concealment. The king walked abroad, unafraid.

With an occasional regal glance to right or left he moved along a narrow game trail until at a turn he came to a sudden stop at what lay revealed before him – Sheeta, the panther, creeping stealthily upon the almost naked body of a Tarmangani lying facedown in the deep dust of the pathway. Numa glared intently at the quiet body in the dust. Recognition came. It was *his* Tarmangani. A low growl of warning rumbled from his throat and Sheeta halted with one paw upon Tarzan's back and turned suddenly to eye the intruder.

What passed within those savage brains? Who may say? The panther seemed to be debating the wisdom of defending his find, for he growled horribly as though warning Numa away from the prey. And Numa? Was the idea of property rights dominating his thoughts? The Tarmangani was his, or he was the Tarmangani's. Had not the Great White Ape mastered and subdued him and, too, had he not fed him? Numa recalled the fear that he had felt of this man-thing and his cruel spear; but in savage brains fear is more likely to engender respect than hatred and so Numa found that he respected the creature who had subdued and mastered him. He saw Sheeta, upon whom he looked with contempt, daring to molest the master of the lion. Jealousy and greed alone might have been sufficient to prompt Numa to drive Sheeta away, even though the lion was not sufficiently hungry to devour the flesh that he thus wrested from the lesser cat; but then, too, there was in the little brain within the massive head a sense of loyalty, and perhaps this it was that sent Numa quickly forward, growling, toward the spitting Sheeta.

For a moment the latter stood his ground with arched back and snarling face, for all the world like a great, spotted tabby.

Numa had not felt like fighting; but the sight of Sheeta daring to dispute his rights kindled his ferocious brain to sudden fire. His rounded eyes glared with rage, his undulating tail snapped to stiff erectness as, with a frightful roar, he charged this presuming vassal.

It came so suddenly and from so short a distance that Sheeta had no chance to turn and flee the rush, and so he met it with raking talons and snapping jaws; but the odds were all against him. To the larger fangs and the more powerful jaws of his adversary were added huge talons and the preponderance of the lion's great weight. At the first clash Sheeta was crushed and, though he deliberately fell upon his back and drew up his powerful hind legs beneath Numa with the intention of disemboweling him, the lion forestalled him and at the same time closed his awful jaws upon Sheeta's throat.

It was soon over. Numa rose, shaking himself, and stood above the torn and mutilated body of his foe. His own sleek coat was cut and the red blood trickled down his flank; though it was but a minor injury, it angered him. He glared down at the dead panther and then, in a fit of rage, he seized and mauled the body only to drop it in a moment, lower his head, voice a single terrific roar, and turn toward the ape-man.

Approaching the still form he sniffed it over from head to foot. Then he placed a huge paw upon it and turned it over with its face up. Again he smelled about the body and at last with his rough tongue licked Tarzan's face. It was then that Tarzan opened his eyes.

Above him towered the huge lion, its hot breath upon his face, its rough tongue upon his cheek. The ape-man had often been close to death; but never before so close as this, he thought, for he was convinced that death was but a matter of seconds. His brain was still numb from the effects of the blow that had felled him, and so he did not, for a moment, recognize the lion that stood over him as the one he had so recently encountered.

Presently, however, recognition dawned upon him and with it a realization of the astounding fact that Numa did not seem bent on devouring him – at least not immediately. His position was a delicate one. The lion stood astraddle Tarzan with his front paws. The ape-man could not rise, therefore, without pushing the lion away and whether Numa would tolerate being pushed was an open question. Too, the beast might consider him already dead and any movement that indicated the contrary was true would, in all likelihood, arouse the killing instinct of the man-eater.

But Tarzan was tiring of the situation. He was in no mood to lie there forever, especially when he contemplated the fact that the girl spy who had tried to brain him was undoubtedly escaping as rapidly as possible.

Numa was looking right into his eyes now evidently aware that he was alive. Presently the lion cocked his head on one side and whined. Tarzan knew the note, and he knew that it spelled neither rage nor hunger, and then he risked all on a single throw, encouraged by that low whine.

'Move, Numa!' he commanded and placing a palm against the tawny shoulder he pushed the lion aside. Then he rose and with a hand on his hunting knife awaited that which might follow. It was then that his eyes fell for the first time on the torn body of Sheeta. He looked from the dead cat to the live one and saw the marks of conflict upon the latter, too, and in an instant realized something of what had happened – Numa had saved him from the panther!

It seemed incredible and yet the evidence pointed clearly to the fact. He turned toward the lion and without fear approached and examined his wounds which he found superficial, and as Tarzan knelt beside him Numa rubbed an itching ear against the naked, brown shoulder. Then the ape-man stroked the great head, picked up his spear, and looked about for the trail of the girl. This he soon found leading toward the east, and as he set out upon it something prompted him to feel for the locket he had hung about his neck. It was gone!

No trace of anger was apparent upon the ape-man's face unless it was a slight tightening of the jaws; but he put his hand ruefully to the back of his head where a bump marked the place where the girl had struck him and a moment later a half-smile played across his lips. He could not help but admit that she had tricked him neatly, and that it must have taken nerve to do the thing she did and to set out armed only with a pistol through the trackless waste that lay between them and the railway and beyond into the hills where Wilhelmstal lies.

Tarzan admired courage. He was big enough to admit it and admire it even in a German spy, but he saw that in this case it only added to her resourcefulness and made her all the more dangerous and the necessity for putting her out of the way paramount. He hoped to overtake her before she reached Wilhelmstal and so he set out at the swinging trot that he could hold for hours at a stretch without apparent fatigue.

That the girl could hope to reach the town on foot in less than two days seemed improbable, for it was a good thirty miles and part of it hilly. Even as the thought crossed his mind he heard the whistle of a locomotive to the east and knew that the railway was in operation again after a shutdown of several days. If the train was going south the girl would signal it if she had reached the right of way. His keen ears caught the whining of brake shoes on wheels and a few minutes later the signal blast for brakes off. The train had stopped and started again and, as it gained headway and greater distance, Tarzan could tell from the direction of the sound that it was moving south.

The ape-man followed the trail to the railway where it ended abruptly on the west side of the track, showing that the girl had boarded the train, just as he thought. There was nothing now but to follow on to Wilhelmstal, where he hoped to find Captain Fritz Schneider, as well as the girl, and to recover his diamond-studded locket.

It was dark when Tarzan reached the little hill town of Wilhelmstal. He loitered on the outskirts, getting his bearings and trying to determine how an almost naked white man might explore the village without arousing suspicion. There were many soldiers about and the town was under guard, for he could see a lone sentinel walking his post scarce a hundred yards from him. To elude this one would not be difficult; but to enter the village and search it would be practically impossible, garbed, or un-garbed, as he was.

Creeping forward, taking advantage of every cover, lying flat and motionless when the sentry's face was toward him, the ape-man at last reached the sheltering shadows of an outhouse just inside the lines. From there he moved stealthily from building to building until at last he was discovered by a large dog in the rear of one of the bungalows. The brute came slowly toward him, growling. Tarzan stood motionless beside a tree. He could see a light in the bungalow and uniformed men moving about and he hoped that the dog would not bark. He did not; but he growled more savagely and, just at the moment that the rear door of the bungalow opened and a man stepped out, the animal charged.

He was a large dog, as large as Dango, the hyena, and he charged with all the vicious impetuosity of Numa, the lion. As he came Tarzan knelt and the dog shot through the air for his throat; but he was dealing with no man now and he found his quickness more than matched by the quickness of the Tarmangani. His teeth never reached the soft flesh – strong fingers, fingers of steel, seized his neck. He voiced a single startled yelp and clawed at the naked breast before him with his talons; but he was powerless. The mighty fingers closed upon his throat; the man rose, snapped the clawing body once, and cast it aside. At the same time a voice from the open bungalow door called: 'Simba!'

There was no response. Repeating the call the man descended the steps and advanced toward the tree. In the light from the doorway Tarzan could see that he was a tall, broad-shouldered man in the uniform of a German officer. The ape-man withdrew into the shadow of the tree's stem. The man came closer, still calling the dog – he did not see the savage beast, crouching now in the shadow, awaiting him. When he had approached within ten feet of the Tarmangani, Tarzan leaped upon him – as Sabor springs to the kill, so sprang the ape-man. The momentum and weight of his body hurled the German to the ground, powerful fingers prevented an outcry and, though the officer struggled, he had no chance and a moment later lay dead beside the body of the dog.

As Tarzan stood for a moment looking down upon his kill and regretting that he could not risk voicing his beloved victory cry, the sight of the uniform suggested a means whereby he might pass to and fro through Wilhelmstal with the minimum chance of detection. Ten minutes later a tall, broad-shouldered officer stepped from the yard of the bungalow leaving behind him the corpses of a dog and a naked man.

He walked boldly along the little street and those who passed him could not guess that beneath Imperial Germany's uniform beat a savage heart that pulsed with implacable hatred for the Hun. Tarzan's first concern was to locate the hotel, for here he guessed he would find the girl, and where the girl was doubtless would be Hauptmann Fritz Schneider, who was either her confederate, her sweetheart, or both, and there, too, would be Tarzan's precious locket.

He found the hotel at last, a low, two-storied building with a veranda. There were lights on both floors and people, mostly officers, could be seen within. The ape-man considered entering and inquiring for those he sought; but his better judgment finally prompted him to reconnoiter first. Passing around the building he looked into all the lighted rooms on the first floor and, seeing neither of those for whom he had come, he swung lightly to the roof of the veranda and continued his investigations through windows of the second story.

At one corner of the hotel in a rear room the blinds were drawn; but he heard voices within and once he saw a figure silhouetted momentarily against the blind. It appeared to be the figure of a woman; but it was gone so quickly that he could not be sure. Tarzan crept close to the window and listened. Yes, there was a woman there and a man – he heard distinctly the tones of their voices although he could overhear no words, as they seemed to be whispering.

The adjoining room was dark. Tarzan tried the window and found it unlatched. All was quiet within. He raised the sash and listened again – still silence. Placing a leg over the sill he slipped within and hurriedly glanced about. The room was vacant. Crossing to the door he opened it and looked out into the hall. There was no one there, either, and he stepped out and approached the door of the adjoining room where the man and woman were.

Pressing close to the door he listened. Now he distinguished words, for the two had raised their voices as though in argument. The woman was speaking.

'I have brought the locket,' she said, 'as was agreed upon between you and General Kraut, as my identification. I carry no other credentials. This was to be enough. You have nothing to do but give me the papers and let me go.'

The man replied in so low a tone that Tarzan could not catch the words and then the woman spoke again – a note of scorn and perhaps a little of fear in her voice.

'You would not dare, Hauptmann Schneider,' she said, and then: 'Do not touch me! Take your hands from me!'

It was then that Tarzan of the Apes opened the door and stepped into the room. What he saw was a huge, bull-necked German officer with one arm about the waist of Fräulein Bertha Kircher and a hand upon her forehead pushing her head back as he tried to kiss her on the mouth. The girl was struggling against the great brute; but her efforts were futile. Slowly the man's lips were coming closer to hers and slowly, step by step, she was being carried backward.

Schneider heard the noise of the opening and closing door behind him and turned. At sight of this strange officer he dropped the girl and straightened up.

'What is the meaning of this intrusion, Lieutenant?' he demanded, noting the other's epaulettes. 'Leave the room at once.'

Tarzan made no articulate reply; but the two there with him heard a low growl break from those firm lips – a growl that sent a shudder through the frame of the girl and brought a pallor to the red face of the Hun and his hand to his pistol; but even as he drew his weapon it was wrested from him and hurled through the blind and window to the yard beyond. Then Tarzan backed against the door and slowly removed the uniform coat.

'You are Hauptmann Schneider,' he said to the German.

'What of it?' growled the latter.

'I am Tarzan of the Apes,' replied the ape-man. 'Now you know why I intrude.'

The two before him saw that he was naked beneath the coat which he threw upon the floor and then slipped quickly from the trousers and stood there clothed only in his loincloth. The girl had recognized him by this time, too.

'Take your hand off that pistol,' Tarzan admonished her. Her hand dropped at her side. 'Now come here!'

She approached and Tarzan removed the weapon and hurled it after the other. At the mention of his name Tarzan had noted the sickly pallor that overspread the features of the Hun. At last he had found the right man. At last his mate would be partially avenged – never could she be entirely avenged. Life was too short and there were too many Germans.

'What do you want of me?' demanded Schneider.

'You are going to pay the price for the thing you did at the little bungalow in the Waziri country,' replied the ape-man.

Schneider commenced to bluster and threaten. Tarzan turned the key in the lock of the door and hurled the former through the window after the pistols. Then he turned to the girl. 'Keep out of the way,' he said in a low voice. 'Tarzan of the Apes is going to kill.'

The Hun ceased blustering and began to plead. 'I have a wife and children at home,' he cried. 'I have done nothing, I—'

'You are going to die as befits your kind,' said Tarzan, 'with blood on your hands and a lie on your lips.' He started across the room toward the burly Hauptmann. Schneider was a large and powerful man – about the height of the ape-man but much heavier. He saw that neither threats nor pleas would avail him and so he prepared to fight as a cornered rat fights for its life with all the maniacal rage, cunning, and ferocity that the first law of nature imparts to many beasts.

Lowering his bull head he charged for the ape-man and in the center of the floor the two clinched. There they stood locked and swaying for a moment until Tarzan succeeded in forcing his antagonist backward over a table which crashed to the floor, splintered by the weight of the two heavy bodies.

The girl stood watching the battle with wide eyes. She saw the two men rolling hither and thither across the floor and she heard with horror the low growls that came from the lips of the naked giant. Schneider was trying to reach his foe's throat with his fingers while, horror of horrors, Bertha Kircher could see that the other was searching for the German's jugular with his teeth!

Schneider seemed to realize this too, for he redoubled his efforts to escape and finally succeeded in rolling over on top of the ape-man and breaking away. Leaping to his feet he ran for the window; but the ape-man was too quick for him and before he could leap through the sash a heavy hand fell upon his shoulder and he was jerked back and hurled across the room to the opposite wall. There Tarzan followed him, and once again they locked, dealing each other terrific blows, until Schneider in a piercing voice screamed, *'Kamerad! Kamerad!'*

Tarzan grasped the man by the throat and drew his hunting knife. Schneider's back was against the wall so that though his knees wobbled he was held erect by the ape-man. Tarzan brought the sharp point to the lower part of the German's abdomen.

'Thus you slew my mate,' he hissed in a terrible voice. 'Thus shall you die!'

The girl staggered forward. 'Oh, God, no!' she cried. 'Not that. You are too brave – you cannot be such a beast as that!'

Tarzan turned at her. 'No,' he said, 'you are right, I cannot do it – I am no German,' and he raised the point of his blade and sunk it deep into the putrid heart of Hauptmann Fritz Schneider, putting a bloody period to the Hun's last gasping cry: 'I did not do it! She is not—'

Then Tarzan turned toward the girl and held out his hand. 'Give me my locket,' he said.

She pointed toward the dead officer. 'He has it.' Tarzan searched him and found the trinket. 'Now you may give me the papers,' he said to the girl, and without a word she handed him a folded document.

For a long time he stood looking at her before he spoke again.

'I came for you, too,' he said. 'It would be difficult to take you back from here and so I was going to kill you, as I have sworn to kill all your kind; but you were right when you said that I was not such a beast as that slayer of women. I could not slay him as he slew mine, nor can I slay you, who are a woman.'

He crossed to the window, raised the sash and an instant later he had stepped out and disappeared into the night. And then Fräulein Bertha Kircher stepped quickly to the corpse upon the floor, slipped her hand inside the blouse and drew forth a little sheaf of papers which she tucked into her waist before she went to the window and called for help.

7
When Blood Told

Tarzan of the Apes was disgusted. He had had the German spy, Bertha Kircher, in his power and had left her unscathed. It is true that he had slain Hauptmann Fritz Schneider, that Underlieutenant von Goss had died at his hands, and that he had otherwise wreaked vengeance upon the men of the German company who had murdered, pillaged, and raped at Tarzan's bungalow in the Waziri country. There was still another officer to be accounted for; but him he could not find. It was Lieutenant Obergatz he still sought, though vainly, for at last he learned that the man had been sent upon some special mission, whether in Africa or back to Europe Tarzan's informant either did not know or would not divulge.

But the fact that he had permitted sentiment to stay his hand when he might so easily have put Bertha Kircher out of the way in the hotel at Wilhelmstal that night rankled in the ape-man's bosom. He was shamed by his weakness, and when he had handed the paper she had given him to the British chief of staff, even though the information it contained permitted the British to frustrate a German flank attack, he was still much dissatisfied with himself. And possibly the root of this dissatisfaction lay in the fact that he realized that were he again to have the same opportunity he would still find it as impossible to slay a woman as it had been in Wilhelmstal that night.

Tarzan blamed this weakness, as he considered it, upon his association with the effeminating influences of civilization, for in the bottom of his savage heart he held in contempt both civilization and its representatives – the men and women of the civilized countries of the world. Always was he comparing their weaknesses, their vices, their hypocrisies, and their little vanities with the open, primitive ways of his ferocious jungle mates, and all the while there battled in that same big heart with these forces another mighty force – Tarzan's love and loyalty for his friends of the civilized world.

The ape-man, reared as he had been by savage beasts amid savage beasts, was slow to make friends. Acquaintances he numbered by the hundreds; but of friends he had few. These few he would have died for as, doubtless, they would have died for him; but there were none of these fighting with the British forces in East Africa, and so, sickened and disgusted by the sight of man waging his cruel and inhuman warfare, Tarzan determined to heed the insistent call of the remote jungle of his youth, for the Germans were now on the run and the war in East Africa was so nearly over that he realized that his further services would be of negligible value.

Never regularly sworn into the service of the King, he was under no obligation to remain now that the moral obligation had been removed, and so it was that he disappeared from the British camp as mysteriously as he had appeared a few months before.

More than once had Tarzan reverted to the primitive only to return again to civilization through love for his mate; but now that she was gone he felt that this time he had definitely departed forever from the haunts of man, and that he should live and die a beast among beasts even as he had been from infancy to maturity.

Between him and destination lay a trackless wilderness of untouched primeval savagery where, doubtless in many spots, his would be the first human foot to touch the virgin turf. Nor did this prospect dismay the Tarmangani – rather was it an urge and an inducement, for rich in his veins flowed that noble strain of blood that has made most of the earth's surface habitable for man.

The question of food and water that would have risen paramount in the mind of an ordinary man contemplating such an excursion gave Tarzan little concern. The wilderness was his natural habitat and woodcraft as inherent to him as breathing. Like other jungle animals he could scent water from a great distance and, where you or I might die of thirst, the ape-man would unerringly select the exact spot at which to dig and find water.

For several days Tarzan traversed a country rich in game and watercourses. He moved slowly, hunting and fishing, or again fraternizing or quarreling with the other savage denizens of the jungle. Now it was little Manu, the monkey, who chattered and scolded at the mighty Tarmangani and in the next breath warned him that Histah, the snake, lay coiled in the long grass just ahead. Of Manu Tarzan inquired concerning the great apes – the Mangani – and was told that few inhabited this part of the jungle, and that even these were hunting farther to the north this season of the year.

'But there is Bolgani,' said Manu. 'Would you like to see Bolgani?'

Manu's tone was sneering, and Tarzan knew that it was because little Manu thought all creatures feared mighty Bolgani, the gorilla. Tarzan arched his great chest and struck it with a clenched fist. 'I am Tarzan,' he cried. 'While Tarzan was yet a balu he slew a Bolgani. Tarzan seeks the Mangani, who are his brothers, but Bolgani he does not seek, so let Bolgani keep from the path of Tarzan.'

Little Manu, the monkey, was much impressed, for the way of the jungle is to boast and to believe. It was then that he condescended to tell Tarzan more of the Mangani.

'They go there and there and there,' he said, making a wide sweep with a brown hand first toward the north, then west, and then south again. 'For there,' and he pointed due west, 'is much hunting; but between lies a great place where there is no food and no water, so they must go that way,' and again he swung his hand through the half-circle that explained to Tarzan the great detour the apes made to come to their hunting ground to the west.

That was all right for the Mangani, who are lazy and do not care to move rapidly; but for Tarzan the straight road would be the best. He would cross the dry country and come to the good hunting in a third of the time that it would take to go far to the north and circle back again. And so it was that he continued on toward the west, and crossing a range of low mountains came in sight of a broad plateau, rock strewn and desolate. Far in the distance he saw another range of mountains beyond which he felt must lie the hunting ground of the Mangani. There he would join them and remain for a while before continuing on toward the coast and the little cabin that his father had built beside the landlocked harbor at the jungle's edge.

Tarzan was full of plans. He would rebuild and enlarge the cabin of his birth, constructing storage houses where he would make the apes lay away food when it was plenty against the times that were lean – a thing no ape ever had dreamed of doing. And the tribe would remain always in the locality and he would be king again as he had in the past. He would try to teach them some of the better things that he had learned from man, yet knowing the ape-mind as only Tarzan could, he feared that his labors would be for naught.

The ape-man found the country he was crossing rough in the extreme, the roughest he ever had encountered. The plateau was cut by frequent canyons the passage of which often entailed hours of wearing effort. The vegetation was sparse and of a faded brown color that lent to the whole landscape a most depressing aspect. Great rocks were strewn in every direction as far as the eye could see, lying partially embedded in an impalpable dust that rose in clouds about him at every step. The sun beat down mercilessly out of a cloudless sky.

For a day Tarzan toiled across this now hateful land and at the going down of the sun the distant mountains to the west seemed no nearer than at morn. Never a sign of living thing had the ape-man seen, other than Ska, that bird of ill omen, that had followed him tirelessly since he had entered this parched waste.

No littlest beetle that he might eat had given evidence that life of any sort existed here, and it was a hungry and thirsty Tarzan who lay down to rest in the evening. He decided now to push on during the cool of the night, for he realized that even mighty Tarzan had his limitations and that where there was no food one could not eat and where there was no water the greatest woodcraft in the world could find none. It was a totally new experience to Tarzan to find so barren and terrible a country in his beloved Africa. Even the Sahara had its oases; but this frightful world gave no indication of containing a square foot of hospitable ground.

However, he had no misgivings but that he would fare forth into the wonder country of which little Manu had told him, though it was certain that he would do it with a dry skin and an empty belly. And so he fought on until daylight, when he again felt the need of rest. He was at the edge of another of those terrible canyons, the eighth he had crossed, whose precipitous sides would have taxed to the uttermost the strength of an untired man well fortified by food and water, and for the first time, as he looked down into the abyss and then at the opposite side that he must scale, misgivings began to assail his mind.

He did not fear death – with the memory of his murdered mate still fresh in his mind he almost courted it, yet strong within him was that primal instinct of self-preservation – the battling force of life that would keep him an active contender against the Great Reaper until, fighting to the very last, he should be overcome by a superior power.

A shadow swung slowly across the ground beside him, and looking up, the ape-man saw Ska, the vulture, wheeling a wide circle above him. The grim and persistent harbinger of evil aroused the man to renewed determination. He arose and approached the edge of the canyon, and then, wheeling, with his face turned upward toward the circling bird of prey, he bellowed forth the challenge of the bull ape.

'I am Tarzan,' he shouted, 'Lord of the Jungle. Tarzan of the Apes is not for Ska, eater of carrion. Go back to the lair of Dango and feed off the leavings of the hyenas, for Tarzan will leave no bones for Ska to pick in this empty wilderness of death.'

But before he reached the bottom of the canyon he again was forced to the realization that his great strength was waning, and when he dropped exhausted at the foot of the cliff and saw before him the opposite wall that must be scaled, he bared his fighting fangs and growled. For an hour he lay resting in the cool shade at the foot of the cliff. All about him reigned utter silence – the silence of the tomb. No fluttering birds, no humming insects, no scurrying reptiles relieved the deathlike stillness. This indeed was the valley of death. He felt the depressing influence of the horrible place setting down upon him; but he staggered to his feet, shaking himself like a great lion, for was he not still Tarzan, mighty Tarzan of the Apes? Yes, and Tarzan the mighty he would be until the last throb of that savage heart!

As he crossed the floor of the canyon he saw something lying close to the base of the side wall he was approaching – something that stood out in startling contrast to all the surroundings and yet seemed so much a part and parcel of the somber scene as to suggest an actor amid the settings of a well-appointed stage, and, as though to carry out the allegory, the pitiless rays of flaming Kudu topped the eastern cliff, picking out the thing lying at the foot of the western wall like a giant spotlight.

And as Tarzan came nearer he saw the bleached skull and bones of a human being about which were remnants of clothing and articles of equipment that, as he examined them, filled the ape-man with curiosity to such an extent that for a time he forgot his own predicament in contemplation of the remarkable story suggested by these mute evidences of a tragedy of a time long past.

The bones were in a fair state of preservation and indicated by their intactness that the flesh had probably been picked from them by vultures as none was broken; but the pieces of equipment bore out the suggestion of their great age. In this protected spot where there were no frosts and evidently but little rainfall, the bones might have lain for ages without disintegrating, for there were here no other forces to scatter or disturb them.

Near the skeleton lay a helmet of hammered brass and a corroded breastplate of steel while at one side was a long, straight sword in its scabbard and an ancient harquebus. The bones were those of a large man – a man of wondrous strength and vitality Tarzan knew he must have been to have penetrated thus far through the dangers of Africa with such a ponderous yet at the same time futile armament.

The ape-man felt a sense of deep admiration for this nameless adventurer of a bygone day. What a brute of a man he must have been and what a glorious tale of battle and kaleidoscopic vicissitudes of fortune must once have been locked within that whitened skull! Tarzan stooped to examine the shreds of clothing that still lay about the bones. Every particle of leather had disappeared, doubtless eaten by Ska. No boots remained, if the man had worn boots, but there were several buckles scattered about suggesting that a great part of his trappings had been of leather, while just beneath the bones of one hand lay a metal cylinder about eight inches long and two inches in diameter. As Tarzan picked it up he saw that it had been heavily lacquered and had withstood the slight ravages of time so well as to be in as perfect a state of preservation today as it had been when its owner dropped into his last, long sleep perhaps centuries ago.

As he examined it he discovered that one end was closed with a friction cover which a little twisting force soon loosened and removed, revealing within a roll of parchment which the ape-man removed and opened, disclosing a number of age-yellowed sheets closely written upon in a fine hand in a language which he guessed to be Spanish but which he could not decipher. Upon the last sheet was a roughly drawn map with numerous reference points marked upon it, all unintelligible to Tarzan, who, after a brief examination of the papers, returned them to their metal case, replaced the top and was about to toss the little cylinder to the ground beside the mute remains of its former possessor when some whim of curiosity unsatisfied prompted him to slip it into the quiver with his arrows, though as he did so it was with the grim thought that possibly centuries hence it might again come to the sight of man beside his own bleached bones.

And then, with a parting glance at the ancient skeleton, he turned to the task of ascending the western wall of the canyon. Slowly and with many rests he dragged his weakening body upward. Again and again he slipped back from sheer exhaustion and would have fallen to the floor of the canyon but for merest chance. How long it took him to scale that frightful wall he could not have told, and when at last he dragged himself over the top it was to lie weak and gasping, too spent to rise or even to move a few inches farther from the perilous edge of the chasm.

At last he arose, very slowly and with evident effort gaining his knees first and then staggering to his feet, yet his indomitable will was evidenced by a sudden straightening of his shoulders and a determined shake of his head as he lurched forward on unsteady legs to take up his valiant fight for survival. Ahead he scanned the rough landscape for sign of another canyon which he knew would spell inevitable doom. The western hills rose closer now though weirdly unreal as they seemed to dance in the sunlight as though mocking him with their nearness at the moment that exhaustion was about to render them forever unattainable.

Beyond them he knew must be the fertile hunting grounds of which Manu had told. Even if no canyon intervened, his chances of surmounting even low hills seemed remote should he have the fortune to reach their base; but with another canyon hope was dead. Above them Ska still circled, and it seemed to the ape-man that the ill-omened bird hovered ever lower and lower as though reading in that failing gait the nearing of the end, and through cracked lips Tarzan growled out his defiance.

Mile after mile Tarzan of the Apes put slowly behind him, borne up by sheer force of will where a lesser man would have lain down to die and rest forever tired muscles whose every move was an agony of effort; but at last his progress became practically mechanical – he staggered on with a dazed mind that reacted numbly to a single urge – on, on, on! The hills were now but a dim, ill-defined blur ahead. Sometimes he forgot that they were hills, and again he wondered vaguely why he must go on forever through all this torture endeavoring to overtake them – the fleeing, elusive hills. Presently he began to hate them and there formed within his half-delirious brain the hallucination that the hills were German hills, that they had slain someone dear to him, whom he could never quite recall, and that he was pursuing to slay them.

This idea, growing, appeared to give him strength – a new and revivifying purpose – so that for a time he no longer staggered; but went forward steadily with head erect. Once he stumbled and fell, and when he tried to rise he found that he could not – that his strength was so far gone that he could only crawl forward on his hands and knees for a few yards and then sink down again to rest.

It was during one of these frequent periods of utter exhaustion that he heard the flap of dismal wings close above him. With his remaining strength he turned himself over on his back to see Ska wheel quickly upward. With the sight Tarzan's mind cleared for a while.

'Is the end so near as that?' he thought. 'Does Ska know that I am so near gone that he dares come down and perch upon my carcass?' And even then a grim smile touched those swollen lips as into the savage mind came a sudden thought – the cunning of the wild beast at bay. Closing his eyes he threw a forearm across them to protect them from Ska's powerful beak and then he lay very still and waited.

It was restful lying there, for the sun was now obscured by clouds and Tarzan was very tired. He feared that he might sleep and something told him that if he did he would never awaken, and so he concentrated all his remaining powers upon the one thought of remaining awake. Not a muscle moved – to Ska, circling above, it became evident that the end had come – that at last he should be rewarded for his long vigil.

Circling slowly he dropped closer and closer to the dying man. Why did not Tarzan move? Had he indeed been overcome by the sleep of exhaustion, or was Ska right – had death at last claimed that mighty body? Was that great, savage heart stilled forever? It was unthinkable.

Ska, filled with suspicions, circled warily. Twice he almost alighted upon the great, naked breast only to wheel suddenly away; but the third time his talons touched the brown skin. It was as though the contact closed an electric circuit that instantaneously vitalized the quiet clod that had lain motionless so long. A brown hand swept downward from the brown forehead and before Ska could raise a wing in flight he was in the clutches of his intended victim.

Ska fought, but he was no match for even a dying Tarzan, and a moment later the ape-man's teeth closed upon the carrion-eater. The flesh was coarse and tough and gave off an unpleasant odor and a worse taste; but it was food and the blood was drink and Tarzan only an ape at heart and a dying ape into the bargain – dying of starvation and thirst.

Even mentally weakened as he was the ape-man was still master of his appetite and so he ate but sparingly, saving the rest, and then, feeling that he now could do so safely, he turned upon his side and slept.

Rain, beating heavily upon his body, awakened him and sitting up he cupped his hands and caught the precious drops which he transferred to his parched throat. Only a little he got at a time; but that was best. The few mouthfuls of Ska that he had eaten, together with the blood and rainwater and the sleep had refreshed him greatly and put new strength into his tired muscles.

Now he could see the hills again and they were close and, though there was no sun, the world looked bright and cheerful, for Tarzan knew that he was saved. The bird that would have devoured him, and the providential rain, had saved him at the very moment that death seemed inevitable.

Again partaking of a few mouthfuls of the unsavory flesh of Ska, the vulture, the ape-man arose with something of his old force and set out with steady gait toward the hills of promise rising alluringly ahead. Darkness fell before he reached them; but he kept on until he felt the steeply rising ground that proclaimed his arrival at the base of the hills proper, and then he lay down and waited until morning should reveal the easiest passage to the land beyond. The rain had ceased, but the sky still was overcast so that even his keen eyes could not penetrate the darkness farther than a few feet. And there he slept, after eating again of what remained of Ska, until the morning sun awakened him with a new sense of strength and well-being.

And so at last he came through the hills out of the valley of death into a land of parklike beauty, rich in game. Below him lay a deep valley through the center of which dense jungle vegetation marked the course of a river beyond which a primeval forest extended for miles to terminate at last at the foot of lofty, snowcapped mountains. It was a land that Tarzan never had looked upon before, nor was it likely that the foot of another white man ever had touched it unless, possibly, in some long-gone day the adventurer whose skeleton he had found bleaching in the canyon had traversed it.

8

Tarzan and the Great Apes

Three days the ape-man spent in resting and recuperating, eating fruits and nuts and the smaller animals that were most easily bagged, and upon the fourth he set out to explore the valley and search for the great apes. Time was a negligible factor in the equation of life – it was all the same to Tarzan if he reached the west coast in a month or a year or three years. All time was his and all Africa. His was absolute freedom – the last tie that had bound him to civilization and custom had been severed. He was alone but he was not exactly lonely. The greater part of his life had been spent thus, and though there was no other of his kind, he was at all times surrounded by the jungle peoples for whom familiarity had bred no contempt within his breast. The least of them interested him, and, too, there were those with whom he always made friends easily, and there were his hereditary enemies whose presence gave a spice to life that might otherwise have become humdrum and monotonous.

And so it was that on the fourth day he set out to explore the valley and search for his fellow-apes. He had proceeded southward for a short distance when his nostrils were assailed by the scent of man, of Gomangani, the black man. There were many of them, and mixed with their scent was another – that of a she Tarmangani.

Swinging through the trees Tarzan approached the authors of these disturbing scents. He came warily from the flank, but paying no attention to the wind, for he knew that man with his dull senses could apprehend him only through his eyes or ears and then only when comparatively close. Had he been stalking Numa or Sheeta he would have circled about until his quarry was upwind from him, thus taking practically all the advantage up to the very moment that he came within sight or hearing; but in the stalking of the dull clod, man, he approached with almost contemptuous indifference, so that all the jungle about him knew that he was passing – all but the men he stalked.

From the dense foliage of a great tree he watched them pass – a disreputable mob of blacks, some garbed in the uniform of German East African native troops, others wearing a single garment of the same uniform, while many had reverted to the simple dress of their forbears – approximating nudity. There were many black women with them, laughing and talking as they kept pace with the men, all of whom were armed with German rifles and equipped with German belts and ammunition.

There were no white officers there, but it was nonetheless apparent to Tarzan that these men were from some German native command, and he guessed that they had slain their officers and taken to the jungle with their women, or had stolen some from native villages through which they must have passed. It was evident that they were putting as much ground between themselves and the coast as possible and doubtless were seeking some impenetrable fastness of the vast interior where they might inaugurate a reign of terror among the primitively armed inhabitants and by raiding, looting, and rape grow rich in goods and women at the expense of the district upon which they settled themselves.

Between two of the black women marched a slender white girl. She was hatless and with torn and disheveled clothing that had evidently once been a trim riding habit. Her coat was gone and her waist half torn from her body. Occasionally and without apparent provocation one or the other of the Negresses struck or pushed her roughly. Tarzan watched through half-closed eyes. His first impulse was to leap among them and bear the girl from their cruel clutches. He had recognized her immediately and it was because of this fact that he hesitated.

What was it to Tarzan of the Apes what fate befell this enemy spy? He had been unable to kill her himself because of an inherent weakness that would not permit him to lay hands upon a woman, all of which of course had no bearing upon what others might do to her. That her fate would now be infinitely more horrible than the quick and painless death that the ape-man would have meted to her only interested Tarzan to the extent that the more frightful the end of a German the more in keeping it would be with what they all deserved.

And so he let the blacks pass with Fräulein Bertha Kircher in their midst, or at least until the last straggling warrior suggested to his mind the pleasures of blackbaiting – an amusement and a sport in which he had grown ever more proficient since that long-gone day when Kulonga, the son of Mbonga, the chief, had cast his unfortunate spear at Kala, the ape-man's foster mother.

The last man, who must have stopped for some purpose, was fully a quarter of a mile in rear of the party. He was hurrying to catch up when Tarzan saw him, and as he passed beneath the tree in which the ape-man perched above the trail, a silent noose dropped deftly about his neck. The main body still was in plain sight, and as the frightened man voiced a piercing shriek of terror, they looked back to see his body rise as though by magic straight into the air and disappear amidst the leafy foliage above.

For a moment the blacks stood paralyzed by astonishment and fear, but presently the burly sergeant, Usanga, who led them, started back along the trail at a run, calling to the others to follow him. Loading their guns as they came the blacks ran to succor their fellow, and at Usanga's command they spread into a thin line that presently entirely surrounded the tree into which their comrade had vanished.

Usanga called but received no reply; then he advanced slowly with rifle at the ready, peering up into the tree. He could see no one – nothing. The circle closed in until fifty blacks were searching among the branches with their keen eyes. What had become of their fellow? They had seen him rise into the tree and since then many eyes had been fastened upon the spot, yet there was no sign of him. One, more venturesome than his fellows, volunteered to climb into the tree and investigate. He was gone but a minute or two and when he dropped to earth again he swore that there was no sign of a creature there.

Perplexed, and by this time a bit awed, the blacks drew slowly away from the spot and with many backward glances and less laughing continued upon their journey until, when about a mile beyond the spot at which their fellow had disappeared, those in the lead saw him peering from behind a tree at one side of the trail just in front of them. With shouts to their companions that he had been found they ran forward; but those who were first to reach the tree stopped suddenly and shrank back, their eyes rolling fearfully first in one direction and then in another as though they expected some nameless horror to leap out upon them.

Nor was their terror without foundation. Impaled upon the end of a brown branch the head of their companion was propped behind the tree so that it appeared to be looking out at them from the opposite side of the bole.

It was then that many wished to turn back, arguing that they had offended some demon of the wood upon whose preserve they had trespassed; but Usanga refused to listen to them, assuring them that inevitable torture and death awaited them should they return and fall again into the hands of their cruel German masters. At last his reasoning prevailed to the end that a much-subdued and terrified band moved in a compact mass, like a drove of sheep, forward through the valley and there were no stragglers.

It is a happy characteristic of the Negro race, which they hold in common with little children, that their spirits seldom remain depressed for a considerable length of time after the immediate cause of depression is removed, and so it was that in half an hour Usanga's band was again beginning to take on to some extent its former appearance of carefree lightheartedness. Thus were the heavy clouds of fear slowly dissipating when a turn in the trail brought them suddenly upon the headless body of their erstwhile companion lying directly in their path, and they were again plunged into the depth of fear and gloomy forebodings.

So utterly inexplicable and uncanny had the entire occurrence been that there was not a one of them who could find a ray of comfort penetrating the dead blackness of its ominous portent. What had happened to one of their number each conceived as being a wholly possible fate for himself – in fact quite his probable fate. If such a thing could happen in broad daylight what frightful thing might not fall to their lot when night had enshrouded them in her mantle of darkness. They trembled in anticipation.

The white girl in their midst was no less mystified than they; but far less moved, since sudden death was the most merciful fate to which she might now look forward. So far she had been subjected to nothing worse than the petty cruelties of the women, while, on the other hand, it had alone been the presence of the women that had saved her from worse treatment at the hands of some of the men – notably the brutal, black sergeant, Usanga. His own woman was of the party – a veritable giantess, a virago of the first magnitude – and she was evidently the only thing in the world of which Usanga stood in awe. Even though she was particularly cruel to the young woman, the latter believed that she was her sole protection from the degraded black tyrant.

Late in the afternoon the band came upon a small palisaded village of thatched huts set in a clearing in the jungle close beside a placid river. At their approach the villagers came pouring out, and Usanga advanced with two of his warriors to palaver with the chief. The experiences of the day had so shaken the nerves of the black sergeant that he was ready to treat with these people rather than take their village by force of arms, as would ordinarily have been his preference; but now a vague conviction influenced him that there watched over this part of the jungle a powerful demon who wielded miraculous power for evil against those who offended him. First Usanga would learn how these villagers stood with this savage god and if they had his goodwill Usanga would be most careful to treat them with kindness and respect.

At the palaver it developed that the village chief had food, goats, and fowl which he would be glad to dispose of for a proper consideration; but as the consideration would have meant parting with precious rifles and ammunition, or the very clothing from their backs, Usanga began to see that after all it might be forced upon him to wage war to obtain food.

A happy solution was arrived at by a suggestion of one of his men – that the soldiers go forth the following day and hunt for the villagers, bringing them in so much fresh meat in return for their hospitality. This the chief agreed to, stipulating the kind and quantity of game to be paid in return for flour, goats, and fowl, and a certain number of huts that were to be turned over to the visitors. The details having been settled after an hour or more of that bickering argument of which the native African is so fond, the newcomers entered the village where they were assigned to huts.

Bertha Kircher found herself alone in a small hut to the palisade at the far end of the village street, and though she was neither bound nor guarded, she was assured by Usanga that she could not escape the village without running into almost certain death in the jungle, which the villagers assured them was infested by lions of great size and ferocity. 'Be good to Usanga,' he concluded, 'and no harm will befall you. I will come again to see you after the others are asleep. Let us be friends.'

As the brute left her the girl's frame was racked by a convulsive shudder as she sank to the floor of the hut and covered her face with her hands. She realized now why the women had not been left to guard her. It was the work of the cunning Usanga, but would not his woman suspect something of his intentions? She was no fool and, further, being imbued with insane jealousy she was ever looking for some overt act upon the part of her ebon lord. Bertha Kircher felt that only she might save her and that she would save her if word could be but gotten to her. But how?

Left alone and away from the eyes of her captors for the first time since the previous night, the girl immediately took advantage of the opportunity to assure herself that the papers she had taken from the body of Hauptmann Fritz Schneider were still safely sewn inside one of her undergarments.

Alas! Of what value could they now ever be to her beloved country? But habit and loyalty were so strong within her that she still clung to the determined hope of eventually delivering the little packet to her chief.

The natives seemed to have forgotten her existence – no one came near the hut, not even to bring her food. She could hear them at the other end of the village laughing and yelling and knew that they were celebrating with food and native beer – knowledge which only increased her apprehension. To be prisoner in a native village in the very heart of an unexplored region of Central Africa – the only white woman among a band of drunken Negroes! The very thought appalled her. Yet there was a slight promise in the fact that she had so far been unmolested – the promise that they might, indeed, have forgotten her and that soon they might become so hopelessly drunk as to be harmless.

Darkness had fallen and still no one came. The girl wondered if she dared venture forth in search of Naratu, Usanga's woman, for Usanga might not forget that he had promised to return. No one was near as she stepped out of the hut and made her way toward the part of the village where the revelers were making merry about a fire. As she approached she saw the villagers and their guests squatting in a large circle about the blaze before which a half-dozen naked warriors leaped and bent and stamped in some grotesque dance. Pots of food and gourds of drink were being passed about among the audience. Dirty hands were plunged into the food pots and the captured portions devoured so greedily that one might have thought the entire community had been upon the point of starvation. The gourds they held to their lips until the beer ran down their chins and the vessels were wrested from them by greedy neighbors. The drink had now begun to take noticeable effect upon most of them, with the result that they were beginning to give themselves up to utter and licentious abandon.

As the girl came nearer, keeping in the shadow of the huts, looking for Naratu she was suddenly discovered by one upon the edge of the crowd – a huge woman, who rose, shrieking, and came toward her. From her aspect the white girl thought that the woman meant literally to tear her to pieces. So utterly wanton and uncalled-for was the attack that it found the girl entirely unprepared, and what would have happened had not a warrior interfered may only be guessed. And then Usanga, noting the interruption, came lurching forward to question her.

'What do you want,' he cried, 'food and drink? Come with me!' and he threw an arm about her and dragged her toward the circle.

'No!' she cried, 'I want Naratu. Where is Naratu?'

This seemed to sober the black for a moment as though he had temporarily forgotten his better half. He cast quick, fearful glances about, and then, evidently assured that Naratu had noticed nothing, he ordered the warrior who was still holding the infuriated black woman from the white girl to take the latter back to her hut and to remain there on guard over her.

First appropriating a gourd of beer for himself the warrior motioned the girl to precede him, and thus guarded she returned to her hut, the fellow squatting down just outside the doorway, where he confined his attentions for some time to the gourd.

Bertha Kircher sat down at the far side of the hut awaiting she knew not what impending fate. She could not sleep so filled was her mind with wild schemes of escape though each new one must always be discarded as impractical. Half an hour after the warrior had returned her to her prison he rose and entered the hut, where he tried to engage in conversation with her. Groping across the interior he leaned his short spear against the wall and sat down beside her, and as he talked he edged closer and closer until at last he could reach out and touch her. Shrinking, she drew away.

'Do not touch me!' she cried. 'I will tell Usanga if you do not leave me alone, and you know what he will do to you.'

The man only laughed drunkenly, and, reaching out his hand, grabbed her arm and dragged her toward him. She fought and cried aloud for Usanga and at the same instant the entrance to the hut was darkened by the form of a man.

'What is the matter?' shouted the newcomer in the deep tones that the girl recognized as belonging to the black sergeant. He had come, but would she be any better off? She knew that she would not unless she could play upon Usanga's fear of his woman.

When Usanga found what had happened he kicked the warrior out of the hut and bade him begone, and when the fellow had disappeared, muttering and grumbling, the sergeant approached the white girl. He was very drunk, so drunk that several times she succeeded in eluding him and twice she pushed him so violently away that he stumbled and fell.

Finally he became enraged and rushing upon her, seized her in his long, apelike arms. Striking at his face with clenched fists she tried to protect herself and drive him away. She threatened him with the wrath of Naratu, and at that he changed his tactics and began to plead, and as he argued with her, promising her safety and eventual freedom, the warrior he had kicked out of the hut made his staggering way to the hut occupied by Naratu.

Usanga, finding that pleas and promises were as unavailing as threats, at last lost both his patience and his head, seizing the girl roughly, and simultaneously there burst into the hut a raging demon of jealousy. Naratu had come. Kicking, scratching, striking, biting, she routed the terrified Usanga in short order, and so obsessed was she by her desire to inflict punishment upon her unfaithful lord and master that she quite forgot the object of his infatuation.

Bertha Kircher heard her screaming down the village street at Usanga's heels and trembled at the thought of what lay in store for her at the hands of these two, for she knew that tomorrow at the latest Naratu would take out upon her the full measure of her jealous hatred after she had spent her first wrath upon Usanga.

The two had departed but a few minutes when the warrior guard returned. He looked into the hut and then entered. 'No one will stop me now, white woman,' he growled as he stepped quickly across the hut toward her.

Tarzan of the Apes, feasting well upon a juicy haunch from Bara, the deer, was vaguely conscious of a troubled mind. He should have been at peace with himself and all the world, for was he not in his native element surrounded by game in plenty and rapidly filling his belly with the flesh he loved best? But Tarzan of the Apes was haunted by the picture of a slight, young girl being shoved and struck by brutal Negresses, and in imagination could see her now camped in this savage country a prisoner among degraded blacks.

Why was it so difficult to remember that she was only a hated German and a spy? Why would the fact that she was a woman and white always obtrude itself upon his consciousness? He hated her as he hated all her kind, and the fate that was sure to be hers was no more terrible than she in common with all her people deserved. The matter was settled and Tarzan composed himself to think of other things, yet the picture would not die – it rose in all its details and annoyed him. He began to wonder what they were doing to her and where they were taking her. He was very much ashamed of himself as he had been after the episode in Wilhelmstal when his weakness had permitted him to spare this spy's life. Was he to be thus weak again? No!

Night came and he settled himself in an ample tree to rest until morning; but sleep would not come. Instead came the vision of a white girl being beaten by black women, and again of the same girl at the mercy of the warriors somewhere in that dark and forbidding jungle.

With a growl of anger and self-contempt Tarzan arose, shook himself, and swung from his tree to that adjoining, and thus, through the lower terraces, he followed the trail that Usanga's party had taken earlier in the afternoon. He had little difficulty as the band had followed a well-beaten path and when toward midnight the stench of a native village assailed his delicate nostrils he guessed that his goal was near and that presently he should find her whom he sought.

Prowling stealthily as prowls Numa, the lion, stalking a wary prey, Tarzan moved noiselessly about the palisade, listening and sniffing. At the rear of the village he discovered a tree whose branches extended over the top of the palisade and a moment later he had dropped quietly into the village.

From hut to hut he went searching with keen ears and nostrils some confirming evidence of the presence of the girl, and at last, faint and almost obliterated by the odor of the Gomangani, he found it hanging like a delicate vapor about a small hut. The village was quiet now, for the last of the beer and the food had been disposed of and the blacks lay in their huts overcome by stupor, yet Tarzan made no noise that even a sober man keenly alert might have heard.

He passed around to the entrance of the hut and listened. From within came no sound, not even the low breathing of one awake; yet he was sure that the girl had been here and perhaps was even now, and so he entered, slipping in as silently as a disembodied spirit. For a moment he stood motionless just within the entranceway, listening. No, there was no one here, of that he was sure, but he would investigate. As his eyes became accustomed to the greater darkness within the hut an object began to take form that presently outlined itself in a human form supine upon the floor.

Tarzan stepped closer and leaned over to examine it – it was the dead body of a naked warrior from whose chest protruded a short spear. Then he searched carefully every square foot of the remaining floor space and at last returned to the body again where he stooped and smelled of the haft of the weapon that had slain the black. A slow smile touched his lips – that and a slight movement of his head betokened that he understood.

A rapid search of the balance of the village assured him that the girl had escaped and a feeling of relief came over him that no harm had befallen her. That her life was equally in jeopardy in the savage jungle to which she must have flown did not impress him as it would have you or me, since to Tarzan the jungle was not a dangerous place – he considered one safer there than in Paris or London by night.

He had entered the trees again and was outside the palisade when there came faintly to his ears from far beyond the village an old, familiar sound. Balancing lightly upon a swaying branch he stood, a graceful statue of a forest god, listening intently. For a minute he stood thus and then there broke from his lips the long, weird cry of ape calling to ape and he was away through the jungle toward the sound of the booming drum of the anthropoids leaving behind him an awakened and terrified village of cringing blacks, who would forever after connect that eerie cry with the disappearance of their white prisoner and the death of their fellow-warrior.

Bertha Kircher, hurrying through the jungle along a well-beaten game trail, thought only of putting as much distance as possible between herself and the village before daylight could permit pursuit of her. Whither she was going she did not know, nor was it a matter of great moment since death must be her lot sooner or later.

Fortune favored her that night, for she passed unscathed through as savage and lion-ridden an area as there is in all Africa – a natural hunting ground which the white man has not yet discovered, where deer and antelope and zebra, giraffe and elephant, buffalo, rhinoceros, and the other herbivorous animals of central Africa abound molested by none but their natural enemies, the great cats which, lured here by easy prey and immunity from the rifles of big-game hunters, swarm the district.

She had fled for an hour or two, perhaps, when her attention was arrested by the sound of animals moving about, muttering and growling close ahead. Assured that she had covered a sufficient distance to insure her a good start in the morning before the blacks could take to her trail, and fearful of what the creatures might be, she climbed into a large tree with the intention of spending the balance of the night there.

She had no sooner reached a safe and comfortable branch when she discovered that the tree stood upon the edge of a small clearing that had been hidden from her by the heavy undergrowth upon the ground below, and simultaneously she discovered the identity of the beasts she had heard.

In the center of the clearing below her, clearly visible in the bright moonlight, she saw fully twenty huge, manlike apes – great, shaggy fellows who went upon their hind feet with only slight assistance from the knuckles of their hands. The moonlight glanced from their glossy coats, the numerous gray-tipped hairs imparting a sheen that made the hideous creatures almost magnificent in their appearance.

The girl had watched them but a minute or two when the little band was joined by others, coming singly and in groups until there were fully fifty of the great brutes gathered there in the moonlight. Among them were young apes and several little ones clinging tightly to their mothers' shaggy shoulders. Presently the group parted to form a circle about what appeared to be a small, flat-topped mound of earth in the center of the clearing. Squatting close about this mound were three old females armed with short, heavy clubs with which they presently began to pound upon the flat top of the earth mound which gave forth a dull, booming sound, and almost immediately the other apes commenced to move about restlessly, weaving in and out aimlessly until they carried the impression of a moving mass of great, black maggots.

The beating of the drum was in a slow, ponderous cadence, at first without time but presently settling into a heavy rhythm to which the apes kept time with measured tread and swaying bodies. Slowly the mass separated into two rings, the outer of which was composed of shes and the very young, the inner of mature bulls. The former ceased to move and squatted upon their haunches, while the bulls now moved slowly about in a circle the center of which was the drum and all now in the same direction.

It was then that there came faintly to the ears of the girl from the direction of the village she had recently quitted a weird and high-pitched cry. The effect upon the apes was electrical – they stopped their movements and stood in attitudes of intent listening for a moment, and then one fellow, huger than his companions, raised his face to the heavens and in a voice that sent the cold shudders through the girl's slight frame answered the far-off cry.

Once again the beaters took up their drumming and the slow dance went on. There was a certain fascination in the savage ceremony that held the girl spellbound, and as there seemed little likelihood of her being discovered, she felt that she might as well remain the balance of the night in her tree and resume her flight by the comparatively greater safety of daylight.

Assuring herself that her packet of papers was safe she sought as comfortable a position as possible among the branches, and settled herself to watch the weird proceedings in the clearing below her.

A half-hour passed, during which the cadence of the drum increased gradually. Now the great bull that had replied to the distant call leaped from the inner circle to dance alone between the drummers and the other bulls. He leaped and crouched and leaped again, now growling and barking, again stopping to raise his hideous face to Goro, the moon, and, beating upon his shaggy breast, uttered a piercing scream – the challenge of the bull ape, had the girl but known it.

He stood thus in the full glare of the great moon, motionless after screaming forth his weird challenge, in the setting of the primeval jungle and the circling apes a picture of primitive savagery and power – a mightily muscled Hercules out of the dawn of life – when from close behind her the girl heard an answering scream, and an instant later saw an almost naked white man drop from a nearby tree into the clearing.

Instantly the apes became a roaring, snarling pack of angry beasts. Bertha Kircher held her breath. What maniac was this who dared approach these frightful creatures in their own haunts, alone against fifty? She saw the brown-skinned figure bathed in moonlight walk straight toward the snarling pack. She saw the symmetry and the beauty of that perfect body – its grace, its strength, its wondrous proportioning, and then she recognized him. It was the same creature whom she had seen carry Major Schneider from General Kraut's headquarters, the same who had rescued her from Numa, the lion; the same whom she had struck down with the butt of her pistol and escaped when he would have returned her to her enemies, the same who had slain Hauptmann Fritz Schneider and spared her life that night in Wilhelmstal.

Fear-filled and fascinated she watched him as he neared the apes. She heard sounds issue from his throat – sounds identical with those uttered by the apes – and though she could scarce believe the testimony of her own ears, she knew that this godlike creature was conversing with the brutes in their own tongue.

Tarzan halted just before he reached the shes of the outer circle. 'I am Tarzan of the Apes!' he cried. 'You do not know me because I am of another tribe; but Tarzan comes in peace or he comes to fight – which shall it be? Tarzan will talk with your king,' and so saying he pushed straight forward through the shes and the young who now gave way before him, making a narrow lane through which he passed toward the inner circle.

Shes and balus growled and bristled as he passed closer, but none hindered him and thus he came to the inner circle of bulls. Here bared fangs menaced him and growling faces hideously contorted. 'I am Tarzan,' he repeated. 'Tarzan comes to dance the Dum-Dum with his brothers. Where is your king?' Again he pressed forward and the girl in the tree clapped her palms to her cheeks as she watched, wide-eyed, this madman going to a frightful death. In another instant they would be upon him, rending and tearing until that perfect form had been ripped to shreds; but again the ring parted, and though the apes roared and menaced him they did not attack, and at last he stood in the inner circle close to the drum and faced the great king ape.

Again he spoke. 'I am Tarzan of the Apes,' he cried. 'Tarzan comes to live with his brothers. He will come in peace and live in peace or he will kill; but he has come and he will stay. Which – shall Tarzan dance the Dum-Dum in peace with his brothers, or shall Tarzan kill first?'

'I am Go-lat, King of the Apes,' screamed the great bull. 'I kill! I kill! I kill!' and with a sullen roar he charged the Tarmangani.

The ape-man, as the girl watched him, seemed entirely unprepared for the charge and she looked to see him born down and slain at the first rush. The great bull was almost upon him with huge hands outstretched to seize him before Tarzan made a move; but when he did move his quickness would have put Ara, the lightning, to shame. As darts forward the head of Histah, the snake, so darted forward the left hand of the man-beast as he seized the left wrist of his antagonist. A quick turn and the bull's right arm was locked beneath the right arm of his foe in a jujutsu hold that Tarzan had learned among civilized men – a hold with which he might easily break the great bones, a hold that left the ape helpless.

'I am Tarzan of the Apes!' screamed the ape-man. 'Shall Tarzan dance in peace or shall Tarzan kill?'

'I kill! I kill! I kill!' shrieked Go-lat.

With the quickness of a cat Tarzan swung the king ape over one hip and sent him sprawling to the ground. 'I am Tarzan, King of all the Apes!' he shouted. 'Shall it be peace?'

Go-lat, infuriated, leaped to his feet and charged again, shouting his war cry: 'I kill! I kill! I kill!' and again Tarzan met him with a sudden hold that the stupid bull, being ignorant of, could not possibly avert – a hold and a throw that brought a scream of delight from the interested audience and suddenly filled the girl with doubts as to the man's madness – evidently he was quite safe among the apes, for she saw him swing Go-lat to his back and then catapult him over his shoulder. The king ape fell upon his head and lay very still.

'I am Tarzan of the Apes!' cried the ape-man. 'I come to dance the Dum-Dum with my brothers,' and he made a motion to the drummers, who immediately took up the cadence of the dance where they had dropped it to watch their king slay the foolish Tarmangani.

It was then that Go-lat raised his head and slowly crawled to his feet. Tarzan approached him. 'I am Tarzan of the Apes,' he cried. 'Shall Tarzan dance the Dum-Dum with his brothers now, or shall he kill first?'

Go-lat raised his bloodshot eyes to the face of the Tarmangani. '*Kagoda!*' he cried. 'Tarzan of the Apes will dance the Dum-Dum with his brothers and Go-lat will dance with him!'

And then the girl in the tree saw the savage man leaping, bending, and stamping with the savage apes in the ancient rite of the Dum-Dum. His roars and growls were more beastly than the beasts'. His handsome face was distorted with savage ferocity. He beat upon his great breast and screamed forth his challenge as his smooth, brown hide brushed the shaggy coats of his fellows. It was weird; it was wonderful; and in its primitive savagery it was not without beauty – the strange scene she looked upon, such a scene as no other human being, probably, ever had witnessed – and yet, withal, it was horrible.

As she gazed, spellbound, a stealthy movement in the tree behind her caused her to turn her head, and there, back of her, blazing in the reflected moonlight, shone two great, yellow-green eyes. Sheeta, the panther, had found her out.

The beast was so close that it might have reached out and touched her with a great, taloned paw. There was no time to think, no time to weigh chances or to choose alternatives. Terror-inspired impulse was her guide as, with a loud scream, she leaped from the tree into the clearing.

Instantly the apes, now maddened by the effects of the dancing and the moonlight, turned to note the cause of the interruption. They saw this she Tarmangani, helpless and alone and they started for her. Sheeta, the panther, knowing that not even Numa, the lion, unless maddened by starvation, dares meddle with the great apes at their Dum-Dum, had silently vanished into the night, seeking his supper elsewhere.

Tarzan, turning with the other apes toward the cause of the interruption, saw the girl, recognized her and also her peril. Here again might she die at the hands of others; but why consider it! He knew that he could not permit it, and though the acknowledgment shamed him, it had to be admitted.

The leading shes were almost upon the girl when Tarzan leaped among them, and with heavy blows scattered them to right and left; and then as the bulls came to share in the kill they thought this new ape-thing was about to make that he might steal all the flesh for himself, they found him facing them with an arm thrown about the creature as though to protect her.

'This is Tarzan's she,' he said. 'Do not harm her.' It was the only way he could make them understand that they must not slay her. He was glad that she could not interpret the words. It was humiliating enough to make such a statement to wild apes about this hated enemy.

So once again Tarzan of the Apes was forced to protect a Hun. Growling, he muttered to himself in extenuation:

'She is a woman and I am not a German, so it could not be otherwise!'

9
Dropped from the Sky

Lieutenant Harold Percy Smith-Oldwick, Royal Air Service, was on reconnaissance. A report, or it would be better to say a rumor, had come to the British headquarters in German East Africa that the enemy had landed in force on the west coast and was marching across the dark continent to reinforce their colonial troops. In fact the new army was supposed to be no more than ten or twelve days' march to the west. Of course the thing was ridiculous – preposterous – but preposterous things often happen in war, and anyway no good general permits the least rumor of enemy activity to go uninvestigated.

Therefore Lieutenant Harold Percy Smith-Oldwick flew low toward the west, searching with keen eyes for signs of a Hun army. Vast forests unrolled beneath him in which a German army corps might have lain concealed, so dense was the overhanging foliage of the great trees. Mountain, meadowland, and desert passed in lovely panorama; but never a sight of man had the young lieutenant.

Always hoping that he might discover some sign of their passage – a discarded lorry, a broken limber, or an old campsite – he continued farther and farther into the west until well into the afternoon. Above a tree-dotted plain through the center of which flowed a winding river he determined to turn about and start for camp. It would take straight flying at top speed to cover the distance before dark; but as he had ample gasoline and a trustworthy machine there was no doubt in his mind that he could accomplish his aim. It was then that his engine stalled.

He was too low to do anything but land, and that immediately, while he had the more open country accessible, for directly east of him was a vast forest into which a stalled engine could only have plunged him to certain injury and probable death; and so he came down in the meadowland near the winding river and there started to tinker with his motor.

As he worked he hummed a tune, some music-hall air that had been popular in London the year before, so that one might have thought him working in the security of an English flying field surrounded by innumerable comrades rather than alone in the heart of an unexplored African wilderness. It was typical of the man that he should be wholly indifferent to his surroundings, although his looks entirely belied any assumption that he was of particularly heroic strain.

Lieutenant Harold Percy Smith-Oldwick was fair-haired, blue-eyed, and slender, with a rosy, boyish face that might have been molded more by an environment of luxury, indolence, and ease than the more strenuous exigencies of life's sterner requirements.

And not only was the young lieutenant outwardly careless of the immediate future and of his surroundings, but actually so. That the district might be infested by countless enemies seemed not to have occurred to him in the remotest degree. He bent assiduously to the work of correcting the adjustment that had caused his motor to stall without so much as an upward glance at the surrounding country. The forest to the east of him, and the more distant jungle that bordered the winding river, might, have harbored an army of bloodthirsty savages, but neither could elicit even a passing show of interest on the part of Lieutenant Smith-Oldwick.

And even had he looked, it is doubtful if he would have seen the score of figures crouching in the concealment of the undergrowth at the forest's edge. There are those who are reputed to be endowed with that which is sometimes, for want of a better appellation, known as the sixth sense – a species of intuition which apprises them of the presence of an unseen danger. The concentrated gaze of a hidden observer provokes a warning sensation of nervous unrest in such as these, but though twenty pairs of savage eyes were gazing fixedly at Lieutenant Harold Percy Smith-Oldwick, the fact aroused no responsive sensation of impending danger in his placid breast. He hummed peacefully and, his adjustment completed, tried out his motor for a minute or two, then shut it off and descended to the ground with the intention of stretching his legs and taking a smoke before continuing his return flight to camp. Now for the first time he took note of his surroundings, to be immediately impressed by both the wildness and the beauty of the scene. In some respects the tree-dotted meadowland reminded him of a parklike English forest, and that wild beasts and savage men could ever be a part of so quiet a scene seemed the remotest of contingencies.

Some gorgeous blooms upon a flowering shrub at a little distance from his machine caught the attention of his aesthetic eye, and as he puffed upon his cigarette, he walked over to examine the flowers more closely. As he bent above them he was probably some hundred yards from his plane and it was at this instant that Numabo, chief of the Wamabo, chose to leap from his ambush and lead his warriors in a sudden rush upon the white man.

The young Englishman's first intimation of danger was a chorus of savage yells from the forest behind him. Turning, he saw a score of naked, black warriors advancing rapidly toward him. They moved in a compact mass and as they approached more closely their rate of speed noticeably diminished. Lieutenant Smith-Oldwick realized in a quick glance that the direction of their approach and their proximity had cut off all chances of retreating to his plane, and he also understood that their attitude was entirely warlike and menacing. He saw that they were armed with spears and with bows and arrows, and he felt quite confident that notwithstanding the fact that he was armed with a pistol they could overcome him with the first rush. What he did not know about their tactics was that at any show of resistance they would fall back, which is the nature of the native Negroes, but that after numerous advances and retreats, during which they would work themselves into a frenzy of rage by much shrieking, leaping, and dancing, they would eventually come to the point of a determined and final assault.

Numabo was in the forefront, a fact which taken in connection with his considerably greater size and more warlike appearance, indicated him as the natural target and it was at Numabo that the Englishman aimed his first shot. Unfortunately for him it missed its target, as the killing of the chief might have permanently dispersed the others. The bullet passed Numabo to lodge in the breast of a warrior behind him and as the fellow lunged forward with a scream the others turned and retreated, but to the lieutenant's chagrin they ran in the direction of the plane instead of back toward the forest so that he was still cut off from reaching his machine.

Presently they stopped and faced him again. They were talking loudly and gesticulating, and after a moment one of them leaped into the air, brandishing his spear and uttering savage war cries, which soon had their effect upon his fellows so that it was not long ere all of them were taking part in the wild show of savagery, which would bolster their waning courage and presently spur them on to another attack.

The second charge brought them closer to the Englishman, and though he dropped another with his pistol, it was not before two or three spears had been launched at him. He now had five shots remaining and there were still eighteen warriors to be accounted for, so that unless he could frighten them off, it was evident that his fate was sealed.

That they must pay the price of one life for every attempt to take his had its effect upon them and they were longer now in initiating a new rush and when they did so it was more skillfully ordered than those that had preceded it, for they scattered into three bands which, partially surrounding him, came simultaneously toward him from different directions, and though he emptied his pistol with good effect, they reached him at last. They seemed to know that his ammunition was exhausted, for they circled close about him now with the evident intention of taking him alive, since they might easily have riddled him with their sharp spears with perfect safety to themselves.

For two or three minutes they circled about him until, at a word from Numabo, they closed in simultaneously, and though the slender young lieutenant struck out to right and left, he was soon overwhelmed by superior numbers and beaten down by the hafts of spears in brawny hands.

He was all but unconscious when they finally dragged him to his feet, and after securing his hands behind his back, pushed him roughly along ahead of them toward the jungle.

As the guard prodded him along the narrow trail, Lieutenant Smith-Oldwick could not but wonder why they had wished to take him alive. He knew that he was too far inland for his uniform to have any significance to this native tribe to whom no inkling of the World War probably ever had come, and he could only assume that he had fallen into the hands of the warriors of some savage potentate upon whose royal caprice his fate would hinge.

They had marched for perhaps half an hour when the Englishman saw ahead of them, in a little clearing upon the bank of the river, the thatched roofs of native huts showing above a crude but strong palisade; and presently he was ushered into a village street where he was immediately surrounded by a throng of women and children and warriors. Here he was soon the center of an excited mob whose intent seemed to be to dispatch him as quickly as possible. The women were more venomous than the men, striking and scratching him whenever they could reach him, until at last Numabo, the chief, was obliged to interfere to save his prisoner for whatever purpose he was destined.

As the warriors pushed the crowd back, opening a space through which the white man was led toward a hut, Lieutenant Smith-Oldwick saw coming from the opposite end of the village a number of Negroes wearing odds and ends of German uniforms. He was not a little surprised at this, and his first thought was that he had at last come in contact with some portion of the army which was rumored to be crossing from the west coast and for signs of which he had been searching.

A rueful smile touched his lips as he contemplated the unhappy circumstances which surrounded the accession of this knowledge for though he was far from being without hope, he realized that only by the merest chance could he escape these people and regain his machine.

Among the partially uniformed blacks was a huge fellow in the tunic of a sergeant and as this man's eyes fell upon the British officer, a loud cry of exultation broke from his lips, and immediately his followers took up the cry and pressed forward to bait the prisoner.

'Where did you get the Englishman?' asked Usanga, the black sergeant, of the chief Numabo. 'Are there many more with him?'

'He came down from the sky,' replied the native chief, 'in a strange thing which flies like a bird and which frightened us very much at first; but we watched for a long time and saw that it did not seem to be alive, and when this white man left it we attacked him and though he killed some of my warriors, we took him, for we Wamabos are brave men and great warriors.'

Usanga's eyes went wide. 'He flew here through the sky?' he asked.

'Yes,' said Numabo. 'In a great thing which resembled a bird he flew down out of the sky. The thing is still there where it came down close to the four trees near the second bend in the river. We left it there because, not knowing what it was, we were afraid to touch it and it is still there if it has not flown away again.'

'It cannot fly,' said Usanga, 'without this man in it. It is a terrible thing which filled the hearts of our soldiers with terror, for it flew over our camps at night and dropped bombs upon us. It is well that you captured this white man, Numabo, for with his great bird he would have flown over your village tonight and killed all your people. These Englishmen are very wicked white men.'

'He will fly no more,' said Numabo. 'It is not intended that a man should fly through the air; only wicked demons do such things as that and Numabo, the chief, will see that this white man does not do it again,' and with the words he pushed the young officer roughly toward a hut in the center of the Village, where he was left under guard of two stalwart warriors.

For an hour or more the prisoner was left to his own devices, which consisted of vain and unremitting attempts to loosen the strands which fettered his wrists, and then he was interrupted by the appearance of the black sergeant Usanga, who entered his hut and approached him.

'What are they going to do with me?' asked the Englishman. 'My country is not at war with these people. You speak their language. Tell them that I am not an enemy, that my people are the friends of the black people and that they must let me go in peace.'

Usanga laughed. 'They do not know an Englishman from a German,' he replied. 'It is nothing to them what you are, except that you are a white man and an enemy.'

'Then why did they take me alive?' asked the lieutenant.

'Come,' said Usanga and he led the Englishman to the doorway of the hut. 'Look,' he said, and pointed a black forefinger toward the end of the village street where a wider space between the huts left a sort of plaza.

Here Lieutenant Harold Percy Smith-Oldwick saw a number of Negresses engaged in laying fagots around a stake and in preparing fires beneath a number of large cooking vessels. The sinister suggestion was only too obvious.

Usanga was eyeing the white man closely, but if he expected to be rewarded by any signs of fear, he was doomed to disappointment and the young lieutenant merely turned toward him with a shrug: 'Really now, do you beggars intend eating me?'

'Not my people,' replied Usanga. 'We do not eat human flesh, but the Wamabos do. It is they who will eat you, but we will kill you for the feast, Englishman.'

The Englishman remained standing in the doorway of the hut, an interested spectator of the preparations for the coming orgy that was so horribly to terminate his earthly existence. It can hardly be assumed that he felt no fear; yet, if he did, he hid it perfectly beneath an imperturbable mask of coolness. Even the brutal Usanga must have been impressed by the bravery of his victim since, though he had come to abuse and possibly to torture the helpless prisoner, he now did neither, contenting himself merely with berating whites as a race and Englishmen especially, because of the terror the British aviators had caused Germany's native troops in East Africa.

'No more,' he concluded, 'will your great bird fly over our people dropping death among them from the skies – Usanga will see to that,' and he walked abruptly away toward a group of his own fighting men who were congregated near the stake where they were laughing and joking with the women.

A few minutes later the Englishman saw them pass out of the village gate, and once again his thoughts reverted to various futile plans for escape.

Several miles north of the village on a little rise of ground close to the river where the jungle, halting at the base of a knoll, had left a few acres of grassy land sparsely wooded, a man and a girl were busily engaged in constructing a small boma, in the center of which a thatched hut already had been erected.

They worked almost in silence with only an occasional word of direction or interrogation between them.

Except for a loincloth, the man was naked, his smooth skin tanned to a deep brown by the action of sun and wind. He moved with the graceful ease of a jungle cat and when he lifted heavy weights, the action seemed as effortless as the raising of empty hands.

When he was not looking at her, and it was seldom that he did, the girl found her eyes wandering toward him, and at such times there was always a puzzled expression upon her face as though she found in him an enigma which she could not solve. As a matter of fact, her feelings toward him were not untinged with awe, since in the brief period of their association she had discovered in this handsome, godlike giant the attributes of the superman and the savage beast closely intermingled. At first she had felt only that unreasoning feminine terror which her unhappy position naturally induced.

To be alone in the heart of an unexplored wilderness of Central Africa with a savage wild man was in itself sufficiently appalling, but to feel also that this man was a blood enemy, that he hated her and her kind and that in addition thereto he owed her a personal grudge for an attack she had made upon him in the past, left no loophole for any hope that he might accord her even the minutest measure of consideration.

She had seen him first months since when he had entered the headquarters of the German high command in East Africa and carried off the luckless Major Schneider, of whose fate no hint had ever reached the German officers; and she had seen him again upon that occasion when he had rescued her from the clutches of the lion and, after explaining to her that he had recognized her in the British camp, had made her prisoner. It was then that she had struck him down with the butt of her pistol and escaped. That he might seek no personal revenge for her act had been evidenced in Wilhelmstal the night that he had killed Hauptmann Fritz Schneider and left without molesting her.

No, she could not fathom him. He hated her and at the same time he had protected her as had been evidenced again when he had kept the great apes from tearing her to pieces after she had escaped from the Wamabo village to which Usanga, the black sergeant, had brought her a captive; but why was he saving her? For what sinister purpose could this savage enemy be protecting her from the other denizens of his cruel jungle? She tried to put from her mind the probable fate which awaited her, yet it persisted in obtruding itself upon her thoughts, though always she was forced to admit that there was nothing in the demeanor of the man to indicate that her fears were well grounded. She judged him perhaps by the standards other men had taught her and because she looked upon him as a savage creature, she felt that she could not expect more of chivalry from him than was to be found in the breasts of the civilized men of her acquaintance.

Fräulein Bertha Kircher was by nature a companionable and cheerful character. She was not given to morbid forebodings, and above all things she craved the society of her kind and that interchange of thought which is one of the marked distinctions between man and the lower animals. Tarzan, on the other hand, was sufficient unto himself. Long years of semisolitude among creatures whose powers of oral expression are extremely limited had thrown him almost entirely upon his own resources for entertainment.

His active mind was never idle, but because his jungle mates could neither follow nor grasp the vivid train of imaginings that his man-mind wrought, he had long since learned to keep them to himself; and so now he found no need for confiding them in others. This fact, linked with that of his dislike for the girl, was sufficient to seal his lips for other than necessary conversation, and so they worked on together in comparative silence. Bertha Kircher, however, was nothing if not feminine and she soon found that having someone to talk to who would not talk was extremely irksome. Her fear of the man was gradually departing, and she was full of a thousand unsatisfied curiosities as to his plans for the future insofar as they related to her, as well as more personal questions regarding himself, since she could not but wonder as to his antecedents and his strange and solitary life in the jungle, as well as his friendly intercourse with the savage apes among which she had found him.

With the waning of her fears she became sufficiently emboldened to question him, and so she asked him what he intended doing after the hut and boma were completed.

'I am going to the west coast where I was born,' replied Tarzan. 'I do not know when. I have all my life before me and in the jungle there is no reason for haste. We are not forever running as fast as we can from one place to another as are you of the outer world. When I have been here long enough I will go on toward the west, but first I must see that you have a safe place in which to sleep, and that you have learned how to provide yourself with necessaries. That will take time.'

'You are going to leave me here alone?' cried the girl; her tones marked the fear which the prospect induced. 'You are going to leave me here alone in this terrible jungle, a prey to wild beasts and savage men, hundreds of miles from a white settlement and in a country which gives every evidence of never having been touched by the foot of civilized men?'

'Why not?' asked Tarzan. 'I did not bring you here. Would one of your men accord any better treatment to an enemy woman?'

'Yes,' she exclaimed. 'They certainly would. No man of my race would leave a defenseless white woman alone in this horrible place.'

Tarzan shrugged his broad shoulders. The conversation seemed profitless and it was further distasteful to him for the reason that it was carried on in German, a tongue which he detested as much as he did the people who spoke it. He wished that the girl spoke English and then it occurred to him that as he had seen her in disguise in the British camp carrying on her nefarious work as a German spy, she probably did speak English and so he asked her.

'Of course I speak English,' she exclaimed, 'but I did not know that you did.'

Tarzan looked his wonderment but made no comment. He only wondered why the girl should have any doubts as to the ability of an Englishman to speak English, and then suddenly it occurred to him that she probably looked upon him merely as a beast of the jungle who by accident had learned to speak German through frequenting the district which Germany had colonized. It was there only that she had seen him and so she might not know that he was an Englishman by birth, and that he had had a home in British East Africa. It was as well, he thought, that she knew little of him, as the less she knew the more he might learn from her as to her activities in behalf of the Germans and of the German spy system of which she was a representative; and so it occurred to him to let her continue to think that he was only what he appeared to be – a savage denizen of his savage jungle, a man of no race and no country, hating all white men impartially; and this in truth, was what she did think of him. It explained perfectly his attacks upon Major Schneider and the major's brother, Hauptmann Fritz.

Again they worked on in silence upon the boma which was now nearly completed, the girl helping the man to the best of her small ability. Tarzan could not but note with grudging approval the spirit of helpfulness she manifested in the ofttimes painful labor of gathering and arranging the thornbushes which constituted the temporary protection against roaming carnivores. Her hands and arms gave bloody token of the sharpness of the numerous points that had lacerated her soft flesh, and even though she was an enemy Tarzan could not but feel compunction that he had permitted her to do this work, and at last he bade her stop.

'Why?' she asked. 'It is no more painful to me than it must be to you, and, as it is solely for my protection that you are building this boma, there is no reason why I should not do my share.'

'You are a woman,' replied Tarzan. 'This is not a woman's work. If you wish to do something, take those gourds I brought this morning and fill them with water at the river. You may need it while I am away.'

'While you are away—' she said. 'You are going away?'

'When the boma is built I am going out after meat,' he replied. 'Tomorrow I will go again and take you and show you how you may make your own kills after I am gone.'

Without a word she took the gourds and walked toward the river. As she filled them, her mind was occupied with painful forebodings of the future. She knew that Tarzan had passed a death sentence upon her, and that the moment that he left her, her doom was sealed, for it could be but a question of time – a very short time – before the grim jungle would claim her, for how could a lone woman hope successfully to combat the savage forces of destruction which constituted so large a part of existence in the jungle?

So occupied was she with the gloomy prophecies that she had neither ears nor eyes for what went on about her. Mechanically she filled the gourds and, taking them up, turned slowly to retrace her steps to the boma only to voice immediately a half-stifled scream and shrank back from the menacing figure looming before her and blocking her way to the hut.

Go-lat, the king ape, hunting a little apart from his tribe, had seen the woman go to the river for water, and it was he who confronted her when she turned back with her filled gourds. Go-lat was not a pretty creature when judged by standards of civilized humanity, though the shes of his tribe and even Go-lat himself, considered his glossy black coat shot with silver, his huge arms dangling to his knees, his bullet head sunk between his mighty shoulders, marks of great personal beauty. His wicked, bloodshot eyes and broad nose, his ample mouth and great fighting fangs only enhanced the claim of this Adonis of the forest upon the affections of his shes.

Doubtless in the little, savage brain there was a well-formed conviction that this strange she belonging to the Tarmangani must look with admiration upon so handsome a creature as Go-lat, for there could be no doubt in the mind of any that his beauty entirely eclipsed such as the hairless white ape might lay claim to.

But Bertha Kircher saw only a hideous beast, a fierce and terrible caricature of man. Could Go-lat have known what passed through her mind, he must have been terribly chagrined, though the chances are that he would have attributed it to a lack of discernment on her part. Tarzan heard the girl's cry and looking up saw at a glance the cause of her terror. Leaping lightly over the boma, he ran swiftly toward her as Go-lat lumbered closer to the girl the while he voiced his emotions in low gutturals which, while in reality the most amicable of advances, sounded to the girl like the growling of an enraged beast. As Tarzan drew nearer he called aloud to the ape and the girl heard from the human lips the same sounds that had fallen from those of the anthropoid.

'I will not harm your she,' Go-lat called to Tarzan.

'I know it,' replied the ape-man, 'but she does not. She is like Numa and Sheeta, who do not understand our talk. She thinks you come to harm her.'

By this time Tarzan was beside the girl. 'He will not harm you,' he said to her. 'You need not be afraid. This ape has learned his lesson. He has learned that Tarzan is lord of the jungle. He will not harm that which is Tarzan's.'

The girl cast a quick glance at the man's face. It was evident to her that the words he had spoken meant nothing to him and that the assumed proprietorship over her was, like the boma, only another means for her protection.

'But I am afraid of him,' she said.

'You must not show your fear. You will be often surrounded by these apes. At such times you will be safest. Before I leave you I will give you the means of protecting yourself against them should one of them chance to turn upon you. If I were you I would seek their society. Few are the animals of the jungle that dare attack the great apes when there are several of them together. If you let them know that you are afraid of them, they will take advantage of it and your life will be constantly menaced. The shes especially would attack you. I will let them know that you have the means of protecting yourself and of killing them. If necessary, I will show you how and then they will respect and fear you.'

'I will try,' said the girl, 'but I am afraid that it will be difficult. He is the most frightful creature I ever have seen.'

Tarzan smiled. 'Doubtless he thinks the same of you,' he said.

By this time other apes had entered the clearing and they were now the center of a considerable group, among which were several bulls, some young shes, and some older ones with their little balus clinging to their backs or frolicking around at their feet. Though they had seen the girl the night of the Dum-Dum when Sheeta had forced her to leap from her concealment into the arena where the apes were dancing, they still evinced a great curiosity regarding her. Some of the shes came very close and plucked at her garments, commenting upon them to one another in their strange tongue. The girl, by the exercise of all the willpower she could command, succeeded in passing through the ordeal without evincing any of the terror and revulsion that she felt. Tarzan watched her closely, a half-smile upon his face. He was not so far removed from recent contact with civilized people that he could not realize the torture that she was undergoing, but he felt no pity for this woman of a cruel enemy who doubtless deserved the worst suffering that could be meted to her. Yet, notwithstanding his sentiments toward her, he was forced to admire her fine display of courage. Suddenly he turned to the apes.

'Tarzan goes to hunt for himself and his she,' he said. 'The she will remain there,' and he pointed toward the hut. 'See that no member of the tribe harms her. Do you understand?'

The apes nodded. 'We will not harm her,' said Go-lat.

'No,' said Tarzan. 'You will not. For if you do, Tarzan will kill you,' and then turning to the girl, 'Come,' he said, 'I am going to hunt now. You had better remain at the hut. The apes have promised not to harm you. I will leave my spear with you. It will be the best weapon you could have in case you should need to protect yourself, but I doubt if you will be in any danger for the short time that I am away.'

He walked with her as far as the boma and when she had entered he closed the gap with thornbushes and turned away toward the forest. She watched him moving across the clearing, noting the easy, catlike tread and the grace of every movement that harmonized so well with the symmetry and perfection of his figure. At the forest's edge she saw him swing lightly into a tree and disappear from view, and then, being a woman, she entered the hut and, throwing herself upon the ground, burst into tears.

10
In the Hands of Savages

Tarzan sought Bara, the deer, or Horta, the boar, for of all the jungle animals he doubted if any would prove more palatable to the white woman, but though his keen nostrils were ever on the alert, he traveled far without being rewarded with even the faintest scent spoor of the game he sought. Keeping close to the river where he hoped to find Bara or Horta approaching or leaving a drinking place he came at last upon the strong odor of the Wamabo village and being ever ready to pay his hereditary enemies, the Gomangani, an undesired visit, he swung into a detour and came up in the rear of the village. From a tree which overhung the palisade he looked down into the street where he saw the preparations going on which his experience told him indicated the approach of one of those frightful feasts the *pièce de résistance* of which is human flesh.

One of Tarzan's chief divertissements was the baiting of the blacks. He realized more keen enjoyment through annoying and terrifying them than from any other source of amusement the grim jungle offered. To rob them of their feast in some way that would strike terror to their hearts would give him the keenest of pleasure, and so he searched the village with his eyes for some indication of the whereabouts of the prisoner. His view was circumscribed by the dense foliage of the tree in which he sat, and, so that he might obtain a better view, he climbed further aloft and moved cautiously out upon a slender branch.

Tarzan of the Apes possessed a woodcraft scarcely short of the marvelous but even Tarzan's wondrous senses were not infallible. The branch upon which he made his way outward from the bole was no smaller than many that had borne his weight upon countless other occasions. Outwardly it appeared strong and healthy and was in full foliage, nor could Tarzan know that close to the stem a burrowing insect had eaten away half the heart of the solid wood beneath the bark.

And so when he reached a point far out upon the limb, it snapped close to the bole of the tree without warning. Below him were no larger branches that he might clutch and as he lunged downward his foot caught in a looped creeper so that he turned completely over and alighted on the flat of his back in the center of the village street.

At the sound of the breaking limb and the crashing body falling through the branches the startled blacks scurried to their huts for weapons, and when the braver of them emerged, they saw the still form of an almost naked white man lying where he had fallen. Emboldened by the fact that he did not move they approached more closely, and when their eyes discovered no signs of others of his kind in the tree, they rushed forward until a dozen warriors stood about him with ready spears. At first they thought that the falling had killed him, but upon closer examination they discovered that the man was only stunned. One of the warriors was for thrusting a spear through his heart, but Numabo, the chief, would not permit it.

'Bind him,' he said. 'We will feed well tonight.'

And so they bound his hands and feet with thongs of gut and carried him into the hut where Lieutenant Harold Percy Smith-Oldwick awaited his fate. The Englishman had also been bound hand and foot by this time for fear that at the last moment he might escape and rob them of their feast. A great crowd of natives were gathered about the hut attempting to get a glimpse of the new prisoner, but Numabo doubled the guard before the entrance for fear that some of his people, in the exuberance of their savage joy, might rob the others of the pleasures of the death dance which would precede the killing of the victims.

The young Englishman had heard the sound of Tarzan's body crashing through the tree to the ground and the commotion in the village which immediately followed, and now, as he stood with his back against the wall of the hut, he looked upon the fellow-prisoner that the blacks carried in and laid upon the floor with mixed feelings of surprise and compassion. He realized that he never had seen a more perfect specimen of manhood than that of the unconscious figure before him, and he wondered to what sad circumstances the man owed his capture. It was evident that the new prisoner was himself as much a savage as his captors if apparel and weapons were any criterion by which to judge; yet it was also equally evident that he was a white man and from his well-shaped head and clean-cut features that he was not one of those unhappy half-wits who so often revert to savagery even in the heart of civilized communities.

As he watched the man, he presently noticed that his eyelids were moving. Slowly they opened and a pair of gray eyes looked blankly about. With returning consciousness the eyes assumed their natural expression of keen intelligence, and a moment later, with an effort, the prisoner rolled over upon his side and drew himself to a sitting position. He was facing the Englishman, and as his eyes took in the bound ankles and the arms drawn tightly behind the other's back, a slow smile lighted his features.

'They will fill their bellies tonight,' he said.

The Englishman grinned. 'From the fuss they made,' he said, 'the beggars must be awfully hungry. They like to have eaten me alive when they brought me in. How did they get you?'

Tarzan shrugged his head ruefully. 'It was my own fault,' he replied. 'I deserve to be eaten. I crawled out upon a branch that would not bear my weight and when it broke, instead of alighting on my feet, I caught my foot in a trailer and came down on my head. Otherwise they would not have taken me – alive.'

'Is there no escape?' asked the Englishman.

'I have escaped them before,' replied Tarzan, 'and I have seen others escape them. I have seen a man taken away from the stake after a dozen spear thrusts had pierced his body and the fire had been lighted about his feet.'

Lieutenant Smith-Oldwick shuddered. 'God!' he exclaimed, 'I hope I don't have to face that. I believe I could stand anything but the thought of the fire. I should hate like the devil to go into a funk before the devils at the last moment.'

'Don't worry,' said Tarzan. 'It doesn't last long and you won't funk. It is really not half as bad as it sounds. There is only a brief period of pain before you lose consciousness. I have seen it many times before. It is as good a way to go as another. We must die sometime. What difference whether it be tonight, tomorrow night, or a year hence, just so that we have lived – and I have lived!'

'Your philosophy may be all right, old top,' said the young lieutenant, 'but I can't say that it is exactly satisfying.'

Tarzan laughed. 'Roll over here,' he said, 'where I can get at your bonds with my teeth.' The Englishman did as he was bid and presently Tarzan was working at the thongs with his strong white teeth. He felt them giving slowly beneath his efforts. In another moment they would part, and then it would be a comparatively simple thing for the Englishman to remove the remaining bonds from Tarzan and himself.

It was then that one of the guards entered the hut. In an instant he saw what the new prisoner was doing and, raising his spear, struck the ape-man a vicious blow across the head with its shaft. Then he called in the other guards and together they fell upon the luckless men, kicking and beating them unmercifully, after which they bound the Englishman more securely than before and tied both men fast on opposite sides of the hut. When they had gone Tarzan looked across at his companion in misery.

'While there is life,' he said, 'there is hope,' but he grinned as he voiced the ancient truism.

Lieutenant Harold Percy Smith-Oldwick returned the other's smile. 'I fancy,' he said, 'that we are getting short on both. It must be close to supper-time now.'

Zu-tag hunted alone far from the balance of the tribe of Go-lat, the great ape. Zu-tag (Big-neck) was a young bull but recently arrived at maturity. He was large, powerful, and ferocious and at the same time far above the average of his kind in intelligence as was denoted by a fuller and less receding forehead. Already Go-lat saw in this young ape a possible contender for the laurels of his kingship and consequently the old bull looked upon Zu-tag with jealousy and disfavor. It was for this reason, possibly, as much as another that Zu-tag hunted so often alone; but it was his utter fearlessness that permitted him to wander far afield away from the protection which numbers gave the great apes. One of the results of this habit was a greatly increased resourcefulness which found him constantly growing in intelligence and powers of observation.

Today he had been hunting toward the south and was returning along the river upon a path he often followed because it led by the village of the Gomangani whose strange and almost apelike actions and peculiar manners of living had aroused his interest and curiosity. As he had done upon other occasions he took up his position in a tree from which he could overlook the interior of the village and watch the blacks at their vocations in the street below.

Zu-tag had scarcely more than established himself in his tree when, with the blacks, he was startled by the crashing of Tarzan's body from the branches of another jungle giant to the ground within the palisade. He saw the Negroes gather about the prostrate form and later carry it into the hut; and once he rose to his full height upon the limb where he had been squatting and raised his face to the heavens to scream out a savage protest and a challenge, for he had recognized in the brown-skinned Tarmangani the strange white ape who had come among them a night or two before in the midst of their Dum-Dum, and who by so easily mastering the greatest among them, had won the savage respect and admiration of this fierce young bull.

But Zu-tag's ferocity was tempered by a certain native cunning and caution. Before he had voiced his protest there formed in his mind the thought that he would like to save this wonderful white ape from the common enemy, the Gomangani, and so he screamed forth no challenge, wisely determined that more could be accomplished by secrecy and stealth than by force of muscle and fang.

At first he thought to enter the village alone and carry off the Tarmangani; but when he saw how numerous were the warriors and that several sat directly before the entrance to the lair into which the prisoner had been carried, it occurred to him that this was work for many rather than one, and so, as silently as he had come, he slipped away though the foliage toward the north.

The tribe was still loitering about the clearing where stood the hut that Tarzan and Bertha Kircher had built. Some were idly searching for food just within the forest's edge, while others squatted beneath the shade of trees within the clearing.

The girl had emerged from the hut, her tears dried and was gazing anxiously toward the south into the jungle where Tarzan had disappeared. Occasionally she cast suspicious glances in the direction of the huge shaggy anthropoids about her. How easy it would be for one of those great beasts to enter the boma and slay her. How helpless she was, even with the spear that the white man had left her, she realized as she noted for the thousandth time the massive shoulders, the bull necks, and the great muscles gliding so easily beneath the glossy coats. Never, she thought, had she seen such personifications of brute power as were represented by these mighty bulls. Those huge hands would snap her futile spear as she might snap a match in two, while their lightest blow could crush her into insensibility and death.

It was while she was occupied with these depressing thoughts that there dropped suddenly into the clearing from the trees upon the south the figure of a mighty young bull. At that time all of the apes looked much alike to Bertha Kircher, nor was it until some time later that she realized that each differed from the others in individual characteristics of face and figure as do individuals of the human races. Yet even then she could not help but note the wondrous strength and agility of this great beast, and as he approached she even found herself admiring the sheen of his heavy, black, silvershot coat.

It was evident that the newcomer was filled with suppressed excitement. His demeanor and bearing proclaimed this even from afar, nor was the girl the only one to note it. For as they saw him coming many of the apes arose and advanced to meet him, bristling and growling as is their way. Go-lat was among these latter, and he advanced stiffly with the hairs upon his neck and down his spine erect, uttering low growls and baring his fighting fangs, for who might say whether Zu-tag came in peace or otherwise? The old king had seen other young apes come thus in his day filled with a sudden resolution to wrest the kingship from their chief. He had seen bulls about to run amuck burst thus suddenly from the jungle upon the members of the tribe, and so Go-lat took no chances.

Had Zu-tag come indolently, feeding as he came, he might have entered the tribe without arousing notice or suspicion, but when one comes thus precipitately, evidently bursting with some emotion out of the ordinary, let all apes beware. There was a certain amount of preliminary circling, growling, and sniffing, stiff-legged and stiff-haired, before each side discovered that the other had no intention of initiating an attack and then Zu-tag told Go-lat what he had seen among the lairs of the Gomangani.

Go-lat grunted in disgust and turned away. 'Let the white ape take care of himself,' he said.

'He is a great ape,' said Zu-tag. 'He came to live in peace with the tribe of Go-lat. Let us save him from the Gomangani.'

Go-lat grunted again and continued to move away.

'Zu-tag will go alone and get him,' cried the young ape, 'if Go-lat is afraid of the Gomangani.'

The king ape wheeled in anger, growling loudly and beating upon his breast. 'Go-lat is not afraid,' he screamed, 'but he will not go, for the white ape is not of his tribe. Go yourself and take the Tarmangani's she with you if you wish so much to save the white ape.'

'Zu-tag will go,' replied the younger bull, 'and he will take the Tarmangani's she and all the bulls of Go-lat who are not cowards,' and so saying he cast his eyes inquiringly about at the other apes. 'Who will go with Zu-tag to fight the Gomangani and bring away our brother,' he demanded.

Eight young bulls in the full prime of their vigor pressed forward to Zu-tag's side, but the old bulls with the conservatism and caution of many years upon their gray shoulders, shook their heads and waddled away after Go-lat.

'Good,' cried Zu-tag. 'We want no old shes to go with us to fight the Gomangani for that is work for the fighters of the tribe.'

The old bulls paid no attention to his boastful words, but the eight who had volunteered to accompany him were filled with self-pride so that they stood around vaingloriously beating upon their breasts, baring their fangs and screaming their hideous challenge until the jungle reverberated to the horrid sound.

All this time Bertha Kircher was a wide-eyed and terrified spectator to what, as she thought, could end only in a terrific battle between these frightful beasts, and when Zu-tag and his followers began screaming forth their fearsome challenge, the girl found herself trembling in terror, for of all the sounds of the jungle there is none more awe inspiring than that of the great bull ape when he issues his challenge or shrieks forth his victory cry.

If she had been terrified before she was almost paralyzed with fear now as she saw Zu-tag and his apes turn toward the boma and approach her. With the agility of a cat Zu-tag leaped completely over the protecting wall and stood before her. Valiantly she held her spear before her, pointing it at his breast. He commenced to jabber and gesticulate, and even with her scant acquaintance with the ways of the anthropoids, she realized that he was not menacing her, for there was little or no baring of fighting fangs and his whole expression and attitude was of one attempting to explain a knotty problem or plead a worthy cause. At last he became evidently impatient, for with a sweep of one great paw he struck the spear from her hand and coming close, seized her by the arm, but not roughly. She shrank away in terror and yet some sense within her seemed to be trying to assure her that she was in no danger from this great beast. Zu-tag jabbered loudly, ever and again pointing into the jungle toward the south and moving toward the boma, pulling the girl with him. He seemed almost frantic in his efforts to explain something to her. He pointed toward the boma, herself, and then to the forest, and then, at last, as though by a sudden inspiration, he reached down and, seizing the spear, repeatedly touched it with his forefinger and again pointed toward the south. Suddenly it dawned upon the girl that what the ape was trying to explain to her was related in some way to the white man whose property they thought she was. Possibly her grim protector was in trouble and with this thought firmly established, she no longer held back, but started forward as though to accompany the young bull. At the point in the boma where Tarzan had blocked the entrance, she started to pull away the thornbushes, and, when Zu-tag saw what she was doing, he fell to and assisted her so that presently they had an opening through the boma through which she passed with the great ape.

Immediately Zu-tag and his eight apes started off rapidly toward the jungle, so rapidly that Bertha Kircher would have had to run at top speed to keep up with them. This she realized she could not do, and so she was forced to lag behind, much to the chagrin of Zu-tag, who constantly kept running back and urging her to greater speed. Once he took her by the arm and tried to draw her along. Her protests were of no avail since the beast could not know that they were protests, nor did he desist until she caught her foot in some tangled grass and fell to the ground. Then indeed was Zu-tag furious and growled hideously. His apes were waiting at the edge of the forest for him to lead them. He suddenly realized that this poor weak she could not keep up with them and that if they traveled at her slow rate they might be too late to render assistance to the Tarmangani, and so without more ado, the giant anthropoid picked Bertha Kircher bodily from the ground and swung her to his back. Her arms were about his neck and in this position he seized her wrists in one great paw so that she could not fall off and started at a rapid rate to join his companions.

Dressed as she was in riding breeches with no entangling skirts to hinder or catch upon passing shrubbery, she soon found that she could cling tightly to the back of the mighty bull and when a moment later he took to the lower branches of the trees, she closed her eyes and clung to him in terror lest she be precipitated to the ground below.

That journey through the primeval forest with the nine great apes will live in the memory of Bertha Kircher for the balance of her life, as clearly delineated as at the moment of its enactment.

The first overwhelming wave of fear having passed, she was at last able to open her eyes and view her surroundings with increased interest and presently the sensation of terror slowly left her to be replaced by one of comparative security when she saw the ease and surety with which these great beasts traveled through the trees; and later her admiration for the young bull increased as it became evident that even burdened with her additional weight, he moved more rapidly and with no greater signs of fatigue than his unburdened fellows.

Not once did Zu-tag pause until he came to a stop among the branches of a tree no great distance from the native village. They could hear the noises of the life within the palisade, the laughing and shouting of the Negroes, and the barking of dogs, and through the foliage the girl caught glimpses of the village from which she had so recently escaped. She shuddered to think of the possibility of having to return to it and of possible recapture, and she wondered why Zu-tag had brought her here.

Now the apes advanced slowly once more and with great caution, moving as noiselessly through the trees as the squirrels themselves until they had reached a point where they could easily overlook the palisade and the village street below.

Zu-tag squatted upon a great branch close to the bole of the tree and by loosening the girl's arms from about his neck, indicated that she was to find a footing for herself and when she had done so, he turned toward her and pointed repeatedly at the open doorway of a hut upon the opposite side of the street below them. By various gestures he seemed to be trying to explain something to her and at last she caught at the germ of his idea – that her white man was a prisoner there.

Beneath them was the roof of a hut onto which she saw that she could easily drop, but what she could do after she had entered the village was beyond her.

Darkness was already falling and the fires beneath the cooking pots had been lighted. The girl saw the stake in the village street and the piles of fagots about it and in terror she suddenly realized the portent of these grisly preparations. Oh, if she but only had some sort of a weapon that might give her even a faint hope, some slight advantage against the blacks. Then she would not hesitate to venture into the village in an attempt to save the man who had upon three different occasions saved her. She knew that he hated her and yet strong within her breast burned the sense of her obligation to him. She could not fathom him. Never in her life had she seen a man at once so paradoxical and dependable. In many of his ways he was more savage than the beasts with which he associated and yet, on the other hand, he was as chivalrous as a knight of old. For several days she had been lost with him in the jungle absolutely at his mercy, yet she had come to trust so implicitly in his honor that any fear she had had of him was rapidly disappearing.

On the other hand, that he might be hideously cruel was evidenced to her by the fact that he was planning to leave her alone in the midst of the frightful dangers which menaced her by night and by day.

Zu-tag was evidently waiting for darkness to fall before carrying out whatever plans had matured in his savage little brain, for he and his fellows sat quietly in the tree about her, watching the preparations of the blacks. Presently it became apparent that some altercation had arisen among the Negroes, for a score or more of them were gathered around one who appeared to be their chief, and all were talking and gesticulating heatedly. The argument lasted for some five or ten minutes when suddenly the little knot broke and two warriors ran to the opposite side of the village from whence they presently returned with a large stake which they soon set up beside the one already in place. The girl wondered what the purpose of the second stake might be, nor did she have long to wait for an explanation.

It was quite dark by this time, the village being lighted by the fitful glare of many fires, and now she saw a number of warriors approach and enter the hut Zu-tag had been watching. A moment later they reappeared, dragging between them two captives, one of whom the girl immediately recognized as her protector and the other as an Englishman in the uniform of an aviator. This, then, was the reason for the two stakes.

Arising quickly she placed a hand upon Zu-tag's shoulder and pointed down into the village. 'Come,' she said, as if she had been talking to one of her own kind, and with the word she swung lightly to the roof of the hut below. From there to the ground was but a short drop and a moment later she was circling the hut upon the side farthest from the fires, keeping in the dense shadows where there was little likelihood of being discovered. She turned once to see that Zu-tag was directly behind her and could see his huge bulk looming up in the dark, while beyond was another one of his eight. Doubtless they had all followed her and this fact gave her a greater sense of security and hope than she had before experienced.

Pausing beside the hut next to the street, she peered cautiously about the corner. A few inches from her was the open doorway of the structure, and beyond, farther down the village street, the blacks were congregating about the prisoners, who were already being bound to the stakes. All eyes were centered upon the victims, and there was only the remotest chance that she and her companions would be discovered until they were close upon the blacks. She wished, however, that she might have some sort of a weapon with which to lead the attack, for she could not know, of course, for a certainty whether the great apes would follow her or not. Hoping that she might find something within the hut, she slipped quickly around the corner and into the doorway and after her, one by one, came the nine bulls. Searching quickly about the interior, she presently discovered a spear, and, armed with this, she again approached the entrance.

Tarzan of the Apes and Lieutenant Harold Percy Smith-Oldwick were bound securely to their respective stakes. Neither had spoken for some time. The Englishman turned his head so that he could see his companion in misery. Tarzan stood straight against his stake. His face was entirely expressionless insofar as either fear or anger were concerned. His countenance portrayed bored indifference though both men knew that they were about to be tortured.

'Goodbye, old top,' whispered the young lieutenant.

Tarzan turned his eyes in the direction of the other and smiled. 'Goodbye,' he said. 'If you want to get it over in a hurry, inhale the smoke and flames as rapidly as you can.'

'Thanks,' replied the aviator and though he made a wry face, he drew himself up very straight and squared his shoulders.

The women and children had seated themselves in a wide circle about the victims while the warriors, hideously painted, were forming slowly to commence the dance of death. Again Tarzan turned to his companion. 'If you'd like to spoil their fun,' he said, 'don't make any fuss no matter how much you suffer. If you can carry on to the end without changing the expression upon your face or uttering a single word, you will deprive them of all the pleasures of this part of the entertainment. Goodbye again and good luck.'

The young Englishman made no reply but it was evident from the set of his jaws that the Negroes would get little enjoyment out of him.

The warriors were circling now. Presently Numabo would draw first blood with his sharp spear which would be the signal for the beginning of the torture after a little of which the fagots would be lighted around the feet of the victims.

Closer and closer danced the hideous chief, his yellow, sharp-filed teeth showing in the firelight between his thick, red lips. Now bending double, now stamping furiously upon the ground, now leaping into the air, he danced step by step in the narrowing circle that would presently bring him within spear reach of the intended feast.

At last the spear reached out and touched the ape-man on the breast and when it came away, a little trickle of blood ran down the smooth, brown hide and almost simultaneously there broke from the outer periphery of the expectant audience a woman's shriek which seemed a signal for a series of hideous screamings, growlings and barkings, and a great commotion upon that side of the circle. The victims could not see the cause of the disturbance, but Tarzan did not have to see, for he knew by the voices of the apes the identity of the disturbers. He only wondered what had brought them and what the purpose of the attack, for he could not believe that they had come to rescue him.

Numabo and his warriors broke quickly from the circle of their dance to see pushing toward them through the ranks of their screaming and terrified people the very white girl who had escaped them a few nights before, and at her back what appeared to their surprised eyes a veritable horde of the huge and hairy forest men upon whom they looked with considerable fear and awe.

Striking to right and left with his heavy fists, tearing with his great fangs, came Zu-tag, the young bull, while at his heels, emulating his example, surged his hideous apes. Quickly they came through the old men and the women and children, for straight toward Numabo and his warriors the girl led them. It was then that they came within range of Tarzan's vision and he saw with unmixed surprise who it was that led the apes to his rescue.

To Zu-tag he shouted: 'Go for the big bulls while the she unbinds me,' and to Bertha Kircher: 'Quick! Cut these bonds. The apes will take care of the blacks.'

Turning from her advance the girl ran to his side. She had no knife and the bonds were tied tightly but she worked quickly and coolly and as Zu-tag and his apes closed with the warriors, she succeeded in loosening Tarzan's bonds sufficiently to permit him to extricate his own hands so that in another minute he had freed himself.

'Now unbind the Englishman,' he cried, and, leaping forward, ran to join Zu-tag and his fellows in their battle against the blacks. Numabo and his warriors, realizing now the relatively small numbers of the apes against them, had made a determined stand and with spears and other weapons were endeavoring to overcome the invaders. Three of the apes were already down, killed or mortally wounded, when Tarzan, realizing that the battle must eventually go against the apes unless some means could be found to break the morale of the Negroes, cast about him for some means of bringing about the desired end. And suddenly his eye lighted upon a number of weapons which he knew would accomplish the result. A grim smile touched his lips as he snatched a vessel of boiling water from one of the fires and hurled it full in the faces of the warriors. Screaming with terror and pain they fell back though Numabo urged them to rush forward.

Scarcely had the first cauldron of boiling water spilled its contents upon them ere Tarzan deluged them with a second, nor was there any third needed to send them shrieking in every direction to the security of their huts.

By the time Tarzan had recovered his own weapons the girl had released the young Englishman, and, with the six remaining apes, the three Europeans moved slowly toward the village gate, the aviator arming himself with a spear discarded by one of the scalded warriors, as they eagerly advanced toward the outer darkness.

Numabo was unable to rally the now thoroughly terrified and painfully burned warriors so that rescued and rescuers passed out of the village into the blackness of the jungle without further interference.

Tarzan strode through the jungle in silence. Beside him walked Zu-tag, the great ape, and behind them strung the surviving anthropoids followed by

Fräulein Bertha Kircher and Lieutenant Harold Percy Smith-Oldwick, the latter a thoroughly astonished and mystified Englishman.

In all his life Tarzan of the Apes had been obliged to acknowledge but few obligations. He won his way through his savage world by the might of his own muscle, the superior keenness of his five senses and his God-given power to reason. Tonight the greatest of all obligations had been placed upon him – his life had been saved by another and Tarzan shook his head, and growled, for it had been saved by one whom he hated above all others.

11

Finding the Airplane

Tarzan of the Apes, returning from a successful hunt, with the body of Bara, the deer, across one sleek, brown shoulder, paused in the branches of a great tree at the edge of a clearing and gazed ruefully at two figures walking from the river to the boma-encircled hut a short distance away.

The ape-man shook his tousled head and sighed. His eyes wandered toward the west and his thoughts to the faraway cabin by the landlocked harbor of the great water that washed the beach of his boyhood home – to the cabin of his long-dead father to which the memories and treasures of a happy childhood lured him. Since the loss of his mate, a great longing had possessed him to return to the haunts of his youth – to the untracked jungle wilderness where he had lived the life he loved best long before man had invaded the precincts of his wild stamping grounds. There he hoped in a renewal of the old life under the old conditions to win surcease from sorrow and perhaps some measure of forgetfulness.

But the little cabin and the landlocked harbor were many long, weary marches away, and he was handicapped by the duty which he felt he owed to the two figures walking in the clearing before him. One was a young man in a worn and ragged uniform of the British Royal Air Forces, the other, a young woman in the even more disreputable remnants of what once had been trim riding togs.

A freak of fate had thrown these three radically different types together. One was a savage, almost naked beast-man, one an English army officer, and the woman, she whom the ape-man knew and hated as a German spy.

How he was to get rid of them Tarzan could not imagine unless he accompanied them upon the weary march back to the east coast, a march that would necessitate his once more retracing the long, weary way he already had covered toward his goal, yet what else could be done? These two had neither the strength, endurance, nor jungle-craft to accompany him through the unknown country to the west, nor did he wish them with him. The man he might have tolerated, but he could not even consider the presence of the girl in the far-off cabin, which had in a way become sacred to him through its memories, without a growl or anger rising to his lips. There remained, then, but the one way, since he could not desert them. He must move by slow and irksome marches back to the east coast, or at least to the first white settlement in that direction.

He had, it is true, contemplated leaving the girl to her fate but that was before she had been instrumental in saving him from torture and death at the hands of the black Wamabos. He chafed under the obligation she had put upon him, but no less did he acknowledge it and as he watched the two, the rueful expression upon his face was lightened by a smile as he thought of the helplessness of them. What a puny thing, indeed, was man! How ill equipped to combat the savage forces of nature and of nature's jungle. Why, even the tiny balu of the tribe of Go-lat, the great ape, was better fitted to survive than these, for a balu could at least escape the numerous creatures that menaced its existence, while with the possible exception of Kota, the tortoise, none moved so slowly as did helpless and feeble man.

Without him these two doubtless would starve in the midst of plenty, should they by some miracle escape the other forces of destruction which constantly threatened them. That morning Tarzan had brought them fruit, nuts, and plantain, and now he was bringing them the flesh of his kill, while the best that they might do was to fetch water from the river. Even now, as they walked across the clearing toward the boma, they were in utter ignorance of the presence of Tarzan near them. They did not know that his sharp eyes were watching them, nor that other eyes less friendly were glaring at them from a clump of bushes close beside the boma entrance. They did not know these things, but Tarzan did. No more than they could he see the creature crouching in the concealment of the foliage, yet he knew that it was there and what it was and what its intentions, precisely as well as though it had been lying in the open.

A slight movement of the leaves at the top of a single stem had apprised him of the presence of a creature there, for the movement was not that imparted by the wind. It came from pressure at the bottom of the stem which communicates a different movement to the leaves than does the wind passing among them, as anyone who has lived his lifetime in the jungle well knows, and the same wind that passed through the foliage of the bush brought to the ape-man's sensitive nostrils indisputable evidence of the fact that Sheeta, the panther, waited there for the two returning from the river.

They had covered half the distance to the boma entrance when Tarzan called to them to stop. They looked in surprise in the direction from which his voice had come to see him drop lightly to the ground and advance toward them.

'Come slowly toward me,' he called to them. 'Do not run for if you run Sheeta will charge.'

They did as he bid, their faces filled with questioning wonderment.

'What do you mean?' asked the young Englishman. 'Who is Sheeta?' but for answer the ape-man suddenly hurled the carcass of Bara, the deer, to the ground and leaped quickly toward them, his eyes upon something in their rear, and then it was that the two turned and learned the identity of Sheeta, for behind them was a devil-faced cat charging rapidly toward them.

Sheeta with rising anger and suspicion had seen the ape-man leap from the tree and approach the quarry. His life's experiences backed by instinct told him that the Tarmangani was about to rob him of his prey and as Sheeta was hungry, he had no intention of being thus easily deprived of the flesh he already considered his own.

The girl stifled an involuntary scream as she saw the proximity of the fanged fury bearing down upon them. She shrank close to the man and clung to him and all unarmed and defenseless as he was, the Englishman pushed her behind him and shielding her with his body, stood squarely in the face of the panther's charge. Tarzan noted the act, and though accustomed as he was to acts of courage, he experienced a thrill from the hopeless and futile bravery of the man.

The charging panther moved rapidly, and the distance which separated the bush in which he had concealed himself from the objects of his desire was not great. In the time that one might understandingly read a dozen words the strong-limbed cat could have covered the entire distance and made his kill, yet if Sheeta was quick, quick too was Tarzan. The English lieutenant saw the ape-man flash by him like the wind. He saw the great cat veer in his charge as though to elude the naked savage rushing to meet him, as it was evidently Sheeta's intention to make good his kill before attempting to protect it from Tarzan.

Lieutenant Smith-Oldwick saw these things and then with increasing wonder he saw the ape-man swerve, too, and leap for the spotted cat as a football player leaps for a runner. He saw the strong, brown arms encircling the body of the carnivore, the left arm in front of the beast's left shoulder and the right arm behind his right foreleg, and with the impact the two together rolling over and over upon the turf. He heard the snarls and growls of bestial combat, and it was with a feeling of no little horror that he realized that the sounds coming from the human throat of the battling man could scarce be distinguished from those of the panther.

The first momentary shock of terror over, the girl released her grasp upon the Englishman's arm. 'Cannot we do something?' she asked. 'Cannot we help him before the beast kills him?'

The Englishman looked upon the ground for some missile with which to attack the panther and then the girl uttered an exclamation and started at a run toward the hut. 'Wait there,' she called over her shoulder. 'I will fetch the spear that he left me.'

Smith-Oldwick saw the raking talons of the panther searching for the flesh of the man and the man on his part straining every muscle and using every artifice to keep his body out of range of them. The muscles of his arms knotted under the brown hide. The veins stood out upon his neck and forehead as with ever-increasing power he strove to crush the life from the great cat. The ape-man's teeth were fastened in the back of Sheeta's neck and now he succeeded in encircling the beast's torso with his legs which he crossed and locked beneath the cat's belly. Leaping and snarling, Sheeta sought to dislodge the ape-man's hold upon him. He hurled himself upon the ground and rolled over and over. He reared upon his hind legs and threw himself backward but always the savage creature upon his back clung tenaciously to him, and always the mighty brown arms crushed tighter and tighter about his chest.

And then the girl, panting from her quick run, returned with the short spear Tarzan had left her as her sole weapon of protection. She did not wait to hand it to the Englishman who ran forward to receive it, but brushed past him and leaped into close quarters beside the growling, tumbling mass of yellow fur and smooth brown hide. Several times she attempted to press the point home into the cat's body, but on both occasions the fear of endangering the ape-man caused her to desist, but at last the two lay motionless for a moment as the carnivore sought a moment's rest from the strenuous exertions of battle, and then it was that Bertha Kircher pressed the point of the spear to the tawny side and drove it deep into the savage heart.

Tarzan rose from the dead body of Sheeta and shook himself after the manner of beasts that are entirely clothed with hair. Like many other of his traits and mannerisms this was the result of environment rather than heredity or reversion, and even though he was outwardly a man, the Englishman and the girl were both impressed with the naturalness of the act. It was as though Numa, emerging from a fight, had shaken himself to straighten his rumpled mane and coat, and yet, too, there was something uncanny about it as there had been when the savage growls and hideous snarls issued from those clean-cut lips.

Tarzan looked at the girl, a quizzical expression upon his face. Again had she placed him under obligations to her, and Tarzan of the Apes did not wish to be obligated to a German spy; yet in his honest heart he could not but admit a certain admiration for her courage, a trait which always greatly impressed the ape-man, he himself the personification of courage.

'Here is the kill,' he said, picking the carcass of Bara from the ground. 'You will want to cook your portion, I presume, but Tarzan does not spoil his meat with fire.'

They followed him to the boma where he cut several pieces of meat from the carcass for them, retaining a joint for himself. The young lieutenant prepared a fire, and the girl presided over the primitive culinary rites of their simple meal. As she worked some little way apart from them, the lieutenant and the ape-man watched her.

'She is wonderful. Is she not?' murmured Smith-Oldwick.

'She is a German and a spy,' replied Tarzan.

The Englishman turned quickly upon him. 'What do you mean?' he cried.

'I mean what I say,' replied the ape-man. 'She is a German and a spy.'

'I do not believe it!' exclaimed the aviator.

'You do not have to,' Tarzan assured him. 'It is nothing to me what you believe. I saw her in conference with the Boche general and his staff at the camp near Taveta. They all knew her and called her by name and she handed him a paper. The next time I saw her she was inside the British lines in disguise, and again I saw her bearing word to a German officer at Wilhelmstal. She is a German and a spy, but she is a woman and therefore I cannot destroy her.'

'You really believe that what you say is true?' asked the young lieutenant. 'My God! I cannot believe it. She is so sweet and brave and good.'

The ape-man shrugged his shoulders. 'She is brave,' he said, 'but even Pamba, the rat, must have some good quality, but she is what I have told you and therefore I hate her and you should hate her.'

Lieutenant Harold Percy Smith-Oldwick buried his face in his hands. 'God forgive me,' he said at last. 'I cannot hate her.'

The ape-man cast a contemptuous look at his companion and arose. 'Tarzan goes again to hunt,' he said. 'You have enough food for two days. By that time he will return.'

The two watched him until he had disappeared in the foliage of the trees at the farther side of the clearing.

When he had gone the girl felt a vague sense of apprehension that she never experienced when Tarzan was present. The invisible menaces lurking in the grim jungle seemed more real and much more imminent now that the ape-man was no longer near. While he had been there talking with them, the little thatched hut and its surrounding thorn boma had seemed as safe a place as the world might afford. She wished that he had remained – two days seemed an eternity in contemplation – two days of constant fear, two days, every moment of which would be fraught with danger. She turned toward her companion.

'I wish that he had remained,' she said. 'I always feel so much safer when he is near. He is very grim and very terrible, and yet I feel safer with him than with any man I ever have known. He seems to dislike me and yet I know that he would let no harm befall me. I cannot understand him.'

'Neither do I understand him,' replied the Englishman; 'but I know this much – our presence here is interfering with his plans. He would like to be rid of us, and I half imagine that he rather hopes to find when he returns that we have succumbed to one of the dangers which must always confront us in this savage land.

'I think that we should try to return to the white settlements. This man does not want us here, nor is it reasonable to assume that we could long survive in such a savage wilderness. I have traveled and hunted in several parts of Africa, but never have I seen or heard of any single locality so overrun with savage beasts and dangerous natives. If we set out for the east coast at once we would be in but little more danger than we are here, and if we could survive a day's march, I believe that we will find the means of reaching the coast in a few hours, for my plane must still be in the same place that I landed just before the blacks captured me. Of course there is no one here who could operate it nor is there any reason why they should have destroyed it. As a matter of fact, the natives would be so fearful and suspicious of so strange and incomprehensible a thing that the chances are they would not dare approach it. Yes, it must be where I left it and all ready to carry us safely to the settlements.'

'But we cannot leave,' said the girl, 'until he returns. We could not go away like that without thanking him or bidding him farewell. We are under too great obligations to him.'

The man looked at her in silence for a moment. He wondered if she knew how Tarzan felt toward her and then he himself began to speculate upon the truth of the ape-man's charges. The longer he looked at the girl, the less easy was it to entertain the thought that she was an enemy spy. He was upon the point of asking her point-blank but he could not bring himself to do so, finally determining to wait until time and longer acquaintance should reveal the truth or falsity of the accusation.

'I believe,' he said as though there had been no pause in their conversation, 'that the man would be more than glad to find us gone when he returns. It is not necessary to jeopardize our lives for two more days in order that we may thank him, however much we may appreciate his services to us. You have more than balanced your obligations to him and from what he told me I feel that you especially should not remain here longer.'

The girl looked up at him in astonishment. 'What do you mean?' she asked.

'I do not like to tell,' said the Englishman, digging nervously at the turf with the point of a stick, 'but you have my word that he would rather you were not here.'

'Tell me what he said,' she insisted. 'I have a right to know.'

Lieutenant Smith-Oldwick squared his shoulders and raised his eyes to those of the girl. 'He said that he hated you,' he blurted. 'He has only aided you at all from a sense of duty because you are a woman.'

The girl paled and then flushed. 'I will be ready to go,' she said, 'in just a moment. We had better take some of this meat with us. There is no telling when we will be able to get more.'

And so the two set out down the river toward the south. The man carried the short spear that Tarzan had left with the girl, while she was entirely unarmed except for a stick she had picked up from among those left after the building of the hut. Before departing she had insisted that the man leave a note for Tarzan thanking him for his care of them and bidding him goodbye. This they left pinned to the inside wall of the hut with a little sliver of wood.

It was necessary that they be constantly on the alert since they never knew what might confront them at the next turn of the winding jungle trail or what might lie concealed in the tangled bushes at either side. There was also the ever-present danger of meeting some of Numabo's black warriors and as the village lay directly in their line of march, there was the necessity for making a wide detour before they reached it in order to pass around it without being discovered.

'I am not so much afraid of the native blacks,' said the girl, 'as I am of Usanga and his people. He and his men were all attached to a German native regiment. They brought me along with them when they deserted, either with the intention of holding me ransom or selling me into the harem of one of the black sultans of the north. Usanga is much more to be feared than Numabo for he has had the advantage of European military training and is armed with more or less modern weapons and ammunition.'

'It is lucky for me,' remarked the Englishman, 'that it was the ignorant Numabo who discovered and captured me rather than the worldly-wise Usanga. He would have felt less fear of the giant flying machine and would have known only too well how to wreck it.'

'Let us pray that the black sergeant has not discovered it,' said the girl.

They made their way to a point which they guessed was about a mile above the village, then they turned into the trackless tangle of undergrowth to the east. So dense was the verdure at many points that it was with the utmost difficulty they wormed their way through, sometimes on hands and knees and again by clambering over numerous fallen tree trunks. Interwoven with dead limbs and living branches were the tough and ropelike creepers which formed a tangled network across their path.

South of them in an open meadowland a number of black warriors were gathered about an object which elicited much wondering comment. The blacks were clothed in fragments of what had once been uniforms of a native

German command. They were a most unlovely band and chief among them in authority and repulsiveness was the black sergeant Usanga. The object of their interest was a British airplane.

Immediately after the Englishman had been brought to Numabo's village Usanga had gone out in search of the plane, prompted partially by curiosity and partially by an intention to destroy it, but when he had found it, some new thought had deterred him from carrying out his design. The thing represented considerable value as he well knew and it had occurred to him that in some way he might turn his prize to profit. Every day he had returned to it, and while at first it had filled him with considerable awe, he eventually came to look upon it with the accustomed eye of a proprietor, so that he now clambered into the fuselage and even advanced so far as to wish that he might learn to operate it.

What a feat it would be indeed to fly like a bird far above the highest tree-top! How it would fill his less favored companions with awe and admiration! If Usanga could but fly, so great would be the respect of all the tribesmen throughout the scattered villages of the great interior, they would look upon him as little less than a god.

Usanga rubbed his palms together and smacked his thick lips. Then indeed, would he be very rich, for all the villages would pay tribute to him and he could even have as many as a dozen wives. With that thought, however, came a mental picture of Naratu, the black termagant, who ruled him with an iron hand. Usanga made a wry face and tried to forget the extra dozen wives, but the lure of the idea remained and appealed so strongly to him that he presently found himself reasoning most logically that a god would not be much of a god with less than twenty-four wives.

He fingered the instruments and the control, half hoping and half fearing that he would alight upon the combination that would put the machine in flight. Often had he watched the British airmen soaring above the German lines and it looked so simple he was quite sure that he could do it himself if there was somebody who could but once show him how. There was, of course, always the hope that the white man who came in the machine and who had escaped from Numabo's village might fall into Usanga's hands and then indeed would he be able to learn how to fly. It was in this hope that Usanga spent so much time in the vicinity of the plane, reasoning as he did that eventually the white man would return in search of it.

And at last he was rewarded, for upon this very day after he had quit the machine and entered the jungle with his warriors, he heard voices to the north and when he and his men had hidden in the dense foliage upon either side of the trail, Usanga was presently filled with elation by the appearance of the British officer and the white girl whom the black sergeant had coveted and who had escaped him.

The Negro could scarce restrain a shout of elation, for he had not hoped that fate would be so kind as to throw these two whom he most desired into his power at the same time.

As the two came down the trail all unconscious of impending danger, the man was explaining that they must be very close to the point at which the plane had landed. Their entire attention was centered on the trail directly ahead of them, as they momentarily expected it to break into the meadowland where they were sure they would see the plane that would spell life and liberty for them.

The trail was broad, and they were walking side by side so that at a sharp turn the parklike clearing was revealed to them simultaneously with the outlines of the machine they sought.

Exclamations of relief and delight broke from their lips, and at the same instant Usanga and his black warriors rose from the bushes all about them.

12

The Black Flier

The girl was almost crushed by terror and disappointment. To have been thus close to safety and then to have all hope snatched away by a cruel stroke of fate seemed unendurable. The man was disappointed, too, but more was he angry. He noted the remnants of the uniforms upon the blacks and immediately he demanded to know where were their officers.

'They cannot understand you,' said the girl and so in the bastard tongue that is the medium of communication between the Germans and the blacks of their colony, she repeated the white man's question.

Usanga grinned. 'You know where they are, white woman,' he replied. 'They are dead, and if this white man does not do as I tell him, he, too, will be dead.'

'What do you want of him?' asked the girl.

'I want him to teach me how to fly like a bird,' replied Usanga.

Bertha Kircher looked her astonishment, but repeated the demand to the lieutenant.

The Englishman meditated for a moment. 'He wants to learn to fly, does he?' he repeated. 'Ask him if he will give us our freedom if I teach him to fly.'

The girl put the question to Usanga, who, degraded, cunning, and entirely unprincipled, was always perfectly willing to promise anything whether he had any intentions of fulfilling his promises or not, and so immediately assented to the proposition.

'Let the white man teach me to fly,' he said, 'and I will take you back close to the settlements of your people, but in return for this I shall keep the great bird,' and he waved a black hand in the direction of the airplane.

When Bertha Kircher had repeated Usanga's proposition to the aviator, the latter shrugged his shoulders and with a wry face finally agreed. 'I fancy there is no other way out of it,' he said. 'In any event the plane is lost to the British government. If I refuse the black scoundrel's request, there is no doubt but what he will make short work of me with the result that the machine will lie here until it rots. If I accept his offer it will at least be the means of assuring your safe return to civilization and that,' he added, 'is worth more to me than all the planes in the British Air Service.'

The girl cast a quick glance at him. These were the first words he had addressed to her that might indicate that his sentiments toward her were more than those of a companion in distress. She regretted that he had spoken as he had and he, too, regretted it almost instantly as he saw the shadow cross her face and realized that he had unwittingly added to the difficulties of her already almost unbearable situation.

'Forgive me,' he said quickly. 'Please forget what that remark implied. I promise you that I will not offend again, if it does offend you, until after we are both safely out of this mess.'

She smiled and thanked him, but the thing had been said and could never be unsaid, and Bertha Kircher knew even more surely than as though he had fallen upon his knees and protested undying devotion that the young English officer loved her.

Usanga was for taking his first lesson in aviation immediately. The Englishman attempted to dissuade him, but immediately the black became threatening and abusive, since, like all those who are ignorant, he was suspicious that the intentions of others were always ulterior unless they perfectly coincided with his wishes.

'All right, old top,' muttered the Englishman, 'I will give you the lesson of your life,' and then turning to the girl: 'Persuade him to let you accompany us. I shall be afraid to leave you here with these devilish scoundrels.' But when she put the suggestion to Usanga the black immediately suspected some plan to thwart him – possibly to carry him against his will back to the German masters he had traitorously deserted, and glowering at her savagely, he obstinately refused to entertain the suggestion.

'The white woman will remain here with my people,' he said. 'They will not harm her unless you fail to bring me back safely.'

'Tell him,' said the Englishman, 'that if you are not standing in plain sight in this meadow when I return, I will not land, but will carry Usanga back to the British camp and have him hanged.'

Usanga promised that the girl would be in evidence upon their return, and took immediate steps to impress upon his warriors that under penalty of death they must not harm her. Then, followed by the other members of his party, he crossed the clearing toward the plane with the Englishman. Once seated within what he already considered his new possession, the black's courage began to wane and when the motor was started and the great propeller commenced to whir, he screamed to the Englishman to stop the thing and permit him to alight, but the aviator could neither hear nor understand the black above the noise of the propeller and exhaust. By this time the plane was moving along the ground and even then Usanga was upon the verge of leaping out, and would have done so had he been able to unfasten the strap from about his waist. Then the plane rose from the ground and in a moment soared gracefully in a wide circle until it topped the trees. The black sergeant was in a veritable collapse of terror. He saw the earth dropping rapidly from beneath him. He saw the trees and river and at a distance the little clearing with the thatched huts of Numabo's village. He tried hard not to think of the results of a sudden fall to the rapidly receding ground below. He attempted to concentrate his mind upon the twenty-four wives which this great bird most assuredly would permit him to command. Higher and higher rose the plane, swinging in a wide circle above the forest, river, and meadowland and presently, much to his surprise, Usanga discovered that his terror was rapidly waning, so that it was not long before there was forced upon him a consciousness of utter security, and then it was that he began to take notice of the manner in which the white man guided and manipulated the plane.

After half an hour of skillful maneuvering, the Englishman rose rapidly to a considerable altitude, and then, suddenly, without warning, he looped and flew with the plane inverted for a few seconds.

'I said I'd give this beggar the lesson of his life,' he murmured as he heard, even above the whir of the propeller, the shriek of the terrified Negro. A moment later Smith-Oldwick had righted the machine and was dropping rapidly toward the earth. He circled slowly a few times above the meadow until he had assured himself that Bertha Kircher was there and apparently unharmed, then he dropped gently to the ground so that the machine came to a stop a short distance from where the girl and the warriors awaited them.

It was a trembling and ashen-hued Usanga who tumbled out of the fuselage, for his nerves were still on edge as a result of the harrowing experience of the loop, yet with terra firma once more underfoot, he quickly regained his composure. Strutting about with great show and braggadocio, he strove to impress his followers with the mere nothingness of so trivial a feat as flying birdlike thousands of yards above the jungle, though it was long until he had thoroughly convinced himself by the force of autosuggestion that he had enjoyed every instant of the flight and was already far advanced in the art of aviation.

So jealous was the black of his newfound toy that he would not return to the village of Numabo, but insisted on making camp close beside the plane, lest in some inconceivable fashion it should be stolen from him. For two days they camped there, and constantly during daylight hours Usanga compelled the Englishman to instruct him in the art of flying.

Smith-Oldwick, in recalling the long months of arduous training he had undergone himself before he had been considered sufficiently adept to be considered a finished flier, smiled at the conceit of the ignorant African who was already demanding that he be permitted to make a flight alone.

'If it was not for losing the machine,' the Englishman explained to the girl, 'I'd let the bounder take it up and break his fool neck as he would do inside of two minutes.'

However, he finally persuaded Usanga to bide his time for a few more days of instruction, but in the suspicious mind of the Negro there was a growing conviction that the white man's advice was prompted by some ulterior motive; that it was in the hope of escaping with the machine himself by night that he refused to admit that Usanga was entirely capable of handling it alone and therefore in no further need of help or instruction, and so in the mind of the black there formed a determination to outwit the white man. The lure of the twenty-four seductive wives proved in itself a sufficient incentive and there, too, was added his desire for the white girl whom he had long since determined to possess.

It was with these thoughts in mind that Usanga lay down to sleep in the evening of the second day. Constantly, however, the thought of Naratu and her temper arose to take the keen edge from his pleasant imaginings. If he could but rid himself of her! The thought having taken form persisted, but always it was more than outweighed by the fact that the black sergeant was actually afraid of his woman, so much afraid of her in fact that he would not have dared to attempt to put her out of the way unless he could do so secretly while she slept. However, as one plan after another was conjured by the strength of his desires, he at last hit upon one which came to him almost with the force of a blow and brought him sitting upright among his sleeping companions.

When morning dawned Usanga could scarce wait for an opportunity to put his scheme into execution, and the moment that he had eaten, he called several of his warriors aside and talked with them for some moments.

The Englishman, who usually kept an eye upon his black captor, saw now that the latter was explaining something in detail to his warriors, and from his gestures and his manner it was apparent that he was persuading them to some new plan as well as giving them instructions as to what they were to do. Several times, too, he saw the eyes of the Negroes turned upon him and once they flashed simultaneously toward the white girl.

Everything about the occurrence, which in itself seemed trivial enough, aroused in the mind of the Englishman a well-defined apprehension that something was afoot that boded ill for him and for the girl. He could not free himself of the idea and so he kept a still closer watch over the black although, as he was forced to admit to himself, he was quite powerless to avert any fate that lay in store for them. Even the spear that he had had when captured had been taken away from him, so that now he was unarmed and absolutely at the mercy of the black sergeant and his followers.

Lieutenant Harold Percy Smith-Oldwick did not have long to wait before discovering something of Usanga's plan, for almost immediately after the sergeant finished giving his instructions, a number of warriors approached the Englishman, while three went directly to the girl.

Without a word of explanation the warriors seized the young officer and threw him to the ground upon his face. For a moment he struggled to free himself and succeeded in landing a few heavy blows among his assailants, but he was too greatly outnumbered to hope to more than delay them in the accomplishment of their object which he soon discovered was to bind him securely hand and foot. When they had finally secured him to their satisfaction, they rolled him over on his side and then it was he saw Bertha Kircher had been similarly trussed.

Smith-Oldwick lay in such a position that he could see nearly the entire expanse of meadow and the airplane a short distance away. Usanga was talking to the girl who was shaking her head in vehement negatives.

'What is he saying?' called the Englishman.

'He is going to take me away in the plane,' the girl called back. 'He is going to take me farther inland to another country where he says that he will be king and I am to be one of his wives,' and then to the Englishman's surprise she turned a smiling face toward him, 'but there is no danger,' she continued, 'for we shall both be dead within a few minutes – just give him time enough to get the machine under way, and if he can rise a hundred feet from the ground I shall never need fear him more.'

'God!' cried the man. 'Is there no way that you can dissuade him? Promise him anything. Anything that you want. I have money, more money than that poor fool could imagine there was in the whole world. With it he can buy anything that money will purchase, fine clothes and food and women, all the women he wants. Tell him this and tell him that if he will spare you I give him my word that I will fetch it all to him.'

The girl shook her head. 'It is useless,' she said. 'He would not understand

and if he did understand, he would not trust you. The blacks are so unprincipled themselves that they can imagine no such thing as principle or honor in others, and especially do these blacks distrust an Englishman whom the Germans have taught them to believe are the most treacherous and degraded of people. No, it is better thus. I am sorry that you cannot go with us, for if he goes high enough my death will be much easier than that which probably awaits you.'

Usanga had been continually interrupting their brief conversation in an attempt to compel the girl to translate it to him, for he feared that they were concocting some plan to thwart him, and to quiet and appease him, she told him that the Englishman was merely bidding her farewell and wishing her good luck. Suddenly she turned to the black. 'Will you do something for me?' she asked. 'If I go willingly with you?'

'What is it you want?' he inquired.

'Tell your men to free the white man after we are gone. He can never catch us. That is all I ask of you. If you will grant him his freedom and his life, I will go willingly with you.'

'You will go with me anyway,' growled Usanga. 'It is nothing to me whether you go willingly or not. I am going to be a great king and you will do whatever I tell you to do.'

He had in mind that he would start properly with this woman. There should be no repetition of his harrowing experience with Naratu. This wife and the twenty-four others should be carefully selected and well trained. Hereafter Usanga would be master in his own house.

Bertha Kircher saw that it was useless to appeal to the brute and so she held her peace though she was filled with sorrow in contemplating the fate that awaited the young officer, scarce more than a boy, who had impulsively revealed his love for her.

At Usanga's order one of the blacks lifted her from the ground and carried her to the machine, and after Usanga had clambered aboard, they lifted her up and he reached down and drew her into the fuselage where he removed the thongs from her wrists and strapped her into her seat and then took his own directly ahead of her.

The girl turned her eyes toward the Englishman. She was very pale but her lips smiled bravely.

'Goodbye!' she cried.

'Goodbye, and God bless you!' he called back – his voice the least bit husky – and then: 'The thing I wanted to say – may I say it now, we are so very near the end?'

Her lips moved but whether they voiced consent or refusal he did not know, for the words were drowned in the whir of the propeller.

The black had learned his lesson sufficiently well so that the motor was started without bungling and the machine was soon under way across the meadowland. A groan escaped the lips of the distracted Englishman as he watched the woman he loved being carried to almost certain death. He saw the plane tilt and the machine rise from the ground. It was a good takeoff – as good as Lieutenant Harold Percy Smith-Oldwick could make himself but he realized that it was only so by chance. At any instant the machine might plunge to earth and even if, by some miracle of chance, the black could succeed in rising above the treetops and make a successful flight, there was not one chance in one hundred thousand that he could ever land again without killing his fair captive and himself.

But what was that? His heart stood still.

13

Usanga's Reward

For two days Tarzan of the Apes had been hunting leisurely to the north, and swinging in a wide circle, he had returned to within a short distance of the clearing where he had left Bertha Kircher and the young lieutenant. He had spent the night in a large tree that overhung the river only a short distance from the clearing, and now in the early morning hours he was crouching at the water's edge waiting for an opportunity to capture Pisah, the fish, thinking that he would take it back with him to the hut where the girl could cook it for herself and her companion.

Motionless as a bronze statue was the wily ape-man, for well he knew how wary is Pisah, the fish. The slightest movement would frighten him away and only by infinite patience might he be captured at all. Tarzan depended upon his own quickness and the suddenness of his attack, for he had no bait or hook. His knowledge of the ways of the denizens of the water told him where to wait for Pisah. It might be a minute or it might be an hour before the fish would swim into the little pool above which he crouched, but sooner or later one would come. That the ape-man knew, so with the patience of the beast of prey he waited for his quarry.

At last there was a glint of shiny scales. Pisah was coming. In a moment he would be within reach and then with the swiftness of light two strong, brown hands would plunge into the pool and seize him, but, just at the moment that the fish was about to come within reach, there was a great crashing in the underbrush behind the ape-man. Instantly Pisah was gone and Tarzan, growling, had wheeled about to face whatever creature might be menacing him. The moment that he turned he saw that the author of the disturbance was Zu-tag.

'What does Zu-tag want?' asked the ape-man.

'Zu-tag comes to the water to drink,' replied the ape.

'Where is the tribe?' asked Tarzan.

'They are hunting for pisangs and scimatines farther back in the forest,' replied Zu-tag.

'And the Tarmangani she and bull –' asked Tarzan, 'are they safe?'

'They have gone away,' replied Zu-tag. 'Kudu has come out of his lair twice since they left.'

'Did the tribe chase them away?' asked Tarzan.

'No,' replied the ape. 'We did not see them go. We do not know why they left.'

Tarzan swung quickly through the trees toward the clearing. The hut and boma were as he had left them, but there was no sign of either the man or the woman. Crossing the clearing, he entered the boma and then the hut. Both were empty, and his trained nostrils told him that they had been gone for at least two days. As he was about to leave the hut he saw a paper pinned upon the wall with a sliver of wood and taking it down, he read:

> After what you told me about Miss Kircher, and knowing that you dislike her, I feel that it is not fair to her and to you that we should impose longer upon you. I know that our presence is keeping you from continuing your journey to the west coast, and so I have decided that it is better for us to try and reach the white settlements immediately without imposing further upon you. We both thank you for your kindness and protection. If there was any way that I might repay the obligation I feel, I should be only too glad to do so.

It was signed by Lieutenant Harold Percy Smith-Oldwick.

Tarzan shrugged his shoulders, crumpled the note in his hand and tossed it aside. He felt a certain sense of relief from responsibility and was glad that they had taken the matter out of his hands. They were gone and would forget, but somehow he could not forget. He walked out across the boma and into the clearing. He felt uneasy and restless. Once he started toward the north in response to a sudden determination to continue his way to the west coast. He would follow the winding river toward the north a few miles where its course turned to the west and then on toward its source across a wooded plateau and up into the foothills and the mountains. Upon the other side of the range he would search for a stream running downward toward the west coast, and thus following the rivers he would be sure of game and water in plenty.

But he did not go far. A dozen steps, perhaps, and he came to a sudden stop. 'He is an Englishman,' he muttered, 'and the other is a woman. They can never reach the settlements without my help. I could not kill her with my own hands when I tried, and if I let them go on alone, I will have killed her just as surely as though I had run my knife into her heart. No,' and again he shook his head. 'Tarzan of the Apes is a fool and a weak, old woman,' and he turned back toward the south.

Manu, the monkey, had seen the two Tarmangani pass two days before. Chattering and scolding, he told Tarzan all about it. They had gone in the direction of the village of the Gomangani, that much had Manu seen with his own eyes, so the ape-man swung on through the jungle in a southerly direction and though with no concentrated effort to follow the spoor of those he trailed, he passed numerous evidences that they had gone this way – faint suggestions of their scent spoor clung lightly to leaf or branch or bole that one or the other had touched, or in the earth of the trail their feet had trod, and where the way wound through the gloomy depth of dank forest, the impress of their shoes still showed occasionally in the damp mass of decaying vegatation that floored the way.

An inexplicable urge spurred Tarzan to increasing speed. The same still, small voice that chided him for having neglected them seemed constantly whispering that they were in dire need of him now. Tarzan's conscience was troubling him, which accounted for the fact that he compared himself to a weak, old woman, for the ape-man, reared in savagery and inured to hardships and cruelty, disliked to admit any of the gentler traits that in reality were his birthright.

The trail made a detour to the east of the village of the Wamabos, and then returned to the wide elephant path nearer to the river, where it continued in a southerly direction for several miles. At last there came to the ears of the ape-man a peculiar whirring, throbbing sound. For an instant he paused, listening intently, 'An airplane!' he muttered, and hastened forward at greatly increased speed.

When Tarzan of the Apes finally reached the edge of the meadowland where Smith-Oldwick's plane had landed, he took in the entire scene in one quick glance and grasped the situation, although he could scarce give credence to the things he saw. Bound and helpless, the English officer lay upon the ground at one side of the meadow, while around him stood a number of the black deserters from the German command. Tarzan had seen these men before and knew who they were. Coming toward him down the meadow was an airplane piloted by the black Usanga and in the seat behind the pilot was the white girl, Bertha Kircher. How it befell that the ignorant savage could operate the plane, Tarzan could not guess nor had he time in which to speculate, upon the subject. His knowledge of Usanga, together with the position of the white man, told him that the black sergeant was attempting to carry off the white girl. Why he should be doing this when he had her in his power and had also captured and secured the only creature in the jungle who might wish to defend her insofar as the black could know, Tarzan could not guess, for he knew nothing of Usanga's twenty-four dream wives nor of the black's fear of the horrid temper of Naratu, his present mate. He did not know, then, that Usanga had determined to fly away with the white girl never to return, and to put so great a distance between himself and Naratu that the latter never could find him again; but it was this very thing that was in the black's mind although not even his own warriors guessed it. He had told them that he would take the captive to a sultan of the north and there obtain a great price for her and that when he returned they should have some of the spoils.

These things Tarzan did not know. All he knew was what he saw – a Negro attempting to fly away with a white girl. Already the machine was slowly leaving the ground. In a moment more it would rise swiftly out of reach. At first Tarzan thought of fitting an arrow to his bow and slaying Usanga, but as quickly he abandoned the idea because he knew that the moment the pilot was slain the machine, running wild, would dash the girl to death among the trees.

There was but one way in which he might hope to succor her – a way which if it failed must send him to instant death and yet he did not hesitate in an attempt to put it into execution.

Usanga did not see him, being too intent upon the unaccustomed duties of a pilot, but the blacks across the meadow saw him and they ran forward with loud and savage cries and menacing rifles to intercept him. They saw a giant white man leap from the branches of a tree to the turf and race rapidly toward the plane. They saw him take a long grass rope from about his shoulders as he ran. They saw the noose swinging in an undulating circle above his head. They saw the white girl in the machine glance down and discover him.

Twenty feet above the running ape-man soared the huge plane. The open noose shot up to meet it, and the girl, half guessing the ape-man's intentions, reached out and caught the noose and, bracing herself, clung tightly to it with both hands. Simultaneously Tarzan was dragged from his feet and the plane lurched sideways in response to the new strain. Usanga clutched wildly at the control and the machine shot upward at a steep angle. Dangling at the end of the rope the ape-man swung pendulumlike in space. The Englishman, lying bound upon the ground, had been a witness of all these happenings. His heart stood still as he saw Tarzan's body hurtling through the air toward the treetops among which it seemed he must inevitably crash; but the plane was rising rapidly, so that the beast-man cleared the topmost branches. Then slowly, hand over hand, he climbed toward the fuselage. The girl, clinging desperately to the noose, strained every muscle to hold the great weight dangling at the lower end of the rope.

Usanga, all unconscious of what was going on behind him, drove the plane higher and higher into the air.

Tarzan glanced downward. Below him the treetops and the river passed rapidly to the rear and only a slender grass rope and the muscles of a frail girl stood between him and the death yawning there thousands of feet below.

It seemed to Bertha Kircher that the fingers of her hands were dead. The numbness was running up her arms to her elbows. How much longer she could cling to the straining strands she could not guess. It seemed to her that those lifeless fingers must relax at any instant and then, when she had about given up hope, she saw a strong brown hand reach up and grasp the side of the fuselage. Instantly the weight upon the rope was removed and a moment later Tarzan of the Apes raised his body above the side and threw a leg over the edge. He glanced forward at Usanga and then, placing his mouth close to the girl's ear he cried: 'Have you ever piloted a plane?' The girl nodded a quick affirmative.

'Have you the courage to climb up there beside the black and seize the control while I take care of him?'

The girl looked toward Usanga and shuddered. 'Yes,' she replied, 'but my feet are bound.'

Tarzan drew his hunting knife from its sheath and, reaching down, severed the thongs that bound her ankles. Then the girl unsnapped the strap that held her to her seat. With one hand Tarzan grasped the girl's arm and steadied her as the two crawled slowly across the few feet which intervened between the two seats. A single slight tip of the plane would have cast them both into eternity. Tarzan realized that only through a miracle of chance could they reach Usanga and effect the change in pilots and yet he knew that that chance must be taken, for in the brief moments since he had first seen the plane, he had realized that the black was almost without experience as a pilot and that death surely awaited them in any event should the black sergeant remain at the control.

The first intimation Usanga had that all was not well with him was when the girl slipped suddenly to his side and grasped the control and at the same instant steellike fingers seized his throat. A brown hand shot down with a keen blade and severed the strap about his waist and giant muscles lifted him bodily from his seat. Usanga clawed the air and shrieked but he was helpless as a babe. Far below the watchers in the meadow could see the airplane careening in the sky, for with the change of control it had taken a sudden dive. They saw it right itself and, turning in a short circle, return in their direction, but it was so far above them and the light of the sun so strong that they could see nothing of what was going on within the fuselage; but presently

Lieutenant Smith-Oldwick gave a gasp of dismay as he saw a human body plunge downward from the plane. Turning and twisting in midair it fell with ever-increasing velocity and the Englishman held his breath as the thing hurtled toward them.

With a muffled thud it flattened upon the turf near the center of the meadow, and when at last the Englishman could gain the courage to again turn his eyes upon it, he breathed a fervent prayer of thanks, for the shapeless mass that lay upon the bloodstained turf was covered with an ebon hide. Usanga had reaped his reward.

Again and again the plane circled above the meadow. The blacks, at first dismayed at the death of their leader, were now worked to a frenzy of rage and a determination to be avenged. The girl and the ape-man saw them gather in a knot about the body of their fallen chief. They saw as they circled above the meadow the black fists shaken at them, and the rifles brandishing a menace toward them. Tarzan still clung to the fuselage directly behind the pilot's seat. His face was close beside Bertha Kircher's, and at the top of his voice, above the noise of propeller, engine and exhaust, he screamed a few words of instruction into her ear.

As the girl grasped the significance of his words she paled, but her lips set in a hard line and her eyes shone with a sudden fire of determination as she dropped the plane to within a few feet of the ground and at the opposite end of the meadow from the blacks and then at full speed bore down upon the savages. So quickly the plane came that Usanga's men had no time to escape it after they realized its menace. It touched the ground just as it struck among them and mowed through them, a veritable juggernaut of destruction. When it came to rest at the edge of the forest the ape-man leaped quickly to the ground and ran toward the young lieutenant, and as he went he glanced at the spot where the warriors had stood, ready to defend himself if necessary, but there was none there to oppose him. Dead and dying they lay strewn for fifty feet along the turf.

By the time Tarzan had freed the Englishman the girl joined them. She tried to voice her thanks to the ape-man but he silenced her with a gesture.

'You saved yourself,' he insisted, 'for had you been unable to pilot the plane, I could not have helped you, and now,' he said, 'you two have the means of returning to the settlements. The day is still young. You can easily cover the distance in a few hours if you have sufficient petrol.' He looked inquiringly toward the aviator.

Smith-Oldwick nodded his head affirmatively. 'I have plenty,' he replied.

'Then go at once,' said the ape-man. 'Neither of you belong in the jungle.' A slight smile touched his lips as he spoke.

The girl and the Englishman smiled too. 'This jungle is no place for us at least,' said Smith-Oldwick, 'and it is no place for any other white man. Why don't you come back to civilization with us?'

Tarzan shook his head. 'I prefer the jungle,' he said.

The aviator dug his toe into the ground and still looking down, blurted something which he evidently hated to say. 'If it is a matter of living, old top,' he said, 'er – money, er – you know –'

Tarzan laughed. 'No,' he said. 'I know what you are trying to say. It is not that. I was born in the jungle. I have lived all my life in the jungle, and I shall die in the jungle. I do not wish to live or die elsewhere.'

The others shook their heads. They could not understand him.

'Go,' said the ape-man. 'The quicker you go, the quicker you will reach safety.'

They walked to the plane together. Smith-Oldwick pressed the ape-man's hand and clambered into the pilot's seat. 'Goodbye,' said the girl as she extended her hand to Tarzan. 'Before I go won't you tell me you don't hate me anymore?' Tarzan's face clouded. Without a word he picked her up and lifted her to her place behind the Englishman. An expression of pain crossed Bertha Kircher's face. The motor started and a moment later the two were being borne rapidly toward the east.

In the center of the meadow stood the ape-man watching them. 'It is too bad that she is a German and a spy,' he said, 'for she is very hard to hate.'

14

The Black Lion

Numa, the lion, was hungry. He had come out of the desert country to the east into a land of plenty but though he was young and strong, the wary grass-eaters had managed to elude his mighty talons each time he had thought to make a kill.

Numa, the lion, was hungry and very savage. For two days he had not eaten and now he hunted in the ugliest of humors. No more did Numa roar forth a rumbling challenge to the world but rather he moved silent and grim, stepping softly that no cracking twig might betray his presence to the keen-eared quarry he sought.

Fresh was the spoor of Bara, the deer, that Numa picked up in the well-beaten game trail he was following. No hour had passed since Bara had come this way; the time could be measured in minutes and so the great lion redoubled the cautiousness of his advance as he crept stealthily in pursuit of his quarry.

A light wind was moving through the jungle aisles, and it wafted down now to the nostrils of the eager carnivore the strong scent spoor of the deer, exciting his already avid appetite to a point where it became a gnawing pain. Yet Numa did not permit himself to be carried away by his desire into any premature charge such as had recently lost him the juicy meat of Pacco, the zebra. Increasing his gait but slightly he followed the tortuous windings of the trail until suddenly just before him, where the trail wound about the bole of a huge tree, he saw a young buck moving slowly ahead of him.

Numa judged the distance with his keen eyes, glowing now like two terrible spots of yellow fire in his wrinkled, snarling face. He could do it – this time he was sure. One terrific roar that would paralyze the poor creature ahead of him into momentary inaction, and a simultaneous charge of lightninglike rapidity and Numa, the lion, would feed. The sinuous tail, undulating slowly at its tufted extremity, whipped suddenly erect. It was the signal for the charge and the vocal organs were shaped for the thunderous roar when, as lightning out of a clear sky, Sheeta, the panther, leaped suddenly into the trail between Numa and the deer.

A blundering charge made Sheeta, for with the first crash of his spotted body through the foliage verging the trail, Bara gave a single startled backward glance and was gone.

The roar that was intended to paralyze the deer broke horribly from the deep throat of the great cat – an angry roar of rage against the meddling Sheeta who had robbed him of his kill, and the charge that was intended for Bara was launched against the panther; but here too Numa was doomed to disappointment, for with the first notes of his fearsome roar Sheeta, considering well the better part of valor, leaped into a nearby tree.

A half-hour later it was a thoroughly furious Numa who came unexpectedly upon the scent of man. Heretofore the lord of the jungle had disdained the unpalatable flesh of the despised man-thing. Such meat was only for the old, the toothless, and the decrepit who no longer could make their kills among the fleet-footed grass-eaters. Bara, the deer, Horta, the boar, and, best and wariest, Pacco, the zebra, were for the young, the strong, and the agile, but Numa was hungry – hungrier than he ever had been in the five short years of his life.

What if he was a young, powerful, cunning, and ferocious beast? In the face of hunger, the great leveler, he was as the old, the toothless, and the decrepit. His belly cried aloud in anguish and his jowls slavered for flesh. Zebra or deer or man, what mattered it so that it was warm flesh, red with the hot juices of life? Even Dango, the hyena, eater of offal, would, at the moment, have seemed a tidbit to Numa.

The great lion knew the habits and frailties of man, though he never before had hunted man for food. He knew the despised Gomangani as the slowest, the most stupid, and the most defenseless of creatures. No woodcraft, no cunning, no stealth was necessary in the hunting of man, nor had Numa any stomach for either delay or silence.

His rage had become an almost equally consuming passion with his hunger, so that now, as his delicate nostrils apprised him of the recent passage of man, he lowered his head and rumbled forth a thunderous roar, and at a swift walk, careless of the noise he made, set forth upon the trail of his intended quarry.

Majestic and terrible, regally careless of his surroundings, the king of beasts strode down the beaten trail. The natural caution that is inherent to all creatures of the wild had deserted him. What had he, lord of the jungle, to fear and, with only man to hunt, what need of caution? And so he did not see or scent what a more wary Numa might readily have discovered until, with the cracking of twigs and a tumbling of earth, he was precipitated into a cunningly devised pit that the wily Wamabos had excavated for just this purpose in the center of the game trail.

Tarzan of the Apes stood in the center of the clearing watching the plane shrinking to diminutive toylike proportions in the eastern sky. He had breathed a sigh of relief as he saw it rise safely with the British flier and Fräulein Bertha Kircher. For weeks he had felt the hampering responsibility of their welfare in this savage wilderness where their utter helplessness would have rendered them easy prey for the savage carnivores or the cruel Wamabos. Tarzan of the Apes loved unfettered freedom, and now that these two were safely off his hands, he felt that he could continue upon his journey toward the west coast and the long-untenanted cabin of his dead father.

And yet, as he stood there watching the tiny speck in the east, another sigh heaved his broad chest, nor was it a sigh of relief, but rather a sensation which Tarzan had never expected to feel again and which he now disliked to admit even to himself. It could not be possible that he, the jungle bred, who had renounced forever the society of man to return to his beloved beasts of the wilds, could be feeling anything akin to regret at the departure of these two, or any slightest loneliness now that they were gone. Lieutenant Harold Percy Smith-Oldwick Tarzan had liked, but the woman whom he had known as a German spy he had hated, though he never had found it in his heart to slay her as he had sworn to slay all Huns. He had attributed this weakness to the fact that she was a woman, although he had been rather troubled by the apparent inconsistency of his hatred for her and his repeated protection of her when danger threatened.

With an irritable toss of his head he wheeled suddenly toward the west as though by turning his back upon the fast disappearing plane he might expunge thoughts of its passengers from his memory. At the edge of the clearing he paused; a giant tree loomed directly ahead of him and, as though actuated by sudden and irresistible impulse, he leaped into the branches and swung himself with apelike agility to the topmost limbs that would sustain his weight. There, balancing lightly upon a swaying bough, he sought in the direction of the eastern horizon for the tiny speck that would be the British plane bearing away from him the last of his own race and kind that he expected ever again to see.

At last his keen eyes picked up the ship flying at a considerable altitude far in the east. For a few seconds he watched it speeding evenly eastward, when, to his horror, he saw the speck dive suddenly downward. The fall seemed interminable to the watcher and he realized how great must have been the altitude of the plane before the drop commenced. Just before it disappeared from sight its downward momentum appeared to abate suddenly, but it was still moving rapidly at a steep angle when it finally disappeared from view behind the far hills.

For half a minute the ape-man stood noting distant landmarks that he judged might be in the vicinity of the fallen plane, for no sooner had he realized that these people were again in trouble than his inherent sense of duty to his own kind impelled him once more to forgo his plans and seek to aid them.

The ape-man feared from what he judged of the location of the machine that it had fallen among the almost impassable gorges of the arid country just beyond the fertile basin that was bounded by the hills to the east of him. He had crossed that parched and desolate country of the dead himself and he knew from his own experience and the narrow escape he had had from succumbing to its relentless cruelty no lesser man could hope to win his way to safety from any considerable distance within its borders. Vividly he recalled the bleached bones of the long-dead warrior in the bottom of the precipitous gorge that had all but proved a trap for him as well. He saw the helmet of hammered brass and the corroded breastplate of steel and the long straight sword in its scabbard and the ancient harquebus – mute testimonials to the mighty physique and the warlike spirit on him who had somehow won, thus illy caparisoned and pitifully armed, to the center of savage, ancient Africa; and he saw the slender English youth and the slight figure of the girl cast into the same fateful trap from which this giant of old had been unable to escape – cast there wounded and broken perhaps, if not killed.

His judgment told him that the latter possibility was probably the fact, and yet there was a chance that they might have landed without fatal injuries, and so upon this slim chance he started out upon what he knew would be an arduous journey, fraught with many hardships and unspeakable peril, that he might attempt to save them if they still lived.

He had covered a mile perhaps when his quick ears caught the sound of rapid movement along the game trail ahead of him. The sound, increasing in volume, proclaimed the fact that whatever caused it was moving in his direction and moving rapidly. Nor was it long before his trained senses convinced him that the footfalls were those of Bara, the deer, in rapid flight. Inextricably confused in Tarzan's character were the attributes of man and of beasts. Long experience had taught him that he fights best or travels fastest who is best nourished, and so, with few exceptions, Tarzan could delay his most urgent business to take advantage of an opportunity to kill and feed. This perhaps was the predominant beast trait in him. The transformation from an English gentleman, impelled by the most humanitarian motives, to that of a wild beast crouching in the concealment of a dense bush ready to spring upon its approaching prey, was instantaneous.

And so, when Bara came, escaping the clutches of Numa and Sheeta, his terror and his haste precluded the possibility of his sensing that other equally formidable foe lying in ambush for him. Abreast of the ape-man came the deer; a light-brown body shot from the concealing verdure of the bush, strong arms encircled the sleek neck of the young buck and powerful teeth fastened themselves in the soft flesh. Together the two rolled over in the trail and a moment later the ape-man rose, and, with one foot upon the carcass of his kill, raised his voice in the victory cry of the bull ape.

Like an answering challenge came suddenly to the ears of the ape-man the thunderous roar of a lion, a hideous angry roar in which Tarzan thought that he discerned a note of surprise and terror. In the breast of the wild things of the jungle, as in the breasts of their more enlightened brothers and sisters of the human race, the characteristic of curiosity is well developed. Nor was Tarzan far from innocent of it. The peculiar note in the roar of his hereditary enemy aroused a desire to investigate, and so, throwing the carcass of Bara, the deer, across his shoulder, the ape-man took to the lower terraces of the forest and moved quickly in the direction from which the sound had come, which was in line with the trail he had set out upon.

As the distance lessened, the sounds increased in volume, which indicated that he was approaching a very angry lion and presently, where a jungle giant overspread the broad game trail that countless thousands of hoofed and padded feet had worn and trampled into a deep furrow during perhaps countless ages, he saw beneath him the lion pit of the Wamabos and in it, leaping futilely for freedom such a lion as even Tarzan of the Apes never before had beheld. A mighty beast it was that glared up at the ape-man – large, powerful and young, with a huge black mane and a coat so much darker than any Tarzan ever had seen that in the depths of the pit it looked almost black – a black lion!

Tarzan who had been upon the point of taunting and reviling his captive foe was suddenly turned to open admiration for the beauty of the splendid beast. What a creature! How by comparison the ordinary forest lion was dwarfed into insignificance! Here indeed was one worthy to be called king of beasts. With his first sight of the great cat the ape-man knew that he had heard no note of terror in that initial roar; surprise doubtless, but the vocal cords of that mighty throat never had reacted to fear.

With growing admiration came a feeling of quick pity for the hapless situation of the great brute rendered futile and helpless by the wiles of the Gomangani. Enemy though the beast was, he was less an enemy to the ape-man than those blacks who had trapped him, for though Tarzan of the Apes claimed many fast and loyal friends among certain tribes of African natives, there were others of degraded character and bestial habits that he looked upon with utter loathing, and of such were the human flesh-eaters of Numabo the chief. For a moment Numa, the lion, glared ferociously at the naked man-thing upon the tree limb above him. Steadily those yellow-green eyes bored into the clear eyes of the ape-man, and then the sensitive nostrils caught the scent of the fresh blood of Bara and the eyes moved to the carcass lying across the brown shoulder, and there came from the cavernous depths of the savage throat a low whine.

Tarzan of the Apes smiled. As unmistakably as though a human voice had spoken, the lion had said to him, 'I am hungry, even more than hungry. I am starving,' and the ape-man looked down upon the lion beneath him and smiled, a slow quizzical smile, and then he shifted the carcass from his shoulder to the branch before him and, drawing the long blade that had been his father's, deftly cut off a hindquarter and, wiping the bloody blade upon Bara's smooth coat, he returned it to its scabbard. Numa, with watering jaws, looked up at the tempting meat and whined again and the ape-man smiled down upon him his slow smile and, raising the hindquarter in his strong brown hands buried his teeth in the tender, juicy flesh.

For the third time Numa, the lion, uttered that low pleading whine and then, with a rueful and disgusted shake of his head, Tarzan of the Apes raised the balance of the carcass of Bara, the deer, and hurled it to the famished beast below.

'Old woman,' muttered the ape-man. 'Tarzan has become a weak old woman. Presently he would shed tears because he has killed Bara, the deer. He cannot see Numa, his enemy, go hungry, because Tarzan's heart is turning to water by contact with the soft, weak creatures of civilization.' But yet he smiled; nor was he sorry that he had given way to the dictates of a kindly impulse.

As Tarzan tore the flesh from that portion of the kill he had retained for himself his eyes were taking in each detail of the scene below. He saw the avidity with which Numa devoured the carcass; he noted with growing admiration the finer points of the beast, and also the cunning construction of the trap. The ordinary lion pit with which Tarzan was familiar had stakes imbedded in the bottom, upon whose sharpened points the hapless lion would be impaled, but this pit was not so made. Here the short stakes were set at intervals of about a foot around the walls near the top, their sharpened points inclining downward so that the lion had fallen unhurt into the trap but could not leap out because each time he essayed it his head came in contact with the sharp end of a stake above him.

Evidently, then, the purpose of the Wamabos was to capture a lion alive. As this tribe had no contact whatsoever with white men insofar as Tarzan knew, their motive was doubtless due to a desire to torture the beast to death that they might enjoy to the utmost his dying agonies.

Having fed the lion, it presently occurred to Tarzan that his act would be futile were he to leave the beast to the mercies of the blacks, and then too it occurred to him that he could derive more pleasure through causing the blacks discomfiture than by leaving Numa to his fate. But how was he to release him? By removing two stakes there would be left plenty of room for the lion to leap from the pit, which was not of any great depth. However, what assurance had Tarzan that Numa would not leap out instantly the way to freedom was open, and before the ape-man could gain the safety of the trees? Regardless of the fact that Tarzan felt no such fear of the lion as you and I might experience under like circumstances, he yet was imbued with the sense of caution that is necessary to all creatures of the wild if they are to survive. Should necessity require, Tarzan could face Numa in battle, although he was not so egotistical as to think that he could best a full-grown lion in mortal combat other than through accident or the utilization of the cunning of his superior man-mind. To lay himself liable to death futilely, he would have considered as reprehensible as to have shunned danger in time of necessity; but when Tarzan elected to do a thing he usually found the means to accomplish it.

He had now fully determined to liberate Numa, and having so determined, he would accomplish it even though it entailed considerable personal risk. He knew that the lion would be occupied with his feeding for some time, but he also knew that while feeding he would be doubly resentful of any fancied interference. Therefore Tarzan must work with caution.

Coming to the ground at the side of the pit, he examined the stakes and as he did so was rather surprised to note that Numa gave no evidence of anger at his approach. Once he turned a searching gaze upon the ape-man for a moment and then returned to the flesh of Bara. Tarzan felt of the stakes and tested them with his weight. He pulled upon them with the muscles of his strong arms, presently discovering that by working them back and forth he could loosen them; and then a new plan was suggested to him so that he fell to work excavating with his knife at a point above where one of the stakes was imbedded. The loam was soft and easily removed, and it was not long until Tarzan had exposed that part of one of the stakes which was imbedded in the wall of the pit to almost its entire length, leaving only enough imbedded to prevent the stake from falling into the excavation. Then he turned his attention to an adjoining stake and soon had it similarly exposed, after which he threw the noose of his grass rope over the two and swung quickly to the branch of the tree above. Here he gathered in the slack of the rope and, bracing himself against the bole of the tree, pulled steadily upward. Slowly the stakes rose from the trench in which they were imbedded and with them rose Numa's suspicion and growling.

Was this some new encroachment upon his rights and his liberties? He was puzzled and, like all lions, being short of temper, he was irritated. He had not minded it when the Tarmangani squatted upon the verge of the pit and looked down upon him, for had not this Tarmangani fed him? But now something else was afoot and the suspicion of the wild beast was aroused. As he watched, however, Numa saw the stakes rise slowly to an erect position, tumble against each other and then fall backward out of his sight upon the surface of the ground above. Instantly the lion grasped the possibilities of the situation, and, too, perhaps he sensed the fact that the man-thing had deliberately opened a way for his escape. Seizing the remains of Bara in his great jaws, Numa, the lion, leaped agilely from the pit of the Wamabos and Tarzan of the Apes melted into the jungles to the east.

On the surface of the ground or through the swaying branches of the trees the spoor of man or beast was an open book to the ape-man, but even his acute senses were baffled by the spoorless trail of the airship. Of what good were eyes, or ears, or the sense of smell in following a thing whose path had lain through the shifting air thousands of feet above the treetops? Only upon his sense of direction could Tarzan depend in his search for the fallen plane. He could not even judge accurately as to the distance it might lie from him, and he knew that from the moment that it disappeared beyond the hills it might have traveled a considerable distance at right angles to its original course before it crashed to earth. If its occupants were killed or badly injured the ape-man might search futilely in their immediate vicinity for some time before finding them.

There was but one thing to do and that was to travel to a point as close as possible to where he judged the plane had landed, and then to follow in ever-widening circles until he picked up their scent spoor. And this he did.

Before he left the valley of plenty he made several kills and carried the choicest cuts of meat with him, leaving all the deadweight of bones behind. The dense vegetation of the jungle terminated at the foot of the western slope, growing less and less abundant as he neared the summit beyond which was a sparse growth of sickly scrub and sunburned grasses, with here and there a gnarled and hardy tree that had withstood the vicissitudes of an almost waterless existence.

From the summit of the hills Tarzan's keen eyes searched the arid landscape before him. In the distance he discerned the ragged tortuous lines that marked the winding course of the hideous gorges which scored the broad plain at intervals – the terrible gorges that had so nearly claimed his life in punishment for his temerity in attempting to invade the sanctity of their ancient solitude.

For two days Tarzan sought futilely for some clue to the whereabouts of the machine or its occupants. He cached portions of his kills at different points, building cairns of rock to mark their locations. He crossed the first deep gorge and circled far beyond it. Occasionally he stopped and called aloud, listening for some response but only silence rewarded him – a sinister silence that his cries only accentuated.

Late in the evening of the second day he came to the well-remembered gorge in which lay the clean-picked bones of the ancient adventurer, and here, for the first time, Ska, the vulture, picked up his trail. 'Not this time, Ska,' cried the ape-man in a taunting voice, 'for now indeed is Tarzan Tarzan. Before, you stalked the grim skeleton of a Tarmangani and even then you lost. Waste not your time upon Tarzan of the Apes in the full of his strength.' But still Ska, the vulture, circled and soared above him, and the ape-man, nothwithstanding his boasts, felt a shudder of apprehension. Through his brain ran a persistent and doleful chant to which he involuntarily set two words, repeated over and over again in horrible monotony: 'Ska knows! Ska knows!' until, shaking himself in anger, he picked up a rock and hurled it at the grim scavenger.

Lowering himself over the precipitous side of the gorge Tarzan half clambered and half slid to the sandy floor beneath. He had come upon the rift at almost the exact spot at which he had clambered from it weeks before, and there he saw, just as he had left it, just, doubtless, as it had lain for centuries, the mighty skeleton and its mighty armor.

As he stood looking down upon this grim reminder that another man of might had succumbed to the cruel powers of the desert, he was brought to startled attention by the report of a firearm, the sound of which came from the depths of the gorge to the south of him, and reverberated along the steep walls of the narrow rift.

15
Mysterious Footprints

As the British plane piloted by Lieutenant Harold Percy Smith-Oldwick rose above the jungle wilderness where Bertha Kircher's life had so often been upon the point of extinction, and sped toward the east, the girl felt a sudden contraction of the muscles of her throat. She tried very hard to swallow something that was not there. It seemed strange to her that she should feel regret in leaving behind her such hideous perils, and yet it was plain to her that such was the fact, for she was also leaving behind something beside the dangers that had menaced her – a unique figure that had entered her life, and for which she felt an unaccountable attraction.

Before her in the pilot's seat sat an English officer and gentleman whom, she knew, loved her, and yet she dared to feel regret in his company at leaving the stamping ground of a wild beast!

Lieutenant Smith-Oldwick, on his part, was in the seventh heaven of elation. He was in possession again of his beloved ship, he was flying swiftly in the direction of his comrades and his duty, and with him was the woman he loved. The fly in the ointment, however, was the accusation Tarzan had made against this woman. He had said that she was a German, and a spy, and from the heights of bliss the English officer was occasionally plunged to the depths of despair in contemplation of the inevitable, were the ape-man's charges to prove true. He found himself torn between sentiments of love and honor. On the one hand he could not surrender the woman he loved to the certain fate that must be meted out to her if she were in truth an enemy spy, while on the other it would be equally impossible for him as an Englishman and an officer to give her aid or protection.

The young man contented himself therefore with repeated mental denials of her guilt. He tried to convince himself that Tarzan was mistaken, and when he conjured upon the screen of recollection the face of the girl behind him, he was doubly reassured that those lines of sweet femininity and character, those clear and honest eyes, could not belong to one of the hated alien race.

And so they sped toward the east, each wrapped in his own thoughts. Below them they saw the dense vegetation of the jungle give place to the scantier growth upon the hillside, and then before them there spread the wide expanse of wastelands marked by the deep scarring of the narrow gorges that long-gone rivers had cut there in some forgotten age.

Shortly after they passed the summit of the ridge which formed the boundary between the desert and the fertile country, Ska, the vulture, winging his way at a high altitude toward his aerie, caught sight of a strange new bird of gigantic proportions encroaching upon the preserves of his aerial domain. Whether with intent to give battle to the interloper or merely impelled by curiosity, Ska rose suddenly upward to meet the plane. Doubtless he misjudged the speed of the newcomer, but be that as it may, the tip of the propeller blade touched him and simultaneously many things happened. The lifeless body of Ska, torn and bleeding, dropped plummetlike toward the ground; a bit of splintered spruce drove backward to strike the pilot on the forehead; the plane shuddered and trembled and as Lieutenant Harold Percy Smith-Oldwick sank forward in momentary unconsciousness the ship dived headlong toward the earth.

Only for an instant was the pilot unconscious, but that instant almost proved their undoing. When he awoke to a realization of their peril it was also to discover that his motor had stalled. The plane had attained frightful momentum and the ground seemed too close for him to hope to flatten out in time to make a safe landing. Directly beneath him was a deep rift in the plateau, a narrow gorge, the bottom of which appeared comparatively level and sand covered.

In the brief instant in which he must reach a decision, the safest plan seemed to attempt a landing in the gorge, and this he did, but not without considerable damage to the plane and a severe shaking-up for himself and his passenger.

Fortunately neither of them was injured but their condition seemed indeed a hopeless one. It was a grave question as to whether the man could repair his plane and continue the journey, and it seemed equally questionable as to their ability either to proceed on foot to the coast or retrace their way to the country they had just left. The man was confident that they could not hope to cross the desert country to the east in the face of thirst and hunger, while behind them in the valley of plenty lay almost equal danger in the form of carnivores and the warlike natives.

After the plane came to its sudden and disastrous stop, Smith-Oldwick turned quickly to see what the effect of the accident had been on the girl. He found her pale but smiling, and for several seconds the two sat looking at each other in silence.

'This is the end?' the girl asked.

The Englishman shook his head. 'It is the end of the first leg, anyway,' he replied.

'But you can't hope to make repairs here,' she said dubiously.

'No,' he said, 'not if they amount to anything, but I may be able to patch it up. I will have to look her over a bit first. Let us hope there is nothing serious. It's a long, long way to the Tanga railway.'

'We would not get far,' said the girl, a slight note of hopelessness in her tone. 'Entirely unarmed as we are, it would be little less than a miracle if we covered even a small fraction of the distance.'

'But we are not unarmed,' replied the man. 'I have an extra pistol here, that the beggars didn't discover,' and, removing the cover of a compartment, he drew forth an automatic.

Bertha Kircher leaned back in her seat and laughed aloud, a mirthless, half-hysterical laugh. 'That popgun!' she exclaimed. 'What earthly good would it do other than to infuriate any beast of prey you might happen to hit with it?'

Smith-Oldwick looked rather crestfallen. 'But it is a weapon,' he said. 'You will have to admit that, and certainly I could kill a man with it.'

'You could if you happened to hit him,' said the girl, 'or the thing didn't jam. Really, I haven't much faith in an automatic. I have used them myself.'

'Oh, of course,' he said ironically, 'an express rifle would be better, for who knows but we might meet an elephant here in the desert.'

The girl saw that he was hurt, and she was sorry, for she realized that there was nothing he would not do in her service or protection, and that it was through no fault of his that he was so illy armed. Doubtless, too, he realized as well as she the futility of his weapon, and that he had only called attention to it in the hope of reassuring her and lessening her anxiety.

'Forgive me,' she said. 'I did not mean to be nasty, but this accident is the proverbial last straw. It seems to me that I have borne all that I can. Though I was willing to give my life in the service of my country, I did not imagine that my death agonies would be so long drawn out, for I realize now that I have been dying for many weeks.'

'What do you mean!' he exclaimed; 'what do you mean by that! You are not dying. There is nothing the matter with you.'

'Oh, not that,' she said, 'I did not mean that. What I mean is that at the moment the black sergeant, Usanga, and his renegade German native troops captured me and brought me inland, my death warrant was signed. Sometimes I have imagined that a reprieve has been granted. Sometimes I have hoped that I might be upon the verge of winning a full pardon, but really in the depths of my heart I have known that I should never live to regain civilization. I have done my bit for my country, and though it was not much I can at least go with the realization that it was the best I was able to offer. All that I can hope for now, all that I ask for, is a speedy fulfillment of the death sentence. I do not wish to linger any more to face constant terror and apprehension. Even physical torture would be preferable to what I have passed through. I have no doubt that you consider me a brave woman, but really my terror has been boundless. The cries of the carnivores at night fill me with a dread so tangible that I am in actual pain. I feel the rending talons in my flesh and the cruel fangs munching upon my bones – it is as real to me as though

I were actually enduring the horrors of such a death. I doubt if you can understand it – men are so different.'

'Yes,' he said, 'I think I can understand it, and because I understand I can appreciate more than you imagine the heroism you have shown in your endurance of all that you have passed through. There can be no bravery where there is no fear. A child might walk into a lion's den, but it would take a very brave man to go to its rescue.'

'Thank you,' she said, 'but I am not brave at all, and now I am very much ashamed of my thoughtlessness for your own feelings. I will try and take a new grip upon myself and we will both hope for the best. I will help you all I can if you will tell me what I may do.'

'The first thing,' he replied, 'is to find out just how serious our damage is, and then to see what we can do in the way of repairs.'

For two days Smith-Oldwick worked upon the damaged plane – worked in the face of the fact that from the first he realized the case was hopeless. And at last he told her.

'I knew it,' she said, 'but I believe that I felt much as you must have; that however futile our efforts here might be, it would be infinitely as fatal to attempt to retrace our way to the jungle we just left or to go on toward the coast. You know and I know that we could not reach the Tanga railway on foot. We should die of thirst and starvation before we had covered half the distance, and if we return to the jungle, even were we able to reach it, it would be but to court an equally certain, though different, fate.'

'So we might as well sit here and wait for death as to uselessly waste our energies in what we know would be a futile attempt at escape?' he asked.

'No,' she replied, 'I shall never give up like that. What I meant was that it was useless to attempt to reach either of the places where we know that there is food and water in abundance, so we must strike out in a new direction. Somewhere there may be water in this wilderness and if there is, the best chance of our finding it would be to follow this gorge downward. We have enough food and water left, if we are careful of it, for a couple of days and in that time we might stumble upon a spring or possibly even reach the fertile country which I know lies to the south. When Usanga brought me to the Wamabo country from the coast he took a southerly route along which there was usually water and game in plenty. It was not until we neared our destination that the country became overrun with carnivores. So there is hope if we can reach the fertile country south of us that we can manage to pull through to the coast.'

The man shook his head dubiously. 'We can try it,' he said. 'Personally, I do not fancy sitting here waiting for death.'

Smith-Oldwick was leaning against the ship, his dejected gaze directed upon the ground at his feet. The girl was looking south down the gorge in the direction of their one slender chance of life. Suddenly she touched him on the arm.

'Look,' she whispered.

The man raised his eyes quickly in the direction of her gaze to see the massive head of a great lion who was regarding them from beyond a rocky projection at the first turning of the gorge.

'Phew!' he exclaimed. 'The beggars are everywhere.'

'They do not go far from water, do they,' asked the girl hopefully.

'I should imagine not,' he replied; 'a lion is not particularly strong on endurance.'

'Then he is a harbinger of hope,' she exclaimed.

The man laughed. 'Cute little harbinger of hope!' he said. 'Reminds me of Cock Robin heralding spring.'

The girl cast a quick glance at him. 'Don't be silly, and I don't care if you do laugh. He fills me with hope.'

'It is probably mutual,' replied Smith-Oldwick, 'as we doubtless fill him with hope.'

The lion evidently having satisfied himself as to the nature of the creatures before him advanced slowly now in their direction.

'Come,' said the man, 'let's climb aboard,' and he helped the girl over the side of the ship.

'Can't he get in here?' she asked.

'I think he can,' said the man.

'You are reassuring,' she returned.

'I don't feel so.' He drew his pistol.

'For heaven's sake,' she cried, 'don't shoot at him with that thing. You might hit him.'

'I don't intend to shoot at him but I might succeed in frightening him away if he attempts to reach us here. Haven't you ever seen a trainer work with lions? He carries a silly little popgun loaded with blank cartridges. With that and a kitchen chair he subdues the most ferocious of beasts.'

'But you haven't a kitchen chair,' she reminded him.

'No,' he said. 'Government is always muddling things. I have always maintained that airplanes should be equipped with kitchen chairs.'

Bertha Kircher laughed as evenly and with as little hysteria as though she were moved by the small talk of an afternoon tea.

Numa, the lion, came steadily toward them; his attitude seemed more that of curiosity than of belligerency. Close to the side of the ship he stopped and stood gazing up at them.

'Magnificent, isn't he?' exclaimed the man.

'I never saw a more beautiful creature,' she replied, 'nor one with such a dark coat. Why, he is almost black.'

The sound of their voices seemed not to please the lord of the jungle, for he suddenly wrinkled his great face into deep furrows as he bared his fangs beneath snarling lips and gave vent to an angry growl. Almost simultaneously he crouched for a spring and immediately Smith-Oldwick discharged his pistol into the ground in front of the lion. The effect of the noise upon Numa seemed but to enrage him further, and with a horrid roar he sprang for the author of the new and disquieting sound that had outraged his ears.

Simultaneously Lieutenant Harold Percy Smith-Oldwick vaulted nimbly out of the cockpit on the opposite side of his plane, calling to the girl to follow his example. The girl, realizing the futility of leaping to the ground, chose the remaining alternative and clambered to the top of the upper plane.

Numa, unaccustomed to the idiosyncrasies of construction of an airship and having gained the forward cockpit, watched the girl clamber out of his reach without at first endeavoring to prevent her. Having taken possession of the plane his anger seemed suddenly to leave him and he made no immediate move toward following Smith-Oldwick. The girl, realizing the comparative safety of her position, had crawled to the other edge of the wing and was calling to the man to try and reach the opposite end of the upper plane.

It was this scene upon which Tarzan of the Apes looked as he rounded the bend of the gorge above the plane after the pistol shot had attracted his attention. The girl was so intent upon watching the efforts of the Englishman to reach a place of safety, and the latter was so busily occupied in attempting to do so that neither at once noticed the silent approach of the ape-man.

It was Numa who first noticed the intruder. The lion immediately evinced his displeasure by directing toward him a snarling countenance and a series of warning growls. His action called the attention of the two upon the upper plane to the newcomer, eliciting a stifled 'Thank God!' from the girl, even though she could scarce credit the evidence of her own eyes that it was indeed the savage man, whose presence always assured her safety, who had come so providentially in the nick of time.

Almost immediately both were horrified to see Numa leap from the cockpit and advance upon Tarzan. The ape-man, carrying his stout spear in readiness, moved deliberately onward to meet the carnivore, which he had recognized as the lion of the Wamabos' pit. He knew from the manner of Numa's approach what neither Bertha Kircher nor Smith-Oldwick knew – that there was more of curiosity than belligerency in it, and he wondered if in that great head there might not be a semblance of gratitude for the kindness that Tarzan had done him.

There was no question in Tarzan's mind but that Numa recognized him, for he knew his fellows of the jungle well enough to know that while they ofttimes forgot certain sensations more quickly than man there are others which remain in their memories for years. A well-defined scent spoor might never be forgotten by a beast if it had first been sensed under unusual circumstances, and so Tarzan was confident that Numa's nose had already reminded him of all the circumstances of their brief connection.

Love of the sporting chance is inherent in the Anglo-Saxon race and it was not now Tarzan of the Apes but rather John Clayton, Lord Greystoke, who smilingly welcomed the sporting chance which he must take to discover how far-reaching was Numa's gratitude.

Smith-Oldwick and the girl saw the two nearing each other. The former swore softly beneath his breath while he nervously fingered the pitiful weapon at his hip. The girl pressed her open palms to her cheeks as she leaned forward in stony-eyed, horror-stricken silence. While she had every confidence in the prowess of the godlike creature who thus dared brazenly to face the king of beasts, she had no false conception of what must certainly happen when they met. She had seen Tarzan battle with Sheeta, the panther, and she had realized then that powerful as the man was, it was only agility, cunning, and chance that placed him upon anywhere near an equal footing with his savage adversary, and that of the three factors upon his side chance was the greatest.

She saw the man and the lion stop simultaneously, not more than a yard apart. She saw the beast's tail whipping from side to side and she could hear his deep-throated growls rumbling from his cavernous breast, but she could read correctly neither the movement of the lashing tail nor the notes of the growl.

To her they seemed to indicate nothing but bestial rage while to Tarzan of the Apes they were conciliatory and reassuring in the extreme. And then she saw Numa move forward again until his nose touched the man's naked leg and she closed her eyes and covered them with her palms. For what seemed an eternity she waited for the horrid sound of the conflict which she knew must come, but all she heard was an explosive sigh of relief from Smith-Oldwick and a half-hysterical 'By Jove! Just fancy it!'

She looked up to see the great lion rubbing his shaggy head against the man's hip, and Tarzan's free hand entangled in the black mane as he scratched Numa, the lion, behind a backlaid ear.

Strange friendships are often formed between the lower animals of different species, but less often between man and the savage felidae, because of the former's inherent fear of the great cats. And so after all, therefore, the friendship so suddenly developed between the savage lion and the savage man was not inexplicable.

As Tarzan approached the plane Numa walked at his side, and when Tarzan stopped and looked up at the girl and the man Numa stopped also.

'I had about given up hope of finding you,' said the ape-man, 'and it is evident that I found you just in time.'

'But how did you know we were in trouble?' asked the English officer.

'I saw your plane fall,' replied Tarzan. 'I was watching you from a tree beside the clearing where you took off. I didn't have much to locate you by other than the general direction, but it seems that you volplaned a considerable distance toward the south after you disappeared from my view behind the hills. I have been looking for you farther toward the north. I was just about to turn back when I heard your pistol shot. Is your ship beyond repair?'

'Yes,' replied Smith-Oldwick, 'it is hopeless.'

'What are your plans, then? What do you wish to do?' Tarzan directed his question to the girl.

'We want to reach the coast,' she said, 'but it seems impossible now.'

'I should have thought so a little while ago,' replied the ape-man, 'but if Numa is here there must be water within a reasonable distance. I ran across this lion two days ago in the Wamabo country. I liberated him from one of their pits. To have reached this spot he must have come by some trail unknown to me – at least I crossed no game trail and no spoor of any animal after I came over the hills out of the fertile country. From which direction did he come upon you?'

'It was from the south,' replied the girl. 'We thought, too, that there must be water in that direction.'

'Let's find out then,' said Tarzan.

'But how about the lion?' asked Smith-Oldwick.

'That we will have to discover,' replied the ape-man, 'and we can only do so if you will come down from your perch.'

The officer shrugged his shoulders. The girl turned her gaze upon him to note the effect of Tarzan's proposal. The Englishman grew suddenly very white, but there was a smile upon his lips as without a word he slipped over the edge of the plane and clambered to the ground behind Tarzan.

Bertha Kircher realized that the man was afraid nor did she blame him, and she also realized the remarkable courage that he had shown in thus facing a danger that was very real to him.

Numa standing close to Tarzan's side raised his head and glared at the young Englishman, growled once, and looked up at the ape-man. Tarzan retained a hold upon the beast's mane and spoke to him in the language of the great apes. To the girl and Smith-Oldwick the growling gutturals falling from human lips sounded uncanny in the extreme, but whether Numa understood them or not they appeared to have the desired effect upon him, as he ceased growling, and as Tarzan walked to Smith-Oldwick's side Numa accompanied him, nor did he offer to molest the officer.

'What did you say to him?' asked the girl.

Tarzan smiled. 'I told him,' he replied, 'that I am Tarzan of the Apes, mighty hunter, killer of beasts, lord of the jungle, and that you are my friends. I have never been sure that all of the other beasts understand the language of the Mangani. I know that Manu, the monkey, speaks nearly the same tongue and I am sure that Tantor, the elephant, understands all that I say to him. We of the jungle are great boasters. In our speech, in our carriage, in every detail of our demeanor we must impress others with our physical power and our ferocity. That is why we growl at our enemies. We are telling them to beware or we shall fall upon them and tear them to pieces. Perhaps Numa does not understand the words that I use but I believe that my tones and my manner carry the impression that I wish them to convey. Now you may come down and be introduced.'

It required all the courage that Bertha Kircher possessed to lower herself to the ground within reach of the talons and fangs of this untamed forest beast, but she did it. Nor did Numa do more than bare his teeth and growl a little as she came close to the ape-man.

'I think you are safe from him as long as I am present,' said the ape-man. 'The best thing to do is simply to ignore him. Make no advances, but be sure to give no indication of fear and, if possible, always keep me between you and him. He will go away presently I am sure and the chances are that we shall not see him again.'

At Tarzan's suggestion Smith-Oldwick removed the remaining water and provisions from the plane and, distributing the burden among them, they set off toward the south. Numa did not follow them, but stood by the plane watching until they finally disappeared from view around a bend in the gorge.

Tarzan had picked up Numa's trail with the intention of following it southward in the belief that it would lead to water. In the sand that floored the bottom of the gorge tracks were plain and easily followed. At first only the fresh tracks of Numa were visible, but later in the day the ape-man discovered the older tracks of other lions and just before dark he stopped suddenly in evident surprise. His two companions looked at him questioningly, and in answer to their implied interrogations he pointed at the ground directly in front of him.

'Look at those,' he exclaimed.

At first neither Smith-Oldwick nor the girl saw anything but a confusion of intermingled prints of padded feet in the sand, but presently the girl discovered what Tarzan had seen, and an exclamation of surprise broke from her lips.

'The imprint of human feet!' she cried.

Tarzan nodded.

'But there are no toes,' the girl pointed out.

'The feet were shod with a soft sandal,' explained Tarzan.

'Then there must be a native village somewhere in the vicinity,' said Smith-Oldwick.

'Yes,' replied the ape-man, 'but not the sort of natives which we would expect to find here in this part of Africa where others all go unshod with the exception of a few of Usanga's renegade German native troops who wear German army shoes. I don't know that you can notice it, but it is evident to me that the foot inside the sandal that made these imprints was not the foot of a Negro. If you will examine them carefully you will notice that the impression of the heel and ball of the foot are well marked even through the sole of the sandal. The weight comes more nearly in the center of a Negro's footprint.'

'Then you think these were made by a white person?'

'It looks that way,' replied Tarzan, and suddenly, to the surprise of both the girl and Smith-Oldwick, he dropped to his hands and knees and sniffed at the tracks – again a beast utilizing the senses and woodcraft of a beast. Over an area of several square yards his keen nostrils sought the identity of the makers of the tracks. At length he rose to his feet.

'It is not the spoor of the Gomangani,' he said, 'nor is it exactly like that of white men. There were three who came this way. They were men, but of what race I do not know.'

There was no apparent change in the nature of the gorge except that it had steadily grown deeper as they followed it downward until now the rocky and precipitous sides rose far above them. At different points natural caves, which appeared to have been eroded by the action of water in some forgotten age, pitted the side walls at various heights. Near them was such a cavity at the ground's level – an arched cavern floored with white sand. Tarzan indicated it with a gesture of his hand.

'We will lair here tonight,' he said, and then with one of his rare, slow smiles: 'We will *camp* here tonight.'

Having eaten their meager supper Tarzan bade the girl enter the cavern.

'You will sleep inside,' he said. 'The lieutenant and I will lie outside at the entrance.'

16

The Night Attack

As the girl turned to bid them goodnight, she thought that she saw a shadowy form moving in the darkness beyond them, and almost simultaneously she was sure that she heard the sounds of stealthy movement in the same direction.

'What is that?' she whispered. 'There is something out there in the darkness.'

'Yes,' replied Tarzan, 'it is a lion. It has been there for some time. Hadn't you noticed it before?'

'Oh!' cried the girl, breathing a sigh of relief, 'is it our lion?'

'No,' said Tarzan, 'it is not our lion; it is another lion and he is hunting.'

'He is stalking us?' asked the girl.

'He is,' replied the ape-man. Smith-Oldwick fingered the grip of his pistol.

Tarzan saw the involuntary movement and shook his head.

'Leave that thing where it is, Lieutenant,' he said.

The officer laughed nervously. 'I couldn't help it, you know, old man,' he said; 'instinct of self-preservation and all that.'

'It would prove an instinct of self-destruction,' said Tarzan. 'There are at least three hunting lions out there watching us. If we had a fire or the moon were up you would see their eyes plainly. Presently they may come after us but the chances are that they will not. If you are very anxious that they should, fire your pistol and hit one of them.'

'What if they do charge?' asked the girl; 'there is no means of escape.'

'Why, we should have to fight them,' replied Tarzan.

'What chance would we three have against them?' asked the girl.

The ape-man shrugged his shoulders. 'One must die sometime,' he said. 'To you doubtless it may seem terrible – such a death; but Tarzan of the Apes has always expected to go out in some such way. Few of us die of old age in the jungle, nor should I care to die thus. Someday Numa will get me, or Sheeta, or a black warrior. These or some of the others. What difference does it make which it is, or whether it comes tonight or next year or in ten years? After it is over it will be all the same.'

The girl shuddered. 'Yes,' she said in a dull, hopeless voice, 'after it is over it will be all the same.'

Then she went into the cavern and lay down upon the sand. Smith-Oldwick sat in the entrance and leaned against the cliff. Tarzan squatted on the opposite side.

'May I smoke?' questioned the officer of Tarzan. 'I have been hoarding a few cigarettes and if it won't attract those bounders out there I would like to have one last smoke before I cash in. Will you join me?' and he proffered the ape-man a cigarette.

'No, thanks,' said Tarzan, 'but it will be all right if you smoke. No wild animal is particularly fond of the fumes of tobacco so it certainly won't entice them any closer.'

Smith-Oldwick lighted his cigarette and sat puffing slowly upon it. He had proffered one to the girl but she had refused, and thus they sat in silence for some time, the silence of the night ruffled occasionally by the faint crunching of padded feet upon the soft sands of the gorge's floor.

It was Smith-Oldwick who broke the silence. 'Aren't they unusually quiet for lions?' he asked.

'No,' replied the ape-man, 'the lion that goes roaring around the jungle does not do it to attract prey. They are very quiet when they are stalking their quarry.'

'I wish they would roar,' said the officer. 'I wish they would do anything, even charge. Just knowing that they are there and occasionally seeing something like a shadow in the darkness and the faint sounds that come to us from them are getting on my nerves. But I hope,' he said, 'that all three don't charge at once.'

'Three?' said Tarzan. 'There are seven of them out there now.'

'Good Lord!' exclaimed Smith-Oldwick.

'Couldn't we build a fire,' asked the girl, 'and frighten them away?'

'I don't know that it would do any good,' said Tarzan, 'as I have an idea that these lions are a little different from any that we are familiar with and possibly for the same reason which at first puzzled me a little – I refer to the apparent docility in the presence of a man of the lion who was with us today. A man is out there now with those lions.'

'It is impossible!' exclaimed Smith-Oldwick. 'They would tear him to pieces.'

'What makes you think there is a man there?' asked the girl.

Tarzan smiled and shook his head. 'I am afraid you would not understand,' he replied. 'It is difficult for us to understand anything that is beyond our own powers.'

'What do you mean by that?' asked the officer.

'Well,' said Tarzan, 'if you had been born without eyes you could not understand sense impressions that the eyes of others transmit to their brains, and as you have both been born without any sense of smell I am afraid you cannot understand how I can know that there is a man there.'

'You mean that you scent a man?' asked the girl.

Tarzan nodded affirmatively.

'And in the same way you know the number of lions?' asked the man.

'Yes,' said Tarzan. 'No two lions look alike, no two have the same scent.'

The young Englishman shook his head. 'No,' he said, 'I cannot understand.'

'I doubt if the lions or the man are here necessarily for the purpose of harming us,' said Tarzan, 'because there has been nothing to prevent their doing so long before had they wished to. I have a theory, but it is utterly preposterous.'

'What is it?' asked the girl.

'I think they are here,' replied Tarzan, 'to prevent us from going some place that they do not wish us to go; in other words we are under surveillance, and possibly as long as we don't go where we are not wanted we shall not be bothered.'

'But how are we to know where they don't want us to go?' asked Smith-Oldwick.

'We can't know,' replied Tarzan, 'and the chances are that the very place we are seeking is the place they don't wish us to trespass on.'

'You mean the water?' asked the girl.

'Yes,' replied Tarzan.

For some time they sat in silence which was broken only by an occasional sound of movement from the outer darkness. It must have been an hour later that the ape-man rose quietly and drew his long blade from its sheath. Smith-Oldwick was dozing against the rocky wall of the cavern entrance, while the girl, exhausted by the excitement and fatigue of the day, had fallen into deep slumber. An instant after Tarzan arose, Smith-Oldwick and the girl were aroused by a volley of thunderous roars and the noise of many padded feet rushing toward them.

Tarzan of the Apes stood directly before the entrance to the cavern, his knife in his hand, awaiting the charge. The ape-man had not expected any such concerted action as he now realized had been taken by those watching them. He had known for some time that other men had joined those who were with the lions earlier in the evening, and when he arose to his feet it was because he knew that the lions and the men were moving cautiously closer to him and his party. He might easily have eluded them, for he had seen that the face of the cliff rising above the mouth of the cavern might be scaled by as good a climber as himself. It might have been wiser had he tried to escape, for he knew that in the face of such odds even he was helpless, but he stood his ground though I doubt if he could have told why.

He owed nothing either of duty or friendship to the girl sleeping in the cavern, nor could he longer be of any protection to her or her companion. Yet something held him there in futile self-sacrifice.

The great Tarmangani had not even the satisfaction of striking a blow in self-defense. A veritable avalanche of savage beasts rolled over him and threw him heavily to the ground. In falling his head struck the rocky surface of the cliff, stunning him.

It was daylight when he regained consciousness. The first dim impression borne to his awakening mind was a confusion of savage sounds which gradually resolved themselves into the growling of lions, and then, little by little, there came back to him the recollections of what had preceded the blow that had felled him.

Strong in his nostrils was the scent of Numa, the lion, and against one naked leg he could feel the coat of some animal. Slowly Tarzan opened his eyes. He was lying on his side and as he looked down his body, he saw that a great lion stood straddling him – a great lion who growled hideously at something which Tarzan could not see.

With the full return of his senses Tarzan's nose told him that the beast above him was Numa of the Wamabo pit.

Thus reassured, the ape-man spoke to the lion and at the same time made a motion as though he would arise. Immediately Numa stepped from above him. As Tarzan raised his head, he saw that he still lay where he had fallen before the opening of the cliff where the girl had been sleeping and that Numa, backed against the cliffside, was apparently defending him from two other lions who paced to and fro a short distance from their intended victim.

And then Tarzan turned his eyes into the cave and saw that the girl and Smith-Oldwick were gone.

His efforts had been for naught. With an angry toss of his head, the ape-man turned upon the two lions who had continued to pace back and forth a few yards from him. Numa of the lion pit turned a friendly glance in Tarzan's direction, rubbed his head against the ape-man's side, and then directed his snarling countenance toward the two hunters.

'I think,' said Tarzan to Numa, 'that you and I together can make these beasts very unhappy.' He spoke in English, which, of course, Numa did not understand at all, but there must have been something reassuring in the tone, for Numa whined pleadingly and moved impatiently to and fro parallel with their antagonists.

'Come,' said Tarzan suddenly and grasping the lion's mane with his left hand he moved toward the other lions, his companion pacing at his side. As the two advanced the others drew slowly back and, finally separating, moved off to either side. Tarzan and Numa passed between them but neither the great black-maned lion nor the man failed to keep an eye upon the beast nearer him so that they were not caught unawares when, as though at some preconcerted signal, the two cats charged simultaneously from opposite directions.

The ape-man met the charge of his antagonist after the same fashion of fighting that he had been accustomed to employing in previous encounters with Numa and Sheeta. To have attempted to meet the full shock of a lion's charge would have been suicidal even for the giant Tarmangani. Instead he resorted to methods of agility and cunning, for quick as are the great cats, even quicker is Tarzan of the Apes.

With outspread, raking talons and bared fangs Numa sprang for the naked chest of the ape-man. Throwing up his left arm as a boxer might ward off a blow, Tarzan struck upward beneath the left forearm of a lion, at the same time rushing in with his shoulder beneath the animal's body and simultaneously drove his blade into the tawny hide behind the shoulder. With a roar of pain Numa wheeled again, the personification of bestial rage. Now indeed would he exterminate this presumptuous man-thing who dared even to think that he could thwart the king of beasts in his desires. But as he wheeled, his intended quarry wheeled with him, brown fingers locked in the heavy mane on the powerful neck and again the blade struck deep into the lion's side.

Then it was that Numa went mad with hate and pain and at the same instant the ape-man leaped full upon his back. Easily before had Tarzan locked his legs beneath the belly of a lion while he clung to its long mane and stabbed it until his point reached its heart. So easy it had seemed before that he experienced a sharp feeling of resentment that he was unable to do so now, for the quick movements of the lion prevented him, and presently, to his dismay, as the lion leaped and threw him about, the ape-man realized that he was swinging inevitably beneath those frightful talons.

With a final effort he threw himself from Numa's back and sought, by his quickness, to elude the frenzied beast for the fraction of an instant that would permit him to regain his feet and meet the animal again upon a more even footing. But this time Numa was too quick for him and he was but partially up when a great paw struck him on the side of the head and bowled him over.

As he fell he saw a black streak shoot above him and another lion close upon his antagonist. Rolling from beneath the two battling lions Tarzan regained his feet, though he was half dazed and staggering from the impact of the terrible blow he had received. Behind him he saw a lifeless lion lying torn and bleeding upon the sand, and before him Numa of the pit was savagely mauling the second lion.

He of the black coat tremendously outclassed his adversary in point of size and strength as well as in ferocity. The battling beasts made a few feints and passes at each other before the larger succeeded in fastening his fangs in the other's throat, and then, as a cat shakes a mouse, the larger lion shook the lesser, and when his dying foe sought to roll beneath and rake his conqueror with his hind claws, the other met him halfway at his own game, and as the great talons buried themselves in the lower part of the other's chest and then were raked downward with all the terrific strength of the mighty hind legs, the battle was ended.

As Numa rose from his second victim and shook himself, Tarzan could not but again note the wondrous proportions and symmetry of the beast. The lions they had bested were splendid specimens themselves and in their coats Tarzan noted a suggestion of the black which was such a strongly marked characteristic of Numa of the pit. Their manes were just a trifle darker than an ordinary black-maned lion but the tawny shade on the balance of their coats predominated. However, the ape-man realized that they were a distinct species from any he had seen as though they had sprung originally from a cross between the forest lion of his acquaintance and a breed of which Numa of the pit might be typical.

The immediate obstruction in his way having been removed, Tarzan was for setting out in search of the spoor of the girl and Smith-Oldwick, that he might discover their fate. He suddenly found himself tremendously hungry and as he circled about over the sandy bottom searching among the tangled network of innumerable tracks for those of his *protégés*, there broke from his lips involuntarily the whine of a hungry beast. Immediately Numa of the pit pricked up his ears and, regarding the ape-man steadily for a moment, he answered the call of hunger and started briskly off toward the south, stopping occasionally to see if Tarzan was following.

The ape-man realized that the beast was leading him to food, and so he followed and as he followed his keen eyes and sensitive nostrils sought for some indication of the direction taken by the man and the girl. Presently out of the mass of lion tracks, Tarzan picked up those of many sandaled feet and the scent spoor of the members of the strange race such as had been with the lions the night before, and then faintly he caught the scent spoor of the girl and a little later that of Smith-Oldwick. Presently the tracks thinned and here those of the girl and the Englishman became well marked.

They had been walking side by side and there had been men and lions to the right and left of them, and men and lions in front and behind. The ape-man was puzzled by the possibilities suggested by the tracks, but in the light of any previous experience he could not explain satisfactorily to himself what his perceptions indicated.

There was little change in the formation of the gorge; it still wound its erratic course between precipitous cliffs. In places it widened out and again it became very narrow and always deeper the farther south they traveled. Presently the bottom of the gorge began to slope more rapidly. Here and there were indications of ancient rapids and waterfalls. The trail became more difficult but was well marked and showed indications of great antiquity, and, in places, the handiwork of man. They had proceeded for a half or three-quarters of a mile when, at a turning of the gorge, Tarzan saw before him a narrow valley cut deep into the living rock of the earth's crust, with lofty mountain ranges bounding it upon the south. How far it extended east and west he could not see, but apparently it was no more than three or four miles across from north to south.

That it was a well-watered valley was indicated by the wealth of vegetation that carpeted its floor from the rocky cliffs upon the north to the mountains on the south.

Over the edge of the cliffs from which the ape-man viewed the valley a trail had been hewn that led downward to the base. Preceded by the lion Tarzan descended into the valley, which, at this point, was forested with large trees. Before him the trail wound onward toward the center of the valley. Raucous-voiced birds of brilliant plumage screamed among the branches while innumerable monkeys chattered and scolded above him.

The forest teemed with life, and yet there was borne in upon the ape-man a sense of unutterable loneliness, a sensation that he never before had felt in his beloved jungles. There was unreality in everything about him – in the valley itself, lying hidden and forgotten in what was supposed to be an arid waste. The birds and the monkeys, while similar in type to many with which he was familiar, were identical with none, nor was the vegetation without its idiosyncrasies. It was as though he had been suddenly transported to another world and he felt a strange restlessness that might easily have been a premonition of danger.

Fruits were growing among the trees and some of these he saw that Manu, the monkey, ate. Being hungry he swung to the lower branches and, amidst a great chattering of the monkeys, proceeded to eat such of the fruit as he saw the monkeys ate in safety. When he had partially satisfied his hunger, for meat alone could fully do so, he looked about him for Numa of the pit to discover that the lion had gone.

17

The Walled City

Dropping to the ground once more he picked up the trail of the girl and her captors, which he followed easily along what appeared to be a well-beaten trail. It was not long before he came to a small stream, where he quenched his thirst, and thereafter he saw that the trail followed in the general direction of the stream, which ran southwesterly. Here and there were cross trails and others which joined the main avenue, and always upon each of them were the tracks and scent of the great cats, of Numa, the lion, and Sheeta, the panther.

With the exception of a few small rodents there appeared to be no other wildlife on the surface of the valley. There was no indication of Bara, the deer, or Horta, the boar, or of Gorgo, the buffalo, Buto, Tantor, or Duro. Histah, the snake, was there. He saw them in the trees in greater numbers than he ever had seen Histah before; and once beside a reedy pool he caught a scent that could have belonged to none other than Gimla, the crocodile, but upon none of these did the Tarmangani care to feed.

And so, as he craved meat, he turned his attention to the birds above him. His assailants of the night before had not disarmed him. Either in the darkness and the rush of the charging lions the human foe had overlooked him or else they had considered him dead; but whatever the reason he still retained his weapons – his spear and his long knife, his bow and arrows, and his grass rope.

Fitting a shaft to his bow Tarzan awaited an opportunity to bring down one of the larger birds, and when the opportunity finally presented itself he drove the arrow straight to its mark. As the gaily plumaged creature fluttered to earth its companions and the little monkeys set up a most terrific chorus of wails and screaming protests. The whole forest became suddenly a babel of hoarse screams and shrill shrieks.

Tarzan would not have been surprised had one or two birds in the immediate vicinity given voice to terror as they fled, but that the whole life of the jungle should set up so weird a protest filled him with disgust. It was an angry face that he turned up toward the monkeys and the birds as there suddenly stirred within him a savage inclination to voice his displeasure and his answer to what he considered their challenge. And so it was that there broke upon this jungle for the first time Tarzan's hideous scream of victory and challenge.

The effect upon the creatures above him was instantaneous. Where before the air had trembled to the din of their voices, now utter silence reigned and a moment later the ape-man was alone with his puny kill.

The silence following so closely the previous tumult carried a sinister impression to the ape-man, which still further aroused his anger. Picking the bird from where it had fallen he withdrew his arrow from the body and returned it to his quiver. Then with his knife he quickly and deftly removed the skin and feathers together. He ate angrily, growling as though actually menaced by a nearby foe, and perhaps, too, his growls were partially induced by the fact that he did not care for the flesh of birds. Better this, however, than nothing and from what his senses had told him there was no flesh in the vicinity such as he was accustomed to and cared most for. How he would have enjoyed a juicy haunch from Pacco, the zebra, or a steak from the loin of Gorgo, the buffalo! The very thought made his mouth water and increased his resentment against this unnatural forest that harbored no such delicious quarry.

He had but partially consumed his kill when he suddenly became aware of a movement in the brush at no great distance from him and downwind, and a moment later his nostrils picked up the scent of Numa from the opposite direction, and then upon either side he caught the fall of padded feet and the brushing of bodies against leafy branches. The ape-man smiled. What stupid creature did they think him, to be surprised by such clumsy stalkers? Gradually the sounds and scents indicated that lions were moving upon him from all directions, that he was in the center of a steadily converging circle of beasts. Evidently they were so sure of their prey that they were making no effort toward stealth, for he heard twigs crack beneath their feet, and the brushing of their bodies against the vegetation through which they forced their way.

He wondered what could have brought them. It seemed unreasonable to believe that the cries of the birds and the monkeys should have summoned them, and yet, if not, it was indeed a remarkable coincidence. His judgment told him that the death of a single bird in this forest which teemed with birds could scarce be of sufficient moment to warrant that which followed. Yet even in the face of reason and past experience he found that the whole affair perplexed him.

He stood in the center of the trail awaiting the coming of the lions and wondering what would be the method of their attack or if they would indeed attack. Presently a maned lion came into view along the trail below him. At sight of him the lion halted. The beast was similar to those that had attacked him earlier in the day, a trifle larger and a trifle darker than the lions of his native jungles, but neither so large nor so black as Numa of the pit.

Presently he distinguished the outlines of other lions in the surrounding brush and among the trees. Each of them halted as it came within sight of the ape-man and there they stood regarding him in silence. Tarzan wondered how long it would be before they charged and while he waited he resumed his feeding, though with every sense constantly alert.

One by one the lions lay down, but always their faces were toward him and their eyes upon him. There had been no growling and no roaring – just the quiet drawing of the silent circle about him. It was all so entirely foreign to anything that Tarzan ever before had seen lions do that it irritated him so that presently, having finished his repast, he fell to making insulting remarks to first one and then another of the lions, after the habit he had learned from the apes of his childhood.

'Dango, eater of carrion,' he called them, and he compared them most unfavorably with Histah, the snake, the most loathed and repulsive creature of the jungle. Finally he threw handfuls of earth at them and bits of broken twigs, and then the lions growled and bared their fangs, but none of them advanced.

'Cowards,' Tarzan taunted them. 'Numa with a heart of Bara, the deer.' He told them who he was, and after the manner of the jungle folk he boasted as to the horrible things he would do to them, but the lions only lay and watched him.

It must have been a half hour after their coming that Tarzan caught in the distance along the trail the sound of footsteps approaching. They were the footsteps of a creature who walked upon two legs, and though Tarzan could catch no scent spoor from that direction he knew that a man was approaching. Nor had he long to wait before his judgment was confirmed by the appearance of a man who halted in the trail directly behind the first lion that Tarzan had seen.

At sight of the newcomer the ape-man realized that here was one similar to those who had given off the unfamiliar scent spoor that he had detected the previous night, and he saw that not only in the matter of scent did the man differ from other human beings with whom Tarzan was familiar.

The fellow was strongly built with skin of a leathery appearance, like parchment yellowed with age. His hair, which was coal black and three or four inches in length, grew out stiffly at right angles to his scalp. His eyes were close set and the irises densely black and very small, so that the white of the eyeball showed around them. The man's face was smooth except for a few straggly hairs on his chin and upper lip. The nose was aquiline and fine, but the hair grew so far down on the forehead as to suggest a very low and brutal type. The upper lip was short and fine while the lower lip was rather heavy and inclined to be pendulous, the chin being equally weak. Altogether the face carried the suggestion of a once strong and handsome countenance entirely altered by physical violence or by degraded habits and thoughts. The man's arms were long, though not abnormally so, while his legs were short, though straight.

He was clothed in tight-fitting nether garments and a loose, sleeveless tunic that fell just below his hips, while his feet were shod in soft-soled sandals, the wrappings of which extended halfway to his knees, closely resembling a modern spiral military legging. He carried a short, heavy spear, and at his side swung a weapon that at first so astonished the ape-man that he could scarcely believe the evidence of his senses – a heavy saber in a leather-covered scabbard. The man's tunic appeared to have been fabricated upon a loom – it was certainly not made of skins, while the garments that covered his legs were quite as evidently made from the hides of rodents.

Tarzan noted the utter unconcern with which the man approached the lions, and the equal indifference of Numa to him. The fellow paused for a moment as though appraising the ape-man and then pushed on past the lions, brushing against the tawny hide as he passed him in the trail.

About twenty feet from Tarzan the man stopped, addressing the former in a strange jargon, no syllable of which was intelligible to the Tarmangani. His gestures indicated numerous references to the lions surrounding them, and once he touched his spear with the forefinger of his left hand and twice he struck the saber at his hip.

While he spoke Tarzan studied the fellow closely, with the result that there fastened itself upon his mind a strange conviction – that the man who addressed him was what might only be described as a rational maniac. As the thought came to the ape-man he could not but smile, so paradoxical the description seemed. Yet a closer study of the man's features, carriage, and the contour of his head carried almost incontrovertibly the assurance that he was insane, while the tones of his voice and his gestures resembled those of a sane and intelligent mortal.

Presently the man had concluded his speech and appeared to be waiting questioningly Tarzan's reply. The ape-man spoke to the other first in the language of the great apes, but he soon saw that the words carried no conviction to his listener. Then with equal futility he tried several native dialects but to none of these did the man respond.

By this time Tarzan began to lose patience. He had wasted sufficient time by the road, and as he had never depended much upon speech in the accomplishment of his ends, he now raised his spear and advanced toward the other. This, evidently, was a language common to both, for instantly the fellow raised his own weapon and at the same time a low call broke from his lips, a call which instantly brought to action every lion in the hitherto silent circle. A volley of roars shattered the silence of the forest and simultaneously lions sprang into view upon all sides as they closed in rapidly upon their quarry. The man who had called them stepped back, his teeth bared in a mirthless grin.

It was then that Tarzan first noticed that the fellow's upper canines were unusually long and exceedingly sharp. It was just a flashing glimpse he got of them as he leaped agilely from the ground and, to the consternation of both the lions and their master, disappeared in the foliage of the lower terrace, flinging back over his shoulder as he swung rapidly away: 'I am Tarzan of the Apes; mighty hunter; mighty fighter! None in the jungle more powerful, none more cunning than Tarzan!'

A short distance beyond the point at which they had surrounded him, Tarzan came to the trail again and sought for the spoor of Bertha Kircher and Lieutenant Smith-Oldwick. He found them quickly and continued upon his search for the two. The spoor lay directly along the trail for another half-mile when the way suddenly debouched from the forest into open land and there broke upon the astonished view of the ape-man the domes and minarets of a walled city.

Directly before him in the wall nearest him Tarzan saw a low-arched gateway to which a well-beaten trail led from that which he had been following. In the open space between the forest and the city walls, quantities of garden stuff was growing, while before him at his feet, in an open man-made ditch, ran a stream of water! The plants in the garden were laid out in well-spaced, symmetrical rows and appeared to have been given excellent attention and cultivation. Tiny streams were trickling between the rows from the main ditch before him and at some distance to his right he could see people at work among the plants.

The city wall appeared to be about thirty feet in height, its plastered expanse unbroken except by occasional embrasures. Beyond the wall rose the domes of several structures and numerous minarets dotted the skyline of the city. The largest and central dome appeared to be gilded, while others were red, or blue, or yellow. The architecture of the wall itself was of uncompromising simplicity. It was of a cream shade and appeared to be plastered and painted. At its base was a line of well-tended shrubs and at some distance toward its eastern extremity it was vine covered to the top.

As he stood in the shadow of the trail, his keen eyes taking in every detail of the picture before him, he became aware of the approach of a party in his rear and there was borne to him the scent of the man and the lions whom he had so readily escaped. Taking to the trees Tarzan moved a short distance to the west and, finding a comfortable crotch at the edge of the forest where he could watch the trail leading through the gardens to the city gate, he awaited the return of his would-be captors. And soon they came – the strange man followed by the pack of great lions. Like dogs they moved along behind him down the trail among the gardens to the gate.

Here the man struck upon the panels of the door with the butt of his spear, and when it opened in response to his signal he passed in with his lions. Beyond the open door Tarzan, from his distant perch, caught but a fleeting glimpse of life within the city, just enough to indicate that there were other human creatures who abode there, and then the door closed.

Through that door he knew that the girl and the man whom he sought to succor had been taken into the city. What fate lay in store for them or whether already it had been meted out to them he could not even guess, nor where, within that forbidding wall, they were incarcerated he could not know. But of one thing he was assured: that if he were to aid them he could not do it from outside the wall. He must gain entrance to the city first, nor did he doubt, that once within, his keen senses would eventually reveal the whereabouts of those whom he sought.

The low sun was casting long shadows across the gardens when Tarzan saw the workers returning from the eastern field. A man came first, and as he came he lowered little gates along the large ditch of running water, shutting off the streams that had run between the rows of growing plants; and behind him came other men carrying burdens of fresh vegetables in great woven baskets upon their shoulders. Tarzan had not realized that there had been so many men working in the field, but now as he sat there at the close of the day he saw a procession filing in from the east, bearing the tools and the produce back into the city.

And then, to gain a better view, the ape-man ascended to the topmost branches of a tall tree where he overlooked the nearer wall. From this point of vantage he saw that the city was long and narrow, and that while the outer walls formed a perfect rectangle, the streets within were winding. Toward the center of the city there appeared to be a low, white building around which the larger edifices of the city had been built, and here, in the fast-waning light, Tarzan thought that between two buildings he caught the glint of water, but of that he was not sure. His experience of the centers of civilization naturally inclined him to believe that this central area was a plaza about which the larger buildings were grouped and that there would be the most logical place to search first for Bertha Kircher and her companion.

And then the sun went down and darkness quickly enveloped the city – a darkness that was accentuated for the ape-man rather than relieved by the artificial lights which immediately appeared in many of the windows visible to him.

Tarzan had noticed that the roofs of most of the buildings were flat, the few exceptions being those of what he imagined to be the more pretentious public structures. How this city had come to exist in this forgotten part of unexplored Africa the ape-man could not conceive. Better than another, he realized something of the unsolved secrets of the Great Dark Continent, enormous areas of which have as yet been untouched by the foot of civilized man. Yet he could scarce believe that a city of this size and apparently thus well constructed could have existed for the generations that it must have been there, without intercourse with the outer world. Even though it was surrounded by a trackless desert waste, as he knew it to be, he could not conceive that generation after generation of men could be born and die there without attempting to solve the mysteries of the world beyond the confines of their little valley.

And yet, here was the city surrounded by tilled land and filled with people!

With the coming of night there arose throughout the jungle the cries of the great cats, the voice of Numa blended with that of Sheeta, and the thunderous roars of the great males reverberated through the forest until the earth trembled, and from within the city came the answering roars of other lions.

A simple plan for gaining entrance to the city had occurred to Tarzan, and now that darkness had fallen he set about to put it into effect. Its success hinged entirely upon the strength of the vines he had seen surmounting the wall toward the east. In this direction he made his way, while from out of the forest about him the cries of the flesh-eaters increased in volume and ferocity. A quarter of a mile intervened between the forest and the city wall – a quarter of a mile of cultivated land unrelieved by a single tree. Tarzan of the Apes realized his limitations and so he knew that it would undoubtedly spell death for him to be caught in the open space by one of the great black lions of the forest if, as he had already surmised, Numa of the pit was a specimen of the forest lion of the valley.

He must, therefore, depend entirely upon his cunning and his speed, and upon the chance that the vine would sustain his weight.

He moved through the middle terrace, where the way is always easiest, until he reached a point opposite the vine-clad portion of the wall, and there he waited, listening and scenting, until he might assure himself that there was no Numa within his immediate vicinity, or, at least, none that sought him. And when he was quite sure that there was no lion close by in the forest, and none in the clearing between himself and the wall, he dropped lightly to the ground and moved stealthily out into the open.

The rising moon, just topping the eastern cliffs, cast its bright rays upon the long stretch of open garden beneath the wall. And, too, it picked out in clear relief for any curious eyes that chanced to be cast in that direction, the figure of the giant ape-man moving across the clearing. It was only chance, of course, that a great lion hunting at the edge of the forest saw the figure of the man half-way between the forest and the wall. Suddenly there broke upon Tarzan's ears a menacing sound. It was not the roar of a hungry lion, but the roar of a lion in rage, and, as he glanced back in the direction from which the sound came, he saw a huge beast moving out from the shadow of the forest toward him.

Even in the moonlight and at a distance Tarzan saw that the lion was huge; that it was indeed another of the black-maned monsters similar to Numa of the pit. For an instant he was impelled to turn and fight, but at the same time the thought of the helpless girl imprisoned in the city flashed through his brain and, without an instant's hesitation, Tarzan of the Apes wheeled and ran for the wall. Then it was that Numa charged.

Numa, the lion, can run swiftly for a short distance, but he lacks endurance. For the period of an ordinary charge he can cover the ground with greater rapidity possibly than any other creature in the world. Tarzan, on the other hand, could run at great speed for long distances, though never as rapidly as Numa when the latter charged.

The question of his fate, then, rested upon whether, with his start, he could elude Numa for a few seconds; and, if so, if the lion would then have sufficient stamina remaining to pursue him at a reduced gait for the balance of the distance to the wall.

Never before, perhaps, was staged a more thrilling race, and yet it was run with only the moon and stars to see. Alone and in silence the two beasts sped across the moonlit clearing. Numa gained with appalling rapidity upon the fleeing man, yet at every bound Tarzan was nearer to the vine-clad wall. Once the ape-man glanced back. Numa was so close upon him that it seemed inevitable that at the next bound he should drag him down; so close was he that the ape-man drew his knife as he ran, that he might at least give a good account of himself in the last moments of his life.

But Numa had reached the limit of his speed and endurance. Gradually he dropped behind but he did not give up the pursuit, and now Tarzan realized how much hinged upon the strength of the untested vines.

If, at the inception of the race, only Goro and the stars had looked down upon the contestants, such was not the case at its finish, since from an embrasure near the summit of the wall two close-set black eyes peered down upon the two. Tarzan was a dozen yards ahead of Numa when he reached the wall. There was no time to stop and institute a search for sturdy stems and safe handholds. His fate was in the hands of chance and with the realization he gave a final spurt and running catlike up the side of the wall among the vines, sought with his hands for something that would sustain his weight. Below him Numa leaped also.

18

Among the Maniacs

As the lions swarmed over her protectors, Bertha Kircher shrank back in the cave in a momentary paralysis of fright superinduced, perhaps, by the long days of terrific nerve strain which she had undergone.

Mingled with the roars of the lions had been the voices of men, and presently out of the confusion and turmoil she felt the near presence of a human being, and then hands reached forth and seized her. It was dark and she could see but little, nor any sign of the English officer or the ape-man. The man who seized her kept the lions from her with what appeared to be a stout spear, the haft of which he used to beat off the beasts. The fellow dragged her from the cavern the while he shouted what appeared to be commands and warnings to the lions.

Once out upon the light sands of the bottom of the gorge objects became more distinguishable, and then she saw that there were other men in the party and that two half led and half carried the stumbling figure of a third, whom she guessed must be Smith-Oldwick.

For a time the lions made frenzied efforts to reach the two captives but always the men with them succeeded in beating them off. The fellows seemed utterly unafraid of the great beasts leaping and snarling about them, handling them much the same as one might handle a pack of obstreperous dogs. Along the bed of the old watercourse that once ran through the gorge they made their way, and as the first faint lightening of the eastern horizon presaged the coming dawn, they paused for a moment upon the edge of a declivity, which appeared to the girl in the strange light of the waning night as a vast, bottomless pit; but as their captors resumed their way and the light of the new day became stronger, she saw that they were moving downward toward a dense forest.

Once beneath the over-arching trees all was again Cimmerian darkness, nor was the gloom relieved until the sun finally arose beyond the eastern cliffs, when she saw that they were following what appeared to be a broad and well-beaten game trail through a forest of great trees. The ground was unusually dry for an African forest and the underbrush, while heavily foliaged, was not nearly so rank and impenetrable as that which she had been accustomed to find in similar woods. It was as though the trees and the bushes grew in a waterless country, nor was there the musty odor of decaying vegetation or the myriads of tiny insects such as are bred in damp places.

As they proceeded and the sun rose higher, the voices of the arboreal jungle life rose in discordant notes and loud chattering about them. Innumerable monkeys scolded and screamed in the branches overhead, while harsh-voiced birds of brilliant plumage darted hither and thither. She noticed presently that their captors often cast apprehensive glances in the direction of the birds and on numerous occasions seemed to be addressing the winged denizens of the forest.

One incident made a marked impression on her. The man who immediately preceded her was a fellow of powerful build, yet, when a brilliantly colored parrot swooped downward toward him, he dropped upon his knees and covering his face with his arms bent forward until his head touched the ground. Some of the others looked at him and laughed nervously. Presently the man glanced upward and seeing that the bird had gone, rose to his feet and continued along the trail.

It was at this brief halt that Smith-Oldwick was brought to her side by the men who had been supporting him. He had been rather badly mauled by one of the lions; but was now able to walk alone, though he was extremely weak from shock and loss of blood.

'Pretty mess, what?' he remarked with a wry smile, indicating his bloody and disheveled state.

'It is terrible,' said the girl. 'I hope you are not suffering.'

'Not as much as I should have expected,' he replied, 'but I feel as weak as a fool. What sort of creatures are these beggars, anyway?'

'I don't know,' she replied; 'there is something terribly uncanny about their appearance.'

The man regarded one of their captors closely for a moment and then, turning to the girl asked, 'Did you ever visit a madhouse?'

She looked up at him in quick understanding and with a horrified expression in her eyes. 'That's it!' she cried.

'They have all the earmarks,' he said. 'Whites of the eyes showing all around the irises, hair growing stiffly erect from the scalp and low down upon the forehead – even their mannerisms and their carriage are those of maniacs.'

The girl shuddered.

'Another thing about them,' continued the Englishman, 'that doesn't appear normal is that they are afraid of parrots and utterly fearless of lions.'

'Yes,' said the girl, 'and did you notice that the birds seem utterly fearless of them – really seem to hold them in contempt? Have you any idea what language they speak?'

'No,' said the man, 'I have been trying to figure that out. It's not like any of the few native dialects of which I have any knowledge.'

'It doesn't sound at all like the native language,' said the girl, 'but there is something familiar about it. You know, every now and then I feel that I am just on the verge of understanding what they are saying, or at least that somewhere I have heard their tongue before, but final recognition always eludes me.'

'I doubt if you ever heard their language spoken,' said the man. 'These people must have lived in this out-of-the-way valley for ages and even if they had retained the original language of their ancestors without change, which is doubtful, it must be some tongue that is no longer spoken in the outer world.'

At one point where a stream of water crossed the trail the party halted while the lions and the men drank. They motioned to their captives to drink too, and as Bertha Kircher and Smith-Oldwick, lying prone upon the ground drank from the clear, cool water of the rivulet, they were suddenly startled by the thunderous roar of a lion a short distance ahead of them. Instantly the lions with them set up a hideous response, moving restlessly to and fro with their eyes always either turned in the direction from which the roar had come or toward their masters, against whom the tawny beasts slunk. The men loosened the sabers in their scabbards, the weapons that had aroused Smith-Oldwick's curiosity as they had Tarzan's, and grasped their spears more firmly.

Evidently there were lions and lions, and while they evinced no fear of the beasts which accompanied them, it was quite evident that the voice of the newcomer had an entirely different effect upon them, although the men seemed less terrified than the lions. Neither, however, showed any indication of an inclination to flee; on the contrary the entire party advanced along the trail in the direction of the menacing roars, and presently there appeared in the center of the path a black lion of gigantic proportions. To Smith-Oldwick and the girl he appeared to be the same lion that they had encountered at the plane and from which Tarzan had rescued them. But it was not Numa of the pit, although he resembled him closely.

The black beast stood directly in the center of the trail lashing his tail and growling menacingly at the advancing party. The men urged on their own beasts, who growled and whined but hesitated to charge. Evidently becoming impatient, and in full consciousness of his might the intruder raised his tail stiffly erect and shot forward. Several of the defending lions made a half-hearted attempt to obstruct his passage, but they might as well have placed themselves in the path of an express train, as hurling them aside the great beast leaped straight for one of the men. A dozen spears were launched at him and a dozen sabers leaped from their scabbards; gleaming, razor-edged weapons they were, but for the instant rendered futile by the terrific speed of the charging beast.

Two of the spears entering his body but served to further enrage him as, with demoniacal roars, he sprang upon the hapless man he had singled out for his prey. Scarcely pausing in his charge he seized the fellow by the shoulder and, turning quickly at right angles, leaped into the concealing foliage that flanked the trail, and was gone, bearing his victim with him.

So quickly had the whole occurrence transpired that the formation of the little party was scarcely altered. There had been no opportunity for flight, even if it had been contemplated; and now that the lion was gone with his prey the men made no move to pursue him. They paused only long enough to recall the two or three of their lions that had scattered and then resumed the march along the trail.

'Might be an everyday occurrence from all the effect it has on them,' remarked Smith-Oldwick to the girl.

'Yes,' she said. 'They seem to be neither surprised nor disconcerted, and evidently they are quite sure that the lion, having got what he came for, will not molest them further.'

'I had thought,' said the Englishman, 'that the lions of the Wamabo country were about the most ferocious in existence, but they are regular tabby cats by comparison with these big black fellows. Did you ever see anything more utterly fearless or more terribly irresistible than that charge?'

For a while, as they walked side by side, their thoughts and conversation centered upon this latest experience, until the trail emerging from the forest opened to their view a walled city and an area of cultivated land. Neither could suppress an exclamation of surprise.

'Why, that wall is a regular engineering job,' exclaimed Smith-Oldwick.

'And look at the domes and minarets of the city beyond,' cried the girl. 'There must be a civilized people beyond that wall. Possibly we are fortunate to have fallen into their hands.'

Smith-Oldwick shrugged his shoulders. 'I hope so,' he said, 'though I am not at all sure about people who travel about with lions and are afraid of parrots. There must be something wrong with them.'

The party followed the trail across the field to an arched gateway which opened at the summons of one of their captors, who beat upon the heavy wooden panels with his spear. Beyond, the gate opened into a narrow street which seemed but a continuation of the jungle trail leading from the forest. Buildings on either hand adjoined the wall and fronted the narrow, winding street, which was only visible for a short distance ahead. The houses were practically all two-storied structures, the upper stories flush with the street while the walls of the first story were set back some ten feet, a series of simple columns and arches supporting the front of the second story and forming an arcade on either side of the narrow thoroughfare.

The pathway in the center of the street was unpaved, but the floors of the arcades were cut stone of various shapes and sizes but all carefully fitted and laid without mortar. These floors gave evidence of great antiquity, there being a distinct depression down the center as though the stone had been worn away by the passage of countless sandaled feet during the ages that it had lain there.

There were few people astir at this early hour, and these were of the same type as their captors. At first those whom they saw were only men, but as they went deeper into the city they came upon a few naked children playing in the soft dust of the roadway. Many they passed showed the greatest surprise and curiosity in the prisoners, and often made inquiries of the guards, which the two assumed must have been in relation to themselves, while others appeared not to notice them at all.

'I wish we could understand their bally language,' exclaimed Smith-Oldwick.

'Yes,' said the girl, 'I would like to ask them what they are going to do with us.'

'That would be interesting,' said the man. 'I have been doing considerable wondering along that line myself.'

'I don't like the way their canine teeth are filed,' said the girl. 'It's too suggestive of some of the cannibals I have seen.'

'You don't really believe they are cannibals, do you?' asked the man. 'You don't think white people are ever cannibals, do you?'

'Are these people white?' asked the girl.

'They're not Negroes, that's certain,' rejoined the man. 'Their skin is yellow, but yet it doesn't resemble the Chinese exactly, nor are any of their features Chinese.'

It was at this juncture that they caught their first glimpse of a native woman. She was similar in most respects to the men though her stature was smaller and her figure more symmetrical. Her face was more repulsive than that of the men, possibly because of the fact that she was a woman, which rather accentuated the idiosyncrasies of eyes, pendulous lip, pointed tusks and stiff, low-growing hair. The latter was longer than that of the men and much heavier. It hung about her shoulders and was confined by a colored bit of some lacy fabric. Her single garment appeared to be nothing more than a filmy scarf which was wound tightly around her body from below her naked breasts, being caught up some way at the bottom near her ankles. Bits of shiny metal resembling gold, ornamented both the headdress and the skirt. Otherwise the woman was entirely without jewelry. Her bare arms were slender and shapely and her hands and feet well proportioned and symmetrical.

She came close to the party as they passed her, jabbering to the guards who paid no attention to her. The prisoners had an opportunity to observe her closely as she followed at their side for a short distance.

'The figure of a houri,' remarked Smith-Oldwick, 'with the face of an imbecile.'

The street they followed was intersected at irregular intervals by cross-roads which, as they glanced down them, proved to be equally as tortuous as that through which they were being conducted. The houses varied but little in design. Occasionally there were bits of color, or some attempt at other architectural ornamentation. Through open windows and doors they could see that the walls of the houses were very thick and that all apertures were quite small, as though the people had built against extreme heat, which they realized must have been necessary in this valley buried deep in an African desert.

Ahead they occasionally caught glimpses of larger structures, and as they approached them, came upon what was evidently a part of the business section of the city. There were numerous small shops and bazaars interspersed among the residences, and over the doors of these were signs painted in characters strongly suggesting Greek origin and yet it was not Greek as both the Englishman and the girl knew.

Smith-Oldwick was by this time beginning to feel more acutely the pain of his wounds and the consequent weakness that was greatly aggravated by loss of blood. He staggered now occasionally and the girl, seeing his plight, offered him her arm.

'No,' he expostulated, 'you have passed through too much yourself to have any extra burden imposed upon you.' But though he made a valiant effort to keep up with their captors he occasionally lagged, and upon one such occasion the guards for the first time showed any disposition toward brutality.

It was a big fellow who walked at Smith-Oldwick's left. Several times he took hold of the Englishman's arm and pushed him forward not ungently, but when the captive lagged again and again the fellow suddenly, and certainly with no just provocation, flew into a perfect frenzy of rage. He leaped upon the wounded man, striking him viciously with his fists and, bearing him to the ground, grasped his throat in his left hand while with his right he drew his long sharp saber. Screaming terribly he waved the blade above his head.

The others stopped and turned to look upon the encounter with no particular show of interest. It was as though one of the party had paused to readjust a sandal and the others merely waited until he was ready to march on again.

But if their captors were indifferent, Bertha Kircher was not. The close-set blazing eyes, the snarling fanged face, and the frightful screams filled her with horror, while the brutal and wanton attack upon the wounded man aroused within her the spirit of protection for the weak that is inherent in all women. Forgetful of everything other than that a weak and defenseless man was being brutally murdered before her eyes, the girl cast aside discretion and, rushing to Smith-Oldwick's assistance, seized the uplifted sword arm of the shrieking creature upon the prostrate Englishman.

Clinging desperately to the fellow she surged backward with all her weight and strength with the result that she overbalanced him and sent him sprawling to the pavement upon his back. In his efforts to save himself he relaxed his grasp upon the grip of his saber which had no sooner fallen to the ground than it was seized upon by the girl. Standing erect beside the prostrate form of the English officer Bertha Kircher, the razor-edged weapon grasped firmly in her hand, faced their captors.

She was a brave figure; even her soiled and torn riding togs and disheveled hair detracted nothing from her appearance. The creature she had felled scrambled quickly to his feet and in the instant his whole demeanor changed. From demoniacal rage he became suddenly convulsed with hysterical laughter although it was a question in the girl's mind as to which was the more terrifying. His companions stood looking on with vacuous grins upon their countenances, while he from whom the girl had wrested the weapon leaped up and down shrieking with laughter. If Bertha Kircher had needed further evidence to assure her that they were in the hands of a mentally deranged people the man's present actions would have been sufficient to convince her. The sudden uncontrolled rage and now the equally uncontrolled and mirthless laughter but emphasized the facial attributes of idiocy.

Suddenly realizing how helpless she was in the event any one of the men should seek to overpower her, and moved by a sudden revulsion of feeling that brought on almost a nausea of disgust, the girl hurled the weapon upon the ground at the feet of the laughing maniac and, turning, kneeled beside the Englishman.

'It was wonderful of you,' he said, 'but you shouldn't have done it. Don't antagonize them: I believe that they are all mad and you know they say that one should always humor a madman.'

She shook her head. 'I couldn't see him kill you,' she said.

A sudden light sprang to the man's eyes as he reached out a hand and grasped the girl's fingers. 'Do you care a little now?' he asked. 'Can't you tell me that you do – just a bit?'

She did not withdraw her hand from his but she shook her head sadly. 'Please don't,' she said. 'I am sorry that I can only like you very much.'

The light died from his eyes and his fingers relaxed their grasp on hers. 'Please forgive me,' he murmured. 'I intended waiting until we got out of this mess and you were safe among your own people. It must have been the shock or something like that, and seeing you defending me as you did. Anyway, I couldn't help it and really it doesn't make much difference what I say now, does it?'

'What do you mean?' she asked quickly.

He shrugged and smiled ruefully. 'I will never leave this city alive,' he said. 'I wouldn't mention it except that I realize that you must know it as well as I. I was pretty badly torn up by the lion and this fellow here has about finished me. There might be some hope if we were among civilized people, but here with these frightful creatures what care could we get even if they were friendly?'

Bertha Kircher knew that he spoke the truth, and yet she could not bring herself to an admission that Smith-Oldwick would die. She was very fond of him, in fact her great regret was that she did not love him, but she knew that she did not.

It seemed to her that it could be such an easy thing for any girl to love Lieutenant Harold Percy Smith-Oldwick – an English officer and a gentleman, the scion of an old family and himself a man of ample means, young, good-looking and affable. What more could a girl ask for than to have such a man love her and that she possessed Smith-Oldwick's love there was no doubt in Bertha Kircher's mind.

She sighed, and then, laying her hand impulsively on his forehead, she whispered, 'Do not give up hope, though. Try to live for my sake and for your sake I will try to love you.'

It was as though new life had suddenly been injected into the man's veins. His face lightened instantly and with strength that he himself did not know he possessed he rose slowly to his feet, albeit somewhat unsteadily. The girl helped him and supported him after he had arisen.

For the moment they had been entirely unconscious of their surroundings and now as she looked at their captors she saw that they had fallen again into their almost habitual manner of stolid indifference, and at a gesture from one of them the march was resumed as though no untoward incident had occurred.

Bertha Kircher experienced a sudden reaction from the momentary exaltation of her recent promise to the Englishman. She knew that she had spoken more for him than for herself but now that it was over she realized, as she had realized the moment before she had spoken, that it was unlikely she would ever care for him the way he wished. But what had she promised? Only that she would try to love him. 'And now?' she asked herself.

She realized that there might be little hope of their ever returning to civilization. Even if these people should prove friendly and willing to let them depart in peace, how were they to find their way back to the coast? With Tarzan dead, as she fully believed him after having seen his body lying lifeless at the mouth of the cave when she had been dragged forth by her captor, there seemed no power at their command which could guide them safely.

The two had scarcely mentioned the ape-man since their capture, for each realized fully what his loss meant to them. They had compared notes relative to those few exciting moments of the final attack and capture and had found that they agreed perfectly upon all that had occurred. Smith-Oldwick had even seen the lion leap upon Tarzan at the instant that the former was awakened by the roars of the charging beasts, and though the night had been dark, he had been able to see that the body of the savage ape-man had never moved from the instant that it had come down beneath the beast.

And so, if at other times within the past few weeks Bertha Kircher had felt that her situation was particularly hopeless, she was now ready to admit that hope was absolutely extinct.

The streets were beginning to fill with the strange men and women of this strange city. Sometimes individuals would notice them and seem to take a great interest in them, and again others would pass with vacant stares, seemingly unconscious of their immediate surroundings and paying no attention whatsoever to the prisoners. Once they heard hideous screams up a side street, and looking they saw a man in the throes of a demoniacal outburst of rage, similar to that which they had witnessed in the recent attack upon Smith-Oldwick. This creature was venting his insane rage upon a child which he repeatedly struck and bit, pausing only long enough to shriek at frequent intervals. Finally, just before they passed out of sight the creature raised the limp body of the child high above his head and cast it down with all his strength upon the pavement, and then, wheeling and screaming madly at the top of his lungs, he dashed headlong up the winding street.

Two women and several men had stood looking on at the cruel attack. They were at too great a distance for the Europeans to know whether their facial expressions portrayed pity or rage, but be that as it may, none offered to interfere.

A few yards farther on a hideous hag leaned from a second-story window where she laughed and jibbered and made horrid grimaces at all who passed her. Others went their ways apparently attending to whatever duties called them, as soberly as the inhabitants of any civilized community.

'God,' muttered Smith-Oldwick, 'what an awful place!'

The girl turned suddenly toward him. 'You still have your pistol?' she asked him.

'Yes,' he replied. 'I tucked it inside my shirt. They did not search me and it was too dark for them to see whether I carried any weapons or not. So I hid it in the hope that I might get through with it.'

She moved closer to him and took hold of his hand. 'Save one cartridge for me, please?' she begged.

Smith-Oldwick looked down at her and blinked his eyes very rapidly. An unfamiliar and disconcerting moisture had come into them. He had realized, of course, how bad a plight was theirs but somehow it had seemed to affect him only: it did not seem possible that anyone could harm this sweet and beautiful girl.

And that she should have to be destroyed – destroyed by him! It was too hideous: it was unbelievable, unthinkable! If he had been filled with apprehension before, he was doubly perturbed now.

'I don't believe I could do it, Bertha,' he said.

'Not even to save me from something worse?' she asked.

He shook his head dismally. 'I could never do it,' he replied.

The street that they were following suddenly opened upon a wide avenue, and before them spread a broad and beautiful lagoon, the quiet surface of which mirrored the clear cerulean of the sky. Here the aspect of all their surroundings changed. The buildings were higher and much more pretentious in design and ornamentation. The street itself was paved in mosaics of barbaric but stunningly beautiful design. In the ornamentation of the buildings there was considerable color and a great deal of what appeared to be gold leaf. In all the decorations there was utilized in various ways the conventional figure of the parrot, and, to a lesser extent, that of the lion and the monkey.

Their captors led them along the pavement beside the lagoon for a short distance and then through an arched doorway into one of the buildings facing the avenue. Here, directly within the entrance was a large room furnished with massive benches and tables, many of which were elaborately hand carved with the figures of the inevitable parrot, the lion, or the monkey, the parrot always predominating.

Behind one of the tables sat a man who differed in no way that the captives could discover from those who accompanied them. Before this person the party halted, and one of the men who had brought them made what seemed to be an oral report. Whether they were before a judge, a military officer, or a civil dignitary they could not know, but evidently he was a man of authority, for, after listening to whatever recital was being made to him the while he closely scrutinized the two captives, he made a single futile attempt to converse with them and then issued some curt orders to him who had made the report.

Almost immediately two of the men approached Bertha Kircher and signaled her to accompany them. Smith-Oldwick started to follow her but was intercepted by one of their guards. The girl stopped then and turned back, at the same time looking at the man at the table and making signs with her hands, indicating, as best she could, that she wished Smith-Oldwick to remain with her, but the fellow only shook his head negatively and motioned to the guards to remove her. The Englishman again attempted to follow but was restrained. He was too weak and helpless even to make an attempt to enforce his wishes. He thought of the pistol inside his shirt and then of the futility of attempting to overcome an entire city with the few rounds of ammunition left to him.

So far, with the single exception of the attack made upon him, they had no reason to believe that they might not receive fair treatment from their captors, and so he reasoned that it might be wiser to avoid antagonizing them until such a time as he became thoroughly convinced that their intentions were entirely hostile. He saw the girl led from the building and just before she disappeared from his view she turned and waved her hand to him:

'Good luck!' she cried, and was gone.

The lions that had entered the building with the party had, during their examination by the man at the table, been driven from the apartment through a doorway behind him. Toward this same doorway two of the men now led Smith-Oldwick. He found himself in a long corridor from the sides of which other doorways opened, presumably into other apartments of the building. At the far end of the corridor he saw a heavy grating beyond which appeared an open courtyard. Into this courtyard the prisoner was conducted, and as he entered it with the two guards he found himself in an opening which was bounded by the inner walls of the building. It was in the nature of a garden in which a number of trees and flowering shrubs grew. Beneath several of the trees were benches and there was a bench along the south wall, but what aroused his most immediate attention was the fact that the lions who had assisted in their capture and who had accompanied them upon the return to the city, lay sprawled about upon the ground or wandered restlessly to and fro.

Just inside the gate his guard halted. The two men exchanged a few words and then turned and reentered the corridor. The Englishman was horror-stricken as the full realization of his terrible plight forced itself upon his tired brain. He turned and seized the grating in an attempt to open it and gain the safety of the corridor, but he found it securely locked against his every effort, and then he called aloud to the retreating figures of the men within. The only reply he received was a high-pitched, mirthless laugh, and then the two passed through the doorway at the far end of the corridor and he was alone with the lions.

19

The Queen's Story

In the meantime Bertha Kircher was conducted the length of the plaza toward the largest and most pretentious of the buildings surrounding it. This edifice covered the entire width of one end of the plaza. It was several stories in height, the main entrance being approached by a wide flight of stone steps, the bottom of which was guarded by enormous stone lions, while at the top there were two pedestals flanking the entrance and of the same height, upon each of which was the stone image of a large parrot. As the girl neared these latter images she saw that the capital of each column was hewn into the semblance of a human skull upon which the parrots perched. Above the arched doorway and upon the walls of the building were the figures of other parrots, of lions, and of monkeys. Some of these were carved in bas-relief; others were delineated in mosaics, while still others appeared to have been painted upon the surface of the wall.

The colorings of the last were apparently much subdued by age with the result that the general effect was soft and beautiful. The sculpturing and mosaic work were both finely executed, giving evidence of a high degree of artistic skill. Unlike the first building into which she had been conducted, the entrance to which had been doorless, massive doors closed the entrance which she now approached. In the niches formed by the columns which supported the door's arch, and about the base of the pedestals of the stone parrots, as well as in various other places on the broad stairway, lolled some score of armed men. The tunics of these were all of a vivid yellow and upon the breast and back of each was embroidered the figure of a parrot.

As she was conducted up the stairway one of these yellow-coated warriors approached and halted her guides at the top of the steps. Here they exchanged a few words and while they were talking the girl noticed that he who had halted them, as well as those whom she could see of his companions, appeared to be, if possible, of a lower mentality than her original captors.

Their coarse, bristling hair grew so low upon their foreheads as, in some instances, to almost join their eyebrows, while the irises were smaller, exposing more of the white of the eyeball.

After a short parley the man in charge of the doorway, for such he seemed to be, turned and struck upon one of the panels with the butt of his spear, at the same time calling to several of his companions, who rose and came forward at his command. Soon the great doors commenced slowly to swing creakingly open, and presently, as they separated, the girl saw behind them the motive force which operated the massive doors – to each door a half-dozen naked Negroes.

At the doorway her two guards were turned back and their places taken by a half-dozen of the yellow-coated soldiery. These conducted her through the doorway which the blacks, pulling upon heavy chains, closed behind them. And as the girl watched them she noted with horror that the poor creatures were chained by the neck to the doors.

Before her led a broad hallway in the center of which was a little pool of clear water. Here again in floor and walls was repeated in new and ever-changing combinations and designs, the parrots, the monkeys, and the lions, but now many of the figures were of what the girl was convinced must be gold. The walls of the corridor consisted of a series of open archways through which, upon either side, other spacious apartments were visible. The hallway was entirely unfurnished, but the rooms on either side contained benches and tables. Glimpses of some of the walls revealed the fact that they were covered with hangings of some colored fabric, while upon the floors were thick rugs of barbaric design and the skins of black lions and beautifully marked leopards.

The room directly to the right of the entrance was filled with men wearing the yellow tunics of her new guard while the walls were hung with numerous spears and sabers. At the far end of the corridor a low flight of steps led to another closed doorway. Here the guard was again halted. One of the guards at this doorway, after receiving the report of one of those who accompanied her, passed through the door, leaving them standing outside. It was fully fifteen minutes before he returned, when the guard was again changed and the girl conducted into the chamber beyond.

Through three other chambers and past three more massive doors, at each of which her guard was changed, the girl was conducted before she was ushered into a comparatively small room, back and forth across the floor of which paced a man in a scarlet tunic, upon the front and back of which was embroidered an enormous parrot and upon whose head was a barbaric headdress surmounted by a stuffed parrot.

The walls of this room were entirely hidden by hangings upon which hundreds, even thousands, of parrots were embroidered. Inlaid in the floor were golden parrots, while, as thickly as they could be painted, upon the ceiling were brilliant-hued parrots with wings outspread as though in the act of flying.

The man himself was larger of stature than any she had yet seen within the city. His parchmentlike skin was wrinkled with age and he was much fatter than any other of his kind that she had seen. His bared arms, however, gave evidence of great strength and his gait was not that of an old man. His facial expression denoted almost utter imbecility and he was quite the most repulsive creature that ever Bertha Kircher had looked upon.

For several minutes after she was conducted into his presence he appeared not to be aware that she was there but continued his restless pacing to and fro. Suddenly, without the slightest warning, and while he was at the far end of the room from her with his back toward her, he wheeled and rushed madly at her. Involuntarily the girl shrank back, extending her open palms toward the frightful creature as though to hold him aloof but a man upon either side of her, the two who had conducted her into the apartment, seized and held her.

Although he rushed violently toward her the man stopped without touching her. For a moment his horrid white-rimmed eyes glared searchingly into her face, immediately following which he burst into maniacal laughter. For two or three minutes the creature gave himself over to merriment and then, stopping as suddenly as he had commenced to laugh, he fell to examining the prisoner. He felt of her hair, her skin, the texture of the garment she wore and by means of signs made her understand she was to open her mouth. In the latter he seemed much interested, calling the attention of one of the guards to her canine teeth and then baring his own sharp fangs for the prisoner to see.

Presently he resumed pacing to and fro across the floor, and it was fully fifteen minutes before he again noticed the prisoner, and then it was to issue a curt order to her guards, who immediately conducted her from the apartment.

The guards now led the girl through a series of corridors and apartments to a narrow stone stairway which led to the floor above, finally stopping before a small door where stood a naked Negro armed with a spear. At a word from one of her guards the Negro opened the door and the party passed into a low-ceilinged apartment, the windows of which immediately caught the girl's attention through the fact that they were heavily barred. The room was furnished similarly to those that she had seen in other parts of the building; the same carved tables and benches, the rugs upon the floor, the decorations upon the walls, although in every respect it was simpler than anything she had seen on the floor below. In one corner was a low couch covered with a rug similar to those on the floor except that it was of a lighter texture, and upon this sat a woman.

As Bertha Kircher's eyes alighted upon the occupant of the room the girl gave a little gasp of astonishment, for she recognized immediately that here was a creature more nearly of her own kind than any she had seen within the city's walls. An old woman it was who looked at her through faded blue eyes, sunken deep in a wrinkled and toothless face. But the eyes were those of a sane and intelligent creature, and the wrinkled face was the face of a white woman.

At sight of the girl the woman rose and came forward, her gait so feeble and unsteady that she was forced to support herself with a long staff which she grasped in both her hands. One of the guards spoke a few words to her and then the men turned and left the apartment. The girl stood just within the door waiting in silence for what might next befall her.

The old woman crossed the room and stopped before her, raising her weak and watery eyes to the fresh young face of the newcomer. Then she scanned her from head to foot and once again the old eyes returned to the girl's face. Bertha Kircher on her part was not less frank in her survey of the little old woman. It was the latter who spoke first. In a thin, cracked voice she spoke, hesitatingly, falteringly, as though she were using unfamiliar words and speaking a strange tongue.

'You are from the outer world?' she asked in English. 'God grant that you may speak and understand this tongue.'

'English?' the girl exclaimed, 'Yes, of course, I speak English.'

'Thank God!' cried the little old woman. 'I did not know whether I myself might speak it so that another could understand. For sixty years I have spoken only their accursed gibberish. For sixty years I have not heard a word in my native language. Poor creature! Poor creature!' she mumbled. 'What accursed misfortune threw you into their hands?'

'You are an English woman?' asked Bertha Kircher. 'Did I understand you aright that you are an English woman and have been here for sixty years?'

The old woman nodded her head affirmatively. 'For sixty years I have never been outside of this palace. Come,' she said, stretching forth a bony hand. 'I am very old and cannot stand long. Come and sit with me on my couch.'

The girl took the proffered hand and assisted the old lady back to the opposite side of the room and when she was seated the girl sat down beside her.

'Poor child! Poor child!' moaned the old woman. 'Far better to have died than to have let them bring you here. At first I might have destroyed myself but there was always the hope that someone would come who would take me away, but none ever comes. Tell me how they got you.'

Very briefly the girl narrated the principal incidents which led up to her capture by some of the creatures of the city.

'Then there is a man with you in the city?' asked the old woman.

'Yes,' said the girl, 'but I do not know where he is nor what are their intentions in regard to him. In fact, I do not know what their intentions toward me are.'

'No one might even guess,' said the old woman. 'They do not know themselves from one minute to the next what their intentions are, but I think you can rest assured, my poor child, that you will never see your friend again.'

'But they haven't slain you,' the girl reminded her, 'and you have been their prisoner, you say, for sixty years.'

'No,' replied her companion, 'they have not killed me, nor will they kill you, though God knows before you have lived long in this horrible place you will beg them to kill you.'

'Who are they –' asked Bertha Kircher, 'what kind of people? They differ from any that I have ever seen. And tell me, too, how you came here.'

'It was long ago,' said the old woman, rocking back and forth on the couch. 'It was long ago. Oh, how long it was! I was only twenty then. Think of it, child! Look at me. I have no mirror other than my bath, I cannot see what I look like for my eyes are old, but with my fingers I can feel my old and wrinkled face, my sunken eyes and these flabby lips drawn in over toothless gums. I am old and bent and hideous, but then I was young and they said that I was beautiful. No, I will not be a hypocrite; I was beautiful. My glass told me that.

'My father was a missionary in the interior and one day there came a band of Arabian slave raiders. They took the men and women of the little native village where my father labored, and they took me, too. They did not know much about our part of the country so they were compelled to rely upon the men of our village whom they had captured to guide them. They told me that they never before had been so far south and that they had heard there was a country rich in ivory and slaves west of us. They wanted to go there and from there they would take us north, where I was to be sold into the harem of some black sultan.

'They often discussed the price I would bring, and that that price might not lessen, they guarded me jealously from one another so the journeys were made as little fatiguing for me as possible. I was given the best food at their command and I was not harmed.

'But after a short time, when we had reached the confines of the country with which the men of our village were familiar and had entered upon a desolate and arid desert waste, the Arabs realized at last that we were lost. But they still kept on, ever toward the west, crossing hideous gorges and marching across the face of a burning land beneath the pitiless sun. The poor slaves they had captured were, of course, compelled to carry all the camp equipage and loot and thus heavily burdened, half starved and without water, they soon commenced to die like flies.

'We had not been in the desert land long before the Arabs were forced to kill their horses for food, and when we reached the first gorge, across which it would have been impossible to transport the animals, the balance of them were slaughtered and the meat loaded upon the poor staggering blacks who still survived.

'Thus we continued for two more days and now all but a handful of blacks were dead, and the Arabs themselves had commenced to succumb to hunger and thirst and the intense heat of the desert. As far as the eye could reach back toward the land of plenty from whence we had come, our route was marked by circling vultures in the sky and by the bodies of the dead who lay down in the trackless waste for the last time. The ivory had been abandoned tusk by tusk as the blacks gave out, and along the trail of death was strewn the camp equipage and the horse trappings of a hundred men.

'For some reason the Arab chief favored me to the last, possibly with the idea that of all his other treasures I could be most easily transported, for I was young and strong and after the horses were killed I had walked and kept up with the best of the men. We English, you know, are great walkers, while these Arabians had never walked since they were old enough to ride a horse.

'I cannot tell you how much longer we kept on but at last, with our strength almost gone, a handful of us reached the bottom of a deep gorge. To scale the opposite side was out of the question and so we kept on down along the sands of what must have been the bed of an ancient river, until finally we came to a point where we looked out upon what appeared to be a beautiful valley in which we felt assured that we would find game in plenty.

'By then there were only two of us left – the chief and myself. I do not need to tell you what the valley was, for you found it in much the same way as I did. So quickly were we captured that it seemed they must have been waiting for us, and I learned later that such was the case, just as they were waiting for you.

'As you came through the forest you must have seen the monkeys and parrots and since you have entered the palace, how constantly these animals, and the lions, are used in the decorations. At home we were all familiar with talking parrots who repeated the things that they were taught to say, but these parrots are different in that they all talk in the same language that the people of the city use, and they say that the monkeys talk to the parrots and the parrots fly to the city and tell the people what the monkeys say. And, although it is hard to believe, I have learned that this is so, for I have lived here among them for sixty years in the palace of their king.

'They brought me, as they brought you, directly to the palace. The Arabian chief was taken elsewhere. I never knew what became of him. Ago XXV was king then. I have seen many kings since that day. He was a terrible man; but then, they are all terrible.'

'What is the matter with them?' asked the girl.

'They are a race of maniacs,' replied the old woman. 'Had you not guessed it? Among them are excellent craftsmen and good farmers and a certain amount of law and order, such as it is.

'They reverence all birds, but the parrot is their chief deity. There is one who is held here in the palace in a very beautiful apartment. He is their god of gods. He is a very old bird. If what Ago told me when I came is true, he must be nearly three hundred years old by now. Their religious rites are revolting in the extreme, and I believe that it may be the practice of these rites through ages that has brought the race to its present condition of imbecility.

'And yet, as I said, they are not without some redeeming qualities. If legend may be credited, their forebears – a little handful of men and women who came from somewhere out of the north and became lost in the wilderness of central Africa – found here only a barren desert valley. To my own knowledge rain seldom, if ever, falls here, and yet you have seen a great forest and luxuriant vegetation outside of the city as well as within. This miracle is accomplished by the utilization of natural springs which their ancestors developed, and upon which they have improved to such an extent that the entire valley receives an adequate amount of moisture at all times.

'Ago told me that many generations before his time the forest was irrigated by changing the course of the streams which carried the spring water to the city but that when the trees had sent their roots down to the natural moisture of the soil and required no further irrigation, the course of the stream was changed and other trees were planted. And so the forest grew until today it covers almost the entire floor of the valley except for the open space where the city stands. I do not know that this is true. It may be that the forest has always been here, but it is one of their legends and it is borne out by the fact that there is not sufficient rainfall here to support vegetation.

'They are peculiar people in many respects, not only in their form of worship and religious rites but also in that they breed lions as other people breed cattle. You have seen how they use some of these lions but the majority of them they fatten and eat. At first, I imagine, they ate lion meat as a part of their religious ceremony but after many generations they came to crave it so that now it is practically the only flesh they eat. They would, of course, rather die than eat the flesh of a bird, nor will they eat monkey's meat, while the herbivorous animals they raise only for milk, hides, and flesh for the lions. Upon the south side of the city are the corrals and pastures where the herbivorous animals are raised. Boar, deer, and antelope are used principally for the lions, while goats are kept for milk for the human inhabitants of the city.'

'And you have lived here all these years,' exclaimed the girl, 'without ever seeing one of your own kind?'

The old woman nodded affirmatively.

'For sixty years you have lived here,' continued Bertha Kircher, 'and they have not harmed you!'

'I did not say they had not harmed me,' said the old woman; 'they did not kill me, that is all.'

'What' – the girl hesitated – 'what,' she continued at last, 'was your position among them? Pardon me,' she added quickly, 'I think I know but I should like to hear from your own lips, for whatever your position was, mine will doubtless be the same.'

The old woman nodded. 'Yes,' she said, 'doubtless; if they can keep you away from the women.'

'What do you mean?' asked the girl.

'For sixty years I have never been allowed near a woman. They would kill me, even now, if they could reach me. The men are frightful, God knows they are frightful! But heaven keep you from the women!'

'You mean,' asked the girl, 'that the men will not harm me?'

'Ago XXV made me his queen,' said the old woman. 'But he had many other queens, nor were they all human. He was not murdered for ten years after I came here. Then the next king took me, and so it has been always. I am the oldest queen now. Very few of their women live to a great age. Not only are they constantly liable to assassination but, owing to their subnormal mentalities, they are subject to periods of depression during which they are very likely to destroy themselves.'

She turned suddenly and pointed to the barred windows. 'You see this room,' she said, 'with the black eunuch outside? Wherever you see these you will know that there are women, for with very few exceptions they are never allowed out of captivity. They are considered and really are more violent than the men.'

For several minutes the two sat in silence, and then the younger woman turned to the older.

'Is there no way to escape?' she asked.

The old woman pointed again to the barred windows and then to the door, saying: 'And there is the armed eunuch. And if you should pass him, how could you reach the street? And if you reached the street, how could you pass through the city to the outer wall? And even if, by some miracle, you should gain the outer wall, and, by another miracle, you should be permitted to pass through the gate, could you ever hope to traverse the forest where the great black lions roam and feed upon men? No!' she exclaimed, answering her own question. 'There is no escape, for after one had escaped from the palace and the city and the forest it would be but to invite death in the frightful desert land beyond.

'In sixty years you are the first to find this buried city. In a thousand no denizen of this valley has ever left it, and within the memory of man, or even in their legends, none had found them prior to my coming other than a single warlike giant, the story of whom has been handed down from father to son.

'I think from the description that he must have been a Spaniard, a giant of a man in buckler and helmet, who fought his way through the terrible forest to the city gate, who fell upon those who were sent out to capture him and slew them with his mighty sword. And when he had eaten of the vegetables from the gardens, and the fruit from the trees and drank of the water from the stream, he turned about and fought his way back through the forest to the mouth of the gorge. But though he escaped the city and the forest he did not escape the desert. For a legend runs that the king, fearful that he would bring others to attack them, sent a party after him to slay him.

'For three weeks they did not find him, for they went in the wrong direction, but at last they came upon his bones picked clean by the vultures, lying a day's march up the same gorge through which you and I entered the valley. I do not know,' continued the old woman, 'that this is true. It is just one of their many legends.'

'Yes,' said the girl, 'it is true. I am sure it is true, for I have seen the skeleton and the corroded armor of this great giant.'

At this juncture the door was thrown open without ceremony and a Negro entered bearing two flat vessels in which were several smaller ones. These he set down on one of the tables near the women, and, without a word, turned and left. With the entrance of the man with the vessels, a delightful odor of cooked food had aroused the realization in the girl's mind that she was very hungry, and at a word from the old woman she walked to the table to examine the viands. The larger vessels which contained the smaller ones were of pottery while those within them were quite evidently of hammered gold. To her intense surprise she found lying between the smaller vessels a spoon and a fork, which, while of quaint design, were quite as serviceable as any she had seen in more civilized communities. The tines of the fork were quite evidently of iron or steel, the girl did not know which, while the handle and the spoon were of the same material as the smaller vessels.

There was a highly seasoned stew with meat and vegetables, a dish of fresh fruit, and a bowl of milk beside which was a little jug containing something which resembled marmalade. So ravenous was she that she did not even wait for her companion to reach the table, and as she ate she could have sworn that never before had she tasted more palatable food. The old woman came slowly and sat down on one of the benches opposite her.

As she removed the smaller vessels from the larger and arranged them before her on the table a crooked smile twisted her lips as she watched the younger woman eat.

'Hunger is a great leveler,' she said with a laugh.

'What do you mean?' asked the girl.

'I venture to say that a few weeks ago you would have been nauseated at the idea of eating cat.'

'Cat?' exclaimed the girl.

'Yes,' said the old woman. 'What is the difference – a lion is a cat.'

'You mean I am eating lion now?'

'Yes,' said the old woman, 'and as they prepare it, it is very palatable. You will grow very fond of it.'

Bertha Kircher smiled a trifle dubiously. 'I could not tell it,' she said, 'from lamb or veal.'

'No,' said the woman, 'it tastes as good to me. But these lions are very carefully kept and very carefully fed and their flesh is so seasoned and prepared that it might be anything so far as taste is concerned.'

And so Bertha Kircher broke her long fast upon strange fruits, lion meat, and goat's milk.

Scarcely had she finished when again the door opened and there entered a yellow-coated soldier. He spoke to the old woman.

'The king,' she said, 'has commanded that you be prepared and brought to him. You are to share these apartments with me. The king knows that I am not like his other women. He never would have dared to put you with them. Herog XVI has occasional lucid intervals. You must have been brought to him during one of these. Like the rest of them he thinks that he alone of all the community is sane, but more than once I have thought that the various men with whom I have come in contact here, including the kings themselves, looked upon me as, at least, less mad than the others. Yet how I have retained my senses all these years is beyond me.'

'What do you mean by prepare?' asked Bertha Kircher. 'You said that the king had commanded I be prepared and brought to him.'

'You will be bathed and furnished with a robe similar to that which I wear.'

'Is there no escape?' asked the girl. 'Is there no way even in which I can kill myself?'

The woman handed her the fork. 'This is the only way,' she said, 'and you will notice that the tines are very short and blunt.'

The girl shuddered and the old woman laid a hand gently upon her shoulder. 'He may only look at you and send you away,' she said. 'Ago XXV sent for me once, tried to talk with me, discovered that I could not understand him and that he could not understand me, ordered that I be taught the language of his people, and then apparently forgot me for a year. Sometimes I do not see the king for a long period. There was one king who ruled for five years whom I never saw. There is always hope; even I whose very memory has doubtless been forgotten beyond these palace walls still hope, though none knows better how futilely.'

The old woman led Bertha Kircher to an adjoining apartment in the floor of which was a pool of water. Here the girl bathed and afterward her companion brought her one of the clinging garments of the native women and adjusted it about her figure. The material of the robe was of a gauzy fabric which accentuated the rounded beauty of the girlish form.

'There,' said the old woman, as she gave a final pat to one of the folds of the garment, 'you are a queen indeed!'

The girl looked down at her naked breasts and but half-concealed limbs in horror. 'They are going to lead me into the presence of men in this half-nude condition!' she exclaimed.

The old woman smiled her crooked smile. 'It is nothing,' she said. 'You will become accustomed to it as did I who was brought up in the home of a minister of the gospel, where it was considered little short of a crime for a woman to expose her stockinged ankle. By comparison with what you will doubtless see and the things that you may be called upon to undergo, this is but a trifle.'

For what seemed hours to the distraught girl she paced the floor of her apartment, awaiting the final summons to the presence of the mad king. Darkness had fallen and the oil flares within the palace had been lighted long before two messengers appeared with instructions that Herog demanded her immediate presence and that the old woman, whom they called Xanila, was to accompany her. The girl felt some slight relief when she discovered that she was to have at least one friend with her, however powerless to assist her the old woman might be.

The messengers conducted the two to a small apartment on the floor below. Xanila explained that this was one of the anterooms off the main throneroom in which the king was accustomed to hold court with his entire retinue. A number of yellow-tunicked warriors sat about upon the benches within the room. For the most part their eyes were bent upon the floor and their attitudes that of moody dejection. As the two women entered several glanced indifferently at them, but for the most part no attention was paid to them.

While they were waiting in the anteroom there entered from another apartment a young man uniformed similarly to the others with the exception that upon his head was a fillet of gold, in the front of which a single parrot feather rose erectly above his forehead. As he entered, the other soldiers in the room rose to their feet.

'That is Metak, one of the king's sons,' Xanila whispered to the girl.

The prince was crossing the room toward the audience chamber when his glance happened to fall upon Bertha Kircher. He halted in his tracks and stood looking at her for a full minute without speaking. The girl, embarrassed by his bold stare and her scant attire, flushed and, dropping her gaze to the floor, turned away. Metak suddenly commenced to tremble from head to foot and then, without warning other than a loud, hoarse scream he sprang forward and seized the girl in his arms.

Instantly pandemonium ensued. The two messengers who had been charged with the duty of conducting the girl to the king's presence danced, shrieking, about the prince, waving their arms and gesticulating wildly as though they would force him to relinquish her, the while they dared not lay hands upon royalty. The other guardsmen, as though suffering in sympathy the madness of their prince, ran forward screaming and brandishing their sabers.

The girl fought to release herself from the horrid embrace of the maniac, but with his left arm about her he held her as easily as though she had been but a babe, while with his free hand he drew his saber and struck viciously at those nearest him.

One of the messengers was the first to feel the keen edge of Metak's blade. With a single fierce cut the prince drove through the fellow's collarbone and downward to the center of his chest. With a shrill shriek that rose above the screaming of the other guardsmen the man dropped to the floor, and as the blood gushed from the frightful wound he struggled to rise once more to his feet and then sank back again and died in a great pool of his own blood.

In the meantime Metak, still clinging desperately to the girl, had backed toward the opposite door. At the sight of the blood two of the guardsmen, as though suddenly aroused to maniacal frenzy, dropped their sabers to the floor and fell upon each other with nails and teeth, while some sought to reach the prince and some to defend him. In a corner of the room sat one of the guardsmen laughing uproariously and just as Metak succeeded in reaching the door and taking the girl through, she thought that she saw another of the men spring upon the corpse of the dead messenger and bury his teeth in its flesh.

During the orgy of madness Xanila had kept closely at the girl's side but at the door of the room Metak had seen her and, wheeling suddenly, cut viciously at her. Fortunately for Xanila she was halfway through the door at the time, so that Metak's blade but dented itself upon the stone arch of the portal, and then Xanila, guided doubtless by the wisdom of sixty years of similar experiences, fled down the corridor as fast as her old and tottering legs would carry her.

Metak, once outside the door, returned his saber to its scabbard and lifting the girl bodily from the ground carried her off in the opposite direction from that taken by Xanila.

20

Came Tarzan

Just before dark that evening, an almost exhausted flier entered the headquarters of Colonel Capell of the Second Rhodesians and saluted.

'Well, Thompson,' asked the superior, 'what luck? The others have all returned. Never saw a thing of Oldwick or his plane. I guess we shall have to give it up unless you were more successful.'

'I was,' replied the young officer. 'I found the plane.'

'No!' ejaculated Colonel Capell. 'Where was it? Any sign of Oldwick?'

'It is in the rottenest hole in the ground you ever saw, quite a bit inland. Narrow gorge. Saw the plane all right but can't reach it. There was a regular devil of a lion wandering around it. I landed near the edge of the cliff and was going to climb down and take a look at the plane. But this fellow hung around for an hour or more and I finally had to give it up.'

'Do you think the lions got Oldwick?' asked the colonel.

'I doubt it,' replied Lieutenant Thompson, 'from the fact that there was no indication that the lion had fed anywhere about the plane. I arose after I found it was impossible to get down around the plane and reconnoitered up and down the gorge. Several miles to the south I found a small, wooded valley in the center of which – please don't think me crazy, sir – is a regular city – streets, buildings, a central plaza with a lagoon, good-sized buildings with domes and minarets and all that sort of stuff.'

The elder officer looked at the younger compassionately. 'You're all wrought up, Thompson,' he said. 'Go and take a good sleep. You have been on this job now for a long while and it must have gotten on your nerves.'

The young man shook his head a bit irritably. 'Pardon me, sir,' he said, 'but I am telling you the truth. I am not mistaken. I circled over the place several times. It may be that Oldwick has found his way there – or has been captured by these people.'

'Were there people in the city?' asked the colonel.

'Yes, I saw them in the streets.'

'Do you think cavalry could reach the valley?' asked the colonel.

'No,' replied Thompson, 'the country is all cut up with these deep gorges. Even infantry would have a devil of a time of it, and there is absolutely no water that I could discover for at least a two days' march.'

It was at this juncture that a big Vauxhall drew up in front of the headquarters of the Second Rhodesians and a moment later General Smuts alighted and entered. Colonel Capell arose from his chair and saluted his superior, and the young lieutenant saluted and stood at attention.

'I was passing,' said the general, 'and I thought I would stop for a chat. By the way, how is the search for Lieutenant Smith-Oldwick progressing? I see Thompson here and I believe he was one of those detailed to the search.'

'Yes,' said Capell, 'he was. He is the last to come in. He found the lieutenant's ship,' and then he repeated what Lieutenant Thompson had reported to him. The general sat down at the table with Colonel Capell, and together the two officers, with the assistance of the flier, marked the approximate location of the city which Thompson had reported he'd discovered.

'It's a mighty rough country,' remarked Smuts, 'but we can't leave a stone unturned until we have exhausted every resource to find that boy. We will send out a small force; a small one will be more likely to succeed than a large one. About one company, Colonel, or say two, with sufficient motor lorries for transport of rations and water. Put a good man in command and let him establish a base as far to the west as the motors can travel. You can leave one company there and send the other forward. I am inclined to believe you can establish your base within a day's march of the city and if such is the case the force you send ahead should have no trouble on the score of lack of water as there certainly must be water in the valley where the city lies. Detail a couple of planes for reconnaissance and messenger service so that the base can keep in touch at all times with the advance party. When can your force move out?'

'We can load the lorries tonight,' replied Capell, 'and march about one o'clock tomorrow morning.'

'Good,' said the general, 'keep me advised,' and returning the others' salutes he departed.

As Tarzan leaped for the vines he realized that the lion was close upon him and that his life depended upon the strength of the creepers clinging to the city walls; but to his intense relief he found the stems as large around as a man's arm, and the tendrils which had fastened themselves to the wall so firmly fixed, that his weight upon the stem appeared to have no appreciable effect upon them.

He heard Numa's baffled roar as the lion slipped downward clawing futilely at the leafy creepers, and then with the agility of the apes who had reared him, Tarzan bounded nimbly aloft to the summit of the wall.

A few feet below him was the flat roof of the adjoining building and as he dropped to it his back was toward the niche from which an embrasure looked out upon the gardens and the forest beyond, so that he did not see the figure crouching there in the dark shadow. But if he did not see he was not long in ignorance of the fact that he was not alone, for scarcely had his feet touched the roof when a heavy body leaped upon him from behind and brawny arms encircled him about the waist.

Taken at a disadvantage and lifted from his feet, the ape-man was, for the time being, helpless. Whatever the creature was that had seized him, it apparently had a well-defined purpose in mind, for it walked directly toward the edge of the roof so that it was soon apparent to Tarzan that he was to be hurled to the pavement below – a most efficacious manner of disposing of an intruder. That he would be either maimed or killed the ape-man was confident; but he had no intention of permitting his assailant to carry out the plan.

Tarzan's arms and legs were free but he was in such a disadvantageous position that he could not use them to any good effect. His only hope lay in throwing the creature off its balance, and to this end Tarzan straightened his body and leaned as far back against his captor as he could, and then suddenly lunged forward. The result was as satisfactory as he could possibly have hoped. The great weight of the ape-man thrown suddenly out from an erect position caused the other also to lunge violently forward with the result that to save himself he involuntarily released his grasp. Catlike in his movements, the ape-man had no sooner touched the roof than he was upon his feet again, facing his adversary, a man almost as large as himself and armed with a saber which he now whipped from its scabbard. Tarzan, however, had no mind to allow the use of this formidable weapon and so he dove for the other's legs beneath the vicious cut that was directed at him from the side, and as a football player tackles an opposing runner, Tarzan tackled his antagonist, carrying him backward several yards and throwing him heavily to the roof upon his back.

No sooner had the man touched the roof than the ape-man was upon his chest, one brawny hand sought and found the sword wrist and the other the throat of the yellow-tunicked guardsman. Until then the fellow had fought in silence but just as Tarzan's fingers touched his throat he emitted a single piercing shriek that the brown fingers cut off almost instantly. The fellow struggled to escape the clutch of the naked creature upon his breast but equally as well might he have fought to escape the talons of Numa, the lion.

Gradually his struggles lessened, his pinpoint eyes popped from their sockets, rolling horribly upward, while from his foam-flecked lips his swollen tongue protruded. As his struggles ceased Tarzan arose, and placing a foot upon the carcass of his kill, was upon the point of screaming forth his victory cry when the thought that the work before him required the utmost caution sealed his lips.

Walking to the edge of the roof he looked down into the narrow, winding street below. At intervals, apparently at each street intersection, an oil flare sputtered dimly from brackets set in the walls a trifle higher than a man's head. For the most part the winding alleys were in dense shadow and even in the immediate vicinity of the flares the illumination was far from brilliant. In the restricted area of his vision he could see that there were still a few of the strange inhabitants moving about the narrow thoroughfares.

To prosecute his search for the young officer and the girl he must be able to move about the city as freely as possible, but to pass beneath one of the corner flares, naked as he was except for a loincloth, and in every other respect markedly different from the inhabitants of the city, would be but to court almost immediate discovery. As these thoughts flashed through his mind and he cast about for some feasible plan of action, his eyes fell upon the corpse upon the roof near him, and immediately there occurred to him the possibility of disguising himself in the raiment of his conquered adversary.

It required but a few moments for the ape-man to clothe himself in the tights, sandals, and parrot emblazoned yellow tunic of the dead soldier. Around his waist he buckled the saber belt but beneath the tunic he retained the hunting knife of his dead father. His other weapons he could not lightly discard, and so, in the hope that he might eventually recover them, he carried them to the edge of the wall and dropped them among the foliage at its base. At the last moment he found it difficult to part with his rope, which, with his knife, was his most accustomed weapon, and the one which he had used for the greatest length of time. He found that by removing the saber belt he could wind the rope about his waist beneath his tunic, and then replacing the belt still retain it entirely concealed from chance observation.

At last, satisfactorily disguised, and with even his shock of black hair adding to the verisimilitude of his likeness to the natives of the city, he sought for some means of reaching the street below. While he might have risked a drop from the eaves of the roof he feared to do so lest he attract the attention of passers-by, and probable discovery. The roofs of the buildings varied in height but as the ceilings were all low he found that he could easily travel along the rooftops and this he did for some little distance, until he suddenly discovered just ahead of him several figures reclining upon the roof of a nearby building.

He had noticed openings in each roof, evidently giving ingress to the apartments below, and now, his advance cut off by those ahead of him, he decided to risk the chance of reaching the street through the interior of one of the buildings. Approaching one of the openings he leaned over the black hole and listened for sounds of life in the apartment below. Neither his ears nor his nose registered evidence of the presence of any living creature in the immediate vicinity, and so without further hesitation the ape-man lowered his body through the aperture and was about to drop when his foot came in contact with the rung of a ladder, which he immediately took advantage of to descend to the floor of the room below.

Here, all was almost total darkness until his eyes became accustomed to the interior, the darkness of which was slightly alleviated by the reflected light from a distant street flare which shone intermittently through the narrow windows fronting the thoroughfare. Finally, assured that the apartment was unoccupied, Tarzan sought for a stairway to the ground floor. This he found in a dark hallway upon which the room opened – a flight of narrow stone steps leading downward toward the street. Chance favored him so that he reached the shadows of the arcade without encountering any of the inmates of the house.

Once on the street he was not at a loss as to the direction in which he wished to go, for he had tracked the two Europeans practically to the gate, which he felt assured must have given them entry to the city. His keen sense of direction and location made it possible for him to judge with considerable accuracy the point within the city where he might hope to pick up the spoor of those whom he sought.

The first need, however, was to discover a street paralleling the northern wall along which he could make his way in the direction of the gate he had seen from the forest. Realizing that his greatest hope of success lay in the boldness of his operations he moved off in the direction of the nearest street flare without making any other attempt at concealment than keeping in the shadows of the arcade, which he judged would draw no particular attention to him in that he saw other pedestrians doing likewise. The few he passed gave him no heed, and he had almost reached the nearest intersection when he saw several men wearing yellow tunics identical to that which he had taken from his prisoner.

They were coming directly toward him and the ape-man saw that should he continue on he would meet them directly at the intersection of the two streets in the full light of the flare. His first inclination was to go steadily on, for personally he had no objection to chancing a scrimmage with them; but a sudden recollection of the girl, possibly a helpless prisoner in the hands of these people, caused him to seek some other and less hazardous plan of action.

He had almost emerged from the shadow of the arcade into the full light of the flare and the approaching men were but a few yards from him, when he suddenly kneeled and pretended to adjust the wrappings of his sandals – wrappings, which, by the way, he was not at all sure that he had adjusted as their makers had intended them to be adjusted. He was still kneeling when the soldiers came abreast of him. Like the others he had passed they paid no attention to him and the moment they were behind him he continued upon his way, turning to the right at the intersection of the two streets.

The street he now took was, at this point, so extremely winding that, for the most part, it received no benefit from the flares at either corner, so that he was forced practically to grope his way in the dense shadows of the arcade. The street became a little straighter just before he reached the next flare, and as he came within sight of it he saw silhouetted against a patch of light the figure of a lion. The beast was coming slowly down the street in Tarzan's direction.

A woman crossed the way directly in front of it and the lion paid no attention to her, nor she to the lion. An instant later a little child ran after the woman and so close did he run before the lion that the beast was forced to turn out of its way a step to avoid colliding with the little one. The ape-man grinned and crossed quickly to the opposite side of the street, for his delicate senses indicated that at this point the breeze stirring through the city streets and deflected by the opposite wall would now blow from the lion toward him as the beast passed, whereas if he remained upon the side of the street upon which he had been walking when he discovered the carnivore, his scent would have been borne to the nostrils of the animal, and Tarzan was sufficiently jungle-wise to realize that while he might deceive the eyes of man and beast he could not so easily disguise from the nostrils of one of the great cats that he was a creature of a different species from the inhabitants of the city, the only human beings, possibly, that Numa was familiar with. In him the cat would recognize a stranger, and, therefore, an enemy, and Tarzan had no desire to be delayed by an encounter with a savage lion. His ruse worked successfully, the lion passing him with not more than a side glance in his direction.

He had proceeded for some little distance and had about reached a point where he judged he would find the street which led up from the city gate when, at an intersection of two streets, his nostrils caught the scent spoor of the girl. Out of a maze of other scent spoors the ape-man picked the familiar odor of the girl and, a second later, that of Smith-Oldwick. He had been forced to accomplish it, however, by bending very low at each street intersection in repeated attention to his sandal wrappings, bringing his nostrils as close to the pavement as possible.

As he advanced along the street through which the two had been conducted earlier in the day he noted, as had they, the change in the type of buildings as he passed from a residence district into that portion occupied by shops and bazaars. Here the number of flares was increased so that they appeared not only at street intersections but midway between as well, and there were many more people abroad. The shops were open and lighted, for with the setting of the sun the intense heat of the day had given place to a pleasant coolness. Here also the number of lions, roaming loose through the thoroughfares, increased, and also for the first time Tarzan noted the idiosyncrasies of the people.

Once he was nearly upset by a naked man running rapidly through the street screaming at the top of his voice. And again he nearly stumbled over a woman who was making her way in the shadows of one of the arcades upon all fours. At first the ape-man thought she was hunting for something she had dropped, but as he drew to one side to watch her, he saw that she was doing nothing of the kind – that she had merely elected to walk upon her hands and knees rather than erect upon her feet. In another block he saw two creatures struggling upon the roof of an adjacent building until finally one of them, wrenching himself free from the grasp of the other, gave his adversary a mighty push which hurled him to the pavement below, where he lay motionless upon the dusty road. For an instant a wild shriek reechoed through the city from the lungs of the victor and then, without an instant's hesitation, the fellow leaped headfirst to the street beside the body of his victim. A lion moved out from the dense shadows of a doorway and approached the two bloody and lifeless things before him. Tarzan wondered what effect the odor of blood would have upon the beast and was surprised to see that the animal only sniffed at the corpses and the hot red blood and then lay down beside the two dead men.

He had passed the lion but a short distance when his attention was called to the figure of a man lowering himself laboriously from the roof of a building upon the east side of the thoroughfare. Tarzan's curiosity was aroused.

21

In the Alcove

As Smith-Oldwick realized that he was alone and practically defenseless in an enclosure filled with great lions he was, in his weakened condition, almost in a state verging upon hysterical terror. Clinging to the grating for support he dared not turn his head in the direction of the beasts behind him. He felt his knees giving weakly beneath him. Something within his head spun rapidly around. He became very dizzy and nauseated and then suddenly all went black before his eyes as his limp body collapsed at the foot of the grating.

How long he lay there unconscious he never knew; but as reason slowly reasserted itself in his semiconscious state he was aware that he lay in a cool bed upon the whitest of linen in a bright and cheery room, and that upon one side close to him was an open window, the delicate hangings of which were fluttering in a soft summer breeze which blew in from a sun-kissed orchard of ripening fruit which he could see without – an old orchard in which soft, green grass grew between the laden trees, and where the sun filtered through the foliage; and upon the dappled greensward a little child was playing with a frolicsome puppy.

'God,' thought the man, 'what a horrible nightmare I have passed through!' and then he felt a hand stroking his brow and cheek – a cool and gentle hand that smoothed away his troubled recollections. For a long minute Smith-Oldwick lay in utter peace and content until gradually there was forced upon his sensibilities the fact that the hand had become rough, and that it was no longer cool but hot and moist; and suddenly he opened his eyes and looked up into the face of a huge lion.

Lieutenant Harold Percy Smith-Oldwick was not only an English gentleman and an officer in name, he was also what these implied – a brave man; but when he realized that the sweet picture he had looked upon was but the figment of a dream, and that in reality he still lay where he had fallen at the foot of the grating with a lion standing over him licking his face, the tears sprang to his eyes and ran down his cheeks. Never, he thought, had an unkind fate played so cruel a joke upon a human being.

For some time he lay feigning death while the lion, having ceased to lick him, sniffed about his body. There are some things than which death is to be preferred; and there came at last to the Englishman the realization that it would be better to die swiftly than to lie in this horrible predicament until his mind broke beneath the strain and he went mad.

And so, deliberately and without haste, he rose, clinging to the grating for support. At his first move the lion growled, but after that he paid no further attention to the man, and when at last Smith-Oldwick had regained his feet the lion moved indifferently away. Then it was that the man turned and looked about the enclosure.

Sprawled beneath the shade of the trees and lying upon the long bench beside the south wall the great beasts rested, with the exception of two or three who moved restlessly about. It was these that the man feared and yet when two more of them had passed him by he began to feel reassured, recalling the fact that they were accustomed to the presence of man.

And yet he dared not move from the grating. As the man examined his surroundings he noted that the branches of one of the trees near the farther wall spread close beneath an open window. If he could reach that tree and had strength to do so, he could easily climb out upon the branch and escape, at least, from the enclosure of the lions. But in order to reach the tree he must pass the full length of the enclosure, and at the very bole of the tree itself two lions lay sprawled out in slumber.

For half an hour the man stood gazing longingly at this seeming avenue of escape, and at last, with a muttered oath, he straightened up and, throwing back his shoulders in a gesture of defiance, he walked slowly and deliberately down the center of the courtyard. One of the prowling lions turned from the side wall and moved toward the center directly in the man's path, but Smith-Oldwick was committed to what he considered his one chance, for even temporary safety, and so he kept on, ignoring the presence of the beast. The lion slouched to his side and sniffed him and then, growling, he bared his teeth.

Smith-Oldwick drew the pistol from his shirt. 'If he has made up his mind to kill me,' he thought, 'I can't see that it will make any difference in the long run whether I infuriate him or not. The beggar can't kill me any deader in one mood than another.'

But with the man's movement in withdrawing the weapon from his shirt the lion's attitude suddenly altered and though he still growled he turned and sprang away, and then at last the Englishman stood almost at the foot of the tree that was his goal, and between him and safety sprawled a sleeping lion.

Above him was a limb that ordinarily he could have leaped for and reached with ease; but weak from his wounds and loss of blood he doubted his ability to do so now. There was even a question as to whether he would be able to ascend the tree at all. There was just one chance: the lowest branch left the bole within easy reach of a man standing on the ground close to the tree's stem, but to reach a position where the branch would be accessible he must step over the body of the lion. Taking a deep breath he placed one foot between the sprawled legs of the beast and gingerly raised the other to plant it upon the opposite side of the tawny body. 'What,' he thought, 'if the beggar should happen to wake now?' The suggestion sent a shudder through his frame but he did not hesitate or withdraw his foot. Gingerly he planted it beyond the lion, threw his weight forward upon it and cautiously brought his other foot to the side of the first. He had passed and the lion had not awakened.

Smith-Oldwick was weak from loss of blood and the hardships he had undergone, but the realization of his situation impelled him to a show of agility and energy which he probably could scarcely have equaled when in possession of his normal strength. With his life depending upon the success of his efforts, he swung himself quickly to the lower branches of the tree and scrambled upward out of reach of possible harm from the lions below – though the sudden movement in the branches above them awakened both the sleeping beasts. The animals raised their heads and looked questioningly up for a moment and then lay back again to resume their broken slumber.

So easily had the Englishman succeeded thus far that he suddenly began to question as to whether he had at any time been in real danger. The lions, as he knew, were accustomed to the presence of men; but yet they were still lions and he was free to admit that he breathed more easily now that he was safe above their clutches.

Before him lay the open window he had seen from the ground. He was now on a level with it and could see an apparently unoccupied chamber beyond, and toward this he made his way along a stout branch that swung beneath the opening. It was not a difficult feat to reach the window, and a moment later he drew himself over the sill and dropped into the room.

He found himself in a rather spacious apartment, the floor of which was covered with rugs of barbaric design, while the few pieces of furniture were of a similar type to that which he had seen in the room on the first floor into which he and Bertha Kircher had been ushered at the conclusion of their journey. At one end of the room was what appeared to be a curtained alcove, the heavy hangings of which completely hid the interior. In the wall opposite the window and near the alcove was a closed door, apparently the only exit from the room.

He could see, in the waning light without, that the close of the day was fast approaching, and he hesitated while he deliberated the advisability of waiting until darkness had fallen, or of immediately searching for some means of escape from the building and the city. He at last decided that it would do no harm to investigate beyond the room, that he might have some idea as how best to plan his escape after dark. To this end he crossed the room toward the door but he had taken only a few steps when the hangings before the alcove separated and the figure of a woman appeared in the opening.

She was young and beautifully formed; the single drapery wound around her body from below her breasts left no detail of her symmetrical proportions unrevealed, but her face was the face of an imbecile. At sight of her Smith-Oldwick halted, momentarily expecting that his presence would elicit screams for help from her. On the contrary she came toward him smiling, and when she was close her slender, shapely fingers touched the sleeve of his torn blouse as a curious child might handle a new toy, and still with the same smile she examined him from head to foot, taking in, in childish wonderment, every detail of his apparel.

Presently she spoke to him in a soft, well-modulated voice which contrasted sharply with her facial appearance. The voice and the girlish figure harmonized perfectly and seemed to belong to each other, while the head and face were those of another creature. Smith-Oldwick could understand no word of what she said, but nevertheless he spoke to her in his own cultured tone, the effect of which upon her was evidently most gratifying, for before he realized her intentions or could prevent her she had thrown both arms about his neck and was kissing him with the utmost abandon.

The man tried to free himself from her rather surprising attentions, but she only clung more tightly to him, and suddenly, as he recalled that he had always heard that one must humor the mentally deficient, and at the same time seeing in her a possible agency of escape, he closed his eyes and returned her embraces.

It was at this juncture that the door opened and a man entered. With the sound from the first movement of the latch, Smith-Oldwick opened his eyes, but though he endeavored to disengage himself from the girl he realized that the newcomer had seen their rather compromising position. The girl, whose back was toward the door, seemed at first not to realize that someone had entered, but when she did she turned quickly and as her eyes fell upon the man whose terrible face was now distorted with an expression of hideous rage she turned, screaming, and fled toward the alcove. The Englishman, flushed and embarrassed, stood where she had left him. With the sudden realization of the futility of attempting an explanation, came that of the menacing appearance of the man, whom he now recognized as the official who had received them in the room below. The fellow's face, livid with insane rage and, possibly, jealousy, was twitching violently, accentuating the maniacal expression that it habitually wore.

For a moment he seemed paralyzed by anger, and then with a loud shriek that rose into an uncanny wail, he drew his curved saber and sprang toward the Englishman. To Smith-Oldwick there seemed no possible hope of escaping the keen-edged weapon in the hands of the infuriated man, and though he felt assured that it would draw down upon him an equally sudden and possibly more terrible death, he did the only thing that remained for him to do – drew his pistol and fired straight for the heart of the oncoming man. Without even so much as a groan the fellow lunged forward upon the floor at Smith-Oldwick's feet – killed instantly with a bullet through the heart. For several seconds the silence of the tomb reigned in the apartment.

The Englishman, standing over the prostrate figure of the dead man, watched the door with drawn weapon, expecting momentarily to hear the rush of feet of those whom he was sure would immediately investigate the report of the pistol. But no sounds came from below to indicate that anyone there had heard the explosion, and presently the man's attention was distracted from the door to the alcove, between the hangings of which the face of the girl appeared. The eyes were widely dilated and the lower jaw dropped in an expression of surprise and awe.

The girl's gaze was riveted upon the figure upon the floor, and presently she crept stealthily into the room and tiptoed toward the corpse. She appeared as though constantly poised for flight, and when she had come to within two or three feet of the body she stopped and, looking up at Smith-Oldwick, voiced some interrogation which he could not, of course, understand. Then she came close to the side of the dead man and kneeling upon the floor felt gingerly of the body.

Presently she shook the corpse by the shoulder, and then with a show of strength which her tenderly girlish form belied, she turned the body over on its back. If she had been in doubt before, one glance at the hideous features set in death must have convinced her that life was extinct, and with the realization there broke from her lips peal after peal of mad, maniacal laughter as with her little hands she beat upon the upturned face and breast of the dead man. It was a gruesome sight from which the Englishman involuntarily drew back – a gruesome, disgusting sight such as, he realized, might never be witnessed outside a madhouse or this frightful city.

In the midst of her frenzied rejoicing at the death of the man, and Smith-Oldwick could attribute her actions to no other cause, she suddenly desisted from her futile attacks upon the insensate flesh and, leaping to her feet, ran quickly to the door, where she shot a wooden bolt into its socket, thus securing them from interference from without. Then she returned to the center of the room and spoke rapidly to the Englishman, gesturing occasionally toward the body of the slain man. When he could not understand, she presently became provoked and in a sudden hysteria of madness she rushed forward as though to strike the Englishman. Smith-Oldwick dropped back a few steps and leveled his pistol upon her. Mad though she must have been, she evidently was not so mad but what she had connected the loud report, the diminutive weapon, and the sudden death of the man in whose house she dwelt, for she instantly desisted and quite as suddenly as it had come upon her, her homicidal mood departed.

Again the vacuous, imbecile smile took possession of her features, and her voice, dropping its harshness, resumed the soft, well-modulated tones with which she had first addressed him. Now she attempted by signs to indicate her wishes, and motioning Smith-Oldwick to follow her she went to the hangings and opening them disclosed the alcove. It was rather more than an alcove, being a fair-sized room heavy with rugs and hangings and soft, pillowed couches. Turning at the entrance she pointed to the corpse upon the floor of the outer room, and then crossing the alcove she raised some draperies which covered a couch and fell to the floor upon all sides, disclosing an opening beneath the furniture.

To this opening she pointed and then again to the corpse, indicating plainly to the Englishman that it was her desire that the body be hidden here. But if he had been in doubt, she essayed to dispel it by grasping his sleeve and urging him in the direction of the body which the two of them then lifted and half carried and half dragged into the alcove. At first they encountered some difficulty when they endeavored to force the body of the man into the small space she had selected for it, but eventually they succeeded in doing so. Smith-Oldwick was again impressed by the fiendish brutality of the girl. In the center of the room lay a bloodstained rug which the girl quickly gathered up and draped over a piece of furniture in such a way that the stain was hidden. By rearranging the other rugs and by bringing one from the alcove she restored the room to order so no outward indication of the tragedy so recently enacted there was apparent.

These things attended to, and the hangings draped once more about the couch that they might hide the gruesome thing beneath, the girl once more threw her arms about the Englishman's neck and dragged him toward the soft and luxurious pillows above the dead man. Acutely conscious of the horror of his position, filled with loathing, disgust, and an outraged sense of decency, Smith-Oldwick was also acutely alive to the demands of self-preservation. He felt that he was warranted in buying his life at almost any price; but there was a point at which his finer nature rebelled.

It was at this juncture that a loud knock sounded upon the door of the outer room. Springing from the couch, the girl seized the man by the arm and dragged him after her to the wall close by the head of the couch. Here she drew back one of the hangings, revealing a little niche behind, into which she shoved the Englishman and dropped the hangings before him, effectually hiding him from observation from the rooms beyond.

He heard her cross the alcove to the door of the outer room, and heard the bolt withdrawn followed by the voice of a man mingled with that of the girl.

The tones of both seemed rational so that he might have been listening to an ordinary conversation in some foreign tongue. Yet with the gruesome experiences of the day behind him, he could not but momentarily expect some insane outbreak from beyond the hangings.

He was aware from the sounds that the two had entered the alcove, and, prompted by a desire to know what manner of man he might next have to contend with, he slightly parted the heavy folds that hid the two from his view and looking out saw them sitting on the couch with their arms about each other, the girl with the same expressionless smile upon her face that she had vouchsafed him. He found he could so arrange the hangings that a very narrow slit between two of them permitted him to watch the actions of those in the alcove without revealing himself or increasing his liability of detection.

He saw the girl lavishing her kisses upon the newcomer, a much younger man than he whom Smith-Oldwick had dispatched. Presently the girl disengaged herself from the embrace of her lover as though struck by a sudden memory. Her brows puckered as in labored thought and then with a startled expression, she threw a glance backward toward the hidden niche where the Englishman stood, after which she whispered rapidly to her companion, occasionally jerking her head in the direction of the niche and on several occasions making a move with one hand and forefinger, which Smith-Oldwick could not mistake as other than an attempt to describe his pistol and its use.

It was evident then to him that she was betraying him, and without further loss of time he turned his back toward the hangings and commenced a rapid examination of his hiding place. In the alcove the man and the girl whispered, and then cautiously and with great stealth, the man rose and drew his curved saber. On tiptoe he approached the hangings, the girl creeping at his side. Neither spoke now, nor was there any sound in the room as the girl sprang forward and with outstretched arm and pointing finger indicated a point upon the curtain at the height of a man's breast. Then she stepped to one side, and her companion, raising his blade to a horizontal position, lunged suddenly forward and with the full weight of his body and his right arm, drove the sharp point through the hangings and into the niche behind for its full length.

Bertha Kircher, finding her struggles futile and realizing that she must conserve her strength for some chance opportunity of escape, desisted from her efforts to break from the grasp of Prince Metak as the fellow fled with her through the dimly lighted corridors of the palace. Through many chambers the prince fled, bearing his prize. It was evident to the girl that, though her captor was the king's son, he was not above capture and punishment for his deeds, as otherwise he would not have shown such evident anxiety to escape with her, as well as from the results of his act.

From the fact that he was constantly turning affrighted eyes behind them, and glancing suspiciously into every nook and corner that they passed, she guessed that the prince's punishment might be both speedy and terrible were he caught.

She knew from their route that they must have doubled back several times although she had quite lost all sense of direction; but she did not know that the prince was as equally confused as she, and that really he was running in an aimless, erratic manner, hoping that he might stumble eventually upon a place of refuge.

Nor is it to be wondered at that this offspring of maniacs should have difficulty in orienting himself in the winding mazes of a palace designed by maniacs for a maniac king. Now a corridor turned gradually and almost imperceptibly in a new direction, again one doubled back upon and crossed itself; here the floor rose gradually to the level of another story, or again there might be a spiral stairway down which the mad prince rushed dizzily with his burden. Upon what floor they were or in what part of the palace even Metak had no idea until, halting abruptly at a closed door, he pushed it open to step into a brilliantly lighted chamber filled with warriors, at one end of which sat the king upon a great throne; beside this, to the girl's surprise, she saw another throne where was seated a huge lioness, recalling to her the words of Xanila which, at the time, had made no impression on her: 'But he had many other queens, nor were they all human.'

At sight of Metak and the girl, the king rose from his throne and started across the chamber, all semblance of royalty vanishing in the maniac's uncontrollable passion. And as he came he shrieked orders and commands at the top of his voice. No sooner had Metak so unwarily opened the door to this hornets' nest than he immediately withdrew and, turning, fled again in a new direction. But now a hundred men were close upon his heels, laughing, shrieking, and possibly cursing. He dodged hither and thither, distancing them for several minutes until, at the bottom of a long runway that inclined steeply downward from a higher level, he burst into a subterranean apartment lighted by many flares.

In the center of the room was a pool of considerable size, the level of the water being but a few inches below the floor. Those behind the fleeing prince and his captive entered the chamber in time to see Metak leap into the water with the girl and disappear beneath the surface, taking his captive with him, nor, though they waited excitedly around the rim of the pool, did either of the two again emerge.

When Smith-Oldwick turned to investigate his hiding place, his hands, groping upon the rear wall, immediately came in contact with the wooden panels of a door and a bolt such as that which secured the door of the outer room.

Cautiously and silently drawing the wooden bar he pushed gently against the panel to find that the door swung easily and noiselessly outward into utter darkness. Moving carefully and feeling forward for each step he passed out of the niche, closing the door behind him.

Feeling about, he discovered that he was in a narrow corridor which he followed cautiously for a few yards to be brought up suddenly by what appeared to be a ladder across the passageway. He felt of the obstruction carefully with his hands until he was assured that it was indeed a ladder and that a solid wall was just beyond it, ending the corridor. Therefore, as he could not go forward and as the ladder ended at the floor upon which he stood, and as he did not care to retrace his steps, there was no alternative but to climb upward, and this he did, his pistol ready in a side pocket of his blouse.

He had ascended but two or three rungs when his head came suddenly and painfully in contact with a hard surface above him. Groping about with one hand over his head he discovered that the obstacle seemed to be the covering to a trapdoor in the ceiling which, with a little effort, he succeeded in raising a couple of inches, revealing through the cracks the stars of a clear African night.

With a sigh of relief, but with unabated caution, he gently slid the trapdoor to one side far enough to permit him to raise his eyes above the level of the roof. A quick glance assured him that there was none near enough to observe his movements, nor, in fact, as far as he could see, was anyone in sight.

Drawing himself quickly through the aperture he replaced the cover and endeavored to regain his bearings. Directly to the south of him the low roof he stood upon adjoined a much loftier portion of the building, which rose several stories above his head. A few yards to the west he could see the flickering light of the flares of a winding street, and toward this he made his way.

From the edge of the roof he looked down upon the nightlife of the mad city. He saw men and women and children and lions, and of all that he saw it was quite evident to him that only the lions were sane. With the aid of the stars he easily picked out the points of the compass, and following carefully in his memory the steps that had led him into the city and to the roof upon which he now stood, he knew that the thoroughfare upon which he looked was the same along which he and Bertha Kircher had been led as prisoners earlier in the day.

If he could reach this he might be able to pass undetected in the shadows of the arcade to the city gate. He had already given up as futile the thought of seeking out the girl and attempting to succor her, for he knew that alone and with the few remaining rounds of ammunition he possessed, he could do nothing against this city full of armed men. That he could live to cross the lion-infested forest beyond the city was doubtful, and having, by some miracle, won to the desert beyond, his fate would be certainly sealed; but yet he was consumed with but one desire – to leave behind him as far as possible this horrid city of maniacs.

He saw that the roofs rose to the same level as that upon which he stood, unbroken to the north to the next street intersection. Directly below him was a flare. To reach the pavement in safety it was necessary that he find as dark a portion of the avenue as possible. And so he sought along the edge of the roofs for a place where he might descend in comparative concealment.

He had proceeded some little way beyond a point where the street curved abruptly to the east before he discovered a location sufficiently to his liking. But even here he was compelled to wait a considerable time for a satisfactory moment for his descent, which he had decided to make down one of the pillars of the arcade. Each time he prepared to lower himself over the edge of the roofs, footsteps approaching in one direction or another deterred him until at last he had almost come to the conclusion that he would have to wait for the entire city to sleep before continuing his flight.

But finally came a moment which he felt propitious and though with inward qualms, it was with outward calm that he commenced the descent to the street below.

When at last he stood beneath the arcade he was congratulating himself upon the success that had attended his efforts up to this point when, at a slight sound behind him, he turned to see a tall figure in the yellow tunic of a warrior confronting him.

22

Out of the Niche

Numa, the lion, growled futilely in baffled rage as he slipped back to the ground at the foot of the wall after his unsuccessful attempt to drag down the fleeing ape-man. He poised to make a second effort to follow his escaping quarry when his nose picked up a hitherto unnoticed quality in the scent spoor of his intended prey. Sniffling at the ground that Tarzan's feet had barely touched, Numa's growl changed to a low whine, for he had recognized the scent spoor of the man-thing that had rescued him from the pit of the Wamabos.

What thoughts passed through that massive head? Who may say? But now there was no indication of baffled rage as the great lion turned and moved majestically eastward along the wall. At the eastern end of the city he turned toward the south, continuing his way to the south side of the wall along which were the pens and corrals where the herbivorous flocks were fattened for the herds of domesticated lions within the city. The great black lions of the forest fed with almost equal impartiality upon the flesh of the grass-eaters and man. Like Numa of the pit they occasionally made excursions across the desert to the fertile valley of the Wamabos, but principally they took their toll of meat from the herds of the walled city of Herog, the mad king, or seized upon some of his luckless subjects.

Numa of the pit was in some respect an exception to the rule which guided his fellows of the forest in that as a cub he had been trapped and carried into the city, where he was kept for breeding purposes, only to escape in his second year. They had tried to teach him in the city of maniacs that he must not eat the flesh of man, and the result of their schooling was that only when aroused to anger or upon that one occasion that he had been impelled by the pangs of hunger, did he ever attack man.

The animal corrals of the maniacs are protected by an outer wall or palisade of upright logs, the lower ends of which are imbedded in the ground, the logs themselves being placed as close together as possible and further reinforced and bound together by withes. At intervals there are gates through which the flocks are turned on to the grazing land south of the city during the daytime. It is at such times that the black lions of the forest take their greatest toll from the herds, and it is infrequent that a lion attempts to enter the corrals at night. But Numa of the pit, having scented the spoor of his benefactor, was minded again to pass into the walled city, and with that idea in his cunning brain he crept stealthily along the outer side of the palisade, testing each gateway with a padded foot until at last he discovered one which seemed insecurely fastened. Lowering his great head he pressed against the gate, surging forward with all the weight of his huge body and the strength of his giant sinews – one mighty effort and Numa was within the corral.

The enclosure contained a herd of goats which immediately upon the advent of the carnivore started a mad stampede to the opposite end of the corral which was bounded by the south wall of the city. Numa had been within such a corral as this before, so that he knew that somewhere in the wall was a small door through which the goatherd might pass from the city to his flock; toward this door he made his way, whether by plan or accident it is difficult to say, though in the light of ensuing events it seems possible that the former was the case.

To reach the gate he must pass directly through the herd which had huddled affrightedly close to the opening so that once again there was a furious rush of hoofs as Numa strode quickly to the side of the portal. If Numa had planned, he had planned well, for scarcely had he reached his position when the door opened and a herder's head was projected into the enclosure, the fellow evidently seeking an explanation of the disturbance among his flock. Possibly he discovered the cause of the commotion, but it is doubtful, for it was dark and the great, taloned paw that reached up and struck downward a mighty blow that almost severed his head from his body, moved so quickly and silently that the man was dead within a fraction of a second from the moment that he opened the door, and then Numa, knowing now his way, passed through the wall into the dimly lighted streets of the city beyond.

Smith-Oldwick's first thought when he was accosted by the figure in the yellow tunic of a soldier was to shoot the man dead and trust to his legs and the dimly lighted, winding streets to permit his escape, for he knew that to be accosted was equivalent to recapture since no inhabitant of this weird city but would recognize him as an alien. It would be a simple thing to shoot the man from the pocket where the pistol lay without drawing the weapon, and with this purpose in mind the Englishman slipped his hand into the side pocket of his blouse, but simultaneously with this action his wrist was seized in a powerful grasp and a low voice whispered in English: 'Lieutenant, it is I, Tarzan of the Apes.'

The relief from the nervous strain under which he had been laboring for so long left Smith-Oldwick suddenly as weak as a babe, so that he was forced to grasp the ape-man's arm for support – and when he found his voice all he could do was to repeat: 'You? You? I thought you were dead!'

'No, not dead,' replied Tarzan, 'and I see that you are not either. But how about the girl?'

'I haven't seen her,' replied the Englishman, 'since we were brought here. We were taken into a building on the plaza close by and there we were separated. She was led away by guards and I was put into a den of lions. I haven't seen her since.'

'How did you escape?' asked the ape-man.

'The lions didn't seem to pay much attention to me and I climbed out of the place by way of a tree and through a window into a room on the second floor. Had a little scrimmage there with a fellow and was hidden by one of their women in a hole in the wall. The loony thing then betrayed me to another bounder who happened in, but I found a way out and up onto the roof where I have been for quite some time now waiting for a chance to get down into the street without being seen. That's all I know, but I haven't the slightest idea in the world where to look for Miss Kircher.'

'Where were you going now?' asked Tarzan.

Smith-Oldwick hesitated. 'I – well, I couldn't do anything here alone and I was going to try to get out of the city and in some way reach the British forces east and bring help.'

'You couldn't do it,' said Tarzan. 'Even if you got through the forest alive you could never cross the desert country without food or water.'

'What shall we do, then?' asked the Englishman.

'We will see if we can find the girl,' replied the ape-man, and then, as though he had forgotten the presence of the Englishman and was arguing to convince himself, 'She may be a German and a spy, but she is a woman – a white woman – I can't leave her here.'

'But how are we going to find her?' asked the Englishman.

'I have followed her this far,' replied Tarzan, 'and unless I am greatly mistaken I can follow her still farther.'

'But I cannot accompany you in these clothes without exposing us both to detection and arrest,' argued Smith-Oldwick.

'We will get you other clothes, then,' said Tarzan.

'How?' asked the Englishman.

'Go back to the roof beside the city wall where I entered,' replied the ape-man with a grim smile, 'and ask the naked dead man there how I got my disguise.'

Smith-Oldwick looked quickly up at his companion. 'I have it,' he exclaimed. 'I know where there is a fellow who doesn't need his clothes anymore, and if we can get back on this roof I think we can find him and get his apparel without much resistance. Only a girl and a young fellow whom we could easily surprise and overcome.'

'What do you mean?' asked Tarzan. 'How do you know that the man doesn't need his clothes anymore?'

'I know he doesn't need them,' replied the Englishman, 'because I killed him.'

'Oh!' exclaimed the ape-man, 'I see. I guess it might be easier that way than to tackle one of these fellows in the street where there is more chance of our being interrupted.'

'But how are we going to reach the roof again, after all?' queried Smith-Oldwick.

'The same way you came down,' replied Tarzan. 'This roof is low and there is a little ledge formed by the capital of each column; I noticed that when you descended. Some of the buildings wouldn't have been so easy to negotiate.'

Smith-Oldwick looked up toward the eaves of the low roof. 'It's not very high,' he said, 'but I am afraid I can't make it. I'll try – I've been pretty weak since a lion mauled me and the guards beat me up, and too, I haven't eaten since yesterday.'

Tarzan thought a moment. 'You've got to go with me,' he said at last. 'I can't leave you here. The only chance you have of escape is through me and I can't go with you now until we have found the girl.'

'I want to go with you,' replied Smith-Oldwick. 'I'm not much good now but at that two of us may be better than one.'

'All right,' said Tarzan, 'come on,' and before the Englishman realized what the other contemplated Tarzan had picked him up and thrown him across his shoulder. 'Now, hang on,' whispered the ape-man, and with a short run he clambered apelike up the front of the low arcade. So quickly and easily was it done that the Englishman scarcely had time to realize what was happening before he was deposited safely upon the roof.

'There,' remarked Tarzan. 'Now, lead me to the place you speak of.'

Smith-Oldwick had no difficulty in locating the trap in the roof through which he had escaped. Removing the cover the ape-man bent low, listening and sniffing. 'Come,' he said after a moment's investigation and lowered himself to the floor beneath. Smith-Oldwick followed him, and together the two crept through the darkness toward the door in the back wall of the niche in which the Englishman had been hidden by the girl. They found the door ajar and opening it Tarzan saw a streak of light showing through the hangings that separated it from the alcove.

Placing his eye close to the aperture he saw the girl and the young man of which the Englishman had spoken seated on opposite sides of a low table upon which food was spread. Serving them was a giant Negro and it was he whom the ape-man watched most closely. Familiar with the tribal idiosyncrasies of a great number of African tribes over a considerable proportion of the Dark Continent, the Tarmangani at last felt reasonably assured that he knew from what part of Africa this slave had come, and the dialect of his people. There was, however, the chance that the fellow had been captured in childhood and that through long years of nonuse his native language had become lost to him, but then there always had been an element of chance connected with nearly every event of Tarzan's life, so he waited patiently until in the performance of his duties the black man approached a little table which stood near the niche in which Tarzan and the Englishman hid.

As the slave bent over some dish which stood upon the table his ear was not far from the aperture through which Tarzan looked. Apparently from a solid wall, for the Negro had no knowledge of the existence of the niche, came to him in the tongue of his own people, the whispered words: 'If you would return to the land of the Wamabo say nothing, but do as I bid you.'

The black rolled terrified eyes toward the hangings at his side. The ape-man could see him tremble and for a moment was fearful that in his terror he would betray them. 'Fear not,' he whispered, 'we are your friends.'

At last the Negro spoke in a low whisper, scarcely audible even to the keen ears of the ape-man. 'What,' he asked, 'can poor Otobu do for the god who speaks to him out of the solid wall?'

'This,' replied Tarzan. 'Two of us are coming into this room. Help us prevent this man and woman from escaping or raising an outcry that will bring others to their aid.'

'I will help you,' replied the Negro, 'to keep them within this room, but do not fear that their outcries will bring others. These walls are built so that no sound may pass through, and even if it did what difference would it make in this village which is constantly filled with the screams of its mad people. Do not fear their cries. No one will notice them. I go to do your bidding.'

Tarzan saw the black cross the room to the table upon which he placed another dish of food before the feasters. Then he stepped to a place behind the man and as he did so raised his eyes to the point in the wall from which the ape-man's voice had come to him, as much as to say, 'Master, I am ready.'

Without more delay Tarzan threw aside the hangings and stepped into the room. As he did so the young man rose from the table to be instantly seized from behind by the black slave. The girl, whose back was toward the ape-man and his companion, was not at first aware of their presence but saw only the attack of the slave upon her lover, and with a loud scream she leaped forward to assist the latter. Tarzan sprang to her side and laid a heavy hand upon her arm before she could interfere with Otobu's attentions to the young man. At first, as she turned toward the ape-man, her face reflected only mad rage, but almost instantly this changed into the vapid smile with which Smith-Oldwick was already familiar and her slim fingers commenced their soft appraisement of the newcomer.

Almost immediately she discovered Smith-Oldwick but there was neither surprise nor anger upon her countenance. Evidently the poor mad creature knew but two principal moods, from one to the other of which she changed with lightninglike rapidity.

'Watch her a moment,' said Tarzan to the Englishman, 'while I disarm that fellow,' and stepping to the side of the young man whom Otobu was having difficulty in subduing Tarzan relieved him of his saber. 'Tell them,' he said to the Negro, 'if you speak their language, that we will not harm them if they leave us alone and let us depart in peace.'

The black had been looking at Tarzan with wide eyes, evidently not comprehending how this god could appear in so material a form, and with the voice of a white Bwana and the uniform of a warrior of this city to which he quite evidently did not belong. But nevertheless his first confidence in the voice that offered him freedom was not lessened and he did as Tarzan bid him.

'They want to know what you want,' said Otobu, after he had spoken to the man and the girl.

'Tell them that we want food for one thing,' said Tarzan, 'and something else that we know where to find in this room. Take the man's spear, Otobu; I see it leaning against the wall in the corner of the room. And you, Lieutenant, take his saber,' and then again to Otobu, 'I will watch the man while you go and bring forth that which is beneath the couch over against this wall,' and Tarzan indicated the location of the piece of furniture.

Otobu, trained to obey, did as he was bid. The eyes of the man and the girl followed him, and as he drew back the hangings and dragged forth the corpse of the man Smith-Oldwick had slain, the girl's lover voiced a loud scream and attempted to leap forward to the side of the corpse. Tarzan, however, seized him and then the fellow turned upon him with teeth and nails. It was with no little difficulty that Tarzan finally subdued the man, and while Otobu was removing the outer clothing from the corpse, Tarzan asked the black to question the young man as to his evident excitement at the sight of the body.

'I can tell you, Bwana,' replied Otobu. 'This man was his father.'

'What is he saying to the girl?' asked Tarzan.

'He is asking her if she knew that the body of his father was under the couch. And she is saying that she did not know it.'

Tarzan repeated the conversation to Smith-Oldwick, who smiled. 'If the chap could have seen her removing all evidence of the crime and arranging the hangings of the couch so that the body was concealed after she had helped me drag it across the room, he wouldn't have very much doubt as to her knowledge of the affair. The rug you see draped over the bench in the corner was arranged to hide the bloodstain – in some ways they are not so loony after all.'

The black man had now removed the outer garments from the dead man, and Smith-Oldwick was hastily drawing them on over his own clothing. 'And now,' said Tarzan, 'we will sit down and eat. One accomplishes little on an empty stomach.' As they ate the ape-man attempted to carry on a conversation with the two natives through Otobu. He learned that they were in the palace which had belonged to the dead man lying upon the floor beside them. He had held an official position of some nature, and he and his family were of the ruling class but were not members of the court.

When Tarzan questioned them about Bertha Kircher, the young man said that she had been taken to the king's palace; and when asked why replied: 'For the king, of course.'

During the conversation both the man and the girl appeared quite rational, even asking some questions as to the country from which their uninvited guests had come, and evidencing much surprise when informed that there was anything but waterless wastes beyond their own valley.

When Otobu asked the man, at Tarzan's suggestion, if he was familiar with the interior of the king's palace, he replied that he was; that he was a friend of Prince Metak, one of the king's sons, and that he often visited the palace and that Metak also came here to his father's palace frequently. As Tarzan ate he racked his brain for some plan whereby he might utilize the knowledge of the young man to gain entrance to the palace, but he had arrived at nothing which he considered feasible when there came a loud knocking upon the door of the outer room.

For a moment no one spoke and then the young man raised his voice and cried aloud to those without. Immediately Otobu sprang for the fellow and attempted to smother his words by clapping a palm over his mouth.

'What is he saying?' asked Tarzan.

'He is telling them to break down the door and rescue him and the girl from two strangers who entered and made them prisoners. If they enter they will kill us all.'

'Tell him,' said Tarzan, 'to hold his peace or I will slay him.'

Otobu did as he was instructed and the young maniac lapsed into scowling silence. Tarzan crossed the alcove and entered the outer room to note the effect of the assaults upon the door. Smith-Oldwick followed him a few steps, leaving Otobu to guard the two prisoners. The ape-man saw that the door could not long withstand the heavy blows being dealt the panels from without. 'I wanted to use that fellow in the other room,' he said to Smith-Oldwick, 'but I am afraid we will have to get out of here the way we came. We can't accomplish anything by waiting here and meeting these fellows. From the noise out there there must be a dozen of them. Come,' he said, 'you go first and I will follow.'

As the two turned back from the alcove they witnessed an entirely different scene from that upon which they had turned their backs but a moment or two before. Stretched on the floor and apparently lifeless lay the body of the black slave, while the two prisoners had vanished completely.

23

The Flight from Xuja

As Metak bore Bertha Kircher toward the edge of the pool, the girl at first had no conception of the deed he contemplated but when, as they approached the edge, he did not lessen his speed she guessed the frightful truth. As he leaped headforemost with her into the water, she closed her eyes and breathed a silent prayer, for she was confident that the maniac had no other purpose than to drown himself and her. And yet, so potent is the first law of nature that even in the face of certain death, as she surely believed herself, she clung tenaciously to life, and while she struggled to free herself from the powerful clutches of the madman, she held her breath against the final moment when the asphyxiating waters must inevitably flood her lungs.

Through the frightful ordeal she maintained absolute control of her senses so that, after the first plunge, she was aware that the man was swimming with her beneath the surface. He took perhaps not more than a dozen strokes directly toward the end wall of the pool and then he arose; and once again she knew that her head was above the surface. She opened her eyes to see that they were in a corridor dimly lighted by gratings set in its roof – a winding corridor, water filled from wall to wall.

Along this the man was swimming with easy powerful strokes, at the same time holding her chin above the water. For ten minutes he swam thus without stopping and the girl heard him speak to her, though she could not understand what he said, as he evidently immediately realized, for, half floating, he shifted his hold upon her so that he could touch her nose and mouth with the fingers of one hand. She grasped what he meant and immediately took a deep breath, whereat he dove quickly beneath the surface, pulling her down with him, and again for a dozen strokes or more he swam thus wholly submerged.

When they again came to the surface, Bertha Kircher saw that they were in a large lagoon and that the bright stars were shining high above them, while on either hand domed and minareted buildings were silhouetted sharply against the starlit sky. Metak swam swiftly to the north side of the lagoon where, by means of a ladder, the two climbed out upon the embankment. There were others in the plaza but they paid but little if any attention to the two bedraggled figures. As Metak walked quickly across the pavement with the girl at his side, Bertha Kircher could only guess at the man's intentions. She could see no way in which to escape and so she went docilely with him, hoping against hope that some fortuitous circumstance might eventually arise that would give her the coveted chance for freedom and life.

Metak led her toward a building which, as she entered, she recognized as the same to which she and Lieutenant Smith-Oldwick had been led when they were brought into the city. There was no man sitting behind the carved desk now, but about the room were a dozen or more warriors in the tunics of the house to which they were attached, in this case white with a small lion in the form of a crest or badge upon the breast and back of each.

As Metak entered and the men recognized him they arose, and in answer to a query he put, they pointed to an arched doorway at the rear of the room. Toward this Metak led the girl, and then, as though filled with a sudden suspicion, his eyes narrowed cunningly and turning toward the soldiery he issued an order which resulted in their all preceding him through the small doorway and up a flight of stairs a short distance beyond.

The stairway and the corridor above were lighted by small flares which revealed several doors in the walls of the upper passageway. To one of these the men led the prince. Bertha Kircher saw them knock upon the door and heard a voice reply faintly through the thick door to the summons. The effect upon those about her was electrical. Instantly excitement reigned, and in response to orders from the king's son the soldiers commenced to beat heavily upon the door, to throw their bodies against it and to attempt to hew away the panels with their sabers. The girl wondered at the cause of the evident excitement of her captors.

She saw the door giving to each renewed assault, but what she did not see just before it crashed inward was the figures of the two men who alone, in all the world, might have saved her, pass between the heavy hangings in an adjoining alcove and disappear into a dark corridor.

As the door gave and the warriors rushed into the apartment followed by the prince, the latter became immediately filled with baffled rage, for the rooms were deserted except for the dead body of the owner of the palace, and the still form of the black slave, Otobu, where they lay stretched upon the floor of the alcove.

The prince rushed to the windows and looked out, but as the suite overlooked the barred den of lions from which, the prince thought, there could be no escape, his puzzlement was only increased. Though he searched about the room for some clue to the whereabouts of its former occupants he did not discover the niche behind the hangings. With the fickleness of insanity he quickly tired of the search, and, turning to the soldiers who had accompanied him from the floor below, dismissed them.

After setting up the broken door as best they could, the men left the apartment and when they were again alone Metak turned toward the girl. As he approached her, his face distorted by a hideous leer, his features worked rapidly in spasmodic twitches. The girl, who was standing at the entrance of the alcove, shrank back, her horror reflected in her face. Step by step she backed across the room, while the crouching maniac crept stealthily after her with clawlike fingers poised in anticipation of the moment they should leap forth and seize her.

As she passed the body of the Negro, her foot touched some obstacle at her side, and glancing down she saw the spear with which Otobu had been supposed to hold the prisoners. Instantly she leaned forward and snatched it from the floor with its sharp point directed at the body of the madman. The effect upon Metak was electrical. From stealthy silence he broke into harsh peals of laughter, and drawing his saber danced to and fro before the girl, but whichever way he went the point of the spear still threatened him.

Gradually the girl noticed a change in the tone of the creature's screams that was also reflected in the changing expression upon his hideous countenance. His hysterical laughter was slowly changing into cries of rage while the silly leer upon his face was supplanted by a ferocious scowl and upcurled lips, which revealed the sharpened fangs beneath.

He now ran rapidly in almost to the spear's point, only to jump away, run a few steps to one side and again attempt to make an entrance, the while he slashed and hewed at the spear with such violence that it was with difficulty the girl maintained her guard, and all the time was forced to give ground step by step. She had reached the point where she was standing squarely against the couch at the side of the room when, with an incredibly swift movement, Metak stooped and grasping a low stool hurled it directly at her head.

She raised the spear to fend off the heavy missile, but she was not entirely successful, and the impact of the blow carried her backward upon the couch, and instantly Metak was upon her.

Tarzan and Smith-Oldwick gave little thought as to what had become of the other two occupants of the room. They were gone, and so far as these two were concerned they might never return. Tarzan's one desire was to reach the street again, where, now that both of them were in some sort of disguise, they should be able to proceed with comparative safety to the palace and continue their search for the girl.

Smith-Oldwick preceded Tarzan along the corridor and as they reached the ladder he climbed aloft to remove the trap. He worked for a moment and then, turning, addressed Tarzan.

'Did we replace the cover on this trap when we came down? I don't recall that we did.'

'No,' said Tarzan, 'it was left open.'

'So I thought,' said Smith-Oldwick, 'but it's closed now and locked. I cannot move it. Possibly you can,' and he descended the ladder.

Even Tarzan's immense strength, however, had no effect other than to break one of the rungs of the ladder against which he was pushing, nearly precipitating him to the floor below. After the rung broke he rested for a moment before renewing his efforts, and as he stood with his head near the cover of the trap, he distinctly heard voices on the roof above him.

Dropping down to Oldwick's side he told him what he had heard. 'We had better find some other way out,' he said, and the two started to retrace their steps toward the alcove. Tarzan was again in the lead, and as he opened the door in the back of the niche, he was suddenly startled to hear, in tones of terror and in a woman's voice, the words: 'O God, be merciful' from just beyond the hangings.

Here was no time for cautious investigation and, not even waiting to find the aperture and part the hangings, but with one sweep of a brawny hand dragging them from their support, the ape-man leaped from the niche into the alcove.

At the sound of his entry the maniac looked up, and as he saw at first only a man in the uniform of his father's soldiers, he shrieked forth an angry order, but at the second glance, which revealed the face of the newcomer, the madman leaped from the prostrate form of his victim and, apparently forgetful of the saber which he had dropped upon the floor beside the couch as he leaped to grapple with the girl, closed with bare hands upon his antagonist, his sharp-filed teeth searching for the other's throat.

Metak, the son of Herog, was no weakling. Powerful by nature and rendered still more so in the throes of one of his maniacal fits of fury he was no mean antagonist, even for the mighty ape-man, and to this a distinct advantage for him was added by the fact that almost at the outset of their battle Tarzan, in stepping backward, struck his heel against the corpse of the man whom Smith-Oldwick had killed, and fell heavily backward to the floor with Metak upon his breast.

With the quickness of a cat the maniac made an attempt to fasten his teeth in Tarzan's jugular, but a quick movement of the latter resulted in his finding a hold only upon the Tarmangani's shoulder. Here he clung while his fingers sought Tarzan's throat, and it was then that the ape-man, realizing the possibility of defeat, called to Smith-Oldwick to take the girl and seek to escape.

The Englishman looked questioningly at Bertha Kircher, who had now risen from the couch, shaking and trembling. She saw the question in his eyes and with an effort she drew herself to her full height. 'No,' she cried, 'if he dies here I shall die with him. Go if you wish to. You can do nothing here, but I – I cannot go.'

Tarzan had now regained his feet, but the maniac still clung to him tenaciously. The girl turned suddenly to Smith-Oldwick. 'Your pistol!' she cried. 'Why don't you shoot him?'

The man drew the weapon from his pocket and approached the two antagonists, but by this time they were moving so rapidly that there was no opportunity for shooting one without the danger of hitting the other. At the same time Bertha Kircher circled about them with the prince's saber, but neither could she find an opening. Again and again the two men fell to the floor, until presently Tarzan found a hold upon the other's throat, against which contingency Metak had been constantly battling, and slowly, as the giant fingers closed, the other's mad eyes protruded from his livid face, his jaws gaped and released their hold upon Tarzan's shoulder, and then in a sudden excess of disgust and rage the ape-man lifted the body of the prince high above his head and with all the strength of his great arms hurled it across the room and through the window where it fell with a sickening thud into the pit of lions beneath.

As Tarzan turned again toward his companions, the girl was standing with the saber still in her hand and an expression upon her face that he never had seen there before. Her eyes were wide and misty with unshed tears, while her sensitive lips trembled as though she were upon the point of giving way to some pent emotion which her rapidly rising and falling bosom plainly indicated she was fighting to control.

'If we are going to get out of here,' said the ape-man, 'we can't lose any time. We are together at last and nothing can be gained by delay. The question now is the safest way. The couple who escaped us evidently departed through the passageway to the roof and secured the trap against us so that we are cut off in that direction. What chance have we below? You came that way,' and he turned toward the girl.

'At the foot of the stairs,' she said, 'is a room full of armed men. I doubt if we could pass that way.'

It was then that Otobu raised himself to a sitting posture. 'So you are not dead after all,' exclaimed the ape-man. 'Come, how badly are you hurt?'

The Negro rose gingerly to his feet, moved his arms and legs and felt of his head.

'Otobu does not seem to be hurt at all, Bwana,' he replied, 'only for a great ache in his head.'

'Good,' said the ape-man. 'You want to return to the Wamabo country?'

'Yes, Bwana.'

'Then lead us from the city by the safest way.'

'There is no safe way,' replied the black, 'and even if we reach the gates we shall have to fight. I can lead you from this building to a side street with little danger of meeting anyone on the way. Beyond that we must take our chance of discovery. You are all dressed as are the people of this wicked city so perhaps we may pass unnoticed, but at the gate it will be a different matter, for none is permitted to leave the city at night.'

'Very well,' replied the ape-man, 'let us be on our way.'

Otobu led them through the broken door of the outer room, and partway down the corridor he turned into another apartment at the right. This they crossed to a passageway beyond, and, finally, traversing several rooms and corridors, he led them down a flight of steps to a door which opened directly upon a side street in rear of the palace.

Two men, a woman, and a black slave were not so extraordinary a sight upon the streets of the city as to arouse comment. When passing beneath the flares the three Europeans were careful to choose a moment when no chance pedestrian might happen to get a view of their features, but in the shadow of the arcades there seemed little danger of detection. They had covered a good portion of the distance to the gate without mishap when there came to their ears from the central portion of the city sounds of a great commotion.

'What does that mean?' Tarzan asked of Otobu, who was now trembling violently.

'Master,' he replied, 'they have discovered that which has happened in the palace of Veza, mayor of the city. His son and the girl escaped and summoned soldiers who have now doubtless discovered the body of Veza.'

'I wonder,' said Tarzan, 'if they have discovered the party I threw through the window.'

Bertha Kircher, who understood enough of the dialect to follow their conversation, asked Tarzan if he knew that the man he had thrown from the window was the king's son. The ape-man laughed. 'No,' he said, 'I did not. That rather complicates matters – at least if they have found him.'

Suddenly there broke above the turmoil behind them the clear strains of a bugle. Otobu increased his pace. 'Hurry, Master,' he cried, 'it is worse than I had thought.'

'What do you mean?' asked Tarzan.

'For some reason the king's guard and the king's lions are being called out. I fear, O Bwana, that we cannot escape them. But why they should be called out for us I do not know.'

But if Otobu did not know, Tarzan at least guessed that they had found the body of the king's son. Once again the notes of the bugle rose high and clear upon the night air. 'Calling more lions?' asked Tarzan.

'No, Master,' replied Otobu. 'It is the parrots they are calling.'

They moved on rapidly in silence for a few minutes when their attention was attracted by the flapping of the wings of a bird above them. They looked up to discover a parrot circling about over their heads.

'Here are the parrots, Otobu,' said Tarzan with a grin. 'Do they expect to kill us with parrots?'

The Negro moaned as the bird darted suddenly ahead of them toward the city wall. 'Now indeed are we lost, Master,' cried the black. 'The bird that found us has flown to the gate to warn the guard.'

'Come, Otobu, what are you talking about?' exclaimed Tarzan irritably. 'Have you lived among these lunatics so long that you are yourself mad?'

'No, Master,' replied Otobu. 'I am not mad. You do not know them. These terrible birds are like human beings without hearts or souls. They speak the language of the people of this city of Xuja. They are demons, Master, and when in sufficient numbers they might even attack and kill us.'

'How far are we from the gate?' asked Tarzan.

'We are not very far,' replied the Negro. 'Beyond this next turn we will see it a few paces ahead of us. But the bird has reached it before us and by now they are summoning the guard,' the truth of which statement was almost immediately indicated by sounds of many voices raised evidently in commands just ahead of them, while from behind came increased evidence of approaching pursuit – loud screams and the roars of lions.

A few steps ahead a narrow alley opened from the east into the thoroughfare they were following and as they approached it there emerged from its dark shadows the figure of a mighty lion. Otobu halted in his tracks and shrank back against Tarzan. 'Look, Master,' he whimpered, 'a great black lion of the forest!'

Tarzan drew the saber which still hung at his side. 'We cannot go back,' he said. 'Lions, parrots, or men, it must be all the same,' and he moved steadily forward in the direction of the gate. What wind was stirring in the city street moved from Tarzan toward the lion and when the ape-man had approached to within a few yards of the beast, who had stood silently eyeing them up to this time, instead of the expected roar, a whine broke from the beast's throat. The ape-man was conscious of a very decided feeling of relief. 'It's Numa of the pit,' he called back to his companions, and to Otobu, 'Do not fear, this lion will not harm us.'

Numa moved forward to the ape-man's side and then turning, paced beside him along the narrow street. At the next turn they came in sight of the gate, where, beneath several flares, they saw a group of at least twenty warriors prepared to seize them, while from the opposite direction the roars of the pursuing lions sounded close upon them, mingling with the screams of numerous parrots which now circled about their heads. Tarzan halted and turned to the young aviator. 'How many rounds of ammunition have you left?' he asked.

'I have seven in the pistol,' replied Smith-Oldwick, 'and perhaps a dozen more cartridges in my blouse pocket.'

'I'm going to rush them,' said Tarzan. 'Otobu, you stay at the side of the woman. Oldwick, you and I will go ahead, you upon my left. I think we need not try to tell Numa what to do,' for even then the great lion was baring his fangs and growling ferociously at the guardsmen, who appeared uneasy in the face of this creature which, above all others, they feared.

'As we advance, Oldwick,' said the ape-man, 'fire one shot. It may frighten them; and after that fire only when necessary. All ready? Let's go!' and he moved forward toward the gate. At the same time, Smith-Oldwick discharged his weapon and a yellow-coated warrior screamed and crumpled forward upon his face. For a minute the others showed symptoms of panic but one, who seemed to be an officer, rallied them. 'Now,' said Tarzan, 'all together!' and he started at a run for the gate. Simultaneously the lion, evidently scenting the purpose of the Tarmangani, broke into a full charge toward the guard.

Shaken by the report of the unfamiliar weapon, the ranks of the guardsmen broke before the furious assault of the great beast. The officer screamed forth a volley of commands in a mad fury of uncontrolled rage but the guardsmen, obeying the first law of nature as well as actuated by their inherent fear of the black denizen of the forest, scattered to right and left to elude the monster. With ferocious growls Numa wheeled to the right, and with raking talons struck right and left among a little handful of terrified guardsmen who were endeavoring to elude him, and then Tarzan and Smith-Oldwick closed with the others.

For a moment their most formidable antagonist was the officer in command. He wielded his curved saber as only an adept might as he faced Tarzan, to whom the similar weapon in his own hand was most unfamiliar. Smith-Oldwick could not fire for fear of hitting the ape-man when suddenly to his dismay he saw Tarzan's weapon fly from his grasp as the Xujan warrior neatly disarmed his opponent. With a scream the fellow raised his saber for the final cut that would terminate the earthly career of Tarzan of the Apes when, to the astonishment of both the ape-man and Smith-Oldwick, the fellow stiffened rigidly, his weapon dropped from the nerveless fingers of his upraised hand, his mad eyes rolled upward and foam flecked his bared lip. Gasping as though in the throes of strangulation the fellow pitched forward at Tarzan's feet.

Tarzan stooped and picked up the dead man's weapon, a smile upon his face as he turned and glanced toward the young Englishman.

'The fellow is an epileptic,' said Smith-Oldwick. 'I suppose many of them are. Their nervous condition is not without its good points – a normal man would have gotten you.'

The other guardsmen seemed utterly demoralized at the loss of their leader. They were huddled upon the opposite side of the street at the left of the gate, screaming at the tops of their voices and looking in the direction from which sounds of reinforcements were coming, as though urging on the men and lions that were already too close for the comfort of the fugitives. Six guardsmen still stood with their backs against the gate, their weapons flashing in the light of the flares and their parchmentlike faces distorted in horrid grimaces of rage and terror.

Numa had pursued two fleeing warriors down the street which paralleled the wall for a short distance at this point. The ape-man turned to Smith-Oldwick. 'You will have to use your pistol now,' he said, 'and we must get by these fellows at once'; and as the young Englishman fired, Tarzan rushed in to close quarters as though he had not already discovered that with the saber he was no match for these trained swordsmen. Two men fell to Smith-Oldwick's first two shots and then he missed, while the four remaining divided, two leaping for the aviator and two for Tarzan.

The ape-man rushed in in an effort to close with one of his antagonists where the other's saber would be comparatively useless. Smith-Oldwick dropped one of his assailants with a bullet through the chest and pulled his trigger on the second, only to have the hammer fall futilely upon an empty chamber. The cartridges in his weapon were exhausted and the warrior with his razor-edged, gleaming saber was upon him.

Tarzan raised his own weapon but once and that to divert a vicious cut for his head. Then he was upon one of his assailants and before the fellow could regain his equilibrium and leap back after delivering his cut, the ape-man had seized him by the neck and crotch. Tarzan's other antagonist was edging around to one side where he might use his weapon, and as he raised the blade to strike at the back of the Tarmangani's neck, the latter swung the body of his comrade upward so that it received the full force of the blow. The blade sank deep into the body of the warrior, eliciting a single frightful scream, and then Tarzan hurled the dying man in the face of his final adversary.

Smith-Oldwick, hard pressed and now utterly defenseless, had given up all hope in the instant that he realized his weapon was empty, when, from his left, a living bolt of black-maned ferocity shot past him to the breast of his opponent. Down went the Xujan, his face bitten away by one snap of the powerful jaws of Numa of the pit.

In the few seconds that had been required for the consummation of these rapidly ensuing events, Otobu had dragged Bertha Kircher to the gate which he had unbarred and thrown open, and with the vanquishing of the last of the active guardsmen, the party passed out of the maniac city of Xuja into the outer darkness beyond. At the same moment a half dozen lions rounded the last turn in the road leading back toward the plaza, and at sight of them Numa of the pit wheeled and charged. For a moment the lions of the city stood their ground, but only for a moment, and then before the black beast was upon them, they turned and fled, while Tarzan and his party moved rapidly toward the blackness of the forest beyond the garden.

'Will they follow us out of the city?' Tarzan asked Otobu.

'Not at night,' replied the black. 'I have been a slave here for five years but never have I known these people to leave the city by night. If they go beyond the forest in the daytime they usually wait until the dawn of another day before they return, as they fear to pass through the country of the black lions after dark. No, I think, Master, that they will not follow us tonight, but tomorrow they will come, and, O Bwana, then will they surely get us, or those that are left of us, for at least one among us must be the toll of the black lions as we pass through their forest.'

As they crossed the garden, Smith-Oldwick refilled the magazine of his pistol and inserted a cartridge in the chamber. The girl moved silently at Tarzan's left, between him and the aviator. Suddenly the ape-man stopped and turned toward the city, his mighty frame, clothed in the yellow tunic of Herog's soldiery, plainly visible to the others beneath the light of the stars. They saw him raise his head and they heard break from his lips the plaintive note of a lion calling to his fellows. Smith-Oldwick felt a distinct shudder pass through his frame, while Otobu, rolling the whites of his eyes in terrified surprise, sank trembling to his knees. But the girl thrilled and she felt her heart beat in a strange exultation, and then she drew nearer to the beast-man until her shoulder touched his arm. The act was involuntary and for a moment she scarce realized what she had done, and then she stepped silently back, thankful that the light of the stars was not sufficient to reveal to the eyes of her companions the flush which she felt mantling her cheek. Yet she was not ashamed of the impulse that had prompted her, but rather of the act itself which she knew, had Tarzan noticed it, would have been repulsive to him.

From the open gate of the city of maniacs came the answering cry of a lion. The little group waited where they stood until presently they saw the majestic proportions of the black lion as he approached them along the trail. When he had rejoined them Tarzan fastened the fingers of one hand in the black mane and started on once more toward the forest. Behind them, from the city, rose a bedlam of horrid sounds, the roaring of lions mingling with the raucous voices of the screaming parrots and the mad shrieks of the maniacs. As they entered the Stygian darkness of the forest the girl once again involuntarily shrank closer to the ape-man, and this time Tarzan was aware of the contact.

Himself without fear, he yet instinctively appreciated how terrified the girl must be. Actuated by a sudden kindly impulse he found her hand and took it in his own and thus they continued upon their way, groping through the blackness of the trail. Twice they were approached by forest lions, but upon both occasions the deep growls of Numa of the pit drove off their assailants. Several times they were compelled to rest, for Smith-Oldwick was constantly upon the verge of exhaustion, and toward morning Tarzan was forced to carry him on the steep ascent from the bed of the valley.

24

The Tommies

Daylight overtook them after they had entered the gorge, but, tired as they all were with the exception of Tarzan, they realized that they must keep on at all costs until they found a spot where they might ascend the precipitous side of the gorge to the floor of the plateau above. Tarzan and Otobu were both equally confident that the Xujans would not follow them beyond the gorge, but though they scanned every inch of the frowning cliffs upon either hand noon came and there was still no indication of any avenue of escape to right or left. There were places where the ape-man alone might have negotiated the ascent but none where the others could hope successfully to reach the plateau, nor where Tarzan, powerful and agile as he was, could have ventured safely to carry them aloft.

For half a day the ape-man had been either carrying or supporting Smith-Oldwick and now, to his chagrin, he saw that the girl was faltering. He had realized well how much she had undergone and how greatly the hardships and dangers and the fatigue of the past weeks must have told upon her vitality. He saw how bravely she attempted to keep up, yet how often she stumbled and staggered as she labored through the sand and gravel of the gorge. Nor could he help but admire her fortitude and the uncomplaining effort she was making to push on.

The Englishman must have noticed her condition too, for some time after noon, he stopped suddenly and sat down in the sand. 'It's no use,' he said to Tarzan. 'I can go no farther. Miss Kircher is rapidly weakening. You will have to go on without me.'

'No,' said the girl, 'we cannot do that. We have all been through so much together and the chances of our escape are still so remote that whatever comes, let us remain together, unless,' and she looked up at Tarzan, 'you, who have done so much for us to whom you are under no obligations, will go on without us. I for one wish that you would. It must be as evident to you as it is to me that you cannot save us, for though you succeeded in dragging us from the path of our pursuers, even your great strength and endurance could never take one of us across the desert waste which lies between here and the nearest fertile country.'

The ape-man returned her serious look with a smile. 'You are not dead,' he said to her, 'nor is the lieutenant, nor Otobu, nor myself. One is either dead or alive, and until we are dead we should plan only upon continuing to live. Because we remain here and rest is no indication that we shall die here. I cannot carry you both to the country of the Wamabos, which is the nearest spot at which we may expect to find game and water, but we shall not give up on that account. So far we have found a way. Let us take things as they come. Let us rest now because you and Lieutenant Smith-Oldwick need the rest, and when you are stronger we will go on again.'

'But the Xujans –?' she asked. 'May they not follow us here?'

'Yes,' he said, 'they probably will. But we need not be concerned with them until they come.'

'I wish,' said the girl, 'that I possessed your philosophy but I am afraid it is beyond me.'

'You were not born and reared in the jungle by wild beasts and among wild beasts, or you would possess, as I do, the fatalism of the jungle.'

And so they moved to the side of the gorge beneath the shade of an overhanging rock and lay down in the hot sand to rest. Numa wandered restlessly to and fro and finally, after sprawling for a moment close beside the ape-man, rose and moved off up the gorge to be lost to view a moment later beyond the nearest turn.

For an hour the little party rested and then Tarzan suddenly rose and, motioning the others to silence, listened. For a minute he stood motionless, his keen ears acutely receptive to sounds so faint and distant that none of the other three could detect the slightest break in the utter and deathlike quiet of the gorge. Finally the ape-man relaxed and turned toward them. 'What is it?' asked the girl.

'They are coming,' he replied. 'They are yet some distance away, though not far, for the sandaled feet of the men and the pads of the lions make little noise upon the soft sands.'

'What shall we do – try to go on?' asked Smith-Oldwick. 'I believe I could make a go of it now for a short way. I am much rested. How about you, Miss Kircher?'

'Oh, yes,' she said, 'I am much stronger. Yes, surely I can go on.'

Tarzan knew that neither of them quite spoke the truth, that people do not recover so quickly from utter exhaustion, but he saw no other way and there was always the hope that just beyond the next turn would be a way out of the gorge.

'You help the lieutenant, Otobu,' he said, turning to the black, 'and I will carry Miss Kircher,' and though the girl objected, saying that he must not waste his strength, he lifted her lightly in his arms and moved off up the canyon, followed by Otobu and the Englishman. They had gone no great distance when the others of the party became aware of the sounds of pursuit, for now the lions were whining as though the fresh scent spoor of their quarry had reached their nostrils.

'I wish that your Numa would return,' said the girl.

'Yes,' said Tarzan, 'but we shall have to do the best we can without him. I should like to find some place where we can barricade ourselves against attack from all sides. Possibly then we might hold them off. Smith-Oldwick is a good shot and if there are not too many men he might be able to dispose of them provided they can only come at him one at a time. The lions don't bother me so much. Sometimes they are stupid animals, and I am sure that these that pursue us, and who are so dependent upon the masters that have raised and trained them, will be easily handled after the warriors are disposed of.'

'You think there is some hope, then?' she asked.

'We are still alive,' was his only answer.

'There,' he said presently, 'I thought I recalled this very spot.' He pointed toward a fragment that had evidently fallen from the summit of the cliff and which now lay imbedded in the sand a few feet from the base. It was a jagged fragment of rock which rose some ten feet above the surface of the sand, leaving a narrow aperture between it and the cliff behind. Toward this they directed their steps and when finally they reached their goal they found a space about two feet wide and ten feet long between the rock and the cliff. To be sure it was open at both ends but at least they could not be attacked upon all sides at once.

They had scarcely concealed themselves before Tarzan's quick ears caught a sound upon the face of the cliff above them, and looking up he saw a diminutive monkey perched upon a slight projection – an ugly-faced little monkey who looked down upon them for a moment and then scampered away toward the south in the direction from which their pursuers were coming. Otobu had seen the monkey too. 'He will tell the parrots,' said the black, 'and the parrots will tell the madmen.'

'It is all the same,' replied Tarzan; 'the lions would have found us here. We could not hope to hide from them.'

He placed Smith-Oldwick, with his pistol, at the north opening of their haven and told Otobu to stand with his spear at the Englishman's shoulder, while he himself prepared to guard the southern approach. 'You will be safe there in the event that they use their spears,' he said.

The minutes that dragged by seemed veritable eternities to Bertha Kircher and then at last, and almost with relief, she knew that the pursuers were upon them. She heard the angry roaring of the lions and the cries of the madmen. For several minutes the men seemed to be investigating the stronghold which their quarry had discovered. She could hear them both to the north and south and then from where she lay she saw a lion charging for the ape-man before her. She saw the giant arm swing back with the curved saber and she saw it fall with terrific velocity and meet the lion as he rose to grapple with the man, cleaving his skull as cleanly as a butcher opens up a sheep.

Then she heard footsteps running rapidly toward Smith-Oldwick and, as his pistol spoke, there was a scream and the sound of a falling body. Evidently disheartened by the failure of their first attempt the assaulters drew off, but only for a short time. Again they came, this time a man opposing Tarzan and a lion seeking to overcome Smith-Oldwick. Tarzan had cautioned the young Englishman not to waste his cartridges upon the lions and it was Otobu with the Xujan spear who met the beast, which was not subdued until both he and Smith-Oldwick had been mauled, and the latter had succeeded in running the point of the saber the girl had carried, into the beast's heart. The man who opposed Tarzan inadvertently came too close in an attempt to cut at the ape-man's head, with the result that an instant later his corpse lay with the neck broken upon the body of the lion.

Once again the enemy withdrew, but again only for a short time, and now they came in full force, the lions and the men, possibly a half dozen of each, the men casting their spears and the lions waiting just behind, evidently for the signal to charge.

'Is this the end?' asked the girl.

'No,' cried the ape-man, 'for we still live!'

The words had scarcely passed his lips when the remaining warriors, rushing in, cast their spears simultaneously from both sides. In attempting to shield the girl, Tarzan received one of the shafts in the shoulder, and so heavily had the weapon been hurled that it bore him backward to the ground. Smith-Oldwick fired his pistol twice when he too was struck down, the weapon entering his right leg midway between hip and knee. Only Otobu remained to face the enemy, for the Englishman, already weak from his wounds and from the latest mauling he had received at the claws of the lion, had lost consciousness as he sank to the ground with this new hurt.

As he fell his pistol dropped from his fingers, and the girl, seeing, snatched it up. As Tarzan struggled to rise, one of the warriors leaped full upon his breast and bore him back as, with fiendish shrieks, he raised the point of his saber above the other's heart. Before he could drive it home the girl leveled Smith-Oldwick's pistol and fired point-blank at the fiend's face.

Simultaneously there broke upon the astonished ears of both attackers and attacked a volley of shots from the gorge. With the sweetness of the voice of an angel from heaven the Europeans heard the sharp-barked commands of an English non-com. Even above the roars of the lions and the screams of the maniacs, those beloved tones reached the ears of Tarzan and the girl at the very moment that even the ape-man had given up the last vestige of hope.

Rolling the body of the warrior to one side Tarzan struggled to his feet, the spear still protruding from his shoulder. The girl rose too, and as Tarzan wrenched the weapon from his flesh and stepped out from behind the concealment of their refuge, she followed at his side. The skirmish that had resulted in their rescue was soon over. Most of the lions escaped but all of the pursuing Xujans had been slain. As Tarzan and the girl came into full view of the group, a British Tommy leveled his rifle at the ape-man. Seeing the fellow's actions and realizing instantly the natural error that Tarzan's yellow tunic had occasioned the girl sprang between him and the soldier. 'Don't shoot,' she cried to the latter, 'we are both friends.'

'Hold up your hands, you, then,' he commanded Tarzan. 'I ain't taking no chances with any duffer with a yellow shirt.'

At this juncture the British sergeant who had been in command of the advance guard approached and when Tarzan and the girl spoke to him in English, explaining their disguises, he accepted their word, since they were evidently not of the same race as the creatures which lay dead about them. Ten minutes later the main body of the expedition came into view. Smith-Oldwick's wounds were dressed, as well as were those of the ape-man, and in half an hour they were on their way to the camp of their rescuers.

That night it was arranged that the following day Smith-Oldwick and Bertha Kircher should be transported to British headquarters near the coast by airplane, the two planes attached to the expeditionary force being requisitioned for the purpose. Tarzan and Otobu declined the offers of the British captain to accompany his force overland on the return march as Tarzan explained that his country lay to the west, as did Otobu's, and that they would travel together as far as the country of the Wamabos.

'You are not going back with us, then?' asked the girl.

'No,' replied the ape-man. 'My home is upon the west coast. I will continue my journey in that direction.'

She cast appealing eyes toward him. 'You will go back into that terrible jungle?' she asked. 'We shall never see you again?'

He looked at her a moment in silence. 'Never,' he said, and without another word turned and walked away.

In the morning Colonel Capell came from the base camp in one of the planes that was to carry Smith-Oldwick and the girl to the east. Tarzan was standing some distance away as the ship landed and the officer descended to the ground. He saw the colonel greet his junior in command of the advance detachment, and then he saw him turn toward Bertha Kircher who was standing a few paces behind the captain. Tarzan wondered how the German spy felt in this situation, especially when she must know that there was one there who knew her real status. He saw Colonel Capell walk toward her with outstretched hands and smiling face and, although he could not hear the words of his greeting, he saw that it was friendly and cordial to a degree.

Tarzan turned away scowling, and if any had been close by they might have heard a low growl rumble from his chest. He knew that his country was at war with Germany and that not only his duty to the land of his fathers, but also his personal grievance against the enemy people and his hatred of them, demanded that he expose the girl's perfidy, and yet he hesitated, and because he hesitated he growled – not at the German spy but at himself for his weakness.

He did not see her again before she entered a plane and was borne away toward the east. He bid farewell to Smith-Oldwick and received again the oft-repeated thanks of the young Englishman. And then he saw him too borne aloft in the high circling plane and watched until the ship became a speck far above the eastern horizon to disappear at last high in the air.

The Tommies, their packs and accouterments slung, were waiting the summons to continue their return march. Colonel Capell had, through a desire to personally observe the stretch of country between the camp of the advance detachment and the base, decided to march back his troops. Now that all was in readiness for departure he turned to Tarzan. 'I wish you would come back with us, Greystoke,' he said, 'and if my appeal carries no inducement possibly that of Smith-Oldwick and the young lady who just left us may. They asked me to urge you to return to civilization.'

'No,' said Tarzan, 'I shall go my own way. Miss Kircher and Lieutenant Smith-Oldwick were only prompted by a sense of gratitude in considering my welfare.'

'Miss Kircher?' exclaimed Capell and then he laughed. 'You know her then as Bertha Kircher, the German spy?'

Tarzan looked at the other a moment in silence. It was beyond him to conceive that a British officer should thus laconically speak of an enemy spy whom he had had within his power and permitted to escape. 'Yes,' he replied, 'I knew that she was Bertha Kircher, the German spy.'

'Is that all you knew?' asked Capell.

'That is all,' said the ape-man.

'She is the Honorable Patricia Canby,' said Capell; 'one of the most valuable members of the British Intelligence Service attached to the East African forces. Her father and I served in India together and I have known her ever since she was born.

'Why, here's a packet of papers she took from a German officer and has been carrying it through all her vicissitudes – single-minded in the performance of her duty. Look! I haven't yet had time to examine them but as you see here is a military sketch map, a bundle of reports, and the diary of one Hauptmann Fritz Schneider.'

'The diary of Hauptmann Fritz Schneider!' repeated Tarzan in a constrained voice. 'May I see it, Capell? He is the man who murdered Lady Greystoke.'

The Englishman handed the little volume over to the other without a word. Tarzan ran through the pages quickly looking for a certain date – the date that the horror had been committed – and when he found it he read rapidly. Suddenly a gasp of incredulity burst from his lips. Capell looked at him questioningly.

'God!' exclaimed the ape-man. 'Can this be true? Listen!' and he read an excerpt from the closely written page:

'"Played a little joke on the English pig. When he comes home he will find the burned body of his wife in her boudoir – but he will only *think* it is his wife. Had von Goss substitute the body of a dead Negress and char it after putting Lady Greystoke's rings on it – Lady G will be of more value to the High Command alive than dead."'

'She lives!' cried Tarzan.

'Thank God!' exclaimed Capell. 'And now?'

'I will return with you, of course. How terribly I have wronged Miss Canby, but how could I know? I even told Smith-Oldwick, who loves her, that she was a German spy.

'Not only must I return to find my wife but I must right this wrong.'

'Don't worry about that,' said Capell; 'she must have convinced him that she is no enemy spy, for just before they left this morning he told me she had promised to marry him.'

TARZAN THE TERRIBLE

1

The Pithecanthropus

Silent as the shadows through which he moved, the great beast slunk through the midnight jungle, his yellow-green eyes round and staring, his sinewy tail undulating behind him, his head lowered and flattened, and every muscle vibrant to the thrill of the hunt. The jungle moon dappled an occasional clearing which the great cat was always careful to avoid. Though he moved through thick verdure across a carpet of innumerable twigs, broken branches, and leaves, his passing gave forth no sound that might have been apprehended by dull human ears.

Apparently less cautious was the hunted thing moving even as silently as the lion a hundred paces ahead of the tawny carnivore, for instead of skirting the moon-splashed natural clearings it passed directly across them, and by the tortuous record of its spoor it might indeed be guessed that it sought these avenues of least resistance, as well it might, since, unlike its grim stalker, it walked erect upon two feet – it walked upon two feet and was hairless except for a black thatch upon its head; its arms were well shaped and muscular; its hands powerful and slender with long tapering fingers and thumbs reaching almost to the first joint of the index fingers. Its legs too were shapely but its feet departed from the standards of all races of men, except possibly a few of the lowest races, in that the great toes protruded at right angles from the foot.

Pausing momentarily in the full light of the gorgeous African moon the creature turned an attentive ear to the rear and then, his head lifted, his features might readily have been discerned in the moonlight. They were strong, clean cut, and regular – features that would have attracted attention for their masculine beauty in any of the great capitals of the world. But was this thing a man? It would have been hard for a watcher in the trees to have decided as the lion's prey resumed its way across the silver tapestry that Luna had laid upon the floor of the dismal jungle, for from beneath the loincloth of black fur that girdled its thighs there depended a long hairless, white tail.

In one hand the creature carried a stout club, and suspended at its left side from a shoulder belt was a short, sheathed knife, while a cross belt supported a pouch at its right hip. Confining these straps to the body and also apparently supporting the loincloth was a broad girdle which glittered in the moonlight as though encrusted with virgin gold, and was clasped in the center of the belly with a huge buckle of ornate design that scintillated as with precious stones.

Closer and closer crept Numa, the lion, to his intended victim, and that the latter was not entirely unaware of his danger was evidenced by the increasing frequency with which he turned his ear and his sharp black eyes in the direction of the cat upon his trail. He did not greatly increase his speed, a long swinging walk where the open places permitted, but he loosened the knife in its scabbard and at all times kept his club in readiness for instant action.

Forging at last through a narrow strip of dense jungle vegetation the man-thing broke through into an almost treeless area of considerable extent. For an instant he hesitated, glancing quickly behind him and then up at the security of the branches of the great trees waving overhead, but some greater urge than fear or caution influenced his decision apparently, for he moved off again across the little plain leaving the safety of the trees behind him. At greater or less intervals leafy sanctuaries dotted the grassy expanse ahead of him and the route he took, leading from one to another, indicated that he had not entirely cast discretion to the winds. But after the second tree had been left behind the distance to the next was considerable, and it was then that Numa walked from the concealing cover of the jungle and, seeing his quarry apparently helpless before him, raised his tail stiffly erect and charged.

Two months – two long, weary months filled with hunger, with thirst, with hardships, with disappointment, and, greater than all, with gnawing pain – had passed since Tarzan of the Apes learned from the diary of the dead German captain that his wife still lived. A brief investigation in which he was enthusiastically aided by the Intelligence Department of the British East African Expedition revealed the fact that an attempt had been made to keep Lady Jane in hiding in the interior, for reasons of which only the German High Command might be cognizant.

In charge of Lieutenant Obergatz and a detachment of native German troops she had been sent across the border into the Congo Free State.

Starting out alone in search of her, Tarzan had succeeded in finding the village in which she had been incarcerated only to learn that she had escaped months before, and that the German officer had disappeared at the same time. From there on the stories of the chiefs and the warriors whom he quizzed were vague and often contradictory. Even the direction that the fugitives had taken Tarzan could only guess at by piecing together bits of fragmentary evidence gleaned from various sources.

Sinister conjectures were forced upon him by various observations which he made in the village. One was incontrovertible proof that these people were man-eaters; the other, the presence in the village of various articles of native German uniforms and equipment. At great risk and in the face of surly objection on the part of the chief, the ape-man made a careful inspection of every hut in the village from which at least a little ray of hope resulted from the fact that he found no article that might have belonged to his wife.

Leaving the village he had made his way toward the southwest, crossing, after the most appalling hardships, a vast waterless steppe covered for the most part with dense thorn, coming at last into a district that had probably never been previously entered by any white man and which was known only in the legends of the tribes whose country bordered it. Here were precipitous mountains, well-watered plateaus, wide plains, and vast swampy morasses, but neither the plains, nor the plateaus, nor the mountains were accessible to him until after weeks of arduous effort he succeeded in finding a spot where he might cross the morasses – a hideous stretch infested by venomous snakes and other larger dangerous reptiles. On several occasions he glimpsed at distances or by night what might have been titanic reptilian monsters, but as there were hippopotami, rhinoceri, and elephants in great numbers in and about the marsh he was never positive that the forms he saw were not of these.

When at last he stood upon firm ground after crossing the morasses he realized why it was that for perhaps countless ages this territory had defied the courage and hardihood of the heroic races of the outer world that had, after innumerable reverses and unbelievable suffering penetrated to practically every other region, from pole to pole.

From the abundance and diversity of the game it might have appeared that every known species of bird and beast and reptile had sought here a refuge wherein they might take their last stand against the encroaching multitudes of men that had steadily spread themselves over the surface of the earth, wresting the hunting grounds from the lower orders, from the moment that the first ape shed his hair and ceased to walk upon his knuckles. Even the species with which Tarzan was familiar showed here either the results of a divergent line of evolution or an unaltered form that had been transmitted without variation for countless ages.

Too, there were many hybrid strains, not the least interesting of which to Tarzan was a yellow and black striped lion. Smaller than the species with which Tarzan was familiar, but still a most formidable beast, since it possessed in addition to sharp saberlike canines the disposition of a devil. To Tarzan it presented evidence that tigers had once roamed the jungles of Africa, possibly giant saber-tooths of another epoch, and these apparently had crossed with lions with the resultant terrors that he occasionally encountered at the present day.

The true lions of this new, Old World differed but little from those with which he was familiar; in size and conformation they were almost identical, but instead of shedding the leopard spots of cubhood, they retained them through life as definitely marked as those of the leopard.

Two months of effort had revealed no slightest evidence that she he sought had entered this beautiful yet forbidding land. His investigation, however, of the cannibal village and his questioning of other tribes in the neighborhood had convinced him that if Lady Jane still lived it must be in this direction that he seek her, since by a process of elimination he had reduced the direction of her flight to only this possibility. How she had crossed the morass he could not guess and yet something within seemed to urge upon him belief that she had crossed it, and that if she still lived it was here that she must be sought. But this unknown, untraversed wild was of vast extent; grim, forbidding mountains blocked his way, torrents tumbling from rocky fastnesses impeded his progress, and at every turn he was forced to match wits and muscles with the great carnivora that he might procure sustenance.

Time and again Tarzan and Numa stalked the same quarry and now one, now the other bore off the prize. Seldom however did the ape-man go hungry for the country was rich in game animals and birds and fish, in fruit and the countless other forms of vegetable life upon which the jungle-bred man may subsist.

Tarzan often wondered why in so rich a country he found no evidences of man and had at last come to the conclusion that the parched, thorn-covered steppe and the hideous morasses had formed a sufficient barrier to protect this country effectively from the inroads of mankind.

After days of searching he had succeeded finally in discovering a pass through the mountains and coming down upon the opposite side, had found himself in a country practically identical with that which he had left. The hunting was good and at a water hole in the mouth of a canyon where it debouched upon a tree-covered plain Bara, the deer, fell an easy victim to the ape-man's cunning.

It was just at dusk. The voices of great four-footed hunters rose now and again from various directions, and as the canyon afforded among its trees no comfortable retreat the ape-man shouldered the carcass of the deer and started downward onto the plain. At its opposite side rose lofty trees – a great forest which suggested to his practiced eye a mighty jungle. Toward this the ape-man bent his step, but when midway of the plain he discovered standing alone such a tree as best suited him for a night's abode, swung lightly to its branches and, presently, a comfortable resting place.

Here he ate the flesh of Bara and when satisfied carried the balance of the carcass to the opposite side of the tree where he deposited it far above the ground in a secure place. Returning to his crotch he settled himself for sleep and in another moment the roars of the lions and the howlings of the lesser cats fell upon deaf ears.

The usual noises of the jungle composed rather than disturbed the ape-man but an unusual sound, however imperceptible to the awakened ear of civilized man, seldom failed to impinge upon the consciousness of Tarzan, however deep his slumber, and so it was that when the moon was high a sudden rush of feet across the grassy carpet in the vicinity of his tree brought him to alert and ready activity. Tarzan does not awaken as you and I with the weight of slumber still upon his eyes and brain, for did the creatures of the wild awaken thus, their awakenings would be few. As his eyes snapped open, clear and bright, so, clear and bright upon the nerve centers of his brain, were registered the various perceptions of all his senses.

Almost beneath him, racing toward his tree was what at first glance appeared to be an almost naked white man, yet even at the first instant of discovery the long, white tail projecting rearward did not escape the ape-man. Behind the fleeing figure, and now so close as to preclude the possibility of its quarry escaping, came Numa, the lion, in full charge. Voiceless the prey, voiceless the killer; as two spirits in a dead world the two moved in silent swiftness toward the culminating tragedy of this grim race.

Even as his eyes opened and took in the scene beneath him – even in that brief instant of perception, followed reason, judgment, and decision, so rapidly one upon the heels of the other that almost simultaneously the ape-man was in midair, for he had seen a white-skinned creature cast in a mold similar to his own, pursued by Tarzan's hereditary enemy. So close was the lion to the fleeing man-thing that Tarzan had no time carefully to choose the method of his attack. As a diver leaps from the springboard headforemost into the waters beneath, so Tarzan of the Apes dove straight for Numa, the lion; naked in his right hand the blade of his father that so many times before had tasted the blood of lions.

A raking talon caught Tarzan on the side, inflicting a long, deep wound and then the ape-man was on Numa's back and the blade was sinking again and again into the savage side. Nor was the man-thing either longer fleeing, or idle. He too, creature of the wild, had sensed on the instant the truth of the miracle of his saving, and turning in his tracks, had leaped forward with raised bludgeon to Tarzan's assistance and Numa's undoing. A single terrific blow upon the flattened skull of the beast laid him insensible and then as Tarzan's knife found the wild heart a few convulsive shudders and a sudden relaxation marked the passing of the carnivore.

Leaping to his feet the ape-man placed his foot upon the carcass of his kill and, raising his face to Goro, the moon, voiced the savage victory cry that had so often awakened the echoes of his native jungle.

As the hideous scream burst from the ape-man's lips the manthing stepped quickly back as in sudden awe, but when Tarzan returned his hunting knife to its sheath and turned toward him the other saw in the quiet dignity of his demeanor no cause for apprehension.

For a moment the two stood appraising each other, and then the man-thing spoke. Tarzan realized that the creature before him was uttering articulate sounds which expressed in speech, though in a language with which Tarzan was unfamiliar, the thoughts of a man possessing to a greater or less extent the same powers of reason that he possessed. In other words, that though the creature before him had the tail and thumbs and great toes of a monkey, it was, in all other respects, quite evidently a man.

The blood, which was now flowing down Tarzan's side, caught the creature's attention. From the pocket-pouch at his side he took a small bag and approaching Tarzan indicated by signs that he wished the ape-man to lie down that he might treat the wound, whereupon, spreading the edges of the cut apart, he sprinkled the raw flesh with powder from the little bag. The pain of the wound was as nothing to the exquisite torture of the remedy but, accustomed to physical suffering, the ape-man withstood it stoically and in a few moments not only had the bleeding ceased but the pain as well.

In reply to the soft and far from unpleasant modulations of the other's voice, Tarzan spoke in various tribal dialects of the interior as well as in the language of the great apes, but it was evident that the man understood none of these. Seeing that they could not make each other understood, the pithecanthropus advanced toward Tarzan and placing his left hand over his own heart laid the palm of his right hand over the heart of the ape-man. To the latter the action appeared as a form of friendly greeting and, being versed in the ways of uncivilized races, he responded in kind as he realized it was doubtless intended that he should. His action seemed to satisfy and please his newfound acquaintance, who immediately fell to talking again and finally, with his head tipped back, sniffed the air in the direction of the tree above them and then suddenly pointing toward the carcass of Bara, the deer, he touched his stomach in a sign language which even the densest might interpret. With a wave of his hand Tarzan invited his guest to partake of the remains of his savage repast, and the other, leaping nimbly as a little monkey to the lower branches of the tree, made his way quickly to the flesh, assisted always by his long, strong sinuous tail.

The pithecanthropus ate in silence, cutting small strips from the deer's loin with his keen knife. From his crotch in the tree Tarzan watched his companion, noting the preponderance of human attributes which were doubtless accentuated by the paradoxical thumbs, great toes, and tail.

He wondered if this creature was representative of some strange race or if, what seemed more likely, but an atavism. Either supposition would have seemed preposterous enough did he not have before him the evidence of the creature's existence. There he was, however, a tailed man with distinctly arboreal hands and feet. His trappings, gold encrusted and jewel studded, could have been wrought only by skilled artisans; but whether they were the work of this individual or of others like him, or of an entirely different race, Tarzan could not, of course, determine.

His meal finished, the guest wiped his fingers and lips with leaves broken from a nearby branch, looked up at Tarzan with a pleasant smile that revealed a row of strong white teeth, the canines of which were no longer than Tarzan's own, spoke a few words which Tarzan judged were a polite expression of thanks and then sought a comfortable place in the tree for the night.

The earth was shadowed in the darkness which precedes the dawn when Tarzan was awakened by a violent shaking of the tree in which he had found shelter. As he opened his eyes he saw that his companion was also astir, and glancing around quickly to apprehend the cause of the disturbance, the ape-man was astounded at the sight which met his eyes.

The dim shadow of a colossal form reared close beside the tree and he saw that it was the scraping of the giant body against the branches that had awakened him. That such a tremendous creature could have approached so closely without disturbing him filled Tarzan with both wonderment and chagrin. In the gloom the ape-man at first conceived the intruder to be an elephant; yet, if so, one of greater proportions than any he had ever before seen, but as the dim outlines became less indistinct he saw on a line with his eyes and twenty feet above the ground the dim silhouette of a grotesquely serrated back that gave the impression of a creature whose each and every spinal vertebra grew a thick, heavy horn. Only a portion of the back was visible to the ape-man, the rest of the body being lost in the dense shadows beneath the tree, from whence there now arose the sound of giant jaws powerfully crunching flesh and bones. From the odors that rose to the ape-man's sensitive nostrils he presently realized that beneath him was some huge reptile feeding upon the carcass of the lion that had been slain there earlier in the night.

As Tarzan's eyes, straining with curiosity, bored futilely into the dark shadows he felt a light touch upon his shoulder, and, turning, saw that his companion was attempting to attract his attention. The creature, pressing a forefinger to his own lips as to enjoin silence, attempted by pulling on Tarzan's arm to indicate that they should leave at once.

Realizing that he was in a strange country, evidently infested by creatures of titanic size, with the habits and powers of which he was entirely unfamiliar, the ape-man permitted himself to be drawn away. With the utmost caution the pithecanthropus descended the tree upon the opposite side from the great nocturnal prowler, and, closely followed by Tarzan, moved silently away through the night across the plain.

The ape-man was rather loath thus to relinquish an opportunity to inspect a creature which he realized was probably entirely different from anything in his past experience; yet he was wise enough to know when discretion was the better part of valor and now, as in the past, he yielded to that law which dominates the kindred of the wild, preventing them from courting danger uselessly, whose lives are sufficiently filled with danger in their ordinary routine of feeding and mating.

As the rising sun dispelled the shadows of the night, Tarzan found himself again upon the verge of a great forest into which his guide plunged, taking nimbly to the branches of the trees through which he made his way with the celerity of long habitude and hereditary instinct, but though aided by a prehensile tail, fingers, and toes, the man-thing moved through the forest with no greater ease or surety than did the giant ape-man.

It was during this journey that Tarzan recalled the wound in his side inflicted upon him the previous night by the raking talons of Numa, the lion, and examining it was surprised to discover that not only was it painless but along its edges were no indications of inflammation, the results doubtless of the antiseptic powder his strange companion had sprinkled upon it.

They had proceeded for a mile or two when Tarzan's companion came to earth upon a grassy slope beneath a great tree whose branches overhung a clear brook. Here they drank and Tarzan discovered the water to be not only deliciously pure and fresh but of an icy temperature that indicated its rapid descent from the lofty mountains of its origin.

Casting aside his loincloth and weapons Tarzan entered the little pool beneath the tree and after a moment emerged, greatly refreshed and filled with a keen desire to breakfast. As he came out of the pool he noticed his companion examining him with a puzzled expression upon his face. Taking the ape-man by the shoulder he turned him around so that Tarzan's back was toward him and then, touching the end of Tarzan's spine with his forefinger, he curled his own tail up over his shoulder and, wheeling the ape-man about again, pointed first at Tarzan and then at his own caudal appendage, a look of puzzlement upon his face, the while he jabbered excitedly in his strange tongue.

The ape-man realized that probably for the first time his companion had discovered that he was tailless by nature rather than by accident, and so he called attention to his own great toes and thumbs to further impress upon the creature that they were of different species.

The fellow shook his head dubiously as though entirely unable to comprehend why Tarzan should differ so from him but at last, apparently giving the problem up with a shrug, he laid aside his own harness, skin, and weapons and entered the pool.

His ablutions completed and his meager apparel redonned he seated himself at the foot of the tree and motioning Tarzan to a place beside him, opened the pouch that hung at his right side taking from it strips of dried flesh and a couple of handfuls of thin-shelled nuts with which Tarzan was unfamiliar. Seeing the other break them with his teeth and eat the kernel, Tarzan followed the example thus set him, discovering the meat to be rich and well flavored. The dried flesh also was far from unpalatable, though it had evidently been jerked without salt, a commodity which Tarzan imagined might be rather difficult to obtain in this locality.

As they ate Tarzan's companion pointed to the nuts, the dried meat, and various other nearby objects, in each instance repeating what Tarzan readily discovered must be the names of these things in the creature's native language. The ape-man could but smile at this evident desire upon the part of his newfound acquaintance to impart to him instructions that eventually might lead to an exchange of thoughts between them. Having already mastered several languages and a multitude of dialects the ape-man felt that he could readily assimilate another even though this appeared one entirely unrelated to any with which he was familiar.

So occupied were they with their breakfast and the lesson that neither was aware of the beady eyes glittering down upon them from above; nor was Tarzan cognizant of any impending danger until the instant that a huge, hairy body leaped full upon his companion from the branches above them.

2

'To the Death!'

In the moment of discovery Tarzan saw that the creature was almost a counterpart of his companion in size and conformation, with the exception that his body was entirely clothed with a coat of shaggy black hair which almost concealed his features, while his harness and weapons were similar to those of the creature he had attacked. Ere Tarzan could prevent the creature had struck the ape-man's companion a blow upon the head with his knotted club that felled him, unconscious, to the earth; but before he could inflict further injury upon his defenseless prey the ape-man had closed with him.

Instantly Tarzan realized that he was locked with a creature of almost superhuman strength. The sinewy fingers of a powerful hand sought his throat while the other lifted the bludgeon above his head. But if the strength of the hairy attacker was great, great too was that of his smooth-skinned antagonist. Swinging a single terrific blow with clenched fist to the point of the other's chin, Tarzan momentarily staggered his assailant and then his own fingers closed upon the shaggy throat, as with the other hand he seized the wrist of the arm that swung the club. With equal celerity he shot his right leg behind the shaggy brute and throwing his weight forward hurled the thing over his hip heavily to the ground, at the same time precipitating his own body upon the other's chest.

With the shock of the impact the club fell from the brute's hand and Tarzan's hold was wrenched from its throat. Instantly the two were locked in a deathlike embrace. Though the creature bit at Tarzan the latter was quickly aware that this was not a particularly formidable method of offense or defense, since its canines were scarcely more developed than his own. The thing that he had principally to guard against was the sinuous tail which sought steadily to wrap itself about his throat and against which experience had afforded him no defense.

Struggling and snarling the two rolled growling about the sward at the foot of the tree, first one on top and then the other but each more occupied at present in defending his throat from the other's choking grasp than in aggressive, offensive tactics. But presently the ape-man saw his opportunity and as they rolled about he forced the creature closer and closer to the pool, upon the banks of which the battle was progressing. At last they lay upon the very verge of the water and now it remained for Tarzan to precipitate them both beneath the surface but in such a way that he might remain on top.

At the same instant there came within range of Tarzan's vision, just behind the prostrate form of his companion the crouching, devil-faced figure of the striped saber-tooth hybrid, eyeing him with snarling, malevolent face.

Almost simultaneously Tarzan's shaggy antagonist discovered the menacing figure of the great cat. Immediately he ceased his belligerent activities against Tarzan and, jabbering and chattering to the ape-man, he tried to disengage himself from Tarzan's hold but in such a way that indicated that as far as he was concerned their battle was over. Appreciating the danger to his unconscious companion and being anxious to protect him from the saber-tooth the ape-man relinquished his hold upon his adversary and together the two rose to their feet.

Drawing his knife Tarzan moved slowly toward the body of his companion, expecting that his recent antagonist would grasp the opportunity for escape. To his surprise, however, the beast, after regaining its club, advanced at his side.

The great cat, flattened upon its belly, remained motionless except for twitching tail and snarling lips where it lay perhaps fifty feet beyond the body of the pithecanthropus. As Tarzan stepped over the body of the latter he saw the eyelids quiver and open, and in his heart he felt a strange sense of relief that the creature was not dead and a realization that without his suspecting it there had arisen within his savage bosom a bond of attachment for this strange new friend.

Tarzan continued to approach the saber-tooth, nor did the shaggy beast at his right lag behind. Closer and closer they came until at a distance of about twenty feet the hybrid charged. Its rush was directed toward the shaggy manlike ape who halted in his tracks with upraised bludgeon to meet the assault. Tarzan, on the contrary, leaped forward and with a celerity second not even to that of the swift-moving cat, he threw himself headlong upon him as might a rugby tackler on an American gridiron. His right arm circled the beast's neck in front of the right shoulder, his left behind the left foreleg, and so great was the force of the impact that the two rolled over and over several times upon the ground, the cat screaming and clawing to liberate itself that it might turn upon its attacker, the man clinging desperately to his hold.

Seemingly the attack was one of mad, senseless ferocity unguided by either reason or skill. Nothing, however, could have been farther from the truth than such an assumption since every muscle in the ape-man's giant frame obeyed the dictates of the cunning mind that long experience had trained to meet every exigency of such an encounter. The long, powerful legs, though seemingly inextricably entangled with the hind feet of the clawing cat, ever as by a miracle, escaped the raking talons and yet at just the proper instant in the midst of all the rolling and tossing they were where they should be to carry out the ape-man's plan of offense. So that on the instant that the cat believed it had won the mastery of its antagonist it was jerked suddenly upward as the ape-man rose to his feet, holding the striped back close against his body as he rose and forcing it backward until it could but claw the air helplessly.

Instantly the shaggy black rushed in with drawn knife which it buried in the beast's heart. For a few moments Tarzan retained his hold but when the body had relaxed in final dissolution he pushed it from him and the two who had formerly been locked in mortal combat stood facing each other across the body of the common foe.

Tarzan waited, ready either for peace or war. Presently two shaggy black hands were raised; the left was laid upon its own heart and the right extended until the palm touched Tarzan's breast. It was the same form of friendly salutation with which the pithecanthropus had sealed his alliance with the ape-man and Tarzan, glad of every ally he could win in this strange and savage world, quickly accepted the proffered friendship.

At the conclusion of the brief ceremony Tarzan, glancing in the direction of the hairless pithecanthropus, discovered that the latter had recovered consciousness and was sitting erect watching them intently. He now rose slowly and at the same time the shaggy black turned in his direction and addressed him in what evidently was their common language. The hairless one replied and the two approached each other slowly. Tarzan watched interestedly the outcome of their meeting. They halted a few paces apart, first one and then the other speaking rapidly but without apparent excitement, each occasionally glancing or nodding toward Tarzan, indicating that he was to some extent the subject of their conversation.

Presently they advanced again until they met, whereupon was repeated the brief ceremony of alliance which had previously marked the cessation of hostilities between Tarzan and the black. They then advanced toward the ape-man addressing him earnestly as though endeavoring to convey to him some important information. Presently, however, they gave it up as an unprofitable job and, resorting to sign language, conveyed to Tarzan that they were proceeding upon their way together and were urging him to accompany them.

As the direction they indicated was a route which Tarzan had not previously traversed he was extremely willing to accede to their request, as he had determined thoroughly to explore this unknown land before definitely abandoning search for Lady Jane therein.

For several days their way led through the foothills parallel to the lofty range towering above. Often were they menaced by the savage denizens of this remote fastness, and occasionally Tarzan glimpsed weird forms of gigantic proportions amidst the shadows of the nights.

On the third day they came upon a large natural cave in the face of a low cliff at the foot of which tumbled one of the numerous mountain brooks that watered the plain below and fed the morasses in the lowlands at the country's edge. Here the three took up their temporary abode where Tarzan's instruction in the language of his companions progressed more rapidly than while on the march.

The cave gave evidence of having harbored other manlike forms in the past. Remnants of a crude, rock fireplace remained and the walls and ceiling were blackened with the smoke of many fires. Scratched in the soot, and sometimes deeply into the rock beneath, were strange hieroglyphics and the outlines of beasts and birds and reptiles, some of the latter of weird form suggesting the extinct creatures of Jurassic times. Some of the more recently made hieroglyphics Tarzan's companions read with interest and commented upon, and then with the points of their knives they too added to the possibly age-old record of the blackened walls.

Tarzan's curiosity was aroused, but the only explanation at which he could arrive was that he was looking upon possibly the world's most primitive hotel register. At least it gave him a further insight into the development of the strange creatures with which Fate had thrown him. Here were men with the tails of monkeys, one of them as hair covered as any fur-bearing brute of the lower orders, and yet it was evident that they possessed not only a spoken, but a written language. The former he was slowly mastering and at this new evidence of unlooked-for civilization in creatures possessing so many of the physical attributes of beasts, Tarzan's curiosity was still further piqued and his desire quickly to master their tongue strengthened, with the result that he fell to with even greater assiduity to the task he had set himself. Already he knew the names of his companions and the common names of the fauna and flora with which they had most often come in contact.

Ta-den, he of the hairless, white skin, having assumed the role of tutor, prosecuted his task with a singleness of purpose that was reflected in his pupil's rapid mastery of Ta-den's mother tongue. Om-at, the hairy black, also seemed to feel that there rested upon his broad shoulders a portion of the burden of responsibility for Tarzan's education, with the result that either one or the other of them was almost constantly coaching the ape-man during his waking hours. The result was only what might have been expected – a rapid assimilation of the teachings to the end that before any of them realized it, communication by word of mouth became an accomplished fact.

Tarzan explained to his companions the purpose of his mission but neither could give him any slightest thread of hope to weave into the fabric of his longing. Never had there been in their country a woman such as he described, nor any tailless man other than himself that they ever had seen.

'I have been gone from A-lur while Bu, the moon, has eaten seven times,' said Ta-den. 'Many things may happen in seven times twenty-eight days; but I doubt that your woman could have entered our country across the terrible morasses which even you found an almost insurmountable obstacle, and if she had, could she have survived the perils that you already have encountered beside those of which you have yet to learn? Not even our own women venture into the savage lands beyond the cities.'

'"A-lur," Light-city, City of Light,' mused Tarzan, translating the word into his own tongue. 'And where is A-lur?' he asked. 'Is it your city, Ta-den, and Om-at's?'

'It is mine,' replied the hairless one; 'but not Om-at's. The Waz-don have no cities – they live in the trees of the forests and the caves of the hills – is it not so, *black man*?' he concluded, turning toward the hairy giant beside him.

'Yes,' replied Om-at, 'we Waz-don are free – only the Ho-don imprison themselves in cities. I would not be a white man!'

Tarzan smiled. Even here was the racial distinction between white man and black man – Ho-don and Waz-don. Not even the fact that they appeared to be equals in the matter of intelligence made any difference – one was white and one was black, and it was easy to see that the white considered himself superior to the other – one could see it in his quiet smile.

'Where is A-lur?' Tarzan asked again. 'You are returning to it?'

'It is beyond the mountains,' replied Ta-den. 'I do not return to it – not yet. Not until Ko-tan is no more.'

'Ko-tan?' queried Tarzan:

'Ko-tan is king,' explained the pithecanthropus. 'He rules this land. I was one of his warriors. I lived in the palace of Ko-tan and there I met O-lo-a, his daughter. We loved, Like-star-light, and I; but Ko-tan would have none of me. He sent me away to fight with the men of the village of Dak-at, who had refused to pay his tribute to the king, thinking that I would be killed, for Dak-at is famous for his many fine warriors. And I was not killed. Instead I returned victorious with the tribute and with Dak-at himself my prisoner; but Ko-tan was not pleased because he saw that O-lo-a loved me even more than before, her love being strengthened and fortified by pride in my achievement.

'Powerful is my father, Ja-don, the Lion-man, chief of the largest village outside of A-lur. Him Ko-tan hesitated to affront and so he could not but praise me for my success, though he did it with half a smile. But you do not understand! It is what we call a smile that moves only the muscles of the face and effects not the light of the eyes – it means hypocrisy and duplicity. I must be praised and rewarded. What better than that he reward me with the hand of O-lo-a, his daughter? But no, he saves O-lo-a for Bu-lot, son of Mo-sar, the chief whose great-grandfather was king and who thinks that he should be king. Thus would Ko-tan appease the wrath of Mo-sar and win the friendship of those who think with Mo-sar that Mo-sar should be king.

'But what reward shall repay the faithful Ta-den? Greatly do we honor our priests. Within the temples even the chiefs and the king himself bow down to them. No greater honor could Ko-tan confer upon a subject – who wished to be a priest; but I did not so wish. Priests other than the high priest must become eunuchs for they may never marry.

'It was O-lo-a herself who brought word to me that her father had given the commands that would set in motion the machinery of the temple. A messenger was on his way in search of me to summon me to Ko-tan's presence. To have refused the priesthood once it was offered me by the king would have been to have affronted the temple and the gods – that would have meant death; but if I did not appear before Ko-tan I would not have to refuse anything. O-lo-a and I decided that I must not appear. It was better to fly, carrying in my bosom a shred of hope, than to remain and, with my priesthood, abandon hope forever.

'Beneath the shadows of the great trees that grow within the palace grounds I pressed her to me for, perhaps, the last time and then, lest by ill-fate I meet the messenger, I scaled the great wall that guards the palace and passed through the darkened city. My name and rank carried me beyond the city gate. Since then I have wandered far from the haunts of the Ho-don but strong within me is the urge to return if even but to look from without her walls upon the city that holds her most dear to me and again to visit the village of my birth, to see again my father and my mother.'

'But the risk is too great?' asked Tarzan.

'It is great, but not too great,' replied Ta-den. 'I shall go.'

'And I shall go with you, if I may,' said the ape-man, 'for I must see this City of Light, this A-lur of yours, and search there for my lost mate even though you believe that there is little chance that I find her. And you, Om-at, do you come with us?'

'Why not?' asked the hairy one. 'The lairs of my tribe lie in the crags above A-lur and though Es-sat, our chief, drove me out I should like to return again, for there is a she there upon whom I should be glad to look once more and who would be glad to look upon me. Yes, I will go with you. Es-sat feared that I might become chief and who knows but that Es-sat was right. But Pan-at-lee! It is she I seek first even before a chieftainship.'

'We three, then, shall travel together,' said Tarzan.

'And fight together,' added Ta-den; 'the three as one,' and as he spoke he drew his knife and held it above his head.

'The three as one,' repeated Om-at, drawing his weapon and duplicating Ta-den's act. 'It is spoken!'

'The three as one!' cried Tarzan of the Apes. 'To the death!' and his blade flashed in the sunlight.

'Let us go, then,' said Om-at; 'my knife is dry and cries aloud for the blood of Es-sat.'

The trail over which Ta-den and Om-at led and which scarcely could be dignified even by the name of trail was suited more to mountain sheep, monkeys, or birds than to man; but the three that followed it were trained to ways which no ordinary man might essay. Now, upon the lower slopes, it led through dense forests where the ground was so matted with fallen trees and overrioting vines and brush that the way held always to the swaying branches high above the tangle; again it skirted yawning gorges whose slippery-faced rocks gave but momentary foothold even to the bare feet that lightly touched them as the three leaped chamois-like from one precarious foothold to the next. Dizzy and terrifying was the way that Om-at chose across the summit as he led them around the shoulder of a towering crag that rose a sheer two thousand feet of perpendicular rock above a tumbling river. And when at last they stood upon comparatively level ground again Om-at turned and looked at them both intently and especially at Tarzan of the Apes.

'You will both do,' he said. 'You are fit companions for Om-at, the Waz-don.'

'What do you mean?' asked Tarzan.

'I brought you this way,' replied the black, 'to learn if either lacked the courage to follow where Om-at led. It is here that the young warriors of Es-sat come to prove their courage. And yet, though we are born and raised upon cliff sides, it is considered no disgrace to admit that Pastar-ul-ved, the Father of Mountains, has defeated us, for of those who try it only a few succeed – the bones of the others lie at the feet of Pastar-ul-ved.'

Ta-den laughed. 'I would not care to come this way often,' he said.

'No,' replied Om-at; 'but it has shortened our journey by at least a full day. So much the sooner shall Tarzan look upon the Valley of Jad-ben-Otho. Come!' and he led the way upward along the shoulder of Pastar-ul-ved until there lay spread below them a scene of mystery and of beauty – a green valley girt by towering cliffs of marble whiteness – a green valley dotted by deep blue lakes and crossed by the blue trail of a winding river. In the center a city of the whiteness of the marble cliffs – a city which even at so great a distance evidenced a strange, yet artistic architecture. Outside the city there were visible about the valley isolated groups of buildings – sometimes one, again two and three and four in a cluster – but always of the same glaring whiteness, and always in some fantastic form.

About the valley the cliffs were occasionally cleft by deep gorges, verdure filled, giving the appearance of green rivers rioting downward toward a central sea of green.

'Jad Pele ul Jad-ben-Otho,' murmured Tarzan in the tongue of the pithecanthropi; '*The Valley of the Great God* – it is beautiful!'

'Here, in A-lur, lives Ko-tan, the king, ruler over all Pal-ul-don,' said Ta-den.

'And here in these gorges live the Waz-don,' exclaimed Om-at, 'who do not acknowledge that Ko-tan is the ruler over all the *Land-of-man*.'

Ta-den smiled and shrugged. 'We will not quarrel, you and I,' he said to Om-at, 'over that which all the ages have not proved sufficient time in which to reconcile the Ho-don and Waz-don; but let me whisper to you a secret, Om-at. The Ho-don live together in greater or less peace under one ruler so that when danger threatens them they face the enemy with many warriors, for every fighting Ho-don of Pal-ul-don is there. But you Waz-don, how is it with you? You have a dozen kings who fight not only with the Ho-don but with one another. When one of your tribes goes forth upon the fighting trail, even against the Ho-don, it must leave behind sufficient warriors to protect its women and its children from the neighbors upon either hand. When we want eunuchs for the temples or servants for the fields or the homes we march forth in great numbers upon one of your villages. You cannot even flee, for upon either side of you are enemies and though you fight bravely we come back with those who will presently be eunuchs in the temples and servants in our fields and homes. So long as the Waz-don are thus foolish the Ho-don will dominate and their king will be king of Pal-ul-don.'

'Perhaps you are right,' admitted Om-at. 'It is because our neighbors are fools, each thinking that his tribe is the greatest and should rule among the Waz-don. They will not admit that the warriors of my tribe are the bravest and our shes the most beautiful.'

Ta-den grinned. 'Each of the others presents precisely the same arguments that you present, Om-at,' he said, 'which, my friend, is the strongest bulwark of defense possessed by the Ho-don.'

'Come!' exclaimed Tarzan; 'such discussions often lead to quarrels and we three must have no quarrels. I, of course, am interested in learning what I can of the political and economic conditions of your land; I should like to know something of your religion; but not at the expense of bitterness between my only friends in Pal-ul-don. Possibly, however, you hold to the same god?'

'There indeed we do differ,' cried Om-at, somewhat bitterly and with a trace of excitement in his voice.

'Differ!' almost shouted Ta-den; 'and why should we not differ? Who could agree with the preposterous—'

'Stop!' cried Tarzan. 'Now, indeed, have I stirred up a hornets' nest. Let us speak no more of matters political or religious.'

'That is wiser,' agreed Om-at; 'but I might mention, for your information, that the one and only god has a long tail.'

'It is sacrilege,' cried Ta-den, laying his hand upon his knife; 'Jad-ben-Otho has no tail!'

'Stop!' shrieked Om-at, springing forward; but instantly Tarzan interposed himself between them.

'Enough!' he snapped. 'Let us be true to our oaths of friendship that we may be honorable in the sight of God in whatever form we conceive Him.'

'You are right, Tailless One,' said Ta-den. 'Come, Om-at, let us look after our friendship and ourselves, secure in the conviction that Jad-ben-Otho is sufficiently powerful to look after himself?'

'Done!' agreed Om-at; 'but—'

'No "buts," Om-at,' admonished Tarzan.

The shaggy black shrugged his shoulders and smiled. 'Shall we make our way down toward the valley?' he asked. 'The gorge below us is uninhabited; that to the left contains the caves of my people. I would see Pan-at-lee once more. Ta-den would visit his father in the valley below and Tarzan seeks entrance to A-lur in search of the mate that would be better dead than in the clutches of the Ho-don priests of Jad-ben-Otho. How shall we proceed?'

'Let us remain together as long as possible,' urged Ta-den. 'You, Om-at, must seek Pan-at-lee by night and by stealth, for three, even we three, may not hope to overcome Es-sat and all his warriors. At any time may we go to the village where my father is chief, for Ja-don always will welcome the friends of his son. But for Tarzan to enter A-lur is another matter, though there is a way and he has the courage to put it to the test – listen, come close for Jad-ben-Otho has keen ears and this he must not hear,' and with his lips close to the ears of his companions Ta-den, the Tall-tree, son of Ja-don, the Lion-man, unfolded his daring plan.

And at the same moment, a hundred miles away, a lithe figure, naked but for a loincloth and weapons, moved silently across a thorn-covered, waterless steppe, searching always along the ground before him with keen eyes and sensitive nostrils.

3

Pan-at-Lee

Night had fallen upon unchartered Pal-ul-don. A slender moon, low in the west, bathed the white faces of the chalk cliffs presented to her in a mellow, unearthly glow. Black were the shadows in Kor-ul-ja, Gorge-of-lions, where dwelt the tribe of the same name under Es-sat, their chief. From an aperture near the summit of the lofty escarpment a hairy figure emerged – the head and shoulders first – and fierce eyes scanned the cliff side in every direction.

It was Es-sat, the chief. To right and left and below he looked as though to assure himself that he was unobserved, but no other figure moved upon the cliff face, nor did another hairy body protrude from any of the numerous cave mouths from the high-flung abode of the chief to the habitations of the more lowly members of the tribe nearer the cliff's base. Then he moved outward upon the sheer face of the white chalk wall. In the half-light of the baby moon it appeared that the heavy, shaggy black figure moved across the face of the perpendicular wall in some miraculous manner, but closer examination would have revealed stout pegs, as large around as a man's wrist protruding from holes in the cliff into which they were driven. Es-sat's four handlike members and his long, sinuous tail permitted him to move with consummate ease whither he chose – a gigantic rat upon a mighty wall. As he progressed upon his way he avoided the cave mouths, passing either above or below those that lay in his path.

The outward appearance of these caves was similar. An opening from eight to as much as twenty feet long by eight high and four to six feet deep was cut into the chalklike rock of the cliff; in the back of this large opening, which formed what might be described as the front veranda of the home, was an opening about three feet wide and six feet high, evidently forming the doorway to the interior apartment or apartments. On either side of this doorway were smaller openings which it were easy to assume were windows through which light and air might find their way to the inhabitants. Similar windows were also dotted over the cliff face between the entrance porches, suggesting that the entire face of the cliff was honeycombed with apartments. From many of these smaller apertures small streams of water trickled down the escarpment, and the walls above others was blackened as by smoke. Where the water ran the wall was eroded to a depth of from a few inches to as much as a foot, suggesting that some of the tiny streams had been trickling downward to the green carpet of vegetation below for ages.

In this primeval setting the great pithecanthropus aroused no jarring discord for he was as much a part of it as the trees that grew upon the summit of the cliff or those that hid their feet among the dank ferns in the bottom of the gorge.

Now he paused before an entranceway and listened and then, noiselessly as the moonlight upon the trickling waters, he merged with the shadows of the outer porch. At the doorway leading into the interior he paused again, listening, and then quietly pushing aside the heavy skin that covered the aperture he passed within a large chamber hewn from the living rock. From the far end, through another doorway, shone a light, dimly. Toward this he crept with utmost stealth, his naked feet giving forth no sound. The knotted club that had been hanging at his back from a thong about his neck he now removed and carried in his left hand.

Beyond the second doorway was a corridor running parallel with the cliff face. In this corridor were three more doorways, one at each end and a third almost opposite that in which Es-sat stood. The light was coming from an apartment at the end of the corridor at his left. A sputtering flame rose and fell in a small stone receptacle that stood upon a table or bench of the same material, a monolithic bench fashioned at the time the room was excavated, rising massively from the floor, of which it was a part.

In one corner of the room beyond the table had been left a dais of stone about four feet wide and eight feet long. Upon this were piled a foot or so of softly tanned pelts from which the fur had not been removed. Upon the edge of this dais sat a young female Waz-don. In one hand she held a thin piece of metal, apparently of hammered gold, with serrated edges, and in the other a short, stiff brush. With these she was occupied in going over her smooth, glossy coat which bore a remarkable resemblance to plucked sealskin. Her loincloth of yellow and black striped *jato*-skin lay on the couch beside her with the circular breastplates of beaten gold, revealing the symmetrical lines of her nude figure in all its beauty and harmony of contour, for even though the creature was jet-black and entirely covered with hair yet she was undeniably beautiful.

That she was beautiful in the eyes of Es-sat, the chief, was evidenced by the gloating expression upon his fierce countenance and the increased rapidity of his breathing. Moving quickly forward he entered the room and as he did so the young she looked up. Instantly her eyes filled with terror and as quickly she seized the loincloth and with a few deft movements adjusted it about her. As she gathered up her breastplates Es-sat rounded the table and moved quickly toward her.

'What do you want?' she whispered, though she knew full well.

'Pan-at-lee,' he said, 'your chief has come for you.'

'It was for this that you sent away my father and my brothers to spy upon the Kor-ul-lul? I will not have you. Leave the cave of my ancestors!'

Es-sat smiled. It was the smile of a strong and wicked man who knows his power – not a pleasant smile at all. 'I will leave, Pan-at-lee,' he said; 'but you shall go with me – to the cave of Es-sat, the chief, to be the envied of the shes of Kor-ul-ja. Come!'

'Never!' cried Pan-at-lee. 'I hate you. Sooner would I mate with a Ho-don than with you, beater of women, murderer of babes.'

A frightful scowl distorted the features of the chief. 'She-*jato*!' he cried. 'I will tame you! I will break you! Es-sat, the chief, takes what he will and who dares question his right, or combat his least purpose, will first serve that purpose and then be broken as I break this,' and he picked a stone platter from the table and broke it in his powerful hands. 'You might have been first and most favored in the cave of the ancestors of Es-sat; but now shall you be last and least and when I am done with you you shall belong to all of the men of Es-sat's cave. Thus for those who spurn the love of their chief!'

He advanced quickly to seize her and as he laid a rough hand upon her she struck him heavily upon the side of his head with her golden breastplates. Without a sound Es-sat, the chief, sank to the floor of the apartment. For a moment Pan-at-lee bent over him, her improvised weapon raised to strike again should he show signs of returning consciousness, her glossy breasts rising and falling with her quickened breathing. Suddenly she stooped and removed Es-sat's knife with its scabbard and shoulder belt. Slipping it over her own shoulder she quickly adjusted her breastplates and keeping a watchful glance upon the figure of the fallen chief, backed from the room.

In a niche in the outer room, just beside the doorway leading to the balcony, were neatly piled a number of rounded pegs from eighteen to twenty inches in length. Selecting five of these she made them into a little bundle about which she twined the lower extremity of her sinuous tail and thus carrying them made her way to the outer edge of the balcony. Assuring herself that there was none about to see, or hinder her, she took quickly to the pegs already set in the face of the cliff and with the celerity of a monkey clambered swiftly aloft to the highest row of pegs which she followed in the direction of the lower end of the gorge for a matter of some hundred yards. Here, above her head, were a series of small round holes placed one above another in three parallel rows. Clinging only with her toes she removed two of the pegs from the bundle carried in her tail and taking one in either hand she inserted them in two opposite holes of the outer rows as far above her as she could reach. Hanging by these new holds she now took one of the three remaining pegs in each of her feet, leaving the fifth grasped securely in her tail. Reaching above her with this member she inserted the fifth peg in one of the holes of the center row and then, alternately hanging by her tail, her feet, or her hands, she moved the pegs upward to new holes, thus carrying her stairway with her as she ascended.

At the summit of the cliff a gnarled tree exposed its time-worn roots above the topmost holes forming the last step from the sheer face of the precipice to level footing. This was the last avenue of escape for members of the tribe hard pressed by enemies from below. There were three such emergency exits from the village and it were death to use them in other than an emergency. This Pan-at-lee well knew; but she knew, too, that it were worse than death to remain where the angered Es-sat might lay hands upon her.

When she had gained the summit, the girl moved quickly through the darkness in the direction of the next gorge which cut the mountainside a mile beyond Kor-ul-ja. It was the Gorge-of-water, Kor-ul-lul, to which her father and two brothers had been sent by Es-sat ostensibly to spy upon the neighboring tribe. There was a chance, a slender chance, that she might find them; if not there was the deserted Kor-ul-gryf several miles beyond, where she might hide indefinitely from man if she could elude the frightful monster from which the gorge derived its name and whose presence there had rendered its caves uninhabitable for generations.

Pan-at-lee crept stealthily along the rim of the Kor-ul-lul. Just where her father and brothers would watch she did not know. Sometimes their spies remained upon the rim, sometimes they watched from the gorge's bottom. Pan-at-lee was at a loss to know what to do or where to go. She felt very small and helpless alone in the vast darkness of the night. Strange noises fell upon her ears. They came from the lonely reaches of the towering mountains above her, from far away in the invisible valley and from the nearer foothills and once, in the distance, she heard what she thought was the bellow of a bull *gryf.* It came from the direction of the Kor-ul-gryf. She shuddered.

Presently there came to her keen ears another sound. Something approached her along the rim of the gorge. It was coming from above. She halted, listening. Perhaps it was her father, or a brother. It was coming closer. She strained her eyes through the darkness. She did not move – she scarcely breathed. And then, of a sudden, quite close it seemed, there blazed through the black night two yellow-green spots of fire.

Pan-at-lee was brave, but as always with the primitive, the darkness held infinite terrors for her. Not alone the terrors of the known but more frightful ones as well – those of the unknown. She had passed through much this night and her nerves were keyed to the highest pitch – raw, taut nerves, they were, ready to react in an exaggerated form to the slightest shock.

But this was no slight shock. To hope for a father and a brother and to see death instead glaring out of the darkness! Yes, Pan-at-lee was brave, but she was not of iron. With a shriek that reverberated among the hills she turned and fled along the rim of Kor-ul-lul and behind her, swiftly, came the devil-eyed lion of the mountains of Pal-ul-don.

Pan-at-lee was lost. Death was inevitable. Of this there could be no doubt, but to die beneath the rending fangs of the carnivore, congenital terror of her kind – it was unthinkable. But there was an alternative. The lion was almost upon her – another instant and he would seize her. Pan-at-lee turned sharply to her left. Just a few steps she took in the new direction before she disappeared over the rim of Kor-ul-lul. The baffled lion, planting all four feet, barely stopped upon the verge of the abyss. Glaring down into the black shadows beneath he mounted an angry roar.

Through the darkness at the bottom of Kor-ul-ja, Om-at led the way toward the caves of his people. Behind him came Tarzan and Ta-den. Presently they halted beneath a great tree that grew close to the cliff.

'First,' whispered Om-at, 'I will go to the cave of Pan-at-lee. Then will I seek the cave of my ancestors to have speech with my own blood. It will not take long. Wait here – I shall return soon. Afterward shall we go together to Ta-den's people.'

He moved silently toward the foot of the cliff up which Tarzan could presently see him ascending like a great fly on a wall. In the dim light the ape-man could not see the pegs set in the face of the cliff. Om-at moved warily. In the lower tier of caves there should be a sentry. His knowledge of his people and their customs told him, however, that in all probability the sentry was asleep. In this he was not mistaken, yet he did not in any way abate his wariness. Smoothly and swiftly he ascended toward the cave of Pan-at-lee while from below Tarzan and Ta-den watched him.

'How does he do it?' asked Tarzan. 'I can see no foothold upon that vertical. Surface and yet he appears to be climbing with the utmost ease.'

Ta-den explained the stairway of pegs. 'You could ascend easily,' he said, 'although a tail would be of great assistance.'

They watched until Om-at was about to enter the cave of Pan-at-lee without seeing any indication that he had been observed and then, simultaneously, both saw a head appear in the mouth of one of the lower caves. It was quickly evident that its owner had discovered Om-at for immediately he started upward in pursuit. Without a word Tarzan and Ta-den sprang forward toward the foot of the cliff. The pithecanthropus was the first to reach it and the ape-man saw him spring upward for a handhold on the lowest peg above him. Now Tarzan saw other pegs roughly paralleling each other in zigzag rows up the cliff face. He sprang and caught one of these, pulled himself upward by one hand until he could reach a second with his other hand; and when he had ascended far enough to use his feet, discovered that he could make rapid progress. Ta-den was outstripping him, however, for these precarious ladders were no novelty to him and, further, he had an advantage in possessing a tail.

Nevertheless, the ape-man gave a good account of himself, being presently urged to redoubled efforts by the fact that the Waz-don above Ta-den glanced down and discovered his pursuers just before the Ho-don overtook him. Instantly a wild cry shattered the silence of the gorge – a cry that was immediately answered by hundreds of savage throats as warrior after warrior emerged from the entrance to his cave.

The creature who had raised the alarm had now reached the recess before Pan-at-lee's cave and here he halted and turned to give battle to Ta-den. Unslinging his club which had hung down his back from a thong about his neck he stood upon the level floor of the entranceway, effectually blocking Ta-den's ascent. From all directions the warriors of Kor-ul-ja were swarming toward the interlopers. Tarzan, who had reached a point on the same level with Ta-den but a little to the latter's left, saw that nothing short of a miracle could save them. Just at the ape-man's left was the entrance to a cave that either was deserted or whose occupants had not as yet been aroused, for the level recess remained unoccupied. Resourceful was the alert mind of Tarzan of the Apes and quick to respond were the trained muscles. In the time that you or I might give to debating an action he would accomplish it and now, though only seconds separated his nearest antagonist from him, in the brief span of time at his disposal he had stepped into the recess, unslung his long rope and leaning far out shot the sinuous noose, with the precision of long habitude, toward the menacing figure wielding its heavy club above Ta-den. There was a momentary pause of the rope-hand as the noose sped toward its goal, a quick movement of the right wrist that closed it upon its victim as it settled over his head and then a surging tug as, seizing the rope in both hands, Tarzan threw back upon it all the weight of his great frame.

Voicing a terrified shriek, the Waz-don lunged headforemost from the recess above Ta-den. Tarzan braced himself for the coming shock when the creature's body should have fallen the full length of the rope and as it did there was a snap of the vertebrae that rose sickeningly in the momentary silence that had followed the doomed man's departing scream. Unshaken by the stress of the suddenly arrested weight at the end of the rope, Tarzan quickly pulled the body to his side that he might remove the noose from about its neck, for he could not afford to lose so priceless a weapon.

During the several seconds that had elapsed since he cast the rope the Waz-don warriors had remained inert as though paralyzed by wonder or by terror. Now, again, one of them found his voice and his head and straightaway, shrieking invectives at the strange intruder, started upward for the ape-man, urging his fellows to attack. This man was the closest to Tarzan. But for him the ape-man could easily have reached Ta-den's side as the latter was urging him to do. Tarzan raised the body of the dead Waz-don above his head, held it poised there for a moment as with face raised to the heavens he screamed forth the horrid challenge of the bull apes of the tribe of Kerchak, and with all the strength of his giant sinews he hurled the corpse heavily upon the ascending warrior. So great was the force of the impact that not only was the Waz-don torn from his hold but two of the pegs to which he clung were broken short in their sockets.

As the two bodies, the living and the dead, hurtled downward toward the foot of the cliff a great cry arose from the Waz-don. 'Jad-guru-don! Jad-guru-don!' he screamed, and then: 'Kill him! Kill him!'

And now Tarzan stood in the recess beside Ta-den. 'Jad-guru-don!' repeated the latter, smiling – 'The terrible man! Tarzan the Terrible! They may kill you, but they will never forget you.'

'They shall not ki – What have we here?' Tarzan's statement as to what 'they' should not do was interrupted by a sudden ejaculation as two figures, locked in deathlike embrace, stumbled through the doorway of the cave to the other porch. One was Om-at, the other a creature of his own kind but with a rough coat, the hairs of which seemed to grow straight outward from the skin, stiffly, unlike Om-at's sleek covering. The two were quite evidently well matched and equally evident was the fact that each was bent upon murder. They fought almost in silence except for an occasional low growl as one or the other acknowledged thus some new hurt.

Tarzan, following a natural impulse to aid his ally, leaped forward to enter the dispute only to be checked by a grunted admonition from Om-at. 'Back!' he said. 'This fight is mine, alone.'

The ape-man understood and stepped aside.

'It is a *gund-bar*,' explained Ta-den, 'a *chief-battle*. This fellow must be Es-sat, the chief. If Om-at kills him without assistance Om-at may become chief.'

Tarzan smiled. It was the law of his own jungle – the law of the tribe of Kerchak, the bull ape – the ancient law of primitive man that needed but the refining influences of civilization to introduce the hired dagger and the poison cup. Then his attention was drawn to the outer edge of the vestibule. Above it appeared the shaggy face of one of Es-sat's warriors. Tarzan sprang to intercept the man; but Ta-den was there ahead of him. 'Back!' cried the Ho-don to the newcomer. 'It is *gund-bar*.' The fellow looked scrutinizingly at the two fighters, then turned his face downward toward his fellows. 'Back!'

he cried. 'It is *gund-bar* between Es-sat and Om-at.' Then he looked back at Ta-den and Tarzan. 'Who are you?' he asked.

'We are Om-at's friends,' replied Ta-den.

The fellow nodded. 'We will attend to you later,' he said and disappeared below the edge of the recess.

The battle upon the ledge continued with unabated ferocity, Tarzan and Ta-den having difficulty in keeping out of the way of the contestants who tore and beat at each other with hands and feet and lashing tails. Es-sat was unarmed – Pan-at-lee had seen to that – but at Om-at's side swung a sheathed knife which he made no effort to draw. That would have been contrary to their savage and primitive code for the chief-battle must be fought with nature's weapons.

Sometimes they separated for an instant only to rush upon each other again with all the ferocity and nearly the strength of mad bulls. Presently one of them tripped the other but in that viselike embrace one could not fall alone – Es-sat dragged Om-at with him, toppling upon the brink of the niche. Even Tarzan held his breath. There they surged to and fro perilously for a moment and then the inevitable happened – the two, locked in murderous embrace, rolled over the edge and disappeared from the ape-man's view.

Tarzan voiced a suppressed sigh for he had liked Om-at and then, with Ta-den, approached the edge and looked over. Far below, in the dim light of the coming dawn, two inert forms should be lying stark in death; but, to Tarzan's amazement, such was far from the sight that met his eyes. Instead, there were the two figures still vibrant with life and still battling only a few feet below him. Clinging always to the pegs with two holds – a hand and a foot, or a foot and a tail, they seemed as much at home upon the perpendicular wall as upon the level surface of the vestibule; but now their tactics were slightly altered, for each seemed particularly bent upon dislodging his antagonist from his holds and precipitating him to certain death below. It was soon evident that Om-at, younger and with greater powers of endurance than Es-sat, was gaining an advantage. Now was the chief almost wholly on the defensive. Holding him by the cross belt with one mighty hand Om-at was forcing his foeman straight out from the cliff, and with the other hand and one foot was rapidly breaking first one of Es-sat's holds and then another, alternating his efforts, or rather punctuating them, with vicious blows to the pit of his adversary's stomach. Rapidly was Es-sat weakening and with the knowledge of impending death there came, as there comes to every coward and bully under similar circumstances, a crumbling of the veneer of bravado which had long masqueraded as courage and with it crumbled his code of ethics. Now was Es-sat no longer chief of Kor-ul-ja – instead he was a whimpering craven battling for life. Clutching at Om-at, clutching at the nearest pegs he sought any support that would save him from that awful fall, and as he strove to push aside the hand of death, whose cold fingers he already felt upon his heart, his tail sought Om-at's side and the handle of the knife that hung there.

Tarzan saw and even as Es-sat drew the blade from its sheath he dropped catlike to the pegs beside the battling men. Es-sat's tail had drawn back for the cowardly fatal thrust. Now many others saw the perfidious act and a great cry of rage and disgust arose from savage throats; but as the blade sped toward its goal, the ape-man seized the hairy member that wielded it, and at the same instant Om-at thrust the body of Es-sat from him with such force that its weakened holds were broken and it hurtled downward, a brief meteor of screaming fear, to death.

4

Tarzan-jad-guru

As Tarzan and Om-at clambered back to the vestibule of Pan-at-lee's cave and took their stand beside Ta-den in readiness for whatever eventuality might follow the death of Es-sat, the sun that topped the eastern hills touched also the figure of a sleeper upon a distant, thorn-covered steppe, awakening him to another day of tireless tracking along a faint and rapidly disappearing spoor.

For a time silence reigned in the Kor-ul-ja. The tribesmen waited, looking now down upon the dead thing that had been their chief, now at one another, and now at Om-at and the two who stood upon his either side. Presently Om-at spoke. 'I am Om-at,' he cried. 'Who will say that Om-at is not *gund* of Kor-ul-ja?'

He waited for a taker of his challenge. One or two of the larger young bucks fidgeted restlessly and eyed him; but there was no reply.

'Then Om-at is *gund*,' he said with finality. 'Now tell me, where are Pan-at-lee, her father, and her brothers?'

An old warrior spoke. 'Pan-at-lee should be in her cave. Who should know that better than you who are there now? Her father and her brothers were sent to watch Kor-ul-lul; but neither of these questions arouse any tumult in our breasts. There is one that does: Can Om-at be chief of Kor-ul-ja and yet stand at bay against his own people with a Ho-don and that terrible man at his side – that terrible man who has no tail? Hand the strangers over to your people to be slain as is the way of the Waz-don and then may Om-at be *gund*.'

Neither Tarzan nor Ta-den spoke then; they but stood watching Om-at and waiting for his decision, the ghost of a smile upon the lips of the ape-man. Ta-den, at least, knew that the old warrior had spoken the truth – the Waz-don entertain no strangers and take no prisoners of an alien race.

Then spoke Om-at. 'Always there is change,' he said. 'Even the old hills of Pal-ul-don appear never twice alike – the brilliant sun, a passing cloud, the moon, a mist, the changing seasons, the sharp clearness following a storm; these things bring each a new change in our hills. From birth to death, day by day, there is constant change in each of us. Change, then, is one of Jad-ben-Otho's laws.

'And now I, Om-at, your *gund*, bring another change. Strangers who are brave men and good friends shall no longer be slain by the Waz-don of Kor-ul-ja!'

There were growls and murmurings and a restless moving among the warriors as each eyed the others to see who would take the initiative against Om-at, the iconoclast.

'Cease your mutterings,' admonished the new *gund*. 'I am your chief. My word is your law. You had no part in making me chief. Some of you helped Es-sat to drive me from the cave of my ancestors; the rest of you permitted it. I owe you nothing. Only these two, whom you would have me kill, were loyal to me. I am *gund* and if there be any who doubts it let him speak – he cannot die younger.'

Tarzan was pleased. Here was a man after his own heart. He admired the fearlessness of Om-at's challenge and he was a sufficiently good judge of men to know that he had listened to no idle bluff – Om-at would back up his words to the death, if necessary, and the chances were that he would not be the one to die. Evidently the majority of the Kor-ul-jaians entertained the same conviction.

'I will make you a good *gund*,' said Om-at, seeing that no one appeared inclined to dispute his rights. 'Your wives and daughters will be safe – they were not safe while Es-sat ruled. Go now to your crops and your hunting. I leave to search for Pan-at-lee. Ab-on will be *gund* while I am away – look to him for guidance and to me for an accounting when I return – and may Jad-ben-Otho smile upon you.'

He turned toward Tarzan and the Ho-don. 'And you, my friends,' he said, 'are free to go among my people; the cave of my ancestors is yours; do what you will.'

'I,' said Tarzan, 'will go with Om-at to search for Pan-at-lee.'

'And I,' said Ta-den.

Om-at smiled. 'Good!' he exclaimed. 'And when we have found her we shall go together upon Tarzan's business and Ta-den's. Where first shall we search?' He turned toward his warriors. 'Who knows where she may be?'

None knew other than that Pan-at-lee had gone to her cave with the others the previous evening – there was no clue, no suggestion as to her whereabouts.

'Show me where she sleeps,' said Tarzan; 'let me see something that belongs to her – an article of her apparel – then, doubtless, I can help you.'

Two young warriors climbed closer to the ledge upon which Om-at stood. They were In-sad and O-dan. It was the latter who spoke.

'*Gund* of Kor-ul-ja,' he said, 'we would go with you to search for Pan-at-lee.'

It was the first acknowledgment of Om-at's chieftainship and immediately following it the tenseness that had prevailed seemed to relax – the warriors spoke aloud instead of in whispers, and the women appeared from the mouths of caves as with the passing of a sudden storm. In-sad and O-dan had taken the lead and now all seemed glad to follow. Some came to talk with Om-at and to look more closely at Tarzan; others, heads of caves, gathered their hunters and discussed the business of the day. The women and children prepared to descend to the fields with the youths and the old men, whose duty it was to guard them.

'O-dan and In-sad shall go with us,' announced Om-at; 'we shall not need more. Tarzan, come with me and I shall show you where Pan-at-lee sleeps, though why you should wish to know I cannot guess – she is not there. I have looked for myself.'

The two entered the cave where Om-at led the way to the apartment in which Es-sat had surprised Pan-at-lee the previous night.

'All here are hers,' said Om-at, 'except the war club lying on the floor – that was Es-sat's.'

The ape-man moved silently about the apartment, the quivering of his sensitive nostrils scarcely apparent to his companion who only wondered what good purpose could be served here and chafed at the delay.

'Come!' said the ape-man, presently, and led the way toward the outer recess.

Here their three companions were awaiting them. Tarzan passed to the left side of the niche and examined the pegs that lay within reach. He looked at them but it was not his eyes that were examining them. Keener than his keen eyes was that marvelously trained sense of scent that had first been developed in him during infancy under the tutorage of his foster mother, Kala, the she-ape, and further sharpened in the grim jungles by that master teacher – the instinct of self-preservation.

From the left side of the niche he turned to the right. Om-at was becoming impatient.

'Let us be off,' he said. 'We must search for Pan-at-lee if we would ever find her.'

'Where shall we search?' asked Tarzan.

Om-at scratched his head. 'Where?' he repeated. 'Why all Pal-ul-don, if necessary.'

'A large job,' said Tarzan. 'Come,' he added, 'she went this way,' and he took to the pegs that led aloft toward the summit of the cliff. Here he followed the scent easily since none had passed that way since Pan-at-lee had fled. At the point at which she had left the permanent pegs and resorted to those carried with her Tarzan came to an abrupt halt. 'She went this way to the summit,' he called back to Om-at who was directly behind him; 'but there are no pegs here.'

'I do not know how you know that she went this way,' said Om-at; 'but we will get pegs. In-sad, return and fetch climbing pegs for five.'

The young warrior was soon back and the pegs distributed. Om-at handed five to Tarzan and explained their use. The ape-man returned one. 'I need but four,' he said.

Om-at smiled. 'What a wonderful creature you would be if you were not deformed,' he said, glancing with pride at his own strong tail.

'I admit that I am handicapped,' replied Tarzan. 'You others go ahead and leave the pegs in place for me. I am afraid that otherwise it will be slow work as I cannot hold the pegs in my toes as you do.'

'All right,' agreed Om-at; 'Ta-den, In-sad, and I will go first, you follow and O-dan bring up the rear and collect the pegs – we cannot leave them here for our enemies.'

'Can't your enemies bring their own pegs?' asked Tarzan.

'Yes; but it delays them and makes easier our defense and – they do not know which of all the holes you see are deep enough for pegs – the others are made to confuse our enemies and are too shallow to hold a peg.'

At the top of the cliff beside the gnarled tree Tarzan again took up the trail. Here the scent was fully as strong as upon the pegs and the ape-man moved rapidly across the ridge in the direction of the Kor-ul-lul.

Presently he paused and turned toward Om-at. 'Here she moved swiftly, running at top speed, and, Om-at, she was pursued by a lion.'

'You can read that in the grass?' asked O-dan as the others gathered about the ape-man.

Tarzan nodded. 'I do not think the lion got her,' he added; 'but that we shall determine quickly. No, he did not get her – look!' and he pointed toward the southwest, down the ridge.

Following the direction indicated by his finger, the others presently detected a movement in some bushes a couple of hundred yards away.

'What is it?' asked Om-at. 'It is she?' and he started toward the spot.

'Wait,' advised Tarzan. 'It is the lion which pursued her.'

'You can see him?' asked Ta-den.

'No, I can smell him.'

The others looked their astonishment and incredulity; but of the fact that it was indeed a lion they were not left long in doubt. Presently the bushes parted and the creature stepped out in full view, facing them. It was a magnificent beast, large and beautifully maned, with the brilliant leopard spots of its kind well marked and symmetrical. For a moment it eyed them and then, still chafing at the loss of its prey earlier in the morning, it charged.

The Pal-ul-donians unslung their clubs and stood waiting the onrushing beast. Tarzan of the Apes drew his hunting knife and crouched in the path of the fanged fury. It was almost upon him when it swerved to the right and leaped for Om-at only to be sent to earth with a staggering blow upon the head. Almost instantly it was up and though the men rushed fearlessly in, it managed to sweep aside their weapons with its mighty paws. A single blow wrenched O-dan's club from his hand and sent it hurtling against Ta-den, knocking him from his feet. Taking advantage of its opportunity the lion rose to throw itself upon O-dan and at the same instant Tarzan flung himself upon its back. Strong, white teeth buried themselves in the spotted neck, mighty arms encircled the savage throat and the sinewy legs of the ape-man locked themselves about the gaunt belly.

The others, powerless to aid, stood breathlessly about as the great lion lunged hither and thither, clawing and biting fearfully and futilely at the savage creature that had fastened itself upon him. Over and over they rolled and now the onlookers saw a brown hand raised above the lion's side – a brown hand grasping a keen blade. They saw it fall and rise and fall again – each time with terrific force and in its wake they saw a crimson stream trickling down *ja*'s gorgeous coat.

Now from the lion's throat rose hideous screams of hate and rage and pain as he redoubled his efforts to dislodge and punish his tormentor; but always the tousled black head remained half buried in the dark brown mane and the mighty arm rose and fell to plunge the knife again and again into the dying beast.

The Pal-ul-donians stood in mute wonder and admiration. Brave men and mighty hunters they were and as such the first to accord honor to a mightier.

'And you would have had me slay him!' cried Om-at, glancing at In-sad and O-dan.

'Jad-ben-Otho reward you that you did not,' breathed In-sad.

And now the lion lunged suddenly to earth and with a few spasmodic quiverings lay still. The ape-man rose and shook himself, even as might *ja*, the leopard-coated lion of Pal-ul-don, had he been the one to survive.

O-dan advanced quickly toward Tarzan. Placing a palm upon his own breast and the other on Tarzan's, he said, 'Tarzan the Terrible, I ask no greater honor than your friendship.'

'And I no more than the friendship of Om-at's friends,' replied the ape-man simply returning the other's salute.

'Do you think,' asked Om-at, coming close to Tarzan and laying a hand upon the other's shoulder, 'that he got her?'

'No, my friend; it was a hungry lion that charged us.'

'You seem to know much of lions,' said In-sad.

'Had I a brother I could not know him better,' replied Tarzan.

'Then where can she be?' continued Om-at.

'We can but follow while the spoor is fresh,' answered the ape-man and again taking up his interrupted tracking he led them down the ridge and at a sharp turning of the trail to the left brought them to the verge of the cliff that dropped into the Kor-ul-lul. For a moment Tarzan examined the ground to the right and to the left, then he stood erect and looking at Om-at pointed into the gorge.

For a moment the Waz-don gazed down into the green rift at the bottom of which a tumultuous river tumbled downward along its rocky bed, then he closed his eyes as to a sudden spasm of pain and turned away.

'You – mean – she jumped?' he asked.

'To escape the lion,' replied Tarzan. 'He was right behind her – look, you can see where his four paws left their impress in the turf as he checked his charge upon the very verge of the abyss.'

'Is there any chance—' commenced Om-at, to be suddenly silenced by a warning gesture from Tarzan.

'Down!' whispered the ape-man, 'many men are coming. They are running – from down the ridge.' He flattened himself upon his belly in the grass, the others following his example.

For some minutes they waited thus and then the others, too, heard the sound of running feet and now a hoarse shout followed by many more.

'It is the war cry of the Kor-ul-lul,' whispered Om-at – 'the hunting cry of men who hunt men. Presently shall we see them and if Jad-ben-Otho is pleased with us they shall not too greatly outnumber us.'

'They are many,' said Tarzan, 'forty or fifty, I should say; but how many are the pursued and how many the pursuers we cannot even guess, except that the latter must greatly outnumber the former, else these would not run so fast.'

'Here they come,' said Ta-den.

'It is An-un, father of Pan-at-lee, and his two sons,' exclaimed O-dan. 'They will pass without seeing us if we do not hurry,' he added looking at Om-at, the chief, for a sign.

'Come!' cried the latter, springing to his feet and running rapidly to intercept the three fugitives. The others followed him.

'Five friends!' shouted Om-at as An-un and his sons discovered them.

'Adenen yo!' echoed O-dan and In-sad.

The fugitives scarcely paused as these unexpected reinforcements joined them but they eyed Ta-den and Tarzan with puzzled glances.

'The Kor-ul-lul are many,' shouted An-un. 'Would that we might pause and fight; but first we must warn Es-sat and our people.'

'Yes,' said Om-at, 'we must warn our people.'

'Es-sat is dead,' said In-sad.

'Who is chief?' asked one of An-un's sons.

'Om-at,' replied O-dan.

'It is well,' cried An-un. 'Pan-at-lee said that you would come back and slay Es-sat.'

Now the enemy broke into sight behind them.

'Come!' cried Tarzan, 'let us turn and charge them, raising a great cry. They pursued but three and when they see eight charging upon them they will think that many men have come to do battle. They will believe that there are more even than they see and then one who is swift will have time to reach the gorge and warn your people.'

'It is well,' said Om-at. 'Id-an, you are swift – carry word to the warriors of Kor-ul-ja that we fight the Kor-ul-lul upon the ridge and that Ab-on shall send a hundred men.'

Id-an, the son of An-un, sped swiftly toward the cliff-dwellings of the Kor-ul-ja while the others charged the oncoming Kor-ul-lul, the war cries of the two tribes rising and falling in a certain grim harmony. The leaders of the Kor-ul-lul paused at sight of the reinforcements, waiting apparently for those behind to catch up with them and, possibly, also to learn how great a force confronted them. The leaders, swifter runners than their fellows, perhaps, were far in advance while the balance of their number had not yet emerged from the brush; and now as Om-at and his companions fell upon them with a ferocity born of necessity they fell back, so that when their companions at last came in sight of them they appeared to be in full rout. The natural result was that the others turned and fled.

Encouraged by this first success Om-at followed them into the brush, his little company charging valiantly upon his either side, and loud and terrifying were the savage yells with which they pursued the fleeing enemy. The brush, while not growing so closely together as to impede progress, was of such height as to hide the members of the party from one another when they became separated by even a few yards. The result was that Tarzan, always swift and always keen for battle, was soon pursuing the enemy far in the lead of the others – a lack of prudence which was to prove his undoing.

The warriors of Kor-ul-lul, doubtless as valorous as their foemen, retreated only to a more strategic position in the brush, nor were they long in guessing that the number of their pursuers was fewer than their own. They made a stand then where the brush was densest – an ambush it was, and into this ran Tarzan of the Apes. They tricked him neatly. Yes, sad as is the narration of it, they tricked the wily jungle lord. But then they were fighting on their own ground, every foot of which they knew as you know your front parlor, and they were following their own tactics, of which Tarzan knew nothing.

A single black warrior appeared to Tarzan a laggard in the rear of the retreating enemy and thus retreating he lured Tarzan on. At last he turned at bay confronting the ape-man with bludgeon and drawn knife and as Tarzan charged him a score of burly Waz-don leaped from the surrounding brush. Instantly, but too late, the giant Tarmangani realized his peril. There flashed before him a vision of his lost mate and a great and sickening regret surged through him with the realization that if she still lived she might no longer hope, for though she might never know of the passing of her lord the fact of it must inevitably seal her doom.

And consequent to this thought there enveloped him a blind frenzy of hatred for these creatures who dared thwart his purpose and menace the welfare of his wife. With a savage growl he threw himself upon the warrior before him twisting the heavy club from the creature's hand as if he had been a little child, and with his left fist backed by the weight and sinew of his giant frame, he crashed a shattering blow to the center of the Waz-don's face – a blow that crushed the bones and dropped the fellow in his tracks. Then he swung upon the others with their fallen comrade's bludgeon striking to right and left mighty, unmerciful blows that drove down their own weapons until that wielded by the ape-man was splintered and shattered. On either hand they fell before his cudgel; so rapid the delivery of his blows, so catlike his recovery that in the first few moments of the battle he seemed invulnerable to their attack; but it could not last – he was outnumbered twenty to one and his undoing came from a thrown club. It struck him upon the back of the head. For a moment he stood swaying and then like a great pine beneath the woodsman's ax he crashed to earth.

Others of the Kor-ul-lul had rushed to engage the balance of Om-at's party. They could be heard fighting at a short distance and it was evident that the Kor-ul-ja were falling slowly back and as they fell Om-at called to the missing one: 'Tarzan the Terrible! Tarzan the Terrible!'

'Jad-guru, indeed,' repeated one of the Kor-ul-lul rising from where Tarzan had dropped him. 'Tarzan-jad-guru! He was worse than that.'

5

In the Kor-ul-gryf

As Tarzan fell among his enemies a man halted many miles away upon the outer verge of the morass that encircles Pal-ul-don. Naked he was except for a loincloth and three belts of cartridges, two of which passed over his shoulders, crossing upon his chest and back, while the third encircled his waist. Slung to his back by its leathern sling-strap was an Enfield, and he carried too a long knife, a bow and a quiver of arrows. He had come far, through wild and savage lands, menaced by fierce beasts and fiercer men, yet intact to the last cartridge was the ammunition that had filled his belts the day that he set out.

The bow and the arrows and the long knife had brought him thus far safely, yet often in the face of great risks that could have been minimized by a single shot from the well-kept rifle at his back. What purpose might he have for conserving this precious ammunition? In risking his life to bring the last bright shining missile to his unknown goal? For what, for whom were these death-dealing bits of metal preserved? In all the world only he knew.

When Pan-at-lee stepped over the edge of the cliff above Kor-ul-lul she expected to be dashed to instant death upon the rocks below; but she had chosen this in preference to the rending fangs of *ja*. Instead, chance had ordained that she make the frightful plunge at a point where the tumbling river swung close beneath the overhanging cliff to eddy for a slow moment in a deep pool before plunging madly downward again in a cataract of boiling foam, and water thundering against rocks.

Into this icy pool the girl shot, and down and down beneath the watery surface until, half choked, yet fighting bravely, she battled her way once more to air. Swimming strongly she made the opposite shore and there dragged herself out upon the bank to lie panting and spent until the approaching dawn warned her to seek concealment, for she was in the country of her people's enemies.

Rising, she moved into the concealment of the rank vegetation that grows so riotously in the well-watered *kors*† of Pal-ul-don.

† I have used the Pal-ul-don word for *gorge* with the English plural, which is not the correct native plural form. The latter, it seems to me, is awkward for us and so I have generally ignored it throughout my manuscript, permitting, for example, Kor-ul-ja to answer for both singular and plural. However, for the benefit of those who may be interested in such things I may say

Hidden amidst the plant life from the sight of any who might chance to pass along the well-beaten trail that skirted the river Pan-at-lee sought rest and food, the latter growing in abundance all about her in the form of fruits and berries and succulent tubers which she scooped from the earth with the knife of the dead Es-sat.

Ah! if she had but known that he was dead! What trials and risks and terrors she might have been saved; but she thought that he still lived and so she dared not return to Kor-ul-ja. At least not yet while his rage was at white heat. Later, perhaps, her father and brothers returned to their cave, she might risk it; but not now – not now. Nor could she for long remain here in the neighborhood of the hostile Kor-ul-lul and somewhere she must find safety from beasts before the night set in.

As she sat upon the bole of a fallen tree seeking some solution of the problem of existence that confronted her, there broke upon her ears from up the gorge the voices of shouting men – a sound that she recognized all too well. It was the war cry of the Kor-ul-lul. Closer and closer it approached her hiding place. Then, through the veil of foliage she caught glimpses of three figures fleeing along the trail, and behind them the shouting of the pursuers rose louder and louder as they neared her. Again she caught sight of the fugitives crossing the river below the cataract and again they were lost to sight. And now the pursuers came into view – shouting Kor-ul-lul warriors, fierce and implacable. Forty, perhaps fifty of them. She waited breathless; but they did not swerve from the trail and passed her, unguessing that an enemy she lay hid within a few yards of them.

Once again she caught sight of the pursued – three Waz-don warriors clambering the cliff face at a point where portions of the summit had fallen away presenting a steep slope that might be ascended by such as these. Suddenly her attention was riveted upon the three. Could it be? O Jad-ben-Otho! had she but known a moment before. When they passed she might have joined them, for they were her father and two brothers. Now it was too late. With bated breath and tense muscles she watched the race. Would they reach the summit? Would the Kor-ul-lul overhaul them? They climbed well, but, oh, so slowly. Now one lost his footing in the loose shale and slipped back! The Kor-ul-lul were ascending – one hurled his club at the nearest fugitive. The Great God was pleased with the brother of Pan-at-lee, for he caused the club to fall short of its target, and to fall, rolling and bounding, back upon its owner carrying him from his feet and precipitating him to the bottom of the gorge.

---

that the plurals are formed simply for all words in the Pal-ul-don language by doubling the initial letter of the word, as *k'kor, gorges*, pronounced as though written *kakor*, the a having the sound of a in *sofa. Lions*, then, would be *j'ja*, or *men d'don*.

Standing now, her hands pressed tight above her golden breastplates, Pan-at-lee watched the race for life. Now one, her older brother, reached the summit and clinging there to something that she could not see he lowered his body and his long tail to the father beneath him. The latter, seizing this support, extended his own tail to the son below – the one who had slipped back – and thus, upon a living ladder of their own making, the three reached the summit and disappeared from view before the Kor-ul-lul overtook them. But the latter did not abandon the chase. On they went until they too had disappeared from sight and only a faint shouting came down to Pan-at-lee to tell her that the pursuit continued.

The girl knew that she must move on. At any moment now might come a hunting party, combing the gorge for the smaller animals that fed or bedded there.

Behind her were Es-sat and the returning party of Kor-ul-lul that had pursued her kin; before her, across the next ridge, was the Kor-ul-gryf, the lair of the terrifying monsters that brought the chill of fear to every inhabitant of Pal-ul-don; below her, in the valley, was the country of the Ho-don, where she could look for only slavery, or death; here were the Kor-ul-lul, the ancient enemies of her people and everywhere were the wild beasts that eat the flesh of man.

For but a moment she debated and then turning her face toward the south-east she set out across the gorge of water toward the Kor-ul-gryf – at least there were no men there. As it is now, so it was in the beginning, back to the primitive progenitor of man which is typified by Pan-at-lee and her kind today, of all the hunters that woman fears, man is the most relentless, the most terrible. To the dangers of man she preferred the dangers of the *gryf*.

Moving cautiously she reached the foot of the cliff at the far side of Kor-ul-lul and here, toward noon, she found a comparatively easy ascent. Crossing the ridge she stood at last upon the brink of Kor-ul-gryf – the horror place of the folklore of her race. Dank and mysterious grew the vegetation below; giant trees waved their plumed tops almost level with the summit of the cliff; and over all brooded an ominous silence.

Pan-at-lee lay upon her belly and stretching over the edge scanned the cliff face below her. She could see caves there and the stone pegs which the ancients had fashioned so laboriously by hand. She had heard of these in the firelight tales of her childhood and of how the *gryfs* had come from the morasses across the mountains and of how at last the people had fled after many had been seized and devoured by the hideous creatures, leaving their caves untenanted for no man living knew how long. Some said that Jad-ben-Otho, who has lived forever, was still a little boy. Pan-at-lee shuddered; but there were caves and in them she would be safe even from the *gryfs*.

She found a place where the stone pegs reached to the very summit of the cliff, left there no doubt in the final exodus of the tribe when there was no longer need of safeguarding the deserted caves against invasion. Pan-at-lee clambered slowly down toward the uppermost cave. She found the recess in front of the doorway almost identical with those of her own tribe. The floor of it, though, was littered with twigs and old nests and the droppings of birds, until it was half choked. She moved along to another recess and still another, but all were alike in the accumulated filth. Evidently there was no need in looking further. This one seemed large and commodious. With her knife she fell to work cleaning away the debris by the simple expedient of pushing it over the edge, and always her eyes turned constantly toward the silent gorge where lurked the fearsome creatures of Pal-ul-don. And other eyes there were, eyes she did not see, but that saw her and watched her every move – fierce eyes, greedy eyes, cunning and cruel. They watched her, and a red tongue licked flabby, pendulous lips. They watched her, and a half-human brain laboriously evolved a brutish design.

As in her own Kor-ul-ja, the natural springs in the cliff had been developed by the long-dead builders of the caves so that fresh, pure water trickled now, as it had for ages, within easy access to the cave entrances. Her only difficulty would be in procuring food and for that she must take the risk at least once in two days, for she was sure that she could find fruits and tubers and perhaps small animals, birds, and eggs near the foot of the cliff, the last two, possibly, in the caves themselves. Thus might she live on here indefinitely. She felt now a certain sense of security imparted doubtless by the impregnability of her high-flung sanctuary that she knew to be safe from all the more dangerous beasts, and this one from men, too, since it lay in the abjured Kor-ul-gryf.

Now she determined to inspect the interior of her new home. The sun, still in the south, lighted the interior of the first apartment. It was similar to those of her experience – the same beasts and men were depicted in the same crude fashion in the carvings on the walls – evidently there had been little progress in the race of Waz-don during the generations that had come and departed since Kor-ul-gryf had been abandoned by men. Of course Pan-at-lee thought no such thoughts, for evolution and progress existed not for her, or her kind. Things were as they had always been and would always be as they were.

That these strange creatures have existed thus for incalculable ages it can scarce be doubted, so marked are the indications of antiquity about their dwellings – deep furrows worn by naked feet in living rock; the hollow in the jamb of a stone doorway where many arms have touched in passing; the endless carvings that cover, ofttimes, the entire face of a great cliff and all the walls and ceilings of every cave and each carving wrought by a different hand, for each is the coat of arms, one might say, of the adult male who traced it.

And so Pan-at-lee found this ancient cave homelike and familiar. There was less litter within than she had found without and what there was was mostly an accumulation of dust. Beside the doorway was the niche in which wood and tinder were kept, but there remained nothing now other than mere dust. She had however saved a little pile of twigs from the debris on the porch. In a short time she had made a light by firing a bundle of twigs and lighting others from this fire she explored some of the inner rooms. Nor here did she find aught that was new or strange nor any relic of the departed owners other than a few broken stone dishes. She had been looking for something soft to sleep upon, but was doomed to disappointment as the former owners had evidently made a leisurely departure, carrying all their belongings with them. Below, in the gorge were leaves and grasses and fragrant branches, but Pan-at-lee felt no stomach for descending into that horrid abyss for the gratification of mere creature comfort – only the necessity for food would drive her there.

And so, as the shadows lengthened and night approached she prepared to make as comfortable a bed as she could by gathering the dust of ages into a little pile and spreading it between her soft body and the hard floor – at best it was only better than nothing. But Pan-at-lee was very tired. She had not slept since two nights before and in the interval she had experienced many dangers and hardships. What wonder then that despite the hard bed, she was asleep almost immediately she had composed herself for rest.

She slept and the moon rose, casting its silver light upon the cliff's white face and lessening the gloom of the dark forest and the dismal gorge. In the distance a lion roared. There was a long silence. From the upper reaches of the gorge came a deep bellow. There was a movement in the trees at the cliffs foot. Again the bellow, low and ominous. It was answered from below the deserted village. Something dropped from the foliage of a tree directly below the cave in which Pan-at-lee slept – it dropped to the ground among the dense shadows. Now it moved, cautiously. It moved toward the foot of the cliff, taking form and shape in the moonlight. It moved like the creature of a bad dream – slowly, sluggishly. It might have been a huge sloth – it might have been a man, with so grotesque a brush does the moon paint – master cubist.

Slowly it moved up the face of the cliff – like a great grub-worm it moved; but now the moon-brush touched it again and it had hands and feet and with them it clung to the stone pegs and raised itself laboriously aloft toward the cave where Pan-at-lee slept. From the lower reaches of the gorge came again the sound of bellowing, and it was answered from above the village.

Tarzan of the Apes opened his eyes. He was conscious of a pain in his head, and at first that was about all. A moment later grotesque shadows, rising and falling, focused his arousing perceptions. Presently he saw that he was in a cave. A dozen Waz-don warriors squatted about, talking. A rude stone cresset containing burning oil lighted the interior and as the flame rose and fell the exaggerated shadows of the warriors danced upon the walls behind them.

'We brought him to you alive, *Gund*,' he heard one of them saying, 'because never before was Ho-don like him seen. He has no tail – he was born without one, for there is no scar to mark where a tail had been cut off. The thumbs upon his hands and feet are unlike those of the races of Pal-ul-don. He is more powerful than many men put together and he attacks with the fearlessness of *ja*. We brought him alive, that you might see him before he is slain.'

The chief rose and approached the ape-man, who closed his eyes and feigned unconsciousness. He felt hairy hands upon him as he was turned over, none too gently. The *gund* examined him from head to foot, making comments, especially upon the shape and size of his thumbs and great toes.

'With these and with no tail,' he said, 'it cannot climb.'

'No,' agreed one of the warriors, 'it would surely fall even from the cliff pegs.'

'I have never seen a thing like it,' said the chief. 'It is neither Waz-don nor Ho-don. I wonder from whence it came and what it is called.'

'The Kor-ul-ja shouted aloud, "Tarzan-jad-guru!" and we thought that they might be calling this one,' said a warrior. 'Shall we kill it now?'

'No,' replied the chief, 'we will wait until its life returns into its head that I may question it. Remain here, In-tan, and watch it. When it can again hear and speak call me.'

He turned and departed from the cave, the others, except In-tan, following him. As they moved past him and out of the chamber Tarzan caught snatches of their conversation which indicated that the Kor-ul-ja reinforcements had fallen upon their little party in great numbers and driven them away. Evidently the swift feet of Id-an had saved the day for the warriors of Om-at. The ape-man smiled, then he partially opened an eye and cast it upon In-tan. The warrior stood at the entrance to the cave looking out – his back was toward his prisoner. Tarzan tested the bonds that secured his wrists. They seemed none too stout and they had tied his hands in front of him! Evidence indeed that the Waz-don took few prisoners – if any.

Cautiously he raised his wrists until he could examine the thongs that confined them. A grim smile lighted his features. Instantly he was at work upon the bonds with his strong teeth, but ever a wary eye was upon In-tan, the warrior of Kor-ul-lul. The last knot had been loosened and Tarzan's hands were free when In-tan turned to cast an appraising eye upon his ward. He saw that the prisoner's position was changed – he no longer lay upon his back as they had left him, but upon his side and his hands were drawn up against his face. In-tan came closer and bent down. The bonds seemed very loose upon the prisoner's wrists. He extended his hands to examine them with his fingers and instantly the two hands leaped from their bonds – one to seize his own wrist, the other his throat. So unexpected the catlike attack that In-tan had not even time to cry out before steel fingers silenced him. The creature pulled him suddenly forward so that he lost his balance and rolled over upon the prisoner and to the floor beyond to stop with Tarzan upon his breast. In-tan struggled to release himself – struggled to draw his knife; but Tarzan found it before him. The Waz-don's tail leaped to the other's throat, encircling it – he too could choke; but his own knife, in the hands of his antagonist, severed the beloved member close to its root.

The Waz-don's struggles became weaker – a film was obscuring his vision. He knew that he was dying and he was right. A moment later he was dead. Tarzan rose to his feet and placed one foot upon the breast of his dead foe. How the urge seized him to roar forth the victory cry of his kind! But he dared not. He discovered that they had not removed his rope from his shoulders and that they had replaced his knife in its sheath. It had been in his hand when he was felled. Strange creatures! He did not know that they held a superstitious fear of the weapons of a dead enemy, believing that if buried without them he would forever haunt his slayers in search of them and that when he found them he would kill the man who killed him.

Against the wall leaned his bow and quiver of arrows.

Tarzan stepped toward the doorway of the cave and looked out. Night had just fallen. He could hear voices from the nearer caves and there floated to his nostrils the odor of cooking food. He looked down and experienced a sensation of relief. The cave in which he had been held was in the lowest tier – scarce thirty feet from the base of the cliff. He was about to chance an immediate descent when there occurred to him a thought that brought a grin to his savage lips – a thought that was born of the name the Waz-don had given him – Tarzan-jad-guru – Tarzan the Terrible – and a recollection of the days when he had delighted in baiting the blacks of the distant jungle of his birth. He turned back into the cave where lay the dead body of In-tan. With his knife he severed the warrior's head and carrying it to the outer edge of the recess tossed it to the ground below, then he dropped swiftly and silently down the ladder of pegs in a way that would have surprised the Kor-ul-lul who had been so sure that he could not climb.

At the bottom he picked up the head of In-tan and disappeared among the shadows of the trees carrying the grisly trophy by its shock of shaggy hair. Horrible? But you are judging a wild beast by the standards of civilization. You may teach a lion tricks, but he is still a lion. Tarzan looked well in a tuxedo, but he was still a Tarmangani and beneath his pleated shirt beat a wild and savage heart.

Nor was his madness lacking in method. He knew that the hearts of the

Kor-ul-lul would be filled with rage when they discovered the thing that he had done and he knew too, that mixed with the rage would be a leaven of fear and it was fear of him that had made Tarzan master of many jungles – one does not win the respect of the killers with bonbons.

Below the village Tarzan returned to the foot of the cliff searching for a point where he could make the ascent to the ridge and thus back to the village of Om-at, the Kor-ul-ja. He came at last to a place where the river ran so close to the rocky wall that he was forced to swim it in search of a trail upon the opposite side and here it was that his keen nostrils detected a familiar spoor. It was the scent of Pan-at-lee at the spot where she had emerged from the pool and taken to the safety of the jungle.

Immediately the ape-man's plans were changed. Pan-at-lee lived, or at least she had lived after the leap from the cliff's summit. He had started in search of her for Om-at, his friend, and for Om-at he would continue upon the trail he had picked up thus fortuitously by accident. It led him into the jungle and across the gorge and then to the point at which Pan-at-lee had commenced the ascent of the opposite cliffs. Here Tarzan abandoned the head of In-tan, tying it to the lower branch of a tree, for he knew that it would handicap him in his ascent of the steep escarpment. Apelike he ascended, following easily the scent spoor of Pan-at-lee. Over the summit and across the ridge the trail lay, plain as a printed page to the delicate senses of the jungle-bred tracker.

Tarzan knew naught of the Kor-ul-gryf. He had seen, dimly in the shadows of the night, strange, monstrous forms and Ta-den and Om-at had spoken of great creatures that all men feared; but always, everywhere, by night and by day, there were dangers. From infancy death had stalked, grim and terrible, at his heels. He knew little of any other existence. To cope with danger was his life and he lived his life as simply and as naturally as you live yours amidst the dangers of the crowded city streets. The black man who goes abroad in the jungle by night is afraid, for he has spent his life since infancy surrounded by numbers of his own kind and safeguarded, especially at night, by such crude means as lie within his powers. But Tarzan had lived as the lion lives and the panther and the elephant and the ape – a true jungle creature dependent solely upon his prowess and his wits, playing a lone hand against creation. Therefore he was surprised at nothing and feared nothing and so he walked through the strange night as undisturbed and unapprehensive as the farmer to the cow lot in the darkness before the dawn.

Once more Pan-at-lee's trail ended at the verge of a cliff; but this time there was no indication that she had leaped over the edge and a moment's search revealed to Tarzan the stone pegs upon which she had made her descent. As he lay upon his belly leaning over the top of the cliff examining the pegs his attention was suddenly attracted by something at the foot of the cliff. He could not distinguish its identity, but he saw that it moved and presently that it was ascending slowly, apparently by means of pegs similar to those directly below him. He watched it intently as it rose higher and higher until he was able to distinguish its form more clearly, with the result that he became convinced that it more nearly resembled some form of great ape than a lower order. It had a tail, though, and in other respects it did not seem a true ape.

Slowly it ascended to the upper tier of caves, into one of which it disappeared. Then Tarzan took up again the trail of Pan-at-lee. He followed it down the stone pegs to the nearest cave and then farther along the upper tier. The ape-man raised his eyebrows when he saw the direction in which it led, and quickened his pace. He had almost reached the third cave when the echoes of Kor-ul-gryf were awakened by a shrill scream of terror.

6

The Tor-o-don

Pan-at-lee slept – the troubled sleep of physical and nervous exhaustion, filled with weird dreamings. She dreamed that she slept beneath a great tree in the bottom of the Kor-ul-gryf and that one of the fearsome beasts was creeping up on her but she could not open her eyes nor move. She tried to scream but no sound issued from her lips. She felt the thing touch her throat, her breast, her arm, and there it closed and seemed to be dragging her toward it. With a superhuman effort of will she opened her eyes. In the instant she knew that she was dreaming and that quickly the hallucination of the dream would fade – it had happened to her many times before. But it persisted. In the dim light that filtered into the dark chamber she saw a form beside her, she felt hairy fingers upon her and a hairy breast against which she was being drawn. Jad-ben-Otho! this was no dream. And then she screamed and tried to fight the thing from her; but her scream was answered by a low growl and another hairy hand seized her by the hair of the head. The beast rose now upon its hind legs and dragged her from the cave to the moonlit recess without and at the same instant she saw the figure of what she took to be a Ho-don rise above the outer edge of the niche.

The beast that held her saw it too and growled ominously but it did not relinquish its hold upon her hair. It crouched as though waiting an attack, and it increased the volume and frequency of its growls until the horrid sounds reverberated through the gorge, drowning even the deep bellowings of the beasts below, whose mighty thunderings had broken out anew with the sudden commotion from the high-flung cave. The beast that held her crouched and the creature that faced it crouched also, and growled – as hideously as the other. Pan-at-lee trembled. This was no Ho-don and though she feared the Ho-don she feared this thing more, with its catlike crouch and its beastly growls. She was lost – that Pan-at-lee knew. The two things might fight for her, but whichever won she was lost. Perhaps, during the battle, if it came to that, she might find the opportunity to throw herself over into the Kor-ul-gryf.

The thing that held her she had recognized now as a Tor-o-don, but the other thing she could not place, though in the moonlight she could see it very distinctly. It had no tail. She could see its hands and its feet, and they were not the hands and feet of the races of Pal-ul-don. It was slowly closing upon the Tor-o-don and in one hand it held a gleaming knife. Now it spoke and to Pan-at-lee's terror was added an equal weight of consternation.

'When it leaves go of you,' it said, 'as it will presently to defend itself, run quickly behind me, Pan-at-lee, and go to the cave nearest the pegs you descended from the cliff top. Watch from there. If I am defeated you will have time to escape this slow thing; if I am not I will come to you there. I am Om-at's friend and yours.'

The last words took the keen edge from Pan-at-lee's terror; but she did not understand. How did this strange creature know her name? How did it know that she had descended the pegs by a certain cave? It must, then, have been here when she came. Pan-at-lee was puzzled.

'Who are you?' she asked, 'and from whence do you come?'

'I am Tarzan,' he replied, 'and just now I came from Om-at, *gund* of Kor-ul-ja, in search of you.'

Om-at, *gund* of Kor-ul-ja! What wild talk was this? She would have questioned him further, but now he was approaching the Tor-o-don and the latter was screaming and growling so loudly as to drown the sound of her voice. And then it did what the strange creature had said that it would do – it released its hold upon her hair as it prepared to charge. Charge it did and in those close quarters there was no room to fence for openings. Instantly the two beasts locked in deadly embrace, each seeking the other's throat. Pan-at-lee watched, taking no advantage of the opportunity to escape which their preoccupation gave her. She watched and waited, for into her savage little brain had come the resolve to pin her faith to this strange creature who had unlocked her heart with those four words – 'I am Om-at's friend!' And so she waited, with drawn knife, the opportunity to do her bit in the vanquishing of the Tor-o-don. That the newcomer could do it unaided she well knew to be beyond the realms of possibility, for she knew well the prowess of the *beast-like man* with whom it fought. There were not many of them in Pal-ul-don, but what few there were were a terror to the women of the Waz-don and the

Ho-don, for the old Tor-o-don bulls roamed the mountains and the valleys of Pal-ul-don between rutting seasons and woe betide the women who fell in their paths.

With his tail the Tor-o-don sought one of Tarzan's ankles, and finding it, tripped him. The two fell heavily, but so agile was the ape-man and so quick his powerful muscles that even in falling he twisted the beast beneath him, so that Tarzan fell on top and now the tail that had tripped him sought his throat as had the tail of In-tan, the Kor-ul-lul. In the effort of turning his antagonist's body during the fall Tarzan had had to relinquish his knife that he might seize the shaggy body with both hands and now the weapon lay out of reach at the very edge of the recess. Both hands were occupied for the moment in fending off the clutching fingers that sought to seize him and drag his throat within reach of his foe's formidable fangs and now the tail was seeking its deadly hold with a formidable persistence that would not be denied.

Pan-at-lee hovered about, breathless, her dagger ready, but there was no opening that did not also endanger Tarzan, so constantly were the two duelists changing their positions. Tarzan felt the tail slowly but surely insinuating itself about his neck though he had drawn his head down between the muscles of his shoulders in an effort to protect this vulnerable part. The battle seemed to be going against him for the giant beast against which he strove would have been a fair match in weight and strength for Bolgani, the gorilla. And knowing this he suddenly exerted a single superhuman effort, thrust far apart the giant hands and with the swiftness of a striking snake buried his fangs in the jugular of the Tor-o-don. At the same instant the creature's tail coiled about his own throat and then commenced a battle royal of turning and twisting bodies as each sought to dislodge the fatal hold of the other, but the acts of the ape-man were guided by a human brain and thus it was that the rolling bodies rolled in the direction that Tarzan wished – toward the edge of the recess.

The choking tail had shut the air from his lungs, he knew that his gasping lips were parted and his tongue protruding; and now his brain reeled and his sight grew dim; but not before he reached his goal and a quick hand shot out to seize the knife that now lay within reach as the two bodies tottered perilously upon the brink of the chasm.

With all his remaining strength the ape-man drove home the blade – once, twice, thrice, and then all went black before him as he felt himself, still in the clutches of the Tor-o-don, topple from the recess.

Fortunate it was for Tarzan that Pan-at-lee had not obeyed his injunction to make good her escape while he engaged the Tor-o-don, for it was to this fact that he owed his life. Close beside the struggling forms during the brief moments of the terrific climax she had realized every detail of the danger to

Tarzan with which the emergency was fraught and as she saw the two rolling over the outer edge of the niche she seized the ape-man by an ankle, at the same time throwing herself prone upon the rocky floor. The muscles of the Tor-o-don relaxed in death with the last thrust of Tarzan's knife and with its hold upon the ape-man released it shot from sight into the gorge below.

It was with infinite difficulty that Pan-at-lee retained her hold upon the ankle of her protector, but she did so and then, slowly, she sought to drag the deadweight back to the safety of the niche. This, however, was beyond her strength and she could but hold on tightly, hoping that some plan would suggest itself before her powers of endurance failed. She wondered if, after all, the creature was already dead, but that she could not bring herself to believe – and if not dead how long it would be before he regained consciousness. If he did not regain it soon he never would regain it, that she knew, for she felt her fingers numbing to the strain upon them and slipping, slowly, slowly, from their hold. It was then that Tarzan regained consciousness. He could not know what power upheld him, but he felt that whatever it was it was slowly releasing its hold upon his ankle. Within easy reach of his hands were two pegs and these he seized upon just as Pan-at-lee's fingers slipped from their hold.

As it was he came near to being precipitated into the gorge – only his great strength saved him. He was upright now and his feet found other pegs. His first thought was of his foe. Where was he? Waiting above there to finish him? Tarzan looked up just as the frightened face of Pan-at-lee appeared over the threshold of the recess.

'You live?' she cried.

'Yes,' replied Tarzan. 'Where is the shaggy one?'

Pan-at-lee pointed downward. 'There,' she said, 'dead.'

'Good!' exclaimed the ape-man, clambering to her side. 'You are unharmed?' he asked.

'You came just in time,' replied Pan-at-lee; 'but who are you and how did you know that I was here and what do you know of Om-at and where did you come from and what did you mean by calling Om-at, *gund?*'

'Wait, wait,' cried Tarzan; 'one at a time. My, but you are all alike – the shes of the tribe of Kerchak, the ladies of England, and their sisters of Pal-ul-don. Have patience and I will try to tell you all that you wish to know. Four of us set out with Om-at from Kor-ul-ja to search for you. We were attacked by the Kor-ul-lul and separated. I was taken prisoner, but escaped. Again I stumbled upon your trail and followed it, reaching the summit of this cliff just as the hairy one was climbing up after you. I was coming to investigate when I heard your scream – the rest you know.'

'But you called Om-at, *gund* of Kor-ul-ja,' she insisted. 'Es-sat is *gund*.'

'Es-sat is dead,' explained the ape-man. 'Om-at slew him and now Om-at is *gund.* Om-at came back seeking you. He found Es-sat in your cave and killed him.'

'Yes,' said the girl, 'Es-sat came to my cave and I struck him down with my golden breastplates and escaped.'

'And a lion pursued you,' continued Tarzan, 'and you leaped from the cliff into Kor-ul-lul, but why you were not killed is beyond me.'

'Is there anything beyond you?' exclaimed Pan-at-lee. 'How could you know that a lion pursued me and that I leaped from the cliff and not know that it was the pool of deep water below that saved me?'

'I would have known that, too, had not the Kor-ul-lul come then and prevented me continuing upon your trail. But now I would ask you a question – by what name do you call the thing with which I just fought?'

'It was a Tor-o-don,' she replied. 'I have seen but one before. They are terrible creatures with the cunning of man and the ferocity of a beast. Great indeed must be the warrior who slays one single-handed.' She gazed at him in open admiration.

'And now,' said Tarzan, 'you must sleep, for tomorrow we shall return to Kor-ul-ja and Om-at, and I doubt that you have had much rest these two nights.'

Pan-at-lee, lulled by a feeling of security, slept peacefully into the morning while Tarzan stretched himself upon the hard floor of the recess just outside her cave.

The sun was high in the heavens when he awoke; for two hours it had looked down upon another heroic figure miles away – the figure of a godlike man fighting his way through the hideous morass that lies like a filthy moat defending Pal-ul-don from the creatures of the outer world. Now waist deep in the sucking ooze, now menaced by loathsome reptiles, the man advanced only by virtue of Herculean efforts gaining laboriously by inches along the devious way that he was forced to choose in selecting the least precarious footing. Near the center of the morass was open water – slimy, green-hued water. He reached it at last after more than two hours of such effort as would have left an ordinary man spent and dying in the sticky mud, yet he was less than halfway across the marsh. Greasy with slime and mud was his smooth, brown hide, and greasy with slime and mud was his beloved Enfield that had shone so brightly in the first rays of the rising sun.

He paused a moment upon the edge of the open water and then throwing himself forward struck out to swim across. He swam with long, easy, powerful strokes calculated less for speed than for endurance, for his was, primarily, a test of the latter, since beyond the open water was another two hours or more of grueling effort between it and solid ground. He was, perhaps, halfway across and congratulating himself upon the ease of the achievement of this portion of his task when there arose from the depths directly in his path a hideous reptile, which, with wide-distended jaws, bore down upon him, hissing shrilly.

Tarzan arose and stretched, expanded his great chest and drank in deep drafts of the fresh morning air. His clear eyes scanned the wondrous beauties of the landscape spread out before them. Directly below lay Kor-ul-gryf, a dense, somber green of gently moving treetops. To Tarzan it was neither grim, nor forbidding – it was jungle, beloved jungle. To his right there spread a panorama of the lower reaches of the Valley of Jad-ben-Otho, with its winding streams and its blue lakes. Gleaming whitely in the sunlight were scattered groups of dwellings – the feudal strongholds of the lesser chiefs of the Ho-don. A-lur, the City of Light, he could not see as it was hidden by the shoulder of the cliff in which the deserted village lay.

For a moment Tarzan gave himself over to that spiritual enjoyment of beauty that only the man-mind may attain and then Nature asserted herself and the belly of the beast called aloud that it was hungry. Again Tarzan looked down at Kor-ul-gryf. There was the jungle! Grew there a jungle that would not feed Tarzan? The ape-man smiled and commenced the descent to the gorge. Was there danger there? Of course. Who knew it better than Tarzan? In all jungles lies death, for life and death go hand in hand and where life teems death reaps his fullest harvest. Never had Tarzan met a creature of the jungle with which he could not cope – sometimes by virtue of brute strength alone, again by a combination of brute strength and the cunning of the man-mind; but Tarzan had never met a *gryf*.

He had heard the bellowings in the gorge the night before after he had lain down to sleep and he had meant to ask Pan-at-lee this morning what manner of beast so disturbed the slumbers of its betters. He reached the foot of the cliff and strode into the jungle and here he halted, his keen eyes and ears watchful and alert, his sensitive nostrils searching each shifting air current for the scent spoor of game. Again he advanced deeper into the wood, his light step giving forth no sound, his bow and arrows in readiness. A light morning breeze was blowing from up the gorge and in this direction he bent his steps. Many odors impinged upon his organs of scent. Some of these he classified without effort, but others were strange – the odors of beasts and of birds, of trees and shrubs and flowers with which he was unfamiliar. He sensed faintly the reptilian odor that he had learned to connect with the strange, nocturnal forms that had loomed dim and bulky on several occasions since his introduction to Pal-ul-don.

And then, suddenly he caught plainly the strong, sweet odor of Bara, the deer. Were the belly vocal, Tarzan's would have given a little cry of joy, for it loved the flesh of Bara. The ape-man moved rapidly, but cautiously forward. The prey was not far distant and as the hunter approached it, he took silently to the trees and still in his nostrils was the faint reptilian odor that spoke of a great creature which he had never yet seen except as a denser shadow among the dense shadows of the night; but the odor was of such a faintness as suggests to the jungle bred the distance of absolute safety.

And now, moving noiselessly, Tarzan came within sight of Bara drinking at a pool where the stream that waters Kor-ul-gryf crosses an open place in the jungle. The deer was too far from the nearest tree to risk a charge, so the ape-man must depend upon the accuracy and force of his first arrow, which must drop the deer in its tracks or forfeit both deer and shaft. Far back came the right hand and the bow, that you or I might not move, bent easily beneath the muscles of the forest god. There was a singing twang and Bara, leaping high in the air, collapsed upon the ground, an arrow through his heart. Tarzan dropped to earth and ran to his kill, lest the animal might even yet rise and escape; but Bara was safely dead. As Tarzan stooped to lift it to his shoulder there fell upon his ears a thunderous bellow that seemed almost at his right elbow, and as his eyes shot in the direction of the sound, there broke upon his vision such a creature as paleontologists have dreamed as having possibly existed in the dimmest vistas of Earth's infancy – a gigantic creature, vibrant with mad rage, that charged, bellowing, upon him.

When Pan-at-lee awoke she looked out upon the niche in search of Tarzan. He was not there. She sprang to her feet and rushed out, looking down into Kor-ul-gryf guessing that he had gone down in search of food and there she caught a glimpse of him disappearing into the forest. For an instant she was panic-stricken. She knew that he was a stranger in Pal-ul-don and that, so, he might not realize the dangers that lay in that gorge of terror. Why did she not call to him to return? You or I might have done so, but no Pal-ul-don, for they know the ways of the *gryf* – they know the weak eyes and the keen ears, and that at the sound of a human voice they come. To have called to Tarzan, then, would but have been to invite disaster and so she did not call. Instead, afraid though she was, she descended into the gorge for the purpose of overhauling Tarzan and warning him in whispers of his danger. It was a brave act, since it was performed in the face of countless ages of inherited fear of the creatures that she might be called upon to face. Men have been decorated for less.

Pan-at-lee, descended from a long line of hunters, assumed that Tarzan would move upwind and in this direction she sought his tracks, which she soon found well marked, since he had made no effort to conceal them. She moved rapidly until she reached the point at which Tarzan had taken to the trees. Of course she knew what had happened; since her own people were semiarboreal; but she could not track him through the trees, having no such well-developed sense of scent as he.

She could but hope that he had continued on upwind and in this direction she moved, her heart pounding in terror against her ribs, her eyes glancing first in one direction and then another. She had reached the edge of a clearing when two things happened – she caught sight of Tarzan bending over a dead deer and at the same instant a deafening roar sounded almost beside her. It terrified her beyond description, but it brought no paralysis of fear. Instead it galvanized her into instant action with the result that Pan-at-lee swarmed up the nearest tree to the very loftiest branch that would sustain her weight. Then she looked down.

The thing that Tarzan saw charging him when the warning bellow attracted his surprised eyes loomed terrifically monstrous before him – monstrous and awe-inspiring; but it did not terrify Tarzan, it only angered him, for he saw that it was beyond even his powers to combat and that meant that it might cause him to lose his kill, and Tarzan was hungry. There was but a single alternative to remaining for annihilation and that was flight – swift and immediate. And Tarzan fled, but he carried the carcass of Bara, the deer, with him. He had not more than a dozen paces' start, but on the other hand the nearest tree was almost as close. His greatest danger lay, he imagined, in the great, towering height of the creature pursuing him, for even though he reached the tree he would have to climb high in an incredibly short time as, unless appearances were deceiving, the thing could reach up and pluck him down from any branch under thirty feet above the ground, and possibly from those up to fifty feet, if it reared up on its hind legs.

But Tarzan was no sluggard and though the *gryf* was incredibly fast despite its great bulk, it was no match for Tarzan, and when it comes to climbing, the little monkeys gaze with envy upon the feats of the ape-man. And so it was that the bellowing *gryf* came to a baffled stop at the foot of the tree and even though he reared up and sought to seize his prey among the branches, as Tarzan had guessed he might, he failed in this also. And then, well out of reach, Tarzan came to a stop and there, just above him, he saw Pan-at-lee sitting, wide-eyed and trembling.

'How came you here?' he asked.

She told him. 'You came to warn me!' he said. 'It was very brave and unselfish of you. I am chagrined that I should have been thus surprised. The creature was upwind from me and yet I did not sense its near presence until it charged. I cannot understand it.'

'It is not strange,' said Pan-at-lee. 'That is one of the peculiarities of the *gryf* – it is said that man never knows of its presence until it is upon him – so silently does it move despite its great size.'

'But I should have smelled it,' cried Tarzan, disgustedly.

'Smelled it!' ejaculated Pan-at-lee. 'Smelled it?'

'Certainly. How do you suppose I found this deer so quickly? And I sensed the *gryf*, too, but faintly as at a great distance.' Tarzan suddenly ceased speaking and looked down at the bellowing creature below them – his nostrils quivered as though searching for a scent. 'Ah!' he exclaimed. 'I have it!'

'What?' asked Pan-at-lee.

'I was deceived because the creature gives off practically no odor,' explained the ape-man. 'What I smelled was the faint aroma that doubtless permeates the entire jungle because of the long presence of many of the creatures – it is the sort of odor that would remain for a long time, faint as it is.

'Pan-at-lee, did you ever hear of a triceratops? No? Well this thing that you call a *gryf* is a triceratops and it has been extinct for hundreds of thousands of years. I have seen its skeleton in the museum in London and a figure of one restored. I always thought that the scientists who did such work depended principally upon an overwrought imagination, but I see that I was wrong. This living thing is not an exact counterpart of the restoration that I saw; but it is so similar as to be easily recognizable, and then, too, we must remember that during the ages that have elapsed since the paleontologist's specimen lived many changes might have been wrought by evolution in the living line that has quite evidently persisted in Pal-ul-don.'

'Triceratops, London, paleo – I don't know what you are talking about,' cried Pan-at-lee.

Tarzan smiled and threw a piece of dead wood at the face of the angry creature below them. Instantly the great bony hood over the neck was erected and a mad bellow rolled upward from the gigantic body. Full twenty feet at the shoulder the thing stood, a dirty slate-blue in color except for its yellow face with the blue bands encircling the eyes, the red hood with the yellow lining and the yellow belly. The three parallel lines of bony protuberances down the back gave a further touch of color to the body, those following the line of the spine being red, while those on either side are yellow. The five- and three-toed hoofs of the ancient horned dinosaurs had become talons in the *gryf*, but the three horns, two large ones above the eyes and a median horn on the nose, had persisted through all the ages. Weird and terrible as was its appearance Tarzan could not but admire the mighty creature looming big below him, its seventy-five feet of length majestically typifying those things which all his life the ape-man had admired – courage and strength. In that massive tail alone was the strength of an elephant.

The wicked little eyes looked up at him and the horny beak opened to disclose a full set of powerful teeth.

'Herbivorous!' murmured the ape-man. 'Your ancestors may have been, but not you,' and then to Pan-at-lee: 'Let us go now. At the cave we will have deer meat and then – back to Kor-ul-ja and Om-at.'

The girl shuddered. 'Go?' she repeated. 'We will never go from here.'

'Why not?' asked Tarzan.

For answer she but pointed to the *gryf.*

'Nonsense!' exclaimed the man. 'It cannot climb. We can reach the cliff through the trees and be back in the cave before it knows what has become of us.'

'You do not know the *gryf,*' replied Pan-at-lee gloomily. 'Wherever we go it will follow and always it will be ready at the foot of each tree when we would descend. It will never give us up.'

'We can live in the trees for a long time if necessary,' replied Tarzan, 'and sometime the thing will leave.'

The girl shook her head. 'Never,' she said, 'and then there are the Tor-o-don. They will come and kill us and after eating a little will throw the balance to the *gryf* – the *gryf* and Tor-o-don are friends, because the Tor-o-don shares his food with the *gryf.*'

'You may be right,' said Tarzan; 'but even so I don't intend waiting here for someone to come along and eat part of me and then feed the balance to that beast below. If I don't get out of this place whole it won't be my fault. Come along now and we'll make a try at it,' and so saying he moved off through the treetops with Pan-at-lee close behind. Below them, on the ground, moved the horned dinosaur and when they reached the edge of the forest where there lay fifty yards of open ground to cross to the foot of the cliff he was there with them, at the bottom of the tree, waiting.

Tarzan looked ruefully down and scratched his head.

7
Jungle Craft

Presently he looked up and at Pan-at-lee. 'Can you cross the gorge through the trees very rapidly?' he questioned.

'Alone?' she asked.

'No,' replied Tarzan.

'I can follow wherever you can lead,' she said then.

'Across and back again?'

'Then come, and do exactly as I bid.' He started back again through the trees, swiftly, swinging monkeylike from limb to limb, following a zigzag course that he tried to select with an eye for the difficulties of the trail beneath. Where the underbrush was heaviest, where fallen trees blocked the way, he led the footsteps of the creature below them; but all to no avail. When they reached the opposite side of the gorge the *gryf* was with them.

'Back again,' said Tarzan, and, turning, the two retraced their high-flung way through the upper terraces of the ancient forest of Kor-ul-gryf. But the result was the same – no, not quite; it was worse, for another *gryf* had joined the first and now two waited beneath the tree in which they stopped.

The cliff looming high above them with its innumerable cave mouths seemed to beckon and to taunt them. It was so near, yet eternity yawned between. The body of the Tor-o-don lay at the cliff's foot where it had fallen. It was in plain view of the two in the tree. One of the *gryfs* walked over and sniffed about it, but did not offer to devour it. Tarzan had examined it casually as he had passed earlier in the morning. He guessed that it represented either a very high order of ape or a very low order of man – something akin to the Java man, perhaps; a truer example of the pithecanthropi than either the Ho-don or the Waz-don; possibly the precursor of them both. As his eyes wandered idly over the scene below his active brain was working out the details of the plan that he had made to permit Pan-at-lee's escape from the gorge. His thoughts were interrupted by a strange cry from above them in the gorge.

'Whee-oo! Whee-oo!' it sounded, coming closer.

The *gryfs* below raised their heads and looked in the direction of the interruption. One of them made a low, rumbling sound in its throat. It was not a bellow and it did not indicate anger. Immediately the 'Whee-oo!' responded. The *gryfs* repeated the rumbling and at intervals the 'Whee-oo!' was repeated, coming ever closer.

Tarzan looked at Pan-at-lee. 'What is it?' he asked.

'I do not know,' she replied. 'Perhaps a strange bird, or another horrid beast that dwells in this frightful place.'

'Ah,' exclaimed Tarzan; 'there it is. Look!'

Pan-at-lee voiced a cry of despair. 'A Tor-o-don!'

The creature, walking erect and carrying a stick in one hand, advanced at a slow, lumbering gait. It walked directly toward the *gryfs*, who moved aside, as though afraid. Tarzan watched intently. The Tor-o-don was now quite close to one of the triceratops. It swung its head and snapped at him viciously. Instantly the Tor-o-don sprang in and commenced to belabor the huge beast across the face with his stick. To the ape-man's amazement the *gryf*, that might have annihilated the comparatively puny Tor-o-don instantly in any of a dozen ways, cringed like a whipped cur.

'Whee-oo! Whee-oo!' shouted the Tor-o-don and the *gryf* came slowly toward him. A whack on the median horn brought it to a stop. Then the Tor-o-don walked around behind it, clambered up its tail and seated himself astraddle of the huge back. 'Whee-oo!' he shouted and prodded the beast with a sharp point of his stick. The *gryf* commenced to move off.

So rapt had Tarzan been on the scene below him that he had given no thought to escape, for he realized that for him and Pan-at-lee time had in these brief moments turned back countless ages to spread before their eyes a page of the dim and distant past. They two had looked upon the first man and his primitive beasts of burden.

And now the ridden *gryf* halted and looked up at them, bellowing. It was sufficient. The creature had warned its master of their presence. Instantly the Tor-o-don urged the beast close beneath the tree which held them, at the same time leaping to his feet upon the horny back. Tarzan saw the bestial face, the great fangs, the mighty muscles. From the loins of such had sprung the human race – and only from such could it have sprung, for only such as this might have survived the horrid dangers of the age that was theirs.

The Tor-o-don beat upon his breast and growled horribly – hideous, uncouth, beastly. Tarzan rose to his full height upon a swaying branch – straight and beautiful as a demigod – unspoiled by the taint of civilization – a perfect specimen of what the human race might have been had the laws of man not interfered with the laws of nature.

The Present fitted an arrow to his bow and drew the shaft far back. The Past basing its claims upon brute strength sought to reach the other and drag him down; but the loosed arrow sank deep into the savage heart and the Past sank back into the oblivion that had claimed his kind.

'Tarzan-jad-guru!' murmured Pan-at-lee, unknowingly giving him out of the fullness of her admiration the same title that the warriors of her tribe had bestowed upon him.

The ape-man turned to her. 'Pan-at-lee,' he said, 'these beasts may keep us treed here indefinitely. I doubt if we can escape together, but I have a plan. You remain here, hiding yourself in the foliage, while I start back across the gorge in sight of them and yelling to attract their attention. Unless they have more brains than I suspect they will follow me. When they are gone you make for the cliff. Wait for me in the cave not longer than today. If I do not come by tomorrow's sun you will have to start back for Kor-ul-ja alone. Here is a joint of deer meat for you.' He had severed one of the deer's hind legs and this he passed up to her.

'I cannot desert you,' she said simply; 'it is not the way of my people to desert a friend and ally. Om-at would never forgive me.'

'Tell Om-at that I commanded you to go,' replied Tarzan.

'It is a command?' she asked.

'It is! Goodbye, Pan-at-lee. Hasten back to Om-at – you are a fitting mate for the chief of Kor-ul-ja.' He moved off slowly through the trees.

'Goodbye, Tarzan-jad-guru!' she called after him. 'Fortunate are my Om-at and his Pan-at-lee in owning such a friend.'

Tarzan, shouting aloud, continued upon his way and the great *gryfs*, lured by his voice, followed beneath. His ruse was evidently proving successful and he was filled with elation as he led the bellowing beasts farther and farther from Pan-at-lee. He hoped that she would take advantage of the opportunity afforded her for escape, yet at the same time he was filled with concern as to her ability to survive the dangers which lay between Kor-ul-gryf and Kor-ul-ja. There were lions and Tor-o-dons and the unfriendly tribe of Kor-ul-lul to hinder her progress, though the distance in itself to the cliffs of her people was not great.

He realized her bravery and understood the resourcefulness that she must share in common with all primitive people who, day by day, must contend face-to-face with nature's law of the survival of the fittest, unaided by any of the numerous artificial protections that civilization has thrown around its brood of weaklings.

Several times during this crossing of the gorge Tarzan endeavored to outwit his keen pursuers, but all to no avail. Double as he would he could not throw them off his track and ever as he changed his course they changed theirs to conform. Along the verge of the forest upon the southeastern side of the gorge he sought some point at which the trees touched some negotiable portion of the cliff, but though he traveled far both up and down the gorge he discovered no such easy avenue of escape. The ape-man finally commenced to entertain an idea of the hopelessness of his case and to realize to the full why the Kor-ul-gryf had been religiously abjured by the races of Pal-ul-don for all these many ages.

Night was falling and though since early morning he had sought diligently a way out of his cul-de-sac he was no nearer to liberty than at the moment the first bellowing *gryf* had charged him as he stooped over the carcass of his kill: but with the falling of night came renewed hope for, in common with the great cats, Tarzan was, to a greater or lesser extent, a nocturnal beast. It is true he could not see by night as well as they, but that lack was largely recompensed for by the keenness of his scent and the highly developed sensitiveness of his other organs of perception. As the blind follow and interpret their Braille characters with deft fingers, so Tarzan reads the book of the jungle with feet and hands and eyes and ears and nose; each contributing its share to the quick and accurate translation of the text.

But again he was doomed to be thwarted by one vital weakness – he did not know the *gryf*, and before the night was over he wondered if the things never slept, for wheresoever he moved they moved also, and always they barred his road to liberty. Finally, just before dawn, he relinquished his immediate effort and sought rest in a friendly tree crotch in the safety of the middle terrace.

Once again was the sun high when Tarzan awoke, rested and refreshed. Keen to the necessities of the moment he made no effort to locate his jailers lest in the act he might apprise them of his movements. Instead he sought cautiously and silently to melt away among the foliage of the trees. His first move, however, was heralded by a deep bellow from below.

Among the numerous refinements of civilization that Tarzan had failed to acquire was that of profanity, and possibly it is to be regretted since there are circumstances under which it is at least a relief to pent emotion. And it may be that in effect Tarzan resorted to profanity if there can be physical as well as vocal swearing, since immediately the bellow announced that his hopes had been again frustrated, he turned quickly and seeing the hideous face of the *gryf* below him seized a large fruit from a nearby branch and hurled it viciously at the horned snout. The missile struck full between the creature's eyes, resulting in a reaction that surprised the ape-man; it did not arouse the beast to a show of revengeful rage as Tarzan had expected and hoped; instead the creature gave a single vicious side snap at the fruit as it bounded from his skull and then turned sulkily away, walking off a few steps.

There was that in the act that recalled immediately to Tarzan's mind similar action on the preceding day when the Tor-o-don had struck one of the creatures across the face with his staff, and instantly there sprung to the cunning and courageous brain a plan of escape from his predicament that might have blanched the cheek of the most heroic.

The gambling instinct is not strong among creatures of the wild; the chances of their daily life are sufficient stimuli for the beneficial excitement of their nerve centers. It has remained for civilized man, protected in a measure from the natural dangers of existence, to invent artificial stimulants in the form of cards and dice and roulette wheels. Yet when necessity bids there are no greater gamblers than the savage denizens of the jungle, the forest, and the hills, for as lightly as you roll the ivory cubes upon the green cloth they will gamble with death – their own lives the stake.

And so Tarzan would gamble now, pitting the seemingly wild deductions of his shrewd brain against all the proofs of the bestial ferocity of his antagonists that his experience of them had adduced – against all the age-old folklore and legend that had been handed down for countless generations and passed on to him through the lips of Pan-at-lee.

Yet as he worked in preparation for the greatest play that man can make in the game of life, he smiled; nor was there any indication of haste or excitement or nervousness in his demeanor.

First he selected a long, straight branch about two inches in diameter at its base. This he cut from the tree with his knife, removed the smaller branches and twigs until he had fashioned a pole about ten feet in length. This he sharpened at the smaller end. The staff finished to his satisfaction he looked down upon the triceratops.

'Whee-oo!' he cried.

Instantly the beasts raised their heads and looked at him. From the throat of one of them came faintly a low rumbling sound.

'Whee-oo!' repeated Tarzan and hurled the balance of the carcass of the deer to them.

Instantly the *gryfs* fell upon it with much bellowing, one of them attempting to seize it and keep it from the other; but finally the second obtained a hold and an instant later it had been torn asunder and greedily devoured. Once again they looked up at the ape-man and this time they saw him descending to the ground.

One of them started toward him. Again Tarzan repeated the weird cry of the Tor-o-don. The *gryf* halted in his track, apparently puzzled, while Tarzan slipped lightly to the earth and advanced toward the nearer beast, his staff raised menacingly and the call of the first-man upon his lips.

Would the cry be answered by the low rumbling of the beast of burden or the horrid bellow of the man-eater? Upon the answer to this question hung the fate of the ape-man.

Pan-at-lee was listening intently to the sounds of the departing *gryfs* as Tarzan led them cunningly from her, and when she was sure that they were far enough away to insure her safe retreat she dropped swiftly from the branches to the ground and sped like a frightened deer across the open space to the foot of the cliff, stepped over the body of the Tor-o-don who had attacked her the night before and was soon climbing rapidly up the ancient stone pegs of the deserted cliff village. In the mouth of the cave near that which she had occupied she kindled a fire and cooked the haunch of venison that Tarzan had left her, and from one of the trickling streams that ran down the face of the escarpment she obtained water to satisfy her thirst.

All day she waited, hearing in the distance, and sometimes close at hand, the bellowing of the *gryfs* which pursued the strange creature that had dropped so miraculously into her life. For him she felt the same keen, almost fanatical loyalty that many another had experienced for Tarzan of the Apes. Beast and human, he had held them to him with bonds that were stronger than steel – those of them that were clean and courageous, and the weak and the helpless; but never could Tarzan claim among his admirers the coward, the ingrate or the scoundrel; from such, both man and beast, he had won fear and hatred.

To Pan-at-lee he was all that was brave and noble and heroic and, too, he was Om-at's friend – the friend of the man she loved. For any one of these reasons Pan-at-lee would have died for Tarzan, for such is the loyalty of the simple-minded children of nature. It has remained for civilization to teach us to weigh the relative rewards of loyalty and its antithesis. The loyalty of the primitive is spontaneous, unreasoning, unselfish and such was the loyalty of Pan-at-lee for the Tarmangani.

And so it was that she waited that day and night, hoping that he would return that she might accompany him back to Om-at, for her experience had taught her that in the face of danger two have a better chance than one. But Tarzan-jad-guru had not come, and so upon the following morning Pan-at-lee set out upon her return to Kor-ul-ja.

She knew the dangers and yet she faced them with the stolid indifference of her race. When they directly confronted and menaced her would be time enough to experience fear or excitement or confidence. In the meantime it was unnecessary to waste nerve energy by anticipating them. She moved therefore through her savage land with no greater show of concern than might mark your sauntering to a corner drugstore for a sundae. But this is your life and that is Pan-at-lee's and even now as you read this Pan-at-lee may be sitting upon the edge of the recess of Om-at's cave while the *ja* and *jaw* roar from the gorge below and from the ridge above, and the Kor-ul-lul threaten upon the south and the Ho-don from the Valley of Jad-ben-Otho far below, for Pan-at-lee still lives and preens her silky coat of jet beneath the tropical moonlight of Pal-ul-don.

But she was not to reach Kor-ul-ja this day, nor the next, nor for many days after though the danger that threatened her was neither Waz-don enemy nor savage beast.

She came without misadventure to the Kor-ul-lul and after descending its rocky southern wall without catching the slightest glimpse of the hereditary enemies of her people, she experienced a renewal of confidence that was little short of practical assurance that she would successfully terminate her venture and be restored once more to her own people and the lover she had not seen for so many long and weary moons.

She was almost across the gorge now and moving with an extreme caution abated no wit by her confidence, for wariness is an instinctive trait of the primitive, something which cannot be laid aside even momentarily if one would survive. And so she came to the trail that follows the windings of Kor-ul-lul from its uppermost reaches down into the broad and fertile Valley of Jad-ben-Otho.

And as she stepped into the trail there arose on either side of her from out of the bushes that border the path, as though materialized from thin air, a score of tall, white warriors of the Ho-don. Like a frightened deer Pan-at-lee cast a single startled look at these menacers of her freedom and leaped quickly toward the bushes in an effort to escape; but the warriors were too close at hand. They closed upon her from every side and then, drawing her knife she turned at bay, metamorphosed by the fires of fear and hate from a startled deer to a raging tiger-cat. They did not try to kill her, but only to subdue and capture her, and so it was that more than a single Ho-don warrior felt the keen edge of her blade in his flesh before they had succeeded in overpowering her by numbers. And still she fought and scratched and bit after they had taken the knife from her until it was necessary to tie her hands and fasten a piece of wood between her teeth by means of thongs passed behind her head.

At first she refused to walk when they started off in the direction of the valley but after two of them had seized her by the hair and dragged her for a number of yards she thought better of her original decision and came along with them, though still as defiant as her bound wrists and gagged mouth would permit.

Near the entrance to Kor-ul-lul they came upon another body of their warriors with which were several Waz-don prisoners from the tribe of Kor-ul-lul. It was a raiding party come up from a Ho-don city of the valley after slaves. This Pan-at-lee knew for the occurrence was by no means unusual. During her lifetime the tribe to which she belonged had been sufficiently fortunate, or powerful, to withstand successfully the majority of such raids made upon them, but yet Pan-at-lee had known of friends and relatives who had been carried into slavery by the Ho-don and she knew, too, another thing which gave her hope, as doubtless it did to each of the other captives – that occasionally the prisoners escaped from the cities of the hairless whites.

After they had joined the other party the entire band set forth into the valley and presently, from the conversation of her captors, Pan-at-lee knew that she was headed for A-lur, the City of Light; while in the cave of his ancestors, Om-at, chief of the Kor-ul-ja, bemoaned the loss of both his friend and she that was to have been his mate.

8

A-lur

As the hissing reptile bore down upon the stranger swimming in the open water near the center of the morass on the frontier of Pal-ul-don it seemed to the man that this indeed must be the futile termination of an arduous and danger-filled journey. It seemed, too, equally futile to pit his puny knife against this frightful creature. Had he been attacked on land it is possible that he might as a last resort have used his Enfield, though he had come thus far through all these weary, danger-ridden miles without recourse to it, though again and again had his life hung in the balance in the face of the savage denizens of forest, jungle, and steppe. For whatever it may have been for which he was preserving his precious ammunition he evidently held it more sacred even than his life, for as yet he had not used a single round and now the decision was not required of him, since it would have been impossible for him to have unslung his Enfield, loaded and fired with the necessary celerity while swimming.

Though his chance for survival seemed slender, and hope at its lowest ebb, he was not minded therefore to give up without a struggle. Instead he drew his blade and awaited the oncoming reptile. The creature was like no living thing he ever before had seen although possibly it resembled a crocodile in some respects more than it did anything with which he was familiar.

As this frightful survivor of some extinct progenitor charged upon him with distended jaws there came to the man quickly a full consciousness of the futility of endeavoring to stay the mad rush or pierce the armor-coated hide with his little knife. The thing was almost upon him now and whatever form of defense he chose must be made quickly. There seemed but a single alternative to instant death, and this he took at almost the instant the great reptile towered directly above him.

With the celerity of a seal he dove headforemost beneath the oncoming body and at the same instant, turning upon his back, he plunged his blade into the soft, cold surface of the slimy belly as the momentum of the hurtling reptile carried it swiftly over him; and then with powerful strokes he swam on beneath the surface for a dozen yards before he rose. A glance showed him the stricken monster plunging madly in pain and rage upon the surface of the water behind him. That it was writhing in its death agonies was evidenced by the fact that it made no effort to pursue him, and so, to the accompaniment of the shrill screaming of the dying monster, the man won at last to the farther edge of the open water to take up once more the almost superhuman effort of crossing the last stretch of clinging mud which separated him from the solid ground of Pal-ul-don.

A good two hours it took him to drag his now weary body through the clinging, stinking muck, but at last, mud covered and spent, he dragged himself out upon the soft grasses of the bank. A hundred yards away a stream, winding its way down from the distant mountains, emptied into the morass, and, after a short rest, he made his way to this and seeking a quiet pool, bathed himself and washed the mud and slime from his weapons, accouterments, and loincloth. Another hour was spent beneath the rays of the hot sun in wiping, polishing, and oiling his Enfield though the means at hand for drying it consisted principally of dry grasses. It was afternoon before he had satisfied himself that his precious weapon was safe from any harm by dirt, or dampness, and then he arose and took up the search for the spoor he had followed to the opposite side of the swamp.

Would he find again the trail that had led into the opposite side of the morass, to be lost there, even to his trained senses? If he found it not again upon this side of the almost impassable bather he might assume that his long journey had ended in failure. And so he sought up and down the verge of the stagnant water for traces of an old spoor that would have been invisible to your eyes or mine, even had we followed directly in the tracks of its maker.

As Tarzan advanced upon the *gryfs* he imitated as closely as he could recall them the methods and mannerisms of the Tor-o-don, but up to the instant that he stood close beside one of the huge creatures he realized that his fate still hung in the balance, for the thing gave forth no sign, either menacing or otherwise. It only stood there, watching him out of its cold, reptilian eyes and then Tarzan raised his staff and with a menacing 'Whee-oo!' struck the *gryf* a vicious blow across the face.

The creature made a sudden side snap in his direction, a snap that did not reach him, and then turned sullenly away, precisely as it had when the Tor-o-don commanded it. Walking around to its rear as he had seen the shaggy first-man do, Tarzan ran up the broad tail and seated himself upon the creature's back, and then again imitating the acts of the Tor-o-don he prodded it with the sharpened point of his staff, and thus goading it forward and guiding it with blows, first upon one side and then upon the other, he started it down the gorge in the direction of the valley.

At first it had been in his mind only to determine if he could successfully assert any authority over the great monsters, realizing that in this possibility lay his only hope of immediate escape from his jailers. But once seated upon the back of his titanic mount the ape-man experienced the sensation of a new thrill that recalled to him the day in his boyhood that he had first clambered to the broad head of Tantor, the elephant, and this, together with the sense of mastery that was always meat and drink to the lord of the jungle, decided him to put his newly acquired power to some utilitarian purpose.

Pan-at-lee he judged must either have already reached safety or met with death. At least, no longer could he be of service to her, while below Kor-ul-gryf, in the soft green valley, lay A-lur, the City of Light, which, since he had gazed upon it from the shoulder of Pastar-ul-ved, had been his ambition and his goal.

Whether or not its gleaming walls held the secret of his lost mate he could not even guess but if she lived at all within the precincts of Pal-ul-don it must be among the Ho-don, since the hairy black men of this forgotten world took no prisoners. And so to A-lur he would go, and how more effectively than upon the back of this grim and terrible creature that the races of Pal-ul-don held in such awe?

A little mountain stream tumbles down from Kor-ul-gryf to be joined in the foothills with that which empties the waters of Kor-ul-lul into the valley, forming a small river which runs southwest, eventually entering the valley's largest lake at the City of A-lur, through the center of which the stream passes. An ancient trail, well marked by countless generations of naked feet of man and beast, leads down toward A-lur beside the river, and along this Tarzan guided the *gryf*. Once clear of the forest which ran below the mouth of the gorge, Tarzan caught occasional glimpses of the city gleaming in the distance far below him.

The country through which he passed was resplendent with the riotous beauties of tropical verdure. Thick, lush grasses grew waist high upon either side of the trail and the way was broken now and again by patches of open parklike forest, or perhaps a little patch of dense jungle where the trees overarched the way and trailing creepers depended in graceful loops from branch to branch.

At times the ape-man had difficulty in commanding obedience upon the part of his unruly beast, but always in the end its fear of the relatively puny goad urged it on to obedience. Late in the afternoon as they approached the confluence of the stream they were skirting and another which appeared to come from the direction of Kor-ul-ja the ape-man, emerging from one of the jungle patches, discovered a considerable party of Ho-don upon the opposite bank. Simultaneously they saw him and the mighty creature he bestrode. For a moment they stood in wide-eyed amazement and then, in answer to the command of their leader, they turned and bolted for the shelter of the nearby wood.

The ape-man had but a brief glimpse of them but it was sufficient indication that there were Waz-don with them, doubtless prisoners taken in one of the raids upon the Waz-don villages of which Ta-den and Om-at had told him.

At the sound of their voices the *gryf* had bellowed terrifically and started in pursuit even though a river intervened, but by dint of much prodding and beating, Tarzan had succeeded in heading the animal back onto the path though thereafter for a long time it was sullen and more intractable than ever.

As the sun dropped nearer the summit of the western hills Tarzan became aware that his plan to enter A-lur upon the back of a *gryf* was likely doomed to failure, since the stubbornness of the great beast was increasing momentarily, doubtless due to the fact that its huge belly was crying out for food. The ape-man wondered if the Tor-o-dons had any means of picketing their beasts for the night, but as he did not know and as no plan suggested itself, he determined that he should have to trust to the chance of finding it again in the morning.

There now arose in his mind a question as to what would be their relationship when Tarzan had dismounted. Would it again revert to that of hunter and quarry or would fear of the goad continue to hold its supremacy over the natural instinct of the hunting flesh-eater? Tarzan wondered but as he could not remain upon the *gryf* forever, and as he preferred dismounting and putting the matter to a final test while it was still light, he decided to act at once.

How to stop the creature he did not know, as up to this time his sole desire had been to urge it forward. By experimenting with his staff, however, he found that he could bring it to a halt by reaching forward and striking the thing upon its beaklike snout. Close by grew a number of leafy trees, in any one of which the ape-man could have found sanctuary, but it had occurred to him that should he immediately take to the trees it might suggest to the mind of the *gryf* that the creature that had been commanding him all day feared him, with the result that Tarzan would once again be held a prisoner by the triceratops.

And so, when the *gryf* halted, Tarzan slid to the ground, struck the creature a careless blow across the flank as though in dismissal and walked indifferently away. From the throat of the beast came a low rumbling sound and without even a glance at Tarzan it turned and entered the river where it stood drinking for a long time.

Convinced that the *gryf* no longer constituted a menace to him the ape-man, spurred on himself by the gnawing of hunger, unslung his bow and selecting a handful of arrows set forth cautiously in search of food, evidence of the near presence of which was being borne up to him by a breeze from downriver.

Ten minutes later he had made his kill, again one of the Pal-ul-don specimens of antelope, all species of which Tarzan had known since childhood as Bara, the deer, since in the little primer that had been the basis of his education the picture of a deer had been the nearest approach to the likeness of the antelope, from the giant eland to the smaller bushbuck of the hunting grounds of his youth.

Cutting off a haunch he cached it in a nearby tree, and throwing the balance of the carcass across his shoulder trotted back toward the spot at which he had left the *gryf*. The great beast was just emerging from the river when Tarzan, seeing it, issued the weird cry of the Tor-o-don. The creature looked in the direction of the sound voicing at the same time the low rumble with which it answered the call of its master. Twice Tarzan repeated his cry before the beast moved slowly toward him, and when it had come within a few paces he tossed the carcass of the deer to it, upon which it fell with greedy jaws.

'If anything will keep it within call,' mused the ape-man as he returned to the tree in which he had cached his own portion of his kill, 'it is the knowledge that I will feed it.' But as he finished his repast and settled himself comfortably for the night high among the swaying branches of his eyrie he had little confidence that he would ride into A-lur the following day upon his prehistoric steed.

When Tarzan awoke early the following morning he dropped lightly to the ground and made his way to the stream. Removing his weapons and loincloth he entered the cold waters of the little pool and after his refreshing bath returned to the tree to breakfast upon another portion of Bara, the deer, adding to his repast some fruits and berries which grew in abundance nearby.

His meal over, he sought the ground again and raising his voice in the weird cry that he had learned, he called aloud on the chance of attracting the *gryf*, but though he waited for some time and continued calling there was no response, and he was finally forced to the conclusion that he had seen the last of his great mount of the preceding day.

And so he set his face toward A-lur, pinning his faith upon his knowledge of the Ho-don tongue, his great strength and his native wit.

Refreshed by food and rest, the journey toward A-lur, made in the cool of the morning along the bank of the joyous river, he found delightful in the extreme. Differentiating him from his fellows of the savage jungle were many characteristics other than those physical and mental. Not the least of these were in a measure spiritual, and one that had doubtless been as strong as another in influencing Tarzan's love of the jungle had been his appreciation of the beauties of nature. The apes cared more for a grubworm in a rotten log than for all the majestic grandeur of the forest giants waving above them. The only beauties that Numa acknowledged were those of his own person as he paraded them before the admiring eyes of his mate, but in all the manifestations of the creative power of nature of which Tarzan was cognizant he appreciated the beauties.

As Tarzan neared the city his interest became centered upon the architecture of the outlying buildings which were hewn from the chalklike limestone of what had once been a group of low hills, similar to the many grass-covered hillocks that dotted the valley in every direction. Ta-den's explanation of the Ho-don methods of house construction accounted for the ofttimes remarkable shapes and proportions of the buildings which, during the ages that must have been required for their construction, had been hewn from the limestone hills, the exteriors chiseled to such architectural forms as appealed to the eyes of the builders while at the same time following roughly the original outlines of the hills in an evident desire to economize both labor and space. The excavation of the apartments within had been similarly governed by necessity.

As he came nearer Tarzan saw that the waste material from these building operations had been utilized in the construction of outer walls about each building or group of buildings resulting from a single hillock, and later he was to learn that it had also been used for the filling of inequalities between the hills and the forming of paved streets throughout the city, the result, possibly, more of the adoption of an easy method of disposing of the quantities of broken limestone than by any real necessity for pavements.

There were people moving about within the city and upon the narrow ledges and terraces that broke the lines of the buildings and which seemed to be a peculiarity of Ho-don architecture, a concession, no doubt, to some inherent instinct that might be traced back to their early cliff-dwelling progenitors.

Tarzan was not surprised that at a short distance he aroused no suspicion or curiosity in the minds of those who saw him, since, until closer scrutiny was possible, there was little to distinguish him from a native either in his general conformation or his color. He had, of course, formulated a plan of action and, having decided, he did not hesitate in the carrying out his plan.

With the same assurance that you might venture upon the main street of a neighboring city Tarzan strode into the Ho-don city of A-lur. The first person to detect his spuriousness was a little child playing in the arched gateway of one of the walled buildings. 'No tail! no tail!' it shouted, throwing a stone at him, and then it suddenly grew dumb and its eyes wide as it sensed that this creature was something other than a mere Ho-don warrior who had lost his tail. With a gasp the child turned and fled screaming into the courtyard of its home.

Tarzan continued on his way, fully realizing that the moment was imminent when the fate of his plan would be decided. Nor had he long to wait since at the next turning of the winding street he came face-to-face with a Ho-don warrior. He saw the sudden surprise in the latter's eyes, followed instantly by a look of suspicion, but before the fellow could speak Tarzan addressed him.

'I am a stranger from another land,' he said; 'I would speak with Ko-tan, your king.'

The fellow stepped back, laying his hand upon his knife. 'There are no strangers that come to the gates of A-lur,' he said, 'other than as enemies or slaves.'

'I come neither as a slave nor an enemy,' replied Tarzan. 'I come directly from Jad-ben-Otho. Look!' and he held out his hands that the Ho-don might see how greatly they differed from his own, and then wheeled about that the other might see that he was tailless, for it was upon this fact that his plan had been based, due to his recollection of the quarrel between Ta-den and Om-at, in which the Waz-don had claimed that Ja-ben-Otho had a long tail while the Ho-don had been equally willing to fight for his faith in the taillessness of his god.

The warrior's eyes widened and an expression of awe crept into them, though it was still tinged with suspicion. 'Jad-ben-Otho!' he murmured, and then, 'It is true that you are neither Ho-don nor Waz-don, and it is also true that Jad-ben-Otho has no tail. Come,' he said, 'I will take you to Ko-tan, for this is a matter in which no common warrior may interfere. Follow me,' and still clutching the handle of his knife and keeping a wary side glance upon the ape-man he led the way through A-lur.

The city covered a large area. Sometimes there was a considerable distance between groups of buildings, and again they were quite close together. There were numerous imposing groups, evidently hewn from the larger hills, often rising to a height of a hundred feet or more. As they advanced they met numerous warriors and women, all of whom showed great curiosity in the stranger, but there was no attempt to menace him when it was found that he was being conducted to the palace of the king.

They came at last to a great pile that sprawled over a considerable area, its western front facing upon a large blue lake and evidently hewn from what had once been a natural cliff. This group of buildings was surrounded by a wall of considerably greater height than any that Tarzan had before seen. His guide led him to a gateway before which waited a dozen or more warriors who had risen to their feet and formed a barrier across the entranceway as Tarzan and his party appeared around the corner of the palace wall, for by this time he had accumulated such a following of the curious as presented to the guards the appearance of a formidable mob.

The guide's story told, Tarzan was conducted into the courtyard where he was held while one of the warriors entered the palace, evidently with the intention of notifying Ko-tan. Fifteen minutes later a large warrior appeared, followed by several others, all of whom examined Tarzan with every sign of curiosity as they approached.

The leader of the party halted before the ape-man. 'Who are you?' he asked. 'What do you want of Ko-tan, the king?'

'I am a friend,' replied the ape-man, 'and I have come from the country of Jad-ben-Otho to visit Ko-tan of Pal-ul-don.'

The warrior and his followers seemed impressed. Tarzan could see the latter whispering among themselves.

'How come you here,' asked the spokesman, 'and what do you want of Ko-tan?'

Tarzan drew himself to his full height. 'Enough!' he cried. 'Must the messenger of Jad-ben-Otho be subjected to the treatment that might be accorded to a wandering Waz-don? Take me to the king at once lest the wrath of Jad-ben-Otho fall upon you.'

There was some question in the mind of the ape-man as to how far he might carry his unwarranted show of assurance, and he waited therefore with amused interest the result of his demand. He did not, however, have long to wait for almost immediately the attitude of his questioner changed. He whitened, cast an apprehensive glance toward the eastern sky and then extended his right palm toward Tarzan, placing his left over his own heart in the sign of amity that was common among the peoples of Pal-ul-don.

Tarzan stepped quickly back as though from a profaning hand, a feigned expression of horror and disgust upon his face.

'Stop!' he cried. 'Who would dare touch the sacred person of the messenger of Jad-ben-Otho? Only as a special mark of favor from Jad-ben-Otho may even Ko-tan himself receive this honor from me. Hasten! Already now have I waited too long! What manner of reception the Ho-don of A-lur would extend to the son of my father!'

At first Tarzan had been inclined to adopt the role of Jad-ben-Otho himself but it occurred to him that it might prove embarrassing and considerable of a bore to be compelled constantly to portray the character of a god, but with the growing success of his scheme it had suddenly occurred to him that the authority of the son of Jad-ben-Otho would be far greater than that of an ordinary messenger of a god, while at the same time giving him some leeway in the matter of his acts and demeanor, the ape-man reasoning that a young god would not be held so strictly accountable in the matter of his dignity and bearing as an older and greater god.

This time the effect of his words was immediately and painfully noticeable upon all those near him. With one accord they shrank back, the spokesman almost collapsing in evident terror. His apologies, when finally the paralysis of his fear would permit him to voice them, were so abject that the ape-man could scarce repress a smile of amused contempt.

'Have mercy, O Dor-ul-Otho,' he pleaded, 'on poor old Dak-lot. Precede me and I will show you to where Ko-tan, the king, awaits you, trembling. Aside, snakes and vermin,' he cried pushing his warriors to right and left for the purpose of forming an avenue for Tarzan.

'Come!' cried the ape-man peremptorily, 'lead the way, and let these others follow.'

The now thoroughly frightened Dak-lot did as he was bid, and Tarzan of the Apes was ushered into the palace of Ko-tan, King of Pal-ul-don.

9

Bloodstained Altars

The entrance through which he caught his first glimpse of the interior was rather beautifully carved in geometric designs, and within the walls were similarly treated, though as he proceeded from one apartment to another he found also the figures of animals, birds, and men taking their places among the more formal figures of the mural decorator's art. Stone vessels were much in evidence as well as ornaments of gold and the skins of many animals, but nowhere did he see an indication of any woven fabric, indicating that in that respect at least the Ho-don were still low in the scale of evolution, and yet the proportions and symmetry of the corridors and apartments bespoke a degree of civilization.

The way led through several apartments and long corridors, up at least three flights of stone stairs and finally out upon a ledge upon the western side of the building overlooking the blue lake. Along this ledge, or arcade, his guide led him for a hundred yards, to stop at last before a wide entranceway leading into another apartment of the palace.

Here Tarzan beheld a considerable concourse of warriors in an enormous apartment, the domed ceiling of which was fully fifty feet above the floor. Almost filling the chamber was a great pyramid ascending in broad steps well up under the dome in which were a number of round apertures which let in the light. The steps of the pyramid were occupied by warriors to the very pinnacle, upon which sat a large, imposing figure of a man whose golden trappings shone brightly in the light of the afternoon sun, a shaft of which poured through one of the tiny apertures of the dome.

'Ko-tan!' cried Dak-lot, addressing the resplendent figure at the pinnacle of the pyramid. 'Ko-tan and warriors of Pal-ul-don! Behold the honor that Jad-ben-Otho has done you in sending as his messenger his own son,' and Dak-lot, stepping aside, indicated Tarzan with a dramatic sweep of his hand.

Ko-tan rose to his feet and every warrior within sight craned his neck to have a better view of the newcomer. Those upon the opposite side of the pyramid crowded to the front as the words of the old warrior reached them. Skeptical were the expressions on most of the faces; but theirs was a skepticism marked with caution. No matter which way fortune jumped they wished to be upon the right side of the fence. For a moment all eyes were centered upon Tarzan and then gradually they drifted to Ko-tan, for from his attitude would they receive the cue that would determine theirs. But Ko-tan was evidently in the same quandary as they – the very attitude of his body indicated it – it was one of indecision and of doubt.

The ape-man stood erect, his arms folded upon his broad breast, an expression of haughty disdain upon his handsome face; but to Dak-lot there seemed to be indications also of growing anger. The situation was becoming strained. Dak-lot fidgeted, casting apprehensive glances at Tarzan and appealing ones at Kotan. The silence of the tomb wrapped the great chamber of the throne-room of Pal-ul-don.

At last Ko-tan spoke. 'Who says that he is Dor-ul-Otho?' he asked, casting a terrible look at Dak-lot.

'He does!' almost shouted that terrified noble.

'And so it must be true?' queried Ko-tan.

Could it be that there was a trace of irony in the chief's tone? Otho forbid! Dak-lot cast a side glance at Tarzan – a glance that he intended should carry the assurance of his own faith; but that succeeded only in impressing the ape-man with the other's pitiable terror.

'O Ko-tan!' pleaded Dak-lot, 'your own eyes must convince you that indeed he is the son of Otho. Behold his godlike figure, his hands, and his feet, that are not as ours, and that he is entirely tailless as is his mighty father.'

Ko-tan appeared to be perceiving these facts for the first time and there was an indication that his skepticism was faltering. At that moment a young warrior who had pushed his way forward from the opposite side of the pyramid to where he could obtain a good look at Tarzan raised his voice.

'Ko-tan,' he cried, 'it must be even as Dak-lot says, for I am sure now that I have seen Dor-ul-Otho before. Yesterday as we were returning with the Kor-ul-lul prisoners we beheld him seated upon the back of a great *gryf*. We hid in the woods before he came too near, but I saw enough to make sure that he who rode upon the great beast was none other than the messenger who stands here now.'

This evidence seemed to be quite enough to convince the majority of the warriors that they indeed stood in the presence of deity – their faces showed it only too plainly, and a sudden modesty that caused them to shrink behind their neighbors. As their neighbors were attempting to do the same thing, the result was a sudden melting away of those who stood nearest the ape-man, until the steps of the pyramid directly before him lay vacant to the very apex and to Ko-tan. The latter, possibly influenced as much by the fearful attitude of his followers as by the evidence adduced, now altered his tone and his manner in such a degree as might comport with the requirements if the stranger was indeed the Dor-ul-Otho while leaving his dignity a loophole of escape should it appear that he had entertained an impostor.

'If indeed you are the Dor-ul-Otho,' he said, addressing Tarzan, 'you will know that our doubts were but natural since we have received no sign from Jad-ben-Otho that he intended honoring us so greatly, nor how could we know, even, that the Great God had a son? If you are he, all Pal-ul-don rejoices to honor you; if you are not he, swift and terrible shall be the punishment of your temerity. I, Ko-tan, King of Pal-ul-don, have spoken.'

'And spoken well, as a king should speak,' said Tarzan, breaking his long silence, 'who fears and honors the god of his people. It is well that you insist that I indeed be the Dor-ul-Otho before you accord me the homage that is my due. Jad-ben-Otho charged me specially to ascertain if you were fit to rule his people. My first experience of you indicates that Jad-ben-Otho chose well when he breathed the spirit of a king into the babe at your mother's breast.'

The effect of this statement, made so casually, was marked in the expressions and excited whispers of the now awestruck assemblage. At last they knew how kings were made! It was decided by Jad-ben-Otho while the candidate was still a suckling babe! Wonderful! A miracle! And this divine creature in whose presence they stood knew all about it. Doubtless he even discussed such matters with their god daily. If there had been an atheist among them before, or an agnostic, there was none now, for had they not looked with their own eyes upon the son of god?

'It is well then,' continued the ape-man, 'that you should assure yourself that I am no impostor. Come closer that you may see that I am not as are men. Furthermore it is not meet that you stand upon a higher level than the son of your god.' There was a sudden scramble to reach the floor of the throneroom, nor was Ko-tan far behind his warriors, though he managed to maintain a certain majestic dignity as he descended the broad stairs that countless naked feet had polished to a gleaming smoothness through the ages. 'And now,' said Tarzan as the king stood before him, 'you can have no doubt that I am not of the same race as you. Your priests have told you that Jad-ben-Otho is tailless. Tailless, therefore, must be the race of gods that spring from his loins. But enough of such proofs as these! You know the power of Jad-ben-Otho; how his lightnings gleaming out of the sky carry death as he wills it; how the rains come at his bidding, and the fruits and the berries and the grains, the grasses, the trees and the flowers spring to life at his divine direction; you have witnessed birth and death, and those who honor their god honor him because he controls these things. How would it fare then with an impostor who claimed to be the son of this all-powerful god? This then is all the proof that you require, for as he would strike you down should you deny me, so would he strike down one who wrongfully claimed kinship with him.'

This line of argument being unanswerable must needs be convincing. There could be no questioning of this creature's statements without the tacit admission of lack of faith in the omnipotence of Jad-ben-Otho. Ko-tan was satisfied that he was entertaining deity, but as to just what form his entertainment should take he was rather at a loss to know. His conception of god had been rather a vague and hazy affair, though in common with all primitive people his god was a personal one as were his devils and demons. The pleasures of Jad-ben-Otho he had assumed to be the excesses which he himself enjoyed, but devoid of any unpleasant reaction. It therefore occurred to him that the Dor-ul-Otho would be greatly entertained by eating – eating large quantities of everything that Ko-tan liked best and that he had found most injurious; and there was also a drink that the women of the Ho-don made by allowing corn to soak in the juices of succulent fruits, to which they had added certain other ingredients best known to themselves. Ko-tan knew by experience that a single draft of this potent liquor would bring happiness and surcease from worry, while several would cause even a king to do things and enjoy things that he would never even think of doing or enjoying while not under the magical influence of the potion, but unfortunately the next morning brought suffering in direct ratio to the joy of the preceding day. A god, Ko-tan reasoned, could experience all the pleasure without the headache, but for the immediate present he must think of the necessary dignities and honors to be accorded his immortal guest.

No foot other than a king's had touched the surface of the apex of the pyramid in the throneroom at A-lur during all the forgotten ages through which the kings of Pal-ul-don had ruled from its high eminence. So what higher honor could Ko-tan offer than to give place beside him to the Dor-ul-Otho? And so he invited Tarzan to ascend the pyramid and take his place upon the stone bench that topped it. As they reached the step below the sacred pinnacle Ko-tan continued as though to mount to his throne, but Tarzan laid a detaining hand upon his arm.

'None may sit upon a level with the gods,' he admonished, stepping confidently up and seating himself upon the throne. The abashed Ko-tan showed his embarrassment, an embarrassment he feared to voice lest he incur the wrath of the king of kings.

'But,' added Tarzan, 'a god may honor his faithful servant by inviting him to a place at his side. Come, Ko-tan; thus would I honor you in the name of Jad-ben-Otho.'

The ape-man's policy had for its basis an attempt not only to arouse the fearful respect of Ko-tan but to do it without making of him an enemy at heart, for he did not know how strong a hold the religion of the Ho-don had upon them, for since the time that he had prevented Ta-den and Om-at from quarreling over a religious difference the subject had been utterly taboo among them. He was therefore quick to note the evident though wordless resentment of Ko-tan at the suggestion that he entirely relinquish his throne to his guest. On the whole, however, the effect had been satisfactory as he could see from the renewed evidence of awe upon the faces of the warriors.

At Tarzan's direction the business of the court continued where it had been interrupted by his advent. It consisted principally in the settling of disputes between warriors. There was present one who stood upon the step just below the throne and which Tarzan was to learn was the place reserved for the higher chiefs of the allied tribes which made up Ko-tan's kingdom. The one who attracted Tarzan's attention was a stalwart warrior of powerful physique and massive, lionlike features. He was addressing Ko-tan on a question that is as old as government and that will continue in unabated importance until man ceases to exist. It had to do with a boundary dispute with one of his neighbors.

The matter itself held little or no interest for Tarzan, but he was impressed by the appearance of the speaker and when Ko-tan addressed him as Ja-don the ape-man's interest was permanently crystallized, for Ja-don was the father of Ta-den. That the knowledge would benefit him in any way seemed rather a remote possibility since he could not reveal to Ja-don his friendly relations with his son without admitting the falsity of his claims to godship.

When the affairs of the audience were concluded Ko-tan suggested that the son of Jad-ben-Otho might wish to visit the temple in which were performed the religious rites coincident to the worship of the Great God. And so the ape-man was conducted by the king himself, followed by the warriors of his court, through the corridors of the palace toward the northern end of the group of buildings within the royal enclosure.

The temple itself was really a part of the palace and similar in architecture. There were several ceremonial places of varying sizes, the purposes of which Tarzan could only conjecture. Each had an altar in the west end and another in the east and were oval in shape, their longest diameter lying due east and west. Each was excavated from the summit of a small hillock and all were without roofs. The western altars invariably were a single block of stone the top of which was hollowed into an oblong basin. Those at the eastern ends were similar blocks of stone with flat tops and these latter, unlike those at the opposite ends of the ovals were invariably stained or painted a reddish brown, nor did Tarzan need to examine them closely to be assured of what his keen nostrils already had told him – that the brown stains were dried and drying human blood.

Below these temple courts were corridors and apartments reaching far into the bowels of the hills, dim, gloomy passages that Tarzan glimpsed as he was led from place to place on his tour of inspection of the temple. A messenger had been dispatched by Ko-tan to announce the coming visit of the son of Jad-ben-Otho with the result that they were accompanied through the temple by a considerable procession of priests whose distinguishing mark of profession seemed to consist in grotesque headdresses; sometimes hideous faces carved from wood and entirely concealing the countenances of their wearers, or again, the head of a wild beast cunningly fitted over the head of a man. The high priest alone wore no such headdress. He was an old man with close-set, cunning eyes and a cruel, thin-lipped mouth.

At first sight of him Tarzan realized that here lay the greatest danger to his ruse, for he saw at a glance that the man was antagonistic toward him and his pretensions, and he knew too that doubtless of all the people of Pal-ul-don the high priest was most likely to harbor the truest estimate of Jad-ben-Otho, and, therefore, would look with suspicion on one who claimed to be the son of a fabulous god.

No matter what suspicion lurked within his crafty mind, Lu-don, the high priest of A-lur, did not openly question Tarzan's right to the tittle of Dor-ul-Otho, and it may be that he was restrained by the same doubts which had originally restrained Ko-tan and his warriors – the doubt that is at the bottom of the minds of all blasphemers even and which is based upon the fear that after all there may be a god. So, for the time being at least Lu-don played safe. Yet Tarzan knew as well as though the man had spoken aloud his inmost thoughts that it was in the heart of the high priest to tear the veil from his imposture.

At the entrance to the temple Ko-tan had relinquished the guidance of the guest to Lu-don and now the latter led Tarzan through those portions of the temple that he wished him to see. He showed him the great room where the votive offerings were kept, gifts from the barbaric chiefs of Pal-ul-don and from their followers. These things ranged in value from presents of dried fruits to massive vessels of beaten gold, so that in the great main storeroom and its connecting chambers and corridors was an accumulation of wealth that amazed even the eyes of the owner of the secret of the treasure vaults of Opar.

Moving to and fro throughout the temple were sleek black Waz-don slaves, fruits of the Ho-don raids upon the villages of their less civilized neighbors. As they passed the barred entrance to a dim corridor, Tarzan saw within a great company of pithecanthropi of all ages and of both sexes, Ho-don as well as Waz-don, the majority of them squatted upon the stone floor in attitudes of utter dejection while some paced back and forth, their features stamped with the despair of utter hopelessness.

'And who are these who lie here thus unhappily?' he asked of Lu-don. It was the first question that he had put to the high priest since entering the temple, and instantly he regretted that he had asked it, for Lu-don turned upon him a face upon which the expression of suspicion was but thinly veiled.

'Who should know better than the son of Jad-ben-Otho?' he retorted.

'The questions of Dor-ul-Otho are not with impunity answered with other questions,' said the ape-man quietly, 'and it may interest Lu-don, the high priest, to know that the blood of a false priest upon the altar of his temple is not displeasing in the eyes of Jad-ben-Otho.'

Lu-don paled as he answered Tarzan's question. 'They are the offerings whose blood must refresh the eastern altars as the sun returns to your father at the day's end.'

'And who told you,' asked Tarzan, 'that Jad-ben-Otho was pleased that his people were slain upon his altars? What if you were mistaken?'

'Then countless thousands have died in vain,' replied Lu-don.

Ko-tan and the surrounding warriors and priests were listening attentively to the dialogue. Some of the poor victims behind the barred gateway had heard and rising, pressed close to the barrier through which one was conducted just before sunset each day, never to return.

'Liberate them!' cried Tarzan with a wave of his hand toward the imprisoned victims of a cruel superstition, 'for I can tell you in the name of Jad-ben-Otho that you are mistaken.'

10
The Forbidden Garden

Lu-don paled. 'It is sacrilege,' he cried; 'for countless ages have the priests of the Great God offered each night a life to the spirit of Jad-ben-Otho as it returned below the western horizon to its master, and never has the Great God given sign that he was displeased.'

'Stop!' commanded Tarzan. 'It is the blindness of the priesthood that has failed to read the messages of their god. Your warriors die beneath the knives and clubs of the Waz-don; your hunters are taken by *ja* and *jato;* no day goes by but witnesses the deaths of few or many in the villages of the Ho-don, and one death each day of those that die are the toll which Jad-ben-Otho has exacted for the lives you take upon the eastern altar. What greater sign of his displeasure could you require, O stupid priest?'

Lu-don was silent. There was raging within him a great conflict between his fear that this indeed might be the son of god and his hope that it was not, but at last his fear won and he bowed his head. 'The son of Jad-ben-Otho has spoken,' he said, and turning to one of the lesser priests: 'Remove the bars and return these people from whence they came.'

He thus addressed did as he was bid and as the bars came down the prisoners, now all fully aware of the miracle that had saved them, crowded forward and throwing themselves upon their knees before Tarzan raised their voices in thanksgiving.

Ko-tan was almost as staggered as the high priest by this ruthless overturning of an age-old religious rite. 'But what,' he cried, 'may we do that will be pleasing in the eyes of Jad-ben-Otho?' turning a look of puzzled apprehension toward the ape-man.

'If you seek to please your god,' he replied, 'place upon your altars such gifts of food and apparel as are most welcome in the city of your people. These things will Jad-ben-Otho bless, when you may distribute them among those of the city who need them most. With such things are your storerooms filled as I have seen with mine own eyes, and other gifts will be brought when the priests tell the people that in this way they find favor before their god,' and Tarzan turned and signified that he would leave the temple.

As they were leaving the precincts devoted to the worship of their deity, the ape-man noticed a small but rather ornate building that stood entirely detached from the others as though it had been cut from a little pinnacle of limestone which had stood out from its fellows. As his interested glance passed over it he noticed that its door and windows were barred.

'To what purpose is that building dedicated?' he asked of Lu-don. 'Who do you keep imprisoned there?'

'It is nothing,' replied the high priest nervously; 'there is no one there. The place is vacant. Once it was used but not now for many years,' and he moved on toward the gateway which led back into the palace. Here he and the priests halted while Tarzan with Ko-tan and his warriors passed out from the sacred precincts of the temple grounds.

The one question which Tarzan would have asked he had feared to ask for he knew that in the hearts of many lay a suspicion as to his genuineness, but he determined that before he slept he would put the question to Ko-tan, either directly or indirectly – as to whether there was, or had been recently within the city of A-lur a female of the same race as his.

As their evening meal was being served to them in the banquet hall of Ko-tan's palace by a part of the army of black slaves upon whose shoulders fell the burden of all the heavy and menial tasks of the city, Tarzan noticed that there came to the eyes of one of the slaves what was apparently an expression of startled recognition, as he looked upon the ape-man for the first time in the banquet hall of Ko-tan. And again later he saw the fellow whisper to another slave and nod his head in his direction. The ape-man did not recall ever having seen this Waz-don before and he was at a loss to account for an explanation of the fellow's interest in him, and presently the incident was all but forgotten.

Ko-tan was surprised and inwardly disgusted to discover that this godly guest had no desire to gorge himself upon rich foods and that he would not even so much as taste the villainous brew of the Ho-don. To Tarzan the banquet was a dismal and tiresome affair, since so great was the interest of the guests in gorging themselves with food and drink that they had no time for conversation, the only vocal sounds being confined to a continuous grunting which, together with their table manners reminded Tarzan of a visit he had once made to the famous Berkshire herd of His Grace, the Duke of Westminster at Woodhouse, Chester.

One by one the diners succumbed to the stupefying effects of the liquor with the result that the grunting gave place to snores, so presently Tarzan and the slaves were the only conscious creatures in the banquet hall.

Rising, the ape-man turned to a tall black who stood behind him. 'I would sleep,' he said; 'show me to my apartment.'

As the fellow conducted him from the chamber the slave who had shown surprise earlier in the evening at sight of him, spoke again at length to one of his fellows. The latter cast a half-frightened look in the direction of the departing ape-man. 'If you are right,' he said, 'they should reward us with our liberty, but if you are wrong, O Jad-ben-Otho, what will be our fate?'

'But I am not wrong!' cried the other.

'Then there is but one to tell this to, for I have heard that he looked sour when this Dor-ul-Otho was brought to the temple and that while the so-called son of Jad-ben-Otho was there he gave this one every cause to fear and hate him. I mean Lu-don, the high priest.'

'You know him?' asked the other slave.

'I have worked in the temple,' replied his companion.

'Then go to him at once and tell him, but be sure to exact the promise of our freedom for the proof.'

And so a black Waz-don came to the temple gate and asked to see Lu-don, the high priest, on a matter of great importance, and though the hour was late Lu-don saw him, and when he had heard his story he promised him and his friend not only their freedom but many gifts if they could prove the correctness of their claims.

And as the slave talked with the high priest in the temple at A-lur the figure of a man groped its way around the shoulder of Pastar-ul-ved and the moonlight glistened from the shiny barrel of an Enfield that was strapped to the naked back, and brass cartridges shed tiny rays of reflected light from their polished cases where they hung in the bandoliers across the broad brown shoulders and the lean waist.

Tarzan's guide conducted him to a chamber overlooking the blue lake where he found a bed similar to that which he had seen in the villages of the Waz-don, merely a raised dais of stone upon which was piled great quantities of furry pelts. And so he lay down to sleep, the question that he most wished to put still unasked and unanswered.

With the coming of a new day he was awake and wandering about the palace and the palace grounds before there was sign of any of the inmates of the palace other than slaves, or at least he saw no others at first, though presently he stumbled upon an enclosure which lay almost within the center of the palace grounds surrounded by a wall that piqued the ape-man's curiosity, since he had determined to investigate as fully as possible every part of the palace and its environs.

This place, whatever it might be, was apparently without doors or windows but that it was at least partially roofless was evidenced by the sight of the waving branches of a tree which spread above the top of the wall near him. Finding no other method of access, the ape-man uncoiled his rope and throwing it over the branch of the tree where it projected beyond the wall, was soon climbing with the ease of a monkey to the summit.

There he found that the wall surrounded an enclosed garden in which grew trees and shrubs and flowers in riotous profusion. Without waiting to ascertain whether the garden was empty or contained Ho-don, Waz-don, or wild beasts, Tarzan dropped lightly to the sward on the inside and without further loss of time commenced a systematic investigation of the enclosure.

His curiosity was aroused by the very evident fact that the place was not for general use, even by those who had free access to other parts of the palace grounds and so there was added to its natural beauties an absence of mortals which rendered its exploration all the more alluring to Tarzan since it suggested that in such a place might he hope to come upon the object of his long and difficult search.

In the garden were tiny artificial streams and little pools of water, flanked by flowering bushes, as though it all had been designed by the cunning hand of some master gardener, so faithfully did it carry out the beauties and contours of nature upon a miniature scale.

The interior surface of the wall was fashioned to represent the white cliffs of Pal-ul-don, broken occasionally by small replicas of the verdure-filled gorges of the original.

Filled with admiration and thoroughly enjoying each new surprise which the scene offered, Tarzan moved slowly around the garden, and as always he moved silently. Passing through a miniature forest he came presently upon a tiny area of flower-studded sward and at the same time beheld before him the first Ho-don female he had seen since entering the palace. A young and beautiful woman stood in the center of the little open space, stroking the head of a bird which she held against her golden breastplate with one hand. Her profile was presented to the apeman and he saw that by the standards of any land she would have been accounted more than lovely.

Seated in the grass at her feet, with her back toward him, was a female Waz-don slave. Seeing that she he sought was not there and apprehensive that an alarm be raised were he discovered by the two women, Tarzan moved back to hide himself in the foliage, but before he had succeeded the Ho-don girl turned quickly toward him as though apprised of his presence by that unnamed sense, the manifestations of which are more or less familiar to us all.

At sight of him her eyes registered only her surprise though there was no expression of terror reflected in them, nor did she scream or even raise her well-modulated voice as she addressed him.

'Who are you,' she asked, 'who enters thus boldly the Forbidden Garden?'

At sound of her mistress's voice the slave maiden turned quickly, rising to her feet. 'Tarzan-jad-guru!' she exclaimed in tones of mingled astonishment and relief.

'You know him?' cried her mistress turning toward the slave and affording Tarzan an opportunity to raise a cautioning finger to his lips lest Pan-at-lee further betray him, for it was Pan-at-lee indeed who stood before him, no less a source of surprise to him than had his presence been to her.

Thus questioned by her mistress and simultaneously admonished to silence by Tarzan, Pan-at-lee was momentarily silenced and then haltingly she groped for a way to extricate herself from her dilemma. 'I thought –' she faltered, 'but no, I am mistaken – I thought that he was one whom I had seen before near the Kor-ul-gryf.'

The Ho-don looked first at one and then at the other, an expression of doubt and questioning in her eyes. 'But you have not answered me,' she continued presently; 'who are you?'

'You have not heard then,' asked Tarzan, 'of the visitor who arrived at your king's court yesterday?'

'You mean,' she exclaimed, 'that you are the Dor-ul-Otho?' And now the erstwhile doubting eyes reflected naught but awe.

'I am he,' replied Tarzan; 'and you?'

'I am O-lo-a, daughter of Ko-tan, the king,' she replied.

So this was O-lo-a, for love of whom Ta-den had chosen exile rather than priesthood. Tarzan had approached more closely the dainty barbarian princess. 'Daughter of Ko-tan,' he said, 'Jad-ben-Otho is pleased with you and as a mark of his favor he has preserved for you through many dangers him whom you love.'

'I do not understand,' replied the girl but the flush that mounted to her cheek belied her words. 'Bu-lat is a guest in the palace of Ko-tan, my father. I do not know that he has faced any danger. It is to Bu-lat that I am betrothed.'

'But it is not Bu-lat whom you love,' said Tarzan.

Again the flush and the girl half turned her face away. 'Have I then displeased the Great God?' she asked.

'No,' replied Tarzan; 'as I told you he is well satisfied and for your sake he has saved Ta-den for you.'

'Jad-ben-Otho knows all,' whispered the girl, 'and his son shares his great knowledge.'

'No,' Tarzan hastened to correct her lest a reputation for omniscience might prove embarrassing. 'I know only what Jad-ben-Otho wishes me to know.'

'But tell me,' she said, 'I shall be reunited with Ta-den? Surely the son of god can read the future.'

The ape-man was glad that he had left himself an avenue of escape. 'I know nothing of the future,' he replied, 'other than what Jad-ben-Otho tells me. But I think you need have no fear for the future if you remain faithful to Ta-den and Ta-den's friends.'

'You have seen him?' asked O-lo-a. 'Tell me, where is he?'

'Yes,' replied Tarzan, 'I have seen him. He was with Om-at, the *gund* of Kor-ul-ja.'

'A prisoner of the Waz-don?' interrupted the girl.

'Not a prisoner but an honored guest,' replied the ape-man.

'Wait,' he exclaimed, raising his face toward the heavens; 'do not speak. I am receiving a message from Jad-ben-Otho, my father.'

The two women dropped to their knees, covering their faces with their hands, stricken with awe at the thought of the awful nearness of the Great God. Presently Tarzan touched O-lo-a on the shoulder.

'Rise,' he said. 'Jad-ben-Otho has spoken. He has told me that this slave girl is from the tribe of Kor-ul-ja, where Ta-den is, and that she is betrothed to Om-at, their chief. Her name is Pan-at-lee.'

O-lo-a turned questioningly toward Pan-at-lee. The latter nodded, her simple mind unable to determine whether or not she and her mistress were the victims of a colossal hoax. 'It is even as he says,' she whispered.

O-lo-a fell upon her knees and touched her forehead to Tarzan's feet. 'Great is the honor that Jad-ben-Otho has done his poor servant,' she cried. 'Carry to him my poor thanks for the happiness that he has brought to O-lo-a.'

'It would please my father,' said Tarzan, 'if you were to cause Pan-at-lee to be returned in safety to the village of her people.'

'What cares Jad-ben-Otho for such as she?' asked O-lo-a, a slight trace of hauteur in her tone.

'There is but one god,' replied Tarzan, 'and he is the god of the Waz-don as well as of the Ho-don; of the birds and the beasts and the flowers and of everything that grows upon the earth or beneath the waters. If Pan-at-lee does right she is greater in the eyes of Jad-ben-Otho than would be the daughter of Ko-tan should she do wrong.'

It was evident that O-lo-a did not quite understand this interpretation of divine favor, so contrary was it to the teachings of the priesthood of her people. In one respect only did Tarzan's teachings coincide with her belief – that there was but one god. For the rest she had always been taught that he was solely the god of the Ho-don in every sense, other than that other creatures were created by Jad-ben-Otho to serve some useful purpose for the benefit of the Ho-don race. And now to be told by the son of god that she stood no higher in divine esteem than the black handmaiden at her side was indeed a shock to her pride, her vanity, and her faith. But who could question the word of Dor-ul-Otho, especially when she had with her own eyes seen him in actual communion with god in heaven?

'The will of Jad-ben-Otho be done,' said O-lo-a meekly, 'if it lies within my power. But it would be best, O Dor-ul-Otho, to communicate your father's wish directly to the king.'

'Then keep her with you,' said Tarzan, 'and see that no harm befalls her.'

O-lo-a looked ruefully at Pan-at-lee. 'She was brought to me but yesterday,' she said, 'and never have I had a slave woman who pleased me better. I shall hate to part with her.'

'But there are others,' said Tarzan.

'Yes,' replied O-lo-a, 'there are others, but there is only one Pan-at-lee.'

'Many slaves are brought to the city?' asked Tarzan.

'Yes,' she replied.

'And many strangers come from other lands?' he asked.

She shook her head negatively. 'Only the Ho-don from the other side of the Valley of Jad-ben-Otho,' she replied, 'and they are not strangers.'

'Am I then the first stranger to enter the gates of A-lur?' he asked.

'Can it be,' she parried, 'that the son of Jad-ben-Otho need question a poor ignorant mortal like O-lo-a?'

'As I told you before,' replied Tarzan, 'Jad-ben-Otho alone is all-knowing.'

'Then if he wished you to know this thing,' retorted O-lo-a quickly, 'you would know it.'

Inwardly the ape-man smiled that this little heathen's astuteness should beat him at his own game, yet in a measure her evasion of the question might be an answer to it. 'There have been other strangers here then recently?' he persisted.

'I cannot tell you what I do not know,' she replied. 'Always is the palace of Ko-tan filled with rumors, but how much fact and how much fancy how may a woman of the palace know?'

'There has been such a rumor then?' he asked.

'It was only rumor that reached the Forbidden Garden,' she replied.

'It described, perhaps, a woman of another race?' As he put the question and awaited her answer he thought that his heart ceased to beat, so grave to him was the issue at stake.

The girl hesitated before replying, and then: 'No,' she said, 'I cannot speak of this thing, for if it be of sufficient importance to elicit the interest of the gods then indeed would I be subject to the wrath of my father should I discuss it.'

'In the name of Jad-ben-Otho I command you to speak,' said Tarzan. 'In the name of Jad-ben-Otho in whose hands lies the fate of Ta-den!'

The girl paled. 'Have mercy,' she cried, 'and for the sake of Ta-den I will tell you all that I know.'

'Tell what?' demanded a stern voice from the shrubbery behind them. The three turned to see the figure of Ko-tan emerging from the foliage. An angry scowl distorted his kingly features but at sight of Tarzan it gave place to an expression of surprise not unmixed with fear. 'Dor-ul-Otho!' he exclaimed. 'I did not know that it was you,' and then, raising his head and squaring his shoulders he said, 'but there are places where even the son of the Great God may not walk and this, the Forbidden Garden of Ko-tan, is one.'

It was a challenge but despite the king's bold front there was a note of apology in it, indicating that in his superstitious mind there flourished the inherent fear of man for his Maker. 'Come, Dor-ul-Otho,' he continued, 'I do not know all this foolish child has said to you but whatever you would know Ko-tan, the king, will tell you. O-lo-a, go to your quarters immediately,' and he pointed with stern finger toward the opposite end of the garden.

The princess, followed by Pan-at-lee, turned at once and left them.

'We will go this way,' said Ko-tan and preceding, led Tarzan in another direction. Close to that part of the wall which they approached Tarzan perceived a grotto in the miniature cliff into the interior of which Ko-tan led him, and down a rocky stairway to a gloomy corridor the opposite end of which opened into the palace proper. Two armed warriors stood at this entrance to the Forbidden Garden, evidencing how jealously were the sacred precincts of the place guarded.

In silence Ko-tan led the way back to his own quarters in the palace. A large chamber just outside the room toward which Ko-tan was leading his guest was filled with chiefs and warriors awaiting the pleasure of their ruler. As the two entered, an aisle was formed for them the length of the chamber, down which they passed in silence.

Close to the farther door and half hidden by the warriors who stood before him was Lu-don, the high priest. Tarzan glimpsed him but briefly but in that short period he was aware of a cunning and malevolent expression upon the cruel countenance that he was subconsciously aware boded him no good, and then with Ko-tan he passed into the adjoining room and the hangings dropped.

At the same moment the hideous headdress of an underpriest appeared in the entrance of the outer chamber. Its owner, pausing for a moment, glanced quickly around the interior and then having located him whom he sought moved rapidly in the direction of Lu-don. There was a whispered conversation which was terminated by the high priest.

'Return immediately to the quarters of the princess,' he said, 'and see that the slave is sent to me at the temple at once.' The underpriest turned and departed upon his mission while Lu-don also left the apartment and directed his footsteps toward the sacred enclosure over which he ruled.

A half-hour later a warrior was ushered into the presence of Ko-tan. 'Lu-don, the high priest, desires the presence of Ko-tan, the king, in the temple,' he announced, 'and it is his wish that he come alone.'

Ko-tan nodded to indicate that he accepted the command which even the king must obey. 'I will return presently, Dor-ul-Otho,' he said to Tarzan, 'and in the meantime my warriors and my slaves are yours to command.'

11
The Sentence of Death

But it was an hour before the king reentered the apartment and in the meantime the ape-man had occupied himself in examining the carvings upon the walls and the numerous specimens of the handicraft of Pal-ul-donian artisans which combined to impart an atmosphere of richness and luxury to the apartment.

The limestone of the country, close-grained and of marble whiteness yet worked with comparative ease with crude implements, had been wrought by cunning craftsmen into bowls and urns and vases of considerable grace and beauty. Into the carved designs of many of these virgin gold had been hammered, presenting the effect of a rich and magnificent cloisonné. A barbarian himself the art of barbarians had always appealed to the ape-man to whom they represented a natural expression of man's love of the beautiful to even a greater extent than the studied and artificial efforts of civilization. Here was the real art of old masters, the other the cheap imitation of the chromo.

It was while he was thus pleasurably engaged that Ko-tan returned. As Tarzan, attracted by the movement of the hangings through which the king entered, turned and faced him he was almost shocked by the remarkable alteration of the king's appearance. His face was livid; his hands trembled as with palsy, and his eyes were wide as with fright. His appearance was one apparently of a combination of consuming anger and withering fear. Tarzan looked at him questioningly.

'You have had bad news, Ko-tan?' he asked.

The king mumbled an unintelligible reply. Behind there thronged into the apartment so great a number of warriors that they choked the entranceway. The king looked apprehensively to right and left. He cast terrified glances at the ape-man and then raising his face and turning his eyes upward he cried: 'Jad-ben-Otho be my witness that I do not this thing of my own accord.' There was a moment's silence which was again broken by Ko-tan. 'Seize him,' he cried to the warriors about him, 'for Lu-don, the high priest, swears that he is an impostor.'

To have offered armed resistance to this great concourse of warriors in the very heart of the palace of their king would have been worse than fatal. Already Tarzan had come far by his wits and now that within a few hours he had had his hopes and his suspicions partially verified by the vague admissions of O-lo-a he was impressed with the necessity of inviting no mortal risk that he could avoid.

'Stop!' he cried, raising his palm against them. 'What is the meaning of this?'

'Lu-don claims he has proof that you are not the son of Jad-ben-Otho,' replied Ko-tan. 'He demands that you be brought to the throneroom to face your accusers. If you are what you claim to be none knows better than you that you need have no fear in acquiescing to his demands, but remember always that in such matters the high priest commands the king and that I am only the bearer of these commands, not their author.'

Tarzan saw that Ko-tan was not entirely convinced of his duplicity as was evidenced by his palpable design to play safe.

'Let not your warriors seize me,' he said to Ko-tan, 'lest Jad-ben-Otho, mistaking their intention, strike them dead.' The effect of his words was immediate upon the men in the front rank of those who faced him, each seeming suddenly to acquire a new modesty that compelled him to self-effacement behind those directly in his rear – a modesty that became rapidly contagious.

The ape-man smiled. 'Fear not,' he said, 'I will go willingly to the audience chamber to face the blasphemers who accuse me.'

Arrived at the great throneroom a new complication arose. Ko-tan would not acknowledge the right of Lu-don to occupy the apex of the pyramid and Lu-don would not consent to occupying an inferior position while Tarzan, to remain consistent with his high claims, insisted that no one should stand above him, but only to the ape-man was the humor of the situation apparent.

To relieve the situation Ja-don suggested that all three of them occupy the throne, but this suggestion was repudiated by Ko-tan who argued that no mortal other than a king of Pal-ul-don had ever sat upon the high eminence, and that furthermore there was not room for three there.

'But who,' said Tarzan, 'is my accuser and who is my judge?'

'Lu-don is your accuser,' explained Ko-tan.

'And Lu-don is your judge,' cried the high priest.

'I am to be judged by him who accuses me then,' said Tarzan. 'It were better to dispense then with any formalities and ask Lu-don to sentence me.' His tone was ironical and his sneering face, looking straight into that of the high priest, but caused the latter's hatred to rise to still greater proportions.

It was evident that Ko-tan and his warriors saw the justice of Tarzan's implied objection to this unfair method of dispensing justice. 'Only Ko-tan can judge in the throneroom of his palace,' said Ja-don; 'let him hear Lu-don's charges and the testimony of his witnesses, and then let Ko-tan's judgment be final.'

Ko-tan, however, was not particularly enthusiastic over the prospect of sitting in trial upon one who might after all very possibly be the son of his god, and so he temporized, seeking for an avenue of escape. 'It is purely a religious matter,' he said, 'and it is traditional that the kings of Pal-ul-don interfere not in questions of the church.'

'Then let the trial be held in the temple,' cried one of the chiefs, for the warriors were as anxious as their king to be relieved of all responsibility in the matter. This suggestion was more than satisfactory to the high priest who inwardly condemned himself for not having thought of it before.

'It is true,' he said, 'this man's sin is against the temple. Let him be dragged thither then for trial.'

'The son of Jad-ben-Otho will be dragged nowhere,' cried Tarzan. 'But when this trial is over it is possible that the corpse of Lu-don, the high priest, will be dragged from the temple of the god he would desecrate. Think well, then, Lu-don, before you commit this folly.'

His words, intended to frighten the high priest from his position failed utterly in consummating their purpose. Lu-don showed no terror at the suggestion the ape-man's words implied.

'Here is one,' thought Tarzan, 'who, knowing more of his religion than any of his fellows, realizes fully the falsity of my claims as he does the falsity of the faith he preaches.'

He realized, however, that his only hope lay in seeming indifference to the charges. Ko-tan and the warriors were still under the spell of their belief in him and upon this fact must he depend in the final act of the drama that Lu-don was staging for his rescue from the jealous priest whom he knew had already passed sentence upon him in his own heart.

With a shrug he descended the steps of the pyramid. 'It matters not to Dor-ul-Otho,' he said, 'where Lu-don enrages his god, for Jad-ben-Otho can reach as easily into the chambers of the temple as into the throneroom of Ko-tan.'

Immeasurably relieved by this easy solution of their problem the king and the warriors thronged from the throneroom toward the temple grounds, their faith in Tarzan increased by his apparent indifference to the charges against him. Lu-don led them to the largest of the altar courts.

Taking his place behind the western altar he motioned Ko-tan to a place upon the platform at the left hand of the altar and directed Tarzan to a similar place at the right.

As Tarzan ascended the platform his eyes narrowed angrily at the sight which met them. The basin hollowed in the top of the altar was filled with water in which floated the naked corpse of a newborn babe. 'What means this?' he cried angrily, turning upon Lu-don.

The latter smiled malevolently. 'That you do not know,' he replied, 'is but added evidence of the falsity of your claim. He who poses as the son of god did not know that as the last rays of the setting sun flood the eastern altar of the temple the lifeblood of an adult reddens the white stone for the edification of Jad-ben-Otho; and that when the sun rises again from the body of its maker it looks first upon this western altar and rejoices in the death of a newborn babe each day, the ghost of which accompanies it across the heavens by day as the ghost of the adult returns with it to Jad-ben-Otho at night.

'Even the little children of the Ho-don know these things, while he who claims to be the son of Jad-ben-Otho knows them not; and if this proof be not enough, there is more. Come, Waz-don,' he cried, pointing to a tall slave who stood with a group of other blacks and priests on the temple floor at the left of the altar.

The fellow came forward fearfully. 'Tell us what you know of this creature,' cried Lu-don, pointing to Tarzan.

'I have seen him before,' said the Waz-don. 'I am of the tribe of Kor-ul-lul, and one day recently a party of which I was one encountered a few of the warriors of the Kor-ul-ja upon the ridge which separates our villages. Among the enemy was this strange creature whom they called Tarzan-jad-guru; and terrible indeed was he for he fought with the strength of many men so that it required twenty of us to subdue him. But he did not fight as a god fights, and when a club struck him upon the head he sank unconscious as might an ordinary mortal.

'We carried him with us to our village as a prisoner but he escaped after cutting off the head of the warrior we left to guard him and carrying it down into the gorge and tying it to the branch of a tree upon the opposite side.'

'The word of a slave against that of a god!' cried Ja-don, who had shown previously a friendly interest in the pseudo godling.

'It is only a step in the progress toward truth,' interjected Lu-don. 'Possibly the evidence of the only princess of the house of Ko-tan will have greater weight with the great chief from the north, though the father of a son who fled the holy offer of the priesthood may not receive with willing ears any testimony against another blasphemer.'

Ja-don's hand leaped to his knife, but the warriors next to him laid detaining fingers upon his arms. 'You are in the temple of Jad-ben-Otho, Ja-don,' they cautioned and the great chief was forced to swallow Lu-don's affront though it left in his heart bitter hatred of the high priest.

And now Ko-tan turned toward Lu-don. 'What knoweth my daughter of this matter?' he asked. 'You would not bring a princess of my house to testify thus publicly?'

'No,' replied Lu-don, 'not in person, but I have here one who will testify for her.' He beckoned to an underpriest. 'Fetch the slave of the princess,' he said.

His grotesque headdress adding a touch of the hideous to the scene, the priest stepped forward dragging the reluctant Pan-at-lee by the wrist.

'The Princess O-lo-a was alone in the Forbidden Garden with but this one slave,' explained the priest, 'when there suddenly appeared from the foliage nearby this creature who claims to be the Dor-ul-Otho. When the slave saw him the princess says that she cried aloud in startled recognition and called the creature by name – Tarzan-jad-guru – the same name that the slave from Kor-ul-lul gave him. This woman is not from Kor-ul-lul but from Kor-ul-ja, the very tribe with which the Kor-ul-lul says the creature was associating when he first saw him. And further the princess said that when this woman, whose name is Pan-at-lee, was brought to her yesterday she told a strange story of having been rescued from a Tor-o-don in the Kor-ul-gryf by a creature such as this, whom she spoke of then as Tarzan-jad-guru; and of how the two were pursued in the bottom of the gorge by two monster *gryfs*, and of how the man led them away while Pan-at-lee escaped, only to be taken prisoner in the Kor-ul-lul as she was seeking to return to her own tribe.

'Is it not plain now,' cried Lu-don, 'that this creature is no god. Did he tell you that he was the son of god?' he almost shouted, turning suddenly upon Pan-at-lee.

The girl shrank back terrified. 'Answer me, slave!' cried the high priest.

'He seemed more than mortal,' parried Pan-at-lee.

'Did he tell you that he was the son of god? Answer my question,' insisted Lu-don.

'No,' she admitted in a low voice, casting an appealing look of forgiveness at Tarzan who returned a smile of encouragement and friendship.

'That is no proof that he is not the son of god,' cried Ja-don. 'Dost think Jad-ben-Otho goes about crying "I am god! I am god!" Hast ever heard him, Lu-don? No, you have not. Why should his son do that which the father does not do?'

'Enough,' cried Lu-don. 'The evidence is clear. The creature is an impostor and I, the head priest of Jad-ben-Otho in the city of A-lur, do condemn him to die.' There was a moment's silence during which Lu-don evidently paused for the dramatic effect of his climax. 'And if I am wrong may Jad-ben-Otho pierce my heart with his lightnings as I stand here before you all.'

The lapping of the wavelets of the lake against the foot of the palace wall was distinctly audible in the utter and almost breathless silence which ensued. Lu-don stood with his face turned toward the heavens and his arms outstretched in the attitude of one who bares his breast to the dagger of an executioner. The warriors and the priests and the slaves gathered in the sacred court awaited the consuming vengeance of their god.

It was Tarzan who broke the silence. 'Your god ignores you, Lu-don,' he taunted, with a sneer that he meant to still further anger the high priest; 'he ignores you and I can prove it before the eyes of your priests and your people.'

'Prove it, blasphemer! How can you prove it?'

'You have called me a blasphemer,' replied Tarzan; 'you have proved to your own satisfaction that I am an impostor, that I, an ordinary mortal, have posed as the son of god. Demand then that Jad-ben-Otho uphold his godship and the dignity of his priesthood by directing his consuming fires through my own bosom.'

Again there ensued a brief silence while the onlookers waited for Lu-don to thus consummate the destruction of this presumptuous impostor.

'You dare not,' taunted Tarzan, 'for you know that I would be struck dead no quicker than were you.'

'You lie,' cried Lu-don, 'and I would do it had I not but just received a message from Jad-ben-Otho directing that your fate be different.'

A chorus of admiring and reverential 'Ahs' arose from the priesthood. Kotan and his warriors were in a state of mental confusion. Secretly they hated and feared Lu-don, but so ingrained was their sense of reverence for the office of the high priest that none dared raise a voice against him.

None? Well, there was Ja-don, fearless old Lion-man of the north. 'The proposition was a fair one,' he cried. 'Invoke the lightnings of Jad-ben-Otho upon this man if you would ever convince us of his guilt.'

'Enough of this,' snapped Lu-don. 'Since when was Ja-don created high priest? Seize the prisoner,' he cried to the priests and warriors, 'and on the morrow he shall die in the manner that Jad-ben-Otho has willed.'

There was no immediate movement on the part of any of the warriors to obey the high priest's command, but the lesser priests on the other hand, imbued with the courage of fanaticism leaped eagerly forward like a flock of hideous harpies to seize upon their prey.

The game was up. That Tarzan knew. No longer could cunning and diplomacy usurp the functions of the weapons of defense he best loved. And so the first hideous priest who leaped to the platform was confronted by no suave ambassador from heaven, but rather a grim and ferocious beast whose temper savored more of hell.

The altar stood close to the western wall of the enclosure. There was just room between the two for the high priest to stand during the performance of the sacrificial ceremonies and only Lu-don stood there now behind Tarzan while before him were perhaps two hundred warriors and priests.

The presumptuous one who would have had the glory of first laying arresting hands upon the blasphemous impersonator rushed forward with outstretched hand to seize the ape-man. Instead it was he who was seized; seized by steel fingers that snapped him up as though he had been a dummy of straw, grasped him by one leg and the harness at his back and raised him with giant arms high above the altar. Close at his heels were others ready to seize the ape-man and drag him down, and beyond the altar was Lu-don with drawn knife advancing toward him.

There was no instant to waste, nor was it the way of the ape-man to fritter away precious moments in the uncertainty of belated decision. Before Lu-don or any other could guess what was in the mind of the condemned, Tarzan with all the force of his great muscles dashed the screaming hierophant in the face of the high priest, and, as though the two actions were one, so quickly did he move, he had leaped to the top of the altar and from there to a hand-hold upon the summit of the temple wall. As he gained a footing there he turned and looked down upon those beneath. For a moment he stood in silence and then he spoke.

'Who dare believe,' he cried, 'that Jad-ben-Otho would forsake his son?' and then he dropped from their sight upon the other side.

There were two at least left within the enclosure whose hearts leaped with involuntary elation at the success of the ape-man's maneuver, and one of them smiled openly. This was Ja-don, and the other, Pan-at-lee.

The brains of the priest that Tarzan had thrown at the head of Lu-don had been dashed out against the temple wall while the high priest himself had escaped with only a few bruises, sustained in his fall to the hard pavement. Quickly scrambling to his feet he looked around in fear, in terror and finally in bewilderment, for he had not been a witness to the ape-man's escape. 'Seize him,' he cried; 'seize the blasphemer,' and he continued to look around in search of his victim with such a ridiculous expression of bewilderment that more than a single warrior was compelled to hide his smiles beneath his palm.

The priests were rushing around wildly, exhorting the warriors to pursue the fugitive but these awaited now stolidly the command of their king or high priest. Ko-tan, more or less secretly pleased by the discomfiture of Lu-don, waited for that worthy to give the necessary directions which he presently did when one of his acolytes excitedly explained to him the manner of Tarzan's escape.

Instantly the necessary orders were issued and priests and warriors sought the temple exit in pursuit of the ape-man. His departing words, hurled at them from the summit of the temple wall, had had little effect in impressing the majority that his claims had not been disproven by Lu-don, but in the hearts of the warriors was admiration for a brave man and in many the same unholy gratification that had risen in that of their ruler at the discomfiture of Lu-don.

A careful search of the temple grounds revealed no trace of the quarry. The secret recesses of the subterranean chambers, familiar only to the priesthood, were examined by these while the warriors scattered through the palace and the palace grounds without the temple. Swift runners were dispatched to the city to arouse the people there that all might be upon the lookout for Tarzan the Terrible. The story of his imposture and of his escape, and the tales that the Waz-don slaves had brought into the city concerning him were soon spread throughout A-lur, nor did they lose aught in the spreading, so that before an hour had passed the women and the children were hiding behind barred doorways while the warriors crept apprehensively through the streets expecting momentarily to be pounced upon by a ferocious demon who, barehanded, did victorious battle with huge *gryfs* and whose lightest pastime consisted in tearing strong men limb from limb.

12
The Giant Stranger

And while the warriors and the priests of A-lur searched the temple and the palace and the city for the vanished ape-man here entered the head of Kor-ul-ja down the precipitous trail from the mountains, a naked stranger bearing an Enfield upon his back. Silently he moved downward toward the bottom of the gorge and there where the ancient trail unfolded more levelly before him he swung along with easy strides, though always with the utmost alertness against possible dangers. A gentle breeze came down from the mountains behind him so that only his ears and his eyes were of value in detecting the presence of danger ahead. Generally the trail followed along the banks of the winding brooklet at the bottom of the gorge, but in some places where the waters tumbled over a precipitous ledge the trail made a detour along the side of the gorge, and again it wound in and out among rocky outcroppings, and presently where it rounded sharply the projecting shoulder of a cliff the stranger came suddenly face-to-face with one who was ascending the gorge.

Separated by a hundred paces the two halted simultaneously. Before him the stranger saw a tall white warrior, naked but for a loincloth, cross belts, and a girdle. The man was armed with a heavy, knotted club and a short knife, the latter hanging in its sheath at his left hip from the end of one of his cross belts, the opposite belt supporting a leathern pouch at his right side. It was Ta-den hunting alone in the gorge of his friend, the chief of Kor-ul-ja. He contemplated the stranger with surprise but no wonder, since he recognized in him a member of the race with which his experience of Tarzan the Terrible had made him familiar and also, thanks to his friendship for the ape-man, he looked upon the newcomer without hostility.

The latter was the first to make outward sign of his intentions, raising his palm toward Ta-den in that gesture which has been a symbol of peace from pole to pole since man ceased to walk upon his knuckles. Simultaneously he advanced a few paces and halted.

Ta-den, assuming that one so like Tarzan the Terrible must be a fellow-tribesman of his lost friend, was more than glad to accept this overture of peace, the sign of which he returned in kind as he ascended the trail to where the other stood. 'Who are you?' he asked, but the newcomer only shook his head to indicate that he did not understand.

By signs he tried to carry to the Ho-don the fact that he was following a trail that had led him over a period of many days from some place beyond the mountains and Ta-den was convinced that the newcomer sought Tarzan-jad-guru. He wished, however, that he might discover whether as friend or foe.

The stranger perceived the Ho-don's prehensile thumbs and great toes and his long tail with an astonishment which he sought to conceal, but greater than all was the sense of relief that the first inhabitant of this strange country whom he had met had proven friendly, so greatly would he have been handicapped by the necessity for forcing his way through a hostile land.

Ta-den, who had been hunting for some of the smaller mammals, the meat of which is especially relished by the Ho-don, forgot his intended sport in the greater interest of his new discovery. He would take the stranger to Om-at and possibly together the two would find some way of discovering the true intentions of the newcomer. And so again through signs he apprised the other that he would accompany him and together they descended toward the cliffs of Om-at's people.

As they approached these they came upon the women and children working under guard of the old men and the youths – gathering the wild fruits and herbs which constitute a part of their diet, as well as tending the small acres of growing crops which they cultivate. The fields lay in small level patches that had been cleared of trees and brush. Their farm implements consisted of metal-shod poles which bore a closer resemblance to spears than to tools of peaceful agriculture. Supplementing these were others with flattened blades that were neither hoes nor spades, but instead possessed the appearance of an unhappy attempt to combine the two implements in one.

At first sight of these people the stranger halted and unslung his bow for these creatures were black as night, their bodies entirely covered with hair. But Ta-den, interpreting the doubt in the other's mind, reassured him with a gesture and a smile. The Waz-don, however, gathered around excitedly jabbering questions in a language which the stranger discovered his guide understood though it was entirely unintelligible to the former. They made no attempt to molest him and he was now sure that he had fallen among a peaceful and friendly people.

It was but a short distance now to the caves and when they reached these

Ta-den led the way aloft upon the wooden pegs, assured that this creature whom he had discovered would have no more difficulty in following him than had Tarzan the Terrible. Nor was he mistaken for the other mounted with ease until presently the two stood within the recess before the cave of Om-at, the chief.

The latter was not there and it was midafternoon before he returned, but in the meantime many warriors came to look upon the visitor and in each instance the latter was more thoroughly impressed with the friendly and peaceable spirit of his hosts, little guessing that he was being entertained by a ferocious and warlike tribe who never before the coming of Ta-den and Tarzan had suffered a stranger among them.

At last Om-at returned and the guest sensed intuitively that he was in the presence of a great man among these people, possibly a chief or king, for not only did the attitude of the other black warriors indicate this but it was written also in the mien and bearing of the splendid creature who stood looking at him while Ta-den explained the circumstances of their meeting. 'And I believe, Om-at,' concluded the Ho-don, 'that he seeks Tarzan the Terrible.'

At the sound of that name, the first intelligible word that had fallen upon the ears of the stranger since he had come among them, his face lightened. 'Tarzan!' he cried. 'Tarzan of the Apes!' and by signs he tried to tell them that it was he whom he sought.

They understood, and also they guessed from the expression of his face that he sought Tarzan from motives of affection rather than the reverse, but of this Om-at wished to make sure. He pointed to the stranger's knife, and repeating Trzan's name, seized Ta-den and pretended to stab him, immediately turning questioningly toward the stranger.

The latter shook his head vehemently and then first placing a hand above his heart he raised his palm in the symbol of peace.

'He is a friend of Tarzan-jad-guru,' exclaimed Ta-den.

'Either a friend or a great liar,' replied Om-at.

'Tarzan,' continued the stranger, 'you know him? He lives? O God, if I could only speak your language.' And again reverting to sign language he sought to ascertain where Tarzan was. He would pronounce the name and point in different directions, in the cave, down the gorge, back toward the mountains, or out upon the valley below, and each time he would raise his brows questioningly and voice the universal 'eh?' of interrogation which they could not fail to understand. But always Om-at shook his head and spread his palms in a gesture which indicated that while he understood the question he was ignorant as to the whereabouts of the ape-man, and then the black chief attempted as best he might to explain to the stranger what he knew of the whereabouts of Tarzan.

He called the newcomer Jar-don, which in the language of Pal-ul-don means 'stranger,' and he pointed to the sun and said *as*. This he repeated several times and then he held up one hand with the fingers outspread and touching them one by one, including the thumb, repeated the word *adenen* until the stranger understood that he meant five. Again he pointed to the sun and describing an arc with his forefinger starting at the eastern horizon and terminating at the western, he repeated again the words *as adenen*. It was plain to the stranger that the words meant that the sun had crossed the heavens five times. In other words, five days had passed. Om-at then pointed to the cave where they stood, pronouncing Tarzan's name and imitating a walking man with the first and second fingers of his right hand upon the floor of the recess, sought to show that Tarzan had walked out of the cave and climbed upward on the pegs five days before, but this was as far as the sign language would permit him to go.

This far the stranger followed him and, indicating that he understood he pointed to himself and then indicating the pegs leading above announced that he would follow Tarzan.

'Let us go with him,' said Om-at, 'for as yet we have not punished the Kor-ul-lul for killing our friend and ally.'

'Persuade him to wait until morning,' said Ta-den, 'that you may take with you many warriors and make a great raid upon the Kor-ul-lul, and this time, Om-at, do not kill your prisoners. Take as many as you can alive and from some of them we may learn the fate of Tarzan-jad-guru.'

'Great is the wisdom of the Ho-don,' replied Om-at. 'It shall be as you say, and having made prisoners of all the Kor-ul-lul we shall make them tell us what we wish to know. And then we shall march them to the rim of Kor-ul-gryf and push them over the edge of the cliff.'

Ta-den smiled. He knew that they would not take prisoner all the Kor-ul-lul warriors – that they would be fortunate if they took one and it was also possible that they might even be driven back in defeat, but he knew too that Om-at would not hesitate to carry out his threat if he had the opportunity, so implacable was the hatred of these neighbors for each other.

It was not difficult to explain Om-at's plan to the stranger or to win his consent since he was aware, when the great black had made it plain that they would be accompanied by many warriors, that their venture would probably lead them into a hostile country and every safeguard that he could employ he was glad to avail himself of, since the furtherance of his quest was the paramount issue.

He slept that night upon a pile of furs in one of the compartments of Om-at's ancestral cave, and early the next day following the morning meal they sallied forth, a hundred savage warriors swarming up the face of the sheer cliff and out upon the summit of the ridge, the main body preceded by two warriors whose duties coincided with those of the point of modern military maneuvers, safeguarding the column against the danger of too sudden contact with the enemy.

Across the ridge they went and down into the Kor-ul-lul and there almost immediately they came upon a lone and unarmed Waz-don who was making his way fearfully up the gorge toward the village of his tribe. Him they took prisoner which, strangely, only added to his terror since from the moment that he had seen them and realized that escape was impossible, he had expected to be slain immediately.

'Take him back to Kor-ul-ja,' said Om-at, to one of his warriors, 'and hold him there unharmed until I return.'

And so the puzzled Kor-ul-lul was led away while the savage company moved stealthily from tree to tree in its closer advance upon the village. Fortune smiled upon Om-at in that it gave him quickly what he sought – a battle royal, for they had not yet come in sight of the caves of the Kor-ul-lul when they encountered a considerable band of warriors headed down the gorge upon some expedition.

Like shadows the Kor-ul-ja melted into the concealment of the foliage upon either side of the trail. Ignorant of impending danger, safe in the knowledge that they trod their own domain where each rock and stone was as familiar as the features of their mates, the Kor-ul-lul walked innocently into the ambush. Suddenly the quiet of that seeming peace was shattered by a savage cry and a hurled club felled a Kor-ul-lul.

The cry was a signal for a savage chorus from a hundred Kor-ul-ja throats with which were soon mingled the war cries of their enemies. The air was filled with flying clubs and then as the two forces mingled, the battle resolved itself into a number of individual encounters as each warrior singled out a foe and closed upon him. Knives gleamed and flashed in the mottling sunlight that filtered through the foliage of the trees above. Sleek black coats were streaked with crimson stains.

In the thick of the fight the smooth brown skin of the stranger mingled with the black bodies of friend and foe. Only his keen eyes and his quick wit had shown him how to differentiate between Kor-ul-lul and Kor-ul-ja since with the single exception of apparel they were identical, but at the first rush of the enemy he had noticed that their loincloths were not of the leopard-marked hides such as were worn by his allies.

Om-at, after dispatching his first antagonist, glanced at Jar-don. 'He fights with the ferocity of *jato*,' mused the chief. 'Powerful indeed must be the tribe from which he and Tarzan-jad-guru come,' and then his whole attention was occupied by a new assailant.

The fighters surged to and fro through the forest until those who survived were spent with exhaustion. All but the stranger who seemed not to know the sense of fatigue. He fought on when each new antagonist would have gladly quit, and when there were no more Kor-ul-lul who were not engaged, he leaped upon those who stood pantingly facing the exhausted Kor-ul-ja.

And always he carried upon his back the peculiar thing which Om-at had thought was some manner of strange weapon but the purpose of which he could not now account for in view of the fact that Jar-don never used it, and that for the most part it seemed but a nuisance and needless incumbrance since it banged and smashed against its owner as he leaped, catlike, hither and thither in the course of his victorious duels. The bow and arrows he had tossed aside at the beginning of the fight but the Enfield he would not discard, for where he went he meant that it should go until its mission had been fulfilled.

Presently the Kor-ul-ja, seemingly shamed by the example of Jar-don, closed once more with the enemy, but the latter, moved no doubt to terror by the presence of the stranger, a tireless demon who appeared invulnerable to their attacks, lost heart and sought to flee. And then it was that at Om-at's command his warriors surrounded a half-dozen of the most exhausted and made them prisoners.

It was a tired, bloody, and elated company that returned victorious to the Kor-ul-ja. Twenty of their number were carried back and six of these were dead men. It was the most glorious and successful raid that the Kor-ul-ja had made upon the Kor-ul-lul in the memory of man, and it marked Om-at as the greatest of chiefs, but that fierce warrior knew that advantage had lain upon his side largely because of the presence of his strange ally. Nor did he hesitate to give credit where credit belonged, with the result that Jar-don and his exploits were upon the tongue of every member of the tribe of Kor-ul-ja and great was the fame of the race that could produce two such as he and Tarzan-jad-guru.

And in the gorge of Kor-ul-lul beyond the ridge the survivors spoke in bated breath of this second demon that had joined forces with their ancient enemy.

Returned to his cave Om-at caused the Kor-ul-lul prisoners to be brought into his presence singly, and each he questioned as to the fate of Tarzan. Without exception they told him the same story – that Tarzan had been taken prisoner by them five days before but that he had slain the warrior left to guard him and escaped, carrying the head of the unfortunate sentry to the opposite side of Kor-ul-lul where he had left it suspended by its hair from the branch of a tree. But what had become of him after, they did not know; not one of them, until the last prisoner was examined, he whom they had taken first – the unarmed Kor-ul-lul making his way from the direction of the Valley of Jad-ben-Otho toward the caves of his people.

This one, when he discovered the purpose of their questioning, bartered with them for the lives and liberty of himself and his fellows. 'I can tell you much of this terrible man of whom you ask, Kor-ul-ja,' he said. 'I saw him yesterday and I know where he is, and if you will promise to let me and my fellows return in safety to the caves of our ancestors I will tell you all, and truthfully, that which I know.'

'You will tell us anyway,' replied Om-at, 'or we shall kill you.'

'You will kill me anyway,' retorted the prisoner, 'unless you make me this promise; so if I am to be killed the thing I know shall go with me.'

'He is right, Om-at,' said Ta-den; 'promise him that they shall have their liberty.'

'Very well,' said Om-at. 'Speak, Kor-ul-lul, and when you have told me all, you and your fellows may return unharmed to your tribe.'

'It was thus,' commenced the prisoner. 'Three days since I was hunting with a party of my fellows near the mouth of Kor-ul-lul not far from where you captured me this morning, when we were surprised and set upon by a large number of Ho-don who took us prisoners and carried us to A-lur where a few were chosen to be slaves and the rest were cast into a chamber beneath the temple where are held for sacrifice the victims that are offered by the Ho-don to Jad-ben-Otho upon the sacrificial altars of the temple at A-lur.

'It seemed then that indeed was my fate sealed and that lucky were those who had been selected for slaves among the Ho-don, for they at least might hope to escape – those in the chamber with me must be without hope.

'But yesterday a strange thing happened. There came to the temple, accompanied by all the priests and by the king and many of his warriors, one whom all did great reverence, and when he came to the barred gateway leading to the chamber in which we wretched ones awaited our fate, I saw to my surprise that it was none other than that terrible man who had so recently been a prisoner in the village of Kor-ul-lul – he whom you call Tarzan-jad-guru but whom they addressed as Dor-ul-Otho. And he looked upon us and questioned the high priest and when he was told of the purpose for which we were imprisoned there he grew angry and cried that it was not the will of Jad-ben-Otho that his people be thus sacrificed, and he commanded the high priest to liberate us, and this was done.

'The Ho-don prisoners were permitted to return to their homes and we were led beyond the City of A-lur and set upon our way toward Kor-ul-lul. There were three of us, but many are the dangers that lie between A-lur and Kor-ul-lul and we were only three and unarmed. Therefore none of us reached the village of our people and only one of us lives. I have spoken.'

'That is all you know concerning Tarzan-jad-guru?' asked Om-at.

'That is all I know,' replied the prisoner, 'other than that he whom they call Lu-don, the high priest at A-lur, was very angry, and that one of the two priests who guided us out of the city said to the other that the stranger was not Dor-ul-Otho at all; that Lu-don had said so and that he had also said that he would expose him and that he should be punished with death for his presumption. That is all they said within my hearing.

'And now, chief of Kor-ul-ja, let us depart.'

Om-at nodded. 'Go your way,' he said, 'and Ab-on, send warriors to guard them until they are safely within the Kor-ul-lul.

'Jar-don,' he said beckoning to the stranger, 'come with me,' and rising he led the way toward the summit of the cliff, and when they stood upon the ridge Om-at pointed down into the valley toward the City of A-lur gleaming in the light of the western sun.

'There is Tarzan-jad-guru,' he said, and Jar-don understood.

13

The Masquerader

As Tarzan dropped to the ground beyond the temple wall there was in his mind no intention to escape from the City of A-lur until he had satisfied himself that his mate was not a prisoner there, but how, in this strange city in which every man's hand must now be against him, he was to live and prosecute his search was far from clear to him.

There was only one place of which he knew that he might find even temporary sanctuary and that was the Forbidden Garden of the king. There was thick shrubbery in which a man might hide, and water and fruits. A cunning jungle creature, if he could reach the spot unsuspected, might remain concealed there for a considerable time, but how he was to traverse the distance between the temple grounds and the garden unseen was a question the seriousness of which he fully appreciated.

'Mighty is Tarzan,' he soliloquized, 'in his native jungle, but in the cities of man he is little better than they.'

Depending upon his keen observation and sense of location he felt safe in assuming that he could reach the palace grounds by means of the subterranean corridors and chambers of the temple through which he had been conducted the day before, nor any slightest detail of which had escaped his keen eyes. That would be better, he reasoned, than crossing the open grounds above where his pursuers would naturally immediately follow him from the temple and quickly discover him.

And so a dozen paces from the temple wall he disappeared from sight of any chance observer above, down one of the stone stairways that led to the apartments beneath. The way that he had been conducted the previous day had followed the windings and turnings of numerous corridors and apartments, but Tarzan, sure of himself in such matters, retraced the route accurately without hesitation.

He had little fear of immediate apprehension here since he believed that all the priests of the temple had assembled in the court above to witness his trial and his humiliation and his death, and with this idea firmly implanted in his mind he rounded the turn of the corridor and came face-to-face with an underpriest, his grotesque headdress concealing whatever emotion the sight of Tarzan may have aroused.

However, Tarzan had one advantage over the masked votary of Jad-ben-Otho in that the moment he saw the priest he knew his intention concerning him, and therefore was not compelled to delay action. And so it was that before the priest could determine on any suitable line of conduct in the premises a long, keen knife had been slipped into his heart.

As the body lunged toward the floor Tarzan caught it and snatched the headdress from its shoulders, for the first sight of the creature had suggested to his ever-alert mind a bold scheme for deceiving his enemies.

The headdress saved from such possible damage as it must have sustained had it fallen to the floor with the body of its owner, Tarzan relinquished his hold upon the corpse, set the headdress carefully upon the floor and stooping down severed the tail of the Ho-don close to its root. Nearby at his right was a small chamber from which the priest had evidently just emerged and into this Tarzan dragged the corpse, the headdress, and the tail.

Quickly cutting a thin strip of hide from the loincloth of the priest, Tarzan tied it securely about the upper end of the severed member and then tucking the tail under his loincloth behind him, secured it in place as best he could. Then he fitted the headdress over his shoulders and stepped from the apartment, to all appearances a priest of the temple of Jad-ben-Otho unless one examined too closely his thumbs and his great toes.

He had noticed that among both the Ho-don and the Waz-don it was not at all unusual that the end of the tail be carried in one hand, and so he caught his own tail up thus lest the lifeless appearance of it dragging along behind him should arouse suspicion.

Passing along the corridor and through the various chambers he emerged at last into the palace grounds beyond the temple. The pursuit had not yet reached this point though he was conscious of a commotion not far behind him. He met now both warriors and slaves but none gave him more than a passing glance, a priest being too common a sight about the palace.

And so, passing the guards unchallenged, he came at last to the inner entrance to the Forbidden Garden and there he paused and scanned quickly that portion of the beautiful spot that lay before his eyes. To his relief it seemed unoccupied and congratulating himself upon the ease with which he had so far outwitted the high powers of A-lur he moved rapidly to the opposite end of the enclosure. Here he found a patch of flowering shrubbery that might safely have concealed a dozen men.

Crawling well within he removed the uncomfortable headdress and sat down to await whatever eventualities fate might have in store for him the while he formulated plans for the future. The one night that he had spent in A-lur had kept him up to a late hour, apprising him of the fact that while there were few abroad in the temple grounds at night, there were yet enough to make it possible for him to fare forth under cover of his disguise without attracting the unpleasant attention of the guards, and, too, he had noticed that the priesthood constituted a privileged class that seemed to come and go at will and unchallenged throughout the palace as well as the temple. Altogether then, he decided, night furnished the most propitious hours for his investigation – by day he could lie up in the shrubbery of the Forbidden Garden, reasonably free from detection. From beyond the garden he heard the voices of men calling to one another both far and near, and he guessed that diligent was the search that was being prosecuted for him.

The idle moments afforded him an opportunity to evolve a more satisfactory scheme for attaching his stolen caudal appendage. He arranged it in such a way that it might be quickly assumed or discarded, and this done he fell to examining the weird mask that had so effectively hidden his features.

The thing had been very cunningly wrought from a single block of wood, very probably a section of a tree, upon which the features had been carved and afterward the interior hollowed out until only a comparatively thin shell remained. Two semicircular notches had been rounded out from opposite sides of the lower edge. These fitted snugly over his shoulders, aprons of wood extending downward a few inches upon his chest and back. From these aprons hung long tassels or switches of hair tapering from the outer edges toward the center which reached below the bottom of his torso. It required but the most cursory examination to indicate to the ape-man that these ornaments consisted of human scalps, taken, doubtless, from the heads of the sacrifices upon the eastern altars. The headdress itself had been carved to depict in formal design a hideous face that suggested both man and *gryf*. There were the three white horns, the yellow face with the blue bands encircling the eyes and the red hood which took the form of the posterior and anterior aprons.

As Tarzan sat within the concealing foliage of the shrubbery meditating upon the hideous priest-mask which he held in his hands he became aware that he was not alone in the garden. He sensed another presence and presently his trained ears detected the slow approach of naked feet across the sward. At first he suspected that it might be one stealthily searching the Forbidden

Garden for him but a little later the figure came within the limited area of his vision which was circumscribed by stems and foliage and flowers. He saw then that it was the princess O-lo-a and that she was alone and walking with bowed head as though in meditation – sorrowful meditation for there were traces of tears upon her lids.

Shortly after his ears warned him that others had entered the garden – men they were and their footsteps proclaimed that they walked neither slowly nor meditatively. They came directly toward the princess and when Tarzan could see them he discovered that both were priests.

'O-lo-a, Princess of Pal-ul-don,' said one, addressing her, 'the stranger who told us that he was the son of Jad-ben-Otho has but just fled from the wrath of Lu-don, the high priest, who exposed him and all his wicked blasphemy. The temple, and the palace, and the city are being searched and we have been sent to search the Forbidden Garden, since Ko-tan, the king, said that only this morning he found him here, though how he passed the guards he could not guess.'

'He is not here,' said O-lo-a. 'I have been in the garden for some time and have seen nor heard no other than myself. However, search it if you will.'

'No,' said the priest who had before spoken, 'it is not necessary since he could not have entered without your knowledge and the connivance of the guards, and even had he, the priest who preceded us must have seen him.'

'What priest?' asked O-lo-a.

'One passed the guards shortly before us,' explained the man.

'I did not see him,' said O-lo-a.

'Doubtless he left by another exit,' remarked the second priest.

'Yes, doubtless,' acquiesced O-lo-a, 'but it is strange that I did not see him.' The two priests made their obeisance and turned to depart.

'Stupid as Buto, the rhinoceros,' soliloquized Tarzan, who considered Buto a very stupid creature indeed. 'It should be easy to outwit such as these.'

The priests had scarce departed when there came the sound of feet running rapidly across the garden in the direction of the princess to an accompaniment of rapid breathing as of one almost spent, either from fatigue or excitement.

'Pan-at-lee,' exclaimed O-lo-a, 'what has happened? You look as terrified as the doe for which you were named!'

'O Princess of Pal-ul-don,' cried Pan-at-lee, 'they would have killed him in the temple. They would have killed the wondrous stranger who claimed to be the Dor-ul-Otho.'

'But he escaped,' said O-lo-a. 'You were there. Tell me about it.'

'The head priest would have had him seized and slain, but when they rushed upon him he hurled one in the face of Lu-don with the same ease that you might cast your breastplates at me; and then he leaped upon the altar and from there to the top of the temple wall and disappeared below. They are searching for him, but, O Princess, I pray that they do not find him.'

'And why do you pray that?' asked O-lo-a. 'Has not one who has so blasphemed earned death?'

'Ah, but you do not know him,' replied Pan-at-lee.

'And you do, then?' retorted O-lo-a quickly. 'This morning you betrayed yourself and then attempted to deceive me. The slaves of O-lo-a do not do such things with impunity. He is then the same Tarzan-jad-guru of whom you told me? Speak woman and speak only the truth.'

Pan-at-lee drew herself up very erect, her little chin held high, for was not she too among her own people already as good as a princess? 'Pan-at-lee, the Kor-ul-ja does not lie,' she said, 'to protect herself.'

'Then tell me what you know of this Tarzan-jad-guru,' insisted O-lo-a.

'I know that he is a wondrous man and very brave,' said Pan-at-lee, 'and that he saved me from the Tor-o-don and the *gryf* as I told you, and that he is indeed the same who came into the garden this morning; and even now I do not know that he is not the son of Jad-ben-Otho for his courage and his strength are more than those of mortal man, as are also his kindness and his honor: for when he might have harmed me he protected me, and when he might have saved himself he thought only of me. And all this he did because of his friendship for Om-at, who is *gund* of Kor-ul-ja and with whom I should have mated had the Ho-don not captured me.'

'He was indeed a wonderful man to look upon,' mused O-lo-a, 'and he was not as are other men, not alone in the conformation of his hands and feet or the fact that he was tailless, but there was that about him which made him seem different in ways more important than these.'

'And,' supplemented Pan-at-lee, her savage little heart loyal to the man who had befriended her and hoping to win for him the consideration of the princess even though it might not avail him; 'and,' she said, 'did he not know all about Ta-den and even his whereabouts. Tell me, O Princess, could a mortal know such things as these?'

'Perhaps he saw Ta-den,' suggested O-lo-a.

'But how would he know that you loved Ta-den,' parried Pan-at-lee. 'I tell you, my princess, that if he is not a god he is at least more than Ho-don or Waz-don. He followed me from the cave of Es-sat in Kor-ul-ja across Kor-ul-lul and two wide ridges to the very cave in Kor-ul-gryf where I hid, though many hours had passed since I had come that way and my bare feet left no impress upon the ground. What mortal man could do such things as these? And where in all Pal-ul-don would virgin maid find friend and protector in a strange male other than he?'

'Perhaps Lu-don may be mistaken – perhaps he is a god,' said O-lo-a, influenced by her slave's enthusiastic championing of the stranger.

'But whether god or man he is too wonderful to die,' cried Pan-at-lee. 'Would that I might save him. If he lived he might even find a way to give you your Ta-den, Princess.'

'Ah, if he only could,' sighed O-lo-a, 'but alas it is too late for tomorrow I am to be given to Bu-lot.'

'He who came to your quarters yesterday with your father?' asked Pan-at-lee.

'Yes; the one with the awful round face and the big belly,' exclaimed the princess disgustedly. 'He is so lazy he will neither hunt nor fight. To eat and to drink is all that Bu-lot is fit for, and he thinks of naught else except these things and his slave women. But come, Pan-at-lee, gather for me some of these beautiful blossoms. I would have them spread around my couch tonight that I may carry away with me in the morning the memory of the fragrance that I love best and which I know that I shall not find in the village of Mo-sar, the father of Bu-lot. I will help you, Pan-at-lee, and we will gather armfuls of them, for I love to gather them as I love nothing else – they were Ta-den's favorite flowers.'

The two approached the flowering shrubbery where Tarzan hid, but as the blooms grew plentifully upon every bush the ape-man guessed there would be no necessity for them to enter the patch far enough to discover him. With little exclamations of pleasure as they found particularly large or perfect blooms the two moved from place to place upon the outskirts of Tarzan's retreat.

'Oh, look, Pan-at-lee,' cried O-lo-a presently; 'there is the king of them all. Never did I see so wonderful a flower – No! I will get it myself – it is so large and wonderful no other hand shall touch it,' and the princess wound in among the bushes toward the point where the great flower bloomed upon a bush above the ape-man's head.

So sudden and unexpected her approach that there was no opportunity to escape and Tarzan sat silently trusting that fate might be kind to him and lead Ko-tan's daughter away before her eyes dropped from the high-growing bloom to him. But as the girl cut the long stem with her knife she looked down straight into the smiling face of Tarzan-jad-guru.

With a stifled scream she drew back and the ape-man rose and faced her.

'Have no fear, Princess,' he assured her. 'it is the friend of Ta-den who salutes you,' raising her fingers to his lips.

Pan-at-lee came now excitedly forward. 'O Jad-ben-Otho, it is he!'

'And now that you have found me,' queried Tarzan, 'will you give me up to Lu-don, the high priest?'

Pan-at-lee threw herself upon her knees at O-lo-a's feet. 'Princess! Princess!' she beseeched. 'Do not discover him to his enemies.'

'But Ko-tan, my father,' whispered O-lo-a fearfully, 'if he knew of my perfidy his rage would be beyond naming. Even though I am a princess Lu-don might demand that I be sacrificed to appease the wrath of Jad-ben-Otho, and between the two of them I should be lost.'

'But they need never know,' cried Pan-at-lee, 'that you have seen him unless you tell them yourself for as Jad-ben-Otho is my witness I will never betray you.'

'Oh, tell me, stranger,' implored O-lo-a, 'are you indeed a god?'

'Jad-ben-Otho is not more so,' replied Tarzan truthfully.

'But why do you seek to escape then from the hands of mortals if you are a god?' she asked.

'When gods mingle with mortals,' replied Tarzan, 'they are no less vulnerable than mortals. Even Jad-ben-Otho, should he appear before you in the flesh, might be slain.'

'You have seen Ta-den and spoken with him?' she asked with apparent irrelevancy.

'Yes, I have seen him and spoken with him,' replied the ape-man. 'For the duration of a moon I was with him constantly.'

'And –' she hesitated – 'he –' she cast her eyes toward the ground and a flush mantled her cheek – 'he still loves me?' and Tarzan knew that she had been won over.

'Yes,' he said, 'Ta-den speaks only of O-lo-a and he waits and hopes for the day when he can claim her.'

'But tomorrow they give me to Bu-lot,' she said sadly.

'May it be always tomorrow,' replied Tarzan, 'for tomorrow never comes.'

'Ah, but this unhappiness will come, and for all the tomorrows of my life I must pine in misery for the Ta-den who will never be mine.'

'But for Lu-don I might have helped you,' said the ape-man. 'And who knows that I may not help you yet?'

'Ah, if you only could, Dor-ul-Otho,' cried the girl, 'and I know that you would if it were possible for Pan-at-lee has told me how brave you are, and at the same time how kind.'

'Only Jad-ben-Otho knows what the future may bring,' said Tarzan. 'And now you two go your way lest someone should discover you and become suspicious.'

'We will go,' said O-lo-a, 'but Pan-at-lee will return with food. I hope that you escape and that Jad-ben-Otho is pleased with what I have done.' She turned and walked away and Pan-at-lee followed while the ape-man again resumed his hiding.

At dusk Pan-at-lee came with food and having her alone Tarzan put the question that he had been anxious to put since his conversation earlier in the day with O-lo-a.

'Tell me,' he said, 'what you know of the rumors of which O-lo-a spoke of the mysterious stranger which is supposed to be hidden in A-lur. Have you too heard of this during the short time that you have been here?'

'Yes,' said Pan-at-lee, 'I have heard it spoken of among the other slaves. It is something of which all whisper among themselves but of which none dares to speak aloud. They say that there is a strange she hidden in the temple and that Lu-don wants her for a priestess and that Ko-tan wants her for a wife and that neither as yet dares take her for fear of the other.'

'Do you know where she is hidden in the temple?' asked Tarzan.

'No,' said Pan-at-lee. 'How should I know? I do not even know that it is more than a story and I but tell you that which I have heard others say.'

'There was only one,' asked Tarzan, 'whom they spoke of?'

'No, they speak of another who came with her but none seems to know what became of this one.'

Tarzan nodded. 'Thank you, Pan-at-lee,' he said. 'You may have helped me more than either of us guess.'

'I hope that I have helped you,' said the girl as she turned back toward the palace.

'And I hope so too,' exclaimed Tarzan emphatically.

14

The Temple of the *Gryf*

When night had fallen Tarzan donned the mask and the dead tail of the priest he had slain in the vaults beneath the temple. He judged that it would not do to attempt again to pass the guard, especially so late at night as it would be likely to arouse comment and suspicion, and so he swung into the tree that overhung the garden wall and from its branches dropped to the ground beyond.

Avoiding too grave risk of apprehension the ape-man passed through the grounds to the court of the palace, approaching the temple from the side opposite to that at which he had left it at the time of his escape. He came thus it is true through a portion of the grounds with which he was unfamiliar but he preferred this to the danger of following the beaten track between the palace apartments and those of the temple. Having a definite goal in mind and endowed as he was with an almost miraculous sense of location he moved with great assurance through the shadows of the temple yard.

Taking advantage of the denser shadows close to the walls and of what shrubs and trees there were he came without mishap at last to the ornate building concerning the purpose of which he had asked Lu-don only to be put off with the assertion that it was forgotten – nothing strange in itself but given possible importance by the apparent hesitancy of the priest to discuss its use and the impression the ape-man had gained at the time that Lu-don lied.

And now he stood at last alone before the structure which was three stories in height and detached from all the other temple buildings. It had a single barred entrance which was carved from the living rock in representation of the head of a *gryf*, whose wide-open mouth constituted the doorway. The head, hood, and front paws of the creature were depicted as though it lay crouching with its lower jaw on the ground between its outspread paws. Small oval windows, which were likewise barred, flanked the doorway.

Seeing that the coast was clear, Tarzan stepped into the darkened entrance where he tried the bars only to discover that they were ingeniously locked in place by some device with which he was unfamiliar and that they also were probably too strong to be broken even if he could have risked the noise which would have resulted. Nothing was visible within the darkened interior and so, momentarily baffled, he sought the windows. Here also the bars refused to yield up their secret, but again Tarzan was not dismayed since he had counted upon nothing different.

If the bars would not yield to his cunning they would yield to his giant strength if there proved no other means of ingress, but first he would assure himself that this latter was the case. Moving entirely around the building he examined it carefully. There were other windows but they were similarly barred. He stopped often to look and listen but he saw no one and the sounds that he heard were too far away to cause him any apprehension.

He glanced above him at the wall of the building. Like so many of the other walls of the city, palace, and temple, it was ornately carved and there were too the peculiar ledges that ran sometimes in a horizontal plane and again were tilted at an angle, giving oft-times an impression of irregularity and even crookedness to the buildings. It was not a difficult wall to climb, at least not difficult for the ape-man.

But he found the bulky and awkward headdress a considerable handicap and so he laid it aside upon the ground at the foot of the wall. Nimbly he ascended to find the windows of the second floor not only barred but curtained within. He did not delay long at the second floor since he had in mind an idea that he would find the easiest entrance through the roof which he had noticed was roughly dome shaped like the throneroom of Ko-tan. Here there were apertures. He had seen them from the ground, and if the construction of the interior resembled even slightly that of the throneroom, bars would not be necessary upon these apertures, since no one could reach them from the floor of the room.

There was but a single question: would they be large enough to admit the broad shoulders of the ape-man.

He paused again at the third floor, and here, in spite of the hangings, he saw that the interior was lighted and simultaneously there came to his nostrils from within a scent that stripped from him temporarily any remnant of civilization that might have remained and left him a fierce and terrible bull of the jungles of Kerchak. So sudden and complete was the metamorphosis that there almost broke from the savage lips the hideous challenge of his kind, but the cunning brute-mind saved him this blunder.

And now he heard voices within – the voice of Lu-don he could have sworn, demanding. And haughty and disdainful came the answering words though utter hopelessness spoke in the tones of this other voice which brought Tarzan to the pinnacle of frenzy.

The dome with its possible apertures was forgotten. Every consideration of stealth and quiet was cast aside as the ape-man drew back his mighty fist and struck a single terrific blow upon the bars of the small window before him, a blow that sent the bars and the casing that held them clattering to the floor of the apartment within.

Instantly Tarzan dove headforemost through the aperture carrying the hangings of antelope hide with him to the floor below. Leaping to his feet he tore the entangling pelt from about his head only to find himself in utter darkness and in silence. He called aloud a name that had not passed his lips for many weary months. 'Jane, Jane,' he cried, 'where are you?' But there was only silence in reply.

Again and again he called, groping with outstretched hands through the Stygian blackness of the room, his nostrils assailed and his brain tantalized by the delicate effluvia that had first assured him that his mate had been within this very room. And he had heard her dear voice combating the base demands of the vile priest. Ah, if he had but acted with greater caution! If he had but continued to move with quiet and stealth he might even at this moment be holding her in his arms while the body of Lu-don, beneath his foot, spoke eloquently of vengeance achieved. But there was no time now for idle self-reproaches.

He stumbled blindly forward, groping for he knew not what till suddenly the floor beneath him tilted and he shot downward into a darkness even more utter than that above. He felt his body strike a smooth surface and he realized that he was hurtling downward as through a polished chute while from above there came the mocking tones of a taunting laugh and the voice of Lu-don screamed after him: 'Return to thy father, O Dor-ul-Otho!'

The ape-man came to a sudden and painful stop upon a rocky floor. Directly before him was an oval window crossed by many bars, and beyond he saw the moonlight playing on the waters of the blue lake below. Simultaneously he was conscious of a familiar odor in the air of the chamber, which a quick glance revealed in the semidarkness as of considerable proportion.

It was the faint, but unmistakable odor of the *gryf*, and now Tarzan stood silently listening. At first he detected no sounds other than those of the city that came to him through the window overlooking the lake; but presently, faintly, as though from a distance he heard the shuffling of padded feet along a stone pavement, and as he listened he was aware that the sound approached.

Nearer and nearer it came, and now even the breathing of the beast was audible. Evidently attracted by the noise of his descent into its cavernous retreat it was approaching to investigate. He could not see it but he knew that it was not far distant, and then, deafeningly there reverberated through those gloomy corridors the mad bellow of the *gryf*.

Aware of the poor eyesight of the beast, and his own eyes now grown accustomed to the darkness of the cavern, the ape-man sought to elude the infuriated charge which he well knew no living creature could withstand. Neither did he dare risk the chance of experimenting upon this strange *gryf* with the tactics of the Tor-o-don that he had found so efficacious upon that other occasion when his life and liberty had been the stakes for which he cast. In many respects the conditions were dissimilar. Before, in broad daylight, he had been able to approach the *gryf* under normal conditions in its natural state, and the *gryf* itself was one that he had seen subjected to the authority of man, or at least of a manlike creature; but here he was confronted by an imprisoned beast in the full swing of a furious charge and he had every reason to suspect that this *gryf* might never have felt the restraining influence of authority, confined as it was in this gloomy pit to serve likely but the single purpose that Tarzan had already seen so graphically portrayed in his own experience of the past few moments.

To elude the creature, then, upon the possibility of discovering some loophole of escape from his predicament seemed to the ape-man the wisest course to pursue. Too much was at stake to risk an encounter that might be avoided – an encounter the outcome of which there was every reason to apprehend would seal the fate of the mate that he had just found, only to lose again so harrowingly. Yet high as his disappointment and chagrin ran, hopeless as his present estate now appeared, there tingled in the veins of the savage lord a warm glow of thanksgiving and elation. She lived! After all these weary months of hopelessness and fear he had found her. She lived!

To the opposite side of the chamber, silently as the wraith of a disembodied soul, the swift jungle creature moved from the path of the charging Titan that, guided solely in the semidarkness by its keen ears, bore down upon the spot toward which Tarzan's noisy entrance into its lair had attracted it. Along the further wall the ape-man hurried. Before him now appeared the black opening of the corridor from which the beast had emerged into the larger chamber. Without hesitation Tarzan plunged into it. Even here his eyes, long accustomed to darkness that would have seemed total to you or to me, saw dimly the floor and the walls within a radius of a few feet – enough at least to prevent him plunging into any unguessed abyss, or dashing himself upon solid rock at a sudden turning.

The corridor was both wide and lofty, which indeed it must be to accommodate the colossal proportions of the creature whose habitat it was, and so Tarzan encountered no difficulty in moving with reasonable speed along its winding trail. He was aware as he proceeded that the trend of the passage was downward, though not steeply, but it seemed interminable and he wondered to what distant subterranean lair it might lead. There was a feeling that perhaps after all he might better have remained in the larger chamber and risked all on the chance of subduing the *gryf* where there was at least sufficient room and light to lend to the experiment some slight chance of success. To be overtaken here in the narrow confines of the black corridor where he was assured the *gryf* could not see him at all would spell almost certain death and now he heard the thing approaching from behind. Its thunderous bellows fairly shook the cliff from which the cavernous chambers were excavated. To halt and meet this monstrous incarnation of fury with a futile *whee-oo!* seemed to Tarzan the height of insanity and so he continued along the corridor, increasing his pace as he realized that the *gryf* was overhauling him.

Presently the darkness lessened and at the final turning of the passage he saw before him an area of moonlight. With renewed hope he sprang rapidly forward and emerged from the mouth of the corridor to find himself in a large circular enclosure the towering white walls of which rose high upon every side – smooth perpendicular walls upon the sheer face of which was no slightest foothold. To his left lay a pool of water, one side of which lapped the foot of the wall at this point. It was, doubtless, the wallow and the drinking pool of the *gryf*.

And now the creature emerged from the corridor and Tarzan retreated to the edge of the pool to make his last stand. There was no staff with which to enforce the authority of his voice, but yet he made his stand for there seemed naught else to do. Just beyond the entrance to the corridor the *gryf* paused, turning its weak eyes in all directions as though searching for its prey. This then seemed the psychological moment for his attempt and raising his voice in peremptory command the ape-man voiced the weird *whee-oo!* of the Tor-o-don. Its effect upon the *gryf* was instantaneous and complete – with a terrific bellow it lowered its three horns and dashed madly in the direction of the sound.

To right nor to left was any avenue of escape, for behind him lay the placid waters of the pool, while down upon him from before thundered annihilation. The mighty body seemed already to tower above him as the ape-man turned and dove into the dark waters.

Dead in her breast lay hope. Battling for life during harrowing months of imprisonment and danger and hardship it had fitfully flickered and flamed only to sink after each renewal to smaller proportions than before and now it had died out entirely leaving only cold, charred embers that Jane Clayton knew would never again be rekindled. Hope was dead as she faced Lu-don, the high priest, in her prison quarters in the Temple of the *Gryf* at A-lur. Both time and hardship had failed to leave their impress upon her physical beauty – the contours of her perfect form, the glory of her radiant loveliness had defied them, yet to these very attributes she owed the danger which now confronted her, for Lu-don desired her. From the lesser priests she had been safe, but from Lu-don, she was not safe, for Lu-don was not as they, since the high priestship of Pal-ul-don may descend from father to son.

Ko-tan, the king, had wanted her and all that had so far saved her from either was the fear of each for the other, but at last Lu-don had cast aside discretion and had come in the silent watches of the night to claim her. Haughtily had she repulsed him, seeking ever to gain time, though what time might bring her of relief or renewed hope she could not even remotely conjecture. A leer of lust and greed shone hungrily upon his cruel countenance as he advanced across the room to seize her. She did not shrink nor cower, but stood there very erect, her chin up, her level gaze freighted with the loathing and contempt she felt for him. He read her expression and while it angered him, it but increased his desire for possession. Here indeed was a queen, perhaps a goddess; fit mate for the high priest.

'You shall not!' she said as he would have touched her. 'One of us shall die before ever your purpose is accomplished.'

He was close beside her now. His laugh grated upon her ears. 'Love does not kill,' he replied mockingly.

He reached for her arm and at the same instant something clashed against the bars of one of the windows, crashing them inward to the floor, to be followed almost simultaneously by a human figure which dove headforemost into the room, its head enveloped in the skin window hangings which it carried with it in its impetuous entry.

Jane Clayton saw surprise and something of terror too leap to the countenance of the high priest and then she saw him spring forward and jerk upon a leather thong that depended from the ceiling of the apartment. Instantly there dropped from above a cunningly contrived partition that fell between them and the intruder, effectively barring him from them and at the same time leaving him to grope upon its opposite side in darkness, since the only cresset the room contained was upon their side of the partition.

Faintly from beyond the wall Jane heard a voice calling, but whose it was and what the words she could not distinguish. Then she saw Lu-don jerk upon another thong and wait in evident expectancy of some consequent happening. He did not have long to wait. She saw the thong move suddenly as though jerked from above and then Lu-don smiled and with another signal put in motion whatever machinery it was that raised the partition again to its place in the ceiling.

Advancing into that portion of the room that the partition had shut off from them, the high priest knelt upon the floor, and down-tilting a section of it, revealed the dark mouth of a shaft leading below. Laughing loudly he shouted into the hole: 'Return to thy father, O Dor-ul-Otho!'

Making fast the catch that prevented the trapdoor from opening beneath the feet of the unwary until such time as Lu-don chose the high priest rose again to his feet.

'Now, Beautiful One!' he cried, and then; 'Ja-don! what do you here?'

Jane Clayton turned to follow the direction of Lu-don's eyes and there she saw framed in the entranceway to the apartment the mighty figure of a warrior, upon whose massive features sat an expression of stern and uncompromising authority.

'I come from Ko-tan, the king,' replied Ja-don, 'to remove the beautiful stranger to the Forbidden Garden.'

'The king defies me, the high priest of Jad-ben-Otho?' cried Lu-don.

'It is the king's command – I have spoken,' snapped Ja-don, in whose manner was no sign of either fear or respect for the priest.

Lu-don well knew why the king had chosen this messenger whose heresy was notorious, but whose power had as yet protected him from the machinations of the priest. Lu-don cast a surreptitious glance at the thongs hanging from the ceiling. Why not? If he could but maneuver to entice Ja-don to the opposite side of the chamber!

'Come,' he said in a conciliatory tone, 'let us discuss the matter,' and moved toward the spot where he would have Ja-don follow him.

'There is nothing to discuss,' replied Ja-don, yet he followed the priest, fearing treachery.

Jane watched them. In the face and figure of the warrior she found reflected those admirable traits of courage and honor that the profession of arms best develops. In the hypocritical priest there was no redeeming quality. Of the two then she might best choose the warrior. With him there was a chance – with Lu-don, none. Even the very process of exchange from one prison to another might offer some possibility of escape. She weighed all these things and decided, for Lu-don's quick glance at the thongs had not gone unnoticed nor uninterpreted by her.

'Warrior,' she said, addressing Ja-don, 'if you would live enter not that portion of the room.'

Lu-don cast an angry glance upon her. 'Silence, slave!' he cried.

'And where lies the danger?' Ja-don asked of Jane, ignoring Lu-don.

The woman pointed to the thongs. 'Look,' she said, and before the high priest could prevent she had seized that which controlled the partition which shot downward separating Lu-don from the warrior and herself.

Ja-don looked inquiringly at her. 'He would have tricked me neatly but for you,' he said; 'kept me imprisoned there while he secreted you elsewhere in the mazes of his temple.'

'He would have done more than that,' replied Jane, as she pulled upon the other thong. 'This releases the fastenings of a trapdoor in the floor beyond the partition. When you stepped on that you would have been precipitated into a pit beneath the temple. Lu-don has threatened me with this fate often. I do not know that he speaks the truth, but he says that a demon of the temple is imprisoned there – a huge *gryf*.'

'There is a *gryf* within the temple,' said Ja-don. 'What with it and the sacrifices, the priests keep us busy supplying them with prisoners, though the victims are sometimes those for whom Lu-don has conceived hatred among our own people. He has had his eyes upon me for a long time. This would have been his chance but for you. Tell me, woman, why you warned me. Are we not all equally your jailers and your enemies?'

'None could be more horrible than Lu-don,' she replied; 'and you have the appearance of a brave and honorable warrior. I could not hope, for hope has died and yet there is the possibility that among so many fighting men, even though they be of another race than mine, there is one who would accord honorable treatment to a stranger within his gates – even though she be a woman.'

Ja-don looked at her for a long minute. 'Ko-tan would make you his queen,' he said. 'That he told me himself and surely that were honorable treatment from one who might make you a slave.'

'Why, then, would he make me queen?' she asked.

Ja-don came closer as though in fear his words might be overheard. 'He believes, although he did not tell me so in fact, that you are of the race of gods. And why not? Jad-ben-Otho is tailless, therefore it is not strange that Ko-tan should suspect that only the gods are thus. His queen is dead leaving only a single daughter. He craves a son and what more desirable than that he should found a line of rulers for Pal-ul-don descended from the gods?'

'But I am already wed,' cried Jane. 'I cannot wed another. I do not want him or his throne.'

'Ko-tan is king,' replied Ja-don simply as though that explained and simplified everything.

'You will not save me then?' she asked.

'If you were in Ja-lur,' he replied, 'I might protect you, even against the king.'

'What and where is Ja-lur?' she asked, grasping at any straw.

'It is the city where I rule,' he answered. 'I am chief there and of all the valley beyond.'

'Where is it?' she insisted. 'Is it far?'

'No,' he replied, smiling, 'it is not far, but do not think of that – you could never reach it. There are too many to pursue and capture you. If you wish to know, however, it lies up the river that empties into Jad-ben-lul whose waters kiss the walls of A-lur – up the western fork it lies with water upon three sides. Impregnable city of Pal-ul-don – alone of all the cities it has never been entered by a foeman since it was built there while Jad-ben-Otho was a boy.'

'And there I would be safe?' she asked.

'Perhaps,' he replied.

Ah, dead Hope; upon what slender provocation would you seek to glow again! She sighed and shook her head, realizing the inutility of Hope – yet the tempting bait dangled before her mind's eye – Ja-lur!

'You are wise,' commented Ja-don interpreting her sigh. 'Come now, we will go to the quarters of the princess beside the Forbidden Garden. There you will remain with O-lo-a, the king's daughter. It will be better than this prison you have occupied.'

'And Ko-tan?' she asked, a shudder passing through her slender frame.

'There are ceremonies,' explained Ja-don, 'that may occupy several days before you become queen, and one of them may be difficult of arrangement.' He laughed, then.

'What?' she asked.

'Only the high priest may perform the marriage ceremony for a king,' he explained.

'Delay!' she murmured; 'blessed delay!' Tenacious indeed of life is Hope even though it be reduced to cold and lifeless char – a veritable phoenix.

15

'The King Is Dead!'

As they conversed Ja-don had led her down the stone stairway that leads from the upper floors of the Temple of the *Gryf* to the chambers and the corridors that honeycomb the rocky hills from which the temple and the palace are hewn and now they passed from one to the other through a doorway upon one side of which two priests stood guard and upon the other two warriors. The former would have halted Ja-don when they saw who it was that accompanied him for well known throughout the temple was the quarrel between king and high priest for possession of this beautiful stranger.

'Only by order of Lu-don may she pass,' said one, placing himself directly in front of Jane Clayton, barring her progress. Through the hollow eyes of the hideous mask the woman could see those of the priest beneath gleaming with the fires of fanaticism. Ja-don placed an arm about her shoulders and laid his hand upon his knife.

'She passes by order of Ko-tan, the king,' he said, 'and by virtue of the fact that Ja-don, the chief, is her guide. Stand aside!'

The two warriors upon the palace side pressed forward. 'We are here, *gund* of Ja-lur,' said one, addressing Ja-don, 'to receive and obey your commands.'

The second priest now interposed. 'Let them pass,' he admonished his companion. 'We have received no direct commands from Lu-don to the contrary and it is a law of the temple and the palace that chiefs and priests may come and go without interference.'

'But I know Lu-don's wishes,' insisted the other.

'He told you then that Ja-don must not pass with the stranger?'

'No – but –'

'Then let them pass, for they are three to two and will pass anyway – we have done our best.'

Grumbling, the priest stepped aside. 'Lu-don will exact an accounting,' he cried angrily.

Ja-don turned upon him. 'And get it when and where he will,' he snapped.

They came at last to the quarters of the Princess O-lo-a where, in the main entranceway, loitered a small guard of palace warriors and several stalwart black eunuchs belonging to the princess, or her women. To one of the latter Ja-don relinquished his charge.

'Take her to the princess,' he commanded, 'and see that she does not escape.'

Through a number of corridors and apartments lighted by stone cressets the eunuch led Lady Greystoke halting at last before a doorway concealed by hangings of *jato* skin, where the guide beat with his staff upon the wall beside the door.

'O-lo-a, Princess of Pal-ul-don,' he called, 'here is the stranger woman, the prisoner from the temple.'

'Bid her enter,' Jane heard a sweet voice from within command.

The eunuch drew aside the hangings and Lady Greystoke stepped within. Before her was a low-ceilinged room of moderate size. In each of the four corners a kneeling figure of stone seemed to be bearing its portion of the weight of the ceiling upon its shoulders. These figures were evidently intended to represent Waz-don slaves and were not without bold artistic beauty. The ceiling itself was slightly arched to a central dome which was pierced to admit light by day, and air. Upon one side of the room were many windows, the other three walls being blank except for a doorway in each. The princess lay upon a pile of furs which were arranged over a low stone dais in one corner of the apartment and was alone except for a single Waz-don slave girl who sat upon the edge of the dais near her feet.

As Jane entered O-lo-a beckoned her to approach and when she stood beside the couch the girl half rose upon an elbow and surveyed her critically.

'How beautiful you are,' she said simply.

Jane smiled, sadly; for she had found that beauty may be a curse.

'That is indeed a compliment,' she replied quickly, 'from one so radiant as the Princess O-lo-a.'

'Ah!' exclaimed the princess delightedly; 'you speak my language! I was told that you were of another race and from some far land of which we of Pal-ul-don have never heard.'

'Lu-don saw to it that the priests instructed me,' explained Jane; 'but I am from a far country, Princess; one to which I long to return – and I am very unhappy.'

'But Ko-tan, my father, would make you his queen,' cried the girl; 'that should make you very happy.'

'But it does not,' replied the prisoner; 'I love another to whom I am already wed. Ah, Princess, if you had known what it was to love and to be forced into marriage with another you would sympathize with me.'

The Princess O-lo-a was silent for a long moment. 'I know,' she said at last, 'and I am very sorry for you; but if the king's daughter cannot save herself from such a fate who may save a slave woman? For such in fact you are.'

The drinking in the great banquet hall of the palace of Ko-tan, king of Pal-ul-don had commenced earlier this night than was usual, for the king was celebrating the morrow's betrothal of his only daughter to Bu-lot, son of Mo-sar, the chief, whose great-grandfather had been king of Pal-ul-don and who thought that he should be king, and Mo-sar was drunk and so was Bu-lot, his son. For that matter nearly all of the warriors, including the king himself, were drunk. In the heart of Ko-tan was no love either for Mo-sar, or Bu-lot, nor did either of these love the king. Ko-tan was giving his daughter to Bu-lot in the hope that the alliance would prevent Mo-sar from insisting upon his claims to the throne, for, next to Ja-don, Mo-sar was the most powerful of the chiefs and while Ko-tan looked with fear upon Ja-don, too, he had no fear that the old Lion-man would attempt to seize the throne, though which way he would throw his influence and his warriors in the event that Mo-sar declared war upon Ko-tan, the king could not guess.

Primitive people who are also warlike are seldom inclined toward either tact or diplomacy even when sober, but drunk they know not the words, if aroused. It was really Bu-lot who started it.

'This,' he said, 'I drink to O-lo-a,' and he emptied his tankard at a single gulp. 'And this,' seizing a full one from a neighbor, 'to her son and mine who will bring back the throne of Pal-ul-don to its rightful owners!'

'The king is not yet dead!' cried Ko-tan, rising to his feet; 'nor is Bu-lot yet married to his daughter – and there is yet time to save Pal-ul-don from the spawn of the rabbit breed.'

The king's angry tone and his insulting reference to Bu-lot's well-known cowardice brought a sudden, sobering silence upon the roistering company. Every eye turned upon Bu-lot and Mo-sar, who sat together directly opposite the king. The first was very drunk though suddenly he seemed quite sober. He was so drunk that for an instant he forgot to be a coward, since his reasoning powers were so effectually paralyzed by the fumes of liquor that he could not intelligently weigh the consequences of his acts. It is reasonably conceivable that a drunk and angry rabbit might commit a rash deed. Upon no other hypothesis is the thing that Bu-lot now did explicable. He rose suddenly from the seat to which he had sunk after delivering his toast and seizing the knife from the sheath of the warrior upon his right hurled it with terrific force at Ko-tan. Skilled in the art of throwing both their knives and their clubs are the warriors of Pal-ul-don and at this short distance and coming as it did without warning there was no defense and but one possible result – Ko-tan, the king, lunged forward across the table, the blade buried in his heart.

A brief silence followed the assassin's cowardly act. White with terror, now, Bu-lot fell slowly back toward the doorway at his rear, when suddenly angry warriors leaped with drawn knives to prevent his escape and to avenge their king. But Mo-sar now took his stand beside his son.

'Ko-tan is dead!' he cried. 'Mo-sar is king! Let the loyal warriors of Pal-ul-don protect their ruler!'

Mo-sar commanded a goodly following and these quickly surrounded him and Bu-lot, but there were many knives against them and now Ja-don pressed forward through those who confronted the pretender.

'Take them both!' he shouted. 'The warriors of Pal-ul-don will choose their own king after the assassin of Ko-tan has paid the penalty of his treachery.'

Directed now by a leader whom they both respected and admired those who had been loyal to Ko-tan rushed forward upon the faction that had surrounded Mo-sar. Fierce and terrible was the fighting, devoid, apparently, of all else than the ferocious lust to kill and while it was at its height Mo-sar and Bu-lot slipped unnoticed from the banquet hall.

To that part of the palace assigned to them during their visit to A-lur they hastened. Here were their servants and the lesser warriors of their party who had not been bidden to the feast of Ko-tan. These were directed quickly to gather together their belongings for immediate departure. When all was ready, and it did not take long, since the warriors of Pal-ul-don require but little impedimenta on the march, they moved toward the palace gate.

Suddenly Mo-sar approached his son. 'The princess,' he whispered. 'We must not leave the city without her – she is half the battle for the throne.'

Bu-lot, now entirely sober, demurred. He had had enough of fighting and of risk. 'Let us get out of A-lur quickly,' he urged, 'or we shall have the whole city upon us. She would not come without a struggle and that would delay us too long.'

'There is plenty of time,' insisted Mo-sar. 'They are still fighting in the *pal-e-don-so*. It will be long before they miss us and, with Ko-tan dead, long before any will think to look to the safety of the princess. Our time is now – it was made for us by Jad-ben-Otho. Come!'

Reluctantly Bu-lot followed his father, who first instructed the warriors to await them just inside the gateway of the palace. Rapidly the two approached the quarters of the princess. Within the entranceway only a handful of warriors were on guard. The eunuchs had retired.

'There is fighting in the *pal-e-don-so*,' Mo-sar announced in feigned excitement as they entered the presence of the guards. 'The king desires you to come at once and has sent us to guard the apartments of the princess. Make haste!' he commanded as the men hesitated.

The warriors knew him and that on the morrow the princess was to be betrothed to Bu-lot, his son. If there was trouble what more natural than that Mo-sar and Bu-lot should be entrusted with the safety of the princess. And then, too, was not Mo-sar a powerful chief to whose orders disobedience might prove a dangerous thing? They were but common fighting men disciplined in the rough school of tribal warfare, but they had learned to obey a superior and so they departed for the banquet hall – the *place-where-men-eat*.

Barely waiting until they had disappeared Mo-sar crossed to the hangings at the opposite end of the entrance-hall and followed by Bu-lot made his way toward the sleeping apartment of O-lo-a and a moment later, without warning, the two men burst in upon the three occupants of the room. At sight of them O-lo-a sprang to her feet.

'What is the meaning of this?' she demanded angrily.

Mo-sar advanced and halted before her. Into his cunning mind had entered a plan to trick her. If it succeeded it would prove easier than taking her by force, and then his eyes fell upon Jane Clayton and he almost gasped in astonishment and admiration, but he caught himself and returned to the business of the moment.

'O-lo-a,' he cried, 'when you know the urgency of our mission you will forgive us. We have sad news for you. There has been an uprising in the palace and Ko-tan, the king, has been slain. The rebels are drunk with liquor and now on their way here. We must get you out of A-lur at once – there is not a moment to lose. Come, and quickly!'

'My father dead?' cried O-lo-a, and suddenly her eyes went wide. 'Then my place is here with my people,' she cried. 'If Ko-tan is dead I am queen until the warriors choose a new ruler – that is the law of Pal-ul-don. And if I am queen none can make me wed whom I do not wish to wed – and Jad-ben-Otho knows I never wished to wed thy cowardly son. Go!' She pointed a slim forefinger imperiously toward the doorway.

Mo-sar saw that neither trickery nor persuasion would avail now and every precious minute counted. He looked again at the beautiful woman who stood beside O-lo-a. He had never before seen her but he well knew from palace gossip that she could be no other than the godlike stranger whom Ko-tan had planned to make his queen.

'Bu-lot,' he cried to his son, 'take you your own woman and I will take – mine!' and with that he sprang suddenly forward and seizing Jane about the waist lifted her in his arms, so that before O-lo-a or Pan-at-lee might even guess his purpose he had disappeared through the hangings near the foot of the dais and was gone with the stranger woman struggling and fighting in his grasp.

And then Bu-lot sought to seize O-lo-a, but O-lo-a had her Pan-at-lee—fierce little tiger-girl of the savage Kor-ul-ja – Pan-at-lee whose name belied her – and Bu-lot found that with the two of them his hands were full. When he would have lifted O-lo-a and borne her away Pan-at-lee seized him around the legs and strove to drag him down. Viciously he kicked her, but she would not desist, and finally, realizing that he might not only lose his princess but be so delayed as to invite capture if he did not rid himself of this clawing, scratching she-*jato*, he hurled O-lo-a to the floor and seizing Pan-at-lee by the hair drew his knife and –

The curtains behind him suddenly parted. In two swift bounds a lithe figure crossed the room and before ever the knife of Bu-lot reached its goal his wrist was seized from behind and a terrific blow crashing to the base of his brain dropped him, lifeless, to the floor. Bu-lot, coward, traitor, and assassin, died without knowing who struck him down.

As Tarzan of the Apes leaped into the pool in the *gryf* pit of the temple at A-lur one might have accounted for his act on the hypothesis that it was the last blind urge of self-preservation to delay, even for a moment, the inevitable tragedy in which each some day must play the leading role upon his little stage; but no – those cool, gray eyes had caught the sole possibility for escape that the surroundings and the circumstances offered – a tiny, moonlit patch of water glimmering through a small aperture in the cliff at the surface of the pool upon its farther side. With swift, bold strokes he swam for speed alone knowing that the water would in no way deter his pursuer. Nor did it. Tarzan heard the great splash as the huge creature plunged into the pool behind him; he heard the churning waters as it forged rapidly onward in his wake. He was nearing the opening – would it be large enough to permit the passage of his body? That portion of it which showed above the surface of the water most certainly would not. His life, then, depended upon how much of the aperture was submerged. And now it was directly before him and the *gryf* directly behind. There was no alternative – there was no other hope. The ape-man threw all the resources of his great strength into the last few strokes, extended his hands before him as a cutwater, submerged to the water's level and shot forward toward the hole.

Frothing with rage was the baffled Lu-don as he realized how neatly the stranger she had turned his own tables upon him. He could of course escape the Temple of the *Gryf* in which her quick wit had temporarily imprisoned him; but during the delay, however brief, Ja-don would find time to steal her from the temple and deliver her to Ko-tan. But he would have her yet – that the high priest swore in the names of Jad-ben-Otho and all the demons of his faith. He hated Ko-tan. Secretly he had espoused the cause of Mo-sar, in whom he would have a willing tool. Perhaps, then, this would give him the opportunity he had long awaited – a pretext for inciting the revolt that would dethrone Ko-tan and place Mo-sar in power – with Lu-don the real ruler of Pal-ul-don. He licked his thin lips as he sought the window through which Tarzan had entered and now Lu-don's only avenue of escape. Cautiously he made his way across the floor, feeling before him with his hands, and when they discovered that the trap was set for him an ugly snarl broke from the priest's lips. 'The she-devil!' he muttered; 'but she shall pay, she shall pay – ah, Jad-ben-Otho; how she shall pay for the trick she has played upon Lu-don!'

He crawled through the window and climbed easily downward to the ground. Should he pursue Ja-don and the woman, chancing an encounter with the fierce chief, or bide his time until treachery and intrigue should accomplish his design? He chose the latter solution, as might have been expected of such as he.

Going to his quarters he summoned several of his priests – those who were most in his confidence and who shared his ambitions for absolute power of the temple over the palace – all men who hated Ko-tan.

'The time has come,' he told them, 'when the authority of the temple must be placed definitely above that of the palace. Ko-tan must make way for Mo-sar, for Ko-tan has defied your high priest. Go then, Pan-sat, and summon Mo-sar secretly to the temple, and you others go to the city and prepare the faithful warriors that they may be in readiness when the time comes.'

For another hour they discussed the details of the coup d'état that was to overthrow the government of Pal-ul-don. One knew a slave who, as the signal sounded from the temple gong, would thrust a knife into the heart of Ko-tan, for the price of liberty. Another held personal knowledge of an officer of the palace that he could use to compel the latter to admit a number of Lu-don's warriors to various parts of the palace. With Mo-sar as the cat's paw, the plan seemed scarce possible of failure and so they separated, going upon their immediate errands to palace and to city.

As Pan-sat entered the palace grounds he was aware of a sudden commotion in the direction of the *pal-e-don-so* and a few minutes later Lu-don was surprised to see him return to the apartments of the high priest, breathless and excited.

'What now, Pan-sat?' cried Lu-don. 'Are you pursued by demons?'

'O master, our time has come and gone while we sat here planning. Ko-tan is already dead and Mo-sar fled. His friends are fighting with the warriors of the palace but they have no head, while Ja-don leads the others. I could learn but little from frightened slaves who had fled at the outburst of the quarrel. One told me that Bu-lot had slain the king and that he had seen Mo-sar and the assassin hurrying from the palace.'

'Ja-don,' muttered the high priest. 'The fools will make him king if we do not act and act quickly. Get into the city, Pan-sat – let your feet fly and raise the cry that Ja-don has killed the king and is seeking to wrest the throne from O-lo-a. Spread the word as you know best how to spread it that Ja-don has threatened to destroy the priests and hurl the altars of the temple into Jad-ben-lul. Rouse the warriors of the city and urge them to attack at once. Lead them into the temple by the secret way that only the priests know and from here we may spew them out upon the palace before they learn the truth. Go, Pan-sat, immediately – delay not an instant.

'But stay,' he called as the underpriest turned to leave the apartment; 'saw or heard you anything of the strange white woman that Ja-don stole from the Temple of the *Gryf* where we have had her imprisoned?'

'Only that Ja-don took her into the palace where he threatened the priests with violence if they did not permit him to pass,' replied Pan-sat. 'This they told me, but where within the palace she is hidden I know not.'

'Ko-tan ordered her to the Forbidden Garden,' said Lu-don; 'doubtless we shall find her there. And now, Pan-sat, be upon your errand.'

In a corridor by Lu-don's chamber a hideously masked priest leaned close to the curtained aperture that led within. Were he listening he must have heard all that passed between Pan-sat and the high priest, and that he had listened was evidenced by his hasty withdrawal to the shadows of a nearby passage as the lesser priest moved across the chamber toward the doorway. Pan-sat went his way in ignorance of the near presence that he almost brushed against as he hurried toward the secret passage that leads from the temple of Jad-ben-Otho, far beneath the palace, to the city beyond, nor did he sense the silent creature following in his footsteps.

16

The Secret Way

It was a baffled *gryf* that bellowed in angry rage as Tarzan's sleek brown body cutting the moonlit waters shot through the aperture in the wall of the *gryf* pool and out into the lake beyond. The ape-man smiled as he thought of the comparative ease with which he had defeated the purpose of the high priest but his face clouded again at the ensuing remembrance of the grave danger that threatened his mate. His sole object now must be to return as quickly as he might to the chamber where he had last seen her on the third floor of the Temple of the *Gryf*, but how he was to find his way again into the temple grounds was a question not easy of solution.

In the moonlight he could see the sheer cliff rising from the water for a great distance along the shore – far beyond the precincts of the temple and the palace – towering high above him, a seemingly impregnable barrier against his return. Swimming close in, he skirted the wall searching diligently for some foothold, however slight, upon its smooth, forbidding surface. Above him and quite out of reach were numerous apertures, but there were no means at hand by which he could reach them. Presently, however, his hopes were raised by the sight of an opening level with the surface of the water. It lay just ahead and a few strokes brought him to it – cautious strokes that brought forth no sound from the yielding waters. At the nearer side of the opening he stopped and reconnoitered. There was no one in sight. Carefully he raised his body to the threshold of the entranceway, his smooth brown hide glistening in the moonlight as it shed the water in tiny sparkling rivulets.

Before him stretched a gloomy corridor, unlighted save for the faint illumination of the diffused moonlight that penetrated it for but a short distance from the opening. Moving as rapidly as reasonable caution warranted, Tarzan followed the corridor into the bowels of the cave. There was an abrupt turn and then a flight of steps at the top of which lay another corridor running parallel with the face of the cliff. This passage was dimly lighted by flickering cressets set in niches in the walls at considerable distances apart. A quick survey showed the ape-man numerous openings upon each side of the corridor and his quick ears caught sounds that indicated that there were other beings not far distant – priests, he concluded, in some of the apartments letting upon the passageway.

To pass undetected through this hive of enemies appeared quite beyond the range of possibility. He must again seek disguise and knowing from experience how best to secure such he crept stealthily along the corridor toward the nearest doorway. Like Numa, the lion, stalking a wary prey he crept with quivering nostrils to the hangings that shut off his view from the interior of the apartment beyond. A moment later his head disappeared within; then his shoulders, and his lithe body, and the hangings dropped quietly into place again. A moment later there filtered to the vacant corridor without a brief, gasping gurgle and again silence. A minute passed; a second, and a third, and then the hangings were thrust aside and a grimly masked priest of the temple of Jad-ben-Otho strode into the passageway.

With bold steps he moved along and was about to turn into a diverging gallery when his attention was aroused by voices coming from a room upon his left. Instantly the figure halted and crossing the corridor stood with an ear close to the skins that concealed the occupants of the room from him, and him from them. Presently he leaped back into the concealing shadows of the diverging gallery and immediately thereafter the hangings by which he had been listening parted and a priest emerged to turn quickly down the main corridor. The eavesdropper waited until the other had gained a little distance and then stepping from his place of concealment followed silently behind.

The way led along the corridor which ran parallel with the face of the cliff for some little distance and then Pan-sat, taking a cresset from one of the wall niches, turned abruptly into a small apartment at his left. The tracker followed cautiously in time to see the rays of the flickering light dimly visible from an aperture in the floor before him. Here he found a series of steps, similar to those used by the Waz-don in scaling the cliff to their caves, leading to a lower level.

First satisfying himself that his guide was continuing upon his way unsuspecting, the other descended after him and continued his stealthy stalking. The passageway was now both narrow and low, giving but bare headroom to a tall man, and it was broken often by flights of steps leading always downward. The steps in each unit seldom numbered more than six and sometimes there was only one or two but in the aggregate the tracker imagined that they had descended between fifty and seventy-five feet from the level of the upper corridor when the passageway terminated in a small apartment at one side of which was a little pile of rubble.

Setting his cresset upon the ground, Pan-sat commenced hurriedly to toss the bits of broken stone aside, presently revealing a small aperture at the base of the wall upon the opposite side of which there appeared to be a further accumulation of rubble. This he also removed until he had a hole of sufficient size to permit the passage of his body, and leaving the cresset still burning upon the floor the priest crawled through the opening he had made and disappeared from the sight of the watcher hiding in the shadows of the narrow passageway behind him.

No sooner, however, was he safely gone than the other followed, finding himself, after passing through the hole, on a little ledge about halfway between the surface of the lake and the top of the cliff above. The ledge inclined steeply upward, ending at the rear of a building which stood upon the edge of the cliff and which the second priest entered just in time to see Pan-sat pass out into the city beyond.

As the latter turned a nearby corner the other emerged from the doorway and quickly surveyed his surroundings. He was satisfied the priest who had led him hither had served his purpose insofar as the tracker was concerned. Above him, and perhaps a hundred yards away, the white walls of the palace gleamed against the northern sky. The time that it had taken him to acquire definite knowledge concerning the secret passageway between the temple and the city he did not count as lost, though he begrudged every instant that kept him from the prosecution of his main objective. It had seemed to him, however, necessary to the success of a bold plan that he had formulated upon overhearing the conversation between Lu-don and Pan-sat as he stood without the hangings of the apartment of the high priest.

Alone against a nation of suspicious and half-savage enemies he could scarce hope for a successful outcome to the one great issue upon which hung the life and happiness of the creature he loved best. For her sake he must win allies and it was for this purpose that he had sacrificed these precious moments, but now he lost no further time in seeking to regain entrance to the palace grounds that he might search out whatever new prison they had found in which to incarcerate his lost love.

He found no difficulty in passing the guards at the entrance to the palace for, as he had guessed, his priestly disguise disarmed all suspicion. As he approached the warriors he kept his hands behind him and trusted to fate that the sickly light of the single torch which stood beside the doorway would not reveal his un-Pal-ul-donian feet. As a matter of fact so accustomed were they to the comings and goings of the priesthood that they paid scant attention to him and he passed on into the palace grounds without even a moment's delay.

His goal now was the Forbidden Garden and this he had little difficulty in reaching though he elected to enter it over the wall rather than to chance arousing any suspicion on the part of the guards at the inner entrance, since he could imagine no reason why a priest should seek entrance there this late at night.

He found the garden deserted, nor any sign of her he sought. That she had been brought hither he had learned from the conversation he had overheard between Lu-don and Pan-sat, and he was sure that there had been no time or opportunity for the high priest to remove her from the palace grounds. The garden he knew to be devoted exclusively to the uses of the princess and her women and it was only reasonable to assume therefore that if Jane had been brought to the garden it could only have been upon an order from Ko-tan. This being the case the natural assumption would follow that he would find her in some other portion of O-lo-a's quarters.

Just where these lay he could only conjecture, but it seemed reasonable to believe that they must be adjacent to the garden, so once more he scaled the wall and passing around its end directed his steps toward an entranceway which he judged must lead to that portion of the palace nearest the Forbidden Garden.

To his surprise he found the place unguarded and then there fell upon his ear from an interior apartment the sound of voices raised in anger and excitement. Guided by the sound he quickly traversed several corridors and chambers until he stood before the hangings which separated him from the chamber from which issued the sounds of altercation. Raising the skins slightly he looked within. There were two women battling with a Ho-don warrior. One was the daughter of Ko-tan and the other Pan-at-lee, the Kor-ul-ja.

At the moment that Tarzan lifted the hangings, the warrior threw O-lo-a viciously to the ground and seizing Pan-at-lee by the hair drew his knife and raised it above her head. Casting the encumbering headdress of the dead priest from his shoulders the ape-man leaped across the intervening space and seizing the brute from behind struck him a single terrible blow.

As the man fell forward dead, the two women recognized Tarzan simultaneously. Pan-at-lee fell upon her knees and would have bowed her head upon his feet had he not, with an impatient gesture, commanded her to rise. He had no time to listen to their protestations of gratitude or answer the numerous questions which he knew would soon be flowing from those two feminine tongues.

'Tell me,' he cried, 'where is the woman of my own race whom Ja-don brought here from the temple?'

'She is but this moment gone,' cried O-lo-a. 'Mo-sar, the father of this thing here,' and she indicated the body of Bu-lot with a scornful finger, 'seized her and carried her away.'

'Which way?' he cried. 'Tell me quickly, in what direction he took her.'

'That way,' cried Pan-at-lee, pointing to the doorway through which Mo-sar had passed. 'They would have taken the princess and the stranger woman to Tu-lur, Mo-sar's city by the Dark Lake.'

'I go to find her,' he said to Pan-at-lee; 'she is my mate. And if I survive I shall find means to liberate you too and return you to Om-at.'

Before the girl could reply he had disappeared behind the hangings of the door near the foot of the dais. The corridor through which he ran was illy lighted and like nearly all its kind in the Ho-don city wound in and out and up and down but at last it terminated at a sudden turn which brought him into a courtyard filled with warriors, a portion of the palace guard that had just been summoned by one of the lesser palace chiefs to join the warriors of Ko-tan in the battle that was raging in the banquet hall.

At sight of Tarzan, who in his haste had forgotten to recover his disguising headdress, a great shout arose. 'Blasphemer!' 'Defiler of the temple!' burst hoarsely from savage throats, and mingling with these were a few who cried, 'Dor-ul-Otho!' evidencing the fact that there were among them still some who clung to their belief in his divinity.

To cross the courtyard armed only with a knife, in the face of this great throng of savage fighting men seemed even to the giant ape-man a thing impossible of achievement. He must use his wits now and quickly too, for they were closing upon him. He might have turned and fled back through the corridor but flight now even in the face of dire necessity would but delay him in his pursuit of Mo-sar and his mate.

'Stop!' he cried, raising his palm against them. 'I am the Dor-ul-Otho and I come to you with a word from Ja-don, who it is my father's will shall be your king now that Ko-tan is slain. Lu-don, the high priest, has planned to seize the palace and destroy the loyal warriors that Mo-sar may be made king – Mo-sar who will be the tool and creature of Lu-don. Follow me. There is no time to lose if you would prevent the traitors whom Lu-don has organized in the city from entering the palace by a secret way and overpowering Ja-don and the faithful band within.'

For a moment they hesitated. At last one spoke. 'What guarantee have we,' he demanded, 'that it is not you who would betray us and by leading us now away from the fighting in the banquet hall cause those who fight at Ja-don's side to be defeated?'

'My life will be your guarantee,' replied Tarzan. 'If you find that I have not spoken the truth you are sufficient in numbers to execute whatever penalty you choose. But come, there is not time to lose. Already are the lesser priests gathering their warriors in the city below,' and without waiting for any further parley he strode directly toward them in the direction of the gate upon the opposite side of the courtyard which led toward the principal entrance to the palace ground.

Slower in wit than he, they were swept away by his greater initiative and that compelling power which is inherent to all natural leaders. And so they followed him, the giant ape-man with a dead tail dragging the ground behind him – a demigod where another would have been ridiculous. Out into the city he led them and down toward the unpretentious building that hid Lu-don's secret passageway from the city to the temple, and as they rounded the last turn they saw before them a gathering of warriors which was being rapidly augmented from all directions as the traitors of A-lur mobilized at the call of the priesthood.

'You spoke the truth, stranger,' said the chief who marched at Tarzan's side, 'for there are the warriors with the priests among them, even as you told us.'

'And now,' replied the ape-man, 'that I have fulfilled my promise I will go my way after Mo-sar, who has done me a great wrong. Tell Ja-don that Jad-ben-Otho is upon his side, nor do you forget to tell him also that it was the Dor-ul-Otho who thwarted Lu-don's plan to seize the palace.'

'I will not forget,' replied the chief. 'Go your way. We are enough to overpower the traitors.'

'Tell me,' asked Tarzan, 'how I may know this city of Tu-lur?'

'It lies upon the south shore of the second lake below A-lur,' replied the chief, 'the lake that is called Jad-in-lul.'

They were now approaching the band of traitors, who evidently thought that this was another contingent of their own party since they made no effort either toward defense or retreat. Suddenly the chief raised his voice in a savage war cry that was immediately taken up by his followers, and simultaneously, as though the cry were a command, the entire party broke into a mad charge upon the surprised rebels.

Satisfied with the outcome of his suddenly conceived plan and sure that it would work to the disadvantage of Lu-don, Tarzan turned into a side street and pointed his steps toward the outskirts of the city in search of the trail that led southward toward Tu-lur.

17
By Jad-bal-lul

As Mo-sar carried Jane Clayton from the palace of Ko-tan, the king, the woman struggled incessantly to regain her freedom. He tried to compel her to walk, but despite his threats and his abuse she would not voluntarily take a single step in the direction in which he wished her to go. Instead she threw herself to the ground each time he sought to place her upon her feet, and so of necessity he was compelled to carry her though at last he tied her hands and gagged her to save himself from further lacerations, for the beauty and slenderness of the woman belied her strength and courage. When he came at last to where his men had gathered he was glad indeed to turn her over to a couple of stalwart warriors, but these too were forced to carry her since Mo-sar's fear of the vengeance of Ko-tan's retainers would brook no delays.

And thus they came down out of the hills from which A-lur is carved, to the meadows that skirt the lower end of Jad-ben-lul, with Jane Clayton carried between two of Mo-sar's men. At the edge of the lake lay a fleet of strong canoes, hollowed from the trunks of trees, their bows and sterns carved in the semblance of grotesque beasts or birds and vividly colored by some master in that primitive school of art, which fortunately is not without its devotees today.

Into the stern of one of these canoes the warriors tossed their captive at a sign from Mo-sar, who came and stood beside her as the warriors were finding their places in the canoes and selecting their paddles.

'Come, Beautiful One,' he said, 'let us be friends and you shall not be harmed. You will find Mo-sar a kind master if you do his bidding,' and thinking to make a good impression on her he removed the gag from her mouth and the thongs from her wrists, knowing well that she could not escape surrounded as she was by his warriors, and presently, when they were out on the lake, she would be as safely imprisoned as though he held her behind bars.

And so the fleet moved off to the accompaniment of the gentle splashing of a hundred paddles, to follow the windings of the rivers and lakes through which the waters of the Valley of Jad-ben-Otho empty into the great morass to the south. The warriors, resting upon one knee, faced the bow and in the last canoe Mo-sar, tiring of his fruitless attempts to win responses from his sullen captive, squatted in the bottom of the canoe with his back toward her and resting his head upon the gunwale sought sleep.

Thus they moved in silence between the verdure-clad banks of the little river through which the waters of Jad-ben-lul emptied – now in the moonlight, now in dense shadow where great trees overhung the stream, and at last out upon the waters of another lake, the black shores of which seemed far away under the weird influence of a moonlight night.

Jane Clayton sat alert in the stern of the last canoe. For months she had been under constant surveillance, the prisoner first of one ruthless race and now the prisoner of another. Since the long-gone day that Hauptmann Fritz Schneider and his band of native German troops had treacherously wrought the Kaiser's work of rapine and destruction on the Greystoke bungalow and carried her away to captivity she had not drawn a free breath. That she had survived unharmed the countless dangers through which she had passed she attributed solely to the beneficence of a kind and watchful Providence.

At first she had been held on the orders of the German High Command with a view of her ultimate value as a hostage and during these months she had been subjected to neither hardship nor oppression, but when the Germans had become hard pressed toward the close of their unsuccessful campaign in East Africa it had been determined to take her farther into the interior and now there was an element of revenge in their motives, since it must have been apparent that she could no longer be of any possible military value.

Bitter indeed were the Germans against that half-savage mate of hers who had cunningly annoyed and harassed them with a fiendishness of persistence and ingenuity that had resulted in a noticeable loss in morale in the sector he had chosen for his operations. They had to charge against him the lives of certain officers that he had deliberately taken with his own hands, and one entire section of trench that had made possible a disastrous turning movement by the British. Tarzan had out-generaled them at every point. He had met cunning with cunning and cruelty with cruelties until they feared and loathed his very name. The cunning trick that they had played upon him in destroying his home, murdering his retainers, and covering the abduction of his wife in such a way as to lead him to believe that she had been killed, they had regretted a thousand times, for a thousandfold had they paid the price for their senseless ruthlessness, and now, unable to wreak their vengeance directly upon him, they had conceived the idea of inflicting further suffering upon his mate.

In sending her into the interior to avoid the path of the victorious British, they had chosen as her escort Lieutenant Erich Obergatz who had been second in command of Schneider's company, and who alone of its officers had escaped the consuming vengeance of the ape-man. For a long time Obergatz had held her in a native village, the chief of which was still under the domination of his fear of the ruthless German oppressors. While here only hardships and discomforts assailed her, Obergatz himself being held in leash by the orders of his distant superior but as time went on the life in the village grew to be a veritable hell of cruelties and oppressions practiced by the arrogant Prussian upon the villagers and the members of his native command – for time hung heavily upon the hands of the lieutenant and with idleness combining with the personal discomforts he was compelled to endure, his none too agreeable temper found an outlet first in petty interference with the chiefs and later in the practice of absolute cruelties upon them.

What the self-sufficient German could not see was plain to Jane Clayton – that the sympathies of Obergatz's native soldiers lay with the villagers and that all were so heartily sickened by his abuse that it needed now but the slightest spark to detonate the mine of revenge and hatred that the pigheaded Hun had been assiduously fabricating beneath his own person.

And at last it came, but from an unexpected source in the form of a German native deserter from the theater of war. Footsore, weary, and spent, he dragged himself into the village late one afternoon, and before Obergatz was even aware of his presence the whole village knew that the power of Germany in Africa was at an end. It did not take long for the lieutenant's native soldiers to realize that the authority that held them in service no longer existed and that with it had gone the power to pay them their miserable wage. Or at least, so they reasoned. To them Obergatz no longer represented aught else than a powerless and hated foreigner, and short indeed would have been his shrift had not a native woman who had conceived a doglike affection for Jane Clayton hurried to her with word of the murderous plan, for the fate of the innocent white woman lay in the balance beside that of the guilty Teuton.

'Already they are quarreling as to which one shall possess you,' she told Jane.

'When will they come for us?' asked Jane. 'Did you hear them say?'

'Tonight,' replied the woman, 'for even now that he has none to fight for him they still fear the white man. And so they will come at night and kill him while he sleeps.'

Jane thanked the woman and sent her away lest the suspicion of her fellows be aroused against her when they discovered that the two whites had learned of their intentions. The woman went at once to the hut occupied by Obergatz. She had never gone there before and the German looked up in surprise as he saw who his visitor was.

Briefly she told him what she had heard. At first he was inclined to bluster arrogantly, with a great display of bravado but she silenced him peremptorily.

'Such talk is useless,' she said shortly. 'You have brought upon yourself the just hatred of these people. Regardless of the truth or falsity of the report which has been brought to them, they believe in it and there is nothing now between you and your Maker other than flight. We shall both be dead before morning if we are unable to escape from the village unseen. If you go to them now with your silly protestations of authority you will be dead a little sooner, that is all.'

'You think it is as bad as that?' he said, a noticeable alteration in his tone and manner.

'It is precisely as I have told you,' she replied. 'They will come tonight and kill you while you sleep. Find me pistols and a rifle and ammunition and we will pretend that we go into the jungle to hunt. That you have done often. Perhaps it will arouse suspicion that I accompany you but that we must chance. And be sure, my dear Herr Lieutenant, to bluster and curse and abuse your servants unless they note a change in your manner and realizing your fear know that you suspect their intention. If all goes well then we can go out into the jungle to hunt and we need not return.

'But first and now you must swear never to harm me, or otherwise it would be better that I called the chief and turned you over to him and then put a bullet into my own head, for unless you swear as I have asked I were no better alone in the jungle with you than here at the mercies of these degraded blacks.'

'I swear,' he replied solemnly, 'in the names of my God and my Kaiser that no harm shall befall you at my hands, Lady Greystoke.'

'Very well,' she said, 'we will make this pact to assist each other to return to civilization, but let it be understood that there is and never can be any semblance even of respect for you upon my part. I am drowning and you are the straw. Carry that always in your mind, German.'

If Obergatz had held any doubt as to the sincerity of her word it would have been wholly dissipated by the scathing contempt of her tone. And so Obergatz, without further parley, got pistols and an extra rifle for Jane, as well as bandoleers of cartridges. In his usual arrogant and disagreeable manner he called his servants, telling them that he and the white *kali* were going out into the brush to hunt. The beaters would go north as far as the little hill and then circle back to the east and in toward the village. The gun carriers he directed to take the extra pieces and precede himself and Jane slowly toward the east, waiting for them at the ford about half a mile distant. The blacks responded with greater alacrity than usual and it was noticeable to both Jane and Obergatz that they left the village whispering and laughing.

'The swine think it is a great joke,' growled Obergatz, 'that the afternoon before I die I go out and hunt meat for them.'

As soon as the gun bearers disappeared in the jungle beyond the village the two Europeans followed along the same trail, nor was there any attempt upon the part of Obergatz's native soldiers, or the warriors of the chief to detain them, for they too doubtless were more than willing that the whites should bring them in one more mess of meat before they killed them.

A quarter of a mile from the village, Obergatz turned toward the south from the trail that led to the ford and hurrying onward the two put as great a distance as possible between them and the village before night fell. They knew from the habits of their erstwhile hosts that there was little danger of pursuit by night since the villagers held Numa, the lion, in too great respect to venture needlessly beyond their stockade during the hours that the king of beasts was prone to choose for hunting.

And thus began a seemingly endless sequence of frightful days and horror-laden nights as the two fought their way toward the south in the face of almost inconceivable hardships, privations, and dangers. The east coast was nearer but Obergatz positively refused to chance throwing himself into the hands of the British by returning to the territory which they now controlled, insisting instead upon attempting to make his way through an unknown wilderness to South Africa where, among the Boers, he was convinced he would find willing sympathizers who would find some way to return him in safety to Germany, and the woman was perforce compelled to accompany him.

And so they had crossed the great thorny, waterless steppe and come at last to the edge of the morass before Pal-ul-don. They had reached this point just before the rainy season when the waters of the morass were at their lowest ebb. At this time a hard crust is baked upon the dried surface of the marsh and there is only the open water at the center to materially impede progress. It is a condition that exists perhaps not more than a few weeks, or even days at the termination of long periods of drought, and so the two crossed the otherwise almost impassable barrier without realizing its latent terrors. Even the open water in the center chanced to be deserted at the time by its frightful denizens which the drought and the receding waters had driven southward toward the mouth of Pal-ul-don's largest river which carries the waters out of the Valley of Jad-ben-Otho.

Their wanderings carried them across the mountains and into the Valley of Jad-ben-Otho at the source of one of the larger streams which bears the mountain waters down into the valley to empty them into the main river just below The Great Lake on whose northern shore lies A-lur. As they had come down out of the mountains they had been surprised by a party of Ho-don hunters. Obergatz had escaped while Jane had been taken prisoner and brought to A-lur. She had neither seen nor heard aught of the German since that time and she did not know whether he had perished in this strange land, or succeeded in successfully eluding its savage denizens and making his way at last into South Africa.

For her part, she had been incarcerated alternately in the palace and the temple as either Ko-tan or Lu-don succeeded in wresting her temporarily from the other by various strokes of cunning and intrigue. And now at last she was in the power of a new captor, one whom she knew from the gossip of the temple and the palace to be cruel and degraded. And she was in the stern of the last canoe, and every enemy back was toward her, while almost at her feet Mo-sar's loud snores gave ample evidence of his unconsciousness to his immediate surroundings.

The dark shore loomed closer to the south as Jane Clayton, Lady Greystoke, slid quietly over the stern of the canoe into the chill waters of the lake. She scarcely moved other than to keep her nostrils above the surface while the canoe was yet discernible in the last rays of the declining moon. Then she struck out toward the southern shore.

Alone, unarmed, all but naked, in a country overrun by savage beasts and hostile men, she yet felt for the first time in many months a sensation of elation and relief. She was free! What if the next moment brought death, she knew again, at least a brief instant of absolute freedom. Her blood tingled to the almost forgotten sensation and it was with difficulty that she restrained a glad triumphant cry as she clambered from the quiet waters and stood upon the silent beach.

Before her loomed a forest, darkly, and from its depths came those nameless sounds that are a part of the nightlife of the jungle – the rustling of leaves in the wind, the rubbing together of contiguous branches, the scurrying of a rodent, all magnified by the darkness to sinister and awe-inspiring proportions; the hoot of an owl, the distant scream of a great cat, the barking of wild dogs, attested the presence of the myriad life she could not see – the savage life, the free life of which she was now a part. And then there came to her, possibly for the first time since the giant ape-man had come into her life, a fuller realization of what the jungle meant to him, for though alone and unprotected from its hideous dangers she yet felt its lure upon her and an exaltation that she had not dared hope to feel again.

Ah, if that mighty mate of hers were but by her side! What utter joy and bliss would be hers! She longed for no more than this. The parade of cities, the comforts and luxuries of civilization held forth no allure half as insistent as the glorious freedom of the jungle.

A lion moaned in the blackness to her right, eliciting delicious thrills that crept along her spine. The hair at the back of her head seemed to stand erect – yet she was unafraid. The muscles bequeathed her by some primordial ancestor reacted instinctively to the presence of an ancient enemy – that was all. The woman moved slowly and deliberately toward the wood. Again the lion moaned; this time nearer. She sought a low-hanging branch and finding it swung easily into the friendly shelter of the tree. The long and perilous journey with Obergatz had trained her muscles and her nerves to such unaccustomed habits. She found a safe resting place such as Tarzan had taught her was best and there she curled herself, thirty feet above the ground, for a night's rest. She was cold and uncomfortable and yet she slept, for her heart was warm with renewed hope and her tired brain had found temporary surcease from worry.

She slept until the heat of the sun, high in the heavens, awakened her. She was rested and now her body was well as her heart was warm. A sensation of ease and comfort and happiness pervaded her being. She rose upon her gently swaying couch and stretched luxuriously, her naked limbs and lithe body mottled by the sunlight filtering through the foliage above combined with the lazy gesture to impart to her appearance something of the leopard. With careful eye she scrutinized the ground below and with attentive ear she listened for any warning sound that might suggest the near presence of enemies, either man or beast. Satisfied at last that there was nothing close of which she need have fear she clambered to the ground. She wished to bathe but the lake was too exposed and just a bit too far from the safety of the trees for her to risk it until she became more familiar with her surroundings. She wandered aimlessly through the forest searching for food which she found in abundance. She ate and rested, for she had no objective as yet. Her freedom was too new to be spoiled by plannings for the future. The haunts of civilized man seemed to her now as vague and unattainable as the half-forgotten substance of a dream. If she could but live on here in peace, waiting, waiting for – *him*. It was the old hope revived. She knew that he would come someday, if he lived. She had always known that, though recently she had believed that he would come too late. If he lived! Yes, he would come if he lived, and if he did not live she were as well off here as elsewhere, for then nothing mattered, only to wait for the end as patiently as might be.

Her wanderings brought her to a crystal brook and there she drank and bathed beneath an overhanging tree that offered her quick asylum in the event of danger. It was a quiet and beautiful spot and she loved it from the first. The bottom of the brook was paved with pretty stones and bits of glassy obsidian. As she gathered a handful of the pebbles and held them up to look at them she noticed that one of her fingers was bleeding from a clean, straight cut. She fell to searching for the cause and presently discovered it in one of the fragments of volcanic glass which revealed an edge that was almost razor-like. Jane Clayton was elated. Here, God-given to her hands, was the first beginning with which she might eventually arrive at both weapons and tools – a cutting edge. Everything was possible to him who possessed it – nothing without.

She sought until she had collected many of the precious bits of stone – until the pouch that hung at her right side was almost filled. Then she climbed into the great tree to examine them at leisure. There were some that looked like knife blades, and some that could easily be fashioned into spearheads, and many smaller ones that nature seemed to have intended for the tips of savage arrows.

The spear she would essay first – that would be easiest. There was a hollow in the bole of the tree in a great crotch high above the ground. Here she cached all of her treasure except a single knifelike sliver. With this she descended to the ground and searching out a slender sapling that grew arrow-straight she hacked and sawed until she could break it off without splitting the wood. It was just the right diameter for the shaft of a spear – a hunting spear such as her beloved Waziri had liked best. How often had she watched them fashioning them, and they had taught her how to use them, too – them and the heavy war spears – laughing and clapping their hands as her proficiency increased.

She knew the arborescent grasses that yielded the longest and toughest fibers and these she sought and carried to her tree with the spear shaft that was to be. Clambering to her crotch she bent to her work, humming softly a little tune. She caught herself and smiled – it was the first time in all these bitter months that song had passed her lips or such a smile.

'I feel,' she sighed, 'I almost feel that John is near – my John – my Tarzan!'

She cut the spear shaft to the proper length and removed the twigs and branches and the bark, whittling and scraping at the nubs until the surface was all smooth and straight. Then she split one end and inserted a spear point, shaping the wood until it fitted perfectly. This done she laid the shaft aside and fell to splitting the thick grass stems and pounding and twisting them until she had separated and partially cleaned the fibers. These she took down to the brook and washed and brought back again and wound tightly around the cleft end of the shaft, which she had notched to receive them, and the upper part of the spearhead which she had also notched slightly with a bit of stone. It was a crude spear but the best that she could attain in so short a time. Later, she promised herself, she should have others – many of them – and they would be spears of which even the greatest of the Waziri spear-men might be proud.

18

The Lion Pit of Tu-lur

Though Tarzan searched the outskirts of the city until nearly dawn he discovered nowhere the spoor of his mate. The breeze coming down from the mountains brought to his nostrils a diversity of scents but there was not among them the slightest suggestion of her whom he sought. The natural deduction was therefore that she had been taken in some other direction. In his search he had many times crossed the fresh tracks of many men leading toward the lake and these he concluded had probably been made by Jane Clayton's abductors. It had only been to minimize the chance of error by the process of elimination that he had carefully reconnoitered every other avenue leading from A-lur toward the southeast where lay Mo-sar's city of Tu-lur, and now he followed the trail to the shores of Jad-ben-lul where the party had embarked upon the quiet waters in their sturdy canoes.

He found many other craft of the same description moored along the shore and one of these he commandeered for the purpose of pursuit. It was daylight when he passed through the lake which lies next below Jad-ben-lul and paddling strongly passed within sight of the very tree in which his lost mate lay sleeping.

Had the gentle wind that caressed the bosom of the lake been blowing from a southerly direction the giant ape-man and Jane Clayton would have been reunited then, but an unkind fate had willed otherwise and the opportunity passed with the passing of his canoe which presently his powerful strokes carried out of sight into the stream at the lower end of the lake.

Following the winding river which bore a considerable distance to the north before doubling back to empty into the Jad-in-lul, the ape-man missed a portage that would have saved him hours of paddling.

It was at the upper end of this portage where Mo-sar and his warriors had debarked that the chief discovered the absence of his captive. As Mo-sar had been asleep since shortly after their departure from A-lur, and as none of the warriors recalled when she had last been seen, it was impossible to conjecture with any degree of accuracy the place where she had escaped. The concensus of opinion was, however, that it had been in the narrow river connecting Jad-ben-lul with the lake next below it, which is called Jad-bal-lul, which freely translated means the lake of gold. Mo-sar had been very wroth and having himself been the only one at fault he naturally sought with great diligence to fix the blame upon another.

He would have returned in search of her had he not feared to meet a pursuing company dispatched either by Ja-don or the high priest, both of whom, he knew, had just grievances against him. He would not even spare a boatload of his warriors from his own protection to return in quest of the fugitive but hastened onward with as little delay as possible across the portage and out upon the waters of Jad-in-lul.

The morning sun was just touching the white domes of Tu-lur when Mo-sar's paddlers brought their canoes against the shore at the city's edge. Safe once more behind his own walls and protected by many warriors, the courage of the chief returned sufficiently at least to permit him to dispatch three canoes in search of Jane Clayton, and also to go as far as A-lur if possible to learn what had delayed Bu-lot, whose failure to reach the canoes with the balance of the party at the time of the flight from the northern city had in no way delayed Mo-sar's departure, his own safety being of far greater moment than that of his son.

As the three canoes reached the portage on their return journey the warriors who were dragging them from the water were suddenly startled by the appearance of two priests, carrying a light canoe in the direction of Jad-in-lul. At first they thought them the advance guard of a larger force of Lu-don's followers, although the correctness of such a theory was belied by their knowledge that priests never accepted the risks or perils of a warriors' vocation, nor even fought until driven into a corner and forced to do so. Secretly the warriors of Pal-ul-don held the emasculated priesthood in contempt and so instead of immediately taking up the offensive as they would have had the two men been warriors from A-lur instead of priests, they waited to question them.

At sight of the warriors the priests made the sign of peace and upon being asked if they were alone they answered in the affirmative.

The leader of Mo-sar's warriors permitted them to approach. 'What do you here,' he asked, 'in the country of Mo-sar, so far from your own city?'

'We carry a message from Lu-don, the high priest, to Mo-sar,' explained one.

'Is it a message of peace or of war?' asked the warrior.

'It is an offer of peace,' replied the priest.

'And Lu-don is sending no warriors behind you?' queried the fighting man.

'We are alone,' the priest assured him. 'None in A-lur save Lu-don knows that we have come upon this errand.'

'Then go your way,' said the warrior.

'Who is that?' asked one of the priests suddenly, pointing toward the upper end of the lake at the point where the river from Jad-bal-lul entered it.

All eyes turned in the direction that he had indicated to see a lone warrior paddling rapidly into Jad-in-lul, the prow of his canoe pointing toward Tu-lur. The warriors and the priests drew into the concealment of the bushes on either side of the portage.

'It is the terrible man who called himself the Dor-ul-Otho,' whispered one of the priests. 'I would know that figure among a great multitude as far as I could see it.'

'You are right, priest,' cried one of the warriors who had seen Tarzan the day that he had first entered Ko-tan's palace. 'It is indeed he who has been rightly called Tarzan-jad-guru.'

'Hasten, priests,' cried the leader of the party. 'You are two paddles in a light canoe. Easily can you reach Tu-lur ahead of him and warn Mo-sar of his coming, for he has but only entered the lake.'

For a moment the priests demurred for they had no stomach for an encounter with this terrible man, but the warrior insisted and even went so far as to threaten them. Their canoe was taken from them and pushed into the lake and they were all but lifted bodily from their feet and put aboard it. Still protesting they were shoved out upon the water where they were immediately in full view of the lone paddler above them. Now there was no alternative. The city of Tu-lur offered the only safety and bending to their paddles the two priests sent their craft swiftly in the direction of the city.

The warriors withdrew again to the concealment of the foliage. If Tarzan had seen them and should come hither to investigate there were thirty of them against one and naturally they had no fear of the outcome, but they did not consider it necessary to go out upon the lake to meet him since they had been sent to look for the escaped prisoner and not to intercept the strange warrior, the stories of whose ferocity and prowess doubtless helped them to arrive at their decision to provoke no uncalled-for quarrel with him.

If he had seen them he gave no sign, but continued paddling steadily and strongly toward the city, nor did he increase his speed as the two priests shot out in full view. The moment the priests' canoe touched the shore by the city its occupants leaped out and hurried swiftly toward the palace gate, casting affrighted glances behind them. They sought immediate audience with Mo-sar, after warning the warriors on guard that Tarzan was approaching.

They were conducted at once to the chief, whose court was a smaller replica of that of the king of A-lur. 'We come from Lu-don, the high priest,' explained the spokesman. 'He wishes the friendship of Mo-sar, who has always been his friend. Ja-don is gathering warriors to make himself king. Throughout the villages of the Ho-don are thousands who will obey the commands of Lu-don, the high priest. Only with Lu-don's assistance can Mo-sar become king, and the message from Lu-don is that if Mo-sar would retain the friendship of Lu-don he must return immediately the woman he took from the quarters of the Princess O-lo-a.'

At this juncture a warrior entered. His excitement was evident. 'The Dor-ul-Otho has come to Tu-lur and demands to see Mo-sar at once,' he said.

'The Dor-ul-Otho!' exclaimed Mo-sar.

'That is the message he sent,' replied the warrior, 'and indeed he is not as are the people of Pal-ul-don. He is, we think, the same of whom the warriors that returned from A-lur today told us and whom some call Tarzan-jad-guru and some Dor-ul-Otho. But indeed only the son of god would dare come thus alone to a strange city, so it must be that he speaks the truth.'

Mo-sar, his heart filled with terror and indecision, turned questioningly toward the priests.

'Receive him graciously, Mo-sar,' counseled he who had spoken before, his advice prompted by the petty shrewdness of his defective brain which, under the added influence of Lu-don's tutorage leaned always toward duplicity. 'Receive him graciously and when he is quite convinced of your friendship he will be off his guard, and then you may do with him as you will. But if possible, Mo-sar, and you would win the undying gratitude of Lu-don, the high priest, save him alive for my master.'

Mo-sar nodded understandingly and turning to the warrior commanded that he conduct the visitor to him.

'We must not be seen by the creature,' said one of the priests. 'Give us your answer to Lu-don, Mo-sar, and we will go our way.'

'Tell Lu-don,' replied the chief, 'that the woman would have been lost to him entirely had it not been for me. I sought to bring her to Tu-lur that I might save her for him from the clutches of Ja-don, but during the night she escaped. Tell Lu-don that I have sent thirty warriors to search for her. It is strange you did not see them as you came.'

'We did,' replied the priests, 'but they told us nothing of the purpose of their journey.'

'It is as I have told you,' said Mo-sar, 'and if they find her, assure your master that she will be kept unharmed in Tu-lur for him. Also tell him that I will send my warriors to join with his against Ja-don whenever he sends word that he wants them. Now go, for Tarzan-jad-guru will soon be here.'

He signaled to a slave. 'Lead the priests to the temple,' he commanded, 'and ask the high priest of Tu-lur to see that they are fed and permitted to return to A-lur when they will.'

The two priests were conducted from the apartment by the slave through a doorway other than that at which they had entered, and a moment later Tarzan-jad-guru strode into the presence of Mo-sar, ahead of the warrior whose duty it had been to conduct and announce him. The ape-man made no sign of greeting or of peace but strode directly toward the chief who, only by the exertion of his utmost powers of will, hid the terror that was in his heart at sight of the giant figure and the scowling face.

'I am the Dor-ul-Otho,' said the ape-man in level tones that carried to the mind of Mo-sar a suggestion of cold steel; 'I am Dor-ul-Otho, and I come to Tu-lur for the woman you stole from the apartments of O-lo-a, the princess.'

The very boldness of Tarzan's entry into this hostile city had had the effect of giving him a great moral advantage over Mo-sar and the savage warriors who stood upon either side of the chief. Truly it seemed to them that no other than the son of Jad-ben-Otho would dare so heroic an act. Would any mortal warrior act thus boldly, and alone enter the presence of a powerful chief and, in the midst of a score of warriors, arrogantly demand an accounting? No, it was beyond reason. Mo-sar was faltering in his decision to betray the stranger by seeming friendliness. He even paled to a sudden thought – Jad-ben-Otho knew everything, even our inmost thoughts. Was it not therefore possible that this creature, if after all it should prove true that he was the Dor-ul-Otho, might even now be reading the wicked design that the priests had implanted in the brain of Mo-sar and which he had entertained so favorably? The chief squirmed and fidgeted upon the bench of hewn rock that was his throne.

'Quick,' snapped the ape-man. 'Where is she?'

'She is not here,' cried Mo-sar.

'You lie,' replied Tarzan.

'As Jad-ben-Otho is my witness, she is not in Tu-lur,' insisted the chief. 'You may search the palace and the temple and the entire city but you will not find her, for she is not here.'

'Where is she, then?' demanded the ape-man. 'You took her from the palace at A-lur. If she is not here, where is she? Tell me not that harm has befallen her,' and he took a sudden threatening step toward Mo-sar, that sent the chief shrinking back in terror.

'Wait,' he cried, 'if you are indeed the Dor-ul-Otho you will know that I speak the truth. I took her from the palace of Ko-tan to save her for Lu-don, the high priest, lest with Ko-tan dead Ja-don seize her. But during the night she escaped from me between here and A-lur, and I have but just sent three canoes full-manned in search of her.'

Something in the chief's tone and manner assured the ape-man that he spoke in part the truth, and that once again he had braved incalculable dangers and suffered loss of time futilely.

'What wanted the priests of Lu-don that preceded me here?' demanded Tarzan chancing a shrewd guess that the two he had seen paddling so frantically to avoid a meeting with him had indeed come from the high priest at A-lur.

'They came upon an errand similar to yours,' replied Mo-sar; 'to demand the return of the woman whom Lu-don thought I had stolen from him, thus wronging me as deeply, O Dor-ul-Otho, as have you.'

'I would question the priests,' said Tarzan. 'Bring them hither.' His peremptory and arrogant manner left Mo-sar in doubt as to whether to be more incensed, or terrified, but ever as is the way with such as he, he concluded that the first consideration was his own safety. If he could transfer the attention and the wrath of this terrible man from himself to Lu-don's priests it would more than satisfy him and if they should conspire to harm him, then Mo-sar would be safe in the eyes of Jad-ben-Otho if it finally developed that the stranger was in reality the son of god. He felt uncomfortable in Tarzan's presence and this fact rather accentuated his doubt, for thus indeed would a mortal feel in the presence of a god. Now he saw a way to escape, at least temporarily.

'I will fetch them myself, Dor-ul-Otho,' he said, and turning, left the apartment. His hurried steps brought him quickly to the temple, for the palace grounds of Tu-lur, which also included the temple as in all of the Ho-don cities, covered a much smaller area than those of the larger city of A-lur. He found Lu-don's messengers with the high priest of his own temple and quickly transmitted to them the commands of the ape-man.

'What do you intend to do with him?' asked one of the priests.

'I have no quarrel with him,' replied Mo-sar. 'He came in peace and he may depart in peace, for who knows but that he is indeed the Dor-ul-Otho?'

'We know that he is not,' replied Lu-don's emissary. 'We have every proof that he is only mortal, a strange creature from another country. Already has Lu-don offered his life to Jad-ben-Otho if he is wrong in his belief that this creature is not the son of god. If the high priest of A-lur, who is the highest priest of all the high priests of Pal-ul-don is thus so sure that the creature is an impostor as to stake his life upon his judgment then who are we to give credence to the claims of this stranger? No, Mo-sar, you need not fear him. He is only a warrior who may be overcome with the same weapons that subdue your own fighting men. Were it not for Lu-don's command that he be taken alive I would urge you to set your warriors upon him and slay him, but the commands of Lu-don are the commands of Jad-ben-Otho himself, and those we may not disobey.'

But still the remnant of a doubt stirred within the cowardly breast of Mo-sar, urging him to let another take the initiative against the stranger.

'He is yours then,' he replied, 'to do with as you will. I have no quarrel with him. What you may command shall be the command of Lu-don, the high priest, and further than that I shall have nothing to do in the matter.'

The priests turned to him who guided the destinies of the temple at Tu-lur. 'Have you no plan?' they asked. 'High indeed will he stand in the counsels of Lu-don and in the eyes of Jad-ben-Otho who finds the means to capture this impostor alive.'

'There is the lion pit,' whispered the high priest. 'It is now vacant and what will hold *ja* and *jato* will hold this stranger if he is not the Dor-ul-Otho.'

'It will hold him,' said Mo-sar; 'doubtless too it would hold a *gryf*, but first you would have to get the *gryf* into it.'

The priests pondered this bit of wisdom thoughtfully and then one of those from A-lur spoke. 'It should not be difficult,' he said, 'if we use the wits that Jad-ben-Otho gave us instead of the worldly muscles which were handed down to us from our fathers and our mothers and which have not even the power possessed by those of the beasts that run about on four feet.'

'Lu-don matched his wits with the stranger and lost,' suggested Mo-sar. 'But this is your own affair. Carry it out as you see best.'

'At A-lur, Ko-tan made much of this Dor-ul-Otho and the priests conducted him through the temple. It would arouse in his mind no suspicion were you to do the same, and let the high priest of Tu-lur invite him to the temple and gathering all the priests make a great show of belief in his kinship to Jad-ben-Otho. And what more natural then than that the high priest should wish to show him through the temple as did Lu-don at A-lur when Ko-tan commanded it, and if by chance he should be led through the lion pit it would be a simple matter for those who bear the torches to extinguish them suddenly and before the stranger was aware of what had happened, the stone gates could be dropped, thus safely securing him.'

'But there are windows in the pit that let in light,' interposed the high priest, 'and even though the torches were extinguished he could still see and might escape before the stone door could be lowered.'

'Send one who will cover the windows tightly with hides,' said the priest from A-lur.

'The plan is a good one,' said Mo-sar, seeing an opportunity for entirely eliminating himself from any suspicion of complicity, 'for it will require the presence of no warriors, and thus with only priests about him his mind will entertain no suspicion of harm.'

They were interrupted at this point by a messenger from the palace who brought word that the Dor-ul-Otho was becoming impatient and if the priests from A-lur were not brought to him at once he would come himself to the temple and get them. Mo-sar shook his head. He could not conceive of such brazen courage in mortal breast and glad he was that the plan evolved for Tarzan's undoing did not necessitate his active participation.

And so, while Mo-sar left for a secret corner of the palace by a roundabout way, three priests were dispatched to Tarzan and with whining words that did not entirely deceive him, they acknowledged his kinship to Jad-ben-Otho and begged him in the name of the high priest to honor the temple with a visit, when the priests from A-lur would be brought to him and would answer any questions that he put to them.

Confident that a continuation of his bravado would best serve his purpose, and also that if suspicion against him should crystallize into conviction on the part of Mo-sar and his followers that he would be no worse off in the temple than in the palace, the ape-man haughtily accepted the invitation of the high priest.

And so he came into the temple and was received in a manner befitting his high claims. He questioned the two priests of A-lur from whom he obtained only a repetition of the story that Mo-sar had told him, and then the high priest invited him to inspect the temple.

They took him first to the altar court, of which there was only one in Tu-lur. It was almost identical in every respect with those at A-lur. There was a bloody altar at the east end and the drowning basin at the west, and the grizzly fringes upon the headdresses of the priests attested the fact that the eastern altar was an active force in the rites of the temple. Through the chambers and corridors beneath they led him, and finally, with torch bearers to light their steps, into a damp and gloomy labyrinth at a low level and here in a large chamber, the air of which was still heavy with the odor of lions, the crafty priests of Tu-lur encompassed their shrewd design.

The torches were suddenly extinguished. There was a hurried confusion of bare feet moving rapidly across the stone floor. There was a loud crash as of a heavy weight of stone falling upon stone, and then surrounding the apeman naught but the darkness and the silence of the tomb.

19

Diana of the Jungle

Jane had made her first kill and she was very proud of it. It was not a very formidable animal – only a hare; but it marked an epoch in her existence. Just as in the dim past the first hunger had shaped the destinies of mankind so it seemed that this event might shape hers in some new mold. No longer was she dependent upon the wild fruits and vegetables for sustenance. Now she might command meat, the giver of the strength and endurance she would require successfully to cope with the necessities of her primitive existence.

The next step was fire. She might learn to eat raw flesh as had her lord and master, but she shrank from that. The thought even was repulsive. She had, however, a plan for fire. She had given the matter thought, but had been too busy to put it into execution so long as fire could be of no immediate use to her. Now it was different – she had something to cook and her mouth watered for the flesh of her kill. She would grill it above glowing embers. Jane hastened to her tree. Among the treasures she had gathered in the bed of the stream were several pieces of volcanic glass, clear as crystal. She sought until she had found the one in mind, which was convex. Then she hurried to the ground and gathered a little pile of powdered bark that was very dry, and some dead leaves and grasses that had lain long in the hot sun. Near at hand she arranged a supply of dead twigs and branches – small and large.

Vibrant with suppressed excitement she held the bit of glass above the tinder, moving it slowly until she had focused the sun's rays upon a tiny spot. She waited breathlessly. How slow it was! Were her high hopes to be dashed in spite of all her clever planning? No! A thin thread of smoke rose gracefully into the quiet air. Presently the tinder glowed and broke suddenly into flame. Jane clasped her hands beneath her chin with a little gurgling exclamation of delight. She had achieved fire!

She piled on twigs and then larger branches and at last dragged a small log to the flames and pushed an end of it into the fire which was crackling merrily. It was the sweetest sound that she had heard for many a month. But she could not wait for the mass of embers that would be required to cook her hare. As quickly as might be she skinned and cleaned her kill, burying the hide and entrails. That she had learned from Tarzan. It served two purposes. One was the necessity for keeping a sanitary camp and the other the obliteration of the scent that most quickly attracts the man-eaters.

Then she ran a stick through the carcass and held it above the flames. By turning it often she prevented burning and at the same time permitted the meat to cook thoroughly all the way through. When it was done she scampered high into the safety of her tree to enjoy her meal in quiet and peace. Never, thought Lady Greystoke, had aught more delicious passed her lips. She patted her spear affectionately. It had brought her this toothsome dainty and with it a feeling of greater confidence and safety than she had enjoyed since that frightful day that she and Obergatz had spent their last cartridge. She would never forget that day – it had seemed one hideous succession of frightful beast after frightful beast. They had not been long in this strange country, yet they thought that they were hardened to dangers, for daily they had had encounters with ferocious creatures; but this day – she shuddered when she thought of it. And with her last cartridge she had killed a black and yellow striped lion-thing with great saber teeth just as it was about to spring upon Obergatz who had futilely emptied his rifle into it – the last shot – his final cartridge. For another day they had carried the now useless rifles; but at last they had discarded them and thrown away the cumbersome bandoleers, as well. How they had managed to survive during the ensuing week she could never quite understand, and then the Ho-don had come upon them and captured her. Obergatz had escaped – she was living it all over again. Doubtless he was dead unless he had been able to reach this side of the valley which was quite evidently less overrun with savage beasts.

Jane's days were very full ones now, and the daylight hours seemed all too short in which to accomplish the many things she had determined upon, since she had concluded that this spot presented as ideal a place as she could find to live until she could fashion the weapons she considered necessary for the obtaining of meat and for self-defense.

She felt that she must have, in addition to a good spear, a knife, and bow and arrows. Possibly when these had been achieved she might seriously consider an attempt to fight her way to one of civilization's nearest outposts. In the meantime it was necessary to construct some sort of protective shelter in which she might feel a greater sense of security by night, for she knew that there was a possibility that any night she might receive a visit from a prowling panther, although she had as yet seen none upon this side of the valley. Aside from this danger she felt comparatively safe in her aerial retreat.

The cutting of the long poles for her home occupied all of the daylight hours that were not engaged in the search for food. These poles she carried high into her tree and with them constructed a flooring across two stout branches, binding the poles together and also to the branches with fibers from the tough arboraceous grasses that grew in profusion near the stream. Similarly she built walls and a roof, the latter thatched with many layers of great leaves. The fashioning of the barred windows and the door were matters of great importance and consuming interest. The windows, there were two of them, were large and the bars permanently fixed; but the door was small, the opening just large enough to permit her to pass through easily on hands and knees, which made it easier to barricade. She lost count of the days that the house cost her; but time was a cheap commodity – she had more of it than anything else. It meant so little to her that she had not even any desire to keep account of it. How long since she and Obergatz had fled from the wrath of the Negro villagers she did not know and she could only roughly guess at the seasons. She worked hard for two reasons; one was to hasten the completion of her little place of refuge, and the other a desire for such physical exhaustion at night that she would sleep through those dreaded hours to a new day. As a matter of fact the house was finished in less than a week – that is, it was made as safe as it ever would be, though regardless of how long she might occupy it she would keep on adding touches and refinements here and there.

Her daily life was filled with her house building and her hunting, to which was added an occasional spice of excitement contributed by roving lions. To the woodcraft that she had learned from Tarzan, that master of the art, was added a considerable store of practical experience derived from her own past adventures in the jungle and the long months with Obergatz, nor was any day now lacking in some added store of useful knowledge. To these facts was attributable her apparent immunity from harm, since they told her when *ja* was approaching before he crept close enough for a successful charge and, too, they kept her close to those never-failing havens of retreat – the trees.

The nights, filled with their weird noises, were lonely and depressing. Only her ability to sleep quickly and soundly made them endurable. The first night that she spent in her completed house behind barred windows and barricaded door was one of almost undiluted peace and happiness. The night noises seemed far removed and impersonal and the soughing of the wind in the trees was gently soothing. Before, it had carried a mournful note and was sinister in that it might hide the approach of some real danger. That night she slept indeed.

She went farther afield now in search of food. So far nothing but rodents had fallen to her spear – her ambition was an antelope, since beside the flesh it would give her, and the gut for her bow, the hide would prove invaluable during the colder weather that she knew would accompany the rainy season. She had caught glimpses of these wary animals and was sure that they always crossed the stream at a certain spot above her camp. It was to this place that she went to hunt them. With the stealth and cunning of a panther she crept through the forest, circling about to get upwind from the ford, pausing often to look and listen for aught that might menace her – herself the personification of a hunted deer. Now she moved silently down upon the chosen spot. What luck! A beautiful buck stood drinking in the stream. The woman wormed her way closer. Now she lay upon her belly behind a small bush within throwing distance of the quarry. She must rise to her full height and throw her spear almost in the same instant and she must throw it with great force and perfect accuracy. She thrilled with the excitement of the minute, yet cool and steady were her swift muscles as she rose and cast her missile. Scarce by the width of a finger did the point strike from the spot at which it had been directed. The buck leaped high, landed upon the bank of the stream, and fell dead. Jane Clayton sprang quickly forward toward her kill.

'Bravo!' A man's voice spoke in English from the shrubbery upon the opposite side of the stream. Jane Clayton halted in her tracks – stunned, almost, by surprise. And then a strange, unkempt figure of a man stepped into view. At first she did not recognize him, but when she did, instinctively she stepped back.

'Lieutenant Obergatz!' she cried. 'Can it be you?'

'It can. It is,' replied the German. 'I am a strange sight, no doubt; but still it is I, Erich Obergatz. And you? You have changed too, is it not?'

He was looking at her naked limbs and her golden breastplates, the loincloth of *jato*-hide, the harness and ornaments that constitute the apparel of a Ho-don woman – the things that Lu-don had dressed her in as his passion for her grew. Not Ko-tan's daughter, even, had finer trappings.

'But why are you here?' Jane insisted. 'I had thought you safely among civilized men by this time, if you still lived.'

'Gott!' he exclaimed. 'I do not know why I continue to live. I have prayed to die and yet I cling to life. There is no hope. We are doomed to remain in this horrible land until we die. The bog! The frightful bog! I have searched its shores for a place to cross until I have entirely circled the hideous country. Easily enough we entered; but the rains have come since and now no living man could pass that slough of slimy mud and hungry reptiles. Have I not tried it! And the beasts that roam this accursed land. They hunt me by day and by night.'

'But how have you escaped them?' she asked.

'I do not know,' he replied gloomily. 'I have fled and fled and fled. I have remained hungry and thirsty in treetops for days at a time. I have fashioned weapons – clubs and spears – and I have learned to use them. I have slain a lion with my club. So even will a cornered rat fight. And we are no better than rats in this land of stupendous dangers, you and I. But tell me about yourself. If it is surprising that I live, how much more so that you still survive.'

Briefly she told him and all the while she was wondering what she might do to rid herself of him. She could not conceive of a prolonged existence with him as her sole companion. Better, a thousand times better, to be alone. Never had her hatred and contempt for him lessened through the long weeks and months of their constant companionship, and now that he could be of no service in returning her to civilization, she shrank from the thought of seeing him daily. And, too, she feared him. Never had she trusted him; but now there was a strange light in his eye that had not been there when last she saw him. She could not interpret it – all she knew was that it gave her a feeling of apprehension – a nameless dread.

'You lived long then in the city of A-lur?' he said, speaking in the language of Pal-ul-don.

'You have learned this tongue?' she asked. 'How?'

'I fell in with a band of half-breeds,' he replied, 'members of a proscribed race that dwells in the rock-bound gut through which the principal river of the valley empties into the morass. They are called Waz-ho-don and their village is partly made up of cave dwellings and partly of houses carved from the soft rock at the foot of the cliff. They are very ignorant and superstitious and when they first saw me and realized that I had no tail and that my hands and feet were not like theirs they were afraid of me. They thought that I was either god or demon. Being in a position where I could neither escape them nor defend myself, I made a bold front and succeeded in impressing them to such an extent that they conducted me to their city, which they call Bu-lur, and there they fed me and treated me with kindness. As I learned their language I sought to impress them more and more with the idea that I was a god, and I succeeded, too, until an old fellow who was something of a priest among them, or medicine-man, became jealous of my growing power. That was the beginning of the end and came near to being the end in fact. He told them that if I was a god I would not bleed if a knife was stuck into me – if I did bleed it would prove conclusively that I was not a god. Without my knowledge he arranged to stage the ordeal before the whole village upon a certain night – it was upon one of those numerous occasions when they eat and drink to Jad-ben-Otho, their pagan deity. Under the influence of their vile liquor they would be ripe for any bloodthirsty scheme the medicine-man might evolve. One of the women told me about the plan – not with any intent to warn me of danger, but prompted merely by feminine curiosity as to whether or not I would bleed if stuck with a dagger. She could not wait, it seemed, for the orderly procedure of the ordeal – she wanted to know at once, and when I caught her trying to slip a knife into my side and questioned her she explained the whole thing with the utmost naïveté. The warriors already had commenced drinking – it would have been futile to make any sort of appeal either to their intellects or their superstitions. There was but one alternative to death and that was flight. I told the woman that I was very much outraged and offended at this reflection upon my godhood and that as a mark of my disfavor I should abandon them to their fate.

'"I shall return to heaven at once!"' I exclaimed.

'She wanted to hang around and see me go, but I told her that her eyes would be blasted by the fire surrounding my departure and that she must leave at once and not return to the spot for at least an hour. I also impressed upon her the fact that should any other approach this part of the village within that time not only they, but she as well, would burst into flames and be consumed.

'She was very much impressed and lost no time in leaving, calling back as she departed that if I were indeed gone in an hour she and all the village would know that I was no less than Jad-ben-Otho himself, and so they must thank me, for I can assure you that I was gone in much less than an hour, nor have I ventured close to the neighborhood of the city of Bu-lur since,' and he fell to laughing in harsh, cackling notes that sent a shiver through the woman's frame.

As Obergatz talked Jane had recovered her spear from the carcass of the antelope and commenced busying herself with the removal of the hide. The man made no attempt to assist her, but stood by talking and watching her, the while he continually ran his filthy fingers through his matted hair and beard. His face and body were caked with dirt and he was naked except for a torn greasy hide about his loins. His weapons consisted of a club and knife of Waz-don pattern, that he had stolen from the city of Bu-lur; but what more greatly concerned the woman than his filth or his armament were his cackling laughter and the strange expression in his eyes.

She went on with her work, however, removing those parts of the buck she wanted, taking only as much meat as she might consume before it spoiled, as she was not sufficiently a true jungle creature to relish it beyond that stage, and then she straightened up and faced the man.

'Lieutenant Obergatz,' she said, 'by a chance of accident we have met again. Certainly you would not have sought the meeting any more than I. We have nothing in common other than those sentiments which may have been engendered by my natural dislike and suspicion of you, one of the authors of all the misery and sorrow that I have endured for endless months. This little corner of the world is mine by right of discovery and occupation. Go away and leave me to enjoy here what peace I may. It is the least that you can do to amend the wrong that you have done me and mine.'

The man stared at her through his fishy eyes for a moment in silence, then there broke from his lips a peal of mirthless uncanny laughter.

'Go away! Leave you alone!' he cried. 'I have found you. We are going to be good friends. There is no one else in the world but us. No one will ever know what we do or what becomes of us and now you ask me to go away and live alone in this hellish solitude.' Again he laughed, though neither the muscles of his eyes or his mouth reflected any mirth – it was just a hollow sound that imitated laughter.

'Remember your promise,' she said.

'Promise! Promise! What are promises? They are made to be broken – we taught the world that at Liége and Louvain. No, no! I will not go away. I shall stay and protect you.'

'I do not need your protection,' she insisted. 'You have already seen that I can use a spear.'

'Yes,' he said; 'but it would not be right to leave you here alone – you are but a woman. No, no; I am an officer of the Kaiser and I cannot abandon you.'

Once more he laughed. 'We could be very happy here together,' he added.

The woman could not repress a shudder, nor, in fact, did she attempt to hide her aversion.

'You do not like me?' he asked. 'Ah, well; it is too sad. But someday you will love me,' and again the hideous laughter.

The woman had wrapped the pieces of the buck in the hide and this she now raised and threw across her shoulder. In her other hand she held her spear and faced the German.

'Go!' she commanded. 'We have wasted enough words. This is my country and I shall defend it. If I see you about again I shall kill you. Do you understand?'

An expression of rage contorted Obergatz's features. He raised his club and started toward her.

'Stop!' she commanded, throwing her spear-hand backward for a cast. 'You saw me kill this buck and you have said truthfully that no one will ever know what we do here. Put these two facts together, German, and draw your own conclusions before you take another step in my direction.'

The man halted and his club-hand dropped to his side. 'Come,' he begged in what he intended as a conciliatory tone. 'Let us be friends, Lady Greystoke. We can be of great assistance to each other and I promise not to harm you.'

'Remember Liége and Louvain,' she reminded him with a sneer. 'I am going now – be sure that you do not follow me. As far as you can walk in a day from this spot in any direction you may consider the limits of my domain. If ever again I see you within these limits I shall kill you.'

There could be no question that she meant what she said and the man seemed convinced for he but stood sullenly eyeing her as she backed from sight beyond a turn in the game trail that crossed the ford where they had met, and disappeared in the forest.

20

Silently in the Night

In A-lur the fortunes of the city had been tossed from hand to hand. The party of Ko-tan's loyal warriors that Tarzan had led to the rendezvous at the entrance to the secret passage below the palace gates had met with disaster. Their first rush had been met with soft words from the priests. They had been exhorted to defend the faith of their fathers from blasphemers. Ja-don was painted to them as a defiler of temples, and the wrath of Jad-ben-Otho was prophesied for those who embraced his cause. The priests insisted that Lu-don's only wish was to prevent the seizure of the throne by Ja-don until a new king could be chosen according to the laws of the Ho-don.

The result was that many of the palace warriors joined their fellows of the city, and when the priests saw that those whom they could influence outnumbered those who remained loyal to the palace, they caused the former to fall upon the latter with the result that many were killed and only a handful succeeded in reaching the safety of the palace gates, which they quickly barred.

The priests led their own forces through the secret passageway into the temple, while some of the loyal ones sought out Ja-don and told him all that had happened. The fight in the banquet hall had spread over a considerable portion of the palace grounds and had at last resulted in the temporary defeat of those who had opposed Ja-don. This force, counseled by underpriests sent for the purpose by Lu-don, had withdrawn within the temple grounds so that now the issue was plainly marked as between Ja-don on the one side and Lu-don on the other.

The former had been told of all that had occurred in the apartments of O-lo-a to whose safety he had attended at the first opportunity and he had also learned of Tarzan's part in leading his men to the gathering of Lu-don's warriors.

These things had naturally increased the old warrior's former inclinations of friendliness toward the ape-man, and now he regretted that the other had departed from the city.

The testimony of O-lo-a and Pan-at-lee was such as to strengthen whatever belief in the godliness of the stranger Ja-don and others of the warriors had previously entertained, until presently there appeared a strong tendency upon the part of this palace faction to make the Dor-ul-Otho an issue of their original quarrel with Lu-don. Whether this occurred as the natural sequence to repeated narrations of the ape-man's exploits, which lost nothing by repetition, in conjunction with Lu-don's enmity toward him, or whether it was the shrewd design of some wily old warrior such as Ja-don, who realized the value of adding a religious cause to their temporal one, it were difficult to determine; but the fact remained that Ja-don's followers developed bitter hatred for the followers of Lu-don because of the high priest's antagonism to Tarzan.

Unfortunately however Tarzan was not there to inspire the followers of Ja-don with the holy zeal that might have quickly settled the dispute in the old chieftain's favor. Instead, he was miles away and because their repeated prayers for his presence were unanswered, the weaker spirits among them commenced to suspect that their cause did not have divine favor. There was also another and a potent cause for defection from the ranks of Ja-don. It emanated from the city where the friends and relatives of the palace warriors, who were largely also the friends and relatives of Lu-don's forces, found the means, urged on by the priesthood, to circulate throughout the palace pernicious propaganda aimed at Ja-don's cause.

The result was that Lu-don's power increased while that of Ja-don waned. Then followed a sortie from the temple which resulted in the defeat of the palace forces, and though they were able to withdraw in decent order withdraw they did, leaving the palace to Lu-don, who was now virtually ruler of Pal-ul-don.

Ja-don, taking with him the princess, her women, and their slaves, including Pan-at-lee, as well as the women and children of his faithful followers, retreated not only from the palace but from the city of A-lur as well and fell back upon his own city of Ja-lur. Here he remained, recruiting his forces from the surrounding villages of the north which, being far removed from the influence of the priesthood of A-lur, were enthusiastic partisans in any cause that the old chieftain espoused, since for years he had been revered as their friend and protector.

And while these events were transpiring in the north, Tarzan-jad-guru lay in the lion pit at Tu-lur while messengers passed back and forth between Mo-sar and Lu-don as the two dickered for the throne of Pal-ul-don. Mo-sar was cunning enough to guess that should an open breach occur between himself and the high priest he might use his prisoner to his own advantage, for he had heard whisperings among even his own people that suggested that there were those who were more than a trifle inclined to belief in the divinity of the stranger and that he might indeed be the Dor-ul-Otho. Lu-don wanted Tarzan himself. He wanted to sacrifice him upon the eastern altar with his own hands before a multitude of people, since he was not without evidence that his own standing and authority had been lessened by the claims of the bold and heroic figure of the stranger.

The method that the high priest of Tu-lur had employed to trap Tarzan had left the ape-man in possession of his weapons though there seemed little likelihood of their being of any service to him. He also had his pouch, in which were the various odds and ends which are the natural accumulation of all receptacles from a gold meshbag to an attic. There were bits of obsidian and choice feathers for arrows, some pieces of flint and a couple of steel, an old knife, a heavy bone needle, and strips of dried gut. Nothing very useful to you or me, perhaps; but nothing useless to the savage life of the ape-man.

When Tarzan realized the trick that had been so neatly played upon him he had awaited expectantly the coming of the lion, for though the scent of *ja* was old he was sure that sooner or later they would let one of the beasts in upon him. His first consideration was a thorough exploration of his prison. He had noticed the hide-covered windows and these he immediately uncovered, letting in the light, and revealing the fact that though the chamber was far below the level of the temple courts it was yet many feet above the base of the hill from which the temple was hewn. The windows were so closely barred that he could not see over the edge of the thick wall in which they were cut to determine what lay close in below him. At a little distance were the blue waters of Jad-in-lul and beyond, the verdure-clad farther shore, and beyond that the mountains. It was a beautiful picture upon which he looked – a picture of peace and harmony and quiet. Nor anywhere a slightest suggestion of the savage men and beasts that claimed this lovely landscape as their own. What a paradise! And someday civilized man would come and – spoil it! Ruthless axes would raze that age-old wood; black, sticky smoke would rise from ugly chimneys against that azure sky; grimy little boats with wheels behind or upon either side would churn the mud from the bottom of Jad-in-lul, turning its blue waters to a dirty brown; hideous piers would project into the lake from squalid buildings of corrugated iron, doubtless, for of such are the pioneer cities of the world.

But would civilized man come? Tarzan hoped not. For countless generations civilization had ramped about the globe; it had dispatched its emissaries to the North Pole and the South; it had circled Pal-ul-don once, perhaps many times, but it had never touched her. God grant that it never would. Perhaps He was saving this little spot to be always just as He had made it, for the scratching of the Ho-don and the Waz-don upon His rocks had not altered the fair face of Nature.

Through the windows came sufficient light to reveal the whole interior to

Tarzan. The room was fairly large and there was a door at each end – a large door for men and a smaller one for lions. Both were closed with heavy masses of stone that had been lowered in grooves running to the floor. The two windows were small and closely barred with the first iron that Tarzan had seen in Pal-ul-don. The bars were let into holes in the casing, and the whole so strongly and neatly contrived that escape seemed impossible. Yet within a few minutes of his incarceration Tarzan had commenced to undertake his escape. The old knife in his pouch was brought into requisition and slowly the ape-man began to scrape and chip away the stone from about the bars of one of the windows. It was slow work but Tarzan had the patience of absolute health.

Each day food and water were brought him and slipped quickly beneath the smaller door which was raised just sufficiently to allow the stone receptacles to pass in. The prisoner began to believe that he was being preserved for something beside lions. However that was immaterial. If they would but hold off for a few more days they might select what fate they would – he would not be there when they arrived to announce it.

And then one day came Pan-sat, Lu-don's chief tool, to the city of Tu-lur. He came ostensibly with a fair message for Mo-sar from the high priest at A-lur. Lu-don had decided that Mo-sar should be king and he invited Mo-sar to come at once to A-lur and then Pan-sat, having delivered the message, asked that he might go to the temple of Tu-lur and pray, and there he sought the high priest of Tu-lur to whom was the true message that Lu-don had sent. The two were closeted alone in a little chamber and Pan-sat whispered into the ear of the high priest.

'Mo-sar wishes to be king,' he said, 'and Lu-don wishes to be king. Mo-sar wishes to retain the stranger who claims to be the Dor-ul-Otho and Lu-don wishes to kill him, and now,' he leaned even closer to the ear of the high priest of Tu-lur, 'if you would be high priest at A-lur it is within your power.'

Pan-sat ceased speaking and waited for the other's reply. The high priest was visibly affected. To be high priest at A-lur! That was almost as good as being king of all Pal-ul-don, for great were the powers of him who conducted the sacrifices upon the altars of A-lur.

'How?' whispered the high priest. 'How may I become high priest at A-lur?'

Again Pan-sat leaned close: 'By killing the one and bringing the other to A-lur,' replied he. Then he rose and departed knowing that the other had swallowed the bait and could be depended upon to do whatever was required to win him the great prize.

Nor was Pan-sat mistaken other than in one trivial consideration. This high priest would indeed commit murder and treason to attain the high office at A-lur; but he had misunderstood which of his victims was to be killed and which to be delivered to Lu-don. Pan-sat, knowing himself all the details of the plannings of Lu-don, had made the quite natural error of assuming that the other was perfectly aware that only by publicly sacrificing the false Dor-ul-Otho could the high priest at A-lur bolster his waning power and that the assassination of Mo-sar, the pretender, would remove from Lu-don's camp the only obstacle to his combining the offices of high priest and king. The high priest at Tu-lur thought that he had been commissioned to kill Tarzan and bring Mo-sar to A-lur. He also thought that when he had done these things he would be made high priest at A-lur, but he did not know that already the priest had been selected who was to murder him within the hour that he arrived at A-lur, nor did he know that a secret grave had been prepared for him in the floor of a subterranean chamber in the very temple he dreamed of controlling.

And so when he should have been arranging the assassination of his chief he was leading a dozen heavily bribed warriors through the dark corridors beneath the temple to slay Tarzan in the lion pit. Night had fallen. A single torch guided the footsteps of the murderers as they crept stealthily upon their evil way, for they knew that they were doing the thing that their chief did not want done and their guilty consciences warned them to stealth.

In the dark of his cell the ape-man worked at his seemingly endless chipping and scraping. His keen ears detected the coming of footsteps along the corridor without – footsteps that approached the larger door. Always before had they come to the smaller door – the footsteps of a single slave who brought his food. This time there were many more than one and their coming at this time of night carried a sinister suggestion. Tarzan continued to work at his scraping and chipping. He heard them stop beyond the door. All was silence broken only by the scrape, scrape, scrape of the ape-man's tireless blade.

Those without heard it and listening sought to explain it. They whispered in low tones making their plans. Two would raise the door quickly and the others would rush in and hurl their clubs at the prisoner. They would take no chances, for the stories that had circulated in A-lur had been brought to Tu-lur – stories of the great strength and wonderful prowess of Tarzan-jad-guru that caused the sweat to stand upon the brows of the warriors, though it was cool in the damp corridor and they were twelve to one.

And then the high priest gave the signal – the door shot upward and ten warriors leaped into the chamber with poised clubs. Three of the heavy weapons flew across the room toward a darker shadow that lay in the shadow of the opposite wall, then the flare of the torch in the priest's hand lighted the interior and they saw that the thing at which they had flung their clubs was a pile of skins torn from the windows and that except for themselves the chamber was vacant.

One of them hastened to a window. All but a single bar was gone and to this was tied one end of a braided rope fashioned from strips cut from the leather window hangings.

To the ordinary dangers of Jane Clayton's existence was now added the menace of Obergatz's knowledge of her whereabouts. The lion and the panther had given her less cause for anxiety than did the return of the unscrupulous Hun, whom she had always distrusted and feared, and whose repulsiveness was now immeasurably augmented by his unkempt and filthy appearance, his strange and mirthless laughter, and his unnatural demeanor. She feared him now with a new fear as though he had suddenly become the personification of some nameless horror. The wholesome, outdoor life that she had been leading had strengthened and rebuilt her nervous system yet it seemed to her as she thought of him that if this man should ever touch her she should scream, and, possibly, even faint. Again and again during the day following their unexpected meeting the woman reproached herself for not having killed him as she would *ja* or *jato* or any other predatory beast that menaced her existence or her safety. There was no attempt at self-justification for these sinister reflections – they needed no justification. The standards by which the acts of such as you or I may be judged could not apply to hers. We have recourse to the protection of friends and relatives and the civil soldiery that upholds the majesty of the law and which may be invoked to protect the righteous weak against the unrighteous strong; but Jane Clayton comprised within herself not only the righteous weak but all the various agencies for the protection of the weak. To her, then, Lieutenant Erich Obergatz presented no different problem than did *ja*, the lion, other than that she considered the former the more dangerous animal. And so she determined that should he ignore her warning there would be no temporizing upon the occasion of their next meeting – the same swift spear that would meet *ja*'s advances would meet his.

That night her snug little nest perched high in the great tree seemed less the sanctuary that it had before. What might resist the sanguinary intentions of a prowling panther would prove no great barrier to man, and influenced by this thought she slept less well than before. The slightest noise that broke the monotonous hum of the nocturnal jungle startled her into alert wakefulness to lie with straining ears in an attempt to classify the origin of the disturbance, and once she was awakened thus by a sound that seemed to come from something moving in her own tree. She listened intently – scarce breathing. Yes, there it was again. A scuffing of something soft against the hard bark of the tree. The woman reached out in the darkness and grasped her spear. Now she felt a slight sagging of one of the limbs that supported her shelter as though the thing, whatever it was, was slowly raising its weight to the branch. It came nearer. Now she thought that she could detect its breathing. It was at the door. She could hear it fumbling with the frail barrier. What could it be? It made no sound by which she might identify it. She raised herself upon her hands and knees and crept stealthily the little distance to the doorway, her spear clutched tightly in her hand. Whatever the thing was, it was evidently attempting to gain entrance without awakening her. It was just beyond the pitiful little contraption of slender boughs that she had bound together with grasses and called a door – only a few inches lay between the thing and her. Rising to her knees she reached out with her left hand and felt until she found a place where a crooked branch had left an opening a couple of inches wide near the center of the barrier. Into this she inserted the point of her spear. The thing must have heard her move within for suddenly it abandoned its efforts for stealth and tore angrily at the obstacle. At the same moment Jane thrust her spear forward with all her strength. She felt it enter flesh. There was a scream and a curse from without, followed by the crashing of a body through limbs and foliage. Her spear was almost dragged from her grasp, but she held to it until it broke free from the thing it had pierced.

It was Obergatz; the curse had told her that. From below came no further sound. Had she, then, killed him? She prayed so – with all her heart she prayed it. To be freed from the menace of this loathsome creature was relief indeed. During all the balance of the night she lay there awake, listening. Below her, she imagined, she could see the dead man with his hideous face bathed in the cold light of the moon – lying there upon his back staring up at her.

She prayed that *ja* might come and drag it away, but all during the remainder of the night she heard never another sound above the drowsy hum of the jungle. She was glad that he was dead, but she dreaded the gruesome ordeal that awaited her on the morrow, for she must bury the thing that had been Erich Obergatz and live on there above the shallow grave of the man she had slain.

She reproached herself for her weakness, repeating over and over that she had killed in self-defense, that her act was justified; but she was still a woman of today, and strong upon her were the iron mandates of the social order from which she had sprung, its interdictions and its superstitions.

At last came the tardy dawn. Slowly the sun topped the distant mountains beyond Jad-in-lul. And yet she hesitated to loosen the fastenings of her door and look out upon the thing below. But it must be done. She steeled herself and untied the rawhide thong that secured the barrier. She looked down and only the grass and the flowers looked up at her. She came from her shelter and examined the ground upon the opposite side of the tree – there was no dead man there, nor anywhere as far as she could see. Slowly she descended, keeping a wary eye and an alert ear ready for the first intimation of danger.

At the foot of the tree was a pool of blood and a little trail of crimson drops upon the grass, leading away parallel with the shore of Jad-ben-lul. Then she had not slain him! She was vaguely aware of a peculiar, double sensation of relief and regret. Now she would be always in doubt. He might return; but at least she would not have to live above his grave.

She thought some of following the bloody spoor on the chance that he might have crawled away to die later, but she gave up the idea for fear that she might find him dead nearby, or, worse yet badly wounded. What then could she do? She could not finish him with her spear – no, she knew that she could not do that, nor could she bring him back and nurse him, nor could she leave him there to die of hunger or of thirst, or to become the prey of some prowling beast. It were better then not to search for him for fear that she might find him.

That day was one of nervous starting to every sudden sound. The day before she would have said that her nerves were of iron; but not today. She knew now the shock that she had suffered and that this was the reaction. Tomorrow it might be different, but something told her that never again would her little shelter and the patch of forest and jungle that she called her own be the same. There would hang over them always the menace of this man. No longer would she pass restful nights of deep slumber. The peace of her little world was shattered forever.

That night she made her door doubly secure with additional thongs of rawhide cut from the pelt of the buck she had slain the day that she met Obergatz. She was very tired for she had lost much sleep the night before; but for a long time she lay with wide-open eyes staring into the darkness. What saw she there? Visions that brought tears to those brave and beautiful eyes – visions of a rambling bungalow that had been home to her and that was no more, destroyed by the same cruel force that haunted her even now in this remote, uncharted corner of the earth; visions of a strong man whose protecting arm would never press her close again; visions of a tall, straight son who looked at her adoringly out of brave, smiling eyes that were like his father's. Always the vision of the crude simple bungalow rather than of the stately halls that had been as much a part of her life as the other. But *he* had loved the bungalow and the broad, free acres best and so she had come to love them best, too.

At last she slept, the sleep of utter exhaustion. How long it lasted she did not know; but suddenly she was wide awake and once again she heard the scuffing of a body against the bark of her tree and again the limb bent to a heavy weight. He had returned! She went cold, trembling as with ague. Was it he, or, O God! had she killed him then and was this –? She tried to drive the horrid thought from her mind, for this way, she knew, lay madness.

And once again she crept to the door, for the thing was outside just as it had been last night. Her hands trembled as she placed the point of her weapon to the opening. She wondered if it would scream as it fell.

21

The Maniac

The last bar that would make the opening large enough to permit his body to pass had been removed as Tarzan heard the warriors whispering beyond the stone door of his prison. Long since had the rope of hide been braided. To secure one end to the remaining bar that he had left for this purpose was the work of but a moment, and while the warriors whispered without, the brown body of the ape-man slipped through the small aperture and disappeared below the sill.

Tarzan's escape from the cell left him still within the walled area that comprised the palace and temple grounds and buildings. He had reconnoitered as best he might from the window after he had removed enough bars to permit him to pass his head through the opening, so that he knew what lay immediately before him – a winding and usually deserted alleyway leading in the direction of the outer gate that opened from the palace grounds into the city.

The darkness would facilitate his escape. He might even pass out of the palace and the city without detection. If he could elude the guard at the palace gate the rest would be easy. He strode along confidently, exhibiting no fear of detection, for he reasoned that thus would he disarm suspicion. In the darkness he easily could pass for a Ho-don and in truth, though he passed several after leaving the deserted alley, no one accosted or detained him, and thus he came at last to the guard of a half-dozen warriors before the palace gate. These he attempted to pass in the same unconcerned fashion and he might have succeeded had it not been for one who came running rapidly from the direction of the temple shouting: 'Let no one pass the gates! The prisoner has escaped from the *pal-ul-ja!*'

Instantly a warrior barred his way and simultaneously the fellow recognized him. '*Xot tor!*' he exclaimed: 'Here he is now. Fall upon him! Fall upon him! Back! Back before I kill you.'

The others came forward. It cannot be said that they rushed forward. If it was their wish to fall upon him there was a noticeable lack of enthusiasm other than that which directed their efforts to persuade someone else to fall upon him. His fame as a fighter had been too long a topic of conversation for the good of the morale of Mo-sar's warriors. It were safer to stand at a distance and hurl their clubs and this they did, but the ape-man had learned something of the use of this weapon since he had arrived in Pal-ul-don. And as he learned great had grown his respect for this most primitive of arms. He had come to realize that the black savages he had known had never appreciated the possibilities of their knob sticks, nor had he, and he had discovered, too, why the Pal-ul-dons had turned their ancient spears into plowshares and pinned their faith to the heavy-ended club alone. In deadly execution it was far more effective than a spear and it answered, too, every purpose of a shield, combining the two in one and thus reducing the burden of the warrior. Thrown as they throw it, after the manner of the hammer-throwers of the Olympian games, an ordinary shield would prove more a weakness than a strength while one that would be strong enough to prove a protection would be too heavy to carry. Only another club, deftly wielded to deflect the course of an enemy missile, is in any way effective against these formidable weapons and, too, the war club of Pal-ul-don can be thrown with accuracy a far greater distance than any spear.

And now was put to the test that which Tarzan had learned from Om-at and Ta-den. His eyes and his muscles trained by a lifetime of necessity moved with the rapidity of light and his brain functioned with an uncanny celerity that suggested nothing less than prescience, and these things more than compensated for his lack of experience with the war club he handled so dexterously. Weapon after weapon he warded off and always he moved with a single idea in mind – to place himself within reach of one of his antagonists. But they were wary for they feared this strange creature to whom the superstitious fears of many of them attributed the miraculous powers of deity. They managed to keep between Tarzan and the gateway and all the time they bawled lustily for reinforcements. Should these come before he had made his escape the ape-man realized that the odds against him would be unsurmountable, and so he redoubled his efforts to carry out his design.

Following their usual tactics, two or three of the warriors were always circling behind him, collecting the thrown clubs when Tarzan's attention was directed elsewhere. He himself retrieved several of them which he hurled with such deadly effect as to dispose of two of his antagonists, but now he heard the approach of hurrying warriors, the patter of their bare feet upon the stone pavement and then the savage cries which were to bolster the courage of their fellows and fill the enemy with fear.

There was no time to lose. Tarzan held a club in either hand and, swinging one he hurled it at a warrior before him and as the man dodged he rushed in and seized him, at the same time casting his second club at another of his opponents. The Ho-don with whom he grappled reached instantly for his knife but the ape-man grasped his wrist. There was a sudden twist, the snapping of a bone and an agonized scream, then the warrior was lifted bodily from his feet and held as a shield between his fellows and the fugitive as the latter backed through the gateway. Beside Tarzan stood the single torch that lighted the entrance to the palace grounds. The warriors were advancing to the succor of their fellow when the ape-man raised his captive high above his head and flung him full in the face of the foremost attacker. The fellow went down and two directly behind him sprawled headlong over their companion as the ape-man seized the torch and cast it back into the palace grounds to be extinguished as it struck the bodies of those who led the charging reinforcements.

In the ensuing darkness Tarzan disappeared in the streets of Tu-lur beyond the palace gate. For a time he was aware of sounds of pursuit but the fact that they trailed away and died in the direction of Jad-in-lul informed him that they were searching in the wrong direction, for he had turned south out of Tu-lur purposely to throw them off his track. Beyond the outskirts of the city he turned directly toward the northwest, in which direction lay A-lur.

In his path he knew lay Jad-bal-lul, the shore of which he was compelled to skirt, and there would be a river to cross at the lower end of the great lake upon the shores of which lay A-lur. What other obstacles lay in his way he did not know but he believed that he could make better time on foot than by attempting to steal a canoe and force his way upstream with a single paddle. It was his intention to put as much distance as possible between himself and Tu-lur before he slept for he was sure that Mo-sar would not lightly accept his loss, but that with the coming of day, or possibly even before, he would dispatch warriors in search of him.

A mile or two from the city he entered a forest and here at last he felt such a measure of safety as he never knew in open spaces or in cities. The forest and the jungle were his birthright. No creature that went upon the ground upon four feet, or climbed among the trees, or crawled upon its belly had any advantage over the ape-man in his native heath. As myrrh and frankincense were the dank odors of rotting vegetation in the nostrils of the great Tarmangani. He squared his broad shoulders and lifting his head filled his lungs with the air that he loved best. The heavy fragrance of tropical blooms, the commingled odors of the myriad-scented life of the jungle went to his head with a pleasurable intoxication far more potent than aught contained in the oldest vintages of civilization.

He took to the trees now, not from necessity but from pure love of the wild freedom that had been denied him so long. Though it was dark and the forest strange yet he moved with a surety and ease that bespoke more a strange uncanny sense than wondrous skill. He heard *ja* moaning somewhere ahead and an owl hooted mournfully to the right of him – long familiar sounds that imparted to him no sense of loneliness as they might to you or to me, but on the contrary one of companionship for they betokened the presence of his fellows of the jungle, and whether friend or foe it was all the same to the ape-man.

He came at last to a little stream at a spot where the trees did not meet above it so he was forced to descend to the ground and wade through the water and upon the opposite shore he stopped as though suddenly his god-like figure had been transmuted from flesh to marble. Only his dilating nostrils bespoke his pulsing vitality. For a long moment he stood there thus and then swiftly, but with a caution and silence that were inherent in him he moved forward again, but now his whole attitude bespoke a new urge. There was a definite and masterful purpose in every movement of those steel muscles rolling softly beneath the smooth brown hide. He moved now toward a certain goal that quite evidently filled him with far greater enthusiasm than had the possible event of his return to A-lur.

And so he came at last to the foot of a great tree and there he stopped and looked up above him among the foliage where the dim outlines of a roughly rectangular bulk loomed darkly. There was a choking sensation in Tarzan's throat as he raised himself gently into the branches. It was as though his heart were swelling either to a great happiness or a great fear.

Before the rude shelter built among the branches he paused, listening. From within there came to his sensitive nostrils the same delicate aroma that had arrested his eager attention at the little stream a mile away. He crouched upon the branch close to the little door.

'Jane,' he called, 'heart of my heart, it is I.'

The only answer from within was as the sudden indrawing of a breath that was half gasp and half sigh, and the sound of a body falling to the floor. Hurriedly Tarzan sought to release the thongs which held the door but they were fastened from the inside, and at last, impatient with further delay, he seized the frail barrier in one giant hand and with a single effort tore it completely away. And then he entered to find the seemingly lifeless body of his mate stretched upon the floor.

He gathered her in his arms; her heart beat; she still breathed, and presently he realized that she had but swooned.

When Jane Clayton regained consciousness it was to find herself held tightly in two strong arms, her head pillowed upon the broad shoulder where so often before her fears had been soothed and her sorrows comforted. At first she was not sure but that it was all a dream. Timidly her hand stole to his cheek.

'John,' she murmured, 'tell me, is it really you?'

In reply he drew her more closely to him. 'It is I,' he replied. 'But there is something in my throat,' he said haltingly, 'that makes it hard for me to speak.'

She smiled and snuggled closer to him. 'God has been good to us, Tarzan of the Apes,' she said.

For some time neither spoke. It was enough that they were reunited and that each knew that the other was alive and safe. But at last they found their voices and when the sun rose they were still talking, so much had each to tell the other; so many questions there were to be asked and answered.

'And Jack,' she asked, 'where is he?'

'I do not know,' replied Tarzan. 'The last I heard of him he was on the Argonne Front.'

'Ah, then our happiness is not quite complete,' she said, a little note of sadness creeping into her voice.

'No,' he replied, 'but the same is true in countless other English homes today, and pride is learning to take the place of happiness in these.'

She shook her head. 'I want my boy,' she said.

'And I too,' replied Tarzan, 'and we may have him yet. He was safe and unwounded the last word I had. And now,' he said, 'we must plan upon our return. Would you like to rebuild the bungalow and gather together the remnants of our Waziri or would you rather return to London?'

'Only to find Jack,' she said. 'I dream always of the bungalow and never of the city, but John, we can only dream, for Obergatz told me that he had circled this whole country and found no place where he might cross the morass.'

'I am not Obergatz,' Tarzan reminded her, smiling. 'We will rest today and tomorrow we will set out toward the north. It is a savage country, but we have crossed it once and we can cross it again.'

And so, upon the following morning, the Tarmangani and his mate went forth upon their journey across the Valley of Jad-ben-Otho, and ahead of them were fierce men and savage beasts, and the lofty mountains of Pal-ul-don; and beyond the mountains the reptiles and the morass, and beyond that the arid, thorn-covered steppe, and other savage beasts and men and weary, hostile miles of untracked wilderness between them and the charred ruins of their home.

Lieutenant Erich Obergatz crawled through the grass upon all fours, leaving a trail of blood behind him after Jane's spear had sent him crashing to the ground beneath her tree. He made no sound after the one piercing scream that had acknowledged the severity of his wound. He was quiet because of a great fear that had crept into his warped brain that the devil woman would pursue and slay him. And so he crawled away like some filthy beast of prey, seeking a thicket where he might lie down and hide.

He thought that he was going to die, but he did not, and with the coming of the new day he discovered that his wound was superficial. The rough obsidian-shod spear had entered the muscles of his side beneath his right arm inflicting a painful, but not a fatal wound. With the realization of this fact came a renewed desire to put as much distance as possible between himself and Jane Clayton. And so he moved on, still going upon all fours because of a persistent hallucination that in this way he might escape observation. Yet though he fled his mind still revolved muddily about a central desire – while he fled from her he still planned to pursue her, and to his lust of possession was added a desire for revenge. She should pay for the suffering she had inflicted upon him. She should pay for rebuffing him, but for some reason which he did not try to explain to himself he would crawl away and hide. He would come back though. He would come back and when he had finished with her, he would take that smooth throat in his two hands and crush the life from her.

He kept repeating this over and over to himself and then he fell to laughing out loud, the cackling, hideous laughter that had terrified Jane. Presently he realized his knees were bleeding and that they hurt him. He looked cautiously behind. No one was in sight. He listened. He could hear no indications of pursuit and so he rose to his feet and continued upon his way a sorry sight – covered with filth and blood, his beard and hair tangled and matted and filled with burrs and dried mud and unspeakable filth. He kept no track of time. He ate fruits and berries and tubers that he dug from the earth with his fingers. He followed the shore of the lake and the river that he might be near water, and when *ja* roared or moaned he climbed a tree and hid there, shivering.

And so after a time he came up the southern shore of Jad-ben-lul until a wide river stopped his progress. Across the blue water a white city glimmered in the sun. He looked at it for a long time, blinking his eyes like an owl. Slowly a recollection forced itself through his tangled brain. This was A-lur, the City of Light. The association of ideas recalled Bu-lur and the Waz-hodon. They had called him Jad-ben-Otho. He commenced to laugh aloud and stood up very straight and strode back and forth along the shore. 'I am Jad-ben-Otho,' he cried, 'I am the Great God. In A-lur is my temple and my high priests. What is Jad-ben-Otho doing here alone in the jungle?'

He stepped out into the water and raising his voice shrieked loudly across toward A-lur. 'I am Jad-ben-Otho!' he screamed. 'Come hither, slaves, and take your god to his temple.' But the distance was great and they did not hear him and no one came, and the feeble mind was distracted by other things – a bird flying in the air, a school of minnows swimming around his feet. He lunged at them trying to catch them, and falling upon his hands and knees he crawled through the water grasping futilely at the elusive fish.

Presently it occurred to him that he was a sea lion and he forgot the fish and lay down and tried to swim by wriggling his feet in the water as though they were a tail. The hardships, the privations, the terrors, and for the past few weeks the lack of proper nourishment had reduced Erich Obergatz to little more than a gibbering idiot.

A water snake swam out upon the surface of the lake and the man pursued it, crawling upon his hands and knees. The snake swam toward the shore just within the mouth of the river where tall reeds grew thickly and Obergatz followed, making grunting noises like a pig. He lost the snake within the reeds but he came upon something else – a canoe hidden there close to the bank. He examined it with cackling laughter. There were two paddles within it which he took and threw out into the current of the river. He watched them for a while and then he sat down beside the canoe and commenced to splash his hands up and down upon the water. He liked to hear the noise and see the little splashes of spray. He rubbed his left forearm with his right palm and the dirt came off and left a white spot that drew his attention. He rubbed again upon the now thoroughly soaked blood and grime that covered his body. He was not attempting to wash himself; he was merely amused by the strange results. 'I am turning white,' he cried. His glance wandered from his body now that the grime and blood were all removed and caught again the white city shimmering beneath the hot sun.

'A-lur – City of Light!' he shrieked and that reminded him again of Tu-lur and by the same process of associated ideas that had before suggested it, he recalled that the Waz-ho-don had thought him Jad-ben-Otho.

'I am Jad-ben-Otho!' he screamed and then his eyes fell again upon the canoe. A new idea came and persisted. He looked down at himself, examining his body, and seeing the filthy loincloth, now water soaked and more bedraggled than before, he tore it from him and flung it into the lake. 'Gods do not wear dirty rags,' he said aloud. 'They do not wear anything but wreaths and garlands of flowers and I am a god – I am Jad-ben-Otho – and I go in state to my sacred city of A-lur.'

He ran his fingers through his matted hair and beard. The water had softened the burrs but had not removed them. The man shook his head. His hair and beard failed to harmonize with his other godly attributes. He was commencing to think more clearly now, for the great idea had taken hold of his scattered wits and concentrated them upon a single purpose, but he was still a maniac. The only difference being that he was now a maniac with a fixed intent. He went out on the shore and gathered flowers and ferns and wove them in his beard and hair – blazing blooms of different colors – green ferns that trailed about his ears or rose bravely upward like the plumes in a lady's hat.

When he was satisfied that his appearance would impress the most casual observer with his evident deity he returned to the canoe, pushed it from shore and jumped in. The impetus carried it into the river's current and the current bore it out upon the lake. The naked man stood erect in the center of the little craft, his arms folded upon his chest. He screamed aloud his message to the city: 'I am Jad-ben-Otho! Let the high priest and the underpriests attend upon me!'

As the current of the river was dissipated by the waters of the lake the wind caught him and his craft and carried them bravely forward. Sometimes he drifted with his back toward A-lur and sometimes with his face toward it, and at intervals he shrieked his message and his commands. He was still in the middle of the lake when someone discovered him from the palace wall, and as he drew nearer, a crowd of warriors and women and children were congregated there watching him and along the temple walls were many priests and among them Lu-don, the high priest. When the boat had drifted close enough for them to distinguish the bizarre figure standing in it and for them to catch the meaning of his words Lu-don's cunning eyes narrowed. The high priest had learned of the escape of Tarzan and he feared that should he join Ja-don's forces, as seemed likely, he would attract many recruits who might still believe in him, and the Dor-ul-Otho, even if a false one, upon the side of the enemy might easily work havoc with Lu-don's plans.

The man was drifting close in. His canoe would soon be caught in the current that ran close to shore here and carried toward the river that emptied the waters of Jad-ben-lul into Jad-bal-lul. The underpriests were looking toward Lu-don for instructions.

'Fetch him hither!' he commanded. 'If he is Jad-ben-Otho I shall know him.'

The priests hurried to the palace grounds and summoned warriors. 'Go, bring the stranger to Lu-don. If he is Jad-ben-Otho we shall know him.'

And so Lieutenant Erich Obergatz was brought before the high priest at A-lur. Lu-don looked closely at the naked man with the fantastic headdress.

'Where did you come from?' he asked.

'I am Jad-ben-Otho,' cried the German. 'I came from heaven. Where is my high priest?'

'I am the high priest,' replied Lu-don.

Obergatz clapped his hands. 'Have my feet bathed and food brought to me,' he commanded.

Lu-don's eyes narrowed to mere slits of crafty cunning. He bowed low until his forehead touched the feet of the stranger. Before the eyes of many priests, and warriors from the palace he did it.

'Ho, slaves!' he cried, rising; 'fetch water and food for the Great God,' and thus the high priest acknowledged before his people the godhood of Lieutenant Erich Obergatz, nor was it long before the story ran like wildfire through the palace and out into the city and beyond that to the lesser villages all the way from A-lur to Tu-lur.

The real god had come – Jad-ben-Otho himself, and he had espoused the cause of Lu-don, the high priest. Mo-sar lost no time in placing himself at the disposal of Lu-don, nor did he mention aught about his claims to the throne. It was Mo-sar's opinion that he might consider himself fortunate were he allowed to remain in peaceful occupation of his chieftainship at Tu-lur, nor was Mo-sar wrong in his deductions.

But Lu-don could still use him and so he let him live and sent word to him to come to A-lur with all his warriors, for it was rumored that Ja-don was raising a great army in the north and might soon march upon the City of Light.

Obergatz thoroughly enjoyed being a god. Plenty of food and peace of mind and rest partially brought back to him the reason that had been so rapidly slipping from him; but in one respect he was madder than ever, since now no power on earth would ever be able to convince him that he was not a god. Slaves were put at his disposal and these he ordered about in godly fashion. The same portion of his naturally cruel mind met upon common ground the mind of Lu-don, so that the two seemed always in accord. The high priest saw in the stranger a mighty force wherewith to hold forever his power over all Pal-ul-don and thus the future of Obergatz was assured so long as he cared to play god to Lu-don's high priest.

A throne was erected in the main temple court before the eastern altar where Jad-ben-Otho might sit in person and behold the sacrifices that were offered up to him there each day at sunset. So much did the cruel, half-crazed mind enjoy these spectacles that at times he even insisted upon wielding the sacrificial knife himself and upon such occasions the priests and the people fell upon their faces in awe of the dread deity.

If Obergatz taught them not to love their god more he taught them to fear him as they never had before, so that the name of Jad-ben-Otho was whispered in the city and little children were frightened into obedience by the mere mention of it. Lu-don, through his priests and slaves, circulated the information that Jad-ben-Otho had commanded all his faithful followers to flock to the standard of the high priest at A-lur and that all others were cursed, especially Ja-don and the base impostor who had posed as the Dor-ul-Otho. The curse was to take the form of early death following terrible suffering, and Lu-don caused it to be published abroad that the name of any warrior who complained of a pain should be brought to him, for such might be deemed to be under suspicion, since the first effects of the curse would result in slight pains attacking the unholy. He counseled those who felt pains to look carefully to their loyalty. The result was remarkable and immediate – half a nation without a pain, and recruits pouring into A-lur to offer their services to Lu-don while secretly hoping that the little pains they had felt in arm or leg or belly would not recur in aggravated form.

22
A Journey on a *Gryf*

Tarzan and Jane skirted the shore of Jad-bal-lul and crossed the river at the head of the lake. They moved in leisurely fashion with an eye to comfort and safety, for the ape-man, now that he had found his mate, was determined to court no chance that might again separate them, or delay or prevent their escape from Pal-ul-don. How they were to recross the morass was a matter of little concern to him as yet – it would be time enough to consider that matter when it became of more immediate moment. Their hours were filled with the happiness and content of reunion after long separation; they had much to talk of, for each had passed through many trials and vicissitudes and strange adventures, and no important hour might go unaccounted for since last they met.

It was Tarzan's intention to choose a way above A-lur and the scattered Ho-don villages below it, passing about midway between them and the mountains, thus avoiding, insofar as possible, both the Ho-don and Waz-don, for in this area lay the neutral territory that was uninhabited by either. Thus he would travel northwest until opposite the Kor-ul-ja where he planned to stop to pay his respects to Om-at and give the *gund* word of Pan-at-lee, and a plan Tarzan had for insuring her safe return to her people. It was upon the third day of their journey and they had almost reached the river that passes through A-lur when Jane suddenly clutched Tarzan's arm and pointed ahead toward the edge of a forest that they were approaching. Beneath the shadows of the trees loomed a great bulk that the ape-man instantly recognized.

'What is it?' whispered Jane.

'A *gryf*,' replied the ape-man, 'and we have met him in the worst place that we could possibly have found. There is not a large tree within a quarter of a mile, other than those among which he stands. Come, we shall have to go back, Jane; I cannot risk it with you along. The best we can do is to pray that he does not discover us.'

'And if he does?'

'Then I shall have to risk it.'

'Risk what?'

'The chance that I can subdue him as I subdued one of his fellows,' replied Tarzan. 'I told you – you recall?'

'Yes, but I did not picture so huge a creature. Why, John, he is as big as a battleship.'

The ape-man laughed. 'Not quite, though I'll admit he looks quite as formidable as one when he charges.'

They were moving away slowly so as not to attract the attention of the beast.

'I believe we're going to make it,' whispered the woman, her voice tense with suppressed excitement. A low rumble rolled like distant thunder from the wood. Tarzan shook his head.

'"The big show is about to commence in the main tent,"' he quoted, grinning. He caught the woman suddenly to his breast and kissed her. 'One can never tell, Jane,' he said. 'We'll do our best – that is all we can do. Give me your spear, and – don't run. The only hope we have lies in that little brain more than in us. If I can control it – well, let us see.'

The beast had emerged from the forest and was looking about through his weak eyes, evidently in search of them. Tarzan raised his voice in the weird notes of the Tor-o-don's cry: 'Whee-oo! Whee-oo! Whee-oo!' For a moment the great beast stood motionless, his attention riveted by the call. The ape-man advanced straight toward him, Jane Clayton at his elbow. 'Whee-oo!' he cried again peremptorily. A low rumble rolled from the *gryf*s cavernous chest in answer to the call, and the beast moved slowly toward them.

'Fine!' exclaimed Tarzan. 'The odds are in our favor now. You can keep your nerve? – but I do not need to ask.'

'I know no fear when I am with Tarzan of the Apes,' she replied softly, and he felt the pressure of her soft fingers on his arm.

And thus the two approached the giant monster of a forgotten epoch until they stood close in the shadow of a mighty shoulder. 'Whee-oo!' shouted Tarzan and struck the hideous snout with the shaft of the spear. The vicious side snap that did not reach its mark – that evidently was not intended to reach its mark – was the hoped-for answer.

'Come,' said Tarzan, and taking Jane by the hand he led her around behind the monster and up the broad tail to the great, horned back. 'Now will we ride in the state that our forebears knew, before which the pomp of modern kings pales into cheap and tawdry insignificance. How would you like to canter through Hyde Park on a mount like this?'

'I am afraid the bobbies would be shocked by our riding habits, John,' she cried, laughingly.

Tarzan guided the *gryf* in the direction that they wished to go. Steep embankments and rivers proved no slightest obstacle to the ponderous creature.

'A prehistoric tank, this,' Jane assured him, and laughing and talking they continued on their way. Once they came unexpectedly upon a dozen Ho-don warriors as the *gryf* emerged suddenly into a small clearing. The fellows were lying about in the shade of a single tree that grew alone. When they saw the beast they leaped to their feet in consternation and at their shouts the *gryf* issued his hideous, challenging bellow and charged them. The warriors fled in all directions while Tarzan belabored the beast across the snout with his spear in an effort to control him, and at last he succeeded, just as the *gryf* was almost upon one poor devil that it seemed to have singled out for its special prey. With an angry grunt the *gryf* stopped and the man, with a single backward glance that showed a face white with terror, disappeared in the jungle he had been seeking to reach.

The ape-man was elated. He had doubted that he could control the beast should it take it into its head to charge a victim and had intended abandoning it before they reached the Kor-ul-ja. Now he altered his plans – they would ride to the very village of Om-at upon the *gryf*, and the Kor-ul-ja would have food for conversation for many generations to come. Nor was it the theatric instinct of the ape-man alone that gave favor to this plan. The element of Jane's safety entered into the matter for he knew that she would be safe from man and beast alike so long as she rode upon the back of Pal-ul-don's most formidable creature.

As they proceeded slowly in the direction of the Kor-ul-ja, for the natural gait of the *gryf* is far from rapid, a handful of terrified warriors came panting into A-lur, spreading a weird story of the Dor-ul-Otho, only none dared call him the Dor-ul-Otho aloud. Instead they spoke of him as Tarzan-jad-guru and they told of meeting him mounted upon a mighty *gryf* beside the beautiful stranger woman whom Ko-tan would have made queen of Pal-ul-don. This story was brought to Lu-don who caused the warriors to be hailed to his presence, when he questioned them closely until finally he was convinced that they spoke the truth and when they had told him the direction in which the two were traveling, Lu-don guessed that they were on their way to Ja-lur to join Ja-don, a contingency that he felt must be prevented at any cost. As was his wont in the stress of emergency, he called Pan-sat into consultation and for long the two sat in close conference. When they arose a plan had been developed. Pan-sat went immediately to his own quarters where he removed the headdress and trappings of a priest to don in their stead the harness and weapons of a warrior. Then he returned to Lu-don.

'Good!' cried the latter, when he saw him. 'Not even your fellow-priests or the slaves that wait upon you daily would know you now. Lose no time, Pan-sat, for all depends upon the speed with which you strike and – remember! Kill the man if you can; but in any event bring the woman to me here, alive. You understand?'

'Yes, master,' replied the priest, and so it was that a lone warrior set out from A-lur and made his way northwest in the direction of Ja-lur.

The gorge next above Kor-ul-ja is uninhabited and here the wily Ja-don had chosen to mobilize his army for its descent upon A-lur. Two considerations influenced him – one being the fact that could he keep his plans a secret from the enemy he would have the advantage of delivering a surprise attack upon the forces of Lu-don from a direction that they would not expect attack, and in the meantime he would be able to keep his men from the gossip of the cities where strange tales were already circulating relative to the coming of Jad-ben-Otho in person to aid the high priest in his war against Ja-don. It took stout hearts and loyal ones to ignore the implied threats of divine vengeance that these tales suggested. Already there had been desertions and the cause of Ja-don seemed tottering to destruction.

Such was the state of affairs when a sentry posted on the knoll of the mouth of the gorge sent word that he had observed in the valley below what appeared at a distance to be nothing less than two people mounted upon the back of a *gryf*. He said that he had caught glimpses of them, as they passed open spaces, and they seemed to be traveling up the river in the direction of the Kor-ul-ja.

At first Ja-don was inclined to doubt the veracity of his informant; but, like all good generals, he could not permit even palpably false information to go uninvestigated and so he determined to visit the knoll himself and learn precisely what it was that the sentry had observed through the distorting spectacles of fear. He had scarce taken his place beside the man ere the fellow touched his arm and pointed. 'They are closer now,' he whispered; 'you can see them plainly.' And sure enough, not a quarter of a mile away Ja-don saw that which in his long experience in Pal-ul-don he had never before seen – two humans riding upon the broad back of a *gryf*.

At first he could scarce credit even this testimony of his own eyes, but soon he realized that the creatures below could be naught else than they appeared, and then he recognized the man and rose to his feet with a loud cry.

'It is he!' he shouted to those about him. 'It is the Dor-ul-Otho himself.'

The *gryf* and his riders heard the shout though not the words. The former bellowed terrifically and started in the direction of the knoll, and Ja-don, followed by a few of his more intrepid warriors, ran to meet him. Tarzan, loath to enter an unnecessary quarrel, tried to turn the animal, but as the beast was far from tractable it always took a few minutes to force the will of its master upon it; and so the two parties were quite close before the ape-man succeeded in stopping the mad charge of his furious mount.

Ja-don and his warriors, however, had come to the realization that this bellowing creature was bearing down upon them with evil intent and they had assumed the better part of valor and taken to trees, accordingly. It was beneath these trees that Tarzan finally stopped the *gryf*. Ja-don called down to him.

'We are friends,' he cried. 'I am Ja-don, Chief of Ja-lur. I and my warriors lay our foreheads upon the feet of Dor-ul-Otho and pray that he will aid us in our righteous fight with Lu-don, the high priest.'

'You have not defeated him yet?' asked Tarzan. 'Why I thought you would be king of Pal-ul-don long before this.'

'No,' replied Ja-don. 'The people fear the high priest and now that he has in the temple one whom he claims to be Jad-ben-Otho many of my warriors are afraid. If they but knew that the Dor-ul-Otho had returned and that he had blessed the cause of Ja-don I am sure that victory would be ours.'

Tarzan thought for a long minute and then he spoke. 'Ja-don,' he said, 'was one of the few who believed in me and who wished to accord me fair treatment. I have a debt to pay to Ja-don and an account to settle with Lu-don, not alone on my own behalf, but principally upon that of my mate. I will go with you, Ja-don, to mete to Lu-don the punishment he deserves. Tell me, chief, how may the Dor-ul-Otho best serve his father's people?'

'By coming with me to Ja-lur and the villages between,' replied Ja-don quickly, 'that the people may see that it is indeed the Dor-ul-Otho and that he smiles upon the cause of Ja-don.'

'You think that they will believe in me more now than before?' asked the ape-man.

'Who will dare doubt that he who rides upon the great *gryf* is less than a god?' returned the old chief.

'And if I go with you to the battle at A-lur,' asked Tarzan, 'can you assure the safety of my mate while I am gone from her?'

'She shall remain in Ja-lur with the Princess O-lo-a and my own women,' replied Ja-don. 'There she will be safe for there I shall leave trusted warriors to protect them. Say that you will come, O Dor-ul-Otho, and my cup of happiness will be full, for even now Ta-den, my son, marches toward A-lur with a force from the northwest and if we can attack, with the Dor-ul-Otho at our head, from the northeast our arms should be victorious.'

'It shall be as you wish, Ja-don,' replied the ape-man; 'but first you must have meat fetched for my *gryf*.'

'There are many carcasses in the camp above,' replied Ja-don, 'for my men have little else to do than hunt.'

'Good,' exclaimed Tarzan. 'Have them brought at once.'

And when the meat was brought and laid at a distance the ape-man slipped from the back of his fierce charger and fed him with his own hand. 'See that there is always plenty of flesh for him,' he said to Ja-don, for he guessed that his mastery might be short-lived should the vicious beast become overhungry.

It was morning before they could leave for Ja-lur, but Tarzan found the *gryf* lying where he had left him the night before beside the carcasses of two antelope and a lion; but now there was nothing but the *gryf*.

'The paleontologists say that he was herbivorous,' said Tarzan as he and Jane approached the beast.

The journey to Ja-lur was made through the scattered villages where Ja-don hoped to arouse a keener enthusiasm for his cause. A party of warriors preceded Tarzan that the people might properly be prepared, not only for the sight of the *gryf* but to receive the Dor-ul-Otho as became his high station. The results were all that Ja-don could have hoped and in no village through which they passed was there one who doubted the deity of the ape-man.

As they approached Ja-lur a strange warrior joined them, one whom none of Ja-don's following knew. He said he came from one of the villages to the south and that he had been treated unfairly by one of Lu-don's chiefs. For this reason he had deserted the cause of the high priest and come north in the hope of finding a home in Ja-lur. As every addition to his forces was welcome to the old chief he permitted the stranger to accompany them, and so he came into Ja-lur with them.

There arose now the question as to what was to be done with the *gryf* while they remained in the city. It was with difficulty that Tarzan had prevented the savage beast from attacking all who came near it when they had first entered the camp of Ja-don in the uninhabited gorge next to the Kor-ul-ja, but during the march to Ja-lur the creature had seemed to become accustomed to the presence of the Ho-don. The latter, however, gave him no cause for annoyance since they kept as far from him as possible and when he passed through the streets of the city he was viewed from the safety of lofty windows and roofs. However tractable he appeared to have become there would have been no enthusiastic seconding of a suggestion to turn him loose within the city. It was finally suggested that he be turned into a walled enclosure within the palace grounds and this was done, Tarzan driving him in after Jane had dismounted. More meat was thrown to him and he was left to his own devices, the awestruck inhabitants of the palace not even venturing to climb upon the walls to look at him.

Ja-don led Tarzan and Jane to the quarters of the Princess O-lo-a who, the moment that she beheld the ape-man, threw herself to the ground and touched her forehead to his feet. Pan-at-lee was there with her and she too seemed happy to see Tarzan-jad-guru again. When they found that Jane was his mate they looked with almost equal awe upon her, since even the most skeptical of the warriors of Ja-don were now convinced that they were entertaining a god and a goddess within the city of Ja-lur, and that with the assistance of the power of these two, the cause of Ja-don would soon be victorious and the old Lion-man set upon the throne of Pal-ul-don.

From O-lo-a Tarzan learned that Ta-den had returned and that they were to be united in marriage with the weird rites of their religion and in accordance with the custom of their people as soon as Ta-den came home from the battle that was to be fought at A-lur.

The recruits were now gathering at the city and it was decided that the next day Ja-don and Tarzan would return to the main body in the hidden camp and immediately under cover of night the attack should be made in force upon Lu-don's forces at A-lur. Word of this was sent to Ta-den where he awaited with his warriors upon the north side of Jad-ben-lul, only a few miles from A-lur.

In the carrying out of these plans it was necessary to leave Jane behind in Ja-don's palace at Ja-lur, but O-lo-a and her women were with her and there were many warriors to guard them, so Tarzan bid his mate goodbye with no feelings of apprehension as to her safety, and again seated upon the *gryf* made his way out of the city with Ja-don and his warriors.

At the mouth of the gorge the ape-man abandoned his huge mount since it had served its purpose and could be of no further value to him in their attack upon A-lur, which was to be made just before dawn the following day when, as he could not have been seen by the enemy, the effect of his entry to the city upon the *gryf* would have been totally lost. A couple of sharp blows with the spear sent the big animal rumbling and growling in the direction of the Kor-ul-gryf nor was the ape-man sorry to see it depart since he had never known at what instant its short temper and insatiable appetite for flesh might turn it upon some of his companions.

Immediately upon their arrival at the gorge the march on A-lur was commenced.

23

Taken Alive

As night fell a warrior from the palace of Ja-lur slipped into the temple grounds. He made his way to where the lesser priests were quartered. His presence aroused no suspicion as it was not unusual for warriors to have business within the temple. He came at last to a chamber where several priests were congregated after the evening meal. The rites and ceremonies of the sacrifice had been concluded and there was nothing more of a religious nature to make call upon their time until the rites at sunrise.

Now the warrior knew, as in fact nearly all Pal-ul-don knew, that there was no strong bond between the temple and the palace at Ja-lur and that Ja-don only suffered the presence of the priests and permitted their cruel and abhorrent acts because of the fact that these things had been the custom of the Ho-don of Pal-ul-don for countless ages, and rash indeed must have been the man who would have attempted to interfere with the priests or their ceremonies.

That Ja-don never entered the temple was well known, and that his high priest never entered the palace, but the people came to the temple with their votive offerings and the sacrifices were made night and morning as in every other temple in Pal-ul-don.

The warriors knew these things, knew them better perhaps than a simple warrior should have known them. And so it was here in the temple that he looked for the aid that he sought in the carrying out of whatever design he had.

As he entered the apartment where the priests were he greeted them after the manner which was customary in Pal-ul-don, but at the same time he made a sign with his finger that might have attracted little attention or scarcely been noticed at all by one who knew not its meaning. That there were those within the room who noticed it and interpreted it was quickly apparent, through the fact that two of the priests rose and came close to him as he stood just within the doorway and each of them, as he came, returned the signal that the warrior had made.

The three talked for but a moment and then the warrior turned and left the apartment. A little later one of the priests who had talked with him left also and shortly after that the other.

In the corridor they found the warrior waiting, and led him to a little chamber which opened upon a smaller corridor just beyond where it joined the larger. Here the three remained in whispered conversation for some little time and then the warrior returned to the palace and the two priests to their quarters.

The apartments of the women of the palace at Ja-lur are all upon the same side of a long, straight corridor. Each has a single door leading into the corridor and at the opposite end several windows overlooking a garden. It was in one of these rooms that Jane slept alone. At each end of the corridor was a sentinel, the main body of the guard being stationed in a room near the outer entrance to the women's quarters.

The palace slept for they kept early hours there where Ja-don ruled. The *pal-e-don-so* of the great chieftain of the north knew no such wild orgies as had resounded through the palace of the king at A-lur. Ja-lur was a quiet city by comparison with the capital, yet there was always a guard kept at every entrance to the chambers of Ja-don and his immediate family as well as at the gate leading into the temple and that which opened upon the city.

These guards, however, were small, consisting usually of not more than five or six warriors, one of whom remained awake while the others slept. Such were the conditions then when two warriors presented themselves, one at either end of the corridor, to the sentries who watched over the safety of Jane Clayton and the Princess O-lo-a, and each of the newcomers repeated to the sentinels the stereotyped words which announced that they were relieved and these others sent to watch in their stead. Never is a warrior loath to be relieved of sentry duty. Where, under different circumstances he might ask numerous questions he is now too well satisfied to escape the monotonies of that universally hated duty. And so these two men accepted their relief without question and hastened away to their pallets.

And then a third warrior entered the corridor and all of the newcomers came together before the door of the ape-man's slumbering mate. And one was the strange warrior who had met Ja-don and Tarzan outside the city of Ja-lur as they had approached it the previous day; and he was the same warrior who had entered the temple a short hour before, but the faces of his fellows were unfamiliar, even to one another, since it is seldom that a priest removes his hideous headdress in the presence even of his associates.

Silently they lifted the hangings that hid the interior of the room from the view of those who passed through the corridor, and stealthily slunk within. Upon a pile of furs in a far corner lay the sleeping form of Lady Greystoke. The bare feet of the intruders gave forth no sound as they crossed the stone floor toward her. A ray of moonlight entering through a window near her couch shone full upon her, revealing the beautiful contours of an arm and shoulder in cameo-distinctness against the dark furry pelt beneath which she slept, and the perfect profile that was turned toward the skulking three.

But neither the beauty nor the helplessness of the sleeper aroused such sentiments of passion or pity as might stir in the breasts of normal men. To the three priests she was but a lump of clay, nor could they conceive aught of that passion which had aroused men to intrigue and to murder for possession of this beautiful American girl, and which even now was influencing the destiny of undiscovered Pal-ul-don.

Upon the floor of the chamber were numerous pelts and as the leader of the trio came close to the sleeping woman he stooped and gathered up one of the smaller of these. Standing close to her head he held the rug outspread above her face. 'Now,' he whispered and simultaneously he threw the rug over the woman's head and his two fellows leaped upon her, seizing her arms and pinioning her body while their leader stifled her cries with the furry pelt. Quickly and silently they bound her wrists and gagged her and during the brief time that their work required there was no sound that might have been heard by occupants of the adjoining apartments.

Jerking her roughly to her feet they forced her toward a window but she refused to walk, throwing herself instead upon the floor. They were very angry and would have resorted to cruelties to compel her obedience but dared not, since the wrath of Lu-don might fall heavily upon whoever mutilated his fair prize.

And so they were forced to lift and carry her bodily. Nor was the task any sinecure since the captive kicked and struggled as best she might, making their labor as arduous as possible. But finally they succeeded in getting her through the window and into the garden beyond where one of the two priests from the Ja-lur temple directed their steps toward a small barred gateway in the south wall of the enclosure.

Immediately beyond this a flight of stone stairs led downward toward the river and at the foot of the stairs were moored several canoes. Pan-sat had indeed been fortunate in enlisting aid from those who knew the temple and the palace so well, or otherwise he might never have escaped from Ja-lur with his captive. Placing the woman in the bottom of a light canoe Pan-sat entered it and took up the paddle. His companions unfastened the moorings and shoved the little craft out into the current of the stream. Their traitorous work completed they turned and retraced their steps toward the temple, while Pan-sat, paddling strongly with the current, moved rapidly down the river that would carry him to the Jad-ben-lul and A-lur.

The moon had set and the eastern horizon still gave no hint of approaching day as a long file of warriors wound stealthily through the darkness into the city of A-lur. Their plans were all laid and there seemed no likelihood of their miscarriage. A messenger had been dispatched to Ta-den whose forces lay northwest of the city. Tarzan, with a small contingent, was to enter the temple through the secret passageway, the location of which he alone knew, while Ja-don, with the greater proportion of the warriors, was to attack the palace gates.

The ape-man, leading his little band, moved stealthily through the winding alleys of A-lur, arriving undetected at the building which hid the entrance to the secret passageway. This spot being best protected by the fact that its existence was unknown to others than the priests, was unguarded. To facilitate the passage of his little company through the narrow winding, uneven tunnel, Tarzan lighted a torch which had been brought for the purpose and preceding his warriors led the way toward the temple.

That he could accomplish much once he reached the inner chambers of the temple with his little band of picked warriors the ape-man was confident since an attack at this point would bring confusion and consternation to the easily overpowered priests, and permit Tarzan to attack the palace forces in the rear at the same time that Ja-don engaged them at the palace gates, while Ta-den and his forces swarmed the northern walls. Great value had been placed by Ja-don on the moral effect of the Dor-ul-Otho's mysterious appearance in the heart of the temple and he had urged Tarzan to take every advantage of the old chieftain's belief that many of Lu-don's warriors still wavered in their allegiance between the high priest and the Dor-ul-Otho, being held to the former more by the fear which he engendered in the breasts of all his followers than by any love or loyalty they might feel toward him.

There is a Pal-ul-donian proverb setting forth a truth similar to that contained in the old Scotch adage that 'The best laid schemes o' mice and men gang aft a-gley.' Freely translated it might read, 'He who follows the right trail sometimes reaches the wrong destination,' and such apparently was the fate that lay in the footsteps of the great chieftain of the north and his godlike ally.

Tarzan, more familiar with the windings of the corridors than his fellows and having the advantage of the full light of the torch, which at best was but a dim and flickering affair, was some distance ahead of the others, and in his keen anxiety to close with the enemy he gave too little thought to those who were to support him. Nor is this strange, since from childhood the ape-man had been accustomed to fight the battles of life single-handed so that it had become habitual for him to depend solely upon his own cunning and prowess.

And so it was that he came into the upper corridor from which opened the chambers of Lu-don and the lesser priests far in advance of his warriors, and as he turned into this corridor with its dim cressets flickering somberly, he saw another enter it from a corridor before him – a warrior half carrying, half dragging the figure of a woman. Instantly Tarzan recognized the gagged and fettered captive whom he had thought safe in the palace of Ja-don at Ja-lur.

The warrior with the woman had seen Tarzan at the same instant that the latter had discovered him. He heard the low beast-like growl that broke from the ape-man's lips as he sprang forward to wrest his mate from her captor and wreak upon him the vengeance that was in the Tarmangani's savage heart. Across the corridor from Pan-sat was the entrance to a smaller chamber. Into this he leaped carrying the woman with him.

Close behind came Tarzan of the Apes. He had cast aside his torch and drawn the long knife that had been his father's. With the impetuosity of a charging bull he rushed into the chamber in pursuit of Pan-sat to find himself, when the hangings dropped behind him, in utter darkness. Almost immediately there was a crash of stone on stone before him followed a moment later by a similar crash behind. No other evidence was necessary to announce to the ape-man that he was again a prisoner in Lu-don's temple.

He stood perfectly still where he had halted at the first sound of the descending stone door. Not again would he easily be precipitated to the *gryf* pit, or some similar danger, as had occurred when Lu-don had trapped him in the Temple of the *Gryf*. As he stood there his eyes slowly grew accustomed to the darkness and he became aware that a dim light was entering the chamber through some opening, though it was several minutes before he discovered its source. In the roof of the chamber he finally discerned a small aperture, possibly three feet in diameter and it was through this that what was really only a lesser darkness rather than a light was penetrating the Stygian blackness of the chamber in which he was imprisoned.

Since the doors had fallen he had heard no sound though his keen ears were constantly strained in an effort to discover a clue to the direction taken by the abductor of his mate. Presently he could discern the outlines of his prison cell. It was a small room, not over fifteen feet across. On hands and knees, with the utmost caution, he examined the entire area of the floor. In the exact center, directly beneath the opening in the roof, was a trap, but otherwise the floor was solid. With this knowledge it was only necessary to avoid this spot insofar as the floor was concerned. The walls next received his attention. There were only two openings. One the doorway through which he had entered, and upon the opposite side that through which the warrior had borne Jane Clayton. These were both closed by the slabs of stone which the fleeing warrior had released as he departed.

Lu-don, the high priest, licked his thin lips and rubbed his bony white hands together in gratification as Pan-sat bore Jane Clayton into his presence and laid her on the floor of the chamber before him.

'Good, Pan-sat!' he exclaimed. 'You shall be well rewarded for this service. Now, if we but had the false Dor-ul-Otho in our power all Pal-ul-don would be at our feet.'

'Master, I have him!' cried Pan-sat.

'What!' exclaimed Lu-don. 'You have Tarzan-jad-guru? You have slain him perhaps. Tell me, my wonderful Pan-sat, tell me quickly. My breast is bursting with a desire to know.'

'I have taken him alive, Lu-don, my master,' replied Pan-sat. 'He is in the little chamber that the ancients built to trap those who were too powerful to take alive in personal encounter.'

'You have done well, Pan-sat, I—'

A frightened priest burst into the apartment. 'Quick, master, quick,' he cried, 'the corridors are filled with the warriors of Ja-don.'

'You are mad,' cried the high priest. 'My warriors hold the palace and the temple.'

'I speak the truth, master,' replied the priest; 'there are warriors in the corridor approaching this very chamber, and they come from the direction of the secret passage which leads hither from the city.'

'It may be even as he says,' exclaimed Pan-sat. 'It was from that direction that Tarzan-jad-guru was coming when I discovered and trapped him. He was leading his warriors to the very holy of holies.'

Lu-don ran quickly to the doorway and looked out into the corridor. At a glance he saw that the fears of the frightened priest were well founded. A dozen warriors were moving along the corridor toward him but they seemed confused and far from sure of themselves. The high priest guessed that deprived of the leadership of Tarzan they were little better than lost in the unknown mazes of the subterranean precincts of the temple.

Stepping back into the apartment he seized a leathern thong that depended from the ceiling. He pulled upon it sharply and through the temple boomed the deep tones of a metal gong. Five times the clanging notes rang through the corridors, then he turned toward the two priests. 'Bring the woman and follow me,' he directed.

Crossing the chamber he passed through a small doorway, the others lifting Jane Clayton from the floor and following him. Through a narrow corridor and up a flight of steps they went, turning to right and left and doubling back through a maze of winding passageways which terminated in a spiral staircase that gave forth at the surface of the ground within the largest of the inner altar courts close beside the eastern altar.

From all directions now, in the corridors below and the grounds above, came the sound of hurrying footsteps. The five strokes of the great gong had summoned the faithful to the defense of Lu-don in his private chambers. The priests who knew the way led the less familiar warriors to the spot and presently those who had accompanied Tarzan found themselves not only leaderless but facing a vastly superior force. They were brave men but under the circumstances they were helpless and so they fell back the way they had come, and when they reached the narrow confines of the smaller passageway their safety was assured since only one foeman could attack them at a time. But their plans were frustrated and possibly also their entire cause lost, so heavily had Ja-don banked upon the success of their venture.

With the clanging of the temple gong Ja-don assumed that Tarzan and his party had struck their initial blow and so he launched his attack upon the palace gate. To the ears of Lu-don in the inner temple court came the savage war cries that announced the beginning of the battle. Leaving Pan-sat and the other priest to guard the woman he hastened toward the palace personally to direct his force and as he passed through the temple grounds he dispatched a messenger to learn the outcome of the fight in the corridors below, and other messengers to spread the news among his followers that the false Dor-ul-Otho was a prisoner in the temple.

As the din of battle rose above A-lur, Lieutenant Erich Obergatz turned upon his bed of soft hides and sat up. He rubbed his eyes and looked about him. It was still dark without.

'I am Jad-ben-Otho,' he cried; 'who dares disturb my slumber?'

A slave squatting upon the floor at the foot of his couch shuddered and touched her forehead to the floor. 'It must be that the enemy have come, O Jad-ben-Otho.' She spoke soothingly for she had reason to know the terrors of the mad frenzy into which trivial things sometimes threw the Great God.

A priest burst suddenly through the hangings of the doorway and falling upon his hands and knees rubbed his forehead against the stone flagging. 'O Jad-ben-Otho,' he cried, 'the warriors of Ja-don have attacked the palace and the temple. Even now they are fighting in the corridors near the quarters of Lu-don, and the high priest begs that you come to the palace and encourage your faithful warriors by your presence.'

Obergatz sprang to his feet. 'I am Jad-ben-Otho,' he screamed. 'With lightning I will blast the blasphemers who dare attack the holy city of A-lur.'

For a moment he rushed aimlessly and madly about the room, while the priest and the slave remained upon hands and knees with their foreheads against the floor.

'Come,' cried Obergatz, planting a vicious kick in the side of the slave girl. 'Come! Would you wait here all day while the forces of darkness overwhelm the City of Light?'

Thoroughly frightened as were all those who were forced to serve the Great God, the two arose and followed Obergatz toward the palace.

Above the shouting of the warriors rose constantly the cries of the temple priests: 'Jad-ben-Otho is here and the false Dor-ul-Otho is a prisoner in the temple.' The persistent cries reached even to the ears of the enemy as it was intended that they should.

24

The Messenger of Death

The sun rose to see the forces of Ja-don still held at the palace gate. The old warrior had seized the tall structure that stood just beyond the palace and at the summit of this he kept a warrior stationed to look toward the northern wall of the palace where Ta-den was to make his attack; but as the minutes wore into hours no sign of the other force appeared, and now in the full light of the new sun upon the roof of one of the palace buildings appeared Lu-don, the high priest, Mo-sar, the pretender, and the strange, naked figure of a man, into whose long hair and beard were woven fresh ferns and flowers. Behind them were banked a score of lesser priests who chanted in unison: 'This is Jad-ben-Otho. Lay down your arms and surrender.' This they repeated again and again, alternating it with the cry: 'The false Dor-ul-Otho is a prisoner.'

In one of those lulls which are common in battles between forces armed with weapons that require great physical effort in their use, a voice suddenly arose from among the followers of Ja-don: 'Show us the Dor-ul-Otho. We do not believe you!'

'Wait,' cried Lu-don. 'If I do not produce him before the sun has moved his own width, the gates of the palace shall be opened to you and my warriors will lay down their arms.'

He turned to one of his priests and issued brief instructions.

The ape-man paced the confines of his narrow cell. Bitterly he reproached himself for the stupidity which had led him into this trap, and yet was it stupidity? What else might he have done other than rush to the succor of his mate? He wondered how they had stolen her from Ja-lur, and then suddenly there flashed to his mind the features of the warrior whom he had just seen with her. They were strangely familiar. He racked his brain to recall where he had seen the man before and then it came to him. He was the strange warrior who had joined Ja-don's forces outside of Ja-lur the day that Tarzan had ridden upon the great *gryf* from the uninhabited gorge next to the Kor-ul-ja down to the capital city of the chieftain of the north. But who could the man be? Tarzan knew that never before that other day had he seen him.

Presently he heard the clanging of a gong from the corridor without and very faintly the rush of feet, and shouts. He guessed that his warriors had been discovered and a fight was in progress. He fretted and chafed at the chance that had denied him participation in it.

Again and again he tried the doors of his prison and the trap in the center of the floor, but none would give to his utmost endeavors. He strained his eyes toward the aperture above but he could see nothing, and then he continued his futile pacing to and fro like a caged lion behind its bars.

The minutes dragged slowly into hours. Faintly sounds came to him as of shouting men at a great distance. The battle was in progress. He wondered if Ja-don would be victorious and should he be, would his friends ever discover him in this hidden chamber in the bowels of the hill? He doubted it.

And now as he looked again toward the aperture in the roof there appeared to be something depending through its center. He came closer and strained his eyes to see. Yes, there was something there. It appeared to be a rope. Tarzan wondered if it had been there all the time. It must have, he reasoned, since he had heard no sound from above and it was so dark within the chamber that he might easily have overlooked it.

He raised his hand toward it. The end of it was just within his reach. He bore his weight upon it to see if it would hold him. Then he released it and backed away, still watching it, as you have seen an animal do after investigating some unfamiliar object, one of the little traits that differentiated Tarzan from other men, accentuating his similarity to the savage beasts of his native jungle. Again and again he touched and tested the braided leather rope, and always he listened for any warning sound from above.

He was very careful not to step upon the trap at any time and when finally he bore all his weight upon the rope and took his feet from the floor he spread them wide apart so that if he fell he would fall astride the trap. The rope held him. There was no sound from above, nor any from the trap below.

Slowly and cautiously he drew himself upward, hand over hand. Nearer and nearer the roof he came. In a moment his eyes would be above the level of the floor above. Already his extended arms projected into the upper chamber and then something closed suddenly upon both his forearms, pinioning them tightly and leaving him hanging in midair unable to advance or retreat.

Immediately a light appeared in the room above him and presently he saw the hideous mask of a priest peering down upon him. In the priest's hands were leathern thongs and these he tied about Tarzan's wrists and forearms until they were completely bound together from his elbows almost to his fingers. Behind this priest Tarzan presently saw others and soon several lay hold of him and pulled him up through the hole.

Almost instantly his eyes were above the level of the floor he understood how they had trapped him. Two nooses had lain encircling the aperture into the cell below. A priest had waited at the end of each of these ropes and at opposite sides of the chamber. When he had climbed to a sufficient height upon the rope that had dangled into his prison below and his arms were well within the encircling snares the two priests had pulled quickly upon their ropes and he had been made an easy captive without any opportunity of defending himself or inflicting injury upon his captors.

And now they bound his legs from his ankles to his knees and picking him up carried him from the chamber. No word did they speak to him as they bore him upward to the temple yard.

The din of battle had risen again as Ja-don had urged his forces to renewed efforts. Ta-den had not arrived and the forces of the old chieftain were revealing in their lessened efforts their increasing demoralization, and then it was that the priests carried Tarzan-jad-guru to the roof of the palace and exhibited him in the sight of the warriors of both factions.

'Here is the false Dor-ul-Otho,' screamed Lu-don.

Obergatz, his shattered mentality having never grasped fully the meaning of much that was going on about him, cast a casual glance at the bound and helpless prisoner, and as his eyes fell upon the noble features of the ape-man, they went wide in astonishment and fright, and his pasty countenance turned a sickly blue. Once before had he seen Tarzan of the Apes, but many times had he dreamed that he had seen him and always was the giant ape-man avenging the wrongs that had been committed upon him and his by the ruthless hands of the three German officers who had led their native troops in the ravishing of Tarzan's peaceful home. Hauptmann Fritz Schneider had paid the penalty of his needless cruelties; Underlieutenant von Goss, too, had paid; and now Obergatz, the last of the three, stood face-to-face with the nemesis that had trailed him through his dreams for long, weary months. That he was bound and helpless lessened not the German's terror – he seemed not to realize that the man could not harm him. He but stood cringing and jibbering and Lu-don saw and was filled with apprehension that others might see and seeing realize that this bewhiskered idiot was no god – that of the two Tarzan-jad-guru was the more godly figure. Already the high priest noted that some of the palace warriors standing near were whispering together and pointing. He stepped closer to Obergatz. 'You are Jad-ben-Otho,' he whispered, 'denounce him!'

The German shook himself. His mind cleared of all but his great terror and the words of the high priest gave him the clue to safety.

'I am Jad-ben-Otho!' he screamed.

Tarzan looked him straight in the eye. 'You are Lieutenant Obergatz of the German Army,' he said in excellent German. 'You are the last of the three I have sought so long and in your putrid heart you know that God has not brought us together at last for nothing.'

The mind of Lieutenant Obergatz was functioning clearly and rapidly at last. He too saw the questioning looks upon the faces of some of those around them. He saw the opposing warriors of both cities standing by the gate inactive, every eye turned upon him, and the trussed figure of the ape-man. He realized that indecision now meant ruin, and ruin, death. He raised his voice in the sharp barking tones of a Prussian officer, so unlike his former maniacal screaming as to quickly arouse the attention of every ear and to cause an expression of puzzlement to cross the crafty face of Lu-don.

'I am Jad-ben-Otho,' snapped Obergatz. 'This creature is no son of mine. As a lesson to all blasphemers he shall die upon the altar at the hand of the god he has profaned. Take him from my sight, and when the sun stands at zenith let the faithful congregate in the temple court and witness the wrath of this divine hand,' and he held aloft his right palm.

Those who had brought Tarzan took him away then as Obergatz had directed, and the German turned once more to the warriors by the gate. 'Throw down your arms, warriors of Ja-don,' he cried, 'lest I call down my lightnings to blast you where you stand. Those who do as I bid shall be forgiven. Come! Throw down your arms.'

The warriors of Ja-don moved uneasily, casting looks of appeal at their leader and of apprehension toward the figures upon the palace roof. Ja-don sprang forward among his men. 'Let the cowards and knaves throw down their arms and enter the palace,' he cried, 'but never will Ja-don and the warriors of Ja-lur touch their foreheads to the feet of Lu-don and his false god. Make your decision now,' he cried to his followers.

A few threw down their arms and with sheepish looks passed through the gateway into the palace, and with the example of these to bolster their courage others joined in the desertion from the old chieftain of the north, but staunch and true around him stood the majority of his warriors and when the last weakling had left their ranks Ja-don voiced the savage cry with which he led his followers to the attack, and once again the battle raged about the palace gate.

At times Ja-don's forces pushed the defenders far into the palace ground and then the wave of combat would recede and pass out into the city again. And still Ta-den and the reinforcements did not come. It was drawing close to noon. Lu-don had mustered every available man that was not actually needed for the defense of the gate within the temple, and these he sent, under the leadership of Pan-sat, out into the city through the secret passageway and there they fell upon Ja-don's forces from the rear while those at the gate hammered them in front.

Attacked on two sides by a vastly superior force the result was inevitable and finally the last remnant of Ja-don's little army capitulated and the old chief was taken a prisoner before Lu-don. 'Take him to the temple court,' cried the high priest. 'He shall witness the death of his accomplice and perhaps Jad-ben-Otho shall pass a similar sentence upon him as well.'

The inner temple court was packed with humanity. At either end of the western altar stood Tarzan and his mate, bound and helpless. The sounds of battle had ceased and presently the ape-man saw Ja-don being led into the inner court, his wrists bound tightly together before him. Tarzan turned his eyes toward Jane and nodded in the direction of Ja-don. 'This looks like the end,' he said quietly. 'He was our last and only hope.'

'We have at least found each other, John,' she replied, 'and our last days have been spent together. My only prayer now is that if they take you they do not leave me.'

Tarzan made no reply for in his heart was the same bitter thought that her own contained – not the fear that they would kill him but the fear that they would not kill her. The ape-man strained at his bonds but they were too many and too strong. A priest near him saw and with a jeering laugh struck the defenseless ape-man in the face.

'The brute!' cried Jane Clayton.

Tarzan smiled. 'I have been struck thus before, Jane,' he said, 'and always has the striker died.'

'You still have hope?' she asked.

'I am still alive,' he said as though that were sufficient answer. She was a woman and she did not have the courage of this man who knew no fear. In her heart of hearts she knew that he would die upon the altar at high noon for he had told her, after he had been brought to the inner court, of the sentence of death that Obergatz had pronounced upon him, and she knew too that Tarzan knew that he would die, but that he was too courageous to admit it even to himself.

As she looked upon him standing there so straight and wonderful and brave among his savage captors her heart cried out against the cruelty of the fate that had overtaken him. It seemed a gross and hideous wrong that that wonderful creature, now so quick with exuberant life and strength and purpose should be presently naught but a bleeding lump of clay – and all so uselessly and wantonly. Gladly would she have offered her life for his but she knew that it was a waste of words since their captors would work upon them whatever it was their will to do – for him, death; for her – she shuddered at the thought.

And now came Lu-don and the naked Obergatz, and the high priest led the German to his place behind the altar, himself standing upon the other's left. Lu-don whispered a word to Obergatz, at the same time nodding in the direction of Ja-don. The Hun cast a scowling look upon the old warrior.

'And after the false god,' he cried, 'the false prophet,' and he pointed an accusing finger at Ja-don. Then his eyes wandered to the form of Jane Clayton.

'And the woman, too?' asked Lu-don.

'The case of the woman I will attend to later,' replied Obergatz. 'I will talk with her tonight after she has had a chance to meditate upon the consequences of arousing the wrath of Jad-ben-Otho.'

He cast his eyes upward at the sun. 'The time approaches,' he said to Lu-don. 'Prepare the sacrifice.'

Lu-don nodded to the priests who were gathered about Tarzan. They seized the ape-man and lifted him bodily to the altar where they laid him upon his back with his head at the south end of the monolith, but a few feet from where Jane Clayton stood. Impulsively and before they could restrain her the woman rushed forward and bending quickly kissed her mate upon the forehead. 'Goodbye, John,' she whispered.

'Goodbye,' he answered, smiling.

The priests seized her and dragged her away. Lu-don handed the sacrificial knife to Obergatz. 'I am the Great God,' cried the German; 'Thus falleth the divine wrath upon all my enemies!' He looked up at the sun and then raised the knife high above his head.

'Thus die the blasphemers of God!' he screamed, and at the same instant a sharp staccato note rang out above the silent, spellbound multitude. There was a screaming whistle in the air and Jad-ben-Otho crumpled forward across the body of his intended victim. Again the same alarming noise and

Lu-don fell, a third and Mo-sar crumpled to the ground. And now the warriors and the people, locating the direction of this new and unknown sound turned toward the western end of the court.

Upon the summit of the temple wall they saw two figures – a Ho-don warrior and beside him an almost naked creature of the race of Tarzan-jad-guru; across his shoulders and about his hips were strange broad belts studded with beautiful cylinders that glinted in the midday sun, and in his hands a shining thing of wood and metal from the end of which rose a thin wreath of blue-gray smoke.

And then the voice of the Ho-don warrior rang clear upon the ears of the silent throng. 'Thus speaks the true Jad-ben-Otho,' he cried, 'through this his Messenger of Death. Cut the bonds of the prisoners. Cut the bonds of the Dor-ul-Otho and of Ja-don, King of Pal-ul-don, and of the woman who is the mate of the son of god.'

Pan-sat, filled with the frenzy of fanaticism, saw the power and the glory of the regime he had served crumpled and gone. To one and only one did he attribute the blame for the disaster that had but just overwhelmed him. It was the creature who lay upon the sacrificial altar who had brought Lu-don to his death and toppled the dreams of power that day by day had been growing in the brain of the underpriest.

The sacrificial knife lay upon the altar where it had fallen from the dead fingers of Obergatz. Pan-sat crept closer and then with a sudden lunge he reached forth to seize the handle of the blade, and even as his clutching fingers were poised above it, the strange thing in the hands of the strange creature upon the temple wall cried out its crashing word of doom and Pan-sat the underpriest, screaming, fell back upon the dead body of his master.

'Seize all the priests,' cried Ta-den to the warriors, 'and let none hesitate lest Jad-ben-Otho's messenger send forth still other bolts of lightning.'

The warriors and the people had now witnessed such an exhibition of divine power as might have convinced an even less superstitious and more enlightened people, and since many of them had but lately wavered between the Jad-ben-Otho of Lu-don and the Dor-ul-Otho of Ja-don it was not difficult for them to swing quickly back to the latter, especially in view of the unanswerable argument in the hands of him whom Ta-den had described as the Messenger of the Great God.

And so the warriors sprang forward now with alacrity and surrounded the priests, and when they looked again at the western wall of the temple court they saw pouring over it a great force of warriors. And the thing that startled and appalled them was the fact that many of these were black and hairy Waz-don.

At their head came the stranger with the shiny weapon and on his right was Ta-den, the Ho-don, and on his left Om-at, the black *gund* of Kor-ul-ja.

A warrior near the altar had seized the sacrificial knife and cut Tarzan's bonds and also those of Ja-don and Jane Clayton, and now the three stood together beside the altar and as the newcomers from the western end of the temple court pushed their way toward them the eyes of the woman went wide in mingled astonishment, incredulity, and hope. And the stranger, slinging his weapon across his back by a leather strap, rushed forward and took her in his arms.

'Jack!' she cried, sobbing on his shoulder. 'Jack, my son!'

And Tarzan of the Apes came then and put his arms around them both, and the King of Pal-ul-don and the warriors and the people kneeled in the temple court and placed their foreheads to the ground before the altar where the three stood.

25
Home

Within an hour of the fall of Lu-don and Mo-sar, the chiefs and principal warriors of Pal-ul-don gathered in the great throneroom of the palace at A-lur upon the steps of the lofty pyramid and placing Ja-don at the apex proclaimed him king. Upon one side of the old chieftain stood Tarzan of the Apes, and upon the other Korak, the Killer, worthy son of the mighty ape-man.

And when the brief ceremony was over and the warriors with upraised clubs had sworn fealty to their new ruler, Ja-don dispatched a trusted company to fetch O-lo-a and Pan-at-lee and the women of his own household from Ja-lur.

And then the warriors discussed the future of Pal-ul-don and the question arose as to the administration of the temples and the fate of the priests, who practically without exception had been disloyal to the government of the king, seeking always only their own power and comfort and aggrandizement. And then it was that Ja-don turned to Tarzan. 'Let the Dor-ul-Otho transmit to his people the wishes of his father,' he said.

'Your problem is a simple one,' said the ape-man, 'if you but wish to do that which shall be pleasing in the eyes of God. Your priests, to increase their power, have taught you that Jad-ben-Otho is a cruel god; that his eyes love to dwell upon blood and upon suffering. But the falsity of their teachings has been demonstrated to you today in the utter defeat of the priesthood.

'Take then the temples from the men and give them instead to the women that they may be administered in kindness and charity and love. Wash the blood from your eastern altar and drain forever the water from the western.

'Once I gave Lu-don the opportunity to do these things but he ignored my commands, and again is the corridor of sacrifice filled with its victims. Liberate these from every temple in Pal-ul-don. Bring offerings of such gifts as your people like and place them upon the altars of your god. And there he will bless them and the priestesses of Jad-ben-Otho can distribute them among those who need them most.'

As he ceased speaking a murmur of evident approval ran through the throng. Long had they been weary of the avarice and cruelty of the priests and now that authority had come from a high source with a feasible plan for ridding themselves of the old religious order without necessitating any change in the faith of the people they welcomed it.

'And the priests,' cried one. 'We shall put them to death upon their own altars if it pleases the Dor-ul-Otho to give the word.'

'No,' cried Tarzan. 'Let no more blood be spilled. Give them their freedom and the right to take up such occupations as they choose.'

That night a great feast was spread in the *pal-e-don-so* and for the first time in the history of ancient Pal-ul-don black warriors sat in peace and friendship with white. And a pact was sealed between Ja-don and Om-at that would ever make his tribe and the Ho-don allies and friends.

It was here that Tarzan learned the cause of Ta-den's failure to attack at the stipulated time. A messenger had come from Ja-don carrying instructions to delay the attack until noon, nor had they discovered until almost too late that the messenger was a disguised priest of Lu-don. And they had put him to death and scaled the walls and come to the inner temple court with not a moment to spare.

The following day O-lo-a and Pan-at-lee and the women of Ja-don's family arrived at the palace at A-lur and in the great throne-room Ta-den and O-lo-a were wed, and Om-at and Pan-at-lee.

For a week Tarzan and Jane and Korak remained the guests of Ja-don, as did Om-at and his black warriors. And then the ape-man announced that he would depart from Pal-ul-don. Hazy in the minds of their hosts was the location of heaven and equally so the means by which the gods traveled between their celestial homes and the haunts of men and so no questionings arose when it was found that the Dor-ul-Otho with his mate and son would travel overland across the mountains and out of Pal-ul-don toward the north.

They went by way of the Kor-ul-ja accompanied by the warriors of that tribe and a great contingent of Ho-don warriors under Ta-den. The king and many warriors and a multitude of people accompanied them beyond the limits of A-lur and after they had bid them goodbye and Tarzan had invoked the blessings of God upon them the three Europeans saw their simple, loyal friends prostrate in the dust behind them until the cavalcade had wound out of the city and disappeared among the trees of the nearby forest.

They rested for a day among the Kor-ul-ja while Jane investigated the ancient caves of these strange people and then they moved on, avoiding the rugged shoulder of Pastar-ul-ved and winding down the opposite slope toward the great morass. They moved in comfort and in safety, surrounded by their escort of Ho-don and Waz-don.

In the minds of many there was doubtless a question as to how the three would cross the great morass but least of all was Tarzan worried by the problem. In the course of his life he had been confronted by many obstacles only to learn that he who will may always pass. In his mind lurked an easy solution of the passage but it was one which depended wholly upon chance.

It was the morning of the last day that, as they were breaking camp to take up the march, a deep bellow thundered from a nearby grove. The ape-man smiled. The chance had come. Fittingly then would the Dor-ul-Otho and his mate and their son depart from unmapped Pal-ul-don.

He still carried the spear that Jane had made, which he had prized so highly because it was her handiwork that he had caused a search to be made for it through the temple in A-lur after his release, and it had been found and brought to him. He had told her laughingly that it should have the place of honor above their hearth as the ancient flintlock of her Puritan grandsire had held a similar place of honor above the fireplace of Professor Porter, her father.

At the sound of the bellowing the Ho-don warriors, some of whom had accompanied Tarzan from Ja-don's camp to Ja-lur, looked questioningly at the ape-man while Om-at's Waz-don looked for trees, since the *gryf* was the one creature of Pal-ul-don which might not be safely encountered even by a great multitude of warriors. Its tough, armored hide was impregnable to their knife thrusts while their thrown clubs rattled from it as futilely as if hurled at the rocky shoulder of Pastar-ul-ved.

'Wait,' said the ape-man, and with his spear in hand he advanced toward the *gryf*, voicing the weird cry of the Tor-o-don. The bellowing ceased and turned to low rumblings and presently the huge beast appeared. What followed was but a repetition of the ape-man's previous experience with these huge and ferocious creatures.

And so it was that Jane and Korak and Tarzan rode through the morass that hems Pal-ul-don, upon the back of a prehistoric triceratops while the lesser reptiles of the swamp fled hissing in terror. Upon the opposite shore they turned and called back their farewells to Ta-den and Om-at and the brave warriors they had learned to admire and respect. And then Tarzan urged their titanic mount onward toward the north, abandoning him only when he was assured that the Waz-don and the Ho-don had had time to reach a point of comparative safety among the craggy ravines of the foothills.

Turning the beast's head again toward Pal-ul-don the three dismounted and a sharp blow upon the thick hide sent the creature lumbering majestically back in the direction of its native haunts. For a time they stood looking back upon the land they had just quit – the land of Tor-o-don and *gryf;* of *ja* and *jato;* of Waz-don and Ho-don; a primitive land of terror and sudden death and peace and beauty; a land that they all had learned to love.

And then they turned once more toward the north and with light hearts and brave hearts took up their long journey toward the land that is best of all – home.

GLOSSARY

From conversations with Lord Greystoke and from his notes, there have been gleaned a number of interesting items relative to the language and customs of the inhabitants of Pal-ul-don that are not brought out in the story. For the benefit of those who may care to delve into the derivation of the proper names used in the text, and thus obtain some slight insight into the language of the race, there is appended an incomplete glossary taken from some of Lord Greystoke's notes.

A point of particular interest hinges upon the fact that the names of all male hairless pithecanthropi begin with a consonant, have an even number of syllables, and end with a consonant, while the names of the females of the same species begin with a vowel, have an odd number of syllables, and end with a vowel. On the contrary, the names of the male hairy black pithecanthropi while having an even number of syllables begin with a vowel and end with a consonant; while the females of this species have an odd number of syllables in their names which begin always with a consonant and end with a vowel.

A. Light.
ab. Boy.
Ab-on. Acting *gund* of Kor-ul-ja.
Ad. Three.
Adad. Six.
Adadad. Nine.
Adaden. Seven.
Aden. Four.
Adenaden. Eight.
Adenen. Five.
A-lur. City of light
An. Spear.
An-un. Father of Pan-at-lee.
As. The sun.
At. Tail.

Bal. Gold or golden.
Bar. Battle.

Ben. Great.
Bu. Moon.
Bu-lot (moon face). Son of chief Mo-sar.
Bu-lur (moon city). The city of the Waz-ho-don.

Dak. Fat.
Dak-at (fat tail). Chief of a Ho-don village.
Dak-lot. One of Ko-tan's palace warriors.
Dan. Rock.
Den. Tree.
Don. Man.
Dor. Son.
Dor-ul-Otho (son of god). Tarzan.

E. Where.
Ed. Seventy.
El. Grace or graceful.
En. One.
Enen. Two.
Es. Rough.
Es-sat (rough skin). Chief of Om-at's tribe of hairy blacks.
Et. Eighty.

Fur. Thirty.

Ged. Forty.
Go. Clear.
Gryf. 'Triceratops. A genus of huge herbivorous dinosaurs of the group Ceratopsia. The skull had two large horns above the eyes, a median horn on the nose, a horny beak, and a great bony hood or transverse crest over the neck. Their toes, five in front and three behind, were provided with hoofs, and the tail was large and strong.' Webster's Dict. The *gryf* of Pal-ul-don is similar except that it is omnivorous, has strong, powerfully armed jaws and talons instead of hoofs. Coloration: face yellow with blue bands encircling the eyes; hood red on top, yellow underneath; belly yellow; body a dirty, slate blue; legs same. Bony protuberances yellow except along the spine – these are red. Tail conforms with body and belly. Horns, ivory.
Gund. Chief.
Guru. Terrible.

Het. Fifty.
Ho. White.

Ho-don. The hairless white men of Pal-ul-don.

Id. Silver.
Id-an. One of Pan-at-lee's two brothers.
In. Dark
In-sad. Kor-ul-ja warrior accompanying Tarzan, Om-at, and Ta-den in search of Pan-at-lee.
In-tan. Kor-ul-lul left to guard Tarzan.

Ja. Lion.
Jad. The.
Jad-bal-lul. The golden lake.
Jad-ben-lul. The big lake.
Jad-ben-Otho. The Great God.
Jad-guru-don. The terrible man.
Jad-in-lul. The dark lake.
Ja-don (the lion-man). Chief of a Ho-don village and father of Ta-den.
Jad Pele ul Jad-ben-Otho. The valley of the Great God.
Ja-lur (lion city). Ja-don's capital.
Jar. Strange.
Jar-don. Name given Korak by Om-at.
Jato. Saber-tooth hybrid.

Ko. Mighty.
Kor. Gorge.
Kor-ul-gryf. Gorge of the *gryf*.
Kor-ul-ja. Name of Es-sat's gorge and tribe.
Kor-ul-lul. Name of another Waz-don gorge and tribe.
Ko-tan. King of the Ho-don.

Lav. Run or running.
Lee. Doe.
Lo. Star.
Lot. Face.
Lu. Fierce.
Lu-don (fierce man). High priest of A-lur.
Lul. Water.
Lur. City.

Ma. Child.
Mo. Short.
Mo-sar (short nose). Chief and pretender.

Mu. Strong.

No. Brook.

O. Like or similar.
Od. Ninety.
O-dan. Kor-ul-ja warrior accompanying Tarzan, Om-at, and Ta-den in search of Pan-at-lee.
Og. Sixty.
O-lo-a (like-star-light). Ko-tan's daughter.
Om. Long.
Om-at (long tail). A black.
On. Ten.
Otho. God.

Pal. Place; land; country.
Pal-e-don-so (place where men eat). Banquet hall.
Pal-ul-don (land of man). Name of the country.
Pal-ul-ja. Place of lions.
Pan. Soft.
Pan-at-lee. Om-at's sweetheart.
Pan-sat (soft skin). A priest.
Pastar. Father.
Pastar-ul-ved. Father of Mountains.
Pele. Valley.

Ro. Flower.

Sad. Forest.
San. One hundred.
Sar. Nose.
Sat. Skin.
So. Eat.
Sod. Eaten.
Sog. Eating.
Son. Ate.

Ta. Tall.
Ta-den (tall tree). A white.
Tan. Warrior.
Tarzan-jad-guru. Tarzan the Terrible.
To. Purple.

Ton. Twenty.
Tor. Beast.
Tor-o-don. Beastlike man.
Tu. Bright.
Tu-lur (bright city). Mo-sar's city.

Ul. Of.
Un. Eye.
Ut. Corn.

Ved. Mountain.

Waz. Black.
Waz-don. The hairy black men of Pal-ul-don.
Waz-ho-don (black white men). A mixed race.

Xot. One thousand.

Yo. Friend.

Za. Girl.

TARZAN AND THE GOLDEN LION

1

The Golden Lion

Sabor, the lioness, suckled her young – a single fuzzy ball, spotted like Sheeta, the leopard. She lay in the warm sunshine before the rocky cavern that was her lair, stretched out upon her side with half closed eyes, yet Sabor was alert. There had been three of these little, fuzzy balls at first – two daughters and a son – and Sabor and Numa, their sire, had been proud of them; proud and happy. But kills had not been plentiful, and Sabor, undernourished, had been unable to produce sufficient milk to nourish properly three lusty cubs, and then a cold rain had come, and the little ones had sickened. Only the strongest survived – the two daughters had died. Sabor had mourned, pacing to and fro beside the pitiful bits of bedraggled fur, whining and moaning. Now and again she would nose them with her muzzle as though she would awaken them from the long sleep that knows no waking. At last, however, she abandoned her efforts, and now her whole savage heart was filled with concern for the little male cub that remained to her. That was why Sabor was more alert than usual.

Numa, the lion, was away. Two nights before he had made a kill and dragged it to their lair and last night he had fared forth again, but he had not returned. Sabor was thinking, as she half dozed, of Wappi, the plump antelope, that her splendid mate might this very minute be dragging through the tangled jungle to her. Or perhaps it would be Pacco, the zebra, whose flesh was the best beloved of her kind – juicy, succulent Pacco. Sabor's mouth watered.

Ah, what was that? The shadow of a sound had come to those keen ears. She raised her head, cocking it first upon one side and then the other, as with up-pricked ears she sought to catch the faintest repetition of that which had disturbed her. Her nose sniffed the air. There was but the suggestion of a breeze, but what there was moved toward her from the direction of the sound she had heard, and which she still heard in a slightly increasing volume that told her that whatever was making it was approaching her. As it drew closer the beast's nervousness increased and she rolled over on her belly, shutting off the milk supply from the cub, which vented its disapproval in miniature growls until a low, querulous whine from the lioness silenced him, then he stood at her side, looking first at her and then in the direction toward which she looked, cocking his little head first on one side and then on the other.

Evidently there was a disturbing quality in the sound that Sabor heard – something that inspired a certain restlessness, if not actual apprehension – though she could not be sure as yet that it boded ill. It might be her great lord returning, but it did not sound like the movement of a lion, certainly not like a lion dragging a heavy kill. She glanced at her cub, breathing as she did so a plaintive whine. There was always the fear that some danger menaced him – this last of her little family – but she, Sabor the lioness, was there to defend him.

Presently the breeze brought to her nostrils the scent-spoor of the thing that moved toward her through the jungle. Instantly the troubled mother-face was metamorphosed into a bare-fanged, glittering-eyed mask of savage rage, for the scent that had come up to her through the jungle was the hated man-scent. She rose to her feet, her head flattened, her sinuous tail twitching nervously. Through that strange medium by which animals communicate with one another she cautioned her cub to lie down and remain where he was until she returned, then she moved rapidly and silently to meet the intruder.

The cub had heard what its mother heard and now he caught the smell of man – an unfamiliar smell that had never impinged upon his nostrils before, yet a smell that he knew at once for that of an enemy – a smell that brought a reaction as typical as that which marked the attitude of the grown lioness, bringing the hairs along his little spine erect and baring his tiny fangs. As the adult moved quickly and stealthily into the underbrush the small cub, ignoring her injunction, followed after her, his hind quarters wobbling from side to side, after the manner of the very young of his kind, the ridiculous gait comporting ill with the dignified bearing of his fore quarters; but the lioness, intent upon that which lay before her, did not know that he followed her.

There was dense jungle before the two for a hundred yards, but through it the lions had worn a tunnel-like path to their lair; and then there was a small clearing through which ran a well-worn jungle trail, out of the jungle at one end of the clearing and into the jungle again at the other. As Sabor reached the clearing she saw the object of her fear and hatred well within it. What if the man-thing were not hunting her or hers? What if he even dreamed not of their presence? These facts were as nothing to Sabor, the lioness, today. Ordinarily she would have let him pass unmolested, so long as he did not come close enough to threaten the safety of her cub; or, cubless, she would have slunk away at the first intimation of his approach. But today the lioness was nervous and fearful – fearful because of the single cub that remained to her – her maternal instinct centered threefold, perhaps, upon this lone and triply loved survivor – and so she did not wait for the man to threaten the safety of her little one; but instead she moved to meet him and to stop him. From the soft mother she had become a terrifying creature of destruction, her brain obsessed by a single thought – to kill.

She did not hesitate an instant at the edge of the clearing, nor did she give the slightest warning. The first intimation that the black warrior had that there was a lion within twenty miles of him, was the terrifying apparition of this devil-faced cat charging across the clearing toward him with the speed of an arrow. The black was not searching for lions. Had he known that there was one near he would have given it a wide berth. He would have fled now had there been anywhere to flee. The nearest tree was farther from him than was the lioness. She could overhaul him before he would have covered a quarter of the distance. There was no hope and there was only one thing to do. The beast was almost upon him and behind her he saw a tiny cub. The man bore a heavy spear. He carried it far back with his right hand and hurled it at the very instant that Sabor rose to seize him. The spear passed through the savage heart and almost simultaneously the giant jaws closed upon the face and skull of the warrior. The momentum of the lioness carried the two heavily to the ground, dead except for a few spasmodic twitchings of their muscles.

The orphaned cub stopped twenty feet away and surveyed the first great catastrophe of his life with questioning eyes. He wanted to approach his dam but a natural fear of the man-scent held him away. Presently he commenced to whine in a tone that always brought his mother to him hurriedly; but this time she did not come – she did not even rise and look toward him. He was puzzled – he could not understand it. He continued to cry, feeling all the while more sad and more lonely. Gradually he crept closer to his mother. He saw that the strange creature she had killed did not move and after a while he felt less terror of it, so that at last he found the courage to come quite close to his mother and sniff at her. He still whined to her, but she did not answer. It dawned on him at last that there was something wrong – that his great, beautiful mother was not as she had been – a change had come over her; yet still he clung to her, crying much until at last he fell asleep, cuddled close to her dead body.

It was thus that Tarzan found him – Tarzan and Jane, his wife, and their son, Korak the Killer, returning from the mysterious land of Pal-ul-don from which the two men had rescued Jane Clayton. At the sound of their approach the cub opened his eyes and rising, flattened his ears and snarled at them, backing close against his dead mother. At sight of him the ape-man smiled.

'Plucky little devil,' he commented, taking in the story of the tragedy at a single glance. He approached the spitting cub, expecting it to turn and run away; but it did nothing of the sort. Instead it snarled more ferociously and struck at his extended hand as he stooped and reached for it.

'What a brave little fellow,' cried Jane. 'Poor little orphan!'

'He's going to make a great lion, or he would have if his dam had lived,' said Korak. 'Look at that back – as straight and strong as a spear. Too bad the rascal has got to die.'

'He doesn't have to die,' returned Tarzan.

'There's not much chance for him – he'll need milk for a couple of months more, and who's going to get it for him?'

'I am,' replied Tarzan.

'You're going to adopt him?'

Tarzan nodded.

Korak and Jane laughed. 'That'll be fine,' commented the former.

'Lord Greystoke, foster mother to the son of Numa,' laughed Jane.

Tarzan smiled with them, but he did not cease his attentions toward the cub. Reaching out suddenly he caught the little lion by the scruff of its neck and then stroking it gently he talked to it in a low, crooning tone. I do not know what he said; but perhaps the cub did, for presently it ceased its struggles and no longer sought to scratch or bite the caressing hand. After that he picked it up and held it against his breast. It did not seem afraid now, nor did it even bare its fangs against this close proximity to the erstwhile hated man-scent.

'How do you do it?' exclaimed Jane Clayton.

Tarzan shrugged his broad shoulders. 'Your kind are not afraid of you – these are really my kind, try to civilize me as you will, and perhaps that is why they are not afraid of me when I give them the signs of friendship. Even this little rascal seems to know it, doesn't he?'

'I can never understand it,' commented Korak. 'I think I am rather familiar with African animals, yet I haven't the power over them or the understanding that you have. Why is it?'

'There is but one Tarzan,' said Lady Greystoke, smiling at her son teasingly, and yet her tone was not without a note of pride.

'Remember that I was born among beasts and raised by beasts,' Tarzan reminded him. 'Perhaps after all my father was an ape – you know Kala always insisted that he was.'

'John! How can you?' exclaimed Jane. 'You know perfectly well who your father and mother were.'

Tarzan looked solemnly at his son and closed one eye. 'Your mother never can learn to appreciate the fine qualities of the anthropoids. One might almost think that she objected to the suggestion that she had mated with one of them.'

'John Clayton, I shall never speak to you again if you don't stop saying such hideous things. I am ashamed of you. It is bad enough that you are an unregenerate wild-man, without trying to suggest that you may be an ape into the bargain.'

The long journey from Pal-ul-don was almost completed – inside the week they should be again at the site of their former home. Whether anything now remained of the ruins the Germans had left was problematical. The barns and outhouses had all been burned and the interior of the bungalow partially wrecked. Those of the Waziri, the faithful native retainers of the Greystokes, who had not been killed by Hauptman Fritz Schneider's soldiers, had rallied to the beat of the war-drum and gone to place themselves at the disposal of the English in whatever capacity they might be found useful to the great cause of humanity. This much Tarzan had known before he set out in search of Lady Jane; but how many of his warlike Waziri had survived the war and what further had befallen his vast estates he did not know. Wandering tribes of natives, or raiding bands of Arab slavers might have completed the demolition inaugurated by the Hun, and it was likely, too, that the jungle had swept up and reclaimed its own, covering his clearings and burying amidst its riot of lush verdure every sign of man's brief trespass upon its world-old preserves.

Following the adoption of the tiny Numa, Tarzan was compelled to an immediate consideration of the needs of his *protégé* in planning his marches and his halts, for the cub must have sustenance and that sustenance could be naught but milk. Lion's milk was out of the question, but fortunately they were now in a comparatively well peopled country where villages were not infrequent and where the great Lord of the Jungle was known, feared, and respected, and so it was that upon the afternoon of the day he had found the young lion Tarzan approached a village for the purpose of obtaining milk for the cub.

At first the natives appeared sullen and indifferent, looking with contempt upon whites who traveled without a large safari – with contempt and without fear. With no safari these strangers could carry no presents for them, nor anything wherewith to repay for the food they would doubtless desire, and with no askari they could not demand food, or rather they could not enforce an order, nor could they protect themselves should it seem worthwhile to molest them. Sullen and indifferent the natives seemed, yet they were scarce unconcerned, their curiosity being aroused by the unusual apparel and ornamentation of these whites. They saw them almost as naked as themselves and armed similarly except that one, the younger man, carried a rifle. All three wore the trappings of Pal-ul-don, primitive and barbaric, and entirely strange to the eyes of the simple blacks.

'Where is your chief?' asked Tarzan as he strode into the village amongst the women, the children, and the yapping dogs.

A few dozing warriors rose from the shadows of the huts where they had been lying and approached the newcomers.

'The chief sleeps,' replied one. 'Who are you to awaken him? What do you want?'

'I wish to speak to your chief. Go and fetch him!'

The warrior looked at him in wide-eyed amaze, and then broke into a loud laugh.

'The chief must be brought to him,' he cried, addressing his fellows, and then, laughing loudly, he slapped his thigh and nudged those nearest him with his elbows.

'Tell him,' continued the ape-man, 'that Tarzan would speak with him.'

Instantly the attitude of his auditors underwent a remarkable transformation – they fell back from him and they ceased laughing – their eyes very wide and round. He who had laughed loudest became suddenly solemn. 'Bring mats,' he cried, 'for Tarzan and his people to sit upon, while I fetch Umanga the chief,' and off he ran as fast as he could as though glad of the excuse to escape the presence of the mighty one he feared he had offended.

It made no difference now that they had no safari, no askari, nor any presents. The villagers were vying with one another to do them honor. Even before the chief came many had already brought presents of food and ornaments. Presently Umanga appeared. He was an old man who had been a chief even before Tarzan of the Apes was born. His manner was patriarchal and dignified and he greeted his guest as one great man might greet another, yet he was undeniably pleased that the Lord of the Jungle had honored his village with a visit.

When Tarzan explained his wishes and exhibited the lion cub Umanga assured him that there would be milk a-plenty so long as Tarzan honored them with his presence – warm milk, fresh from the chiefs own goats. As they palavered the apeman's keen eyes took in every detail of the village and its people, and presently they alighted upon a large bitch among the numerous curs that overran the huts and the street. Her udder was swollen with milk and the sight of it suggested a plan to Tarzan. He jerked a thumb in the direction of the animal. 'I would buy her,' he said to Umanga.

'She is yours, Bwana, without payment,' replied the chief. 'She whelped two days since and last night her pups were all stolen from her nest, doubtless by a great snake; but if you will accept them I will give you instead as many younger and fatter dogs as you wish, for I am sure that this one would prove poor eating.'

'I do not wish to eat her,' replied Tarzan. 'I will take her along with me to furnish milk for the cub. Have her brought to me.'

Some boys then caught the animal and tying a thong about its neck dragged it to the ape-man. Like the lion, the dog was at first afraid, for the scent of the Tarmangani was not as the scent of the blacks, and it snarled and snapped at its new master; but at length he won the animal's confidence so that it lay quietly beside him while he stroked its head. To get the lion close to it was, however, another matter, for here both were terrified by the enemy scent of the other – the lion snarling and spitting and the dog bare-fanged and growling. It required patience – infinite patience – but at last the thing was an accomplished fact and the cur bitch suckled the son of Numa. Hunger had succeeded in overcoming the natural suspicion of the lion, while the firm yet kindly attitude of the ape-man had won the confidence of the canine, which had been accustomed through life to more of cuffs and kicks than kindness.

That night Tarzan had the dog tied in the hut he occupied, and twice before morning he made her lie while the cub fed. The next day they took leave of Umanga and his people and with the dog still upon a leash trotting beside them they set off once more toward home, the young lion cuddled in the hollow of one of Tarzan's arms or carried in a sack slung across his shoulder.

They named the lion Jad-bal-ja, which in the language of the pithecanthropi of Pal-ul-don, means the Golden Lion, because of his color. Every day he became more accustomed to them and to his foster mother, who finally came to accept him as flesh of her flesh. The bitch they called Za, meaning girl. The second day they removed her leash and she followed them willingly through the jungle, nor ever after did she seek to leave them, nor was happy unless she was near one of the three.

As the moment approached when the trail should break from the jungle onto the edge of the rolling plain where their home had been, the three were filled with suppressed excitement, though none uttered a syllable of the hope and fear that was in the heart of each. What would they find? What *could* they find other than the same tangled mass of vegetation that the ape-man had cleared away to build his home when first he had come there with his bride?

At last they stepped from the concealing verdure of the forest to look out across the plain where, in the distance, the outlines of the bungalow had once been clearly discernible nestled amidst the trees and shrubs that had been retained or imported to beautify the grounds.

'Look!' cried Lady Jane. 'It is there – it is still there!'

'But what are those other things to the left, beyond it?' asked Korak.

'They are the huts of natives,' replied Tarzan.

'The fields are being cultivated!' exclaimed the woman.

'And some of the outbuildings have been rebuilt,' said Tarzan. 'It can mean but one thing – the Waziri have come back from the war – my faithful Waziri. They have restored what the Hun destroyed and are watching over our home until we return.'

2
The Training of Jad-bal-ja

And so Tarzan of the Apes, and Jane Clayton, and Korak came home after a long absence and with them came Jad-bal-ja, the golden lion, and Za, the bitch. Among the first to meet them and to welcome them home was old Muviro, father of Wasimbu, who had given his life in defense of the home and wife of the ape-man.

'Ah, Bwana,' cried the faithful black, 'my old eyes are made young again by the sight of you. It has been long that you have been gone, but though many doubted that you would return, old Muviro knew that the great world held nothing that might overcome his master. And so he knew, too, that his master would return to the home of his love and the land where his faithful Waziri awaited him; but that she, whom we have mourned as dead, should have returned is beyond belief, and great shall be the rejoicing in the huts of the Waziri tonight. And the earth shall tremble to the dancing feet of the warriors and the heavens ring with the glad cries of their women, since the three they love most on earth have come back to them.'

And in truth, great indeed was the rejoicing in the huts of the Waziri. And not for one night alone, but for many nights did the dancing and the rejoicing continue until Tarzan was compelled to put a stop to the festivities that he and his family might gain a few hours of unbroken slumber. The ape-man found that not only had his faithful Waziri, under the equally faithful guidance of his English foreman, Jervis, completely rehabilitated his stables, corrals, and outbuildings as well as the native huts, but had restored the interior of the bungalow, so that in all outward appearances the place was precisely as it had been before the raid of the Germans.

Jervis was at Nairobi on the business of the estate, and it was some days after their arrival that he returned to the ranch. His surprise and happiness were no less genuine than those of the Waziri. With the chief and warriors he sat for hours at the feet of the Big Bwana, listening to an account of the strange land of Pal-ul-don and the adventures that had befallen the three during Lady Greystoke's captivity there, and with the Waziri he marveled at the queer pets the ape-man had brought back with him. That Tarzan might have fancied a mongrel native cur was strange enough, but that he should have adopted a cub of his hereditary enemies, Numa and Sabor, seemed beyond all belief. And equally surprising to them all was the manner of Tarzan's education of the cub.

The golden lion and his foster mother occupied a corner of the ape-man's bedroom, and many was the hour each day that he spent in training and educating the little spotted, yellow ball – all playfulness and affection now, but one day to grow into a great, savage beast of prey.

As the days passed and the golden lion grew, Tarzan taught it many tricks – to fetch and carry, to lie motionless in hiding at his almost inaudible word of command, to move from point to point as he indicated, to hunt for hidden things by scent and to retrieve them, and when meat was added to its diet he fed it always in a way that brought grim smiles to the savage lips of the Waziri warriors, for Tarzan had built for him a dummy in the semblance of a man and the meat that the lion was to eat was fastened always at the throat of the dummy. Never did the manner of feeding vary. At a word from the ape-man the golden lion would crouch, belly to the ground, and then Tarzan would point at the dummy and whisper the single word 'kill.' However hungry he might be, the lion learned never to move toward his meat until that single word had been uttered by its master; and then with a rush and a savage growl it drove straight for the flesh. While it was little it had difficulty at first in clambering up the dummy to the savory morsel fastened at the figure's throat, but as it grew older and larger it gained the objective more easily, and finally a single leap would carry it to its goal and down would go the dummy upon its back with the young lion tearing at its throat.

There was one lesson that, of all the others, was most difficult to learn and it is doubtful that any other than Tarzan of the Apes, reared by beasts, among beasts, could have overcome the savage blood-lust of the carnivore and rendered his natural instinct subservient to the will of his master. It took weeks and months of patient endeavor to accomplish this single item of the lion's education, which consisted in teaching him that at the word 'fetch' he must find any indicated object and return with it to his master, even the dummy with raw meat tied at its throat, and that he must not touch the meat nor harm the dummy nor any other article that he was fetching, but place them carefully at the ape-man's feet. Afterward he learned always to be sure of his reward, which usually consisted in a double portion of the meat that he loved best.

Lady Greystoke and Korak were often interested spectators of the education of the golden lion, though the former expressed mystification as to the purpose of such elaborate training of the young cub and some misgivings as to the wisdom of the ape-man's program.

'What in the world can you do with such a brute after he is grown?' she asked. 'He bids fair to be a mighty Numa. Being accustomed to men he will be utterly fearless of them, and having fed always at the throat of a dummy he will look there at the throat of living men for his food hereafter.'

'He will feed only upon what I tell him to feed,' replied the ape-man.

'But you do not expect him to feed always upon men?' she interrogated, laughingly.

'He will never feed upon men.'

'But how can you prevent it, having taught him from cub-hood always to feed upon men?'

'I am afraid, Jane, that you under-estimate the intelligence of a lion, or else I very much over-estimate it. If your theory is correct the hardest part of my work is yet before me, but if I am right it is practically complete now. However, we will experiment a bit and see which is right. We shall take Jad-bal-ja out upon the plain with us this afternoon. Game is plentiful and we shall have no difficulty in ascertaining just how much control I have over young Numa after all.'

'I'll wager a hundred pounds,' said Korak, laughing, 'that he does just what he jolly well pleases after he gets a taste of live blood.'

'You're on, my son,' said the ape-man. 'I think I am going to show you and your mother this afternoon what you or anyone else never dreamed could be accomplished.'

'Lord Greystoke, the world's premier animal trainer!' cried Lady Greystoke, and Tarzan joined them in their laughter.

'It is not animal training,' said the ape-man. 'The plan upon which I work would be impossible to anyone but Tarzan of the Apes. Let us take a hypothetical case to illustrate what I mean. There comes to you some creature whom you hate, whom by instinct and heredity you consider a deadly enemy. You are afraid of him. You understand no word that he speaks. Finally, by means sometimes brutal he impresses upon your mind his wishes. You may do the thing he wants, but do you do it with a spirit of unselfish loyalty? You do not – you do it under compulsion, hating the creature that forces his will upon you. At any moment that you felt it was in your power to do so, you would disobey him. You would even go further – you would turn upon him and destroy him. On the other hand, there comes to you one with whom you are familiar; he is a friend, a protector. He understands and speaks the language that you understand and speak. He has fed you, he has gained your confidence by kindness and protection, he asks you to do something for him. Do you refuse? No, you obey willingly. It is thus that the golden lion will obey me.'

'As long as it suits his purpose to do so,' commented Korak.

'Let me go a step farther then,' said the ape-man. 'Suppose that this creature, whom you love and obey, has the power to punish, even to kill you, if it is necessary so to do to enforce his commands. How then about your obedience?'

'We'll see,' said Korak, 'how easily the golden lion will make one hundred pounds for me.'

That afternoon they set out across the plain, Jad-bal-ja following Tarzan's horse's heels. They dismounted at a little clump of trees some distance from the bungalow and from there proceeded onward warily toward a swale in which antelopes were usually to be found, moving up which they came cautiously to the heavy brush that bordered the swale upon their side. There was Tarzan, Jane, and Korak, and close beside Tarzan the golden lion – four jungle hunters – and of the four Jad-bal-ja, the lion, was the least accomplished. Stealthily they crawled through the brush, scarce a leaf rustling to their passage, until at last they looked down into the swale upon a small herd of antelope grazing peacefully below. Closest to them was an old buck, and him Tarzan pointed out in some mysterious manner to Jad-bal-ja.

'Fetch him,' he whispered, and the golden lion rumbled a scarce audible acknowledgment of the command.

Stealthily he worked his way through the brush. The antelopes fed on, unsuspecting. The distance separating the lion from his prey was over great for a successful charge, and so Jad-bal-ja waited, hiding in the brush, until the antelope should either graze closer to him or turn its back toward him. No sound came from the four watching the grazing herbivora, nor did the latter give any indication of a suspicion of the nearness of danger. The old buck moved closer to Jad-bal-ja. Almost imperceptibly the lion was gathering for the charge. The only noticeable movement was the twitching of his tail's tip, and then, as lightning from the sky, as an arrow from a bow, he shot from immobility to tremendous speed in an instant. He was almost upon the buck before the latter realized the proximity of danger, and then it was too late, for scarcely had the antelope wheeled than the lion rose upon its hind legs and seized it, while the balance of the herd broke into precipitate flight.

'Now,' said Korak, 'we shall see.'

'He will bring the antelope to me,' said Tarzan confidently.

The golden lion hesitated a moment, growling over the carcass of his kill. Then he seized it by the back and with his head turned to one side dragged it along the ground beside him, as he made his way slowly back toward Tarzan. Through the brush he dragged the slain antelope until he had dropped it at the feet of his master, where he stood, looking up at the face of the ape-man with an expression that could not have been construed into aught but pride in his achievement and a plea for commendation.

Tarzan stroked his head and spoke to him in a low voice, praising him, and then, drawing his hunting knife, he cut the jugular of the antelope and let the blood from the carcass. Jane and Korak stood close, watching Jad-bal-ja – what would the lion do with the smell of fresh, hot blood in his nostrils? He sniffed at it and growled, and with bared fangs he eyed the three wickedly. The ape-man pushed him away with his open palm and the lion growled again angrily and snapped at him.

Quick is Numa, quick is Bara, the deer, but Tarzan of the Apes is lightning. So swiftly did he strike, and so heavily, that Jad-bal-ja was falling on his back almost in the very instant that he had growled at his master. Swiftly he came to his feet again and the two stood facing one another.

'Down!' commanded the ape-man. 'Lie down, Jad-bal-ja!' His voice was low and firm. The lion hesitated but for an instant, and then lay down as Tarzan of the Apes had taught him to do at the word of command. Tarzan turned and lifted the carcass of the antelope to his shoulder.

'Come,' he said to Jad-bal-ja. 'Heel!' and without another glance at the carnivore he moved off toward the horses.

'I might have known it,' said Korak, with a laugh, 'and saved my hundred pounds.'

'Of course you might have known it,' said his mother.

3
A Meeting of Mystery

A rather attractive-looking, though over-dressed, young woman was dining in a second-rate chop-house in London. She was noticeable, not so much for her fine figure and coarsely beautiful face as for the size and appearance of her companion, a large, well-proportioned man in the mid-twenties, with such a tremendous beard that it gave him the appearance of hiding in ambush. He stood fully three inches over six feet. His shoulders were broad, his chest deep, and his hips narrow. His physique, his carriage, everything about him, suggested indubitably the trained athlete.

The two were in close conversation, a conversation that occasionally gave every evidence of bordering upon heated argument.

'I tell you,' said the man, 'that I do not see what we need of the others. Why should they share with us – why divide into six portions that which you and I might have alone?'

'It takes money to carry the plan through,' she replied, 'and neither you nor I have any money. *They* have it and they will back us with it – me for my knowledge and you for your appearance and your strength. They searched for you, Esteban, for two years, and, now that they have found you, I should not care to be in your shoes if you betrayed them. They would just as soon slit your throat as not, Esteban, if they no more than thought they couldn't use you, now that you have all the details of their plan. But if you should try to take all the profit from them—' She paused, shrugging her shoulders. 'No, my dear, I love life too well to join you in any such conspiracy as that.'

'But I tell you, Flora, we ought to get more out of it than they want to give.

You furnish all the knowledge and I take all the risk – why shouldn't we have more than a sixth apiece?'

'Talk to them yourself, then, Esteban,' said the girl, with a shrug, 'but if you will take my advice you will be satisfied with what you are offered. Not only have I the information, without which they can do nothing, but I found you into the bargain, yet I do not ask it all – I shall be perfectly satisfied with one-sixth, and I can assure you that if you do not muddle the thing, one-sixth of what you bring out will be enough for any one of us for the rest of his natural life.'

The man did not seem convinced, and the young woman had a feeling that he would bear watching. Really, she knew very little about him, and had seen him in person only a few times since her first discovery of him some two months before, upon the screen of a London cinema house in a spectacular feature in which he had played the rôle of a Roman soldier of the Pretorian Guard.

Here his heroic size and perfect physique had alone entitled him to consideration, for his part was a minor one, and doubtless of all the thousands who saw him upon the silver sheet Flora Hawkes was the only one who took more than a passing interest in him, and her interest was aroused, not by his histrionic ability, but rather because for some two years she and her confederates had been searching for such a type as Esteban Miranda so admirably represented. To find him in the flesh bade fair to prove difficult of accomplishment, but after a month of seemingly fruitless searching she finally discovered him among a score of extra men at the studio of one of London's lesser producing companies. She needed no other credentials than her good looks to form his acquaintance, and while that was ripening into intimacy she made no mention to him of the real purpose of her association with him.

That he was a Spaniard and apparently of good family was evident to her, and that he was unscrupulous was to be guessed by the celerity with which he agreed to take part in the shady transaction that had been conceived in the mind of Flora Hawkes, and the details of which had been perfected by her and her four confederates. So, therefore, knowing that he was unscrupulous, she was aware that every precaution must be taken to prevent him taking advantage of the knowledge of their plan that he must one day have in detail, the key to which she, up to the present moment, had kept entirely to herself, not even confiding it to any one of her four other confederates.

They sat for a moment in silence, toying with the empty glasses from which they had been drinking. Presently she looked up to find his gaze fixed upon her and an expression in his eyes that even a less sophisticated woman than Flora Hawkes might readily have interpreted.

'You can make me do anything you want, Flora,' he said, 'for when I am with you I forget the gold, and think only of that other reward which you continually deny me, but which one day I shall win.'

'Love and business do not mix well,' replied the girl. 'Wait until you have succeeded in this work, Esteban, and then we may talk of love.'

'You do not love me,' he whispered, hoarsely. 'I know – I have seen – that each of the others loves you. That is why I could hate them. And if I thought that you loved one of them, I could cut his heart out. Sometimes I have thought that you did – first one of them and then another. You are too familiar with them, Flora. I have seen John Peebles squeeze your hand when he thought no one was looking, and when you dance with Dick Throck he holds you too close and you dance cheek to cheek. I tell you I do not like it, Flora, and one of these days I shall forget all about the gold and think only of you, and then something will happen and there will not be so many to divide the ingots that I shall bring back from Africa. And Bluber and Kraski are almost as bad; perhaps Kraski is the worst of all, for he is a good-looking devil and I do not like the way in which you cast sheep's eyes at him.'

The fire of growing anger was leaping to the girl's eyes. With an angry gesture she silenced him.

'What business is it of yours, *Señor* Miranda, who I choose for my friends, or how I treat them or how they treat me? I will have you understand that I have known these men for years, while I have known you for but a few weeks, and if any has a right to dictate my behavior, which, thank God, none has, it would be one of them rather than you.'

His eyes blazed angrily.

'It is as I thought!' he cried. 'You love one of them.' He half rose from the table and leaned across it toward her, menacingly. 'Just let me find out which one it is and I will cut him into pieces!'

He ran his fingers through his long, black hair until it stood up on end like the mane of an angry lion. His eyes were blazing with a light that sent a chill of dread through the girl's heart. He appeared a man temporarily bereft of reason – if he were not a maniac he most certainly looked one, and the girl was afraid and realized that she must placate him.

'Come, come, Esteban,' she whispered softly, 'there is no need for working yourself into a towering rage over nothing. I have not said that I loved one of these, nor have I said that I do not love you, but I am not used to being wooed in such fashion. Perhaps your Spanish *señoritas* like it, but I am an English girl and if you love me treat me as an English lover would treat me.'

'You have not said that you loved one of these others – no, but on the other hand you have not said that you do not love one of them – tell me, Flora, which one of them is it that you love?'

His eyes were still blazing, and his great frame trembling with suppressed passion.

'I do not love any of them, Esteban,' she replied, 'nor, as yet, do I love you. But I could, Esteban, that much I will tell you. I could love you, Esteban, as I could never love another, but I shall not permit myself to do so until after you have returned and we are free to live where and how we like. Then, maybe – but, even so, I do not promise.'

'You had better promise,' he said, sullenly, though evidently somewhat mollified. 'You had better promise, Flora, for I care nothing for the gold if I may not have you also.'

'Hush,' she cautioned, 'here they come now, and it is about time; they are fully a half-hour late.'

The man turned his eyes in the direction of her gaze, and the two sat watching the approach of four men who had just entered the chop-house. Two of them were evidently Englishmen – big, meaty fellows of the middle class, who looked what they really were, former pugilists; the third, Adolph Bluber, was a short, fat German, with a round, red face and a bull neck; the other, the youngest of the four, was by far the best looking. His smooth face, clear complexion, and large dark eyes might of themselves have proven sufficient grounds for Miranda's jealousy, but supplementing these were a mop of wavy, brown hair, the figure of a Greek god and the grace of a Russian dancer, which, in truth, was what Carl Kraski was when he chose to be other than a rogue.

The girl greeted the four pleasantly, while the Spaniard vouchsafed them but a single, surly nod, as they found chairs and seated themselves at the table.

'Ale!' cried Peebles, pounding the table to attract the attention of a waiter, 'let's 'ave ale.'

The suggestion met with unanimous approval, and as they waited for their drink they spoke casually of unimportant things; the heat, the circumstance that had delayed them, the trivial occurrences since they had last met; throughout which Esteban sat in sullen silence, but after the waiter had returned and they drank to Flora, with which ceremony it had long been their custom to signalize each gathering, they got down to business.

'Now,' cried Peebles, pounding the table with his meaty fist, ''ere we are, and that's that! We 'ave everything, Flora – the plans, the money, *Señor* Miranda – and are jolly well ready, old dear, for your part of it.'

'How much money have you?' asked Flora. 'It is going to take a lot of money, and there is no use starting unless you have plenty to carry on with.'

Peebles turned to Bluber. 'There,' he said, pointing a pudgy finger at him, 'is the bloomin' treasurer. 'E can tell you 'ow much we 'ave, the fat rascal of a Dutchman.'

Bluber smiled an oily smile and rubbed his fat palms together. 'Veil,' he said, 'how much you t'ink, Miss Flora, ve should have?'

'Not less than two thousand pounds to be on the safe side,' she replied quickly.

'Ach, weh!' exclaimed Bluber. 'But dat is a lot of money – two t'ousand pounds.'

The girl made a gesture of disgust. 'I told you in the first place that I wouldn't have anything to do with a bunch of cheap screws, and that until you had enough money to carry the thing out properly I would not give you the maps and directions, without which you cannot hope to reach the vaults, where there is stored enough gold to buy this whole, tight, little island if half that what I have heard them say about it is true. You can go along and spend your own money, but you've got to show me that you have at least two thousand pounds to spend before I give up the information that will make you the richest men in the world.'

'The blighter's got the money,' growled Throck. 'Blime if I know what he's beefin' about.'

'He can't help it,' growled the Russian, 'he's that kind of chap; Bluber would try to bargain with the marriage license clerk if he were going to get married.'

'Oh, veil,' sighed Bluber, 'for vy should we spend more money than is necessary? If ve can do it for von t'ousand pounds so much the better.'

'Certainly,' snapped the girl, 'and if it doesn't take but one thousand, that is all that you will have to spend, but you've got to have the two thousand in case of emergencies, and from what I have seen of that country you are likely to run up against more emergencies than anything else.'

'Ach, weh!' cried Bluber.

''E's got the money all right,' said Peebles, 'now let's get busy.'

'He may have it, but I want to see it first,' replied the girl.

'Vat you t'ink; I carry all dat money around in my pocket?' cried Bluber.

'Can't you take our word for it?' grumbled Throck.

'You're a nice bunch of crooks to ask me that,' she replied, laughing in the face of the burly ruffians. 'I'll take Carl's word for it, though; if he tells me that you have it, and that it is in such shape that it can, and will, be used to pay all the necessary expenses of our expedition, I will believe him.'

Peebles and Throck scowled angrily, and Miranda's eyes closed to two narrow, nasty slits, as he directed his gaze upon the Russian. Bluber, on the contrary, was affected not at all; the more he was insulted, the better, apparently, he liked it. Toward one who treated him with consideration or respect he would have become arrogant, while he fawned upon the hand that struck him. Kraski, alone, smiled a self-satisfied smile that set the blood of the Spaniard boiling.

'Bluber has the money, Flora,' he said; 'each of us has contributed his share. We'll make Bluber treasurer, because we know that he will squeeze the last farthing until it shrieks before he will let it escape him. It is our plan now to set out from London in pairs.'

He drew a map from his pocket, and unfolding it, spread it out upon the table before them. With his finger he indicated a point marked X. 'Here we will meet and here we will equip our expedition. Bluber and Miranda will go first; then Peebles and Throck. By the time that you and I arrive everything will be in shape for moving immediately into the interior, where we shall establish a permanent camp, off the beaten track and as near our objective as possible. Miranda will disport himself behind his whiskers until he is ready to set out upon the final stage of his long journey. I understand that he is well schooled in the part that he is to play and that he can depict the character to perfection. As he will have only ignorant natives and wild beasts to deceive it should not tax his histrionic ability too greatly.' There was a veiled note of sarcasm in the soft, drawling tone that caused the black eyes of the Spaniard to gleam wickedly.

'Do I understand,' asked Miranda, his soft tone belying his angry scowl, 'that you and Miss Hawkes travel alone to X?'

'You do, unless your understanding is poor,' replied the Russian.

The Spaniard half rose from the table and leaned across it menacingly toward Kraski. The girl, who was sitting next to him, seized his coat.

'None of that!' she said, dragging him back into his chair. 'There has been too much of it among you already, and if there is any more I shall cut you all and seek more congenial companions for my expedition.'

'Yes, cut it out; 'ere we are, and that's that!' exclaimed Peebles belligerently.

'John's right,' rumbled Throck, in his deep bass, 'and I'm here to back him up. And if there is any more of it, blime if I don't bash a couple of you pretty 'uns,' and he looked first at Miranda and then at Kraski.

'Now,' soothed Bluber, 'let's all shake hands and be good friends.'

'Right-o,' cried Peebles, 'that's the talk. Give 'im your 'and, Esteban. Come, Carl, bury the 'atchet. We can't start in on this thing with no hanimosities, and 'ere we are, and that's that.'

The Russian, feeling secure in his position with Flora, and therefore in a magnanimous mood, extended his hand across the table toward the Spaniard. For a moment Esteban hesitated.

'Come, man, shake!' growled Throck, 'or you can go back to your job as an extra man, blime, and we'll find someone else to do your work and divvy the swag with.'

Suddenly the dark countenance of the Spaniard was lighted by a pleasant smile. He extended his hand quickly and clasped Kraski's. 'Forgive me,' he said, 'I am hot-tempered, but I mean nothing. Miss Hawkes is right, we must all be friends, and here's my hand on it, Kraski, as far as I am concerned.'

'Good,' said Kraski, 'and I am sorry if I offended you;' but he forgot that the other was an actor, and if he could have seen into the depths of that dark soul he would have shuddered.

'Und now, dat we are all good friends,' said Bluber, rubbing his hands together unctuously, 'vy not arrange for vhen ve shall commence starting to finish up everyt'ings? Miss Flora, she gives me the map und der directions und we start commencing immediately.'

'Loan me a pencil, Carl,' said the girl, and when the man had handed her one she searched out a spot upon the map some distance into the interior from X, where she drew a tiny circle. 'This is O,' she said. 'When we all reach here you shall have the final directions and not before.'

Bluber threw up his hands. '*Ach!* Miss Flora, vat you t'ink, ve spend two t'ousand pounds to buy a pig in a poke? *Ach, weh!* you vouldn't ask us to do dat? Ve must see everyt'ing, ve must know everyt'ing before ve spend vun farthing.'

'Yes, and 'ere we are, and that's that!' roared John Peebles, striking the table with his fist.

The girl rose leisurely from her seat. 'Oh, very well,' she said with a shrug. 'If you feel that way about it we might as well call it all off.'

'Oh, vait, vait, Miss Flora,' cried Bluber, rising hurriedly. 'Don't be ogcited. But can't you see vere ve are? Two t'ousand pounds is a lot of money, and ve are good business men. Ve shouldn't be spending it all vit'out getting not'ings for it.'

'I am not asking you to spend it and get nothing for it,' replied the girl, tartly; 'but if anyone has got to trust anyone else in this outfit, it is you who are going to trust me. If I give you all the information I have, there is nothing in the world that could prevent you from going ahead and leaving me out in the cold, and I don't intend that that shall happen.'

'But we are not fools, Miss Flora,' insisted Bluber. 'Ve vould not t'ink for vun minute of cheating you.'

'You're not angels, either, Bluber, any of you,' retorted the girl. 'If you want to go ahead with this you've got to do it in my way, and I am going to be there at the finish to see that I get what is coming to me. You've taken my word for it, up to the present time, that I had the dope, and now you've got to take it the rest of the way or all bets are off. What good would it do me to go over into a bally jungle and suffer all the hardships that we are bound to suffer, dragging you along with me, if I were not going to be able to deliver the goods when I got there? And I am not such a softy as to think I could get away with it with a bunch of bandits like you if I tried to put anything of that kind over on you. And as long as I do play straight I feel perfectly safe, for I know that either Esteban or Carl will look after me, and I don't know but what the rest of you would, too. Is it a go or isn't it?'

'Vell, John, vot do you und Dick t'ink?' asked Bluber, addressing the two ex-prize-fighters. 'Carl, I know he vill t'ink vhatever Flora t'inks. Hey? Vat?'

'Blime,' said Throck, 'I never was much of a hand at trusting nobody unless I had to, but it looks now as though we had to trust Flora.'

'Same 'ere,' said John Peebles. 'If you try any funny work, Flora –' He made a significant movement with his finger across his throat.

'I understand, John,' said the girl with a smile, 'and I know that you would do it as quickly for two pounds as you would for two thousand. But you are all agreed, then, to carry on according to my plans? You too, Carl?'

The Russian nodded. 'Whatever the rest say goes with me,' he remarked.

And so the gentle little coterie discussed their plans in so far as they could – each minutest detail that would be necessary to place them all at the O which the girl had drawn upon the map.

4

What the Footprints Told

When Jad-bal-ja, the golden lion, was two years old, he was as magnificent a specimen of his kind as the Greystokes had ever looked upon. In size he was far above the average of that attained by mature males; in conformation he was superb, his noble head and his great black mane giving him the appearance of a full-grown male, while in intelligence he far outranked his savage brothers of the forest.

Jad-bal-ja was a never-ending source of pride and delight to the ape-man who had trained him so carefully, and nourished him cunningly for the purpose of developing to the full all the latent powers within him. The lion no longer slept at the foot of his master's bed, but occupied a strong cage that Tarzan had constructed for him at the rear of the bungalow, for who knew better than the ape-man that a lion, wherever he may be or however he may have been raised, is yet a lion – a savage flesh-eater. For the first year he had roamed at will about the house and grounds; after that he went abroad only in the company of Tarzan. Often the two roamed the plain and the jungle hunting together. In a way the lion was almost equally as familiar with Jane and Korak, and neither of them feared or mistrusted him, but toward Tarzan of the Apes did he show the greatest affection. The blacks of Tarzan's household he tolerated, nor did he ever offer to molest any of the domestic animals or fowl, after Tarzan had impressed upon him in his early cubhood that appropriate punishment followed immediately upon any predatory excursion into the corrals or henhouses. The fact that he was never permitted to become ravenously hungry was doubtless the deciding factor in safeguarding the livestock of the farm.

The man and the beast seemed to understand one another perfectly. It is doubtful that the lion understood all that Tarzan said to him, but be that as it may the ease with which he communicated his wishes to the lion bordered upon the uncanny. The obedience that a combination of sternness and affection had elicited from the cub had become largely habit in the grown lion. At Tarzan's command he would go to great distances and bring back antelope or zebra, laying his kill at his master's feet without offering to taste the flesh himself, and he had even retrieved living animals without harming them. Such, then, was the golden lion that roamed the primeval forest with his god-like master.

It was at about this time that there commenced to drift in to the ape-man rumors of a predatory band to the west and south of his estate; ugly stories of ivory-raiding, slave-running and torture, such as had not disturbed the quiet of the ape-man's savage jungle since the days of Sheik Amor Ben Khatour, and there came other tales, too, that caused Tarzan of the Apes to pucker his brows in puzzlement and thought, and then a month elapsed during which Tarzan heard no more of the rumors from the west.

The war had reduced the resources of the Greystokes to but a meager income. They had given practically all to the cause of the Allies, and now what little had remained to them had been all but exhausted in the rehabilitation of Tarzan's African estate.

'It looks very much, Jane,' he said to his wife one night, 'as though another trip to Opar were on the books.'

'I dread to think of it. I do not want you to go,' she said. 'You have come away from that awful city twice, but barely with your life. The third time you may not be so fortunate. We have enough, John, to permit us to live here in comfort and in happiness. Why jeopardize those two things which are greater than all wealth in another attempt to raid the treasure vaults?'

'There is no danger, Jane,' he assured her. 'The last time Werper dogged my footsteps, and between him and the earthquake I was nearly done for. But there is no chance of any such combination of circumstances thwarting me again.'

'You will not go alone, John?' she asked. 'You will take Korak with you?'

'No,' he said, 'I shall not take him. He must remain here with you, for really my long absences are more dangerous to you than to me. I shall take fifty of the Waziri, as porters, to carry the gold, and thus we should be able to bring out enough to last us for a long time.'

'And Jad-bal-ja,' she asked, 'shall you take him?'

'No, he had better remain here; Korak can look after him and take him out for a hunt occasionally. I am going to travel light and fast and it would be too hard a trip for him – lions don't care to move around too much in the hot sun, and as we shall travel mostly by day I doubt if Jad-bal-ja would last long.'

And so it befell that Tarzan of the Apes set out once more upon the long trail that leads to Opar. Behind him marched fifty giant Waziri, the pick of the warlike tribe that had adopted Tarzan as its Chief. Upon the veranda of the bungalow stood Jane and Korak waving their adieux, while from the rear of the building there came to the ape-man's ears the rumbling roar of Jad-bal-ja, the golden lion. And as they marched away the voice of Numa accompanied them out upon the rolling plain, until at last it trailed off to nothingness in the distance.

His speed determined by that of the slowest of the blacks, Tarzan made but comparatively rapid progress. Opar lay a good twenty-five days' trek from the farm for men traveling light, as were these, but upon the return journey, laden as they would be with the ingots of gold, their progress would be slower. And because of this the ape-man had allotted two months for the venture. His safari, consisting of seasoned warriors only, permitted of really rapid progress. They carried no supplies, for they were all hunters and were moving through a country in which game was abundant – no need then for burdening themselves with the cumbersome inpedimenta of white huntsmen.

A thorn boma and a few leaves furnished their shelter for the night, while spears and arrows and the powers of their great white chief insured that their bellies would never go empty. With the picked men that he had brought with him Tarzan expected to make the trip to Opar in twenty-one days, though had he been traveling alone he would have moved two or three times as fast, since, when Tarzan elected to travel with speed, he fairly flew through the jungle, equally at home in it by day or by night and practically tireless.

It was on a mid-afternoon the third week of the march that Tarzan, ranging far ahead of his blacks in search of game, came suddenly upon the carcass of Bara, the deer, a feathered arrow protruding from its flank. It was evident that Bara had been wounded at some little distance from where it had lain down to die, for the location of the missile indicated that the wound could not have caused immediate death. But what particularly caught the attention of the ape-man, even before he had come close enough to make a minute examination, was the design of the arrow, and immediately he withdrew it from the body of the deer he knew it for what it was, and was filled with such wonderment as might come to you or to me were we to see a native Swazi headdress upon Broadway or the Strand, for the arrow was precisely such as one may purchase in most any sporting-goods house in any large city of the world – such an arrow as is sold and used for archery practice in the parks and suburbs. Nothing could have been more incongruous than this silly toy in the heart of savage Africa, and yet that it had done its work effectively was evident by the dead body of Bara, though the ape-man guessed that the shaft had been sped by no practiced, savage hand.

Tarzan's curiosity was aroused and also his inherent jungle caution. One must know his jungle well to survive long in it, and if one would know it well he must let no unusual occurrence or circumstance go unexplained. And so it was that Tarzan set out upon the back track of Bara for the purpose of ascertaining, if possible, the nature of Bara's slayer. The bloody spoor was easily followed and the ape-man wondered why it was that the hunter had not tracked and overtaken his quarry, which had evidently been dead since the previous day. He found that Bara had traveled far, and the sun was already low in the west before Tarzan came upon the first indications of the slayer of the animal. These were in the nature of footprints that filled him with quite as much surprise as had the arrow. He examined them carefully, and, stooping low, even sniffed at them with his sensitive nostrils. Improbable, nay impossible though it seemed, the naked footprints were those of *a white man* – a large man, probably as large as Tarzan himself. As the foster-son of Kala stood gazing upon the spoor of the mysterious stranger he ran the fingers of one hand through his thick, black hair in a characteristic gesture indicative of deep puzzlement.

What naked white man could there be in Tarzan's jungle who slew Tarzan's game with the pretty arrow of an archery club? It was incredible that there should be such a one, and yet there recurred to the ape-man's mind the vague rumors that he had heard weeks before. Determined to solve the mystery he set out now upon the trail of the stranger – an erratic trail which wound about through the jungle, apparently aimlessly, prompted, Tarzan guessed, by the ignorance of an inexperienced hunter. But night fell before he had arrived at a solution of the riddle, and it was pitch dark as the ape-man turned his steps toward camp.

He knew that his Waziri would be expecting meat and it was not Tarzan's intention to disappoint them, though he then discovered that he was not the only carnivore hunting the district that night. The coughing grunt of a lion close by apprised him of it first, and then, from the distance, the deep roar of another. But of what moment was it to the ape-man that others hunted? It would not be the first time that he had pitted his cunning, his strength, and his agility against the other hunters of his savage world – both man and beast.

And so it was that Tarzan made his kill at last, snatching it almost from under the nose of a disappointed and infuriated lion – a fat antelope that the latter had marked as his own. Throwing his kill to his shoulder almost in the path of the charging Numa, the ape-man swung lightly to the lower terraces and with a taunting laugh for the infuriated cat, vanished noiselessly into the night.

He found the camp and his hungry Waziri without trouble, and so great was their faith in him that they not for a moment doubted but that he would return with meat for them.

Early the following morning Tarzan set out again toward Opar, and directing his Waziri to continue the march in the most direct way, he left them that he might pursue further his investigations of the mysterious presence in his jungle that the arrow and the footsteps had apprised him of. Coming again to the spot at which darkness had forced him to abandon his investigations, he took up the spoor of the stranger. Nor had he followed it far before he came upon further evidence of the presence of this new and malign personality – stretched before him in the trail was the body of a giant ape, one of the tribe of great anthropoids among whom Tarzan had been raised. Protruding from the hairy abdomen of the Mangani was another of the machine-made arrows of civilization. The ape-man's eyes narrowed and a scowl darkened his brow. Who was this who dared invade his sacred preserves and slaughter thus ruthlessly Tarzan's people?

A low growl rumbled in the throat of the ape-man. Sloughed with the habiliments of civilization was the thin veneer of civilization that Tarzan wore among white men. No English lord was this who looked upon the corpse of his hairy cousin, but another jungle beast in whose breast raged the unquenchable fire of suspicion and hatred for the man-thing that is the heritage of the jungle-bred. A beast of prey viewed the bloody work of ruthless man. Nor was there in the consciousness of Tarzan any acknowledgement of his blood relationship to the killer.

Realizing that the trail had been made upon the second day before, Tarzan hastened on in pursuit of the slayer. There was no doubt in his mind but that plain murder had been committed, for he was sufficiently familiar with the traits of the Mangani to know that none of them would provoke assault unless driven to it.

Tarzan was traveling upwind, and some half-hour after he had discovered the body of the ape his keen nostrils caught the scent-spoor of others of its kind. Knowing the timidity of these fierce denizens of the jungle he moved forward now with great wariness, lest, warned of his approach, they take flight before they were aware of his identity. He did not see them often, yet he knew that there were always those among them who recalled him, and that through these he could always establish amicable relations with the balance of the tribe.

Owing to the denseness of the undergrowth Tarzan chose the middle terraces for his advance, and here, swinging freely and swiftly among the leafy boughs, he came presently upon the giant anthropoids. There were about twenty of them in the band, and they were engaged, in a little natural clearing, in their never-ending search for caterpillars and beetles, which formed important items in the diet of the Mangani.

A faint smile overspread the ape-man's face as he paused upon a great branch, himself hidden by the leafy foliage about him, and watched the little band below him. Every action, every movement of the great apes, recalled vividly to Tarzan's mind the long years of his childhood, when, protected by the fierce mother-love of Kala, the she-ape, he had ranged the jungle with the tribe of Kerchak. In the romping young, he saw again Neeta and his other childhood playmates and in the adults all the great, savage brutes he had feared in youth and conquered in manhood. The ways of man may change but the ways of the ape are the same, yesterday, today and forever.

He watched them in silence for some minutes. How glad they would be to see him when they discovered his identity! For Tarzan of the Apes was known the length and the breadth of the great jungle as the friend and protector of the Mangani. At first they would growl at him and threaten him, for they would not depend solely on either their eyes or their ears for confirmation of his identity. Not until he had entered the clearing, and bristling bulls with bared fighting fangs had circled him stiffly until they had come close enough for their nostrils to verify the evidence of their eyes and ears, would they finally accept him. Then doubtless there would be great excitement for a few minutes, until, following the instincts of the ape mind, their attention was weaned from him by a blowing leaf, a caterpillar, or a bird's egg, and then they would move about their business, taking no further notice of him more than of any other member of the tribe. But this would not come until after each individual had smelled of him, and perhaps, pawed his flesh with calloused hands.

Now it was that Tarzan made a friendly sound of greeting, and as the apes looked up stepped from his concealment into plain view of them. 'I am Tarzan of the Apes,' he said, 'mighty fighter, friend of the Mangani. Tarzan comes in friendship to his people,' and with these words he dropped lightly to the lush grass of the clearing.

Instantly pandemonium reigned. Screaming warnings, the shes raced with the young for the opposite side of the clearing, while the bulls, bristling and growling, faced the intruder.

'Come,' cried Tarzan, 'do you not know me? I am Tarzan of the Apes, friend of the Mangani, son of Kala, and king of the tribe of Kerchak.'

'We know you,' growled one of the old bulls; 'yesterday we saw you when you killed Gobu. Go away or we shall kill you.'

'I did not kill Gobu,' replied the ape-man. 'I found his dead body yesterday and I was following the spoor of his slayer, when I came upon you.'

'We saw you,' repeated the old bull; 'go away or we shall kill you. You are no longer the friend of the Mangani.'

The ape-man stood with brows contracted in thought. It was evident that these apes really believed that they had seen him kill their fellow. What was the explanation? How could it be accounted for? Did the naked footprints of the great white man whom he had been following mean more, then, than he had guessed? Tarzan wondered. He raised his eyes and again addressed the bulls.

'It was not I who killed Gobu,' he insisted. 'Many of you have known me all your lives. You know that only in fair fight, as one bull fights another, have I ever killed a Mangani. You know that, of all the jungle people, the Mangani are my best friends, and that Tarzan of the Apes is the best friend the Mangani have. How, then, could I slay one of my own people?'

'We only know,' replied the old bull, 'that we saw you kill Gobu. With our own eyes we saw you kill him. Go away quickly, therefore, or we shall kill you. Mighty fighter is Tarzan of the Apes, but mightier even than he are all the great bulls of Pagth. I am Pagth, king of the tribe of Pagth. Go away before we kill you.'

Tarzan tried to reason with them but they would not listen, so confident were they that it was he who had slain their fellow, the bull Gobu. Finally, rather than chance a quarrel in which some of them must inevitably be killed, he turned sorrowfully away. But more than ever, now, was he determined to seek out the slayer of Gobu that he might demand an accounting of one who dared thus invade his life-long domain.

Tarzan trailed the spoor until it mingled with the tracks of many men – barefooted blacks, mostly, but among them the footprints of booted white men, and once he saw the footprints of a woman or a child, which, he could not tell. The trail led apparently toward the rocky hills which protected the barren valley of Opar.

Forgetful now of his original mission and imbued only with a savage desire to wrest from the interlopers a full accounting for their presence in the jungle, and to mete out to the slayer of Gobu his just desserts, Tarzan forged ahead upon the now broad and well-marked trail of the considerable party which could not now be much more than a half-day's march ahead of him, which meant that they were now already upon the rim of the valley of Opar, if this was their ultimate destination. And what other they could have in view Tarzan could not imagine.

He had always kept closely to himself the location of Opar. In so far as he knew no white person other than Jane, and their son, Korak, knew of the location of the forgotten city of the ancient Atlantians. Yet what else could have drawn these white men, with so large a party, into the savage, unexplored wilderness which hemmed Opar upon all sides?

Such were the thoughts that occupied Tarzan's mind as he followed swiftly the trail that led toward Opar. Darkness fell, but so fresh was the spoor that the ape-man could follow it by scent even when he could not see the imprints upon the ground, and presently, in the distance, he saw the light of a camp ahead of him.

5

The Fatal Drops

At home, the life in the bungalow and at the farm followed its usual routine as it had before the departure of Tarzan. Korak, sometimes on foot and sometimes on horseback, followed the activities of the farm hands and the herders, sometimes alone, but more often in company with the white foreman, Jervis, and often, especially when they rode, Jane accompanied them.

The golden lion Korak exercised upon a leash, since he was not at all confident of his powers of control over the beast, and feared lest, in the absence of his master, Jad-bal-ja might take to the forest and revert to his natural savage state. Such a lion, abroad in the jungle, would be a distinct menace to human life, for Jad-bal-ja, reared among men, lacked that natural timidity of men that is so marked a trait of all wild beasts. Trained as he had been to make his kill at the throat of a human effigy, it required no considerable powers of imagination upon the part of Korak to visualize what might occur should the golden lion, loosed from all restraint, be thrown upon his own resources in the surrounding jungle.

It was during the first week of Tarzan's absence that a runner from Nairobi brought a cable message to Lady Greystoke, announcing the serious illness of her father in London. Mother and son discussed the situation. It would be five or six weeks before Tarzan could return, even if they sent a runner after him, and, were Jane to await him, there would be little likelihood of her reaching her father in time. Even should she depart at once, there seemed only a faint hope that she should see him alive. It was decided, therefore, that she should set out immediately, Korak accompanying her as far as Nairobi, and then returning to the ranch and resuming its general supervision until his father's return.

It is a long trek from the Greystoke estate to Nairobi, and Korak had not yet returned when, about three weeks after Tarzan's departure, a black, whose duty it was to feed and care for Jad-bal-ja, carelessly left the door of the cage unfastened while he was cleaning it. The golden lion paced back and forth while the black wielded his broom within the cage. They were old friends, and the Waziri felt no fear of the great lion, with the result that his back was as often turned to him as not. The black was working in the far corner of the cage when Jad-bal-ja paused a moment at the door at the opposite end. The beast saw that the gate hung slightly ajar upon its hinges. Silently he raised a great padded paw and inserted it in the opening – a slight pull and the gate swung in. Instantly the golden lion inserted his snout in the widened aperture, and as he swung the barrier aside the horrified black looked up to see his charge drop softly to the ground outside.

'Stop, Jad-bal-ja! Stop!' screamed the frightened black, leaping after him. But the golden lion only increased his pace, and leaping the fence, loped off in the direction of the forest.

The black pursued him with brandishing broom, emitting loud yells that brought the inmates of the Waziri huts into the open, where they joined their fellow in pursuit of the lion. Across the rolling plains they followed him, but might as well have sought to snare the elusive will-o'-the-wisp as this swift and wary fugitive, who heeded neither their blandishments nor their threats. And so it was that they saw the golden lion disappear into the primeval forest and, though they searched diligently until almost dark, they were forced at length to give up their quest and return crestfallen to the farm.

'Ah,' cried the unhappy black, who had been responsible for the escape of Jad-bal-ja, 'what will the Big Bwana say to me, what will he do to me when he finds that I have permitted the golden lion to get away!'

'You will be banished from the bungalow for a long time, Keewazi,' old Muviro assured him. 'And doubtless you will be sent to the grazing ground far to the east to guard the herd there, where you will have plenty of lions for company, though they will not be as friendly as was Jad-bal-ja. It is not half what you deserve, and were the heart of the Big Bwana not filled with love for his black children – were he like other white Bwanas old Muviro has seen – you would be lashed until you could not stand, perhaps until you died.'

'I am a man,' replied Keewazi. 'I am a warrior and a Waziri. Whatever punishment the Big Bwana inflicts I will accept as a man should.'

It was that same night that Tarzan approached the campfires of the strange party he had been tracking. Unseen by them, he halted in the foliage of a tree directly in the center of their camp, which was surrounded by an enormous thorn boma, and brilliantly lighted by numerous fires which blacks were diligently feeding with branches from an enormous pile of firewood that they had evidently gathered earlier in the day for this purpose. Near the center of the camp were several tents, and before one, in the light of a fire, sat four white men. Two of them were great, bull-necked, red-faced fellows, apparently Englishmen of the lower class, the third appeared to be short, fat, and Teutonic, while the fourth was a tall, slender, handsome fellow, with dark, wavy brown hair and regular features. He and the German were most meticulously garbed for Central African traveling, after the highly idealized standard of motion pictures, in fact either one of them might have stepped directly from a screening of the latest jungle thriller. The young man was evidently not of English descent and Tarzan mentally cataloged him, almost immediately, as a Slav. Shortly after Tarzan's arrival this one arose and entered one of the nearby tents, from which Tarzan immediately heard the sound of voices in low conversation. He could not distinguish the words, but the tones of one seemed quite distinctly feminine. The three remaining at the fire were carrying on a desultory conversation, when suddenly from near at hand beyond the boma wall, a lion's roar broke the silence of the jungle.

With a startled shriek Bluber leaped to his feet, so suddenly that he cleared the ground a good foot, and then, stepping backward, he lost his balance, tripped over his camp-stool, and sprawled upon his back.

'My Gord, Adolph!' roared one of his companions. 'If you do that again, damn me if I don't break your neck. 'Ere we are, and that's that.'

'Blime if 'e ain't worse'n a bloomin' lion,' growled the other.

Bluber crawled to his feet. '*Mein Gott!*' he cried, his voice quavering, 'I t'ought sure he vas coming over der fence. S'elp me if I ever get out of diss, neffer again – not for all der gold in Africa vould I go t'rough vat I haf been t'rough dese past t'ree mont's. *Ach, weh!* ven I t'ink of it, *Ach, du lieber!* Lions, und leopards, und rhinoceroses und hippopotamuses.'

His companions laughed. 'Dick and I tells you right along from the beginning that you 'adn't oughter come into the interior,' said one of them.

'But for vy I buy all dese clo's?' wailed the German. '*Mein Gott*, dis suit, it stands me tventy guineas, vot I stand in. Ach, had I know somet'ing, vun guinea vould have bought me my whole vardrobe – tventy guineas for dis und no vun to see it but savages und lions.'

'And you look like 'ell in it, besides,' commented one of his friends.

'Und look at it, it's all dirty and torn. How should I know it I spoil dis suit? Mit mine own eyes I see it at der Princess Teayter, how der hero spend t'ree mont's in Africa hunting lions und killing cannibals, und ven he comes oud he hasn't even got a greast spot on his pants – how should I know it Africa was so dirty und full of thorns?'

It was at this point that Tarzan of the Apes elected to drop quietly into the circle of firelight before them. The two Englishmen leaped to their feet, quite evidently startled, and Bluber turned and took a half step as though in flight, but immediately his eyes rested upon the ape-man he halted, a look of relief supplanting that of terror which had overspread his countenance, as Tarzan had dropped upon them apparently from the heavens.

'*Mein Gott*, Esteban,' shrilled the German, 'vy you come back so soon, and for vy you come back like dot, sudden – don't you suppose ve got nerves?'

Tarzan was angry, angry at these raw intruders, who dared enter without his permission, the wide domain in which he kept peace and order. When Tarzan was angry there flamed upon his forehead the scar that Bolgani, the gorilla, had placed there upon that long-gone day when the boy Tarzan had met the great beast in mortal combat, and first learned the true value of his father's hunting knife – the knife that had placed him, the comparatively weak little Tarmangani, upon an even footing with the great beasts of the jungle.

His gray eyes were narrowed, his voice came cold and level as he addressed them. 'Who are you,' he demanded, 'who dare thus invade the country of the Waziri, the land of Tarzan, without permission from the Lord of the Jungle?'

'Where do you get that stuff, Esteban,' demanded one of the Englishmen, 'and wat in 'ell are you doin' back 'ere alone and so soon? Where are your porters, and where is the bloomin' gold?'

The ape-man eyed the speaker in silence for a moment. 'I am Tarzan of the Apes,' he said. 'I do not know what you are talking about. I only know that I come in search of him who slew Gobu, the great ape; him who slew Bara, the deer, without my permission.'

'Oh, 'ell,' exploded the other Englishman, 'stow the guff, Esteban – if you're tryin' for to be funny we don't see the joke, 'ere we are, and that's that.'

Inside the tent, which the fourth white man had entered while Tarzan was watching the camp from his hiding place in the tree above, a woman, evidently suddenly stirred by terror, touched the arm of her companion frantically, and pointed toward the tall, almost naked figure of the ape-man as he stood revealed in the full light of the beast fires. 'God, Carl,' she whispered, in trembling tones, 'look!'

'What's wrong, Flora?' inquired her companion. 'I see only Esteban.'

'It is not Esteban,' hissed the girl. 'It is Lord Greystoke himself – it is Tarzan of the Apes!'

'You are mad, Flora,' replied the man, 'it cannot be he.'

'It is he, though,' she insisted. 'Do you suppose that I do not know him? Did I not work in his town house for years? Did I not see him nearly every day? Do you suppose that I do not know Tarzan of the Apes? Look at that red scar flaming on his forehead – I have heard the story of that scar and I have seen it burn scarlet when he was aroused to anger. It is scarlet now, and Tarzan of the Apes is angry.'

'Well, suppose it *is* Tarzan of the Apes, what can he do?'

'You do not know him,' replied the girl. 'You do not guess the tremendous power he wields here – the power of life and death over man and beast. If he knew our mission here not one of us would ever reach the coast alive. The very fact that he is here now makes me believe that he may have discovered our purpose, and if he has, God help us – unless – unless—'

'Unless what?' demanded the man.

The girl was silent in thought for a moment. 'There is only one way,' she said finally. 'We dare not kill him. His savage blacks would learn of it, and no power on earth could save us then. There is a way, though, if we act quickly.' She turned and searched for a moment in one of her bags, and presently she handed the man a small bottle, containing liquid. 'Go out and talk to him,' she said, 'make friends with him. Lie to him. Tell him anything. Promise anything. But get on friendly enough terms with him so that you can offer him coffee. He does not drink wine or anything with alcohol in it, but I know that he likes coffee. I have often served it to him in his room late at night upon his return from the theater or a ball. Get him to drink coffee and then you will know what to do with this.' And she indicated the bottle which the man still held in his hand.

Kraski nodded. 'I understand,' he said, and, turning, left the tent.

He had taken but a step when the girl recalled him. 'Do not let him see me. Do not let him guess that I am here or that you know me.'

The man nodded and left her. Approaching the tense figures before the fire he greeted Tarzan with a pleasant smile and a cheery word.

'Welcome,' he said, 'we are always glad to see a stranger in our camp. Sit down. Hand the gentleman a stool, John,' he said to Peebles.

The ape-man eyed Kraski as he had eyed the others. There was no answering friendly light in his eyes responding to the Russian's greeting.

'I have been trying to find out what your party is doing here,' he said sharply to the Russian, 'but they still insist that I am someone whom I am not. They are either fools or knaves, and I intend to find out which, and deal with them accordingly.'

'Come, come,' cried Kraski, soothingly. 'There must be some mistake, I am sure. But tell me, who are you?'

'I am Tarzan of the Apes,' replied the ape-man. 'No hunters enter this part of Africa without my permission. That fact is so well known that there is no chance of your having passed the coast without having been so advised. I seek an explanation, and that quickly.'

'Ah, you are Tarzan of the Apes,' exclaimed Kraski. 'Fortunate indeed are we, for now may we be set straight upon our way, and escape from our frightful dilemma is assured. We are lost, sir, inextricably lost, due to the ignorance or knavery of our guide, who deserted us several weeks ago. Surely we knew of you; who does not know of Tarzan of the Apes? But it was not our intention to cross the boundaries of your territory. We were searching farther south for specimens of the fauna of the district, which our good friend and employer, here, Mr Adolph Bluber, is collecting at great expense for presentation to a museum in his home city in America. Now I am sure that, you can tell us where we are and direct us upon our proper course.'

Peebles, Throck, and Bluber stood fascinated by Kraski's glib lies, but it was the German who first rose to the occasion. Too thick were the skulls of the English pugs to grasp quickly the clever ruse of the Russian.

'Vy yes,' said the oily Bluber, rubbing his palms together, 'dot iss it, yust vot I vas going to tell you.'

Tarzan turned sharply upon him. 'Then what was all this talk about Esteban?' he asked. 'Was it not by that name that these others addressed me?'

'Ah,' cried Bluber, 'John will haf his leetle joke. He iss ignorant of Africa; he has neffer been here before. He t'ought perhaps dat you vere a native. John he calls all der natives Esteban, und he has great jokes by himself mit dem, because he knows dey cannot onderstand vot he says. Hey John, iss it not so, vot it iss I say?' But the shrewd Bluber did not wait for John to reply. 'You see,' he went on, 've are lost, und you take us oud mit dis jungle, ve pay you anyt'ing – you name your own price.'

The ape-man only half believed him, yet he was somewhat mollified by their evidently friendly intentions. Perhaps after all they were telling him a half-truth and had, really, wandered into his territory unwittingly. That, however, he would find out definitely from their native carriers, from whom his own Waziri would wean the truth. But the matter of his having been mistaken for Esteban still piqued his curiosity, also he was still desirous of learning the identity of the slayer of Gobu, the great ape.

'Please sit down,' urged Kraski. 'We were about to have coffee and we should be delighted to have you join us. We meant no wrong in coming here, and I can assure you that we will gladly and willingly make full amends to you, or to whomever else we may have unintentionally wronged.'

To take coffee with these men would do no harm. Perhaps he had wronged them, but however that might be a cup of their coffee would place no great obligation upon him. Flora had been right in her assertion that if Tarzan of the Apes had any weakness whatsoever it was for an occasional cup of black coffee late at night. He did not accept the proffered camp stool, but squatted, ape-fashion, before them, the flickering light of the beast fires playing upon his bronzed hide and bringing into relief the gracefully contoured muscles of his godlike frame. Not as the muscles of the blacksmith or the professional strong man were the muscles of Tarzan of the Apes, but rather as those of Mercury or Apollo, so symmetrically balanced were their proportions, suggesting only the great strength that lay in them. Trained to speed and agility were they as well as to strength, and thus, clothing as they did his giant frame, they imparted to him the appearance of a demi-god.

Throck, Peebles, and Bluber sat watching him in spellbound fascination, while Kraski walked over to the cook fire to arrange for the coffee. The two Englishmen were as yet only half awakened to the fact that they had mistaken this newcomer for another, and as it was, Peebles still scratched his head and grumbled to himself in inarticulate half-denial of Kraski's assumption of the new identity of Tarzan. Bluber was inwardly terror-stricken. His keener intelligence had quickly grasped the truth of Kraski's recognition of the man for what he was rather than for what Peebles and Throck thought him to be, and, as Bluber knew nothing of Flora's plan, he was in quite a state of funk as he tried to visualize the outcome of Tarzan's discovery of them at the very threshold of Opar. He did not realize, as did Flora, that their very lives were in danger – that it was Tarzan of the Apes, a beast of the jungle, with whom they had to deal, and not John Clayton, Lord Greystoke, an English peer. Rather was Bluber considering the two thousand pounds that they stood to lose through this deplorable termination of their expedition, for he was sufficiently familiar with the reputation of the ape-man to know that they would never be permitted to take with them the gold that Esteban was very likely, at this moment, pilfering from the vaults of Opar. Really Bluber was almost upon the verge of tears when Kraski returned with the coffee, which he brought himself.

From the dark shadows of the tent's interior Flora Hawkes looked nervously out upon the scene before her. She was terrified at the possibility of discovery by her former employer, for she had been a maid in the Greystokes' London town house as well as at the African bungalow and knew that Lord Greystoke would recognize her instantly should he chance to see her. She entertained for him, now, in his jungle haunts, a fear that was possibly greater than Tarzan's true character warranted, but none the less real was it to the girl whose guilty conscience conjured all sorts of possible punishments for her disloyalty to those who had always treated her with uniform kindliness and consideration.

Constant dreaming of the fabulous wealth of the treasure vaults of Opar, concerning which she had heard so much in detail from the conversations of the Greystokes, had aroused within her naturally crafty and unscrupulous mind a desire for possession, and in consequence thereof she had slowly visualized a scheme whereby she might loot the treasure vaults of a sufficient number of the golden ingots to make her independently wealthy for life. The entire plan had been hers. She had at first interested Kraski, who had in turn enlisted the cooperation of the two Englishmen and Bluber, and these four had raised the necessary money to defray the cost of the expedition. It had been Flora who had searched for a type of man who might successfully impersonate Tarzan in his own jungle, and she had found Esteban Miranda, a handsome, powerful, and unscrupulous Spaniard, whose histrionic ability aided by the art of make-up, of which he was a past master, permitted him to impersonate almost faultlessly the character they desired him to portray, in so far, at least, as outward appearances were concerned.

The Spaniard was not only powerful and active, but physically courageous as well, and since he had shaved his beard and donned the jungle habiliments of a Tarzan, he had lost no opportunity for emulating the ape-man in every way that lay within his ability. Of jungle craft he had none of course, and personal combats with the more savage jungle beasts caution prompted him to eschew, but he hunted the lesser game with spear and arrow and practiced continually with the grass rope that was a part of his make-up.

And now Flora Hawkes saw all her well-laid plans upon the verge of destruction. She trembled as she watched the men before the fire, for her fear of Tarzan was very real, and then she became tense with nervous anticipation as she saw Kraski approaching the group with the coffee pot in one hand and cups in the other. Kraski set the pot and the cups upon the ground a little in the rear of Tarzan, and, as he filled the latter, she saw him pour a portion of the contents of the bottle she had given him into one of the cups. A cold sweat broke out upon her forehead as Kraski lifted this cup and offered it to the ape-man. Would he take it? Would he suspect? If he did suspect what horrible punishment would be meted to them all for their temerity? She saw Kraski hand another cup to Peebles, Throck, and Bluber, then return to the circle with the last one for himself. As the Russian raised it before his face and bowed politely to the ape-man, she saw the five men drink. The reaction which ensued left her weak and spent. Turning, she collapsed upon her cot, and lay there trembling, her face buried in her arm. And, outside, Tarzan of the Apes drained his cup to the last drop.

6

Death Steals Behind

During the afternoon of the day that Tarzan discovered the camp of the conspirators, a watcher upon the crumbling outer wall of the ruined city of Opar descried a party of men moving downward into the valley from the summit of the encircling cliff. Tarzan, Jane Clayton, and their black Waziri were the only strangers that the denizens of Opar had ever seen within their valley during the lifetime of the oldest among them, and only in half-forgotten legends of a by-gone past was there any suggestion that strangers other than these had ever visited Opar. Yet from time immemorial a guard had always remained upon the summit of the outer wall. Now a single knurled and crippled man-like creature was all that recalled the numerous, lithe warriors of lost Atlantis. For down through the long ages the race had deteriorated and finally, through occasional mating with the great apes, the men had become the beast-like things of modern Opar. Strange and inexplicable had been the providence of nature that had confined this deterioration almost solely to the males, leaving the females straight, well-formed, often of comely and even beautiful features, a condition that might be largely attributable to the fact that female infants possessing ape-like characteristics were immediately destroyed, while, on the other hand, boy babies who possessed purely human attributes were also done away with.

Typical indeed of the male inhabitants of Opar was the lone watcher upon the outer city wall, a short, stocky man with matted hair and beard, his tangled locks growing low upon a low, receding forehead; small, close-set eyes and fang-like teeth bore evidence of his simian ancestry, as did his short, crooked legs and long, muscular ape-like arms, all scantily hair-covered as was his torso.

As his wicked, blood-rimmed eyes watched the progress of the party across the valley toward Opar, evidences of his growing excitement were manifested in the increased rapidity of his breathing, and low, almost inaudible growls that issued from his throat. The strangers were too far distant to be recognizable only as human beings, and their number roughly to be approximated as between two and three score. Having assured himself of these two facts the watcher descended from the outer wall, crossed the space between it and the inner wall, through which he passed, and at a rapid trot crossed the broad avenue beyond and disappeared within the crumbling but still magnificent temple beyond.

Cadj, the High Priest of Opar, squatted beneath the shade of the giant trees which now overgrew what had once been one of the gardens of the ancient temple. With him were a dozen members of the lesser priesthood, the intimate cronies of the High Priest, who were startled by the sudden advent of one of the inferior members of the clan of Opar. The fellow hurried breathlessly to Cadj.

'Cadj,' he cried, 'strange men descend upon Opar! From the northwest they have come into the valley from beyond the barrier cliffs – fifty of them at least, perhaps half again that number. I saw them as I watched from the summit of the outer wall, but further than they are men I cannot say, for they are still a great distance away. Not since the great Tarmangani came among us last have there been strangers within Opar.'

'It has been many moons since the great Tarmangani who called himself Tarzan of the Apes was among us,' said Cadj. 'He promised us to return before the rain to see that no harm had befallen La, but he did not come back and La has always insisted that he is dead. Have you told any other of what you have seen?' he demanded, turning suddenly upon the messenger.

'No,' replied the latter.

'Good!' exclaimed Cadj. 'Come, we will all go to the outer wall and see who it is who dares enter forbidden Opar, and let no one breathe a word of what Blagh has told us until I give permission.'

'The word of Cadj is law until La speaks,' murmured one of the priests.

Cadj turned a scowling face upon the speaker. 'I am High Priest of Opar,' he growled. 'Who dares disobey me?'

'But La is High Priestess,' said one, 'and the High Priestess is the queen of Opar.'

'But the High Priest can offer whom he will as sacrifice in the Chamber of the Dead or to the Flaming God,' Cadj reminded the other meaningly.

'We shall keep silence, Cadj,' replied the priest, cringing.

'Good!' growled the High Priest and led the way from the garden through the corridors of the temple back toward the outer wall of Opar. From here they watched the approaching party that was in plain view of them, far out across the valley. The watchers conversed in low gutturals in the language of the great apes, interspersed with which were occasional words and phrases of a strange tongue that were doubtless corrupted forms of the ancient language of Atlantis handed down through countless generations from their human progenitors – that now extinct race whose cities and civilization lie buried deep beneath the tossing waves of the Atlantic, and whose adventurous spirit had, in remote ages, caused them to penetrate into the heart of Africa in search of gold and to build there, in duplication of their far home cities, the magnificent city of Opar.

As Cadj and his followers watched from beneath shaggy brows the strangers plodding laboriously beneath the now declining equatorial sun across the rocky, barren valley, a gray little monkey eyed them from amidst the foliage of one of the giant trees that had forced its way through the pavement of the ancient avenue behind them. A solemn, sad-faced little monkey it was, but like all his kind overcome by curiosity, and finally to such an extent that his fear of the fierce males of Opar was so considerably overcome that he at last swung lightly from the tree to the pavement, made his way through the inner wall and up the inside of the outer wall to a position in their rear where he could hide behind one of the massive granite blocks of the crumbling wall in comparative safety from detection, the while he might overhear the conversation of the Oparians, all of which that was carried on in the language of the great apes he could understand perfectly.

The afternoon was drawing to a close before the slowly moving company approaching Opar was close enough for individuals to be recognizable in any way, and then presently one of the younger priests exclaimed excitedly:

'It is he, Cadj. It is the great Tarmangani who calls himself Tarzan of the Apes. I can see him plainly; the others are all black men. He is urging them on, prodding them with his spear. They act as though they were afraid and very tired, but he is forcing them forward.'

'You are sure,' demanded Cadj, 'you are sure that it is Tarzan of the Apes?'

'I am positive,' replied the speaker, and then another of the priests joined his assurances to that of his fellow. At last they were close enough so that Cadj himself, whose eye-sight was not as good as that of the younger members of the company, realized that it was indeed Tarzan of the Apes who was returning to Opar. The High Priest scowled angrily in thought. Suddenly he turned upon the others.

'He must not come,' he cried; 'he must not enter Opar. Hasten and fetch a hundred fighting men. We will meet them as they come through the outer wall and slay them one by one.'

'But La,' cried he who had aroused Cadj's anger in the garden, 'I distinctly recall that La offered the friendship of Opar to Tarzan of the Apes upon that time, many moons ago, that he saved her from the tusks of infuriated Tantor.'

'Silence,' growled Cadj, 'he shall not enter; we shall slay them all, though we need not know their identity until it is too late. Do you understand? And know, too, that whosoever attempts to thwart my purpose shall die – and he die not as a sacrifice, he shall die at my hands, but die he shall. You hear me?' And he pointed an unclean finger at the trembling priest.

Manu, the monkey, hearing all this, was almost bursting with excitement. He knew Tarzan of the Apes – as all the migratory monkeys the length and breadth of Africa knew him – he knew him for a friend and protector. To Manu the males of Opar were neither beast, nor man, nor friend. He knew them as cruel and surly creatures who ate the flesh of his kind, and he hated them accordingly. He was therefore greatly exercised at the plot that he had heard discussed which was aimed at the life of the great Tarmangani. He scratched his little gray head, and the root of his tail, and his belly, as he attempted mentally to digest what he had heard, and bring forth from the dim recesses of his little brain a plan to foil the priests and save Tarzan of the Apes. He made grotesque grimaces that were aimed at the unsuspecting Cadj and his followers, but which failed to perturb them, possibly because a huge granite block hid the little monkey from them. This was quite the most momentous thing that had occurred in the life of Manu. He wanted to jump up and down and dance and screech and jabber – to scold and threaten the hated Oparians, but something told him that nothing would be gained by this, other than, perhaps, to launch in his direction a shower of granite missiles, which the priests knew only too well how to throw with accuracy. Now Manu is not a deep thinker, but upon this occasion he quite outdid himself, and managed to concentrate his mind upon the thing at hand rather than permit its being distracted by each falling leaf or buzzing insect. He even permitted a succulent caterpillar to crawl within his reach and out again with impunity.

Just before darkness fell, Cadj saw a little gray monkey disappear over the summit of the outer wall fifty paces from where he crouched with his fellows, waiting for the coming of the fighting men. But so numerous were the monkeys about the ruins of Opar that the occurrence left Cadj's mind almost as quickly as the monkey disappeared from his view, and in the gathering gloom he did not see the little gray figure scampering off across the valley toward the band of intruders who now appeared to have stopped to rest at the foot of a large kopje that stood alone out in the valley, about a mile from the city.

Little Manu was very much afraid out there alone in the growing dusk, and he scampered very fast with his tail bowed up and out behind him. All the time he cast affrightened glances to the right and left. The moment he reached the kopje he scampered up its face as fast as he could. It was really a huge, precipitous granite rock with almost perpendicular sides, but sufficiently weather-worn to make its ascent easy to little Manu. He paused a moment at the summit to get his breath and still the beatings of his frightened little heart, and then he made his way around to a point where he could look down upon the party beneath.

There, indeed, was the great Tarmangani Tarzan, and with him were some fifty Gomangani. The latter were splicing together a number of long, straight poles, which they had laid upon the ground in two parallel lines. Across these two, at intervals of a foot or more, they were lashing smaller straight branches about eighteen inches in length, the whole forming a crude but substantial ladder. The purpose of all this Manu, of course, did not understand, nor did he know that it had been evolved from the fertile brain of Flora Hawkes as a means of scaling the precipitous kopje, at the summit of which lay the outer entrance to the treasure vaults of Opar. Nor did Manu know that the party had no intention of entering the city of Opar and were therefore in no danger of becoming victims of Cadj's hidden assassins. To him, the danger to Tarzan of the Apes was very real, and so, having regained his breath, he lost no time in delivering his warning to the friend of his people.

'Tarzan,' he cried, in the language that was common to both.

The white man and the blacks looked up at the sound of his chattering voice.

'It is Manu, Tarzan,' continued the little monkey, 'who has come to tell you not to go to Opar. Cadj and his people await within the outer wall to slay you.'

The blacks, having discovered that the author of the disturbance was nothing but a little gray monkey, returned immediately to their work, while the white man similarly ignored his words of warning. Manu was not surprised at the lack of interest displayed by the blacks, for he knew that they did not understand his language, but he could not comprehend why Tarzan failed to pay any attention whatsoever to him. Again and again he called Tarzan by name. Again and again he shrieked his warning to the ape-man, but without eliciting any reply or any information that the great Tarmangani had either heard or understood him. Manu was mystified. What had occurred to render Tarzan of the Apes so indifferent to the warnings of his old friend?

At last the little monkey gave it up and looked longingly back in the direction of the trees within the walled city of Opar. It was now very dark and he trembled at the thought of recrossing the valley, where he knew enemies might prowl by night. He scratched his head and he hugged his knees, then sat there whimpering, a very forlorn and unhappy little ball of a monkey. But however uncomfortable he was upon the high kopje, he was comparatively safe, and so he decided to remain there during the night rather than venture the terrifying return trip through the darkness. Thus it was that he saw the ladder completed and erected against the side of the kopje; and when the moon rose at last and lighted the scene, he saw Tarzan of the Apes urging his men to mount the ladder. He had never seen Tarzan thus rough and cruel with the blacks who accompanied him. Manu knew how ferocious the great Tarmangani could be with an enemy, whether man or beast, but he had never seen him accord such treatment to the blacks who were his friends.

One by one and with evident reluctance the blacks ascended the ladder, continually urged forward to greater speed by the sharp spear of the white man; when they had all ascended Tarzan followed, and Manu saw them disappear apparently into the heart of the great rock.

It was only a short time later that they commenced to reappear, and now each was burdened by two heavy objects which appeared to Manu to be very similar to some of the smaller stone blocks that had been used in the construction of the buildings in Opar. He saw them take the blocks to the edge of the kopje and cast them over to the ground beneath, and when the last of the blacks had emerged with his load and cast it to the valley below, one by one the party descended the ladder to the foot of the kopje. But this time Tarzan of the Apes went first. Then they lowered the ladder and took it apart and laid its pieces close to the foot of the cliff, after which they took up the blocks which they had brought from the heart of the kopje, and following Tarzan, who set out in the lead, they commenced to retrace their steps toward the rim of the valley.

Manu would have been very much mystified had he been a man, but being only a monkey he saw only what he saw without attempting to reason very much about it. He knew that the ways of men were peculiar, and oftentimes unaccountable. For example, the Gomangani who could not travel through the jungle and the forest with the ease of any other of the animals which frequented them, added to their difficulties by loading themselves down with additional weights in the form of metal anklets and armlets, with necklaces and girdles, and with skins of animals, which did nothing more than impede their progress and render life much more complicated than that which the untrammeled beasts enjoyed. Manu, whenever he gave the matter a thought, congratulated himself that he was not a man – he pitied the foolish, unreasonable creatures.

Manu must have slept. He thought that he had only closed his eyes a moment, but when he opened them the rosy light of dawn had overspread the desolate valley. Just disappearing over the cliffs to the northeast he could see the last of Tarzan's party commencing the descent of the barrier, then Manu turned his face toward Opar and prepared to descend from the kopje, and scamper back to the safety of his trees within the walls of Opar. But first he would reconnoiter – Sheeta, the panther, might be still abroad, and so he scampered around the edge of the kopje to a point where he could see the entire valley floor between himself and Opar. And there it was that he saw again that which filled him with greatest excitement. For, debouching from the ruined outer wall of Opar was a large company of Opar's frightful men – fully a hundred of them Manu could have counted had Manu been able to count.

They seemed to be coming toward the kopje, and he sat and watched them as they approached, deciding to defer his return to the city until after the path was cleared of hated Oparians. It occurred to him that they were coming after him, for the egotism of the lower animals is inordinate. Because he was a monkey, the idea did not seem at all ridiculous and so he hid behind a jutting rock, with only one little, bright eye exposed to the enemy. He saw them come closer and he grew very much excited, though he was not at all afraid, for he knew that if they ascended one side of the kopje he could descend the other and be halfway to Opar before they could possibly locate him again.

On and on they came, but they did not stop at the kopje – as a matter of fact they did not come very close to it, but continued on beyond it. Then it was that the truth of the matter flashed into the little brain of the monkey – Cadj and his people were pursuing Tarzan of the Apes to slay him. If Manu had been offended by Tarzan's indifference to him upon the night before, he had evidently forgotten it, for now he was quite as excited about the danger which he saw menace the ape-man as he had been upon the afternoon previous. At first he thought of running ahead, and again warning Tarzan, but he feared to venture so far from the trees of Opar, even if the thought of having to pass the hated Oparians had not been sufficient to deter him from carrying out this plan. For a few minutes he sat watching them, until they had all passed the kopje, and then it became quite clear to him that they were heading directly for the spot at which the last of Tarzan's party had disappeared from the valley – there could be no doubt that they were in pursuit of the ape-man.

Manu scanned the valley once more toward Opar. There was nothing in sight to deter him from an attempted return, and so, with the agility of his kind, he scampered down the vertical face of the kopje and was off at great speed toward the city's wall. Just when he formulated the plan that he eventually followed it is difficult to say. Perhaps he thought it all out as he sat upon the kopje, watching Cadj and his people upon the trail of the ape-man, or perhaps it occurred to him while he was scampering across the barren waste toward Opar. It may just have popped into his mind from a clear sky after he had regained the leafy sanctuary of his own trees. Be that however as it may, the fact remains that as La, High Priestess and princess of Opar, in company with several of her priestesses, was bathing in a pool in one of the temple gardens, she was startled by the screaming of a monkey, swinging frantically by his tail from the branch of a great tree which overspread the pool – it was a little gray monkey with a face so wise and serious that one might easily have imagined that the fate of nations lay constantly upon the shoulders of its owner.

'La, La,' it screamed, 'they have gone to kill Tarzan. They have gone to kill Tarzan.'

At the sound of that name La was instantly all attention. Standing waist deep in the pool she looked up at the little monkey questioningly. 'What do you mean, Manu?' she asked. 'It has been many moons since Tarzan was at Opar. He is not here now. What are you talking about?'

'I saw him,' screamed Manu, 'I saw him last night with many Gomangani. He came to the great rock that lies in the valley before Opar; with all his men he climbed to the top of it, went into the heart of it, and came out with stones which they threw down into the valley. Afterward they descended from the rock, and picked up the stones again and left the valley – there,' and Manu pointed toward the northeast with one of his hairy little fingers.

'How do you know it was Tarzan of the Apes?' asked La.

'Does Manu not know his cousin and his friend?' demanded the monkey. 'With my eyes I saw him – it was Tarzan of the Apes.'

La of Opar puckered her brows in thought. Deep in her heart smoldered the fires of her great love for Tarzan. Fires that had been quenched by the necessity that had compelled her marriage with Cadj since last she had seen the ape-man. For it is written among the laws of Opar that the high Priestess of the Flaming God must take a mate within a certain number of years after her consecration. For many moons La longed to make Tarzan that mate. The ape-man had not loved her, and finally she had come to a realization that he could never love her. Afterward she had bowed to the frightful fate that had placed her in the arms of Cadj.

As month after month had passed and Tarzan had not returned to Opar, as he had promised he would do, to see that no harm befell La, she had come to accept the opinion of Cadj that the ape-man was dead, and though she hated the repulsive Cadj none the less, her love for Tarzan had gradually become little more than a sorrowful memory. Now to learn that he was alive and had been so near was like reopening an old wound. At first she comprehended little else than that Tarzan had been close to Opar, but presently the cries of Manu aroused her to a realization that the ape-man was in danger – just what the danger was, she did not know.

'Who has gone to kill Tarzan of the Apes?' she demanded suddenly.

'Cadj, Cadj!' shrieked Manu. 'He has gone with many, many men, and is following upon the spoor of Tarzan.'

La sprang quickly from the pool, seized her girdle and ornaments from her attendant and adjusting them hurriedly, sped through the garden and into the temple.

7

'You Must Sacrifice Him'

Warily Cadj and his hundred frightful followers, armed with their bludgeons and knives, crept stealthily down the face of the barrier into the valley below, upon the trail of the white man and his black companions. They made no haste, for they had noted from the summit of Opar's outer wall, that the party they were pursuing moved very slowly, though why, they did not know, for they had been at too great a distance to see the burden that each of the blacks carried. Nor was it Cadj's desire to overtake his quarry by daylight, his plans contemplating a stealthy night attack, the suddenness of which, together with the great number of his followers, might easily confuse and overwhelm a sleeping camp.

The spoor they followed was well marked. There could be no mistaking it, and they moved slowly down the now gentle declivity, toward the bottom of the valley. It was close to noon that they were brought to a sudden halt by the discovery of a thorn boma recently constructed in a small clearing just ahead of them. From the center of the boma arose the thin smoke of a dying fire. Here, then, was the camp of the ape-man.

Cadj drew his followers into the concealment of the thick bushes that bordered the trail, and from there he sent ahead a single man to reconnoiter. It was but a few moments later that the latter returned to say that the camp was deserted, and once again Cadj moved forward with his men. Entering the boma they examined it in an effort to estimate the size of the party that accompanied Tarzan. As they were thus occupied Cadj saw something lying half concealed by bushes at the far end of the boma. Very warily he approached it, for there was that about it which not only aroused his curiosity but prompted him to caution, for it resembled indistinctly the figure of a man, lying huddled upon the ground.

With ready bludgeons a dozen of them approached the thing that had aroused Cadj's curiosity, and when they had come close to it they saw lying before them the lifeless figure of Tarzan of the Apes.

'The Flaming God has reached forth to avenge his desecrated altar,' cried the High Priest, his eyes glowing with the maniacal fires of fanaticism. But another priest, more practical, perhaps, or at least more cautious, kneeled beside the figure of the ape-man and placed his ear against the latter's heart.

'He is not dead,' he whispered; 'perhaps he only sleeps.'

'Seize him, then, quickly,' cried Cadj, and an instant later Tarzan's body was covered by the hairy forms of as many of the frightful men as could pile upon him. He offered no resistance – he did not even open his eyes, and presently his arms were securely bound behind him.

'Drag him forth where the eye of the Flaming God may rest upon him,' cried Cadj. They dragged Tarzan out into the center of the boma into the full light of the sun, and Cadj, the High Priest, drawing his knife from his loin cloth, raised it above his head and stood over the prostrate form of his intended victim. Cadj's followers formed a rough circle about the ape-man and some of them pressed close behind their leader. They appeared uneasy, looking alternately at Tarzan and their High Priest, and then casting furtive glances at the sun, riding high in a cloud-mottled sky. But whatever the thoughts that troubled their half-savage brains, there was only one who dared voice his, and he was the same priest who, upon the preceding day, had questioned Cadj's proposal to slay the ape-man.

'Cadj,' he said now, 'who are you to offer up a sacrifice to the Flaming God? It is the privilege alone of La, our High Priestess and our queen, and indeed will she be angry when she learns what you have done.'

'Silence, Dooth!' cried Cadj; 'I, Cadj, am the High Priest of Opar. I, Cadj, am the mate of La, the queen. My word, too, is law in Opar. And you would remain a priest, and you would remain alive, keep silence.'

'Your word is not law,' replied Dooth, angrily, 'and if you anger La, the High Priestess, or if you anger the Flaming God, you may be punished as another. If you make this sacrifice both will be angry.'

'Enough,' cried Cadj; 'the Flaming God has spoken to me and has demanded that I offer up as sacrifice this defiler of his temple.'

He knelt beside the ape-man and touched his breast above the heart with the point of his sharp blade, and then he raised the weapon high above him, preparatory to the fatal plunge into the living heart. At that instant a cloud passed before the face of the sun and a shadow rested upon them. A murmur rose from the surrounding priests.

'Look,' cried Dooth, 'the Flaming God is angry. He has hidden his face from the people of Opar.'

Cadj paused. He cast a half-defiant, half-frightened look at the cloud obscuring the face of the sun. Then he rose slowly to his feet, and extending his arms upward toward the hidden god of day, he remained for a moment silent in apparently attentive and listening attitude. Then, suddenly, he turned upon his followers.

'Priests of Opar,' he cried, 'the Flaming God has spoken to his High Priest, Cadj. He is not angered. He but wishes to speak to me alone, and he directs that you go away into the jungle and wait until he has come and spoken to Cadj, after which I shall call you to return. Go!'

For the most part they seemed to accept the word of Cadj as law, but Dooth and a few others, doubtless prompted by a certain skepticism, hesitated.

'Be gone!' commanded Cadj. And so powerful is the habit of obedience that the doubters finally turned away and melted into the jungle with the others. A crafty smile lighted the cruel face of the High Priest as the last of them disappeared from sight, and then he once again turned his attention to the ape-man. That, deep within his breast however, lurked an inherent fear of his deity, was evidenced by the fact that he turned questioning glances toward the sky. He had determined to slay the ape-man while Dooth and the others were absent, yet the fear of his god restrained his hand until the light of his deity should shine forth upon him once more and assure him that the thing he contemplated might meet with favor.

It was a large cloud that overcast the sun, and while Cadj waited his nervousness increased. Six times he raised his knife for the fatal blow, yet in each instance his superstition prevented the consummation of the act. Five, ten, fifteen minutes passed, and still the sun remained obscured. But now at last Cadj could see that it was nearing the edge of the cloud, and once again he took his position kneeling beside the ape-man with his blade ready for the moment that the sunlight should flood again, for the last time, the living Tarzan. He saw it sweeping slowly across the boma toward him, and as it came a look of demoniacal hatred shone in his close-set, wicked eyes. Another instant and the Flaming God would have set the seal of his approval upon the sacrifice. Cadj trembled in anticipation. He raised the knife a trifle higher, his muscles tensed for the downward plunge, and then the silence of the jungle was broken by a woman's voice, raised almost to a scream.

'Cadj!' came the single word, but with all the suddenness and all the surprising effect of lightning from a clear sky.

His knife still poised on high, the High Priest turned in the direction of the interruption to see at the clearing's edge the figure of La, the High Priestess, and behind her Dooth and a score of the lesser priests.

'What means this, Cadj?' demanded La, angrily, approaching rapidly toward him across the clearing. Sullenly the High Priest rose.

'The Flaming God demanded the life of this unbeliever,' he cried.

'Speaker of lies,' retorted La, 'the Flaming God communicates with men through the lips of his High Priestess only. Too often already have you attempted to thwart the will of your queen. Know, then, Cadj, that the power of life and death which your queen holds is as potent over you as another. During the long ages that Opar has endured, our legends tell us that more than one High Priest has been offered upon the altar to the Flaming God. And it is not unlikely that yet another may go the way of the presumptuous. Curb, therefore, your vanity and your lust for power, lest they prove your undoing.'

Cadj sheathed his knife and turned sullenly away, casting a venomous look at Dooth, to whom he evidently attributed his undoing. That he was temporarily abashed by the presence of his queen was evident, but to those who knew Cadj there was little doubt that he still harbored his intention to despatch the ape-man, and if the opportunity ever presented itself that he would do so, for Cadj had a strong following among the people and priests of Opar. There were many who doubted that La would ever dare to incur the displeasure and anger of so important a portion of her followers as to cause the death or degradation of their high priest, who occupied his office by virtue of laws and customs so old that their origin had been long lost in antiquity.

For years she had found first one excuse and then another to delay the ceremonies that would unite her in marriage to the High Priest. She had further aroused the antagonism of her people by palpable proofs of her infatuation for the ape-man, and even though at last she had been compelled to mate with Cadj, she had made no effort whatsoever to conceal her hatred and loathing for the man. How much further she could go with impunity was a question that often troubled those whose position in Opar depended upon her favor, and, knowing all these conditions as he did, it was not strange that Cadj should entertain treasonable thoughts toward his queen. Leagued with him in his treachery was Oah, a priestess who aspired to the power and offices of La. If La could be done away with, then Cadj had the influence to see that Oah became High Priestess. He also had Oah's promise to mate with him and permit him to rule as king, but as yet both were bound by the superstitious fear of their flaming deity, and because of this fact was the life of La temporarily made safe. It required, however, but the slightest spark to ignite the flames of treason that were smoldering about her.

So far, she was well within her rights in forbidding the sacrifice of Tarzan by the High Priest. But her fate, her very life, perhaps, depended upon her future treatment of the prisoner. Should she spare him, should she evidence in any way a return of the great love she had once almost publicly avowed for him, it was likely that her doom would be sealed. It was even questionable whether or not she might with impunity spare his life and set him at liberty.

Cadj and the others watched her closely now as she crossed to the side of Tarzan. Standing there silently for several moments she looked down upon him.

'He is already dead?' she asked.

'He was not dead when Cadj sent us away,' volunteered Dooth. 'If he is dead now it is because Cadj killed him while we were away.'

'I did not kill him,' said Cadj. 'That remains, as La, our queen, has told you, for her to do. The eye of the Flaming God looks down upon you, High Priestess of Opar. The knife is at your hip, the sacrifice lies before you.'

La ignored the man's words and turned toward Dooth. 'If he still lives,' she said, 'construct a litter and bear him back to Opar.'

Thus, once more, came Tarzan of the Apes into the ancient colonial city of the Atlantians. The effects of the narcotic that Kraski had administered to him did not wear off for many hours. It was night when he opened his eyes, and for a moment he was bewildered by the darkness and the silence that surrounded him. All that he could scent at first was that he lay upon a pile of furs and that he was uninjured, for he felt no pain. Slowly there broke through the fog of his drugged brain recollection of the last moment before unconsciousness had overcome him, and presently he realized the trick that had been played upon him. For how long he had been unconscious and where he then was he could not imagine. Slowly he arose to his feet, finding that except for a slight dizziness he was quite himself. Cautiously he felt around in the darkness, moving with care, a hand outstretched, and always feeling carefully with his feet for secure footing. Almost immediately a stone wall stopped his progress, and this he followed around four sides of what he soon realized was a small room in which there were but two openings, a door upon each of the opposite sides. Only his senses of touch and smell were of value to him here. These told him only at first that he was imprisoned in a subterranean chamber, but as the effects of the narcotic diminished, the keenness of the latter returned, and with its return there was borne in upon Tarzan's brain an insistent impression of familiarity in certain fragrant odors that impinged upon his olfactory organs – a haunting suggestion that he had known them before under similar circumstances. Presently from above, through earth and masonry, came the shadow of an uncanny scream – just the faintest suggestion of it reached the keen ears of the ape-man, but it was sufficient to flood his mind with vivid recollections, and, by association of ideas, to fix the identity of the familiar odors about him. He knew at last that he was in the dark pit beneath Opar.

Above him, in her chamber in the temple, La, the High, Priestess, tossed upon a sleepless couch. She knew all too well the temper of her people and the treachery of the High Priest, Cadj. She knew the religious fanaticism which prompted the ofttime maniacal actions of her bestial and ignorant followers, and she guessed truly that Cadj would inflame them against her should she fail this time in sacrificing the ape-man to the Flaming God. And it was the effort to find an escape from her dilemma that left her sleepless, for it was not in the heart of La to sacrifice Tarzan of the Apes. High Priestess of a horrid cult though she was, the queen of a race of half-beasts, yet she was a woman, too, a woman who had loved but once and given that love to the godlike ape-man who was again within her power. Twice before had he escaped her sacrificial knife; in the final instance love had at last triumphed over jealousy and fanaticism, and La, the woman, had realized that never again could she place in jeopardy the life of the man she loved, however hopeless she knew that love to be.

Tonight she was faced with a problem that she felt almost beyond her powers of solution. The fact that she was mated with Cadj removed the last vestige of hope that she had ever had of becoming the wife of the ape-man. Yet she was no less determined to save Tarzan if it were possible. Twice had he saved her life, once from a mad priest, and once from Tantor in *must*. Then, too, she had given her word that when Tarzan came again to Opar he came in friendship and would be received in friendship. But the influence of Cadj was great, and she knew that that influence had been directed unremittingly against the ape-man – she had seen it in the attitude of her followers from the very moment that they had placed Tarzan upon a litter to bear him back to Opar – she had seen it in the evil glances that had been cast at her. Sooner or later they would dare denounce her – all that they needed was some slight, new excuse, that, she knew, they eagerly awaited in her forthcoming attitude toward Tarzan. It was well after midnight when there came to her one of the priestesses who remained always upon guard outside her chamber door.

'Dooth would speak with you,' whispered the hand-maiden.

'It is late,' replied La, 'and men are not permitted in this part of the temple. How came he here, and why?'

'He says that he comes in the service of La, who is in great danger,' replied the girl.

'Fetch him here then,' said La, 'and as you value your life see that you tell no one.'

'I shall be as voiceless as the stones of the altar,' replied the girl, as she turned and left the chamber.

A moment later she returned bringing Dooth, who halted a few feet from the High Priestess and saluted her. La signaled to the girl who had brought him, to depart, and then she turned questioningly to the man.

'Speak, Dooth!' she commanded.

'We all know,' he said, 'of La's love for the strange ape-man, and it is not for me, a lesser priest, to question the thoughts or acts of my High Priestess. It is only for me to serve, as those would do better to serve who now plot against you.'

'What do you mean, Dooth? Who plots against me?'

'Even at this minute are Cadj and Oah and several of the priests and priestesses carrying out a plan for your undoing. They are setting spies to watch you, knowing that you would liberate the ape-man, because there will come to you one who will tell you that to permit him to escape will be the easiest solution of your problem. This one will be sent by Cadj, and then those who watch you will report to the people and to the priests that they have seen you lead the sacrifice to liberty. But even that will avail you nothing, for Cadj and Oah and the others have placed upon the trail from Opar many men in hiding, who will fall upon the ape-man and slay him before the Flaming God has descended twice into the western forest. In but one way only may you save yourself, La of Opar.'

'And what is that way?' she asked.

'You must, with your own hands, upon the altar of our temple, sacrifice the ape-man to the Flaming God.'

8

Mystery of the Past

La had breakfasted the following morning, and had sent Dooth with food for Tarzan, when there came to her a young priestess, who was the sister of Oah. Even before the girl had spoken La knew that she was an emissary from Cadj, and that the treachery of which Dooth had warned her was already under way. The girl was ill at ease and quite evidently frightened, for she was young and held in high revere the queen whom she had good reason to know was all-powerful, and who might even inflict death upon her if she so wished. La, who had already determined upon a plan of action that she knew would be most embarrassing to Cadj and his conspirators, waited in silence for the girl to speak. But it was some time before the girl could muster up her courage or find a proper opening. Instead, she spoke of many things that had no bearing whatsoever upon her subject, and La, the High Priestess, was amused at her discomfiture.

'It is not often,' said La, 'that the sister of Oah comes to the apartments of her queen unless she is bidden. I am glad to see that she at last realizes the service that she owes to the High Priestess of the Flaming God.'

'I come,' said the girl, at last, speaking almost as one who has learned a part, 'to tell you that I have overheard that which may be of interest to you, and which I am sure that you will be glad to hear.'

'Yes?' interrogated La, raising her arched eyebrows.

'I overheard Cadj speaking with the lesser priests,' the girl continued, 'and I distinctly heard him say that he would be glad if the ape-man escaped, as that would relieve you, and Cadj as well, of much embarrassment. I thought that La, the queen, would be glad to know this, for it is known by all of us that La has promised friendship to the ape-man and therefore does not wish to sacrifice him upon the altar of the Flaming God.'

'My duty is plain to me,' replied La, in a haughty voice, 'and I do not need Cadj nor any hand-maiden to interpret it to me. I also know the prerogatives of a High Priestess, and that the right of sacrifice is one of them. For this reason I prevented Cadj from sacrificing the stranger. No other hand than mine may offer his heart's blood to the Flaming God, and upon the third day he shall die beneath my knife upon the altar of our temple.'

The effect of these words upon the girl were precisely what La had anticipated. She saw disappointment and chagrin written upon the face of Cadj's messenger, who now had no answer, for her instructions had not foreseen this attitude upon the part of La. Presently the girl found some lame pretext upon which to withdraw, and when she had left the presence of the High Priestess, La could scarcely restrain a smile. She had no intention of sacrificing Tarzan, but this, of course, the sister of Oah did not know. So she returned to Cadj and repeated as nearly as she could recall it, all that La had said to her. The High Priest was much chagrined, for his plan had been now, not so much to encompass the destruction of Tarzan as to lead La into the commission of an act that would bring upon her the wrath of the priests and people of Opar, who, properly instigated, would demand her life in expiation. Oah, who was present when her sister returned, bit her lips, for great was her disappointment. Never before had she seen so close at hand the longed-for possibility of becoming High Priestess. For several minutes she paced to and fro in deep thought, and then, suddenly, she halted before Cadj.

'La loves this ape-man,' she said, 'and even though she may sacrifice him, it is only because of fear of her people. She loves him still – loves him better, Cadj, than she has ever loved you. The ape-man knows it, and trusts her, and because he knows it there is a way. Listen, Cadj, to Oah. We will send one to the ape-man who shall tell him that she comes from La, and that La has instructed her to lead him out of Opar and set him free. This one shall lead him into our ambush and when he is killed we shall go, many of us, before La, and accuse her of treachery. The one who led the ape-man from Opar shall say that La ordered her to do it, and the priests and the people will be very angry, and then you shall demand the life of La. It will be very easy and we shall be rid of both of them.'

'Good!' exclaimed Cadj. 'We shall do this thing at dawn upon the morrow, and before the Flaming God goes to his rest at night he shall look upon a new High Priestess in Opar.'

That night Tarzan was aroused from his sleep by a sound at one of the doors of his prison cell. He heard the bolt slipped back and the door creak slowly open upon its ancient hinges. In the inky darkness he could discern no presence, but he heard the stealthy movement of sandaled feet upon the concrete floor, and then, out of the darkness, his name was whispered, in a woman's voice.

'I am here,' he replied. 'Who are you and what do you want of Tarzan of the Apes?'

'Your life is in danger,' replied the voice. 'Come, follow me.'

'Who sent you?' demanded the ape-man, his sensitive nostrils searching for a clue to the identity of the nocturnal visitor, but so heavily was the air laden with the pungent odor of some heavy perfume with which the body of the woman seemed to have been anointed, that there was no distinguishing clue by which he might judge as to whether she was one of the priestesses he had known upon the occasion of his former visits to Opar, or an entire stranger to him.

'La sent me,' she said, 'to lead you from the pits of Opar to the freedom of the outside world beyond the city's walls.' Groping in the darkness she finally found him. 'Here are your weapons,' she said, handing them to him, and then she took his hand, turned and led him from the dungeon, through a long, winding, and equally black corridor, down flights of age-old concrete steps, through passages and corridors, opening and closing door after door that creaked and groaned upon rusty hinges. How far they traveled thus, and in what direction, Tarzan could not guess. He had gleaned enough from Dooth, when the latter brought him his food, to believe that in La he had a friend who would aid him, for Dooth had told him that she had saved him from Cadj when the latter had discovered him unconscious in the deserted boma of the Europeans who had drugged and left him. And so, the woman having said that she came from La, Tarzan followed her willingly. He could not but recall Jane's prophecy of the evils that he might expect to befall him should he persist in undertaking this third trip to Opar, and he wondered if, after all, his wife were right, that he should never again escape from the toils of the fanatical priests of the Flaming God. He had not, of course, expected to enter Opar, but there seemed to hang over the accursed city a guardian demon that threatened the life of whosoever dared approach the forbidden spot or wrest from the forgotten treasure vaults a portion of their great hoard.

For more than an hour his guide led him through the Stygian darkness of underground passages, until ascending a flight of steps they emerged into the center of a clump of bushes, through which the pale light of the moon was barely discernible. The fresh air, however, told him that they had reached the surface of the ground, and now the woman, who had not spoken a word since she had led him from his cell, continued on in silence, following a devious trail that wound hither and thither in an erratic fashion through a heavy forest choked with undergrowth, and always upward.

From the location of the stars and moon, and from the upward trend of the trail, Tarzan knew that he was being led into the mountains that lie behind Opar – a place he had never thought of visiting, since the country appeared rough and uninviting, and not likely to harbor game such as Tarzan cared most to hunt. He was already surprised by the nature of the vegetation, for he had thought the hills barren except for stunted trees and scraggy bush. As they continued upon their way, climbing ever upward, the moon rose higher in the heavens, until its soft light revealed more clearly to the keen eyes of the ape-man the topography of the country they were traversing, and then it was that he saw they were ascending a narrow, thickly wooded gorge, and he understood why the heavy vegetation had been invisible from the plain before Opar. Himself naturally uncommunicative, the woman's silence made no particular impression upon Tarzan. Had he had anything to say he should have said it, and likewise he assumed that there was no necessity for her speaking unless there was some good reason for speaking, for those who travel far and fast have no breath to waste upon conversation.

The eastern stars were fading at the first hint of coming dawn when the two scrambled up a precipitous bank that formed the upper end of the ravine, and came out upon comparatively level ground. As they advanced the sky lightened, and presently the woman halted at the edge of a declivity, and as the day broke Tarzan saw below him a wooded basin in the heart of the mountain, and, showing through the trees at what appeared to be some two or three miles distant, the outlines of a building that glistened and sparkled and scintillated in the light of the new sun. Then he turned and looked at his companion, and surprise and consternation were writ upon his face, for standing before him was La, the High Priestess of Opar.

'You?' he exclaimed. 'Now indeed will Cadj have the excuse that Dooth said he sought to put you out of the way.'

'He will never have the opportunity to put me out of the way,' replied La, 'for I shall never return to Opar.'

'Never return to Opar!' he exclaimed, 'then where are you going? Where can you go?'

'I am going with you,' she replied. 'I do not ask that you love me. I only ask that you take me away from Opar and from the enemies who would slay me. There was no other way. Manu, the monkey, overheard them plotting, and he came to me and told me all that they would do. Whether I saved you or sacrificed you, it had all been the same with me. They were determined to do away with me, that Oah might be High Priestess and Cadj king of Opar. But I should not have sacrificed you, Tarzan, under any circumstances, and this, then, seemed the only way in which we might both be saved. We could not go to the north or the west across the plain of Opar for there Cadj has placed warriors in ambush to waylay you, and though you be Tarzan and a mighty fighter, they would overwhelm you by their very numbers and slay you.'

'But where are you leading me?' asked Tarzan.

'I have chosen the lesser of two evils; in this direction lies an unknown country, filled for us Oparians with legends of grim monsters and strange people. Never has an Oparian ventured here and returned again to Opar. But if there lives in all the world a creature who could win through this unknown valley, it be you, Tarzan of the Apes.'

'But if you know nothing of this country, or its inhabitants,' demanded Tarzan, 'how is it that you so well know the trail that leads to it?'

'We well know the trail to the summit, but that is as far as I have ever been before. The great apes and the lions use this trail when they come down into Opar. The lions, of course, cannot tell us where it leads, and the great apes will not, for usually we are at war with them. Along this trail they come down into Opar to steal our people, and upon this trail we await to capture them, for often we offer a great ape in sacrifice to the Flaming God, or rather that was our former custom, but for many years they have been too wary for us, the toll being upon the other side, though we do not know for what purpose they steal our people, unless it be that they eat them. They are a very powerful race, standing higher than Bolgani, the gorilla, and infinitely more cunning, for, as there is ape blood in our veins, so is there human blood in the veins of these great apes that dwell in the valley above Opar.'

'Why is it, La, that we must pass through this valley in order to escape from Opar? There must be some other way.'

'There is no other way, Tarzan of the Apes,' she replied. 'The avenues across the valley are guarded by Cadj's people. Our only chance of escape lies in this direction, and I have brought you along the only trail that pierces the precipitous cliffs that guard Opar upon the south. Across or around this valley we must go in an attempt to find an avenue across the mountain and down upon the other side.'

The ape-man stood gazing down into the wooded basin below them, his mind occupied with the problems of the moment. Had he been alone he would not have come this way, for he was sufficiently confident of his own prowess to believe that he might easily have crossed the valley of Opar in comparative safety, regardless of Cadj's plans to the contrary. But he was not alone. He had now to think of La, and he realized that in her efforts to save him she had placed him under a moral obligation which he might not disregard.

To skirt the basin, keeping as far as possible from the building, which he could see in the distance, seemed the wisest course to pursue, since, of course, his sole purpose was to find a way across the mountain and out of this inhospitable country. But the glimpses he caught of the edifice, half concealed as it was amid the foliage of great trees, piqued his curiosity to such an extent that he felt an almost irresistible urge to investigate. He did not believe that the basin was inhabited by other than wild beasts, and he attributed the building which he saw to the handiwork of an extinct or departed people, either contemporaneous with the ancient Atlantians who had built Opar or, perhaps, built by the original Oparians themselves, but now forgotten by their descendants. The glimpses which he caught of the building suggested such size and magnificence as might belong to a palace.

The ape-man knew no fear, though he possessed to a reasonable extent that caution which is inherent in all wild beasts. He would not have hesitated to pit his cunning and his prowess against the lower orders, however ferocious they might be, for, unlike man, they could not band together to his undoing. But should men elect to hunt him in numbers he knew that a real danger would confront him, and that, in the face of their combined strength and intelligence, his own might not avail him. There was little likelihood, however, he reasoned, that the basin was inhabited by human beings. Doubtless closer investigation of the building he saw would reveal that it was but a deserted ruin, and that the most formidable foes he would encounter would be the great apes and the lions. Of neither of these had he any fear; with the former it was even reasonable to imagine that he might establish amicable relations. Believing as he did that he must look for egress from the basin upon its opposite side, it was only natural that he should wish to choose the most direct route across the basin. Therefore his inclinations to explore the valley were seconded by considerations of speed and expediency.

'Come,' he said to La, and started down the declivity which led into the basin in the direction of the building ahead of them.

'You are not going that way?' she cried in astonishment.

'Why not?' he said. 'It is the shortest way across the valley, and in so far as I can judge our trail over the mountains is more likely to lie in that direction than elsewhere.'

'But I am afraid,' she said. 'The Flaming God alone knows what hideous dangers lurk in the depths of that forest below us.'

'Only Numa and the Mangani,' he said. 'Of these we need have no fear.'

'You fear nothing,' she said, 'but I am only a woman.'

'We can die but once,' replied Tarzan, 'and that once we must die. To be always fearing, then, would not avert it, and would make life miserable. We shall go the short way, then, and perhaps we shall see enough to make the risk well worthwhile.'

They followed a well-worn trail downward among the brush, the trees increasing in both size and number as they approached the floor of the basin, until at last they were walking beneath the foliage of a great forest. What wind there was was at their back, and the ape-man, though he moved at a swinging walk, was constantly on the alert. Upon the hard-packed earth of the trail there were few signs to indicate the nature of the animals that had passed to and fro, but here and there the spoor of a lion was in evidence. Several times Tarzan stopped and listened, often he raised his head and his sensitive nostrils dilated as he sought for whatever the surrounding air might hold for him.

'I think there are men in this valley,' he said presently. 'For some time I have been almost positive that we are being watched. But whoever is stalking us is clever beyond words, for it is only the barest suggestion of another presence that I can scent.'

La looked about apprehensively and drew close to his side. 'I see no one,' she said, in a low voice.

'Nor I,' he replied. 'Nor can I catch any well-defined scent spoor, yet I am positive that someone is following us. Someone or something that trails by scent, and is clever enough to keep its scent from us. It is more than likely that, whatever it is, it is passing through the trees, at a sufficient height to keep its scent spoor always above us. The air is right for that, and even if he were upwind from us we might not catch his scent at all. Wait here, I will make sure,' and he swung lightly into the branches of a nearby tree and swarmed upward with the agility of Manu, the monkey. A moment later he descended to the girl's side.

'I was right,' he said, 'there is someone, or something, not far off. But whether it is man or Mangani I cannot say, for the odor is a strange one to me, suggesting neither, yet both. But two can play at that game. Come!' And he swung the girl to his shoulder and a moment later had carried her high into the trees. 'Unless he is close enough to watch us, which I doubt,' he said, 'our spoor will be carried over his head and it will be some time before he can pick it up again, unless he is wise enough to rise to a higher level.'

La marveled at the strength of the ape-man as he carried her easily from tree to tree, and at the speed with which he traversed the swaying, leafy trail.

For half an hour he continued onward, and then quite suddenly he stopped, poised high upon a swaying bough.

'Look!' he said, pointing ahead and below them. Looking in the direction that he indicated the girl saw through the leafy foliage a small, heavily stockaded compound, in which were some dozen huts that immediately riveted her surprised attention, nor no less was the ape-man's curiosity piqued by what he glimpsed vaguely through the foliage. Huts they evidently were, but they seemed to be moving to and fro in the air, some moving gently backward and forward, while others jumped up and down in more or less violent agitation. Tarzan swung to a nearer tree and descended to a sturdy branch, to which he lowered La from his shoulder. Then he crept forward stealthily, the girl following, for she was, in common with the other Oparians, slightly arboreal. Presently they reached a point where they could see plainly the village below them, and immediately the seeming mystery of the dancing huts was explained.

They were of the bee-hive type, common to many African tribes, and were about seven feet in diameter by six or seven in height, but instead of resting on the ground, each hut was suspended by a heavy hawser-like grass rope to a branch of one of the several giant trees that grew within the stockade. From the center of the bottom of each hut trailed another lighter rope. From his position above them Tarzan saw no openings in any of the huts large enough to admit the body of a man, though there were several openings four or five inches in diameter in the sides of each hut about three feet above the floor. Upon the ground, inside the compound, were several of the inhabitants of the village, if the little collection of swinging houses could be dignified by such a name. Nor were the people any less strange to Tarzan than their peculiar domiciles. That they were negroes was evident, but of a type entirely unfamiliar to the ape-man. All were naked, and without any ornamentation whatsoever other than a few daubs of color, placed apparently at random upon their bodies. They were tall, and very muscular appearing, though their legs seemed much too short and their arms too long for perfect symmetry, while their faces were almost bestial in contour, their jaws being exaggeratedly prognathous while above their beetling brows there was no forehead, the skull running back in an almost horizontal plane to a point.

As Tarzan stood looking at them he saw another descend one of the ropes that dangled from the bottom of a hut, and immediately he understood the purpose of the ropes and the location of the entrances to the dwellings. The creatures squatting about upon their haunches were engaged in feeding. Several had bones from which they were tearing the uncooked flesh with their great teeth, while others ate fruit and tubers. There were individuals of both sexes and of various ages, from childhood to maturity, but there was none that seemed very old. They were practically hairless, except for scraggy, reddish brown locks upon their heads. They spoke but seldom and then in tones which resembled the growling of beasts, nor once, while Tarzan watched them, did he see one laugh or even smile, which, of all their traits, rendered them most unlike the average native of Africa. Though Tarzan's eyes searched the compound carefully he saw no indication of cooking utensils or of any fire. Upon the ground about them lay their weapons, short javelin-like spears and a sort of battle-axe with a sharpened, metal blade. Tarzan of the Apes was glad that he had come this way, for it had permitted him to see such a type of native as he had not dreamed existed – a type that bordered closely upon the brute. Even the Waz-dons and Ho-dons of Pal-ul-don were far advanced in the scale of evolution compared to these.

As he looked at them he could not but wonder that they were sufficiently intelligent to manufacture the weapons they possessed, which he could see, even at a distance, were of fine workmanship and design. Their huts, too, seemed well and ingeniously made, while the stockade which surrounded the little compound was tall, strong, and well-built, evidently for the purpose of safeguarding them against the lions which infested the basin.

As Tarzan and La watched these people they became presently aware of the approach of some creature from their left, and a moment later they saw a man similar to those of the compound swing from a tree that overhung the stockade and drop within. The others acknowledged his coming with scarce more than indifferent glances. He came forward and, squatting among them, appeared to be telling them of something, and though Tarzan could not hear his words he judged from his gestures and the sign language which he used to supplement his meager speech, that he was telling his fellows of the strange creatures he had seen in the forest a short time before, and the ape-man immediately judged that this was the same whom he had been aware was following them and whom he had successfully put off the scent. The narration evidently excited them, for some of them arose, and leaping up and down with bent knees, slapped their arms against their sides grotesquely. The expressions upon their faces scarcely changed, however, and after a moment each squatted down again as he had been before.

It was while they were thus engaged that there echoed through the forest a loud scream that awakened in the mind of the ape-man many savage memories.

'Bolgani,' he whispered to La.

'It is one of the great apes,' she said, and shuddered.

Presently they saw him, swinging down the jungle trail toward the compound. A huge gorilla, but such a gorilla as Tarzan of the Apes had never looked on before. Of almost gigantic stature, the creature was walking erect with the stride of a man, not ever once touching his knuckles to the ground. His head and face were almost those of a gorilla, and yet there was a difference, as Tarzan could note as the creature came nearer – it was Bolgani, with the soul and brain of a man – nor was this all that rendered the creature startling and unique. Stranger perhaps than aught else was the fact that it wore ornaments – and such ornaments! Gold and diamonds sparkled against its shaggy coat, above its elbows were numerous armlets and there were anklets upon its legs, while from a girdle about its middle there depended before and behind a long narrow strip that almost touched the ground and which seemed to be entirely constructed of golden spangles set with small diamonds. Never before had John Clayton, Lord Greystoke, seen such a display of barbaric finery, nor even amidst the jewels of Opar such a wealth of priceless stones.

Immediately after the hideous scream had first broken the comparative silence of the forest, Tarzan had noticed its effects upon the inmates of the compound. Instantly they had arisen to their feet. The women and children scurried behind the boles of the trees or clambered up the ropes into their swinging cages, while some of the men advanced to what Tarzan now saw was the gate of the compound. Outside this gate the gorilla halted and again raised his voice, but this time in speech rather than his hideous scream.

9

The Shaft of Death

As the huge, man-like gorilla entered the compound the warriors closed the gate, and fell back respectfully as he advanced to the center of the village where he stood for a moment, looking about.

'Where are the shes and the balus?' he asked, tersely. 'Call them.'

The women and the children must have heard the command, but they did not emerge from their hiding places. The warriors moved about uneasily, evidently torn by the conflicting emotions of fear of the creature who had issued the order, and reluctance to fulfil his commands.

'Call them,' he repeated, 'or go and fetch them.' But at last one of the warriors mustered the courage to address him.

'This village has already furnished one woman within the moon,' he said. 'It is the turn of another village.'

'Silence!' roared the gorilla-man, advancing threateningly toward him. 'You are a rash Gomangani to threaten the will of a Bolgani – I speak with the voice of Numa, the Emperor; obey or die.'

Trembling, the black turned and called the women and children, but none responded to his summons. The Bolgani gestured impatiently.

'Go and fetch them,' he demanded. And the blacks, cringing, moved sullenly across the compound toward the hiding places of their women and children. Presently they returned, dragging them with them, by the arms sometimes, but usually by the hair. Although they had seemed loath to give them up, they showed no gentleness toward them, nor any indication of affection. Their attitude toward them, however, was presently explained to Tarzan by the next words of the warrior who had spoken previously.

'Great Bolgani,' he said, addressing the gorilla-man, 'if Numa takes always from this village, there will soon be not enough women for the warriors here, and there will be too few children, and in a little time there will be none of us left.'

'What of that?' growled the gorilla-man. 'There are already too many Gomangani in the world. For what other purpose were you created than to serve Numa, the emperor, and his chosen people, the Bolgani?' As he spoke he was examining the women and children, pinching their flesh and pounding upon their chests and backs. Presently he returned to a comparatively young woman, straddling whose hip was a small child.

'This one will do,' he said, snatching the child from its mother and hurling it roughly across the compound, where it lay against the face of the palisade, moaning pitifully, and perchance broken and dying. The poor, stupid mother, apparently more beast than human, stood for a moment trembling in dumb anguish, and then she started to rush forward to her child. But the gorilla-man seized her with one of his great hands and hurled her to the ground. Simultaneously there arose from the silent foliage above them the fierce and terrible scream of the challenging bull ape. In terror the simple blacks cast affrighted glances upward, while the gorilla-man raised his hideous face in snarling anger toward the author of the bestial cry.

Swaying upon a leafy bough they beheld such a creature as none of them had ever looked upon before – a white man, a Tarmangani, with hide as hairless as the body of Histah, the snake. In the instant that they looked they saw the spear hand of the stranger drive forward, and the shaft, speeding with the swiftness of thought, bury itself in the breast of the Bolgani. With a single scream of rage and pain, the gorilla-man crumpled to the earth, where he struggled spasmodically for a moment and then lay still, in death.

The ape-man held no great love for the Gomangani as a race, but inherent in his English brain and heart was the spirit of fair play, which prompted him to spontaneous espousal of the cause of the weak. On the other hand Bolgani was his hereditary enemy. His first battle had been with Bolgani, and his first kill.

The poor blacks were still standing in stupefied wonderment when he dropped from the tree to the ground among them. They stepped back in terror, and simultaneously they raised their spears menacingly against him.

'I am a friend,' he said. 'I am Tarzan of the Apes. Lower your spears.' And then he turned and withdrew his own weapon from the carcass of Bolgani. 'Who is this creature, that may come into your village and slay your balus and steal your shes? Who is he, that you dare not drive your spears through him?'

'He is one of the great Bolgani,' said the warrior, who seemed to be spokesman, and the leader in the village. 'He is one of the chosen people of Numa, the Emperor, and when Numa learns that he has been killed in our village we shall all die for what you have done.'

'Who is Numa?' demanded the ape-man, to whom Numa, in the language of the great apes, meant only lion.

'Numa is the Emperor,' replied the black, 'who lives with the Bolgani in the Palace of Diamonds.'

He did not express himself in just these words, for the meager language of the great apes, even though amplified by the higher intelligence and greater development of the Oparians, is still primitive in the extreme. What he had really said was more nearly 'Numa, the king of kings, who lives in the king's hut of glittering stones,' which carried to the ape-man's mind the faithful impression of the fact. Numa, evidently, was the name adopted by the king of the Bolgani, and the title *emperor*, indicated merely his preeminence among the chiefs.

The instant that Bolgani had fallen the bereaved mother rushed forward and gathered her injured infant into her arms. She squatted now against the palisade, cuddling it to her breast, and crooning softly to pacify its cries, which Tarzan suddenly discovered were more the result of fright than injury. At first the mother had been frightened when he had attempted to examine the child, drawing away and baring her fighting fangs, much after the manner of a wild beast. But presently there had seemed to come to her dull brain a realization that this creature had saved her from Bolgani, that he had permitted her to recover her infant and that he was making no effort to harm either of them. Convinced at last that the child was only bruised, Tarzan turned again toward the warriors, who were talking together in an excited little group a few paces away. As they saw him advancing, they spread into a semi-circle and stood facing him.

'The Bolgani will send and slay us all,' they said, 'when they learn what has happened in our village, unless we can take to them the creature that cast the spear. Therefore, Tarmangani, you shall go with us to the Palace of Diamonds, and there we shall give you over to the Bolgani and perhaps Numa will forgive us.'

The ape-man smiled. What kind of creature did the simple blacks think him, to believe that he would permit himself to be easily led into the avenging hands of Numa, the Emperor of the Bolgani. Although he was fully aware of the risk that he had taken in entering the village, he knew too that because he was Tarzan of the Apes there was a greater chance that he would be able to escape than that they could hold him. He had faced savage spearmen before and knew precisely what to expect in the event of hostilities. He preferred, however, to make peace with these people, for it had been in his mind to find some means of questioning them the moment that he had discovered their village hidden away in this wild forest.

'Wait,' he said, therefore. 'Would you betray a friend who enters your village to protect you from an enemy?'

'We will not slay you, Tarmangani. We will take you to the Bolgani for Numa, the Emperor.'

'But that would amount to the same thing,' returned Tarzan, 'for you well know that Numa, the Emperor, will have me slain.'

'That we cannot help,' replied the spokesman. 'If we could save you we would, but when the Bolgani discover what has happened in our village, it is we who must suffer, unless, perhaps, they are satisfied to punish you instead.'

'But why need they know that the Bolgani has been slain in your village?' asked Tarzan.

'Will they not see his body next time they come?' asked the spokesman.

'Not if you remove his body,' replied Tarzan.

The blacks scratched their heads. Into their dull, ignorant minds had crept no such suggestion of a solution of their problem. What the stranger said was true. None but they and he knew that Bolgani had been slain within their palisade. To remove the body, then, would be to remove all suspicion from their village. But where were they to take it? They put the question to Tarzan.

'I will dispose of him for you,' replied the Tarmangani. 'Answer my questions truthfully and I will promise to take him away and dispose of him in such a manner that no one will know how he died, or where.'

'What are your questions?' asked the spokesman.

'I am a stranger in your country. I am lost here,' replied the ape-man. 'And I would find a way out of the valley in that direction.' And he pointed toward the southeast.

The black shook his head. 'There may be a way out of the valley in that direction,' he said, 'but what lies beyond no man knows, nor do I know whether there be a way out or whether there be anything beyond. It is said that all is fire beyond the mountain, and no one dares to go and see. As for myself, I have never been far from my village – at most only a day's march to hunt for game for the Bolgani, and to gather fruit and nuts and plantains for them. If there is a way out I do not know, nor would any man dare take it if there were.'

'Does no one ever leave the valley?' asked Tarzan.

'I know not what others do,' replied the spokesman, 'but those of this village never leave the valley.'

'What lies in that direction?' asked Tarzan, pointing toward Opar.

'I do not know,' replied the black, 'only that sometimes the Bolgani come from that way, bringing with them strange creatures; little men with white skins and much hair, with short, crooked legs and long arms, and sometimes white shes, who do not look at all like the strange little Tarmangani. But where they get them I do not know, nor do they ever tell us. Are these all the questions that you wish to ask?'

'Yes, that is all,' replied Tarzan, seeing that he could gain no information whatsoever from these ignorant villagers. Realizing that he must find his own way out of the valley, and knowing that he could do so much more quickly and safely if he were alone, he decided to sound the blacks in relation to a plan that had entered his mind.

'If I take the Bolgani away, so that the others will not know that he was slain in your village, will you treat me as a friend?' he asked.

'Yes,' replied the spokesman.

'Then,' said Tarzan, 'will you keep here for me my white she until I return again to your village? You can hide her in one of your huts if a Bolgani comes, and no one need ever know that she is among you. What do you say?'

The blacks looked around. 'We do not see her,' said the spokesman. 'Where is she?'

'If you will promise to protect her and hide her, I will bring her here,' replied the ape-man.

'I will not harm her,' said the head man, 'but I do not know about the others.'

Tarzan turned toward the others who were clustered about, listening. 'I am going to bring my mate into your village,' he said, 'and you are going to hide her, and feed her, and protect her until I return. I shall take away the body of Bolgani, so that no suspicion shall fall upon you, and when I come back I shall expect to find my mate safe and unharmed.'

He had thought it best to describe La as his mate, since thus they might understand that she was under his protection, and if they felt either gratitude or fear toward him, La would be safer. Raising his face toward the tree where she was hidden, he called to La to descend, and a moment later she clambered down to the lower branches of one of the trees in the compound and dropped into Tarzan's arms.

'This is she,' he said to the assembled blacks, 'guard her well and hide her from the Bolgani. If, upon my return, I find that any harm has befallen her, I shall take word to the Bolgani that it was you who did this,' and he pointed to the corpse of the gorilla-man.

La turned appealingly toward him, fear showing in her eyes. 'You are not going to leave me here?' she asked.

'Temporarily only,' replied Tarzan. 'These poor people are afraid that if the death of this creature is traced to their village they shall all suffer the wrath of his fellows, and so I have promised that I will remove the evidence in such a way as to direct suspicion elsewhere. If they are sufficiently high in the scale of evolution to harbor sentiments of gratitude, which I doubt, they will feel obligated to me for having slain this beast, as well as for preventing suspicion falling upon them. For these reasons they should protect you, but to make assurance doubly sure I have appealed also to their fear of the Bolgani – a characteristic which I know they possess. I am sure that you will be as safe here as with me until I return, otherwise I would not leave you. But alone I can travel much faster, and while I am gone I intend to find a way out of this valley, then I shall return for you and together we may make our escape easily, or at least with greater assurance of success than were we to blunder slowly about together.'

'You will come back?' she asked, a note of fear, longing, and appeal in her voice.

'I will come back,' he replied, and then turning to the blacks: 'Clear out one of these huts for my mate, and see that she is not molested, and that she is furnished with food and water. And remember what I said, upon her safety your lives depend.'

Stooping, Tarzan lifted the dead gorilla-man to his shoulder, and the simple blacks marveled at his prowess. Of great physical strength themselves, there was not one of them but would have staggered under the weight of Bolgani, yet this strange Tarmangani walked easily beneath his burden, and when they had opened the gate in the palisade he trotted down the jungle trail as though he carried nothing but his own frame. A moment later he disappeared at a turn and was swallowed by the forest.

La turned to the blacks: 'Prepare my hut,' she said, for she was very tired and longed to rest. They eyed her askance and whispered among themselves. It was evident to her that there was a difference of opinion among them, and presently from snatches of conversation which she overheard she realized that while some of the blacks were in favor of obeying Tarzan's injunctions implicitly, there were others who objected strenuously and who wished to rid their village of her, lest she be discovered there by the Bolgani, and the villagers be punished accordingly.

'It would be better,' she heard one of the blacks say, 'to turn her over to the Bolgani at once and tell them that we saw her mate slay the messenger of Numa. We will say that we tried to capture the Tarmangani but that he escaped, and that we were only able to seize his mate. Thus will we win the favor of Numa, and perhaps then he will not take so many of our women and children.'

'But the Tarmangani is great,' replied one of the others. 'He is more powerful even than Bolgani. He would make a terrible enemy, and, as the chances are that the Bolgani would not believe us we should then have not only them but the Tarmangani to fear.'

'You are right,' cried La, 'the Tarmangani is great. Far better will it be for you to have him for friend than enemy. Single-handed he grapples with Numa, the lion, and slays him. You saw with what ease he lifted the body of the mighty Bolgani to his shoulder. You saw him trot lightly down the jungle trail beneath his burden. With equal ease will he carry the corpse through the trees of the forest, far above the ground. In all the world there is no other like him, no other like Tarzan of the Apes. If you are wise, Gomangani, you will have Tarzan for a friend.'

The blacks listened to her, their dull faces revealing nothing of what was passing in their stupid brains. For a few moments they stood thus in silence, the hulking, ignorant blacks upon one side, the slender, beautiful white woman upon the other. Then La spoke.

'Go,' she cried imperiously, 'and prepare my hut.' It was the High Priestess of the Flaming God; La, the queen of Opar, addressing slaves. Her regal mien, her commanding tones, wrought an instant change in the villagers, and La knew then that Tarzan was right in his assumption that they could be moved only through fear, for now they turned quickly, cowering like whipped dogs, and hastened to a nearby hut, which they quickly prepared for her, fetching fresh leaves and grasses for its floor, and fruit and nuts and plantains for her meal.

When all was ready, La clambered up the rope and through the circular opening in the floor of the hanging hut, which she found large and airy, and now reasonably clean. She drew the rope up after her and threw herself upon the soft bed they had prepared for her, and soon the gentle swaying of the swinging hut, the soft murmur of the leaves above her, the voices of the birds and insects combined with her own physical exhaustion to lull her into deep slumber.

10

Mad Treachery

To the northwest of the valley of Opar the smoke rose from the cook fires of a camp in which some hundred blacks and six whites were eating their evening meal. The negroes squatted sullen and morose, mumbling together in low tones over their meager fare, the whites, scowling and apprehensive, kept their firearms close at hand. One of them, a girl, and the only member of her sex in the party, was addressing her fellows:

'We have Adolph's stinginess and Esteban's braggadocio to thank for the condition in which we are,' she said.

The fat Bluber shrugged his shoulder, the big Spaniard scowled.

'For vy,' asked Adolph, 'am I to blame?'

'You were too stingy to employ enough carriers. I told you at the time that we ought to have had two hundred blacks in our party, but you wanted to save a little money, and now what is the result? Fifty men carrying eighty pounds of gold apiece and the other carriers are overburdened with camp equipment, while there are scarce enough left for askari to guard us properly. We have to drive them like beasts to make any progress and to keep them from throwing away their loads, and they are fagged out and angry. They don't require much of an excuse to kill us all on the spot. On top of all this they are underfed. If we could keep their bellies filled we could probably keep them happy and reasonably contented, but I have learned enough about natives to know that if they are hungry they are neither happy nor contented, even in idleness. If Esteban had not bragged so much about his prowess as a hunter we should have brought enough provisions to last us through, but now, though we are barely started upon our return journey, we are upon less than half rations.'

'I can't kill game when there isn't any game,' growled the Spaniard.

'There is plenty of game,' said Kraski, the Russian. 'We see the tracks of it every day.'

The Spaniard eyed him venomously. 'If there is so much game,' he said, 'go out and get it yourself.'

'I never claimed to be a hunter,' replied Kraski, 'though I could go out with a sling shot and a pea shooter and do as well as you have.'

The Spaniard leaped to his feet menacingly, and instantly the Russian covered him with a heavy service revolver.

'Cut that business,' cried the girl, sharply, leaping between them.

'Let the blighters fight,' growled John Peebles. 'If one of 'em kills the hother there'll be fewer to split the swag, and 'ere we are 'n that's that.'

'For vy should ve quarrel?' demanded Bluber. 'Dere is enough for all – over forty-tree t'ousand pounds apiece. Ven you get mad at me you call me names und say dat I am stingy, but *Mein Gott!* you English are vorser. You vould kill vun of your friends to get more money. *Ja wohl*, tank *Gott* dat I am not an Englisher.'

'Shut up,' growled Throck, 'or we'll have forty-three thousand pounds more to divide.'

Bluber eyed the big Englishman fearfully. 'Come, come, Dick,' he oozed, in his oiliest tones, 'you vouldn't get mad at a leedle choke vould you, und me your best friend?'

'I'm sick of all this grousin',' said Throck. 'I ain't no high-brow, I ain't nothin' but a pug. But I got sense enough to know that Flora's the only one in the bloomin' bunch whose brains wouldn't rattle around in a peanut shell. John, Bluber, Kraski and me, we're here because we could raise the money to carry out Flora's plan. The actor there' – and he indicated Esteban – 'because his face and his figure filled the bill. There don't any of us need no brains for this work, and there ain't any of us got any more brains than we need. Flora's the brains of this outfit, and the sooner everyone understands that and takes orders from her, the better off we'll all be. She's been to Africa with this Lord Greystoke feller before – you wuz his wife's maid, wasn't you, Flora? And she knows somethin' about the country and the natives and the animals, and there don't none of us know nuttin'.'

'Throck is right,' said Kraski, quickly, 'we've been muddling long enough. We haven't had a boss, and the thing to do is to make Flora boss from now on. If anyone can get us out of this, she can, and from the way those fellows over there are acting,' and he nodded toward the blacks, 'we'll be lucky if we ever get out with our skins, let alone taking any of the gold with us.'

'*Ach, nein!* You don't mean to leave der gold?' almost shrieked Bluber.

'I mean that we do whatever Flora thinks best,' replied Kraski. 'If she says to leave the gold, we'll leave it.'

'That we do,' seconded Throck.

'I'm for it,' said Peebles. 'Whatever Flora says goes.'

The Spaniard nodded his assent sullenly.

'The rest of us are all for it, Bluber. How about you?' asked Kraski.

'O vell – sure – if you say so,' said Bluber, 'und as John says "und here ve ain't und vat's dat."'

'And now, Flora,' said Peebles, 'you're the big 'un. What you say goes. What'll we do next?'

'Very well,' said the girl; 'we shall camp here until these men are rested, and early tomorrow we'll start out intelligently and systematically, and get meat for them. With their help we can do it. When they are rested and well fed we will start on again for the coast, moving very slowly, so as not to tire them too much. This is my first plan, but it hinges upon our ability to get meat. If we do not find it I shall bury the gold here, and we will do our best to reach the coast as quickly as possible. There we shall recruit new porters – twice as many as we have now – and purchase enough provisions to carry us in and out again. As we come back in, we will cache provisions at every camping place for our return trip, thus saving the necessity of carrying heavy loads all the way in and out again. In this way we can come out light, with twice as many porters as we actually need. And by working them in shifts we will travel much faster and there will be no grumbling. These are my two plans. I am not asking you what you think of them, because I do not care. You have made me chief, and I am going to run this from now on as I think best.'

'Bully for you,' roared Peebles; 'that's the kind of talk I likes to hear.'

'Tell the head man I want to see him, Carl,' said the girl, turning to Kraski, and a moment later the Russian returned with a burly native.

'Owaza,' said the girl, as the black halted before her, 'we are short of food and the men are burdened with loads twice as heavy as they should carry. Tell them that we shall wait here until they are rested and that tomorrow we shall all go out and hunt for meat. You will send your boys out under three good men, and they will act as beaters and drive the game in to us. In this way we should get plenty of meat, and when the men are rested and well fed we will move on slowly. Where game is plentiful we will hunt and rest. Tell them that if they do this and we reach the coast in safety and with all our loads, I shall pay them twice what they agreed to come for.'

'*Himmel!*' spluttered Bluber. 'Twice vat dey agreed to come for! Oh, Flora, vy not offer dem ten per cent? Dat would be fine interest on their money.'

'Shut up, you fool,' snapped Kraski, and Bluber subsided, though he rocked back and forth, shaking his head in disapproval.

The black, who had presented himself for the interview with sullen and scowling demeanor, brightened visibly now. 'I will tell them,' he said, 'and I think that you will have no more trouble.'

'Good,' said Flora, 'go and tell them now,' and the black turned and left.

'There,' said the girl, with a sigh of relief, 'I believe that we can see light ahead at last.'

'Twice vat ve promised to pay them!' bawled Bluber.

Early the following morning they prepared to set out upon the hunt. The blacks were now smiling and happy in anticipation of plenty of meat, and as they tramped off into the jungle they were singing gayly. Flora had divided them into three parties, each under a head man, with explicit directions for the position each party was to take in the line of beaters. Others had been detailed to the whites as gun-bearers, while a small party of the askari were left behind to guard the camp. The whites, with the exception of Esteban, were armed with rifles. He alone seemed inclined to question Flora's authority, insisting that he preferred to hunt with spear and arrows in keeping with the part he was playing. The fact that, though he had hunted assiduously for weeks, yet had never brought in a single kill, was not sufficient to dampen his egotism. So genuinely had he entered his part that he really thought he was Tarzan of the Apes, and with such fidelity had he equipped himself in every detail, and such a master of the art of make-up was he, that, in conjunction with his splendid figure and his handsome face that were almost a counterpart of Tarzan's, it was scarcely to be wondered at that he almost fooled himself as successfully as he had fooled others, for there were men among the carriers who had known the great ape-man, and even these were deceived, though they wondered at the change in him, since in little things he did not deport himself as Tarzan, and in the matter of kills he was disappointing.

Flora Hawkes, who was endowed with more than a fair share of intelligence, realized that it would not be well to cross any of her companions unnecessarily, and so she permitted Esteban to hunt that morning in his own way, though some of the others grumbled a little at her decision.

'What is the difference?' she asked them, after the Spaniard had set out alone. 'The chances are that he could use a rifle no better than he uses his spear and arrows. Carl and Dick are really the only shots among us, and it is upon them we depend principally for the success of our hunt today. Esteban's egotism has been so badly bumped that it is possible that he will go to the last extremity to make a kill today – let us hope that he is successful.'

'I hope he breaks his fool neck,' said Kraski. 'He has served our purpose and we would be better off if we were rid of him.'

The girl shook her head negatively. 'No,' she said, 'we must not think or speak of anything of that kind. We went into this thing together, let us stick together until the end. If you are wishing that one of us is dead, how do you know that others are not wishing that you were dead?'

'I haven't any doubt but that Miranda wishes I were dead,' replied Kraski. 'I never go to bed at night without thinking that the damned greaser may try to stick a knife into me before morning. And it don't make me feel any kinder toward him to hear you defending him, Flora. You've been a bit soft on him from the start.'

'If I have, it's none of your business,' retorted the girl.

And so they started out upon their hunt, the Russian scowling and angry, harboring thoughts of vengeance or worse against Esteban, and Esteban, hunting through the jungle, was occupied with his hatred and his jealousy. His dark mind was open to every chance suggestion of a means for putting the other men of the party out of the way, and taking the woman and the gold for himself. He hated them all; in each he saw a possible rival for the affections of Flora, and in the death of each he saw not only one less suitor for the girl's affections, but forty-three thousand additional pounds to be divided among fewer people. His mind was thus occupied to the exclusion of the business of hunting, which should have occupied him solely, when he came through a patch of heavy underbrush, and stepped into the glaring sunlight of a large clearing, face to face with a party of some fifty magnificent ebon warriors. For just an instant Esteban stood frozen in a paralysis of terror, forgetting momentarily the part he was playing – thinking of himself only as a lone white man in the heart of savage Africa facing a large band of war-like natives – cannibals, perhaps. It was that moment of utter silence and inaction that saved him, for, as he stood thus before them, the Waziri saw in the silent, majestic figure their beloved lord in a characteristic pose.

'O Bwana, Bwana,' cried one of the warriors, rushing forward, 'it is indeed you, Tarzan of the Apes, Lord of the Jungle, whom we had given up as lost. We, your faithful Waziri, have been searching for you, and even now we were about to dare the dangers of Opar, fearing that you might have ventured there without us and had been captured.'

The black, who had at one time accompanied Tarzan to London as a body servant, spoke broken English, an accomplishment of which he was inordinately proud, losing no opportunity to air his attainment before his less fortunate fellows. The fact that it had been he whom fate had chosen to act as spokesman was indeed a fortunate circumstance to Miranda. Although the latter had applied himself assiduously to mastering the dialect of the west coast carriers, he would have been hard put to it to carry on a conversation with one of them, while he understood nothing of the Waziri tongue. Flora had schooled him carefully and well in the lore of Tarzan, so that he realized now that he was in the presence of a band of the ape-man's faithful Waziri. Never before had he seen such magnificent blacks – clean-cut, powerful men, with intelligent faces and well molded features, appearing as much higher in the scale of evolution as were the west coast blacks above the apes. Lucky indeed was Esteban Miranda that he was quick-witted and a consummate actor. Otherwise must he have betrayed his terror and his chagrin upon learning that this band of Tarzan's fierce and faithful followers was in this part of the country. For a moment longer he stood in silence before them, gathering his wits, and then he spoke, realizing that his very life depended upon his plausibility. And as he thought a great light broke upon the shrewd brain of the unscrupulous Spaniard.

'Since I last saw you,' he said, 'I discovered that a party of white men had entered the country for the purpose of robbing the treasure vaults of Opar. I followed them until I found their camp, and then I came in search of you, for there are many of them and they have many ingots of gold, for they have already been to Opar. Follow me, and we will raid their camp and take the gold from them. Come!' and he turned back toward the camp that he had just quitted.

As they made their way along the jungle trail, Usula, the Waziri who had spoken English to him, walked at Esteban's side. Behind them the Spaniard could hear the other warriors speaking in their native tongue, no word of which he understood, and it occurred to him that his position would be most embarrassing should he be addressed in the Waziri language, which, of course, Tarzan must have understood perfectly. As he listened to the chatter of Usula his mind was working rapidly, and presently, as though it were an inspiration, there recurred to him the memory of an accident that had befallen Tarzan, which had been narrated to him by Flora – the story of the injury he had received in the treasure vaults of Opar upon the occasion that he had lost his memory because of a blow upon the head. Esteban wondered if he had committed himself too deeply at first to attribute to amnesia any shortcomings in the portrayal of the rôle he was acting. At its worst, however, it seemed to him the best that he could do. He turned suddenly upon Usula.

'Do you remember,' he asked, 'the accident that befell me in the treasure vaults of Opar, depriving me of my memory?'

'Yes, Bwana, I remember it well,' replied the black.

'A similar accident has befallen me,' said Esteban. 'A great tree fell in my path, and in falling a branch struck me upon the head. It has not caused me to lose my memory entirely, but since then it is with difficulty that I recall many things, and there are others which I must have forgotten entirely, for I do not know your name, nor do I understand the words that my other Waziri are speaking about me.'

Usula looked at him compassionately. 'Ah, Bwana, sad indeed is the heart of Usula to hear that this accident has befallen you. Doubtless it will soon pass away as did the other, and in the meantime I, Usula, will be your memory for you.'

'Good,' said Esteban, 'tell the others that they may understand, and tell them also that I have lost the memory of other things besides. I could not now find my way home without you, and my other senses are dull as well. But as you say, Usula, it will soon pass off, and I shall be myself again.'

'Your faithful Waziri will rejoice indeed with the coming of that moment,' said Usula.

As they approached the camp, Miranda cautioned Usula to warn his followers to silence, and presently he halted them at the outskirts of the clearing where they could attain a view of the boma and the tents, guarding which was a little band of a half-dozen askari.

'When they see our greater numbers they will make no resistance,' said Esteban. 'Let us surround the camp, therefore, and at a signal from me we will advance together, when you shall address them, saying that Tarzan of the Apes comes with his Waziri for the gold they have stolen, but that he will spare them if they will leave the country at once and never return.'

Had it fulfilled his purpose as well, the Spaniard would have willingly ordered his Waziri to fall upon the men guarding the camp and destroy them all, but to his cunning brain had been born a cleverer scheme. He wanted these men to see him with the Waziri and live to tell the others that they had seen him, and to repeat to Flora and her followers the thing that Esteban had in his mind to tell one of the askari, while the Waziri were gathering up the gold ingots from the camp.

In directing Usula to station his men about the camp, Esteban had to warn them that they were not to show themselves until he had crept out into the clearing and attracted the attention of the askari on guard. Fifteen minutes, perhaps, were consumed in stationing his men, and then Usula returned to Esteban to report that all was ready.

'When I raise my hand then you will know that they have recognized me and that you are to advance,' Esteban cautioned him, and stepped forward slowly into the clearing. One of the askari saw him and recognized him as Esteban. The Spaniard took a few steps closer to the boma and then halted.

'I am Tarzan of the Apes,' he said; 'your camp is entirely surrounded by my warriors. Make no move against us and we shall not hurt you.'

He waved his hand. Fifty stalwart Waziri stepped into view from the concealing verdure of the surrounding jungle. The askari eyed them in ill-concealed terror, fingering their rifles nervously.

'Do not shoot,' cautioned Esteban, 'or we shall slay you all.' He approached more closely and his Waziri closed in about him, entirely surrounding the boma.

'Speak to them, Usula,' said Esteban. The black stepped forward.

'We are the Waziri,' he cried, 'and this is Tarzan of the Apes, Lord of the Jungle, our master. We have come to recover the gold of Tarzan that you have stolen from the treasure vaults of Opar. This time we shall spare you on condition that you leave the country and never return. Tell this word to your masters; tell them that Tarzan watches, and that his Waziri watch with him. Lay down your rifles.'

The askari, glad to escape so easily, complied with the demands of Usula, and a moment later the Waziri had entered the boma, and at Esteban's direction were gathering up the golden ingots. As they worked, Esteban approached one of the askari, whom he knew spoke broken English.

'Tell your master,' he said, 'to give thanks for the mercy of Tarzan who has exacted a toll of but one life for this invasion of his country and theft of his treasure. The creature who presumes to pose as Tarzan I have slain, and his body I shall take away with me and feed to the lions. Tell them that Tarzan forgives even their attempt to poison him upon the occasion that he visited their camp, but only upon the condition that they never return to Africa, and that they divulge the secret of Opar to no others. Tarzan watches and his Waziri watch, and no man may enter Africa without Tarzan's knowledge. Even before they left London I knew that they were coming. Tell them that.'

It took but a few minutes for the Waziri to gather up the golden ingots, and before the askari had recovered from the surprise of their appearance, they had gone again into the jungle, with Tarzan, their master.

It was late in the afternoon before Flora and the four white men returned from their hunt, surrounded by happy, laughing blacks, bearing the fruits of a successful chase.

'Now that you are in charge, Flora,' Kraski was saying, 'fortune is smiling upon us indeed. We have enough meat here for several days, and with plenty of meat in their bellies they ought to make good progress.'

'I vill say it myself dot tings look brighter,' said Bluber.

'Blime, they do that,' said Throck. 'I'm tellin' you Flora's a bright one.'

'What the devil is this?' demanded Peebles, 'what's wrong with them beggars?' And he pointed toward the boma which was now in sight, and from which the askari were issuing at a run, jabbering excitedly as they raced toward them.

'Tarzan of the Apes has been here,' they cried excitedly. 'He has been here with all his Waziri – a thousand great warriors – and though we fought, they overcame us, and taking the gold they went away. Tarzan of the Apes spoke strange words to me before they left. He said that he had killed one of your number who had dared to call himself Tarzan of the Apes. We do not understand it. He went away alone to hunt when you went in the morning, and he came back shortly with a thousand warriors, and he took all the gold and he threatened to kill us and you if you ever return to this country again.'

'Vot, vot?' cried Bluber, 'der gold iss gone? *Ach! Ach!*' And then they all commenced to ask questions at once until Flora silenced them.

'Come,' she said to the leader of the askari, 'we will return to the boma and then you shall tell me slowly and carefully all that has happened since we left.'

She listened intently to his narrative, and then questioned him carefully upon various points several times. At last she dismissed him. Then she turned to her confederates.

'It is all clear to me,' she said. 'Tarzan recovered from the effects of the drug we administered. Then he followed us with his Waziri, caught Esteban and killed him and, finding the camp, has taken the gold away. We shall be fortunate indeed if we escape from Africa with our lives.'

'*Ach, weh!*' almost shrieked Bluber, 'der dirty crook. He steals all our gold, und ve lose our two t'ousand pounds into der bargain.'

'Shut up, you coward,' growled Throck. 'If it hadn't 'a' been for you and the actor there 'ere thing would never 'a' 'appened. With 'im abraggin' about 'is 'unting and not bein' able to kill anything, and you a-squeezin' every bloomin' hapenny, we're in a rotten mess – that we are. This 'ere Tarzan bounder he bumped off Esteban, which is the best work what 'e ever done. Too bloody bad you weren't 'ere to get it too, and what I got a good mind to do is to slit your throat meself.'

'Stow the guff, Dick,' roared Peebles; 'it wasn't nobody's fault, as far as I can see. Instead of talkin' what we oughter do is to go after this 'ere Tarzan feller and take the bloomin' gold away from 'im.'

Flora Hawkes laughed. 'We haven't a chance in the world,' she said. 'I know this Tarzan bloke. If he was all alone we wouldn't be a match for him, but he's got a bunch of his Waziri with him, and there are no finer warriors in Africa than they. And they'd fight for him to the last man. You just tell Owaza that you're thinking of going after Tarzan of the Apes and his Waziri to take the gold away from them, and see how long it'd be before we wouldn't have a single porter with us. The very name of Tarzan scares these west coast blacks out of a year's growth. They would sooner face the devil. No, sir, we've lost, and all we can do is to get out of the country, and thank our lucky stars if we manage to get out alive. The ape-man will watch us. I should not be surprised if he were watching us this minute.' Her companions looked around apprehensively at this, casting nervous glances toward the jungle. 'And he'd never let us get back to Opar for another load, even if we could prevail upon our blacks to return there.'

'Two t'ousand pounds, two t'ousand pounds!' wailed Bluber. 'Und all dis suit, vat it cost me tventy guineas vat I can't vear it again in England unless I go to a fancy dress ball, vich I never do.'

Kraski had not spoken, but had sat with eyes upon the ground, listening to the others. Now he raised his head. 'We have lost our gold,' he said, 'and before we get back to England we stand to spend the balance of our two thousand pounds – in other words our expedition is a total loss. The rest of you may be satisfied to go back broke, but I am not. There are other things in Africa besides the gold of Opar, and when we leave the country there is no reason why we shouldn't take something with us that will repay us for our time and investment.'

'What do you mean?' asked Peebles.

'I have spent a lot of time talking with Owaza,' replied Kraski, 'trying to learn their crazy language, and I have come to find out a lot about the old villain. He's as crooked as they make 'em, and if he were to be hanged for all his murders, he'd have to have more lives than a cat, but notwithstanding all that, he's a shrewd old fellow, and I've learned a lot more from him than just his monkey talk – I have learned enough, in fact, so that I feel safe in saying that if we stick together we can go out of Africa with a pretty good sized stake. Personally, I haven't given up the gold of Opar yet. What we've lost, we've lost, but there's plenty left where that came from, and some day after this blows over, I'm coming back to get my share.'

'But how about this other thing?' asked Flora. 'How can Owaza help us?'

'There's a little bunch of Arabs down here,' explained Kraski, 'stealing slaves and ivory. Owaza knows where they are working and where their main camp is. There are only a few of them, and their blacks are nearly all slaves who would turn on them in a minute. Now the idea is this: we have a big enough party to overpower them and take their ivory away from them if we can get their slaves to take our side. We don't want the slaves; we couldn't do anything with them if we had them, so we can promise them their freedom for their help, and give Owaza and his gang a share in the ivory.'

'How do you know Owaza will help us?' asked Flora.

'The idea is his; that's the reason I know,' replied Kraski.

'It sounds good to me,' said Peebles; 'I ain't fer goin' 'ome empty 'anded.' And in turn the others signified their approval of the scheme.

11

Strange Incense Burns

As Tarzan carried the dead Bolgani from the village of the Gomangani, he set his steps in the direction of the building he had seen from the rim of the valley, the curiosity of the man overcoming the natural caution of the beast. He was traveling upwind and the odors wafted down to his nostrils told him that he was approaching the habitat of the Bolgani. Intermingled with the scent spoor of the gorilla-men was that of Gomangani and the odor of cooked food, and the suggestion of a heavily sweet scent, which the ape-man could connect only with burning incense, though it seemed impossible that such a fragrance could emanate from the dwellings of the Bolgani. Perhaps it came from the great edifice he had seen – a building which must have been constructed by human beings, and in which human beings might still dwell, though never among the multitudinous odors that assailed his nostrils did he once catch the faintest suggestion of the man scent of whites.

When he perceived from the increasing strength of their odor, that he was approaching close to the Bolgani, Tarzan took to the trees with his burden, that he might thus stand a better chance of avoiding discovery, and presently, through the foliage ahead, he saw a lofty wall, and, beyond, the outlines of the weird architecture of a strange and mysterious pile – outlines that suggested a building of another world, so unearthly were they, and from beyond the wall came the odor of the Bolgani and the fragrance of the incense, intermingled with the scent spoor of Numa, the lion. The jungle was cleared away for fifty feet outside the wall surrounding the building, so that there was no tree overhanging the wall, but Tarzan approached as closely as he could, while still remaining reasonably well-concealed by the foliage. He had chosen a point at a sufficient height above the ground to permit him to see over the top of the wall.

The building within the enclosure was of great size, its different parts appearing to have been constructed at various periods, and each with utter disregard to uniformity, resulting in a conglomeration of connecting buildings and towers, no two of which were alike, though the whole presented a rather pleasing, if somewhat bizarre appearance. The building stood upon an artificial elevation about ten feet high, surrounded by a retaining wall of granite, a wide staircase leading to the ground level below. About the building were shrubbery and trees, some of the latter appearing to be of great antiquity, while one enormous tower was almost entirely covered by ivy. By far the most remarkable feature of the building, however, lay in its rich and barbaric ornamentation. Set into the polished granite of which it was composed was an intricate mosaic of gold and diamonds; glittering stones in countless thousands scintillated from façades, minarets, domes, and towers.

The enclosure, which comprised some fifteen or twenty acres, was occupied for the most part by the building. The terrace upon which it stood was devoted to walks, flowers, shrubs, and ornamental trees, while that part of the area below, which was within the range of Tarzan's vision, seemed to be given over to the raising of garden truck. In the garden and upon the terrace were naked blacks, such as he had seen in the village where he had left La. There were both men and women, and these were occupied with the care of growing things within the enclosure. Among them were several of the gorilla-like creatures such as Tarzan had slain in the village, but these performed no labor, devoting themselves rather, it seemed, to directing the work of the blacks, toward whom their manner was haughty and domineering, sometimes even brutal. These gorilla-men were trapped in rich ornaments, similar to those upon the body which now rested in a crotch of the tree behind the ape-man.

As Tarzan watched with interest the scene below him, two Bolgani emerged from the main entrance, a huge portal, some thirty feet in width, and perhaps fifteen feet high. The two wore head-bands, supporting tall, white feathers. As they emerged they took post on either side of the entrance, and cupping their hands before their mouths gave voice to a series of shrill cries that bore a marked resemblance to trumpet calls. Immediately the blacks ceased work and hastened to the foot of the stairs descending from the terrace to the garden. Here they formed lines on either side of the stairway, and similarly the Bolgani formed two lines upon the terrace from the main portal to the stairway, forming a living aisle from one to the other. Presently from the interior of the building came other trumpet-like calls, and a moment later Tarzan saw the head of a procession emerging. First came four Bolgani abreast, each bedecked with an ornate feather headdress, and each carrying a huge bludgeon erect before him. Behind these came two trumpeters, and twenty feet behind the trumpeters paced a huge, black-maned lion, held in leash by four sturdy blacks, two upon either side, holding what appeared to be golden chains that ran to a scintillant diamond collar about the beast's neck. Behind the lion marched twenty more Bolgani, four abreast. These carried spears, but whether they were for the purpose of protecting the lion from the people or the people from the lion Tarzan was at a loss to know.

The attitude of the Bolgani lining either side of the way between the portal and the stairway indicated extreme deference, for they bent their bodies from their waists in a profound bow while Numa was passing between their lines. When the beast reached the top of the stairway the procession halted, and immediately the Gomangani ranged below prostrated themselves and placed their foreheads on the ground. Numa, who was evidently an old lion, stood with lordly mien surveying the prostrate humans before him. His evil eyes glared glassily, the while he bared his tusks in a savage grimace, and from his deep lungs rumbled forth an ominous roar, at the sound of which the Gomangani trembled in unfeigned terror. The ape-man knit his brows in thought. Never before had he been called upon to witness so remarkable a scene of the abasement of man before a beast. Presently the procession continued upon its way descending the staircase and turning to the right along a path through the garden, and when it had passed them the Gomangani and the Bolgani arose and resumed their interrupted duties.

Tarzan remained in his concealment watching them, trying to discover some explanation for the strange, paradoxical conditions that he had witnessed. The lion, with his retinue, had turned the far corner of the palace and disappeared from sight. What was he to these people, to these strange creatures? What did he represent? Why this topsy-turvy arrangement of species? Here man ranked lower than the half-beast, and above all, from the deference that had been accorded him, stood a true beast – a savage carnivore.

He had been occupied with his thoughts and his observations for some fifteen minutes following the disappearance of Numa around the eastern end of the palace, when his attention was attracted to the opposite end of the structure by the sound of other shrill trumpet calls. Turning his eyes in that direction, he saw the procession emerging again into view, and proceeding toward the staricase down which they had entered the garden. Immediately the notes of the shrill call sounded upon their ears the Gomangani and the Bolgani resumed their original positions from below the foot of the staircase to the entrance to the palace, and once again was homage paid to Numa as he made his triumphal entry into the building.

Tarzan of the Apes ran his fingers through his mass of tousled hair, but finally he was forced to shake his head in defeat – he could find no explanation whatsoever for all that he had witnessed. His curiosity, however, was so keenly piqued that he determined to investigate the palace and surrounding grounds further before continuing on his way in search of a trail out of the valley.

Leaving the body of Bolgani where he had cached it, he started slowly to circle the building that he might examine it from all sides from the concealing foliage of the surrounding forest. He found the architecture equally unique upon all sides, and that the garden extended entirely around the building, though a portion upon the south side of the palace was given over to corrals and pens in which were kept numerous goats and a considerable flock of chickens. Upon this side, also, were several hundred swinging, bee-hive huts, such as he had seen in the native village of the Gomangani. These he took to be the quarters of the black slaves, who performed all the arduous and menial labor connected with the palace.

The lofty granite wall which surrounded the entire enclosure was pierced by but a single gate which opened opposite the east end of the palace. This gate was large and of massive construction, appearing to have been built to withstand the assault of numerous and well-armed forces. So strong did it appear that the ape-man could not but harbor the opinion that it had been constructed to protect the interior against forces equipped with heavy battering rams. That such a force had ever existed within the vicinity in historic times seemed most unlikely, and Tarzan conjectured, therefore, that the wall and the gate were of almost unthinkable antiquity, dating, doubtless, from the forgotten age of the Atlantians, and constructed, perhaps, to protect the builders of the Palace of Diamonds from the well-armed forces that had come from Atlantis to work the gold mines of Opar and to colonize central Africa.

While the wall, the gate, and the palace itself, suggested in many ways almost unbelievable age, yet they were in such an excellent state of repair that it was evident that they were still inhabited by rational and intelligent creatures; while upon the south side Tarzan had seen a new tower in process of construction, where a number of blacks working under the direction of Bolgani were cutting and shaping granite blocks and putting them in place.

Tarzan had halted in a tree near the east gate to watch the life passing in and out of the palace grounds beneath the ancient portal, and as he watched, a long cavalcade of powerful Gomangani emerged from the forest and entered the enclosure. Swung in hides between two poles, this party was carrying rough-hewn blocks of granite, four men to a block. Two or three Bolgani accompanied the long line of carriers, which was preceded and followed by a detachment of black warriors, armed with battle-axes and spears. The demeanor and attitude of the black porters, as well as of the Bolgani, suggested to the ape-man nothing more nor less than a caravan of donkeys, plodding their stupid way at the behest of their drivers. If one lagged he was prodded with the point of a spear or struck with its haft. There was no greater brutality shown than in the ordinary handling of beasts of burden the world around, nor in the demeanor of the blacks was there any more indication of objection or revolt than you see depicted upon the faces of a long line of burden-bearing mules; to all intents and purposes they were dumb, driven cattle. Slowly they filed through the gateway and disappeared from sight.

A few moments later another party came out of the forest and passed into the palace grounds. This consisted of fully fifty armed Bolgani and twice as many black warriors with spears and axes. Entirely surrounded by these armed creatures were four brawny porters, carrying a small litter, upon which was fastened an ornate chest about two feet wide by four feet long, with a depth of approximately two feet. The chest itself was of some dark, weather-worn wood, and was reinforced by bands and corners of what appeared to be virgin gold in which were set many diamonds. What the chest contained Tarzan could not, of course, conceive, but that it was considered of great value was evidenced by the precautions for safety with which it had been surrounded. The chest was borne directly into the huge, ivy-covered tower at the northeast corner of the palace, the entrance to which, Tarzan now first observed, was secured by doors as large and heavy as the east gate itself.

At the first opportunity that he could seize to accomplish it undiscovered, Tarzan swung across the jungle trail and continued through the trees to that one in which he had left the body of the Bolgani. Throwing this across his shoulder he returned to a point close above the trail near the east gate, and seizing upon a moment when there was a lull in the traffic he hurled the body as close to the portal as possible.

'Now,' thought the ape-man, 'let them guess who slew their fellow if they can.'

Making his way toward the southeast, Tarzan approached the mountains which lie back of the Valley of the Palace of Diamonds. He had often to make detours to avoid native villages and to keep out of sight of the numerous parties of Bolgani that seemed to be moving in all directions through the forest. Late in the afternoon he came out of the hills into full view of the mountains beyond – rough, granite hills they were, whose precipitous peaks rose far above the timber line. Directly before him a well-marked trail led into a canyon, which he could see wound far upward toward the summit. This, then, would be as good a place to commence his investigations as another. And so, seeing that the coast was clear, the ape-man descended from the trees, and taking advantage of the underbrush bordering the trail, made his way silently, yet swiftly, into the hills. For the most part he was compelled to worm his way through thickets, for the trail was in constant use by Gomangani and Bolgani, parties passing up it empty-handed and, returning, bearing blocks of granite. As he advanced more deeply into the hills the heavy underbrush gave way to a lighter growth of scrub, through which he could pass with far greater ease though with considerable more risk of discovery. However, the instinct of the beast that dominated Tarzan's jungle craft permitted him to find cover where another would have been in full view of every enemy. Halfway up the mountain the trail passed through a narrow gorge, not more than twenty feet wide and eroded from solid granite cliffs. Here there was no concealment whatsoever, and the ape-man realized that to enter it would mean almost immediate discovery. Glancing about, he saw that by making a slight detour he could reach the summit of the gorge, where, amid tumbled, granite boulders and stunted trees and shrubs, he knew that he could find sufficient concealment, and perhaps a plainer view of the trail beyond.

Nor was he mistaken, for, when he had reached a vantage point far above the trail, he saw ahead an open pocket in the mountain, the cliffs surrounding which were honeycombed with numerous openings, which, it seemed to Tarzan, could be naught else than the mouths of tunnels. Rough wooden ladders reached to some of them, closer to the base of the cliffs, while from others knotted ropes dangled to the ground below. Out of these tunnels emerged men carrying little sacks of earth, which they dumped in a common pile beside a rivulet which ran through the gorge. Here other blacks, supervised by Bolgani, were engaged in washing the dirt, but what they hoped to find or what they did find, Tarzan could not guess.

Along one side of the rocky basin many other blacks were engaged in quarrying the granite from the cliffs, which had been cut away through similar operations into a series of terraces running from the floor of the basin to the summit of the cliff. Here naked blacks toiled with primitive tools under the supervision of savage Bolgani. The activities of the quarrymen were obvious enough, but what the others were bringing from the mouths of the tunnels Tarzan could not be positive, though the natural assumption was that it was gold. Where, then, did they obtain their diamonds? Certainly not from these solid granite cliffs.

A few minutes' observation convinced Tarzan that the trail he had followed from the forest ended in this little cul-de-sac, and so he sought a way upward and around it, in search of a pass across the range.

The balance of that day and nearly all the next he devoted to his efforts in this direction, only in the end to be forced to admit that there was no egress from the valley upon this side. To points far above the timber line he made his way, but there, always, he came face to face with sheer, perpendicular cliffs of granite towering high above him, upon the face of which not even the ape-man could find foothold. Along the southern and eastern sides of the basin he carried his investigation, but with similar disappointing results, and then at last he turned his steps back toward the forest with the intention of seeking a way out through the valley of Opar with La, after darkness had fallen.

The sun had just risen when Tarzan arrived at the native village in which he had left La, and no sooner did his eyes rest upon it than he became apprehensive that something was amiss, for not only was the gate wide open but there was no sign of life within the palisade, nor was there any movement of the swinging huts that would indicate that they were occupied. Always wary of ambush, Tarzan reconnoitered carefully before descending into the village. To his trained observation it became evident that the village had been deserted for at least twenty-four hours. Running to the hut in which La had been hidden he hastily ascended the rope and examined the interior – it was vacant, nor was there any sign of the High Priestess. Descending to the ground, the ape-man started to make a thorough investigation of the village in search of clews to the fate of its inhabitants and of La. He had examined the interiors of several huts when his keen eyes noted a slight movement of one of the swinging, cage-like habitations some distance from him. Quickly he crossed the intervening space, and as he approached the but he saw that no rope trailed from its doorway. Halting beneath, Tarzan raised his face to the aperture, through which nothing but the roof of the but was visible.

'Gomangani,' he cried, 'it is I, Tarzan of the Apes. Come to the opening and tell me what has become of your fellows and of my mate, whom I left here under the protection of your warriors.'

There was no answer, and again Tarzan called, for he was positive that someone was hiding in the hut.

'Come down,' he called again, 'or I will come up after you.'

Still there was no reply. A grim smile touched the ape-man's lips as he drew his hunting knife from its sheath and placed it between his teeth, and then, with a cat-like spring, leaped for the opening, and catching its sides, drew his body up into the interior of the hut.

If he had expected opposition, he met with none, nor in the dimly lighted interior could he at first distinguish any presence, though, when his eyes became accustomed to the semi-darkness, he descried a bundle of leaves and grasses lying against the opposite wall of the structure. Crossing to these he tore them aside revealing the huddled form of a terrified woman. Seizing her by a shoulder he drew her to a sitting position.

'What has happened?' he demanded. 'Where are the villagers? Where is my mate?'

'Do not kill me! Do not kill me!' she cried. 'It was not I. It was not my fault.'

'I do not intend to kill you,' replied Tarzan. 'Tell me the truth and you shall be safe.'

'The Bolgani have taken them away,' cried the woman. 'They came when the sun was low upon the day that you arrived, and they were very angry, for they had found the body of their fellow outside the gate of the Palace of Diamonds. They knew that he had come here to our village, and no one had seen him alive since he had departed from the palace. They came, then, and threatened and tortured our people, until at last the warriors told them all.

I hid. I do not know why they did not find me. But at last they went away, taking all the others with them; taking your mate, too. They will never come back.'

'You think that the Bolgani will kill them?' asked Tarzan.

'Yes,' she replied, 'they kill all who displease them.'

Alone, now, and relieved of the responsibility of La, Tarzan might easily make his way by night through the valley of Opar and to safety beyond the barrier. But perhaps such a thought never entered his head. Gratitude and loyalty were marked characteristics of the ape-man. La had saved him from the fanaticism and intrigue of her people. She had saved him at a cost of all that was most dear to her, power and position, peace and safety. She had jeopardized her life for him, and became an exile from her own country. The mere fact then that the Bolgani had taken her with the possible intention of slaying her, was not sufficient for the ape-man. He must know whether or not she lived, and if she lived he must devote his every energy to winning her release and her eventual escape from the dangers of this valley.

Tarzan spent the day reconnoitering outside the palace grounds, seeking an opportunity of gaining entrance without detection, but this he found impossible inasmuch as there was never a moment that there were not Gomangani or Bolgani in the outer garden. But with the approach of darkness the great east gate was closed, and the inmates of the huts and palace withdrew within their walls, leaving not even a single sentinel without – a fact that indicated clearly that the Bolgani had no reason to apprehend an attack. The subjugation of the Gomangani, then, was apparently complete, and so the towering wall surrounding their palace, which was more than sufficient to protect them from the inroads of lions, was but the reminder of an ancient day when a once-powerful, but now vanished, enemy threatened their peace and safety.

When darkness had finally settled Tarzan approached the gate, and throwing the noose of his grass rope over one of the carved lions that capped the gate posts, ascended quickly to the summit of the wall, from where he dropped lightly into the garden below. To insure an avenue for quick escape in the event that he found La, he unlatched the heavy gates and swung them open. Then he crept stealthily toward the ivy-covered east tower, which he had chosen after a day of investigation as offering easiest ingress to the palace. The success of his plan hinged largely upon the age and strength of the ivy which grew almost to the summit of the tower, and, to his immense relief, he found that it would easily support his weight.

Far above the ground, near the summit of the tower, he had seen from the trees surrounding the palace an open window, which, unlike the balance of those in this part of the palace, was without bars. Dim lights shone from several of the tower windows, as from those of other parts of the palace. Avoiding these lighted apertures, Tarzan ascended quickly, though carefully, toward the unbarred window above, and as he reached it and cautiously raised his eyes above the level of the sill, he was delighted to find that it opened into an unlighted chamber, the interior of which, however, was so shrouded in darkness that he could discern nothing within. Drawing himself carefully to the level of the sill he crept quietly into the apartment beyond. Groping through the blackness, he cautiously made the rounds of the room, which he found to contain a carved bedstead of peculiar design, a table, and a couple of benches. Upon the bedstead were stuffs of woven material, thrown over the softly tanned pelts of antelopes and leopards.

Opposite the window through which he had entered was a closed door. This he opened slowly and silently, until, through a tiny aperture he could look out upon a dimly lighted corridor or circular hallway, in the center of which was an opening about four feet in diameter, passing through which and disappearing beyond a similar opening in the ceiling directly above was a straight pole with short crosspieces fastened to it at intervals of about a foot – quite evidently the primitve staircase which gave communication between the various floors of the tower. Three upright columns, set at equal intervals about the circumference of the circular opening in the center of the floor helped to support the ceiling above. Around the outside of this circular hallway there were other doors, similar to that opening into the apartment in which he was.

Hearing no noise and seeing no evidence of another than himself, Tarzan opened the door and stepped into the hallway. His nostrils were now assailed strongly by the same heavy fragrance of incense that had first greeted him upon his approach to the palace several days before. In the interior of the tower, however, it was much more powerful, practically obliterating all other odors, and placing upon the ape-man an almost prohibitive handicap in his search for La. In fact as he viewed the doors upon this single stage of the tower, he was filled with consternation at the prospect of the well-nigh impossible task that confronted him. To search this great tower alone, without any assistance whatever from his keen sense of scent, seemed impossible of accomplishment, if he were to take even the most ordinary precautions against detection.

The ape-man's self-confidence was in no measure blundering egotism. Knowing his limitations, he knew that he would have little or no chance against even a few Bolgani were he to be discovered within their palace, where all was familiar to them and strange to him. Behind him was the open window, and the silent jungle night, and freedom. Ahead danger, predestined failure; and, quite likely, death. Which would he choose? For a moment he stood in silent thought, and then, raising his head and squaring his great shoulders, he shook his black locks defiantly and stepped boldly toward the nearest door. Room after room he had investigated until he had made the entire circle of the landing, but in so far as La or any clew to her were concerned his search was fruitless. He found quaint furniture and rugs and tapestries, and ornaments of gold and diamonds, and in one dimly lighted chamber he came upon a sleeping Bolgani, but so silent were the movements of the ape-man that the sleeper slept on undisturbed, even though Tarzan passed entirely around his bed, which was set in the center of the chamber, and investigated a curtained alcove beyond.

Having completed the rounds of this floor, Tarzan determined to work upward first and then, returning, investigate the lower stages later. Pursuant to this plan, therefore, he ascended the strange stairway. Three landings he passed before he reached the upper floor of the tower. Circling each floor was a ring of doors, all of which were closed, while dimly lighting each landing were feebly burning cressets – shallow, golden bowls – containing what appeared to be tallow, in which floated a tow-like wick.

Upon the upper landing there were but three doors, all of which were closed. The ceiling of this hallway was the dome-like roof of the tower, in the center of which was another circular opening, through which the stairway protruded into the darkness of the night above.

As Tarzan opened the door nearest him it creaked upon its hinges, giving forth the first audible sound that had resulted from his investigations up to this point The interior of the apartment before him was unlighted and as Tarzan stood there in the entrance in statuesque silence for a few seconds following the creaking of the hinge, he was suddenly aware of movement – of the faintest shadow of a sound – behind him. Wheeling quickly he saw the figure of a man standing in an open doorway upon the opposite site of the landing.

12

The Golden Ingots

Esteban Miranda had played the rôle of Tarzan of the Apes with the Warizi as his audience for less than twenty-four hours when he began to realize that, even with the lee-way that his supposedly injured brain gave him, it was going to be a very difficult thing to carry on the deception indefinitely. In the first place Usula did not seem at all pleased at the idea of merely taking the gold away from the intruders and then running from them. Nor did his fellow warriors seem any more enthusiastic over the plan than he. As a matter of fact they could not conceive that any number of bumps upon the head could render their Tarzan of the Apes a coward, and to run away from these west coast blacks and a handful of inexperienced whites seemed nothing less than cowardly.

Following all this, there had occurred in the afternoon that which finally decided the Spaniard that he was building for himself anything other than a bed of roses, and that the sooner he found an excuse for quitting the company of the Waziri the greater would be his life expectancy.

They were passing through rather open jungle at the time. The brush was not particularly heavy and the trees were at considerable distances apart, when suddenly, without warning, a rhinoceros charged them. To the consternation of the Waziri, Tarzan of the Apes turned and fled for the nearest tree the instant his eyes alighted upon the charging Buto. In his haste Esteban tripped and fell, and when at last he reached the tree instead of leaping agilely into the lower branches, he attempted to shin up the huge bole as a schoolboy shins up a telegraph pole, only to slip and fall back again to the ground.

In the meantime Buto, who charges either by scent or hearing, rather than by eyesight, his powers of which are extremely poor, had been distracted from his original direction by one of the Waziri, and after missing the fellow had gone blundering on to disappear in the underbrush beyond.

When Esteban finally arose and discovered that the rhinoceros was gone, he saw surrounding him a semi-circle of huge blacks, upon whose faces were written expressions of pity and sorrow, not unmingled, in some instances, with a tinge of contempt. The Spaniard saw that he had been terrified into a practically irreparable blunder, yet he seized despairingly upon the only excuse he could conjure up.

'My poor head,' he cried, pressing both palms to his temples.

'The blow was upon your *head*, Bwana,' said Usula, 'and your faithful Waziri thought that it was the *heart* of their master that knew no fear.'

Esteban made no reply, and in silence they resumed their march. In silence they continued until they made camp before dark upon the bank of the river just above a waterfall. During the afternoon Esteban had evolved a plan of escape from his dilemma, and no sooner had he made camp than he ordered the Waziri to bury the treasure.

'We shall leave it here,' he said, 'and tomorrow we shall set forth in search of the thieves, for I have decided to punish them. They must be taught that they may not come into the jungle of Tarzan with impunity. It was only the injury to my head that prevented me from slaying them immediately I discovered their perfidy.'

This attitude pleased the Waziri better. They commenced to see a ray of hope. Once again was Tarzan of the Apes becoming Tarzan. And so it was that with lighter hearts and a new cheerfulness they set forth the next morning in search of the camp of the Englishmen, and by shrewd guessing on Usula's part they cut across the jungle to intercept the probable march of the Europeans to such advantage that they came upon them just as they were making camp that night. Long before they reached them they smelled the smoke of their fires and heard the songs and chatter of the west coast carriers.

Then it was that Esteban gathered the Waziri about him. 'My children,' he said, addressing Usula in English, 'these strangers have come here to wrong Tarzan. To Tarzan, then, belongs the vengeance. Go, therefore, and leave me to punish my enemies alone and in my own way. Return home, leave the gold where it is, for it will be a long time before I shall need it.'

The Waziri were disappointed, for this new plan did not at all accord with their desires, which contemplated a cheerful massacre of the west coast blacks. But as yet the man before them was Tarzan, their Big Bwana, to whom they had never failed in implicit obedience. For a few moments following Esteban's declaration of his intention, they stood in silence shifting uneasily, and then at last they commenced to speak to one another in Waziri. What they said the Spaniard did not know, but evidently they were urging something upon Usula, who presently turned toward him.

'Oh, Bwana,' cried the black. 'How can we return home to the Lady Jane and tell her that we left you injured and alone to face the rifles of the white men and their askari? Do not ask us to do it, Bwana. If you were yourself we should not fear for your safety, but since the injury to your head you have not been the same, and we fear to leave you alone in the jungle. Let us, then, your faithful Waziri, punish these people, after which we will take you home in safety, where you may be cured of the evils that have fallen upon you.'

The Spaniard laughed. 'I am entirely recovered,' he said, 'and I am in no more danger alone than I would be with you,' which he knew, even better than they, was but a mild statement of the facts. 'You will obey my wishes,' he continued sternly. 'Go back at once the way that we have come. After you have gone at least two miles you may make camp for the night, and in the morning start out again for home. Make no noise, I do not want them to know that I am here. Do not worry about me. I am all right, and I shall probably overtake you before you reach home. Go!'

Sorrowfully the Waziri turned back upon the trail they had just covered and a moment later the last of them disappeared from the sight of the Spaniard.

With a sigh of relief Esteban Miranda turned toward the camp of his own people. Fearing that to surprise them suddenly might invite a volley of shots from the askari he whistled, and then called aloud as he approached.

'It is Tarzan!' cried the first of the blacks who saw him. 'Now indeed shall we all be killed.'

Esteban saw the growing excitement among the carriers and askari – he saw the latter seize their rifles and that they were fingering the triggers nervously.

'It is I, Esteban Miranda,' he called aloud. 'Flora! Flora, tell those fools to lay aside their rifles.'

The whites, too, were standing watching him, and at the sound of his voice Flora turned toward the blacks. 'It is all right,' she said, 'that is not Tarzan. Lay aside your rifles.'

Esteban entered the camp, smiling. 'Here I am,' he said.

'We thought that you were dead,' said Kraski. 'Some of these fellows said that Tarzan said that he had killed you.'

'He captured me,' said Esteban, 'but as you see he did not kill me. I thought that he was going to, but he did not, and finally he turned me loose in the jungle. He may have thought that I could not survive and that he would accomplish his end just as surely without having my blood upon his hands.'

''E must have knowed you,' said Peebles. 'You'd die, all right, if you were left alone very long in the jungle – you'd starve to death.'

Esteban made no reply to the sally but turned toward Flora. 'Are you not glad to see me, Flora?' heasked.

The girl shrugged her shoulders. 'What is the difference?' she asked. 'Our expedition is a failure. Some of them think you were largely to blame.' She nodded her head in the general direction of the other whites.

The Spaniard scowled. None of them cared very much to see him. He did not care about the others, but he had hoped that Flora would show some enthusiasm about his return. Well, if she had known what he had in his mind, she might have been happier to see him, and only too glad to show some kind of affection. But she did not know. She did not know that Esteban Miranda had hidden the golden ingots where he might go another day and get them. It had been his intention to persuade her to desert the others, and then, later, the two would return and recover the treasure, but now he was piqued and offended – none of them would have a shilling of it – he would wait until they left Africa and then he would return and take it all for himself. The only fly in the ointment was the thought that the Waziri knew the location of the treasure, and that, sooner or later, they would return with Tarzan and get it. This weak spot in his calculations must be strengthened, and to strengthen it he must have assistance which would mean sharing his secret with another, but whom?

Outwardly oblivious of the sullen glances of his companions he took his place among them. It was evident to him that they were far from being glad to see him, but just why he did not know, for he had not heard of the plan that Kraski and Owaza had hatched to steal the loot of the ivory raiders, and that their main objection to his presence was the fear that they would be compelled to share the loot with him. It was Kraski who first voiced the thought that was in the minds of all but Esteban.

'Miranda,' he said, 'it is the consensus of opinion that you and Bluber are largely responsible for the failure of our venture. We are not finding fault. I just mention it as a fact. But since you have been away we have struck upon a plan to take something out of Africa that will partially recompense us for the loss of the gold. We have worked the thing all out carefully and made our plans. We don't need you to carry them out. We have no objection to your coming along with us, if you want to, for company, but we want to have it understood from the beginning that you are not to share in anything that we get out of this.'

The Spaniard smiled and waved a gesture of unconcern. 'It is perfectly all right,' he said. 'I shall ask for nothing. I would not wish to take anything from any of you.' And he grinned inwardly as he thought of the more than quarter of a million pounds in gold which he would one day take out of Africa for himself, alone.

At this unexpected attitude of acquiescence upon Esteban's part the others were greatly relieved, and immediately the entire atmosphere of constraint was removed.

'You're a good fellow, Esteban,' said Peebles. 'I've been sayin' right along that you'd want to do the right thing, and I want to say that I'm mighty glad to see you back here safe an' sound. I felt terrible when I 'eard you was croaked, that I did.'

'Yes,' said Bluber, 'John he feel so bad he cry himself to sleep every night, ain't it, John?'

'Don't try to start nothin', Bluber,' growled Peebles, glaring at the fat man.

'I vasn't commencing to start nodding,' replied Adolph, seeing that the big Englishman was angry; 'of course ve vere all sorry dat ve t'ought Esteban was killed und ve is all glad dat he is back.'

'And that he don't want any of the swag,' added Throck.

'Don't worry,' said Esteban, 'If I get back to London I'll be happy enough – I've had enough of Africa to last me all the rest of my life.'

Before he could get to sleep that night, the Spaniard spent a wakeful hour or two trying to evolve a plan whereby he might secure the gold absolutely to himself, without fear of its being removed by the Waziri later. He knew that he could easily find the spot where he had buried it and remove it to another close by, provided that he could return immediately over the trail along which Usula had led them that day, and he could do this alone, insuring that no one but himself would know the new location of the hiding place of the gold, but he was equally positive that he could never again return later from the coast and find where he had hidden it. This meant that he must share his secret with another – one familiar with the country who could find the spot again at any time and from any direction. But who was there whom he might trust! In his mind he went carefully over the entire personnel of their safari, and continually his mind reverted to a single individual – Owaza. He had no confidence in the wily old scoundrel's integrity, but there was no other who suited his purpose as well, and finally he was forced to the conclusion that he must share his secret with this black, and depend upon avarice rather than honor for his protection. He could repay the fellow well – make him rich beyond his wildest dreams, and this the Spaniard could well afford to do in view of the tremendous fortune at stake. And so he fell asleep dreaming of what gold, to the value of over a quarter of a million pounds sterling, would accomplish in the gay capitals of the world.

The following morning while they were breakfasting Esteban mentioned casually that he had passed a large herd of antelope not far from their camp the previous day, and suggested that he take four or five men and do a little hunting, joining the balance of the party at camp that night. No one raised any objection, possibly for the reason that they assumed that the more he hunted and the further from the safari he went the greater the chances of his being killed, a contingency that none of them would have regretted, since at heart they had neither liking nor trust for him.

'I will take Owaza,' he said. 'He is the cleverest hunter of them all, and five or six men of his choosing.' But later, when he approached Owaza, the black interposed objections to the hunt.

'We have plenty of meat for two days,' he said. 'Let us go on as fast as we can, away from the land of the Waziri and Tarzan. I can find plenty of game anywhere between here and the coast. March for two days, and then I will hunt with you.'

'Listen,' said Esteban, in a whisper. 'It is more than antelope that I would hunt. I cannot tell you here in camp, but when we have left the others I will explain. It will pay you better to come with me today than all the ivory you can hope to get from the raiders.' Owaza cocked an attentive ear and scratched his woolly head.

'It is a good day to hunt, Bwana,' he said. 'I will come with you and bring five boys.'

After Owaza had planned the march for the main party and arranged for the camping place for the night, so that he and the Spaniard could find them again, the hunting party set out upon the trail that Usula had followed from the buried treasure the preceding day. They had not gone far before Owaza discovered the fresh spoor of the Waziri.

'Many men passed here late yesterday,' he said to Esteban, eyeing the Spaniard quizzically.

'I saw nothing of them,' replied the latter. 'They must have come this way after I passed.'

'They came almost to our camp, and then they turned about and went away again,' said Owaza. 'Listen, Bwana, I carry a rifle and you shall march ahead of me. If these tracks were made by your people, and you are leading me into ambush, you shall be the first to die.'

'Listen, Owaza,' said Esteban, 'we are far enough from camp now so that I may tell you all. These tracks were made by the Waziri of Tarzan of the Apes, who buried the gold for me a day's march from here. I have sent them home, and I wish you to go back with me and move the gold to another hiding place. After these others have gotten their ivory and returned to England, you and I will come back and get the gold, and then, indeed, shall you be well rewarded.'

'Who are you, then?' asked Owaza. 'Often I have doubted that you are Tarzan of the Apes. The day that we left the camp outside of Opar one of my men told me that you had been poisoned by your own people and left in the camp. He said that he saw it with his own eyes – your body lying hidden behind some bushes – and yet you were with us upon the march that day. I thought that he lied to me, but I saw the consternation in his face when he saw you, and so I have often wondered if there were two Tarzans of the Apes.'

'I am not Tarzan of the Apes,' said Esteban. 'It was Tarzan of the Apes who was poisoned in our camp by the others. But they only gave him something that would put him to sleep for a long time, possibly with the hope that he would be killed by wild animals before he awoke. Whether or not he still lives we do not know. Therefore you have nothing to fear from the Waziri or Tarzan on my account, Owaza, for I want to keep out of their way even more than you.'

The black nodded. 'Perhaps you speak the truth,' he said, but still he walked behind, with his rifle always ready in his hand.

They went warily, for fear of overtaking the Waziri, but shortly after passing the spot where the latter had camped they saw that they had taken another route and that there was no danger of coming in contact with them.

When they had reached a point within about a mile of the spot where the gold had been buried, Esteban told Owaza to have his boys remain there while they went ahead alone to effect the transfer of the ingots.

'The fewer who know of this,' he said to the black, 'the safer we shall be.'

'The Bwana speaks words of wisdom,' replied the wily black.

Esteban found the spot near the waterfall without difficulty, and upon questioning Owaza he discovered that the latter knew the location perfectly, and would have no difficulty in coming directly to it again from the coast. They transferred the gold but a short distance, concealing it in a heavy thicket near the edge of the river, knowing that it would be as safe from discovery there as though they had transported it a hundred miles, for the chances were extremely slight that the Waziri or anyone else who should learn of its original hiding place would imagine that anyone would go to the trouble of removing it but a matter of a hundred yards.

When they had finished Owaza looked at the sun.

'We will never reach camp tonight,' he said, 'and we will have to travel fast to overtake them even tomorrow.'

'I did not expect to,' replied Esteban, 'but could not tell them that. If we never find them again I shall be satisfied.' Owaza grinned. In his crafty mind an idea was formed.

'Why,' he thought, 'risk death in a battle with the Arab ivory raiders on the chance of securing a few tusks, when all this gold awaits only transportation to the coast to be ours?'

13

A Strange, Flat Tower

Tarzan, turning, discovered the man standing behind him on the top level of the ivy-covered east tower of the Palace of Diamonds. His knife leaped from its sheath at the touch of his quick fingers. But almost simultaneously his hand dropped to his side, and he stood contemplating the other, with an expression of incredulity upon his face that but reflected a similar emotion registered upon the countenance of the stranger. For what Tarzan saw was no Bolgani, nor a Gomangani, but a white man, bald and old and shriveled, with a long, white beard – a white man, naked but for barbaric ornaments of gold spangles and diamonds.

'God!' exclaimed the strange apparition.

Tarzan eyed the other quizzically. That single English word opened up such tremendous possibilities for conjecture as baffled the mind of the ape-man.

'What are you? Who are you?' continued the old man, but this time in the dialect of the great apes.

'You used an English word a moment ago,' said Tarzan. 'Do you speak that language?' Tarzan himself spoke in English.

'Ah, dear God!' cried the old man, 'that I should have lived to hear that sweet tongue again.' And he, too, now spoke in English, halting English, as might one who was long unaccustomed to voicing the language.

'Who are you?' asked Tarzan, 'and what are you doing here?'

'It is the same question that I asked you,' replied the old man. 'Do not be afraid to answer me. You are evidently an Englishman, and you have nothing to fear from me.'

'I am here after a woman, captured by the Bolgani,' replied Tarzan.

The other nodded. 'Yes,' he said, 'I know. She is here.'

'Is she safe?' asked Tartan.

'She has not been harmed. She will be safe until tomorrow or the next day,' replied the old man. 'But who are you, and how did you find your way here from the outer world?'

'I am Tarzan of the Apes,' replied the ape-man. 'I came into this valley looking for a way out of the valley of Opar where the life of my companion was in danger. And you?'

'I am an old man,' replied the other, 'and I have been here ever since I was a boy. I was a stowaway on the ship that brought Stanley to Africa after the establishment of the station on Stanley Pool, and I came into the interior with him. I went out from camp to hunt, alone, one day. I lost my way and later was captured by unfriendly natives. They took me farther into the interior to their village from which I finally escaped, but so utterly confused and lost that I had no idea what direction to take to find a trail to the coast. I wandered thus for months, until finally, upon an accursed day I found an entrance to this valley. I do not know why they did not put me to death at once, but they did not, and later they discovered that my knowledge could be turned to advantage to them. Since then I have helped them in their quarrying and mining and in their diamond cutting. I have given them iron drills with hardened points and drills tipped with diamonds. Now I am practically one of them, but always in my heart has been the hope that some day I might escape from the valley – a hopeless hope, though, I may assure you.'

'There is no way out?' asked Tarzan.

'There is a way, but it is always guarded.'

'Where is it?' queried Tarzan.

'It is a continuation of one of the mine tunnels, passing entirely through the mountain to the valley beyond. The mines have been worked by the ancestors of this race for an almost incalculable length of time. The mountains are honeycombed with their shafts and tunnels. Back of the gold-bearing quartz lies an enormous deposit of altered peridotite, which contains diamonds, in the search for which it evidently became necessary to extend one of the shafts to the opposite side of the mountain, possibly for purposes of ventilation. This tunnel and the trail leading down into Opar are the only means of ingress to the valley. From time immemorial they have kept the tunnel guarded, more particularly, I imagine, to prevent the escape of slaves than to thwart the inroads of an enemy, since they believe that there is no fear of the latter emergency. The trail to Opar they do not guard, because they no longer fear the Oparians, and know quite well that none of their Gomangani slaves would dare enter the valley of the sunworshipers. For the same reason, then, that the slaves cannot escape, we, too, must remain prisoners here forever.'

'How is the tunnel guarded?' asked Tarzan.

'Two Bolgani and a dozen or more Gomangani warriors are always upon duty there,' replied the old man.

'The Gomangani would like to escape?'

'They have tried it many times in the past, I am told,' replied the old man, 'though never since I have lived here, and always they were caught and tortured. And all their race was punished and worked the harder because of these attempts upon the part of a few.'

'They are numerous – the Gomangani?'

'There are probably five thousand of them in the valley,' replied the old man.

'And how may Bolgani?' the ape-man asked.

'Between ten and eleven hundred.'

'Five to one,' murmured Tarzan, 'and yet they are afraid to attempt to escape.'

'But you must remember,' said the old man, 'that the Bolgani are the dominant and intelligent race – the others are intellectually little above the beasts of the forest.'

'Yet they are men,' Tarzan reminded him.

'In figure only,' replied the old man. 'They cannot band together as men do. They have not as yet reached the community plane of evolution. It is true that families reside in a single village, but that idea, together with their weapons, was given to them by the Bolgani that they might not be entirely exterminated by the lions and panthers. Formerly, I am told, each individual Gomangani, when he became old enough to hunt for himself, constructed a hut apart from others and took up his solitary life, there being at that time no slightest semblance of family life. Then the Bolgani taught them how to build palisaded villages and compelled the men and women to remain in them and rear their children to maturity, after which the children were required to remain in the village, so that now some of the communities can claim as many as forty or fifty people. But the death rate is high among them, and they cannot multiply as rapidly as people living under normal conditions of peace and security. The brutalities of the Bolgani kill many; the carnivora take a considerable toll.'

'Five to one, and still they remain in slavery – what cowards they must be,' said the ape-man.

'On the contrary, they are far from cowardly,' replied the old man. 'They will face a lion with the utmost bravery. But for so many ages have they been subservient to the will of the Bolgani, that it has become a fixed habit in them – as the fear of God is inherent in us, so is the fear of the Bolgani inherent in the minds of the Gomangani from birth.'

'It is interesting,' said Tarzan. 'But tell me now where the woman is of whom I have come in search.'

'She is your mate?' asked the old man.

'No,' replied Tarzan. 'I told the Gomangani that she was, so that they would protect her. She is La, queen of Opar, High Priestess of the Flaming God.'

The old man looked his incredulity. 'Impossible!' he cried. 'It cannot be that the queen of Opar has risked her life by coming to the home of her hereditary enemies.'

'She was forced to it,' replied Tarzan, 'her life being threatened by a part of her people because she had refused to sacrifice me to their god.'

'If the Bolgani knew this there would be great rejoicing,' replied the old man.

'Tell me where she is,' demanded Tarzan. 'She preserved me from her people, and I must save her from whatever fate the Bolgani contemplate for her.'

'It is hopeless,' said the old man. 'I can tell you where she is, but you cannot rescue her.'

'I can try,' replied the ape-man.

'But you will fail and die.'

'If what you tell me is true, that there is absolutely no chance of my escaping from the valley, I might as well die,' replied the ape-man. 'However, I do not agree with you.'

The old man shrugged. 'You do not know the Bolgani,' he said.

'Tell me where the woman is,' said Tarzan.

'Look,' replied the old man, motioning Tarzan to follow him into his apartment, and approaching a window which faced toward the west, he pointed towards a strange flat tower which rose above the roof of the main building near the west end of the palace. 'She is probably somewhere in the interior of that tower,' said the old man to Tarzan, 'but as far as you are concerned, she might as well be at the north pole.'

Tarzan stood in silence for a moment, his keen eyes taking in every salient detail of the prospect before him. He saw the strange, flat-topped tower, which it seemed to him might be reached from the roof of the main building. He saw, too, branches of the ancient trees that sometimes topped the roof itself, and except for the dim light shining through some of the palace windows he saw no signs of life. He turned suddenly upon the old man.

'I do not know you,' he said, 'but I believe I may trust you, since after all blood ties are strong, and we are the only men of our race in this valley. You might gain something in favor by betraying me, but I cannot believe that you will do it.'

'Do not fear,' said the old man, 'I hate them. If I could help you I would, but I know that there is no hope of success for whatever plan you may have in mind – the woman will never be rescued; you will never leave the Valley of the Palace of Diamonds – you will never leave the palace itself unless the Bolgani wish it.'

The ape-man grinned. 'You have been here so long,' he said, 'that you are beginning to assume the attitude of mind that keeps the Gomangani in perpetual slavery. If you want to escape, come with me. We may not succeed, but at least you will have a better chance if you try than as if you remained forever in this tower.'

The old man shook his head. 'No,' he said, 'it is hopeless. If escape had been possible I should have been away from here long ago.'

'Goodbye then,' said Tarzan, and swinging out of the window he clambered toward the roof below, along the stout stem of the old ivy.

The old man watched him for a moment until he saw him make his way carefully across the roof toward the flat-topped tower where he hoped to find and liberate La. Then the old fellow turned and hurried rapidly down the crude stairway that rose ladder-like to the center of the tower.

Tarzan made his way across the uneven roof of the main building, clambering up the sides of its higher elevations and dropping again to its lower levels as he covered a considerable distance between the east tower and that flat-topped structure of peculiar design in which La was supposed to be incarcerated. His progress was slow, for he moved with the caution of a beast of prey, stopping often in dense shadows to listen.

When at last he reached the tower, he found that it had many openings letting upon the roof – openings which were closed only with hangings of the heavy tapestried stuff which he had seen in the tower. Drawing one of these slightly aside he looked within upon a large chamber, bare of furnishings, from the center of which there protruded through a circular aperture the top of a stairway similar to that he had ascended in the east tower. There was no one in sight within the chamber, and Tarzan crossed immediately to the stairway. Peering cautiously into the opening Tarzan saw that the stairway descended for a great distance, passing many floors. How far it went he could not judge, except it seemed likely that it pierced subterranean chambers beneath the palace. Sounds of life came up to him through the shaft, and odors, too, but the latter largely nullified, in so far as the scent impressions which they offered Tarzan were concerned, by the heavy incense which pervaded the entire palace.

It was this perfume that was to prove the ape-man's undoing, for otherwise his keen nostrils would have detected the scent of a nearby Gomangani. The fellow lay behind one of the hangings at an aperture in the tower wall. He had been lying in such a position that he had seen Tarzan enter the chamber, and he was watching him now as the ape-man stood looking down the shaft of the stairway. The eyes of the black had at first gone wide in terror at sight of this strange apparition, the like of which he had never seen before. Had the creature been of sufficient intelligence to harbor superstition, he would have thought Tarzan a god descended from above. But being of too low an order to possess any imagination whatsoever, he merely knew that he saw a strange creature, and that all strange creatures must be enemies, he was convinced. His duty was to apprise his masters of this presence in the palace, but he did not dare to move until the apparition had reached a sufficient distance from him to insure that the movements of the Gomangani would not be noticed by the intruder – he did not care to call attention to himself, for he had found that the more one effaced oneself in the presence of the Bolgani, the less one was likely to suffer. For a long time the stranger peered down the shaft of the stairway, and for a long time the Gomangani lay quietly watching him. But at last the former descended the stairs and passed out of sight of the watcher, who immediately leaped to his feet and scurried away across the roof of the palace toward a large tower arising at its western end.

As Tarzan descended the ladder the fumes of the incense became more and more annoying. Where otherwise he might have investigated quickly by scent he was now compelled to listen for every sound, and in many cases to investigate the chambers opening upon the central corridor by entering them. Where the doors were locked, he lay flat and listened close to the aperture at their base. On several occasions he risked calling La by name, but in no case did he receive any reply.

He had investigated four landings and was descending to the fifth when he saw standing in one of the doorways upon this level an evidently much excited and possibly terrified black. The fellow was of giant proportions and entirely unarmed. He stood looking at the ape-man with wide eyes as the latter jumped lightly from the stairway and stood facing him upon the same level.

'What do you want?' finally stammered the black. 'Are you looking for the white she, your mate, whom the Bolgani took?'

'Yes,' replied Tarzan. 'What do you know of her?'

'I know where she is hidden,' replied the black, 'and if you will follow me I will lead you to her.'

'Why do you offer to do this for me?' asked Tarzan, immediately suspicious. 'Why is it that you do not go at once to your masters and tell them that I am here that they may send men to capture me?'

'I do not know the reason that I was sent to tell you this,' replied the black. 'The Bolgani sent me. I did not wish to come for I was afraid.'

'Where did they tell you to lead me?' asked Tarzan.

'I am to lead you into a chamber, the door of which will be immediately bolted upon us. You will then be a prisoner.'

'And you?' inquired Tarzan.

'I, too, shall be a prisoner with you. The Bolgani do not care what becomes of me. Perhaps you will kill me, but they do not care.'

'If you lead me into a trap I shall kill you,' replied Tarzan. 'But if you lead me to the woman perhaps we shall all escape. You would like to escape, would you not?'

'I should like to escape, but I cannot.'

'Have you ever tried?'

'No, I have not. Why should I try to do something that cannot be done?'

'If you lead me into the trap I shall surely kill you. If you lead me to the woman, you at least have the chance that I do to live. Which will you do?'

The black scratched his head in thought, the idea slowly filtering through his stupid mind. At last he spoke.

'You are very wise,' he said. 'I will lead you to the woman.'

'Go ahead, then,' said Tarzan, 'and I will follow you.' The black descended to the next level and opening the door entered a long, straight corridor. As the ape-man followed his guide he had leisure to reflect upon the means through which the Bolgani had learned of his presence in the tower, and the only conclusion he could arrive at was that the old man had betrayed him, since in so far as Tarzan was aware he alone knew that the ape-man was in the palace. The corridor along which the black was leading him was very dark, receiving a dim and inadequate illumination from the dimly lighted corridor they had just left, the door into which remained open behind them. Presently the black stopped, before a closed door.

'The woman is in there,' said the black, pointing to the door.

'She is alone?' asked Tarzan.

'No,' replied the black. 'Look,' and he opened the door, revealing a heavy hanging, which he gently separated, revealing to Tarzan the interior of the chamber beyond.

Seizing the black by the wrist, that he might not escape, Tarzan stepped forward and put his eyes to the aperture. Before him lay a large chamber, at one end of which was a raised dais, the base of which was of a dark, ornately carved wood. The central figure upon this dais was a huge, blackmaned lion – the same that Tarzan had seen escorted through the gardens of the palace. His golden chains were now fastened to rings in the floor, while the four blacks stood in statuesque rigidity, two upon either side of the beast. Upon golden thrones behind the lion sat three magnificently ornamented Bolgani. At the foot of the steps leading to the stair stood La, between two Gomangani guards. Upon either side of a central aisle were carved benches facing the dais, and occupying the front section of these were some fifty Bolgani, among whom Tarzan almost immediately espied the little, old man that he had met in the tower, the sight of whom instantly crystallized the ape-man's conviction of the source of his betrayal.

The chamber was lighted by hundreds of cressets, burning a substance which gave forth both light and the heavy incense that had assailed Tarzan's nostrils since first he had entered the domain of the Bolgani. The long, cathedralesque windows upon one side of the apartment were thrown wide, admitting the soft air of the jungle summer night. Through them Tarzan could see the palace grounds and that this chamber was upon the same level as the terrace upon which the palace stood. Beyond those windows was an open gateway to the jungle and freedom, but interposed between him and the windows were fifty armed gorilla-men. Perhaps, then, strategy would be a better weapon than force with which to carve his way to freedom with La. Yet to the forefront of his mind was evidently a belief in the probability that in the end it would be force rather than strategy upon which he must depend. He turned to the black at his side.

'Would the Gomangani guarding the lion like to escape from the Bolgani?' he asked.

'The Gomangani would all escape if they could,' replied the black.

'If it is necessary for me to enter the room, then,' said Tarzan to the black, 'will you accompany me and tell the other Gomangani that if they will fight for me I will take them out of the valley?'

'I will tell them, but they will not believe,' replied the black.

'Tell them that they will die if they do not help me, then,' said Tarzan.

'I will tell them.'

As Tarzan turned his attention again to the chamber before him he saw that the Bolgani occupying the central golden throne was speaking.

'Nobles of Numa, King of Beasts, Emperor of All Created Things,' he said in deep, growling tones, 'Numa has heard the words that this she has spoken, and it is the will of Numa that she die. The Great Emperor is hungry. He, himself, will devour her here in the presence of his Nobles and the Imperial Council of Three. It is the will of Numa.'

A growl of approval arose from the beast-like audience, while the great lion bared his hideous fangs and roared until the palace trembled, his wicked, yellow-green eyes fixed terribly upon the woman before him, evidencing the fact that these ceremonies were of sufficient frequency to have accustomed the lion to what he might expect as the logical termination of them.

'Day after tomorrow,' continued the speaker, 'the mate of of this creature, who is by this time safely imprisoned in the Tower of the Emperors, will be brought before Numa for judgment. Slaves,' he cried suddenly in a loud voice, rising to his feet and glaring at the guards holding La, 'drag the woman to your emperor.'

Instantly the lion became frantic, lashing its tail and straining at its stout chains, roaring and snarling as it reared upon its hind feet and sought to leap upon La, who was now being forcibly conducted up the steps of the dais toward the bejeweled man-eater so impatiently awaiting her.

She did not cry out in terror, but she sought to twist herself free from the detaining hands of the powerful Gomangani – all futilely, however.

They had reached the last step, and were about to push La into the claws of the lion, when they were arrested by a loud cry from one side of the chamber – a cry that halted the Gomangani and brought the assembled Bolgani to their feet in astonishment and anger, for the sight that met their eyes was well-qualified to arouse the latter within them. Leaping into the room with raised spear was the almost naked white man of whom they had heard, but whom none of them had as yet seen. And so quick was he that in the very instant of entry – even before they could rise to their feet – he had launched his spear.

14

The Chamber of Horrors

A black-maned lion moved through the jungle night. With majestic unconcern for all other created things he took his lordly way through the primeval forest. He was not hunting, for he made no efforts toward stealth, nor, on the other hand, did he utter any vocal sound. He moved swiftly, though sometimes stopping with uplifted nose to scent the air and to listen. And thus at last he came to a high wall, along the face of which he sniffed, until the wall was broken by a half-opened gateway, through which he passed into the enclosure.

Before him loomed a great building, and presently as he stood watching it and listening, there broke from the interior the thunderous roar of an angry lion.

He of the black mane cocked his head upon one side and moved stealthily forward.

At the very instant that La was about to be thrust into the clutches of Numa, Tarzan of the Apes leaped into the apartment with a loud cry that brought to momentary pause the Gomangani that were dragging her to her doom, and in that brief instant of respite which the ape-man knew would follow his interruption the swift spear was launched. To the rage and consternation of the Bolgani they saw it bury itself in the heart of their Emperor – the great, blackmaned lion.

At Tarzan's side stood the Gomangani whom he had terrified into service, and as Tarzan rushed forward toward La the black accompanied him, crying to his fellows that if they would help this stranger they might be free and escape from the Bolgani forever.

'You have permitted the great Emperor to be slain,' he cried to the poor Gomangani who guarded Numa. 'For this the Bolgani will kill you. Help to save the strange Tarmangani and his mate and you have at least a chance for life and freedom. And you,' he added, addressing the two who had been guarding La, 'they will hold you responsible also – your only hope lies with us.'

Tarzan had reached La's side and was dragging her up the steps of the dais where he hoped that he might make a momentary stand against the fifty Bolgani who were now rushing forward from their seats toward him.

'Slay the three who sit upon the dais,' cried Tarzan to the Gomangani, who were now evidently hesitating as to which side they would cast their lot with. 'Slay them if you wish your freedom! Slay them if you wish to live!'

The authoritative tones of his voice, the magnetic appeal of his personality, his natural leadership won them to him for the brief instant that was necessary to turn them upon the hated authority that the three Bolgani upon the dais represented, and as they drove their spears into the shaggy black bodies of their masters they became then and forever the creatures of Tarzan of the Apes, for there could be no future hope for them in the land of the Bolgani.

With one arm around La's waist the ape-man carried her to the summit of the dais, where he seized his spear and drew it from the body of the dead lion. Then, turning about, and facing the advancing Bolgani, he placed one foot upon the carcass of his kill and raised his voice in the terrifying victory cry of the apes of Kerchak.

Before him the Bolgani paused, behind him the Gomangani quailed in terror.

'Stop!' cried Tarzan, raising a palm toward the Bolgani. 'Listen! I am Tarzan of the Apes. I sought no quarrel with your people. I but look for a passage through your country to my own. Let me go my way in peace with this woman, taking these Gomangani with me.'

For answer a chorus of savage growls arose from the Bolgani as they started forward again toward the dais. From their ranks there suddenly leaped the old man of the east tower, who ran swiftly toward Tarzan.

'Ah, traitor,' cried the ape-man, 'you would be the first, then, to taste the wrath of Tarzan?' He spoke in English and the old man replied in the same tongue.

'Traitor?' he exclaimed in surprise.

'Yes, traitor,' thundered Tarzan. 'Did you not hurry here to tell the Bolgani that I was in the palace, that they might send the Gomangani to lure me to a trap?'

'I did nothing of the kind,' replied the other. 'I came here to place myself near the white woman, with the thought that I might be of service to her or you if I were needed. I come now, Englishman, to stand at your side and die at your side, for die you shall, as sure as there is a God in heaven. Nothing can save you now from the wrath of the Bolgani whose Emperor you have killed.'

'Come, then,' cried Tarzan, 'and prove your loyalty. It were better to die now than to live in slavery forever.'

The six Gomangani had ranged themselves, three upon either side of Tarzan and La, while the seventh, who had entered the chamber with Tarzan unarmed, was taking weapons from the body of one of the three Bolgani who had been slain upon the dais.

Before this array of force so new to them, the Bolgani paused at the foot of the steps leading to the dais. But only for a moment they paused, for there were but nine against fifty, and as they surged up the steps, Tarzan and his Gomangani met them with battle-axe, and spear, and bludgeon. For a moment they pressed them back, but the numbers against them were too great, and once again a wave swept up that seemed likely to overwhelm them, when there broke upon the ears of the contestants a frightful roar, which, coming from almost at their sides, brought a sudden, momentary cessation of the battle.

Turning their eyes in the direction of the sound they saw a huge, black-maned lion standing upon the floor of the apartment, just within one of the windows. For an instant he stood like a statue of golden bronze, and then again the building trembled to the reverberations of his mighty roar.

Towering above them all Tarzan of the Apes looked down from the dais upon the great beast below them, and then in quick elation he raised his voice above the growlings of the Bolgani.

'Jad-bal-ja,' he cried, and pointing toward the Bolgani, 'Kill! Kill!'

Scarcely had the words been uttered ere the huge monster, a veritable devil incarnate, was upon the hairy gorilla-men. And simultaneously there occurred to the mind of the ape-man a daring plan of salvation for himself and the others who were dependent upon him.

'Quick,' he cried to the Gomangani, 'fall upon the Bolgani. Here at last is the true Numa, King of Beasts, and ruler of all creation. He slays his enemies but he will protect Tarzan of the Apes and the Gomangani, who are his friends.'

Seeing their hated masters falling back before the terrific onslaughts of the lion, the Gomangani rushed in with battle-axes and clubs, while Tarzan, casting aside his spear, took his place among them with drawn knife, and, keeping close to Jad-bal-ja, directed the lion from one victim to another, lest he fall by mistake upon the Gomangani or the little, old, white man, or even La herself. Twenty of the Bolgani lay dead upon the floor before the balance managed to escape from the chamber, and then Tarzan, turning to Jad-bal-ja, called him to heel.

'Go!' he said, turning toward the Gomangani, 'and drag the body of the false Numa from the dias. Remove it from the room, for the true Emperor has come to claim his throne.'

The old man and La were eyeing Tarzan and the lion in amazement.

'Who are you,' asked the former, 'that you can work such miracles with a savage beast of the jungle? Who are you, and what do you intend to do?'

'Wait and see,' said Tarzan with a grim smile. 'I think that we shall all be safe now, and that the Gomangani may live in comfort for a long time hereafter.'

When the blacks had removed the carcass of the lion from the dias and thrown it from one of the windows of the chamber, Tarzan sent Jad-bal-ja to sit in the place upon the dais that had formerly been occupied by the lion, Numa.

'There,' he said, turning to the Gomangani, 'you see the true Emperor, who does not have to be chained to his throne. Three of you will go to the huts of your people behind the palace and summon them to the throne room, that they, too, may see what has transpired. Hurry, that we may have many warriors here before the Bolgani return in force.'

Filled with an excitement which almost shook their dull minds into a semblance of intelligence three of the Gomangani hastened to do Tarzan's bidding, while the others stood gazing at Tarzan with expressions of such awe that might only be engendered by the sight of deity. La came then and stood beside Tarzan, looking up into his face with eyes that reflected a reverence fully as deep as that held by the blacks.

'I have not thanked you, Tarzan of the Apes,' she said, 'for what you have risked and done for me. I know that you must have come here in search of me, to save me from these creatures, and I know that it was not love that impelled you to this heroic and well-nigh hopeless act. That you have succeeded thus far is little short of miraculous, but I, in the legends of whose people are recounted the exploits of the Bolgani, know that there can be no hope of eventual escape for us all, and so I beseech that you go at once and make good your escape alone, if possible, for you alone of us have any possible chance of escape.'

'I do not agree with you that we have no chance to escape, La,' replied the ape-man. 'It seems to me that now we not only have every reason to believe that we are practically assured of escape, but that we may insure also to these poor Gomangani freedom from slavery and from the tyranny of the Bolgani. But this is not all. With this I shall not be satisfied. Not only must these people who show no hospitality to strangers be punished, but your own disloyal priests as well. To this latter end I intend to march out of the Valley of the Palace of Diamonds, down upon the city of Opar with a force of Gomangani sufficient to compel Cadj to relinquish the power he has usurped and replace you upon the throne of Opar. Nothing less than this shall satisfy me, and nothing less than this shall I accomplish before I leave.'

'You are a brave man,' said the old man, 'and you have succeeded beyond what I thought could be possible, but La is right, you do not know the ferocity or the resources of the Bolgani, or the power which they wield over the Gomangani. Could you raise from the stupid minds of the blacks the incubus of fear that rests so heavily upon them you might win over a sufficient number to make good your escape from the valley, but that, I fear, is beyond even you. Our only hope, therefore, is to escape from the palace while they are momentarily disorganized, and trust to fleetness and to luck to carry us beyond the limits of the valley before we are apprehended.'

'See,' cried La, pointing; 'even now it is too late – they return.'

Tarzan looked in the direction that she indicated and saw through the open doorway at the far end of the chamber a large number of gorilla-men approaching. His eyes moved swiftly to the windows in the other wall. 'But wait,' he said, 'behold another factor in the equation!'

The others looked toward the windows which opened upon the terrace, and they saw beyond them what appeared to be a crowd of several hundred blacks running rapidly toward the windows. The other blacks upon the dais cried out excitedly: 'They come! They come! We shall be free, and no longer shall the Bolgani be able to make us work until we drop from exhaustion, or beat us, or torture us, or feed us to Numa.'

As the first of the Bolgani reached the doorway leading into the chamber, the Gomangani commenced to pour through the several windows in the opposite wall. They were led by the three who had been sent to fetch them, and to such good effect had these carried their message that the blacks already seemed like a new people, so transfigured were they by the thought of immediate freedom. At sight of them the leader of the Bolgani cried aloud for them to seize the intruders upon the dais, but his answer was a spear hurled by the nearest black, and as he lunged forward, dead, the battle was on.

The Bolgani in the palace greatly outnumbered the blacks, but the latter had the advantage of holding the interior of the throne room in sufficient numbers to prevent the entry of many Bolgani simultaneously. Tarzan, immediately he recognized the temper of the blacks, called Jad-bal-ja to follow him, and, descending from the dais, he took command of the Gomangani. At each opening he placed sufficient men to guard it, and at the center of the room he held the balance in reserve. Then he called the old man into consultation.

'The gate in the east wall is open,' he said. 'I left it so when I entered. Would it be possible for twenty or thirty blacks to reach it in safety and, entering the forest, carry word to the villagers of what is transpiring here in the palace, and prevail upon them to send all of their warriors immediately to complete the work of emancipation that we have begun?'

'It is an excellent plan,' replied the old man. 'The Bolgani are not upon that side of the palace between us and the gate, and if it may ever be accomplished, now is the time. I will pick your men for you. They must be headmen, whose words will carry some weight with the villagers outside the palace walls.'

'Good!' exclaimed Tarzan. 'Select them immediately; tell them what we want and urge upon them the necessity for haste.'

One by one the old man chose thirty warriors, whose duty he carefully explained to each. They were delighted with the plan and assured Tarzan that in less than an hour the first of the reinforcements would come.

'As you leave the enclosure,' said the ape-man, 'destroy the lock if you can, so that the Bolgani may not lock it again and bar out our reinforcements. Carry also the word that the first who come are to remain outside the wall until a sufficient number have arrived to make entry into the palace grounds reasonably safe – at least as many as are within this room now.'

The blacks signified their understanding, and a moment later passed out of the room through one of the windows and disappeared into the darkness of the night beyond.

Shortly after the blacks had left the Bolgani made a determined rush upon the Gomangani guarding the main entrance to the throne room, with the result that a score or more of the gorilla-men succeeded in cutting their way into the room. At this first indication of reversal the blacks showed signs of faltering, the fear of the Bolgani that was inherent in them showing in their wavering attitude and seeming reluctance to force a counter attack. As Tarzan leaped forward to assist in checking the rush of the Bolgani into the throne room he called to Jad-bal-ja, and as the great lion leaped from the dais the ape-man, pointing to the nearest Bolgani, cried: 'Kill! Kill!'

Straight for the throat of the nearest leaped Jad-bal-ja. The great jaws closed upon the snarling face of the frightened gorilla-man but once, and then, at the command of his master the golden lion dropped the carcass after a single shake and leaped upon another. Three had died thus in quick succession when the balance of the Bolgani turned to flee this chamber of horrors; but the Gomangani, their confidence restored by the ease with which this fierce ally brought death and terror to the tyrants, interposed themselves between the Bolgani and the doorway, shutting off their retreat.

'Hold them! Hold them!' cried Tarzan. 'Do not kill them!' And then to the Bolgani: 'Surrender and you will not be harmed!'

Jad-bal-ja clung close to the side of his master, glaring and growling at the Bolgani, and casting an occasional beseeching look at the ape-man which said plainer than words, 'Send me among them.'

Fifteen of the Bolgani who had entered the room survived. For a moment they hesitated, and then one of them threw his weapons upon the floor. Immediately the others followed suit.

Tarzan turned toward Jad-bal-ja. 'Back!' he said, pointing toward the dais, and as the lion wheeled and slunk away toward the platform, Tarzan turned again toward the Bolgani.

'Let one of your number go,' he said, 'and announce to your fellows that I demand their immediate surrender.'

The Bolgani whispered among themselves for a few moments and finally one of them announced that he would go and see the others. After he had left the room the old man approached Tarzan.

'They will never surrender,' he said. 'Look out for treachery.'

'It is all right,' said Tarzan. 'I am expecting that, but I am gaining time, and that is what we need most. If there were a place near where I might confine these others I should feel better, for it would cut down our antagonists by at least that many.'

'There is a room there,' said the old man, pointing toward one of the doorways in the throne room, 'where you can confine them – there are many such rooms in the Tower of the Emperors.'

'Good,' said Tarzan, and a moment later, following his instructions the Bolgani were safely locked in a room adjoining the throne room. In the corridors without they could hear the main body of the gorilla-men in argument. It was evident that they were discussing the message sent to them by Tarzan. Fifteen minutes passed, and finally thirty, with no word from the Bolgani and no resumption of hostilities, and then there came to the main entrance of the throne room the fellow whom Tarzan had despatched with his demand for surrender.

'Well,' asked the ape-man, 'what is their answer?'

'They will not surrender,' replied the Bolgani, 'but they will permit you to leave the valley provided that you will release those whom you have taken prisoner and harm no others.'

The ape-man shook his head. 'That will not do,' he replied. 'I hold the power to crush the Bolgani of the Valley of Diamonds. Look,' and he pointed toward Jad-bal-ja, 'here is the true Numa. The creature you had upon your throne was but a wild beast, but this is Numa, King of Beasts, Emperor of All Created Things. Look at him. Must he be held in leash by golden chains like some prisoner or slave? No! He is indeed an Emperor. But there is one yet greater than he, one from whom he takes commands. And that one is I, Tarzan of the Apes. Anger me and you shall feel not only the wrath of Numa, but the wrath of Tarzan as well. The Gomangani are my people, the Bolgani shall be my slaves. Go and tell your fellows that, and that if they would live at all they had best come soon and sue for mercy. Go!'

When the messenger had again departed Tarzan looked at the old man, who was eyeing him with an expression which might have denoted either awe or reverence, were it not for the vaguest hint of a twinkle in the corners of the eyes. The ape-man breathed a deep sigh of relief. 'That will give us at least another half hour,' he said.

'We shall need it, and more, too,' replied the old man, 'though, at that, you have accomplished more than I had thought possible, for at least you have put a doubt in the minds of the Bolgani, who never before have had cause to question their own power.'

Presently from the outer corridors the sounds of argument and discussion gave place to that of movement among the Bolgani. A company, comprising some fifty of the gorilla-men, took post directly outside the main entrance of the throne room where they stood in silence, their weapons ready, as though for the purpose of disputing any effort upon the part of the inmates of the room to escape. Beyond them the balance of the gorilla-men could be seen moving away and disappearing through doorways and corridors leading from the main hallway of the palace. The Gomangani, together with La and the old man, watched impatiently for the coming of the black reinforcements, while Tarzan sat upon the edge of the dais half-reclining, with an arm about the neck of Jad-bal-ja.

'They are up to something,' said the old man. 'We must watch carefully against a surprise. If the blacks would but come now, while the doorway is held by only fifty, we should overcome them easily, and have, I do verily believe, some slight chance of escaping from the palace grounds.'

'Your long residence here,' said Tarzan, 'has filled you with the same senseless fear of the Bolgani that the Gomangani hold. From the attitude of mind which you hold toward them one would think them some manner of supermen – they are only beasts, my friend, and if we remain loyal to our cause we shall overcome them.'

'Beasts they may be,' replied the old man, 'but they are beasts with the brains of men – their cunning and their cruelty are diabolical.'

A long silence ensued, broken only by the nervous whisperings of the Gomangani, whose morale, it was evident, was slowly disintegrating under the nervous strain of the enforced wait, and the failure of their fellows of the forest to come quickly to their aid. To this was added the demoralizing effect of speculation upon what the Bolgani were planning or what plan they already were putting into effect. The very silence of the gorilla-men was more terrible than the din of actual assault. La was the first of the whites to break the silence.

'If thirty of the Gomangani could leave the palace so easily, why might not we leave also?' she asked.

'There were two reasons,' replied Tarzan. 'One was that should we have left simultaneously the Bolgani, greatly outnumbering us as they did, could have harassed us and detained us for a sufficient length of time to have permitted their messengers to reach the villagers ahead of us, with the result that in a short time we should have been surrounded by thousands of hostile warriors. The second reason is that I desire to punish the creatures, so that in future a stranger may be safe in the Valley of the Palace of Diamonds.' He paused. 'And now I shall give you a third reason why we may not seek to escape at this moment.' He pointed toward the windows overlooking the terrace. 'Look,' he said, 'the terrace and the gardens are filled with Bolgani. Whatever their plan I think its success depends upon our attempt to escape from this room through the windows, for, unless I am mistaken, the Bolgani upon the terrace and in the gardens are making an attempt to hide themselves from us.'

The old man walked to a part of the room from which he could see the greater part of the terrace and gardens upon which the windows of the throne room looked.

'You are right,' he said when he returned to the ape-man's side; 'the Bolgani are all massed outside these windows with the exception of those who guard the entrance, and possibly some others at the doorways at other portions of the throne room. That, however, we must determine.' He walked quickly to the opposite side of the chamber and drew back the hangings before one of the apertures, disclosing beyond a small band of Bolgani. They stood there motionless, not making any effort to seize or harm him. To another exit, and another, he went, and beyond each discovered to the occupants of the chamber the same silent gorilla guardians. He made the circle of the room, passing over the dais behind the three thrones, and then he came back to Tarzan and La.

'It is as I suspected,' he said, 'we are entirely surrounded. Unless help comes soon we are lost.'

'But their force is divided,' Tarzan reminded him.

'Even so, it is sufficient to account for us,' replied the old man.

'Perhaps you are right,' said Tarzan, 'but at least we shall have a bully fight.'

'What is that!' exclaimed La, and simultaneously, attracted by the same noise, the inmates of the throne room raised their eyes to the ceiling above them, where they saw that traps had been lifted from a dozen openings, revealing the scowling faces of several score of gorilla-men.

'What are they up to now!' exclaimed Tarzan, and as though in answer to the query the Bolgani above began hurling bundles of burning, oil-soaked rags, tied in goat skins, into the throne room, which immediately commenced to fill it with a thick, suffocating smoke, accompanied by the stench of burning hide and hair.

15
The Map of Blood

After Esteban and Owaza had buried the gold they returned to the spot where they had left their five boys, and proceeding with them to the river made camp for the night. Here they discussed their plans, deciding to abandon the balance of the party to reach the coast as best they might, while they returned to another section of the coast where they could recruit sufficient porters to carry out the gold.

'Instead of going way back to the coast for porters,' asked Esteban, 'why could we not just as well recruit them from the nearest village?'

'Such men would not go with us way to the coast,' replied Owaza. 'They are not porters. At best they would but carry our gold to the next village.'

'Why not that, then?' inquired the Spaniard. 'And at the next village we could employ porters to carry us on still farther, until we could employ other men to continue on with us.'

Owaza shook his head. 'It is a good plan, Bwana, but we cannot do it, because we have nothing with which to pay our porters.'

Esteban scratched his head. 'You are right,' he said, 'but it would save us that damnable trip to the coast and return.' They sat for some moments in silence, thinking. 'I have it!' at last exclaimed the Spaniard. 'Even if we had the porters now we could not go directly to the coast for fear of meeting Flora Hawkes's party – we must let them get out of Africa before we take the gold to the coast. Two months will be none too long to wait, for they are going to have a devil of a time getting to the coast at all with that bunch of mutinous porters. While we are waiting, therefore, let us take one of the ingots of gold to the nearest point at which we can dispose of it for trade goods. Then we can return and hire porters to carry it from village to village.'

'The Bwana speaks words of wisdom,' replied Owaza. 'It is not as far to the nearest trading post as it is back to the coast, and thus we shall not only save time, but also many long, hard marches.'

'In the morning, then, we shall return and unearth one of the ingots, but we must be sure that none of your men accompanies us, for no one must know until it is absolutely necessary where the gold is buried. When we return for it, of course, then others must know, too, but inasmuch as we shall be with it constantly thereafter there will be little danger of its being taken from us.'

And so upon the following morning the Spaniard and Owaza returned to the buried treasure, where they unearthed a single ingot.

Before he left the spot the Spaniard drew upon the inner surface of the leopard skin that he wore across his shoulder an accurate map of the location of the treasure, making the drawing with a sharpened stick, dipped in the blood of a small rodent he had killed for the purpose. From Owaza he obtained the native names of the river and of such landmarks as were visible from the spot at which the treasure was buried, together with as explicit directions as possible for reaching the place from the coast. This information, too, he wrote below the map, and when he had finished he felt much relieved from the fear that should aught befall Owaza he might never be able to locate the gold.

When Jane Clayton reached the coast to take passage for London she found awaiting her a wire stating that her father was entirely out of danger, and that there was no necessity for her coming to him. She, therefore, after a few days of rest, turned her face again toward home, and commenced to retrace the steps of the long, hot, weary journey that she had just completed. When, finally, she arrived at the bungalow she learned, to her consternation, that Tarzan of the Apes had not yet returned from his expedition to the city of Opar after the gold from the treasure vaults. She found Korak, evidently much exercised, but unwilling to voice a doubt as to the ability of his father to care for himself. She learned of the escape of the golden lion with regret, for she knew that Tarzan had become much attached to the noble beast.

It was the second day after her return that the Waziri who had accompanied Tarzan returned without him. Then, indeed, was her heart filled with fear for her lord and master. She questioned the men carefully, and when she learned from them that Tarzan had suffered another accident that had again affected his memory, she immediately announced that she would set out on the following day in search of him, commanding the Waziri who had just returned to accompany her.

Korak attempted to dissuade her, but failing in that insisted upon accompanying her.

'We must not all be away at once,' she said. 'You remain here, my son. If I fail I shall return and let you go.'

'I cannot let you go alone, Mother,' replied Korak.

'I am not alone when the Waziri are with me,' she laughed. 'And you know perfectly well, boy, that I am as safe anywhere in the heart of Africa with them as I am here at the ranch.'

'Yes, yes, I suppose so,' he replied, 'but I wish I might go, or that Meriem were here.'

'Yes, I, too, wish that Meriem were here,' replied Lady Greystoke. 'However, do not worry. You know that my jungle-craft, while not equal to that of

Tarzan or Korak, is by no means a poor asset, and that, surrounded by the loyalty and bravery of the Waziri, I shall be safe.'

'I suppose you are right,' replied Korak, 'but I do not like to see you go without me.'

And so, notwithstanding his objections, Jane Clayton set out the next morning with fifty Waziri warriors in search of her savage mate.

When Esteban and Owaza had not returned to camp as they had promised, the other members of the party were at first inclined to anger, which was later replaced by concern, not so much for the safety of the Spaniard but for fear that Owaza might have met with an accident and would not return to take them in safety to the coast, for of all the blacks he alone seemed competent to handle the surly and mutinous carriers. The negroes scouted the idea that Owaza had become lost and were more inclined to the opinion that he and Esteban had deliberately deserted them. Luvini, who acted as headman in Owaza's absence, had a theory of his own.

'Owaza and the Bwana have gone after the ivory raiders alone. By trickery they may accomplish as much as we could have accomplished by force, and there will only be two among whom to divide the ivory.'

'But how may two men overcome a band of raiders?' inquired Flora, skeptically.

'You do not know Owaza,' answered Luvini. 'If he can gain the ears of their slaves he will win them over, and when the Arabs see that he who accompanies Owaza and who fights at the head of the mutinous slaves is Tarzan of the Apes, they will flee in terror.'

'I believe he is right,' muttered Kraski, 'it sounds just like the Spaniard,' and then suddenly he turned upon Luvini. 'Can you lead us to the raiders' camp?' he demanded.

'Yes,' replied the negro.

'Good,' exclaimed Kraski; 'and now, Flora, what do you think of this plan? Let us send a swift runner to the raiders, warning them against Owaza and the Spaniard, and telling them that the latter is not Tarzan of the Apes, but an impostor. We can ask them to capture and hold the two until we come, and after we arrive we can make such further plans as the circumstances permit. Very possibly we can carry out our original design after we have once entered their camp as friends.'

'Yes, that sounds good,' replied Flora, 'and it is certainly crooked enough – just like you, yourself.'

The Russian blushed. '"Birds of a feather" –' he quoted.

The girl shrugged her shoulders indifferently, but Bluber, who, with Peebles and Throck, had been silent listeners to the conversation, blustered.

'Vot do you mean birds vit fedders?' he demanded. 'Who vas a crook? I tell you, Master Carl Kraski, I am an honest man, dot is von t'ing dot no man don't say about Adolph Bluber, he is a crook.'

'O shut up,' snapped Kraski, 'if there's anything in it you'll be for it – if there's no risk. These fellows stole the ivory themselves, and killed a lot of people, probably, to do it. In addition they have taken slaves, which we will free.'

'O vell,' said Bluber, 'if it is fair und eqvitable, vy, all right, but just remember, Mister Kraski, dot *I* am an honest man.'

'Blime!' exclaimed Throck, 'we're all honest; I've never seen such a downy bunch of parsons in all me life.'

'Sure we're honest,' roared John Peebles, 'and anyone 'at says we ain't gets 'is bally 'ead knocked off, and 'ere we are, 'n that's that.'

The girl smiled wearily. 'You can always tell honest men,' she said. 'They go around telling the world how honest they are. But never mind that; the thing now is to decide whether we want to follow Kraski's suggestion or not. It's something we've got all pretty well to agree upon before we undertake it. There are five of us. Let's leave it to a vote. Do we, or don't we?'

'Will the men accompany us?' asked Kraski, turning to Luvini.

'If they are promised a share of the ivory they will,' replied the black.

'How many are in favor of Carl's plan?' asked Flora.

They were unanimously for it, and so it was decided that they would undertake the venture, and a half hour later a runner was despatched on the trail to the raiders' camp with a message for the raider chief. Shortly after, the party broke camp and took up its march in the same direction.

A week later, when they reached the camp of the raiders they found that their messenger had arrived safely and that they were expected. Esteban and Owaza had not put in an appearance nor had anything been seen or heard of them in the vicinity. The result was that the Arabs were inclined to be suspicious and surly, fearing that the message brought to them had been but a ruse to permit this considerable body of whites and armed blacks to enter their stockade in safety.

Jane Clayton and her Waziri moving rapidly, picked up the spoor of Flora Hawkes's safari at the camp where the Waziri had last seen Esteban, whom they still thought to have been Tarzan of the Apes. Following the plainly marked trail, and moving much more rapidly than the Hawkes safari, Jane and the Waziri made camp within a mile of the ivory raiders only about a week after the Hawkes party had arrived and where they still remained, waiting either for the coming of Owaza and Esteban, or for a propitious moment in which they could launch their traitorous assault upon the Arabs. In the meantime, Luvini and some of the other blacks had succeeded in secretly spreading the propaganda of revolt among the slaves of the Arabs. Though he reported his progress daily to Flora Hawkes, he did not report the steady growth and development of a little private plan of his own, which contemplated, in addition to the revolt of the slaves, and the slaying of the Arabs, the murder of all the whites in the camp, with the exception of Flora Hawkes, whom Luvini wished to preserve either for himself or for sale to some black sultan of the north. It was Luvini's shrewd plan first to slay the Arabs, with the assistance of the whites, and then to fall upon the whites and slay them, after their body servants had stolen their weapons from them.

That Luvini would have been able to carry out his plan with ease there is little doubt, had it not been for the loyalty and affection of a young black boy attached to Flora Hawkes for her personal service.

The young white woman, notwithstanding the length to which she would go in the satisfaction of her greed and avarice, was a kind and indulgent mistress. The kindnesses she had shown this ignorant little black boy were presently to return her dividends far beyond her investment.

Luvini had been to her upon a certain afternoon to advise her that all was ready, and that the revolt of the slaves and the murder of the Arabs should take place that evening, immediately after dark. The cupidity of the whites had long been aroused by the store of ivory possessed by the raiders, with the result that all were more than eager for the final step in the conspiracy that would put them in possession of considerable wealth.

It was just before the evening meal that the little negro boy crept into Flora Hawkes's tent. He was very wide-eyed, and terribly frightened.

'What is the matter?' she demanded.

'S-sh!' he cautioned. 'Do not let them hear you speak to me, but put your ear close to me while I tell you in a low voice what Luvini is planning.'

The girl bent her head close to the lips of the little black. 'You have been kind to me,' he whispered, 'and now that Luvini would harm you I have come to tell you.'

'What do you mean?' exclaimed Flora, in a low voice.

'I mean that Luvini, after the Arabs are killed, has given orders that the black boys kill all the white men and take you prisoner. He intends either to keep you for himself or to sell you in the north for a great sum of money.'

'But how do you know all this?' demanded the girl.

'All the blacks in camp know it,' replied the boy. 'I was to have stolen your rifle and your pistol, as each of the boys will steal the weapons of his white master.'

The girl sprang to her feet. 'I'll teach that traitor a lesson,' she cried, seizing her pistol and striding toward the flap of the tent.

The boy seized her about the knees and held her. 'No! no!' he cried. 'Do not do it. Do not say anything. It will only mean that they will kill the white men sooner and take you prisoner just the same. Every black boy in the camp is against you. Luvini has promised that the ivory shall be divided equally among them all. They are ready now, and if you should threaten Luvini, or if in any other way they should learn that you were aware of the plot, they would fall upon you immediately.'

'What do you expect me to do then?' she asked.

'There is but one hope, and that is in flight. You and the white men must escape into the jungle. Not even I may accompany you.'

The girl stood looking at the little boy in silence for a moment, and then finally she said, 'Very well, I will do as you say. You have saved my life. Perhaps I may never be able to repay you, and perhaps, again, I may. Go, now, before suspicion alights upon you.'

The black withdrew from the tent, crawling beneath the back wall to avoid being seen by any of his fellows who were in the center of the camp from which the front of the tent was in plain view. Immediately he was gone Flora walked casually into the open and went to Kraski's tent, which the Russian occupied in common with Bluber. She found the two men and in low whispers apprised them of what the black had told her. Kraski then called Peebles and Throck, it being decided that they should give no outward sign of holding any suspicion that aught was wrong. The Englishmen were for jumping in upon the blacks and annihilating them, but Flora Hawkes dissuaded them from any such rash act by pointing out how greatly they were outnumbered by the natives, and how hopeless it would be to attempt to overpower them.

Bluber, with his usual cunning and shrewdness which inclined always to double dealing where there was the slightest possibility for it, suggested that they secretly advise the Arabs of what they had learned, and joining forces with them take up as strong a position in the camp as possible and commence to fire into the blacks without waiting for their attack.

Again Flora Hawkes vetoed the suggestion. 'It will not do,' she said, 'for the Arabs are at heart as much our enemies as the blacks. If we were successful in subduing the latter it would be but a question of minutes before the Arabs knew every detail of the plot that we had laid against them, after which our lives would not be worth *that*,' and she snapped her fingers.

'I guess Flora is right, as usual,' growled Peebles, 'but what in 'ell are we goin' to do wanderin' around in this 'ere jungle without nobody to hunt for us, or cook for us, or carry things for us, or find our way for us, that's wot I'd like to know, and 'ere we are, 'n that's that.'

'I guess there ain't nothin' else to do,' said Throck; 'but blime if I likes to run away.'

There came then to the ears of the whites, rumbling from the far distance in the jungle, the roar of a lion.

'*Ach, weh!*' cried Bluber. 'Ve go out all alone in dot jungle? *Mein Gott!* I just as soon stay here und get killed like a vite man.'

'They won't kill you like a white man,' said Kraski. 'They'll torture you if you stay.'

Bluber wrung his hands, and the sweat of fear rolled down his oily face. '*Ach!* vy did I done it? Vy did I done it?' he wailed. 'Vy didn't I stay home in London vere I belong?'

'Shut up!' snapped Flora. 'Don't you know that if you do anything to arouse the suspicion of these fellows they will be on us at once? There is only one thing for us to do and that is to wait until they precipitate the attack upon the Arabs. We will still have our weapons, for they do not plan to steal them from us until after the Arabs are killed. In the confusion of the fight, we must make our escape into the jungle, and after that – God knows – and God help us.'

'Yes,' blubbered Bluber, who was in a blue funk, '*Gott* help us!'

A moment later Luvini came to them. 'All is ready, Bwanas,' he said. 'As soon as the evening meal has been eaten, be in readiness. You will hear a shot, that will be the signal. Then open fire upon the Arabs.'

'Good,' said Kraski; 'we have just been talking about it and we have decided that we will take our stand near the gate to prevent their escape.'

'It is well,' said Luvini, 'but you must remain here.' He was addressing Flora. 'It would not be safe for you to be where there is to be fighting. Remain here in your tent, and we will confine the fighting to the other side of the village and possibly to the gate, if any of them makes a break for escape.'

'All right,' said Flora, 'I will remain here where it is safe.'

Satisfied that things could not have worked into his hands to better advantage the black left them, and presently the entire camp was occupied with the evening meal. There was an atmosphere of restraint, and high, nervous tension throughout the entire camp that must have been noticeable, even to the Arabs, though they, alone of the entire company, were ignorant as to its cause. Bluber was so terrified that he could not eat, but sat white and trembling with his eyes roving wildly about the camp – first to the blacks, then to the Arabs, and then to the gate, the distance to which he must have measured a hundred times as he sat there waiting for the shot that was to be the signal for the massacre that was to send him out into the jungle to be, he surely thought, the immediate prey of the first hunting lion that passed.

Peebles and Throck ate their meal stolidly, much to Bluber's disgust. Kraski, being of a highly nervous temperament, ate but little, but he showed no signs of fear. Nor did Flora Hawkes, though at heart she realized the hopelessness of their situation.

Darkness had fallen. Some of the blacks and Arabs were still eating, when suddenly the silence was shattered by the sharp staccato report of a rifle. An Arab sank silently to the earth. Kraski rose and grasped Flora by the arm. 'Come!' he cried.

Followed by Peebles and Throck, and preceded by Bluber, to whose feet fright had lent wings, they hurried toward the gate of the palisade.

By now the air was filled with the hoarse cries of fighting men and the report of rifles. The Arabs, who had numbered but about a dozen, were putting up a game fight, and being far better marksmen than the blacks, the issue of the battle was still in doubt when Kraski opened the gate and the five whites fled into the darkness of the jungle.

The outcome of the fight within the camp could not have been other than it was, for so greatly did the blacks outnumber the Arabs, that eventually, notwithstanding their poor marksmanship, they succeeded in shooting down the last of the nomads of the north. Then it was that Luvini turned his attention to the other whites only to discover that they had fled the village. The black realized two things instantly. One was that someone had betrayed him, and the other, that the whites could not have gone far in the short time since they had left the camp.

Calling his warriors about him he explained to them what had happened, and impressing upon them that the whites, if permitted to escape, would eventually return with reinforcements to punish the blacks, he aroused his followers, who now numbered over two hundred warriors, to the necessity of setting out immediately upon the trail of the fugitives and overtaking them before they could carry word even to a neighboring village, the nearest of which was not more than a day's march distant.

16

The Diamond Hoard

As the primitive smoke bombs filled the throne room of the Tower of the Emperors with their suffocating fumes, the Gomangani clustered about Tarzan begging him to save them, for they, too, had seen the massed Bolgani before every entrance and the great body of them that awaited in the gardens and upon the terrace without

'Wait a minute,' said Tarzan, 'until the smoke is thick enough to hide our movements from the Bolgani, and then we will rush the windows overlooking the terrace, for they are nearer the east gate than any other exit, and thus some of us will have a better chance for escape.'

'I have a better plan,' said the old man. 'When the smoke conceals us, follow me. There is one exit that is unguarded, probably because they do not dream that we would use it. When I passed over the dais behind the throne I took occasion to note that there were no Bolgani guarding it.'

'Where does it lead?' asked Tarzan.

'Into the basement of the Tower of Diamonds – the tower in which I discovered you. That portion of the palace is nearest to the east gate, and if we can reach it before they suspect our purpose there will be little doubt that we can reach the forest at least.'

'Splendid!' ejaculated the ape-man. 'It will not be long now before the smoke hides us from the Bolgani.'

In fact it was so thick by this time that the occupants of the throne room were finding difficulty in breathing. Many of them were coughing and choking and the eyes of all were watering from the effects of the acrid smoke. And yet they were not entirely hidden from the observation of the watchers all about them.

'I don't know how much more of this we can stand,' said Tarzan. 'I have about all I care for, now.'

'It *is* thickening up a bit,' said the old man. 'Just a moment more and I think we can make it unseen.'

'I can stand it no longer,' cried La. 'I am suffocating and I am half-blinded.'

'Very well,' said the old man; 'I doubt if they can see us now. It is pretty thick. Come, follow me,' and he led the way up the steps of the dais and through an aperture behind the thrones – a small opening hidden by hangings. The old man went first, and then La, followed by Tarzan and Jad-bal-ja, who had about reached the limit of his endurance and patience, so that it had been with difficulty that Tarzan had restrained him, and who now was voicing his anger in deep growls which might have apprised the Bolgani of their avenue of escape. Behind Tarzan and the lion crowded the coughing Gomangani; but because Jad-bal-ja was just in front of them they did not crowd as closely upon the party ahead of them as they probably would have done otherwise.

The aperture opened into a dark corridor which led down a flight of rough steps to a lower level, and then straight through utter darkness for the rather considerable distance which separated the Tower of Diamonds from the Tower of the Emperors. So great was their relief at escaping the dense smoke of the throne room that none of the party minded the darkness of the corridor, but followed patiently the lead of the old man who had explained that the first stairs down which they had passed were the only obstacles to be encountered in the tunnel.

At the corridor's end the old man halted before a heavy door, which after considerable difficulty he managed to open.

'Wait a moment,' he said, 'until I find a cresset and make a light.'

They heard him moving about beyond the doorway for a moment and then a dim light flared, and presently the wick in a cresset flickered. In the dim rays Tarzan saw before them a large rectangular chamber, the great size of which was only partially suggested in the wavering light of the cresset.

'Get them all in,' said the old man, 'and close the door,' and when that had been done he called to Tarzan. 'Come!' he said. 'Before we leave this chamber I want to show you such a sight as no other human eyes have ever rested upon.'

He led him to the far side of the chamber where, in the light of the cresset, Tarzan saw tier after tier of shelves, upon which were stacked small sacks made of skins. The old man set the cresset upon one of the shelves and taking a sack opened it and spilled a portion of the contents into the palm of his hand. 'Diamonds,' he said. 'Each of these packages weighs five pounds and each contains diamonds. They have been accumulating them for countless ages, for they mine far more than they can use themselves. In their legends is the belief that some day the Atlantians will return and they can sell the diamonds to them. And so they continue to mine them and store them as though there was a constant and ready market for them. Here, take one of the bags with you,' he said. He handed one to Tarzan and another to La.

'I do not believe that we shall ever leave the valley alive, but we might,' and he took a third bag for himself.

From the diamond vault the old man led them up a primitive ladder to the floor above, and quickly to the main entrance of the Tower. Only two heavy doors, bolted upon the inside, now lay between them and the terrace, a short distance beyond which the east gate swung open. The old man was about to open the doors when Tarzan stopped him.

'Wait a moment,' he said, 'until the rest of the Gomangani come. It takes them some time to ascend the ladder. When they are all here behind us, swing the doors open, and you and La, with this ten or a dozen Gomangani that are immediately around us, make a break for the gate. The rest of us will bring up the rear and hold the Bolgani off in case they attack us. Get ready,' he added a moment later, 'I think they are all up.'

Carefully Tarzan explained to the Gomangani the plan he had in mind, and then, turning to the old man, he commanded 'Now!' The bolt slipped, the doors swung open, and simultaneously the entire party started at a run toward the east gate.

The Bolgani, who were still massed about the throne room, were not aware that their victims had eluded them until Tarzan, bringing up the rear with Jad-bal-ja was passing through the east gate. Then the Bolgani discovered him, and immediately set up a hue and cry that brought several hundred of them on a mad run in pursuit.

'Here they come,' cried Tarzan to the others, 'make a run of it – straight down the valley toward Opar, La.'

'And you?' demanded the young woman.

'I shall remain a moment with the Gomangani, and attempt to punish these fellows.'

La stopped in her tracks. 'I shall not go a step without you, Tarzan of the Apes,' she said. 'Too great already are the risks you have taken for me. No; I shall not go without you.'

The ape-man shrugged. 'As you will,' he said. 'Here they come.'

With great difficulty he rallied a portion of the Gomangani who, once through the gate, seemed imbued but with a single purpose, and that to put as much distance between the Palace of Diamonds and themselves as possible. Perhaps fifty warriors rallied to his call, and with these he stood in the gateway toward which several hundred Bolgani were now charging.

The old man came and touched Tarzan on the arm. 'You had better fly,' he said. 'The Gomangani will break and run at the first assault.'

'We will gain nothing by flying,' said Tarzan, 'for we should only lose what we have gained with the Gomangani, and then we should have the whole valley about us like hornets.'

He had scarcely finished speaking when one of the Gomangani cried: 'Look! Look! They come,' and pointed along the trail into the forest.

'And just in time, too,' remarked Tarzan, as he saw the first of a swarm of Gomangani pouring out of the forest toward the east gate. 'Come!' he cried to the advancing blacks, 'the Bolgani are upon us. Come, and avenge your wrongs!' Then he turned, and calling to the blacks around him, leaped forward to meet the onrushing gorilla-men. Behind them wave after wave of Gomangani rolled through the east gate of the Palace of Diamonds, carrying everything before them to break at last like surf upon the wavering wall of Bolgani that was being relentlessly hurled back against the palace walls.

The shouting and the fighting and the blood worked Jad-bal-ja into such a frenzy of excitement that Tarzan with difficulty restrained him from springing upon friend and foe alike, with the result that it required so much of the ape-man's time to hold in leash his ferocious ally that he was able to take but little part in the battle, yet he saw that it was going his way, and that, but for the occurrence of some untoward event, the complete defeat of the Bolgani was assured.

Nor were his deductions erroneous. So frantic were the Gomangani with the blood-lust of revenge and so enthused by the first fruits of victory, that they went fully as mad as Jad-bal-ja himself. They neither gave nor asked quarter, and the fighting ended only when they could find no more Bolgani to slay.

The fighting over, Tarzan, with La and the old man, returned to the throne room, from which the fumes of the smoke bombs had now disappeared. To them they summoned the headman of each village, and when they had assembled before the dais, above which stood the three whites, with the great, black-maned lion Jad-bal-ja, Tarzan addressed them.

'Gomangani of the Valley of the Palace of Diamonds,' he said, 'you have this night won your freedom from the tyrannical masters that have oppressed you since far beyond the time the oldest of you may remember. For so many countless ages have you been oppressed that there has never developed among you a leader capable of ruling you wisely and justly. Therefore you must select a ruler from another race than your own.'

'You! You!' cried voice after voice as the headmen clamored to make Tarzan of the Apes their king.

'No,' cried the ape-man, holding up his hand for silence, 'but there is one here who has lived long among you, and who knows your habits and your customs, your hopes and your needs better than any other. If he will stay with you and rule you he will, I am sure, make you a good king,' and Tarzan pointed to the old man.

The old man looked at Tarzan in bewilderment. 'But I want to go away from here,' he said; 'I want to get back into the world of civilization, from which I have been buried all these years.'

'You do not know what you are talking about,' replied the ape-man. 'You have been gone very long. You will find no friends left back there from whence you came. You will find deceit, and hypocrisy, and greed, and avarice, and cruelty. You will find that no one will be interested in you and that you will be interested in no one there. I, Tarzan of the Apes, have left my jungle and gone to the cities built by men, but always I have been disgusted and been glad to return to my jungle – to the noble beasts that are honest in their loves and in their hates – to the freedom and genuineness of nature.

'If you return you will be disappointed, and you will realize that you have thrown away an opportunity of accomplishing a work well worth your while. These poor creatures need you. I cannot remain to guide them out of darkness, but you may, and you may so mold them that they will be an industrious, virtuous, and kindly people, not untrained, however, in the arts of warfare, for when we have that which is good, there will always be those who are envious and who, if they are more powerful than we, will attempt to come and take what we have by force. Therefore, you must train your people to protect their country and their rights, and to protect them they must have the ability and the knowledge to fight successfully, and the weapons wherewith to wage their wars.'

'You speak the truth, Tarzan of the Apes,' replied the old man. 'There is nothing for me in that other world, so, if the Gomangani wish me to be their chief I will remain here.'

The headmen, when he questioned them, assured Tarzan that if they could not have him for chief they would be very glad to have the old man, whom they all knew, either by sight or reputation, as one who had never perpetrated any cruelties upon the Gomangani.

The few surviving Bolgani who had taken refuge in various parts of the palace were sought out and brought to the throne room. Here they were given the option of remaining in the valley as slaves, or leaving the country entirely. The Gomangani would have fallen upon them and slain them, but that their new king would not permit.

'But where shall we go if we leave the Valley of the Palace of Diamonds?' asked one of the Bolgani. 'Beyond the city of Opar we know not what exists, and in Opar may we find only enemies.'

Tarzan sat eyeing them quizzically, and in silence. For a long time he did not speak, while several of the Gomangani headmen, and others of the Bolgani, made suggestions for the future of the gorilla-men. Finally the ape-man arose and nodded toward the Bolgani.

'There are about a hundred of you,' he said. 'You are powerful creatures and should be ferocious fighters. Beside me sits La, the High Priestess and queen of Opar. A wicked priest, usurping her power, has driven her from her throne, but tomorrow we march upon Opar with the bravest Gomangani of the Valley of the Palace of Diamonds, and there we punish Cadj, the High Priest, who has proven a traitor to his queen; and La, once more, ascends the throne of Opar. But where the seeds of treason have once been broadcast the plant may spring up at any time and where least expected. It will be long, therefore, before La of Opar may have full confidence in the loyalty of her people – a fact which offers you an opportunity and a country. Accompany us, therefore, to Opar, and fight with us to replace La upon her throne, and then, when the fighting is over, remain there as La's bodyguard to protect her, not only from enemies without, but from enemies within.'

The Bolgani discussed the matter for several minutes, and then one of them came to Tarzan. 'We will do as you suggest,' he said.

'And you will be loyal to La?' asked the ape-man.

'A Bolgani is never a traitor,' replied the gorilla-man.

'Good!' exclaimed Tarzan, 'and you, La, are you satisfied with this arrangement?'

'I accept them in my service,' replied she.

Early the next morning Tarzan and La set out with three thousand Gomangani and a hundred Bolgani to punish the traitorous Cadj. There was little or no attempt at strategy or deception. They simply marched down through the Valley of the Palace of Diamonds, descended the rocky ravine into the valley of Opar, and made straight for the rear of the palace of La.

A little gray monkey, sitting among the vines and creepers upon the top of the temple walls, saw them coming. He cocked his head, first upon one side and then upon the other, and became so interested and excited that for a moment he forgot to scratch his belly – an occupation he had been assiduously pursuing for some time. The closer the column approached the more excited became Manu, the monkey, and when he realized vaguely the great numbers of the Gomangani he was fairly beside himself, but the last straw that sent him scampering madly back to the palace of Opar was the sight of the Bolgani – the ogres of his little world.

Cadj was in the courtyard of the inner temple, where at sunrise he had performed a sacrifice to the Flaming God. With Cadj were a number of the lesser priests, and Oah and her priestesses. That there was dissension among them was evident by the scowling faces fully as much as by the words which Oah directed at Cadj.

'Once again have you gone too far, Cadj,' she cried bitterly. 'Only may the High Priestess of the Flaming God perform the act of sacrifice. Yet again and again do you persist in defiling the sacred knife with your unworthy hand.'

'Silence, woman,' growled the High Priest. 'I am Cadj, King of Opar, High Priest of the Flaming God. You are what you are only because of the favor of Cadj. Try not my patience too far or you shall indeed know the feel of the sacred knife.' There could be no mistaking the sinister menace in his words. Several of those about him could ill conceal the shocked surprise they felt at his sacrilegious attitude toward their High Priestess. However little they thought of Oah, the fact remained that she had been elevated to the highest place among them, and those that believed that La was dead, as Cadj had taken great pains to lead them all to believe, gave in full to Oah the reverence which her high office entitled her to.

'Have a care, Cadj,' warned one of the older priests. 'There is a limit beyond which not even you may pass.'

'You dare threaten me?' cried Cadj, the maniacal fury of fanaticism gleaming in his eyes. 'You dare threaten *me*, Cadj, the High Priest of the Flaming God?' And as he spoke he leaped toward the offending man, the sacrificial knife raised menacingly above his head, and just at that moment a little gray monkey came chattering and screaming through an embrasure in the wall overlooking the court of the temple.

'The Bolgani! The Bolgani!' he shrieked. 'They come! They come!'

Cadj stopped and wheeled toward Manu, the hand that held the knife dropping at his side. 'You saw them, Manu?' he asked. 'You are speaking the truth? If this is another of your tricks you will not live to play another joke upon Cadj.'

'I speak the truth,' chattered the little monkey. 'I saw them with my own eyes.'

'How many of them are there?' asked Cadj. 'And how near to Opar have they come?'

'They are as many as the leaves upon the trees,' replied Manu, 'and they are already close to the temple wall – the Bolgani and the Gomangani, they come as the grasses that grow in the ravines where it is cool and damp.'

Cadj turned and raised his face toward the sun, and throwing back his head gave voice to a long-drawn scream that ended in a piercing shriek. Three times he voiced the hideous cry, and then with a command to the others in the court to follow him he started at a brisk trot toward the palace proper. As Cadj directed his steps toward the ancient avenue, upon which the palace of Opar faced, there issued from every corridor and doorway groups of the knurled and hairy men of Opar, armed with their heavy bludgeons and their knives. Screaming and chattering in the trees above them were a score or more of little gray monkeys.

'Not here,' they cried, 'not here,' and pointed toward the south side of the city.

Like an undisciplined mob the horde of priests and warriors reentered the palace at Cadj's heels, and retraced their steps toward the opposite side of the edifice. Here they scrambled to the summit of the lofty wall which guards the palace, just as Tarzan's forces came to a halt outside.

'Rocks! Rocks!' screamed Cadj, and in answer to his commands the women in the courtyard below commenced to gather the loose fragments of stone that had crumbled from the wall and from the palace, and to toss them up to the warriors above.

'Go away!' screamed Cadj to the army outside his gates. 'Go away! I am Cadj, High Priest of the Flaming God, and this is his temple. Defile not the temple of the Flaming God or you shall know his wrath.'

Tarzan stepped forward a little ahead of the others, and raised his hand for silence.

'La, your High Priestess and your queen, is here,' he cried to the Oparians upon the wall. 'Cadj is a traitor and an impostor. Open your gates and receive your queen. Give up the traitors to justice, and no harm will befall you; but refuse La entry to her city and we shall take by force and with bloodshed that which belongs to La rightfully.'

As he ceased speaking La stepped to his side that all her people might see her, and immediately there were scattering cries for La and a voice or two raised against Cadj. Evidently realizing that it would not take much to turn the scale against him, Cadj shrieked to his men to attack, and simultaneously launched a stone at Tarzan. Only the wondrous agility that he possessed saved the ape-man, and the missile passed by, and striking a Gomangani over the heart, felled him. Instantly a shower of missiles fell upon them, and then Tarzan called to his followers to charge. Roaring and growling, the Bolgani and the Gomangani leaped forward to the attack. Cat-like they ran up the rough wall in the face of the menacing bludgeons above. Tarzan, who had chosen Cadj as his objective, was among the first to reach the summit. A hairy, crooked warrior struck at him with a bludgeon, and hanging to the summit of the wall with one hand, Tarzan caught the weapon in the other and wrested it from his assailant. At the same time he saw Cadj turn and disappear into the courtyard beyond. Then Tarzan drew himself to the top where he was immediately engaged by two other warriors of Opar. With the weapon he had wrested from their fellow he knocked them to right and left, so great an advantage his great height and strength gave him over them, and then, remembering only that Cadj, who was the ring-leader of the revolt against La, must not be permitted to escape Tarzan leaped to the pavement below just as the High Priest disappeared through an archway at the opposite end of the courtyard.

Some priests and priestesses sought to impede his progress. Seizing one of the former by the ankles he swung the body in circles about him, clearing his own pathway as he ran for the opposite end of the courtyard, and there he halted and wheeled and putting all the strength of his great muscles into the effort, he swung the body of the priest once more and hurled it back into the faces of his pursuers.

Without waiting to note the effect of his act he turned again and continued in pursuit of Cadj. The fellow kept always just ahead of him, because Cadj knew his way through the labyrinthian mazes of the palace and temple and courtyards better than Tarzan. That the trail was leading toward the inner courts of the temple Tarzan was convinced. There Cadj would find easy ingress to the pits beneath the palace and a hiding place from which it would be difficult to dislodge him, so numerous and winding were the dark subterranean tunnels. And so Tarzan put forth every effort to reach the sacrificial court in time to prevent Cadj from gaining the comparative safety of the underground passages; but as he finally leaped through the doorway into the court, a noose, cunningly laid, closed about one of his ankles and he was hurled heavily to the ground. Almost instantly a number of the crooked little men of Opar leaped upon him, where he lay, half-stunned by the fall, and before he had fully regained his faculties they had trussed him securely.

Only about half conscious, he felt them raise him from the ground and carry him, and presently he was deposited upon a cold stone surface. Then it was that full consciousness returned to him, and he realized that he lay outstretched once more upon the sacrificial altar of the inner court of the Temple of the Flaming God and above him stood Cadj, the High Priest, his cruel face contorted in a grimace of hate and the anticipation of revenge long deferred.

'At last!' gloated the creature of hate. 'This time, Tarzan of the Apes, you shall know the fury not of the Flaming God, but of Cadj, the man; nor shall there be any wait nor any interference.'

He swung the sacrificial knife high above his head. Beyond the point of the knife Tarzan of the Apes saw the summit of the courtyard wall, and just surmounting it the head and shoulders of a mighty, black-maned lion.

'Jad-bal-ja!' he cried. 'Kill! Kill!'

Cadj hesitated, his knife poised on high. He saw the direction of the ape-man's eyes and followed them, and in that instant the golden lion leaped to the pavement, and with two mighty bounds was upon the High Priest of Opar. The knife clattered to the floor and the great jaws closed upon the horrid face.

The lesser priests who had seized Tarzan, and who had remained to witness his death at the hands of Cadj, had fled screaming from the court the instant that the golden lion had leaped upon their master, and now Tarzan and Jad-bal-ja and the corpse of Cadj were the sole occupants of the sacrificial courtyard of the temple.

'Come, Jad-bal-ja,' commanded Tarzan; 'let no one harm Tarzan of the Apes.'

An hour later the victorious forces of La were overrunning the ancient palace and temples of Opar. The priests and warriors who had not been killed had quickly surrendered and acknowledged La as their queen and High Priestess, and now at La's command the city was being searched for Tarzan and Cadj. It was thus that La herself, leading a searching party, entered the sacrificial courtyard.

The sight that met her eyes brought her to a sudden halt, for there, bound upon the altar, lay Tarzan of the Apes, and standing above him, his snarling face and gleaming eyes glaring directly at her was Jad-bal-ja, the golden lion.

'Tarzan!' shrieked La, taking a step toward the altar. 'Cadj has had his way at last. God of my fathers have pity on me – Tarzan is dead.'

'No,' cried the ape-man; 'far from dead. Come and release me. I am only bound, but had it not been for Jad-bal-ja I had been dead beneath your sacrificial knife.'

'Thank God,' cried La, and started to approach the altar, but paused before the menacing attitude of the growling lion.

'Down!' cried Tarzan, 'let her approach'; and Jad-bal-ja lay down beside his master and stretched his whiskered chin across the ape-man's breast.

La came then, and picking up the sacrificial knife, cut the bonds that held the lord of the jungle captive, and then she saw beyond the altar the corpse of Cadj.

'Your worst enemy is dead,' said Tarzan, 'and for his death you may thank Jad-bal-ja, as I thank him for my life. You should rule now in peace and happiness and in friendship with the people of the Valley of the Palace of Diamonds.'

That night Tarzan and the Bolgani and the headmen of the Gomangani, and the priests and priestesses of Opar, sat in the great banquet hall of the Palace of Opar, as the guests of La, the queen, and ate from the golden platters of the ancient Atlantians – platters that had been fashioned on a continent that exists today only in the legends of antiquity. And the following morning Tarzan and Jad-bal-ja set forth upon their return journey to the land of the Waziri and home.

17
The Torture of Fire

Flora Hawkes and her four confederates, pursued by Luvini and his two hundred warriors, stumbled through the darkness of the jungle night. They had no objective, for, guided entirely as they had been by the blacks, they knew not where they were and were completely lost. The sole idea dominating the mind of each was to put as much distance between themselves and the camp of the ivory raiders as possible, for no matter what the outcome of the battle there might have been, their fate would be the same should the victorious party capture them. They had stumbled on for perhaps half an hour when, during a momentary rest, they heard plainly behind them the sound of pursuit, and again they plunged on in their aimless flight of terror.

Presently, to their surprise, they discerned the glow of a light ahead. What could it be? Had they made a complete circle, and was this again the camp they had been fleeing? They pushed on to reconnoiter, until at last they saw before them the outlines of a camp surrounded by a thorn boma, in the center of which was burning a small camp-fire. About the fire were congregated half-a-hundred black warriors, and as the fugitives crept closer they saw among the blacks a figure standing out clearly in the light of the camp-fire – a white woman – and behind them rose louder and louder the sound of pursuit.

From the gestures and gesticulations of the blacks around the camp-fire it was evident that they were discussing the sounds of the battle they had recently heard in the direction of the raiders' camp, for they often pointed in that direction, and now the woman raised her hand for silence and they all listened, and it was evident that they, too, heard the coming of the warriors who were pursuing Flora Hawkes and her confederates.

'There is a white woman there,' said Flora to the others.

'We do not know who she is, but she is our only hope, for those who are pursuing us will overtake us quickly. Perhaps this woman will protect us.

Come, I am going to find out,' and without waiting for an answer she walked boldly toward the boma.

They had come but a short distance when the keen eyes of the Waziri discovered them, and instantly the boma wall was ringed with bristling spears.

'Stop!' cried one of the warriors. 'We are the Waziri of Tarzan. Who are you?'

'I am an Englishwoman,' called Flora in reply. 'I and my companions are lost in the jungle. We have been betrayed by our safari – our headman is pursuing us now with warriors. There are but five of us and we ask your protection.'

'Let them come,' said Jane to the Waziri.

As Flora Hawkes and the four men entered the boma beneath the scrutiny of Jane Clayton and the Waziri, another pair of eyes watched from the foliage of the great tree that overhung the camp upon the opposite side – gray eyes to which a strange light came as they recognized the girl and her companions.

As the newcomers approached Lady Greystoke the latter gave an exclamation of surprise. 'Flora!' she exclaimed, in astonishment. 'Flora Hawkes, what in the world are you doing here?'

The girl, startled too, came to a full stop. 'Lady Greystoke!' she ejaculated.

'I do not understand,' continued Lady Greystoke. 'I did not know that you were in Africa.'

For a moment the glib Flora was overcome by consternation, but presently her native wit came to her assistance. 'I am here with Mr Bluber and his friends,' she said, 'who came to make scientific researches, and brought me along because I had been to Africa with you and Lord Greystoke, and knew something of the manners and customs of the country, and now our boys have turned against us and unless you can help us we are lost.'

'Are they west coast boys?' asked Jane.

'Yes,' replied Flora.

'I think my Waziri can handle them. How many of them are there?'

'About two hundred,' said Kraski.

Lady Greystoke shook her head. 'The odds are pretty heavy,' she commented, and then she called to Usula, who was in charge. 'There are two hundred west coast boys coming after these people,' she said; 'we shall have to fight to defend them.'

'We are Waziri,' replied Usula, simply, and a moment later the van of Luvini's forces broke into view at the outer rim of the camp-fire's reach.

At sight of the glistening warriors ready to receive them the west coast boys halted. Luvini, taking in the inferior numbers of the enemy at a glance, stepped forward a few paces ahead of his men and commenced to shout taunts and insults, demanding the return of the whites to him. He accompanied his words with fantastic and grotesque steps, at the same time waving his rifle and shaking his fist. Presently his followers took up the refrain until the whole band of two hundred was shrieking and yelling and threatening, the while they leaped up and down as they worked themselves into a frenzy of excitement that would impart to them the courage necessary for the initiating of a charge.

The Waziri, behind the boma wall, schooled and disciplined by Tarzan of the Apes, had long since discarded the fantastic overture to battle so dear to the hearts of other warlike tribes and, instead, stood stolid and grim awaiting the coming of the foe.

'They have a number of rifles,' commented Lady Grey-stoke; 'that looks rather bad for us.'

'There are not over half-a-dozen who can hit anything with their rifles,' said Kraski.

'You men are all armed. Take your places among my Waziri. Warn your men to go away and leave us alone. Do not fire until they attack, but at the first overt act, commence firing, and keep it up – there is nothing that so discourages a west coast black as the rifle fire of white men. Flora and I will remain at the back of the camp, near that large tree.' She spoke authoritatively, as one who is accustomed to command and knows whereof she speaks. The men obeyed her; even Bluber, though he trembled pitiably as he moved forward to take his place in the front ranks among the Waziri.

Their movements, in the light of the camp-fire, were all plainly discernible to Luvini, and also to that other who watched from the foliage of the tree beneath which Jane Clayton and Flora Hawkes took refuge. Luvini had not come to fight. He had come to capture Flora Hawkes. He turned to his men. 'There are only fifty of them,' he said. 'We can kill them easily, but we did not come to make war. We came to get the white girl back again. Stay here and make a great show against those sons of jackals. Keep them always looking at you. Advance a little and then fall back again, and while you are thus keeping their attention attracted in this direction I will take fifty men and go to the rear of their camp and get the white girl, and when I have her I will send word to you and immediately you can return to the village, where, behind the palisade, we shall be safe against attack.'

Now this plan well suited the west coast blacks, who had no stomach for the battle looming so imminent, and so they danced and yelled and menaced more vociferously than before, for they felt they were doing it all with perfect impunity, since presently they should retire, after a bloodless victory, to the safety of their palisade.

As Luvini, making a detour, crept through the concealment of the dense jungles to the rear of the camp while the din of the west coast blacks arose to almost deafening proportions, there dropped suddenly to the ground before the two white women from the tree above them, the figure of a white giant, naked except for loin cloth and leopard skin – his godlike contour picked out by the flickering light of the beast fire.

'John!' exclaimed Lady Greystoke. 'Thank God it is you.'

'S-s-sh!' cautioned the white giant, placing a forefinger to his lips, and then suddenly he wheeled upon Flora Hawkes. 'It is you I want,' he cried, and seizing the girl he threw her lightly across his shoulders, and before Lady Greystoke could interfere – before she half-realized what had occurred – he had lightly leaped the protecting boma in the rear of the camp and disappeared into the jungle beyond.

For a moment Jane Clayton stood reeling as one stunned by an unexpected blow, and then, with a stifled moan, she sank sobbing to the ground, her face buried in her arms.

It was thus that Luvini and his warriors found her as they crept stealthily over the boma and into the camp in the rear of the defenders upon the opposite side of the beast fire. They had come for a white woman and they had found one, and roughly dragging her to her feet, smothering her cries with rough and filthy palms, they bore her out into the jungle toward the palisaded village of the ivory raiders.

Ten minutes later the white men and the Waziri saw the west coast blacks retire slowly into the jungle, still yelling and threatening, as though bent on the total annihilation of their enemies – the battle was over without a shot fired or a spear hurled.

'Blime,' said Throck, 'what was all the bloomin' fuss about anyhow? I thought they was goin' to eat us up, an' the blighters never done nothin' but yell, an' 'ere we are, 'n that's that.'

Bluber swelled out his chest. 'It takes more as a bunch of natives to bluff Adolph Bluber,' he said pompously.

Kraski looked after the departing blacks, and then, scratching his head, turned back toward the camp-fire. 'I can't understand it,' he said, and then, suddenly, 'Where are Flora and Lady Greystoke?'

It was then that they discovered that the two women were missing.

The Waziri were frantic. They called the name of their mistress aloud, but there was no reply. 'Come!' cried Usula, 'we, the Waziri, shall fight, after all,' and running to the boma he leaped it, and, followed by his fifty blacks, set out in pursuit of the west coast boys.

It was but a moment or two before they overtook them, and that which ensued resembled more a rout than a battle. Fleeing in terror toward their palisade with the Waziri at their heels the west coast blacks threw away their rifles that they might run the faster, but Luvini and his party had had sufficient start so that they were able to reach the village and gain the safety of the palisade before pursued and pursuers reached it. Once inside the gate the defenders made a stand, for they realized that if the Waziri entered they should all be massacred, and so they fought as a cornered rat will fight, with the result that they managed to hold off the attackers until they could close and bar the gate. Built as it had been as a defense against far greater numbers the village was easy to defend, for there were less than fifty Waziri now, and nearly two hundred fighting men within the village to defend it against them.

Realizing the futility of blind attack Usula withdrew his forces a short distance from the palisade, and there they squatted, their fierce, scowling faces glaring at the gateway while Usula pondered schemes for outwitting the enemy, which he realized he could not overcome by force alone.

'It is only Lady Greystoke that we want,' he said; 'vengeance can wait until another day.'

'But we do not even know that she is within the village,' reminded one of his men.

'Where else could she be, then?' asked Usula. 'It is true that you may be right – she may not be within the village, but that I intend to find out. I have a plan. See; the wind is from the opposite side of the village. Ten of you will accompany me, the others will advance again before the gate and make much noise, and pretend that you are about to attack. After awhile the gate will open and they will come out. That I promise you. I will try to be here before that happens, but if I am not, divide into two parties and stand upon either side of the gateway and let the west coast blacks escape; we do not care for them. Watch only for Lady Greystoke, and when you see her take her away from those who guard her. Do you understand?' His companions nodded. 'Then come,' he said, and selecting ten men disappeared into the jungle.

Luvini had carried Jane Clayton to a hut not far from the gateway to the village. Here he had bound her securely and tied her to a stake, still believing that she was Flora Hawkes, and then he had left her to hurry back toward the gate that he might take command of his forces in defense of the village.

So rapidly had the events of the past hour transpired that Jane Clayton was still half dazed from the series of shocks that she had been called upon to endure. Dwarfing to nothingness the menace of her present position was the remembrance that her Tarzan had deserted her in her hour of need, and carried off into the jungle another woman. Not even the remembrance of what Usula had told her concerning the accident that Tarzan had sustained, and which had supposedly again affected his memory, could reconcile her to the brutality of his desertion, and now she lay, face down, in the filth of the Arab hut, sobbing as she had not for many years.

As she lay there torn by grief, Usula and his ten crept stealthily and silently around the outside of the palisade to the rear of the village. Here they found great quantities of dead brush left from the clearing which the Arabs had made when constructing their village. This they brought and piled along the palisade, close against it, until nearly three-quarters of the palisade upon that side of the village was banked high with it. Finding that it was difficult to prosecute their work in silence, Usula despatched one of his men to the main body upon the opposite side of the village, with instructions that they were to keep up a continuous din of shouting to drown the sound of the operations of their fellows. The plan worked to perfection, yet even though it permitted Usula and his companions to labor with redoubled efforts, it was more than an hour before the brush pile was disposed to his satisfaction.

Luvini, from an aperture in the palisade, watched the main body of the Waziri who were now revealed by the rising of the moon, and finally he came to the conclusion that they did not intend to attack that night, and therefore he might relax his watchfulness and utilize the time in another and more agreeable manner. Instructing the bulk of his warriors to remain near the gate and ever upon the alert, with orders that he be summoned the moment that the Waziri showed any change in attitude, Luvini repaired to the hut in which he had left Lady Greystoke.

The black was a huge fellow, with low, receding forehead and prognathous jaw. As he entered the hut with a lighted torch which he stuck in the floor, his bloodshot eyes gazed greedily at the still form of the woman lying prone before him. He licked his thick lips and, coming closer, reached out and touched her. Jane Clayton looked up, and recoiling in revulsion shrunk away. At sight of the woman's face the black looked his surprise.

'Who are you?' he demaned in the pidgin English of the coast.

'I am Lady Greystoke, wife of Tarzan of the Apes,' replied Jane Clayton. 'If you are wise you will release me at once.'

Surprise and terror showed in the eyes of Luvini, and another emotion as well, but which would dominate the muddy brain it was difficult, then, to tell. For a long time he sat gazing at her, and slowly the greedy, gloating expression upon his face dominated and expunged the fear that had at first been written there, and in the change Jane Clayton read her doom.

With fumbling fingers Luvini untied the knots of the bonds that held Jane Clayton's wrists and ankles. She felt his hot breath upon her and saw his bloodshot eyes and the red tongue that momentarily licked the thick lips. The instant that she felt the last thong with which she was tied fall away she leaped to her feet and sprang for the entrance to the hut, but a great hand reached forth and seized her, and as Luvini dragged her back toward him, she wheeled like a mad tigress and struck repeatedly at his grinning, ugly face. By brute force, ruthless and indomitable, he beat down her weak resistance and slowly and surely dragged her closer to him. Oblivious to aught else, deaf to the cries of the Waziri before the gate and to the sudden new commotion that arose in the village, the two struggled on, the woman, from the first, foredoomed to defeat.

Against the rear palisade Usula had already put burning torches to his brush pile at half-a-dozen different places. The flames, fanned by a gentle jungle breeze, had leaped almost immediately into a roaring conflagration, before which the dry wood of the palisade crumbled in a shower of ruddy sparks which the wind carried to the thatched roofs of the huts beyond, until in an incredibly short period of time the village was a roaring inferno of flames. And even as Usula had predicted the gate swung open and the west coast blacks swarmed forth in terror toward the jungle. Upon either side of the gateway the Waziri stood, looking for their mistress, but though they waited and watched in silence until no more came from the gateway of the village, and until the interior of the palisade was a seething hell of fire, they saw nothing of her.

Long after they were convinced that no human being could remain alive in the village they still waited and hoped; but at last Usula gave up the useless vigil.

'She was never there,' he said, 'and now we must pursue the blacks and capture some of them, from whom we may learn the whereabouts of Lady Greystoke.'

It was daylight before they came upon a small band of stragglers, who were in camp a few miles toward the west. These they quickly surrounded, winning their immediate surrender by promises of immunity in the event that they would answer truthfully the questions that Usula should propound.

'Where is Luvini?' demanded Usula, who had learned the name of the leader of the west coast boys from the Europeans the evening before.

'We do not know; we have not seen him since we left the village,' replied one of the blacks. 'We were some of the slaves of the Arabs, and when we escaped the palisade last night we ran away from the others, for we thought that we should be safer alone than with Luvini, who is even crueller than the Arabs.'

'Did you see the white women that he brought to the camp last night?' demanded Usula.

'He brought but one white woman,' replied the other.

'What did he do with her? Where is she now?' asked Usula.

'I do not know. When he brought her he bound her hand and foot and put her in the hut which he occupied near the village gate. We have not seen her since.'

Usula turned and looked at his companions. A great fear was in his eyes, a fear that was reflected in the countenances of the others.

'Come!' he said, 'we shall return to the village. And you will go with us,' he added, addressing the west coast blacks, 'and if you have lied to us—' he made a significant movement with his forefinger across his throat.

'We have not lied to you,' replied the others.

Quickly they retraced their steps toward the ruins of the Arab village, nothing of which was left save a few piles of smouldering embers.

'Where was the hut in which the white woman was confined?' demanded Usula, as they entered the smoking ruins.

'Here,' said one of the blacks, and walked quickly a few paces beyond what had been the village gateway. Suddenly he halted and pointed at something which lay upon the ground.

'There,' he said, 'is the white woman you seek.'

Usula and the others pressed forward. Rage and grief contended for mastery of them as they beheld, lying before them, the charred remnants of a human body.

'It is she,' said Usula, turning away to hide his grief as the tears rolled down his ebon cheeks. The other Waziri were equally affected, for they all had loved the mate of the Big Bwana.

'Perhaps it is not she,' suggested one of them; 'perhaps it is another.'

'We can tell quickly,' cried a third. 'If her rings are among the ashes it is indeed she,' and he knelt and searched for the rings which Lady Greystoke habitually wore.

Usula shook his head despairingly. 'It is she,' he said, 'there is the very stake to which she was fastened' – he pointed to the blackened stub of a stake close beside the body – 'and as for the rings, even if they are not there it will mean nothing, for Luvini would have taken them away from her as soon as he captured her. There was time for everyone else to leave the village except she, who was bound and could not leave – no, it cannot be another.'

The Waziri scooped a shallow grave and reverently deposited the ashes there, marking the spot with a little cairn of stones.

18

The Spoor of Revenge

As Tarzan of the Apes, adapting his speed to that of Jad-bal-ja, made his comparatively slow way toward home, he reviewed with varying emotions the experiences of the past week. While he had been unsuccessful in raiding the treasure vaults of Opar, the sack of diamonds which he carried compensated several-fold for this miscarriage of his plans. His only concern now was for the safety of his Waziri, and, perhaps, a troublesome desire to seek out the whites who had drugged him and mete out to them the punishment they deserved. In view, however, of his greater desire to return home he decided to make no effort at apprehending them for the time being at least.

Hunting together, feeding together, and sleeping together, the man and the great lion trod the savage jungle trails toward home. Yesterday they had shared the meat of Bara, the deer, today they feasted upon the carcass of Horta, the boar, and between them there was little chance that either would go hungry.

They had come within a day's march of the bungalow when Tarzan discovered the spoor of a considerable body of warriors. As some men devour the latest stock-market quotations as though their very existence depended upon an accurate knowledge of them, so Tarzan of the Apes devoured every scrap of information that the jungle held for him, for, in truth, an accurate knowledge of all that this information could impart to him had been during his lifetime a *sine qua non* to his existence. So now he carefully examined the spoor that lay before him, several days old though it was and partially obliterated by the passage of beasts since it had been made, but yet legible enough to the keen eyes and nostrils of the ape-man. His partial indifference suddenly gave way to keen interest, for among the footprints of the great warriors he saw now and again the smaller one of a white woman – a loved footprint that he knew as well as you know your mother's face.

'The Waziri returned and told her that I was missing,' he soliloquized, 'and now she has set out with them to search for me.' He turned to the lion. 'Well, Jad-bal-ja, once again we turn away from home – but no, where she is is home.'

The direction that the trail led rather mystified Tarzan of the Apes, as it was not along the direct route toward Opar, but in a rather more southerly direction. On the sixth day his keen ears caught the sound of approaching men, and presently there was wafted to his nostrils the spoor of blacks. Sending Jad-bal-ja into a thicket to hide, Tarzan took to the trees and moved rapidly in the direction of the approaching negroes. As the distance between them lessened the scent became stronger, until, even before he saw them, Tarzan knew that they were Waziri, but the one effluvium that would have filled his soul with happiness was lacking.

It was a surprised Usula who, at the head of the sad and dejected Waziri, came at the turning of the trail suddenly face to face with his master.

'Tarzan of the Apes!' cried Usula. 'Is it indeed you?'

'It is none other,' replied the ape-man, 'but where is Lady Greystoke?'

'Ah, master, how can we tell you!' cried Usula.

'You do not mean—' cried Tarzan. 'It cannot be. Nothing could happen to her while she was guarded by my Waziri!'

The warriors hung their heads in shame and sorrow. 'We offer our lives for hers,' said Usula, simply. He threw down his spear and shield and, stretching his arms wide apart, bared his great breast to Tarzan. 'Strike, Bwana,' he said.

The ape-man turned away with bowed head. Presently he looked at Usula again. 'Tell me how it happened,' he said, 'and forget your foolish speech as I have forgotten the suggestion which prompted it.'

Briefly Usula narrated the events which had led up to the death of Jane, and when he was done Tarzan of the Apes spoke but three words, voicing a question which was typical of him.

'Where is Luvini?' he asked.

'Ah, that we do not know,' replied Usula.

'But I shall know,' said Tarzan of the Apes. 'Go upon your way, my children, back to your huts, and your women and your children, and when next you see Tarzan of the Apes you will know that Luvini is dead.'

They begged permission to accompany him, but he would not listen to them.

'You are needed at home at this time of year,' he said. 'Already have you been gone too long from the herds and fields. Return, then, and carry word to Korak, but tell him that it is my wish that he, too, remains at home – if I fail, then may he come and take up my unfinished work if he wishes to do so.' As he ceased speaking he turned back in the direction from which he had come, and whistled once a single, low, long-drawn note, and a moment later Jad-bal-ja, the golden lion, bounded into view along the jungle trail.

'The golden lion!' cried Usula. 'When he escaped from Keewazi it was to search for his beloved Bwana.'

Tarzan nodded. 'He followed many marches to a strange country until he found me,' he said, and then he bid the Waziri goodbye and bent his steps once more away from home in search of Luvini and revenge.

John Peebles, wedged in the crotch of a large tree, greeted the coming dawn with weary eyes. Near him was Dick Throck, similarly braced in another crotch, while Kraski, more intelligent and therefore possessing more inventive genius, had rigged a small platform of branches across two parallel boughs, upon which he lay in comparative comfort. Ten feet above him Bluber swung, half exhausted and wholly terrified, to a smaller branch, supported in something that approximated safety by a fork of the branch to which he clung.

'Gord,' groaned Peebles, 'hi'll let the bloody lions 'ave me before hi'll spend another such a night as this, an' 'ere we are, 'n that's that!'

'And blime, too,' said Throck, 'hi sleeps on the ground hafter this, lions or no lions.'

'If the combined intelligence of the three of you was equal to that of a walrus,' remarked Kraski, 'we might have slept in comparative safety and comfort last night on the ground.'

'Hey there, Bluber, *Mister* Kraski is spikin' to yer,' called Peebles in fine sarcasm, accenting the Mister.

'*Ach, weh!* I don't care vat nobody says,' moaned Bluber.

''E wants us to build a 'ouse for 'im hevery night,' continued Peebles, 'while 'e stands abaht and tells us bloomin' well 'ow to do it, and 'im, bein' a fine gentleman, don't do no work.'

'Why should I do any work with my hands when you two big beasts haven't got anything else to work with?' asked Kraski. 'You would all have starved by this time if I hadn't found food for you. And you'll be lion meat in the end, or die of exhaustion if you don't listen to me – not that it would be much loss.'

The others paid no attention to his last sally. As a matter of fact they had all been quarreling so much for such a long time that they really paid little attention to one another. With the exception of Peebles and Throck they all hated one another cordially, and only clung together because they were afraid to separate. Slowly Peebles lowered his bulk to the ground. Throck followed him, and then came Kraski, and then, finally, Bluber, who stood for a moment in silence, looking down at his disreputable clothing.

'*Mein Gott!*' he exclaimed at last. 'Look at me! Dis suit, vat it cost me twenty guineas, look at it. Ruined. Ruined. It vouldn't bring vun penny in der pound.'

'The hell with your clothes!' exclaimed Kraski. 'Here we are, lost, half starved, constantly menaced by wild animals, and maybe, for all we know, by cannibals, with Flora missing in the jungle, and you can stand there and talk about your "tventy guinea" suit. You make me tired, Bluber. But come on, we might as well be moving.'

'Which way?' asked Throck.

'Why, to the west, of course,' replied Kraski. 'The coast is there, and there is nothing else for us to do but try to reach it.'

'We can't reach it by goin' east,' roared Peebles, 'an' 'ere we are, 'n that's that.'

'Who said we could?' demanded Kraski.

'Well, we was travelin' east all day yesterday,' said Peebles. 'I knew all the time that there was somethin' wrong, and I just got it figured out.'

Throck looked at his partner in stupid surprise. 'What do you mean?' he growled. 'What makes you think we was travelin' east?'

'It's easy enough,' replied Peebles, 'and I can prove it to you. Because this party here knows so much more than the rest of us we've been travelin' straight toward the interior ever since the natives deserted us.' He nodded toward the Russian, who stood with his hands on his hips, eyeing the other quizzically.

'If you think I'm taking you in the wrong direction, Peebles,' said Kraski, 'you just turn around and go the other way; but I'm going to keep on the way we've been going, which is the right way.'

'It ain't the right way,' retorted Peebles, 'and I'll show yer. Listen here. When you travel west the sun is at your left side, isn't it – that is, all durin' the middle of the day. Well, ever since we've been travelin' without the natives the sun has been on our right. I thought all the time there was somethin' wrong, but I could never figure it out until just now. It's plain as the face on your nose. We've been travelin' due east right along.'

'Blime,' cried Throck, 'that we have, due east, and this blighter thinks as 'ow 'e knows it all.'

'*Ach!*' groaned Bluber, 'und ve got to valk it all back again yet, once more?'

Kraski laughed and turned away to resume the march in the direction he had chosen. 'You fellows go on your own way if you want to,' he said, 'and while you're traveling, just ponder the fact that you're south of the equator and that therefore the sun is always in the north, which, however, doesn't change its old-fashioned habit of setting in the west.'

Bluber was the first to grasp the truth of Kraski's statement. 'Come on, boys,' he said, 'Carl vas right,' and he turned and followed the Russian.

Peebles stood scratching his head, entirely baffled by the puzzling problem, which Throck, also, was pondering deeply. Presently the latter turned after Bluber and Kraski. 'Come on, John,' he said to Peebles, 'hi don't hunderstand it, but hi guess they're right. They are headin' right toward where the sun set last night, and that sure must be west.'

His theory tottering, Peebles followed Throck, though he remained unconvinced.

The four men, hungry and footsore, had dragged their weary way along the jungle trail toward the west for several hours in vain search for game. Unschooled in jungle craft they blundered on. There might have been on every hand fierce carnivore or savage warriors, but so dull are the perceptive faculties of civilized man, the most blatant foe might have stalked them unperceived.

And so it was that shortly after noon, as they were crossing a small clearing, the zip of an arrow that barely missed Bluber's head, brought them to a sudden, terrified halt. With a shrill scream of terror Adolph crumpled to the ground. Kraski threw his rifle to his shoulder and fired.

'There!' he cried, 'behind those bushes,' and then another arrow, from another direction, pierced his forearm. Peebles and Throck, beefy and cumbersome, got into action with less celerity than the Russian, but, like him, they showed no indication of fear.

'Down,' cried Kraski, suiting the action to the word. 'Lie down and let them have it.'

Scarcely had the three men dropped among the long grass when a score of pigmy hunters came into the open, and a volley of arrows whizzed above the prone men, while from a nearby tree two steel-gray eyes looked down upon the ambush.

Bluber lay upon his belly with his face buried in his arms, his useless rifle lying at his side, but Kraski, Peebles, and Throck, fighting for their lives, pumped lead into the band of yelling pigmies.

Kraski and Peebles each dropped a native with his rifle and then the foe withdrew into the concealing safety of the surrounding jungle. For a moment there was a cessation of hostilities. Utter silence reigned, and then a voice broke the quiet from the verdure of a nearby forest giant.

'Do not fire until I tell you to,' it said, in English, 'and I will save you.'

Bluber raised his head. 'Come qvick! Come qvick!' he cried. 'Ve vill not shoot. Safe me, safe me, und I giff you five pounds.'

From the tree from which the voice had issued there came a single, low, long-drawn, whistled note, and then silence for a time.

The pigmies, momentarily surprised by the mysterious voice emanating from the foliage of a tree, ceased their activities, but presently, hearing nothing to arouse their fear, they emerged from the cover of the bushes and launched another volley of arrows toward the four men lying among the grasses in the clearing. Simultaneously the figure of a giant white leaped from the lower branches of a patriarch of the jungle, as a great black-maned lion sprang from the thicket below.

'Ach!' shrieked Bluber, and again buried his face in his arms.

For an instant the pigmies stood terrified, and then their leader cried: 'It is Tarzan!' and turned and fled into the jungle.

'Yes, it is Tarzan – Tarzan of the Apes,' cried Lord Greystoke. 'It is Tarzan and the golden lion,' but he spoke in the dialect of the pigmies, and the whites understood no word of what he said. Then he turned to them. 'The Gomangani have gone,' he said; 'get up.'

The four men crawled to their feet. 'Who are you, and what are you doing here?' demanded Tarzan of the Apes. 'But I do not need to ask who you are. You are the men who drugged me, and left me helpless in your camp, a prey to the first passing lion or savage native.'

Bluber stumbled forward, rubbing his palms together and cringing and smiling. '*Ach, nein!* Mr Tarzan, ve did not know you. Neffer vould ve did vat ve done, had ve known it vas Tarzan of der Apes. Safe me! Ten pounds – tventy pounds – anyt'ing. Name your own price. Safe me, und it is yours.'

Tarzan ignored Bluber and turned toward the others. 'I am looking for one of your men,' he said; 'a black named Luvini. He killed my wife. Where is he?'

'We know nothing of that,' said Kraski. 'Luvini betrayed us and deserted us. Your wife and another white woman were in our camp at the time. None of us knows what became of them. They were behind us when we took our post to defend the camp from our men and the slaves of the Arabs. Your Waziri were there. After the enemy had withdrawn we found that the two women had disappeared. We do not know what became of them. We are looking for them now.'

'My Waziri told me as much,' said Tarzan, 'but have you seen aught of Luvini since?'

'No, we have not,' replied Kraski.

'What are you doing here?' demanded Tarzan.

'We came with Mr Bluber on a scientific expedition,' replied the Russian. 'We have had a great deal of trouble. Our headmen, askari, and porters have mutinied and deserted. We are absolutely alone and helpless.'

'Ja, Ja!' cried Bluber. 'Safe us! Safe us! But keep dat lion avay. He makes me nerfous.'

'He will not hurt you – unless I tell him to,' said Tarzan.

'Den please don't tell him to,' cried Bluber.

'Where do you want to go?' asked Tarzan.

'We are trying to get back to the coast,' replied Kraski, 'and from there to London.'

'Come with me,' said Tarzan, 'possibly I can help you. You do not deserve it, but I cannot see white men perish here in the jungle.'

They followed him toward the west, and that night they made camp beside a small jungle stream.

It was difficult for the four Londoners to accustom themselves to the presence of the great lion, and Bluber was in a state of palpable terror.

As they squatted around the fire after the evening meal, which Tarzan had provided, Kraski suggested that they set to and build some sort of a shelter against the wild beasts.

'It will not be necessary,' said Tarzan. 'Jad-bal-ja will guard you. He will sleep here beside Tarzan of the Apes, and what one of us does not hear the other will.'

Bluber sighed. *'Mein Gott!'* he cried. 'I should giff ten pounds for vun night's sleep.'

'You may have it tonight for less than that,' replied Tarzan, 'for nothing shall befall you while Jad-bal-ja and I are here.'

'Vell, den I t'ink I say goodnight,' said Bluber, and moving a few paces away from the fire he curled up and was soon asleep. Throck and Peebles followed suit, and shortly after Kraski, too.

As the Russian lay, half dozing, his eyes partially open, he saw the ape-man rise from the squatting position he had maintained before the fire, and turn toward a nearby tree. As he did so something fell from beneath his loin cloth – a little sack made of hides – a little sack, bulging with its contents.

Kraski, thoroughly awakened now, watched it as the ape-man moved off a short distance, accompanied by Jad-bal-ja, and lay down to sleep.

The great lion curled beside the prostrate man, and presently the Russian was assured that both slept. Immediately he commenced crawling, stealthily and slowly toward the little package lying beside the fire. With each forward move that he made he paused and looked at the recumbent figures of the two ferocious beasts before him, but both slept on peacefully. At last the Russian could reach out and grasp the sack, and drawing it toward him he stuffed it quickly inside his shirt. Then he turned and crawled slowly and carefully back to his place beyond the fire. There, lying with his head upon one arm as though in profound slumber, he felt carefully of the sack with the fingers of his left hand.

'They feel like pebbles,' he muttered to himself, 'and doubtless that is what they are, for the barbaric ornamentation of this savage barbarian who is a peer of England. It does not seem possible that this wild beast has sat in the House of Lords.'

Noiselessly Kraski undid the knot which held the mouth of the sack closed, and a moment later he let a portion of the contents trickle forth into his open palm.

'My God!' he cried, 'diamonds!'

Greedily he poured them all out and gloated over them – great scintillating stones of the first water – five pounds of pure, white diamonds, representing so fabulous a fortune that the very contemplation of it staggered the Russian. 'My God!' he repeated, 'the wealth of Crœsus in my own hand.'

Quickly he gathered up the stones and replaced them in the sack, always with one eye upon Tarzan and Jad-bal-ja; but neither stirred, and presently he had returned them all to the pouch and slipped the package inside his shirt.

'Tomorrow,' he muttered, 'tomorrow – would to God that I had the nerve to attempt it tonight.'

In the middle of the following morning Tarzan, with the four Londoners, approached a good sized, stockaded village, containing many huts. He was received not only graciously, but with the deference due an emperor.

The whites were awed by the attitude of the black chief and his warriors as Tarzan was conducted into their presence.

After the usual ceremony had been gone through, Tarzan turned and waved his hand toward the four Europeans. 'These are my friends,' he said to the black chief, 'and they wish to reach the coast in safety. Send with them, then, sufficient warriors to feed and guard them during the journey. It is I, Tarzan of the Apes, who requests this favor.'

'Tarzan of the Apes, the great chief, Lord of the Jungle, has but to command,' replied the black.

'Good!' exclaimed Tarzan, 'feed them well and treat them well. I have other business to attend to and may not remain.'

'Their bellies shall be filled, and they shall reach the coast unscrathed,' replied the chief.

Without a word of farewell, without even a sign that he realized their existence, Tarzan of the Apes passed from the sight of the four Europeans, while at his heels paced Jad-bal-ja, the golden lion.

19

A Barbed Shaft Kills

Kraski spent a sleepless night. He could not help but realize that sooner or later Tarzan would discover the loss of his pouch of diamonds, and that he would return and demand an accounting of the four Londoners he had befriended. And so it was that as the first streak of dawn lighted the eastern horizon, the Russian arose from his pallet of dried grasses within the hut that had been assigned him and Bluber by the chief, and crept stealthily out into the village street.

'God!' he muttered to himself. 'There is only one chance in a thousand that I can reach the coast alone, but this,' and he pressed his hand over the bag of diamonds that lay within his shirt – 'but this, this is worth every effort, even to the sacrifice of life – the fortune of a thousand kings – my God, what could I not do with it in London, and Paris, and New York!'

Stealthily he slunk from the village, and presently the verdure of the jungle beyond closed about Carl Kraski, the Russian, as he disappeared forever from the lives of his companions.

Bluber was the first to discover the absence of Kraski, for, although there was no love between the two, they had been thrown together owing to the friendship of Peebles and Throck.

'Have you seen Carl dis morning?' he asked Peebles as the three men gathered around the pot containing the unsavory stew that had been brought to them for their breakfast.

'No,' said Peebles. 'He must be asleep yet.'

'He is not in der hut,' replied Bluber. 'He vas not dere ven I woke up.'

'He can take care of himself,' growled Throck, resuming his breakfast. 'You'll likely find him with some of the ladies,' and he grinned in appreciation of his little joke on Kraski's well-known weakness.

They had finished their breakfast and were attempting to communicate with some of the warriors, in an effort to learn when the chief proposed that they should set forth for the coast, and still Kraski had not made an appearance. By this time Bluber was considerably concerned, not at all for Kraski's safety, but for his own, since, if something could happen to Kraski in this friendly village in the still watches of the night, a similar fate might overtake him, and when he made this suggestion to the others it gave them food for thought, too, so that there were three rather apprehensive men who sought an audience with the chief.

By means of signs and pidgin English, and distorted native dialect, a word or two of which each of the three understood, they managed to covey to the chief the information that Kraski had disappeared, and they wanted to know what had become of him.

The chief was, of course, as much puzzled as they, and immediately instituted a thorough search of the village, with the result that it was soon found that Kraski was not within the palisade, and shortly afterward footprints were discovered leading through the village gateway into the jungle.

'*Mein Gott!*' exclaimed Bluber. 'He vent out dere, und he vent alone, in der middle of der night. He must have been crazy.'

'Gord!' cried Throck. 'What did he want to do that for?'

'You ain't missed nothin', have you?' asked Pebbles of the other two. ''E might 'ave stolen somethin'.'

'*Ach, weh!* Vot have ve got to steal?' cried Bluber. 'Our guns, our ammunition – dey are here beside us. He did not take them. Beside dose ve have nothing of value except my tventy guinea suit.'

'But what did 'e do it for?' demanded Peebles.

''E must 'ave been walkin' in 'is bloomin' sleep,' said Throck. And that was as near to an explanation of Kraski's mysterious disappearance as the three could reach. And hour later they set out toward the coast under the protection of a company of the chief's warriors.

Kraski, his rifle slung over his shoulder, moved doggedly along the jungle trail, a heavy automatic pistol grasped in his right hand. His ears were constantly strained for the first intimation of pursuit as well as for whatever other dangers might lurk before or upon either side. Alone in the mysterious jungle he was experiencing a nightmare of terror, and with each mile that he traveled the value of the diamonds became less and less by comparison with the frightful ordeal that he realized he must pass through before he could hope to reach the coast.

One Histah, the snake, swinging from a low-hung branch across the trail, barred his way, and the man dared not fire at him for fear of attracting the attention of possible pursuers to his position. He was forced, therefore, to make a detour through the tangled mass of underbrush which grew closely upon either side of the narrow trail. When he reached it again, beyond the snake, his clothing was more torn and tattered than before, and his flesh was scratched and cut and bleeding from the innumerable thorns past which he had been compelled to force his way. He was soaked with perspiration and panting from exhaustion, and his clothing was filled with ants whose vicious attacks upon his flesh rendered him half mad with pain.

Once again in the clear he tore his clothing from him and sought frantically to rid himself of the torturing pests.

So thick were the myriad ants upon his clothing that he dared not attempt to reclaim it. Only the sack of diamonds, his ammunition and his weapons did he snatch from the ravening horde whose numbers were rapidly increasing, apparently by millions, as they sought again to lay hold upon him and devour him.

Shaking the bulk of the ants from the articles he had retrieved, Kraski dashed madly along the trail as naked as the day he was born, and when, a half hour later, stumbling and at last falling exhausted, he lay panting upon the damp jungle earth, he realized the utter futility of his mad attempt to reach the coast alone, even more fully than he ever could have under any other circumstances, since there is nothing that so paralyzes the courage and self-confidence of a civilized man as to be deprived of his clothing.

However scant the protection that might have been afforded by the torn and tattered garments he had discarded, he could not have felt more helpless had he lost his weapons and ammunition instead, for to such an extent are we the creatures of habit and environment. It was, therefore, a terrified Kraski, already foredoomed to failure, who crawled fearfully along the jungle trail.

That night, hungry and cold, he slept in the crotch of a tree while the hunting carnivore roared, and coughed, and growled through the blackness of the jungle about him. Shivering with terror he started momentarily to fearful wakefulness, and when, from exhaustion, he would doze again it was not to rest but to dream of horrors that a sudden roar would merge into reality. Thus the long hours of a frightful night dragged out their tedious length, until it seemed that dawn would never come. But come it did, and once again he took up his stumbling way toward the west.

Reduced by fear and fatigue and pain to a state bordering upon half consciousness, he blundered on, with each passing hour becoming perceptibly weaker, for he had been without food or water since he had deserted his companions more than thirty hours before.

Noon was approaching. Kraski was moving but slowly now with frequent rests, and it was during one of these that there came to his numbed sensibilities an insistent suggestion of the voices of human beings not far distant.

Quickly he shook himself and attempted to concentrate his waning faculties. He listened intently, and presently with a renewal of strength he arose to his feet.

There was no doubt about it. He heard voices but a short distance away and they sounded not like the tones of natives, but rather those of Europeans. Yet he was still careful, and so he crawled cautiously forward, until at a turning of the trail he saw before him a clearing dotted with trees which bordered the banks of a muddy stream. Near the edge of the river was a small hut thatched with grasses and surrounded by a rude palisade protected by an outer boma of thorn bushes.

It was from the direction of the hut that the voices were coming, and now he clearly discerned a woman's voice raised in protest and in anger, and replying to it the deep voice of a man.

Slowly the eyes of Carl Kraski went wide in incredulity, not unmixed with terror, for the tones of the voice of the man he heard were the tones of the dead Esteban Miranda, and the voice of the woman was that of the missing Flora Hawkes, whom he had long since given up as dead also. But Carl Kraski was no great believer in the supernatural. Disembodied spirits need no huts or palisades, or bomas of thorns. The owners of those voices were as live – as material – as he.

He started forward toward the hut, his hatred of Esteban and his jealousy almost forgotten in the relief he felt in the realization that he was to again have the companionship of creatures of his own kind. He had moved, however, but a few steps from the edge of the jungle when the woman's voice came again to his ear, and with it the sudden realization of his nakedness. He paused in thought, looking about him, and presently he was busily engaged gathering the long, broad-leaved jungle grasses, from which he fabricated a rude but serviceable skirt, which he fastened about his waist with a twisted rope of the same material. Then with a feeling of renewed confidence he moved forward toward the hut. Fearing that they might not recognize him at first, and, taking him for an enemy, attack him, Kraski, before he reached the entrance to the palisade, called Esteban by name. Immediately the Spaniard came from the hut, followed by the girl. Had Kraski not heard his voice and recognized him by it, he would have thought him Tarzan of the Apes, so close was the remarkable resemblance.

For a moment the two stood looking at the strange apparition before them.

'Don't you know me?' asked Kraski. 'I am Carl – Carl Kraski. You know me, Flora.'

'Carl!' exclaimed the girl, and started to leap forward, but Esteban grasped her by the wrist and held her back.

'What are you doing here, Kraski?' asked the Spaniard in a surly tone.

'I am trying to make my way to the coast,' replied the Russian. 'I am nearly dead from starvation and exposure.'

'The way to the coast is there,' said the Spaniard, and pointed down the trail toward the west. 'Keep moving, Karski, it is not healthy for you here.'

'You mean to say that you will send me on without food or water?' demanded the Russian.

'There is water,' said Esteban, pointing at the river, 'and the jungle is full of food for one with sufficient courage and intelligence to gather it.'

'You cannot send him away,' cried the girl. 'I did not think it possible that even you could be so cruel,' and then, turning to the Russian, 'O Carl,' she cried 'do not go. Save me! Save me from this beast!'

'Then stand aside,' cried Kraski, and as the girl wrenched herself free from the grasp of Miranda the Russian leveled his automatic and fired point-blank at the Spaniard. The bullet missed its target; the empty shell jammed in the breach and as Kraski pulled the trigger again with no result he glanced at his weapon and, discovering its uselessness, hurled it from him with an oath. As he strove frantically to bring his rifle into action Esteban threw back his spear hand with the short, heavy spear that he had learned by now so well to use, and before the other could press the trigger of his rifle the barbed shaft tore through his chest and heart. Without a sound Carl Kraski sank dead at the foot of his enemy and his rival, while the woman both had loved, each in his own selfish or brutal way, sank sobbing to the ground in the last and deepest depths of despair.

Seeing that the other was dead, Esteban stepped forward and wrenched his spear from Kraski's body and also relieved his dead enemy of his ammunition and weapons. As he did so his eyes fell upon a little bag made of skins which Kraski had fastened to his waist by the grass rope he had recently fashioned to uphold his primitive skirt.

The Spaniard felt of the bag and tried to figure out the nature of its contents, coming to the conclusion that it was ammunition, but he did not examine it closely until he had carried the dead man's weapons into his hut, where he had also taken the girl, who crouched in a corner, sobbing.

'Poor Carl! Poor Carl!' she moaned, and then to the man facing her: 'You beast!'

'Yes,' he cried, with a laugh, 'I am a beast. I am Tarzan of the Apes, and that dirty Russian dared to call me Esteban. I am Tarzan! I am Tarzan of the Apes!' he repeated in a loud scream. 'Who dares call me otherwise dies. I will show them. I will show them,' he mumbled

The girl looked at him with wide and flaming eyes and shuddered.

'Mad,' she muttered. 'Mad! My God – alone in the jungle with a maniac!' And, in truth, in one respect was Esteban Miranda mad – mad with the madness of the artist who lives the part he plays. And for so long, now, had

Esteban Miranda played the part, and so really proficient had he become in his interpretation of the noble character, that he believed himself Tarzan, and in outward appearance he might have deceived the ape-man's best friend. But within that godlike form was the heart of a cur and the soul of a craven.

'He would have stolen Tarzan's mate,' muttered Esteban. 'Tarzan, Lord of the Jungle! Did you see how I slew him, with a single shaft? You could love a weakling, could you, when you could have the love of the great Tarzan!'

'I loathe you,' said the girl. 'You are indeed a beast. You are lower than the beasts.'

'You are mine, though,' said the Spaniard, 'and you shall never be another's – first I would kill you – but let us see what the Russian had in his little bag of hides, it feels like ammunition enough to kill a regiment,' and he untied the thongs that held the mouth of the bag closed and let some of the contents spill out upon the floor of the hut. As the sparkling stones rolled scintillant before their astonished eyes, the girl gasped in incredulity.

'Holy Mary!' exclaimed the Spaniard. 'They are diamonds.'

'Hundreds of them,' murmured the girl. 'Where could he have gotten them?'

'I do not know and I do not care,' said Esteban. 'They are mine. They are all mine – I am rich, Flora. I am rich, and if you are a good girl you shall share my wealth with me.'

Flora Hawkes's eyes narrowed. Awakened within her breast was the always-present greed that dominated her being, and beside it, and equally as powerful now to dominate her, her hatred for the Spaniard. Could he have known it, possession of those gleaming baubles had crystallized at last in the mind of the woman a determination she had long fostered to slay the Spaniard while he slept. Heretofore she had been afraid of being left alone in the jungle, but now the desire to possess this great wealth overcame her terror.

Tarzan, ranging the jungle, picked up the trail of the various bands of west coast boys and the fleeing slaves of the dead Arabs, and overhauling each in turn he prosecuted his search for Luvini, awing the blacks into truthfulness and leaving them in a state of terror when he departed. Each and every one, they told him the same story. There was none who had seen Luvini since the night of the battle and the fire, and each was positive that he must have escaped with some other band.

So thoroughly occupied had the ape-man's mind been during the past few days with his sorrow and his search that lesser considerations had gone neglected, with the result that he had not noted that the bag containing the diamonds was missing. In fact, he had practically forgotten the diamonds when, by the merest vagary of chance his mind happened to revert to them, and then it was that he suddenly realized that they were missing, but when he had lost them, or the circumstances surrounding the loss, he could not recall.

'Those rascally Europeans,' he muttered to Jad-bal-ja, 'they must have taken them,' and suddenly with the thought the scarlet scar flamed brilliantly upon his forehead, as just anger welled within him against the perfidy and ingratitude of the men he had succored. 'Come,' he said to Jad-bal-ja, 'as we search for Luvini we shall search for these others also.' And so it was that Peebles and Throck and Bluber had traveled but a short distance toward the coast when, during a noon-day halt, they were surprised to see the figure of the ape-man moving majestically toward them while, at his side, paced the great, black-maned lion.

Tarzan made no acknowledgment of their exuberant greeting, but came forward in silence to stand at last with folded arms before them. There was a grim, accusing expression upon his countenance that brought the chill of fear to Bluber's cowardly heart, and blanched the faces of the two hardened English pugs.

'What is it?' they chorused. 'What is wrong? What has happened?'

'I have come for the bag of stones you took from me,' said Tarzan simply.

Each of the three eyed his companion suspiciously.

'I do not understand vot you mean, Mr Tarzan,' purred Bluber, rubbing his palms together. 'I am sure dere is some mistake, unless –' he cast a furtive and suspicious glance in the direction of Peebles and Throck.

'I don't know nothin' about no bag of stones,' said Peebles, 'but I will say as 'ow you can't trust the likes of you.'

'I don't trust any of you,' said Tarzan. 'I will give you five seconds to hand over the bag of stones, and if you don't produce it in that time I shall have you thoroughly searched.'

'Sure,' cried Bluber, 'search me, search me, by all means. Vy, Mr Tarzan, I vouldn't take notting from you for notting.'

'There's something wrong here,' growled Throck. 'I ain't got nothin' of yours and I'm sure these two haven't neither.'

'Where is the other?' asked Tarzan.

'Oh, Kraski? He disappeared the same night you brought us to that village. We hain't seen him since – that's it; I got it now – we wondered why he left, and now I see it as plain as the face on me nose. It was him that stole that bag of stones. That's what he done. We've been tryin' to figure out ever since he left what he stole, and now I see it plain enough.'

'Sure,' exclaimed Peebles. 'That's it, and 'ere we are, 'n that's that.'

'Ve might have knowed it, ve might have knowed it,' agreed Bluber.

'But nevertheless I'm going to have you all searched,' said Tarzan, and when the headman came and Tarzan had explained what he desired, the three whites were quickly stripped and searched. Even their few belongings were thoroughly gone through, but no bag of stones was revealed.

Without a word Tarzan turned back toward the jungle, and in another moment the blacks and the three Europeans saw the leafy sea of foliage swallow the ape-man and the golden lion.

'Gord help Kraski!' exclaimed Peebles.

'Wot do yer suppose he wants with a bag o' stones?' inquired Throck. ''E must be a bit balmy, I'll say.'

'Balmy nudding,' exclaimed Bluber. 'Dere is but vun kind of stones in Africa vot Kraski would steal and run off into der jungle alone mit – diamonds.'

Peebles and Throck opened their eyes in surprise. 'The damned Russian!' exclaimed the former. 'He double-crossed us, that's what 'e did.'

'He likely as not saved our lives, says hi,' said Throck. 'If this ape feller had found Kraski and the diamonds with us we'd of all suffered alike – you couldn't 'a' made 'im believe we didn't 'ave a 'and in it. And Kraski wouldn't 'a' done nothin' to help us out.'

'I 'opes 'e catches the beggar!' exclaimed Peebles, fervently.

They were startled into silence a moment later by the sight of Tarzan returning to the camp, but he paid no attention to the whites, going instead directly to the headman, with whom he conferred for several minutes. Then, once more, he turned and left.

Acting on information gained from the headman, Tarzan struck off through the jungle in the general direction of the village where he had left the four whites in charge of the chief, and from which Kraski had later escaped alone. He moved rapidly, leaving Jad-bal-ja to follow behind, covering the distance to the village in a comparatively short time, since he moved almost in an air line through the trees, where there was no matted undergrowth to impede his progress.

Outside the village gate he took up Kraski's spoor, now almost obliterated, it is true, but still legible to the keen perceptive faculties of the ape-man. This he followed swiftly, since Kraski had clung tenaciously to the open trail that wound in a general westward direction.

The sun had dropped almost to the western treetops, when Tarzan came suddenly upon a clearing beside a sluggish stream, near the banks of which stood a small, rude hut, surrounded by a palisade and a thorn boma.

The ape-man paused and listened, sniffing the air with his sensitive nostrils, and then on noiseless feet he crossed the clearing toward the hut. In the grass outside the palisade lay the dead body of a white man, and a single glance told the ape-man that it was the fugitive whom he sought. Instantly he realized the futility of searching the corpse for the bag of diamonds, since it was a foregone conclusion that they were now in the possession of whoever had slain the Russian. A perfunctory examination revealed the fact that he was right in so far as the absence of the diamonds was concerned.

Both inside the hut and outside the palisade were indications of the recent presence of a man and woman, the spoor of the former tallying with that of the creature who had killed Gobu, the great ape, and hunted Bara, the deer, upon the preserves of the ape-man. But the woman – who was she? It was evident that she had been walking upon sore, tired feet, and that in lieu of shoes she wore bandages of cloth.

Tarzan followed the spoor of the man and the woman where it led from the hut into the jungle. As it progressed it became apparent that the woman had been lagging behind, and that she had commenced to limp more and more painfully. Her progress was very slow, and Tarzan could see that the man had not waited for her, but that he had been, in some places, a considerable distance ahead of her.

And so it was that Esteban had forged far ahead of Flora Hawkes, whose bruised and bleeding feet would scarce support her.

'Wait for me, Esteban,' she had pleaded. 'Do not desert me. Do not leave me alone here in this terrible jungle.'

'Then keep up with me,' growled the Spaniard. 'Do you think that with this fortune in my possession I am going to wait here forever in the middle of the jungle for someone to come and take it away from me? No, I am going on to the coast as fast as I can. If you can keep up, well and good. If you cannot, that is your own lookout.'

'But you could not desert me. Even you, Esteban, could not be such a beast after all that you have forced me to do for you.'

The Spaniard laughed. 'You are nothing more to me,' he said, 'than an old glove. With this,' and he held the sack of diamonds before him, 'I can purchase the finest gloves in the capitals of the world – new gloves,' and he laughed grimly at his little joke.

'Esteban, Esteban,' she cried, 'come back, come back. I can go no farther. Do not leave me. Please come back and save me.' But he only laughed at her, and as a turn of the trail shut him from her sight, she sank helpless and exhausted to the ground.

20
The Dead Return

That night Esteban made his lonely camp beside a jungle trail that wound through the dry wash of an old river bed, along which a tiny rivulet still trickled, according the Spaniard the water which he craved.

The obsession which possessed him that he was in truth Tarzan of the Apes, imparted to him a false courage, so that he could camp alone upon the ground without recourse to artificial protection of any kind, and fortune had favored him in this respect in that it had sent no prowling beasts of prey to find him upon those occasions that he had dared too much. During the period that Flora Hawkes had been with him he had built shelters for her, but now that he had deserted her and was again alone, he could not, in the rôle that he had assumed, consider so effeminate an act as the building of even a thorn boma for protection during the darkness of the night.

He did, however, build a fire, for he had made a kill and had not yet reached a point of primitive savagery which permitted him even to imagine that he enjoyed raw meat.

Having devoured what meat he wanted and filled himself at the little rivulet, Esteban came back and squatted before his fire, where he drew the pouch of diamonds from his loin cloth and, opening it, spilled a handful of the precious gems into his palm. The flickering firelight playing upon them sent scintillant gleams shooting into the dark of the surrounding jungle night as the Spaniard let a tiny stream of the sparkling stones trickle from one hand to the other, and in the pretty play of light the Spaniard saw visions of the future – power, luxury, beautiful women – all that great wealth might purchase for a man. With half closed eyes he dreamed of the ideal that he should search the world over to obtain – the dream-woman for whom he had always searched – the dream-woman he had never found, the fit companion for such as Esteban Miranda imagined himself to be. Presently through the dark lashes that veiled his narrowed lids the Spaniard seemed to see before him in the flickering light of his campfire a vague materialization of the figure of his dream – a woman's figure, clothed in flowing diaphanous white which appeared to hover just above him at the outer rim of his firelight at the summit of the ancient river bank.

It was strange how the vision persisted. Esteban closed his eyes tightly, and then opened them ever so little, and there, as it had been before he closed them, the vision remained. And then he opened his eyes wide, and still the figure of the woman in white floated above him.

Esteban Miranda went suddenly pale. 'Mother of God!' he cried. 'It is Flora. She is dead and has come back to haunt me.'

With staring eyes he slowly rose to his feet to confront the apparition, when in soft and gentle tones it spoke.

'Heart of my heart,' it cried, 'it is really you!'

Instantly Esteban realized that this was no disembodied spirit, nor was it Flora – but who was it? Who was this vision of beauty, alone in the savage African wilderness?

Very slowly now it was descending the embankment and coming toward him. Esteban returned the diamonds to the pouch and replaced it inside his loin cloth.

With outstretched arms the girl came toward him. 'My love, my love,' she cried, 'do not tell me that you do not know me.' She was close enough now for the Spaniard to see her rapidly rising and falling breasts and her lips trembling with love and passion. A sudden wave of hot desire swept over him, so with outstretched arms he sprang forward to meet her and crush her to his breast.

Tarzan, following the spoor of the man and the woman, moved in a leisurely manner along the jungle trail, for he realized that no haste was essential to overtake these two. Nor was he at all surprised when he came suddenly upon the huddled figure of a woman, lying in the center of the pathway. He knelt beside her and laid a hand upon her shoulder, eliciting a startled scream.

'God!' she cried, 'this is the end!'

'You are in no danger,' said the ape-man. 'I will not harm you.'

She turned her eyes and looked up at him. At first she thought he was Esteban. 'You have come back to save me, Esteban?' she asked.

'Esteban!' he exclaimed. 'I am not Esteban. That is not my name.' And then she recognized him.

'Lord Greystoke!' she cried. 'It is really you?'

'Yes,' he said, 'and who are you?'

'I am Flora Hawkes. I was Lady Greystoke's maid.'

'I remember you,' he said. 'What are you doing here?'

'I am afraid to tell you,' she said. 'I am afraid of your anger.'

'Tell me,' he commanded. 'You should know, Flora, that I do not harm women.'

'We came to get gold from the vaults of Opar,' she said. 'But that you know.'

'I know nothing of it,' he replied. 'Do you mean that you were with those Europeans who drugged me and left me in their camp?'

'Yes,' she said, 'we got the gold, but you came with your Waziri and took it from us.'

'I came with no Waziri and took nothing from you,' said Tarzan. 'I do not understand you.'

She raised her eyebrows in surprise, for she knew that Tarzan of the Apes did not lie.

'We became separated,' she said, 'after our men turned against us. Esteban stole me from the others, and then, after a while Kraski found us. He was the Russian. He came with a bagful of diamonds and then Esteban killed him and took the diamonds.'

It was now Tarzan's turn to experience surprise.

'And Esteban is the man who is with you?' he asked.

'Yes,' she said, 'but he has deserted me. I could not walk farther on my sore feet. He has gone and left me here to die and he has taken the diamonds with him.'

'We shall find him,' said the ape-man. 'Come.'

'But I cannot walk,' said the girl.

'That is a small matter,' he said, and stooping lifted her to his shoulder.

Easily the ape-man bore the exhausted girl along the trail. 'It is not far to water,' he said, 'and water is what you need. It will help revive you and give you strength, and perhaps I shall be able to find food for you soon.'

'Why are you so good to me?' asked the girl.

'You are a woman. I could not leave you alone in the jungle to die, no matter what you may have done,' replied the ape-man. And Flora Hawkes could only sob a broken plea for forgiveness for the wrong she had done him.

It grew quite dark, but still they moved along the silent trail until presently Tarzan caught in the distance the reflection of firelight.

'I think we shall soon find your friend,' he whispered. 'Make no noise.'

A moment later his keen ears caught the sound of voices. He halted and lowered the girl to her feet.

'If you cannot follow,' he said, 'wait here. I do not wish him to escape. I will return for you. If you can follow on slowly, do so.' And then he left her and made his way cautiously forward toward the light and the voices. He heard Flora Hawkes moving directly behind him. It was evident that she could not bear the thought of being left alone again in the dark jungle. Almost simultaneously Tarzan heard a low whine a few paces to his right. 'Jad-bal-ja,' he whispered in a low voice, 'heel,' and the great black-maned lion crept close to him, and Flora Hawkes, stifling a scream, rushed to his side and grasped his arms.

'Silence,' he whispered; 'Jad-bal-ja will not harm you.'

An instant later the three came to the edge of the ancient river bank, and through the tall grasses growing there looked down upon the little camp beneath.

Tarzan, to his consternation, saw a counterpart of himself standing before a little fire, while slowly approaching the man, with outstretched arms, was a woman, draped in flowing white. He heard her words; soft words of love and endearment, and at the sound of the voice and the scent spoor that a vagrant wind carried suddenly to his nostrils, a strange complex of emotion overwhelmed him – happiness, despair, rage, love, and hate.

He saw the man at the fire step forward with open arms to take the woman to his breast, and then Tarzan separated the grasses and stepped to the very edge of the embankment, his voice shattering the jungle with a single word.

'Jane!' he cried, and instantly the man and woman turned and looked up at him, where his figure was dimly revealed in the light of the campfire. At sight of him the man wheeled and raced for the opposite side of the river, and then Tarzan leaped to the bottom of the wash below and ran toward the woman.

'Jane,' he cried, 'it is you, it is you!'

The woman showed her bewilderment. She looked first at the retreating figure of the man she had been about to embrace and then turned her eyes toward Tarzan. She drew her fingers across her brow and looked back toward Esteban, but Esteban was no longer in sight. Then she took a faltering step toward the ape-man.

'My God,' she cried, 'what does it mean? Who are you, and if you are Tarzan who was he?'

'I am Tarzan, Jane,' said the ape-man.

She looked back and saw Flora Hawkes approaching. 'Yes,' she said, 'you are Tarzan. I saw you when you ran off into the jungle with Flora Hawkes. I cannot understand, John. I could not believe that you, even had you suffered an accident to your head, could have done such a thing.'

'I, run off into the jungle with Flora Hawkes?' he asked, in unfeigned surprise.

'I saw you,' said Jane.

The ape-man turned toward Flora. 'I do not understand it,' he said.

'It was Esteban who ran off into the jungle with me, Lady Greystoke,' said the girl. 'It was Esteban who was about to deceive you again. This is indeed Lord Greystoke. The other was an impostor, who only just deserted me and left me to die in the jungle. Had not Lord Greystoke come when he did I should be dead by now.'

Lady Greystoke took a faltering step toward her husband. 'Ah, John,' she said, 'I knew it could not have been you. My heart told me, but my eyes deceived me. Quick,' she cried, 'that impostor must be captured. Hurry, John, before he escapes.'

'Let him go,' said the ape-man. 'As much as I want him, as much as I want that which he has stolen from me, I will not leave you alone again in the jungle, Jane, even to catch him.'

'But Jad-bal-ja,' she cried. 'What of him?'

'Ah,' cried the ape-man, 'I had forgotten,' and turning to the lion he pointed toward the direction in which the Spaniard had escaped. 'Fetch him, Jad-bal-ja,' he cried; and, with a bound, the tawny beast was off upon the spoor of his quarry.

'He will kill him?' asked Flora Hawkes, shuddering. And yet at heart she was glad of the just fate that was overtaking the Spaniard.

'No, he will not kill him,' said Tarzan of the Apes. 'He may maul him a bit, but he will bring him back alive if it is possible.' And then, as though the fate of the fugitive were already forgotten, he turned toward his mate.

'Jane,' he said, 'Usula told me that you were dead. He said that they found your burned body in the Arab village and that they buried it there. How is it, then, that you are here alive and unharmed? I have been searching the jungles for Luvini to avenge your death. Perhaps it is well that I did not find him.'

'You would never have found him,' replied Jane Clayton, 'but I cannot understand why Usula should have told you that he had found my body and buried it.'

'Some prisoners that he took,' replied Tarzan, 'told him that Luvini had taken you bound hand and foot into one of the Arab huts near the village gateway, and that there he had further secured you to a stake driven into the floor of the hut. After the village had been destroyed by fire Usula and the other Waziri returned to search for you with some of the prisoners they had taken who pointed out the location of the hut, where the charred remains of a human body were found beside a burned stake to which it had apparently been tied.'

'Ah!' exclaimed the girl, 'I see. Luvini did bind me hand and foot and tie me to the stake, but later he came back into the hut and removed the bonds. He attempted to attack me – how long we fought I do not know, but so engrossed were we in our struggle that neither one of us was aware of the burning of the village about us. As I persistently fought him off I caught a glimpse of a knife in his belt, and then I let him seize me and as his arms encircled me I grasped the knife and, drawing it from its sheath, plunged it into his back, below his left shoulder – that was the end. Luvini sank lifeless to the floor of the hut. Almost simultaneously the rear and roof of the structure burst into flames.

'I was almost naked, for he had torn nearly all my clothing from me in our struggles. Hanging upon the wall of the hut was this white burnoose, the property, doubtless, of one of the murdered Arabs. I seized it, and throwing it about me ran into the village street. The huts were now all aflame, and the last of the natives was disappearing through the gateway. To my right was a section of palisade that had not yet been attacked by the flames. To escape into the jungle by the gateway would have meant running into the arms of my enemies, and so, somehow, I managed to scale the palisade and and drop into the jungle unseen by any.

'I have had considerable difficulty eluding the various bands of blacks who escaped the village. A part of the time I have been hunting for the Waziri and the balance I have had to remain in hiding. I was resting in the crotch of a tree, about half a mile from here, when I saw the light of this man's fire, and when I came to investigate I was almost stunned by joy to discover that I had, as I imagined, stumbled upon my Tarzan.'

'It was Luvini's body, then, and not yours that they buried,' said Tarzan.

'Yes,' said Jane, 'and it was this man who just escaped whom I saw run off into the jungle with Flora, and not you, as I believed.'

Flora Hawkes looked up suddenly. 'And it must have been Esteban who came with the Waziri and stole the gold from us. He fooled our men and he must have fooled the Waziri, too.'

'He might have fooled anyone if he could deceive me,' said Jane Clayton. 'I should have discovered the deception in a few minutes I have no doubt, but in the flickering light of the campfire, and influenced as I was by the great joy of seeing Lord Greystoke again, I believed quickly that which I wanted to believe.'

The ape-man ran his fingers through his thick shock of hair in a characteristic gesture of meditation. 'I cannot understand how he fooled Usula in broad daylight,' he said with a shake of his head.

'I can,' said Jane. 'He told him that he had suffered an injury to his head which had caused him to lose his memory partially – an explanation which accounted for many lapses in the man's interpretation of your personality.'

'He was a clever devil,' commented the ape-man.

'He was a devil, all right,' said Flora.

It was more than an hour later that the grasses at the river bank suddenly parted and Jad-bal-ja emerged silently into their presence. Grasped in his jaws was a torn and bloody leopard skin which he brought and laid at the feet of his master.

The ape-man picked the thing up and examined it, and then he scowled. 'I believe Jad-bal-ja killed him after all,' he said.

'He probably resisted,' said Jane Clayton, 'in which event Jad-bal-ja could do nothing else in self-defense but slay him.'

'Do you suppose he ate him?' cried Flora Hawkes, drawing fearfully away from the beast.

'No,' said Tarzan, 'he has not had time. In the morning we will follow the spoor and find his body. I should like to have the diamonds again.' And then he told Jane the strange story connected with his acquisition of the great wealth represented by the little bag of stones.

The following morning they set out in search of Esteban's corpse. The trail led through dense brush and thorns to the edge of the river farther down stream, and there it disappeared, and though the ape-man searched both sides of the river for a couple of miles above and below the point at which he had lost the spoor, he found no further sign of the Spaniard. There was blood along the tracks that Esteban had made and blood upon the grasses at the river's brim.

At last the ape-man returned to the two women. 'That is the end of the man who would be Tarzan,' he said.

'Do you think he is dead?' asked Jane.

'Yes, I am sure of it,' said the ape-man. 'From the blood I imagine that Jad-bal-ja mauled him, but that he managed to break away and get into the river. The fact that I can find no indication of his having reached the bank within a reasonable distance of this spot leads me to believe that he has been devoured by crocodiles.'

Again Flora Hawkes shuddered. 'He was a wicked man,' she said, 'but I would not wish even the wickedest such a fate as that.'

The ape-man shrugged. 'He brought it upon himself, and, doubtless, the world is better off without him.'

'It was my fault,' said Flora. 'It was my wickedness that brought him and the others here. I told them of what I had heard of the gold in the treasure vaults of Opar – it was my idea to come here and steal it and to find a man who could impersonate Lord Greystoke. Because of my wickedness many men have died, and you, Lord Greystoke, and your lady, have almost met your death – I do not dare to ask for forgiveness.'

Jane Clayton put her arm about the girl's shoulder. 'Avarice has been the cause of many crimes since the world began,' she said, 'and when crime is invoked in its aid it assumes its most repulsive aspect and brings most often its own punishment, as you, Flora, may well testify. For my part I forgive you. I imagine that you have learned your lesson.'

'You have paid a heavy price for your folly,' said the ape-man. 'You have been punished enough. We will take you to your friends who are on their way to the coast under escort of a friendly tribe. They cannot be far distant, for, from the condition of the men when I saw them, long marches are beyond their physical powers.'

The girl dropped to her knees at his feet. 'How can I thank you for your kindness?' she said. 'But I would rather remain here in Africa with you and Lady Greystoke, and work for you and show by my loyalty that I can redeem the wrong I did you.'

Tarzan glanced at his wife questioningly, and Jane Clayton signified her assent to the girl's request.

'Very well, then,' said the ape-man, 'you may remain with us, Flora.'

'You will never regret it,' said the girl. 'I will work my fingers off for you.'

The three, and Jad-bal-ja, had been three days upon the march toward home when Tarzan, who was in the lead, paused, and, raising his head, sniffed the jungle air. Then he turned to them with a smile. 'My Waziri are disobedient,' he said. 'I sent them home and yet here they are, coming toward us, directly away from home.'

A few minutes later they met the van of the Waziri, and great was the rejoicing of the blacks when they found both their master and mistress alive and unscathed.

'And now that we have found you,' said Tarzan, after the greetings were over, and innumerable questions had been asked and answered, 'tell me what you did with the gold that you took from the camp of the Europeans.'

'We hid it, O Bwana, where you told us to hide it,' replied Usula.

'I was not with you, Usula,' said the ape-man. 'It was another, who deceived Lady Greystoke even as he deceived you – a bad man – who impersonated Tarzan of the Apes so cleverly that it is no wonder that you were imposed upon.'

'Then it was not you who told us that your head had been injured and that you could not remember the language of the Waziri?' demanded Usula.

'It was not I,' said Tarzan, 'for my head has not been injured, and I remember well the language of my children.'

'Ah,' cried Usula, 'then it was not our Big Bwana who ran from Buto, the rhinoceros?'

Tarzan laughed. 'Did the other run from Buto?'

'That he did,' cried Usula; 'he ran in great terror.'

'I do not know that I blame him,' said Tarzan, 'for Buto is no pleasant playfellow.'

'But our Big Bwana would not run from him,' said Usula, proudly.

'Even if another than I hid the gold it was you who dug the hole. Lead me to the spot then, Usula.'

The Waziri constructed rude yet comfortable litters for the two white women, though Jane Clayton laughed at the idea that it was necessary that she be carried and insisted upon walking beside her bearers more often than she rode. Flora Hawkes, however, weak and exhausted as she was, could not have proceeded far without being carried, and was glad of the presence of the brawny Waziri who bore her along the jungle trail so easily.

It was a happy company that marched in buoyant spirits toward the spot where the Waziri had cached the gold for Esteban. The blacks were overflowing with good nature because they had found their master and their mistress, while the relief and joy of Tarzan and Jane were too deep for expression.

When at last they came to the place beside the river where they had buried the gold the Waziri, singing and laughing, commenced to dig for the treasure, but presently their singing ceased and their laughter was replaced by expressions of puzzled concern.

For a while Tarzan watched them in silence and then a slow smile overspread his countenance. 'You must have buried it deep, Usula,' he said.

The black scratched his head. 'No, not so deep as this, Bwana,' he cried. 'I cannot understand it. We should have found the gold before this.'

'Are you sure you are looking in the right place?' asked Tarzan.

'This is the exact spot, Bwana,' the black assured him, 'but the gold is not here. Someone has removed it since we buried it.'

'The Spaniard again,' commented Tarzan. 'He was a slick customer.'

'But he could not have taken it alone,' said Usula. 'There were many ingots of it.'

'No,' said Tarzan, 'he could not, and yet it is not here.'

The Waziri and Tarzan searched carefully about the spot where the gold had been buried, but so clever had been the woodcraft of Owaza that he had obliterated even from the keen senses of the ape-man every vestige of the spoor that he and the Spaniard had made in carrying the gold from the old hiding place to the new.

'It is gone,' said the ape-man, 'but I shall see that it does not get out of Africa,' and he despatched runners in various directions to notify the chiefs of the friendly tribes surrounding his domain to watch carefully every safari crossing their territory, and to let none pass who carried gold.

'That will stop them,' he said after the runners had departed.

That night as they made their camp upon the trail toward home, the three whites were seated about a small fire with Jad-bal-ja lying just behind the ape-man, who was examining the leopard skin that the golden lion had retrieved in his pursuit of the Spaniard, when Tarzan turned to his wife.

'You were right, Jane,' he said. 'The treasure vaults of Opar are not for me. This time I have lost not only the gold but a fabulous fortune in diamonds as well, beside risking that greatest of all treasures – yourself.'

'Let the gold and the diamonds go, John,' she said; 'we have one another, and Korak.'

'And a bloody leopard skin,' he supplemented, 'with mysterious map painted upon it in blood.'

Jad-bal-ja sniffed the hide and licked his chops in – anticipation or retrospection – which?

21

An Escape and a Capture

At sight of the true Tarzan, Esteban Miranda turned and fled blindly into the jungle. His heart was cold with terror as he rushed on in blind fear. He had no objective in mind. He did not know in what direction he was going. His only thought – the thought which dominated him – was based solely upon a desire to put as much distance as possible between himself and the ape-man, and so he blundered on, forcing his way through dense thickets of thorns that tore and lacerated his flesh until at every step he left a trail of blood behind him.

At the river's edge the thorns reached out and seized again, as they had several times before, the precious leopard skin to which he clung with almost the same tenacity as he clung to life itself. But this time the thorns would not leave go their hold, and as he struggled to tear it away from them his eyes turned back in the direction from which he had come. He heard the sound of a great body moving rapidly through the thicket toward him, and an instant later saw the baleful glare of two gleaming, yellow-green spots of flame. With a stifled cry of terror the Spaniard relinquished his hold upon the leopard skin and, wheeling, dived into the river.

As the black waters closed above his head Jad-bal-ja came to the edge of the bank and looked down upon the widening circles which marked the spot of his quarry's disappearance, for Esteban, who was a strong swimmer, struck boldly for the opposite side of the stream, keeping himself well submerged.

For a moment the golden lion scanned the surface of the river, and then he turned and sniffed at the hide the Spaniard had been forced to leave behind, and grasping it in his jaws tore it from the thorns that held it and carried it back to lay it at the feet of his master.

Forced at last to come to the surface for air the Spaniard arose amid a mass of tangled foliage and branches. For a moment he thought that he was lost, so tightly held was he by the entangling boughs, but presently he forced his way upward, and as his head appeared above the surface of the water amidst the foliage he discovered that he had arisen directly beneath a fallen tree that was floating down the center of the stream. After considerable effort he managed to draw himself up to the boughs and find a place astride the great bole, and thus he floated down stream in comparative safety.

He breathed a deep sigh of relief as he realized with what comparative ease he had escaped the just vengeance of the ape-man. It is true that he bemoaned the loss of the hide which carried the map to the location of the hidden gold, but he still retained in his possession a far greater treasure, and as he thought of it his hands gloatingly fondled the bag of diamonds fastened to his loin cloth. Yet, even though he possessed this great fortune in diamonds, his avaricious mind constantly returned to the golden ingots by the waterfall.

'Owaza will get it,' he muttered to himself. 'I never trusted the black dog, and when he deserted me I knew well enough what his plans were.'

All night long Esteban Miranda floated down stream upon the fallen tree, seeing no sign of life, until shortly after daybreak he passed a native village upon the shore.

It was the village of Obebe, the cannibal, and at sight of the strange figure of the white giant floating down the stream upon the bole of a tree, the young woman who espied him raised a great hue and cry until the population of the village lined the shore watching him pass.

'It is a strange god,' cried one.

'It is the river devil,' said the witch doctor. 'He is a friend of mine. Now, indeed, shall we catch many fish if for each ten that you catch you give one to me.'

'It is not the river devil,' rumbled the deep voice of Obebe, the cannibal. 'You are getting old,' he said to the witch doctor, 'and of late your medicine has been poor medicine, and now you tell me that Obebe's greatest enemy is the river devil. That is Tarzan of the Apes. Obebe knows him well.' And in truth every cannibal chief in the vicinity knew Tarzan of the Apes well and feared and hated him, for relentless had been the ape-man's war against them.

'It is Tarzan of the Apes,' repeated Obebe, 'and he is in trouble. Perhaps it is our chance to capture him.'

He called his warriors about him, and presently half a hundred brawny young bucks started at a jog trot down the trail that paralleled the river. For miles they followed the slowly moving tree which carried Esteban Miranda until at last at a bend in the river the tree was caught in the outer circle of a slow-moving eddy, which carried it beneath the overhanging limbs of the trees growing close to the river's edge.

Cramped and chilled and hungry as he was, Esteban was glad of the opportunity to desert his craft and gain the shore. And so, laboriously, he drew himself up among the branches of the tree that momentarily offered him a haven of retreat from the river, and crawling to its stem lowered himself to the ground beneath, unconscious of the fact that in the grasses around him squatted half a hundred cannibal warriors.

Leaning against the bole of the tree the Spaniard rested for a moment. He felt for the diamonds and found that they were safe.

'I am a lucky devil, after all,' he said aloud, and almost simultaneously the fifty blacks arose about him and leaped upon him. So sudden was the attack, so overwhelming the force, that the Spaniard had no opportunity to defend himself against them, with the result that he was down and securely bound almost before he could realize what was happening to him.

'Ah, Tarzan of the Apes, I have you at last,' gloated Obebe, the cannibal, but Esteban did not understand a word the man said, and so he could make no reply. He talked to Obebe in English, but that language the latter did not understand.

Of only one thing was Esteban certain; that he was a prisoner and that he was being taken back toward the interior. When they reached Obebe's village there was great rejoicing on the part of the women and the children and the warriors who had remained behind. But the witch doctor shook his head and made wry faces and dire prophecies.

'You have seized the river devil,' he said. 'We shall catch no more fish, and presently a great sickness will fall upon Obebe's people and they will all die like flies.' But Obebe only laughed at the witch doctor for, being an old man and a great king, he had accumulated much wisdom and, with the acquisition of wisdom, man is more inclined to be skeptical in matters of religion.

'You may laugh now, Obebe,' said the witch doctor, 'but later you will not laugh. Wait and see.'

'When, with my own hands, I kill Tarzan of the Apes, then indeed shall I laugh,' replied the chief, 'and when I and my warriors have eaten his heart and his flesh, then, indeed, shall we no longer fear any of your devils.'

'Wait,' cried the witch doctor angrily, 'and you shall see.'

They took the Spaniard, securely bound, and threw him into a filthy hut, through the doorway of which he could see the women of the village preparing cooking fires and pots for the feast of the coming night. A cold sweat stood out upon the brow of Esteban Miranda as he watched these grewsome preparations, the significance of which he could not misinterpret, when coupled with the gestures and the glances that were directed toward the hut where he lay, by the inhabitants of the village.

The afternoon was almost spent and the Spaniard felt that he could count the hours of life remaining to him upon possibly two fingers of one hand, when there came from the direction of the river a series of piercing screams which shattered the quiet of the jungle, and brought the inhabitants of the village to startled attention, and an instant later sent them in a mad rush in the direction of the fear-laden shrieks. But they were too late and reached the river only just in time to see a woman dragged beneath the surface by a huge crocodile.

'Ah, Obebe, what did I tell you?' demanded the witch doctor, exultantly. 'Already has the devil god commenced his revenge upon your people.'

The ignorant villagers, steeped in superstition, looked fearfully from their witch doctor to their chief. Obebe scowled. 'He is Tarzan of the Apes,' he insisted.

'He is the river devil who has taken the shape of Tarzan of the Apes,' insisted the witch doctor.

'We shall see,' replied Obebe. 'If he is the river devil he can escape our bonds. If he is Tarzan of the Apes he cannot. If he is the river devil he will not die a natural death, like men die, but will live on forever. If he is Tarzan of the Apes some day he will die. We will keep him, then, and see, and that will prove whether or not he is Tarzan of the Apes or the river devil.'

'How?' asked the witch doctor.

'It is very simple,' replied Obebe. 'If some morning we find that he has escaped we will know that he is the river devil, and because we have not harmed him but have fed him well while he has been here in our village, he will befriend us and no harm will come of it. But if he does not escape we will know that he is Tarzan of the Apes, provided he dies a natural death. And so, if he does not escape, we shall keep him until he dies and then we shall know that he was, indeed, Tarzan of the Apes.'

'But suppose he does not die?' asked the witch doctor, scratching his woolly head.

'Then,' exclaimed Obebe triumphantly, 'we will know that you are right, and that he was, indeed, the river devil.'

Obebe went and ordered women to take food to the Spaniard while the witch doctor stood, where Obebe had left him, in the middle of the street, still scratching his head in thought.

And thus was Esteban Miranda, possessor of the most fabulous fortune in diamonds that the world had ever known, condemned to life imprisonment in the village of Obebe, the cannibal.

While he had been lying in the hut his traitorous confederate, Owaza, from the opposite bank of the river from the spot where he and Esteban had hidden the golden ingots, saw Tarzan and his Waziri come and search for the gold and go away again, and the following morning Owaza came with fifty men whom he had recruited from a neighboring village and dug up the gold and started with it toward the coast.

That night Owaza made camp just outside a tiny village of a minor chief, who was weak in warriors. The old fellow invited Owaza into his compound, and there he fed him and gave him native beer, while the chief's people circulated among Owaza's boys plying them with innumerable questions until at last the truth leaked out and the chief knew that Owaza's porters were carrying a great store of yellow gold.

When the chief learned this for certain he was much perturbed, but finally a smile crossed his face as he talked with the half-drunken Owaza.

'You have much gold with you,' said the old chief, 'and it is very heavy. It will be hard to get your boys to carry it all the way back to the coast.'

'Yes,' said Owaza, 'but I shall pay them well.'

'If they did not have to carry it so far from home you would not have to pay them so much, would you?' asked the chief.

'No,' said Owaza, 'but I cannot dispose of it this side of the coast.'

'I know where you can dispose of it within two days' march,' replied the old chief.

'Where?' demanded Owaza. 'And who here in the interior will buy it?'

'There is a white man who will give you a little piece of paper for it and you can take that paper to the coast and get the full value of your gold.'

'Who is this white man?' demanded Owaza, 'and where is he?'

'He is a friend of mine,' said the chief, 'and if you wish I will take you to him on the morrow, and you can bring with you all your gold and get the little piece of paper.'

'Good,' said Owaza, 'and then I shall not have to pay the carriers but a very small amount.'

The carriers were glad, indeed, to learn the next day that they were not to go all the way to the coast, for even the lure of payment was not sufficient to overcome their dislike to so long a journey, and their fear of being at so great a distance from home. They were very happy, therefore, as they set forth on a two days' march toward the northeast. And Owaza was happy and so was the old chief, who accompanied them himself, though why he was happy about it Owaza could not guess.

They had marched for almost two days when the chief sent one of his own men forward with a message.

'It is to my friend,' he said, 'to tell him to come and meet us and lead us to his village.' And a few hours later, as the little caravan emerged from the jungle onto a broad, grassy plain, they saw not far from them, and approaching rapidly, a large band of warriors. Owaza halted.

'Whose are those?' he demanded.

'Those are the warriors of my friend,' replied the chief, 'and he is with them. See?' and he pointed toward a figure at the head of the blacks, who were approaching at a trot, their spears and white plumes gleaming in the sunshine.

'They come for war and not for peace,' said Owaza fearfully.

'That depends upon you, Owaza,' replied the chief.

'I do not understand you,' said Owaza.

'But you will in a few minutes after my friend has come.'

As the advancing warriors approached more closely Owaza saw a giant white at their head – a white whom he mistook for Esteban – the confederate he had so traitorously deserted. He turned upon the chief. 'You have betrayed me,' he cried.

'Wait,' said the old chief; 'nothing that belongs to you shall be taken from you.'

'The gold is not his,' cried Owaza. 'He stole it,' and he pointed at Tarzan who had approached and halted before him, but who ignored him entirely and turned to the chief.

'Your runner came,' he said to the old man, 'and brought your message, and Tarzan and his Waziri have come to see what they could do for their old friend.'

The chief smiled. 'Your runner came to me, O Tarzan, four days since, and two days later came this man with his carriers, bearing golden ingots toward the coast. I told him that I had a friend who would buy them, giving him a little piece of paper for them, but that, of course, only in case the gold belonged to Owaza.'

The ape-man smiled. 'You have done well, my friend,' he said. 'The gold does not belong to Owaza.'

'It does not belong to you, either,' cried Owaza. 'You are not Tarzan of the Apes. I know you. You came with the four white men and the white woman to steal the gold from Tarzan's country, and then you stole it from your own friends.'

The chief and the Waziri laughed. The ape-man smiled one of his slow smiles.

'The other was an impostor, Owaza,' he said, 'but I am Tarzan of the Apes, and I thank you for bringing my gold to me. Come,' he said, 'it is but a few more miles to my home,' and the ape-man compelled Owaza to direct his carriers to bear the golden ingots to the Greystoke bungalow. There Tarzan fed the carriers and paid them, and the next morning sent them back to their own country. He sent Owaza with them, but not without a gift of value, accompanied with an admonition that the black never again return to Tarzan's country.

When they had departed, and Tarzan, Jane and Korak were standing upon the veranda of the bungalow with Jad-bal-ja lying at their feet, the ape-man threw an arm about his mate's shoulders.

'I shall have to retract what I said about the gold of Opar not being for me, for you see before you a new fortune that has come all the way from the treasure vaults of Opar without any effort on my part.'

'Now, if someone would only bring your diamonds back,' laughed Jane.

'No chance of that,' said Tarzan. 'They are unquestionably at the bottom of the Ugogo River,' and far away, upon the banks of the Ugogo, in the village of Obebe, the cannibal, Esteban Miranda lay in the filth of the hut that had been assigned to him, gloating over the fortune that he could never utilize as he entered upon a life of captivity that the stubbornness and superstition of Obebe had doomed him to undergo.

TARZAN AND THE ANT MEN

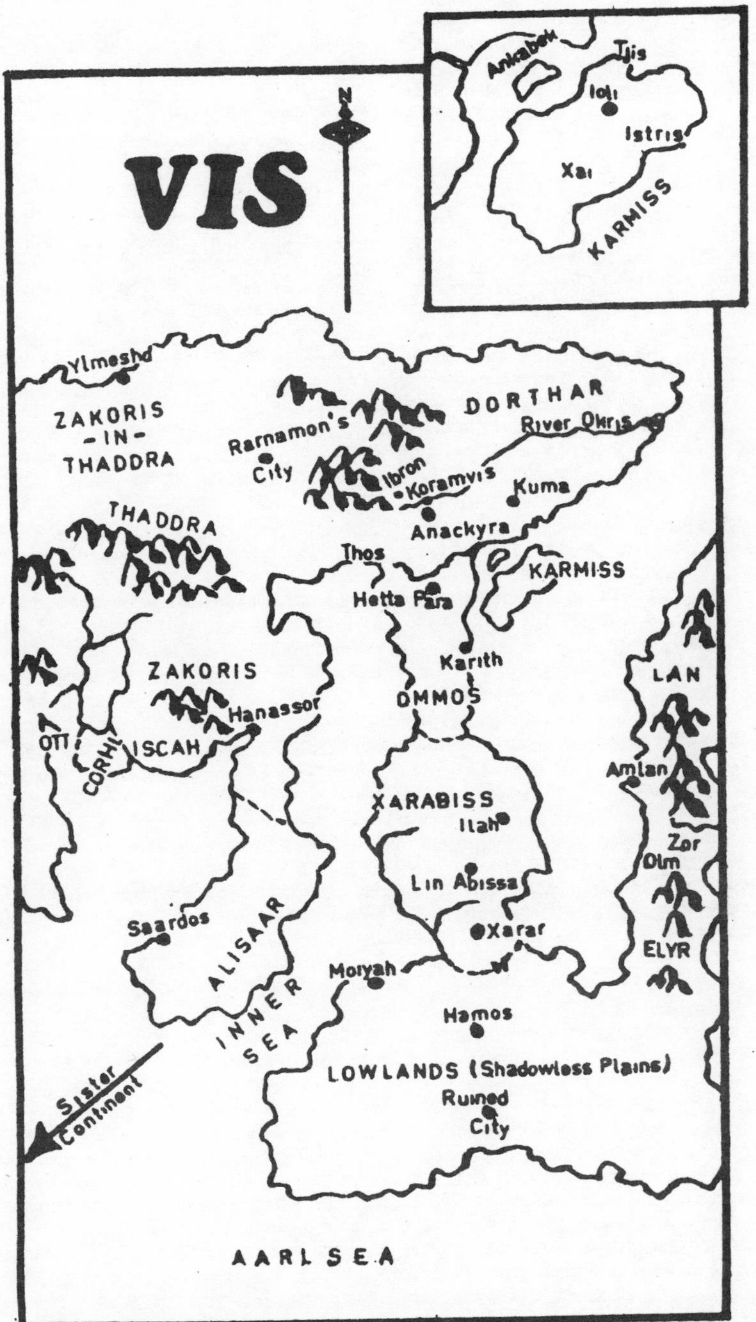
VIS
N
Ankabek
Tijis
Ioli
Istris
Xai
KARMISS
Ylmeshd
ZAKORIS
-IN-
THADDRA
Rarnamon's
City
DORTHAR
River Okris
Ibron
Koramvis
Kuma
Anackyra
THADDRA
Thos
Hetta Para
KARMISS
Karith
LAN
ZAKORIS
Hanassor
OMMOS
OTT
CORHL
ISCAH
Amlan
XARABISS
Ilah
Zor
Olm
Lin Abissa
Saardos
Xarar
ELYR
ALISAAR
Moiyah
INNER
SEA
Hamos
LOWLANDS (Shadowless Plains)
Sister Continent
Ruined
City
AARL SEA

1

The Age-old Barrier

Three persons stepped from the veranda of Lord Greystoke's African bungalow and walked slowly towards the gate along a rose-embowered path that swung in a graceful curve through the well-ordered, though unpretentious grounds surrounding the ape-man's rambling, one-storey home. There were two men and a woman, all in khaki, the older man carrying a flier's helmet and a pair of goggles in one hand. He was smiling quietly as he listened to the younger man.

'You wouldn't be doing this now if mother were here,' said the latter; 'she would never permit it.'

'I'm afraid you are right, my son,' replied Tarzan of the Apes; 'but only this one flight alone and then I'll promise not to go up again until she returns. You have said yourself that I am an apt pupil, and if you are any sort of an instructor you should have perfect confidence in me after having said that I was perfectly competent to pilot a ship alone. Eh, Meriem, isn't that true?' he demanded of the young woman.

She shook her head. 'Like my dear husband, I am always afraid for you, *man père*,' she replied. 'You take such risks that one would think you considered yourself immortal. You should be more careful.'

The younger man threw his arm about his wife's shoulders. 'Meriem is right,' he said: 'you *should* be more careful, father.'

Tarzan shrugged. 'If you and mother had your way my nerves and muscles would have atrophied long since. They were given to me to use and I intend using them – with discretion. Doubtless I shall be old and useless soon enough, and long enough, as it is.'

A child burst suddenly from the bungalow, pursued by a perspiring governess, and raced to Meriem's side.

'Muvver,' he cried, 'Dackie doe? Dackie doe?'

'Let him come along as far as the biplane,' urged Tarzan.

Out on the level plain, that stretched away from the bungalow to the distant jungle, the verdant masses and deep shadows of which were vaguely discernible to the north-west, lay a biplane. In its shade lolled two Waziri warriors who had been trained by Korak, the son of Tarzan, in the duties of mechanics, and, later, to pilot the ship themselves.

This fact had not been without weight in determining Tarzan of the Apes to perfect himself in the art of flying, since, as chief of the Waziri, it was not mete that the lesser warriors of his tribe should excel him in any particular feat. Adjusting his helmet and goggles, Tarzan climbed into the cockpit.

'Better take me along,' advised Korak.

Tarzan shook his head, smiling good-naturedly.

'Then one of the boys, here,' urged his son. 'You might develop some trouble that would force you to make a landing, and if you have no mechanic along to make repairs what are you going to do?'

'Walk,' replied the ape-man. 'Turn her over, Andua!' he directed one of the blacks.

A moment later the ship was bumping over the veldt, from which, directly, it arose in smooth and graceful flight; circled, climbing to a greater altitude, and then sped away in an air line, while on the ground below the six strained their eyes until the wavering speck that it had dwindled to disappeared entirely.

'Where do you suppose he is going?' asked Meriem.

Korak shook his head. 'He isn't supposed to be going anywhere in particular,' he replied; 'just making his first practice flight alone; but, knowing him as I do, I wouldn't be surprised to learn that he had taken it into his head to fly to London and see mother.'

'But he could never do it!' cried Meriem.

'No ordinary man could, with no more experience than he has had; but then, you will have to admit, father is no ordinary man.'

For an hour and a half Tarzan flew without altering his course and without realizing the flight of time or the great distance he had covered, so delighted was he with the ease with which he controlled the ship, and so thrilled by this new power that gave him the freedom and mobility of the birds, the only denizens of his beloved jungle that he ever had had cause to envy.

Presently, ahead, he discerned a great basin, or what might better be described as a series of basins, surrounded by wooded hills, and immediately he recognized to the left of it the winding Ugogo; but the country of the basins was new to him and he was puzzled. He recognized, simultaneously, another fact: that he was more than a hundred miles from home, and he determined to put back at once; but the mystery of the basins lured him on – he could not bring himself to return home without a closer view of them.

Why was it that he had never come upon this country in his many wanderings? Why had he never even heard of it from the natives living within easy access to it. He dropped to a lower level the better to inspect the basins, which now appeared to him as a series of shallow craters of long extinct volcanoes. He saw forests, lakes, and rivers the very existence of which he had never dreamed, and then quite suddenly he discovered a solution of the seeming mystery that there should exist in a country with which he was familiar so large an area of which he had been in total ignorance. He recognized it now – the so-called Great Thorn Forest. For years he had been familiar with that impenetrable thicket that was supposed to cover a vast area of territory into which only the smallest of animals might venture, and now he saw it was but a relatively narrow fringe encircling a pleasant, habitable country, but a fringe so cruelly barbed as to have protected since time immemorial the secret that it held from the eyes of man.

Tarzan determined to circle this long-hidden land of mystery before setting the nose of his ship toward home, and, to obtain a closer view, he accordingly dropped nearer the earth. Beneath him was a great forest and beyond that an open veldt that ended at the foot of precipitous, rocky hills.

He saw that, absorbed as he had been in the strange new country, he had permitted the plane to drop too low. With the realization, before he could move the control within his hand, the ship touched the leafy crown of some old monarch of the jungle, veered, swung completely around, and crashed downward through the foliage amid the snapping and rending of broken branches and the splintering of its own woodwork. Just for a second this, and then silence.

2

The Alali

Along a forest trail slouched a mighty creature, manlike in its physical attributes, yet vaguely inhuman: a great brute that walked erect upon two feet and carried a club in one horny, calloused hand. Its long hair fell, unkempt, about its shoulders, and there was hair upon its chest and a little upon its arms and legs, though no more than is found upon many males of civilized races.

A strip of hide about its waist supported the ends of a narrow G-string, as well as numerous raw-hide strands, to the lower ends of which were fastened round stones from one to two inches in diameter. Close to each stone were attached several smaller feathers, for the most part of brilliant hues. The strands supporting the stones being fastened to the belt at intervals of one to two inches, and the strands themselves being about eighteen inches long, the whole formed a skeleton skirt, fringed with round stones and feathers, that fell almost to the creature's knees.

Its large feet were bare and its white skin tanned to a light brown by exposure to the elements. The illusion of great size was suggested more by the massiveness of the shoulders and the development of the muscles of the back and arms than by height, although the creature measured close to six feet.

Its face was massive, with a broad nose and a wide, full-lipped mouth. The eyes, of normal size, were set beneath heavy beetling brows, topped by a wide, low forehead.

As it walked it flapped its large, flat ears and occasionally moved rapidly portions of its skin on various parts of its head and body to dislodge flies, as does a horse with the muscles along its sides and flanks. It moved silently, its dark eyes constantly on the alert, while the flapping ears were often momentarily stilled as the woman – for such was the creature's sex – listened for sounds of quarry or foe.

She stopped now, her ears bent forward, her nostrils expanded to sniff the air. Some scent or sound that our feeble sensitory organs could not have perceived had attracted her attention. Warily she crept forward along the trail, until, at a turning, she saw before her a figure lying face downward in the path.

It was Tarzan of the Apes. Unconscious he lay, while above him the splintered wreckage of his plane was wedged among the branches of the great tree that had caused its downfall.

The woman gripped her club more firmly and approached. Her expression reflected the puzzlement the discovery of this strange creature had engendered in her elementary mind, but she evinced no fear. She walked directly to the side of the prostrate man, her club raised to strike; but something stayed her hand.

She knelt beside him and fell to examining his clothing. She turned him over on his back and placed one of her ears above his heart. Then she fumbled with the front of his shirt for a moment, and suddenly taking it in her two mighty hands, tore it apart. Again she listened, her ear this time against his naked flesh. She arose and looked about, sniffing and listening, then she stooped and lifting the body of the ape-man she swung it lightly across one of her broad shoulders and continued along the trail in the direction she had been going.

The trail, winding through the forest, broke presently from the leafy shade into an open, park-like strip of rolling land that stretched at the foot of rocky hills, and, crossing this, disappeared within the entrance of a narrow gorge eroded by the elements, from the native sandstone, fancifully as the capricious architecture of a dream, among whose grotesquely domed and minareted rocks the woman bore her burden along a well-worn course. A half-mile from the entrance to the gorge the trail entered a roughly circular amphitheatre, the precipitous walls of which were pierced by numerous cave-mouths, before several of which squatted creatures similar to that which bore Tarzan into this strange, savage environment.

As she entered the amphitheatre all eyes were upon her, for the large, sensitive ears had warned them of her approach long before she had arrived within scope of their vision. Immediately they beheld her and her burden several of them arose and came to meet her. All females, these, similar in physique and scant garb to the captor of the ape-man, though differing in proportions and physiognomy as do the individuals of all races differ from their fellows.

They spoke no words nor uttered any sounds, nor did she whom they approached as she moved straight along her way, which was evidently directed toward one of the cave-mouths, but she gripped her bludgeon firmly and swung it to and fro, while her eyes, beneath their scowling brows, kept sullen surveillance upon every move of her fellows.

She had approached close to the cave, which was quite evidently her destination, when one of those who followed her darted forward and clutched at Tarzan. With the quickness of a cat the woman dropped her burden, turned upon the temerarious one, and, swinging her bludgeon with lightning-like celerity, felled her with a heavy blow on the head.

Then, standing astride the prostrate Tarzan, she glared about her like a lioness at bay, questioning dumbly who would be next to attempt to wrest her prize from her. The others slunk back to their caves, leaving the vanquished one lying, unconscious, in the hot sand.

The victor thereupon shouldered her burden, undisputed, and continued her way to the cave, where she dumped the ape-man unceremoniously upon the ground just within the shadow of the entrance-way. There, squatting beside him, she faced outward, so that she might not be taken unaware by any of her fellows, and proceeded to examine her find minutely. Tarzan's clothing either piqued her curiosity or aroused her disgust, for she began almost immediately to divest him of it, and having had no former experience of buttons and buckles she tore it away by main force. The heavy, cordovan boots troubled her for a moment, but finally their seams gave way to her powerful muscles. Only the diamond-studded, golden bracelet that had been his mother's she left untouched upon its golden chain about his neck.

For a moment she sat contemplating him and then she arose and tossing him once more to her shoulder she walked toward the centre of the amphitheatre, the greater portion of which was covered by low buildings constructed of enormous slabs of stone, some set on the edge to form the walls, while others, lying across these, constituted the roofs. Joined end to end, with occasional wings at irregular intervals running out into the amphitheatre, they enclosed a rough oval of open ground that formed a large courtyard. The several outer entrances to the buildings were closed with two slabs of stone, one of which, standing on edge, covered the aperture, while the other, leaning against the first upon the outside, held it securely in place against any efforts that might be made to dislodge it from the interior of the building.

To one of these entrances the woman carried her unconscious captive, laid him on the ground, removed the slabs that closed the aperture, and dragged him into the dim and gloomy interior, where she deposited him upon the floor and clapped her palms together sharply three times, with the result that there presently slouched into the room a half-dozen children of both sexes, who ranged in age from one year to sixteen or seventeen. The very youngest of them walked easily and seemed as fit to care for itself as the young of most lower orders at a similar age. The girls, even the smallest, were armed with clubs, but the boys carried no weapons either of offence or defence.

At sight of them the woman pointed to Tarzan, struck her head with her clenched fist, and gestured toward herself, touching her breast several times with a calloused thumb. She made several other motions with her hands, so eloquent of meaning that one entirely unfamiliar with her sign-language could almost guess their purport; then she turned and left the building, replaced the stones before the entrance, and slouched back to her cave, passing, apparently without notice, the woman she had recently struck down and who was now regaining consciousness.

As she took her seat before her cave-mouth her victim suddenly sat erect, rubbed her head for a moment, and then, after looking dully, rose unsteadily to her feet. For just an instant she swayed and staggered, but presently she mastered herself, and with only a glance at the author of her hurt moved off in the direction of her own cave.

Before she had reached it her attention, together with that of all the others of this strange community, or at least of all those who were in the open, was attracted by the sound of approaching footsteps. She halted in her tracks, her great ears up-pricked, her eyes directed toward the trail leading up from the valley. The others were similarly watching and listening and a moment later their vigil was rewarded by sight of another of their kind as she appeared in the entrance to the amphitheatre.

A huge creature this, even larger than she who captured the ape-man – broader and heavier, although little, if any, taller – carrying upon one shoulder the carcase of an antelope and upon the other the body of a creature that might have been half human and half beast, yet, assuredly, was not entirely the one or the other. The antelope was dead, but not so the other creature. It wriggled weakly – its futile movements could not have been termed struggles – as it hung, its middle across the bare brown shoulder of its captor, its arms and legs dangling limply before and behind. The captive was either in partial unconsciousness or in the paralysis of fear.

The woman who had brought Tarzan to the amphitheatre arose and stood before the entrance to her cave. We shall have to call her the First Woman, for she had no name; in her sluggish brain she never had sensed even the need for a distinctive appellation, and among her fellows she was equally nameless, as were they, and so, that we may differentiate her from the others, we shall call her the First Woman. Similarly, we shall know the creature that she felled with her bludgeon as the Second Woman, and she who now entered the amphitheatre with a burden upon each shoulder, as the Third Woman.

So the First Woman arose, her eyes fixed upon the newcomer, her ears up-pricked. And the Second Woman arose, and all the others that were in sight, and all stood glaring at the Third Woman, who moved steadily along with her burden, her watchful eyes ever upon the menacing figures of her fellows.

She was very large, this Third Woman, so for a while the others only stood and glared at her, but presently the First Woman took a step forward and turning cast a long look at the Second Woman, and then she took another step forward and stopped and looked again at the Second Woman, and this time she pointed at herself, at the Second Woman, and then at the Third Woman, who now quickened her pace in the direction of her cave, for she understood the menace in the attitude of the First Woman.

The Second Woman understood too, and moved forward now with the First Woman. No word was spoken, no sound issued from those savage lips – lips that never had parted to a smile; lips that never had known laughter, nor ever would.

As the two approached her the Third Woman dropped her spoils in a heap at her feet, gripped her cudgel more firmly, and prepared to defend her rights. The others, brandishing their own weapons, charged her. The remaining women were now but onlookers, their hands stayed, perhaps by some ancient tribal custom that gauged the numbers of attackers by the quantity of spoils awarding the right of contest to whoever initiated it.

When the First Woman had been attacked by the Second Woman the others had all held aloof, for it had been the Second Woman that had advanced first to try conclusions for the possession of Tarzan. And now the Third Woman had come with two prizes, and since the First Woman and the Second Woman had stepped out to meet her the others had held back. As the three women came together it seemed inevitable that the Third Woman would go down beneath the bludgeons of the others; but she warded off both blows with the skill and celerity of a trained fencer and, stepping quickly into the opening she had made, dealt the First Woman a terrific blow upon the head. It stretched her motionless upon the ground, where a little pool of blood attested the terrible strength of the wielder of the bludgeon, the while it marked the savage, unmourned passing of the First Woman.

And now the Third Woman could devote her undivided attention to the Second Woman, but the Second Woman, seeing the fate of her companion, did not wait to discuss the matter further. She broke and ran for her cave.

The creature that the Third Woman had been carrying along with the carcass of the antelope, apparently believing that it saw a chance for escape while its captor was engaged with her assailants was crawling stealthily away in the opposite direction. Its attempt might have proved successful had the fight lasted longer; but the skill and ferocity of the Third Woman had terminated the whole thing in a matter of seconds, and now, turning about, she espied her prey seeking to escape and sprang quickly after it.

As she did so the Second Woman wheeled and darted back to seize the carcass of the antelope, while the crawling fugitive leaped to its feet and raced swiftly down the trail that led through the mouth of the amphitheatre toward the valley.

As the thing arose to its feet it became apparent that it was a man, or at least a male, and evidently of the same species as the women of this peculiar race, though much shorter and of proportionately lighter build. It stood about five feet in height, had a few hairs on its upper lip and chin, a much lower forehead than the women, and its eyes were set closer together. Its legs were much longer and more slender than those of the women, who seemed to have been designed for strength rather than speed, and it was apparent from the start that the Third Woman could have no hope of overhauling her escaping quarry, and then it was that the utility of the strange skirt of thongs and pebbles and feathers became apparent. Seizing one of the thongs she disengaged it easily and quickly from the girdle that supported them about her hips, and grasping the end of the thong between a thumb and forefinger she whirled it rapidly in a vertical plane until the feathered pebble at its end was moving with great rapidity – then she let go the thong.

Like an arrow the missile sped toward the racing fugitive. The pebble, as large as an English walnut, struck the man on the back of his head, dropping him unconscious to the ground.

Then the Third Woman turned upon the Second Woman, who by this time had seized the antelope, and brandishing her bludgeon bore down upon her. The Second Woman, possessing more courage than good sense, prepared to defend her stolen flesh and took her stand, her bludgeon ready.

As the Third Woman bore down upon her, a veritable mountain of muscle, the Second Woman met her with threatening cudgel, but so terrific was the blow dealt by her mighty adversary that her weapon, splintered, was swept from her hands, and she found herself at the mercy of the creature she would have robbed. Evidently she knew how little mercy she might expect.

She did not fall upon her knees in an attitude of supplication – not she. Instead she tore a handful of the pebble missiles from her girdle in a vain attempt to defend herself. Futilest of futilities! The huge destroying bludgeon had not even paused, but swinging in a great circle fell upon the skull of the Second Woman. The Third Woman paused and looked about questioningly, as if to ask, 'Is there another who wishes to take my antelope or my man? If so, let her step forward.' But no one accepted the gage, and presently the woman turned and walked back to the prostrate man.

Roughly she jerked him to his feet and shook him. Consciousness was returning slowly and he tried to stand. His efforts, however, were a failure and so she threw him across her shoulder again and walked back to the dead antelope, which she flung to the opposite shoulder and, continuing her interrupted way to her cave, dumped the two unceremoniously to the ground. Here, in the cave-mouth, she kindled a fire, twirling a fire stick dexterously amid dry tinder in a bit of hollowed wood, and, cutting generous strips from the carcass of the antelope, ate ravenously. While she was thus occupied the man regained consciousness and, sitting up, looked about, dazed. Presently his nostrils caught the aroma of the cooking meat and he pointed at it.

The woman handed him the rude stone knife that she had tossed back to the floor of the cave and motioned toward the meat. The man seized the implement and was soon broiling a generous cut above the fire. Half burned and half raw as it was he ate it with seeming relish, and as he ate the woman sat and watched him.

He was not much to look at, yet she may have thought him handsome. Unlike the woman, who wore no ornaments, the man had bracelets, and anklets as well as a necklace of teeth and pebbles, while in his hair, which was wound into a small knot above his forehead, were thrust several wooden skewers, ten or twelve inches long, which protruded in various directions in a horizontal plane.

When the man had eaten his fill the woman arose and, seizing him by the hair dragged him into the cave. He scratched and bit at her, trying to escape, but he was no match for his captor. Such is the situation of the sexes – among the Alali.

Upon the floor of the amphitheatre, before the entrances to the caves, lay the bodies of the First Woman and the Second Woman, and black upon them swarmed the circling scavengers of the sky. Ska, the vulture, is first always to the feast.

3

The Lion

Within the dim interior of the strange, rocky chamber where he had been so ruthlessly deposited, Tarzan immediately became the centre of interest to the several Alali young that crowded about him. They examined him carefully, turned him over, pawed him, pinched him, and at last one of the young males, attracted by the golden locket, removed it from the ape-man's neck and placed it about his own.

Lowest, perhaps, in the order of human evolution, nothing held their interest over-long, so that they soon tired of Tarzan and trooped out into the sunlit courtyard, leaving the ape-man to regain consciousness as best he could, or not at all. It was immaterial to them which he did.

Fortunately for the Lord of the Jungle, the fall through the roof of the forest had been broken by the fortuitous occurrence of supple branches directly in the path of his descent, with the result that he suffered only from slight concussion of the brain. Already he was slowly regaining consciousness, and not long after the Alali young had left him his eyes opened, rolled dully about the dim interior of his prison, and closed again. His breathing was normal, and when again he opened his eyes it was as if he had emerged from a deep and natural slumber, the only reminder of his accident being a dull aching of the head.

Sitting up, he looked about him, his eyes gradually accustoming themselves to the faint light of the chamber. He found himself in a rude shelter constructed of great slabs of rock. A single opening led into what appeared to be another similar chamber, the interior of which, however, was much lighter than that in which he lay.

Slowly he arose to his feet and crossed to the opening. Across the second chamber he beheld another doorway leading to the fresh air and the sunshine. Except for filthy heaps of dead grasses on the floor the rooms were unfurnished and devoid of any suggestion that they were utilized as places of human habitation.

From the second doorway, to which he crossed, he looked out upon a narrow courtyard walled by great slabs of stone, the lower ends of which, embedded in the ground, caused them to remain erect. Here he saw the young Alali squatting about, some in the sun, others in the shadow. Tarzan looked at them in evident puzzlement. What were they? What was this place in which he was, all too evidently, incarcerated? Were these his keepers or were they his fellow prisoners? How had he come hither?

Running his fingers through his shock of black hair in a characteristic gesture of perplexity, he shook his head. He recalled the unfortunate termination of the flight; he even remembered falling through the foliage of the great tree, but beyond all that was blank. He stood for a moment examining the Alali, who were all unconscious of his near presence or his gaze upon them, and then he stepped boldly out into the courtyard before them, as a lion, fearless, ignores the presence of jackals.

Immediately they saw him they arose and clustered about him, the girls pushing the boys aside and coming boldly close. Tarzan spoke to them, first in one native dialect and then in another, but they seemed not to understand, for they made no reply. Then, as a last resort, he addressed them in the primitive language of the great apes, the language of Manu the monkey, the first language that Tarzan had learned when, as a babe, he suckled at the hairy breast of Kala the she-ape and listened to the gutturals of the savage members of the tribe of Kerchak. But again his auditors made no response – at least no audible response, although they moved their hands and shoulders and bodies, and jerked their heads in what the ape-man soon recognized as a species of sign-language, nor did they utter any vocal sounds that might indicate that they were communicating with one another through the medium of a spoken language. Presently they again lost interest in the newcomer and resumed their indolent lounging about the walls of the courtyard, while Tarzan paced to and fro its length, his keen eyes searching for whatever avenue of escape chance might provide, and he saw it in the height of the walls, to the top of which a long, running jump would take his outstretched fingers, he was sure; but not yet! – he must wait for darkness to shield his attempt from those within the enclosure and those without.

And as darkness approached the actions of the other occupants of the courtyard became noticeably altered; they walked back and forth, constantly passing and repassing the entrance to the shelter at the end of the courtyard, and occasionally entering the first room and often passing to the second room, where they listened for a moment before the great slab that closed the outer aperture; then back into the courtyard again and back and forth in restless movement. Finally one stamped a foot upon the ground, and this was taken up by the others until, in regular cadence, the *thud, thud, thud* of their naked feet must have been audible for some distance beyond the confines of their narrow prison yard.

Whatever this procedure might have been intended to accomplish, nothing, apparently, resulted, and presently one of the girls, her sullen face snarling in anger, seized her bludgeon more firmly in her two hands and stepping close to one of the walls began to pound violently upon one of its huge stone slabs. At once the other girls followed her example, while the young males continued beating time with their heels. For a while Tarzan was puzzled for an explanation of their behaviour, but it was his own stomach that at last suggested an answer – the creatures were hungry and were attempting to attract the attention of their jailers; and their method of doing so suggested something else, as well – something of which his past, brief experience with them had already partly convinced him: the creatures were without speech, even totally unvocal, perhaps.

The girl who had started the pounding upon the wall suddenly stopped and pointed at Tarzan. The others looked at him and then back at her, whereby she pointed at her bludgeon and then at Tarzan again, after which she acted out a little pantomime, very quickly, very briefly, but none the less remarkably realistically, The pantomime depicted the bludgeon falling upon Tarzan's head, following which the pantomimist, assisted by her fellows, were to devour the ape-man.

The bludgeons ceased to fall upon the wall, the heels no longer smote the earth – the assemblage was interested in the new suggestion. They eyed Tarzan hungrily. The mother who should have brought them food, the First Woman, was dead. They did not know this; all they knew was that they were hungry. They were not cannibals. Only in the last stages of hunger would they have devoured one another, even as shipwrecked sailors of civilized races have been known to do; but they did not look upon the stranger as one of their own kind. He was as unlike them as some of the other creatures that the First Woman had brought them to feed upon. It was no more wrong to devour him than it would have been to devour an antelope.

The thought, however, would not have occurred to most of them: the older girl it was who had suggested it; nor would it have occurred to her had there been other food, for she knew that he had not been brought here for that purpose – he had been brought as the mate of the First Woman, who in common with the other women of this primitive race hunted a new mate each season among the forests and the jungles where the timid males lived their solitary lives, except for the brief weeks that they were held captive in the stone corrals of the dominant sex, and where they were treated with great brutality and contempt even by the children of their temporary spouses. Sometimes they managed to escape, although rarely, but eventually they were turned loose, since it was easier to hunt a new one the following season than to feed one in captivity for a whole year. There was nothing approximating love in the family relations of these savage half brutes. The young, conceived without love, knowing not their own fathers, possessed not even an elemental affection for one another, nor for any other living thing.

A certain tie bound them to their savage mothers, at whose breasts they suckled for a few short months and to whom they looked for food until themselves sufficiently developed to go forth into the forests and make their own kills or secure whatever other food bountiful nature provided for them.

Somewhere between the ages of fifteen and seventeen the young males were liberated and chased into the forest, after which their mothers knew them not from any other male; and at a similar age the females were taken to the maternal cave, where they lived, accompanying their mothers on the daily hunt, until they had succeeded in capturing a first mate. After that they took up their abodes in separate caves and the tie between parent and child was cut as cleanly as though it never had existed, and they might, the following season even become rivals for the same man, or at any time quarrel to the death.

The building of the stone shelters and corrals into which the children and the males were kept was the only community activity in which the women engaged, and this work they were compelled to do alone, since the men would have escaped into the forest at the first opportunity had they been released from the corrals to take part in the work of construction, while the children, as soon as they had become strong enough to be of any assistance, would doubtless have done likewise; but the great shes were amply able to accomplish their titanic labours alone.

Equipped by nature with mighty frames and thews of steel they quarried the great slabs from a side hill overlooking the amphitheatre, slid them to the floor of the little valley, and pulled and pushed them into position by main strength.

It was seldom necessary to add to the shelters and corrals already built, since the high rate of mortality among the females ordinarily left plenty of vacant enclosures for maturing girls. Jealousy, greed, the hazards of the hunt, the contingencies of intertribal wars all took heavy toll among the adult shes. Even the despised male, fighting for his freedom, sometimes slew his captor. The hideous life of the Alalus was the natural result of the unnatural reversal of sex dominance. It is the province of the male to initiate love and by his masterfulness to inspire first respect, then admiration, in the breast of the female he seeks to attract, love itself developing postliminary to these other emotions.

Having no love for her mate and having become a more powerful brute, the savage Alalus woman soon came to treat the members of the opposite sex with contempt and brutality, with the result that the power, or at least the desire, to initiate love ceased to exist in the heart of the male – he could not love a creature he feared and hated, he could not respect or admire the fierce creatures that the Alali women had become, and so he fled into the forests and the jungles, and there the dominant females hunted him lest their race perish from the earth.

It was the offspring of such savage and perverted creatures that Tarzan faced, fully aware of their cannibalistic intentions. The males did not attack him at once, but busily engaged themselves in fetching dry grass and small pieces of wood from one of the covered rooms, and while the three girls, one of them scarcely seven years of age, approached the ape-man warily with ready bludgeons, they prepared a fire, over which they expected soon to be broiling juicy cuts from the strange creature that their hairy dam had brought them.

One of the males, a lad of sixteen, held back, making excited signs with hand, head, and body. He appeared to be trying to dissuade or prevent the girls from the carrying out of their plan; he even appealed to the other boys for backing, but they merely glanced at the girls and continued their culinary preparations. At last, however, as the girls deliberately approached the ape-man he placed himself directly in their path and attempted to stop them.

Instantly the three little demons swung their bludgeons and sprang forward to destroy him. The boy dodged, plucked several of the feathered stones from his girdle and flung them at his assailants. So swift and so accurate did the missiles speed that two girls dropped, howling to the ground.

The third missed, striking one of the other boys on the temple, killing him instantly. He was the youth who had stolen Tarzan's locket, and, like all his fellow-males, being a timid creature, he had kept it continually covered by a palm since the ape-man's return to consciousness had brought him out into the courtyard among them. The older girl, nothing daunted, leaped forward, her face hideous in a snarl of rage. The boy cast another stone at her and then turned and ran toward the ape-man. What reception he expected he himself probably did not know.

Perhaps it was the recrudescence of a long dead emotion of fellowship that prompted him to place himself at Tarzan's side – possibly Tarzan himself, in whom loyalty to kind was strong, had inspired this reawakening of an atrophied soul sense. However that may be, the fact remains that the boy came and stood at Tarzan's side, while the girl, evidently sensing danger to herself in this strange, new temerity of her brother, advanced more cautiously.

In signs she seemed to be telling him what she would do to him if he did not cease to interpose his weak will between her and her gastronomic desires but he signed back at her defiantly and stood his ground. Tarzan reached over and patted him on the back, smiling. The boy bared his teeth horribly, but it seemed evident that he was trying to return the ape-man's smile. And now the girl was almost upon them. Tarzan was quite at a loss as to how to proceed against her. His natural chivalry restrained him from attacking her and made it seem most repellent to injure her even in self-preservation; but he knew that before he was done with her he might possibly have to kill her, and so, while looking for an alternative, he steeled himself for the deed he loathed; but yet he hoped to escape without that.

The Third Woman, conducting her new mate from the cave to the corral where she would keep him imprisoned for a week or two, had heard the cadenced beating of naked heels and heavy bludgeons arising from the corral of the First Woman, and immediately guessed their import. The welfare of the offspring of the First Woman concerned her not as an individual.

Community instinct, however, prompted her to release them that they might search for food and their services not be lost to the tribe through starvation. She would not feed them, of course, as they did not belong to her, but she would open their prison gate and turn them loose to fend for themselves.

But the Third Woman took her time. Her powerful fingers entangled in the hair of her snarling spouse, she dragged the protesting creature to her corral, removed the great slab from before the entrance, pushed the man roughly within, accelerating his speed with a final kick, replaced the slab and turned leisurely toward the nearby corral of the First Woman.

Removing the stone door she passed through the two chambers and entered the corral at the moment that the oldest girl was advancing upon Tarzan. Pausing by the entrance-way she struck her bludgeon against the stone wall of the shelter, evidently to attract the attention of those within the corral. Instantly all looked in her direction.

She was the first adult female, other than their own dam, that the children of the First Woman had seen. They shrunk from her in evident terror. The youth at Tarzan's side slunk behind the ape-man, nor did Tarzan wonder at their fear. The Third Woman was the first adult Alalus he had seen, since all the time that he had been in the hands of the First Woman he had been unconscious.

The girl who had been theatening him with her great club appeared now to have forgotten him, and instead stood with snarling face and narrowed eyes confronting the newcomer. Of all the children she seemed the least terrified.

The ape-man scrutinized the huge brutish female standing at the far end of the corral with her savage eyes upon him. She had not seen him before, as she had been in the forest hunting at the time that the First Woman had brought her prize back to the amphitheatre. She had not known that the First Woman had any male in her corral other than her own spawn. Here, indeed, was a prize. She would remove him to her own corral. With this idea in mind, and knowing that, unless he succeeded in dodging past her and reaching the entrance-way ahead of her, he could not escape her, she moved very slowly toward him ignoring now the other occupants of the corral.

Tarzan, not guessing her real purpose, thought that she was about to attack him as a dangerous alien in the sacred precincts of her home. He viewed her great bulk, her enormous muscular development, and the huge bludgeon swinging in her hamlike hand, and compared them with his own defenceless nakedness. To the jungle born, flight from useless and uneven combat carries with it no stigma of cowardice, and not only was Tarzan of the Apes jungle born and jungle raised, but the stripping of his clothes from him had now, as always before, stripped also away the thin and unnatural veneer of his civilization. It was, then, a savage beast that faced the oncoming Alalus woman – a cunning beast as well as a powerful one – a beast that knew when to fight and when to flee.

Tarzan cast a quick glance behind him. There crouched the Alalus lad, trembling in fear. Beyond was the rear wall of the corral, one of the great stone slabs of which tilted slightly outward. Slow is the mind of man, slower his eye by comparison with the eye and the mind of the trapped beast seeking escape. So quick was the ape-man that he was gone before the Third

Woman had guessed that he was contemplating flight, and with him had gone the eldest Alalus boy. Wheeling in a single motion, Tarzan had swung the young male to his shoulder, leaped swiftly the few paces that had separated him from the rear wall of the corral, and catlike, run up the smooth surface of the slightly tilted slab until his fingers closed upon the top, drawn himself over without a single backward glance, dropped the youth to the ground upon the opposite side, following him so quickly that they alighted almost together. Then he glanced about.

For the first time he saw the natural amphitheatre and the caves, before several of which women still squatted. It would soon be dark. The sun was dropping behind the crest of the western hills.

Tarzan saw only a single avenue of escape – the opening at the lower end of the amphitheatre through which the trail led down into the valley and the forest below. Toward this he ran, followed by the youth.

Presently a woman, sitting before the entrance to her cave, saw him. Seizing her cudgel she leaped to her feet and gave immediate chase. Attracted by her, another and another took up the pursuit, until five or six of them thundered along the trail.

The youth, pointing the way, raced swiftly ahead of the ape-man, but, swift as he was, he could not outdistance the lithe muscles that had so often in the past carried their master safely from the swift rush of maddened Numa, or win him a meal against the fleetness of Bara the deer.

The heavy lumbering women behind them had no chance of overhauling this swift pair if they were to depend entirely upon speed, but that they had no intention of doing. They had their stone missiles with which, almost from birth, they had practised until approximate perfection was attained in casting them at either stationary or moving targets.

It was growing dark, the trail twisted and turned, and the speed of the quarry made them elusive marks at which to cast an accurate missile that would be so timed as to stun rather than to kill. Of course, more often than not a missile intended to stun did actually kill, but the quarry must take that chance.

Instinct warned the women against killing the males, though it did not warn them against treating them with the utmost brutality.

Had Tarzan realized why the women were pursuing him he would have run even faster than he did, and when the missiles began to fly past his head perhaps he did accelerate his speed a trifle. Had one hit him then Tarzan of the Apes had ceased to be, for the women realizing that darkness would soon drop its protecting mantle over the forms of the fugitives, were throwing viciously, indifferent to whether their missiles killed or not.

It was then that the ape-man reached the forest and, as if he had dissolved into thin air, disappeared from the astonished view of his pursuers, for now, indeed, was he in his own element. While they looked for him upon the ground he swung swiftly through the lower terraces, keeping in view the Alalus boy racing along the trail beneath him.

But, with the man escaped, the women stopped and turned back toward their caves. The youth they did not want. For two or three years he would roam the forests unmolested by his own kind, and if he escaped the savage beasts and the spears and arrows of the ant-people he would come to man's estate and be fair prey for any of the great shes during the mating season. For the time being, at least, he would lead a comparatively safe and happy existence.

His chances of survival had been materially lessened by his early escape into the forest. Had the First Woman lived she would have kept him safely within the walls of her corral for another year at least, when he would have been better fitted to cope with the dangers and emergencies of the savage life of the forest and the jungle.

The boy had keen ears telling him that the women had given up the pursuit, halted and looked back for the strange creature that had freed him from the hated corral, but he could see only a short distance through the darkness of the growing forest night. The stranger was not in sight. The youth up-pricked his great ears and listened intently. There was no sound of human footsteps other than the rapidly diminishing ones of the retreating women. There were other sounds, however – unfamiliar forest sounds that filled his muddy brain with vague terrors: sounds that came from the surrounding underbush; sounds that came from the branches above his head, and, too, there were terrifying odours.

Darkness, complete and impenetrable, had closed in upon him with a suddenness that left him trembling. He could almost feel it weighing down upon him – crushing him and at the same time leaving him exposed to nameless terrors. He looked about him and could see naught, so that it seemed to him that he was without eyes, and being without voice he could not call out either to frighten his enemies or attract the attention of the strange creature that had befriended him once, and whose presence had so strangely aroused in his own breast an inexplicable emotion – a pleasurable emotion.

He could not explain it – he had no word for it who had no word for anything – but he felt it, and it still warmed his bosom and he wished in his turbid way that he could make a noise that would attract that strange creature to him again. He was very lonely and very much afraid.

A crackling of the bushes nearby aroused him to new and more intimate terror. Something large was approaching through the black night. The youth stood with his back against a great tree. He dare not move. He sniffed, but what movement of the air there was took course from him in the direction of the thing that was creeping upon him out of the terrible forest, and so he could not identify it; but his instinct told him that the creature had identified him and was doubtless creeping closer to leap upon him and devour him.

He knew naught of lions, unless instinct carries with it a picture of the various creatures of which the denizens of the wild are instinctively afraid. In all his life he had never been outside the corral of the First Woman, and, as his people are without speech, his dam could have told him nothing of the outside world; yet when the lion roared as it sprang suddenly toward him he knew that it was a lion.

4

Naked Hunters

The sun beating down upon the hot corral of the First Woman found it deserted of life. Only the corpse of a youth lay sprawled where it had fallen the previous evening.

A speck appeared in the distant blue. It grew larger as it approached until it took upon itself the form of a bird gliding easily upon motionless wings. Nearer and nearer it came, now and again winging great, slow circles, until at last it swung above the corral of the First Woman. Once again it circled and then dropped to earth within the enclosure – Ska, the vulture, had come.

Within the hour the body of the youth was hidden by a mantle of the great birds. When they left only the clean-picked bones remained, and entangled about the neck of one of the birds was a golden chain from which depended a diamond-encrusted locket. Ska fought the bauble that swung annoyingly beneath him when he flew and impeded his progress when he walked upon the ground, but it was looped twice about his neck and he was unable to dislodge it, and so he winged away across the Great Thorn Forest, the bright gems gleaming and scintillating in the sun.

Tarzan of the Apes, after eluding the women that had chased him and the Alalus youth into the forest, halted in the tree beneath which the frightened son of the First Woman had come to a terrified pause. He was there, close above him, when Numa charged, and reaching quickly down had seized the youth by the hair and dragged him to safety as the lion's raking talons embraced thin air beneath the feet of the Alalus. The following day the ape-man concerned himself seriously in the hunt for food, weapons, and apparel. Naked and unarmed as he was, it might have gone hard with him had he been other than Tarzan of the Apes; and it had gone hard, too, with the Alalus had it not been for the ape-man. Fruits and nuts Tarzan found, and birds' eggs; but he craved meat, and for meat he hunted assiduously, not alone because of the flesh of the kill, but for the skin and the gut and the tendons that he could use in the fabrication of the things he required for the safety and comfort of his primitive existence.

As he searched for the spoor of his prey he searched also for the proper woods for a spear and for bow and arrows; nor were they difficult to find in this forest of familiar trees, but the day was almost done before the gentle wind, up which he had been hunting, carried to his sensitive nostrils the scent of Bara the deer. Swinging into a tree he motioned the Alalus to follow him, but so inept and awkward was the creature that Tarzan was compelled to drag him to a place among the branches, where, by signs, he attempted to impart to him the fact that he wished him to remain where he was, watching the materials that the ape-man had collected for his weapons, while the latter continued the hunt alone.

That the youth understood him, he was not at all sure but at least he did not follow when Tarzan swung off silently through the branches of the forest along the elusive trail of the ruminant, the scent of which was always translated to the foster-son of Kala the she-ape as *Bara the deer,* though, in fact, as practically always, the animal was an antelope. But strong are the impressions of childhood, and since that long-gone day upon which he had pored over the coloured alphabet primer in the far-off cabin of his dead father beside the land-locked harbour on the west coast and learned that 'D stands for Deer,' and had admired the picture of the pretty animal, the thing that most closely resembled it, with which he was familiar in his daily life, the antelope, became to him then, and always remained, Bara the deer. To approach sufficiently close to Bara to bring him down with spear or arrow requires cunning and woodcraft far beyond the limited range of civilized man's ability. The native hunter loses more often than he wins in this game of wits and percipience. Tarzan, however, must excel them both, and the antelope, too, in the keenness of his perceptive faculties and in co-ordination of mind and muscle if he were to lay Bara low with only the weapons with which nature had endowed him at birth.

As Tarzan sped silently through the jungle guided by his nostrils in the direction of Bara the increasing strength of the familiar effluvium apprised him that not far ahead Bara forgathered in numbers, and the mouth of the savage ape-man watered in anticipation of the feast that but awaited his coming. And as the strength of the scent increased, more warily went the great hunting creature, moving silently, a shadow among the shadows of the forest, until he came at last to the verge of a park-like opening in which he saw a dozen antelope grazing.

Squatting motionless upon a low hanging limb the ape-man watched the movements of the herd against the moment that one might come close enough to the encircling trees to give a forthright charge at least a shadow of a chance for success. To wait patiently, oftentimes hour upon hour, for the quarry to expose itself to more certain death is a part of the great game that the hunters of the wild must play. Tarzan remained in statuesque immobility waiting for chance to send one of the antelope within striking distance, and while he waited there came to his nostrils, faintly, the scent of Numa the lion. Tarzan scowled.

He was downwind from Bara and the lion was not between him and the antelope. It must, therefore, be upwind from the quarry as well as from himself; but why had not the sensitive nostrils of the herbivora caught the scent of their arch enemy before it had reached the ape-man; that they had not was evinced by their placidity as they grazed contentedly, their tails switching and occasionally a head raised to look about with up-pricked ears though with no symptom of the terror that would immediately follow the discovery of Numa in their vicinity.

The ape-man concluded that one of those freaks of the air currents that so often leaves a motionless pocket of air directly in the path of the flow had momentarily surrounded the antelope, insulating them, as it were, from their immediate surroundings. And while he was thinking these things and wishing that Numa would go away he was shocked to hear a sudden crashing in the underbrush upon the opposite side of the clearing beyond the antelope, which were instantly upon the alert and poised for flight. Almost simultaneously there broke into view a young lion, which, upon coming in sight of the antelope, set up a terrific roaring as it charged.

Tarzan could have torn his hair in rage and disappointment. The blundering stupidity of a young lion had robbed him of his meat – the ruminants were scattering in all directions. The lion, charging futilely, had lost his own meat and Tarzan's too. But wait! – what was this?

A terrified buck, blind to all save the single thought of escape from the talons of the dread carnivore, was bolting straight for the tree in which Tarzan sat. As it came beneath him a sleek brown body shot headforemost from the foliage, steel fingers gripped the throat of the buck, strong teeth fastened in its neck. The weight of the savage hunter carried the quarry to its knees, and before it could stumble to its feet again a quick wrench with those powerful hands had twisted and broken its neck. Without a backward glance the ape-man threw the carcase to a shoulder and leaped into the nearest tree. He had no need to waste time in looking back to know what Numa would be doing, for he realized that he leaped upon Bara in full sight of the king of beasts. Scarce had he drawn himself to safety ere the great cat crashed across the spot where he had stood.

Numa, baffled, roared terribly as he returned to glare up at the ape-man perched above him. Tarzan smiled.

'Son of Dango, the hyena,' he taunted, 'go hungry until you learn to hunt,' and casting a broken branch contemptuously in the lion's face the ape-man vanished among the leafy branches bearing his kill lightly across one broad shoulder.

It was still daylight when Tarzan returned to where the Alalus was awaiting him. The youth had a small stone knife, and with this the ape-man hacked off a generous portion of the antelope for the whelp of the First Woman and another for himself. Into the raw flesh, hungrily, sank the strong white teeth of the English lord, while the Alalus youth, gazing at him in surprise, sought materials for fire-making.

Amused, Tarzan watched him until the other had succeeded in preparing his food as he thought it should be prepared – the outside burned to a cinder, the inside raw; yet it was cooked food, and doubtless imparted to its partaker a feeling of great superiority over the low beasts that devoured their meat raw.

Tarzan smiled as he thought how vague, after all, is the line that separates primitive from civilized man in matters pertaining to their instincts and their appetites. Some of his French friends, with whom he was dining upon a certain occasion, were horrified when they learned that in common with many of the African tribes and the apes he ate caterpillars, and they voiced their horror between mouthfuls of the snails they were eating with relish at the time.

The provincial American scoffs at the French for eating frogs' legs, the while he munches upon the leg of a muskrat. The Eskimos eat raw blubber, the Amazonians, both white and native, eat the contents of the stomachs of parrots and monkeys and consider them delicacies, and there is a man in New York, an estimable and otherwise harmless individual, who eats Limburger cheese on Bartlett pears.

The following morning, with sufficient meat to last them several days, Tarzan set to work upon his weapons and his loin cloth. Showing the Alalus how to scrape the antelope hide with his stone knife the ape-man set to work, with nothing more in the way of tools than bits of stone picked from the bed of a stream, to fashion weapons with which to cope successfully with the Alali women, the great carnivores, and whatever other enemies time might reveal to him. And as he worked he watched the Alalus youth and wondered of what use the poor creature could be to him in finding his way through the encircling thorn forest that he must pass to reach familiar country and the trail for home. That the poor thing was timid had been evidenced by its manner when fleeing from the Alali women and its terror when confronted by

Numa. Its speechlessness made it useless as a companion and it was entirely without woodcraft other than a certain crude, instinctive kind that was of no use to Tarzan.

But it had placed itself at his side during the altercation in the corral, and, although it could not have been of any help to him, yet it had won a right to his consideration by its act. It was evident, quite evident, that it had attached itself to Tarzan and intended to remain with him. An idea occurred to Tarzan as he worked upon his weapons and thought upon the Alalus – he would make similar weapons for the youth and teach him how to use them. He had seen that the crude weapons of the Alali would be no match against one armed with a bow and arrows, or even a good spear. Accurately they could not hope to throw their missiles as far as a good bowman could speed his shaft and their bludgeons were helpless in the face of a well-thrown spear.

Yes, he would make weapons for the youth and train him in their use, and then he could be made of service in the hunt and, if necessary, in the fight. As Tarzan of the Apes thought upon the matter, the Alalus suddenly paused in his work and bent an ear close to the ground, then he lifted his head and turned his eyes upon Tarzan, pointing at him, at his ear, and then at the ground. The ape-man understood that he was to listen as the other had, and when he did so he distinctly heard approaching footsteps resounding upon a hard-worn trail.

Gathering up his belongings he carried them high among the trees to a safe cache with the remnants of Bara the deer, and then returning helped the youth into the tree beside him. Slowly, already, the Alalus was becoming more at ease in the trees and could help himself to a greater extent in climbing into them, but he was still virtually helpless in Tarzan's estimation.

The two had not long to wait before there swung down the trail one of the terrible women of the amphitheatre, and behind her at ten or fifteen paces another, and behind the second, a third. It was not often that they travelled thus, for theirs was a solitary existence, the Alali being almost devoid of gregarious instincts; yet they did occasionally start out upon their hunts together, especially when they were hunting some dangerous beast, that had encroached upon their rights, or when, failing to collect sufficient men from the forest during the mating season, the unsuccessful ones banded together to make a raid upon the corrals of a neighbouring tribe.

The three slouching along the trail, passed directly beneath the tree from which Tarzan and the youth watched them. The great, flat ears flapped lazily, the dark eyes wandered from side to side, and from time to time they moved rapidly the skin upon some portion of their bodies as they sought to dislodge annoying insects.

The two in the tree remained motionless while the three brute-women passed down the trail, to be presently lost to their view at a turning of the forest highway; then, after a short interval of listening, they descended to the ground and resumed their interrupted labours. The ape-man smiled as he idly pondered the events of the last few minutes – Tarzan of the Apes, Lord of the Jungle, hiding among the trees to escape the notice of three women!

But such women! He knew little about them or their ways as yet, but what he did know was sufficient to convince him that they were as formidable foes as ever he had encountered, and that while he remained weaponless he was no match against their great bludgeons and swiftly thrown missiles.

The days passed; the ape-man and his silent companion perfected the weapons that would more easily give them food, the latter working mechanically, following the instructions of his master. At last the time came when Tarzan and the Alalus were fully equipped, and then they hunted together, the man training the youth in the use of the bow and spear and the long grass rope that from boyhood had formed a unique feature of the ape-man's armament.

During these days of hunting there came over the Alalus youth, quite abruptly, a great change. It had been his habit to glide stealthily through the forest, stopping often to look this way and that, fearful apparently, of every creature that roamed the shadowy trails – his one great fear the ferocious females of his kind; but suddenly all this changed as by magic.

Slowly he was mastering the bow and the spear; with deep interest and a sense of awe and respect he had watched Tarzan bring down many animals, great and small for food. Once he had seen him dispatch Sabor the lioness with a single thrust of his great spear when she had caught the ape-man in a clearing too far from the sanctuary of his beloved trees.

And then the boy's own day came. He and Tarzan were hunting when the former disturbed a small herd of wild pigs, bringing down two with his arrows. The others scattered in all directions, and one of these, a boar, sighting the Alalus, charged him.

The youth was of a mind to flee, for ages of inherited instinct prompted him to flight. Always the male Alalus fled from danger and between fleeing from carnivorous animals and from their own women they had become very swift – so swift that no dangerous enemy could overtake them.

He could have escaped the boar by flight, and for an instant he was upon the verge of flight, but a sudden thought checked him – back flew his spear hand as the ape-man had taught him and then forward, with all the weight of his body behind the cast. The boar was coming straight for him. The spear struck in front of the left shoulder and ranged downward through the heart. Horta the boar dropped in his tracks.

A new expression came into his eyes and spread over the countenance of the Alalus. No longer wore he that hunted expression; no longer slunk he through the forest casting fearful glances from side to side.

Now he walked erect, boldly and with fearless mien, and, perhaps, instead of dreading the appearance of a female he rather courted the event. He was the personification of avenging manhood. Within him rankled countless ages of contemptuous treatment and abuse at the hands of his shes.

Doubtless he never thought of the matter in this way at all, but the fact remained, and Tarzan realized it, that the first woman unfortunate enough to stumble upon this youth was going to get the surprise of her life.

5

New Friends

With doglike devotion the Alalus youth clung to Tarzan. The latter had mastered the meagre sign-language of his protégé, giving them a means of communication that was adequate for all their needs. The former, gaining confidence with a growing familiarity with his new weapons, became more independent, with the result that the two more often separated for the hunt, thus insuring a more fully stocked larder. It was on one of these occasions that Tarzan came suddenly upon a strange sight. He had been following the scent spoor of Bara the deer when it was suddenly crossed by that of one of the great female Alali. That probably meant that another would try to rob him of his prey.

The savage instinct of the jungle beast now predominated in the guidance of the breech-clouted ape-man. It was not the polished Lord Greystoke of London whose snarling upper lip revealed two gleaming fighting fangs – it was a primordial hunting brute about to be robbed of its quarry.

Taking to the trees he moved rapidly in the direction of the Alalus woman, but before he came within sight of her a new scent impinged upon his nostrils – a strange, new scent that puzzled him. It was the scent of man, yet strange and unfamiliar to a degree. Never before had anything like it arrested his attention.

It was very faint, and yet, somehow, he knew that it was close, and then, ahead of him, he heard voices – low musical voices, that came faintly to his ears; and although they were low and musical there was something in the quality and pitch of them that suggested excitement. Now Tarzan went more carefully; Bara the deer all but forgotten.

As he drew nearer he realized that there were many voices and much commotion, and then he came upon a large, parklike plain that stretched away to the distant hills, and in the foreground, not a hundred yards from him, he looked upon a sight that might well have caused him to doubt the veracity of his own eyes. The only familiar figure was a giant Alalus woman.

Surrounding her was a horde of diminutive men – tiny white warriors – mounted upon what appeared to be a form of the Royal Antelope of the West Coast. Armed with lances and swords, they repeatedly charged at the huge legs of the Alalus, who, backing slowly toward the forest, kicked viciously at her assailants and struck at them with her heavy bludgeon.

It quickly became evident to Tarzan that they were attempting to hamstring her, and had they been successful they might easily have slain her then, but although there must have been fully a hundred of them their chances of success appeared small since, with a single kick of her mighty foot, the woman could lay low a dozen or more of her assailants at a time. Already at least fifty of the force were casualties.

The courage of the survivors, however, filled Tarzan with admiration as he watched them hurl themselves upon almost certain death in their stubborn efforts to bring down the giant female; and then it was that the ape-man saw the reason, or the apparent reason, for the mad sacrifice of life – in her left hand the Alalus clutched one of the tiny warriors. It was to rescue him, evidently, that the others were maintaining this forlorn hope.

If the warriors filled Tarzan with admiration, to scarcely a lesser extent did their courageous and agile mounts. Always had he thought of the Royal Antelope, the smallest known member of its family, as the most timid of creatures, but not so these cousins of theirs. Slightly larger, standing perhaps fifteen inches at the withers, they were in all other outward respects identical; yet, at the guidance of their riders, they leaped fearlessly into close range of those enormous feet and the great, slashing bludgeon.

Perfectly reined, were they, too – so perfectly that their muscles seemed to have co-ordinated with the minds of their riders. In and out they bounded, scarcely touching the ground before they were out of harm's way again. A half-dozen feet they covered at a leap, so that Tarzan wondered not only at their agility but at the almost marvellous riding ability of the warriors who could keep their seats so perfectly upon those leaping, bounding, turning, twisting mounts.

It was a pretty sight and an inspiring one, and however unreal it had at first appeared to him he was not long in realizing that he was looking upon a race of real pygmies – not members of the black tribe with which all African explorers are more or less familiar, but with that lost white race of diminutive men reference to which is occasionally to be found in ancient manuscripts of travel and exploration, of myth and legend.

While the encounter interested him and he viewed it at first as a disinterested neutral, he soon found his sympathies gravitating to the tiny warriors, and when it became evident that the Alalus woman was going to make good her escape into the forest with her captive, the ape-man decided to take a hand.

As he stepped from the concealment of the forest the little warriors were the first to see him. Evidently they mistook him at first for another of their giant enemies, for a great cry of disappointment arose from them and they fell back for the first time since Tarzan had been watching the unequal struggle.

Wishing to make his intentions clear before the little men set upon him with the intention of ham-stringing him he moved quickly in the direction of the woman, who, the instant that her eyes fell upon him, made imperative signs for him to join her in dispatching the balance of the pygmies. She was accustomed to being feared and obeyed by her mankind, when she had them in her power.

As Tarzan advanced he commanded her in the sign-language he had learned from the youth that she was to release her captive and go away, molesting the little men no more. At this she made an ugly grimace and came forward to meet him. The ape-man fitted an arrow to his bow.

'Go back!' he signalled her. 'Go back, or I will kill you. Go back, and put down the little man.'

She snarled ferociously and increased her pace. Tarzan raised the arrow to the level of his eye and drew it back until the bow bent. The pygmies, realizing that for the moment at least this strange giant was their ally, sat their mounts and awaited the outcome of the duel.

The ape-man hoped that the woman would obey his commands before he was compelled to take her life, but even a cursory glance at her face revealed anything but an intention to relinquish her purpose, which now seemed to be to annihilate this presumptuous meddler. On she came. Already she was too close to make further delay safe and the ape-man released his shaft; straight into her savage heart it drove, and as she stumbled forward Tarzan leaped to meet her, seizing the warrior from her grasp before she might fall upon the tiny body and crush it.

As he did so the other warriors, evidently mistaking his intentions, spurred forward with loud shouts and brandished weapons, but before they reached him he had set the rescued man upon the ground and released him.

Instantly the attitude of the charging pygmies changed again, and from war-cries their tone turned to cheers. Riding forward they drew rein before the warrior that Tarzan had rescued, and several of their number leaped from their mounts and, kneeling, raised his hand to their lips. It was now revealed that none of them was more than eighteen inches in height.

It was evident too, to the ape man that he had rescued one who stood high among them – their chief perhaps; and now he wondered what would be their attitude toward him, as, with a look of amused tolerance upon his grim features, he watched them as one might watch the interesting doings of a swarm of ants.

As they felicitated their fellow upon his miraculous escape, Tarzan had an opportunity to inspect them more closely. Their skins were tanned by exposure to a shade a trifle darker than his own, yet there was no question but that they were white men; their features were regular and well proportioned so that by any standards of our race they would have been considered handsome.

There were, of course, variations and exceptions, but on the whole those that he saw before him were fine-looking men. All were smooth-faced, and there appeared to be no very old men among them, while he whom Tarzan had saved from the Alalus woman was apparently younger than the average, and much younger than those who had dismounted to do him homage.

As Tarzan watched them the young man bade the others rise, and then addressed them for a moment, after which he turned towards the ape-man and directed his remarks to him, none of which, of course, Tarzan could understand. By his manner, however, he guessed that the other was thanking him, and possibly too asking his further intentions toward them, and in reply the ape-man endeavoured to assure them that he desired their friendship. Further to emphasize his peaceful intentions, he cast his weapons aside and took a step toward them, his arms thrown slightly outward, his open palms in their direction.

The young man seemed to understand his friendly overtures for, he too advanced, offering his hand to Tarzan. The ape-man knew that the other meant that he should kiss it, but this he did not do, preferring to assume a role of equality with their highest.

Instead, he kneeled upon one knee that he might more easily reach the proffered hand of the pygmy, and, pressing the tiny fingers gently, inclined his head slightly in a formal bow, which carried no suggestion of servility. The other seemed satisfied, returned the bow with equal dignity, and then attempted to convey to the ape-man that he and his party were about to ride off across the plain, inviting him to accompany them.

Rather curious to see more of these remarkable little people, Tarzan was nothing loath to accept the invitation. Before the party set out, however, they dispersed to gather up their dead and wounded and put out of their misery any of the injured antelopes that were too severely hurt to travel. This they did with the relatively long, straight sword which was part of the armament of each. Their lances they left resting in cylindrical boots attached to the right side of their saddles.

For other weapons Tarzan could discover nothing but a tiny knife carried in a scabbard at the right side of each warrior. The blade, like the blade of the rapier, was two-edged, but only about an inch and a half long, with a very sharp point.

Having gathered the dead and wounded, the latter were examined by the young leader of the party, who was accompanied by the five or six who had gathered about him at the time that Tarzan had released him. These Tarzan took to be lieutenants or under-chiefs. He saw them question the wounded as they examined them, and in three cases, each evidently a hopeless one, the leader ran his sword quickly through the hearts of the unhappy men.

While this seemingly cruel, yet unquestionably sound, military measure was being carried out, the balance of the warriors, directed by under-officers, were excavating a long trench beside the dead, of which there were about twenty, their tool being a stout shovel blade, which is carried attached to the saddle and may be quickly fitted to the butt of the spear or lance. The men worked with extreme rapidity and under a plan that appeared to eliminate lost motion, so that in an incredibly short time they had excavated a trench fifty inches in length, eighteen inches wide, and nine inches deep, the equivalent of which to men of normal size, would have been nearly seventeen feet long, six feet wide, and three feet in depth. Into this they packed the dead like sardines and in two layers. They then shovelled back sufficient earth to fill the interstices between the bodies and to come to a level with the top layer, after which loose pebbles were rolled in until the bodies were entirely covered by two inches of stone.

By the time this work was completed the loose antelopes had been caught and the wounded men strapped to their backs. At a word from their commander the party formed with military precision, a detail started ahead with the wounded, and a moment later the balance of the troop was mounted and on the way. The method of mounting and taking up the march was unique and a source of considerable interest to Tarzan. The dismounted warriors were standing in line facing the young leader, who was mounted as were the several officers who accompanied him. Each warrior held his mount by the bridle.

The commander made a rapid signal with the raised point of his sword – here was no spoken word of command – immediately after which he dropped the point quickly to his side, simultaneously wheeling his mount, which leaped quickly off in the direction that the troop was facing, the mounts of his officers wheeling with him as if actuated by a single brain, and at the same instant the mount of each alternate warrior in the line leaped forward, and as it leaped its rider swung to his saddle, vaulting to his seat as lightly as a feather.

The instant the first line had cleared them the antelopes of the second line leaped in pursuit, their riders mounted, as had the others before them, and with a second and longer leap the intervals were closed and the whole troop raced forward in a compact line. It was most clever and practical.

As the troops galloped away, ten warriors wheeled from the left flank and, following one of the officers who had detached himself from the party of the commander of the troop, returned to Tarzan. By signs the officer conveyed to the ape-man the intelligence that he was to follow this party, which would guide him to their destination. Already the main body was far away across the open plain, their lithe mounts clearing as many as five or six feet in a single bound. Even the swift Tarzan could not have kept pace with them. As the ape-man started away under the guidance of the detachment his thoughts reverted to the Alalus youth, who was hunting alone in the forest behind them, but he soon put the creature from his mind with the realization that it was better equipped to defend itself than any of its kind, and that when he had made his visit to the country of the pygmies he could doubtless return and find the Alalus, if he so desired.

Tarzan, inured to hardship and to long and rapid marches, fell into a dog trot such as he could keep up for hours without rest, while his guides, galloping their graceful mounts, kept just ahead of him. The plain was more rolling than it had appeared from the edge of the forest, with here and there a clump of trees; the grass was plentiful, and there were bands of the larger species of antelope grazing at intervals.

At sight of the approaching riders and the comparatively giantlike figure of Tarzan they broke and ran. Once the party passed a rhinoceros, making only a slight detour to avoid it, and later, in a clump of trees, the leader halted his detachment suddenly, and seizing his lance, advanced again slowly toward several bushes, at the same time transmitting an order to his men which caused them to spread and surround the thicket.

Tarzan halted and watched the proceedings. The wind was blowing from him in the direction of the thicket, so that he could not determine, what manner of creature had attracted the attention of the officer.

Presently, when the warriors had completely surrounded the bushes and those upon the other side had ridden into it, their spears couched and ready he heard an ugly snarl issuing from the centre of the thicket, and an instant later an African wild-cat sprang into view, leaping directly at the officer waiting with ready spear to receive it.

The weight and momentum of the beast all but unseated the little rider, the point of whose spear had met the cat full in the chest. There were a few spasmodic struggles before death ensued, during which, had the spear broken, the man would have been badly mauled and perhaps killed, for the cat was relatively as formidable a beast as is the lion to us. The instant that it died four warriors leaped forward and with their sharp knives removed the head and skin in an incredibly short time.

Tarzan could not but note that everything these people did was accomplished with maximum efficiency. Never did there seem to be any lost motion, never was one at a loss as to what to do, never did one worker get in the way of another.

The officer who commanded the detachment was a young fellow, not much, if any, older than the commander of the troop. That he was courageous Tarzan could bear witness for the manner in which he had faced what must have been, to so diminutive a people, a most deadly and ferocious beast; but then, the entire party's hopeless attack upon the Alalus woman had proved that they were all courageous, and the ape-man admired and respected courage.

Already he liked these little men, though it was at times still difficult for him to accept them as a reality, so prone are we to disbelieve in the possibility of the existence of any form of life with which we are not familiar by association or credible repute.

They had been travelling for nearly six hours across the plain; the wind had changed, and there was borne to Tarzan's nostrils clearly the scent of Bara, the deer, ahead. The ape-man, who had tasted no food that day, was ravenous, with the result that the odour of meat aroused all the savage instincts fostered by his strange upbringing.

Springing forward abreast the leader of the detachment that was escorting him, he signed to them to halt, and then as clearly as he could through the comparatively laborious and never quite satisfactory medium of further signs explained that he was hungry, and there was meat ahead, and that they should remain in the rear until he had stalked his prey and made his kill.

The officer having understood and signified his assent, Tarzan crept stealthily forward toward a small clump of trees, beyond which his keen scent told him there were several antelopes, and behind Tarzan followed the detachment, so noiselessly that even the keen ears of the ape-man heard them not.

Sheltered by the trees Tarzan saw a dozen or more antelopes grazing a short distance beyond, the nearest being scarcely a hundred feet from the small grove. Unslinging his bow and taking a handful of arrows from his quiver, the ape-man moved noiselessly to the tree nearest the antelopes. The detachment was not far behind him, although it had stopped the moment the officer saw the game that Tarzan was stalking, lest it be frightened away.

The pygmies watched with deep interest every move of the ape-man with his bow and arrows. As when he slew the she Alalus, they saw him fit an arrow to his bow, draw it far back, and release it almost in a single moment, so quick with this weapon was he.

Then they saw the antelope leap to the impact of the missile, which was followed in rapid succession by a second and a third, and as he shot his bolts

Tarzan leaped forward in pursuit of his prey; but there was no danger that he would lose it. With the second arrow the buck was upon his knees, and when Tarzan reached him he was already dead.

The warriors who had followed close behind Tarzan the instant that there was no further need for caution were already surrounding the antelope, where they were talking with much more excitement than Tarzan had seen them previously display. Their interest seemingly centred about the death-dealing projectiles that had so easily laid this great animal low, for to them this antelope was as large as would be the largest elephant to us.

Having withdrawn his arrows and returned them to his quiver, Tarzan signed to the leader of the detachment that he would borrow his rapier. For an instant the man seemed to hesitate, and all his fellows watched him intently, but he drew the sword and passed it hilt foremost to the ape-man.

If you are going to eat flesh raw while it is still warm, you do not bleed the carcass, nor did Tarzan in this instance. Instead, he merely cut off a hind quarter, sliced off what he wanted, and fell to devouring it hungrily.

The little men viewed his act with surprise, not unmixed with horror, and when he offered them some of the flesh they refused it and drew away. What their reaction was he could not know, but he guessed that they held a strong aversion to the eating of raw meat.

Later he was to learn that their revulsion was due to the fact that within the entire range of their experience heretofore the only creatures that devoured raw meat devoured the pygmies as well. When, therefore, they saw this mighty giant eating the flesh of his kill raw they could not but draw the conclusion that should he become sufficiently hungry he would eat them.

Wrapping some of the meat of the antelope in its own skin, Tarzan secured it to his back, and the party resumed its journey. The warriors now appeared troubled, and as they conversed in low tones they cast many backward glances in the direction of the ape-man. They were not afraid for themselves, for these warriors scarcely knew the meaning of fear. The question that caused them apprehension related to the wisdom of leading among their people such a huge devourer of raw flesh, who at a single hurried meal had eaten nearly the equivalent of a grown man.

The afternoon was drawing to a close when Tarzan discerned in the far distance what appeared to be a group of symmetrical, dome-shaped hillocks, and later, as they approached these, he saw a body of mounted warriors galloping to meet them. From his greater height he saw these before the others saw them, and attracting the officer's attention made signs apprising the latter of his discovery, but the oncoming warriors were hidden from the view of their fellows by the inequalities of the ground.

Realizing this, Tarzan stooped and, before the officer could guess his intention, had gathered the antelope and rider gently in his powerful hands and lifted them high above the ground. For an instant consternation held the remaining warriors. Swords flashed and a warning cry arose, and even the plucky pygmy in his grasp drew his own diminutive weapon; but a smile from the ape-man assured them all, and an instant later the officer saw why Tarzan had raised him aloft. He called down to the others below him then, and from their manner, as from that of him whom he held, the ape-man guessed that the approaching party was composed of friends of his escort, and so, a few minutes later, it proved when he was surrounded by several hundreds of the pygmies, all friendly, eager, and curious. Among them was the leader whom he had rescued from the Alalus woman and him he greeted with a handshake.

A consultation now took place between the leader of the detachment that had escorted the ape-man, the young commander of the larger party, and several older warriors. By the expressions of their faces and the tone of their voices Tarzan judged that the matter was serious, and that it concerned him he was sure from the numerous glances that were cast in his direction.

He could not know, though, that the subject of their discussion was based upon the report of the commander of the escort that their mighty guest was an eater of raw flesh and the consequent danger of bringing him among their people.

The chief among them, the young commander, settled the question, however, by reminding them that although the giant must have been very hungry to have devoured so much flesh, nevertheless he had travelled for many hours with only a small number of their warriors always within easy reach of him and had not offered to molest them. This seemed a conclusive argument of his good intentions, and consequently the cavalcade set forth without further delay in the direction of the hillocks that were now in plain view a mile or two away.

As they neared them Tarzan saw what appeared to be literally innumerable little men moving about among the hillocks, and as he came nearer still he realized that these seeming hillocks were symmetrical mounds of small stones quite evidently built by the pygmies themselves. The hordes of pygmies moving about among them were workers, for here was a long line all moving in one direction, emerging from a hole in the ground and following a well-defined path to a half-completed hillock that was evidently in course of construction.

Another line moved, empty-handed, in the opposite direction, entering the ground through a second hole, and upon the flanks of each line and at frequent intervals marched armed warriors, while other similar lines of guarded workers moved in and out of openings in each of the other dome-like structures, carrying to the mind of the ape-man a suggestion of ants labouring about their hills.

6

Trohanadalmakus

Ska, the vulture, winged his way leisurely in great circles far above the right bank of the Ugogo. The pendant locket, sparkling in the sunlight, had ceased to annoy him while on the wing; only when he alighted and walked upon the ground did it become an encumbrance and then he stepped upon it and tripped, but long since had he ceased to fight it, accepting it now as a necessary and inescapable evil. Beneath him he presently descried the still, recumbent form of Gorgo, the buffalo, whose posture proclaimed that he was already fit food for Ska. The great bird dropped, alighting in a nearby tree. All was well; no foes were in evidence.

Satisfied of this, Ska flapped to the head of the fallen beast, alighting upon one horn, where it is as well for effete, civilized nerves to leave him with his procedure undescribed.

In the village of the ant-men Tarzan found a warm welcome, and having decided to remain with them for a while that he might study them and their customs he set to work, as was his wont when thrown among strange peoples, to learn their language as quickly as possible. Having already mastered several languages and numerous dialects the ape-man never found it difficult to add to his linguistic attainments, and so it was only a matter of a comparatively short time before he found it possible to understand his hosts and to make himself understood by them.

It was then that he learned that they had at first thought that he was some form of Alalus, and had consequently believed that it ever would be impossible to communicate with him by other means than signs. They were greatly delighted, therefore, when it had become apparent that he could utter vocal sounds identical to theirs; and when they comprehended that he desired to learn their tongue, Adendrohahkis, the king, placed several instructors at his disposal and gave orders that all his people, with whom the giant stranger came into contact, should aid him to an early understanding of their language.

Adendrohahkis was particularly well-inclined toward the ape-man, because of the fact that it had been the king's son, Komodoflorensal, whom Tarzan had rescued from the clutches of the Alalus woman, and so it was that everything was done to make the giant's stay among them a pleasant one. A hundred slaves brought his food to him where he had taken up his abode beneath the shade of a great tree that grew in lonely majesty just outside the city.

When he walked among the group of dome-houses a troop of cavalry galloped ahead to clear a path for him, lest he trod upon some of the people of the city, but always was Tarzan careful of his hosts, so that no harm ever befell one of them because of him.

As he mastered the language he learned many things concerning these remarkable people. Prince Komodoflorensal almost daily took it upon himself to assist in the instruction of his colossal guest, and it was from him that Tarzan learned most. Nor were his eyes idle as he strolled around the city. Particularly interesting was the method of construction used in erecting the comparatively gigantic dome-houses which towered high above even the great Tarzan.

The first step in the construction was to outline the periphery of the base with boulders of uniform size and weight, perhaps, fifty pounds each. Two slaves easily carried such a boulder when it was slung in a rope hammock, and as thousands of slaves were employed the work progressed with rapidity.

The circular base, with a diameter of one hundred and fifty to two hundred feet, having been outlined, another, smaller circle was laid about ten feet inside the first, four openings being left in each circle to mark the location of the four entrances to the completed building and corresponding to the four principal cardinal points of the compass. The walls of the entrances were then outlined upon the ground with similar large boulders, these being a little more carefully selected for uniformity, after which the four enclosures thus formed were packed closely with boulders. The corridors and chambers of the first floor were then outlined and the spaces between filled with boulders, each being placed with the utmost care and nicety in relation to those touching it and those that should rest upon it when the second course was laid, for these were to support a tremendous weight when the edifice was completed. The corridors were generally three feet wide, the equivalent of twelve feet by our standards, while the chambers varied in dimensions according to the uses to which they were to be put. In the exact centre of the building a circular opening was left that measured ten feet in diameter, and this was carried upward as the building progressed until the whole formed an open shaft from ground floor to roof in the completed edifice.

The lower course having been built up in this manner to a height of six inches, wooden arches were placed at intervals the lengths of the corridors, which were now ceiled over by the simple expedient of fastening thin wooden strips lengthwise of the corridors from arch to arch until the corridors were entirely roofed. The strips, or boards, which overlapped one another, were fastened in place by wooden dowels driven through them into the peripheries of the arches.

As this work was progressing, the walls of the various chambers and the outer wall of the building were raised to a height of twenty-four inches, bringing them to the level of the ceilings of the arched corridors, and the spaces between chambers and corridors were packed with boulders, the interstices between which were filled with smaller stones and gravel. The ceiling beams were then placed across the other chambers, timber six inches square hewn from a hard, tough wood being used, and in the larger chambers these were further supported, at intervals, by columns of the same dimensions and material.

The ceiling beams being in place they were covered over with tight-fitting boards, dowelled to place. The ceilings of the chambers now projected six inches above the surrounding course of the structure, and at this juncture hundreds of cauldrons were brought in which a crude asphaltum was heated until it became liquid and the interstices of the next six-inch course were filled with it, bringing the entire completed course to the same level at a height of thirty inches, over all of which a second six-inch course of rock and asphaltum was laid, and the second story was laid out and completed in a similar manner.

The palace of Adendrohahkis, constructed in this way, was two hundred and twenty feet in diameter, and one hundred and ten feet high, with thirty-six floors capable of housing eighty thousand people: a veritable ant-hill of humanity. The city consisted of ten similar domes, although each slightly smaller than the king's, housing a total of five hundred thousand people, two-thirds of whom were slaves – these being for the most part the artisans and the body servants of the ruling class.

Another half million slaves, the unskilled labourers of the city, dwelt in the subterranean chambers of the quarries from which the building material was obtained. The passageways and chambers of these mines were carefully shored and timbered as the work progressed, resulting in fairly commodious and comfortable quarters for the slaves, upon the upper levels at least; and as the city was built upon the surface of an ancient ground moraine, because of the accessibility of building material, the drainage was perfect, the slaves suffering no inconvenience because of living underground.

The domes themselves were well ventilated through the large central air-shaft and the numerous windows that pierced the outer walls at frequent intervals at each level above the ground floor, in which, as previously explained, there are but four openings. The windows, which are six and one-quarter inches wide by eighteen and a half inches high, admit a certain amount of light as well as air; but the interior of the dome, especially the gloomy chambers mid-way between the windows and the central light and air-shaft, is illuminated by slow-burning, smokeless candles.

Tarzan watched the construction of the new dome with keenest interest, realising that it was the only opportunity that he ever would have to see the interior of one of these remarkable human hives, and as he was thus engaged Komodoflorensal and his friends hastened to initiate him into the mysteries of their language; and as he learned the language of his hosts he learned many other things of interest about them. The slaves, he discovered, were either prisoners of war or the descendants of prisoners of war. Some had been in bondage for so many generations that all trace of their origin had become lost and they considered themselves as much citizens of Trohanadalmakus, the city of King Adendrohahkis, as did any of the nobility. On the whole they were treated with kindness and were not overworked after the second generation.

The recent prisoners and their children were, for the most part, included in the caste of unskilled labour, from which the limit of human endurance was exacted. They were the miners, the quarriers, and the builders, and fully fifty per cent of them were literally worked to death. With the second generation the education of the children commenced, those who showed aptitude for any skilled crafts being immediately transferred from the quarries to the domes, where they took up the relatively easy life of a prosperous and indulged middle-class.

In another manner might an individual escape the quarries – by marriage, or rather by selection, as they choose to call it, with a member of the ruling class. In a community where class consciousness was so ingrained a characteristic of the people and where caste was almost a fetish, it was rather remarkable that such connections brought no odium upon either, but on the contrary, automatically elevated the lesser to the caste of the higher contracting party.

'It is thus, Deliverer of the Son of Adendrohahkis,' explained Komodoflorensal, in reply to Tarzan's inquiry relative to this rather peculiar exception to the rigid class distinctions the king's son had so often impressed upon him: 'Ages ago, during the reign of Klamataamorosal in the city of Trohanadalmakus, the warriors of Veltotishago, king of the city of Veltoptismakus, marched upon our fair capital and in the battle that ensued the troops of our ancestors were all but annihilated. Thousands of our men and women were carried away into slavery, and all that saved us from being totally wiped out was the courageous defence that our own slaves waged for their masters.

'Klamataamorosal, from whom I am descended, fighting in the thick of the fray, noted the greater stamina of the slaves; they were stronger than the warriors of either city and seemed not to tire at all, while the high caste nobility of the fighting clans, although highly courageous, became completely exhausted after a few minutes of fighting. After the battle was over Klamataamorosal called together all the chief officers of the city, or rather all who had not been killed or taken prisoner, and pointed out to them that the reason our city had been defeated was not so much because of the greater numbers of the forces of the king Veltotishago as to the fact that our own warriors were physical weaklings, and he asked them why this should be and what could be done to remedy so grievous a fault. The youngest man among them, wounded and weak from loss of blood, was the only one who could offer a reasonable explanation, or suggest a means of correcting the one obvious weakness of the city.

'He called their attention to the fact that of all the race of the Minunians the people of the city of Trohanadalmakus were the most ancient, and that for ages there had been no infusion of new blood, since they were not permitted to mate outside their own caste, while their slaves, recruited from all the cities of Minuni, had inter-bred, with the result that they had become strong and robust while their masters, through inbreeding, had grown correspondingly weaker.

'He exhorted Klamataamorosal to issue a decree elevating to the warrior class any slave that was chosen as mate by either a man or woman of that class, and further to obligate each and every warrior to select at least one mate from among their slaves. At first, of course, the objections to so iconoclastic a suggestion were loud and bitter, but Klamataamorosal was quick to sense the wisdom of the idea, and not only did he issue the decree, but he was the first to espouse a slave woman, and what the king did all were anxious to do also.

'The very next generation showed the wisdom of the change, and each succeeding generation has more than fulfilled the expectations of Klamataamorosal, until now you see the people of Trohanadalmakus the most powerful and warlike of the Minunians.

'Our ancient enemy, Veltoptismakus, was the next city to adopt the new order, having learned of it through slaves taken in raids upon our own community, but they were several generations behind us. Now all the cities of Minuni wed their warriors with their slave women. Time has made some slight changes in the manner of the selection of these new mates, and now it is often customary to make war upon another city for the sole purpose of capturing their noblest born and most beautiful women.

'For us of the royal family it has been nothing less than salvation from extinction. Our ancestors were transmitting disease and insanity to their progeny. The new, pure, virile blood of the slaves has washed the taint from our veins, and so altered has our point of view become that whereas, in the past, the child of a slave woman and a warrior was without caste – the lowest of the low – now they rank highest of the high, since it is considered immoral for one of the royal family to wed other than a slave.'

'And your wife,' replied Tarzan. 'You took her in a battle with some other city?'

'I have no wife,' replied Komodoflorensal. 'We are preparing now to make war upon Veltoptismakus, the daughter of whose king, we are told by slaves from that city, is the most beautiful creature in the world. Her name is Janzara, and as she is not related to me, except possibly very remotely, she is a fit mate for the son of Adendrohahkis.'

'How do you know she is not related to you?' asked the ape-man.

'We keep as accurate a record of the royal families of Veltoptismakus and several other of the nearer cities of Minuni as we do of our own,' replied Komodoflorensal, 'obtaining our information from captives, usually from those who are chosen in marriage by our own people.

'For several generations the kings of Veltoptismakus have not been sufficiently powerful or fortunate to succeed in taking royal princesses from us either by force of arms or strategy, though they have never ceased attempting to do so, and the result has been that they have been forced to find their mates in other and oftentimes distant cities.

'The present king of Veltoptismakus, Elkomoelhago, the father of the princess Janzara, took his mate, the mother of the princess, from a far distant city that has never, within historic times, taken slaves from Trohanadalmakus, nor have our warriors visited that city within the memory of any living man. Janzara, therefore, should make me an excellent mate.'

'But what about love – suppose you should not care for each other?' asked Tarzan.

Komodoflorensal shrugged his shoulders. 'She will bear me a son who will some day be King of Trohanadalmakus,' he replied, 'and that is all that can be asked.' While the preparations for the expedition against Veltoptismakus were being carried on Tarzan was left much to his own devices. The activities of these diminutive people were a never-ending source of interest to him.

He watched the endless lines of slaves struggling with their heavy burdens toward the new dome that was rising with almost miraculous speed, or he strolled to the farmlands just beyond the city where other slaves tilled the rich soil, which they scratched with tiny ploughs drawn by teams of diadets, the diminutive antelope that was their only beast of burden.

Always were the slaves accompanied by armed warriors if they were slaves of the first or second generation, lest they should attempt escape or revolution, as well as a protection against beasts of prey and human enemies.

The slaves of the first and second generations were easily recognisable by the vivid green tunic, reaching almost to the knees, which was the single garment of their caste, and which carried upon both its front and back an emblem or character in black that denoted the city of the slave's birth and the individual to whom he now belonged. All the slaves employed upon public works belonged to the king, Adendrohahkis, but in the fields many families were represented by their chattels.

Moving about the city upon their various duties were thousands of white-tunicked slaves. They exercised the mounts of their masters, they oversaw much of the more menial and laborious work of the lower caste slaves, they plied their trades and sold their wares in perfect freedom, but, like the other slaves, they wore but a single garment, other than rough sandals, which were common to both classes, and on their breasts and backs in red were only the emblems of their masters, which was also true of the second generation slaves of the green tunics, these having been born in the city and being consequently considered a part of it.

There were other, although minor, distinguishing marks upon the tunics of the higher caste slaves: small insignia on one shoulder or both, or on a sleeve, denoted the occupation of the wearer. Groom, body servant, major domo, cook, hairdresser, worker in gold and silver, potter – one could tell at a glance the vocation of each, and each belonged, body and soul to his master, who was compelled to feed and clothe these dependants, the fruits of whose labours belonged exclusively to him.

The wealth of one warrior family might lie in the beauty and perfection of the gold and silver ornaments it sold to its wealthy fellows, and in such an instance all its skilled slaves, other than those required for personal and household duties, would be employed in the designing and fabrication of these articles. Another family might devote its attention to agriculture, another to the raising of diadets, but all the work was done by the slaves, with the single exception of the breaking of diadets that were bred for riding, an occupation that was not considered beneath the dignity of the warrior class.

As an interested spectator Tarzan whiled the lazy days away. To his repeated queries as to the possibility of a way out of this bizarre, thorn-invested world, his hosts replied that it was naught to penetrate the forest of thorn trees, but that as it continued indefinitely to the uttermost extremities of matter it were quite useless to attempt to penetrate it at all, their conception of the world being confined to what they had actually seen – a land of hills, valleys and forests surrounded by thorn trees.

To creatures of their size the thorn forest was far from impenetrable, but Tarzan was not their size. Still he never ceased to plan on a means of escape, although he was in no great haste to attempt it, since he found the Minunians interesting, and it suited his present primitive mood to loll in lazy ease in the city of Trohanadalmakus. But suddenly a change came, early one morning, just as the first, faint promise of dawn was tinging the eastern sky.

7
War

The Alalus youth, son of the First Woman, ranged the forest in search of the ape-man, the only creature that had ever stirred within his savage, primitive breast any emotion even slightly akin to affection; but he did not find him. Instead he fell in with two older males of his own species, and these three hunted together, as was occasionally the custom of these inoffensive creatures.

His new acquaintances showed little interest in his strange armament – they were quite content with a stick and a stone knife. To them an occasional rodent fell, and they found many a luscious grub and insect beneath the mould that floored the forest or hidden under the bark of a tree. For the most part, however, they fed upon fruits, nuts, and tubers.

Not so the son of the First Woman, however. He brought in many birds and an occasional antelope, for he was becoming daily more proficient with the bow and the spear; and as he often brought in more than he could eat and left the remainder to his two fellows, they were permanently attached to him, or at least until such time as some fearsome woman should appear upon the scene to shatter their idyllic existence and drag one of them away to her corral.

They wondered a little at him in their slow and stupid minds, for he seemed to differ in some vague, intangible way from them and all others of their sex that they had known. He held his chin higher for one thing and his gaze was far less shifty and apologetic.

He strode with a firmer step and with less caution, but perhaps they smiled inwardly as they cogitated muddily upon that inevitable moment that would discover one of their coarse, brutal hairy shes felling him with her bludgeon and dragging him off toward the caves by the hair of his head.

And then one day the thing happened, or at least a part of it happened: they met a huge she suddenly in an open place in the forest. The two who accompanied the son of the First Woman turned in flight but when they had reached the vantage ground of close-growing timber they paused and looked back to see if the woman was pursuing them and what had become of their companion.

To their relief they saw that the woman was not following them and, to their consternation, that their fellow had not fled, but was facing her defiantly, and motioning her to go away, or be killed. Such crass stupidity! He must have been whelped without brains.

It never occurred to them to attribute his act to courage. Courage was for the shes; the male spent his life in fleeing danger and the female of his species.

But they were grateful to him, for his rash act would save them, since the she would take but one of them, and that one would be he who thus foolishly remained behind to defy her.

The woman, unaccustomed to having her rights challenged by mere man, was filled with surprise and righteous anger. Her surprise brought her to a sudden halt twenty paces from the young man, and her anger caused her to reach for one of the stone missiles hanging at her girdle. That was her undoing.

The son of the First Woman, standing before her with an arrow already fitted to his bow, waited not to discover her further intentions, but even as the woman's fingers loosed the feathered messenger of defeat from the leathern thong of her girdle he drew the shaft to his cheek and released it.

His two companions watching from the seclusion of the wood, saw the woman stiffen, her face contorted in a spasm of pain; they saw her clutch frantically at a feathered shaft protruding from her chest, sink to her knees and then sprawl to the earth, where she lay kicking with her feet and clutching with her fingers for a brief moment before she relapsed into eternal quiet. Then the watchers emerged from their concealment, and as the son of the First Woman approached his victim and wrenched the arrow from her heart they joined him, half stunned as they were by surprise, and gazed first at the corpse of the she with expressions of incredulity and then at him with what was close akin to awe and reverence.

They examined his bow and arrows, and again and again they returned to the wound in the woman's chest. It was all quite too amazing.

And the son of the First Woman? He held his head high and his chest out and strutted proudly. Never before had he or any other man of the Alali been cast in the role of hero, and he enjoyed it.

But he would impress them further. Seizing the corpse of the woman he dragged it to a nearby tree, where he propped it in a sitting posture against the bole. Then he walked away some twenty feet and, signing to his fellows to observe him closely, he raised his heavy spear and hurled it at his realistic target, through which it passed to embed itself in the tree behind. The others were greatly excited. One of them wanted to attempt this wondrous feat, and when he had thrown, and missed, his fellow insisted upon having a turn. Later they craved practice with the bow and arrow.

For hours the three remained before their grisly target, nor did they desist until hunger prompted them to move on, and the son of the First Woman had promised to show them how to fashion weapons similar to his own. It was a momentous occurrence in the history of the Alali, although these three sensed it as little as did the hundreds of Alali women repairing to their caves that night in blissful ignorance of the blow that had been struck at their supremacy by the militant male suffragist of Minuni.

And as suddenly the even tenor of Tarzan's existence in the city of Trohanadalmakus was altered and events were initiated that were to lead to the maddest and most unbelievable result.

The ape-man lay upon a bed of grasses beneath a great tree that grew beside the city of King Adendrohahkis. The pink dawn was flushing the sky above the forest to the east of Trohanadalmakus, when Tarzan, his ear close to the ground, was suddenly awakened by a strange reverberation that appeared to hum faintly from the bowels of the earth.

It was such a dim and distant sound that it would scarce have been appreciable to you or to me had we placed an ear flat against the ground after having been told that the noise existed, but to Tarzan it was an interruption of the ordinary noises of the night, and, therefore, however slight, of sufficient import to impinge upon his consciousness, even in sleep.

Awakened, he still lay listening intently. He knew that the sound did not come from the bowels of the earth, but from the surface, and he guessed that it originated at no great distance, and also he knew that it was coming closer rapidly. For just a moment it puzzled him, and then a great light dawned upon him and he sprang to his feet.

The dome of the king, Adendrohahkis, lay a hundred yards away, and toward it he bent his steps. Just before the south entrance he was challenged by a tiny sentinel.

'Take word to your king,' the ape-man directed him, 'that Tarzan hears many diadets galloping toward Trohanadalmakus, and that, unless he is much mistaken, each carries a hostile warrior upon its back.'

The sentinel turned and hallooed down the corridor leading from the entrance, and a moment later an officer and several other warriors appeared. At sight of Tarzan they halted.

'What is wrong?' demanded the officer.

'The king's guest says that he hears many diadets approaching,' replied the sentinel.

'From what direction?' demanded the officer, addressing Tarzan.

'From that direction the sounds appeared to come,' replied the ape-man, pointing toward the west.

'The Veltoptismakusians!' exclaimed the officer, and then, turning to those who had accompanied him from the interior of the king's dome: 'Quick, arouse Trohanadalmakus – I will warn the king's dome and the king!' and he wheeled and ran quickly within, while others sped away to awaken the city.

In an incredibly short space of time Tarzan saw thousands of warriors streaming from the ten domes. From the north and the south doors of each dome rode mounted men, and from the east and west marched the foot soldiers. There was no confusion; everything moved with military precision and evidently in accordance with a plan of defence in which each unit had been thoroughly drilled.

Small detachments of cavalry galloped quickly to the four points of the compass – scouts were these, each detail of which spread fanwise just beyond the limits of the domes until the city was encircled by a thin line of mounted men that would halt when it had reached a predetermined distance from the city and fall back with the information before an advancing enemy.

Following these, stronger detachments of mounted men moved out to north and south and east and west, to take positions just inside the line of scouts. These detachments were strong enough to engage the enemy and impede his progress as they fell back upon the main body of the cavalry, which might by this plan be summoned in time to the point at which the enemy was making his boldest effort to reach the city.

And then the main body of the cavalry moved out, and in this instance toward the west, from which point they were already assured the foe was approaching, while the infantry, which had not passed since it emerged from the domes, marched likewise toward the four points of the compass in four compact bodies of which by far the largest moved toward the west.

The advance foot troops took their stations but a short distance outside the city, while within the area of the domes the last troops to emerge from them, both cavalry and infantry, remained evidently as a reserve force, and it was with these troops that Adendrohahkis took his post that he might be centrally located for the purpose of directing the defence of his city to better advantage.

Komodoflorensal, the prince, had gone out in command of the main body of cavalry that was to make the first determined stand against the oncoming foe. This body consisted of seven thousand and five hundred men and its position lay two miles outside the city, half a mile behind a cavalry patrol of five hundred men, of which there were four groups, one at each point of the compass, and totalling two thousand men. The remainder of the ten thousand advance mounted troops consisted of the five hundred mounted scouts or vedettes who, in turn, were half a mile in advance of the picket patrols, at two hundred foot intervals, entirely surrounding the city at a distance of three miles. Inside the city fifteen thousand mounted men were held in reserve.

In the increasing light of dawn Tarzan watched these methodical preparations for defence with growing admiration for the tiny Minunians. There was no shouting and no singing, but on the face of every warrior who passed close enough for the ape-man to discern his features was an expression of exalted rapture. No need here for war cries or battle-hymns to bolster the questionable courage of the weak – there were no weak.

The pounding of the hoofs of the advancing Veltoptismakusian horde had ceased. It was evident that their scouts had discovered that the intended surprise had failed. Were they altering the plan or point of attack, or had they merely halted the main body temporarily to await the result of a reconnaissance?

Tarzan asked a nearby officer if, perchance, the enemy had abandoned their intention of attacking at all. The man smiled and shook his head.

'Minunians never abandon an attack,' he said.

As Tarzan's eyes wandered over the city's ten domes, illuminated now by the rays of the rising sun, he saw in each of the numerous window embrasures that pierced the homes at regular intervals at each of their thirty odd floors a warrior stationed, at whose side lay a great bundle of short javelins, while just to his rear was piled a quantity of small, round stones. The ape-man smiled.

'They overlook no possible contingency,' he thought. 'But the quarry slaves! What of them? Would they not turn against their masters at the first opportunity for escape that an impending battle such as this would be almost certain to present to them?' He turned to an officer and put the question to him.

The latter turned and pointed toward the entrance to the nearest quarry where Tarzan saw hundreds of white-tunicked slaves piling rocks upon it, while a detachment of infantry leaned idly upon their spears as their officers directed the labour of the slaves.

'There is another detachment of warriors bottled up inside the quarry entrance,' explained the officer to Tarzan. 'If the enemy gains the city and this outer guard is driven into the domes or killed or captured, the inner guard can hold off an entire army, as only one man can attack them at a time. Our slaves are safe, therefore, unless the city falls, and that has not happened to any Minunian city within the memory of man.

'The best that the Veltoptismakusians can hope for now is to pick up a few prisoners, but they will doubtless leave behind as many as they take. Had their surprise been successful they might have forced their way into one of the domes and made away with many women and much loot.

'Now, though, our forces are too well disposed to make it possible for any but a greatly superior force to seriously threaten the city itself, I even doubt if our infantry is engaged at all.'

'How is the infantry disposed?' asked Tarzan.

'Five thousand men are stationed within the windows of the domes,' replied the officer; 'five thousand more comprise the reserve which you see about you, and from which detachments have been detailed to guard the quarries. A mile from the city are four other bodies of infantry – those to the east, north, and south having a strength of one thousand men each, while the one to the west, facing the probable point of attack, consists of seven thousand warriors.'

'Then you think the fighting will not reach the city?' asked Tarzan.

'No. The lucky men today are in the advance cavalry – they will get whatever fighting there is. I doubt if an infantryman draws a sword or casts a spear; but that is usually the case – it is the cavalry that fights, always.'

'I take it that you feel unfortunate in not being attached to a cavalry unit. Could you not be transferred?'

'Oh, we must all take our turns of duty in each branch,' explained the officer. 'We are all mounted except for defence of the city, and for that purpose we are assigned to the foot troops for four moons, followed by five moons in the cavalry' (the word he used was *diadetax*), 'five thousand men being transferred from one to the other the night of each new moon.'

Tarzan turned and looked out across the plain toward the west. He could see the nearer troops standing at ease, awaiting the enemy. Even the main body of cavalry two miles away, he could discern, because there were so many of them, but the distant pickets and vedettes were invisible.

As he stood leaning upon his spear watching the scene – a scene such as no other man of his race ever had witnessed – and realized the seriousness of these little men in the business of war that confronted them, he could not but think of the people of his own world lining up their soldiers for purposes usually far less momentous to them than the call to arms that had brought the tough little warriors of Adendrohahkis swarming from their pallets in the defence of home and city.

No chicanery of politics here, no thinly veiled ambition of some potential tyrant, no mad conception of hare-brained dreamers seized by the avaricous criminal for self-aggrandisement and riches; none of these, but patriotism of purest strain energized by the powerful urge of self-preservation. The perfect fighters, the perfect warriors, the perfect heroes these. No need for blaring trumpets; of no use to them the artificial aids to courage conceived by captains of the outer world.

During the lull that followed the departure from the city of the last of the advance troops Tarzan approached Adendrohahkis where he sat astride his diadet surrounded by a number of his high officers. The king was resplendent in golden jerkin, a leathern garment upon which small disks of gold were sewn, overlapping one another.

About his waist was a wide belt of heavy leather, held in place by three buckles of gold, and of such dimensions as to have almost the appearance of a corset. This belt supported his rapier and knife, the scabbards of which were heavily inlaid with gold and baser metals in intricate and beautiful designs.

Leather cuisses protected his upper legs in front, covering the thighs to the knees, while his forearms were encased in metal armlets from wrists almost to elbows. Upon his feet were strapped tough sandals, with a circular golden plate protecting each ankle bone. A well-shaped leather casque fitted his head closely.

As Tarzan stopped before him the king recognized the ape-man with a pleasant greeting. 'The captain of the guard reports that it is to you we owe the first warning of the coming of the Veltoptismakusians. Once again have you placed the people of Trohanadalmakus under deep obligations. However are we to repay our debt?'

Tarzan gestured deprecatively. 'You owe me nothing, King of Trohanadalmakus,' he replied. 'Give me your friendship and tell me that I may go forward and join your noble son, the prince; then all the obligations shall be upon my head.'

'Until death devour me I shall be your friend always, Tarzan,' returned the king graciously. 'Go where you will, and that you choose to go where there should be fighting surprises me not.'

It was the first time that any Minunian had addressed him by his name. Always he had been called Saviour of the Prince, Guest of the King, Giant of the Forest, and by other similar impersonal appellations. Among the Minunians a man's name is considered a sacred possession, the use of which is permitted only his chosen friends and the members of his family, and to be called 'Tarzan' by Adendrohahkis was equivalent to an invitation, or a command, to the closest personal friendship with the king.

The ape-man acknowledged the courtesy with a bow. 'The friendship of Adendrohahkis is a sacred honour, ennobling those who wear it. I shall guard it always with my life, as my most treasured possession,' he said in a low voice; nor was the Lord of the Jungle moved by any maudlin sentimentality as he addressed the king. For these little people he had long since acknowledged to himself a keen admiration, and for the personal character of Adendrohahkis he had come to have the most profound respect. Never since he had learned their language had he ceased his inquiries concerning the manners and the customs of these people, and he had found the personality of Adendrohahkis so inextricably interwoven with the lives of his subjects that in receiving the answers to his questions he could not but absorb unquestionable evidence of the glories of the king's character.

Adendrohahkis seemed pleased with his words, which he acknowledged graciously, and then the ape-man withdrew and started toward the front. On the way he tore a leafy bough from a tree that grew beside his path, for the thought had occurred to him that such a weapon might be useful against Minunians, and he knew not what the day might hold.

He had just passed the advanced infantry when a courier sped by him on a mad race toward the city. Tarzan strained his eyes ahead, but he could see no sign of battle, and when he reached the main cavalry advance there was still no indication of an enemy as far ahead as he could see.

Prince Komodoflorensal greeted him warmly and looked a little wonderingly, perhaps, at the leafy branch he carried across one shoulder.

'What news?' asked Tarzan.

'I have just sent a messenger to the king,' replied the prince, 'reporting that our scouts have come in touch with those of the enemy, who are, as we thought, the Veltoptismakusians. A strong patrol from the outpost in our front pushed through the enemy's scout line, and one courageous warrior even managed to penetrate as far as the summit of the Hill of Gartolas, from which he saw the entire main body of the enemy forming for attack. He says there are between twenty thousand and thirty thousand of them.'

As Komodoflorensal ceased speaking a wave of sound came rolling toward them from the west.

'They are coming,' announced the prince.

8

Outnumbered

Ska, perched upon the horn of dead Gorgo, became suddenly aware of a movement in a nearby thicket. He turned his head in the direction of the sound and saw Sabor, the lioness, emerge from the foliage and walk slowly toward him. Ska was not terrified. He would leave, but he would leave with dignity. He crouched to spring upward, and extended his great wings to aid him in taking off.

But Ska, the vulture, never arose. As he essayed to do so something pulled sharply upon his neck and held him down. He scrambled to his feet and, violently this time, strove to fly away. Again he was dragged back. Now Ska was terrified. The hateful thing that had been dangling about his neck for so long was holding him to earth – the swinging loop of the golden chain had caught around the horn of Gorgo, the buffalo. Ska was trapped.

He struggled, beating his wings. Sabor stopped to regard him and his wild antics. Ska was flopping around in a most surprising manner. Sabor had never seen Ska behave thus before, and lions are sensitive, temperamental animals; so Sabor was not only surprised, she was inclined to be frightened.

For another moment she watched the unaccountable antics of Ska, and then she turned tail and slunk back into the undergrowth, turning an occasional growling countenance back upon the vulture, as if to say, 'Pursue me at your peril!' But Ska had no thought of pursuing. Never again would Ska, the vulture, pursue aught.

'They are coming! They are coming!' announced Komodoflorensal, Prince of Trohanadalmakus.

As Tarzan looked out across the rolling country in the direction of the enemy, he presently saw, from his greater height, the advance of the Veltoptismakusians.

'Our scouts are falling back,' he announced to Komodoflorensal.

'You can see the enemy?' demanded the prince.

'Yes.'

'Keep me advised as to their movements.'

'They are advancing in several long lines, deploying over a considerable front,' reported the ape-man. 'The scouts are falling back upon the outpost, which seems to be standing its ground to receive them. It will be overwhelmed – if not by the first line then by those that succeed it.'

Komodoflorensal gave a short command. A thousand mounted men leaped forward, urging their diadets into bounding leaps that cleared six or seven feet at a time. Straight for the outpost ahead of them they raced, deploying as they went.

Another thousand moved quickly toward the right and a third toward the left of the advance cavalry's position following Tarzan's announcement that the enemy had divided into two bodies just before it engaged the outpost, and that one of these was moving as if with the intention of turning the right flank of the main cavalry of Trohanadalmakus, while the other circled in the direction of the left flank.

'They are striking boldly and quickly for prisoners,' said the prince to Tarzan.

'Their second and third lines are ploying upon the centre and moving straight for us,' said Tarzan. 'They have reached the outpost, which is racing forward with them, giving battle vigorously with rapiers,' Komodoflorensal was despatching messengers toward the rear.

'It is thus we fight,' he said, evidently in explanation of the action of the outpost. 'It is time that you returned to the rear, for in another few moments you will be surrounded by the enemy if you remain. When they reach us we, too, will turn and fight them hand-to-hand back toward the city.

'If it still is their intention to enter the city the battle will resemble more a race than aught else, for the speed will be too great for effective fighting; but if they have abandoned that idea and intend contenting themselves with prisoners there will be plenty of fighting before we reach the infantry, past which I doubt if they will advance.

'With their greatly superior numbers they will take some prisoners, and we shall take some. But, quick! you must get back to the city, if already it is not too late.'

'I think I shall remain here,' replied the ape-man.

'But they will take you prisoner, or kill you.'

Tarzan of the Apes smiled and shook his leafy branch. 'I do not fear them,' he said simply.

'That is because you do not know them,' replied the prince. 'Your great size makes you over-confident, but remember that you are only four times the size of a Minunian and there may be thirty thousand seeking to overthrow you.'

The Veltoptismakusians were driving swiftly forward. The prince could give no more time to what he saw was but a futile attempt to persuade Tarzan to retreat, and while he admired the strange giant's courage he likewise deplored his ignorance. Komodoflorensal had grown fond of their strange guest, and he would have saved him had it been possible, but now he must turn to the command of his troops, since the enemy was almost upon them.

Tarzan watched the coming of the little men on their agile wiry mounts. Line after line poured across the rolling country towards him, carrying to his mind an inescapable suggestion of the incoming rollers of the ocean's surf, each drop of which was soft and harmless, but in their countless numbers combined into a relentless and terrifying force of destruction. The ape-man glanced at his leafy bough and smiled, albeit a trifle ruefully.

But now his whole attention was riveted by the fighting in the first two lines of the advancing horde. Racing neck and neck with the Veltoptismakusian warriors were the men of Adendrohahkis's outpost and the thousand who had reinforced them. Each had selected an enemy rider whom he sought to strike from his saddle, and at top speed each duel was carried on with keen rapiers, though here and there was a man wielding his spear, and sometimes to good effect.

A few riderless diadets leaped forward with the vanguard, while others, seeking to break back or to the flanks, fouled the racing ranks, often throwing beasts and riders to the ground; but more frequently the warriors leaped their mounts entirely over these terrified beasts. The riding of the Minunians was superb, and their apparently effortless control of their swift and nervous steeds bordered upon the miraculous.

Now a warrior, lifting his mount high into the air, cleared an adversary, and as he rose above him cut down viciously with his rapier at his foe-man's head, striking him from the saddle, but there was scarce time to catch more than a fleeting, kaleidoscopic impression of the swift-moving spectacle before the great horde swarmed down upon the giant observer.

With his leafy bough, Tarzan had thought to sweep the little men from his path but now friend and foe were so intermingled that he dared not attempt it for fear of unseating and injuring some of the warriors of his hosts. He raised the bough above their heads and waited until the first lines should have passed him and then, with only the enemies of Adendrohahkis about him, he would brush them aside and break the centre of their charge.

He saw the surprised expressions on the faces of the men of Veltoptismakus as they passed near him – surprise but no fear – and he heard their shouts as one more fortunate than his fellows was able to rein closer to him and cut viciously at his legs as he sped past. Then, indeed, it became naught other than a matter of self-preservation to attempt to fend these off with his bough, nor was this impossible as the first lines moved past in loose ranks, but presently the solid mass of the Veltoptismakusian cavalry was upon him. There was no veering aside to avoid him. In unbroken ranks, file after file, they bore down upon this titanic enemy. He threw aside his useless bough before him to impede their progress and grappled them with his fingers, tearing the riders from their mounts and hurling them back upon their onrushing fellows, but still they came.

They jumped their diadets over every obstruction. One rider, leaping straight for Tarzan, struck him head on in the pit of the stomach, half winding him and sending him back a step. Another and another struck his legs and sides.

Again and again the needle-like points of their rapiers pierced his brown hide, until from hips to feet he was red with his own blood, and always there were more thousands bearing down upon him. His weapons, useless against them, he made no attempt to use, and although he wrought havoc among them with his bare hands there were always a hundred to take the place of each that he disposed of.

He smiled grimly as he realized that in these little people, scarce one-fourth his size, he, the incomparable Tarzan, the Lord of the Jungle, had met his conqueror. He realized that he now was entirely surrounded by the Veltoptismakusians.

The warriors of Trohanadalmakus, having engaged the advancing enemy, were racing onward with them toward the seven thousand dismounted men who were to receive the brunt of that terrific charge. Tarzan wished that he might have witnessed this phase of the battle, but he had fighting enough and to spare to engage all his attention where he was.

Again he was struck in the stomach by a charging rider and again the blow staggered him. Before he could recover himself another struck him in the same place, and this time he went down, and instantly he was covered, buried, by warriors and diadets swarming over him, like ants in countless numbers. He tried to rise and that was the last that he remembered before he sank into unconsciousness.

9

Princess Janzara

When Tarzan of the Apes regained his senses he found himself lying upon an earthen floor in a large chamber. As he first opened his eyes, before a complete consciousness returned, he noticed that the room was well but not brilliantly lighted, and that there were others there beside himself. Later, as he commenced to collect and dominate his faculties of thought, he saw that the room was illuminated by two immense candles that appeared to be fully three feet in diameter and although evidently partly melted away yet at least five feet tall. Each supported a wick fully as large as a man's wrist, and although the manner of their burning was similar to the candles with which he was familiar, yet they gave off no smoke, nor were the beams and boards of the ceiling directly above them smoke blackened.

The lights, being the most noticeable things in the room, had been the first to attract the ape-man's attention, but now his eyes wandered to the other occupants of the room. There were nearly a hundred men of about his own height, but they were garbed and armed as had been the little men of Trohanadalmakus and Veltoptismakus.

Tarzan knit his brows and looked long and steadily at them. Who were they? Where was he?

As consciousness spread slowly throughout his body he realized that he was in pain and that his arms felt heavy and numb. He tried to move them, only to discover that he could not – they were securely bound behind his back. He moved his feet – they were not secured.

At last, after considerable effort, for he found that he was very weak, he raised himself to a sitting posture and looked about him. The room was filled with warriors who looked precisely like the little Veltoptismakusians, but they were as large as normal men, and the room itself was immense.

There were a number of benches and tables standing about the floor, and most of the men either were seated upon the benches or lay stretched upon the hard earth. A few men moved about among them and seemed to be working over them.

Then it was that Tarzan saw that nearly all within the chamber were suffering from wounds, many of them severe ones. The men who moved about among them were evidently attending to the wounded, and those, who might have been the nurses, were garbed in white tunics like the high caste slaves of Trohanadalmakus. In addition to the wounded and the nurses there were a half-dozen armed warriors who were uninjured. One of these was the first to spy Tarzan after he had raised himself to a sitting posture.

'Ho!' shouted he. 'The giant has come into his senses,' and crossing the room he approached the ape-man. Standing before him, his feet wide spread, he eyed Tarzan with a broad grin upon his face. 'Your great bulk availed you little,' he taunted, 'and now we are as large as you. We, too, are giants, eh?' and he turned to his fellows with a laugh in which they joined him.

Seeing that he was a prisoner, surrounded by enemies, the ape-man fell back upon that lifelong characteristic of the wild beast – sullen silence. He made no reply, but only sat there regarding them with the savage, level gaze of the brute at bay.

'He is dumb like the great beast-women of the caves,' said the warrior to his fellows.

'Perhaps he is one of them,' suggested another.

'Yes,' seconded a third, 'perhaps he is one of the Zertalacolols.'

'But their men are all cowards,' urged the first speaker; 'and this one fought like a warrior born.'

'Yes, with his bare hands he fought until he went down.'

'You should have seen how he threw diadets and warriors as one might pick up the tiny pebbles and hurl them afar.'

'He does not look like the men of the Zertalacolols; ask him if he is.'

He who had first addressed him put the question to Tarzan, but the ape-man only continued to glare at them.

'He does not understand me,' said the warrior, 'I do not think that he is a Zertalacolol, though. What he is, however, I do not know.'

He approached and examined Tarzan's wounds. 'These will soon be healed. In seven days, or less, he will be fit for the quarries.' They sprinkled a brown powder upon his wounds and brought him food and water and the milk of antelopes, and when they found that his arms were swelling badly and becoming discoloured they brought an iron chain and, fastening one end about his waist with a clumsy padlock, secured him to a ring in the stone wall of the chamber, and cut the bonds from his wrists.

As they believed that he did not understand their language they spoke freely before him, but as their tongue was almost identical with that employed by the Trohanadalmakusians, Tarzan understood everything that they said, and thus he learned that the battle before the city of Adendrohahkis had not gone as well for the Veltoptismakusians as Elkomoelhago, their king, had desired. They had lost many in killed and prisoners and in return had not killed nearly so many of the enemy and had taken comparatively few prisoners, although Elkomoelhago, he learned, considered Tarzan worth the entire cost of the brief war.

How they had changed themselves into men of his own stature Tarzan could not comprehend, nor did any of the remarks he overheard shed any light upon this mystery of mysteries. But the climax of improbability was attained a few days later when he saw pass through the corridor, upon which the room of his incarceration was located, a file of warriors as large as he, each of whom was mounted upon a huge antelope fully as tall at the shoulder as the Giant Eland, although obviously, from its contour and markings, a Royal Antelope, which is the smallest known. Tarzan ran his brown fingers through his thatch of black hair and gave up attempting to solve the enigmas that surrounded him.

His wounds healed quickly, as did those of the Veltoptismakusians who were convalescing about him, and upon the seventh day a half-dozen warriors came for him and the chain was removed from about his waist that he might accompany them. His captors had long since ceased to address him, believing that he was ignorant of their language, which meant to them that he was speechless as an Alalus, since they could conceive of no language other than their own. But from their conversation, as they led him from the chamber and along a circular corridor, he discovered that he was being taken before their king.

The long corridor, through which they were proceeding, was lighted partly by small candles set in niches and by the light from illuminated chambers, the doors of which opened upon it. Slaves and warriors moved in two continuous and opposing lines through this corridor and every one that crossed it.

There were high caste slaves in white tunics with the red emblems of their owners and their own occupation insignia upon them; there were green-tunicked slaves of the second generation with their master's insignia upon breast and back in black, and green-tunicked slaves of the first generation with a black emblem upon their breasts, denoting the city of their nativity and their master's emblem upon their backs; there were warriors of every rank and position; there were the plain leather trappings of the young and poor, and the jewel-studded harness of the rich, and passing all these in both directions and often at high speed were the other warriors mounted upon the mighty antelopes that were still the greatest wonder that had confronted Tarzan since his incarceration in the city of Veltoptismakus.

At intervals along the corridor Tarzan saw ladders extending to a floor above, but as he never saw one descending to a lower level he assumed that they were then upon the lowest floor of the structure. From the construction that he noted he was convinced that the building was similar to the dome he had seen in the course of construction in the city of Adendrohahkis, but when he permitted his mind to dwell upon the tremendous proportions of such a dome capable of housing men of his own size he was staggered.

Had Adendrohahkis's dome been duplicated in these greater dimensions, although in the same proportions, it would have been eight hundred and eighty feet in diameter and four hundred and forty feet high. It seemed preposterous to think that any race existed capable of accomplishing such an architectural feat with only the primitive means that these people might be able to command, yet here were the corridors with the arched roofs, the walls of neatly laid boulders, and the great chambers with their heavy ceiling beams and stout columns, all exactly as he had seen in the dome in Trohanadalmakus, but on a vastly larger scale.

As his eyes and mind dwelt upon these enigmas which confronted them his escort led him from the circular corridor into one that ran at right angles to it, where presently they stopped at the entrance to a chamber filled with row upon row of shelving packed full with all manner of manufactured articles. There were large candles and small candles, candles of every conceivable size and shape; there were helmets, belts, sandals, tunics; bowls, jars, vases and the thousand other articles in the daily life of the Minunians with which Tarzan had become more or less familiar during his sojourn among the Trohanadalmakusians.

As they halted before the entrance to this room a white-tunicked slave came forward in response to the summons of one of the warriors of the escort.

'A green tunic for this fellow from Trohanadalmakus,' he ordered.

'Whose insignia upon his back?' inquired the slave.

'He belongs to Zoanthrohago,' replied the warrior.

The slave ran quickly to one of the shelves, from which he selected a green tunic. From another he took two large wooden blocks upon the face of each was carved a different device, These he covered evenly with some sort of paint or ink, slipped a smooth board inside the tunic, placed one of the dies face downward upon the cloth, tapped it smartly with a wooden mallet several times and then repeated the operation with the other die upon the reverse side of the tunic. When he handed the garment to Tarzan with instructions to don it the ape-man saw that it bore a device in black upon the breast and another upon the back, but he could not read them – his education had not progressed thus far.

The slave then gave him a pair of sandals, and when he had strapped these to his feet the warriors motioned him on down the corridor, which, as they proceeded, he was aware changed rapidly in appearance. The rough boulder walls were plastered now and decorated with coloured paintings portraying, most often, battle scenes and happenings of the hunt, usually framed in panels bordered in intricate, formal designs. Vivid colourings predominated. Many-hued candles burned in frequent niches.

Gorgeously trapped warriors predominated. The green-tunicked slave almost disappeared, while the white tunics of the higher caste bondsmen were of richer material and the slaves themselves often richly trapped with jewels and fine leather.

The splendour of the scene, the brilliancy of the lighting, increased until the corridor came to an abrupt end before two massive doors or hammered gold, in front of which stood splendidly trapped warriors who halted them and questioned the commander of the escort as to their business.

'By the king's command we bring the slave of Zoanthrohago,' replied the commander; 'the giant who was taken prisoner at Trohanadalmakus.'

The warrior who had challenged them turned to one of his fellows. 'Go with this message and deliver it to the king!' he said.

After the messenger had departed the warriors fell to examining Tarzan and asking many questions concerning him, to few of which could his guard give more than speculative answers; and then, presently, the messenger returned with word that the party was immediately to be admitted to the king's presence. The heavy doors were swung wide and Tarzan found himself upon the threshold of an enormous chamber, the walls of which converged toward the opposite end, where a throne stood upon a dais.

Massive wooden columns supported the ceiling, which was plastered between its beams. The beams as well as the columns were ornamented with carving, while the plastered portions of the ceiling carried gorgeous arabesques in brilliant colours. The walls were panelled to half their height, and above the panelling of wood were painted panels which Tarzan assumed depicted historical events from the history of Veltoptismakus and her kings. The room was vacant, except for two warriors, who stood before doors that flanked the throne dais, and as the party moved down the broad centre aisle toward the throne one of these warriors signalled the leader and motioned to the door which he was guarding and which he now threw open before them, revealing a small antechamber, in which were a half-dozen handsomely arrayed warriors seated on small, carved benches.

A seventh lolled in a high-backed arm-chair, his fingers tapping upon its broad arms as he listened to the conversation of the others, into which he threw an occasional word that always was received with deepest attention. If he scowled when he spoke the others scowled still more deeply; if he smiled they broke into laughter, and scarcely for an instant did their eyes leave his face, lest they miss some fleeting index of his changing moods.

Just inside the doorway the warriors who were conducting Tarzan halted, where they remained in silence until the man in the high-backed arm-chair deigned to notice them, then the leader knelt upon one knee, raised his arms, palms forward, high above his head, leaned as far back as he could, and in a monotonous dead level intoned his salutation.

'Oh! Elkomoelhago, King of Veltoptismakus, Ruler of All Men, Master of Created Things, All-Wise, All-Courageous, All-Glorious! We bring thee as thou hast commanded the slave of Zoanthrohago.'

'Arise and bring the slave closer,' commanded the man in the high-backed arm-chair; and then to his companions, 'this is the giant that Zoanthrohago brought back from Trohanadalmakus.'

'We have heard of him, All-Glorious,' they replied.

'And of Zoanthrohago's wager?' questioned the king.

'And of Zoanthrohago's wager, All-Wise!' replied one.

'What think you of it?' demanded Elkomoelhago.

'Even as you think, Ruler of All Men,' quickly spoke another.

'And how is that?' asked the king.

The six looked quickly and uneasily, one at the others. 'How *does* he think?' whispered he who was furthest from Elkomoelhago to his neighbour, who shrugged his shoulders hopelessly and looked to another.

'What was that, Gofoloso?' demanded the king. 'What was that you said?'

'I was about to remark that unless Zoanthrohago first consulted our august and all-wise ruler and is now acting upon his judgment he must almost of necessity lose the wager,' replied Gofoloso glibly.

'Of course,' said the king, 'there is something in what you say, Gofolso. Zoanthrohago did consult me. It was I who discovered the vibratory principle which made the thing possible. It was I who decided just how the first experiments were to be carried out. Heretofore it has not been enduring: but we believe that the new formula will have a persistency of thirty-nine moons at least – it is upon this that Zoanthrohago has made his wager. If he is wrong he loses a thousand slaves to Dalfastomalo.'

'Wonderful!' exclaimed Gofoloso. 'Blessed indeed are we above all other peoples with a king so learned and so wise as Elkomoelhago.'

'You have much to be thankful for, Gofoloso,' agreed the king: 'but nothing compared to what will follow the success of my efforts to apply this principle of which we have been speaking, but with results diametrically opposite to those we have so far achieved; but we work upon it, we work upon it! Some day it will come, and then I shall give to Zoanthrohago the formula that will revolutionize Minuni – then with a hundred men might we go forth and conquer the world!'

Elkomoelhago now turned his attention suddenly upon the green-tunicked slave standing a short distance before him. He scrutinized him closely and in silence for several minutes.

'From what city do you come?' demanded the king, at last.

'Oh, All-Glorious Elkomoelhago,' spoke up the leader of the guard, 'the poor ignorant creature is without speech.'

'Utters he any sound?' inquired the king

'None since he was captured, Master of Men,' replied the warrior.

'He is a Zertalacolol,' stated Elkomoelhago, 'Why all this silly excitement over one of these low, speechless creatures?'

'See now!' exclaimed Gofoloso, 'how quickly and surely the father of wisdom grasps all things, probing to the bottom of all mysteries, revealing their secrets. Is it not marvellous!'

'Now that the Sun of Science has shone upon him even the dullest may see that the creature is indeed a Zertalacolol,' cried another of the king's companions. 'How simple, how stupid of us all! Ah, what would become of us were it not for the glorious intelligence of the All-Wise?'

Elkomoelhago was examining Tarzan closely. He appeared not to have heard the eulogies of his courtiers. Presently he spoke again.

'He has not the features of the Zertalacolols,' he pondered, musingly. 'See his ears. They are not the ears of the speechless ones, nor his hair. His body is not formed as theirs, and his head is shaped for the storing of knowledge and the functioning of reason. No, he cannot be a Zertalacolol.'

'Marvellous!' cried Gofoloso. 'Did I not tell you! Elkomoelhago, our king, is always right.'

'The most stupid of us may easily see that he is not a Zertalacolol, now that the king's divine intelligence has made it so plain.' exclaimed the second courtier.

At this juncture a door, opposite that through which Tarzan had been brought into the apartment, opened and a warrior appeared. 'Oh, Elkomoelhago, King of Veltoptismakus,' he droned, 'thy daughter, the Princess Janzara, has come. She would see the strange slave that Zoanthrohago brought from Trohanadalmakus, and craves the royal permission to enter.' Elkomoelhago nodded his assent. 'Conduct the princess to us!' he commanded.

The princess must have been waiting within earshot immediately outside the door, for scarcely had the king spoken when she appeared upon the threshold, followed by two other young women, behind whom were a half-dozen warriors. At sight of her the courtiers arose, but not the king.

'Come in, Janzara,' he said, 'and behold the strange giant who is more discussed in Veltoptismakus than Veltoptismakus's king.'

The princess crossed the room and stood directly in front of the ape-man, who remained standing, as he had since he had entered the chamber, with his arms folded across his broad chest, an expression of absolute indifference upon his face. He glanced at the princess as she approached him and saw that she was a very beautiful young woman. Except for an occasional distant glimpse of some of the women of Trohanadalmakus she was the first

Minunian female Tarzan had seen. Her features were faultlessly chiselled, her soft, dark hair becomingly arranged beneath a gorgeous jewelled headdress, her clear skin shaming the down of the peach in its softness. She was dressed entirely in white, befitting a virgin princess in the palace of her sire; her gown, of a soft, clinging stuff, fell in straight and simple lines to her arched insteps.

Tarzan looked into her eyes. They were grey, but the shadows of her heavy lashes made them appear much darker than they were. He sought there an index to her character, for here was the young woman whom his friend, Komodoflorensal, hoped some day to espouse and make queen of Trohanadalmakus, and for this reason the ape-man was interested. He saw the beautiful brows knit into a sudden frown.

'What is the matter with the beast?' cried the princess. 'Is it made of wood?'

'It speaks no language, nor understands any,' explained her father. 'It has uttered no sound since it was captured.'

'It is a sullen, ugly brute,' said the princess. 'I'll wager to make it utter a sound, and that quickly.' With which she snatched a thin dagger from her belt and plunged it into Tarzan's arm. With such celerity had she moved that her act had taken all who witnessed it by surprise; but she had given the Lord of the Jungle an instant's warning in the few words she had spoken before she struck and these had been sufficient for him.

He could not avoid the blow, but he could and did avoid giving her the satisfaction of seeing her cruel experiment succeed, for he uttered no sound. Perhaps she would have struck again, for she was very angry now, but the king spoke sharply to her.

'Enough, Janzara,' he cried. 'We would have no harm befall this slave upon whom we are conducting an experiment that means much to the future of Veltoptismakus.'

'He has dared to stare into my eyes,' cried the princess, 'and he has refused to speak when he knew that it would give me pleasure. He should be killed!'

'He is not yours to kill,' returned the king. 'He belongs to Zoanthrohago.'

'I will buy him,' and, turning to one of her warriors, 'fetch Zoanthrohago!'

10
Gefasto

The Princess Janzara of Veltoptismakus did not purchase the slave of Zoanthrohago. Her father, the king, would not permit it, and so, very angry, she walked from the apartment where she had come to examine the captive, and when she had passed into the next room and was out of her royal sire's range of vision, she turned and made a face in his direction, at which all her warriors and the two handmaidens laughed.

'Fool!' she whispered in the direction of her unsuspecting father. 'I shall own the slave yet and kill him, too, if I mind.'

The warriors and the handmaidens nodded their heads approvingly. King Elkomoelhago arose languidly from his chair. 'Take it to the quarries.' he said, indicating Tarzan with a motion of his thumb, 'but tell the officer in charge that it is the king's wish that it be not overworked, nor injured,' and as the ape-man was led away through one doorway, the king quitted the chamber by another, his six courtiers bowing until he was gone.

Then one of them tiptoed quickly to the doorway through which Elkomoelhago had disappeared, flattened himself against the wall beside the door and listened for a moment. Apparently satisfied, he cautiously insinuated his head beyond the doorframe until he could view the chamber adjoining with one eye, then he turned back toward his fellows.

'The old half-wit has gone,' he announced, although in a whisper that could have been inaudible beyond the chamber in which it was breathed, for even in Minuni they have learned that the walls have ears, although they express it differently, saying instead: *Trust not too far the loyalty of even the stones of your chamber*.

'Saw you ever a creature endowed with such inordinate vanity!' exclaimed one.

'He believes that he is wiser than, not any man, but all men combined,' said another. 'Sometimes I feel that I can abide his arrogance no longer.'

'But you will, Gefasto,' said Gofoloso. 'To be Chief of Warriors of Veltoptismakus is too rich a berth to be lightly thrown aside.'

'When one might simultaneously throw away one's life at the same time,' added Torndali, Chief of Quarries.

'But the colossal effrontery of the man!' ejaculated another, Makahago, Chief of Buildings. 'He has had no more to do with Zoanthrohago's success than I have, and yet he claims the successes all for himself and blames the failures upon Zoanthrohago.'

'The glory of Veltoptismakus is threatened by his egotism,' cried Throwaldo, Chief of Agriculture. 'He has chosen us as his six advisers, six princes, whose knowledge of their several departments should be greater than that of any other individuals, and whose combined knowledge of the needs of Veltoptismakus and the affairs of state should form a bulwark against the egregious errors that he is constantly committing, but never will he heed our advice. To offer it he considers a usurpation of his royal prerogatives; to urge it, little short of treason. To question his judgment spells ruin.

'Of what good are we to Veltoptismakus? What must the people think of us?'

'It is well known what they think of us,' snapped Gofoloso. 'They say that we were chosen, not for what we know, but for what we do not know. Nor can you blame them. I, a breeder of diadets, master of ten thousand slaves who till the soil and raise a half of all the food that the city consumes, am chosen Chief of Chiefs, filling an office for which I have no liking and no training, while Throwaldo, who scarce knows the top of a vegetable from its roots, is Chief of Agriculture.

'Makahago worked the quarry slaves for a hundred moons and is made Chief of Buildings, while Torndali, who is acclaimed the greatest builder of our time, is Chief of Quarries. Gefasto and Vestako alone are masters of their bureaus.

'Vestako the king chose wisely as Chief of the Royal Dome, that his royal comfort and security might be assured; but in Gefasto, behold his greatest blunder! He elevated a gay young pleasure-seeker to the command of the army of Veltoptismakus and discovered in his new Chief of Warriors as great a military genius as Veltoptismakus has ever produced.'

Gefasto bowed his acknowledgment.

'Had it not been for Gefasto the Trohanadalmakusians would have trapped us fairly the other day,' continued Gofoloso.

'I advised the king against pushing the assault,' interjected Gefasto, 'as soon as it became evident that we had failed to surprise them. We should have withdrawn. It was only after we had advanced and I was free from him that I could direct the affair without interference, and then, as you saw, I quickly extricated our troops and withdrew them with as little loss of men and prestige as possible.'

'It was nobly done, Gefasto,' said Torndali. 'The troops worship you. They would like a king who led them in battle as you might lead them.'

'And let them have their wine as of old,' interjected Makahago.

'We would all rally around a king who permitted us the innocent pleasure of our wine,' said Gofoloso; 'what say you, Vestako?'

The Chief of the Royal Dome, the king's major-domo, who had remained silent throughout the arraignment of his master, shook his head.

'It is not wise to speak treason,' he said.

The three looked sharply at him and glanced quickly at one another.

'Who has spoken treason, Vestako?' demanded Gofoloso.

'You have all come too close to it for safety,' said the oily Vestako. He spoke in a much louder voice than the others had spoken, as if, far from being fearful of being overheard, he rather hoped that he would be. 'Elkomoelhago has been good to us. He has heaped honours and riches upon us. We are very powerful. He is a wise ruler. Who are we to question the wisdom of his acts?'

The others looked uneasily about. Gofoloso laughed nervously. 'You were ever slow to appreciate a joke, my good Vestako,' he said. 'Could you not see that we were hoaxing you?'

'I could not,' replied Vestako; 'but the king has a fine sense of humour. I will repeat the joke to him, and if he laughs then I shall laugh too, for I shall know that it was indeed a joke. But I wonder upon whom it will be!'

'Oh, Vestako, do not repeat what we have said – not to the king. He might not understand. We are good friends and it was said among friends.' Gofoloso was quite evidently perturbed in spirit – he spoke rapidly. 'By the way, my good Vestako, I just happened to recall that the other day you admired one of my slaves. I have intended giving him to you. If you will accept him he is yours.'

'I admire a hundred of your slaves,' said Vestako softly.

'They are yours, Vestako,' said Gofoloso. 'Come with me now and select them. It is a pleasure to make my good friend so trifling a present.'

Vestako looked steadily at the other four. They shifted uneasily in momentary silence, which was broken by Throwaldo, Chief of Agriculture. 'If Vestako would accept a hundred of my poor slaves I should be overwhelmed with delight,' he said.

'I hope they will be slaves of the white tunic,' said Vestako.

'They will,' said Throwaldo.

'I cannot be outdone in generosity,' said Torndali; 'you must accept a hundred slaves from me.'

'And from me!' cried Makahago, Chief of Buildings.

'If you will send them to my head slave at my quarters before the sun enters the Warriors' Corridor I shall be overwhelmed with gratitude,' said Vestako, rubbing his palms and smiling unctuously. Then he looked quickly and meaningly at Gefasto, Chief of Warriors of Veltoptismakus.

'Best can I show my friendship for the noble Vestako,' said Gefasto, unsmiling, 'by assuring him that I shall, if possible, prevent my warriors from slipping a dagger between his ribs. Should aught of harm befall me, however, I fear that I cannot be responsible for the acts of these men, who, I am told, love me.' For a moment longer he stood looking straight into the eyes of Vestako, then he turned upon his heel and strode from the room.

Of the six men who composed the Royal Council, Gefasto and Gofoloso were the most fearless, though even they flattered the vain and arrogant Elkomoelhago, whose despotic powers rendered him a most dangerous enemy. Custom and inherent loyalty to the royal family, in addition to that most potent of human instrumentalities – self-interest – held them to the service of their king, but so long had they been plotting against him now, and so rife was discontent throughout the city, that each now felt that he might become bolder with impunity.

Tordali, Makahago and Throwaldo, having been chosen by the king for their supposed pliability and having, unlike Gefasto and Gofoloso, justified his expectations, counted for little one way or another. Like the majority of the Veltoptismakusian nobles under the reign of Elkomoelhago they had become corrupt, and self-interest guided their every act and thought. Gefasto did not trust them, for he knew that they could be bought even while professing their virtue, and Gefasto had taken to the study of men since his success with the warriors of his city – a success that was fully as much a surprise to him as to others – and his knowledge of the mounting restlessness of the people had implanted in the fertile soil of a virile brain the idea that Veltoptismakus was ripe for a new dynasty.

Vestako he knew for a self-acknowledged and shameless bribe-taker. He did not believe that there was an honest hair in the man's head, but he had been surprised at the veiled threat of exposure he had used to mulct his fellows.

'Low indeed have fallen the fortunes of Veltoptismakus,' he said to Gofoloso as the two walked along the Warriors' Corridor after quitting the council chamber of the king.

'As exemplified by?' queried the Chief of Chiefs. 'By Vestako's infamy. He cares neither for king nor for people. For slaves or gold he would betray either and Vestako is typical of the majority of us. No longer is friendship sacred, for even from Throwaldo he exacted the toll of his silence, and Throwaldo has ever been accounted his best friend.'

'What has brought us to such a pass, Gefasto,' asked Gofoloso, thoughtfully. 'Some attribute it to one cause and some to another, and though there should be no man in Veltoptismakus better able than myself to answer my own question, I confess that I am at a loss. There are many theories, but I doubt me the right one has yet been expounded.'

'If one should ask me, Gofoloso – and you have asked me – I should say to him as I am about to say to you, that the trouble with Veltoptismakus is too much peace. The material prosperity that has followed peace has given us the means to gratify our every whim. We have become satiated with the things we looked upon in the days of yesterday as luxuries to be sparingly enjoyed upon rare occasion. Consequently we have been forced to invent new whims to be gratified, and you may rest assured that these have become more and more extravagant and exaggerated in form and idea until even our wondrous prosperity has been taxed to meet the demands of our appetites.

'Extravagance reigns supreme. It rests, like a malign incubus, upon the king and his government. To mend its inroads upon the treasury the burden of the incubus is shifted from the belly of the government to the backs of the people in the form of outrageous taxes which no man can meet honestly and have sufficient remaining wherewith to indulge his appetites, and so, by one means or another, he passes the burden on to those less fortunate or less shrewd.'

'But the heaviest taxation falls upon the rich,' Gofoloso reminded him.

'In theory, but not in fact,' replied Gefasto. 'It is true that the rich pay the bulk of the taxes into the treasury of the king, but first they collect it from the poor in higher prices and other forms of extortion, in the proportion of two *jetaks* for every one that they pay to the tax collector. The cost of collecting this tax added to the loss in revenue to the government by the abolition of wine and the cost of preventing the unscrupulous from making and selling wine illicitly would, if turned back into the coffers of the government, reduce our taxes so materially that they would fall as a burden upon none.'

'And that, you think, would solve our problems and restore happiness to Veltoptismakus?' asked Gofoloso

'No,' replied his fellow prince. 'We must have war. As we have found that there is no enduring happiness in peace or virtue, let us have a little war and a little sin. A pudding that is all of one ingredient is nauseating – it must be seasoned, it must be spiced; and before we can enjoy the eating of it to the fullest we must be forced to strive for it.'

'War and work, the two most distasteful things in the world are nevertheless, the most essential to the happiness and the existence of a people. Peace reduces the necessity for labour, and induces slothfulness. War compels labour, that her ravages may be effaced. Peace turns us into fat worms. War makes men of us.'

'War and wine, then, would restore Veltoptismakus to her former pride and happiness, you think?' laughed Gofoloso. 'What a firebrand you have become since you came to the command of all the warriors of our city!'

'You misunderstand me, Gofoloso,' said Gefasto patiently. 'War and wine will accomplish nothing but our ruin. I have no quarrel with peace or virtue or temperance. My quarrel is with the misguided theorists who think that peace alone, or virtue alone, or temperance alone will make a strong, a virile, a contented nation. They must be mixed with war and wine and sin and a great measure of hard work – especially hard work; and with nothing but peace and prosperity there is little necessity for hard work, and only the exceptional man works hard when he docs not have to.

'But come, you must hasten to deliver the hundred slaves to Vestako before the sun enters the Warriors' Corridor, or he will tell your little joke to Elkomoelhago.'

Gofoloso smiled ruefully. 'Some day he shall pay for these hundred slaves,' he said, 'and the price will be very high.'

'If his master falls,' said Gefasto.

'*When* his master falls!' Gofoloso corrected.

The Chief of Warriors shrugged his shoulders, but he smiled contentedly and he was still smiling after his friend had turned into an intersecting corridor and gone his way.

11

The Slave Girl

Tarzan of the Apes was led directly from the Royal Dome to the quarries of Veltoptismakus, which lie a quarter of a mile from the nearer of the eight domes which constitute the city. A ninth dome was in course of construction, and it was toward this that the line of burdened slaves wound from the entrance to the quarry to which the ape-man was conducted. Just below the surface, in a well-lighted chamber, he was turned over to the officer in charge of the quarry guard, to whom the king's instructions concerning him were communicated. 'Your name?' demanded the officer, opening a large book that lay upon the table at which he was seated.

'He is as dumb as the Zertalacolols,' explained the commander of the escort that had brought him to the quarry. 'Therefore he has no name.'

'We will call him "Giant," then,' said the officer, 'for such he has been known since his capture,' and he wrote in his book, Zuanthrol, with Zoanthrohago as the owner, and Trohanadalmakus as the city of his origin, and then he turned to one of the warriors lolling upon a nearby bench. 'Take him to the timbering crew in the extension of tunnel thirteen at the thirty-sixth level, and tell the Vental in charge to give him light work and see that no harm befalls him, for such are the commands of the thagosto. Go! But wait! Here is his number. Fasten it upon his shoulder.'

The warrior took the circular piece of fabric with black hieroglyphics stamped upon it and affixed it with a metal clasp to the left shoulder of Tarzan's green tunic, and then, motioning the ape-man to precede him, left the chamber.

Tarzan now found himself in a short, dark corridor which presently opened into a wider and lighter one, along which innumerable unladen slaves were moving in the same direction that his guard escorted him. He noticed that the floor of the corridor had a constant downward gradient and that it turned ever to the right, forming a great spiral leading downward into the earth. The walls and ceiling were timbered and the floor paved with flat stones, worn smooth by the millions of sandalled feet that had passed over them. At sufficiently frequent intervals candles were set in niches in the left-hand wall and, also at regular intervals, other corridors opened out of it. Over each of these openings were more of the strange hieroglyphics of Minuni. As Tarzan was to learn later these designated the levels at which the tunnels lay and led to circular corridors which surround the main spiral runway.

From these circular corridors ran the numerous horizontal tunnels leading to the workings at each level. Shafts for ventilation and emergency exits pierced these tunnels at varying distances, running from the surface to the lowest levels of the quarry.

At nearly every level a few slaves turned off into these lateral tunnels, which were well lighted, though not quite as brilliantly as the spiral. Shortly after they had commenced the descent Tarzan, accustomed from infancy to keen observation, had taken note of the number of tunnel entrances they passed, but he could only conjecture at the difference in the depths of the levels into which they opened.

A rough guess placed them at fifteen feet, but before they reached the thirty-sixth, into which they turned, Tarzan felt that there must be an error in his calculations, for he was sure that they could not be five hundred and forty feet below the earth's surface with open flames and no forced ventilation.

The horizontal corridor they now entered, after leaving the spiral, curved sharply to the right and then back to the left. Shortly afterward it crossed a wide, circular corridor, in which were both laden and unladen slaves, beyond which were two lines, those laden with rock moving back in the direction from which Tarzan had come, while others, bearing lumber, moved in the same direction that he did. With both lines there were unladen slaves.

After traversing the horizontal tunnel for a considerable distance they came at last upon the working party, and here Tarzan was turned over to the Vental, a warrior who, in the military organisation of the Minunians, commands ten men.

'So this is the giant!' exclaimed the Vental. 'And we are not to work him too hard.' His tone was sneering and disagreeable. 'Such a giant!' he cried. 'Why he is no larger than I and they are afraid to let him work into the bargain. Mark you, he will work here or get the lash. Kalfastoban permits no sluggards,' and the fellow struck his chest vauntingly.

He who brought Tarzan appeared disgusted. 'You will do well, Kalfastoban,' he said as he turned away to retrace his steps to the guardroom, 'to heed the king's commands. I should hate to be wearing your harness if aught befell this speechless slave that has set every tongue in Veltoptismakus going and made Elkomoelhago so jealous of Zoanthrohago that he could slip steel between his ribs were it not that he could then no longer steal the great wizard's applause.'

'Kalfastoban fears no king,' blustered the Vental, 'least of all the sorry specimen that befouls the throne of Veltoptismakus. He fools no one but himself. We all know that Zoanthrohago is his brain and Gefasto his sword.'

Kalfastoban Vental set the new slave to work upon the timbering of the tunnel as it was excavated from the great moraine that formed the quarry. The line of slaves coming from the surface empty handed passed down one side of the tunnel to the end, loosened each a rock, or if heavy a rock to two men, and turned back up the tunnel's opposite side, carrying their burdens to the spiral runway used by those leaving the workings, and so up and out to the new dome.

The earth, a light clay, that filled the interstices between the rocks in the moraine was tamped into the opening behind the wall timbers, the tunnel being purposely made sufficiently large to permit of this. Certain slaves were detailed for this work, others carried timbers cut to the right dimensions down to the timbering crews, of which Tarzan was one.

It was only necessary for this crew of three to scoop a narrow, shallow trench in which to place the foot of each wall board, set them in place, and slip the ceiling board on top of them. At each end of the ceiling boards was a cleat, previously attached at the surface, which kept the wall boards from falling in after being set in place. The dirt tamped behind them fastened them solidly in their places, the whole making a quickly erected and substantial shoring.

The work was light for the ape-man, although he was still weak from the effects of his wounds, and he had opportunities constantly to observe all that went on around him and to gather new information relative to the people in whose power he found himself. Kalfastoban he soon set down as a loud-mouthed braggart, from whom one need have nothing to fear during the routine of their everyday work, but who would bear watching if ever opportunity came for him to make a show of authority or physical prowess before the eyes of his superiors.

The slaves about him worked steadily, but seemed not to be overtaxed, while the guards, which accompanied them constantly in the ratio of about one warrior to every fifty slaves, gave no indications of brutality in the treatment they gave their charges.

The fact that puzzled him most now, as it had since the moment of his first return to consciousness, was the stature of these people. They were no pygmies, but men fully as large as the usual run of Europeans. There was none quite as tall as the ape-man, but there were many who missed it by only a fraction of an inch.

He knew that they were Veltoptismakusians, the same people he had seen battling with the Trohanadalmakusians; they spoke of having captured him in the battle that he had seen waged; and they called him Zuanthrol, the Giant, yet they were as large as he, and as he had passed from the Royal Dome to the quarry he had seen their gigantic dome dwellings rising fully four hundred feet above his head. It was all preposterous and impossible, yet he had the testimony of his faculties that it was true.

Contemplation of it only tended to confuse him more, and so he gave over all attempts to solve the mystery and set himself to the gathering of information concerning his captors and his prison against the time, which he well knew must some day come, when the means of escape should offer itself to the alert and cunning instincts of the wild beast that, at heart, he always considered himself.

Wherever he had been in Veltoptismakus, whoever he had heard refer to the subject, he had had it borne in upon him that the people were generally dissatisfied with their king and his government, and he knew that among a discontented people efficiency would be at low ebb and discipline demoralized to such an extent that, should he watch carefully, he must eventually discover the opportunity he sought, through the laxity of those responsible for his safe keeping.

He did not expect it today or tomorrow, but today and tomorrow were the days upon which to lay the foundation of observation that would reveal an avenue of escape.

When the long working day at last drew to a close the slaves were conducted to their quarters, which, as Tarzan discovered, were always on levels near to those in which they laboured. He, with several other slaves, was conducted to the thirty-fifth level and into a tunnel, the far end of which had been widened to the proportions of a large chamber, the narrow entrance to which had been walled up with stone except for a small aperture through which the slaves were forced to pass in and out of their chamber upon all fours, and when the last of them was within this was closed and secured by a heavy door, outside which two warriors watched throughout the night. Once inside and standing upon his feet the ape-man looked about him to discover himself within a chamber so large that it appeared easily to accommodate the great throng of slaves that must have numbered fully five thousand souls of both sexes. The women were preparing food over small fires, the smoke of which found its way from the chamber through openings in the ceiling.

For the great number of fires the amount of smoke was noticeably little, a fact which was, however, accounted for by the nature of the fuel, a clean, hard charcoal; but why the liberated gases did not asphyxiate them all was quite beyond the ape-man, as was still the riddle of the open flames and the pure air at the depth the workings lay.

The slaves were of all ages from infancy to middle age, but there were no aged or venerables among them. The skins of the women and children were the whitest Tarzan had ever seen, and he marvelled at them until he came to know that some of the former and all of the latter had never seen daylight since birth. The children who were born here would go up into the daylight sometime when they were of age that warranted beginning their training.

But the women who had been captured from other cities would remain here until death claimed them, unless that rarest of miracles occurred – they should be chosen by a Veltoptismakusian warrior as his mate; but that was scarce even a remote possibility, since the warriors almost invariably chose their mates from the slaves of the white tunic, with whom they came in daily contact in the domes above ground

The faces of the women bore the imprint of a sadness that brought a spontaneous surge of sympathy to the breast of the savage ape-man. Never in his life had he seen such abject hopelessness depicted upon any face.

As he crossed the room many were the glances that were cast upon him, for it was obvious from his deep tan that he was a newcomer, and, too, there was that about him that marked him of different clay from them, and soon there were whispers running through the throng, for the slaves who had entered with him had passed the word of his identity to the others.

Presently a young girl, kneeling above a brazier over which she was grilling a cut of flesh, caught his eye and motioned him to her. As he came he saw that she was very beautiful, with a pale, translucent skin, the whiteness of which was accentuated by the blue-black of a wealth of lustrous hair.

'You are the giant?' she asked.

'I am Zuanthrol,' he replied.

'He has told me about you,' said the girl. 'I will cook for you, too. I cook for him. Unless,' she added, with a trace of embarrassment, 'there is another you would rather have cook for you.'

'There is no one I would rather have cook for me,' Tarzan told her; 'but who are you and who is *he?*'

'I am Talaskar,' she replied, 'but I know him only by his number. He says that while he remains a slave he has no name, but will go always by his number, which is Eight Hundred Cubed, Plus Nineteen. I see that you are Eight Hundred Cubed, Plus Twenty-One.' She was looking at the hieroglyphics that had been fastened upon his shoulder. 'Have you a name?'

'They call me Zuanthrol.'

'Ah,' she said, 'you are a large man, but I should scarcely call you a giant.

He, too, is from Trohanadalmakus, and he is about your height. I never heard that there were any giants in Minuni except the people they call Zertalacolols.'

'I thought you were a Zertalacolol,' said a man's voice at Tarzan's ear.

The ape-man turned to see one of the slaves eyeing him quizzically, and smiled.

'I am a Zertalacolol to my masters,' he replied.

The other raised his brows. 'I see,' he said. 'Perhaps you are wise. I shall not be the one to betray you,' and passed on.

'What did he mean?' asked the girl.

'I have never spoken until now since they took me prisoner,' he explained, 'and they think that I am speechless, though I am sure that I do not look like a Zertalacolol, yet some of them insist that I am one.'

'I have never seen one,' said the girl.

'You are fortunate,' Tarzan told her. 'They are neither pleasant to see nor to meet.'

'But I should like to see them,' she insisted. 'I should like to see anything that was different from these slaves whom I see all day and every day.'

'Do not lose hope,' he encouraged her, 'for who knows but that it may be very soon that you will return to the surface.'

'Return,' she repeated. 'I have never been there.'

'Never been to the surface! You mean since you were captured.'

'I was born in this chamber,' she told him, 'and never have I been out of it.'

'You are a slave of the second generation and are still confined to the quarries! I do not understand it. In all Minunian cities, I have been told, slaves of the second generation are given the white tunic and comparative freedom above ground.'

'It was not for me. My mother would not permit it. She would rather I had died than mated with a Veltoptismakusian or another slave, as I must do if I go into the city above.'

'But how do you avoid it? Your masters certainly do not leave such things to the discretion of their slaves.'

'Where there are so many one or two may go unaccounted for indefinitely, and women, if they be ill-favoured, cause no comment upon the part of our masters. My birth was never reported, and so they have no record of me. My mother took a number for me from the tunic of one who died, and in this way I attract no attention upon the few occasions that our masters or the warriors enter our chamber.'

'But you are not ill-favoured – your face would surely attract attention anywhere,' Tarzan reminded her.

For just an instant she turned her back upon him, putting her hands to her face and to her hair, and then she faced him again and the ape-man saw before him a hideous and wrinkled hag, upon whose crooked features no man would look a second time.

'God!' ejaculated Tarzan.

Slowly the girl's face relaxed, assuming its normal lines of beauty, and with quick, deft touches she arranged her dishevelled hair.

'My mother taught me this,' she said, 'so that when they came and looked upon me they would not want me.'

'But would it not be better to be mated with one of them and live a life of comfort above ground than to eke out a terrible existence below ground?' he demanded. 'The warriors of Veltoptismakus are, doubtless, but little different from those of your own country.'

She shook her head. 'It cannot be, for me,' she said. 'My father is of far Mandalamakus. My mother was stolen from him only a couple of moons before I was born in this horrid chamber, far from the air and sunlight that my mother never tired of telling me about.'

'And your mother?' asked Tarzan. 'Is she here?'

The girl shook her head sadly. 'They came for her over twenty moons since and took her away. I do not know what became of her.'

'And these others, they never betray you?' he inquired.

'Never! Whatever slave betrayed another would be torn to pieces by his fellows. But come, you must be hungry,' and she offered him of the flesh she had been cooking.

Tarzan would have preferred his meat raw. but he did not wish to offend her, and so he thanked her and ate that which she offered him, squatting on his haunches across the brazier from her.

'It is strange that he does not come,' she remarked, referring to Eight Hundred Cubed, Plus Nineteen. 'Never before has he been so late.'

A brawny slave, who had approached from behind her, had halted and was looking scowlingly at Tarzan.

'Perhaps this is he,' said Tarzan to the girl, indicating the man with a gesture.

Talaskar turned quickly, an almost happy light in her eyes, but when she saw who it was that stood behind her she rose quickly and stepped back, her expression altered to one of disgust.

'No,' she said, 'it is not he.'

'You are cooking for him?' demanded the fellow, pointing at Tarzan. 'But you would not cook for me,' he accused, not waiting for a reply to his question, the answer to which was all too obvious.

'There are plenty to cook for you, Caraftap,' replied Talaskar, 'and I do not wish to. Go to some other woman. Until there are too many men we are permitted to choose those whom we shall cook for. I do not choose to cook for you.'

'If you know what is well for you you will cook for me,' growled the man. 'You will be my mate, too. I have a right to you, because I have asked you many times before these others came. Rather than let them have you I will tell the Vental tomorrow the truth about you and he will take you away. Have you ever seen Kalfastoban?'

The girl shuddered.

'I will see that Kalfastoban gets you,' continued Caraftap. 'They will not permit you to remain here when they find that you refuse to produce more slaves.'

'I should prefer Kalfastoban to you,' sneered the girl, 'but neither one nor the other shall have me.'

'Do not be too sure of that,' he cried, and stepping forward, quickly, seized her by the arm before she could elude him. Dragging her toward him the man attempted to kiss her – but he did not succeed.

Steel fingers closed upon his shoulder, he was torn roughly from his prey and hurled ruthlessly a dozen paces, stumbling and falling to the floor. Between him and the girl stood the grey-eyed stranger with the shock of black hair.

Almost roaring in his rage, Caraftap scrambled to his feet and charged Tarzan – charged as a mad bull charges, with lowered head and bloodshot eyes. 'For this you shall die,' he screamed.

12

Caraftap the Bully

The son of the First Woman strode proudly through the forest. He carried a spear, jauntily, and there was a bow and arrows slung to his back. Behind him came ten other males of his species, similarly armed, and each walked as if he owned the earth he trod. Toward them along the trail, although still beyond their sight, or hearing, or smell, came a woman of their kind. She, too, walked with fearless step. Presently her eyes narrowed and she paused, up-pricking her great, flat ears to listen; sniffing the air. Men!

She increased her gait to a trot, bearing down upon them. There was more than one – there were several. If she came upon them suddenly they would be startled, filled with confusion, and no doubt she could seize one of them before they took to flight. If not – the feathered pebbles at her girdle would seek one out.

For some time men had been scarce. Many women of her tribe who had gone out into the forest to capture mates had never returned. She had seen the corpses of several of these herself, lying in the forest. She had wondered what had killed them. But here were men at last, the first she had discovered in two moons, and this time she would not return empty handed to her cave.

At a sudden turning of the forest trail she came within sight of them, but saw, to her dismay, that they were still a long way off. They would be sure to escape if they saw her, and she was upon the point of hiding when she realized that already it was too late. One of them was pointing at her,

Loosening a missile from her girdle and grasping her cudgel more firmly she started toward them at a rapid, lumbering run. She was both surprised and pleased when she saw that they made no attempt to escape. How terrified they must be to stand thus docilely while she approached them.

But what was this? They were advancing to meet her! And now she saw the expressions upon their faces. No fear there – only rage and menace. What were the strange things they carried in their hands? One who was running toward her, the nearest, paused and hurled a long pointed stick at her. It was sharp, and when it grazed her shoulder, it brought blood. Another paused, and holding a little stick across a longer stick, the ends of which were bent back with a piece of gut, suddenly released the smaller stick, which leaped through the air and pierced the flesh beneath one of her arms.

And behind these two the others were rushing upon her with similar weapons. She recalled the corpses of women she had seen in the forest and the dearth of men for the last several moons, and although she was dull of wit yet she was not without reasoning faculties, and so she compared these facts with the occurrences of the last few seconds with a resultant judgment that sent her lumbering away, in the direction from which she had come, as fast as her hairy legs would carry her. Nor did she once pause in her mad flight until she sank exhausted at the mouth of her own cave.

The men did not pursue her. As yet they had not reached that stage in their emancipation that was to give them sufficient courage and confidence in themselves to overcome entirely their hereditary fear of women. To chase one away was sufficient.

When the other women of the tribe saw their sister-brute stagger to her cave and sensed that her condition was the result of terror and the physical strain of long flight, they seized their cudgels and ran forth, prepared to meet and vanquish her pursuers, which they immediately assumed to be a lion. But no lion appeared, and then some of them wandered to the side of the woman, who lay panting on her threshold.

'From what did you run?' they asked her in their simple sign-language.

'Men,' she replied.

Disgust showed plainly upon every face, and one of them kicked her and another spat upon her.

'There were many,' she told them, 'and they would have killed me with flying sticks. Look!' and she showed them the spear wound and the arrow still embedded in the flesh beneath the arm. 'They did not run from me, but came forward to attack me. Thus have all the women been killed whose corpses we have seen in the forest during the past few moons.'

This troubled them. They ceased to annoy the prostrate woman. Their leader, the fiercest of them, paced to and fro, making hideous faces. Suddenly she halted. 'Come!' she signalled. 'We shall go forth together and find these men, and bring them back and punish them.' She shook her cudgel above her head and grimaced horribly.

The others danced about her, imitating her expression and her actions, and when she started off toward the forest, they trooped behind her, a savage, bloodthirsty company – all but the woman who still lay panting where she had fallen. She had had enough of man – she was through with him forever.

'For this you shall die!' screamed Caraftap, as he rushed upon Tarzan of the Apes in the long gallery of the slaves' quarters in the quarry of Elkomoelhago, King of Veltoptismakus.

The ape-man stepped quickly aside, avoiding the other, and tripped him with a foot, sending him sprawling, face downward, upon the floor. Caraftap, before he rose, looked about as though in search of a weapon, and his eyes alighting upon the hot brazier he reached forth to seize it. A murmur of disapproval rose from the slaves who having been occupied nearby, had seen the inception of the quarrel.

'No weapons!' cried one. 'It is not permitted among us. Fight with your bare hands or not at all.' But Caraftap was too drunk with hate and jealousy to hear them, or to heed had he heard, and so he grasped the brazier, and, rising, rushed at Tarzan to hurl it in his face. Now it was another who tripped him, and this time two slaves leaped upon him and wrenched the brazier from his hand. 'Fight fair!' they admonished him, and dragged him to his feet.

Tarzan had stood smiling and indifferent, for the rage of the others amused him where it was greater than circumstances warranted, and now he waited for Caraftap, and when his adversary saw the smile upon his face it but increased his spleen, so that he fairly leaped upon the ape-man in his madness to destroy him. Tarzan met him with the most surprising defence that Caraftap, who for long had been a bully among the slaves, ever had encountered. It was a doubled fist at the end of a straight arm, and it caught Caraftap upon the point of the chin, stretching him upon his back. The slaves, who had by this time gathered in considerable numbers to watch the quarrel, voiced their approval in the shrill, 'Ee-ah-ee-ah,' that constituted their form of applause.

Dazed and groggy, Caraftap staggered to his feet once more and with lowered head looked about him as if in search of his enemy. The girl, Talaskar, had come to Tarzan's side and was standing there looking up into his face.

'You are very strong,' she said, but the expression on her eyes said more, or at least it appeared to Caraftap to say more. It seemed to speak of love, whereas it was only the admiration that a normal woman always feels for strength exercised in a worthy cause.

Caraftap made a noise in his throat that sounded much like the squeal of an angry pig and once again he rushed upon the ape-man. Behind them some slaves were being let into the corridor, and as the aperture was open one of the warriors beyond it, who chanced to be stooping down at the time, could see within. He saw but little, although what he saw was enough – a large slave with a shock of black hair raising another large slave high above his head and dashing him to the hard floor.

The warrior, pushing the slaves aside, scrambled through into the corridor and ran forward toward its centre. Before they were aware of his presence he stood facing Tarzan and Talaskar. It was Kalfastoban.

'What is the meaning of this?' he cried in a loud voice, and then, 'Ah, ha! I see. It is the giant. He would show the other slaves how strong he is, would he?' He glanced at Caraftap, struggling to rise from the floor, and his face grew very dark – Caraftap was a favourite of his.

'Such things are not permitted here, fellow!' he cried, shaking his fist in the ape-man's face, and forgetting in his anger that the new slave neither spoke nor understood. But presently he recollected and motioned Tarzan to follow him. 'A hundred lashes will explain to him that he must not quarrel,' he said aloud, to no one in particular, but he was looking at Talaskar.

'Do not punish him,' cried the girl, still forgetful of herself. 'It was all Caraftap's fault. Zuanthrol acted in self-defence.'

Kalfastoban could not take his eyes from the girl's face, and presently she sensed her danger, and flushed, but still she stood her ground, interceding for the ape-man. A crooked smile twisted Kalfastoban's mouth as he laid a familiar hand upon her shoulder.

'How old are you?' he asked.

She told him, shuddering.

'I shall see your master, and purchase you,' he announced. 'Take no mate.'

Tarzan was looking at Talaskar, and it seemed that he could see her wilt, as a flower wilts in noxious air, and then Kalfastoban turned upon him.

'You cannot understand me, you stupid beast,' he said: 'but I can tell you, and those around you may listen and, perhaps guide you from danger. This time I shall let you off, but let it happen again and you shall have a hundred lashes, or worse, maybe. And if I hear that you have aught to do with this girl, whom I intend to purchase and take to the surface, it will go still harder with you,' with which he strode to the entrance and passed through into the corridor beyond.

After the Vental had departed and the door of the chamber been closed a hand was laid upon Tarzan's shoulder from behind and a man's voice called him by name: 'Tarzan!' It sounded strange in his ears, far down in this buried chamber beneath the ground, in an alien city and among an alien people, not one of whom ever had heard his name; but as he turned to face the man who had greeted him a look of recognition and a smile of pleasure overpread his features.

'Kom –' he started to ejaculate, but the other placed a finger to his lips. 'Not here,' he said. 'Here I am Aoponato or Eight Hundred Cubed Plus Nineteen.'

'But your stature! You are as large as I. It is beyond me. What has happened to swell the race of Minunians to such relatively gigantic proportions?'

Komodoflorensal smiled. 'Human egotism would not permit you to attribute this change to an opposite cause from that to which you have ascribed it,' he said.

Tarzan knit his brows and gazed long and thoughtfully at his royal friend. An expression that was of mingled incredulity and amusement crept gradually over his countenance.

'You mean,' he asked slowly, 'that I – have been – reduced in size to the stature of a Minunian?'

Komodoflorensal nodded. 'Is it not easier to believe that than to think that an entire race of people and all their belongings, even their dwellings and the stones that they were built of, and all their weapons and their diadets, had been increased in size to your own stature?'

'But I tell you it is impossible!' cried the ape-man.

'I should have said the same thing a few moons ago,' replied the prince. 'Even when I heard the rumour here that they had reduced you I did not believe it, not for a long time, and I was still a bit sceptical until I entered this chamber and saw you with my own eyes.'

'How was it accomplished?' demanded Tarzan.

'The greatest mind in Veltoptismakus, and perhaps in all Minuni, is Zoanthrohago,' explained Komodoflorensal. 'We have recognized this for many moons, for, during the occasional intervals that we are at peace with Veltoptismakus, there is some exchange of ideas as well as goods between the two cities, and thus we heard of the many marvels attributed to this greatest of walmaks.'

'I have never heard a wizard spoken of in Minuni until now,' said Tarzan, for he thought that that was the meaning of the word 'walmak,' and perhaps it is, as nearly as it can be translated into English. A scientist who works miracles would be, perhaps, a truer definition.

'It was Zoanthrohago who captured you,' continued Aopanato, 'encompassing your fall by means at once scientific and miraculous. After you had fallen he caused you to lose consciousness, and while you were in that condition you were dragged hither by a score of diadets hitched to a hastily improvised litter built of small trees tied securely one to the other, after their branches had been removed.

'It was after they had you safely within Veltoptismakus that Zoanthrohago set to work upon you to reduce your stature, using apparatus that he has built himself. I have heard them discussing it, and they say that it did not take him over-long.'

'I hope that Zoanthrohago has the power to undo that which he has done,' said the ape-man.

'They say that that is doubtful. He has never been able to make a creature larger than it formerly was, although in his numerous experiments he has reduced the size of many of the lower animals. The fact of the matter is,' continued Aoponato, 'that he has been searching for a means to enlarge the Veltoptismakusians so that they may overcome all the other peoples of Minuni, but he has only succeeded in developing a method that gives precisely opposite results from that which they seek, so, if he cannot make others larger, I doubt if he can make you any larger than you are now.'

'I would be rather helpless among the enemies of my own world,' said Tarzan ruefully.

'You need not worry about that, my friend,' said the prince gently.

'Why?' asked the ape-man.

'Because your chances of reaching your own world again are virtually non-existent,' said Komodoflorensal, a trifle sadly. 'I have no hope of ever seeing Trohanadalmakus again. Only by the utter overthrow of Veltoptismakus by my father's warriors could I hope for rescue, since nothing less could overcome the guard in the quarry mouth.

'While we often capture slaves of the white tunic from the enemies' cities, it is seldom that we gather in any of the green tunic. Only in the rare cases of utter surprise attacks by daylight do any of us catch an enemy's green slaves above ground, and surprise day attacks may occur once in the lifetime of a man or never.'

'You believe that we will spend the rest of our lives in this underground hole?' demanded Tarzan.

'Unless we chance to be used for labour above ground during the daytime, occasionally,' replied Komodoflorensal.

The ape-man shrugged. 'We shall see,' he said.

After Kalfastoban had left, Caraftap had limped away to the far end of the chamber, muttering to himself, his ugly face black and scowling.

'I am afraid that he will make you trouble,' Talaskar said to Tarzan, indicating the disgruntled slave with a nod of her shapely head, 'and I am sorry for it is all my fault.'

'Your fault?' demanded Komodoflorensal.

'Yes,' said the girl. 'Caraftap was threatening me when Zuanthrol interfered and punished him.'

'And it was on account of Talaskar that you were fighting? I thank you, my friend. I am sorry that I was not here to protect her. Talaskar cooks for me. She is a good girl.'

Komodoflorensal was looking at the girl as he spoke and Tarzan saw how her eyes lowered beneath his gaze and the delicate flush that mounted her cheeks, and he realized that he was downwind from an idea, and smiled.

'So this is the Aoponato of whom you told me?' he said to Talaskar.

'Yes, this is he.'

'I am sorry that he was captured, but it is good to find a friend here,' said the ape-man. 'We three should be able to hit upon some plan of escape,' but the twain shook their heads, smiling sadly.

For a while, after they had eaten, they sat talking together, being joined occasionally by other slaves, for Tarzan had many friends here now since he had chastised Caraftap, and they would have talked all night had not the ape-man questioned Komodoflorensal as to the sleeping arrangements of the slaves.

Komodoflorensal laughed, and pointed here and there about the chamber at recumbent figures lying upon the hard, earthen floor: men, women and children sleeping, for the most part where they had eaten their evening meal.

'The green slaves are not pampered,' he remarked laconically.

'I can sleep anywhere,' said Tarzan, 'but more easily when it is dark. I shall wait until the lights are extinguished.'

'You will wait for ever, then,' Komodoflorensal told him.

'The lights are never extinguished?' demanded the ape-man.

'Were they, we should all be soon dead,' replied the prince. 'These flames serve two purposes – they dissipate the darkness and consume the foul gases that would otherwise quickly asphyxiate us. Unlike the ordinary flame, that consumes oxygen, these candles, perfected from the discoveries and inventions of an ancient Minunian scientist, consume the deadly gases and liberate oxygen.'

'It is because of this even more than for the light they give that they are used exclusively throughout Minuni. Even our domes would be dark, ill-smelling noxious places were it not for them, while the quarries would be absolutely unworkable.'

'Then I shall not wait for them to be extinguished,' said Tarzan, stretching himself at full length upon the earth floor with a nod and a 'Tuano!' a Minunian 'goodnight,' to Talaskar and Komodoflorensal.

13
In the Royal Dome

As Talaskar was preparing their breakfast the following morning Komodoflorensal remarked to Tarzan that he wished they could be employed upon the same work, that they might be always together.

'If there is ever the chance for escape that you seem to think will some day present itself,' he said, 'then it will be well if we are together.'

'When we go,' replied Tarzan, 'we must take Talaskar with us.'

Komodoflorensal cast a swift glance at the ape-man, but made no comment upon his suggestion.

'You would take me with you!' exclaimed Talaskar. 'Ah, if such a dream could be but realized! I would go with you to Trohanadalmakus and be your slave, for I know that you would not harm me. But, alas it can be nothing more than a pleasant day-dream, enduring for a brief time, for Kalfastoban has spoken for me, and doubtless my master will be glad to sell me to him, for I have heard it said among the slaves that he sells many of his each year to raise the money to pay his taxes.'

'We will do what we can, Talaskar,' said Tarzan, 'and if Aoponato and I find a means of escape we will take you with us; but first he and I must find a way to be together more.'

'I have a plan,' said Komodoflorensal, 'that might prove successful. They believe that you neither speak nor understand their language. To work a slave with whom they cannot communicate is, to say the least, annoying. I shall tell them that I can communicate with you, when it is quite probable that they will assign us to the same crew.'

'But how will you communicate with me without using the Minunian language?' demanded the ape-man.

'Leave that to me,' replied Komodoflorensal. 'Until they discover in some other way that you speak Minunian I can continue to deceive them.'

It was not long before the fruits of Komodorflorensal's plan ripened. The guards had come for the slaves and the various parties had gone forth from the sleeping chamber, joining in the outside corridors the thousands of others wending their way to the scene of their daily labour.

The ape-man joined the timbering crew at the extension of the thirteenth tunnel at the thirty-sixth level, where he once more attacked the monotonous work of shoring the sides and roof of the shaft with an enthusiasm that elicited commendation from even the surly Kalfastoban, although Caraftap, who was removing rocks just ahead of Tarzan, often shot venomous looks at the ape-man.

The work had been progressing for perhaps two or three hours when two warriors descended the tunnel and halted beside Kalfastoban. They were escorting a green-tunicked slave, to whom Tarzan paid no more attention than he did to the warriors until a scrap of their conversation reached his ears; then he shot a quick glance in the direction of the four and saw that the slave was Komodoflorensal, Prince of Trohanadalmakus, known in the quarries of Veltoptismakus as Slave Aoponato.

As Tarzan looked up Komodoflorensal caught his eye and winked, then Kalfastoban beckoned to the ape-man, who crossed the corridor and stood in silence before the Vental.

'Let us hear you talk to him,' cried Kalfastoban to Komodoflorensal. 'I don't believe that he will understand you. How could he when he cannot understand us? The fellow could not conceive of another language than his own.'

'I will ask him in his own language,' said Komodoflorensal, 'if he understands me, and you will see that he nods his head affirmatively.'

'Very good,' cried Kalfastoban; 'ask him.'

Komodoflorensal turned toward Tarzan and voiced a dozen syllables of incomprehensible gibberish and when he was done the ape-man nodded his head.

'You see?' demanded Komodoflorensal.

Kalfastoban scratched his head. 'It is even as he says,' he admitted, ruefully, 'the Zertalacolol has a language.'

Tarzan did not smile, although he should have liked to, at the clever manner in which Komodoflorensal had deceived the Veltoptismakusians into believing that he had communicated with Tarzan in a strange language. As long as he could contrive to put all his communications into questions that could be answered by yes or no, the deception would be easily maintained; but under circumstances that made this impossible some embarrassments might be expected to arise, and he wondered how the resourceful Trohanadalmakusian would handle these.

'Tell him,' said one of the warriors to Komodoflorensal, 'that his master. Zoanthrohago, has sent for him, and ask him if he fully understands that he is a slave, and that upon his good behaviour depends his comfort – yes, even his life; for Zoanthrohago has the power of life and death over him – as much so as have the royal family. If he comes docilely to his master and is obedient he will not fare ill, but if he be lazy, impudent, or threatening he may expect to taste the point of a freeman's sword.'

Komodoflorensal strung out, this time, a much longer series of senseless syllables, until he could scarce compose his features to comport with the seriousness of his mien. 'Tell them,' said Tarzan, in English, which of course, not one of them understood, 'that at the first opportunity I shall break the neck of my master; that it would require but little incentive to cause me to seize one of these timbers and crack the skull of Kalfastoban and the rest of the warriors about us; and that I shall run away at the first opportunity and take you and Talaskar with me.'

Komodoflorensal listened intently until Tarzan had ceased speaking and then turned to the two warriors who had come with him to find the ape-man.

'Zuanthrol says that he fully understands his position and that he is glad to serve the noble and illustrious Zoanthrohago, from whom he claims but a single boon,' translated the Trohanadalmakusian prince, rather freely.

'And what boon is that?' demanded one of the warriors.

'That I may be permitted to accompany him that he may thus better fulfil the wishes of his master, since without me he could not even know what was desired of him,' explained Aoponato.

Tarzan understood now how Komodoflorensal would surmount whatever difficulties of communication might arise, and he felt that he would be safe in the hands of his quick-witted friend for as long as he cared to pretend ignorance of the Minunian tongue.

'The thought was even in our minds, slave, when we heard that you could communicate with this fellow,' said the warrior to whom Komodoflorensal had addressed the suggestion. 'You shall both be taken to Zoanthrohago, who will doubtless decide his wishes without consulting you or any other slave. Come! Kalfastoban Vental, we assume responsibility for the slave Zuanthrol,' and they handed the Vental a slip of paper upon which they had marked some curious hieroglyphics.

Then, with swords drawn, they motioned Komodoflorensal and Tarzan to precede them along the corridor, for the story of Tarzan's handling of Caraftap had reached even to the guardroom of the quarry, and these warriors were taking no chances.

The way led through a straight corridor and up a winding spiral runway to the surface, where Tarzan greeted the sunlight and the fresh air almost with a sob of gratitude, for to be shut away from them for even a brief day was to the ape-man cruel punishment, indeed. Here he saw again the vast multitude of slaves bearing endlessly their heavy burdens to and fro, the trim warriors who paced haughtily upon either flank of the long lines of toiling serfs, the richly trapped nobles of the higher castes and the innumerable white-tunicked slaves who darted hither and thither upon the errands of their masters, or upon their own business or pleasure, for many of these had a certain freedom and independence that gave them almost the standing of freedom.

Always were these slaves of the white tunic owned by a master, but, especially in the case of skilled artisans, about the only allegiance they owed to this master was to pay him a certain percentage of their incomes. They constituted the bourgeoisie of Minuni and also the higher caste serving class. Unlike the green-tunicked slaves, no guard was placed over them to prevent their escape, since there was no danger that they would attempt to escape, there being no city in Minuni where their estate would be improved, for any other city than that of their birth would treat them as alien prisoners, reducing them immediately to the green tunic and lifelong hard labour. The domes of Veltoptismakus were as imposing as those of Trohanadalmakus. In fact, to Tarzan, they appeared infinitely larger since he now was one-fourth the size he had been when he left Trohanadalmakus. There were eight of them fully occupied and another in course of construction, for the surface population of Veltoptismakus was already four hundred and eighty thousand souls, and as overcrowding was not permitted in the king's dome the remaining seven were packed densely with humanity.

It was to the royal dome that Tarzan and Komodoflorensal were conducted, but they did not enter by way of the King's Corridor, before the gates of which fluttered the white and gold of the royal standards. Instead they were escorted to the Warrior's Corridor, which opens toward the west. Unlike the city of Trohanadalmakus, Veltoptismakus was beautiful in the areas between the domes with flowers and shrubbery and trees, among which wound gravelled walks and broad roadways.

The royal dome faced upon a large parade where a body of mounted warriors was at drill. There were a thousand of them, forming an amak, consisting of four ovands of two hundred and fifty men each, the larger body being commanded by a kamak and the smaller by a novand. Five entex of fifty men each compose an ovand, there being five entals of ten men each to an entex – these latter units commanded by a vental and a ventax, respectively. The evolutions of the amak were performed with kaleidoscopic rapidity, so quick upon their feet and so well trained were the tiny diadets.

There was one evolution in particular, performed while he was passing, that greatly interested the ape-man. Two ovands formed line at one end of the parade and two at the other, and at the command of the kamak the thousand men charged swiftly down the field in two solid ranks that approached each other with the speed of an express train. Just when it appeared impossible that a serious accident could be averted, when it seemed that in another instant diadets and riders must crash together in a bloody jumble of broken bones, the warriors rushing so swiftly toward the east raised their agile mounts which fairly flew above the heads of the opposing force and, alighting upon the other side in an unbroken line, continued to the far end of the field.

Tarzan was commenting on this manoeuvre and upon the beauties of the landscaping of the city of Veltoptismakus to Komodoflorensal as they proceeded along the Warrior's Corridor, sufficiently ahead of their escort that Tarzan might speak in a low tone without the guard being cognizant of the fact that he was using the language of Minuni.

'It is a beautiful evolution,' replied Komodoflorensal, 'and it was performed with a precision seldom attained. I have heard that Elkomoelhago's troops are famous for the perfection of their drill, and as justly so as is Veltoptismakus for the beauty of her walks and gardens; but, my friend, these very things constitute the weakness of the city.

'While Elkomoelhago's warriors are practising to perfect their appearance upon parade, the warriors of my father, Adendrohahkis, are far afield, out of sight of admiring women and spying slaves, practising the art of war under the rough conditions of the field and camp. The amaks of Elkomoelhago might easily defeat those of Adendrohahkis in a contest for the most beautiful; but it was not long since you saw less than fifteen thousand Trohanadalmakusians repulse fully thirty thousand warriors of Veltoptismakus, for they never passed the infantry line that day.

'Yes, they can drill beautifully upon parade and they are courageous – all Minunians are that – but they have not been trained in the sterner arts of war: it is not the way of Elkomoelhago. He is soft and effeminate. He cares not for war. He listens to the advice he likes best – the advice of the weaklings and the women who urge him to refrain from war entirely, which would be not altogether bad if he could persuade the other fellow to refrain also.

'The beautiful trees and shrubs that almost make a forest of Veltoptismakus, and which you so much admire! I, too, admire them – especially do I admire them in the city of an enemy. How easy it would be for a Trohanadalmakusian army to creep through the night, hidden by the beautiful trees and shrubs, to the very gateways of the domes of Veltoptismakus! Do you understand now, my friend, why you saw less perfect manoeuvres upon the parade grounds of my city than you have seen here, and why, although we love trees and shrubbery, we have none planted within the city of Trohanadalmakus?'

One of the guards who had approached him quickly from the rear touched Komodoflorensal upon the shoulder. 'You said the Zuanthrol does not understand our language. Why then do you speak to him in this tongue which he cannot understand?' the fellow demanded.

Komodoflorensal did not know how much the warrior had overheard. If he had heard Tarzan speak in Minuni it might be difficult to persuade the fellow that the 'giant' did not understand the language: but he must act on the assumption that he alone had been overheard.

'He wishes to learn it, and I am trying to teach him,' replied Komodoflorensal quickly.

'Has he learned anything of it?' asked the warrior.

'No,' said Komodoflorensal, 'he is very stupid.'

And after this they went in silence, winding up long, gentle inclines, or again scaling the primitive ladders that the Minunians use to reach the upper levels of their dome houses between the occasional levels that are not connected by the inclined runways, which are thus frequently broken for purposes of defence, the ladders being easily withdrawn upward behind hard-pressed defenders, and the advance of the enemy thus more easily checked.

The royal dome of Elkomoelhago was of vast proportions, its summit rising to an equivalent of more than four hundred feet, had it been built upon a scale corresponding to the relatively larger size of ordinary mankind. Tarzan ascended until he was almost as far above ground as he had been below ground in the quarry. Where the corridors on lower levels had been crowded with humanity, those which they now traversed were almost devoid of life.

Occasionally they passed a tenanted chamber, but far more generally the rooms were utilized for storage purposes, especially for food, great quantities of which, cured, dried and neatly wrapped, were packed ceiling high in many large chambers.

The decorations of the walls were less ornate and the corridors narrower, on the whole, than those at lower levels. However, they passed through many large chambers, or halls, which were gorgeously decorated, and in several of which were many people of both sexes and all ages variously occupied, either with domestic activities or with the handiwork of one art or another. Here was a man working in silver, perhaps fashioning a bracelet of delicate filigree, or another carving beautiful arabesques upon leather. There were makers of pottery, weavers of cloth, metal stampers, painters, makers of candles, and these appeared to predominate, for the candle was in truth life to these people.

And then, at last, they reached the highest level, far above the ground, where the rooms were much closer to daylight because of the diminished thickness of the walls near the summit of the dome; but even here were the ever present candles. Suddenly the walls of the corridor became gorgeously decorated, the number of candles increased, and Tarzan sensed that they were approaching the quarters of a rich or powerful noble. They halted, now, before a doorway where stood a sentinel, with whom one of the warriors conducting them communicated.

'Tell Zoanthrohago Zertol that we have brought Zuanthrol and another slave who can communicate with him in a strange tongue.' The sentinel struck a heavy gong with his lance, and presently, from the interior of the chamber a man appeared to whom the sentinel repeated the warrior's message.

'Let them enter,' said the newcomer, who was a white-tunicked slave; 'my glorious master, Zoanthrohago Zertol, expects his slave Zuanthrol. Follow me!'

They followed him through several chambers until at last he led them into the presence of a gorgeously garbed warrior, who was seated behind a large table, or desk, upon which were numerous strange instruments, large, cumbersome-looking volumes, pads of heavy Minunian writing paper, and the necessary implements for writing. The man looked up as they entered the room.

'It is your slave, Zuanthrol, Zertol,' announced the fellow who had led them hither.

'But the other?' Prince Zoanthrohago pointed at Komodoflorensal.

'He speaks the strange language that Zuanthrol speaks, and he was brought along that you might communicate with Zuanthrol if you so wished.'

Zoanthrohago nodded and turned to Komodoflorensal. 'Ask him,' he ordered, 'if he feels any differently since I reduced his size.'

When the question was put to Tarzan by Komodoflorensal in the imaginary language with which they were supposed to communicate, the ape-man shook his head, at the same time speaking a few words in English. 'He says no, illustrious prince,' translated Komodoflorensal out of his imagination, 'and he asks when you will restore him to his normal size and permit him to return to his own country, which is far from Minuni.'

'As a Minunian he should know,' replied the Zertol, 'that he never will be permitted to return to his own country – Trohanadalmakus never will see him again.'

'But he is not of Trohanadalmakus, nor is he a Minunian,' explained Komodoflorensal. 'He came to us and we did not make a slave of him, but treated him as a friend, because he is from a far country with which we have never made war.'

'What country is that?' demanded Zoanthrohago.

'That we do not know, but he says that there is a great country beyond the thorns where dwell many millions as large as was he. He says that his people would not be unfriendly to ours and for this reason we should not enslave him, but treat him as a guest.'

Zoanthrohago smiled. 'If you believe this you must be a simple fellow, Trohanadalmakusian,' he said. 'We all know that there is naught beyond Minuni but impenetrable forests of thorn to the very uttermost wall of the blue dome, within which we all dwell. I can well believe that the fellow is no Trohanadalmakusian, but he most certainly is a Minunian, since all creatures of whatever kind dwell in Minuni.

'Doubtless he is a strange form of Zertalacolol, a member of a tribe inhabiting some remote mountain fastness, which we have never previously discovered; but be that as it may, he will never—'

At this juncture the prince was interrupted by the clanging of the great gong at the outer entrance to his apartments. He paused to count the strokes, and when they reached five and ceased he turned to the warriors who had conducted Tarzan and Komodoflorensal to his presence.

'Take the slaves into that chamber,' he instructed, pointing to a doorway in the rear of the apartment in which he had received them. When the king has gone I will send for them.'

As they were crossing toward the doorway Zoanthrohago had indicated a warrior halted in the main entrance to the chamber. 'Elkomoelhago,' he announced, 'Thagosto of Veltoptismakus, Ruler of All Men, Master of Created Things, All-Wise, All-Courageous, All-Glorious! Down before the Thagosto!'

Tarzan glanced back as he was quitting the chamber to see Zoanthrohago and the others in the room kneel and lean far back with arms raised high above their heads as Elkomoelhago entered with a guard of a dozen gorgeous warriors, and he could not but compare this ruler with the simple and dignified soldier who ruled Trohanadalmakus and who went about his city without show or pomp, and oftentimes with no other escort than a single slave; a ruler to whom no man bent his knee, yet to whom was accorded the maximum of veneration and respect. And Elkomoelhago had seen the slaves and warriors leave the chamber as he had entered it. He acknowledged the salutes of Zoanthrohago and his people with a curt wave of the hand and commanded them to rise.

'Who quitted the apartment as I entered?' he demanded, looking suspiciously at Zoanthrohago.

'The slave Zuanthrol and another who interprets his strange language for me,' explained the Zertol.

'Have them back,' commanded the thagosto; 'I would speak with you concerning Zuanthrol.'

Zoanthrohago instructed one of his slaves to fetch them, and in the few moments that it required Elkomoelhago took a chair behind the desk at which his host had been sitting. When Tarzan and Komodoflorensal entered the chamber the guard who had accompanied them brought them to within a few paces of the desk behind which the king sat, and there he bade them kneel and make their obeisance to the thagosto. Familiar since childhood was every tradition of slavery to Komodoflorensal the Trohanadalmakusian. Almost in a spirit of fatalism had he accepted the conditions of this servitude that the fortunes of war had thrust him into, and so it was that, without question or hesitation, he dropped to one knee in servile salute to this alien king;

but not so Tarzan of the Apes. He was thinking of Adendrohahkis. He had bent no knee to him and he did not propose to do greater honour to Elkomoelhago. whose very courtiers and slaves despised him, than he had done to a really great king.

Elkomoelhago glared at him. 'The fellow is not kneeling,' he whispered to Zoanthrohago, who had been leaning back so far that he had not noticed the new slave's act of disrespect.

The Zertol glanced toward Tarzan. 'Down fellow!' he cried, and then recalling that he understood no Minunian, he commanded Komodoflorensal to order him to kneel, but when the Trohanadalmakusian Zertolosto pretended so to do Tarzan only shook his head. Elkomoelhago signalled the others to rise. 'We will let it pass this time,' he said, for something in the attitude of the slave told him that Zuanthrol never would kneel to him, and as he was valuable because of the experiment of which he was the subject the king preferred to swallow his pride rather than risk having the slave killed in an effort to compel him to kneel. 'He is but an ignorant Zertalacolol. See that he is properly instructed before we observe him again.'

14

The Secret Formula

The Alali women, fifty strong, sallied forth into the forest to chastise their recalcitrant males. They carried their heavy bludgeons and many feathered pebbles, but most formidable of all was their terrible rage.

Never in the memory of one of them had man dared to question their authority, never had he presumed to show aught but fear of them; and now, instead of slinking away at their approach, he dared defy them to attack them, to slay them! but such a condition was too preposterous, too unnatural, to exist, nor would it exist much longer.

Had they had speech they would have said that and a number of other things. It was looking black for the men: the women were in an ugly mood – but what else could be expected of women who were denied the power of speech?

And in this temper they came upon the men in a large clearing, where the renegades had built a fire and were cooking the flesh of a number of antelope. Never had the women seen their men so sleek and trim. Always before they had appeared skinny to the verge of cadaverousness, for in the past they had never fared so well as since the day that Tarzan of the Apes had given weapons to the son of the First Woman.

Where before they had spent their lives fleeing in terror from their terrible women, with scarcely time to hunt for decent food, now they had leisure and peace of mind, and their weapons brought them flesh that otherwise they might not have tasted once in a year. From caterpillars and grubs and worms they had graduated to an almost steady diet of antelope meat. But the women gave very little heed at the moment to the physical appearance of the men. They had found them. That was enough.

The shes were creeping nearer when one of the men looked up and discovered them, and so insistent are the demands of habit that he forgot his new-found independence and, leaping to his feet, bolted for the trees. The others, hardly waiting to know the cause of his precipitancy, followed close upon his heels. The women raced across the clearing as the men disappeared among the trees upon the opposite side. They knew what the men would do. Once in the forest they would stop behind the nearest trees and look back to see if their pursuers were coming in their direction. It was this silly habit of the males that permitted their being easily caught by the less agile females

But all the men had not disappeared. One had taken a few steps in the mad race for safety, and had then halted and wheeled about, facing the oncoming women. He was the son of the First Woman, and to him Tarzan had imparted something more than knowledge of new weapons, for from the Lord of the Jungle, whom he worshipped with doglike devotion, he had acquired the first rudiments of courage.

And so it now happened that when his more timorous fellows paused behind the trees and looked back they saw this one standing alone facing the charge of fifty infuriated shes. They saw him fit an arrow to bow, and the women saw too, but they did not understand – not immediately – and then the bowstring twanged and the foremost woman collapsed with an arrow in her heart; but the others did not pause, because the thing had been done so quickly that the full purport of it had not as yet penetrated their thick skulls.

The son of the First Woman fitted a second arrow and sped it. Another woman fell, rolling over and over, and now the others hesitated – hesitated and were lost, for that momentary pause gave courage to the other men peering from behind the trees. If one of their number could face fifty women and bring them to a halt what might not eleven men banded together accomplish? They rushed forth then with spears and arrows just as the women renewed their assault. The feathered pebbles flew thick and fast, but faster and more accurately flew the feathered arrows of the men. The leading women rushed courageously forward to close quarters, where they might use their bludgeons and lay hold of the men with their mighty hands, but they learned then that spears were more formidable weapons than bludgeons, with the result that those who did not fall wounded turned and fled.

It was then that the son of the First Woman revealed possession of a spark of generalship that decided the issue of that day, and, perhaps, for all time. His action was epochal in the existence of the Zertalacolols. Instead of being satisfied with repulsing the women, instead of resting upon laurels gloriously won, he turned the tables upon the hereditary foe and charged the women, signalling his fellows to accompany him; and when they saw the women running from them, so inspired were they by this reversal of a custom ages old, they leaped swiftly in pursuit.

They thought the son of the First Woman intended that they should slay all the enemy, and so they were surprised when they saw him overhaul a comely, young female and, seizing her by the hair, disarm her. So remarkable did it seem to them that one of their number, having a woman in his power, did not immediately slay her, they were constrained to pause and gather around him, asking questions in their strange sign-language.

'Why do you hold her?' 'Why do you not kill her?'

'I am going to keen her,' replied the son of the First Woman. 'I do not like to cook. She shall cook for me. If she refuses I shall stick her with this,' and he made a jab toward the young woman's ribs with his spear, a gesture that caused her to cower and drop fearfully upon one knee.

The men jumped up and down in excitement as the value of this plan and the evident terror of the woman for the man sank into their dull souls.

'Where are the women?' they signed to one another; but the women had disappeared.

One of the men started off in the direction they had gone. 'I go!' he signalled. 'I come back with a woman of my own, to cook for me!' In a mad rush the others followed him, leaving the son of the First Woman alone with his she. He turned upon her.

'You will cook for me?' he demanded.

To his signs she but returned a sullen, snarling visage. The son of the First Woman raised his spear and with the heavy shaft struck the girl upon the head, knocking her down, and he stood over her, himself snarling and scowling, menacing her with further punishment, while she cowered where she had fallen. He kicked her in the side.

'Get up!' he commanded.

Slowly she crawled to her knees and embracing his legs gazed up into his face with an expression of cowlike adulation and devotion.

'You will cook for me?' he demanded again.

'Forever!' she replied in the sign-language of their people.

Tarzan had remained but a short time in the little room adjoining that in which Zoanthrohago had received Elkomoelhago when he was summoned to appear before them alone, and as he entered the room his master motioned him to approach the desk behind which the two men sat. There was no other person in the room, even the warriors having been dismissed.

'You are quite positive that he understands nothing of our language?' demanded the king.

'He has not spoken a word since he was captured,' replied Zoanthrohago. 'We had supposed him some new form of Zertolacolol until it was discovered that he possessed a language through which he was able to communicate with the other Trohanadalmakusian slave. It is perfectly safe to speak freely before him, All-Wise.'

Elkomoelhago cast a quick, suspicious glance at his companion. He would have preferred that Zoanthrohago, of all men, address him as All-Glorious – it was less definite in its implication. He might deceive others, even himself, as to his wisdom, but he could not fool Zoanthrohago.

'We have never discussed fully,' said the king, 'the details of this experiment. It was for this purpose that I came to the laboratory today. Now that we have the subject here let us go into the matter fully and determine what next step we should take.'

'Yes, All-Wise,' replied Zoanthrohago.

'Call me Thagosto,' snapped Elkomoelhago.

'Yes, Thagosto,' said the prince, using the Minunian word for Chief-Royal, or King, as Elkomoelhago had commanded. 'Let us discuss the matter, by all means. It presents possibilities of great importance to your throne.'

He knew that what Elkomoelhago meant by *discussing* the matter consisted only in receiving from Zoanthrohago a detailed explanation of how he had reduced the stature of the slave Zuanthrol to one quarter its original proportions, but he proposed, if possible, to obtain value received for the information, which he knew the king would use for his own aggrandisement, giving Zoanthrohago no credit whatever for his discoveries or for all the long moons he had devoted to accomplishing this marvellous scientific miracle.

'Before we enter into this discussion, O'Thagosto,' he said, 'I beg that you will grant me one boon, which I have long desired and have hitherto hesitated to request, knowing that I did not deserve the recognition I crave for my poor talents and my mean service to thy illustrious and justly-renowned rule.'

'What boon do you wish?' demanded Elkomoelhago crustily. At heart he feared this wisest of men, and, like the coward that he was, with him to fear was to hate. If he could have destroyed Zoanthrohago he would gladly have done so; but he could not afford to do this, since from this greatest of walmaks came whatever show of scientific ability the king could make, as well as all the many notable inventions for the safeguarding of the royal person.

'I would sit at the royal council,' said Zoanthrohago, simply.

The king fidgeted. Of all the nobles of Veltoptismakus here was the very last he would wish to see numbered among the royal councillors, whom he had chosen with especial reference to the obtuseness of their minds.

'There are no vacancies,' he said, at last.

'The Ruler of all Men might easily make a vacancy,' suggested Zoanthrohago, 'or create a new post – Assistant Chief of Chiefs, for example, so that when Gofoloso was absent there would be one to take his place. Otherwise, I should not have to attend upon your council meetings, but devote my time to the perfection of our discoveries and inventions.'

Here was a way out and Elkomoelhago seized it. He had no objections to Zoanthrohago being a royal councillor and thus escaping the burdensome income tax, which the makers of the tax had been careful to see proved no burden to themselves, and he knew that probably that was the only reason that Zoanthrohago wished to be a councillor.

No, the king had no objection to the appointment provided it could be arranged that the new minister was not present at council meetings, for even Elkomoelhago would have shrunk a bit from claiming as his own all the great discoveries of Zoanthrohago had Zoanthrohago been present.

'Very well,' said the king, 'you shall be appointed this very day – and when I want you at council meetings I will send for you.'

Zoanthrohago bowed. 'And now,' he said, 'to the discussion of our experiments, which we hope will reveal a method for increasing the stature of our warriors when they go forth to battle with our enemies, and of reducing them to normal size once more when they return.'

'I hate the mention of battles,' cried the king, with a shudder.

'But we must be prepared to win them when they are forced upon us,' suggested Zoanthrohago.

'I suppose so.' assented the king; 'but once we perfect this method of ours we shall need but few warriors and the rest may be turned to peaceful and useful occupations. However, go on with the discussion.' Zoanthrohago concealed a smile and, rising, walked around the end of the table and stopped beside the ape-man.

'Here,' he said, placing a finger at the base of Tarzan's skull, 'there lies, as you know, a small, oval, reddish grey body containing a liquid which influences the growth of tissues and organs. It long ago occurred to me that interference with the normal functioning of this gland would alter the growth of the subject to which it belonged.

'I experimented with small rodents and achieved remarkable results, but the thing I wished to accomplish – the increase of man's stature – I have been unable to achieve. I have tried many methods and some day I shall discover the right one. I think I am on the right track, and that it is merely now a matter of experimentation.

'You know that stroking your face lightly with a smooth bit of stone produces a pleasurable sensation. Apply the same stone to the same face in the same manner, but with greatly increased force, and you produce a diametrically opposite sensation. Rub the stone slowly across the face and back again many times, and then repeat the same motion rapidly for the same number of times, and you will discover that the results are quite different. I am that close to a solution; I have the correct method but not quite, as yet, the correct application.

'I can reduce creatures in size, but I cannot enlarge them; and although I can reduce them with great ease I cannot determine the period or endurance of their reduction. In some cases subjects have not regained their normal size under thirty-one moons, and in others they have done so in as short a period as three moons.'

'There have been cases where normal stature was regained gradually during a period of seven suns, and others where the subject passed suddenly from a reduced size to normal size in less than a hundred heart beats; this latter phenomenon being always accompanied by fainting and unconsciousness when it occurred during waking hours.'

'Of course,' commented Elkomoelhago. 'Now, let us see. I believe the thing is simpler than you imagine. You say that to reduce the size of this subject you struck him with a rock upon the base of the skull. Therefore, to enlarge his size, the most natural and scientific thing to do would be to strike him a similar blow upon the forehead. Fetch the rock and we will prove the correctness of my theory.'

For a moment Zoanthrohago was at a loss as to how best to circumvent the stupid intention of the king without humiliating his pride and arousing his resentment, but the courtiers of Elkomoelhago were accustomed to thinking quickly in similar emergencies, and Zoanthrohago speedily found an avenue of escape from his dilemma.

'Your sagacity is the pride of your people, Thagosto,' he said, 'and your brilliant hyperbole the despair of your courtiers. In a clever figure of speech you suggest the way of achievement. By reversing the manner in which we reduced the stature of Zuanthrol we should be able to increase it; but alas! I have tried this and failed. But wait, let us repeat the experiment precisely as it was originally carried out, and then, by reversing it, we shall, perhaps, be enabled to determine why I have failed in the past.'

He stepped quickly across the room to one of a series of large cabinets that lined the wall, and opening the door of it revealed a cage in which were a number of rodents. Selecting one of these he returned to the table, where with wooden pegs and bits of cord he fastened the animal securely to a smooth board, its legs spread out and its body flattened, the under side of the lower jaw resting firmly upon a small metal plate set flush with the surface of the board. He then brought forth a small wooden box and a large metal disk, the latter mounted vertically between supports that permitted it be revolved rapidly by means of a hand crank. Mounted rigidly upon the same axis as the revolving disk was another which remained stationary. The latter disk appeared to have been constructed of seven segments, each of a different material from all the others, and from each of these segments, a pad or brush, protruded sufficiently to press lightly against the revolving disk.

To the reverse side of each of the seven segments of the stationary disk a wire was attached, and these wires Zoanthrohago now connected to seven posts projecting from the upper surface of the wooden box. A single wire attached to a post upon the side of the box had at its other extremity a small, curved metal plate attached to the inside of a leather collar. This collar Zoanthrohago adjusted about the neck of the rodent so that the metal plate came into contact with its skin at the base of the skull and as close to the hypophysis gland as possible.

He then turned his attention once more to the wooden box, upon the top of which, in addition to the seven binding posts, was a circular instrument consisting of a dial about the periphery of which were a series of hieroglyphics. From the centre of this dial projected seven tubular, concentric shafts, each of which supported a needle which was shaped or painted in some distinguishing manner, while beneath the dial seven small metal disks were set in the cover of the box so that they lay in the arc of a circle, from the centre of which a revolving metal shaft was so arranged that its free end might be moved to any one of the seven metal disks at the will of the operator.

The connexions having all been made, Zoanthrohago moved the free end of the shaft from one of the metal disks to another, keeping his eyes at all times intently upon the dial, the seven needles of which moved variously as he shifted the shaft from point to point. Elkomoelhago was an intent, if somewhat bewildered observer, and the slave Zuanthrol, unobserved, had moved nearer the table that he might better watch this experiment, which might mean so much to him.

Zoanthrohago continued to manipulate the revolving shaft, and the needles moved hither and thither from one series of hieroglyphics to another, until at last the walmak appeared satisfied.

'It is not always easy,' he said, 'to attune the instrument to the frequency of the organ upon which we are working. From all matter, and even from such incorporeal a thing as thought, there emanate identical particles, so infinitesimal as to be scarcely noted by the most delicate of my instruments. These particles constitute the basic structure of all things, whether animate or inanimate, corporeal or incorporeal. The frequency, quantity, and rhythm of the emanations determine the nature of the substance.

'Having located upon this dial the coefficient of the gland under discussion it now becomes necessary, in order so to interfere with its proper functioning that the growth of the creature involved will not be only stopped but actually reversed, that we decrease the frequency, increase the quantity, and compound the rhythm of these emanations. This I shall now proceed to do,' and he forthwith manipulated several small buttons upon one side of the box, and grasping the crank handle of the free disk revolved it rapidly. The result was instantaneous and startling. Before their eyes Elkomoelhago, the king, and Zuanthrol, the slave, saw the rodent shrink rapidly in size, while retaining its proportions unchanged. Tarzan, who had followed every move and every word of the walmak, leaned far over that he might impress indelibly upon his memory the position of the seven needles. Elkomoelhago glanced up and discovered his interest.

'We do not need this fellow now,' he said, addressing Zoanthrohago. 'Have him sent away.'

'Yes, Thagosto,' replied Zoanthrohago, summoning a warrior, whom he directed to remove Tarzan and also Komodoflorensal to a chamber where they could be secured until their presence was again required.

15

The Dungeon

Through several chambers and corridors they were conducted toward the centre of the dome on the same level as the chamber in which they had left the king and the walmak, until finally they were thrust into a small chamber and a heavy door slammed and barred behind them. There was no candle in the chamber. A faint light, however, relieved the darkness, so that the interior of the room was discernible. The chamber contained two benches and a table – that was all. The light which faintly illuminated it entered through a narrow embrasure, which was heavily barred, but it was quite evidently daylight.

'We are alone,' whispered Komodoflorensal, 'and at last we can converse; but we must be cautious,' he added. 'Trust not too far the loyalty of even the stones of your chamber.'

'Where are we?' asked Tarzan. 'You are more familiar with Minunian dwellings than I.'

'We are upon the highest level of the Royal Dome of Elkomoelhago,' replied the prince. 'With no such informality does a king visit the other domes of his city. You may rest assured that this is Elkomoelhago's. We are in one of the innermost chambers, next to the central shaft that pierces the dome from its lowest level to its roof. For this reason we do not need a candle to support life – we will obtain sufficient air through this embrasure. And now, tell me what happened within the room with Elkomoelhago and Zoanthrohago.'

'I discovered how they reduced my stature,' replied Tarzan, 'and furthermore, that at almost any time I may regain my full size – an occurrence that may eventuate from three to thirty-nine moons after the date of my reduction. Even Zoanthrohago cannot determine when this thing will happen.'

'Let us hope that it does not occur while you are in this small chamber,' exclaimed Komodoflorensal.

'I would have a devil of a time getting out,' agreed Tarzan.

'You would never get out,' his friend assured him. 'While you might before your reduction, have crawled through some of the larger corridors upon the first level, or even upon many of the lower levels, you could not squeeze into the smaller corridors of the upper levels, which are reduced in size as the necessity for direct supports for the roof increases as we approach the apex of the dome.'

'Then it behoves me to get out of here as quickly as possible,' said Tarzan. Komodoflorensal shook his head. 'Hope is a beautiful thing, my friend,' he said, 'but if you were a Minunian you would know that under such circumstances as we find ourselves it is a waste of mental energy. Look at these bars,' and he walked to the window and shook the heavy irons that spanned the embrasure. 'Think you that you could negotiate these?'

'I haven't examined them,' replied the ape-man, 'but I shall never give up hope of escaping; that your people do is doubtless the principal reason that they remain for ever in bondage. You are too much a fatalist, Komodoflorensal.'

As he spoke Tarzan crossed the room and standing at the prince's side took hold of the bars at the window. 'They do not seem over heavy,' he remarked, and at the same time exerted pressure upon them.

They bent! Tarzan was interested now, and Komodoflorensal as well. The ape-man threw ail his strength and weight into the succeeding effort, with the result that two bars, bent almost double, were torn from their setting.

Komodoflorensal gazed at him in astonishment. 'Zoanthrohago reduced your size, but left you with your former physical prowess,' he cried.

'In no other way can it be accounted for,' replied Tarzan, who now, one by one, was removing the remaining bars from the window embrasure. He straightened one of the shorter ones and handed it to Komodoflorensal. 'This will make a good weapon,' he said, 'if we are forced to fight for our liberty,' and then he straightened another for himself.

The Trohanadalmakusian gazed at him in wonder. 'And you intend,' he demanded, 'to defy a city of four hundred and eighty thousand people, armed only with a bit of iron rod?'

'And my wits,' added Tarzan.

'You will need them,' said the prince.

'And I shall use them.' Tarzan assured him.

'When shall you start?' asked Komodoflorensal, chaffingly.

'Tonight, tomorrow, next moon – who knows?' replied the ape-man. 'Conditions must be ripe. All the time I shall be watching and planning. In that sense I started to escape the instant I regained consciousness and knew that I was a prisoner.'

Komodoflorensal shook his head.

'You have no faith in me?' demanded Tarzan.

'That is precisely what I have – faith,' replied Komodoflorensal. 'My judgment tells me that you cannot succeed, and yet I shall cast my lot with you, hoping for success – yes, believing in success. If that is not faith I do not know what it might be called.' The ape-man smiled. He seldom, if ever, laughed aloud.

'Let us commence,' he said. 'First we will arrange these rods so that they will have the appearance, from the doorway, of not having been disturbed, for I take it we shall have an occasional visitor. Someone will bring us food, at least, and whoever comes must suspect nothing.'

Together they arranged the rods so that they might be quickly removed and as quickly replaced. By that time it was getting quite dark within the chamber. Shortly after they had finished with the rods their door opened and two warriors, lighting their way with candles, appeared escorting a slave who bore food in bucket-like receptacles and water in bottles of glazed pottery.

As they were going away again, after depositing the food and drink just inside the doorway, taking their candles with them, Komodoflorensal addressed them.

'We are without candles, warrior,' he said to the nearer. 'Will you not leave us one of yours?'

'You need no candle in this chamber,' replied the man. 'One night in darkness will do you good, and tomorrow you return to the quarry. Zoanthrohago is done with you.'

The two slaves heard the heavy bolt shot into place upon the opposite side of the door. It was very dark now. With difficulty they found the receptacles containing the food and water.

'Well?' inquired Komodoflorensal, dipping into one of the food jars. 'Do you think it is going to be so easy when tomorrow you will be back in the quarry, perhaps five hundred huals below ground?'

'But I shall not be,' replied Tarzan, 'and neither shall you.'

'Why not?' asked the prince.

'Because, since they expect to remove us to the quarries tomorrow, it follows that we must escape tonight,' explained Tarzan.

Komodoflorensal only laughed.

When Tarzan had eaten his fill he arose and walked to the window, where he removed the bars, and, taking the one that he had selected for himself, crawled through the passage that led to the opposite end of the embrasure, for even so close to the apex of the dome the wall was quite thick, perhaps ten huals.

The hual, which is about three inches in length by our standards, constitutes the Minunian basic unit of measurement, corresponding most closely to our foot. At this high level the embrasure was much smaller than those opening at lower levels, practically all of which were of sufficient size to permit a warrior to walk erect within them; but here Tarzan was forced to crawl about upon all fours.

At the far end he found himself looking out into a black void, above which the stars were shining and about the sides of which were dotted vague reflections of inner lights, marking the lighted chambers within the dome. Above him it was but a short distance to the apex of the dome, below was a sheer drop of four hundred huals.

Tarzan, having seen all that could be seen from the mouth of the embrasure, returned to the chamber. 'How far is it, Komodoflorensal,' he asked, 'from the floor of this embrasure to the roof of the dome?'

'Twelve huals, perhaps,' replied the Trohanadalmakusian.

Tarzan took the longest of the bars from the embrasure and measured it as best he could. 'Too far,' he said.

'What is too far?' demanded Komodoflorensal.

'The roof,' explained Tarzan.

'What difference does it make where the roof is – you did not expect to escape by way of the roof of the dome, did you?'

'Most certainly, had it been accessible,' replied the ape-man; 'but now we shall have to go by way of the shaft, which will mean crossing entirely through the dome from the interior shaft to the outer periphery. The other route would have entailed less danger of detection.'

Komodoflorensal laughed aloud. 'You seem to think to escape a Minunian city it is only necessary to walk out and away. It cannot be done. What of the sentries? What of the outer patrols? You would be discovered before you were halfway down the outside of the dome, provided that you could get that far without falling to your death.'

'Then perhaps the shaft would be safer,' said Tarzan. 'There will be less likelihood of discovery before we reach the bottom, for from what I could see it is as dark as pitch in the shaft.'

'Clamber down the inside of the shaft!' exclaimed Komodoflorensal. 'You are mad! You could not clamber from this level to the next without falling, and it must be a full four hundred huals to the bottom.'

'Wait!' Tarzan admonished him.

Komodoflorensal could hear his companion moving around in the dark chamber. He heard a scraping of metal on stone and presently a pounding, not loud, but heavy.

And Komodoflorensal waited, wondering. It was Tarzan who spoke next.

'Could you find the chamber in which Talaskar is confined in the quarry,' he asked.

'Why,' demanded the prince.

'We are going after her,' explained Tarzan. 'We promised that we would not leave without her.'

'I can find it,' said Komodoflorensal, rather sullenly, Tarzan thought.

For some time the ape-man worked on in silence, except for the muffled pounding and the scraping of iron on stone, or of iron on iron.

'Do you know everyone in Trohanadalmakus?' Tarzan asked suddenly.

'Why, no,' replied Komodoflorensal. 'There are a million souls, including all the slaves. I could not know them all.'

'Did you know by sight all those that dwelt in the royal dome?' continued the ape-man.

'No, not even those who lived in the royal dome,' replied the Trohanadalmakusian; 'though, doubtless I knew practically all of the nobles, and the warrior class by sight if not by name.'

'Did anyone?' asked Tarzan.

'I doubt it,' was. the reply.

'Good,' exclaimed Tarzan.

Again there was a silence, broken again by the Englishman.

'Can a warrior go anywhere without question in any dome of his own city?' he inquired.

'Anywhere, under ordinary circumstances, except into the king's dome, in the daytime.'

'One could not go about at night then?' asked Tarzan.

'No,' replied his companion.

'By day, might a warrior go and come in the quarries as he pleased?'

'If he appeared to be employed upon some message or other duty he would not be questioned, ordinarily.' Tarzan worked a little longer in silence. 'Come!' he said presently; 'we are ready to go.'

'I shall go with you,' said Komodoflorensal, 'because I like you and because I think it would be better to be dead than a slave. At least we shall have some pleasure out of what remains to us of life, even though it be not a long life.'

'I think we shall have some pleasure, my friend,' replied Zuanthrol. 'We may not escape; but, like you, I should rather die now than remain a slave for life. I have chosen to-night for our first step toward freedom, because I realize that once returned to the quarry our chances for a successful break for liberty will be reduced to almost nothing, and to-night is our only night above ground.'

'How do you propose that we escape from this chamber?'

'By way of the central shaft,' replied Tarzan; 'but first tell me, may a white-tunicked slave enter the quarries freely by day?'

Komodoflorensal wondered what bearing all these seemingly immaterial questions had upon the problem of their escape; but he answered patiently.

'No, white tunics are never seen in the quarries.'

'Have you the iron bar I straightened for you?'

'Yes.'

'Then follow me through the embrasure. Bring the other rods that I shall leave in the opening. I will carry the bulk of them. Come!'

Komodoflorensal heard Tarzan crawling into the embrasure, the iron rod that he carried breaking the silence of the little chamber. Then he followed. In the mouth of the embrasure he found the rods that Tarzan had left for him to carry. There were four rods, the ends of each bent into hooks. It had been upon this work that Tarzan had been engaged in the darkness – Komodoflorensal wondered to what purpose. Presently his further movement was halted by Tarzan's body.

'Just a moment,' said the ape-man. 'I am making a hole in the window-ledge. When that is done we shall be ready.' A moment later he turned his head back towards his companion. 'Pass along the rods,' he said.

After Komodoflorensal had handed the hooked rods to Tarzan he heard the latter working with them, very quietly, for several minutes, and then he heard him move his body about in the narrow confines of the embrasure, and presently when the ape-man spoke again the Trohanadalmakusian realised that he had turned around and that his head was close to that of his companion.

'I shall go first, Komodoflorensal,' he said. 'Come to the edge of the embrasure and when you hear me whistle once, follow me.'

'Where?' asked the prince.

'Down the shaft to the first embrasure that will give us foothold, and let us pray that there is no one directly below this within the next eighteen huals. I have hooked the rods together, the upper end hooked into the hole I made in the ledge, the lower end dangling down a distance of eighteen huals.'

'Goodbye, my friend,' said Komodoflorensal.

Tarzan smiled and slipped over the edge of the embrasure. In one hand he carried the rod that he had retained as a weapon, with the other he clung to the window ledge. Below him for eighteen huals dangled the slender ladder of iron hooks, and below this four hundred huals of pitchy darkness hid the stone flagging of the inner courtyard.

Perhaps it roofed the great central throne-room of the king, as was true in the royal dome of Adendrohahkis; perhaps it was but an open court. The truth was immaterial if the frail support slipped from the shallow hole in the ledge above, or if one of the hooks straightened under his weight.

Now he grasped the upper section of his ladder with the hand that held his improvised weapon, removed the hand from the ledge, and grasped the rod again, still lower down.

In this way he lowered his body a few inches at a time. He moved very slowly for two reasons, the more important of which was that he feared that any sudden strain upon his series of hooks might straighten one of them and precipitate him into the abyss below; the other was the necessity for silence.

It was very dark even thus close to the summit of the dome, but that was rather an advantage than otherwise, for it hid his presence from any chance observer who might glance through one of the embrasures in the opposite wall of the shaft.

As he descended he felt in both directions for an embrasure, but he was almost at the end of his ladder before he felt himself swing slightly into one. When he had lowered himself still further and could look into the opening he saw that it was dark, an indication that it did not lead into an inhabitated chamber, a fact for which he was thankful. He hoped, too, that the inner end of the embrasure was not barred, nor the door beyond bolted upon the outside.

He whistled once, very low, for Komodoflorensal, and an instant later he felt the movement on the iron ladder that told him his companion had commenced the descent. The embrasure in which he stood was higher than the one they had just quitted, permitting him to stand erect. There he waited for the Trohanadalmakusian, who was soon standing upon the ledge beside him.

'Whew!' exclaimed the prince in a whisper. 'I should hate to have had to do that in the daytime when I could have seen all the way to the bottom. What next? We have come further already than ever I dreamed would be possible. Now I am commencing to believe that escape may lay within the realm of possibilities.'

'We haven't started yet,' Tarzan assured him; 'but we are going to now. Come!'

Grasping their rude weapons the two walked stealthily the length of the embrasure. There were no bars to impede their progress and they stepped to the floor of the chamber beyond. Very carefully, feeling each step before he planted a foot and with his weapon extended before him, Tarzan groped his way about the chamber, which he found was fairly well filled with casks and bottles, the latter in wooden and wicker cases. Komodoflorensal was directly behind him.

'We are in one of the rooms where the nobles charged with enforcing the laws against wine have hidden confiscated liquor,' whispered the Trohanadalmakusian. 'I have heard much talk concerning the matter since I was made prisoner – the warriors and the slaves, too, seem to talk of nothing else but this and the high taxes. The chances are that the door is heavily barred – they guard these forbidden beverages as never they guarded their gold or jewels.'

'I have found the passageway leading to the door,' whispered Tarzan, 'and I can see a light beneath it.'

They crept stealthily the length of the passage. Each grasped his weapon more firmly as Tarzan gently tried the latch. It gave! Slowly the ape-man pushed the door ajar. Through the tiny aperture thus opened he could see a portion of the room. Its floor was strewn with gorgeous carpets, thick and soft. That portion of the wall that was revealed to him was hung with heavy fabrics woven in many colours and strange patterns – splendid, barbaric. Directly in the line of his vision the body of a man lay sprawled, face down, upon the floor – a pool of red stained a white rug beneath his head.

Tarzan opened the door a little further, revealing the bodies of three other men. Two lay upon the floor, the third upon a low divan. The scene, gorgeous in its colourings, tragic in its suggestion of mystery and violent death, held the eyes of the ape-man yet a moment longer before he opened the door still wider and leaped quickly to the centre of the room, his weapon raised and ready.

A quick glance about the apartment showed the bodies of six men that had not been visible from the partly opened door. These were lying in a pile in one corner of the room.

16

The Masqueraders

Komodoflorensal stood at Tarzan's side, his weapon ready to take issue with any who might question their presence here; but presently the end of his iron rod dropped to the floor and a broad smile overspread his features.

Tarzan looked at him. 'Who are they?' he demanded, 'and why have they been killed?'

'They are not dead, my friend,' replied Komodoflorensal. 'They are the nobles whose duty it is to prevent the use of wine. They are not dead – they are drunk.'

'But the blood beneath the head of this one at my feet!' demanded the ape-man.

'It is red wine, not blood,' his companion assured him. Then Tarzan smiled.

'They could not have chosen a better night for their orgy,' he said. 'Had they remained sober the door through which we entered from the store room would have been securely fastened, I imagine.'

'Assuredly, and we would have had a sober guard of warriors to deal with in this chamber, instead of ten drunken nobles. We are very fortunate, Zuanthrol.'

He had scarcely ceased speaking when a door in the opposite side of the room swung open, revealing two warriors, who stepped immediately into the chamber. They eyed the two who faced them and then glanced about the room at the inert forms of its other occupants.

'What do you here, slaves?' demanded one of the newcomers. 'Sh-sh!' cautioned Tarzan, placing a finger to his lips. 'Enter and close the door, lest others hear.'

'There is no one near to hear,' snapped one of them, but they entered and he closed the door. 'What is the meaning of this?'

'That you are our prisoners,' cried the ape-man, leaping past them and placing himself before the door, his iron rod in readiness.

A sneer twisted the mouths of the two Veltoptismakusians as they whipped out their rapiers and leaped toward the ape-man, ignoring for the moment the Trohanadalmakusian, who, seizing upon the opportunity thus afforded him, threw aside his iron rod and snatched a rapier from the side of one of the drunken nobles – a substitution of weapons that would render Komodoflorensal a dangerous opponent anywhere in Minuni, for there was no better swordsman among all the warlike clans of Trohanadalmakus. Facing, with only an iron rod, two skilled swordsmen placed Tarzan of the Apes at a disadvantage that might have proved his undoing had it not been for the presence of Komodoflorensal, who, no sooner than he had appropriated a weapon, leaped forward and engaged one of the warriors. The other pressed Tarzan fiercely.

'Your prisoner, eh, slave?' he sneered as he lunged for his opponent; but though less skilled, perhaps, in sword play than his antagonist, the Lord of the Jungle had not faced Bolgani and Numa for nothing. His movements were as lightning, his strength as great as before Zoanthrohago had reduced his stature.

At the first onslaught of the warriors he had leaped to one side to avoid the thrust of a blade, and as much to his own astonishment as to theirs, what he had intended but for a nimble sidestep had carried him the length of the room, and then the man had been at him again, while the other was having his time well occupied with the Zertolosto of Trohanadalmakus.

Twice Tarzan parried cuts with his cumbersome bar, and then a thrust but missed him by a hair's breadth, his sidestep coming only in the nick of time. It was a close call, for the man had lunged at his abdomen – a close call for Tarzan and death for his opponent, for as the point slipped harmlessly by him the ape-man swung his rod upon the unguarded head of the Veltoptismakusian, and with a grunt the fellow slumped to the floor, his skull crushed.

Then Tarzan turned to aid Komodoflorensal, but the son of Adendrohahkis needed no aid. He had his man against the wall and was running him through the heart as Tarzan turned in their direction. As he fell, Komodoflorensal swung toward the centre of the room, and as his eye fell upon the ape-man a smile crossed his face.

'With an iron bar you bested a swordsman of Minuni!' he cried. 'I would not have believed it possible, and so I hastened to dispatch my man that I might come to your rescue before it was too late.'

Tarzan laughed. 'I had the same thought in mind concerning you,' he said.

'And you could have well held it had I not been able to secure this rapier,' Komodoflorensal assured him. 'But what now? We have again come much further than it seems possible we can have. Naught will surprise me hereafter.'

'We are going to trade apparel with these two unfortunate gentlemen,' said Tarzan, divesting himself of the green tunic as he spoke.

Komodoflorensal chuckled as he followed the example of his companion. 'There are other peoples as great as the Minunians,' he declared, 'though until I met you, my friend, I should never have believed it.'

A few moments later the two stood garbed in the habiliments of Veltoptismakusian warriors and Tarzan was slipping his green tunic upon the corpse of him whom he had slain.

'But why are you doing that?' asked the prince.

'Do likewise with yours and you will see presently,' Tarzan replied. Komodoflorensal did as the other bid him, and when the change had been completed the ape-man threw one of the corpses across his shoulder and carried it into the storeroom, followed closely by Komodoflorensal with the other. Walking through the window embrasure to the edge of the shaft Tarzan hurled his burden out into space, and reaching back took Komodoflorensal's from him and pitched it after the first.

'If they do not examine them too closely,' he said, 'the ruse may serve to convince them that we died attempting to escape.' As he spoke he detached two of the hooks from the ladder down which they had clambered from the window of their dungeon and dropped them after the corpses. 'These will lend colour to the suggestion,' he added in explanation.

Together they returned to the room where the drunken nobles lay, where Komodoflorensal began to rifle the fat money pouches of the unconscious men. 'We shall need all of this that we can get if we are to pose as Veltoptismakusian warriors for any length of time,' he said. 'I know these people by reputation and that gold will buy many of the things that we may require – the blindness of guards and the complaisance of officials, if they do not guess too close to the truth concerning us.'

'That part of it you must attend to, Komodoflorensal,' said Tarzan, 'for I am unfamiliar with the ways of your people; but we may not remain here. These gentlemen have served us well, and themselves, too, for their faithlessness and debauchery saved their lives, while the two who followed in sobriety the path of duty were destroyed.'

'Matters are strangely ordered,' commented Komodoflorensal.

'In Minuni as elsewhere,' agreed Tarzan, leading the way to the door of the chamber, which they found opened into a corridor instead of into another chamber, as they had rather expected would be the fact at a point thus close to the central shaft. In silence they proceeded along the passageway, which at this hour of the morning was deserted. They passed lighted chambers where men and women were sleeping peacefully in the glare of many candles. They saw a sentry asleep before the door of a noble's quarters.

No one discovered them, and thus they passed down a series of inclined runways and along interminable corridors until they were far from that portion of the royal dome in which they had been incarcerated and where it would be most natural for the search for them to commence in the event that the bodies they had hurled into the shaft were not immediately discovered, or were identified for what they really were rather than for what the two fugitives had tried to make them appear.

And now a white-tunicked slave was approaching them along the corridor. He passed without paying any heed, and presently another and another appeared, until the two realized that morning was approaching and the corridors would soon be filled with the inhabitants of the dome.

'It will be best,' said Komodoflorensal, 'to find a hiding place until there are more people abroad. We shall be safer in a crowd than among just a few, where we shall be the more noticeable.'

Nearly all the chambers they passed now were occupied by families, while those that were untenanted were without candles, and therefore unsafe as hiding places for any length of time; but presently Komodoflorensal touched Tarzan's arm and pointed to a hieroglyphic beside a door they were approaching.

'Just the place,' he said.

'What is it?' asked Tarzan, and, as they came opposite the open door. 'Why it is filled with men. When they awake we shall be discovered.'

'But not recognized,' returned the Trohanadalmakusian; 'or at least the chances are slight that we shall be. This is a common chamber where any man may purchase lodgings overnight. Doubtless, there are visitors from other domes, and strangers will not be particularly remarked on this account.'

He entered the room, followed by Tarzan. A white-tunicked slave approached them. 'Candles for two,' demanded Komodoflorensal, handing the slave one of the smaller golden coins he had filched from the sleeping nobles.

The fellow led them to a far corner of the room where there was plenty of space upon the floor, lit two candles, and left them. A moment later they were stretched at full length, their faces toward the wall as a further protection against recognition, and were soon asleep.

When Tarzan awoke he saw that he and Komodoflorensal were the only remaining occupants of the chamber, other than the slave who had admitted them, and he awoke his companion, believing that they should do nothing that might even in a slight degree call more than ordinary attention to them. A bucket of water was brought them, and they performed their ablutions at a gutter which encircled the chamber, passing along the foot of each wall, as is the custom throughout Minuni, the waste water being carried away in pipes to the fields beyond the cities, where it was used for irrigating the crops.

As all the water has to be carried into the domes and to the different levels in buckets, the amount used for ablutions is reduced to the minimum, the warrior and noble class getting the bulk of it, while the white-tunicked slaves depend principally upon the rivers, near which domes are always erected, for their baths.

The green slaves fare the worst, and suffer a real hardship through lack of bathing facilities, for the Minunians are a cleanly people; but they managed to alleviate their plight to some extent, where the quarry masters are more kindly disposed, by the use of stagnant, seepage water that accumulates in every quarry at the lower levels, and which, not being fit for drinking purposes, may be used by the slaves for bathing when they are permitted the time to obtain it.

Having washed, Tarzan and Komodoflorensal passed out into the corridor, a broad thoroughfare of the dome city, where there were now passing two solid lines of humanity moving in opposite directions, the very numbers of the people proving the fugitives' greatest safeguard against detection. Candles at frequent intervals diffused a brilliant light and purified the air. Open doorways revealed shops of various descriptions, within which men and women were bartering for goods, and now Tarzan had his first real glimpse of Veltoptismakusian life. All the shops were conducted by white-tunicked slaves, but slaves and warriors intermingled as customers, both sexes of each class being represented.

It was Tarzan's first opportunity, also, to see the women of the warriors' class outside their own homes. He had seen the Princess Janzara in the palace quarters and, through the doorways in various portions of the dome, he had seen other women of varying stations in life, but they were the first that he had seen abroad at close hand.

Their faces were painted deep vermilion, their ears blue, and their apparel so arranged that the left leg and left arm were bare, although if even so much as the right ankle or wrist became uncovered they hastily readjusted their garments to hide them, giving every evidence of confusion and embarrassment. As the ape-man watched them he was reminded of fat dowagers he had seen at home whose evening gowns had left them naked of back to their kidneys, yet who would rather have died than expose a knee. The fronts of the shops were covered with brilliant paintings, usually depicting the tools that were on sale, together with hieroglyphics describing the wares and advertising the name of the proprietor. One of these finally held the attention of the Trohanadalmakusian, and he touched Tarzan's arm and pointed toward it.

'A place where food is served,' he said. 'Let us eat.'

'Nothing would suit me better. I am famished,' Tarzan assured him, and so the two entered the little shop, where several customers were already sitting upon the floor with small benches pulled close to them, upon which food was being served in wooden dishes. Komodoflorensal found a space near the rear of the shop, not far from a doorway leading into another chamber, which was also a shop of a different character, not all the places of business being fortunately located upon a corridor, but having their entrances, like this one, through another place of business.

Having seated themselves and dragged a bench before them they looked about while waiting to be served. It was evidently a poor shop, Komodoflorensal told Tarzan, catering to the slave caste and the poorer warriors, of which there were several sitting at benches in different parts of the room. By their harness and apparel, which was worn and shabby, one might easily guess at their poverty. In the adjoining shop were several more of the same class of unfortunate warriors mending their own clothes with materials purchased from the poor shopkeeper.

The meal was served by a slave in a white tunic of very cheap material, who was much surprised when payment for the meal and the service was offered in gold. 'It is seldom,' he said, 'that warriors rich enough to possess gold come to our poor shop. Pieces of iron and bits of lead, with much wooden money, pass into my coffers, but rarely do I see gold. Once I did, and many of my customers were formerly the richest of the city.

'Yonder, see that tall man with the heavily wrinkled face. Once he was rich – the richest warrior in his dome. Look at him now! And see them in that next room performing menial services, men who once owned slaves so prosperous that they, in turn, hired other slaves to do the meaner duties for them. Victims, all of them, of the tax that Elkomoelhago has placed upon industry.

'To be poor,' he continued, 'assures one an easier life than being rich, for the poor have no tax to pay, while those who work hard and accumulate property have only their labour for their effort, since the government takes all from them in taxes.'

'Over there is a man who was very rich. He worked hard all his life and accumulated a vast fortune. For several years after Elkomoelhago's new tax law was enforced he struggled to earn enough to ensure that his income would be at least equal to his taxes and the cost of his living; but he found that it was impossible.

'He had *one* enemy, a man who had wronged him grievously. This man was very poor, and to him he gave all of what remained of his great fortune and his property. It was a terrible revenge. From being a contended man, this victim of another's spleen is now a haggard wreck, labouring unceasingly eighteen hours each day in a futile attempt to ensure himself an income that will defray his taxes.'

Having finished their meal the two fugitives returned to the corridor and continued their way downward through the dome toward the first level, keeping always to the more crowded corridors, where detection seemed least likely. Now mounted men were more frequently encountered, and so rapidly and recklessly did the warriors ride along the narrow corridors that it was with difficulty that the pedestrians avoided being ridden down and trampled, and it appeared to Tarzan but little less than a miracle that any of them arrived at their destinations uninjured.

Having at last come to the lowest level, they were engaged in searching for one of the four corridors that would lead them from the dome, when their way was completely blocked by a great throng that had congregated at the intersection of two corridors. Those in the rear were stretching their necks to observe what was going on in the centre of the gathering. Every one was asking questions of his neighbour, but as yet no one upon the outskirts of the mob appeared to know what had occurred until at last fragments of rumours filtered to the furthermost. Tarzan and Komodoflorensal dared ask no questions, but they kept their ears open, and presently they were rewarded by overhearing repeated what seemed to be an authoritative account of what had occurred to cause this congestion. In answer to a question put by one of the throng, a fellow who was elbowing his way out from the centre of the jam explained that those in front of him had halted to view the remains of two slaves who had been killed while trying to escape.

'They were locked in one of Zoanthrohago's slave cells at the very highest level,' he told his questioner, 'and they tried to escape by climbing down an improvised ladder into the central shaft. Their ladder broke and they were precipitated to the roof of the throne room, where their bodies, terribly mangled, were but just found. They are being carried out to the beasts now. One of them was a great loss to Zoanthrohago as it was the slave Zuanthrol, upon whom he was experimenting.'

'Ah,' exclaimed a listener, 'I saw them but yesterday!'

'You would not know them today,' vouchsafed the informer, 'so terribly are their faces disfigured.'

When the press of humanity had been relieved Tarzan and Komodoflorensal continued their way, finding that the Slaves' Corridor lay just before them, and that it was down this avenue that the bodies of their victims of the previous night were being carried.

'What,' asked the ape-man, 'did he mean by saying that they were being carried to the beasts?'

'It is the way in which we dispose of the bodies of slaves,' replied the Trohanadalmakusian. 'They are carried to the edge of the jungle, where they are devoured by wild beasts. There are old and toothless lions near Trohanadalmakus that subsist entirely upon slave meat. They are our scavengers and so accustomed are they to being fed that they often come to meet the parties who bring out the corpses, pacing beside them, roaring and growling, until the spot is reached where the bodies are to be deposited.'

'You dispose of all your dead in this manner?'

'Only the slave dead. The bodies of warriors and nobles are burned.'

'In a short time then,' continued Tarzan, 'there will be no danger of there ever being a correct identification of those two.' He jerked his thumb toward the corridor ahead, where the bodies of the two dead warriors were being jounced and jolted along upon the backs of diadets.

17
Betrayed

'Where now?' demanded Komodoflorensal, as the two emerged from the mouth of the Slaves' Corridor and stood for a moment in the brilliant sunlight without.

'Lead the way to the quarry where we were confined and to the chamber in which we slept.'

'You must be weary of your brief liberty,' remarked the Trohanadalmakusian.

'We are returning for Talaskar, as I promised,' Tarzan reminded him.

'I know,' said the Zertolosto, 'and I commend your loyalty and valour, while deprecating your judgment. It will be impossible to rescue Talaskar. Were it otherwise I should be the first to her assistance, but I know, and she knows, that for her escape is beyond hope. We will but succeed in throwing ourselves again into the hands of our masters.'

'Let us hope not,' said Tarzan; 'but, if you feel as you say, that our effort is foredoomed to failure, and that we shall but be recaptured, do not accompany me. My only real need of you is to guide me to the apartment where Talaskar is confined. If you can direct me to it, that is all I ask.'

'Think you I was attempting to evade the danger?' demanded Komodoflorensal. 'No! Where you go, I will go. If you are captured, I shall be captured.'

'Good,' commented Tarzan. 'Now lead the way to the quarry and use your knowledge of things Minunian and your best wits to gain us entrance.'

They passed, unchallenged, along the shaded walks between the domes of Veltoptismakus and past the great parade where gorgeously caparisoned warriors were executing intricate evolutions with the nicest precision, and out beyond the domes along well-worn trails filled with toiling slaves and their haughty guards. Here they fell in beside the long column moving in the direction of the quarry in which they had been imprisoned, taking their places in the column of flanking guards, and thus they came to the entrance of the quarry. Perfunctorily the numbers of the slaves were taken, as they passed in, and entered in a great book, but to Tarzan's relief he noted that no attention was paid to the guards, who moved along beside their charges and down into the interior without being checked or even counted, and with them went Komodoflorensal, Prince Royal of Trohanadalmakus, and Tarzan of the Apes.

Once inside the quarry and past the guardroom, the two fell gradually to the rear of the column and so that when it turned into a level above that which they wished to reach they were enabled to detach themselves from it without being noticed. To leave one column was but to join another, for there was no break in them, and often there were several moving abreast, but when they reached the thirty-fifth level and entered the tunnel leading to the chamber in which Talaskar was confined they found themselves alone, since there is little or no activity in these corridors leading to slave quarters except early in the morning when the men are led forth to their labours and again at night when they are brought back. Before the door of the chamber they found a single warrior on guard. He was squatting on the floor of the tunnel leaning against the wall, but at their approach he rose and challenged them.

Komodoflorensal, who was in the lead, approached him and halted. 'We have come for the slave girl, Talaskar,' he said.

Tarzan, who was just behind Komodoflorensal, saw a sudden light leap to the eyes of the warrior. Was it recognition?

'Who sent you?' demanded the warrior.

'Her master, Zoanthrohago,' replied the Trohanadalmakusian.

The expression upon the face of the warrior changed to one of cunning.

'Go in and fetch her,' he said, and unbolted the door, swinging it open.

Komodoflorensal dropped upon his hands and knees and crawled through the low aperture, but Tarzan stood where he was.

'Go in,' said the guard to him.

'I will remain where I am,' replied the ape-man. 'It will not require two of us to find a single slave and fetch her to the corridor.'

For an instant the warrior hesitated, then he closed the door hurriedly and shot the heavy bolts. When he turned toward Tarzan again, who was now alone with him in the corridor, he turned with a naked sword in his hand; but he found Zuanthrol facing him with a drawn rapier.

'Surrender!' cried the warrior. 'I recognised you both instantly.'

'I thought as much,' said Zuanthrol. 'You are clever, with the exception of your eyes – they are fools, for they betrayed you.'

'But my sword is no fool,' snapped the fellow as he thrust viciously at the ape-man's breast.

Now, Lieutenant Paul D'Arnot, of the French navy, had been recognized as one of the cleverest swordsmen in the service, and to his friend, Lord Greystoke, he had imparted a great measure of his skill during many hours that the two had whiled away with the foils, and today Tarzan of the Apes breathed a prayer of gratitude to the far-distant friend whose careful training was, after many long years, to serve the ape-man in such good stead, for he soon realized that, although his antagonist was a master of the art of fence, he was not wholly out-classed, and to his skill was added his great strength and his agility. They had fought for only a minute or two when the

Veltoptismakusian realized that he was facing no mean antagonist and that he was labouring at a disadvantage in being unable to fall back when Tarzan rushed him, while his foeman had at his back the whole length of the tunnel. He tried then to force Tarzan back, but in this he failed, receiving a thrust in the shoulder for his pains, and then he commenced to call for help, and the ape-man realized that he must silence him and that quickly.

Awaiting the opportunity that was presently afforded by a feint that evoked a wild lunge, Tarzan stepped quickly in and passed his sword through the heart of the Veltoptismakusian, and as he withdrew his blade from the body of his antagonist he released the bolts that held the door and swung it open. Beyond it, white of face, crouched Komodoflorensal, but as his eyes fell upon Tarzan and the body of the guard behind him, a smile curved his lips, and an instant later he was in the corridor beside his friend.

'How did it happen?' he demanded.

'He recognized us; but what of Talaskar? Is she not coming?'

'She is not here, Kalfastoban took her away today. He has purchased her from Zoanthrohago.'

Tarzan wheeled. 'Rebolt the door and let us get out of here,' he said.

Komodoflorensal closed and fastened the door. 'Where now?' he asked.

'To find Kalfastoban's quarters,' replied the ape-man.

Komodoflorensal shrugged his shoulders and followed on behind his friend. They retraced their steps toward the surface without incident until they were opposite the sixteenth level, when a face was suddenly turned toward them from a column of slaves crossing the runway from one lateral to another. Just for an instant did the eyes of the slave meet those of Tarzan, and then the fellow had passed into the mouth of the lateral and disappeared.

'We must hurry,' whispered Tarzan to his companion.

'Why now more than before?' demanded Komodoflorensal.

'Did you not see the fellow who just passed us and turned to look a second time at me?'

'No. Who was it?'

'Caraftap,' replied Tarzan.

'Did he recognize you?'

'As to that I cannot say, but he evidently found something familiar in my appearance. Let us hope that he did not place me, though I fear that he did.'

'Then we must lose no time in getting out of here, and out of Veltoptismakus as well.'

They hurried on. 'Where are Kalfastoban's quarters?' asked Tarzan.

'I do not know. In Trohanadalmakus, warriors are detailed to the quarries for but short periods and do not transfer their quarters or their slaves during the time that they are there. I do not know the custom here. Kalfastoban may have finished his tour of duty in the quarries. On the other hand it may be for a long period that they are detailed for that service, and his quarters may lie on the upper level of the quarry. We shall have to inquire.'

Soon after this Tarzan stepped up to a warrior moving in the same direction as he and Komodoflorensal. 'Where can I find Kalfastoban Vental?' he asked.

'They will tell you in the guardroom if it is any of your affair,' he replied, shooting a quick glance at the two. 'I do not know.'

After that they passed the fellow, and at the first turn that hid them from him they increased their speed, for both were becoming suspicious of every least untoward incident, and their one wish now was to escape the quarry in safety. Nearing the entrance they attached themselves to a column of slaves toiling upward with their heavy burdens of rocks for the new dome, and with them they came to the guardroom where the slaves were checked out. The officer and the clerks laboured in a mechanical manner, and it appeared that it was to be as easy to leave the quarry as it had been to enter it, when the officer suddenly drew his brows together and commenced to count.

'How many slaves in this crew?' he asked.

'One hundred,' replied one of the warriors accompanying them.

'Then why four guards?' he demanded.

'There are but two of us,' rejoined the warrior.

'We are not with them,' Komodoflorensal spoke up quickly.

'What do you here?' demanded the officer.

'And we can see you alone we can explain that quickly,' replied the Trohanadalmakusian.

The officer waved the crew of slaves upon their way and beckoned to Komodoflorensal and Tarzan to follow him into an adjoining chamber, which they found a small ante-room in which the commander of the guard slept.

'Now,' he said, 'let me see your passes.'

'We have none,' replied Komodoflorensal.

'No passes! That will be difficult to explain, will it not?'

'Not to one of your discrimination,' replied the prince, accidentally jingling the golden coins in his pouch. 'We are in search of Kalfastoban. We understand he owns a slave we wish to purchase, and, not being able to obtain a pass to the quarry in the short time at our disposal, we ventured to come upon so simple an errand without one. Could you direct us to Kalfastoban?' Again he jingled the coins.

'I shall be delighted,' replied the officer. 'His quarters are upon the fifth level of the Royal Dome, upon the central corridor, and about midway between the King's Corridor and the Warriors' Corridor. As he was relieved from duty in the quarry this very morning, I have no doubt but that you will find him there.'

'We thank you,' said Komodoflorensal, leaning far back in the Minunian bow. 'And now,' he added, as though it was an afterthought, 'if you will accept it we shall be filled with gratitude if you will permit us to leave this slight token of our appreciation,' and he drew a large gold coin from the pouch and proffered it to the officer.

'Rather than seem ungrateful,' replied the officer, 'I must accept your gracious gift, with which I may alleviate the sufferings of the poor. May the shadow of disaster never fall upon you!'

The three then bowed, and Tarzan and Komodoflorensal quitted the guardroom and a moment later were in the free, fresh air of the surface.

'Even in Minuni!' breathed Tarzan.

'What was that?' asked his friend.

'I was just thinking of my simple, honest jungle and its God's creatures that men call brutes and beasts.'

'What should they call them?' demanded Komodoflorensal.

'If judged by the standards that men themselves make, and fail to observe, they should be called demi-gods,' replied the ape-man.

'I believe I get your point,' laughed the other; 'but think? Had a lion guarded the entrance to this quarry, no gold piece would have let us pass. The frailties of man are not without their virtues; because of them right has just triumphed over wrong, and bribery has worn the vestments of virtue.'

Returning to the Royal Dome, they passed around the east side of the structure to the north front, where lies the Slaves' Corridor in every dome. In quitting the dome they had come from the Warriors' Corridor on the west, and they felt that it would be only increasing the chances of detection were they to pass too often along the same route where someone, half recognizing them in one instance might do so fully after a second or third inspection.

To reach the fifth level required only a few minutes after they had gained entrance to the dome. With every apparance of boldness they made their way toward the point in the central corridor at which the officer of the guard had told them they would find Kalfastoban's quarters, and perhaps Kalfastoban himself, but they were constantly on the alert, for both recognized the greatest danger of detection lay through the chance that Kalfastoban would recall their features, as he of all Veltoptismakusians would be most apt to, since he had seen the most of them, or at least the most of Tarzan, since he had donned the slave's green.

They had reached a point about midway between the Slaves' Corridor and the Warriors' Corridor when Komodoflorensal halted a young female slave and asked her where the quarters of Kalfastoban were located: 'It is necessary to pass through the quarters of Hamadalban to reach those of Kalfastoban,' replied the girl. 'Go to the third entrance,' and she pointed along the corridor in the direction they had been going.

After they had left her Tarzan asked Komodoflorensal if he thought there would be any difficulty in gaining entrance to Kalfastoban's quarters.

'No,' he replied; 'the trouble will arise in knowing what to do after we get there.'

'We know what we have come for,' replied the ape-man. 'It is only necessary to carry out our design, removing all obstacles as they intervene.'

'Quite simple,' laughed the prince.

Tarzan was forced to smile. 'To be candid,' he admitted, 'I haven't the remotest idea what we are going to do after we get in there, or after we get out either, if we are succssful in finding Talaskar and bringing her away with us; but that is not strange, since I know nothing, or practically nothing, of what conditions I may expect to confront me from moment to moment in this strange city of a strange world.

'All that we can do is to do our best. We have come thus far much more easily that I expected – perhaps we will go the whole distance with no greater friction – or we may stop within the next dozen steps, for ever.'

Pausing before the third entrance, they glanced in, discovering several women squatting upon the floor. Two of them were of the warrior class, the others slaves of the white tunic. Komodoflorensal entered boldly.

'These are the quarters of Hamadalban?' he asked.

'They are,' replied one of the women.

'And Kalfastoban's are beyond?'

'Yes.'

'And beyond Kalfastoban's?' inquired the Trohanadalmakusian.

'A long gallery leads to the outer corridor. Upon this gallery open many chambers where live hundreds of people. I do not know them all. Whom do you seek?'

'Palastokar,' replied Komodoflorensal quickly, choosing the first name that presented itself to his memory.

'I do not recall the name,' said the woman, knitting her brows in thought.

'But I shall find him now, thanks to you,' said Komodoflorensal, 'for my directions were to pass through the quarters of Hamadalban and Kalfastoban, when I should come upon a gallery into which opened the quarters of Palastokar; but perhaps if Kalfastoban is in he will be able to direct me more exactly.'

'Kalfastoban has gone out with Hamadalban,' replied the woman, 'but I expect them back momentarily. If you will wait they will soon be here.'

'Thank you,' said Komodoflorensal hastily, 'but I am sure that we shall have no trouble finding the quarters of Palastokar. May your candles burn long and brilliantly!' And without waiting on further ceremony, he crossed the room and entered the quarters of Kalfastoban, into which Tarzan of the Apes followed at his heels. 'I think, my friend,' said the prince, 'that we shall have to work rapidly.'

Tarzan glanced quickly around the first chamber that they entered. It was vacant. Several doors opened from it. They were all closed either with wooden doors or with hangings. The ape-man stepped quickly to the nearer and tried the latch. It gave and he pushed the door ajar. All was darkness within.

'Bring a candle, Komodoflorensal,' he said.

The prince brought two from their niches in the wall. 'A storeroom,' he said, as the rays of the candles illuminated the interior of the room. 'Food and candles and raiment. Kalfastoban is no pauper. The tax-collector has not ruined him yet.'

Tarzan, standing in the doorway of the storeroom, just behind Komodoflorensal, turned suddenly and looked out across the other chamber. He had heard voices in the quarters of Hamadalban beyond – men's voices. One of them he recognized an instant later – it was the voice of Kalfastoban Vental.

'Come!' roared the bull voice of the Vental. 'Come to my quarters Hamadalban and I will show you this new slave of mine.'

Tarzan pushed Komodoflorensal into the storeroom and, following him, closed the door. 'Did you hear?' he whispered.

'Yes; it was Kalfastoban!'

The storeroom door was ornamented with a small open grille covered with a hanging of some heavy stuff upon the inside. By drawing the hanging aside the two could obtain a view of most of the interior of the outer chamber, and they could hear all that was said by the two men who now entered from Hamadalban's quarters.

'I tell you she is the greatest bargain I have ever seen,' cried Kalfastoban. 'But wait – I'll fetch her!' And he stepped to another door, which he unlocked with a key. 'Come out!' he roared, flinging the door wide. With the haughty bearing of a queen, a girl stepped slowly into the larger room – no cowering servility of the slave here. Her chin was high, her gaze level. She glanced almost with contempt upon the Vental. And she was beautiful.

It was Talaskar. Komodoflorensal realized that he had never before appreciated how really beautiful was the little slave girl who had cooked for him. Kalfastoban had given her a white tunic of good quality, which set off the texture of her skin and the rich blackness of her hair to better effect than had the cheap green thing that he had always seen her in.

'She belonged to Zoanthrohago,' Kalfastoban explained to his friend, 'but I doubt that he ever saw her, else he never would have parted with her for the paltry sum I paid.'

'You will take her for your own woman and raise her to our class?' asked Hamadalban.

'No,' replied Kalfastoban, 'for then she would no longer be a slave, and I could not sell her. Women are too expensive. I shall keep her for a time and then sell her while her value is still high. I should make a pretty good profit from her.'

Tarzan's fingers closed tightly, as if upon the throat of an enemy, and the right hand of Komodoflorensal crept to the hilt of his rapier.

A woman came from the quarters of Hamadalban and stood in the doorway.

'Two of the guards from the quarry are here with a green slave inquiring for Kalfastoban,' she said. 'Send them in,' directed the Vental.

A moment later the three entered – the slave was Caraftap. 'Aha!' exclaimed Kalfastoban. 'My good slave, Caraftap; the best in the quarry. Why is he brought here?'

'He says that he has information of great value,' replied one of the guards; 'but he will divulge it to none but you. He has staked his life against the worth of his information, and the Novand of the guard ordered him brought hither.'

'What information have you?' demanded Kalfastoban.

'It is of great moment,' cried Caraftap. 'Noble Zoanthrohago, and even the king, will be grateful for it, but were I to give it and have to return to the quarries the other slaves would kill me. You were always good to me, Kalfastoban Vental, and so I asked to be brought to you, for I know that if you promise that I shall be rewarded with the white tunic I shall be safe.'

'You know that I cannot do that,' replied Kalfastoban.

'But the king can, and if you intercede with him he will not refuse.'

'I can promise to intercede with the king on your behalf if the information you bring is of value; but that is all I can do.'

'That is enough – if you promise,' said Caraftap.

'Very well; I promise. What do you know that the king would like?'

'News travels fast in Veltoptismakus,' said Caraftap, 'and so it was that we in the quarry heard of the death of the two slaves, Aoponato and Zuanthrol, within a short time after their bodies were discovered As both had been slaves of Zoanthrohago, we were all confined together in one chamber, and thus I knew them both well. Imagine then my surprise when, while crossing one of the main spirals with a crew of other slaves, I beheld both Zuanthrol and Aoponato, in the habiliments of warriors, ascending toward the surface.'

'What is the appearance of these two?' suddenly demanded one of the warriors who had accompanied Caraftap from the quarry.

The slave described them as fully as he could.

'The same!' cried the warrior. 'These very two stopped me upon the spiral and inquired the whereabouts of Kalfastoban.'

A crowd of women and men had gathered in the doorway of Kalfastoban's chamber, having been attracted by the presence of a green slave accompanied by members of the quarry guard. One of them was a young slave girl.

'I too was questioned by these very men,' she exclaimed, 'only a short time ago. They asked me the same question.'

One of Hamadalban's women voiced a little scream. 'They passed through our quarters but a moment since,' she cried, 'and entered Kalfastoban's but they asked not where lay the quarters of Kalfastoban, the name they mentioned was unknown to me – a strange name.'

'Palastokar,' one of her companions reminded her.

'Yes, Palastokar, and they said he had his quarters upon the gallery leading from Kalfastoban's to the outer corridor.'

'There is no one of such a name in the Royal Dome,' said Kalfastoban. 'It was but a ruse to enter my quarters.'

'Or to pass through them,' suggested one of the quarry guard.

'We must hurry after them,' said the other.

'Keep Caraftap here until we return, Kalfastoban,' said the first guard, 'and also search your own quarters and those adjoining carefully. Come!' And motioning to the other guard, he crossed the chamber and departed along the gallery that led to the outer corridor, followed not alone by his fellow but by Hamadalban and all the other men who had congregated in the chamber, leaving Kalfastoban and Caraftap, with the women, in the Vental's quarters.

18

The Voice from The Wall

Kalfastoban turned immediately to a search of the various chambers of his quarters, but Caraftap laid a restraining hand upon his arm.

'Wait, Vental,' he begged. 'If they be here, would it not be best to ensure their capture by fastening the doors leading from your quarters?'

'A good thought, Caraftap,' replied Kalfastoban; 'and then we may take our time searching for them. Out of here, all you women!' he cried, waving the females back into Hamadalban's quarters. A moment later the two doors leading from the chamber to Hamadalban's quarters and the gallery were closed and locked. 'And now, master,' suggested Caraftap, 'as there be two of them, would it not be well to supply me with a weapon?'

Kalfastoban smote his chest. 'A dozen such could Kalfastoban overcome alone,' he cried: 'but for your own protection get you a sword from yonder room, while I lock this proud she-cat in her cell again.'

As Kalfastoban followed Talaskar to the room in which she had been imprisoned, Caraftap crossed to the door of the storeroom where the Vental had told him he would find a weapon.

The Vental reached the door of the room just behind the girl, and reaching out, caught her by the arm.

'Not so fast my pretty!' he cried. 'A kiss before you leave me; but fret not! The moment we are sure that those villainous slaves are not within these rooms I shall join you: so do not pine for your Kalfastoban.'

Talaskar wheeled and struck the Vental in the face. 'Lay not your filthy hands upon me, beast!' she cried.

'So-ho! a cat indeed!' exclaimed the man; but he did not release her, and so they struggled until they disappeared from sight within the cell, and at the same moment Caraftap the slave laid his hand upon the latch of the store-room door, and, opening it, stepped within.

As he did so steel fingers reached forth out of the darkness and closed upon his throat. He would have screamed with terror, but no sound could he force through his tight-closed throat. He struggled and struck at the thing that held him – a thing so powerful that he knew it could not be human; and then a low voice, cold and terrifying, whispered in his ear:

'Die, Caraftap!' it said. 'Meet the fate that you deserve, and that you we'll know you deserved when you said that you dared not return to the quarters of the slaves of Zoanthrohago after betraying two of your number. Die, Caraftap, and know before you die that he whom you would have betrayed is your slayer. You searched for Zuanthrol and – you have found him!' With the last words the terrible fingers closed upon the man's neck. Spasmodically the slave struggled, lighting for air. Then the two hands that gripped him turned slowly in opposite directions and the head of the traitor was twisted from his neck.

Throwing the corpse aside, Tarzan sprang into the main chamber of the Vental's quarters and ran quickly toward the door of Talaskar's cell, Komodo-florensal but half a pace behind him. The door of the little room had been pushed to by the struggles of the couple within, and as Tarzan pushed it open he saw the girl in the clutches of the huge Vental, who, evidently maddened by her resistance, had lost his temper completely and was attempting to rain blows upon her face which she sought to ward off clutching at his arms and hands.

A heavy hand fell upon the shoulder of the Vental. 'You seek us!' a low voice whispered in his ear. 'Here we are!'

Kalfastoban released the girl and swung around, at the same time reaching for his sword. Facing him were the two slaves, and both were armed, though only Aoponato had drawn his weapon. Zuanthrol, who held him, had not yet drawn.

'"A dozen such could Kalfastoban overcome alone",' quoted Tarzan. 'Here we are, braggart, and we are only two; but we cannot wait while you show us how mighty you be. We are sorry. Had you not molested this girl, I should merely have locked you in your quarters, from which you would soon have been released; but your brutality deserves but one punishment – death.'

'Caraftap!' screamed Kalfastoban. No longer was he a blusterer, deep-toned and swaggering. His voice was shrill with terror and he shook in the hands of the ape-man. 'Caraftap! Help!' he cried.

'Caraftap is dead,' said Tarzan. 'He died because he betrayed his fellows. You shall die because you were brutal to a defenceless slave girl. Run him through Komodoflorensal! We have no time to waste here.'

As the Trohanadalmakusian withdrew his sword from the heart of Kalfastoban Vental and the corpse slid to the floor of the cell, Talaskar ran forward and fell at the feet of the ape-man.

'Zuanthrol and Aoponato!' she cried. 'Never did I think to see you again. What has happened? Why are you here? You have saved me, but now you will be lost. Fly – I know not where you may fly, but go from here! Do not let them find you here. I cannot understand why you are here, anyway.'

'We are trying to escape,' explained Komodoflorensal, 'and Zuanthrol would not go without you. He searched the quarry for you and now the Royal Dome. He has performed the impossible, but he has found you.'

'Why did you this for me?' asked Talaskar, looking wonderingly at Tarzan.

'Because you were kind to me, when I was brought to the chamber of Zoanthrohago's slaves,' replied the ape-man, 'and because I promised that when the time for escape came we three should go together.'

He had lifted her to her feet and led her into the main chamber. Komodoflorensal stood a little aside, his eyes upon the floor. Tarzan glanced at him and an expression of puzzlement came into the eyes of the ape-man, but whatever thought had caused it he must have put it quickly aside for the consideration of more pressing matters.

'Komodoflorensal, you know best what avenues of escape should be the least beset by the dangers of discovery. Whether to go by way of Hamadalban's quarters or through the gallery they mentioned? These are questions I cannot answer to my own satisfaction; and look' – his eyes had been roving about the chamber – 'there is an opening in the ceiling! Where might that lead?'

'It might lead almost anywhere, or nowhere at all,' replied the Trohanadalmakusian. 'Many chambers have such openings. Sometimes they lead into small lofts that are not connected with any other chamber; again they lead into secret chambers, or even into corridors upon another level.'

There came a pounding upon the door leading into Hamadalban's quarters, and a woman's voice called aloud: 'Kalfastoban, open!' she cried. 'There has come an ental from the quarry guard in search of Caraftap. The sentry at the entrance to the quarters of the slaves of Zoanthrohago has been found slain and they wish to question Caraftap, believing that there is a conspiracy among the slaves.'

'We must go by the gallery,' whispered Komodoflorensal, stepping quickly to the door leading thereto. As he reached it someone laid a hand upon the latch from the opposite side and attempted to open the door, which was locked.

'Kalfastoban!' cried a voice from the gallery beyond. 'Let us in! The slaves went not this way. Come, open quickly!'

Tarzan of the Apes glanced quickly about. Upon his face was a half snarl, for once again was he the cornered beast. He measured the distance from the floor to the trap in the ceiling, and then with a little run he sprang lightly upward. He had forgotten to what extent the reduction of his weight had affected his agility. He had hoped to reach a handhold upon the upper edge of the opening, but instead he shot entirely through it, alighting upon his feet in a dark chamber.

Turning, he looked down at his friends below. Consternation was writ large upon the countenance of each, but at that he could not wonder. He was almost as much surprised himself.

'Is it too far for you to jump?' he asked.

'Too far!' they replied.

He swung, then, head downward through the opening, catching the edge of the trap in the hollow of his knees. At the gallery door the knocking was becoming insistent, and now at that leading into the quarters of Hamadalban a man's voice had supplanted that of the woman. The fellow was demanding entrance, angrily. 'Open!' he shouted. 'In the name of the king, open!'

'Open yourself!' shouted the fellow who had been hammering at the opposite door, thinking that the demand to open came from the interior of the chamber to which he sought admission.

'How can I open?' screamed back the other. 'The door is locked upon your side!'

'It is not locked upon my side. It is locked upon yours,' cried the other, angrily.

'You lie!' shouted he who sought entrance from Hamadalban's quarters, 'and you will pay well when this is reported to the king.'

Tarzan swung, head downward, into the chamber, his hands extended toward his companions. 'Lift Talaskar to me,' he directed Komodoflorensal, and as the other did so he grasped the girl's wrists and raised her as far as he could until she could seize upon a part of his leather harness and support herself alone without falling. Then he took another hold upon her, lower down, and lifted still higher, and in this way she managed to clamber into the chamber above. The angry warriors at the two doors were now evidently engaged in an attempt to batter their way into the chamber. Heavy blows were falling upon the substantial panels that threatened to splinter them at any moment.

'Fill your pouch with candles, Komodoflorensal,' said Tarzan, 'and then jump for my hands.'

'I took all the candles I could carry while we were in the storeroom,' replied the other. 'Brace yourself! I am going to jump.'

A panel splintered and bits of wood flew to the centre of the floor from the door at the gallery just as Tarzan seized the outstretched hands of Komodoflorensal and an instant later, as both men knelt in the darkness of the loft and looked down into the chamber below, the opposite door flew open and the ten warriors who composed the ental burst in at the heels of their Vental.

For an instant they looked about in blank surprise and their attention was attracted by the pounding upon the other door. A smile crossed the face of the Vental as he stepped quickly to the gallery door and unlocked it. Angry warriors rushed in upon him, but when he had explained the misapprehension under which both parties had been striving for entrance to the chamber they all joined in the laughter, albeit a trifle shamefacedly.

'But who was in here?' demanded the Vental who had brought the soldiers.

'Kalfastoban and the green slave Caraftap,' proffered a woman belonging to Hamadalban.

'They must be hiding,' said a warrior.

'Search the quarters!' commanded the Vental.

'It will not take too long to find one,' said another warrior, pointing at the floor just inside the storeroom doorway. The others looked and there they saw a human hand resting upon the floor. The fingers seemed frozen into the semblance of clutching claws. Mutely they proclaimed death. One of the warriors stepped quickly to the storeroom, opened the door and dragged forth the body of Caraftap, to which the head was clinging by a shred of flesh. Even the warriors stepped back, aghast. They looked quickly around the chamber.

'Both doors were barred upon the inside,' said the Vental. 'Whatever did this must still be here.'

'It could have been nothing human,' whispered a woman who had followed them from the adjoining quarters. 'Search carefully,' said the Vental, and as he was a brave man, he went first into one chamber and then another. In the last one they found Kalfastoban, run through the heart.

'It is time we got out of here if there is any way out,' whispered Tarzan to Komodoflorensal. 'One of them will espy this hole directly.'

Very cautiously the two men felt their way in opposite directions around the walls of the dark, stuffy loft. Deep dust, the dust of ages, rose about them chokingly, evidencing the fact that the room had not been used for years, perhaps for ages. Presently Komodoflorensal heard a 'Hs-s-t-!' from the ape-man, who called them to him. 'Come here both of you. I have found something.'

'What have you found?' asked Talaskar, coming close.

'An opening near the bottom of the wall,' replied Tarzan. 'It is large enough for a man to crawl through. Think you, Komodoflorensal, that it would be safe to light a candle?'

'No, not now,' replied the prince.

'I will go without it then,' announced the ape-man, 'for we must see where this tunnel leads, if anywhere.'

He dropped upon his hands and knees, then, and Talaskar, who had been standing next him, felt him move away. She could not see him – it was too dark in the gloomy loft.

The two waited, but Zuanthrol did not return. They heard voices in the room below. They wondered if the searchers would soon investigate the loft, but really there was no need for apprehension. The searchers had determined to invest the place – it would be safer than crawling up into that dark hole after an unknown thing that could tear the head from a man's body. When it came down, as come down it would have to, they would be prepared to destroy or capture it, but in the meantime they were content to wait.

'What has become of him?' whispered Talaskar, anxiously.

'You care very much for him, do you not?' asked Komodoflorensal.

'Why should I not?' asked the girl. 'You do, too, do you not?'

'Yes,' replied Komodoflorensal.

'I wish he would come back,' said the girl.

'Yes,' said Komodoflorensal.

As if in answer to their wish they heard a low whistle from the depths of the tunnel into which Tarzan had crawled. 'Come!' whispered the ape-man. Talaskar first, they followed him crawling upon hands and knees through a winding tunnel, feeling their way through the darkness, until at last a light flared before them and they saw Zuanthrol lighting a candle in a small chamber, that was only just high enough to permit a tall man to sit erect within it.

'I got this far,' he said to them, 'and as it offered a fair hiding-place where we might have light without fear of discovery I came back after you. Here we can stop a while in comparative comfort and safety until I can explore the tunnel further. From what I have been able to judge it has never been used during the lifetime of any living Veltoptismakusian, so there is little likelihood that anyone will think of looking here for us.'

'Do you think they will follow us?' asked Talaskar.

'I think they will,' replied Komodoflorensal, 'and as we cannot go back it will be better if we push on at once, as it is reasonable to assume that the opposite end of this tunnel opens into another chamber. Possibly there we shall find an avenue of escape.'

'You are right, Komodoflorensal,' agreed Tarzan.

'Nothing can be gained by remaining here. I will go ahead. Let Talaskar follow me, and you bring up the rear. If the place proves a blind alley we shall be no worse off for having investigated it.'

Lighting their way this time with candles the three crawled laboriously and painfully over the uneven rock floor of the tunnel, which turned often, this way and that, as though passing around chambers until, to their relief, the passageway abruptly enlarged, both in width and height, so that now they could proceed in an erect position. The tunnel now dropped in a steep declivity to a lower level, and a moment later the three emerged into a small chamber, where Talaskar suddenly placed a hand upon Tarzan's arm, with a little intaking of her breath in a half gasp.

'What is that, Zuanthrol?' she whispered, pointing into the darkness ahead.

Upon the floor at one side of the room a crouching figure was barely discernible close to the wall.

'And that!' exclaimed the girl, pointing to another portion of the room.

The ape-man shook her hand from his arm and stepped quickly forward, his candle held high in his left hand, his right upon his sword. He came close to the crouching figure and bent to examine it. He laid his hand upon it and it fell into a heap of dust.

'What was it?' demanded the girl.

'It *was* a man,' replied Tarzan; 'but it has been dead many years. It was chained to this wall. Even the chain has rusted away.'

'And the other, too?' asked Talaskar.

'There are several of them,' said Komodoflorensal. 'See? There and there.'

'At least they cannot detain us,' said Tarzan, and moved on again across the chamber toward a doorway on the opposite side.

'But they tell us something, possibly,' ventured Komodoflorensal.

'What do they say?' asked the ape-man.

'That this corridor connected with the quarters of a very powerful Veltoptismakusian,' replied the prince. 'So powerful was he that he might dispose of his enemies thus, without question; and it also tells *us* that all this happened long years ago.'

'The condition of the bodies told us that,' said Tarzan.

'Not entirely,' replied Komodoflorensal. 'The ants would have reduced them to that state in a short time. In past ages the dead were left within the domes, and the ants, who were then our scavengers, soon disposed of them, but the ants sometimes attacked the living. They grew from a nuisance to a menace, and then every precaution had to be taken to keep from attracting them. Also we fought them.

'There were great battles waged in Trohanadalmakus between the Minunians and the ants and thousands of our warriors were devoured alive, and though we slew billions of ants their queens could propagate faster than we could kill the sexless workers who attacked us with their soldiers. But at last we turned our attention to their nests. Here the carnage was terrific, but we succeeded in slaying their queens, and since then no ants have come into our domes. They live about us, but they fear us. However, we do not risk attracting them again by leaving our dead within the domes.'

'Then you believe that this corridor leads to the quarters of some great noble?' inquired Tarzan.

'I believe that it once did. The ages bring change. Its end may now be walled up. The chamber to which it leads may have housed a king's son when these bones were quick; today it may be a barrack-room for soldiers or a stable for diadets. All that we know definitely about it,' concluded Komodoflorensal, 'is that it has not been used by man for a long time, and probably therefore, is unknown to present-day Veltoptismakusians.'

Beyond the chamber of death the tunnel dropped rapidly to lower levels, entering, at last, a third chamber larger than either of the others. Upon the floor lay the bodies of many men.

'These were not chained to the walls,' remarked Tarzan.

'No, they died fighting as one may see by their naked swords and the position of their bones.'

As the three paused a moment to look about the chamber there sounded upon their ears the tones of a human voice.

19

Janzara's Boudoir

As the days passed and Tarzan did not return to his home, his son became more and more apprehensive Runners were sent to nearby villages, but each returned with the same report. No one had seen the Big Bwana.

Korak dispatched messages, then, to the nearest telegraph inquiring from all the principal points in Africa, where the ape-man might have made a landing, if aught had been seen or heard of him, but always again were the answers in the negative.

And at last, stripped to G-string and carrying naught but his primitive weapons, Korak the Killer took the trail, with a score of the swiftest and bravest of the Waziri, in search of his father. Long and diligently they searched the jungle and the forest, often enlisting the friendly services of the villages near which they chanced to be carrying on their quest, until they had covered as with a fine-toothed comb a vast area of country, covered it as could have no other body of men; but for all their care and all their diligence they uncovered no single clue as to the fate or whereabouts of Tarzan of the Apes. And so, disheartened yet indefatigable, they searched on and on through tangled miles of steaming jungle or across rocky uplands as inhospitable as the stunted thorns that dotted them.

And in the Royal Dome of Elkomoelhago, Thagosto of Veltoptismakus, three persons halted in a rock-walled hidden chamber and listened to a human voice that appeared to come to them out of the very rock of the walls surrounding them. Upon the floor about them lay the bones of men long dead. About them arose the impalpable dust of ages.

The girl pressed closer to Tarzan. 'Who is it?' she whispered. Tarzan shook his head.

'It is a woman's voice,' said Komodoflorensal.

The ape-man raised his candle high above his head and took a step closer to the left-hand wall; then he stopped and pointed. The others looked and saw an opening in the wall a hual or two above his head. Tarzan handed his candle to Komodoflorensal, removed his sword and laid it on the floor, and then sprang lightly for the opening. For a moment he clung to its edge listening, and then he dropped back into the chamber.

'It is pitch black beyond,' he murmured. 'Whoever owns that voice is in another chamber beyond that into which I was just looking. There was no human being in the next apartment.'

'If it was absolutely dark, how could you know that?' Komodoflorensal asked.

'Had there been anyone there I should have smelled him,' replied the ape-man.

The others looked at him in astonishment. 'I am sure of it,' said Tarzan, 'because I could plainly feel a draught sucking up from the chamber through the aperture and into this chamber. Had there been a human being there his effluvium would have been carried directly to my nostrils.'

'And you could have detected it?' demanded Komodoflorensal. 'My friend, I can believe much of you, but not that.'

Tarzan smiled. 'I at least have the courage of my convictions,' he said, 'for I am going over there to investigate. From the clearness with which the voice comes to us I am certain that it comes through no solid wall. There must be an opening into the chamber where the woman is, and as we should investigate every possible avenue of escape, I shall investigate this.' He stepped again toward the wall below the aperture.

'Oh, let us not separate,' cried the girl. 'Where one goes, let us all go!'

'Two swords are better than one,' said Komodoflorensal, though his tone was only half-hearted.

'Very well,' replied Tarzan. 'I will go first, then you can pass Talaskar up.'

Komodoflorensal nodded. A minute or two later the three stood upon the opposite side of the wall. Their candles revealed a narrow passage that showed indications of much more recent use than those through which they had passed from the quarters of Kalfastoban. The wall they had passed through to reach it was of stone, but that upon the opposite side was of studding and rough boards.

'This is a passage built along the side of a panelled room,' whispered Komodoflorensal. 'The other side of these rough boards support beautifully polished panels of brilliant woods or burnished metals.'

'Then there should be a door, you think, opening from this passage into that adjoining chamber?' asked Tarzan.

'A secret panel, more likely,' he replied.

They walked along the passage, listening intently. At first they had just been able to distinguish that the voice they heard was that of a woman, but now they heard the words:

'… Had they let me have him,' was the first that they distinguished.

'Most glorious mistress this would not have happened then,' replied another female voice.

'Zoanthrohago is a fool and deserves to die, but my illustrious father, the king, is a bigger fool,' spoke the first voice. 'He will kill Zoanthrohago, and with him the chance of discovering the secret of making our warriors giants. Had they let me buy this Zuanthrol he would not have escaped. They thought that I would kill him but that was farthest from my intentions.'

'What would you have done with him, wondrous Princess?'

'That is not for a slave to ask or know,' snapped the mistress.

'That is the Princess Janzara speaking,' whispered Tarzan to Komodoflorensal. 'It is the daughter of Elkomoelhago whom you could have captured and made your princess, but you would have had a handful.'

'Is she as beautiful as they say?' asked Komodoflorensal.

'She is very beautiful, but she is a devil.'

'It would have been my duty to take her,' said Komodoflorensal.

Tarzan was silent. A plan was unfolding itself within his mind. The voice from beyond the partition spoke again. 'He was very wonderful,' it said; 'much more wonderful than our warriors,' and then, after a silence: 'You may go, slave, and see to it that I am not disturbed before the sun stands midway between the Women's Corridor and the King's Corridor.'

'May your candles burn as deathlessly as your beauty, Princess,' said the slave, as she backed across the apartment. An instant later the three behind the panelling heard a door close.

Tarzan crept stealthily along the passage, seeking the secret panel that connected with the apartment where the Princess Janzara lay composed for the night, but it was Talaskar who found it.

'Here!' she whispered, and together the three examined the fastening.

It was simple and could evidently be opened from the opposite side by pressure upon a certain spot in the panel.

'Wait here!' said Tarzan to his companions. 'I am going to fetch the Princess Janzara. If we cannot escape with her we should be able to buy our liberty with such a hostage.'

Without waiting to discuss the advisability of his action with the others, Tarzan gently slid back the catch that held the panel and pushed it slightly ajar. Before him was the apartment of Janzara – a creation of gorgeous barbarity, in the centre of which, upon a marble slab, the princess lay, a gigantic candle burning at her head and another at her feet.

Regardless of the luxuriousness of their surroundings, of their wealth, or their positions in life, the Minunians never sleep upon a substance softer than a single thickness of fabric, which they throw upon the ground, or upon wooden, stone or marble sleeping slabs, according to their caste or their wealth. Leaving the panel open, the ape-man stepped quietly into the apartment and moved directly toward the princess, who lay with closed eyes, either already asleep, or assiduously wooing Morpheus. He had crossed halfway to her cold couch when a sudden draft closed the panel with a noise that might well have awakened the dead.

Instantly the princess was on her feet and facing him. For a moment she stood in silence, gazing at him, and then she moved slowly toward him, the sinuous undulations of her graceful carriage suggesting to the Lord of the Jungle a similarity to the savage majesty of Sabor, the lioness.

'It is you, Zuanthrol!' breathed the princess. 'You have come for me?'

'I have come for you, princess,' replied the ape-man. 'Make no outcry and no harm will befall you.'

'I will make no outcry,' whispered Janzara as with half-closed lids she glided toward him and threw her arms about his neck.

Tarzan drew back and gently disengaged himself. 'You do not understand, princess,' he told her. 'You are my prisoner. You are coming with me.'

'Yes,' she breathed, 'I am your prisoner, but it is you who do not understand. I love you. It is my right to choose whatever slave I will to be my prince. I have chosen you.' Tarzan shook his head impatiently. 'You do not love me,' he said. 'I am sorry that you think you do, for I do not love you. I have no time to waste. Come!' And he stepped closer to take her by the wrist.

'Are you mad?' she demanded. 'Or can it be that you do not know who I am?'

'You are Janzara, daughter of Elkomoelhago,' replied Tarzan. 'I know well who you are.'

'And you dare to spurn my love!' She was breathing heavily, her bosom rising and falling to the tumultuous urge of her emotions.

'It is no question of love between us,' replied the ape-man. 'To me it is only a question of liberty and life for myself and my companions.'

'You love another? "asked Janzara.

'Yes.' Tarzan told her.

'Who is she?' demanded the princess.

'Will you come quietly, or shall I be compelled to carry you away by force?'

For a moment the woman stood silently before him, her every muscle tensed, her dark eyes two blazing wells of fire, and then slowly her expression changed. Her face softened, and she stretched one hand toward him.

'I will help you, Zuanthrol,' she said. 'I will help you to escape. Because I love you I shall do this. Come! Follow me!' She turned and moved softly across the apartment.

'But my companions,' said the ape-man. 'I cannot go without them.'

'Where are they?'

He did not tell her, for as yet he was none too sure of her motives. 'Show me the way,' he said, 'and I can return for them.'

'Yes,' she replied, 'I will show you, and then perhaps you will love me better than you love the other.' In the passage behind the panelling Talaskar and Komodoflorensal awaited the outcome of Tarzan's venture. Distinctly to their ears came every word of the conversation between the ape-man and the princess.

'He loves you,' said Komodoflorensal. 'You see, he loves you.'

'I see nothing of the kind,' returned Talaskar. 'Because he does not love the Princess Janzara is no proof that he loves me.'

'But he does love you – and you love him! I have seen it since first he came. Would that he were not my friend, for then I might run him through.'

'Why would you run him through because he loves me – if he does?' demanded the girl. 'Am I so low that you would rather see your friend dead than mated with me?'

'I' – he hesitated – 'I cannot tell you what I mean.' The girl laughed and then suddenly sobered. 'She is leading him from her apartment,' she said. 'We had better follow.'

As Talaskar laid her fingers upon the spring that actuated the lock holding the panel in place, Janzara led Tarzan across the chamber toward a doorway in one of the side walls – not the doorway through which her slave had departed.

'Follow me,' whispered the princess, 'and you will see what the love of Janzara means.'

Tarzan, not entirely assured of her intentions, followed her warily.

'You are afraid,' she said. 'You do not trust me. Well, come here then and look, yourself, into this chamber before you enter.'

Komodoflorensal and Talaskar had but just stepped into the apartment when Tarzan approached the door to one side of which Janzara stood. They saw the floor give suddenly beneath his feet and an instant later Zuanthrol had disappeared. As he shot down a polished chute he heard a wild laugh from Janzara following him into the darkness of the unknown.

Komodoflorensal and Talaskar leaped quickly across the chamber, but too late. The floor that had given beneath Tarzan's feet had slipped quietly back into place. Janzara stood above the spot trembling with anger and staring down at the place where the ape-man had disappeared. She shook as an aspen shakes in the breeze – shook in the mad tempest of her own passions.

'If you will not come to me, you shall never go to another!' she screamed, and then she turned and saw Komodoflorensal and Talaskar running toward her. What followed occurred so quickly that it would be impossible to record the facts in the brief time that they actually consumed. It was over almost before Tarzan reached the bottom of the chute and picked himself from the earthen floor upon which he had been deposited.

The room in which he found himself was lighted by several candles burning in iron-barred niches. Opposite him was a heavy gate of iron bars, through which he could see another lighted apartment in which a man, his chin sagging dejectedly upon his breast, was seated on a low bench. At the sound of Tarzan's precipitate entrance into the adjoining chamber the man looked up, and, at sight of Zuanthrol, leaped to his feet.

'Quick! To your left!' he cried; and Tarzan, turning saw two huge, green eyed beasts crouching to spring. His first impulse was to rub his eyes as one might to erase the phantom figures of a disquieting dream, for what he saw were two ordinary African wildcats – ordinary in contour and markings, but in size gigantic. For an instant the ape-man forgot that he was only one-fourth his normal size and that the cats, which appeared to him as large as full-grown lions, were in reality but average specimens of their kind.

As they came toward him he whipped out his sword, prepared to battle for his life with these great felines as he had so often before with their mighty cousins of his own jungle.

'If you can hold them off until you reach this gate,' cried the man in the next chamber, 'I can let you through. The bolt is upon this side.' But even as he spoke one of the cats charged.

Komodoflorensal, brushing past Janzara, leaped for the spot upon the floor at which Tarzan had disappeared, and as it gave beneath him he heard a savage cry break from the lips of the Princess of Veltoptismakus.

'So it is you he loves?' she screamed. 'But he shall not have you – no, not even in death!' And that was all that Komodoflorensal heard as the chute swallowed him.

Talaskar, confronted by the infuriated Janzara, halted, and then stepped back, for the princess was rushing upon her with drawn dagger.

'Die, slave!' she screamed, as she lunged for the white breast of Talaskar; but the slave girl caught the other's wrist, and a moment later they dropped, locked in each other's embrace. Together they rolled about the floor, the daughter of Elkomoelhago seeking to drive her slim blade into the breast of the slave girl, while Talaskar fought to hold off the menacing steel.

As the first cat charged, the other followed, not to be robbed of its share of the flesh of the kill, for both were ravenous, and as the ape-man met the charge of the first, side-stepping its rush and springing in again to thrust at its side. Komodoflorensal, who had drawn his sword as he entered the apartment of Janzara, shot into the subterranean den almost into the teeth of the second beast. This savage cat was so disconcerted by the sudden appearance of a second human that it wheeled and sprang to the far end of the den before it could gather its courage for another attack.

In the chamber above, Talaskar and Janzara fought savagely, two she-tigers in human form. They rolled to and fro about the room, straining and striking; Janzara screaming, 'Die, slave! You shall not have him!'

But Talaskar held her peace and saved her breath, so that slowly she was overcoming the other when they chanced to roll upon the very spot that had let Tarzan and Komodoflorensal down to the pit beneath.

As Janzara realized what had happened she uttered a scream of terror. 'The cats! The cats!' she cried; and then the two disappeared into the black shaft.

Komodoflorensal did not follow the cat that had retreated to the far end of the pit, but sprang at once to Tarzan's aid, and together they drove off the first beast as they backed toward the gate, where the man in the adjoining chamber stood ready to admit them to the safety of his own apartment.

The two cats charged and then retreated, springing in quickly and away again as quickly, for they had learned the taste of the sharp steel with which the humans were defending themselves. The two men were almost at the gate, another instant and they could spring through. The cats charged again, and were again driven to the far corner of the pit. The man in the next chamber swung open the gate. 'Quick!' he cried; and at the same instant the two figures shot from the mouth of the shaft and, locked tightly in each other's embrace, rolled to the floor of the pit directly in the path of the charging cats.

20
Fugitives

As Tarzan and Komodoflorensal realized that Talaskar and Janzara lay exposed to the savage assault of the hungry beasts they both sprang quickly toward the two girls. As had been the case when Komodoflorensal had shot into the pit, the cats were startled by the sudden appearance of the two new humans, and in the first instant of their surprise had leaped again to the far end of the chamber.

Janzara had lost her dagger as the two girls had fallen into the shaft, and now Talaskar saw it lying on the floor beside her. Releasing her hold upon the princess, she seized the weapon and leaped to her feet. Already Tarzan and Komodoflorensal were at her side, and the cats were returning to the attack.

Janzara arose slowly and half bewildered. She looked about, terror disfiguring her marvellous beauty, and as she did so the man in the adjoining chamber saw her. 'Janzara!' he cried. 'My princess, I come!' And seizing the bench upon which he had been sitting, and the only thing within the chamber that might be converted into a weapon, he swung wide the gate and leaped into the chamber, where the four were now facing the thoroughly infuriated cats.

Both animals, bleeding from many wounds, were mad with pain, rage, and hunger. Screaming and growling, they threw themselves upon the swords of the two men. who had pushed the girls behind them and were backing slowly toward the gate, and then the man with the bench joined Tarzan and Komodoflorensal, and the three fought back the charges of the infuriated cats.

The bench proved fully as good a weapon of defence as the swords, and so together the five drew slowly back until quite suddenly and without the slightest warning, both cats leaped quickly to one side and darted behind the party as if sensing that the women would prove easier prey. One of them came near to closing upon Janzara had not the man with the bench, imbued apparently with demoniacal fury, leaped upon it with his strange weapon and beaten it back so desperately that it was forced to abandon the princess.

Even then the man did not cease to follow it, but, brandishing the bench, pursued it and its fellow with such terrifying cries and prodigious blows that, to escape him, both cats suddenly dodged into the chamber that the man had occupied, and before they could return to the attack he with the bench had slammed the gate and fastened them upon its opposite side. Then he wheeled and faced the four.

'Zoanthrohago!' cried the princess.

'Your slave!' replied the noble, dropping to one knee and leaning far back with outstretched arms. 'You have saved my life, Zoanthrohago,' said Janzara, 'and after all the indignities that I have heaped upon you! How can I reward you?'

'I love you, princess, as you have long known.' replied the man, 'but now it is too late, for tomorrow I die by the king's will. Elkomoelhago has spoken, and, even though you be his daughter, I do not hesitate to say his very ignorance prevents him ever changing a decision once reached.'

'I know,' said Janzara. 'He is my sire, but I love him not. He killed my mother in a fit of unreasoning jealousy. He is a fool – the fool of fools.'

Suddenly she turned upon the others.

'These slaves would escape, Zoanthrohago,' she cried. 'With my aid they might accomplish it. With their company we might succeed in escaping too, and in finding an asylum in their own land.'

'If any one of them is of sufficient power in his own native city,' replied Zoanthrohago.

'This one,' said Tarzan, seeing a miraculous opportunity for freedom, 'is the son of Adendrohahkis, King of Trohanadalmakus – the oldest son, and Zertolosto.' Janzara looked at Tarzan a moment after he had done speaking. 'I was wicked, Zuanthrol,' she said; 'but I thought that I wanted you, and being the daughter of a king I have seldom been denied aught that I craved.' And then to Talaskar: 'Take your man, my girl, and may you be happy with him.' And she pushed Talaskar gently toward the ape-man; but Talaskar drew back.

'You are mistaken, Janzara,' she said; 'I do not love Zuanthrol, nor does he love me.'

Komodoflorensal looked at Tarzan as if expecting that he would quickly deny the truth of Talaskar's statement, but the ape-man only nodded his head in assent. 'Do you mean,' demanded Komodoflorensal, 'that you do not love Talaskar?' And he looked straight into the eyes of his friend.

'On the contrary I love her very much,' replied Tarzan; 'but not in the way you have believed – or should I say feared? I love her because she is a good girl and a kind girl and a loyal friend, and also because she was in trouble and needed the love and protection which you and I alone could give her; but as a man loves his mate, I do not love her, for I have a mate of my own in my country beyond the thorns.' Komodoflorensal said no more, but he thought a great deal. He thought of what it would mean to return to his own city where he was the Zertolosto, and where, by all the customs of ages, he would be supposed to marry the princess from another city. But he did not want a princess; he wanted Talaskar, the little girl slave of Veltoptismakus, who scarcely know the name of her own mother and most probably had never heard that of her father.

He wanted Talaskar, but he could only have her in Trohanadalmakus as a slave. His love for her was real, and so he would not insult her by thinking such a thing as that. If he could not make her his princess, he would not have her at all; and so Komodoflorensal, the son of Adendrohahkis, was sad. But he had none too much time to dwell upon his sorrow now, for the others were planning the best means for escape.

'The keepers come down to feed the cats upon this side,' said Zoanthrohago, indicating a small door in the wall of the pit opposite that which led into the chamber in which he had been incarcerated. 'Doubtless it is not locked, either,' said Janzara, 'for a prisoner could not reach it without crossing through this chamber where the two cats were kept.'

'We will see,' said Tarzan, and crossed to the door. A moment sufficed to force it open, revealing a narrow corridor beyond. One after another the five crawled through the small aperture and, following the corridor, ascended an acclivity, lighting their way with candles taken from the den of the carnivores. At the top a door opened into a wide corridor, a short distance down which stood a warrior, evidently on guard before a door.

Janzara looked through the tiny crack that Tarzan had opened the door and saw the corridor and the man.

'Good!' she exclaimed. 'It is my own corridor, and the warrior is on guard before my door. I know him well. Through me he has escaped payment of his taxes for the past thirty moons. He would die for me. Come! We have nothing to fear.' And stepping boldly into the corridor, she approached the sentry, the others following behind her.

Until he recognized her there was danger that the fellow would raise an alarm, but the moment he saw who it was he was as wax in her hands.

'You are blind,' she told him.

'If the Princess Janzara wishes it,' he replied.

She told him what she wished – five diadets and some warriors' heavy wraps. He eyed those who were with her, and evidently recognized Zoanthrohago, and guessed who the two other men were.

'Not only shall I be blind for my princess,' he said, 'but tomorrow I shall be dead for her.'

'Fetch six diadets, then,' said the princess; and he understood her and smiled his gratitude.

Then she turned toward Komodoflorensal. 'You are Prince Royal of Trohanadalmakus?' she asked.

'I am,' he replied.

'And if we show you the way to liberty you will not enslave us?'

'I shall take you to the city as my own slaves and then liberate you,' he replied.

'It is something that has seldom if ever been done,' she mused; 'not in the memory of living man in Veltoptismakus. I wonder if your sire will permit it.'

'The thing is not done without precedent,' replied Komodoflorensal. 'It has been done but rarely, yet it *has* been done. I think you may feel assured of a friendly welcome at the court of Adendrohahkis, where the wisdom of the Zoanthrohago will not go unappreciated or unrewarded.'

It was a long time before the warrior returned with the diadets. His face was covered with perspiration and his hands with blood.

'I had to fight for them,' he said, 'and we shall have to fight to use them if we do not hurry. Here, prince, I brought you weapons,' and he handed a sword and dagger to Zoanthrohago.

They mounted quickly. It was Tarzan's first experience upon one of the wiry, active little mounts of the Minunians, but he found the saddle well designed and the diadet easily controlled.

'They will be following me from the King's Corridor,' explained Oratharc, the warrior who had fetched the diadets. 'It would be best, then, to leave by one of the others.'

'Trohanadalmakus is east of Veltoptismakus,' said Zoanthrohago, 'and if we leave by the Women's Corridor with two slaves from Trohanadalmakus they will assume that we are going there; but if we leave by another corridor they will not be sure, and if they lose even a little time in starting the pursuit it will give us just that much of an advantage. If we go straight toward Trohanadalmakus we shall almost certainly be overtaken, as the swiftest of diadets will be used in our pursuit.

'Our only hope lies in deceiving them as to our route or destination, and to accomplish this I believe that we should leave either by the Warriors' Corridor or the Slaves' Corridor, cross the hills north of the city, circle far out to the north and east, not turning south until we are well past Trohanadalmakus. In this way we can approach that city from the east while our pursuers are patrolling the country west of Trohanadalmakus to Veltoptismakus.'

'Let us leave by the Warriors' Corridor, then,' suggested Janzara.

'The trees and shrubbery will conceal us while we pass around to the north of the city,' said Komodoflorensal.

'We should leave at once,' urged Oratharc.

'Go first, then, with the princess,' said Zoanthrohago, 'for there is a possibility that the guard at the entrance will let her pass with her party. We will muffle ourselves well with our warriors' cloaks. Come, lead the way!'

With Janzara and Oratharc ahead and the others following closely, they moved at a steady trot along the circular corridor toward the Warriors' Corridor, and it was not until they had turned into the latter that any sign of pursuit developed. Even then, although they heard the voices of men behind them, they hesitated to break into a faster gait lest they arouse the suspicions of the warriors in the guardroom, which they must pass near the mouth of the corridor.

Never had the Warriors' Corridor seemed so long to any of the Veltoptismakusians in the party as it did this night: never had they so wished to race their diadets as now; but they held their mounts to an even pace that would never have suggested to the most suspicious that here were six persons seeking to escape, most of them from death.

They had come almost to the exit when they were aware that the pursuit had turned into the Warriors' Corridor behind them, and that their pursuers were advancing at a rapid gait.

Janzara and Oratharc drew up beside the sentry at the mouth of the corridor as he stepped out to bar their progress.

'The Princess Janzara!' announced Oratharc. 'Aside for the Princess Janzara!'

The princess drew back the hood of the warriors' cloak she wore, revealing her features, well known to every warrior in the Royal Dome – and well feared. The fellow hesitated. 'Aside, man,' cried the princess, 'or I ride you down!'

A great shout arose behind them. Warriors on swiftly galloping diadets leaped along the corridor toward them. The warriors were shouting something, the sense of which was hidden by the distance and the noise, but the sentry was suspicious.

'Wait until I call the Novand of the Guard, princess,' he cried. 'Something is amiss, and I dare let no one pass without authority; but wait! here he is.' And the party turned in their saddles to see a Novand emerging from the door of the guardroom followed by a number of warriors.

'Ride!' cried Janzara, and spurred her diadet straight for the single sentry in their path.

The others lifted their mounts quickly in pursuit. The sentry went down striking valiantly with his rapièr at the legs and bellies of flying diadets. The Novand and his men rushed from the guardroom just in time to collide with the pursuers, whom they immediately assumed were belated members of the fleeing party. The brief minutes that these fought, before explanations could be made and understood gave the fugitives time to pass among the trees to the west side of the city and turning north, make for the hills that were dimly visible in the light of a clear but moonless night.

Oratharc, who said that he knew the hill trails perfectly, led the way, the others following as closely as they could, Komodoflorensal and Tarzan bringing up the rear Thus they moved on in silence through the night, winding along precipitous mountain trails, leaping now and again from rock to rock where the trail itself had been able to find no footing; sliding into dank ravines, clambering through heavy brush and timber along tunnel-like trails that followed their windings, or crept up their opposite sides to narrow ridge or broad plateau; and all night long no sign of pursuit developed.

The morning came at last, and with it, from the summit of a lofty ridge, a panorama of broad plain stretching to the north, of distant hills, of forests, and of streams. They decided then to descend to one of the numerous park-like glades that they could see nestling in the hills below them, and there rest their mounts and permit them to feed, for the work of the night had been hard upon them. They knew that in the hills they might hide almost indefinitely, so wild and so little travelled were they, and so they went into camp an hour after sunrise in a tiny cuplike valley surrounded by great trees, and watered and fed their mounts with a sense of security greater than they had felt since they left Veltoptismakus.

Oratharc went out on foot and killed a couple of quail, and Tarzan speared a large fish in the stream. These they prepared and ate, and then, the men taking turns on guard, they slept until afternoon, for none had had sleep the night before.

Taking up their flight again in mid-afternoon, they were well out upon the plain when darkness overtook them. Komodoflorensal and Zoanthrohago were riding on the flanks, and all were searching for a suitable camping-place. It was Zoanthrohago who found it, and when they all gathered about him Tarzan saw nothing in the waning light of day that appeared any more like a good camping-place than any other spot on the open plain. There was a little clump of trees, but they had passed many such clumps, and there was nothing about this one that appeared to offer any greater security than another.

As a matter of fact, to Tarzan it was anything but a desirable camp site. There was no water; there was little shelter from the wind and none from an enemy; but perhaps they were going into the trees. That would be better. He looked up at the lofty branches lovingly. How enormous these trees seemed! He knew them for what they were, and that they were trees of average size, yet to him now they reared their heads aloft like veritable giants.

'I will go in first,' he heard Komodoflorensal say, and turned to learn what he referred to.

The three other men were standing at the mouth of a large hole, into which they were looking. Tarzan knew that the opening was the mouth of the burrow of a ratel, the African member of the badger family, and he wondered why any of them wished to enter it.

Tarzan had never cared for the flesh of the ratel. He stepped over and joined the others, and as he did so he saw Komodoflorensal crawl into the opening, his drawn sword in his hand.

'Why is he doing that?' he asked Zoanthrohago.

'To drive out or kill the cambon, if he is there,' replied the prince, giving the ratel its Minunian name.

'And why?' asked Tarzan. 'Surely you do not eat its flesh?'

'No, but we want its home for the night,' replied Zoanthrohago. 'I had forgotten that you are not a Minunian. We will spend the night in the underground chambers of the cambon, safe from the attacks of the cat or the lion. It would be better were we there now – this is a bad hour of the night for Minunians to be abroad on the plain or in the forest. for it is at this hour that the lion hunts.'

A few minutes later Komodoflorensal emerged from the hole. 'The cambon is not there,' he said. 'The burrow is deserted. I found only a snake, which I killed. Go in, Oratharc, and Janzara and Talaskar will follow you. You have candles?'

They had, and one by one they disappeared into the mouth of the hole, until Tarzan, who had asked to remain until last, stood alone in the gathering night, gazing at the mouth of the ratel's burrow, a smile upon his lips. It seemed ridiculous to him that Tarzan of the Apes should ever be contemplating hiding from Numa in the hole of a ratel, or, worse still, hiding from little Skree, the wild-cat. And, as he stood there smiling, a bulk loomed dimly among the trees; the diadets, standing near, untethered, snorted and leaped away; and Tarzan, wheeled to face the largest lion he ever had seen – a lion that towered more than twice the ape-man's height above him.

How tremendous, how awe-inspiring Numa appeared to one the size of a Minunian!

The lion crouched, its tail extended, the tip moving ever so gently, but the ape-man was not deceived. He guessed what was coming, and even as the great cat sprang he turned and dived headforemost down the hole of the ratel. Behind him rattled the loose earth pushed into the burrow's mouth by Numa as he alighted upon the spot where Tarzan had stood.

21

The Son of the First Woman

For three days the six travelled toward the east and then, upon the fourth, they turned south. A great forest loomed upon the distant southern horizon, sweeping also wide upon the east.

To the south-west lay Trohanadalmakus, a good two days' journey for their tired diadets.

Tarzan often wondered what rest the little creatures obtained. At night they were turned loose to graze, but his knowledge of the habits of the carnivora assured him that the tiny antelope must spend the greater part of each night in terrified watching or in flight, yet every morning they were back at the camp awaiting the pleasure of their masters.

That they did not escape, never to return, is doubtless due to two principal facts. One is that they have been for ages bred in the domes of the Minunians – they know no other life than with their masters, to whom they look for food and care – and the other is the extreme kindness and affection which the Minunians accord their beautiful beasts of burden, and which have won the love and confidence of the little animals to such an extent that the diadet is most contented when in the company of man.

It was during the afternoon of the fourth day of their flight that Talaskar suddenly called their attention to a small cloud of dust far to their rear. For a while all six watched it intently as it increased in size and drew nearer.

'It may be the long awaited pursuit,' said Zoanthrohago.

'Or some of my own people from Trohanadalmakus,' suggested Komodoflorensal.

'Whoever they are they greatly outnumber us,' said Janzara, 'and I think we should find shelter until we know their identity.'

'We can reach the forest before they overtake us,' said Oratharc, 'and in the forest we may elude them if it is necessary to do so.'

'I fear the forest,' said Janzara.

'We have no alternative,' said Zoanthrohago; 'but even now I doubt that we can reach it ahead of them. Come, we must be quick!'

Never before had Tarzan of the Apes covered ground so rapidly upon the back of an animal. The diadets flew through the air in great bounds. Behind them the nucleus of the dust cloud had resolved itself into a dozen mounted warriors, against whom their four blades would be helpless. Their one hope, therefore, lay in reaching the forest ahead of their pursuers, and now it appeared that they would not.

The recently distant wood seemed to be rushing toward him as Tarzan watched ahead between the tiny horns of his graceful mount, and, behind, the enemy was gaining. They were Veltoptismakusians – they were close enough now for the devices upon their helmets to be seen – and they had recognized their quarry, for they cried aloud upon them to stop calling several of them by name.

One of the pursuers forged further ahead than the others. He came now close behind Zoanthrohago, who rode neck and neck with Tarzan in the rear of their party. A half length ahead of Zoanthrohago was Janzara. The fellow called aloud to her.

'Princess!' he cried. 'The king's pardon for you all if you return the slaves to us. Surrender and all will be forgiven.'

Tarzan of the Apes heard and he wondered what the Veltoptismakusians would do. It must have been a great temptation and he knew it. Had it not been for Talaskar he would have advised them to fall back among their friends, but he would not see the slave girl sacrificed. He drew his sword then and dropped back beside Zoanthrohago, although the other never guessed his purpose.

'Surrender and all will be forgiven!' shouted the pursuer again.

'Never!' cried Zoanthrohago.

'Never!' echoed Janzara.

'The consequences are yours,' cried the messenger, and on they rushed, pursuers and pursued, toward the dark forest, while from just within its rim savage eyes watched the mad race, and red tongues licked hungry lips in anticipation.

Tarzan had been glad to hear the reply given by both Zoanthrohago and Janzara, whom he had found likeable companions and good comrades. Janzara's whole attitude had changed since the very instant she had joined them in their attempted escape.

No longer was she the spoiled daughter of a despot, but a woman seeking happiness through the new love that she had found, or the old love that she had but just discovered, for she often told Zoanthrohago that she knew now that she always had loved him.

She seemed now to be trying to make up to Talaskar for the cruelty of her attack upon her when she had first seen her. Her mad infatuation for Tarzan she now knew in its true light – because she had been refused him she wanted him, and she would have taken him as her prince to spite her father, whom she hated.

Komodoflorensal and Talaskar always rode together, but no words of love did the Trohanadalmakusian speak in the ear of the little slave girl. A great resolve was crystallizing in his mind, but it had as yet taken on no definite form. And Talaskar, happy just to be near him, rode blissfully through the first days of the only freedom she had ever known, but now all was forgotten except the instant danger of capture and its alternative concomitants, death or slavery.

The six urged their straining mounts ahead. The forest was so near now. Ah, if they could but reach it! There, one warrior might be as good as three and the odds against them would be reduced, for in the forest the whole twelve could not engage them at once and by careful manoeuvring they doubtless could separate their pursuers.

They were going to make it! A great shout arose to the lips of Oratharc as his diadet leaped into the shadows of the first trees, and the others took it up for a brief instant, and then it died upon their lips as they saw a giant hand reach down and snatch Oratharc from his saddle. They tried to stop and wheel their mounts, but it was too late.

Already they were in the forest and all about them was a horde of the hideous Zertalacolols. One by one they were snatched from their diadets, while their pursuers, who must have seen what was taking place just inside the forest, wheeled and galloped away.

Talaskar, writhing in the grip of a she Alali, turned toward Komodoflorensal.

'Goodbye!' she cried. 'This, at last, is the end, but I can die near you and so I am happier dying than I have been living until you came to Veltoptismakus.'

'Goodbye, Talaskar!' he replied. 'Living I dared not tell you, but dying I can proclaim my love. Tell me that you love me.'

'With all my heart, Komodoflorensal!' They seemed to have forgotten that another existed but themselves. In death they were alone with their love.

Tarzan found himself in the hand of a male, and he also found himself wondering, even as he faced certain death, how it occurred that this great band of male and female Alali should be hunting together, and then he noticed the weapons of the males. They were not the crude bludgeon and the slinging stones that they had formerly carried, but long, trim spears, and bows and arrows.

And now the creature that held him had lifted him even with his face and was scrutinizing him and Tarzan saw a look of recognition and amazement cross the bestial features, and he, in turn, recognized his captor. It was the son of the First Woman.

Tarzan did not wait to learn the temper of his old acquaintance. Possibly their relations were altered now. Possibly they were not. He recalled the dog-like devotion of the creature when last he had seen him and he put him to the test at once.

'Put me down!' he signed, peremptorily. 'And tell your people to put down all of my people. Harm them not!'

Instantly the great creature set Tarzan gently upon the ground and immediately signalled his fellows to do the same with their captives. The men did immediately as they were bid and all of the women but one. She hesitated. The son of the First Woman leaped towards her, his spear raised like a whip, and the female cowered and set Talaskar down upon the ground.

Very proud, the son of the First Woman explained to Tarzan as best he could the great change that had come upon the Alali since the ape-man had given the men weapons and the son of the First Woman had discovered what a proper use of them would mean to the males of his kind. Now each male had a woman cooking for him – at least one, and some of them, the stronger, had more than one.

To entertain Tarzan and to show him what great strides civilization had taken in the land of the Zertalacolols, the son of the First Woman seized a female by the hair and, dragging her to him, struck her heavily about the head and face with his clenched fist, and the woman fell upon her knees and fondled his legs, looking wistfully into his face, her own eloquent with love and admiration.

That night the six slept in the open surrounded by the great Zertalacolols and the next day they started across the plain toward Trohanadalmakus where Tarzan had resolved to remain until he regained his normal size, when he would make a determined effort to cut his way through the thorn forest to his own country.

The Zertalacolols went a short distance out into the plain with them, and both men and women tried in their crude, savage way, to show Tarzan their gratitude for the change that he had wrought among them, and the new happiness he had given them.

Two days later the six fugitives approached the domes of Trohanadalmakus. They had been seen by sentries when they were still a long way off, and a body of warriors rode forth to meet them, for it is always well to learn the nature of a visitor's business in Minuni before he gets too close to your home.

When the warriors discovered that Komodoflorensal and Tarzan had returned they shouted for joy and a number of them galloped swiftly back to the city to spread the news. The fugitives were conducted at once to the throne-room of Adendrohahkis, and there that great ruler took his son in his arms and wept, so great was his happiness at having him returned safely to him. Nor did he forget Tarzan, although it was some time before he or the other Trohanadalmakusians could accustom themselves to the fact that this man, no bigger than they, was the giant who had dwelt among them a few moons since.

Adendrohahkis called Tarzan to the foot of the throne, and there, before the nobles and warriors of Trohanadalmakus, he made him a zertol, or prince, and he gave him diadets and riches and allotted him quarters fitted to his rank, begging him to stay among them always.

Janzara, Zoanthrohago, and Oratharc he gave their liberty and permission to remain in Trohanadalmakus, and then Komodoflorensal drew Talaskar to the foot of the throne.

'And now for myself I ask a boon, Adendrohahkis,' he said. 'As Zertolosto, I am bound by custom to wed a prisoner princess taken from another city; but in this slave girl have I found the one I love. Let me renounce my rights to the throne and have her instead.'

Talaskar raised her hand as if to demur, but Komodoflorensal would not let her speak, and then Adendrohahkis arose and descended the steps at the foot of which Talaskar stood and, taking her by the hand, led her to a place beside the throne.

'You are bound by custom only, Komodoflorensal,' he said, 'to wed a princess, but custom is not law. A Trohanadalmakusian may wed whom he pleases.'

'And even though he were bound by law,' said Talaskar, 'to wed a princess, still might he wed me, for I am the daughter of Talaskhago, King of Mandalmakus. My mother was captured by the Veltoptismakusians but a few moons before my birth, which took place in the very chamber in which Komodoflorensal found me.

'She charged me to take my life before mating with anyone less than a prince, but I would have forgotten her teachings had Komodoflorensal been but the son of a slave.

'That he was the son of a king I did not dream until the night we left Veltoptismakus, and I had already given him my heart long before, although he did not know it.'

Weeks passed, and still no change came to Tarzan of the Apes. He was happy in his life with the Minunians, but he longed for his own people and the mate who would be grieving for him, and so he determined to set forth as he was, pass through the thorn forest, and make his way toward home, trusting to chance that he might escape the countless dangers that would infest his way. Perhaps he would come to his normal size somewhere during the long journey.

His friends sought to dissuade him, but he was determined, and at last, brooking no further delay, he set out toward the south-east in the direction that he thought lay the point where he had entered the land of the Minuni. A kamak, a body consisting of one thousand mounted warriors, accompanied him to the great forest, and there, after some days' delay, the son of the First Woman found him. The Minunians bade him goodbye, and as he watched them ride away upon their graceful mounts something arose in his throat that only came upon those few occasions in his life that Tarzan of the Apes knew the meaning of homesickness.

The son of the First Woman and his savage band escorted Tarzan to the edge of the thorn forest. Farther than that they could not go. A moment later they saw him disappear among the thorns, with a wave of farewell to them.

For two days Tarzan, no larger than a Minunian, made his way through the thorn forest. He met small animals that now were large enough to be dangerous to him, but he met nothing that he could not cope with. By night he slept in the underground dens of the larger burrowing animals. Birds and eggs formed his food supply.

During the second night he awoke with a feeling of nausea suffusing him.

A premonition of danger assailed him. It was dark as the grave in the burrow he had selected for the night.

Suddenly the thought smote him that he might be about to pass through the ordeal of regaining his normal stature. To have this thing happen while he lay buried in this tiny burrow would mean death, for he would be crushed or suffocated before he regained consciousness. Already he felt dizzy, as one might feel who was upon the verge of unconsciousness. He stumbled to his knees and clawed his way up the steep acclivity that led to the surface. Would he be able to reach it in time?

He stumbled on, and then, abruptly, a burst of fresh night air smote his nostrils. He staggered to his feet. He was out! He was free!

Behind him he heard a low growl. Grasping his sword, he lunged forward among the thorn trees. How far he went, or in what direction, he did not know, but as he ran he instinctively tore his clothing from his feverish body. It was still dark when he stumbled and fell unconscious to the ground.

22
The River Devil

Khamis, the witch doctor, searched untiringly for Uhha, his young daughter. A tribal rumour had arisen that a River Devil had stolen her from their home village of Obebe, the cannibal. The father suspected that a ravenous lion or a marauding leopard had taken the child, but he doggedly made pilgrimages to other villages, some of them remote from his own country. So far he had found no slightest trace of the girl or her abductor.

Khamis was returning from another fruitless search that had extended far to the east of the village of Obebe, skirting the Great Thorn Forest a few miles north of the Ugogo. It was early morning. He had just broken his lonely camp and set out upon the last leg of his homeward journey when his keen old eyes discovered something unusual lying at the edge of a small open space a hundred yards away.

He did not know what it was, but instinct bade him to investigate. Cautiously moving nearer, he presently identified the thing as a human knee showing above the low grass that covered the clearing. He crept closer, and suddenly his eyes narrowed and his breath made a single, odd little sound as it sucked rapidly between his lips in mechanical reaction to surprise. For that which he saw was the body of what could be naught but a River Devil – a naked, brown-skinned, beautifully proportioned man; which is one of the water-fiend's disguises, of course. It was upon its back with one knee flexed – the knee that he had seen above the grasses.

His spear advanced and ready, he approached until he stood above the motionless form. Was the River Devil dead, or was he asleep? Placing the point of his spear against the brown breast, Khamis prodded. The Devil did not awaken. He was not asleep, then; nor did he appear to be dead. Khamis knelt and placed an ear above the creature's heart. He was not dead! The witch doctor thought quickly. In his heart he did not believe in River Devils, yet there was a chance that there might be such things, and perhaps this one was shamming unconsciousness, or temporarily absent from the flesh it assumed as a disguise so that it might go among men without arousing suspicion.

But, too, it probably was the abductor of his missing daughter. That thought filled him with rage and with courage. He must force the truth from those lips even though the creature were a fiend.

He unwound a bit of fibre rope from about his waist and, turning the helpless form over, quickly bound the wrists behind it. Then he sat down beside it to wait. An hour passed before signs of returning consciousness appeared, then the River Devil opened his eyes and looked up at Khamis.

'Where is Uhha, my daughter?' demanded the witch doctor.

The River Devil tried to free his arms, but they were too tightly bound. He made no reply to Khamis's question. It was as if he had not heard it. He ceased struggling and lay back again, resting. After a while he open his eyes once more and lay looking up at Khamis; but he did not speak.

'Get up!' commanded the witch doctor, and prodded him with a spear.

The River Devil rolled over on his side, flexed his right knee, raised on one elbow and finally got to his feet. Khamis prodded him in the direction of the trail. Toward dusk they arrived at the village of Obebe, the cannibal.

When the warriors and the women and the children saw what Khamis was bringing to the village they became very much excited, and had it not been for the witch doctor, of whom they were afraid, they would have knifed and stoned the prisoner to death before he was fairly inside the village gates; but Khamis did not want the River Devil killed – not yet. He wanted first to force from him the truth concerning Uhha. So far he had been unable to get a word out of his prisoner. Incessant questioning, emphasized by many prods of the spear point, had elicited nothing.

Khamis led his prisoner into a hut, bound him even more securely, and placed two warriors on guard. Obebe came to see him. He, too, questioned him, but the River Devil only looked blankly in the face of the chief.

'I will make him speak,' said Obebe. 'After we have finished eating we will have him out and make him speak. I know many ways.'

'You must not kill him,' said the witch doctor. 'He knows what became of Uhha, and until he tells me no one shall kill him.'

'He will speak before he dies,' said Obebe.

'He is a River Devil, and will never die,' said Khamis, reverting to an old tribal controversy.

After the cannibals had eaten they heated irons in a fire near the hut of the witch doctor, who was squatting before the entrance working rapidly with numerous charms – bits of wood wrapped in leaves, pieces of stone, some pebbles, a zebra's tail.

Villagers were congregating about Khamis until presently the prisoner could no longer see him. A little later he was taken out and pushed roughly towards the hut of the witch doctor.

Obebe was there, as he saw after the guards had opened a way through the throng, and he stood beside the fire in the centre of the circle. It was only a small fire – just enough to keep a couple of irons hot.

'Where, is Uhha, my daughter?' demanded Khamis.

The River Devil did not answer. Not once had he spoken since Khamis had captured him.

'Burn out one of his eyes,' said Obebe. 'That will make him speak'

The witch doctor arose and put the question again, but received no reply. Then he struck the River Devil a heavy blow in the face. Khamis had lost his temper, so that he did not fear even the sinister silence of this fiend.

'You will answer me now!' he screamed, and, stooping, he seized a red hot iron.

'The right eye first!' shrilled Obebe.

Suddenly the muscles upon the back and shoulders of the prisoner leaped into action, rolling beneath his brown hide. For just an instant he appeared to exert a terrific physical force, there was a snapping sound at his back as the strands about his wrists parted, and then steel-thewed fingers fell upon the right wrist of the witch doctor.

Blazing eyes burned into his. Khamis dropped the red hot rod, his fingers paralysed by the pressure upon his wrist, and he screamed, for he saw death in the angry face of the River Devil.

Obebe leaped frantically to his feet. Warriors pressed forward – but not near enough to be within reach of the River Devil. They had never been certain of the safety of tempting fate in any such manner as Khamis and Obebe had been about to do. Now here was the result!

The wrath of the River Devil would fall upon them all. They fell back, some of them, and that was a cue for others to fall back. In the minds of all was the same thought: 'If I have no hand in this, the River Devil will not be angry with me.' Then they turned and fled to their huts, stumbling over women and children who were trying to out-distance their lords and masters.

Obebe turned now to flee also, and the River Devil picked Khamis up and held him in his two hands high above his head, and ran after the chief. Obebe dodged into his own hut. He had scarce reached the centre of it when there came a terrific crash upon the light, thatched roof, which gave way beneath a heavy weight. A body descending upon the chief filled him with terror.

The River Devil must have leaped in through the roof of his hut to destroy him! The instinct of self-preservation arose temporarily above his fear of the supernatural, for now he was convinced that Khamis had been right and the creature they had held prisoner was indeed the River Devil.

And Obebe drew the knife at his side and lunged it again and again into the creature that had leaped upon him, and when he knew that life was extinct he stood proudly erect and, dragging the body after him, stepped out of his hut into the light of the moon and the fires.

'Come, my people!' he cried. 'You have nothing to fear, for I, Obebe, your chief, have slain the River Devil with my own hands,' and then he looked down at the thing trailing behind him, and gave a gasp, and sat down suddenly in the dust of the village street. For the body at his heels was that of Khamis, the witch doctor.

His people came, and when they saw what had happened they said nothing, but looked terrified. Obebe examined his hut and the ground around it. He took several warriors and searched the village. The stranger had departed. They went to the gates. These were closed, but in the dust before them was the imprint of naked feet – the naked feet of a white man. Then Obebe came back to his hut, where his frightened people stood waiting him.

'Khamis was mistaken,' he said. 'The creature was not the River Devil. It must have been the man that I have heard called Tarzan of the Apes, for only he could hurl Khamis so high above his head that he would fall through the roof of a hut, and only he could pass unaided over our gates.'

23

The Subtlest Vibration

A Waziri, returning from the village of Obebe the cannibal, encountered a hungry python on the trail. In making a wide and discreet detour through the jungle, he discovered a human skeleton. This find, in itself, was nothing remarkable. Many bones lie alongside savage trails in Africa.

But this skeleton caused him to pause. It was that of a child. Yet this alone was not enough to delay a warrior hastening through an unfriendly country back toward his own people.

But Usula, the spearman, had heard strange tales in the village of Obebe the cannibal, where a vague hint had brought him in search of his beloved master, the Big Bwana. Obebe had promptly denied that he had seen or heard anything of the giant white man, Tarzan of the Apes. He spoke much and argumentatively of a River Devil instead.

From other members of the tribe, however, the Waziri learned that the terrible creature whom the chief foolishly tried to torture had left in the dust the footprints of a white man, lacking the callouses and the prehensile, outspread toes of the natives. Usula, therefore, was on the lookout for any clue that would fit the story of Obebe, or give that cannibal chieftain the lie.

When he saw the small skeleton near the trail he recalled the story of the missing Uhha; poked among the bones with the blade of his spear and retrieved a copper necklace which a woman of the cannibal tribe had described as belonging to the daughter of the ill-fated witch doctor. And then Usula knew that Obebe had lied. A River Devil leaves behind no trace of the human victim.

So now the warrior renewed his eager search for the white man who had pressed straight, firm toes in the dust of Obebe's village path. This identification, coupled with the tale of his terrific strength, pointed to none other than Tarzan of the Apes.

Usula sought his missing master with all the hunting skill of his meat-eating tribe. He climbed trees to take observations of the wide veldt where grazed the antelope herds.

If, miles away, he saw a flurried movement among the grazing animals he made his way there. But always the alarm had been from some beast of prey, perhaps a hunting leopard or cheetah, or maybe only the scent of lion brought down on the wind.

And ever the warrior cast a raging glance aloft at the arching sky to where the vultures moved in their sentinel circles. He had a sullen bitter fear of seeing these slow, feathery windings turn into an aerial funnel that should touch the earth where Tarzan of the Apes might lie helpless or even beyond help.

Three days after finding the child's skeleton, as he moved silently along the trail close to the Great Thorn Forest, he came suddenly to a halt, the hand grasping his heavy spear tensing in readiness. In a little open place he saw a man, an almost naked man, lying upon the ground. The man was alive – he saw him move – but what was he doing?

Usula crept closer, making no noise. He moved around until he could observe the man from another angle, and then he saw a horrid sight. This man was white and he lay beside the carcass of a long-dead buffalo, greedily devouring the dried remnants of hide that clung to the bleaching bones.

The man raised his head a little, and Usula, catching a better view of his face, gave a cry of horror. Then the man looked up and grinned foolishly. It was the Big Bwana! Usula ran to him and raised him upon his knees, but the man only smiled and grinned like an infant as yet without the power of speech.

At his side, caught over one of the horns of the buffalo, was the Big Bwana's golden locket with the great diamonds set in it. Usula replaced it about the master's neck.

He then built a strong shelter for him near by and hunted food, and for many days he remained until Tarzan's strength came back; but his mind did not come back, nor did his speech. And thus, in this condition, the faithful Usula led his master home.

They found many wounds and bruises upon his body and his head; some old, some new, some trivial, some serious; and they sent to England for a great surgeon to come out to Africa to seek to mend the poor thing that once had been Tarzan of the Apes. The dogs that had once loved Lord Greystoke slunk uneasily from this brainless creature. Jad-bal-ja, the Golden Lion, growled when the man was brought near his cage.

Korak, the Killer, paced the floor in dumb despair, for his mother was on her way from England, and what would be the effect upon her of this awful blow? He hesitated even to contemplate it.

The surgeon arrived first at the bungalow of the ape-man. He examined his patient at great length, paying particular attention to the skull. And the puzzled shaking of the scientist's head was an added terror to the hearts of Korak and Meriem, his wife.

Being a truly great surgeon, he did not operate at once. Instead, he discoursed learnedly of 'fictitious imbecility,' 'amnesia,' and 'aphasia,' and the like, and then courteously translated the terms into common phrases for his lay hearers.

'Tarzan has sustained some subtle shock,' he declared, 'and there probably is lacking only a slight vibration to restore him to his normal senses. You will observe that he has not the true signs of imbecility – his head does not loll on his neck; he does not drool at the mouth.

'His amnesia – loss of memory – is complete for the moment, as is his aphasia – loss of speech. As opposed to these disabilities is the fact that he reacts swiftly to a brusque touch or harsh sound.

'Undoubtedly, he fled for many hours in the jungle from pursuing beasts of prey, and perhaps imaginary dangers, until he dropped exhausted. Those hardships, however, do not account for his mental condition. I shall await the arrival of his wife before operating on the head.'

Lady Greystoke was a tired and dusty traveller as she alighted before the rose-embowered entrance of the bungalow. Korak, her son, would have detained her in the hope that his words of warning might prepare her for the worst. He had not dared to put all the truth in his cable and radio messages.

She gently put his hands aside.

'Take me to my man, at once!' she said, softly but imperiously.

Her distressed son motioned to Meriem and the surgeon to accompany them, and so the four entered the room where Tarzan of the Apes sat staring dully at the shining world visible through the window. He glanced with a blank air at the intruders, and turned again to his brainless contemplation.

'He does not know any of us,' Korak whispered to his mother. 'Wait until after the operation before you see him again. You can do him no good, and to see him this way is too hard a strain upon you.' Again Lady Greystoke calmly disregarded the plea of her son. It was as if she instinctively knew more of the ailing human before her than did the great surgeon.

With a cautionary finger on her proud lips to enforce silence on the spectators, she stole silently toward the unsuspecting ape-man. Here she clapped her slender hands on to his eyelids and called out, laughingly:

'Guess!'

At the touch of these trembling, loving hands, an electric shock appeared to course through Tarzan of the Apes. His lips spread in a smile – a human, understanding amusement; and he laughed the deep-throated note of his normal days.

'As if I wouldn't know the touch of your fingers, my dear wife, in this world or the next!' he said triumphantly.

TARZAN, LORD OF THE JUNGLE

1

Tantor the Elephant

His great bulk swaying to and fro as he threw his weight first upon one side and then upon the other, Tantor the elephant lolled in the shade of the father of forests. Almost omnipotent, he, in the realm of his people. Dango, Sheeta, even Numa the mighty were as naught to the pachyderm. For a hundred years he had come and gone up and down the land that had trembled to the comings and the goings of his forebears for countless ages. In peace he had lived with Dango the hyena, Sheeta the leopard and Numa the lion. Man alone had made war upon him. Man, who holds the unique distinction among created things of making war on all created things, even to his own kind. Man, the ruthless; man, the pitiless; man, the most hated living organism that Nature has evolved.

Always, during the long hundred years of his life, Tantor had known man. There had been black men, always. Big black warriors with spears and arrows; little black warriors; swart Arabs with crude muskets, white men with powerful express rifles and elephant guns. The white men had been the last to come – and were the worst. Yet Tantor did not hate men – not even white men. Hate, vengeance, envy, avarice, lust are a few of the delightful emotions reserved exclusively for Nature's noblest work – the *lower* animals do not know them. Neither do they know fear as man knows it, but rather a certain bold caution that sends the antelope and the zebra, watchful and wary, to the water-hole with the lion.

Tantor shared this caution with his fellows and avoided men – especially white men and so, had there been other eyes there that day to see, their possessor might almost have questioned their veracity, or attributed their error to the half-light of the forest as they scanned the figure sprawling prone upon the rough back of the elephant, half dozing in the heat to the swaying of the great body, for, despite the sun-bronzed hide, the figure was quite evidently that of a white man. But there were no other eyes to see; Tantor drowsed in the heat of mid-day, and Tarzan, Lord of the Jungle, dozed upon the back of his mighty friend. A sultry air-current moved sluggishly from the North, bringing to the keen nostrils of the ape-man no disquieting perception. Peace lay upon the jungle and the two beasts were content.

In the forest, Fahd and Motlog, of the tribe el Harb, hunted north from the menzil of Sheik Ibn Jad of the Beny Sâlem fendy el-Guâd. With them were black slaves. They advanced warily and in silence upon the fresh spoor of el-fîl the elephant; the thoughts of the swart 'Aarab dwelt upon ivory, those of the black slaves upon fresh meat. The 'abd Fejjuân, black Galla slave, sleek, ebon warrior, eater of raw meat, famed hunter, led the others. Fejjuân, as his comrades, thought of fresh meat, but also he thought of el-Hábash, the land from which he had been stolen as a boy. He thought of coming again to the lonely Galla hut of his parents. Perhaps el-Hábash was not far off now. For months Ibn Jad had been travelling south and now he had come east for a long distance. El-Hábash must be near. When he was sure of that, his days of slavery would be over and Ibn Jad would have lost his best Galla slave.

Two marches to the north, in the southern extremity of Abyssinia, stood the round dwelling of the father of Fejjuân, almost on the roughly mapped route that Ibn Jad had planned nearly a year since when he had undertaken this mad adventure upon the advice of a learned Séhar, a magician of repute. But of either the exact location of his father's house or the exact plans of Ibn Jad, Fejjuân was equally ignorant. He but dreamed, and his dreams were flavoured with raw meat.

The leaves of the forest drowsed in the heat above the heads of the hunters. Beneath the drowsing leaves of other trees a stone's throw ahead of them, Tarzan and Tantor drowsed, their perceptive faculties momentarily dulled by the soothing influence of fancied security and the somnolence that is a corollary of equatorial mid-day.

Fejjuân, the Galla slave, stopped in his tracks, stopping those behind him by the silent mandate of an upraised hand. Directly before him, seen dimly between the boles and through the foliage, swayed the giant bulk of el-fîl. Fejjuân motioned to Fahd, who moved stealthily to the side of the black. The Galla slave pointed through the foliage toward a patch of grey hide. Fahd raised el-Lazzáry, his ancient matchlock, to his shoulder. There was a flash of flame, a burst of smoke, a roar and el-fîl, unhit, was bolting through the forest.

As Tantor surged, forward at the sound of the report, Tarzan started to spring to an upright position and at the same instant the pachyderm passed beneath a low-hanging limb which struck the ape-man squarely across the side of his head, sweeping him to the ground, where he lay stunned and unconscious.

Terrified, Tantor thought only of escape as he ran north through the forest, leaving in his wake felled trees, trampled or uptorn bushes. Perhaps he did not know that his friend lay helpless and injured, at the mercy of the common enemy, man. Tantor never thought of Tarzan as one of the Tarmangani, for the white man was synonymous with discomfort, pain, annoyance, whereas Tarzan of the Apes meant to him restful companionship, peace, happiness. Of all the jungle beasts except his own kind he fraternised with Tarzan only.

'Billah! Thou missed,' exclaimed Fejjuân.

'Gluck!' ejaculated Fahd. 'Sheytân guided the bullet. But let us see – perhaps el-fîl is hit.'

'Nay, thou missed.'

The two men pushed forward, followed by their fellows, looking for the hoped-for carmine spoor. Fahd was in the lead now. Suddenly he stopped.

'Wellah! What have we here?' he cried. 'I fired at el-fîl and killed a Nasrâny.'

The others crowded about. 'It is indeed a Christian dog, and naked, too,' said Motlog.

'Or some wild man of the forest,' suggested another. 'Where didst thy bullet strike him, Fahd?'

They stooped and rolled Tarzan over. 'There is no mark of bullet upon him.'

'Is he dead? Perhaps he, too, hunted el-fîl and was slain by the great beast.'

'He is not dead,' announced Fejjuân, who had kneeled and placed an ear above the ape-man's heart. 'He lives and from the mark upon his head I think but temporarily out of his wits from a blow. See, he lies in the path that el-fîl made when he ran away – he was struck down in the brute's flight.'

'I will finish him,' said Fahd, drawing his khûsa.

'By Ullah, no! Put back thy knife, Fahd,' said Motlog. 'Let the sheik say if he shall be killed. Thou art always too eager to let the blood of another.'

'It is but a Nasrâny,' insisted Fahd. 'Think thou to carry him back to the menzil?'

'He moves,' said Fejjuân. 'Presently he will be able to walk there without help. But perhaps he will not come with us and look, he hath the size and muscles of a giant. Wellah! What a man!'

'Bind him,' commanded Fahd, and with thongs of camel hide they made the ape-man's two wrists secure together across his belly, nor was the work completed any too soon. They had scarce done when Tarzan opened his eyes and looked them slowly over. He shook his head, like some great lion, and presently his senses cleared. He recognised the 'Aarab instantly for what they were.

'Why are my wrists bound?' he asked them in their own tongue. 'Remove the thongs!'

Fahd laughed. 'Thinkest thou, Nasrâny, that thou art some great sheik that thou canst order about the Beduw as they were dogs?'

'I am Tarzan,' replied the ape-man, as one might say, 'I am the sheik of sheiks.'

'Tarzan!' exclaimed Motlog. He drew Fahd aside. 'Of all men,' he said, lowering his voice, 'that it should be our ill-fortune to offend this one! In every village that we have entered in the past two weeks we have heard his name. "Wait," they have said, "until Tarzan, Lord of the Jungle, returns. He will slay you when he learns that you have taken slaves in his country".'

'When I drew my khûsa thou shouldst not have stopped my hand, Motlog,' complained Fahd; 'but it is not too late yet.' He placed his hand upon the hilt of his knife.

'Billah, nay!' cried Motlog. 'We have taken slaves in this country. They are with us now and some of them will escape. That you know as well as I. Suppose they carry word to the fendy of this great sheik that we have slain him? Not one of us will live to return to Béled el-Guâd.'

'Let us then take him before Ibn Jad that the responsibility may be his,' said Fahd.

'Wellah, you speak wisely,' replied Motlog. 'What the sheik doeth with this man is the sheik's business. Come!'

As they returned to where Tarzan stood he eyed them questioningly.

'What have you decided to do with me?' he demanded. 'If you are wise you will cut these bonds and lead me to your sheik. I wish a word with him.'

'We are only poor men,' said Motlog. 'It is not for us to say what shall be done and so we shall take you to our sheik, who will decide.'

The Sheik Ibn Jad of the fendy el-Guâd squatted in the open men's compartment of his beyt es-sh'ar and beside him in the mukaad of his house of hair sat Tollog, his brother, and a young Beduin, Zeyd, who, doubtless, found less attraction in the company of the sheik than in the proximity of the sheik's hareem, whose quarters were separated from the mukaad only by a breast-high curtain suspended between the waist poles of the beyt, affording thus an occasional glimpse of Ateja, the daughter of Ibn Jad. That it also afforded an occasional glimpse of Hirfa, his wife, raised not the temperature of Zeyd an iota.

As the men talked, the two women were busy within their apartment at their housewifely duties. In a great brazen jidda, Hirfa was placing mutton to be boiled for the next meal, while Ateja fashioned sandals from an old bag of camel leather impregnated with the juice of the dates that it had borne upon many a ráhla; and meanwhile they missed naught of the conversation that passed in the mukaad.

'We have come a long way without mishap from our own Béled,' Ibn Jad was remarking, 'and the way has been longer because I wished not to pass through el-Hábash lest we be set upon or followed by the people of that country. Now may we turn north again and enter el-Hábash close to the spot where the magician foretold we should find the treasure city of Nímmr.'

'And thinkest thou to find this fabled city easily, once we are within the boundaries of el-Hábash?' asked Tollog, his brother.

'Wellah, yes. It is known to the people of this far south Hábash. Fejjuân, himself an Hábashy, though he has never been there, heard of it as a boy. We shall take prisoners among them, and, by the grace of Allah, we shall find the means to loose their tongues and have the truth from them.'

'By Ullah, I hope it does not prove like the treasure that lies upon the great rock el-Howwâra in the plain of Medáin Sâlih,' said Zeyd. 'An afrit guards it where it lies sealed in a stone tower and they say that should it be removed, disaster would befall mankind, for men would turn upon their friends, and even upon their brothers, the sons of their fathers and mothers, and the kings of the world would give battle one against another.'

'Yea,' testified Tollog, 'I had it from one of the fendy Hazim that a wise Móghreby came by there in his travels and consulting the cabalistic signs in his book of magic discovered that indeed the treasure lay there.'

'But none dared take it up,' said Zeyd.

'Billah!' exclaimed Ibn Jad. 'There be no afrit guarding the treasures of Nímmr. Naught but flesh and blood Habûsh that may be laid low with ball and powder. The treasure is ours for the taking.'

'Ullah grant that it may be as easily found as the treasure of Geryeh,' said Zeyd, 'which lies a journey north of Tebuk in the ancient ruins of a walled city. There, each Friday, the pieces of money roll out of the ground and run about over the desert until sunset.'

'Once we are come to Nimmr there will be no difficulty finding the treasure,' Ibn Jad assured them. 'The difficulty will lie in getting out of el-Hábash with the treasure and the woman, and if she is as beautiful as the Séhar said, the men of Nímmr may protect her even more savagely than they would the treasure.'

'Often do magicians lie,' said Tollog.

'Who comes?' exclaimed Ibn Jad, looking toward the jungle that hemmed the menzil upon all sides.

'Billah! It is Fahd and Motlog returning from the hunt,' said Tollog. 'Ullah grant that they bring ivory and meat.'

'They return too soon,' said Zeyd.

'But they do not come empty-handed,' and Ibn Jad pointed toward the naked giant that accompanied the returning hunters.

The group surrounding Tarzan approached the sheik's beyt and halted. Wrapped in his soiled calico thôb, his head kerchief drawn across the lower part of his face, Ibn Jad exposed two villainous eyes to the intent scrutiny of the ape-man which simultaneously included the pock-marked, shifty-eyed visage of Tollog, the sheik's brother, and the not ill-favoured countenance of the youthful Zeyd.

'Who is sheik here?' demanded Tarzan in tones of authority that belied the camel-leather thongs about his wrists.

Ibn Jad permitted his thorrîb to fall from before his face. 'Wellah, I am sheik,' he said, 'and by what name art thou known, Nasrâny?'

'They call me Tarzan of the Apes, Moslem.'

'Tarzan of the Apes,' mused Ibn Jad. 'I have heard the name.'

'Doubtless. It is not unknown to 'Aarab slave raiders. Why, then, came you to my country, knowing that I do not permit my people to be taken into slavery?'

'We do not come for slaves,' Ibn Jad assured him. 'We do but trade in peace for ivory.'

'Thou liest in thy beard, Moslem,' returned Tarzan, quietly. 'I recognise both Manyuema and Galla slaves in thy menzil and I know that they are not here of their own choosing. Then, too, was I not present when your henchmen fired a shot at el-fîl? Is that peaceful trading for ivory? No! It is poaching, and that Tarzan of the Apes does not permit in his country. You are raiders and poachers.'

'By Ullah! we are honest men,' cried Ibn Jad. 'Fahd and Motlog did but hunt for meat. If they shot el-fîl it must be that they mistook him for another beast.'

'Enough!' cried Tarzan. 'Remove the thongs that bind me and prepare to return north whence thou came. Thou shalt have an escort and bearers to the Sudan. These will I arrange for.'

'We have come a long way and wish only to trade in peace,' insisted Ibn Jad. 'We shall pay our bearers for their labour and take no slaves, nor shall we again fire upon el-fîl. Let us go our way and when we return we will pay you well for permission to pass through your country.'

Tarzan shook his head. 'No! You shall go at once. Come, cut these bonds!'

Ibn Jad's eyes narrowed. 'We have offered thee peace and profits, Nasrâny;' he said, 'but if thou wouldst have war let it be war. Thou art in our power and remember that dead enemies are harmless. Think it over,' and to Fahd: 'Take him away and bind his feet also.'

'Be careful, Moslem,' warned Tarzan. 'The arms of the ape-man are long – they may reach out even in death and their fingers encircle your throat.'

'Thou shalt have until dark to decide, Nasrâny, and thou mayest know that Ibn Jad will not turn back until he hath that for which he came.'

They took Tarzan then and at a distance from the beyt of Ibn Jad they pushed him into a small héjra, but once within this tent it required three men to throw him to the ground and bind his ankles, even though his wrists were already bound.

In the beyt of the sheik the Bedúins sipped their coffee, sickish with clove, cinnamon and other spice, the while they discussed the ill-fortune that had befallen them, for, regardless of his bravado, Ibn Jad knew full well that only speed and most propitious circumstances could now place the seal of success upon his venture.

'But for Motlog,' said Fahd, 'we would have had no cause for worry concerning the Nasrâny, for I had my knife ready to slit the dog's throat when Motlog interfered.'

'And had word of his slaying spread broadcast over his country before another sunset and all his people at our heels,' countered Motlog.

'Wellah,' said Tollog, the sheik's brother, 'I wish Fahd had done the thing he wished. After all, how much better off are we if we permit the Nasrâny to live? Should we free him we know that he will gather his people and drive us from the country. If we keep him prisoner and an escaped slave carries word of it to his people will they not be upon us even more surely than as though we had slain him?'

'Tollog, thou speakest words of wisdom,' said Ibn Jad, nodding appreciatively.

'But wait,' said Tollog, 'I have within me, unspoken, words of even greater worth.' He leaned forward motioning the others closer and lowered his voice. 'Should this one whom they call Tarzan of the Apes escape during the night, or should we set him free, there would be no bad word for an escaped slave to bear to his people.'

'Billah!' exclaimed Fahd disgustedly. 'There would be no need for an escaped slave to bring word to his people – the Nasrâny himself would do that and lead them upon us in person. Bah! The brains of Tollog are as camel's dung.'

'Thou hast not heard all that I would say, brother,' continued Tollog, ignoring Fahd. 'It would only *seem* to the slaves that this man had escaped, for in the morning he would be gone and we would make great lamentation over the matter, or we would say: "Wellah, it is true that Ibn Jad made peace with the stranger, who departed into the jungle, blessing him".'

'I do not follow thee, brother,' said Ibn Jad.

'The Nasrâny lies bound in yonder héjra. The night will be dark. A slim knife between his ribs were enough. There be faithful Habûsh among us who will do our bidding, nor speak of the matter after. They can prepare a trench from the bottom of which a dead Tarzan may not reach out to harm us.'

'By Ullah, it is plain that thou art of sheikly blood, Tollog,' exclaimed Ibn Jad. 'The wisdom of thy words proclaims it. Thou shalt attend to the whole matter. Then will it be done secretly and well. The blessings of Ullah be upon thee!' and Ibn Jad arose and entered the quarters of his hareem.

2
Comrades of the Wild

Darkness fell upon the menzil of Ibn Jad the sheik. Beneath the small flitting tent where his captors had left him, Tarzan still struggled with the bonds that secured his wrists, but the tough camel-leather withstood even the might of his giant thews. At times he lay listening to the night noises of the jungle, many of them noises that no other human ear could have heard, and always he interpreted each correctly. He knew when Numa passed and Sheeta the leopard, and then from afar and so faintly that it was but the shadow of a whisper there came down the wind the trumpeting of a bull elephant.

Without the beyt of Ibn Jad, Ateja, the sheik's daughter, loitered and with her was Zeyd, a young Bedúin of the tribe. They stood very close to one another and the man held the maiden's hands in his.

'Tell me, Ateja,' he said, 'that you love no other than Zeyd.'

'How many times must I tell you that?' whispered the girl.

'And you do not love Fahd?' insisted the man.

'Billah, no!' she ejaculated.

'Yet your father gives the impression that one day you will be Fahd's.'

'My father wishes me to be of the hareem of Fahd, but I mistrust the man and I could not belong to one whom I neither loved nor trusted.'

'I, too, mistrust Fahd,' said Zeyd. 'Listen, Ateja! I doubt his loyalty to thy father, and not his alone, but another whose name I durst not even whisper. Upon occasions I have seen them whispering together when they thought that there were no others about.'

The girl nodded her head. 'I know. It is not necessary even to whisper the name to me – and I hate him even as I hate Fahd.'

'But he is of thine own kin,' the youth reminded her.

'What of that? Is he not also my father's brother? If that bond does not hold him loyal to Ibn Jad, who hath treated him well, why should I pretend loyalty to him? Nay, I think him a traitor to my father, but Ibn Jad seems blind to the fact. We are a long way from our own country and if aught should befall the sheik, Tollog, being next of blood, would assume the sheikly duties and honours. I think he hath won Fahd's support by a promise to further his suit for me with Ibn Jad, for I have noticed that Tollog exerts himself to praise Fahd in the hearing of my father.'

'And perhaps a division of the spoils of the ghrazzu upon the treasure city,' suggested Zeyd.

'It is not unlikely,' replied the girl, 'and – Ullah! what was that?'

The Bedúins seated about the coffee fire leaped to their feet. The black slaves, startled, peered out into the darkness from their rude shelters. Muskets were seized. Silence fell again upon the tense, listening menzil. The weird, uncanny cry that had unnerved them was not repeated.

'Billah!' ejaculated Ibn Jad. 'It came from the midst of the menzil, and it was the voice of a beast, where there are only men and a few domestic animals.'

'Could it have been—?' The speaker stopped as though fearful that the thing he would suggest might indeed be true.

'But he is a man and that was the voice of a beast,' insisted Ibn Jad. 'It could not have been he.'

'But he is a Nasrâny,' reminded Fahd. 'perhaps he has league with Sheytan.'

'And the sound came from the direction where he lies bound in a héjra,' observed another.

'Come!' said Ibn Jad. 'Let us investigate.'

With muskets ready the 'Aarab, lighting the way with paper lanterns, approached the héjra where Tarzan lay. Fearfully, the foremost looked within.

'He is here,' he reported.

Tarzan, who was sitting in the centre of the tent, surveyed the 'Aarab somewhat contemptuously. Ibn Jad pressed forward.

'You heard a cry?' he demanded of the ape-man.

'Yes, I heard it. Camest thou, Sheik Ibn Jad, to disturb my rest upon so trivial an errand, or camest thou to release me?'

'What manner of cry was it? What did it signify?' asked Ibn Jad.

Tarzan of the Apes smiled grimly. 'It was but the call of a beast to one of its kind,' he replied. 'Does the noble Bedùwy tremble thus always when he hears the voices of the jungle people?'

'Gluck!' growled Ibn Jad. 'The Beduw fear naught. We thought the sound came from this héjra and we hastened hither believing some jungle beast had crept within the menzil and attacked thee. Tomorrow it is the thought of Ibn Jad to release thee.'

'Why not tonight?'

'My people fear thee. They would that when you are released you depart hence immediately.'

'I shall. I have no desire to remain in thy lice-infested menzil.'

'We could not send thee alone into the jungle at night where el-adrea is abroad hunting,' protested the sheik!

Tarzan of the Apes smiled again, one of his rare smiles. 'Tarzan is more secure in his teeming jungle than are the Beduw in their desert,' he replied; 'the jungle night has no terrors for Tarzan.'

'Tomorrow,' snapped the sheik and then, motioning to his followers, he turned and departed.

Tarzan watched their paper lanterns bobbing across the camp to the sheik's beyt and then he stretched himself at full length and pressed an ear to the ground.

When the inhabitants of the 'Aarab menzil heard the cry of the beast shatter the quiet of the new night it aroused within their breasts a certain vague unrest, but otherwise it was meaningless to them. Yet there was one far off in the jungle who caught the call faintly and understood – a huge beast, the great, grey dreadnought of the jungle, Tantor the elephant. Again he raised his trunk aloft and trumpeted loudly. His little eyes gleamed redly wicked as, a moment later, he swung off through the forest at a rapid trot.

Slowly silence fell upon the menzil of Sheik Ibn Jad as the 'Aarab and their slaves sought their sleeping mats. Only the sheik and his brother sat smoking in the sheik's beyt – smoking and whispering in low tones.

'Do not let the slaves see you slay the Nasrâny, Tollog,' cautioned Ibn Jad. 'Attend to that yourself first in secrecy and in silence, then quietly arouse two of the slaves. Fejjuân would be as good as another, as he has been among us since childhood and is loyal. He will do well for one.'

'Abbas is loyal, too, and strong,' suggested Tollog.

'Yea, let him be the second,' agreed Ibn Jad; 'but it is well that they do not know how the Nasrâny came to die. Tell them that you heard a noise in the direction of his héjra and that when you had come to learn the nature of it you found him thus dead.'

'You may trust to my discretion, brother,' Tollog assured.

'And warn them to secrecy,' continued the sheik. 'No man but we four must ever know of the death of the Nasrâny, nor of his place of burial. In the morning we shall tell the others that he escaped during the night. Leave his cut bonds within the héjra as proof. You understand?'

'By Ullah, fully.'

'Good! Now go. The people sleep.' The sheik rose and Tollog, also. The former entered the apartment of his hareem and the latter moved silently through the darkness of the night in the direction of the héjra where his victim lay.

Through the jungle came Tantor the elephant and from his path fled gentle beasts and fierce. Even Numa the lion slunk growling to one side as the mighty pachyderm passed.

Into the darkness of the héjra crept Tollog, the sheik's brother, but Tarzan, lying with an ear to the ground, had heard him approaching from the moment that he had left the beyt of Ibn Jad. Tarzan heard other sounds as well, and, as he interpreted these others, he interpreted the stealthy approach of Tollog and was convinced when the footsteps turned into the tent where he lay – convinced of the purpose of his visitor. For what purpose but the taking of his life would a Bedúin visit Tarzan at this hour of the night?

As Tollog, groping in the dark, entered the tent Tarzan sat erect and again there smote upon the ears of the Bedúin the horrid cry that had disturbed the menzil earlier in the evening, but this time it arose in the very héjra in which Tollog stood.

The Bedúin halted, aghast. 'Ullah!' he cried, stepping back. 'What beast is here? Nasrâny! Art thou being attacked?'

Others in the camp were awakened, but none ventured forth to investigate. Tarzan smiled and remained silent.

'Nasrâny!' repeated Tollog, but there was no reply.

Cautiously, his knife ready in his hand, the Bedúin backed from the héjra. He listened but heard no sound from within. Running quickly to his own beyt he made a light in a paper lantern and hastened back to the héjra and this time he carried his musket and it was at full cock. Peering within, the lantern held above his head, Tollog saw the ape-man sitting upon the ground looking at him. There was no wild beast! Then the truth flashed into the mind of the Bedúin.

'Billah! It wast thou, Nasrâny, who made the fearful cries.'

'Bedùwy, thou comest to kill the Nasrâny, eh?' demanded Tarzan.

From the jungle came the roar of a lion and the trumpeting of a bull elephant, but the boma was high and sharp with thorns and there were guards and beast fire, so Tollog gave no thought to these familiar noises of the night. He did not answer Tarzan's question but laid aside his musket and drew his khûsa, which after all was answer enough.

In the dim light of the paper lantern Tarzan watched these preparations. He saw the cruel expression upon the malevolent face. He saw the man approaching slowly, the knife ready in his hand.

The man was almost upon him now, his eyes glittering in the faint light. To the ears of the ape-man came the sound of a commotion at the far edge of the menzil followed by an Arab oath. Then Tollog launched a blow at Tarzan's breast. The prisoner swung his bound wrists upward and struck the Bedúin's knife-arm away and simultaneously he struggled to his knees. With an oath, Tollog struck again, and again Tarzan fended the blow, and this time he followed swiftly with a mighty sweep of his arms that struck the Bedúin upon the side of the head and sent him sprawling across the héjra; but Tollog was instantly up and at him again, this time with the ferocity of a maddened bull, yet at the same time with far greater cunning, for instead of attempting a direct frontal attack Tollog leaped quickly around Tarzan to strike him from behind.

In his effort to turn upon his knees that he might face his antagonist the ape-man lost his balance, his feet being bound together, and fell prone at Tollog's mercy. A vicious smile bared the yellow teeth of the Bedúin.

'Die, Nasrâny!' he cried, and then: 'Billah! What was that?' as, of a sudden, the entire tent was snatched from above his head and hurled off into the night. He turned quickly and a shriek of terror burst from his lips as he saw, red-eyed and angry, the giant form of el-fîl towering above him, and in that very instant a supple trunk encircled his body and Tollog, the sheik's brother, was raised high aloft and hurled off into the darkness as the tent had been.

For an instant Tantor stood looking about, angrily, defiantly, then he reached down and lifted Tarzan from the ground, raised him high above his head, wheeled about and trotted rapidly across the menzil toward the jungle. A frightened sentry fired once and fled. The other sentry lay crushed and dead where Tantor had hurled him when he entered the camp. An instant later Tarzan and Tantor were swallowed by the jungle and the darkness.

The menzil of Sheik Ibn Jad was in an uproar. Armed men hastened hither and thither seeking the cause of the disturbance, looking for an attacking enemy. Some came to the spot where had stood the héjra where the Nasrâny had been confined, but héjra and Nasrâny both had disappeared. Nearby, the beyt of one of Ibn Jad's cronies lay flattened. Beneath it were screaming women and a cursing man. On top of it was Tollog, the sheik's brother, his mouth filled with vile Bedúin invective, whereas it should have contained only praises of Allah and thanksgiving, for Tollog was indeed a most fortunate man. Had he alighted elsewhere than upon the top of a sturdily-pegged beyt he had doubtless been killed or badly injured when Tantor hurled him thus rudely aside.

Ibn Jad, searching for information, arrived just as Tollog was extricating himself from the folds of the tent.

'Billah!' cried the sheik. 'What has come to pass? What, O brother, art thou doing upon the beyt of Abd-el-Aziz?'

A slave came running to the sheik. 'The Nasrâny is gone and he hath taken the héjra with him,' he cried.

Ibn Jad turned to Tollog. 'Canst thou not explain, brother?' he demanded. 'Is the Nasrâny truly departed?'

'The Nasrâny is indeed gone,' replied Tollog. 'He is in league with Sheytan, who came in the guise of el-fîl and carried the Nasrâny into the jungle, after throwing me upon the top of the beyt of Abd-el-Aziz whom I still hear squealing and cursing beneath as though it had been he who was attacked rather than I.'

Ibn Jad shook his head. Of course he knew that Tollog was a liar – that he always had known – yet he could not understand how his brother had come to be upon the top of the beyt of Abd-el-Aziz.

'What did the sentries see?' demanded the sheik. 'Where were they?'

'They were at their posts,' spoke up Motlog. 'I was just there. One of them is dead, the other fired upon the intruder as it escaped.'

'And what said he of it?' demanded Ibn Jad.

'Wellah, he said that el-fîl came and entered the menzil, killing Yémeny and rushing to the héjra where the Nasrâny lay bound, ripping it aside, throwing Tollog high into the air. Then he seized the prisoner and bore him off into the jungle and as he passed him Hásan fired.'

'And missed,' guessed Ibn Jad.

For several moments the sheik stood in thought, then he turned slowly toward his own beyt. 'Tomorrow, early, is the ráhla,' he said, and the word spread quickly that early upon the morrow they would break camp.

Far into the forest Tantor bore Tarzan until they had come to a small clearing well carpeted with grass, and here the elephant deposited his burden gently upon the ground and stood guard above.

'In the morning,' said Tarzan, 'when Kudu the Sun hunts again through the heavens and there is light by which to see, we shall discover what may be done about removing these bonds, Tantor, but for now let us sleep.'

Numa the lion, Dango the hyena, Sheeta the leopard passed near that night, and the scent of the helpless man-thing was strong in their nostrils, but when they saw who stood guard above Tarzan and heard the mutterings of the big bull they passed on about their business while Tarzan of the Apes slept.

With the coming of dawn all was quickly astir in the menzil of Ibn Jad. Scarce was the meagre breakfast eaten ere the beyt of the sheik was taken down by his women and at this signal the other houses of hair came tumbling to the ground and within the hour the 'Aarab were winding northward toward el-Hábash.

The Bedúins and their women were mounted upon the desert ponies that had survived the long journey from the north, while the slaves that they had brought with them from their own country marched afoot at the front and rear of the column in the capacity of askari, and these were armed with muskets. Their bearers were the natives that they had impressed into their service along the way. These carried the impedimenta of the camp and herded the goats and sheep along the trail.

Zeyd rode beside Ateja, the daughter of the sheik, and more often were his eyes upon her profile than upon the trail ahead. Fahd, who rode near Ibn Jad, cast an occasional angry glance in the direction of the two. Tollog, the sheik's brother, saw and grinned.

'Zeyd is a bolder suitor than thou, Fahd,' he whispered to the young man.

'He has whispered lies into her ears and she will have none of me,' complained Fahd.

'If the sheik favoured thy suit though,' suggested Tollog.

'But he does not,' snapped Fahd. 'A word from you might aid. You promised it.'

'Wellah, yes, but my brother is an over-indulgent sire,' explained Tollog. 'He doth not mislike you, Fahd, but rather he would have his bint happy and so leaves the selection of her mate to her.'

'What is there to do, then?' demanded Fahd.

'If I were sheik, now,' suggested Tollog, 'but alas I am not.'

'If you were sheik, what then?'

'My niece would go to the man of my own choosing.'

'But you are not sheik,' Fahd reminded him.

Tollog leaned close and whispered in Fahd's ear. 'A suitor as bold as Zeyd would find the way to make me sheik.'

Fahd made no reply, but only rode on in silence, his head bowed and his brows contracted in thought.

3

The Apes of Toyat

Three days crawled slowly out of the east and followed one another across the steaming jungle and over the edge of the world beyond. For three days the 'Aarab moved slowly northward toward el-Hábash. For three days Tarzan of the Apes lay in the little clearing, bound and helpless while Tantor the elephant stood guard above him. Once each day the great bull brought the ape-man food and water.

The camel-leather thongs held securely and no outside aid appeared to release Tarzan from the ever-increasing discomfort and danger of his predicament. He had called to Manu the monkey to come and gnaw the strands apart, but Manu, ever irresponsible, had only promised and forgotten. And so the ape-man lay uncomplaining, as is the way of beasts, patiently waiting for release, knowing that it might come in the habiliment of death.

Upon the morning of the fourth day Tantor gave evidences of restlessness. His brief foragings had exhausted the nearby supply of food for himself and his charge. He wanted to move on and take Tarzan with him, but the ape-man was now convinced that to be carried farther into the elephant country would lessen his chances for succour, for he felt that the only one of the jungle people who could release him was Mangani the great ape. Already Tarzan knew that he was practically at the outer limits of the Mangani country, yet there was a remote chance that a band of the great anthropoids might pass this way and discover him, while, should Tantor carry him farther north, even this meagre likelihood of release would be gone for ever.

Tantor wanted to be gone. He nudged Tarzan with his trunk and rolled him over. He raised him from the ground.

'Put me down, Tantor,' said the ape-man, and the pachyderm obeyed, but he turned and walked away. Tarzan watched him across the clearing to the trees upon the far side. There Tantor hesitated, stopped, turned. He looked back at Tarzan and trumpeted. He dug up the earth with a great tusk and appeared angry.

'Go and feed,' said Tarzan, 'and then return. Tomorrow the Mangani may come.'

Tantor trumpeted again and, wheeling about, disappeared in the jungle. For a long time the ape-man lay listening to the retreating footfalls of his old friend.

'He is gone,' he mused. 'I cannot blame him. Perhaps it is as well. What matter whether it be today, tomorrow, or the day after?'

The morning passed. The noonday silence lay upon the jungle. Only the insects were abroad. They annoyed Tarzan as they did the other jungle beasts, but to the poison of their stings he was immune through a lifetime of inoculation.

Suddenly there came a great scampering through the trees. Little Manu and his brothers, his sisters and his cousins came trooping madly through the middle terrace, squealing, chattering and scolding.

'Manu!' called Tarzan. 'What comes?'

'The Mangani! The Mangani!' shrieked the monkeys.

'Go and fetch them, Manu!' commanded the ape-man.

'We are afraid.'

'Go and call to them from the upper terraces,' urged Tarzan. 'They cannot reach you there. Tell them that one of their people lies helpless here. Tell them to come and release me.'

'We are afraid.'

'They cannot reach you in the upper terraces. Go! They will be your friends then.'

'They cannot climb to the upper terraces,' said an old monkey. 'I will go.'

The others, halted in their flight, turned and watched the greybeard as he scampered quickly off amongst the loftiest branches of the great trees and Tarzan waited.

Presently he heard the deep gutturals of his own people, the great apes, the Mangani. Perhaps there would be those among them who knew him. Perhaps, again, the band may have come from afar and have no knowledge of him, though that he doubted. In them, however, lay his only hope. He lay there listening, waiting. He heard Manu screaming and chattering as he scampered about high above the Mangani, then, of a sudden, silence fell upon the jungle. There was only the sound of insects, buzzing, humming.

The ape-man sat cross-legged looking in the direction from which had come the sounds of the approaching anthropoids. He knew what was transpiring behind that dense wall of foliage. He knew that presently a pair of fierce eyes would be examining him, surveying the clearing, searching for an enemy, warily probing for a trick or a trap. He knew that the first sight of him might arouse distrust, fear, rage; for what reason had they to love or trust the cruel and merciless Tarmangani?

There lay great danger in the possibility that, seeing him, they might quietly withdraw without showing themselves. That, then, would be the end, for there were no others than the Mangani to whom he might look for rescue. With this in mind he spoke.

'I am a friend,' he called to them. 'The Tarmangani caught me and bound my wrists and ankles. I cannot move. I cannot defend myself. I cannot get food nor water. Come and remove my bonds.'

From just behind the screen of foliage a voice replied. 'You are a Tarmangani.'

'I am Tarzan of the Apes,' replied the ape-man.

'Yes,' screamed Manu, 'he is Tarzan of the Apes. The Tarmangani and the Gomangani bound him and Tantor brought him here. Four times has Kudu hunted across the sky while Tarzan of the Apes lay bound.'

'I know Tarzan,' said another voice from behind the foliage and presently the leaves parted and a huge, shaggy ape lumbered into the clearing. Swinging along with knuckles to the ground the brute came close to Tarzan.

'M'walat!' exclaimed the ape-man.

'It is Tarzan of the Apes,' said the great ape, but the others did not understand.

'What?' they demanded.

'Whose band is this?' asked Tarzan.

'Toyat is king,' replied M'walat.

'Then do not tell them it is really I,' whispered Tarzan, 'until you have cut these bonds. Toyat hates me. He will kill me if I am defenceless.'

'Yes,' agreed M'walat.

'Here,' said Tarzan, raising his bound wrists. 'Bite these bonds in two.'

'You are Tarzan of the Apes, the friend of M'walat. M'walat will do as you ask,' replied the ape.

Of course, in the meagre language of the apes, their conversation did not sound at all like a conversation between men, but was rather a mixture of growls and grunts and gestures which, however, served every purpose that could have been served by the most formal and correct of civilised speech, since it carried its messages clearly to the minds of both the Mangani and the Tarmangani, the Great Ape and the Great White Ape.

As the other members of the band pressed forward into the clearing, seeing that M'walat was not harmed, the latter stooped and with powerful teeth severed the camel-leather thongs that secured the wrists of the ape-man, and similarly he freed his ankles.

As Tarzan came to his feet the balance of the fierce and shaggy band swung into the clearing. In the lead was Toyat, king ape, and at his heels eight more full-grown males with perhaps six or seven females and a number of young. The young and the shes hung back, but the bulls pressed forward to where Tarzan stood with M'walat at his side.

The king ape growled menacingly. 'Tarmangani!' he cried. Wheeling in a circle he leaped into the air and came down on all fours, he struck the ground savagely with his clenched fists, he growled and foamed, and leaped again and again. Toyat was working himself to a pitch of rage that would nerve him to attack the Tarmangani and by these manoeuvres he hoped also to arouse the savage fighting spirit of his fellows.

'It is Tarzan of the Apes, friend of the Mangani,' said M'walat.

'It is a Tarmangani, enemy of the Mangani,' cried Toyat. 'They come with great thunder-sticks and kill us. They make our shes and our balus dead with a loud noise. Kill the Tarmangani!'

'It is Tarzan of the Apes,' growled Gayat. 'When I was a little balu he saved me from Numa. Tarzan of the Apes is the friend of the Mangani.'

'Kill the Tarmangani!' shrieked Toyat, leaping high into the air.

Several of the other bulls were now circling and leaping into the air as Gayat placed himself at Tarzan's side. The ape-man knew them well. He knew that sooner or later one of them would have excited himself to such a pitch of maniacal frenzy that he would leap suddenly upon him. M'walat and Gayat would attack in his defence; several more bulls would launch themselves into the battle and there would ensue a free-for-all fight from which not all of them would emerge alive and none without more or less serious injuries, and Tarzan of the Apes did not wish to battle with his friends.

'Stop!' he commanded raising his opened palm to attract attention.

'I am Tarzan of the Apes, mighty hunter, mighty fighter; long did I range with the tribe of Kerchak; when Kerchak died I became king ape; many of you know me; all know that I am first a Mangani; that I am friend to all Mangani. Toyat would have you kill me because Toyat hates Tarzan of the Apes. He hates him, not because he is a Tarmangani, but because Tarzan once kept Toyat from becoming king. That was many rains ago when some of you were still balus. If Toyat has been a good king Tarzan is glad, but now he is not acting like a good king for he is trying to turn you against your best friend.

'You, Zutho!' he exclaimed, suddenly pointing a finger at a huge bull. 'You leap and growl and foam at the mouth. You would sink your fangs into the flesh of Tarzan. Have you forgotten, Zutho, the time that you were sick and the other members of the tribe left you to die? Have you forgotten who brought you food and water? Have you forgotten who it was that kept Sabor the lioness and Sheeta the panther and Dango the hyena from you during those long nights?'

As Tarzan spoke, his tone one of quiet authority, the apes gradually paused to listen to his words. It was a long speech for the jungle folk. The great apes nor the little monkeys long concentrate upon one idea. Already, before he had finished, one of the bulls was overturning a rotted log in search of succulent insects. Zutho was wrinkling his brows in unaccustomed recollection. Presently he spoke.

'Zutho remembers,' he said. 'He is the friend of Tarzan,' and ranged himself beside M'walat and with this the other bulls, except Toyat, appeared to lose interest in the proceedings and either wandered off in search of food or squatted down in the grass.

Toyat still fumed, but as he saw his cause deserted he prosecuted his war dance at a safer distance from Tarzan and his defenders and it was not long before he, too, was attracted by the more profitable business of bug-hunting.

And so Tarzan ranged again with the great apes and as he loafed lazily through the forest with the shaggy brutes he thought of his foster mother, Kala, the great she-ape, the only mother he had ever known; he recalled with a thrill of pride her savage defence of him against all their natural enemies of the jungle and against the hate and jealousy of old Tublat, her mate, and against the enmity of Kerchak the terrible old king ape.

As it had been but yesterday since he had seen him, Tarzan's memory projected again upon the screen of recollection the huge bulk and the ferocious features of old Kerchak. What a magnificent beast he had been! To the childish mind of the ape-boy Kerchak had been the personification of savage ferocity and authority and even today he recalled him almost with a sensation of awe. That he had overthrown and slain this gigantic ruler still seemed to Tarzan almost incredible.

He fought again his battles with Terkoz and with Bolgani the gorilla. He thought of Teeka, whom he had loved, and of Thaka and Tana, and of the little black boy, Tibo, whom he had endeavoured to adopt, and so he dreamed through lazy daylight hours while Ibn Jad crept slowly northward toward the leopard city of Nimmr and in another part of the jungle events were transpiring that were to entangle Tarzan in the meshes of a great adventure.

4

Bolgani the Gorilla

A black porter caught his foot in an entangling creeper and stumbled, throwing his load to the ground. Of such trivialities are crises born. This one altered the entire life of James Hunter Blake, young, rich American, hunting big game for the first time in Africa with his friend Wilbur Stimbol who, having spent three weeks in the jungle two years before, was naturally the leader of the expedition and an infallible authority on all matters pertaining to big game, African jungle safari, food, weather and negroes. The further fact that Stimbol was twenty-five years Blake's senior naturally but augmented his claims to omniscience.

These factors did not in themselves constitute the basis for the growing differences between the two men, for Blake was a phlegmatically inclined young man of twenty-five who was rather amused at Stimbol's egotism than otherwise. The first rift had occurred at railhead when, through Stimbol's domineering manner and ill temper, the entire purpose of the expedition had been abandoned by necessity and what was to have been a quasi-scientific motion picture camera study of wild African life had resolved itself into an ordinary big game hunt.

At railhead, while preparations were going on to secure equipment and a safari, Stimbol had so offended and insulted the cameraman that he had left them flat and returned to the coast. Blake was disappointed, but he made up his mind to go on through and get what pictures he could with a still camera. He was not a man who enjoyed killing for the mere sport of taking life and as originally planned there was to have been no shooting of half a dozen trophies that Stimbol particularly wished to add to his collection.

There had since been one or two altercations relative to Stimbol's treatment of the black porters, but these matters, Blake was hopeful, had been ironed out and Stimbol had promised to leave the handling of the safari entirely to Blake and refrain from any further abuse of the men.

They had come into the interior even farther than they had planned, had had the poorest of luck in the matter of game and were about to turn back towards railhead. It seemed now to Blake that after all they were going to pull through without further difficulty and that he and Stimbol would return to America together to all intent and purpose still friends; but just then a black porter caught his foot in an entangling creeper and stumbled, throwing his load to the ground.

Directly in front of the porter Stimbol and Blake were walking side by side and, as though guided by a malevolent power, the load crashed into Stimbol, hurling him to the ground. Stimbol and the porter scrambled to their feet amidst the laughter of the negroes who had witnessed the accident. The porter was grinning. Stimbol was flushed with anger.

'You damned clumsy nigger!' he cried and before Blake could interfere or the porter protect himself, the angry white man stepped quickly over the fallen load and struck the black a terrific blow in the face that felled him and as he lay there, stunned, Stimbol kicked him in the side; but only once. Before he could repeat the outrage Blake seized him by the shoulder, wheeled him about and struck him precisely as he had struck the black.

Stimbol fell, rolled over on his side and reached for the automatic that hung at his hip, but quick as he was, Blake was quicker. 'Cut that!' said Blake, crisply, covering Stimbol with a .45. Stimbol's hand dropped from the grip of his gun. 'Get up!' ordered Blake, and when the other had risen: 'Now, listen to me, Stimbol – this is the end. You and I are through. Tomorrow morning we split the safari and equipment and whichever way you go with your half, I'll go in the opposite direction.'

Blake had returned his gun to its holster as he spoke, the black had arisen and was nursing a bloody nose, the other blacks were looking on sullenly. Blake motioned to the porter to pick up his load and presently the safari was again on the move – a sullen safari without laughter or song.

Blake made camp at the first available ground shortly before noon in order that the division of equipment, food and men could be made during the afternoon and the two safaris thus be enabled to make an early start the following morning.

Stimbol, sullen, would give no assistance, but taking a couple of the askari, the armed natives who act as soldiers for the safari, started out from camp to hunt. He had proceeded scarcely a mile along a mould-padded game trail which gave forth no sound in answer to their falling footsteps when one of the natives in the lead held up his hand in warning as he halted in his tracks.

Stimbol advanced cautiously and the black pointed toward the left, through the foliage. Dimly, Stimbol saw a black mass moving slowly away from them.

'What is it?' he whispered.

'Gorilla,' replied the black.

Stimbol raised his rifle and fired at the retreating figure. The black was not surprised that he missed.

'Hell!' ejaculated the white. 'Come on, get after him! I've got to have him. Gad! what a trophy he'll make.'

The jungle was rather more open than usual and again and again they came within sight of the retreating gorilla. Each time Stimbol fired and each time he missed. Secretly the blacks were amused and pleased. They did not like Stimbol.

At a distance Tarzan of the Apes, hunting with the tribe of Toyat, heard the first shot and immediately took to the trees and was racing in the direction of the sound. He felt sure that the weapon had not been discharged by the Bedúins, for he well knew and could differentiate between the reports of their muskets and those made by modern weapons.

Perhaps, he thought, there may be among them such a rifle, because such was not impossible, but more likely it meant white men and in Tarzan's country it was his business to know what strangers were there and why. Seldom they came even now, though once they had never come. It was those days that Tarzan regretted, for when the white man comes peace and happiness depart.

Racing through the trees, swinging from limb to limb, Tarzan of the Apes unerringly followed the direction of the sound of the succeeding shots and as he approached more closely the scene of the pursuit of Bolgani the gorilla he heard the crashing of underbrush and the voices of men.

Bolgani, fleeing with greater haste than caution, his mind and attention occupied by thoughts of escape from the hated Tarmangani and the terrifying thunder-stick that roared each time the Tarmangani came within sight of him, abandoned his accustomed wariness and hurried through the jungle forgetful of what few other enemies might beset his path: and so it was that he failed to see Histah the snake draped in sinuous loops along an overhanging branch of a nearby patriarch of the forest.

The huge python, naturally short-tempered and irritable, had been disturbed and annoyed by the crashing sounds of pursuit and escape and the roaring voice of the rifle. Ordinarily he would have permitted a full-grown bull gorilla to pass unmolested, but in his present state of mind he might have attacked even Tantor himself.

His beady eyes glaring fixedly he watched the approach of the shaggy Bolgani and as the gorilla passed beneath the limb to which he clung Histah launched himself upon his prey.

As the great coils, powerful, relentless, silent, encircled him, Bolgani sought to tear the hideous folds from about him. Great is the strength of Bolgani, but even greater is that of Histah the snake. A single hideous, almost human scream burst from the lips of Bolgani with the first realisation of the disaster that had befallen him and then he was on the ground tearing futilely at the steadily-tightening bands of living steel that would crush the life from him, crush until his bones gave to the tremendous pressure, until only broken pulp remained within a sausage-like thing that would slip between the distended jaws of the serpent.

It was upon this sight that Stimbol and Tarzan came simultaneously – Stimbol stumbling awkwardly through the underbrush, Tarzan of the Apes, demi-god of the forest, swinging gracefully through the foliage of the middle terraces.

They arrived simultaneously but Tarzan was the only one of the party whose presence was unsuspected by the others, for, as always, he had moved silently and with the utmost wariness because of the unknown nature of the conditions he might discover.

As he looked down upon the scene below his quick eye and his knowledge of the jungle revealed at a glance the full story of the tragedy that had overtaken Bolgani and then he saw Stimbol raise his rifle, intent upon bagging two royal specimens with a single shot.

In the heart of Tarzan was no great love for Bolgani the gorilla. Since childhood the shaggy, giant man-beast had been the natural foe of the ape-man. His first mortal combat had been with Bolgani. For years he had feared him, or rather avoided him through caution, for of fear Tarzan was ignorant, and since he had emerged from childhood he had continued to avoid Bolgani for the simple reason that his own people, the great apes, avoided him.

But now when he saw the huge brute beset by two of the natural enemies of both the Mangani and the Bolgani there flared within his breast a sudden loyalty that burned away the personal prejudices of a lifetime.

He was directly above Stimbol and with such celerity do the mind and muscles of the ape-man co-ordinate that even as the American raised his weapon to his shoulder Tarzan had dropped upon his back, felling him to the earth and before Stimbol could discover what had happened to him, long before he could stumble, cursing, to his feet, Tarzan, who had been unarmed, had snatched the hunter's knife from its scabbard and leaped full upon the writhing, struggling mass of python and gorilla.

Stimbol came to his feet ready to kill but what he saw before him temporarily drove the desire for vengeance from his mind as surprise and awe replaced the baser craving.

Naked but for a loin cloth, bronzed, black-haired, a giant white man battled with the dread python, and as Stimbol watched he shuddered as he became aware that the low, beastlike growls he heard came not alone from the savage lips of the gorilla but from the throat of the god-like man-thing that battled with him against the snake.

Steel fingers encircled the snake just back of its head, while those of the free hand drove Stimbol's hunting knife again and again into the coiling, writhing body of the serpent. With the projection of a new and more menacing enemy into the battle, Histah was forced partially to release his hold upon Bolgani with, at first, the intention of including Tarzan in the same embrace that he might crush them both at once, but soon he discovered that the hairless man-thing constituted a distinct menace to his life that would necessitate his undivided attention and so he quickly uncoiled from about Bolgani and in a frenzy of rage and pain that whipped his great length into a lashing fury of destruction he sought to encircle the ape-man; but wheresoever his coils approached the keen knife bit deep into tortured flesh.

Bolgani, the spark of life all but crushed from him, lay gasping upon the ground, unable to come to the aid of his preserver, while Stimbol, goggle-eyed with awe and terror, kept at a safe distance, momentarily forgetful both of his lust for trophies and his bent for revenge.

Thus was Tarzan pitted, single-handed, against one of the mightiest of Nature's creations in a duel to the death the result of which seemed to the watching American already a foregone conclusion, for what man born of woman could hope, unaided, to escape from the embrace of the deadly coils of a python?

Already Histah had encircled the torso and one leg of the ape-man, but his powers of constriction, lessened by the frightful wounds he had received, had as yet been unable to crush his adversary into helplessness and Tarzan was now concentrating his attention and the heavy blade of the hunting knife upon a single portion of the weakening body in an attempt to cut Histah in two.

Man and serpent were red with blood and crimson were the grasses and the brush for yards in all directions as, with a final effort, Histah closed his giant coils spasmodically about his victim at the instant that Tarzan with a mighty upward heave cut through the vertebrae of the great snake.

Lashing and writhing, the nether portion, headless, flopped aside while the ape-man, still fighting with what remained, exerting his superhuman strength to its ultimate utmost, slowly forced the coils from about his body and cast the dying Histah from him. Then, without a glance at Stimbol, he turned to Bolgani.

'You are hurt to death?' he asked in the language of the great apes.

'No,' replied the gorilla. 'I am Bolgani! I kill, Tarmangani!'

'I am Tarzan of the Apes,' said the ape-man. 'I saved you from Histah.'

'You did not come to kill Bolgani?' inquired the gorilla.

'No. Let us be friends.'

Bolgani frowned in an effort to concentrate upon this remarkable problem. Presently he spoke. 'We will be friends,' he said. 'The Tarmangani behind you will kill us both with his thunder-stick. Let us kill him first.' Painfully he staggered to his feet.

'No,' remonstrated Tarzan. 'I will send the Tarmangani away.'

'You? He will not go.'

'I am Tarzan, Lord of the Jungle,' replied the ape-man. 'The word of Tarzan is law in the jungle.'

Stimbol, who had been watching, was under the impression that the man and the beast were growling at one another and that a new duel impended. Had he guessed the truth, that they considered him a common enemy, he would have felt far less at ease. Now, his rifle regained, he started toward Tarzan just as the latter turned to address him.

'Stand to one side, young fellow,' said Stimbol, 'while I finish that gorilla. After the experience you just had with the snake I doubt if you want that fellow to jump you, too.' The American was none too sure of what the attitude of the white giant might be, for all too fresh in his mind was the startling and disconcerting manner of the wild man's introduction, but he felt safe because he held a rifle, while the other was unarmed and he guessed that the giant might be only too glad to be saved from the attentions of the gorilla, which, from Stimbol's imagined knowledge of such beasts appeared to him to be quite evidently threatening.

Tarzan halted directly between Bolgani and the hunter and eyed the latter appraisingly for a moment. 'Lower your rifle,' he said, presently. 'You are not going to shoot the gorilla.'

'The hell I'm not!' ejaculated Stimbol. 'What do you suppose I've been chasing him through the jungle for?'

'Under a misapprehension,' replied Tarzan.

'What misapprehension?' demanded Stimbol.

'That you were going to shoot him. You are not.'

'Say, young man, do you know who I am?' demanded Stimbol.

'I am not interested,' replied Tarzan, coldly.

'Well, you'd better be. I'm Wilbur Stimbol of Stimbol & Company, brokers, New York!' That was a name to conjure with – in New York. Even in Paris and London it had opened many a door, bent many a knee. Seldom had it failed the purpose of this purse-arrogant man.

'What are you doing in my country?' demanded the ape-man, ignoring Stimbol's egotistical statement of his identity.

'Your country? Who the hell are you?'

Tarzan turned toward the two blacks who had been standing a little in the rear of Stimbol and to one side. 'I am Tarzan of the Apes,' he said to them in their own dialect. 'What is this man doing in my country? How many are there in his party – how many white men?'

'Big Bwana,' replied one of the men with sincere deference, 'we knew that you were Tarzan of the Apes when we saw you swing from the trees and slay the great snake. There is no other in all the jungle who could do that. This white man is a bad master. There is one other white man with him. The other is kind. They came to hunt Simba the lion and other big game. They have had no luck. Tomorrow they turn back.'

'Where is their camp?' demanded Tarzan.

The black who had spoken pointed. 'It is not far,' he said.

The ape-man turned to Stimbol. 'Go back to your camp,' he said. 'I shall come there later this evening and talk with you and your companion. In the meantime hunt no more except for food in Tarzan's country.'

There was something in the voice and manner of the stranger that had finally gone through Stimbol's thick sensibilities and impressed him with a species of awe – a thing he had scarcely ever experienced in the past except in the presence of wealth that was grossly superior to his own. He did not reply. He just stood and watched the bronzed giant turn to the gorilla. He heard them growl at one another for a moment and then, to his vast surprise, he saw them move off through the jungle together, shoulder to shoulder, and as the foliage closed about them he removed his helmet and wiped the sweat from his forehead with a silk handkerchief as he stood staring at the green branches that had parted to receive this strangely assorted pair.

Finally he turned to his men with an oath. 'A whole day wasted!' he complained. 'Who is this fellow? You seemed to know him.'

'He is Tarzan,' replied one of the blacks.

'Tarzan? Never heard of him,' snapped Stimbol.

'All who know the jungle, know Tarzan.'

'Humph!' sneered Stimbol. 'No lousy wild man is going to tell Wilbur Stimbol where he can hunt and where he can't.'

'Master,' said the black who had first spoken, 'the word of Tarzan is the law of the jungle. Do not offend him.'

'I'm not paying you damned niggers for advice,' snapped Stimbol. 'If I say hunt, we hunt, and don't you forget it,' but on their return to camp they saw no game, or at least Stimbol saw none. What the blacks saw was their own affair.

5

The Tarmangani

During Stimbol's absence from camp Blake had been occupied in dividing the food and equipment into two equal parts which were arranged for Stimbol's inspection and approval, but the division of the porters and askari he had left until the other's return and was writing in his diary when the hunting party entered the camp.

He could see at a glance that Stimbol was in bad humour, but as that was the older man's usual state of temper it caused Blake no particular anxiety, but rather gave him cause for added relief that on the morrow he would be rid of his ill-natured companion for good.

Blake was more concerned, however, by the sullen demeanour of the askari who had accompanied Stimbol, for it meant to the younger man that his companion had found some new occasion for bullying, abusing or insulting them and the difficulty of dividing the safari thus increased. Blake felt from the moment that he had definitely reached the decision to separate from Stimbol, that one of the greatest obstacles they would have to overcome to carry out the plan would be to find sufficient men, willing to submit themselves to Stimbol's ideas of discipline, properly to transport his luggage and provisions and guard them and him.

As Stimbol passed and saw the two piles of equipment the frown upon his face deepened. 'I see you've got the stuff laid out,' he remarked, as he halted before Blake.

'Yes, I wanted you to look it over and see that it is satisfactorily divided before I have it packed.'

'I don't want to be bothered with it,' replied the other. 'I know you wouldn't take any advantage of me on the division.'

'Thanks,' replied Blake.

'How about the niggers?'

'That's not going to be so easy. You know you haven't treated them very well and there will not be many of them anxious to return with you.'

'There's where you're dead wrong, Blake. The trouble with you is that you don't know anything about niggers. You're too easy with 'em. They haven't any respect for you and the man they don't respect they don't like. They know that a fellow who beats 'em is their master and they know that a master is going to look after them. They wouldn't want to trust themselves on a long trek with you. You divided the junk, now let me handle the niggers – that's more in my line – and I'll see that you get a square deal and a good, safe bunch and I'll put the fear of God into 'em so they won't dare be anything but loyal to you.'

'Just how do you propose selecting the men?' asked Blake.

'Well, in the first place I'd like you to have those men who may wish to accompany you – I'll grant there are a few – so we'll just have 'em all up, explain that we are separating and I'll tell all those who wish to return with your safari to step forward, then I'll choose some good men from what are left and make up enough that way to complete your quota – see? That's fair enough, isn't it?'

'It's quite fair,' agreed Blake. He was hoping that the plan would work out as easily as Stimbol appeared to believe that it would, but he was far from believing and so he thought it best to suggest an alternative that he was confident would have to be resorted to in the end.

'In the event that one of us has difficulty in securing the requisite number of volunteers,' he said, 'I believe that we can enlist the necessary men by offering a bonus to be paid upon safe arrival at railhead. If I am short of men I shall be willing to do so.'

'Not a bad idea if you're afraid you can't hold 'em together after I leave you,' said Stimbol. 'It will be an added factor of safety for you, too; but as for me my men will live up to their original agreement or there'll be some mighty sick niggers in these parts. What say we have 'em up and find out just how much of a job we've got on our hands?' He glanced about until his eyes fell on a headman. 'Here, you!' he called. 'Come here and make it snappy.'

The black approached and stopped before the two white men. 'You called me, Bwana?' he asked.

'Gather up everyone in camp,' directed Stimbol. 'Have them up here in five minutes for a palaver – every last man-jack of them.'

'Yes, Bwana.'

As the headman withdrew, Stimbol turned to Blake. 'Any stranger in camp today?' he asked.

'No, why?'

'Ran across a wild man while I was hunting,' replied Stimbol. 'He ordered me out of the jungle. What do you know about that?' and Stimbol laughed.

'A wild man?'

'Yes. Some crazy nut I suppose. The niggers seemed to know about him.'

'Who is he?'

'Calls himself Tarzan.'

Blake elevated his brows. 'Ah!' he exclaimed; 'You have met Tarzan of the Apes and he has ordered you out of the jungle?'

'You've heard of him?'

'Certainly, and if he ever orders me out of his jungle, I'll go.'

'You would, but not Wilbur Stimbol.'

'Why did he order you out?' asked Blake.

'He just ordered me out, that's all. Wouldn't let me shoot a gorilla I'd been stalking. The fellow saved the gorilla from a python, killed the python, ordered me out of the jungle, said he'd visit us in camp later and walked away with the gorilla like they were old pals. I never saw anything to match it, but it doesn't make any difference to me who or what he thinks he is, I know who and what I am and it's going to take more than a half-wit to scare me out of this country till I'm good and ready to go.'

'So you think Tarzan of the Apes is a half-wit?'

'I think anyone's a half-wit who'd run about this jungle naked and unarmed.'

'You'll find he's not a half-wit, Stimbol, and unless you want to get in more trouble than you ever imagined existed you'll do just as Tarzan of the Apes tells you to do.'

'What do you know about him? Have you ever seen him?'

'No,' replied Blake. 'But I have heard a lot about him from our men. He's as much a part of this locality as the jungle, or the lions. Very few, if any, of our men have seen him, but he has the same hold upon their imaginations and superstitions as any of their demons and they are even more fearful of incurring his displeasure. If they think Tarzan has it in for us we're out of luck.'

'Well, all I've got to say is that if this monkey-man knows when he's well off he'll not come butting into the affairs of Wilbur Stimbol.'

'And he's coming to visit us, is he?' said Blake. 'Well, I certainly want to see him. I've heard of nothing much else since we struck his country.'

'It's funny I never heard of him,' said Stimbol.

'You never talk with the men,' Blake reminded him.

'Gad, it seems as though I'm doing nothing but talk to them,' grumbled Stimbol.

'I said, talk *with* them.'

'I don't chum with niggers,' sneered Stimbol.

Blake grinned.

'Here are the men,' said Stimbol. He turned toward the waiting porters and askari and cleared his throat. 'Mr Blake and I are going to separate,' he announced. 'Everything has been divided. I am going to hunt a little farther to the west, make a circle toward the south and return to the coast by a new route. I do not know what Mr Blake's plans are, but he is going to get half the porters and half the askari and I want to tell you niggers right now that there isn't going to be any funny business about it. Half of you are going with Mr Blake, whether you like it or not.' He paused, impressively, to let the full weight of his pronouncement sink home. 'As usual,' he continued, 'I wish to keep everyone contented and happy, so I'm going to give you who may want to go with Mr Blake an opportunity to do so. Now listen! The packs over on that side are Mr Blake's; those on this side are mine. All those who are willing to accompany Mr Blake go over on that side!'

There was a moment's hesitation upon the part of the men and then some of them moved quietly over among Blake's packs. Others followed as their understandings slowly grasped the meaning of Stimbol's words until all of the men stood upon Blake's side.

Stimbol turned to Blake with a laugh and a shake of his head. 'Gad!' he exclaimed. 'Did you ever see such a dumb bunch? No one could have explained the thing more simply than I and yet look at em! Not one of them understood me!'

'Are you quite sure of that, Stimbol?' inquired Blake.

Stimbol did not immediately grasp the insinuation. When he did he scowled. 'Don't be a fool,' he snapped. 'Of course they misunderstood me.' He turned angrily toward the men. 'You thick-skulled, black idiots! Can't you understand anything?' he demanded. 'I did not say that you all had to go with Mr Blake – only those who wished to. Now the rest of you – those who wish to accompany me – get back over here on this side with my packs, and step lively!'

No one moved in the direction of Stimbol's packs. The man flushed.

'This is mutiny!' he stormed. 'Whoever is at the bottom of this is going to suffer. Come here, you!' He motioned to a headman. 'Who put you fellows up to this? Has Mr Blake been telling you what to do?'

'Don't be a fool, Stimbol,' said Blake. 'No one has influenced the men and there is no mutiny. The plan was yours. The men have done just what you told them to. If it had not been for your insufferable egotism you would have known precisely what the outcome would be. These black men are human beings. In some respects they are extremely sensitive human beings and in many ways they are like children. You strike them, you curse them, you insult them and they will fear you and hate you. You have done all these things to them and they do fear you and hate you. You have sowed and now you are reaping. I hope to God that it will teach you a lesson. There is just one way to get your men and that is to offer them a big bonus. Are you willing to do that?'

Stimbol, his self-assurance momentarily shaken at last, wilted in the face of the realisation that Blake was right. He looked about helplessly for a moment. The blacks, sullen-faced, stood there like dumb beasts, staring at him. In all those eyes there was no single friendly glance. He turned back to Blake. 'See what you can do with them,' he said.

Blake faced the men. 'It will be necessary for half of you to accompany Mr Stimbol back to the coast,' he said. 'He will pay double wages to all those who go with him, provided that you serve him loyally. Talk it over among yourselves and send word to us later by your headmen. That is all. You may go.'

The balance of the afternoon passed, the two white men keeping to their respective tents; the blacks gathered in groups, whispering. Blake and Stimbol no longer messed together, but after the evening meal each appeared with his pipe to await the report of the headmen. After half an hour Blake sent his boy to summon them and presently they came and stood before the young man.

'Well, have the men decided who will accompany Mr Stimbol?' he asked.

'No one will accompany the old Bwana,' replied their spokesman. 'All will go with the young Bwana.'

'But Mr Stimbol will pay them well,' Blake reminded, 'and half of you must go with him.'

The black shook his head. 'He could not make the pay big enough,' he said. 'No boy will go with him.'

'You agreed to come out with us and return with us,' said Blake. 'You must fulfil your agreement.'

'We agreed to come out with both of you and return with both of you. There was nothing said about returning separately. We will live up to our agreement and the old Bwana may return in safety with the young Bwana.' There was finality in the tone of the spokesman.

Blake thought for a moment before replying. 'You may go,' he said. 'I will talk with you again in the morning.'

The blacks had departed but a moment when the figure of a man appeared suddenly out of the darkness into the light of the camp fire.

'Who the – oh, it's you is it?' exclaimed Stimbol. 'Here's the wild man, Blake.'

The young American turned and surveyed the figure of the bronze giant who was standing just within the circle of the firelight. He noted the clean-cut features, the quiet dignity, the majestic mien and smiled inwardly at recollection of Stimbol's description of this god-like creature – half-wit!

'So you are Tarzan of the Apes!' he said.

Tarzan inclined his head. 'And you?' he asked.

'I am Jim Blake, of New York,' replied the American.

'Hunting, of course?'

'With a camera.'

'Your companion was using a rifle,' Tarzan reminded him.

'I am not responsible for his acts. I cannot control them,' replied Blake.

'Nor anyone else,' snapped Stimbol.

Tarzan permitted his gaze to move to Stimbol for an instant, but ignored his boast.

'I overheard the conversation between you and the headmen,' he said, addressing Blake. 'Some of your blacks had already told me something about your companion and twice today I have had an opportunity to form an estimate of my own from personal observation, so I assume that you are separating because you cannot agree. Am I right?'

'Yes,' acknowledged Blake.

'And after you separate – what are your plans?'

'I intend to push in a little farther west and then swing—' commenced Stimbol.

'I was speaking to Blake,' interrupted Tarzan; 'my plans concerning you are already made.'

'Well, who the—'

'Silence!' admonished the ape-man. 'Go ahead, Blake!'

'We have not had much luck so far,' replied Blake, 'principally because we never can agree on methods. The result is that I have scarcely a single decent wild animal study. I had planned to go north a way in search of lion pictures. I dislike going back without anything to show for the time and money I have put into the expedition, but now that the men have refused to accompany us separately there is nothing for it but to return to the coast by the shortest route.'

'You two don't seem to be taking me into consideration at all,' grumbled Stimbol. 'I've got as much money and time in this trip as Blake. You forget that I'm here to hunt, and what's more I'm going to hunt and I'm not going straight back to the coast by a damned sight, monkey man or no monkey man.'

Again Tarzan ignored Stimbol. 'Get ready to move out about an hour after sunrise,' he said to Blake. 'There will be no trouble about dividing the safari. I shall be here to attend to that and give you your final instructions,' and as he spoke he turned and disappeared in the darkness.

6

Ara the Lightning

Before dawn the camp was astir and by the appointed hour the packs were made and all was in readiness. The porters loitered, awaiting the word that would start the safari upon its eastward journey toward the coast. Blake and Stimbol smoked in silence. The foliage of a nearby tree moved to the swaying of a branch and Tarzan of the Apes dropped lightly into the camp. Exclamation of surprise broke from the lips of the negroes – surprise clearly tinged with terror. The ape-man turned toward them and addressed them in their own dialect.

'I am Tarzan of the Apes,' he said, 'Lord of the Jungle. You have brought white men into my country to kill my people: I am displeased. Those of you who wish to live to return to your villages and your families will listen well and do as Tarzan commands.

'You,' he pointed at the chief headman, 'shall accompany the younger white man whom I will permit to make pictures in my country where and when he will. Select half the men of the safari to accompany the young Bwana.

'And you,' he addressed another headman, 'take those men that remain and escort the older Bwana to railhead by the most direct route and without delay. He is not permitted to hunt and there will be no killing except for food or self-defence. Do not fail me. Remember always that Tarzan watches and Tarzan never forgets.'

He turned then to the white men. 'Blake,' he said, 'the arrangements are made. You may leave when you please, with your own safari, and go where you please. The question of hunting is left to your own discretion – you are the guest of Tarzan.'

'And you,' he addressed Stimbol, 'will be taken directly out of the country by the shortest route. You will be permitted to carry firearms for use in self-defence. If you abuse this permission they will be taken away from you. Do not hunt, even for food – your headman will attend to that.'

'Now just hold your horses,' blustered Stimbol. 'If you think I'm going to put up with any such high-handed interference with my rights as an American citizen you're very much mistaken. Why I could buy and sell you and your damned jungle forty times and not know that I'd spent a cent. For God's sake, Blake, tell this poor fool who I am before he gets himself into a lot of trouble.'

Tarzan turned to the headman he had selected for Stimbol. 'You may up-load and march,' he said. 'If this white man does not follow you, leave him behind. Take good care of him if he obeys me and deliver him safely at rail-head. Obey his orders if they do not conflict with those that I have given you. Go!'

A moment later Stimbol's safari was preparing to depart and, at Tarzan's request, Blake's too was moving out of camp. Stimbol swore and threatened, but his men, sullenly ignoring him, filed off into the jungle toward the east. Tarzan had departed, swinging into the trees and disappearing among the foliage, and at last Stimbol stood alone in the deserted camp.

Thwarted, humiliated, almost frothing with rage, he ran after his men, screaming commands and threats that were ignored. Later in the day, sullen and silent, he marched near the head of the long file of porters and askari, convinced at last that the power of the ape-man was greater than his, but in his heart burned resentment and in his mind rioted plans for vengeance – plans that he knew were futile.

Tarzan, wishing to assure himself that his instructions were being carried out, had swung far ahead and was waiting in the crotch of a tree that over-hung the trail along which Stimbol must pass. In the distance he could hear the sounds that arose from the marching safari. Along the trail from the opposite direction something was approaching. The ape-man could not see it but he knew what it was. Above the tree tops black clouds rolled low, but no air stirred in the jungle.

Along the trail came a great, shaggy, black man-thing. Tarzan of the Apes hailed it as it came in sight of his arboreal perch.

'Bolgani!' he called in low tones.

The gorilla stopped. He stood erect upon his hind feet and looked about.

'I am Tarzan,' said the ape-man.

Bolgani grunted. 'I am Bolgani,' he replied.

'The Tarmangani comes,' warned Tarzan.

'I kill!' growled Bolgani.

'Let the Tarmangani pass,' said Tarzan. 'He and his people have many thunder-sticks. I have sent this Tarmangani out of the jungle. Let him pass. Go a little way from the trail – the stupid Gomangani and the Tarmangani, who is stupider, will pass by without knowing that Tarzan and Bolgani are near.'

From the darkening sky distant thunder boomed and the two beasts looked upward toward the broad field of Nature's powers, more savage and destructive than their own.

'Pand the thunder hunts in the sky,' remarked the ape-man.

'Hunts for Usha the wind,' said Bolgani.

'Presently we shall hear Usha fleeing through the trees to escape.' Tarzan viewed the lowering, black clouds. 'Even Kudu the sun fears Pand, hiding his face when Pand hunts.'

Ara the lightning shot through the sky. To the two beasts it was a bolt from Pand's bow and the great drops of rain that commenced to fall shortly after was Meeta, the blood of Usha the wind, pouring from many a wound.

The jungle bent to a great pressure but as yet there was no other noise than the rolling thunder. The trees whipped back and Usha tore through the forest. The darkness increased. The rain fell in great masses. Leaves and branches hurtled through the air, trees crashed amongst their fellows. With deafening roars the elements unleashed their pent anger. The beasts cowered beneath the one awe-inspiring power that they acknowledged as supreme.

Tarzan crouched in the crotch of a great tree with his shoulders arched against the beating rain. Just off the trail Bolgani squatted in drenched and bedraggled misery. They waited. There was nothing else that they could do.

Above them the storm broke again with maniacal fury. The thunder crashed with deafening reverberation. There was a blinding flash of light and the branch upon which Tarzan squatted sagged and hurtled to the trail beneath.

Stunned, the ape-man lay where he had fallen, the great branch partially across his body.

As quickly as it had come, the storm departed. Kudu the sun burst through the clouds. Bolgani, dejected and still terrified, remained where he had squatted, motionless and silent. Bolgani had no desire to attract the attention of Pand the thunder.

Soaked with water, cold, furious, Stimbol slopped along the slippery, muddy trail. He did not know that his safari was some little distance behind him, for he had forged ahead during the storm while they had taken refuge beneath the trees.

At a turn in the trail he came suddenly upon a fallen branch that blocked the way. At first he did not see the body of the man lying beneath it, but when he did he recognised it instantly and a new hope sprang to life within his breast. With Tarzan dead he would be free to do as he pleased; but was the ape-man dead?

Stimbol ran forward, and, kneeling, placed an ear to the breast of the prostrate figure. An expression of disappointment crossed his face – Tarzan was not dead. The expression upon Stimbol's face changed – a cunning look came into his eyes as he glanced back down the trail. His men were not in sight! He looked quickly about him. He was alone with the unconscious author of his humiliation!

He thought he was alone. He did not see the shaggy figure that had silently arisen as the sound of Stimbol's approach had come to its sensitive ears and was now peering at him through the foliage – peering at him and at the silent figure of the ape-man.

Stimbol drew his hunting knife from its scabbard. He could slip its point into the wild man's heart and run back down the trail. His men would find him waiting for them. Later they would come upon the dead Tarzan, but they would not guess how he had met his end.

The ape-man moved – consciousness was returning. Stimbol realised that he must act quickly and at the same instant a great hairy arm reached out through the foliage and a mighty hand closed upon his shoulder. With a screaming curse he turned to look into the hideous face of Bolgani. He tried to strike at the shaggy breast of his antagonist with his hunting knife, but the puny weapon was torn from his grasp and hurled into the bushes.

The great yellow fangs were bared against his throat as Tarzan opened his eyes.

'Kreeg-ah!' cried the ape-man, in warning.

Bolgani paused and looked at his fellow beast.

'Let him go,' said Tarzan.

'The Tarmangani would have killed Tarzan,' explained the gorilla. 'Bolgani stopped him. Bolgani kill!' He growled horribly.

'No!' snapped Tarzan. 'Free the Tarmangani!'

The gorilla released his grasp upon Stimbol just as the first of the hunter's men came in sight of them and as Bolgani saw the blacks and how numerous they were his nervousness and irritability increased.

'Take to the jungle, Bolgani,' said Tarzan. 'Tarzan will take care of this Tarmangani and the Gomangani.'

With a parting growl the gorilla merged with the foliage and the shadows of the jungle as Tarzan of the Apes faced Stimbol and his boys.

'You had a close call then, Stimbol,' said the ape-man. 'It is fortunate for you that you didn't succeed in killing me. I was here for two reasons. One was to see that you obeyed my instructions and the other to protect you from your men. I did not like the way they eyed you in camp this morning. It would not be a difficult thing to lose you in the jungle, you know, and that would put a period to you as surely as poison or a knife. I felt a certain responsibility for you because you are a white man, but you have just now released me from whatever obligation racial ties may have influenced me to acknowledge.

'I shall not kill you, Stimbol, as you deserve; but from now on you may reach the coast on your own and you will doubtless discover that one cannot make too many friends in the jungle or afford a single unnecessary enemy.' He wheeled upon Stimbol's black boys. 'Tarzan of the Apes goes his way. You will not see him again, perhaps. Do your duty by this white man as long as he obeys the word of Tarzan; *but see that he does not hunt*!'

With this final admonition the ape-man swung into the lower branches and was gone.

When Stimbol, after repeatedly questioning his men, discovered that Tarzan had practically assured them that they would see no more of him he regained much of his former assurance and egotistical bluster. Once more he was the leader of men, shouting at the blacks in a loud tone, cursing them, ridiculing them. He thought that it impressed them with his greatness. He believed that they were simple people whom he could deceive into thinking that he was not afraid of Tarzan, and by flaunting Tarzan's commands win their respect. Now that Tarzan had promised not to return Stimbol felt safer in ignoring his wishes and so it befell that just before they reached a camping ground Stimbol came upon an antelope and without an instant's hesitation fired and killed it.

It was a sullen camp that Stimbol made that night. The men gathered in groups and whispered. 'He has shot an antelope and Tarzan will be angry with us,' said one.

'He will punish us,' said a headman.

'The Bwana is a bad man,' said another. 'I wish he was dead.'

'We may not kill him. Tarzan has said that.'

'If we leave him in the jungle he will die.'

'Tarzan told us to do our duty.'

'He said to do it as long as the bad Bwana obeyed the commands of Tarzan.'

'He has disobeyed them!'

'Then we may leave him.'

Stimbol, exhausted by the long march, slept like a log. When he awoke the sun was high. He shouted for his boy. There was no response. Again he shouted and louder, adding an oath. No one came. There was no sound in camp.

'The lazy niggers,' he grumbled. 'They'll step a little livelier when I get out there.'

He arose and dressed, but as he was dressing the silence of the camp came to impress him as something almost menacing, so that he hastened to be through and out of the tent. As he stepped into the open the truth was revealed at almost the first quick glance about. Not a human being was in sight, and all but one of the packs containing provisions were gone. He had been deserted in the heart of Africa!

His first impulse was to seize his rifle and start after the blacks, but second thought impressed him with the danger of such procedure and convinced him that the last thing he should now do was to place himself again in the power of these men who had once demonstrated that they felt no compunction in abandoning him to almost certain death. If they wanted to be rid of him they could easily find even a quicker means if he returned and forced himself upon them again.

There was but a single alternative and that was to find Blake and remain with him. He knew that Blake would not abandon him to death in the jungle.

The blacks had not left him without provisions, nor had they taken his rifle or ammunition, but the difficulty that now confronted Stimbol was largely in the matter of transportation for his food. There was plenty of it to last many days, but he knew that he could not carry it through the jungle together with his rifle and ammunition. To remain where the food was would be equally futile. Blake was returning to the coast by another route; the ape-man had said that he would not follow Stimbol's safari further; it might be years, therefore, before another human being chanced along this little used game trail.

He knew that he and Blake were now separated by about two marches and if he travelled light and Blake did not march too rapidly he might hope to overtake him inside a week. Perhaps Blake would find good camera-hunting soon and make a permanent camp. In that case Stimbol would find him even more quickly.

He felt better when he had definitely decided upon a plan of action, and after a good breakfast he made up a small pack of provisions – enough to last him a week, filled his belts and pockets with ammunition and started off along the back trail.

It was easy going for the trail of the day before was plain and this was the third time that Stimbol had been over it, so he had no difficulty in reaching the camp at which he and Blake had parted company.

As he entered the little clearing early in the afternoon he determined to keep on and cover as much ground on Blake's trail as he could before dark, but for a few minutes he would rest. As he sat down with his back against the bole of a tree he did not notice a movement of the tops of a clump of jungle grasses a few yards distant, and if he had he would, doubtless, have attached no importance to the matter.

Finishing a cigarette Stimbol arose, rearranged his pack and started off in the direction Blake's men had taken early the preceding morning; but he had covered but a yard or two when he was brought to a sudden halt by an ominous growl that arose from a little clump of jungle grasses close in front of him. Almost simultaneously the fringing grasses parted and there appeared in the opening the head of a great, black-maned lion.

With a scream of fear, Stimbol dropped his pack, threw aside his rifle and started on a run for the tree beneath which he had been sitting. The, lion, itself somewhat surprised, stood for an instant watching him and then started in pursuit at an easy lope.

Stimbol, casting an affrighted glance rearward, was horrified – the lion seemed so close and the tree so far away. If distance lends enchantment to the view proximity may also at times have its advantage. In this instance it served to accelerate the speed of the fleeing man to a most surprising degree and though he was no longer young he clawed his way to the lower branches of the tree with speed, if not with grace, that would have done justice to a trained athlete.

Nor was he an instant too speedy. Numa's raking talons touched his boot and sent him swarming up among the higher branches, where he clung weak and panting looking down into the snarling visage of the carnivore.

For a moment Numa growled up at him and then, with a coughing grunt, turned away and strode majestically in the direction of the clump of grasses from which he had emerged. He stopped to sniff at the pack of provisions Stimbol had discarded and, evidently piqued by the man scent clinging to it, cuffed at it angrily. It rolled to one side and Numa stepped back, eyeing it warily, then, with a growl, he leaped upon it and commenced to maul the insensate thing, ripping and tearing until its contents were scattered about upon the ground. He bit into tins and boxes until scarcely an article remained intact and Stimbol crouched in the tree and watched the destruction of his provisions, utterly helpless to interfere.

A dozen times he cursed himself for having thrown away his rifle and even more frequently he vowed vengeance. He consoled himself, however, with the realisation that Blake could not be far away and that with Blake there were ample provisions which could be augmented by trading and hunting. When the lion left he would descend and follow Blake's trail.

Numa, tired of the contents of the pack, resumed his way toward the long grass, but again his attention was distracted – this time by the thunder-stick of the Tarmangani. The lion smelled at the discarded rifle. Pawed it and finally picked it up between his jaws. Stimbol looked on, horrified. What if the beast damaged the weapon? He would be left without means for defence or for obtaining food!

'Drop it!' shouted Stimbol. 'Drop it!'

Numa, ignoring the ravings of the despised man-thing, strode into his lair, carrying the rifle with him.

That afternoon and night spelled an eternity of terror for Wilbur Stimbol. While daylight lasted the lion remained in the nearby patch of grass effectually deterring the unhappy man from continuing his search for Blake's camp and after night fell no urge whatever could have induced Stimbol to descend to the paralysing terrors of the jungle night even had he known that the lion had departed and no sounds had apprised him of the near presence of danger; but sounds did apprise him. From shortly after dark until nearly dawn a perfect bedlam of howls and growls and coughs and grunts and barks arose from directly beneath him as there had been held a convention of all the horrid beasts of the jungle at the foot of the tree that seemed at best an extremely insecure sanctuary.

When morning came the jungle lay silent and peaceful about him and only torn canvas and empty tins bore mute evidence to the feast of the hyenas that had passed into jungle history. Numa had departed leaving the remains of the kill upon which he had lain as the *pièce de résistance* of the hyenian banquet for which Stimbol had furnished the *hors d'œuvres*.

Stimbol, trembling, descended. Through the jungle, wild-eyed, startled by every sound, scurried a pitiful figure of broken, terror-stricken old age. Few could have recognised in it Wilbur Stimbol of Stimbol and Company, Brokers, New York.

7

The Cross

The storm that had overtaken Stimbol's safari wrought even greater havoc with the plans of Jim Blake, altering in the instant of a single blinding flash of lightning the course of his entire life.

Accompanied by a single black, who carried his camera and an extra rifle, Blake had struck out from the direct route of his safari in search of lion pictures, there being every indication that the great carnivores might be found in abundance in the district through which they were passing.

It was his intention to parallel the route of his main body and rejoin it in camp in the afternoon. The boy who accompanied him was intelligent and resourceful, the direction and speed of the marching safari were mutually agreed upon and the responsibility for bringing Blake into camp safely was left entirely to the negro. Having every confidence in the boy, Blake gave no heed to either time or direction, devoting all his energies to the fascinating occupation of searching for photographic studies.

Shortly after leaving the safari Blake and his companion encountered a herd of seven or eight lions, which included a magnificent old male, an old lioness and five or six young, ranging from half to full grown.

At sight of Blake and his companion the lions took off leisurely through rather open forest and the men followed awaiting patiently the happy coincidence of time, light and grouping that would give the white man such a picture as he desired.

In the mind of the black man was pictured the route of the safari and its relation to the meanderings of the quarry. He knew how far and in what directions he and his companion were being led from their destination. To have returned to the trail of the safari would have been a simple matter to him, but Blake, depending entirely upon the black, gave no heed either to time or direction.

For two hours they clung doggedly to the spoor, encouraged by occasional glimpses of now one, now several members of the regal group, but never was the opportunity afforded for a successful shot. Then the sky became rapidly overcast by black clouds and a few moments later the storm broke in all the terrific fury that only an equatorial storm can achieve, and an instant later amidst the deafening roar of thunder and a blinding flash of lightning utter disaster engulfed James Hunter Blake.

How long he lay, stunned by the shock of the bolt that had struck but a few feet from him, he did not know. When he opened his eyes the storm had passed and the sun was shining brightly through the leafy canopy of the forest. Still dazed, uncomprehending the cause or extent of the catastrophe, he raised himself slowly upon an elbow and looked about him.

One of the first sights that met his eyes aided materially in the rapid recovery of his senses. Less than a hundred feet from him stood a group of lions, seven of them, solemnly regarding him. The characteristics of individual lions differ as greatly from those of their fellows as do the characteristics of individuals of the human race and, even as a human being, a lion may have his moods as well as his personal idiosyncrasies.

These lions that gravely inspected the man-thing had been spared any considerable experience of the human species; they had seen but few men; they had never been hunted; they were well fed; Blake had done nothing greatly to upset their easily irritated nervous systems. Fortunately for him they were merely curious.

But Blake did not know all this. He knew only that seven lions were standing within a hundred feet of him, that they were not in a cage and that while he had pursued them to obtain photographs the thing that he most desired at the moment was not his camera but his rifle.

Stealthily, that he might not annoy them, he looked about him for the weapon. To his consternation it was nowhere in sight, nor was his gun bearer with the extra rifle. Where could the boy be? Doubtless, frightened by the lions, he had decamped. Twenty feet away was a most inviting tree. Blake wondered if the lions would charge the moment that he rose to his feet. He tried to remember all that he had heard about lions and he did recall one fact that applies with almost axiomatic verity to all dangerous animals – if you run from them they will pursue you. To reach the tree it would be necessary to walk almost directly toward the lions.

Blake was in a quandary and then one of the younger lions moved a few steps nearer! That settled the matter as far as Blake was concerned for the closer the lions came the shorter his chance of gaining the tree ahead of them in the event that they elected to prevent.

In the midst of a tremendous forest, entirely surrounded by trees. Nature had chosen to strike him down almost in the centre of a natural clearing. There was a good tree a hundred feet away and on the opposite side of the clearing from the lions. Blake stole a longing glance at it and then achieved some rapid mental calculations. If he ran for the farther tree the lions would have to cover two hundred feet while he was covering one hundred, while if he chose the nearer tree, they must come eighty feet while he was going twenty. There seemed, therefore, no doubt as to the greater desirability of the nearer tree which ruled favourite by odds of two to one. Against it, however, loomed the mental hazard that running straight into the face of seven lions involved.

Jim Blake was sincerely, genuinely and honestly scared; but unless the lions were psycho-analysts they would never have dreamed the truth as he started nonchalantly and slowly toward them – and the tree. The most difficult feat that he had ever accomplished lay in making his legs behave themselves. They wanted to run. So did his feet and his heart and his brain. Only his will held them in leash.

Those were tense moments for Jim Blake – the first half dozen steps he took with seven great lions watching his approach. He saw that they were becoming nervous. The lioness moved uneasily. The old male growled. A younger male, he who had started forward, lashed his sides with his tail, flattened his head, bared his fangs and came stealthily to meet the man.

Blake was almost at the tree when something happened – he never knew what the cause, but inexplicably the lioness turned and bounded away, voicing a low whine, and after her went the other six.

The man leaned against the bole of the tree and fanned himself with his helmet. 'Whew!' he breathed; 'I hope the next lion I see is in the Central Park Zoo.'

But even lions were forgotten in the developments that the next few moments revealed after repeated shouts for the black boy had brought no response and Blake had determined that he must set out in search of him. Nor did he have far to go. On the back track, just inside the clearing Blake found a few remnants of charred flesh and a blackened and half-molten rifle barrel. Of the camera not a vestige remained. The bolt that had bowled Blake over must have squarely struck his gun bearer, killing him instantly, exploding all the ammunition he carried, destroying the camera and ruining the rifle that he had carried.

But what had become of the rifle that had been in Blake's hands? The man searched in all directions, but could not find it and was finally forced to the conclusion that its disappearance could be attributed only to one of those freakish tricks which severe electrical storms so often play upon helpless and futile humanity.

Frankly aware that he was lost and had not the faintest conception of the direction in which lay the proposed camp of his safari, Blake started blindly off on what he devoutly hoped would prove the right route. It was not. His safari was moving north east. Blake headed north.

For two days he trudged on through dense forest, sleeping at night among the branches of trees. Once his fitful slumbers were disturbed by the swaying of a branch against which he was braced. As he awoke he felt it sag as to the weight of some large animal. He looked and saw two fiery eyes gleaming in the dark. Blake knew it to be a leopard as he drew his automatic and fired point blank. With a hideous scream the great cat sprang or fell to the ground. Blake never knew if he hit it. It did not return and there were no signs of it in the morning.

He found food and water in abundance and upon the morning of the third day he emerged from the forest at the foot of a range of lofty mountains and for the first time in weeks revelled in an unobstructed view of the blue sky and saw the horizon again and all that lay between himself and it. He had not realised that he had been depressed by the darkness and the crowding pressure of the trees, but now he experienced all the spiritual buoyancy of a released convict long immured from freedom and the light of day. Rescue was no longer problematical, merely a matter of time. He wanted to sing and shout; but he conserved his energies and started toward the mountains. There had been no native villages in the forest and so, he reasoned, as there must be native villages in a well-watered country stocked with game he would find them upon the mountain slopes.

Topping a rise he saw below him the mouth of a canyon in the bed of which ran a small stream. A village would be built on water. If he followed the water he would come to the village. Quite easy! He descended to the stream where he was deeply gratified to find that a well-worn patch paralleled it. Encouraged by the belief that he would soon encounter natives, and believing that he would have no difficulty in enlisting their services in aiding him to relocate his safari, Blake followed the path upward into the canyon.

He had covered something like three miles without having discovered any sign of habitation when, at a turn in the path, he found himself at the foot of a great white cross of enormous proportions. Hewn from limestone, it stood directly in the centre of the trail and towered above him fully sixty feet. Checked and weatherworn, it gave an impression of great antiquity, which was further borne out by the remains of an almost obliterated inscription upon the face of its massive base.

Blake examined the carved letters, but could not decipher their message. The characters appeared of early English origin, but he dismissed such a possibility as too ridiculous to entertain. He knew that he could not be far from the southern boundary of Abyssinia and that the Abyssinians are Christians. Thus he explained the presence of the cross; but he could not explain the suggestion of sinister menace that this lonely, ancient symbol of the crucifix held for him. Why was it? What was it?

Standing there, tongueless, hoary with age, it seemed to call upon him to stop, to venture not beyond it into the unknown; it warned him back, but not, seemingly, out of a spirit of kindliness and protection, but rather with arrogance and hate.

With a laugh Blake threw off the mood that had seized him and went on, but as he passed the great white monolith he crossed himself, though he was not a Catholic. He wondered what had impelled him to the unfamiliar act, but he could no more explain it than he could the strange and uncanny suggestion of power and personality that seemed to surround the crumbling cross.

Another turn in the path and the trail narrowed where it passed between two huge boulders that might have fallen from the cliff top towering far above. Cliffs closed in closely now in front and upon two sides. Apparently he was close to the canyon's head and yet there was no slightest indication of a village. Yet where did the trail lead? It had an end and a purpose. He would discover the former and, if possible, the latter.

Still under the depressing influence of the cross, Blake passed between the two boulders and the instant that he had passed them a man stepped out behind him and another in front. They were negroes, stalwart, fine-featured fellows and in themselves nothing to arouse wonder or surprise. Blake had expected to meet negroes in Africa; but not negroes wearing elaborately decorated leather jerkins upon the breasts of which red crosses were emblazoned, close fitting nether garments and sandals held by doeskin thongs, cross gartered halfway to their knees; not negroes wearing close fitting bassinets of leopard skin that fitted their heads closely and reached to below their ears;

not negroes armed with two-handed broadswords and elaborately tipped pikes.

Blake was acutely aware of the pike tips as there was one pressing against his belly and another in the small of his back.

'Who be ye?' demanded the negro that faced Blake.

Had the man addressed him in Greek Blake would have been no more surprised than he was by the incongruity of this archaic form of speech falling from the lips of a twentieth century central African black. He was too dumbfounded for an instant to reply.

'Doubtless the fellow be a Saracen, Paul,' said the black behind Blake, 'and understands not what thou sayest – a spy, perchance.'

'Nay, Peter Wiggs, as my name be Paul Bodkin he be no infidel – that I know of mine own good eyes.'

'Whatsoe'er he be it is for ye to fetch him before the captain of the gate who will question him, Paul Bodkin.'

'Natheless there be no hurt in questioning him first, and he will answer.'

'Stop thy tongue and take him to the captain,' said Peter. 'I will abide here and guard the way until thou returnest.'

Paul stepped aside and motioned for Blake to precede him. Then he fell in behind and the American did not need to glance behind to know that the ornate tip of the pike was ever threateningly ready.

The way lay plain before him and Blake followed the trail toward the cliffs where there presently appeared the black mouth of a tunnel leading straight into the rocky escarpment. Leaning against the sides of a niche just within the entrance were several torches made of reeds or twigs bound tightly together and dipped in pitch. One of these Paul Bodkin selected, took some tinder from a metal box he carried in a pouch at his side, struck a spark to it with flint and steel and having thus ignited the tinder and lighted the torch he pushed Blake on again with the tip of his pike and the two entered the tunnel, which the American found to be narrow and winding, well-suited to defence. Its floor was worn smooth until the stones of which it was composed shone polished in the flaring light of the torch. The sides and roof were black with the soot of countless thousands, perhaps, of torch-lighted passages along this strange way that led to – what?

8
The Snake Strikes

Unversed in jungle craft, overwhelmed by the enormity of the catastrophe that had engulfed him, his reasoning faculties numbed by terror, Wilbur Stimbol slunk through the jungle, the fleeing quarry of every terror that imagination could conjure. Matted filth caked the tattered remnants of his clothing that scarce covered the filth of his emaciated body. His once greying hair had turned to white, matching the white stubble of a four-days' beard.

He followed a broad and well-marked trail along which men and horses, sheep and goats had passed within the week and with the blindness and ignorance of the city dweller he thought that he was on the spoor of Blake's safari, and thus it came that he stumbled, exhausted, into the menzil of the slow moving Ibn Jad.

Fejjuân, the Galla slave, discovered him and took him at once to the sheik's beyt where Ibn Jad, with his brother, Tollog, and several others were squatting in the mukaad sipping coffee.

'By Ullah! What strange creature has thou captured now, Fejjuân?' demanded the sheik.

'Perhaps a holy man,' replied the black, 'for he is very poor and without weapons and very dirty – yes, surely he must be a very holy man.'

'Who art thou?' demanded Ibn Jad.

'I am lost and starving. Give me food,' begged Stimbol.

But neither understood the language of the other.

'Another Nasrâny,' said Fahd, contemptuously. 'A Frenjy, perhaps.'

'He looks more like one of el-Engleys,' remarked Tollog.

'Perhaps he is from Fransa,' suggested Ibn Jad. 'Speak to him that vile tongue, Fahd, which thou didst come by among the soldiers in Algeria.'

'Who are you, stranger?' demanded Fahd, in French.

'I am an American,' replied Stimbol, relieved and delighted to have discovered a medium of communication with the Arabs. 'I have been lost in the jungle and I am starving.'

'He is from the New World and he has been lost and is starving,' translated Fahd.

Ibn Jad directed that food be brought and as the stranger ate they carried on a conversation through Fahd. Stimbol explained that his men had deserted him and that he would pay well to be taken to the coast. The Bedúin had no desire to be further hampered by the presence of a weak old man and was inclined to have Stimbol's throat slit as the easiest solution of the problem, but Fahd, who was impressed by the man's boastings of his great wealth, saw the possibilities of a great reward or ransom and prevailed upon the sheik to permit Stimbol to remain among them for a time at least, promising to take him into his own beyt and be responsible for him.

'Ibn Jad would have slain you, Nasrâny,' said Fahd to Stimbol later, 'but Fahd saved you. Remember that when the time comes for distributing the reward, and remember, too, that Ibn Jad will be as ready to kill you tomorrow as he was today and that always your life is in the hands of Fahd. What is it worth?'

'I will make you rich,' replied the American.

During the days that followed Fahd and Stimbol became much better acquainted and with returning strength and a feeling of security Stimbol's old boastfulness returned. He succeeded in impressing the young Bedúin with his vast wealth and importance, and so lavish were his promises that Fahd soon commenced to see before him a life of luxury, ease and power; but with growing cupidity and ambition developed an increasing fear that someone might wrest his good fortune from him. Ibn Jad being the most logical and powerful competitor for the favours of the Nasrâny, Fahd lost no opportunity to impress upon Stimbol that the sheik was still thirsting for his blood, though, as a matter of fact, Ibn Jad was so little concerned over the affairs of Wilbur Stimbol that he would have forgotten his presence entirely were he not occasionally reminded of it by seeing the man upon the march or about the camps.

One thing, however, that Fahd accomplished was to acquaint Stimbol with the fact that there was dissension and treachery in the ranks of the Bedúins and this he determined to put to his own advantageous uses should necessity demand.

And ever, though slowly, the 'Aarab drew closer to the fabled Leopard city of Nímmr, and as they marched Zeyd found opportunity to forward his suit for the hand of Ateja the daughter of Sheik Ibn Jad, while Tollog sought by insinuation to advance the claims of Fahd in the eyes of the sheik. This he did always and only when Fahd might hear as, in reality, his only wish was to impress upon the young traitor the depth of the latter's obligation to him. When Tollog should become sheik he would not care who won the hand of Ateja.

But Fahd was not satisfied with the progress that was being made. Jealousy rode him to distraction until he could not look upon Zeyd without thoughts of murder seizing his mind and at last they obsessed him. He schemed continually to rid himself and the world of his more successful rival. He spied upon him and upon Ateja and at last a plan unfolded itself with opportunity treading upon its heels.

Fahd had noticed that nightly Zeyd absented himself from the gatherings of the men in the mukaad of the sheik's tent and that when the simple household duties were performed Ateja slipped out into the night. Fahd followed and confirmed what was really too apparent to be dignified by the name of suspicion – Zeyd and Ateja met.

And then one night, Fahd was not at the meeting in the sheik's beyt. Instead he hid near the tent of Zeyd and when the latter had left to keep his tryst Fahd crept in and seized the matchlock of his rival. It was already loaded and he had but to prime it with powder. Stealthily he crept by back ways through the camp to where Zeyd awaited his light of love and sneaked up behind him.

At a little distance, sitting in his mukaad with his friends beneath the light of paper lanterns, Ibn Jad the sheik was plainly visible to the two young men standing in the outer darkness. Ateja and Hirfa were still engaged in housewifely duties.

Fahd, standing behind Zeyd, raised the ancient matchlock to his shoulder and aimed – very carefully he aimed, but not at Zeyd. No, for the cunning of Fahd was as the cunning of the fox. Had Zeyd been murdered naught could ever convince Ateja that Fahd was not the murderer. Fahd knew that and he was equally sure that Ateja would have naught of the slayer of her lover.

Beyond Zeyd was Ibn Jad, but Fahd was not aiming at Ibn Jad either. At whom was he aiming? No one. Not yet was the time ripe to slay the sheik. First must they have their hands upon the treasure, the secret of which he alone was supposed to hold.

Fahd aimed at one of the am'dán of the sheik's tent. He aimed with great care, and then he pulled the trigger. The prop splintered and broke a foot above the level of Ibn Jad's head and simultaneously Fahd threw down the musket and leaped upon the startled Zeyd, at the same time crying loudly for help.

Startled by the shot and the cries men ran from all directions and with them was the sheik. He found Zeyd being held tightly from behind by Fahd.

'What is the meaning of this?' demanded Ibn Jad.

'By Ullah, Ibn Jad, he would have slain thee!' cried Fahd. 'I came upon him just in time and as he fired I leaped upon his back, else he would have killed you.'

'He lies!' cried Zeyd. 'The shot came from behind me. If any fired upon Ibn Jad it was Fahd himself.'

Ateja, wide-eyed, ran to her lover. 'Thou didst not do it, Zeyd; tell me that thou didst not do it.'

'As Allah is my God and Mohammed his prophet I did not do it,' swore Zeyd.

'I would not have thought it of him,' said Ibn Jad.

Cunning Fahd did not mention the matchlock. Shrewdly he guessed that its evidence would be more potent if discovered by another than he and that it would be discovered he was sure. Nor was he wrong. Tollog found it.

'Here,' he exclaimed, 'is the weapon.'

'Let us examine it beneath the light,' said Ibn Jad. 'It should dispel our doubts more surely than any lying tongue.'

As the party moved in the direction of the sheik's beyt Zeyd experienced the relief of one reprieved from death, for he knew that the testimony of the matchlock would exonerate him. It could not be his. He pressed the hand of Ateja, walking at his side.

Beneath the light of the paper lanterns in the mukaad Ibn Jad held the weapon beneath his gaze as, with craning necks, the others pressed about him. A single glance sufficed. With stern visage the sheik raised his eyes.

'It is Zeyd's,' he said.

Ateja gasped and drew away from her lover.

'I did not do it! It is some trick,' cried Zeyd.

'Take him away!' commanded Ibn Jad. 'See that he is tightly bound.'

Ateja rushed to her father and fell upon her knees. 'Do not slay him!' she cried. 'It could not have been he. I know it was not he.'

'Silence, girl,' commanded the sheik sternly. 'Go to thy quarters and remain there!'

They took Zeyd to his own beyt and bound him securely and in the mukaad of the sheik the elders sat in judgment while from behind the curtains of the women's quarters Ateja listened.

'At dawn, then, he shall be shot!' This was the sentence that Ateja heard passed upon her lover.

Behind his greasy thorrîb Fahd smiled a crooked smile. In his black house of hair Zeyd struggled with the bonds that held him, for though he had not heard the sentence he was well aware of what his fate would be. In the quarters of the hareem of the Sheik Ibn Jad the sheik's daughter lay sleepless and suffering. Her long lashes were wet with tears but her grief was silent. Wide-eyed she waited, listening, and presently her patience was rewarded by the sounds of the deep, regular breathing of Ibn Jad and his wife, Hirfa. They slept!

Ateja stirred. Stealthily she raised the lower edge of the tent cloth beside which lay her sleeping mat and rolled quietly beneath it into the mukaad, now deserted. Groping, she found the matchlock of Zeyd where Ibn Jad had left it. She carried also a bundle wrapped in an old thorrîb, the contents of which she had gathered earlier in the evening when Hirfa, occupied with her duties, had been temporarily absent from the women's quarters.

Ateja emerged from the tent of her father and crept cautiously along the single, irregular street formed by the pitched tents of the 'Aarab until she came to the beyt of Zeyd. For a moment she paused at the opening, listening, then she entered softly on sandalled feet.

But Zeyd, sleepless, struggling with his bonds, heard her. 'Who comes?' he demanded.

'S-s-sh!' cautioned the girl. 'It is I, Ateja.' She crept to his side.

'Beloved!' he murmured.

Deftly the girl cut the bonds that held his wrists and ankles. 'I have brought thee food and thy musket,' she told him. 'These and freedom I give thee – the rest thou must do thyself. Thy mare stands tethered with the others. Far is the Béled el-Guâd, beset with dangers is the way, but night and day will Ateja pray to Allah to guide thee safely. Haste, my loved one!'

Zeyd pressed her tightly to his breast, kissed her and was gone into the night.

9

Sir Richard

The floor of the tunnel along which Paul Bodkin conducted Blake inclined ever upwards and again and again it was broken by flights of steps which carried them always to higher levels. To Blake the way seemed interminable. Even the haunting mystery of the long tunnel failed to overcome the monotony of its unchanging walls that slipped silently into the torch's dim ken for a brief instant and as silently back into the Cimmerian oblivion behind to make place for more wall, unvaryingly identical.

But, as there ever is to all things, there was an end to the tunnel. Blake first glimpsed it in a little patch of distant daylight ahead and presently he stepped out into the sunlight and looked out across a wide valley that was tree-dotted and beautiful. He found himself standing upon a wide ledge, or shelf, some hundred feet above the base of the mountain through which the tunnel had been cut. There was a sheer drop before him and to his right the ledge terminated abruptly at a distance of a hundred feet or less. Then he glanced to the left and his eyes went wide in astonishment.

Across the shelf stood a solid wall of masonry flanked at either side by great, round towers pierced by long, narrow embrasures. In the centre of the wall was a lofty gateway which was closed by a massive and handsomely wrought portcullis behind which Blake saw two negroes standing guard. They were clothed precisely as his captors, but held great battle-axes, the butts of which rested upon the ground.

'What ho, the gate!' shouted Paul Bodkin. 'Open to the outer guard and a prisoner!'

Slowly the portcullis rose and Blake and his captor passed beneath. Directly inside the gateway and at the left, built into the hillside, was what was evidently a guard house. Before it loitered a score or so soldiers, all uniformed like Paul Bodkin, upon the breast of each the red cross. To a heavy wooden rail gaily caparisoned horses were tethered, their handsome trappings recalling to Blake's memory paintings he had seen of mounted knights of medieval England.

There was so much of unreality in the strangely-garbed blacks, the massive barbican that guarded the way, the trappings of the horses, that Blake was no longer capable of surprise when one of the two doors in the guard house opened and there stepped out a handsome young man clad in a hauberk of chain mail over which was a light surcoat of rough stuff, dyed purple. Upon the youth's head fitted a leopard skin bassinet from the lower edge of which depended a camail or gorget of chain mail that entirely surrounded and protected his throat and neck. He was armed only with a heavy sword and a dagger, but against the side of the guard house, near the doorway where he paused to look at Blake, leaned a long lance, and near it was a shield with a red cross emblazoned upon its boss.

'Od zounds!' exclaimed the young man. 'What hast thou there, varlet?'

'A prisoner, an' it please thee, noble lord,' replied Paul Bodkin, deferentially.

'A Saracen, of a surety,' stated the young man.

'Nay, an' I may make so bold, Sir Richard,' replied Paul; 'but methinks he be no Saracen.'

'And why?'

'With mine own eyes I didst see him make the sign before the Cross.'

'Fetch him hither, lout!'

Bodkin prodded Blake in the rear with his pike, but the American scarce noticed the offence, so occupied was his mind by the light of truth that had so suddenly illuminated it. In the instant he had grasped the solution. He laughed inwardly at himself for his denseness. Now he understood everything – and these fellows thought they could put it over on him, did they? Well, they had come near to doing it, all right.

He stepped quickly toward the young man and halted, upon his lips a faintly sarcastic smile. The other eyed him with haughty arrogance.

'Whence comest thou,' he asked, 'and what doest thou in the Valley of the Sepulchre, varlet?'

Blake's smile faded – too much was too much. 'Cut the comedy, young fellow,' he drawled in his slow way. 'Where's the director?'

'Director? Forsooth, I know not what thou meanest.'

'Yes you don't!' snapped Blake, with fine sarcasm. 'But let me tell you right off the bat that no seven-fifty a day extra can't pull anything like that with me, you cheap ham!'

'Oddsbud, fellow! I ken not the meaning of all the words, but I mislike thy tone and "cheap ham" savours o'er much of insult to fall sweetly upon the ears of Richard Montmorency.'

'Be yourself,' advised Blake, 'If the director isn't handy send for the assistant director, or the camera man – even the continuity writer may have more sense than you seem to have.'

'Be myself? and who thinkest thee I would be other than Richard Montmorency, a noble sir Knight of Nímmr.'

Blake shook his head in despair, then he turned to the soldiers who were standing about listening to the conversation. He thought some of them would be grinning at the joke that was being played on him, but he saw only solemn, serious faces.

'Look here,' he said, addressing Paul Bodkin, 'don't any of you know where the director is?'

'"Director,"' repeated Bodkin, shaking his head. 'There be none in Nímmr thus yclept, nay, nor in all the Valley of the Sepulchre that I wot.'

'I'm sorry,' said Blake; 'the mistake is mine; but if there is no director there must be a keeper. May I see him?'

'Ah, keeper!' cried Bodkin, his face lighting with understanding. 'Sir Richard is the keeper.'

'My gawd!' exclaimed Blake, turning to the young man. 'I beg your pardon, I thought that you were one of the inmates.'

'Inmates? Indeed thou speakest a strange tongue and yet withal it hath the flavour of England,' replied the young man gravely. 'But yon varlet be right – I am indeed this day the Keeper of the Gate.'

Blake was commencing to doubt his own sanity, or at least his judgment. Neither the young white man nor any of the negroes had any of the facial characteristics of mad men. He looked up suddenly at the Keeper of the Gate.

'I am sorry,' he said, flashing one of the frank smiles that was famous among his acquaintances. 'I have acted like a boor, but I've been under considerable nervous strain for a long time and on top of that I've been lost in the jungle for days without proper or sufficient food.

'I thought that you were trying to play some sort of a joke on me and, well, I wasn't in any mood for jokes when I expected friendship and hospitality instead.

'Tell me, where am I? What country is this?'

'Thou art close upon the city of Nímmr,' replied the young man.

'I suppose this is something of a national holiday or something?' suggested Blake.

'I do not understand thee,' replied the young man.

'Why, you're all in a pageant or something, aren't you?'

'Odsbodikins! the fellow speaks an outlandish tongue! Pageant?'

'Yes, those costumes.'

'What be amiss with this apparel? True, 'tis not of any wondrous newness, but methinks it be at least more fair than thine. At least it well suffices the daily service of a Knight.'

'You don't mean that you dress like this every day?' demanded Blake.

'And why not? But enough of this. I have no wish to bandy further words with thee. Fetch him within, two of thee. And thou, Bodkin, return to the outer guard!' The young man turned and re-entered the building, while two of the soldiers seized Blake, none too gently, and hustled him within.

He found himself in a high-ceilinged room with walls of cut stone and great hand hewn beams and rafters blackened with age. Upon the stone floor stood a table behind which, upon a bench, the young man seated himself while Blake was placed facing him with a guard on either hand.

'Thy name,' demanded the young man.

'Blake.'

'That be all – just Blake?'

'James Hunter Blake.'

'What title bearest thou in thine own country?'

'I have no title.'

'Ah, thou art not a gentleman, then?'

'I am called one.'

'What is thy country?'

'America.'

'America! There be no such country, fellow.'

'And why not?'

'I never heard of it. What doest thou near the Valley of Sepulchre? Didst not know 'tis forbidden?'

'I told you I was lost. I didn't know where I was. All I want is to get back to my safari or to the coast.'

'That be impossible. We be surrounded by Saracens. For seven hundred and thirty five years we have been invested by their armies. How came you through the enemy's lines? How passed you through his vast army?'

'There isn't any army.'

'Givest thou the lie to Richard Montmorency, varlet? An' thou wert of gentle blood thou shouldst account to me that insult upon the field of honour. Methink'st thou beest some low-born spy sent hither by the Saracen sultan. 'Twould be well an' thou confessed all to me, for if I take thee before the Prince he will wrest the truth from thee in ways that are far from pleasant. What say?'

'I have nothing to confess. Take me before the Prince, or whoever your boss is; perhaps he will at least give me food.'

'Thou shalt have food here. Never shall it be said that Richard Montmorency turned a hungry man from his doorway. Hey! Michel! Michel! Where is the lazy brat? Michel!'

A door opened from an inner apartment to admit a boy, sleepy-eyed, digging a grimy fist into one eye. He was clothed in a short tunic, his legs encased in green tights. In his cap was a feather.

'Sleeping again, eh?' demanded Sir Richard. 'Thou lazy knave! Fetch bread and meat for this poor wayfarer and be not until the morrow at it!'

Wide-eyed and rather stupidly, the boy stared at Blake. 'A Saracen, master?' he asked.

'What boots it?' snapped Sir Richard. 'Did not our Lord Jesus feed the multitude, nor ask if there were unbelievers among them? Haste, churl! the stranger be of a great hunger.'

The youth turned and shuffled from the room, wiping his nose upon his sleeve, and Sir Richard's attention came back to Blake.

'Thou art not ill favoured, fellow,' he said. ''Tis a pity that thou beest not of noble blood, for thy mien appeareth not like that of one low born.'

'I never considered myself low born,' said Blake, with a grin.

'Thy father, now – was he not at least a sir Knight?'

Blake was thinking quickly now. He was far from being able as yet to so much as hazard a guess that might explain his host's archaic costume and language, but he was sure the man was in earnest, whether sane or not, and were he not sane it seemed doubly wise to humour him.

'Yes, indeed,' he replied, 'my father is a thirty second degree Mason and a Knight Templar.'

'Sblud! I knew it,' cried Sir Richard.

'And so am I,' added Blake, when he realised the happy effect his statement had produced.

'Ah, I knew it! I knew it!' cried Sir Richard. 'Thy bearing proclaimed thy noble blood; but why didst thou seek to deceive me? And so thou art one of the Poor Knights of Christ and of the Temple of Solomon who guard the way of the pilgrims to the Holy Land! This explaineth thy poor raiment and glorifies it.'

Blake was mystified by the allusion as the picture always suggested by a reference to Knights Templars was of waving white plumes, gorgeous aprons and glittering swords. He did not know that in the days of their origin they were clothed in any old garments that the charity of others might bequeath them.

At this moment Michel returned bearing a wooden trencher containing cold mutton and several pieces of simnel bread and carrying in one hand a flagon of wine. These he set upon the table before Blake and going to a cupboard fetched two metal goblets into which he decanted a portion of the contents of the flagon.

Sir Richard arose and taking one of the goblets raised it before him on a level with his head.

'Hail Sir James!' he cried; 'and welcome to Nímmr and the Valley of the Sepulchre.'

'Here's looking at you!' replied Blake.

'A quaint saying,' remarked Sir Richard. 'Methinks the ways of England must be changed since the days of Richard the Lion Hearted when my noble ancestor set forth upon the great crusade in the company of his king. Here's looking at you! Odsbodikins! I must not let that from my memory. Here's looking at you! Just wait thou 'til some fair knight doth drink my health – I shall lay him flat with that!

'But stay! Here, Michel, fetch you stool for Sir James, and eat, sir knight. Thou must be passing hungry.'

'I'll tell the world I am,' replied Blake, feelingly, as he sat down on the stool that Michel brought. There were no knives or forks, but there were fingers, and these Blake used to advantage while his host sat smiling happily at him from across the rude table.

'Thou art better than a minstrel for pleasure,' cried Sir Richard. '"I'll tell the world I am!" Ho, ho! Thou wilt be a gift from heaven in the castle of the prince. "I'll tell the world I am!"'

When Blake had satisfied his hunger, Sir Richard ordered Michel to prepare horses. 'We ride down to the castle, Sir James,' he explained. 'No longer art thou my prisoner, but my friend and guest. That I should have received thee so scurvily shalt ever be to my discredit.'

Mounted upon prancing chargers and followed at a respectful distance by Michel the two rode down the winding mountain road. Sir Richard now carried his shield and lance, a pennon fluttering bravely in the wind from just below the tip of the lance, the sun glancing from the metal of his hauberk, a smile upon his brave face as he chatted with his erstwhile prisoner. To Blake he seemed a gorgeous picture ridden from out the pages of a story book. Yet, belying his martial appearance, there was a childlike simplicity about the man that won Blake's liking from the first, for there was that about him that made it impossible for one to conceive him as the perpetrator of a dishonourable act.

His ready acceptance of Blake's statements about himself bespoke a credulity that seemed incompatible with the high intelligence reflected by his noble countenance and the American preferred to attribute it to a combination of unsophistication and an innate integrity which could not conceive of perfidy in others.

As the road rounded the shoulder of a hill, Blake saw another barbican barring the way and, beyond, the towers and battlements of an ancient castle. At a command from Sir Richard the warders of the gate opened to them and the three rode through into the ballium. This space between the outer and inner walls appeared unkept and neglected. Several old trees flourished within it and beneath the shade of one of these, close to the outer gateway, lolled several men-at-arms two of whom were engaged in a game that resembled draughts.

At the foot of the inner wall was a wide moat, the waters of which reflected the grey stones of the wall and the ancient vines that, growing upon its inner side, topped it to form a leafy coping that occasionally hung low upon the outer side.

Directly opposite the barbican was the great gateway in the inner wall and here a drawbridge spanned the moat and a heavy portcullis barred the way into the great court of the castle; but at a word from Sir Richard the gate lifted and, clattering across the drawbridge, they rode within.

Before Blake's astonished eyes loomed a mighty castle of rough hewn stone, while to the right and left, within the great court, spread broad gardens, not ill kept, in which were gathered a company of men and women who might have but just stepped from Arthur's court.

At sight of Sir Richard and his companion the nearer members of the company regarded Blake with interest and evident surprise. Several called greetings and questions to Sir Richard as the two men dismounted and turned their horses over to Michel.

'Ho, Richard!' cried one. 'What bringest thou – a Saracen?'

'Nay,' replied Richard. 'A fair sir knight who would do his devoir to the prince. Where be he?'

'Yonder,' and they pointed toward the far end of the court where a larger company was assembled.

'Come, Sir James!' directed Richard, and led him down the courtyard, the knights and ladies following closely, asking questions, commenting with a frankness that brought a flush to Blake's face. The women openly praised his features and his carriage, while the men, perhaps prompted by jealousy, made unflattering remarks about his soiled and torn apparel and its, to them, ridiculous cut, and indeed the contrast was great between their gorgeous dalmaticas of villosa or cyclas, their close-fitting tights, their coloured caps and Blake's drab shirt, whip-cord breeches and cordovan boots, now soiled, torn and scratched.

The women were quite as richly dressed as the men, wearing clinging mantles of rich stuff, their hair and shoulders covered with dainty wimples of various colours and often elaborately embroidered.

None of these men, nor any of those in the assemblage they were approaching wore armour, but Blake had seen an armoured knight at the outer gateway and another at the inner, and he judged that only when engaged in military duties did they wear this heavy and uncomfortable dress.

When they reached the party at the end of the court Sir Richard elbowed his way among them to the centre of the group where stood a tall man of imposing appearance, chatting with those about him. As Sir Richard and Blake halted before him the company fell silent.

'My lord prince,' said Richard, bowing, 'I bring thee Sir James, a worthy Knight Templar who hath come under the protection of God through the lines of the enemy to the gates of Nímmr.'

The tall man eyed Blake searchingly and he had not the appearance of great credulity.

'Thou sayest that thou comest from the Temple of Solomon in the Kingdom of Jerusalem?' he demanded.

'Sir Richard must have misunderstood me,' replied Blake.

'Then thou art no Knight Templar?'

'Yes, but I am not from Jerusalem.'

'Perchance he is one of those doughty sir knights that guard the pilgrims' way to the Holy Land,' suggested a young woman standing near the prince.

Blake glanced quickly at the speaker and as their eyes met, hers fell, but not before he had seen that they were very beautiful eyes set in an equally beautiful, oval face.

'More like it haps he be a Saracen spy sent among us by the Sultan,' snapped a dark man who stood beside the girl.

The latter raised her eyes to the prince. 'He looketh not like a Saracen, my father,' she said.

'What knowest thou of the appearance of a Saracen, child?' demanded the prince. 'Hast seen so many?' The party laughed and the girl pouted.

'Verily an' I hast seen full as many a Saracen as has Sir Malud or thyself, my lord prince,' she snapped, haughtily. 'Let Sir Malud describe a Saracen.'

The dark young man flushed angrily. 'At least,' he said, 'my lord prince, I knowest an English knight when I seest one, an' if here be an English knight then Sir Malud be a Saracen!'

'Enough,' said the prince and then, turning to Blake: 'If thou art not from Jerusalem where art thou from?'

'New York,' replied the American.

'Ha,' whispered Sir Malud to the girl; 'didst I not tell you?'

'Tell me what – that he is from New York? Where is that?' she demanded.

'Some stronghold of the infidel,' asserted Malud.

'New York?' repeated the prince. 'Be that in the Holy Land?'

'It is sometimes called New Jerusalem,' explained Blake.

'And thou comest to Nímmr through the lines of the enemy? Tell me, sir knight, had they many men-at-arms? And how were their forces disposed? Be they close upon the Valley of the Sepulchre? Thinkest thou they plan an early attack? Come, tell me all – thou canst be of great service.'

'I have come for days through the forest and seen no living man,' said Blake. 'No enemy surrounds you.'

'What?' cried the prince.

'Didst I not tell thee?' demanded Malud. 'He is an enemy spy. He wouldst lead us into the belief that we are safe, that the forces of the sultan may find us off our guard and take Nímmr and the Valley.'

'Odsblud! Methinks thou beest right, Sir Malud,' cried the prince. 'No enemy indeed! Why else then hast the Knights of Nímmr lain here seven and a half centuries if there be no horde of infidels surrounding our stronghold?'

'Search me,' said Blake.

'Eh, what?' demanded the prince.

'He hath a quaint manner of speech, my lord prince,' explained Richard, 'but I do not think him an enemy of England. Myself will vouch for him an' you will take him into your service, my lord prince.'

'Wouldst enter my service, sir?' demanded the prince.

Blake glanced at Sir Malud and looked dubious – then his eyes wandered to those of the girl. 'I'll tell the world I would!' he said.

10

The Return of Ulala

Numa was hungry. For three days and three nights he had hunted but always the prey had eluded him. Perhaps Numa was growing old. Not so keen were his scent and his vision, not so swift his charges, nor quick well-timed the spring that heretofore had brought down the quarry. So quick the food of Numa that a fraction of a second, a hair's breadth, might mark the difference between a full belly and starvation.

Perhaps Numa was growing old, yet he still was a mighty engine of destruction and now the pangs of hunger had increased his ferocity many-fold, stimulated his cunning, emboldened him to take great risks that his belly might be filled. It was a nervous, irascible, ferocious Numa that crouched beside the trail. His up-pricked ears, his intent and blazing eyes, his quivering nostrils, the gently moving tail-tip, evidenced his awareness of another presence.

Down the wind to the nostrils of Numa the lion came the man-scent. Four days ago, his belly full, Numa had doubtless slunk away at the first indication of the presence of man, but today is another day and another Numa.

Zeyd, three days upon the back track from the menzil of the sheik Ibn Jad, thought of Ateja, of far Guâd, congratulated himself upon the good fortune that had thus far smiled upon his escape and flight. His mare moved slowly along the jungle trail, unurged, for the way was long; and just ahead a beast of prey waited in ambush.

But Numa's were not the only ears to hear, nor his nostrils the only nostrils to scent the coming of the man-thing – another beast crouched near, unknown to Numa.

Over-anxious, fearful of being cheated of his meat, Numa made a false move. Down the trail came the mare. She must pass within a yard of Numa, but Numa could not wait. Before she was within the radius of his spring he charged, voicing a horrid roar. Terrified, the mare reared and, rearing, tried to turn and bolt. Overbalanced, she toppled backward and fell and in falling unhorsed Zeyd; but in the instant she was up and flying back along the trail, leaving her master alone in the path of the charging lion.

Horrified, the man saw the snarling face, the bared fangs almost upon him. Then he saw something else – something equally awe-inspiring – a naked giant that leaped from a swaying branch full upon the back of the great cat. He saw a bronzed arm encircle the neck of the beast of prey as the lion was borne to earth by the weight and impact of the man's body. He saw a heavy knife flashing in the air, striking home again and again as the frenzied lion threw itself about in futile effort to dislodge the thing upon its back. He heard the roars and the growls of el-adrea and mingled with them were growls and snarls that turned his blood cold, for he saw that they came from the lips of the man-beast.

Then Numa went limp and the giant arose and stood above the carcass. He placed one foot upon it and, raising his face toward the heavens, voiced a hideous scream that froze the marrow in the bones of the Bedúin – a scream that few men have heard: the victory cry of the bull ape.

It was then that Zeyd recognised his saviour and shuddered again as he saw that it was Tarzan of the Apes. The ape-man looked down at him.

'Thou art from the menzil of Ibn Jad,' he said.

'I am but a poor man,' replied Zeyd. 'I but followed where my sheik led. Hold it not against Zeyd, sheik of the jungle, that he be in thy Béled. Spare my poor life I pray thee and may Allah bless thee.'

'I have no wish to harm thee, Bedùwy,' replied Tarzan. 'What wrong hath been done in my country is the fault of Ibn Jad alone. Is he close by?'

'Wellah, nay, he be many marches from here.'

'Where art thy companions?' demanded the ape-man.

'I have none.'

'Thou art alone?'

'Billah, yes.'

Tarzan frowned. 'Think well, Bedùwy, before lying to Tarzan,' he snapped.

'By Ullah, I speak the truth! I am alone.'

'And why?'

'Fahd did plot against me to make it appear that I tried to take the life of Ibn Jad, which, before Allah, is a lie that stinketh to heaven, and I was to be shot; but Ateja, the daughter of the sheik, cut my bonds in the night and I escaped.'

'What is thy name?'

'Zeyd.'

'Whither goest thou – to thine own country?'

'Yes, to Béled el-Guâd, a Beny Sâlem fendy of el-Harb.'

'Thou canst not, alone, survive the perils of the way,' Tarzan warned him.

'Of that I be fearful, but death were certain had I not escape the wrath of Ibn Jad.'

For a moment Tarzan was silent in thought. 'Great must be the love of Ateja, the daughter of the sheik, and great her belief in you,' he said.

'Wellah, yes, great is our love and, too, she knew that I would not slay her father, whom she loves.'

Tarzan nodded. 'I believe thee and shall help thee. Thou canst not go on alone. I shall take thee to the nearest village and there the chief will furnish you with warriors who will take you to the next village and thus from village to village you will be escorted to the Sudan.'

'May Allah ever watch over and guard thee!' exclaimed Zeyd.

'Tell me,' said Tarzan, as the two moved along the jungle trail in the direction of the nearest village which lay two marches to the south of them. 'Tell me what Ibn Jad doth in this country. It is not true that he came for ivory alone. Am I not right?'

'Wellah, yes, Sheik Tarzan,' admitted Zeyd. 'Ibn Jad came for treasure, but not for ivory.'

'What, then?'

'In el-Hábash lies the treasure city of Nímmr,' explained Zeyd. 'This Ibn Jad was told by a learned Sáhar. So great is the wealth of Nímmr that a thousand camels could carry away not a tenth part of it. It consists of gold and jewels and – a woman.'

'A woman?'

'Yes, a woman of such wondrous beauty that in the north she alone would bring a price that would make Ibn Jad rich beyond dreams. Surely thou must have heard of Nímmr.'

'Sometimes the Gallas speak of it,' said Tarzan, 'but always I thought it of no more reality than the other places of their legends. And Ibn Jad undertook this long and dangerous journey on no more than the word of a magician?'

'What could be better than the word of a learned Sáhar?' demanded Zeyd.

Tarzan of the Apes shrugged.

During the two days that it took them to reach the village, Tarzan learned of the white man who had come to the camp of Ibn Jad, but from Zeyd's description of him he was not positive whether it was Blake or Stimbol.

As Tarzan travelled south with Zeyd, Ibn Jad trekked northward into el-Hábash and Fahd plotted with Tollog, and Stimbol plotted with Fahd, while Fejjuân the Galla slave waited patiently for the moment of his delivery from bondage and Ateja mourned for Zeyd.

'As a boy thou wert raised in this country, Fejjuân,' she said one day to the Galla slave. 'Tell me, dost thou think Zeyd could make his way alone to el-Guâd?'

'Billah, nay,' replied the black. 'Doubtless he be dead by now.'

The girl stifled a sob.

'Fejjuân mourns with thee, Ateja,' said the black, 'for Zeyd was a kindly man. Would that Allah had spared your lover and taken him who was guilty.'

'What do you mean?' asked Ateja. 'Knowest thou, Fejjuân, who fired the shot at Ibn Jad, my father? It was not Zeyd! Tell me it was not Zeyd; but thy words tell me that which I well knew before. Zeyd could not have sought the life of my father!'

'Nor did he,' replied Fejjuân.

'Tell me what you know of this thing.'

'And you will not tell another who told you?' he asked. 'It would go hard with me if one I am thinking of knew that I had seen what I did see.'

'I swear by Allah that I wilt not betray you, Fejjuân,' cried the girl. 'Tell me, what didst thou see?'

'I did not see who fired the shot at thy father, Ateja,' replied the black, 'but something else I saw before the shot was fired.'

'Yes, what was it?'

'I saw Fahd creep into the beyt of Zeyd and come out again bearing Zeyd's matchlock. That I saw.'

'I knew it! I knew it!' cried the girl.

'But Ibn Jad will not believe if you tell him.'

'I know; but now that I am convinced perhaps I shall find a way to have Fahd's blood for the blood of Zeyd,' cried the girl bitterly.

For days Ibn Jad skirted the mountains behind which he thought lay the fabled city of Nímmr, as he searched for an entrance which he hoped to find without having recourse to the natives whose haunts he had sedulously avoided lest through them opposition to his venture might develop.

The country was sparsely settled, which rendered it easy for the 'Aarab to avoid coming into close contact with the natives, though it was impossible that the Gallas were ignorant of their presence. If, however, the blacks were willing to leave them alone Ibn Jad had no intention of molesting them unless he found that it would be impossible to carry his project to a successful issue without their assistance, in which event he was equally ready to approach them with false promises or ruthless cruelty, whichever seemed the more likely to best serve his purpose.

As the days passed Ibn Jad waxed increasingly impatient for, search as he would, he could locate no pass across the mountains, nor any entrance to the fabled valley wherein lay the treasure city of Nímmr.

'Billah!' he exclaimed one day; 'There be a city of Nímmr and there be an entrance to it, and, by Allah, I will find it! Summon the Habush, Tollog! From them or through them we shall have a clue in one way or another.'

When Tollog had fetched the Galla slaves to the beyt of Ibn Jad the old sheik questioned them but there was none who had definite knowledge of the trail leading to Nímmr.

'Then, by Allah,' exclaimed Ibn Jad, 'we shall have it from the native Habush!'

'They be mighty warriors, brother,' cried Tollog, 'and we be far within their country. Should we anger them and they set upon us it might fare ill with us.'

'We be Bedùwy,' said Ibn Jad proudly, 'and we be armed with muskets. "What could their simple spears and arrows avail against us?"

'But they be many and we be few,' insisted Tollog.

'We shall not fight unless we be driven to it,' said Ibn Jad. 'First we shall seek, by friendly overtures, to win their confidence and cajole the secret from them.

'Fejjuân!' he exclaimed, turning to the great black. 'Thou art a Habashy. I have heard thee say that thou well rememberest the days of thy childhood in the hut of thy father and the story of Nímmr was no new story to you. Go, then, and seek out thy people. Make friends with them. Tell them that the great Sheik Ibn Jad comes among them in friendliness and that he hath gifts for their chiefs. Tell them also that he would visit the city of Nímmr and if they will lead him there he will reward them well.'

'I but await thy commands,' said Fejjuân, elated at this opportunity to do what he had long dreamed of doing. 'When shall I set forth?'

'Prepare thyself tonight and when dawn comes depart,' replied the sheik.

And so it was that Fejjuân, the Galla slave, set forth early the following morning from the menzil of Ibn Jad, sheik of the fendy el-Guâd, to search for a village of his own people.

By noon he had come upon a well-worn trail leading toward the west and this he followed boldly guessing that he would best disarm suspicion thus than by attempting to approach a Galla village by stealth. Also he well knew that there was little likelihood that he could accomplish the latter in any event. Fejjuân was no fool. He knew that it might be difficult to convince the Gallas that he was of their blood and there was against him not alone his 'Aarab garments and weapons but the fact that he would be able to speak the Galla tongue but lamely after all these years.

That he was a brave man was evidenced by the fact that he well knew the suspicious and warlike qualities of his people and their inborn hatred of the 'Aarab and yet gladly embraced this opportunity to go amongst them.

How close he had approached a village Fejjuân did not know. There were neither sounds nor odours to enlighten him when there suddenly appeared in the trail ahead of him three husky Galla warriors and behind him he heard others, though he did not turn.

Instantly Fejjuân raised his hands in sign of peace and at the same time he smiled.

'What are you doing in the Galla country?' demanded one of his warriors.

'I am seeking the house of my father,' replied Fejjuân.

'The house of your father is not in the country of the Gallas,' growled the warrior. 'You are one of these who come to rob us of our sons and daughters.'

'No,' replied Fejjuân. 'I am a Galla.'

'If you were a Galla you would speak the language of the Gallas better. We understand you, but you do not speak as a Galla speaks.'

'That is because I was stolen away when I was a child and have lived among the Bedùwy since, speaking only their tongue.'

'What is your name?'

'The Bedùwy call me Fejjuân, but my Galla name was Ulala.'

'Do you think he speaks the truth?' demanded one of the blacks of a companion. 'When I was a child I had a brother whose name was Ulala.'

'Where is he?' asked the other warrior.

'We do not know. Perhaps Simba the lion devoured him. Perhaps the desert people took him. Who knows?'

'Perhaps he speaks the truth,' said the second warrior. 'Perhaps he is your brother. Ask him his father's name.'

'What was your father's name?' demanded the first warrior.

'Naliny,' replied Fejjuân.

At this reply the Galla warriors became much excited and whispered among themselves for several seconds. Then the first warrior turned again to Fejjuân.

'Did you have a brother?' he demanded.

'Yes,' replied Fejjuân.

'What was his name?'

'Tabo,' answered Fejjuân without hesitation.

The warrior who had questioned him leaped into the air with a wild shout.

'It is Ulala!' he cried. 'It is my brother. I am Tabo, Ulala. Do you not remember me?'

'Tabo!' cried Fejjuân. 'No, I would not know you, for you were a little boy when I was stolen away and now you are a great warrior. Where are our father and mother? Are they alive? Are they well?'

'They are alive and well, Ulala,' replied Tabo. 'Today they are in the village of the chief, for there is a great council because of the presence of some desert people in our country. Came you with them?'

'Yes, I am a slave to the desert people,' replied Fejjuân. 'Is it far to the village of the chief? I would see my mother and my father and, too, I would talk with the chief about the desert people who have come to the country of the Gallas.'

'Come brother!' cried Tabo. 'We are not far from the village of the chief. Ah, my brother, that I should see you again whom we thought to be dead all these years! Great will be the joy of our father and mother.

'But, tell me, have the desert people turned you against your own people? You have lived with them many years. Perhaps you have taken a wife among them. Are you sure that you do not love them better than you love those whom you have not seen for many years?'

'I do not love the Bedùwy,' replied Fejjuân, 'nor have I taken wife among them. Always in my heart has been the hope of returning to the mountains of my own country, to the house of my father. I love my own people, Tabo. Never again shall I leave them.'

'The desert people have been unkind to you – they have treated you with cruelty?' demanded Tabo.

'Nay, on the contrary they have treated me well,' replied Fejjuân. 'I do not hate them, but neither do I love them. They are not of my own blood. I am a slave among them.'

As they talked the party moved along the trail toward the village while two of the warriors ran ahead to carry the glad tidings to the father and mother of the long missing Ulala, and so it was that when they came within sight of the village they were met by a great crowd of laughing, shouting Gallas, and in the fore rank were the father and mother of Fejjuân, their eyes blinded by tears of love and joy that welled at sight of this long-lost child.

After the greetings were over, and every man, woman and child in the company must crowd close and touch the returned wanderer, Tabo conducted Fejjuân into the village and the presence of the chief.

Batando was an old man. He had been chief when Ulala was stolen away. He was inclined to be sceptical, fearing a ruse of the desert people, and he asked many questions of Fejjuân concerning matters that he might hold in his memory from the days of his childhood. He asked him about the house of his father and the names of his playmates and other intimate things that an impostor might not know, and when he had done he arose and took Fejjuân in his arms and rubbed his cheek against the cheek of the prodigal.

'You are indeed Ulala,' he cried. 'Welcome back to the land of your people. Tell me now what the desert people do here. Have they come for slaves?'

'The desert people will always take slaves when they can get them, but Ibn Jad has not come first for slaves, but for treasure.'

'Ai! What treasure?' demanded Batando.

'He has heard of the treasure city of Nímmr,' replied Fejjuân. 'It is a way into the valley where lies Nímmr that he seeks. For this he sent me to find Gallas who would lead him to Nímmr. He will make gifts and he promises rich rewards when he shall have wrested the treasure from Nímmr.'

'Does he speak true words?' demanded Batando.

'There is no truth in the beards of the desert dwellers,' replied Fejjuân.

'And if he does not find the treasure of Nímmr, perhaps he will try to find treasure and slaves in the Galla country to repay the expense of the long journey he has undertaken from the desert country?' asked Batando.

'Batando speaks out of the great wisdom of many years,' replied Fejjuân.

'What does he know of Nímmr?' asked the old chief.

'Naught other than what an old medicine man of the 'Aarab told him,' replied Fejjuân. 'He said to Ibn Jad that great treasure lay hoarded in the city of Nímmr, and that there was a beautiful woman who would bring a great price in the far north.'

'Nothing more he told him?' demanded Batando. 'Did he not tell him of the difficulties of entering the forbidden valley?'

'Nay.'

'Then we can guide him to the entrance to the valley,' said Batando, smiling slyly.

11

Sir James

As Tarzan and Zeyd journeyed toward the village in which the ape-man purposed to enlist an escort for the Arab upon the first stage of his return journey toward his desert home, the Bedúin had time to meditate much upon many matters and having come to trust and respect his savage guide he at last unbosomed himself to Tarzan.

'Great Sheik of the Jungle,' he said one day, 'by thy kindness thou hast won the undying loyalty of Zeyd who begs that thou wilt grant him one more favour.'

'And what is that?' asked the ape-man.

'Ateja, whom I love, remains here in the savage country in constant danger so long as Fahd be near her. I dare not now return to the menzil of Ibn Jad even could I find it, but later, when the heat of Ibn Jad's anger will have had time to cool, then I might come again among them and convince him of my innocence, and be near Ateja and protect her from Fahd.'

'What, then, would you do?' demanded Tarzan.

'I would remain in the village to which you are taking me until Ibn Jad returns this way toward el-Guâd. It is the only chance that I have to see Ateja again in this life as I could not cross the Sudan alone and on foot should you compel me to leave your country now.'

'You are right,' replied the ape-man. 'You shall remain here six months. If Ibn Jad has not returned in that time I shall leave word that you be sent to my home. From there I can find a way to return you in safety to your own country.'

'May the blessings of Allah be upon thee!' cried Zeyd.

And when they came at last to the village Tarzan received the promise of the chief to keep Zeyd until Ibn Jad returned.

After he had left the village again the ape-man headed north, for he was concerned over the report that Zeyd had given him of the presence of a European prisoner among the 'Aarab. That Stimbol, whom he had sent eastward toward the coast, should be so far north and west as Zeyd had reported appeared inconceivable, and so it seemed more probable that the prisoner was young Blake, for whom Tarzan had conceived a liking. Of course, the prisoner might not be either Stimbol or Blake, but whoever he was Tarzan could not readily brook the idea of a white man being permitted to remain a prisoner of the Bedúins.

But Tarzan was in no hurry, for Zeyd had told him that the prisoner was to be held for ransom. He would have a look about for Blake's camp first, and then follow up the spoor of the Arabs. His progress, therefore, was leisurely. On the second day he met the apes of Toyat and for two days he hunted with them, renewing his acquaintance with Gayat and Zutho, listening to the gossip of the tribe, often playing with the balus.

Leaving them, he loafed on through the jungle, stopping once for half a day to bait Numa where he lay upon a fresh kill, until the earth trembled to the thunderous roars of the maddened king of beasts as the ape-man taunted and annoyed him.

Sloughed was the thin veneer of civilisation that was Lord Greystoke; back to primitive, back to the savage beast the ape-man reverted as naturally, as simply, as one changes from one suit to another. It was only in his beloved jungle, surrounded by its savage denizens that Tarzan of the Apes was truly Tarzan, for always in the presence of civilised men there was a certain restraint that was the outcome of that inherent suspicion that creatures of the wild ever feel for man.

Tired of throwing ripe fruit at Numa, Tarzan swung away through the middle terraces of the forest, lay up for the night far away and in the morning, scenting Bara the deer, made a kill and fed. Lazy, he slept again, until the breaking of twigs and the rustle of down-trampled grasses awoke him.

He sniffed the air with sensitive nostrils, and listened with ears that could hear an ant walk, and then he smiled. Tantor was coming.

For half a day he lolled on the huge back, listening to Manu the monkey chattering and scolding among the trees. Then he moved on again.

A day or two later he came upon a large band of monkeys. They seemed much excited and at sight of him they all commenced to jabber and chatter.

'Greetings, Manu!' cried the ape-man. 'I am Tarzan, Tarzan of the Apes. What happens in the jungle?'

'Gomangani! Gomangani!' cried one.

'Strange Gomangani!' cried another.

'Gomangani with thunder-sticks!' chattered a third.

'Where?' asked the ape-man.

'There! There!' they shouted in chorus, pointing toward the north east.

'Many sleeps away?' asked Tarzan.

'Close! Close!' the monkeys answered.

'There is one Tarmangani with them?'

'No, only Gomangani. With their thunder-sticks they kill little Manu and eat him. Bad Gomangani!'

'Tarzan will talk with them,' said the ape-man.

'They will kill Tarzan with their thunder-sticks and eat him,' prophesied an old grey-beard.

The ape-man laughed and swung off through the trees in the direction Manu had indicated. He had not gone far when the scent spoor of blacks came faintly to his nostrils and this spoor he followed until presently he could hear their voices in the distance.

Silently, warily Tarzan came through the trees, noiseless as the shadows that kept him company, until he stood upon a swaying limb directly above a camp of negroes.

Instantly Tarzan recognised the safari of the young American, Blake, and a second later he dropped to the ground before the astonished eyes of the blacks. Some of them would have run, but others recognised him.

'It is Big Bwana!' they cried. 'It is Tarzan of the Apes.'

'Where is your headman?' demanded Tarzan.

A stalwart negro approached him. 'I am headman,' he said.

'Where is your master?'

'He is gone, many days,' replied the black.

'Where?'

'We do not know. He hunted with a single askar. There was a great storm. Neither of them ever returned. We searched the jungle for them, but could not find them. We waited in camp where they were to have joined us. They did not come. We did not know what to do. We would not desert the young Bwana, who was kind to us; but we feared that he was dead. We have not provisions to last more than another moon. We decided to return home and tell our story to the friends of the young Bwana.'

'You have done well,' said Tarzan. 'Have you seen a company of the desert people in the jungle?'

'We have not seen them,' replied the headman, 'but while we were searching for the young Bwana we saw where desert people had camped. It was a fresh camp.'

'Where?'

The black pointed. 'It was on the trail to the north Galla country in Abyssinia and when they broke camp they went north.'

'You may return to your villages,' said Tarzan, 'but first take those things which are the young Bwana's to his friends to keep for him and send a runner to the home of Tarzan with this message: Send one hundred Waziri to Tarzan in the north Galla country. From the water hole of the smooth, round rocks follow the trail of the desert people.'

'Yes, Big Bwana, it will be done,' said the headman.

'Repeat my message.'

The black boy did as he was bidden.

'Good!' said Tarzan. 'I go. Kill not Manu the monkey if you can find other food, for Manu is the cousin of Tarzan and of you.'

'We understand, Big Bwana.'

In the castle of Prince Gobred in the city of Nímmr, James Hunter Blake was being schooled in the duties of a Knight of Nímmr. Sir Richard had taken him under his protection and made himself responsible for his training and his conduct.

Prince Gobred, quick to realise Blake's utter ignorance of even the simplest observance of knighthood, was frankly sceptical and Sir Malud was almost openly antagonistic, but the loyal Sir Richard was a well-beloved knight and so he had his way. Perhaps, too, the influence of the Princess Guinalda was not without its effect upon her sire, for first among the treasures of the Prince of Nímmr ranked his daughter Guinalda, and Guinalda's curiosity and interest had been excited by the romance of the coming of this fair stranger knight to the buried and forgotten city of Nímmr.

Sir Richard had clothed Blake from his own wardrobe until a weaver, a cutter of cloth, a seamstress and an armourer could fashion one for him. Nor did it take long. A week found Sir James clothed, armoured and horsed as befitted a Knight of Nímmr, and when he spoke to Sir Richard of payment for all this he found that money was almost unknown among them. There were, Sir Richard told him, a few pieces of coin that their ancestors had brought here seven hundred and thirty five years before, but payment was made by service.

The knights served the prince and he kept them. They protected the labourers and the artisans and in return received what they required from them. The slaves received their food and clothing from the prince or from whichever knight they served. Jewels and precious metals often changed hands in return for goods or service, but each transaction was a matter of individual barter as there were no standards of value.

They cared little for wealth. The knights valued most highly their honour and their courage upon which there could be no price. The artisan found his reward in the high perfection of his handicraft and in the honours that it brought him.

The valley provided food in plenty for all, the slaves tilled the ground, the freemen were the artisans, the men-at-arms, the herders of cattle, the knights defended Nímmr against its enemies, contended against one another in tourneys, and hunted the wild game that abounded in the valley and its surrounding mountains.

As the days passed, Blake found himself rapidly acquiring a certain proficiency in knightly arts under the wise tutorage of Sir Richard. The use of sword and buckler he found most difficult notwithstanding the fact that he had been proficient with the foils in his college days, for the knights of Nímmr knew naught of the defensive use of their two-edged weapons and seldom used the point for other purpose than the *coup de grâce*. For them the sword was almost wholly a cutting weapon, the buckler their sole defence; but as Blake practised with this weapon it dawned upon him that his knowledge of fencing might be put to advantage should the necessity arise, to the end that his awkwardness with the buckler should be outweighed by his nicer defensive handling of his sword and his offensive improved by the judicious use of the point, against which they had developed little or no defence.

The lance he found less difficult, its value being so largely dependent upon the horsemanship of him who wielded it and that Blake was a splendid horseman was evidenced by his polo rating as an eight goal man.

The ballium, or outer court, which lay between the inner and outer walls of the castle and entirely surrounded it, was, upon the north or valley side given over entirely to knightly practise and training. Here the ballium was very wide and against the inner wall was built a wooden grand-stand that could be quickly removed in the event of an attack upon the castle.

Jousts and tilts were held here weekly, while the great tourneys that occurred less often were given upon a field outside the castle wall upon the floor of the valley.

Daily many knights and ladies came to watch the practise and training that filled the ballium with life and action and colour during the morning hours. Good-natured banter flew back and forth, wagers were laid, and woe betide the contender who was unhorsed during these practise bouts, for the thing that a knight dreaded even more than he dreaded death was ridicule.

In the formal jousts that were held weekly, greater decorum was observed by the audience, but during the daily practise their raillery verged upon brutality.

It was before such an audience as this that Blake received his training and because he was a novelty the audiences were larger than ordinarily and because the friends of Sir Malud and the friends of Sir Richard had tacitly acknowledged him as an issue both the applause and the ridicule were loud and boisterous.

Even the Prince came often, and Guinalda always was there. It was soon apparent that Prince Gobred leaned slightly to the side of Sir Malud with the natural result that Malud's party immediately acquired numerous recruits.

The training of the lads who were squires to the knights and who would one day be admitted to the charmed circle of knighthood occupied the earlier hours of the morning. This was followed by practise tilts between knights, during which Sir Richard or one of his friends undertook the training of Blake at the far side of the ballium and it was during this practise that the American's outstanding horsemanship became apparent, even Gobred being led to applause.

'Odsbodikins,' he exclaimed, 'the man be a part of his charger!'

''Twas but chance that saved him from a fall,' said Malud.

'Mayhap,' agreed Gobred, 'but at that melikes the looks of him within a saddle.'

'He doeth not too ill with his lance,' admitted Malud, 'but, odsblud! didst ever see a more awkward lout with a buckler? Methinks he hath had more use for a trencher,' a sally which elicited roars of laughter in which the Princess Guinalda did not join, a fact which Malud, whose eyes were often upon her, was quick to note. 'Thou still believest this churl to be a knight, Princess Guinalda?' he demanded.

'Have I said aught?' she asked.

'Thou didst not laugh,' he reminded her.

'He is a stranger knight, far from his own country, and it seemeth not a knightly nor a gentle thing to ridicule him,' she replied. 'Therefore I did not laugh, for I was not amused.'

Later that day as Blake joined the others in the great court he ran directly into Malud's party nor was it at all an accident, as he never made any effort to avoid Malud or his friends and was, seemingly, oblivious to their thinly-veiled taunts and insinuations. Malud himself attributed this to the density and ignorance of a yokel, which he insisted Blake to be, but there were others who rather admired Blake for his attitude, seeing in it studied affront that Malud was too dense to perceive.

Most of the inmates of the grim castle of Nímmr were inclined pleasantly toward the newcomer. He had brought with him an air of freshness and newness that was rather a relief from the hoary atmosphere that had surrounded Nímmr for nearly seven and a half centuries. He had brought them new words and new expressions and new views, which many of them were joyously adopting, and had it not been for the unreasoning antagonism of the influential Sir Malud, Blake had been accepted with open arms.

Sir Richard was far more popular than Malud, but lacked the latter's wealth in horses, arms and retainers, and consequently had less influence with Prince Gobred. However, there were many independent souls who either followed Sir Richard because they were fond of him or arrived at their own decisions without reference to the dictates of policy, and many of these were staunch friends to Blake.

Not all of those who surrounded Malud this afternoon were antagonistic to the American, but the majority of them laughed when Malud laughed and frowned when he frowned, for in the courts of kings and princes flourished the first order of 'yes' men.

Blake was greeted by many a smile and nod as he advanced and bowed low before the Princess Guinalda who was one of the company, and, being of princely blood, entitled to his first devoirs.

'Thou didst well this morning, Sir James,' said the Princess, kindly. 'It pleases me greatly to see thee ride.'

'Methinketh 'twould be a rarer treat to see him serve a side of venison,' sneered Malud.

This provoked so much laughter that Malud was encouraged to seek further applause.

'Odzooks!' he cried; 'Arm him with a trencher and carving knife and he would be at home!'

'Speaking of serving,' said Blake, 'and Sir Malud's mind seems to be more occupied with that than with more knightly things, does any of you know what is necessary quickly to serve fresh pig?'

'Nay, fair sir knight,' said Guinalda, 'we know not. Prithee tell us.'

'Yes, tell us,' roared Malud; 'thou, indeed, shouldst know.'

'You said a mouthful, old scout, I do know!'

'And what be necessary that you may quickly serve fresh pig?' demanded Malud, looking about him and winking.

'A trencher, a carving knife and you, Sir Malud,' replied Blake.

It was several seconds before the thrust penetrated their simple minds and it was the Princess Guinalda who first broke into merry laughter and soon all were roaring, while some explained the quip to others.

No, not all were laughing – not Sir Malud. When he grasped the significance of Blake's witticism he first turned very red and then went white, for the great Sir Malud liked not to be the butt of ridicule, which is ever the way of those most prone to turn ridicule upon others.

'Sirrah!' he cried; 'Darest thou affront Malud? Odsblud, fellow! Low-born varlet! Only thy blood canst atone this affront!'

'Hop to it, old thing!' replied Blake. 'Name your poison!'

'I knowest not the meaning of thy silly words,' cried Malud; 'but I know that an thou dost not meet me in fair tilt upon the morrow I shalt whip thee across the Valley of the Holy Sepulchre with a barrel stave.'

'You're on!' snapped back Blake. 'Tomorrow morning in the south ballium with—'

'Thou mayst choose the weapons, sirrah,' said Malud.

'Don't call me sirrah, I don't like it,' said Blake very quietly, and now he was not smiling. 'I want to tell you something, Malud, that may be good for your soul. You are really the only man in Nímmr who didn't want to treat me well and give me a chance, a fair chance, to prove that I am all right.

'You think you are a great knight, but you are not. You have no intelligence, no heart, no chivalry. You are not what we would call in my country a good sport. You have a few horses and few men-at-arms. That is all you have, for without them you would not have the favour of the Prince, and without his favour you would have no friends.

'You are not so good or great a man in any way as is Sir Richard, who combines all the qualities of chivalry that for centuries have glorified the order of knighthood; nor are you so good a man as I, who, with your own weapons, will best you on the morrow, when, in the north ballium, I meet you on horseback with sword and buckler!'

The members of the party, upon seeing Malud's wrath had gradually fallen away from Blake until, as he concluded his speech, he stood alone a few paces apart from Malud and those who surrounded him. Then it was that one stepped from among those at Malud's side and walked to Blake. It was the Princess Guinalda.

'Sir James,' she said with a sweet smile, 'thou spokest with thy mouth full!' and then she broke into a merry laugh. 'Walk with me in the garden, sir knight!' and taking his arm she guided him toward the south end of the eastern court.

'You're wonderful!' was all that Blake could find to say.

'Dost really think I be wonderful?' she demanded. ''Tis hard to know if men speak the truth to such as I. The truth, as people see it, is spoke more oft to slaves than princes.'

'I hope to prove it by my conduct,' he said.

They had drawn a short distance away from the others now and the girl suddenly laid her hand impulsively upon his arm.

'I brought thee away, Sir James, that I might speak with thee alone,' she said.

'I do not care what the reason was so long as you did it,' he replied, smiling.

'Thou art a stranger among us, unaccustomed to our ways, unversed in knightly practise – so much so that there are many who doubt thy claims to knighthood. Yet thou are a brave man, or else a very simple one, or thou wouldst never have chosen to meet Sir Malud with sword and buckler, for he be skilled with these while thou art clumsy with them.

'Because I thinkest that thou goest to thy death tomorrow I have brought thee aside to speak with thee.'

'What can be done about it now?' asked Blake.

'Thou art passing fair with thy lance,' she said, 'and it is still not too late to change thy selection of weapons. I beg thee to do so.'

'You care?' he asked. There can be a world of meaning in two words.

The girl's eyes dropped for an instant and then flashed up to his and there was a touch of hauteur in them. 'I am the daughter of the Prince of Nímmr,' she said. 'I care for the humblest of my father's subjects.'

'I guess that will hold you for a while, Sir James,' thought Blake, but to the girl he said nothing, only smiled.

Presently she stamped her foot. 'Thou has an impudent smile, sirrah!' she exclaimed angrily. 'Meliketh it not. Then thou art too forward with the daughter of a prince.'

'I merely asked you if you cared whether I was killed. Even a cat could ask that.'

'And I replied. Why then didst thou smile?'

'Because your eyes had answered me before your lips had spoken and I knew that your eyes had told the truth.'

Again she stamped her foot angrily. 'Thou art indeed a forward boor,' she exclaimed. 'I shall not remain to be insulted further.'

Her head held high she turned and walked haughtily away to rejoin the other party.

Blake stepped quickly after her. 'Tomorrow,' he whispered, 'I meet Sir Malud with sword and buckler. With your favour upon my helm I could overthrow the best sword in Nímmr.'

The Princess Guinalda did not deign to acknowledge that she had heard his words as she walked on to join the others clustered about Sir Malud.

12

'Tomorrow Thou Diest!'

There was a great celebration in the village of Batando the chief, the night that Ulala returned. A goat was killed and many chickens and there were fruit and cassava bread and native beer in plenty for all. There was music, too, and dancing. With all of which it was morning before they sought their sleeping mat, with the result that it was after noon the following day before Fejjuân had an opportunity to speak of serious matters with Batando.

When finally he sought him out he found the old chief squatting in the shade before his hut, slightly the worse for the orgy of the preceding night.

'I have come to talk with you, Batando,' he said, 'of the desert people.'

Batando grunted. His head ached.

'Yesterday you said that you would lead them to the entrance to the forbidden valley,' said Fejjuân. 'You mean, then, that you will not fight them?'

'We shall not have to fight them if we lead them to the entrance to the forbidden valley,' replied Batando.

'You speak in riddles,' said Fejjuân.

'Listen, Ulala,' replied the old chief. 'In childhood you were stolen from your people and taken from your country. Being young, there were many things you did not know and there are others that you have forgotten.

'It is not difficult to enter the forbidden valley, especially from the north. Every Galla knows how to find the northern pass through the mountains or the tunnel beyond the great cross that marks the southern entrance. There are only these two ways in – every Galla knows them; but every Galla also knows that there is no way out of the forbidden valley.'

'What do you mean, Batando?' demanded Fejjuân. 'If there are two ways in there must be two ways out.'

'No – there is no way out,' insisted the chief. 'As far back as goes the memory of man or the tales of our fathers and our fathers' fathers, it is known that many men have entered the forbidden valley and it, is also known that no man has ever come out of it.'

'And why have they not come out.'

Batando shook his head. 'Who knows?' he asked. 'We cannot even guess what their fate is.'

'What sort of people inhabit the valley?' asked Fejjuân.

'Not even that is known. No man has seen them and returned to tell. Some say they are the spirits of the dead, others that the valley is peopled by leopards; but no one knows.

'Go, therefore, Ulala, and tell the chief of the desert people that we will lead him to the entrance to the valley. If we do this we shall not have to fight him and his people, nor shall we ever again be bothered by them,' and Batando laughed at his little joke.

'Will you send guides back with me to lead the Bedùwy to the valley?' asked Fejjuân.

'No,' replied the chief. 'Tell them we shall come in three days. In the meantime I shall gather together many warriors from other villages, for I do not trust the desert people. Thus we shall conduct them through our country. Explain this to their chief and also that in payment he must release to us all the Galla slaves he has with him – before he enters the valley.'

'That Ibn Jad will not do.' said Fejjuân.

'Perhaps, when he sees himself surrounded by Galla warriors, he will be glad to do even more,' replied Batando.

And so Fejjuân, the Galla slave, returned to his masters and reported all that Batando had told him to report.

Ibn Jad at first refused to give up his slaves, but when Fejjuân had convinced him that under no other terms would Batando lead him to the entrance to the valley and that his refusal to liberate the slaves would invite the hostile attentions of the Gallas, he finally consented, but in the back of his mind was the thought that before his promise was consummated he might find an opportunity to evade it.

Only one regret had Fejjuân in betraying the Bedùwy, and that was caused by his liking for Ateja, but being a fatalist, he was consoled by the conviction that whatever was to be, would be, regardless of what he might do.

And as Ibn Jad waited and Batando gathered his black warriors from far and near, Tarzan of the Apes came to the water hole of the smooth, round rocks and took up the trail of the Bedúins.

Since he had learned from Blake's blacks that the young American was missing and also that they had seen nothing of Stimbol since the latter had separated from Blake and started for the coast, the ape-man was more convinced than ever that the white prisoner among the Arabs was Blake.

Still he felt no great concern for the man's safety, since had the Bedúins sufficient hopes of reward to spare his life at all he was in no great danger from them. Reasoning thus, Tarzan made no pretence of speed as he followed the spoor of Ibn Jad and his people.

Two men sat upon rough benches at opposite sides of a rude table. Between them a cresset of oil with a cotton wick lying in it burned feebly, slightly illuminating the stone flagging of the floor and casting weird shadows of themselves upon the rough stone walls.

Through a narrow window, innocent of glass, the night air blew, driving the flame of the cresset now this way, now that. Upon the table, between the men, lay a square board blocked off into squares and within some of these were several wooden pieces.

'It is your move, Richard,' said one of the men. 'You don't appear to be very keen about the game tonight. What's the matter?'

'I be thinking of the morrow, James, and my heart be heavy within me,' replied the other.

'And why?' demanded Blake.

'Malud is not the best swordsman in Nímmr,' replied Sir Richard, 'but—' he hesitated.

'I am the worst,' Blake finished the sentence for him, laughingly.

Sir Richard looked up and smiled, 'Thou wilt always joke, even in the face of death,' he said. 'Art all the men of this strange country thou tell'st of alike?'

'It is your move, Richard,' said Blake.

'Hide not his sword from thine eyes with thy buckler, James,' cautioned Richard. 'Ever keep thine eyes upon his eyes until thou knowest whereat he striketh, then, with thy buckler ready, thou mayst intercept the blow, for he be over slow and always his eyes proclaim where his blade will fall. Full well I knoweth that for often have I exercised against him.'

'And he hasn't killed you,' Blake reminded him.

'Ah, we did but practise, but on the morrow it will be different, for Malud engages thee to the death in mortal combat, my friend, to wash away in blood the affront thou didst put upon him.'

'He wants to kill me, just for that?' asked Blake. 'I'll tell the world he's a touchy little rascal!'

'Were it only that, he might be satisfied merely to draw blood, but there is more that he hath against thee.'

'More? What? I've scarcely spoken to him a dozen times,' said Blake.

'He be jealous.'

'Jealous? Of whom?'

'He would wed the Princess and he hath seen in what manner thou lookest at her,' explained Richard.

'Poppycock!' cried Blake, but he flushed.

'Nay, he be not the only one who hath marked it,' insisted Richard.

'You're crazy,' snapped Blake.

'Often men look thus at the princess, for she be beautiful beyond compare, but—'

'Has he killed them all?' demanded the American.

'No, for the princess didst not look back at *them* in the same manner.'

Blake leaned back upon his bench and laughed. 'Now I know you're crazy,' he cried, 'all of you. I'll admit that I think the princess is a mighty sweet kid, but say young fellow, she can't see me a little bit.'

'Enough of thy outlandish speech I grasp to gather thy meaning, James, but thou canst not confuse me upon the one subject, nor deceive me upon the other. The eyes of the princess seldom leave thee whilst thou art at practise upon the lists, and the look in thine when they rest upon her – hast ever seen a hound adoring his master?'

'Run along and sell your papers,' admonished Blake.

'For this Malud wouldst put thee out of the way, and it is because I know this that I grieve, for I have learned to like thee over-well, my friend.'

Blake arose and came around the end of the table. 'You're a good old scout, Richard,' he said, placing a hand affectionately upon the other's shoulder; 'but do not worry – I am not dead yet. I know I seem awkward with the sword, but I have learned much about its possibilities within the past few days, and I think that Sir Malud has a surprise awaiting him.'

'Thy courage and thy vast assurance should carry thee far, James, but they may not overcome a lifetime of practise with the sword, and that is just the advantage that Malud hath over thee.'

'Does Prince Gobred favour Malud's suit?' demanded Blake.

'Why not? Malud is a powerful knight, with a great castle of his own and many horses and retainers. Besides a dozen knights he hath fully an hundred men-at-arms.'

'There are several knights who have their own castles and following, are there not?' asked Blake.

'Twenty, perchance,' replied Richard.

'And they live close to Gobred's castle?'

'At the edge of the hills, within three leagues upon either hand of Gobred's castle,' explained Richard.

'And no others live in all this great Valley?' demanded Blake.

'You have heard mention made of Bohun?' asked Richard.

'Yes, often – why?'

'He calls himself king, but never will we refer to him as king. He and his followers dwell upon the opposite side of the valley. They number, perchance, as many as we and we be always at war against them.'

'But I've been hearing quite a bit about a great tournament for which the knights are practising now. I thought that Bohun and his knights were to take part in it.'

'They be. Once each year, commencing upon the first Sunday of Lent, and extending over a period of three days there hath been from time immemorial a truce declared between the Fronters and the Backers, during which is held The Great Tourney, one year in the plain before the city of Nímmr and the next year in the plain before the city of the Sepulchre, as they call it.'

'Fronters and Backers! What in heck do those mean?' demanded Blake.

'Thou art a Knight of Nímmr and know not that?' exclaimed Richard.

'What I know about knighting would rattle around in a peanut shell,' admitted Blake.

'Thou shouldst know, and I shalt tell thee. Hark thee well, then,' said Richard, 'for I must need go back to the beginning.' He poured two goblets of wine from a flagon standing on the floor beside him, took a long drink and proceeded with his tale. 'Richard I. sailed from Sicily in the spring of 1191 with all his great following bound for Acre, where he was to meet the French king, Philip Augustus, and wrest the Holy Land from the power of the Saracen. But Richard tarried upon the way to conquer Cyprus and punish the vile despot who had placed an insult upon Berengaria, whom Richard was to wed.

'When the great company again set their sails for Acre there were many Cyprian maidens hidden away upon the ships by knights who had taken a fancy to their lovely faces, and it so befell that two of these ships, encountering a storm, were blown from their course and wrecked upon the Afric shore.

'One of these companies was commanded by a knight yclept Bohun and the other by one Gobred and though they marched together they kept separate other than when attacked by an enemy.

'Thus, searching for Jerusalem, they came upon this valley which the followers of Bohun declared was the Valley of the Holy Sepulchre, and that the crusade was over. Their crosses, that they had worn upon their breasts as do all crusaders who have not reached their goal, they removed and placed upon their backs to signify that the crusade was over and that they were returning home.

'Gobred insisted that this was not the Valley of the Holy Sepulchre and that the crusade was not accomplished. He, therefore, and all his followers retained their crosses upon their breasts and built a city and a strong castle to defend the entrance to the valley that Bohun and his followers might be prevented from returning to England until they had accomplished their mission.

'Bohun crossed the valley and built a city and a castle to prevent Gobred from pushing on in the direction in which the latter knew that the true Sepulchre lay, and for nearly seven and a half centuries the descendants of Bohun have prevented the descendants of Gobred from pushing on and rescuing the Holy Land from the Saracen, while the descendants of Gobred have prevented the descendants of Bohun from returning to England, to the dishonour of knighthood.

'Gobred took the title of prince and Bohun that of king, and these titles have been handed down from father to son during the centuries, while the followers of Gobred still wear the cross upon their breasts and are called, therefrom, the Fronters, and the followers of Bohun wear theirs upon their backs and are called Backers.'

'And you would still push on and liberate the Holy Land?' asked Blake.

'Yes,' replied Richard, 'and the Backers would return to England; but long since have we realised the futility of either hope, since we be surrounded by a vast army of Saracens and our numbers be too few to pit against them.

'Thinkest thou not that we are wise to remain here under such stress?' he demanded.

'Well, you'd certainly surprise 'em if you rode into Jerusalem, or London, either,' admitted Blake. 'On the whole, Richard, I'd remain right here, if I were you. You see, after seven hundred and thirty six years most of the home folks may have forgotten you and even the Saracens might not know what it was all about if you came charging into Jerusalem.'

'Mayhap you speak wisely, James,' said Richard, 'and then, too, we be content here, knowing no other country.'

For a while both men were silent, in thought. Blake was the first to speak. 'This big tourney interests me,' he said. 'You say it starts the first Sunday in Lent. That's not far away.'

'No, not far. Why?'

'I was wondering if you thought I'd be in shape to have a part in it. I'm getting better and better with the lance every day.'

Sir Richard looked sadly at him and shook his head. 'Tomorrow thou wilt be dead,' he said.

'Say! You're a cheerful party,' exclaimed Blake.

'I am only truthful, good friend,' replied Richard. 'It grieveth my heart sorely and it should be true, but true it be – thou canst not prevail over Sir Malud on the morrow. Wouldst that I might take thy place in the lists against him, but that may not be. But I console myself with the thought that thou wilt comport thyself courageously and die as a good sir knight should with no stain upon thy escutcheon. Greatly will it solace the Princess Guinalda to know that thou didst die thus.'

'You think so?' ventured Blake.

'Verily.'

'And if I don't die – will she be put out?'

'Put out! Put out of what?' demanded Richard.

'Will she be sore vexed, then,' corrected Blake.

'I should not go so far as to say that,' admitted Richard; 'but natheless it appears certain that no lady would rejoice to see her promised husband overthrown and killed, and if thou art not slain it may only be because thou hast slain Malud.'

'She is his affianced wife?' demanded Blake.

''Tis understood, that be all. As yet no formal marriage banns have been proclaimed.'

'I'm going to turn in,' snapped Blake. 'If I've got to be killed tomorrow I ought to get a little sleep tonight.'

As he stretched himself upon a rough wool blanket that was spread over a bed of rushes upon the stone floor in one corner of the room, and drew another similar blanket over him, he felt less like sleep than he had ever felt before. The knowledge that on the morrow he was to meet a medieval knight in mortal combat naturally gave him considerable concern, but Blake was too self-reliant and too young seriously to harbour the belief that he would be the one to be killed. He knew it was possible but he did not intend to permit the thought to upset him. There was, however, another that did. It upset him very much and, too, it made him angry when he realised that he was concerned about it – about the proposed marriage of Sir Malud of West Castle and Guinalda, Princess of Nímmr.

Could it be that he had been ass enough, he soliloquised, to have fallen in love with this little medieval princess who probably looked upon him as dirt beneath her feet? And what was he going to do about Malud? Suppose he should get the better of the fellow on the morrow? Well, what about it? If he killed him that would make Guinalda unhappy. If he didn't kill him – what? Sir James did not know.

13

In the Beyt of Zeyd

Ibn Jad waited three days in his menzil but no Galla guides arrived to lead him into the valley as Batando had promised and so he sent Fejjuân once more to the chief to urge him to hasten for always in the mind of Ibn Jad was the fear of Tarzan of the Apes, and the thought that he might return to thwart and punish him.

He knew he was out of Tarzan's country now, but he also knew that where boundaries were so vague he could not definitely count upon this fact as an assurance of safety from reprisal. His one hope was that Tarzan was awaiting his return through Tarzan's country and this Ibn Jad had definitely decided not to attempt. Instead he was planning upon moving directly west, passing north of the ape-man's stamping grounds, until he picked up the trail to the north down which he had travelled from the desert country.

In the mukaad of the sheik with Ibn Jad sat Tollog, his brother, and Fahd and Stimbol, besides some other 'Aarab. They were speaking of Batando's delay in sending guides and they were fearful of treachery, for it had long been apparent to them that the old chief was gathering a great army of warriors and though Fejjuân assured them that they would not be used against the 'Aarab if Ibn Jad resorted to no treachery, yet they were all apprehensive of danger.

Ateja, employed with the duties of the hareem, did not sing or smile as had been her wont, for her heart was heavy with mourning for her lover. She heard the talk in the mukaad, but it did not interest her. Seldom did her eyes glance above the curtain that separated the women's quarters from the mukaad, and when they did the fires of hatred blazed within them as they crossed the countenance of Fahd.

She chanced to be thus glancing when she saw Fahd's eyes, which were directed outward across the menzil, go suddenly wide with astonishment.

'Billah, Ibn Jad!' cried the man. 'Look!'

With the others Ateja turned her glance in the direction Fahd was staring, and with the others she voiced a little gasp of astonishment, though those of the men were rounded into oaths.

Walking straight across the menzil toward the sheik's beyt strode a bronzed giant armed with a spear, arrows and a knife. Upon his back was suspended an oval shield and across one shoulder and his breast was coiled a rope, hand plaited from long fibres.

'Tarzan of the Apes!' ejaculated Ibn Jad. 'The curse of Ullah be upon him!'

'He must have brought his black warriors with him and left them hidden in the forest,' whispered Tollog. 'Not else would he dare enter the menzil of the Beduw.'

Ibn Jad was heart sick and he was thinking fast when the ape-man halted directly in the outer opening of the mukaad. Tarzan let his eyes run quickly over the assemblage. They stopped upon Stimbol, finally.

'Where is Blake?' he demanded of the American.

'You ought to know,' growled Stimbol.

'Have you seen him since you and he separated?'

'No.'

'You are sure of that?' insisted the ape-man.

'Of course I am.'

Tarzan turned to Ibn Jad. 'You have lied to me. You are not here to trade but to find and sack a city; to take its treasure and steal its women.'

'That is a lie!' cried Ibn Jad. 'Whoever told thee that, lied.'

'I do not think he lied,' replied Tarzan. 'He seemed an honest youth.'

'Who was he?' demanded Ibn Jad.

'His name is Zeyd.' Ateja heard and was suddenly galvanised to new interest. 'He says all this and more, and I believe him.'

'What else did he tell thee, Nasrâny?'

'That another stole his musket and sought to slay thee, Ibn Jad, and then put the blame upon him.'

'That is a lie, like all he hath told thee!' cried Fahd.

Ibn Jad sat in thought, his brows contracted in a dark scowl, but presently he looked up at Tarzan with a crooked smile. 'Doubtless the poor youth thought that he spoke the truth,' he said, 'just as he thought that he should slay his sheik and for the same reason. Always hath his brain been sick, but never before did I think him dangerous.

'He hath deceived thee, Tarzan of the Apes, and that I can prove by all my people as well as by this Nasrâny I have befriended, for all will tell thee that I am seeking to obey thee and leave thy country. Why else then should I have travelled north back in the direction of my own Béled?'

'If thou wished to obey me why didst thou hold me prisoner and send thy brother to slay me in the night?' asked Tarzan.

'Again thou wrongst Ibn Jad,' said the sheik, sadly. 'My brother came to cut thy bonds and set thee free, but thou set upon him and then came el-fîl and carried thee away.'

'And what meant thy brother when he raised his knife and cried: "Die, Nasrâny!"?' demanded the ape-man. 'Sayeth a man thus who cometh to do a kindness?'

'I did but joke,' mumbled Tollog.

'I am here again,' said Tarzan, 'but not to joke. My Waziri are coming. Together we shall see you well on your way towards the desert.'

'It is what we wish,' said the sheik quickly. 'Ask this other Nasrâny if it be not true that we are lost and would be but too glad to have thee lead us upon the right way. Here we be beset by Galla warriors. Their chief hath been gathering them for days and momentarily we fear that we shall be attacked. Is that not true, Nasrâny?' he turned to Stimbol as he spoke.

'Yes, it is true,' said Stimbol.

'It is true that you are going to leave the country,' said Tarzan, 'and I shall remain to see that you do so. Tomorrow you will start. In the meantime set aside a beyt for me – and let there be no more treachery.'

'Thou needst fear nothing,' Ibn Jad assured him, then he turned his face towards the women's quarters. 'Hirfa! Ateja!' he called. 'Make ready the beyt of Zeyd for the sheik of the jungle.'

To one side but at no great distance from the beyt of Ibn Jad the two women raised the black tent for Tarzan and when the am'dán had been placed and straightened and the tunb el-beyt made fast to the pegs that Ateja drove into the earth, Hirfa returned to her household duties, leaving her daughter to stretch the side curtains.

The instant that Hirfa was out of ear-shot Ateja ran to Tarzan.

'Oh, Nasrâny,' she cried, 'thou hast seen my Zeyd? He is safe?'

'I left him in a village where the chief will care for him until such time as thy people come upon thy return to the desert country. He is quite safe and well.'

'Tell me of him, oh, Nasrâny, for my heart hungers for word of him,' implored the girl. 'How came you upon him? Where was he?'

'His mare had been dragged down by el-adrea who was about to devour your lover. I chanced to be there and slew el-adrea. Then I took Zeyd to the village of a chief who is my friend, for I knew that he could not survive the perils of the jungle should I leave him afoot and alone. It was my thought to send him from the country in safety, but he begged to remain until you returned that way. This I have permitted. In a few weeks you will see your lover.'

Tears were falling from Ateja's long, black lashes – tears of joy – as she seized Tarzan's hand and kissed it. 'My life is thine, Nasrâny,' she cried, 'for thou hast given me back my lover.'

That night as the Galla slave, Fejjuân, walked through the menzil of his masters he saw Ibn Jad and Tollog sitting in the sheik's mukaad whispering together and Fejjuân, well aware of the inherent turpitude of this precious pair, wondered what might be the nature of their plotting.

Behind the curtain of the hareem Ateja lay huddled upon her sleeping mat, but she did not sleep. Instead she was listening to the whispered conversation of her father and her uncle.

'He must be put out of the way,' Ibn Jad insisted.

'But his Waziri are coming,' objected Tollog. 'If they do not find him here what can we say? They will not believe us, whatever we say. They will set upon us. I have heard that they are terrible men.'

'By Ullah!' cried Ibn Jad. 'If he stays we are undone. Better risk something than to return empty-handed to our own country after all that we have passed through.'

'If thou thinkest that I shall again take this business upon myself thou art mistaken, brother,' said Tollog. 'Once was enough.'

'No, not thee; but we must find a way. Is there none among us who might wish more than another to be rid of the Nasrâny?' asked Ibn Jad, but to himself as though he were thinking aloud.

'The other Nasrâny!' exclaimed Tollog. 'He hateth him.'

Ibn Jad clapped his hands together. 'Thou hast it, brother!'

'But still shall we be held responsible,' reminded Tollog.

'What matter if he be out of the way. We can be no worse off than we now are. Suppose Batando came tomorrow with the guides? Then indeed would the jungle sheik know that we have lied to him and it might go hard with us. No, we must be rid of him this very night.'

'Yes, but how?' asked Tollog.

'Hold! I have a plan. Listen well, O brother!' and Ibn Jad rubbed his palms together and smiled, but he would not have smiled, perhaps, had he known that Ateja listened or had he seen the silent figure crouching in the dark just beyond the outer curtain of his beyt.

'Speak, Ibn Jad,' urged Tollog; 'tell me thy plan.'

'Wellah, it is known by all that the Nasrâny Stimbol hates the sheik of the jungle. With loud tongue he hath proclaimed it many times before all when many were gathered in my mukaad.'

'You would send Stimbol to slay Tarzan of the Apes?'

'Thou hast guessed aright,' admitted Ibn Jad.

'But how wilt that relieve us of responsibility? He will have been slain by thy order in thine own menzil,' objected Tollog.

'Wait! I shall not command the one Nasrâny to slay the other; I shall but suggest it and when it is done I shall be filled with rage and horror that this murder hath been done in my menzil. And to prove my good faith I shall order that the murderer be put to death in punishment for his crime. Thus we shall be rid of two unbelieving dogs and at the same time be able to convince the Waziri that we were indeed the friends of their sheik, for we shall mourn him with loud lamentations – when the Waziri shall have arrived.'

'Allah be praised for such a brother!' exclaimed Tollog, enraptured.

'Go thou now, at once, and summon the Nasrâny Stimbol,' directed Ibn Jad. 'Send him to me alone, and after I have spoken with him and he hath departed upon his errand come thee back to my beyt.'

Ateja trembled upon her sleeping mat, while the silent figure crouching outside the sheik's tent arose after Tollog had departed and disappeared in the darkness of the night.

Hastily summoned from the beyt of Fahd, Stimbol, cautioned to stealth by Tollog, moved silently through the darkness to the mukaad of the sheik, where he found Ibn Jad awaiting him.

'Sit, Nasrâny,' invited the Bedúin.

'What in hell do you want of me this time of night?' demanded Stimbol.

'I have been talking with Tarzan of the Apes,' said Ibn Jad, 'and because you are my friend and he is not I have sent for you to tell you what he plans for you. He has interfered in all my designs and is driving me from the country, but that is as nothing compared with what he intends for you.'

'What in hell is he up to now?' demanded Stimbol. 'He's always butting into someone else's business.'

'Thou dost not like him?' asked Ibn Jad.

'Why should I?' and Stimbol applied a vile epithet to Tarzan.

'Thou wilt like him less when I tell thee,' said Ibn Jad.

'Well, tell me.'

'He says that thou hast slain thy companion, Blake,' explained the sheik, 'and for that Tarzan is going to kill thee on the morrow.'

'Eh? What? Kill me?' demanded Stimbol. 'Why, he can't do it! What does he think he is – a Roman emperor?'

'Nevertheless he will do as he says,' insisted Ibn Jad. 'He is all powerful here. No one questions the acts of this great jungle sheik. Tomorrow he will kill thee.'

'But – you won't let him, Ibn Jad! Surely, you won't let him?' Stimbol was already trembling with terror.

Ibn Jad elevated his palms. 'What can I do?' he asked.

'You can – you can – why there must be something that you can do,' wailed the frightened man.

'There is naught that any can do – save yourself,' whispered the sheik.

'What do you mean?'

'He lies asleep in yon beyt and – thou hast a sharp khûsa.'

'I have never killed a man,' whimpered Stimbol.

'Nor hast thou ever been killed,' reminded the sheik; 'but tonight thou must kill or tomorrow thou wilt be killed.'

'God!' gasped Stimbol.

'It is late,' said Ibn Jad, 'and I go to my sleeping mat. I have warned thee – do what thou wilt in the matter,' and he arose as though to enter the women's quarters.

Trembling, Stimbol staggered out into the night. For a moment he hesitated, then he crouched and crept silently through the darkness toward the beyt that had been erected for the ape-man.

But ahead of him ran Ateja to warn the man who had saved her lover from the fangs of el-adrea. She was almost at the beyt she had helped to erect for the ape-man when a figure stepped from another tent and clapping a palm across her mouth and an arm about her waist held her firmly.

'Where goest thou?' whispered a voice in her ear, a voice that she recognised at once as belonging to her uncle; but Tollog did not wait for a reply – he answered for her. 'Thou goest to warn the Nasrâny because he befriended thy lover! Get thee back to thy father's beyt. If he knew this he would slay thee. Go!' and he gave her a great shove in the direction from which she had come.

There was a nasty smile upon Tollog's lips as he thought how neatly he had foiled the girl, and he thanked Allah that chance had placed him in a position to intercept her before she had been able to ruin them all, and even as Tollog, the brother of the sheik, smiled in his beard, a hand reached out of the darkness behind him and seized him by the throat – fingers grasped him and he was dragged away.

Trembling, bathed in cold sweat, grasping in tightly-clenched fingers the hilt of a keen knife, Wilbur Stimbol crept through the darkness toward the tent of his victim.

Stimbol had been an irritable man, a bully and a coward; but he was no criminal. Every fibre of his being revolted at the thing he contemplated. He did not want to kill, but he was a cornered human rat, and he thought that death stared him in the face, leaving open only this one way of escape.

As he entered the beyt of the ape-man he steeled himself to accomplish that for which he had come, and he was indeed a very dangerous, a very formidable man as he crept to the side of the figure lying in the darkness, wrapped in an old burnous.

14

Sword and Buckler

As the sun touched the turrets of the castle of the Prince of Nímmr a youth rolled from between his blankets, rubbed his eyes and stretched. Then he reached over and shook another youth of about his own age who slept beside him.

'Awaken, Edward! Awaken, thou sluggard!' he cried.

Edward rolled over on his back and essayed to say 'Eh?' and to yawn at the same time.

'Up, lad!' urged Michel. 'Forgettest thou that thy master fares forth to be slain this day?'

Edward sat up, now fully awake. His eyes flashed. ''Tis a lie!' he cried, loyally. 'He will cleave Sir Malud from poll to breast plate with a single blow. Livest no sir knight with such mighty thews as hast Sir James. Thou art disloyal, Michel, to Sir Richard's friend who hath been a good and kindly friend to us as well.'

Michel patted the other lad upon the shoulder. 'Nay, I did but jest, Edward,' he said. 'My hopes be all for Sir James, and yet—' he paused, 'I fear—'

'Fear what?' demanded Edward.

'That Sir James be not well enough versed in the use of sword and buckler to overcome Sir Malud, for even were his strength the strength of ten men it shall avail him naught without the skill to use it.'

'Thou shalt see!' maintained Edward, stoutly.

'I see that Sir James hath a loyal squire,' said a voice behind them, and turning they saw Sir Richard standing in the doorway, 'and may all his friends wish him well this day thus loyally!'

'I fell asleep last night praying to our Lord Jesus to guide his blade through Sir Malud's helm,' said Edward.

'Good! And get thee up now and look to thy master's mail and to the trappings of his steed, that he may enter the lists bedight as befits a noble sir knight of Nímmr,' instructed Richard, and left them.

It was eleven o'clock of this February morning. The sun shone down into the great north ballium of the castle of Nímmr, glinting from the polished mail of noble knights and from pike and battle-axe of men-at-arms; picking out the gay colours of the robes of the women gathered in the grand-stand below the inner wall.

Upon a raised dais at the front and centre of the grand-stand sat Prince Gobred and his party and upon either side of them and extending to the far ends of the stand were ranged the noble knights and ladies of Nímmr, while behind them sat men-at-arms who were off duty, then the freedmen and, last of all, the serfs, for under the beneficent rule of the house of Gobred these were accorded many privileges.

At either end of the lists was a tent, gay with pennons and the colours and devices of its owner; one with the green and gold of Sir Malud and the other with the blue and silver of Sir James.

Before each of these tilts stood two men-at-arms, resplendent in new apparel, the metal of their battle-axes gleaming brightly and here a groom held a restive, richly-caparisoned charger, while the squire of each of the contestants busied himself with last-minute preparations for the encounter.

A trumpeter, statuesque, the bell of his trumpet resting upon his hip, waited for the signal to sound the fanfare that would announce the entrance of his master into the lists.

A few yards to the rear a second charger champed upon his bit as he nuzzled the groom that held him in waiting for the knight who would accompany each of the contestants upon the field.

In the blue and silver tilt sat Blake and Sir Richard, the latter issuing instructions and advice and of the two he was the more nervous. Blake's hauberk, gorget and bassinet were of heavy chain mail, the latter lined inside and covered outside, down to the gorget, with leopard skin, offering fair protection for his head from an ordinary, glancing blow; upon his breast was sewn a large, red cross and from one shoulder depended the streamers of a blue and silver rosette. Hanging from the pole of the tilt, upon a wooden peg, were Blake's sword and buckler.

The grand-stand was filled. Prince Gobred glanced up at the sun and spoke to a knight at his side. The latter gave a brief command to a trumpeter stationed at the princely loge, and presently loud and clear, the notes of a trumpet rang in the ballium. Instantly the tilts at either end of the lists were galvanised to activity, while the grand-stand seemed to spring to new life as necks were craned first toward the tent of Sir Malud and then toward that of Sir James.

Edward, flushed with excitement, ran into the tilt and seizing Blake's sword passed the girdle about his hips and buckled it in place at his left side, then, with the buckler, he followed his master out of the tilt.

As Blake prepared to mount, Edward held his stirrup while the groom sought to quiet the nervous horse. The lad pressed Blake's leg after he had swung into the saddle (no light accomplishment, weighed down as he was by heavy chain mail) and looked up into his face.

'I have prayed for thee, Sir James,' he said. 'I know that thou wilt prevail.'

Blake saw tears in the youth's eyes as he looked down at him and he caught a choking note in his voice. 'You're a good boy, Eddie,' he said. 'I'll promise that you won't have to be ashamed of me.'

'Ah, Sir James, how could I? Even in death thou wilt be a noble figure of a knight. An fairer one it hath never been given one to see, methinks,' Edward assured him as he handed him his round buckler.

Sir Richard had by now mounted and at a signal from him that they were ready there was a fanfare from the trumpet at Sir Malud's tilt and that noble sir knight rode forward, followed by a single knight.

Blake's trumpeter now announced his master's entry and the American rode out close along the front of the grand-stand, followed by Sir Richard. There was a murmur of applause for each contestant, which increased as they advanced and met before Prince Gobred's loge.

Here the four knights reined in and faced the Prince and each raised the hilt of his sword to his lips and kissed it in salute. As Gobred cautioned them to fight honourably, as true knights, and reminded them of the rules governing the encounter, Blake's eyes wandered to the face of Guinalda.

The little princess sat stiffly erect, looking straight before her. She seemed very white, Blake thought, and he wondered if she were ill.

How beautiful, thought Blake, and though she did not once appear to look at him he was not cast down, for neither did she look at Malud.

Again the trumpet sounded and the four knights rode slowly back to opposite sides of the lists and the principals waited for the final signal to engage. Blake disengaged his arm from the leather loop of his buckler and tossed the shield upon the ground.

Edward looked at him aghast. 'My lord knight!' he cried. 'Art ill? Art fainting? Didst drop thy buckler?' and he snatched it up and held it aloft to Blake, though he knew full well that his eyes had not deceived him and that his master had cast aside his only protection.

To the horrified Edward there seemed but one explanation and that his loyalty would not permit him to entertain for an instant – that Blake was preparing to dismount and refuse to meet Sir Malud, giving the latter the victory by default and assuring himself of the contempt and ridicule of all Nímmr.

He ran to Richard who had not seen Blake's act. 'Sir Richard! Sir Richard!' he cried in a hoarse whisper. 'Some terrible affliction hath befallen Sir James!'

'Hey, what?' exclaimed Richard. 'What meaneth thou, lad?'

'He has cast aside his buckler,' cried the youth. 'He must be stricken sore ill, for it cannot be that otherwise he would refuse combat.'

Richard spurred to Blake's side. 'Hast gone mad, man?' he demanded. 'Thou canst not refuse the encounter now unless thou wouldst bring dishonour upon thy friends!'

'Where did you get that line?' demanded Blake. 'Who said I was going to quit?'

'But thy buckler?' cried Sir Richard.

The trumpet at the Prince's loge rang out peremptorily. Sir Malud spurred forward to a fanfare from his own trumpeter.

'Let her go!' cried Blake to his.

'Thy buckler!' screamed Sir Richard.

'The damned thing was in my way,' shouted Blake as he spurred forward to meet the doughty Malud, Richard trailing behind him, as did Malud's second behind that knight.

There was a confident smile upon the lips of Sir Malud and he glanced often at the knights and ladies in the grand-stand, but Blake rode with his eyes always upon his antagonist.

Both horses had broken immediately into a gallop and as they neared one another Malud spurred forward at a run and Blake saw that the man's aim was doubtless to overthrow him at the first impact, or at least to so throw him out of balance as to make it easy for Malud to strike a good blow before he could recover himself.

Malud rode with his sword half raised at his right side, while Blake's was at guard, a position unknown to the Knights of Nímmr, who guarded solely with their bucklers.

The horsemen approached to engage upon each other's left and as they were about to meet Sir Malud rose in his stirrups and swung his sword hand down, to gain momentum, described a circle with his blade and launched a terrific cut at Blake's head.

It was at that instant that some few in the grand-stand realised that Blake bore no buckler.

'His buckler! Sir James hath no buckler! He hath lost his buckler!' rose now from all parts of the stand, and from right beside him, where the two knights met before the loge of Gobred, Blake heard a woman scream, but he could not look to see if it were Guinalda.

As they met Blake reined his horse suddenly toward Malud's, so that the two chargers' shoulders struck and at the same time he cast all his weight in the same direction, whereas Malud, who was standing in his stirrups to deliver his blow, was almost in a state of equilibrium and having his buckler ready for defence was quite helpless insofar as manoeuvring his mount was concerned.

Malud, overbalanced, lost the force and changed the direction of his blow, which fell, much to the knight's surprise, upon Blake's blade along which it spent its force and was deflected from its target.

Instantly, his horse well in hand by reason that his left arm was unencumbered by a buckler, Blake reined in and simultaneously cut to the left and rear, his point opening the mail on Malud's left shoulder and biting into the flesh before the latter's horse had carried him out of reach.

A loud shout of approbation arose from the stands for the thing had been neatly done and then Malud's second spurred to the Prince's loge and entered a protest.

'Sir James hath no buckler!' he cried. ''Tis no fair combat!'

''Tis fairer for thy knight than for Sir James,' said Gobred.

'We would not take that advantage of him,' parried Malud's second, Sir Jarred.

'What sayest thou?' demanded Gobred of Sir Richard who had quickly ridden to Jarred's side. 'Is Sir James without a buckler through some accident that befell before he entered the lists?'

'Nay, he cast it aside,' replied Richard, 'and averred that the "damned thing" did annoy him; but if Sir Jarred feeleth that, because of this, they be not fairly matched, we are willing that Sir Malud, also, should cast aside his buckler.'

Gobred smiled. 'That be fair,' he said.

The two men, concerned with their encounter, and not with the argument of their seconds, had engaged once more. Blood was showing upon Malud's shoulder and trickling down his back, staining his skirts and the housing of his charger.

The stand was in an uproar, for many were still shouting aloud about the buckler and others were screaming with delight over the neat manner in which Sir James had drawn first blood. Wagers were being freely made and though Sir Malud still ruled favourite in the betting odds against Blake were not so great, and while men had no money to wager they had jewels and arms and horses. One enthusiastic adherent of Sir Malud bet three chargers against one that his champion would be victorious and the words were scarce out of his mouth ere he had a dozen takers, whereas before the opening passage at arms offers as high as ten to one had found no takers.

Now the smile was gone from Malud's lips and he glanced no more at the grand-stand. There was rage in his eyes as he spurred again toward Blake, who he thought had profited by a lucky accident.

Unhampered by a buckler Blake took full advantage of the nimbleness of the wiry horse he rode and which he had ridden daily since his arrival in Nímmr, so that man and beast were well-accustomed to one another.

Again Sir Malud saw his blade glance harmlessly from the sword of his antagonist and then, to his vast surprise, the point of Sir James' blade leaped quickly beneath his buckler and entered his side. It was not a deep wound, but it was painful and again it brought blood.

Angrily Malud struck again, but Blake had reined his charger quickly to the rear and before Malud could gather his reins Blake had struck him again, this time a heavy blow upon the helm.

Half stunned and wholly infuriated, Malud wheeled and charged at full tilt, once again determined to ride his adversary down. They met with a crash directly in front of Gobred's loge, there was a quick play of swords that baffled the eyesight of the onlookers, and then to the astonishment of all, most particularly Malud, that noble sir knight's sword flew from his grasp and hurtled to the field, leaving him entirely to the mercy of his foe.

Malud reined in and sat erect, waiting. He knew and Blake knew that under the rules that governed their encounter Blake was warranted in running him through unless Malud sued for mercy, and no one, Blake least of all, expected this of so proud and haughty a knight.

Sir Malud sat proudly on his charger waiting for Blake to advance and kill him. Utter silence had fallen upon the stands, so that the champing of Malud's horse upon its bit was plainly audible. Blake turned to Sir Jarred.

'Summon a squire, sir knight,' he said, 'to return Sir Malud's sword to him.'

Again the stands rocked to the applause, but Blake turned his back upon them and rode to Richard's side to wait until his adversary was again armed.

'Well, old top,' he inquired of Sir Richard, 'just how much a dozen am I offered for bucklers now?'

Richard laughed. 'Thou hast been passing fortunate, James,' he replied; 'but methinks a good swordsman would long since have cut thee through.'

'I know Malud would have if I had packed that chopping bowl along on the party,' Blake assured him, though it is doubtful if Sir Richard understood what he was talking about, as was so often the case when Blake discoursed that Richard had long since ceased to even speculate as to the meaning of much that his friend said.

But now Sir Malud was re-armed and riding toward Blake. He stopped his horse before the American and bowed low. 'I do my devoirs to a noble and generous knight,' he said, graciously.

Blake bowed. 'Are you ready, sir?' he asked.

Malud nodded.

'On guard, then!' snapped the American.

For a moment the two jockeyed for position. Blake feinted and Malud raised his buckler before his face to catch the blow, but as it did not fall he lowered his shield, just as Blake had known that he would, and as he did so the edge of the American's weapon fell heavily upon the crown of his bassinet.

Malud's arms dropped at his side, he slumped in his saddle and then toppled forward and rolled to the ground. Agile, even in his heavy armour, Blake dismounted and walked to where his foe lay, stretched upon his back almost in front of Gobred's loge. He placed his foot upon Malud's breast and pressed the point of his sword against his throat.

The crowd leaned forward to see the *coup de grâce* administered, but Blake did not drive his point home. He looked up at Prince Gobred and addressed him.

'Here is a brave knight,' he said, 'with whom I have no real quarrel. I spare him to your service, Prince, and to those who love him,' and his eyes went straight to the eyes of the Princess Guinalda. Then he turned and walked back along the front of the grand-stand to his own tilt, while Richard rode behind him, and the knights and the ladies, the men-at-arms, the freedmen and the serfs stood upon their seats and shouted their applause.

Edward was beside himself with joy, as was Michel. The former knelt and embraced Blake's legs; he kissed his hand, and wept, so great were his happiness and his excitement.

'I knew it! I knew it!' he cried. 'Didst I not tell thee, Michel, that my own sir knight would overthrow Sir Malud?'

The men-at-arms, the trumpeter and the grooms at Blake's tilt wore grins that stretched from ear to ear. Whereas a few minutes before they had felt ashamed to have been detailed to the losing side, now they were most proud and looked upon Blake as the greatest hero of Nímmr. Great would be their boasting among their fellows as they gathered with their flagons of ale about the rough deal table in their dining-hall.

Edward removed Blake's armour and Michel got Richard out of his amidst babbling upon the part of the youths who could not contain themselves, so doubly great was their joy because so unexpected.

Blake went directly to his quarters and Richard accompanied him and when the two men were alone Richard placed a hand upon Blake's shoulder.

'Thou hast done a noble and chivalrous thing, my friend,' he said, 'but I know not that it be a wise one.'

'And why?' demanded Blake. 'You didn't think I could stick the poor mutt when he was lying there defenceless?'

Richard shook his head. ''Tis but what he would have done for thee had thy positions been reversed,' said he.

'Well, I couldn't do it. We're not taught to believe that it is exactly ethical to hit a fellow when he's down, where I come from,' explained Blake.

'Had your quarrel been no deeper than appeared upon the surface thou might well have been thus magnanimous; but Malud be jealous of thee and that jealousy will be by no means lessened by what has transpired this day. Thou might have been rid of a powerful and dangerous enemy had thou given him the *coup de grâce*, as was thy right; but now thou hast raised up a greater enemy since to his jealousy is added hatred and envy against thee for thy prowess over him. Thou didst make him appear like a monkey, James, and that Sir Malud wilt never forgive, and I know the man.'

The knights and ladies attached to the castle of Gobred ate together at a great table in the huge hall of the castle. Three hundred people could be accommodated at the single board and it took quite a company of serving men to fill their needs. Whole pigs, roasted, were carried in upon great trenchers and there were legs of mutton and sides of venison and bowls of vegetables with wine and ale, and at the end, immense puddings.

There was much laughter and loud talking and it all presented a wild and fascinating picture to Sir James Blake as he sat at the lower end of the table, far below the salt that night, in his accustomed place as one of the latest neophytes in the noble ranks of the knighthood of Nímmr.

The encounter between himself and Malud was the subject of the moment, and many were the compliments bestowed upon him and many the questions as to where and how he had acquired his strange technique of swordsmanship. Although they had seen him accomplish it yet they still appeared to believe it inconceivable that a man might prevail without a buckler over one who carried this essential article of defence.

Prince Gobred and his family sat, with the higher nobles of Nímmr, at a table slightly raised above the rest of the board and running across its upper end, the whole forming a huge T. When he wished to speak to anyone farther down the table he resorted to the simple expedient of raising his voice, so that if several were so inclined at the same time the room became a bedlam for uproar and confusion.

And as Blake sat at the farthest end of the table it was necessary for one at Gobred's end to scream to attract attention, though when it was discovered that it was the prince who was speaking the rest of the company lapsed into silence out of respect for him, unless they were too far gone in drink.

Shortly after the feasters were seated Gobred had arisen and lifted his goblet high in air and silence had fallen upon the whole company as knights and ladies rose and faced their prince.

'Hail to our King!' cried Gobred. 'Hail to our liege lord, Richard of England!'

And in a great chorus rose the answering 'Hail!' as the company drank the health of Richard Cœur de Lion seven hundred and twenty eight years after his death!

Then they drank the health of Gobred and of the Princess Brynilda, his wife, and of the Princess Guinalda and each time a voice boomed from just below the daïs of the prince: 'Here I be looking at thee!' as Sir Richard with a proud smile displayed his newly acquired knowledge.

Again Prince Gobred rose. 'Hail!' he cried, 'to that worthy sir knight who hath most nobly and chivalrously acquitted himself in the lists this day! Hail to Sir James, Knight Templar and, now, Knight of Nímmr!'

Not even the name of Richard I of England had aroused the enthusiasm that followed the drinking to Sir James. The length of the long hall Blake's eyes travelled straight to where Guinalda stood. He saw her drink to him and he saw that her eyes were regarding him, but the distance was too great and the light of the pitch torches and the oil cressets too dim for him to see whether her glance carried a message of friendship or dislike.

When the noise had partially subsided and the drinkers had retaken their seats, Blake arose.

'Prince Gobred,' he called the length of the room, 'knights and ladies of Nímmr, I give you another toast! To Sir Malud!'

For a moment there was silence, the silence of surprise, and then the company arose and drank the health of the absent Sir Malud.

'Thou art a strange sir knight, with strange words upon thy lips and strange ways, Sir James,' shouted Gobred, 'but though thou callest a hail a "toast" and thy friends be "old top" and "kid" yet withal it seemeth that we understand thee and would know more about thy country and the ways of the noble knights that do abide there.

'Tell us, are they all thus chivalrous and magnanimous to their fallen foes?'

'If they're not they get the raspberry,' explained Blake.

'"Get the raspberry"!' repeated Gobred. ''Tis some form of punishment, methinks.'

'You said it, Prince!'

'Of a surety I said it, Sir James!' snapped Gobred with asperity.

'I mean, Prince, that you hit the nail on the head – you guessed it the first time. You see the raspberry is about the only form of punishment that the Knights of the Squared Circle, or the Knights of the Diamond can understand.'

'"Knights of the Squared Circle"! "Knights of the Diamond"! Those be knightly orders of which I wot not. Be they doughty knights?'

'Some of them are dotty, but a lot of them are regulars. Take Sir Dempsey, for instance. There's the heavyweight champion knight of the Squared Circle. He took the count to Sir Tunney once, but, take it from me, Prince, he showed 'em all he was a regular knight in defeat, which is much more difficult than being a regular knight in victory.'

'Be there other orders of knighthood these days?' demanded Gobred.
'We're lousy with them!'

'What?' cried Gobred.

'We're all knights these days,' explained Blake.

'All knights! Be there no serfs nor yeomen? 'Tis incredible!'

'Well, there are some yeomen in the navy, I think; but all the rest of us, pretty much, are knights. You see things have changed a lot since the days of Richard. The people have sort of overthrown the old order of things. They poked a lot of ridicule at knights and wanted to get rid of knighthood and as soon as they had they all wanted to be knights themselves, so we have Knights Templars now and Knights of Pythias and Knights of Columbus and Knights of Labour and a lot more I can't recall just now.'

'Methinks it must be a fine and a noble world,' cried Gobred, 'for what with so many noble sir knights it would seemeth that they must often contend, one against another – is that not true?'

'Well, they do scrap some,' Blake admitted.

15
The Lonely Grave

Within the dark interior of the beyt Stimbol could see nothing. Just before him he heard a man breathing heavily as might one in a troubled sleep. The would-be murderer paused to steady his nerves, for he was trembling like a leaf. Then, on hands and knees, he crept forward inch by inch.

Presently one of his hands touched the prostrate figure of the sleeper. Lightly, cautiously, Stimbol groped until he had definitely discovered the position in which his victim lay. In one hand, ready, he grasped the keen knife. He scarce dared breathe for fear he might awaken the ape-man. He prayed that Tarzan was a sound sleeper and he prayed that the first blow of his weapon would reach that savage heart.

Now he was ready! He had located the exact spot where he must strike! He raised his knife and struck. His victim shuddered spasmodically. Again and again with savage maniacal force and speed the knife was plunged into the soft flesh. Stimbol felt the warm blood spurt out upon his hand and wrist.

At length, satisfied that his mission had been accomplished, he scurried from the beyt. Now he was trembling so that he could scarcely stand – terrified, revolted by the horrid crime he had committed.

Wild eyed, haggard, he stumbled to the mukaad of Ibn Jad's beyt and there he collapsed. The sheik stepped from the women's quarters and looked down upon the trembling figure that the dim light of a paper lantern revealed.

'What doest thou here, Nasrâny?' he demanded.

'I have done it, Ibn Jad!' muttered Stimbol.

'Done what?' cried the sheik.

'Slain Tarzan of the Apes.'

'Ai! Ai!' screamed Ibn Jad. 'Tollog! Where art thou? Hirfa! Ateja! Come! Didst hear what the Nasrâny sayeth?'

Hirfa and Ateja rushed into the mukaad.

'Didst hear him?' repeated Ibn Jad. 'He hath slain my good friend the great sheik of the Jungle. Motlog! Fahd! Haste!' His voice had been rising until now he was screaming at the top of his lungs and 'Aarab were streaming toward his beyt from all directions.

Stimbol, stunned by what he had done, dumb from surprise and terror at the unexpected attitude of Ibn Jad, crouched speechless in the centre of the mukaad.

'Seize him!' cried the sheik to the first men that arrived. 'He hath slain Tarzan of the Apes, our great friend, who was to preserve us and lead us from this land of dangers. Now all wilt be our enemies. The friends of Tarzan wilt fall upon us and slay us. Allah, bear witness that I be free from guilt in this matter, and let thy wrath and the wrath of the friends of Tarzan fall upon this guilty man!'

By this time the entire population of the menzil was gathered in front of the sheik's beyt, and if they were surprised by the protestations of sudden affection for Tarzan which marked the words of their sheik they gave no evidence of it.

'Take him away!' commanded Ibn Jad. 'In the morning we shall gather and decide what we must do.'

They dragged the terrified Stimbol to Fahd's beyt, where they bound him hand and foot and left him for Fahd to guard. When they had gone the Bedúin leaned low over Stimbol and whispered in his ear.

'Didst really slay the jungle sheik?' he demanded.

'Ibn Jad forced me to do so and now he turns against me,' whimpered Stimbol.

'And tomorrow he will have you killed so that he may tell the friends of Tarzan that he hath punished the slayer of Tarzan,' said Fahd.

'Save me, Fahd!' begged Stimbol. 'Save me and I will give you twenty million francs – I swear it! Once I am safe in the nearest European colony I will get the money for you. Think of it, Fahd – twenty million francs!'

'I am thinking of it, Nasrâny,' replied the Bedúin, 'and I think that thou liest. There be not that much money in the world!'

'I swear that I have ten times that amount. If I have lied to you you may kill me. Save me! Save me!'

'Twenty million francs!' murmured Fahd. 'Perchance he does not lie! Listen, Nasrâny. I do not know that I can save thee, but I shall try and if I succeed and thou forgettest the twenty million francs I shall kill thee if I have to follow thee across the world – dost understand?'

Ibn Jad called two ignorant slaves to him and commanded them to go to the beyt that had been Zeyd's and carry Tarzan's body to the edge of the menzil where they were to dig a grave and bury it.

With paper lanterns they went to the beyt of death, and wrapping the dead man in the old burnous that already covered him they carried him across the menzil and laid him down while they dug a shallow grave, and so, beneath a forest giant in the land that he loved the grave of Tarzan of the Apes was made.

Roughly the slaves rolled the corpse into the hole they had made, shovelled the dirt upon it, and left it in its lonely, unmarked tomb.

Early the next morning Ibn Jad called about him the elders of the tribe and when they were gathered it was noted that Tollog was missing and though a search was made he could not be found. Fahd suggested that he had gone forth early to hunt.

Ibn Jad explained to them that if they were to escape the wrath of the friends of Tarzan they must take immediate steps to disprove their responsibility for the slaying of the ape-man, and that they might only do this and express their good faith by punishing the murderer.

It was not difficult to persuade them to take the life of a Christian and there was only one that demurred. This was Fahd.

'There are two reasons, Ibn Jad, why we should not now take the life of this Nasrâny,' he said.

'By Ullah, there never be any reason why a true believer should not take the life of a Nasrâny!' cried one of the old men.

'Listen,' admonished Fahd, 'to what I have in my mind and then I am sure that you will agree that I am right.'

'Speak, Fahd,' said Ibn Jad.

'This Nasrâny is a rich and powerful man in his own Béled. If it be possible to spare his life he will command a great ransom – dead he is worth nothing to us. If, by chance, the friends of Tarzan do not learn of his death before we are safely out of this accursed land it will have profited us naught to have killed Stimbol and, billah, if we kill him now they may not believe us when we say that he slew Tarzan and we took his life in punishment.

'But if we keep him alive until we are met with the friends of Tarzan, should it so befall that they overtake us, then we may say that we did hold him prisoner that Tarzan's own people might mete out their vengeance to him, which would suit them better.'

'Thy words are not without wisdom,' admitted Ibn Jad, 'but suppose the Nasrâny spoke lies concerning us and said that it was we who slew Tarzan? Wouldst they not believe him above us?'

'That be easily prevented,' said the old man who had spoken before. 'Let us cut his tongue out forthwith that he may not bear false witness against us.'

'Wullah, thou hast it!' exclaimed Ibn Jad.

'Billah, nay!' cried Fahd. 'The better we treat him the larger will be the reward that he will pay us.'

'We can wait until the last moment,' said Ibn Jad, 'and we see that we are to lose him and our reward then may we cut out his tongue.'

Thus the fate of Wilbur Stimbol was left to the gods, and Ibn Jad, temporarily freed from the menace of Tarzan, turned his attention once more to his plans for entering the valley. With a strong party he went in person and sought a palaver with the Galla chief.

As he approached the village of Batando he passed through the camps of thousands of Galla warriors and realised fully what he had previously sensed but vaguely – that his position was most precarious and that with the best grace possible he must agree to what ever terms the old chief might propose.

Batando received him graciously enough, though with all the majesty of a powerful monarch, and assured him that on the following day he would escort him to the entrance to the valley, but that first he must deliver to Batando all the Galla slaves that were with his party.

'But that will leave us without carriers or servants and will greatly weaken the strength of my party,' cried Ibn Jad.

Batando but shrugged his black shoulders.

'Let them remain with us until we have returned from the valley,' implored the sheik.

'No Galla man may accompany you,' said Batando with finality.

Early the next morning the tent of Ibn Jad was struck in signal that all were to prepare for the ráhla, and entirely surrounded by Galla warriors they started toward the rugged mountains where lay the entrance to the valley of Ibn Jad's dreams.

Fejjuân and the other Galla slaves that the 'Aarab had brought with them from Béled el-Guâd marched with their own people, happy in their new-found freedom. Stimbol, friendless, fearful, utterly cowed, trudged wearily along under guard of two young Bedųins, his mind constantly reverting to the horror of the murdered man lying in his lonely grave behind them.

Winding steadily upward along what at times appeared to be an ancient trail and again no trail at all the 'Aarab and their escort climbed higher and higher into the rugged mountains that rim the Valley of the Sepulchre upon the north, and at the close of the second day, after they had made camp beside a mountain brook, Batando came to Ibn Jad and pointed to the entrance to a rocky side ravine that branched from the main canyon directly opposite the camp.

'There,' he said, 'lies the trail into the Valley. Here we leave you and return to our villages. Upon the morrow we go.'

When the sun rose the following morning Ibn Jad discovered that the Gallas had departed during the night, but he did not know that it was because of the terror they felt for the mysterious inhabitants of the mysterious valley from which no Galla ever had returned.

That day Ibn Jad spent in making a secure camp in which to leave the women and children until the warriors had returned from their adventure in the valley or had discovered that they might safely fetch their women, and the next, leaving a few old men and boys to protect the camp, he set forth with those who were accounted the fighting men among them and presently the watchers in the camp saw the last of them disappear in the rocky ravine that lay opposite the menzil.

16
The Great Tourney

King Bohun with many knights and squires and serving men had ridden down from his castle above the City of The Sepulchre two days ago to take his way across the valley to the field before the city of Nímmr for The Great Tourney that is held once each year, commencing upon the first Sunday in Lent.

Gay pennons fluttered from a thousand lance tips and gay with colour were the housings of the richly caparisoned chargers that proudly bore the Knights of The Sepulchre upon whose backs red crosses were emblazoned to denote that they had completed the pilgrimage to The Holy Land and were returning to home and England.

Their bassinets, unlike those of the Knights of Nímmr, were covered with bullock hide and the devices upon their bucklers differed, and their colours. But for these and the crosses upon their backs they might have been Gobred's own good knights and true.

Sturdy sumpter beasts, almost as richly trapped as the knight's steeds, bore the marquees and tilts that were to house the knights during the tourney as well as their personal belongings, their extra arms and their provisions for the three days of the tourney, for custom, over seven centuries old, forbade the Knights of Nímmr and the Knights of The Sepulchre breaking bread together.

The Great Tourney was merely a truce during which they carried on their ancient warfare under special rules which transformed it into a gorgeous pageant and an exhibition of martial prowess which non-combatants might witness in comfort and with impunity. It did not permit friendly intercourse between the two factions as this was not compatible with the seriousness of the event, in which knights of both sides often were killed, or the spirit in which the grand prize was awarded.

This prize as much as any other factor had kept open the breach of seven and a half centuries' duration that separated the Fronters from the Backers, for it consisted of five maidens whom the winners took back with them to their own city and who were never again seen by their friends or relatives.

Though the sorrow was mitigated by the honourable treatment that custom and the laws of knighthood decreed should be accorded these unfortunate maidens it was still bitter because attached to it was the sting of defeat.

Following the tournament the maidens became the especial charges of Gobred or Bohun, dependent of course upon whether the honours of the tourney had fallen to the Fronters or the Backers, and in due course were given in honourable marriage to knights of the victorious party.

The genesis of the custom, which was now fully seven centuries old, doubtless lay in the wise desire of some ancient Gobred or Bohun to maintain the stock of both factions strong and virile by the regular infusion of new blood, as well, perhaps, as to prevent the inhabitants of the two cities from drifting too far apart in manners, customs and speech.

Many a happy wife of Nímmr had been born in the City of The Sepulchre, and seldom was it that the girls themselves repined for long. It was considered an honour to be chosen and there were always many more volunteered than the requisite number of five that annually made the sacrifice.

The five who constituted the prize offered by the City of The Sepulchre this year rode on white palfreys and were attended by a guard of honour in silver mail. The girls, selected for their beauty thus to honour the city of their birth, were gorgeously attired and weighed down with ornaments of gold and silver and precious stones.

Upon the plain before the city of Nímmr preparations for the tourney had been in progress for many days. The lists were being dragged and rolled with heavy wooden rollers, the ancient stands of stone from which the spectators viewed the spectacle were undergoing their annual repairs and cleansing, a frame superstructure was being raised to support the canopies that would shade the choice seats reserved for the nobility, and staffs for a thousand pennons had been set around the outer margin of the lists – these and a hundred other things were occupying a company of workmen, and in the walled city and in the castle that stood above it, the hammers of armourers and smiths rang far into the nights forging iron shoes and mail and lance tips.

Blake had been assured that he was to have a part in The Great Tourney, and was as keen for it as he had been for the big game of the season during his football days at college. He had been entered in two sword contests – one in which five Knights of Nímmr met five Knights of The Sepulchre, and another in which he was pitted against a single antagonist, but his only contest with the lance was to be in the grand finale when a hundred Fronters faced a hundred Backers, since whereas before his encounter with Malud he had been considered hopeless with sword and buckler now Prince Gobred looked to him to win many points with these, his lance work being held but mediocre.

King Bohun and his followers were camped in a grove of oaks about a mile north of the lists, nor did the laws governing The Great Tourney permit them to come nearer until the hour appointed for their entrance upon the first day of the spectacle.

Blake, in preparing for the tourney, had followed the custom adopted by many of the knights of wearing distinctive armour and trapping his charger similarly. His chain mail was all of solid black relieved only by the leopard skin of his bassinet and the blue and silver pennon upon his lance. The housings of his mount were of black, edged with silver and blue, and there were, of course, the prescribed red crosses upon his breast and upon his horse housings.

As he came from his quarters upon the opening morning of the tourney, followed by Edward bearing his lance and buckler, he appeared a sombre figure among the resplendently caparisoned knights and the gorgeously-dressed women that were gathered in the great court awaiting the word to mount their horses which were being held in the north ballium by the grooms.

That his black mail was distinctive was evidenced by the attention he immediately attracted and that he had quickly become popular among the knights and ladies of Nímmr was equally apparent by the manner in which they clustered about him, but opinion was divided in the matter of his costume, some holding that it was too dismal and depressing.

Guinalda was there but she remained seated upon a bench where she was conversing with one of the maidens that had been chosen as Nímmr's prize. Blake quickly disengaged himself from those who had crowded about him and crossed the court to where Guinalda sat. At his approach the princess looked up and inclined her head slightly in recognition of his bow, and then she resumed her conversation with the maiden.

The rebuff was too obvious to permit of misunderstanding, but Blake was not satisfied to accept it and go his way without an explanation. He could scarce believe, however, that the princess was still vexed merely because he had intimated that he had believed that she took a greater interest in him than she had admitted. There must be some other reason.

He did not turn and walk away, then, although she continued to ignore him, but stood quietly before her, waiting patiently until she should again notice him.

Presently he noted that she was becoming nervous, as was also the maiden with whom she spoke. There were lapses in their conversation; one of Guinalda's feet was tapping the flagging irritably; a slow flush was creeping upward into her cheeks. The maiden fidgeted, she plucked at the ends of the wimple that lay about her shoulders, she smoothed the rich cyclas of her mantle and finally arose and bowing low before the princess asked if she might go and bid farewell to her mother.

Guinalda bade her begone and then, alone with Blake, and no longer able to ignore him, nor caring to, she turned angrily upon him.

'I was right!' she snapped. 'Thou beest a forward boor. Why standeth thou thus staring at me when I have made it plain that I wouldst not be annoyed by thee? Go!'

'Because –' Blake hesitated, 'because I love you.'

'Sirrah!' cried Guinalda, springing to her feet. 'How darest thou!'

'I would dare anything for you, my princess,' replied Blake, 'because I love you.'

Guinalda looked straight at him for a moment in silence, then her short upper lip curved in a contemptuous sneer and she laughed in his face.

'Thou liest!' she said. 'I have heard what thou hast said concerning me!' and without waiting for a reply she brushed past him and walked away.

Blake hurried after her. 'What I have said about you?' he demanded. 'I have said nothing that I would not repeat before all Nímmr. Not even have I presumed to tell my best friend, Sir Richard, that I love you. No other ears than yours have heard that.'

'I have heard differently,' said Guinalda, haughtily, 'and I care not to discuss the matter further.'

'But—' commenced Blake, but at that instant a trumpet sounded from the north gate leading into the ballium. It was the signal for the knights to mount. Guinalda's page came running to her to summon her to her father's side. Sir Richard appeared and seized Blake by the arm.

'Come, James!' he cried. 'We should have been mounted before now, for we ride in the fore rank of the knights today,' and so Blake was dragged away from the princess before he could obtain an explanation of her, to him inexplicable, attitude.

The north ballium presented a scene of colour and activity, crowded as it was with knights and ladies, pages, squires, grooms, men-at-arms and horses, nor would it accommodate them all, so that the overflow stretched into the east and south balliums and even through the great east gate out upon the road that leads down into the valley.

For half an hour something very like chaos reigned about the castle of the Prince of Nímmr, but eventually perspiring marshals and shouting heralds whipped the cortege into shape as it took its slow and imposing way down the winding mountain road toward the lists.

First rode the marshals and heralds and behind them a score of trumpeters; then came Prince Gobred, riding alone, and following was a great company of knights, their coloured pennons streaming in the wind. They rode just before the ladies and behind the ladies was another company of knights, while in the rear marched company after company of men-at-arms, some armed with crossbows, others with pikes and still others again with battle-axes of huge proportions.

Perhaps a hundred knights and men-at-arms all told were left behind to guard the castle and the entrance to the Valley of The Sepulchre, but these would be relieved to witness the second and third days' exercises.

As the Knights of Nimmr wound down to the lists the Knights of The Sepulchre moved out from their camp among the oaks and the marshals of the two parties timed their approach so that both entered the lists at the same time.

The ladies of Nímmr dropped out of the procession and took their places in the stand, the five maidens of Nímmr and the five from the City of The Sepulchre were escorted to a dais at one end of the lists, after which the knights lined up in solid ranks, the Knights of Nímmr upon the south side of the lists, the Knights of The Sepulchre upon the north.

Gobred and Bohun rode forward and met in the centre of the field, where, in measured and imposing tones, Bohun delivered the ancient challenge prescribed by custom and the laws of The Great Tourney and handed Gobred the gage, the acceptance of which constituted an acceptance of the challenge and marked the official opening of the tourney.

As Gobred and Bohun reined about and faced their own knights these rode out of the lists, those who were not to take part in the encounters of the day seeking places in the stands after turning their chargers over to grooms, while those who were formed again for the purpose of riding once around the lists, for the double purpose of indicating to their opponents and the spectators the entrants for that day and of viewing the prizes offered by their opponents.

In addition to the maidens there were many minor prizes consisting of jewelled ornaments, suits of mail, lances, swords, bucklers, splendid steeds and the many articles that were valued by knights or might find favour in the eyes of their ladies.

The Knights of The Sepulchre paraded first, with Bohun at their head and it was noticeable that the eyes of the king were often upon the women in the stands as he rode past. Bohun was a young man, having but just ascended the throne following the recent death of his father. He was arrogant and tyrannical and it had been common knowledge in Nímmr that for years he had been at the head of a faction that was strong for war with Nímmr, that the city might be reduced and the entire Valley of The Sepulchre brought under the rule of the Bohuns.

His charger prancing, his colours flying, his great company of knights at his back, King Bohun rode along the stands reserved for the people of Nímmr, and when he came to the central loge in which sat Prince Gobred with the Princess Brynilda and Princess Guinalda his eyes fell upon the face of the daughter of Gobred.

Bohun reined in his charger and stared straight into the face of Guinalda, Gobred flushed angrily, for Bohun's act was a breach of courtesy, and half-rose from his seat, but at that moment Bohun, bowing low across his mount's withers, moved on, followed by his knights.

That day the honours went to the Knights of The Sepulchre, for they scored two hundred and twenty seven points against one hundred and six that the Knights of Nímmr were able to procure.

Upon the second day the tourney opened with the riding past of the entrants who, ordinarily, were conducted by a herald, but to the surprise of all Bohun again led his knights past the stands and again he paused and looked full at the Princess Guinalda.

This day the Knights of Nimmr fared a little better, being for the day but seven points behind their opponents, though the score for two days stood two hundred and sixty nine to three hundred and ninety seven in favour of the Knights of The Sepulchre.

So the third day opened with the knights from the north boasting what seemed an insuperable lead of one hundred and twenty eight points and the Knights of Nímmr spurred to greater action by the knowledge that to win the tourney they must score two hundred and thirty two of the remaining three hundred and thirty four points.

Once again, contrary to age-old custom, Bohun led his entrants about the lists as they paraded before the opening encounter, and once again he drew rein before the loge of Gobred and his eyes rested upon the beautiful face of Guinalda for an instant before he addressed her sire.

'Prince Gobred of Nímmr,' he said in his haughty and arrogant voice, 'as ye well know, my valiant sir knights have bested thine by more than six score points and the Great Tourney be as good as ours already.

'Yet we would make thee a proposition.'

'Speak, Bohun! The Great Tourney is yet far from won, but and ye have any proposition that an honourable prince may consider, thou hast my assurance that 'twill be given consideration.'

'Thy five maidens are as good as ours,' said Bohun; 'but give me thy daughter to be queen of The Valley of The Sepulchre and I will grant thee the tourney.'

Gobred went white with anger, but when he replied his voice was low and even, for he was master of his own emotions, as befitted a princely man.

'Sir Bohun,' he said, refusing to accord to his enemy the title of king, 'thy words are an offence in the ears of honourable men, implying as they do that the daughter of a Gobred be for sale and that the honour of the knighthood of Nímmr may be bartered for.

'Get thee hence to thine own side of the lists before I set serfs upon ye to drive ye there with staves.'

'So that be thine answer, eh?' shouted Bohun. 'Then know ye that I shall take the five maidens by the rules of The Great Tourney and thy daughter by force of arms!' and with this threat delivered he wheeled his steed and spurred away.

Word of Bohun's proposition and his rebuff spread like wildfire throughout the ranks of the Knights of Nímmr so that those who were to contend this last day of the Tourney were keyed to the highest pitch of derring do in the defence of the honour of Nímmr and the protection of the Princess Guinalda.

The great lead attained by the Knights of The Sepulchre during the first two days was but an added incentive to greater effort, provoking them, as a spur, to the utmost limits of daring and exertion. There was no need that their marshals should exhort them. The youth and chivalry of Nímmr had heard the challenge and would answer it in the lists!

Blake's sword and buckler encounter with a Knight of The Sepulchre was scheduled for the first event of the day and when the lists were cleared he rode in to a fanfare of trumpets, moving parallel with the south stands while his adversary rode along the front of the north stands, the latter halting before the loge of Bohun as Blake drew rein in front of that of Gobred, where he raised the hilt of his sword to his lips to the Prince, though his eyes were upon Guinalda.

'Conduct thyself as a true knight this day to the glory and honour of Nímmr,' charged Gobred, 'and may the blessings of our Lord Jesus be upon thee and thy sword, our well beloved Sir Tames!'

'To the glory and honour of Nímmr I pledge my sword and my life!' should have been Blake's reply according to the usages of The Great Tourneys.

'To the glory and honour of Nímmr and to the protection of my Princess I pledge my sword and my life!' is what he said, and it was evident from the expression on Gobred's face that he was not displeased, while the look of haughty disdain which had been upon Guinalda's face softened.

Slowly she arose and tearing a ribbon from her gown stepped to the front of the loge. 'Receive this favour from thy lady, sir knight,' she said, 'bearing it with honour and to victory in thy encounter.'

Blake reined close to the rail of the loge and bent low while Guinalda pinned the ribbon upon his shoulder. His face was close to hers; he sensed the intoxicating perfume of her hair; he felt her warm breath upon his cheek.

'I love you,' he whispered, so low that no other ears than hers could hear.

'Thou art a boor,' she replied in a voice as low as his. 'It be for the sake of the five maidens that I encourage ye with this favour.'

Blake looked straight into her eyes. 'I love you, Guinalda,' he said, 'and – you love me!'

Before she could reply he had wheeled away, the trumpets had sounded, and he was cantering slowly toward the end of the field where the tilts of the Knights of Nímmr stood.

Edward, very much excited, was there and Sir Richard and Michel, with a marshal, heralds, trumpeters, men-at-arms – a martial company to urge him on with encouragement and advice.

Blake cast aside his buckler, nor was there any to reprove him now. Instead they smiled proudly and knowingly, for had they not seen him best Sir Malud without other defence than his horsemanship and his sword?

The trumpets blared again. Blake turned and put spurs to his charger, straight down the centre of the lists he rode and from the opposite end came a knight of The Sepulchre to meet him!

'Sir James! Sir James!' cried the spectators in the stands upon the south side, while the north stands answered with the name of their companion.

'Who is the black knight?' asked many a man in the north stands of his neighbour.

'He hath no buckler!' cried some. 'He be mad!' 'Sir Guy wilt cleave him open at the first pass!' 'Sir Guy! Sir Guy!'

17

'The Saracens!'

Just as the second day of The Great Tourney had opened in The Valley of The Sepulchre upon the plains below the city of Nimmr a band of swart men in soiled thôbs and carrying long matchlocks topped the summit of the pass upon the north side of the valley and looked down upon the City of The Sepulchre and the Castle of King Bohun.

They had followed upward along what may once have been a trail, but for so long a time, or so infrequently had it been used that it was scarce distinguishable from the the surrounding brush; but below them now Ibn Jad saw at a short distance a better marked road and, beyond, what appeared to him a fortress. Beyond that again he glimpsed the battlements of Bohun's castle.

What he saw in the foreground was the barbican guarding the approach to the castle and the city, both of which were situated in much the same relative position as were the barbican and castle upon the south side of the valley where Prince Gobred guarded the city of Nímmr and the valley beyond it against the daily expected assault of the Saracens.

Seeking cover, Ibn Jad and his Bedúins crept down toward the barbican where an old knight and a few men-at-arms kept perfunctory ward. Hiding in the mountain brush the 'Aarab saw two strangely-apparelled blacks hunting just outside the great gateway. They were armed with crossbows and arrows and their prey was rabbits. For years they had seen no stranger come down this ancient road, and for years they had hunted between the gate and the summit of the mountains, though further than this they were not permitted to wander, nor had they any great desire to do so, for, though they were descendants of Gallas who lived just beyond this mountain top, they thought that they were Englishmen and that a horde of Saracens awaited to annihilate them should they venture too far afield.

Today they hunted as they had often hunted when they chanced to be placed in the guard at the outer barbican. They moved silently forward, warily awaiting the break of a rabbit. They did not see the dark-faced men, hiding in the brush.

Ibn Jad saw the great gateway was open and that the gate that closed it raised and lowered vertically. It was raised now. Great was the laxity of the old knight and the men-at-arms, but King Bohun was away and there was none to reprove them.

Ibn Jad motioned those nearest him to follow and crept closer to the gateway. What of the old knight and the other watchers? The former was partaking of a late breakfast just within one of the great towers of the barbican and the latter were taking advantage of the laxity of his discipline to catch a few more winks of sleep as they stretched beneath the shade of some trees within the ballium.

Ibn Jad won to within a few yards of the gateway and waited for the others to reach his side. When they were all there he whispered to them and then trotted on silent sandals toward the gate, his matchlock ready in his hands. Behind him came his fellows and they were all within the ballium before the men-at-arms were aware that there was an enemy this side of Palestine.

With crossbow and battle-axe the men-at-arms sprang to defend the gate and their cries of 'The Saracens! The Saracens!' brought the old sir knight and the hunters running toward the ballium.

Below, at the castle of King Bohun, the men at the gates and the other retainers who had been left while Bohun sallied forth to The Great Tourney heard strange noises from the direction of the outer barbican. The shouts of men floated down to them and strange, sharp sounds that were like thunder and yet unlike it. Such sounds they had never heard before, nor any of their forebears. They rallied at the outer castle gate and the knights with them consulted as to what was best to be done.

Being brave knights there seemed but one thing open for them. If those at the far outer barbican had been attacked they must hasten to their defence. Summoning all but four of the knights and men-at-arms at his disposal the marshal of the castle mounted and rode forth toward the outer gate.

Halfway there they were espied by Ibn Jad and his men who, having overcome the poorly-armed soldiers at the gate, were advancing down the road toward the castle. At sight of these reinforcements Ibn Jad hastened to secrete his followers and himself in the bushes that lined the roadway and so it fell that the marshal rode by them and did not see them and, when they had passed, Ibn Jad and his followers came out of the bushes and continued down the winding mountain road toward the castle of the King.

The men at the castle gate, now fully upon the alert, stood ready with the portcullis raised as the marshal had instructed them, so that in the event that those who had ridden out should be hard pressed upon their return by an enemy at their rear they could still find sanctuary within the ballium, the plan being, in such event, to lower the portcullis behind the men of The Sepulchre and in the faces of the pursuing Saracens, for that an enemy must be such was a foregone conclusion – had not they and their ancestors waited for near seven and a half centuries now for this momentarily expected assault?

They wondered if it really had come at last and while they discussed the question Ibn Jad watched them from a concealing clump of bushes a few yards away.

The wily Bedúin knew the purpose of that portcullis and he was trying to plan how best he might enter the enclosure beyond ere it could be dropped before his face. At last he found a plan and smiled. He beckoned three men to come close and into their ears he whispered that which he had in mind.

There were four men-at-arms ready to drop the portcullis at the psychological moment and all four of them stood in plain sight of Ibn Jad and the three that were beside him. Carefully, cautiously, noiselessly the four 'Aarab raised their ancient matchlocks and took careful aim.

'Now!' whispered Ibn Jad and four matchlocks belched forth flame and black powder and slugs of lead.

The four men-at-arms dropped to the stone flagging and Ibn Jad and all his followers raced forward and stood within the ballium of the castle of King Bohun. Before them, across the ballium, was another gate and a broad moat, but the drawbridge was lowered, the portcullis raised and the gateway unguarded.

The marshal and his followers had ridden unhindered into the ballium of the outer barbican and there they had found all its defenders lying in their own blood, even to the little squire of the old knight who should have watched the gate and did not.

One of the men-at-arms still lived and in his dying breath he gasped the terrible truth. The Saracens had come at last!

'Where are they?' demanded the marshal.

'Didst thou not see them, sir?' asked the dying man. 'They marched down the road toward the castle.'

'Impossible!' cried the marshal, 'we didst but ride along that very road and saw no one.'

'They marched down toward the castle,' gasped the man.

The marshal knit his brows. 'Were there many?' he demanded.

'There are few,' replied the man-at-arms. 'It was but the advance guard of the armies of the Sultan.'

Just then the volley that laid low the four warders at the castle gate crashed upon the ears of the marshal and his men.

'Odsblud!' he cried.

'They must have hid themselves in the bush as we passed,' exclaimed a knight at the marshal's side, 'for of a surety they be there and we be here and there be but one road from there to here.'

'There be but four men at the castle gate,' said the marshal, 'and I bid them keep the 'cullis up till we returned. God pity me! I have given over The Sepulchre to the Saracens. Slay me, Sir Morley!'

'Nay, man! We need every lance and sword and crossbow that we may command. This be no time to think of taking thy life when thou canst give it to our Lord Jesus in defence of His Sepulchre against the infidels!'

'Thou are right, Morley,' cried the marshal. 'Remain you here, then, with six men and hold this gate. I shall return with the others and give battle at the castle!'

But when the marshal came again to the castle gate he found the portcullis down and a dark-faced bearded Saracen glaring at him through the iron bars. The marshal gave the order for crossbowmen to shoot the fellow down, but as they raised their weapons to their shoulders there was a loud explosion that almost deafened them and flame leaped from a strange thing that the Saracen held against his shoulder and pointed at them. One of the cross-bowmen screamed and lunged forward upon his face and the others turned and fled.

They were brave men in the face of dangers that were natural and to be expected, but in the presence of the supernatural, the weird, the uncanny, they reacted as most men do, and what could have been more weird than death leaping in flame and with a great noise through space to strike their fellow down?

But Sir Bulland, the marshal, was a Knight of The Sepulchre. He might wish to run away fully as much as the simple and lowly men-at-arms, but there was something that held him there that was more potent than fear of death. It is called Honour.

Sir Bulland could not run away and so he sat there on his great horse and challenged the Saracens to mortal combat; challenged them to send their doughtiest sir knight to meet him and thus decide who should hold the gate.

But the 'Aarab already held it. Furthermore they did not understand him; and in addition to all this they were without honour as Sir Bulland knew it, and perhaps as any other than a Bedúin knows it, and would but have laughed at his silly suggestion.

One thing they did know – two things they knew – that he was a Nasrâny and that he was unarmed. They did not count his great lance and his sword as weapons, for he could not reach them with either. So one of them took careful aim and shot Sir Bulland through his chain mail where it covered his noble and chivalrous heart.

Ibn Jad had the run of the castle of King Bohun and he was sure that he had discovered the fabled city of Nímmr that the Sáhar had told him of. He herded together the women and children and the few men that remained and held them under guard. For a while he was minded to slay them, since they were but Nasrâny, but he was so pleased at having found and taken the treasured city that he let them live – for the time at least.

At his command his followers ransacked the castle in search of the treasure nor were they disappointed, for the riches of Bohun were great. There is gold in the hills of the Valley of The Sepulchre and there are precious stones to be found there, also. For seven and a half centuries the slaves of The Sepulchre and of Nímmr have been washing gold from the creek beds and salvaging precious stones from the same source. The value of these things is not to the men of The Sepulchre and Nímmr what it would be to men of the outer world. They but esteemed these things as trinkets, yet they liked them and saved them and even bartered for them on occasion, but they did not place them in vaults under lock and key, and why should they in a land where such things were not stolen. Their women and their horses they kept under guard, but not their gold or their jewels.

And so Ibn Jad had gathered a great sackful of treasure, enough to satisfy his wildest imaginings of cupidity. He gathered all that he could find in the castle of King Bohun, more than he had hoped in find in this fabled city; and then a strange thing happened. Having more wealth than he possibly could use he wanted more. No, not so strange after all, for Ibn Jad was human.

He spent the night with his followers in the castle of King Bohun and during the night he planned, for he had seen a wide valley stretching far away to other mountains and at the base of those mountains he had seen that which appeared to be a city. 'Perhaps,' thought Ibn Jad, 'it is a richer city than this. I shall start on the morrow to see.'

18

The Black Knight

Down the field thundered the two chargers. Silence fell upon the stands. They were almost met when Sir Guy realised that his adversary bore no shield. But what of that? He had been sent into the lists by his own people – the responsibility was theirs, the advantage Sir Guy's. Had they sent him in without a sword Sir Guy might still have slain him without besmirching his knightly honour, for such were the laws of The Great Tourney.

Yet his discovery had its effect upon the knight of The Sepulchre as just for an instant it had distracted his attention from the thought that should have been uppermost in his mind – gaining the primary advantage by the skill of his opening attack.

He saw his antagonist's horse swing out just before they met; he stood in his stirrups, as had Sir Malud, to deliver a terrific cut; then Blake threw his horse straight into the shoulder of Sir Guy's, the latter's sword fell and with a loud, clanging noise slipped harmlessly from the blade of the knight of Nímmr. Guy had raised his buckler to protect his own head and neck and could not see Sir James. Guy's horse stumbled and nearly fell and as it recovered itself Blake's blade slipped beneath the buckler of the knight of The Sepulchre and its point pierced the gorget of his adversary and passed through his throat.

With a cry that ended in a blood-choked gurgle Sir Guy of The Sepulchre toppled backward upon his horse's rump and rolled upon the ground, while the south stands went mad with joy.

The laws of The Great Tourney account the knight slain who is unhorsed, so the *coup de grâce* is never given and no knight is killed unnecessarily. The victor rides to the tilt of the vanquished, wheels about and gallops to his own tilt, the full length of the lists where he waits until a herald of the opposing side fetches the prize to him.

And so it was that as Blake swung from his saddle, sword in hand, and approached the fallen Sir Guy, a gasp arose from the south stands and a roar of angry protest from the north.

Marshals and heralds galloped madly from the tilt of the fallen Backer and, seeing this, Sir Richard, fearing that Blake would be set upon and slain, led a similar party from his end of the field.

Blake approached the fallen knight, who lay upon his back, feebly struggling to arise and when the spectators looked to see him run Sir Guy through with his sword they saw him instead toss the weapon to the ground and kneel beside the wounded man.

With an arm beneath Sir Guy's shoulders he raised him and held him against his knee while he tore off his helm and gorget, and when the marshals and the heralds and the others drew rein beside him Blake was trying to staunch the flow of blood.

'Quick!' he cried to them; 'a chirurgeon! His jugular is not touched, but this flow of blood must be stopped.'

Several of the knights dismounted and gathered about and among them was Sir Richard. A herald of Sir Guy's faction kneeled and took the youth from Blake's arms.

'Come!' said Richard. 'Leave the sir knight to his own friends.'

Blake arose. He saw how peculiar were the expressions upon the faces of the knights about him, but as he drew away one of them spoke. An older man, who was one of Bohun's marshals.

'Thou art a generous and chivalrous knight,' he said to Blake – 'and a courageous one too who would thus set at naught the laws of The Great Tourney and the customs of centuries.'

Blake faced him squarely. 'I do not give a damn for your laws or your customs,' he said. 'Where I come from a decent man wouldn't let a yellow dog bleed to death without trying to save him, much less a brave and gallant boy like this, and because he fell by my hand by the customs of my country I should be compelled to aid him.'

'Yes,' explained Sir Richard, 'as otherwise he would be punished with a raspberry.'

The winning of the first event of the day was but a forerunner of a series of successes on the part of the Knights of Nímmr until, at the opening of the last event, the score showed four hundred fifty two points for them against four hundred forty eight for their opponents; but a margin of four points was as nothing at this stage of the tourney, as the final event held one hundred points which Fate might allot almost entirely to one side.

This was the most spectacular event of the whole tourney and one which the spectators always looked forward to with the greatest anticipation. Two hundred knights were engaged in it, one hundred Knights of Nímmr against one hundred Knights of The Sepulchre. They formed at opposite ends of the lists and as the trumpets sounded the signal they charged with lances and thus they fought until all of one side had been unhorsed or had retired from the field because of wounds. Broken lances could be replaced as a polo player may ride out and obtain a fresh mallet when he breaks his. Otherwise there were few rules to govern this concluding number of The Great Tourney, which more nearly approximated a battle scene than any other event of the three days of conflict.

Blake had won his fifteen points for the Knights of Nímmr in the opening event of the day and again with four other comrades, pitted against five mounted swordsmen from the north, he had helped to add still further points to the growing score of the Fronters.

He was entered in the last event largely because the marshals appreciated the value of his horsemanship and felt that it would more than compensate for his inexperience with the lance.

The two hundred mailed knights had paraded for the final event and were forming lines at opposite ends of the lists, one hundred Knights of The Sepulchre at one end and one hundred Knights of Nímmr at the other. Their chargers, especially selected for this encounter, were powerful and fleet; chosen for their courage, too, as were the youths who bestrode them.

The knights, with few exceptions, were youths in their twenties, for to youth went the laurels of this great sport of the Middle Ages as they still do in the sports of today. Here and there was a man of middle age, a hardened veteran whose heart and hand had withstood the march of years and whose presence exerted a steadying influence upon the young knights the while it spurred them to their utmost efforts, for these were champions whose deeds were sung by minstrels in the great halls of the castles of Nímmr.

In proud array, with upright lances and fluttering pennons, the sunlight glinting from burnished mail and bit and boss and shining brightly upon the gorgeous housings of their mounts, the two hundred presented a proud and noble spectacle as they awaited the final summons of the trumpet.

Rearing and plunging, eager to be off, many a war horse broke the line as will a thoroughbred at the barrier, while at one side and opposite the centre of the lists a herald waited for the moment that both lines should be formed before he gave the signal that would send these iron men hurtling into combat.

Blake found himself well toward the centre of the line of Nímmr's knights, beneath him a great black that fretted to be off, before him the flower of the knighthood of The Sepulchre. In his right hand he grasped a heavy, iron-shod lance, the butt of which rested in a boot at his stirrup, and upon his left arm he bore a great shield, nor had he any wish to discard it in the face of all those sturdy, iron-tipped lances.

As he looked down the long length of the lists upon the hundred knights that would presently be racing towards him in solid array with lance points projecting far ahead of their horses Blake felt that his shield was entirely inadequate and he experienced a certain nervousness that reminded him of similar moments of tense waiting for the referee's whistle during his football days – those seemingly long gone days of another life that he sensed now as a remote and different incarnation.

At last came the signal! He saw the herald raise his sword on high. With the two hundred he gathered his restive charger and couched his lance. The sword fell! From the four corners of the lists trumpets blared; from two hundred throats rose the *cri de guerre*; four hundred spurs transmitted the awaited signal from man to horse.

The thundering lines bore down the field; a score of heralds raced along the flanks and rear to catch any infraction of the sole regulation that bore upon the final tumultuous collision. Each knight must engage the foe upon his bridle hand, for to couch his lance upon the one upon his right was an unknightly act, since thus a single knight might have two lances set upon him at once, against which there could be no defence.

From above the rim of his shield Blake saw the solid front of lances, iron shod chargers and great shields almost upon him. The speed, the weight, the momentum seemed irresistible and, metaphorically, with deep respect Blake took his hat off to the knights of old.

And now the two lines were about to meet! The spectators sat in spellbound silence; the riders, grim-jawed, with tight-set lips, were voiceless now.

Blake, his lance across his horse's withers, picked the knight racing towards him upon his left hand; for an instant he caught the other's eyes and then each crouched behind his shield as the two lines came together with a deafening crash.

Blake's shield smashed back against his face and body with such terrific force that he was almost carried from his saddle. He felt his own lance strike and splinter and then, half stunned, he was through the iron line, his charger, frantic and uncontrolled, running wildly towards the tilts of Bohun's knights.

With an effort Blake pulled himself together, gathered his reins and finally managed to get his horse under control and it was not until he had reined him about that he got his first glimpse of the result of the opening encounter. A half dozen chargers were scrambling to their feet and nearly a score more were galloping, riderless, about the lists. A full twenty-five knights lay upon the field and twice that many squires and serving men were running on foot to succour their masters.

Already several of the knights had again set their lances against an enemy and Blake saw one of the Knights of The Sepulchre bearing down upon him, but he raised his broken spear shaft above his head to indicate that he was momentarily *hors de combat* and galloped swiftly back to his own end of the lists where Edward was awaiting him with a fresh weapon.

'Thou didst nobly well, beloved master,' cried Edward.

'Did I get my man?' asked Blake.

'That thou didst, sir,' Edward assured him, beaming with pride and pleasure, 'and albeit thou breakest thy lance upon his shield thou didst e'en so unhorse him.'

Armed anew, Blake turned back toward the centre of the lists where many individual encounters were taking place. Already several more knights were down and the victors looking for new conquests in which the stands were assisting with hoarse cries and advice, and as Blake rode back into the lists he was espied by many in the north stands occupied by the knights and followers of The Sepulchre.

'The black knight!' they cried. 'Here! Here! Sir Wildred! Here is the black knight that overthrew Sir Guy. Have at him, Sir Wildred!'

Sir Wildred, a hundred yards away, couched his lance. 'Have at thee, Sir Black Knight!' he shouted.

'You're on!' Blake shouted back, putting spurs to the great black.

Sir Wildred was a large man and he bestrode a raw-boned roan with the speed of a deer and the heart of a lion. The pair would have been a match for the best of Nímmr's knighthood.

Perhaps it was as well for Blake's peace of mind that Wildred appeared to him like any other knight and that he did not know that he was the most sung of all the heroes of The Sepulchre.

As a matter of fact any knight looked formidable to Blake, who was still at a loss to understand how he had unhorsed his man in the first encounter of this event.

'The bird must have lost both stirrups,' is what he had mentally assured himself when Edward had announced his victory.

But he couched his lance like a good sir knight and true and bore down upon the redoubtable Sir Wildred. The Knight of The Sepulchre was charging diagonally across the field from the south stands and beyond him Blake caught a glimpse of a slim, girlish figure standing in the central loge. He could not see her eyes, but he knew that they were upon him.

'For my Princess!' he whispered as Sir Wildred loomed large before him.

Lance smote on shield as the two knights crashed together with terrific force and Blake felt himself lifted clear of his saddle and hurled heavily to the ground. He was neither stunned nor badly hurt and as he sat up a sudden grin wreathed his face, for there, scarce a lance length from him, sat Sir Wildred; but Sir Wildred did not smile.

''Sdeath!' he cried. 'Thou laughest at me, sirrah?'

'If I look as funny as you do,' Blake assured him, 'you've got a laugh coming too.'

Sir Wildred knit his brows. 'Odsblud!' he exclaimed. 'And thou beest a knight of Nímmr I be a Saracen! Who beest thou? Thy speech savoureth not of The Valley.'

Blake had arisen. 'Hurt much?' he asked stepping forward. 'Here, I'll give you a hand up.'

'Thou art, of a certainty, a strange sir knight,' said Wildred. 'I recall now that thou didst offer succour to Sir Guy when thou hadst fairly vanquished him.'

'Well, what's wrong with that?' asked Blake. 'I haven't anything against you. We've had a bully good scrap and are out of it. Why should we sit here and make faces at one another?'

Sir Wildred shook his head. 'Thou art beyond my comprehension,' he admitted.

By this time their squires and a couple of serving men had arrived, but neither of the fallen knights was so badly injured that he could not walk without assistance and as they started for their respective tilts Blake turned and smiled at Wildred.

'So long, old man!' he cried cheerily. 'Hope we meet again some day.'

Still shaking his head Sir Wildred limped away, followed by the two who had come to assist him.

At his tilt Blake learned that the outcome of The Great Tourney still hung in the balance and it was another half hour before the last of the knights of Nímmr went down in defeat, leaving two knights of The Sepulchre victorious upon the field; but this was not enough to overcome the lead of four points that the Fronters had held at the opening of the last event and a moment later the heralds announced that the knights of Nímmr had won The Great Tourney by the close margin of two points.

Amidst the shouting of the occupants of the stands at the south the knights of Nímmr who had taken part in the tourney and had won points for the Fronters formed to ride upon the lists and claim the grand prize. Not all were there, as some had been killed or wounded in encounters that had followed their victories, though the toll on both sides had been much smaller than Blake had imagined that it would be. Five men were dead and perhaps twenty too badly injured to ride, the casualties being about equally divided.

As the knights of Nímmr rode down the field to claim the five maidens from the City of The Sepulchre, Bohun gathered all his knights at his side of the lists as though preparing to ride back to his camp and at the same time a knight of The Sepulchre, wearing the leopard skin bassinet of Nímmr, entered the stands upon the south side of the field and made his way toward the loge of Prince Gobred.

Bohun watched. The Knights of Nímmr were at the far end of the field engrossed in the ritualistic rites that the laws of The Great Tourney prescribed for the reception of the five maidens.

Close beside Bohun two young knights sat their chargers, their eyes upon their king, and one of them held the bridle reins of a riderless horse.

Suddenly Bohun raised his hand and spurred across the field followed by his knights. They moved a little toward the end of the field where the knights of Nímmr were congregated so that the bulk of them were between this end of the field and Gobred's loge.

The young knight who had sat close beside Bohun, and his companion leading the riderless horse, spurred at a run straight for the stands of Nímmr and the loge of the Prince. As they drew abreast of it a knight leaped into the loge from the rear, swept Guinalda into his arms, tossed her quickly to the young knight waiting to receive her, sprang to the edge of the rail and leaped into the saddle of the spare horse being held in readiness for him; then they both wheeled and spurred away before the surprised Gobred or those about him could raise a hand to stay them. Behind them swept Bohun and the knights of The Sepulchre out toward the camp among the oaks.

Instantly all was pandemonium. A trumpeter in Gobred's loge sounded the alarm; the prince ran from the stands to the spot where his horse was being held by a groom; the Knights of Nímmr, ignorant of what had occurred, not knowing where to rally or against whom, milled about the lists for a few moments.

Then Gobred came, spurring swiftly before them. 'Bohun has stolen the Princess Guinalda!' he cried. 'Knights of Nímmr—' but before he could say more, or issue orders to his followers, a black knight on a black charger spurred roughly through the ranks of surrounding knights and was away after the retreating knights of The Sepulchre.

19

Lord Tarzan

There was a nasty smile upon Tollog's lips as he thought how neatly he had foiled Ateja, who would have warned Nasrâny of the plot to slay him, and he thanked Allah that chance had placed him in a position to intercept her before she had been able to ruin them all, and even as Tollog, the brother of the sheik, smiled in his beard a hand reached out of the darkness behind him and seized him by the throat – fingers grasped him and he was dragged away.

Into the beyt that had been Zeyd's and which had been set up for the Nasrâny, Tollog was dragged. He struggled and tried to scream for help, but he was powerless in the grip of steel that held him and choked him.

Inside the beyt a voice whispered in his ear. 'Cry out, Tollog,' it said, 'and I shall have to kill you,' and then the grasp upon his throat relaxed, but Tollog did not call for help, for he had recognised the voice that spoke and he knew that it had made no idle threat.

He lay still while the bonds were drawn tight about his wrists and ankles and a gag fastened securely in his mouth. He felt the folds of his burnous drawn across his face and then – silence.

He heard Stimbol creep into the beyt, but he thought that it was still he who had bound him. And thus died Tollog, the brother of Ibn Jad, died as he had planned that Tarzan of the Apes should die.

And, knowing that he would die thus, there was a smile upon the lips of the ape-man as he swung through the forest toward the south east.

Tarzan's quest was not for Bedúins but for Blake, and having assured himself that the white man in the menzil of Ibn Jad was Stimbol and that none knew the whereabouts of the other American he was hastening back to the locality where Blake's boys had told him their Bwana had disappeared, in the hope of picking up his trail, if unable to assist him, at least to learn what fate had overtaken him.

Tarzan moved swiftly and his uncanny senses of sight and smell aided him greatly in wresting its secrets from the jungle, yet it was three days before he found the spot where Ara the lightning had struck down Blake's gun bearer.

Here he discovered Blake's faint spoor leading toward the north. Tarzan shook his head, for he knew that there was a stretch of uninhabited forest lying between this place and the first Galla villages and he knew, too, that if Blake survived hunger and the menace of wild beasts he might only live to fall victim to a Galla spear.

For two days Tarzan followed a spoor that no other human eye might have discerned and upon the afternoon of the second day he came upon a great stone cross built directly in the centre of an ancient trail; but Tarzan saw the cross from the concealment of bushes for he moved as beasts of prey moved, taking advantage of every cover, suspicious of every strange object, always ready for flight or battle as occasion might demand.

And so it was that he did not walk blindly into the clutches of the two men-at-arms that guarded the outer way to the City of Nímmr. To his keen ears was borne the sound of their voices long before he saw them.

Even as Sheeta or Numa approached their prey so Tarzan of the Apes crept through the brush until he lay within a few yards of the men-at-arms and to his vast astonishment heard them conversing in a quaint form of English that, while understandable to him, seemed yet a foreign tongue. He marvelled at their antiquated costumes and obsolete weapons and in them he saw an explanation of Blake's disappearance and a suggestion of his fate.

For a time Tarzan lay watching the two with steady, unblinking eyes – it might have been Numa, himself weighing the chances of a sudden charge. He saw that each was armed with a sturdy pike and a sword. They could speak English, after a fashion; therefore, he argued, they might be able to give him word of Blake. But would they receive him in a friendly spirit or would they attempt to set upon and slay him?

He determined that he could never ascertain what their attitude would be by lying hidden among the brush and so he gathered himself, as Numa does when he is about to spring.

The two blacks were idly gossipping, their minds as far from thoughts of danger as it were possible they could be, when suddenly and without warning Tarzan launched himself full upon the back of the nearer, hurling him to the ground and before the other could gather his wits the ape-man had dragged his victim into the concealment of the bush from which he had sprung, while the fellow's companion turned and fled in the direction of the tunnel.

The man in Tarzan's grasp fought and struggled to be free but the ape-man held him as easily as he might have held a child.

'Lie still,' he advised; 'I shall not harm you.'

'Odsblud!' cried the black. 'What manner of creature be thou?'

'One who will not harm you if you will tell him the truth,' replied Tarzan.

'What wouldst thou know?' demanded the black.

'A white man came this way many weeks ago. Where is he?'

'Thou speakest of Sir James?' asked the soldier.

'Sir James!' mused Tarzan and then he recollected that Blake's first name was James. 'His name was James,' he replied; 'James Blake.'

'Verily, 'tis the same,' said the other.

'You have seen him? Where is he now?'

'He be defending the honour of Our Lord Jesus and the Knights of Nímmr in The Great Tourney in the lists upon the plain below the city, and have ye come to wreak despite upon our good Sir James thou wilt find many doughty knights and men-at-arms who will take up the gage in his behalf.'

'I am his friend,' said Tarzan.

'Then why didst thou leap upon me thus, if thou beest a friend to Sir James?' demanded the man.

'I did not know how you had received him or how you would receive me!'

'A friend of Sir James will be received well in Nímmr,' said the man.

Tarzan took the man's sword from him and permitted him to rise – his pike he had dropped before being dragged among the bushes.

'Go before me and lead me to your master,' commanded the ape-man, 'and remember that your life will be the forfeit that you must pay for treachery.'

'Do not make me leave the road unguarded against the Saracens,' begged the man. 'Soon my companion will return with others and then I shall beg them to take thee where thou wilt.'

'Very well,' agreed the ape-man and they had not waited long before he heard the sound of hastening footsteps and a strange jingling and clanking that might have been caused by the shaking of many chains and the striking against them of objects of metal.

Shortly afterwards he was surprised to see a white man clothed in chain mail and carrying a sword and buckler descending the trail at a trot, a dozen pikemen at his back.

'Tell them to halt!' commanded Tarzan, placing the point of the man's sword in the small of his back. 'Tell them I would talk with them before they approach too closely.'

'Stop, I pray thee!' cried the fellow. 'This be a friend of Sir James, but he wilt run me through with my own sword and ye press him too close. Parley with him, most noble sir knight, for I wouldst live at least to know the result of The Great Tourney.'

The knight halted a few paces from Tarzan and looked him up and down from feet to head. 'Thou art truly a friend to Sir James?' he demanded.

Tarzan nodded. 'I have been seeking him for days.'

'And some mishap befell thee and thou lost thy apparel.'

The ape-man smiled. 'I go thus, in the jungle,' he said.

'Art thou a sir knight and from the same country as Sir James?'

'I am an Englishman,' replied Tarzan of the Apes.

'An Englishman! Thrice welcome then to Nímmr. I be Sir Bertram and a good friend to Sir James.'

'And I am called Tarzan,' said the ape-man.

'And thy rank?' inquired Sir Bertram.

Tarzan was mystified by the strange manners and garb of his seemingly friendly inquisitor, but he sensed that whatever the man might be he took himself quite seriously and would be more impressed if he knew that Tarzan was a man of position, and so he answered him truthfully, in his quiet way.

'A Viscount,' he said.

'A peer of the realm!' exclaimed Sir Bertram. 'Prince Gobred wilt be o'er pleased to greet thee, Lord Tarzan. Come thou with me and I wilt furnish thee with apparel that befits thee.'

At the outer barbican Bertram took Tarzan into the quarters reserved for the knight commanding the warders and kept him there while he sent his squire to the castle to fetch raiment and a horse and while they waited Bertram told Tarzan all that had befallen Blake since his arrival in Nímmr and, too, much of the strange history of this unknown British colony.

When the squire returned with the clothing it was found that it fitted the ape-man well, for Bertram was a large man, and presently Tarzan of the Apes was garbed as a knight of Nímmr and was riding down toward the castle with Sir Bertram. Here the knight announced him at the gate as The Lord Viscount Tarzan and once within introduced him to another knight whom he persuaded to relieve him at the gate while he conducted Tarzan to the lists that he might be presented to Gobred and witness the final scenes of the tourney, were it not concluded before they arrived.

And so it was that Tarzan of the Apes, clad in chain mail and armed with lance and sword rode down into the Valley of The Sepulchre just as Bohun put his foul scheme into execution and carried off the Princess Guinalda.

Long before they reached the lists Bertram was aware that something was amiss, for they could see the dust clouds racing rapidly north, away from the lists as though one body of knights pursued another. He put spur to his mount and Tarzan followed suit and so they came at a stiff run to the lists and there found all pandemonium.

The women were mounting preparatory to riding back to Nímmr under escort of a few knights that Gobred had sent back to guard them. The men-at-arms were forming themselves into companies, but all was being done in a confused manner since every now and then a great part of the company would rush to the highest part of the stands and peer off toward the north after the clouds of dust that revealed nothing to them.

Sir Bertram accosted one of his fellows. 'What hath befallen?' he demanded.

'Bohun hath seized the Princess Guinalda and carried her away,' came the astounding reply.

'Zounds!' cried Bertram, reining about. 'Wilt ride with me in the service of our princess, Lord Tarzan?'

For answer Tarzan spurred his horse alongside of Bertram's and stirrup to stirrup the two set out across the plain, while far ahead of them Blake drew gradually closer and closer to the fleeing knights of The Sepulchre.

So thick the cloud of dust they threw up that they were hid from their pursuer even as he was hid from them and so were unaware that Blake was near them.

The American carried no lance nor shield, but his sword clattered and clashed at his side and at his right hip swung his forty-five. Whenever he had been armed, since he entered Nímmr, he had carried this weapon of another world and another age. To their queries he had answered that it was but a lucky talisman that he carried, but in his heart was the thought that some day it might stand him in better stead even than these simple knights and ladies could dream.

He knew that he would never use it except in battle, or as a last resort against overwhelming odds or unfair tactics; but he was glad that he carried it today as it might mean the difference between liberty and captivity for the woman he loved.

Slowly he drew closer to the rearmost knights of The Sepulchre. Their mounts, bred and trained to the utmost endurance and to carry great weight of man and mail, kept to a brisk canter even after the first long spurt of speed that had carried them away from the lists of Nímmr.

The dust rolled up in clouds from iron-shod feet. Through it Blake groped, catching vague glimpses of mounted men just ahead. The black – powerful, fleet, courageous – showed no sign of fatigue. The rider carried his sword in his hand, ready. He was no longer a black knight, but a grey. Bassinet, hauberk, all the rich caparisons of his horse, the horse itself, were grey with dust.

Blake glimpsed a knight toward whom he was slowly drawing closer. This knight was grey! Like a flash Blake realised the value of the camouflage that chance had laid upon him. He might ride among them and they would not suspect that he was not of them!

Instantly he sheathed his sword and pressed forward, but he edged off a little from the knight before he passed him. Urging the black ever a little faster than the others' chargers were going Blake crept up through the ranks of Bohun's knights. Somewhere a knight was carrying double and this knight he sought.

The nearer the head of the column he forged the greater became the danger of discovery, for now the dust was less thick and men could see farther; but yet his own armour, his face, the leopard skin of his bassinet were coated thick with grey, and though knights peered intently at him as he passed, none recognised him.

Once one hailed him. 'Ist thou, Percival?' he demanded.

'Nay,' replied Blake and spurred on a trifle faster.

Now, dimly, just ahead, he saw several knights bunched close and once he thought he glimpsed the fluttering garments of a woman in their midst. Pressing on, he drew close behind these and there, surrounded by knights, he saw a woman held before one of the riders.

Drawing his sword he spurred straight between two knights who rode close behind he who carried Guinalda and as he passed he cut to the right and left and the two knights rolled from their saddles.

At a touch of the spurs the black leaped abreast the young knight that was bearing off the princess. So quickly was the thing accomplished that happened then that the knights who rode scarce an arm's length from him had not the time to realise what was occurring and prevent it.

Blake slipped his left arm about the girl and at the same time thrust to the left above his left forearm, driving his blade far into the body of the youthful knight; then he spurred forward carrying Guinalda from the dead arms as the knight pitched headlong from his saddle.

Blake's sword was wrenched from his grasp, so far had he driven it into the body of the man who had dared commit this wrong against the woman Blake loved.

Cries of rage arose about him as knights spurred in pursuit and the black ran free with no guiding hand upon the reins. A huge fellow loomed close just at Blake's rear and another was closing in from the other side. The first man swung his sword as he stood in his stirrups and the second was already reaching for Blake with his point.

Strange oaths were on their lips and their countenances were contorted by rage as they strove to have the life of the rash man who had almost thwarted them in their design; but that he could succeed they had not the slightest belief, for he was one against a thousand.

Then something happened the like of which had never been known to them or their progenitors. A blue barrelled forty-five flashed from the holster at Blake's hip, there was a loud report and the knight upon Blake's right rear lunged headforemost to the ground. Blake turned in his saddle and shot the knight upon his other side between the eyes.

Terrified, the horses of other knights close by, who might have menaced him, bolted, as did the great black that Blake bestrode; but while the American was trying to replace his weapon in its holster and gather the reins in his right hand he leaned to the left and thus forced the horse slowly around in one direction he wished him to go, Blake's plan being to cut across the front of the knights of The Sepulchre and then turn southward toward Nímmr.

He was sure that Gobred and his followers must be close behind and that it would be but a matter of minutes before he would have Guinalda safe behind a thousand or more knights, any one of whom would lay down his life for her.

But the knights of The Sepulchre had spread out over a very much greater front than Blake had anticipated and now, presently, he saw them coming rapidly up upon his left and was forced to swerve in a more northerly direction.

Closer and closer they came and once more the American found it necessary to drop his reins and draw his forty-five. One shot sent the horses of the menacing knights rearing and plunging away from the terrifying sound, and it sent the black into a new paroxysm of terror that almost resulted in Blake and the girl being unhorsed.

But when the man finally brought the animal again under control the dust cloud that marked the position of the knights of The Sepulchre was far behind and close upon Blake's left was a great forest, whose dark depths offered concealment for the moment at least.

Reining quickly within, Sir James drew up and gently lowered Guinalda to the ground. Then he dismounted and tied the black to a tree, for Blake was spent after what he had been through this day since his first entry upon the lists, and the black was spent as well.

He slipped the housing and the heavy saddle from the horse's back and took the great bit from his mouth, replacing a portion of the housing to serve as a cooler until the horse should be less heated; nor once did he glance at the princess until he had finished caring for his horse.

Then he turned and faced her. She was standing leaning against a tree, looking at him.

'Thou art a brave, sir knight,' she said softly, and then added, arrogantly, 'but still a boor.'

Blake smiled, wanly. He was very tired and had no wish to argue.

'I'm sorry to ask you to do it,' he said, ignoring what she had said to him, 'but Sir Galahad here will have to be kept moving about a bit until he cools off and I'm too fagged to do it.'

The Princess Guinalda looked at him in wide-eyed amaze. 'Ye – ye,' she stammered, 'ye mean that I should lead the beast? I, a princess!'

'I can't do it Guinalda,' replied Blake. 'I tell you I'm just about all in, lugging all these skid chains about since sunrise. I guess you'll have to do it.'

'Have to! Durst thou command, knave?'

'Snap out of it, kid!' advised Blake curtly. 'I'm responsible for your safety and it may all depend on this horse. Get busy, and do as I tell you! Lead him back and forth slowly.'

There were tears of rage in the eyes of the Princess Guinalda as she prepared to make an angry retort, but there was something in Blake's eyes that silenced her. She looked at him for a long moment and then turned and walked to the black. Untying the rope that tethered him to the tree she led him slowly to and fro, while Blake sat with his back against a great tree and watched out across the plain for the first sign of pursuit.

But there was no pursuit, for the knights of Nímmr had overtaken the knights of The Sepulchre and the two forces were engaging in a running fight that was leading them farther and farther away towards the City of The Sepulchre upon the north side of the valley.

Guinalda led the black for half an hour. She led him in silence and in silence Blake sat gazing out across the valley. Presently he turned toward the girl and rose to his feet.

'That'll be good,' he said, approaching her. 'Thank you. I'll rub him a bit now. I was too exhausted to do it before.'

Without a word she turned the black over to him and with dry leaves he rubbed the animal from muzzle to dock. When he had finished he threw the housing over him again and came and sat down beside the girl.

He let his eyes wander to her profile – to her straight nose, her short upper lip, her haughty chin. 'She is beautiful,' thought Blake, 'but selfish, arrogant and cruel;' but when she turned her eyes toward him, even though they passed over him as though he had not been there, they seemed to belie all the other evidence against her.

He noticed that her eyes were never quiet. Her glances roved from place to place, but most often into the depths of the wood and upward among the branches of the trees. Once she started and turned suddenly to gaze intently into the forest.

'What is it?' asked Blake.

'Methought something moved within the wood,' she said. 'Let us be gone.'

'It is almost dusk,' he replied. 'When it is dark we can ride to Nímmr in safety. Some of Bohun's knights may still be searching for you.'

'What!' she exclaimed. 'Remain here until dark? Knowest thou not where we be?'

'Why, what's wrong with this place?' demanded the man.

She leaned toward him, her eyes wide with terror. 'It be The Wood of the Leopards!' she whispered.

'Yes?' he queried casually.

'Here lair the great leopards of Nímmr,' she continued, 'and after night falls only a camp with many guards and beast-fires be safe from them, and even so not always then, for they have been known to leap upon a warder and, dragging him into the wood, devour him within hearing of the camp.

'But,' suddenly her eyes responded to a new thought, 'I hadst forgot the strange, roaring weapon with which thou slew the knights of Bohun! Of a surety with that thou coulds't slay all the leopards of the wood!'

Blake hesitated to undeceive her and add to her alarm. 'Perhaps,' he said, 'it will be as well to start now, for we have a long ride and it will soon be dark.'

As he spoke he started towards Sir Galahad. He had almost reached the horse when the animal suddenly raised its head and with up-pricked ears and dilated nostrils looked into the gathering shadows of the wood. For an instant Sir Galahad trembled like a leaf and then, with a wild snort, he lay back with all his weight upon the tether and as it parted with a snap he wheeled and raced out upon the plain.

Blake drew his gun and peered into the wood, but he saw nothing nor could his atrophied sense of smell catch the scent that had come so clearly to the nostrils of Sir Galahad.

Eyes that he could not see were watching him, but they were not the eyes of Sheeta the leopard.

20

'I Love You!'

Lord Tarzan rode with Sir Bertram in the wake of the knights of Nímmr, nor did they overtake them until after Blake had borne Guinalda out of the battle which had followed immediately the hosts of Gobred had overhauled the knights of The Sepulchre.

As the two approached, Tarzan saw opposing knights paired off in mortal combat. He saw a knight of Nímmr go down before an adversary's lance and then the victor espied Tarzan.

'Have at you, sir knight!' cried he of The Sepulchre, and couched his lance and put spurs to his charger.

This was a new experience for the ape-man, a new adventure, a new thrill. He knew as much about jousting as he did about ping-pong, but from childhood he had wielded a spear, and so he smiled as the iron knight thundered down upon him.

Lord Tarzan waited and the knight of The Sepulchre was disconcerted to see his adversary awaiting him, motionless, his spear not even couched to receive him.

Lord Bertram had reined in his horse to watch the combat and observe how this English peer accounted for himself in battle and he too was perplexed. Was the man mad, or was he fearful of the issue?

As his antagonist approached him Tarzan rose in his stirrups and carried his lance hand above and behind his head and when the tip of the other's lance was yet five paces from him the ape-man launched the heavy weapon as he had so often launched his hunting spear and his war spear in the chase and in battle.

It was not Viscount Greystoke who faced the knight of The Sepulchre; it was not the king of the great apes; it was the chief of the Waziri and no other arm in all the world could cast a war spear as could his.

Forward his spear hand shot; straight as an arrow sped the great lance. It struck the shield of the knight of the Sepulchre just above the boss and, splitting the heavy wood, drove into the heart of Tarzan's foe, and at the same instant the ape-man reined his horse aside as that of his fallen antagonist thundered past.

Sir Bertram shook his head and spurred to meet an antagonist that had just challenged him. He was not sure that the act of Lord Tarzan had been entirely ethical, but he had to admit that it had been magnificent.

The fortunes of the battle carried Tarzan toward the west. His lance gone, he fought with his sword. Luck and his great strength and wondrous agility carried him through two encounters. By this time the battle had drawn off toward the north east.

Tarzan had accounted for his second man since he had lost his lance and a knight of The Sepulchre had slain a knight of Nímmr. Now these two remained alone upon the field, nor did the other lose a moment in shouting his challenge at the ape-man.

Never in his life had Tarzan seen such fierce, bold men, such gluttons for battle. That they gloried in conflict and in death with a fierce lust that surpassed the maddest fanaticism he had ever witnessed filled Tarzan's breast with admiration. What men! What warriors!

Now the last knight was upon him. Their swords clashed on ready buckler. They wheeled and turned and struck back. They passed and spurred once more to close quarters. Each rose in his stirrups to deliver a terrific cut, each sought to cleave the other's skull.

The blade of the knight of The Sepulchre glanced from Tarzan's buckler and bit into the skull of the ape-man's charger, but Tarzan's edge smote true.

As his horse went down Tarzan leaped free, his antagonist falling dead at his feet, while the riderless horse of the slain knight galloped swiftly off in the direction in which lay The City of The Sepulchre.

Tarzan looked about him. He was alone upon the field. Far to the north and east he saw the dust of battle. The City of Nímmr lay across the plain toward the south. When the battle was over it was there that Blake would ride and it was Blake whom Tarzan wanted to find. The sun was sinking behind the western hills as Tarzan turned toward Nímmr.

The chain mail that he wore was heavy, hot and uncomfortable and Tarzan had not gone far before he discarded it. He had his knife and his rope. These he always kept with him, but he left the sword with the armour and with a sigh of relief continued on his way.

Ibn Jad, as he had come across the valley from The City of The Sepulchre towards the city that he had seen upon the opposite side, had been perturbed by the great clouds of dust that had been raised by the knights of The Sepulchre and the pursuing Nímmrians.

Seeing a forest close upon his right hand he had thought it wiser to seek its concealing shadows until he could learn more concerning that which caused so great a dust cloud, which he saw was rapidly approaching.

Within the forest it was cool and here Ibn Jad and his followers rested.

'Let us remain here,' suggested Abd-el-Aziz, 'until evening, when we may approach the city under cover of darkness.'

Ibn Jad approved the plan and so they camped just within the forest and waited. They watched the dust cloud pass and continue on toward The City of The Sepulchre.

'Billah, it is well we did escape that village before yon host returned,' said Ibn Jad.

They saw a horseman enter the forest, or pass to the south of it – they could not know which – but they were not interested in single horsemen, or in any horseman, so they did not investigate. He seemed to be either carrying another person upon his horse with him, or some great bundle. At a distance they could not see which.

'Perhaps,' said Abd-el-Aziz, 'we shall find greater treasure in the city to the south.'

'And perhaps the beautiful woman of whom the Sáhar spoke,' added Ibn Jad, 'for she was not within the city we left this morning.'

'There were some there that were beautiful,' said Fahd.

'The one I seek is more beautiful than a houri,' said Ibn Jad.

When they took up their march again just before dark they moved cautiously just within the edge of the forest. They had covered a mile, perhaps, when those in the lead heard voices ahead. Ibn Jad sent one to investigate.

The man was soon back. His eyes were bright with excitement. 'Ibn Jad,' he whispered, 'thou needst seek no farther – the houri is just ahead!'

Following the suggestion of the scout Ibn Jad, followed by his companions, went deeper into the woods and approached Blake and Guinalda from the west. When Sir Galahad broke loose and Blake drew his forty-five Ibn Jad knew that they could remain in concealment no longer. He called Fahd to him.

'Many of the Nasrânys speak the language thou didst learn among the soldiers of the North,' he said; 'speak thou therefore to this one in the same tongue, telling him we are friends and that we are lost.'

When Fahd saw the Princess Guinalda his eyes narrowed and he trembled almost as might a man with ague. Never in his life had Fahd seen so beautiful a woman; never had he dreamed that a houri might be so lovely.

'Do not fire upon us,' he called to Blake from the concealment of some bushes. 'We are friends. We are lost.'

'Who are you?' demanded Blake, surprised to hear French spoken in The Valley of The Sepulchre.

'We are poor men from the desert country,' replied Fahd. 'We are lost. Help us to find our way and the blessings of Allah shall be upon thee.'

'Come out and let me see you,' said Blake. 'If you are friendly you need not fear me. I've had all the trouble I'm looking for.'

Fahd and Ibn Jad stepped out into view and at sight of them Guinalda voiced a little scream and seized Blake's arm. 'The Saracens!' she gasped.

'I guess they're Saracens all right,' said Blake, 'but you needn't worry – they won't hurt you.'

'Not harm a Crusader?' she demanded incredulously.

'These fellows never heard of a Crusader.'

'Melikes not the way they look at me,' whispered Guinalda.

'Well, neither do I, but perhaps they mean no harm.'

With many smiles the 'Aarab gathered around the two and through Fahd, Ibn Jad repeated his protestations of friendship and his delight at meeting one who could direct him from the valley. He asked many questions about the City of Nímmr and all the while his followers pressed closer to Blake.

Of a sudden the smiles vanished from their faces as, at a signal from their sheik, four stalwart Bedúins leaped upon the American and bore him to the ground, snatching his gun from him; while simultaneously two others seized the Princess Guinalda.

In a moment Blake was securely bound and the 'Aarab were debating what disposition to make of him. Several wanted to slit his throat, but Ibn Jad counselled against it since they were in a valley filled with the man's friends and should the fortunes of war decide to throw some of the Beduw into the hands of the enemy such would fare better if they spared this one's life.

Blake threatened, promised, begged that they give Guinalda her liberty, but Fahd only laughed at him and spit upon him. For a time it seemed almost certain that they were going to kill Blake, as one of the Bedúins stood over him with a keen khûsa in his hand, awaiting the word from Ibn Jad.

It was then that Guinalda tore free from those who held her and threw herself upon Blake to shield his body from the blade with her own.

'Thou shalt not slay him!' she cried. 'Take my life an' thou must have Christian blood, but spare him.'

'They cannot understand you, Guinalda,' said Blake. 'Perhaps they will not kill me; but that does not matter. You must escape them.'

'Oh, they must not kill thee – they shall not! Canst ever forgive me the cruel words I spoke? I did not mean them. My pride was hurt that thou shouldst say of me what Malud told me thou didst say and so I spoke to hurt thee and not from my heart. Canst forgive me?'

'Forgive you? God love you, I could forgive you murder! But what did Malud tell you I had said?'

'Oh, mind not now. I care not what thou said. I tell thee I forgive it! Say to me again thy words that thou didst speak when I pinned my favour upon they hauberk and I can forgive thee anything.'

'What did Malud say?' insisted Blake.

'That thou hadst bragged that thou wouldst win me and then cast my love aside,' she whispered.

'The cur! You must know that he lied, Guinalda.'

'Say what I have asked and I shall know he lied,' she insisted.

'I love you! I love you, Guinalda!' cried Blake.

The Arabs laid heavy hands upon the girl and dragged her to her feet. Ibn Jad and the others still argued about the disposition to be made of Blake.

'By Ullah!' exclaimed the sheik, at last, 'we shall leave the Nasrâny where he lies and if he die none can say that the Beduw did slay him.

'Abd-el-Aziz,' he continued, 'let thou take men and continue across the valley to that other city. Come, I shall accompany you a way and we will talk out of hearing of this Nasrâny who, perchance, understandeth more of our tongue than he would have us guess.'

As they moved away toward the south Guinalda tried to free herself again from the grasp of her captors, but they dragged her with them. Yet until the last Blake saw her struggling and saw her dear face turned toward him and as they passed out of sight among the trees she called back through the falling night three words that meant more to him than all the languages of all the world combined – 'I love you!'

At a distance from Blake the 'Aarab halted. 'I leave thee here, Abdel-Aziz,' said Ibn Jad. 'Go thou and see if the city appears to be a rich place and if it be too strongly guarded make no attempt to loot it, but return to the menzil that will be just beyond the northern summit where it now is, or, if we move it, we shall make our trail plain that you may follow us.

'I shall hasten from the valley with this rich treasure that we now have, not the least of which is the woman. Billah! In the north she will fetch the ransom of a dozen sheik.

'Go, Abd-el-Aziz, and may Allah be with thee!'

Ibn Jad turned directly north. His belief that the great body of horsemen he had glimpsed amid the distant dust were returning to the city he had sacked argued against his attempting to leave the valley by the same route that he had entered it, and so he had determined to attempt to scale the steep mountains at a point west of The City of The Sepulchre, avoiding the castle and its defenders entirely.

Blake heard the retreating footsteps of the Bedúins die away in the distance. He struggled with his bonds, but the camel-leather held securely. Then he lay quiet. How silent, how lonely the great, black wood – the Wood of the Leopards! Blake listened. Momentarily he expected to hear the fall of padded feet, the sound of a great, furred body approaching through the underbrush. The slow minutes dragged. An hour had passed.

The moon rose – a great, swollen, red moon that floated silently up from behind distant mountains. This moon was looking down upon Guinalda as it was on him. He whispered a message to it – a message for his princess. It was the first time that Blake ever had been in love and he almost forgot his bonds and the leopards in recalling those three words that Guinalda had tossed back at the instant of their separation.

What was that? Blake strained his eyes into the darkness of the shadowy wood. Something was moving! Yes, it was the sound of stealthy, padded feet – the scraping of a furred body against leaves and twigs. The leopard of the wood was coming!

Hark! There must be another in a nearby tree, for he was sure that he could see a shadowy form almost above him.

The moonlight, shining from the low moon near the eastern horizon, crept beneath the trees and lighted the ground upon which Blake lay and beyond him for a dozen yards and more.

Presently into this moonlit space stepped a great leopard.

Blake saw the blazing eyes, felt them burning into him like fire. He could not tear his own from the great snarling figure, where it was held in awful fascination.

The carnivore crouched and crept closer. Inch by inch it crept upon him as though with the studied cruelty of premeditated torture. He saw the sinuous tail lashing from side to side. He saw the great fangs bared. He saw the beast flatten itself against the ground, its muscles tensed. It was about to spring! Helpless, horrified, Blake could not take his eyes from the hideous, snarling face.

He saw it leap suddenly with the lightness and agility of a house cat and at the same instant he saw something flash through the air. The leopard stopped in mid-leap and was jerked backward and then Blake's astonished eyes saw it being hauled upward into a tree that overhung the spot.

He saw the shadowy form that he had seen before, but now he saw that it was a man and that it was hauling the leopard upward by a rope that had been cast about its neck at the instant that it had risen to leap upon him.

Screaming, pawing with raking talons, Sheeta the leopard was dragged upward. A mighty hand reached out and grasped the great cat by the scruff of the neck and another hand drove a knife blade into the savage heart.

When Sheeta ceased to struggle, and hung quiet, the hand released its grasp and the dead body of the carnivore thudded to the ground beside Blake. Then the god-like figure of an almost naked white man dropped lightly to the leafy mould.

Blake voiced an exclamation of surprised delight. 'Tarzan of the Apes!' he cried.

'Blake?' demanded the ape-man, and then: 'At last! And I didn't find you much too soon, either.'

'I'll tell the world you didn't!' exclaimed Blake.

Tarzan cut the bonds that held the American.

'You've been looking for me?' asked Blake.

'Ever since I learned that you had become separated from your safari.'

'By George, that was white of you!'

'Who left you trussed up here?'

'A bunch of Arabs.'

Something like a growl escaped the lips of the ape-man. 'That villainous old Ibn Jad here?' he demanded incredulously.

'They took a girl who was with me,' said Blake. 'I do not need to ask you to help me rescue her, I know.'

'Which way did they go?' asked Tarzan.

'There,' and Blake pointed toward the south.

'When?'

'About an hour ago.'

'You'd better shed that armour,' advised Tarzan, 'it makes walking a punishment – I just tried it.'

With the ape-man's help Blake got out of his coat of mail and then the two set out upon the plain trail of the 'Aarab. At the point where Ibn Jad had turned back toward the north they were at a loss to know which of the two spoors to follow, for here the footprints of Guinalda, that the ape-man had been able to pick up from time to time since they left the spot where the girl had been seized, disappeared entirely.

They wondered what had become of them and they could not know that here, when she found that Ibn Jad was going to turn back with her away from Nímmr, she had refused to walk farther. It had been all right as long as they were approaching Nímmr, but she refused absolutely to be a party to her own abduction when it led away from home.

What breeze there was blowing from the east, nullifying the value of Tarzan's sense of smell and even the great ape-man could not know in what direction or with which party Guinalda had been carried off.

'The most reasonable assumption,' said Tarzan, 'is that your princess is with the party that has gone north, for I know that Ibn Jad's menzil must lie in that direction. He did not enter the valley from the south. That I know because I just came in that way myself and Sir Bertram assured me that there are only two entrances – the one through which I came and a pass above the City of The Sepulchre.

'Ibn Jad would want to get the girl out of the valley and into his camp as soon as possible whether he is going to hold her for ransom or take her north to sell her. The party that went south toward Nímmr may have been sent to treat with her people for a ransom; but the chances are that she is not with that party.

'However, it is at best but a matter of conjecture. We must ascertain definitely and I suggest that you follow the northern spoor, which is, I am certain, the one that will lead to the girl, while I overtake the party to the south.

'I can travel faster than you and if I am right and the girl is with the northern party I'll turn back and overtake you without much loss of time. If you catch up with the other band and find that the girl is not with them, you can turn back and join me, but if she is with them you'd better not risk trying to recover her until you have help, for you are unarmed and those Bedúins would think no more of cutting your throat than they would of drinking a cup of coffee.

'Now, goodbye and good luck!' and Tarzan of the Apes was off at a trot upon the trail of the party that had gone in the direction of Nímmr, while Blake turned northward to face a dismal journey through the black depths of The Wood of the Leopards.

21

'For Every Jewel a Drop of Blood!'

All night Ibn Jad and his party marched northward and though they were hampered by the refusal of Guinalda to walk, yet they made rapid progress for they were spurred on by their great desire to escape from the valley with their booty before they should be discovered and set upon by the great host of fighting men they were now convinced were quartered in the castle and city they had been fortunate enough to find almost deserted.

Avarice gave them strength and endurance far beyond that which they normally displayed, with the result that dawn found them at the foot of the ragged mountains that Ibn Jad had determined to scale rather than attempt an assault upon the castle which guarded the easy way from the valley.

It was a jaded party that won eventually to the pass just above the outer barbican that guards the road to The City of The Sepulchre, nor were they discovered by the warders there until the last man of them was safely on the trail leading to the low saddle at the summit of the mountains, beyond which lay the menzil of the Bedúins.

The defenders of the barbican made a sortie against them and approached their rear so closely that the sir knight who commanded saw Guinalda and recognised her, but a volley from the matchlocks of the desert people sent the crudely-armed soldiers of Bohun back in retreat, though the brave knight couched his lance and charged again until his horse was brought down by a bullet and he lay pinned beneath the carcass of the animal.

It was afternoon before Ibn Jad with his fagged company staggered into the menzil and though they dropped in their tracks from sheer exhaustion he allowed them but an hour of sleep before he gave the signal for the ráhla, for the sheik of the fendy el-Guâd was filled with an ever increasing fear that the treasure and the woman would be taken away from him before he could reach the sandy wastes of his own barren Béled.

The heavy weight of the treasure had been divided into several bundles and these were distributed among his least mistrusted followers, while the custody of the girl captive was placed in the hands of Fahd, whose evil eyes filled the princess with fear and loathing.

Stimbol, who had secretly scoffed at the stories of treasure and the mad tales of a beautiful woman that the 'Aarab expected to find in some fabulous, hidden city, was dumbfounded when he viewed the spoils of the Bedúin raid, and at first was inclined to attribute them to the hallucinations of his fever-racked brain.

Weak, he staggered feebly along the trail, keeping as close to Fahd as he could, for he knew that of all the company this unscrupulous scoundrel would be most likely to assist him, for to Fahd a live Stimbol meant great wealth; nor was Fahd unmindful of the fact. And now there was another purpose in the evil mind of the Bedúin who had conceived for the white girl an infatuation that was driving him to the verge of madness.

With the wealth that Stimbol had promised him Fahd realised that he could afford to possess this lovely houri whom otherwise a poor Bedùwy must sell for the great price that she would bring, and so there revolved in the mind of Fahd many schemes whereby he might hope to gain sole possession of both Guinalda and Stimbol; but always there loomed in the path of every plan that he considered the dour figure of his greedy sheik.

At the foot of the Mountains of The Sepulchre Ibn Jad turned toward the east, planning to thus avoid passing again through the country of Batando. Beyond the eastern end of the range he would turn south again and later strike west just above the northern limits of the territory that was nominally Tarzan's, for though he knew that the Lord of the Jungle was dead he yet feared the vengeance of his people.

It was late before Ibn Jad made camp. The preparations for the evening meal were hurried. The light from the cooking fire and the paper lanterns in the beyt of the sheik was dim and flickering, yet not so dim but that Ateja saw Fahd drop something into the bowl of food that she had prepared for Ibn Jad and which stood upon the ground between him and his would-be assassin.

As the sheik reached for the receptacle Ateja stepped from the women's quarters and struck it from his hand, but before she could explain her act or charge Fahd with his villainy the culprit, realising that his perfidy had been discovered leaped to his feet and seizing his matchlock sprang into the women's quarters where Guinalda had been left under the watchful care of Hirfa and Ateja.

Seizing the girl by the wrist and dragging her after him Fahd broke through the curtains at the rear of the beyt and ran in the direction of his own tent. By this time the mukaad of Ibn Jad was in an uproar. The sheik was demanding an explanation from Ateja and still unaware that Fahd had escaped through the rear of the beyt no one had followed him into the women's quarters.

'He placed *simm* in thy food!' cried Ateja. 'I saw him and the proof of it be that he fled when he knew that I had seen.'

'Billah!' exclaimed Ibn Jad. 'The son of a jackal would poison me? Seize him and fetch him to me!'

'He hath fled through the beyt!' cried Hirfa, 'and taken the Nasrawîa with him.'

The Bedúins sprang to their feet and took after Fahd but at his own beyt he stopped them with a bullet and they retreated. In his own tent he seized Stimbol who was lying upon a filthy sleeping mat and dragged him to his feet.

'Hasten!' he hissed in the American's ear. 'Ibn Jad has ordered that thou be slain! Quick! follow me and I will save thee.'

Again Fahd had recourse to the rear curtains of a beyt and as his fellows approached the front in anger but with caution, Fahd, dragging Guinalda and followed by Stimbol, sneaked through the darkness of the menzil and turned toward the west.

It was dusk when James Blake, following the plain trail of Ibn Jad, finally clambered over the final escarpment and stood upon the trail that led through the pass toward the outer world beyond the Valley of The Sepulchre.

A hundred yards to his right loomed the grey towers of the barbicans; to his left was the trail that led in the direction of his heart's desire and all about him concealed in the bushes, were the men-at-arms of King Bohun of The Sepulchre; but this he did not guess, for how could he know that for hours the eyes of the warders had been watching his slow ascent toward the pass trail?

Spent by the long climb following hours of gruelling exertion without food or rest, unarmed, Blake was helpless to resist or to attempt escape when a dozen armed men stepped from the surrounding bushes and encircled him in a band of steel, and so Sir James of Nímmr was seized and haled before King Bohun and when he was questioned and Bohun found that he was the same black knight that had thwarted his plan to abduct the Princess Guinalda he could scarce contain himself.

Assuring Blake only of the fact that he would be put to death as soon as Bohun could determine upon a fate commensurate with the heinousness of the crime, the king ordered him to be placed in chains and the American was led away by guards to a black hole beneath the castle, where by the light of flares a smith forged a heavy iron band about one ankle and he was chained to a damp stone wall.

In the light of the flare Blake saw two emaciated, naked creatures similarly chained and in a far corner glimpsed a skeleton among the bones of which rusted a length of chain and a great anklet. Then they left him, taking the flares with them, and James Blake was left in darkness and despair.

Upon the plain, below the City of Nímmr, Tarzan had overtaken the party of Bedúins led by Abd-el-Aziz and after assuring himself that the girl was not with them he had turned without revealing himself to them and hurried northward to take up the trail of the other party.

Requiring food and rest he lay up in The Wood of the Leopards during the heat of the day after stalking Horta the boar and making a quick kill. His belly filled, the ape-man found a high flung tree crotch where there was little likelihood of the heavy leopards of Nímmr disturbing his slumbers and here he slept until the sun was sinking behind the western mountains and early the following morning he reached the deserted menzil where Ibn Jad's people had camped during his incursion of the Valley of The Sepulchre.

Some time since, he had lost the spoor of Blake, but that of the girl frequently recurred and as her rescue now took precedence over other considerations he followed doggedly along the trail of Ibn Jad. For a time he was mystified by the fact that Guinalda's spoor, well marked by the imprints of the tiny sandals of medieval design, did not appear among the footprints of those who left the Bedúin menzil and he lost some time searching about in an effort to discover a clue to the riddle and presently he hit upon the truth, which lay in the fact that Guinalda's light sandals having been badly worn by her journey and far too tight for comfortable walking she had been given a pair belonging to Ateja and thus it became difficult to differentiate between the spoor of the two girls, who were of equal weight and of a similarity of carriage that rendered their footprints practically identical.

Tarzan therefore contented himself with following the spoor of the party and so it was that he passed their first night's camp, where Fahd had stolen Guinalda from the sheik, without discovering that three of its members had there turned to the west, while the main body of the 'Aarab marched toward the east.

And as Tarzan followed the spoor of Ibn Jad a hundred stalwart Waziri moved northward from the water hole of the smooth, round rocks upon the old trail of the Bedúins.

With them was Zeyd, who had begged so hard to accompany them when they passed the village where he had been waiting that at last the sub-chief consented.

When Tarzan overtook the 'Aarab they had already turned south around the eastern end of the Mountains of The Sepulchre. He saw the bags they carried and the evident concern with which Ibn Jad watched and guarded them and he shrewdly guessed that the wily old thief had indeed found the treasure he had sought; but he saw no evidence of the presence of the Princess, and Stimbol, too, was missing.

Tarzan was furious. He was furious at the thieving Bedúins for daring to invade his country and he was furious at himself because he felt that in some way he had been tricked.

Tarzan had his own methods of inflicting punishment upon his enemies and he had, as well, his own grim and grisly sense of humour. When men were doing wrong it pleased him to take advantage of whatever might cause them the greater suffering and in this he was utterly ruthless with his enemies.

He was confident that the 'Aarab thought him dead and it did not suit his whim to reveal their error to them at this time, but it did accord with his fancy to let them commence to feel the weight of his displeasure and taste the first fruits of their villainy.

Moving silently through the trees Tarzan paralleled the course of the 'Aarab. They were often plainly visible to him, but none saw Tarzan, nor dreamed that savage eyes were watching their every move.

Five men carried the treasure, though its weight was not so great but that one powerful man might have borne it for a short distance. Tarzan watched these men most often, these and the Sheik Ibn Jad.

The trail was wide and the sheik walked beside one of those who bore the treasure. It was very quiet in the jungle. Even the 'Aarab, garrulous among themselves, were quiet, for they were very tired and the day was hot and they were unused to the burdens they were forced to carry since Batando had robbed them of their slaves.

Of a sudden, without warning and with only the swish of its flight through the air to announce it, an arrow passed through the neck of the Bedúin who walked beside Ibn Jad.

With a scream the man lunged forward upon his face and the 'Aarab, warned by their sheik, cocked their muskets and prepared to receive an attack, but look where they would they saw no sign of an enemy. They waited, listening, but there was no sound other than the droning of insects and the occasional raucous cry of a bird; but when they moved on again, leaving their fellow dead upon the trail, a hollow voice called to them from a distance.

'For every jewel a drop of blood!' it wailed dismally, for its author knew well the intensely superstitious nature of the desert dwellers and how best to affright them.

It was a shaken column that continued on its way, nor was there any mention of making camp until almost sunset, so anxious were they all to leave behind this gloomy wood and the horrid afrit that inhabited it; but the forest persisted and at length it became necessary to make camp.

Here the camp fires and food relieved the tension upon their overwrought nerves and their spirits had revived to such an extent that there were again singing and laughter in the menzil of Ibn Jad.

The old Sheik himself sat in his mukaad surrounded by the five bags of treasure, one of which he had opened and beneath the light of a lantern was fondling the contents. About him were his cronies, sipping their coffee.

Something fell heavily upon the ground before the beyt and rolled into the mukaad among them. It was the severed head of a man! Glaring up at them were the dead eyes of their fellow, whose corpse they had left lying in the trail earlier in the day.

Horror-struck, spellbound, they sat staring at the gruesome thing when, from out of the dark forest, came the hollow voice again: 'For every jewel a drop of blood!'

Ibn Jad shook as a man with ague. The men of the camp gathered close together in front of the beyt of the sheik. Each grasped a musket in one hand and searched for his hijab with the other, for each carried several of these amulets and that in demand this night was the one written against the jan, for certainly none but a djin could have done this thing.

Hirfa stood half within the mukaad staring at the dead face of her fellow while Ateja crouched upon a sleeping mat in the quarters of the women. She did not see the back curtain rise, nor the figure that crept within. It was dark in the quarters of the hareem since little light filtered in from the lanterns in the mukaad.

Ateja felt a hand clapped across her mouth at the same instant that another grasped her by the shoulder. A voice whispered in her ear. 'Make no sound! I shall not hurt thee. I am a friend to Zeyd. Tell me the truth and no harm will befall you or him. Where is the woman Ibn Jad brought from the valley?'

He who held her placed his ear close to her lips and removed his hand from them. Ateja trembled like a leaf. She had never seen a djin; she could not see the creature that leaned close above her; but she knew that it was one of those fearsome creatures of the night.

'Answer!' whispered the voice in her ear. 'If thou wouldst save Zeyd, speak and speak the truth!'

'Fahd took the woman from our menzil last night,' she gasped. 'I do not know where they went.'

As it came, in silence the presence left the side of the terrified girl. When Hirfa sought her a moment later she found her in a swoon.

22
Bride of the Ape

Blake squatted upon the stone floor in the utter darkness of his dungeon. After his jailers had left he had spoken to his fellow-prisoners, but only one had replied and his jibbering tones assured the American that the poor wretch had been reduced to stark insanity by the horrors of imprisonment in this foul hole.

The young man, accustomed to freedom, light, activity, already felt the hideousness of his position and wondered how long it would be before he, too, jibbered incoherently at the end of a rusting chain; how long before he, too, was but mildewed bones upon a clammy floor.

In utter darkness and in utter silence there is no time, for there is no means by which one may compute the passage of time. How long Blake crouched in the stifling air of his dank dungeon he could not know. He slept once; but whether he had dozed for an instant or slept the clock around he could not even hazard a guess. And of what moment was it? A second, a day, a year meant nothing here. There were only two things that could mean anything to Jim Blake now – freedom or death. He knew that it would not be long before he would welcome the latter.

A sound disturbed the silence of the buried vault. Footsteps were approaching. Blake listened as they came nearer. Presently he discerned a flickering light that grew in intensity until a pine torch illuminated the interior of his prison. At first it blinded his eyes so that he could not see who came, bearing the light; but whoever it was crossed and stopped before him.

Blake looked up, his eyes more accustomed to the unwonted brilliance, and saw two knights standing before him.

'It be he,' said one.

'Dost thou not know us, Sir Black Knight?' demanded the other.

Blake looked at them closely. A slow smile lighted his face, as he saw a great bandage wrapped about the neck of the younger of the two.

'I suppose,' he said, 'here is where I get mine.'

'Get thine! What meanest thou?' demanded the older man.

'Well, you two certainly haven't come to pin any medals on me, Sir Wildred,' said Blake, with a wry smile.

'Thou speakest in riddles,' said Wildred. 'We have come to free thee that the young king may not bring disgrace upon the Knights of The Sepulchre by carrying out his wicked will with thee. Sir Guy and I heard that he would burn thee at the stake, and we said to one another that while blood flowed in our bodies we would not let so valorous a knight be thus shamelessly wronged by any tyrant.'

As he spoke Wildred stooped and with a great rasp commenced filing upon the iron rivets that held the hinged anklet in place.

'You are going to help me to escape!' exclaimed Blake. 'But suppose you are discovered – will not the king punish you?'

'We shall not be discovered,' said Wildred, 'though I would take that chance for so noble a sir knight as thee. Sir Guy be upon the outer barbican this night and 'twill be no trick to get thee that far. He can pass thee through and thou canst make thy way down the mountain side and cross to Nímmr. We cannot get thee through the city gates for these be held by two of Bohun's basest creatures; but perchance upon the morrow Sir Guy or I may find the way to ride out upon the plain with a led horse and that we shall if so it hap that it be possible.'

'Tell us of a thing that hath filled us with questioning,' said Sir Guy.

'I don't follow you,' said Blake.

'Thou didst, and mighty prettily too, take the Princess Guinalda from under the very nose of Bohun,' continued Guy, 'and yet later she was seen in the clutches of the Saracens. How came this to pass?'

'She was seen?' demanded Blake. 'Where?'

'Beyond the outer barbican she was and the Saracens carried her away through the pass that leadeth no man knoweth where,' said Wildred.

Blake told them of all that had transpired since he had taken Guinalda from Bohun and by the time he had finished the rivets had been cut and he stood again a free man.

Wildred smuggled him through secret passages to his own quarters and there gave him food and new clothing and a suit of armour, for now that they knew he was riding out over the pass into the strange country they had decided that he could only be permitted to do so properly armoured, armed and mounted.

It was midnight when Wildred smuggled Blake through the castle gate and rode with him toward the outer barbican. Here Sir Guy met them and a few minutes later Blake bid these chivalrous enemies goodbye and, mounted on a powerful charger, his own colours flying from his lance tip, rode beneath the portcullis and out upon the starlit road that led to the summit of the Mountains of The Sepulchre.

Toyat, the king ape, picked a succulent beetle from the decaying bark of a fallen tree. About him were the great, savage people of his tribe. It was afternoon and the apes loafed in the shade of great trees beside a little natural clearing in the jungle. They were content and at peace with all the world.

Coming toward them were three people, but the wind blew from the apes toward the people and so neither Toyat nor any of his fellows caught the scent spoor of the Tarmangani. The jungle trail was soft with damp mould, for it had rained the night before, and the feet of the three gave forth no sound that the apes heard as yet. Then, too, the three were moving cautiously for they had not eaten for two days and they were hunting for food.

There was a grey old man, emaciated by fever, tottering along with the aid of a broken tree branch; there was a wicked-eyed Bedúin carrying a long musket; and the third was a girl whose strange garmenture of splendid stuffs was torn and soiled. Her face was streaked with dirt and was drawn and thin, yet still it was a face of almost heavenly beauty. She walked with an effort and though she sometimes stumbled from weariness never did she lose a certain regality of carriage, nor lower the haughty elevation of her well-moulded chin.

The Bedúin was in the lead. It was he who first sighted a young ape playing at the edge of the clearing, farthest from the great bulls of the tribe of Toyat. Here was food! The Bedúin raised his ancient weapon and took aim. He pressed the trigger and the ensuing roar mingled with the scream of pain and terror that burst from the wounded balu.

Instantly the great bulls leaped to action. Would they flee the feared and hated thunder-stick of the Tarmangani, or would they avenge the hurting of the balu? Who might know? Today they might do the one, tomorrow, under identical circumstances, the other. Today they chose vengeance.

Led by Toyat, growling hideously, the bulls lumbered forward to investigate. It was this sight that met the horrified gaze of the three as they followed up Fahd's shot to learn if at last they were to eat or if they must plod on hopelessly, weakened by the hunger gnawing at their vitals.

Fahd and Stimbol turned and bolted back down the trail, the Arab, in his cowardly haste, pushing Guinalda to one side and hurling her to the ground. The leading bull, seeing the girl, leaped upon her and was about to sink his teeth into her neck when Toyat seized him and dragged him from her, for Toyat had recognised her for what she was and the king ape had once seen another Tarmangani she, and had decided that he would like to have one as a wife.

The other ape, a huge bull, seeing that Toyat wanted the prey and angered by the bullying manner of the king, immediately decided to contest Toyat's right to what he had first claimed. Baring his fangs he advanced menacingly toward Toyat who had dragged the girl back into the clearing.

Toyat snarled back at him. 'Go away,' said Toyat. 'This is Toyat's she.'

'It is Go-yad's,' replied the other, advancing.

Toyat turned back. 'I kill!' he screamed.

Go-yad came on and suddenly Toyat seized Guinalda in his hairy arms and fled into the jungle. Behind him, bellowing and screaming, pursued Go-yad.

The Princess Guinalda, wide-eyed with horror, fought to free herself from the hideous, hairy creature that was bearing her off. She had never seen or even heard of such a thing as a great ape and she thought them now some hideous, low inhabitant of that outer world that she had always been taught consisted of encircling armies of Saracens and beyond and at a great distance a wonderful country known as England. What else was there she had not even tried to guess, but evidently it was a horrid place peopled by hideous creatures, including dragons.

Toyat had run no great distance when he realised that he could not escape while burdened with the she and as he had no mind to give her up he turned suddenly and faced the roaring Go-yad. Go-yad did not stop. He came on frothing at the mouth, bristling, snarling – a picture of bestial savagery, power and frenzied rage.

Toyat, relinquishing his hold upon the girl, advanced to meet the charge of his rebellious subject, while Guinalda, weakened by unaccustomed exertion and lack of nourishment, appalled by the hideous circumstances of her plight, sank panting to the ground.

Toyat and Go-yad, immersed in the prospect of battle, were oblivious to all else. Could Guinalda have taken advantage of this temporary forgetfulness of her she might have escaped; but she was too stunned, too exhausted to take advantage of her opportunity. Spellbound, fascinated by the horror of it, she watched these terrifying, primordial man-beasts preparing to do battle for possession of her.

Nor was Guinalda the sole witness of these savage preliminaries. From the concealment of a low bush behind which he lay another watched the scene with steady, interested eyes. Absorbed by their own passion neither Toyat nor Go-yad noted the occasional movement of the outer leaves of the bush behind which this other watcher lay, a movement imparted by the body of the watcher with each breath and with each slightest change of position.

Perhaps the watcher discovered no sporting interest in the impending duel, for just as the two apes were about to engage he arose and stepped into the open – a great black-maned lion, whose yellow coat gleamed golden in the sunlight.

Toyat saw him first and with a growl of rage turned and fled leaving his adversary and their prize to whatever fate Providence might hold in store for them.

Go-yad, thinking his rival had abandoned the field through fear of him, beat loudly upon his breast and roared forth the victory cry of the bull ape; then, swaggering as became a victor and a champion, he turned to claim the prize.

Between himself and the girl he saw the lion standing, gazing with serious mien straight into his eyes. Go-yad halted. Who would not have? The lion was within springing distance but he was not crouched. Go-yad backed away, snarling, and when the lion made no move to follow, the great ape suddenly turned and lumbered off into the jungle, casting many a backward glance in the direction of the great cat until intervening foliage shut him from his view.

Then the lion turned toward the girl. Poor little Princess! Hopeless, resigned, she lay upon the ground staring, wide-eyed, at this new engine of torture and destruction. The king of beasts surveyed her for a moment and then walked slowly toward her. Guinalda clasped her hands and prayed – not for life, for hope of that she had long since resigned, but for death, speedy and painless.

The tawny beast came close. Guinalda closed her eyes to shut out the fearsome sight. She felt hot breath upon her cheek, its fetid odour assailed her nostrils. The lion sniffed about her. God! why did he not end it? Tortured nerves could endure no more and Guinalda swooned. Merciful surcease of her sufferings.

23

Jad-Bal-Ja ...

Nerve shaken, the remnants of Ibn Jad's company turned toward the west and hastened by forced marches to escape the hideous forest of the djin. Abd-el-Aziz and those who had accompanied him from The Wood of the Leopards toward Nímmr had not rejoined them, nor ever would they, for upon the plain below the treasure city of the Bedúins' dreaming the knights of Gobred had discovered them and, despite the thundering havoc of the ancient matchlocks, the iron knights of Nímmr had couched their spears against the Saracens and once again the victorious *cri de guerre* of the Crusaders had rung out after seven centuries of silence to announce a new engagement in the hoary war for the possession of The Holy Land – the war that is without end.

From the north a mailed knight rode down through the forests of Galla land. A blue and silver pennon fluttered from his lance. The housings of his great charger were rich with gold and silver from the treasure vaults of Wildred of The Sepulchre. Wide-eyed Galla warriors viewed this solitary anachronism from afar, and fled.

Tarzan of the Apes, ranging westward, came upon the spoor of Fahd and Stimbol and Guinalda and followed it toward the south.

Northward marched a hundred ebon giants, veterans of a hundred battles – the famed Waziri – and with them came Zeyd, the lover of Ateja. One day they came upon a fresh spoor crossing their line of march diagonally toward the south west. It was the spoor of Arab sandals – those of two men and a woman – and when the Waziri pointed them out to Zeyd the young Bedúin swore that he recognised those of the woman as belonging to Ateja, for who knew better the shape and size of her little foot, or the style of the sandals she fabricated? He begged the Waziri to turn aside for a time and aid him in finding his sweetheart, and while the sub-chief was debating the question in his mind the sound of something hurrying through the jungle attracted the attention of every ear.

While they listened a man staggered into view. It was Fahd. Zeyd recognised him instantly and as immediately became doubly positive that the footprints of the woman had been made by Ateja.

Zeyd approached Fahd menacingly. 'Where is Ateja?' he demanded.

'How should I know? I have not seen her for days,' replied Fahd, truthfully enough.

'Thou liest!' cried Zeyd, and pointed at the ground. 'Here lie her own footprints beside thine!'

A cunning expression came into the eyes of Fahd. Here he saw an opportunity to cause suffering to the man he hated. He shrugged his shoulders.

'Wellah, if you know, you know,' he said.

'Where is she?' demanded Zeyd.

'She is dead. I would have spared you,' answered Fahd.

'Dead?' The suffering in that single word would have melted a heart of stone – but not Fahd's.

'I stole her from her father's beyt,' continued Fahd, wishing to inflict as much torture as possible upon his rival. 'For days and nights she was mine; then a huge ape stole her from me. By now she must be dead.'

But Fahd had gone too far. He had encompassed his own undoing. With a scream of rage Zeyd leaped upon him and with drawn khûsa and before the Waziri could interfere or Fahd defend himself the keen blade had drank thrice in the heart of the lying Bedúin.

With bent head and dull eyes Zeyd marched on northward with the Waziri, as, a mile behind them, a wasted old man, burning with fever, stumbled in the trail and fell. Twice he tried to regain his feet, only to sink weakly back to earth. A filthy, ragged bundle of old bones, he lay – sometimes raving in delirium, sometimes so still that he seemed dead.

Down from the north came Tarzan of the Apes upon the spoor of Guinalda and the two who had accompanied her. Knowing well the windings of the trail he took short cuts, swinging through the branches of the trees, and so it happened that he missed the Waziri at the point where their trail had encountered that of Fahd, where Zeyd had slain his rival, and presently his nostrils picked up the scent of the Mangani in the distance.

Toward the great apes he made his way swiftly for he feared that harm might befall the girl should she, by any mischance, fall into the hands of the anthropoids and he arrived in the clearing where they lazed, a short time after the return of Toyat and Go-yad, who, by now, had abandoned their quarrel, since the prize had been taken by one stronger than either of them.

The preliminaries of meeting over and the apes having recognised and acknowledged Tarzan he demanded if any had seen the Tarmangani she who had recently passed through the jungle.

M'walat pointed at Toyat and Tarzan turned toward the king.

'You have seen the she?' demanded Tarzan, fearful, for he did not like the manner of the king ape.

Toyat jerked a thumb toward the south. 'Numa,' he said and went on hunting for food, but Tarzan knew what the ape meant as surely as though he had spoken a hundred words of explanation.

'Where?' asked Tarzan.

Toyat pointed straight to where he had abandoned Guinalda to the lion and the ape-man, moving straight through the jungle along the line indicated by the king ape, went sadly to investigate, although he already guessed what he would find. At least he could drive Numa from his kill and give decent burial to the unfortunate girl.

Slowly consciousness returned to Guinalda. She did not open her eyes, but lay very quiet wondering if this were death. She felt no pain.

Presently a sickly sweet and pungent odour assailed her nostrils and something moved very close to her, so close that she felt it against her body, pressing gently, and where it pressed she felt heat as from another body.

Fearfully she opened her eyes and the horror of her predicament again swept over her for she saw that the lion had lain down almost against her. His back was toward her, his noble head was lifted, his black mane almost brushed her face. He was looking off, intently, toward the north.

Guinalda lay very quiet. Presently she felt, rather than heard, a low rumbling growl that seemed to have its origin deep in the cavernous chest of the carnivore.

Something was coming! Even Guinalda sensed that; but it could not be succour, for what in all the world could succour her from this hideous beast?

There was a rustling among the branches of the trees a hundred feet away and suddenly the giant figure of a demi-god dropped to the ground. The lion rose and faced the man. The two stood thus, eyeing one another for a brief moment. Then the man spoke.

'Jad-bal-ja!' he exclaimed, and then: 'Come to heel!'

The great, golden lion whined and strode across the open space, stopping before the man. Guinalda saw the beast look up into the face of the demi-god and saw the latter stroke the tawny head affectionately; but meanwhile the eyes of the man, or god, or whatever he was, were upon Guinalda and she saw the sudden relief that came to them as Tarzan realised that the girl was unharmed.

Leaving the lion the ape-man crossed to where the princess lay and knelt beside her.

'You are the Princess Guinalda?' he asked.

The girl nodded, wondering how he knew her. As yet she was too stunned to command her own voice.

'Are you hurt?' he asked.

She shook her head.

'Do not be afraid,' he assured her in a gentle voice. 'I am your friend. You are safe now.'

There was something in the way he said it that filled Guinalda with such a sense of safety as all the mailed knights of her father's realm had scarce imparted.

'I am not afraid – any more,' she said simply.

'Where are your companions?' he asked.

She told him all that had happened.

'You are well rid of them,' said the ape-man, 'and we shall not attempt to find them. The jungle will account for them in its own way and in its own good time.'

'Who art thou?' asked the girl.

'I am Tarzan.'

'How didst thou know my name?' she queried.

'I am a friend of one whom you know as Sir James,' he explained. 'He and I were searching for you.'

'Thou art his friend?' she cried. 'Oh, sweet sir, then thou art mine as well!'

The ape-man smiled. 'Always!' he said.

'Why did the lion not kill thee, Sir Tarzan?' she demanded, thinking him a simple knight, for in her land there were only these beside the members of her princely house and the pseudo king of The City of The Sepulchre, for in the original company that had been wrecked upon the coast of Africa at the time of the Third Crusade there were only knights, except one bastard son of Henry II who had been the original Prince Gobred. Never having been in contact with an English king since they parted from Richard at Cyprus no Gobred had assumed the right to issue patents of nobility to his followers, solely the prerogative, of the king.

'Why did the lion not kill me!' repeated Tarzan. 'Because he is Jad-bal-ja, The Golden Lion, whom I raised from cubhood. All his life he has known me only as friend and master. He would not harm me and it was because of his life-long association with human beings that he did not harm you; though I was fearful, when I saw him beside you that he had, for a lion is always a lion!'

'Thou dwellest nearby?' asked the girl.

'Far away,' said Tarzan; 'but there must be some of my people nearby, else Jad-bal-ja would not be here. I sent for my warriors and doubtless he has accompanied them.'

Finding that the girl was hungry Tarzan bade The Golden Lion remain and guard her while he went in search of food.

'Do not fear him,' he told her, 'and remember that you could not have a protector more competent than he to discourage the approach of enemies.'

'And well mayst I believe it,' admitted Guinalda.

Tarzan returned with food and then, as the day was not done, he started back towards Nímmr with the rescued girl, carrying her, as she was now too weak to walk and beside them strode the great, black-maned lion of gold.

During that journey Tarzan learned much of Nímmr and also discovered that Blake's love for his princess was apparently fully reciprocated by the girl, for she seemed never so content as when talking about her Sir James and asking questions concerning his far country and his past life, of which, unfortunately, Tarzan could tell her nothing.

Upon the second day the three came to the great cross and here Tarzan hailed the warders and bade them come and take their princess.

She urged the ape-man to accompany her to the castle and receive the thanks of her father and mother, but he told her that he must leave at once to search for Blake, and at that she ceased her urging.

'And thou findst him,' she said, 'tell him that the gates of Nímmr be always open to him and that the Princess Guinalda awaits his return.'

Down from The Cross went Tarzan and Jad-bal-ja and before she turned back to enter the tunnel that led to her father's castle the Princess Guinalda stood watching them until a turn in the trail hid them from her view.

'May Our Lord Jesus bless thee, sweet sir knight,' she murmured, 'and watch o'er thee and fetch thee back once more with my beloved!'

24

Where Trails Met

Down through the forest rode Blake searching for some clue to the whereabouts of the Arabs, ranging this way and that, following trails and abandoning them.

Late one day he came suddenly in to a large clearing where once a native village had stood. The jungle had not yet reclaimed it and as he entered it he saw a leopard crouching upon the far side and before the leopard lay the body of a human being. At first Blake thought the poor creature dead, but presently he saw it attempt to rise and crawl away.

The great cat growled and advanced toward it. Blake shouted and spurred forward, but Sheeta paid no attention to him, evidently having no mind to give up its prey; but as Blake came nearer the cat turned to face him with an angry growl.

The American wondered if his horse would dare the close proximity of the beast of prey, but he need not have feared, nor would he had he been more fully acquainted with the customs of The Valley of The Sepulchre, where one of the greatest sports of the knights of the two enemy cities is hunting the giant cats with lance alone when they venture from the sanctuary of The Wood of the Leopards.

The charger that Blake bestrode had faced many a savage cat, and larger, too, by far than this one and so he fell into his charging stride with no show of fear or nervousness and the two thundered down upon Sheeta while the creature that was to have been its prey looked on with wide, astounded eyes.

Within the length of its spring Sheeta rose swiftly to meet the horse and man. He leaped and as he leaped he struck full on the metal tip of the great lance and the wooden shaft passed through him so far that it was with difficulty that the man forced the carcass from it.

When he had he turned and rode to the side of the creature lying helpless on the ground.

'My God!' he cried as his eyes rested on the face below him. 'Stimbol!'

'Blake!'

The younger man dismounted.

'I'm dying, Blake,' whispered Stimbol. 'Before I go I want to tell you that I'm sorry. I acted like a cad. I guess I've got what was coming to me.'

'Never mind that, Stimbol,' said Blake. 'You're not dead yet. The first thing is to get you where there are food and water.' He stooped and lifted the emaciated form and placed the man in his saddle. 'I passed a small native village a few miles back. They all ran when they saw me, but we'll try there for food.'

'What are you doing here?' asked Stimbol. 'And, in the name of King Arthur, where did you get that outfit?'

'I'll tell you about it when we get to the village,' said Blake. 'It's a long story. I'm looking for a girl that was stolen by the Arabs a few days ago.'

'God!' ejaculated Stimbol.

'You know something about her?' demanded Blake.

'I was with the man that stole her,' said Stimbol; 'or at least who stole her from the other Arabs.'

'Where is she?'

'She's dead, Blake!'

'Dead?'

'A bunch of those big anthropoid apes got her. The poor child must have been killed immediately.'

Blake was silent for a long time, walking with bowed head as, weighed down by heavy armour, he led the horse along the trail.

'Did the Arabs harm her?' he asked presently.

'No,' said Stimbol. 'The sheik stole her either for ransom or to sell her in the north, but Fahd stole her for himself. He took me along because I had promised him a lot of money if he'd save me and I kept him from harming the girl by telling him that he'd never get a cent from me if he did. I felt sorry for the poor child and I made up my mind that I was going to save her if I could.'

When Blake and Stimbol approached the village the blacks again fled, leaving the white men in full possession of the place and it did not take Blake long to find food for them both.

Making Stimbol as comfortable as possible, Blake found fodder for his horse and presently returned to the old man. He was engaged in narrating his experiences when he was suddenly aware of the approach of many people. He could hear voices and the pad of naked feet. Evidently the villagers were returning.

Blake prepared to meet them with friendly overtures, but the first glimpse he had of the approaching party gave him a distinct shock, for these were not the frightened villagers he had seen scurrying into the jungle a short time before.

With white plumes waving above their heads a company of stalwart warriors came swinging down the trail. Great oval shields were upon their backs, long war spears in their hands.

'Well,' said Blake. 'I guess we're in for it. The villagers must have sent for their big brothers.'

The warriors entered the village and when they saw Blake they halted in evident surprise. One of their number approached him and to Blake's surprise addressed him in fairly good English.

'We are the Waziri of Tarzan,' he said. 'We search for our chief and master. Have you seen him, Bwana?'

The Waziri! Blake could have hugged them. He had been at his wits end to know what he was to do with Stimbol. Alone he never could have brought the man to civilisation, but now he knew that his worries were over.

Had it not been for the grief of Blake and Zeyd it had been a merry party that made free with the cassava and beer of the villagers that night, for the Waziri were not worrying about their chief.

'Tarzan cannot die,' said the sub-chief to Blake, when the latter asked if the other felt any fear as to the safety of his master, and the simple conviction of the quiet words almost succeeded in convincing Blake of their truth.

Along the trail plodded the weary 'Aarab of the Beny Sâlem fendy el-Guâd. Tired men staggered beneath the weight of half-loads. The women carried even more. Ibn Jad watched the treasure with greedy eyes. An arrow came from nowhere and pierced the heart of a treasure-bearer close before Ibn Jad. A hollow voice sounded from the jungle: 'For every jewel a drop of blood!'

Terrified, the Bedúins hastened on. Who would be next? They wanted to cast aside the treasure, but Ibn Jad, greedy, would not let them. Behind them they caught a glimpse of a great lion. He terrified them because he did not either come nearer or go away – he just stalked silently along behind. There were no stragglers.

An hour passed; the lion paced just within sight of the tail end of the column. Never had the head of one of Ibn Jad's columns been so much in demand. Everyone wished to go in the lead.

A scream burst from another treasure carrier. An arrow had passed through his lungs. 'For every jewel a drop of blood!'

The men threw down the treasure. 'We will not carry the accursed thing more!' they cried, and again the voice spoke.

'Take up the treasure, Ibn Jad!' it said. 'Take up the treasure! It is thou who murdered to acquire it. Pick it up, thief and murderer, and carry it thyself!'

Together the 'Aarab made the treasure into one load and lifted it to Ibn Jad's back. The old sheik staggered beneath the weight.

'I cannot carry it!' he cried aloud. 'I am old and I am not strong.'

'Thou canst carry it, or – die!' boomed the hollow voice, while the lion stood in the trail behind them, his steady eyes glaring fixedly at them.

Ibn Jad staggered on beneath the great load. He could not now travel as fast as the others and so he was left behind with only the lion as company; but only for a short time. Ateja saw his predicament and came back to his side, bearing a musket in her hands.

'Fear not,' she said, 'I am not the son thou didst crave, but yet I shall protect thee even as a son!'

It was almost dusk when the leaders of the Bedúin company stumbled upon a village. They were in it and surrounded by a hundred warriors before they realised that they were in the midst of the one tribe of all others they most feared and dreaded – the Waziri of Tarzan.

The sub-chief disarmed them at once.

'Where is Ibn Jad?' demanded Zeyd.

'He cometh!' said one.

They looked back along the trail and presently Zeyd saw two figures approaching. One was a man bent beneath a great load and the other was that of a young girl. What he did not see was the figure of a great lion in the shadows behind them.

Zeyd held his breath because, for an instant, his heart had stopped beating.

'Ateja!' he cried and ran forward to meet her and clasp her in his arms.

Ibn Jad staggered into the village. He took one look at the stern visages of the dread Waziri and sank weakly to the ground, the treasure almost burying him as it fell upon his head and shoulders.

Hirfa voiced a sudden scream as she pointed back along the trail and as every eye turned in that direction a great golden lion stepped into the circle of the firelight in the village and at its side strode Tarzan, Lord of the Jungle.

As Tarzan entered the village Blake came forward and grasped his hand.

'We were too late!' said the American sadly.

'What do you mean?' asked the ape-man.

'The Princess Guinalda is dead!'

'Nonsense!' exclaimed Tarzan. 'I left her this morning at the entrance to the city of Nímmr.'

A dozen times Tarzan was forced to assure Blake that he was not playing a cruel joke upon him. A dozen times Tarzan had to repeat Guinalda's message: 'And thou findst him tell him that the gates of Nímmr be always open to him and that the Princess Guinalda awaits his return!'

Later in the evening Stimbol, through Blake, begged Tarzan to come to the hut in which he lay.

'Thank God!' exclaimed the old man fervently. 'I thought that I had killed you. It has preyed on my mind and now that I know that it was not you I believe that I can recover.'

'You will be taken care of properly, Stimbol,' said the ape-man, 'and as soon as you are well enough you will be taken to the coast,' then he walked away. He would do his duty by the man who had disobeyed him and tried to kill him, but he would not feign a friendship he did not feel.

The following morning they prepared to leave the village. Ibn Jad and his Arabs, with the exception of Zeyd and Ateja, who had asked to come and serve Tarzan in his home, were being sent to the nearest Galla village under escort of a dozen Waziri. Here they would be turned over to the Galla and doubtless sold into slavery in Abyssinia.

Stimbol was borne in a litter by four stout Waziri as the party prepared to take up its march toward the south and the country of Tarzan. Four others carried the treasure of The City of The Sepulchre.

Blake, dressed again in his iron mail, bestrode his great charger as the column started out of the village and down the trail into the south. Tarzan and the Golden Lion stood beside him. Blake reached down and extended his hand to the ape-man.

'Goodbye, sir!' he said.

'Goodbye?' demanded Tarzan. 'Aren't you coming home with us?'

Blake shook his head.

'No,' he said, 'I am going back into the Middle Ages with the woman I love!'

Tarzan and Jad-bal-ja stood in the trail watching as Sir James rode out toward the city of Nímmr, the blue and silver of his pennon fluttering bravely from the iron tip of his great lance.

TARZAN AND THE LOST EMPIRE

1

Nkima danced excitedly upon the naked, brown shoulder of his master.

He chattered and scolded, now looking up inquiringly into Tarzan's face and then off into the jungle.

'Something is coming, Bwana,' said Muviro, sub-chief of the Waziri. 'Nkima has heard it.'

'And Tarzan,' said the ape-man.

'The Big Bwana's ears are as keen as the ears of Bara the antelope,' said Muviro.

'Had they not been, Tarzan would not be here today,' replied the ape-man, with a smile. 'He would not have grown to manhood had not Kala, his mother, taught him to use all of the senses that Mulungu gave him.'

'What comes?' asked Muviro.

'A party of men,' replied Tarzan.

'Perhaps they are not friendly,' suggested the black. 'Shall I warn the warriors.'

Tarzan glanced about the little camp where a score of his black fighting men were busy preparing their evening meal and saw that, as was the custom of the Waziri, their weapons were in order and at hand.

'No,' he said. 'It will, I believe, be unnecessary, as these people who are approaching do not come stealthily as enemies would, nor are their numbers so great as to cause us any apprehension.'

But Nkima, a born pessimist, expected only the worst, and as the approaching party came nearer his excitement increased. He leaped from Tarzan's shoulder to the ground, jumped up and down several times and then, springing back to Tarzan's side, seized his arm and attempted to drag him to his feet.

'Run, run!' he cried, in the language of the apes. 'Strange Gomangani are coming. They will kill little Nkima.'

'Do not be afraid, Nkima,' said the ape-man. 'Tarzan and Muviro will not let the strangers hurt you.'

'I smell a strange Tarmangani,' chattered Nkima. 'There is a Tarmangani with them. The Tarmangani are worse than the Gomangani. They come with thundersticks and kill little Nkima and all his brothers and sisters. They kill the Mangani. They kill the Gomangani. They kill everything with their thundersticks. Nkima does not like the Tarmangani. Nkima is afraid.'

To Nkima, as to the other denizens of the jungle, Tarzan was no Tarmangani, no white man. He was of the jungle. He was one of them, and if they thought of him as being anything other than just Tarzan it was as Mangani, a great ape, that they classified him.

The advance of the strangers was now plainly audible to everyone in the camp. The Waziri warriors glanced into the jungle in the direction from which the sounds were coming and then back to Tarzan and Muviro, but when they saw that their leaders were not concerned they went quietly on with their cooking.

A tall, black warrior was the first of the party to come within sight of the camp. When he saw the Waziri he halted and an instant later a bearded white man stopped beside him.

For an instant the white man surveyed the camp and then he came forward, making the sign of peace. Out of the jungle a dozen or more blacks followed him. Most of them were porters, there being but three or four rifles in evidence.

Tarzan and the Waziri realized at once that it was a small and harmless party, and even Nkima, who had retreated to the safety of a nearby tree, showed his contempt by scampering fearlessly back to climb to the shoulder of his master.

'Doctor von Harben!' exclaimed Tarzan, as the bearded stranger approached. 'I scarcely recognized you at first.'

'God has been kind to me, Tarzan of the Apes,' said von Harben, extending his hand. 'I was on my way to see you and I have found you a full two days' march sooner than I expected.'

'We are after a cattle-killer,' explained Tarzan. 'He has come into our kraal several nights of late and killed some of our best cattle, but he is very cunning: I think he must be an old lion to outwit Tarzan for so long.

'But what brings you into Tarzan's country, Doctor? I hope it is only a neighbourly visit and that no trouble has come to my good friend, though your appearance belies my hope.'

'I, too, wish that it were nothing more than a friendly call,' said von Harben, 'but as a matter of fact I am here to seek your help because I am in trouble – very serious trouble, I fear.'

'Do not tell me that the Arabs have come down again to take slaves or to steal ivory, or is it that the leopard men are waylaying your people upon the jungle trails at night?'

'No, it is neither the one nor the other. I have come to see you upon a more personal matter. It it about my son, Erich. You have never met him.'

'No,' said Tarzan; 'but you are tired and hungry. Let your men make camp here. My evening meal is ready; while you and I eat you shall tell me how Tarzan may serve you.'

As the Waziri, at Tarzan's command, assisted von Harben's blacks in making their camp, the doctor and the ape-man sat cross-legged upon the ground and ate the rough fare that Tarzan's Waziri cook had prepared.

Tarzan saw that his guest's mind was filled with the trouble that had brought him in search of the ape-man, and so he did not wait until they had finished the meal to reopen the subject, but urged von Harben to continue his story at once.

'I wish to preface the real object of my visit with a few words of explanation,' commenced von Harben. 'Erich is my only son. Four years ago, at the age of nineteen, he completed his university course with honours and received his first degree. Since then he has spent the greater part of his time in pursuing his studies in various European universities, where he has specialized in archæology and the study of dead languages. His one hobby, outside of his chosen field, has been mountain-climbing and during successive summer vacations he scaled every important Alpine peak.

'A few months ago he came here to visit me at the mission and immediately became interested in the study of the various Bantu dialects that are in use by the several tribes in our district and those adjacent thereto.

'While pursuing his investigation among the natives he ran across that old legend of The Lost Tribe of the Wiramwazi Mountains, with which we are all so familiar. Immediately his mind became imbued, as have the minds of so many others, with the belief that this fable might have originated in fact and that if he could trace it down he might possibly find descendants of one of the lost tribes of Biblical history.'

'I know the legend well,' said Tarzan, 'and because it is so persistent and the details of its narration by the natives so circumstantial, I have thought that I should like to investigate it myself, but in the past no necessity has arisen to take me close to the Wiramwazi Mountains.'

'I must confess,' continued the doctor, 'that I also have had the same urge many times. I have upon two occasions talked with men of the Bagego tribe that live upon the slopes of the Wiramwazi Mountains and in both instances I have been assured that a tribe of white men dwells somewhere in the depths of that great mountain range. Both of these men told me that their tribe has carried on trade with these people from time immemorial and each assured me that he had often seen members of The Lost Tribe both upon occasions of peaceful trading and during the warlike raids that the mountaineers occasionally launched upon the Bagego.

'The result was that when Erich suggested an expedition to the Wiramwazi I rather encouraged him, since he was well fitted to undertake the adventure. His knowledge of Bantu and his intensive, even though brief, experience among the natives gave him an advantage that few scholars otherwise equipped by education to profit by such an expedition would have, while his considerable experience as a mountain-climber would, I felt, stand him in good stead during such an adventure.

'On the whole I felt that he was an ideal man to lead such an expedition, and my only regret was that I could not accompany him, but this was impossible at the time. I assisted him in every way possible in the organization of his safari and in equipping and provisioning it.

'He has not been gone a sufficient length of time to accomplish any considerable investigation and return to the mission, but recently a few of the members of his safari were reported to me as having returned to their villages. When I sought to interview them thy avoided me, but rumours reached me that convinced me that all was not well with my son. I therefore determined to organise a relief expedition, but in all my district I could find only these few men who dared accompany me to the Wiramwazi Mountains, which, their legends assure them, are inhabited by malign spirits – for, as you know, they consider The Lost Tribe of the Wiramwazi to be a band of bloodthirsty ghosts. It became evident to me that the deserters of Erich's safari had spread terror through the district.

'Under the circumstances I was compelled to look elsewhere for help and naturally I turned, in my perplexity, to Tarzan, Lord of the Jungle … Now you know why I am here.'

'I will help you, Doctor,' said Tarzan, after the other had concluded.

'Good!' exclaimed von Harben; 'but I knew that you would. You have about twenty men here, I should judge, and I have about fourteen. My men can act as carriers, while yours, who are acknowledged to be the finest fighting men in Africa, can serve as askaris. With you to guide us we can soon pick up the trail and with such a force, small though it be, there is no country that we cannot penetrate.'

Tarzan shook his head. 'No, Doctor,' he said, 'I shall go alone. That is always my way. Alone I may travel much more rapidly and when I am alone the jungle holds no secrets from me – I shall be able to obtain more information along the way than would be possible were I accompanied by others. You know the jungle people consider me as one of themselves. They do not run away from me as they would from you and these blacks.'

'You know best,' said von Harben. 'I should like to accompany you. I should like to feel that I am doing my share, but if you say no I can only abide by your decision.'

'Return to your mission, Doctor, and wait there until you hear from me.'

'And in the morning you leave for the Wiramwazi Mountains?' asked von Harben.

'I leave at once,' said the ape-man.

'But it is already dark,' objected von Harben.

'There is a full moon and I wish to take advantage of it,' explained the other. 'I can lie up in the heat of the day for what rest I need.' He turned and called Muviro to him. 'Return home with my warriors, Muviro,' he instructed, 'and hold every fighting man of the Waziri in readiness in the event that I find it necessary to send for you.'

'Yes, Bwana,' replied Muviro; 'and how long shall we wait for a message before we set out for the Wiramwazi Mountains in search of you?'

'I shall take Nkima with me and if I need you I shall send him back to fetch and to guide you.'

'Yes, Bwana,' replied Muviro. 'They will be in readiness – all the fighting men of the Waziri. Their weapons will be at hand by day and by night and fresh war-paint will be ready in every pot.'

Tarzan swung his bow and his quiver of arrows across his back. Over his left shoulder and under his right arm lay the coils of his grass rope and at his hip dangled the hunting-knife of his long-dead sire. He picked up his short spear and stood for a moment with head up, sniffing the breeze. The firelight played upon his bronzed skin.

For a moment he stood thus, every sense alert. Then he called to Nkima in the tongue of the ape folk and as the little monkey scampered toward him, Tarzan of the Apes turned without a word of farewell and moved silently off into the jungle, his lithe carriage, his noiseless tread, his majestic mien suggesting to the mind of von Harben, a personification of another mighty jungle animal, Numa the lion, king of beasts.

2

Erich von Harben stepped from his tent upon the slopes of the Wiramwazi Mountains to look upon a deserted camp.

When he had first awakened, the unusual quiet of his surroundings had aroused within him a presentiment of ill, which was augmented when repeated calls for his body-servant, Gabula, elicited no response.

For weeks, as the safari had been approaching the precincts of the feared Wiramwazi, his men had been deserting by twos and threes until the preceding evening when they had made this camp well upon the mountain slopes only a terrified remnant of the original safari had remained with him. Now even these, overcome during the night by the terrors of ignorance and superstition, had permitted fear to supplant loyalty and had fled from the impending and invisible terrors of this frowning range, leaving their master alone with the bloodthirsty spirits of the dead.

A hasty survey of the camp site revealed that the blacks had stripped von Harben of everything. All of his supplies were gone and his gun carriers had decamped with his rifles and all of his ammunition, with the exception of a single Luger pistol and its belt of ammunition that had been in the tent with him.

Erich von Harben had had sufficient experience with these natives to understand fairly well the mental processes based upon their deep-rooted superstition that had led them to this seemingly inhuman and disloyal act and so he did not place so much blame upon them as might another less familiar with them.

While they had known their destination when they embarked upon the undertaking, their courage had been high in direct proportion to the great distance that they had been from the Wiramwazi, but in proportion as the distance lessened with each day's march their courage had lessened until now upon the very threshold of horrors beyond the ken of human minds the last vestige of self-control had deserted them and they had fled precipitately.

That they had taken his provisions, his rifles and his ammunition might have seemed the depth of baseness had von Harben not realized the sincerity of their belief that there could be no possible hope for him and that his immediate death was a foregone conclusion.

He knew that they had reasoned that under the circumstances it would be a waste of food to leave it behind for a man who was already as good as dead when they would need it for their return journey to their villages, and likewise, as the weapons of mortal man could avail nothing against the ghosts of Wiramwazi, it would have been a needless extravagance to have surrendered fine rifles and quantities of ammunition that von Harben could not use against his enemies of the spirit world.

Von Harben stood for some time looking down the mountain slope toward the forest, somewhere in the depths of which his men were hastening toward their own country. That he might overtake them was a possibility, but by no means a certainty, and if he did not he would be no better off alone in the jungle than he would be on the slopes of the Wiramwazi.

He faced about and looked up toward the rugged heights above him. He had come a long way to reach his goal, which now lay somewhere just beyond that serrated skyline, and he was of no mind to turn back now in defeat. A day or a week in these rugged mountains might reveal the secret of The Lost Tribe of legend, and surely a month would be sufficient to determine beyond a reasonable doubt that the story had no basis in fact, for von Harben believed that in a month he could fairly well explore such portions of the range as might naturally lend themselves to human habitation, where he hoped at best to find relics of the fabled tribe in the form of ruins or burial mounds. For to a man of von Harben's training and intelligence there could be no thought that The Lost Tribe of legend, if it had ever existed, could be anything more than a vague memory surrounding a few mouldy artifacts and some crumbling bones.

It did not take the young man long to reach a decision and presently he turned back to his tent and, entering it, packed a few necessities that had been left to him in a light haversack, strapped his ammunition belt about him, and stepped forth once more to turn his face upward toward the mystery of the Wiramwazi.

In addition to his Luger, von Harben carried a hunting-knife and with this he presently cut a stout staff from one of the small trees that grew sparsely upon the mountainside against the time when he might find an alpenstock indispensable.

A mountain rill furnished him pure, cold water to quench his thirst, and he carried his pistol cocked, hoping that he might bag some small game to satisfy his hunger. Nor had he gone far before a hare broke cover, and as it rolled over to the crack of the Luger, von Harben gave thanks that he had devoted much time to perfecting himself in the use of small arms.

On the spot he built a fire and grilled the hare, after which he lit his pipe and lay at ease while he smoked and planned. His was not a temperament to be depressed or discouraged by seeming reverses, and he was determined not to be hurried by excitement, but to conserve his strength at all times during the strenuous days that he felt must lie ahead of him.

All day he climbed, choosing the long way when it seemed safer, exercising all the lore of mountain-climbing that he had accumulated, and resting often. Night overtook him well up toward the summit of the highest ridge that had been visible from the base of the range. What lay behind, he could not even guess, but experience suggested that he would find other ridges and frowning peaks before him.

He had brought a blanket with him from the last camp and in this he rolled up on the ground. From below there came the noises of the jungle subdued by distance – the yapping of jackals and faintly from afar the roaring of a lion.

Toward morning he was awakened by the scream of a leopard, not from the jungle far below, but somewhere upon the mountain slopes near by. He knew that this savage night prowler constituted a real menace, perhaps the greatest he would have to face, and he regretted the loss of his heavy rifle.

He was not afraid, for he knew that after all there was little likelihood that the leopard was hunting him or that it would attack him, but there was always that chance and so to guard against it he started a fire of dry wood that he had gathered for the purpose the night before. He found the warmth of the blaze welcome, for the night had grown cold, and he sat for some time warming himself.

Once he thought he heard an animal moving in the darkness beyond the range of the firelight, but he saw no shining eyes and the sound was not repeated. And then he must have slept, for the next thing he knew it was daylight and only embers remained to mark where the beast fire had blazed.

Cold and without breakfast, von Harben continued the ascent from his cheerless camp, his eyes, under the constant urging of his stomach, always alert for food. The terrain offered few obstacles to an experienced mountain climber, and he even forgot his hunger in the thrill of expectancy in which he anticipated the possibilities hidden by the ridge whose summit now lay but a short distance ahead of him.

It is the summit of the ridge that ever lures the explorer onward. What new sights lie just beyond? What mysteries will its achievement unveil to the eager eyes of the adventurer? Judgment and experience joined forces to asure him that when his eyes surmounted the ridge ahead they would be rewarded with nothing more startling that another similar ridge to be negotiated; yet there was always that other hope hanging like a shining beacon just below the next horizon, above which the rays of its hidden light served to illuminate the figments of his desire, and his imagination transformed the figments into realities.

Von Harben, sane and phlegmatic as he was, was now keyed to the highest pitch of excitement as he at last scaled the final barrier and stood upon the crest of the ridge. Before him stretched a rolling plateau, dotted with stunted wind-swept trees, and in the distance lay the next ridge that he had anticipated, but indistinct and empurpled by the haze of distance. What lay between him and those far hills? His pulse quickened at the thought of the possibilities for exploration and discovery that lay before him for the terrain that he looked upon was entirely different from what he had anticipated. No lofty peaks were visible except in the far distance, and between him and them there must lie intriguing ravines and valleys – virgin fields at the feet of the explorer.

Eagerly, entirely forgetful of his hunger or his solitude, von Harben moved northward across the plateau. The land was gently rolling, rock-strewn, sterile, and uninteresting, and when he had covered a mile of it he commenced to have misgivings, for if it continued on without change to the dim hills in the distance, as it now seemed was quite likely the case, it could offer him neither interest nor sustenance.

As these thoughts were commencing to oppress him, he became suddenly conscious of a vague change in the appearance of the terrain ahead. It was only an impression of unreality. The hills far away before him seemed to rise out of a great void, and it was as though between him and them there existed nothing. He might have been looking across an inland sea to distant, hazy shores – a waterless sea, for nowhere was there any suggestion of water – and then suddenly he came to a halt, startled, amazed. The rolling plateau ceased abruptly at his feet, and below him, stretching far to the distant hills, lay a great abyss – a mighty canyon similar to that which has made the gorge of the Colorado world-famous.

But here there was a marked difference. There were indications of erosion. The grim walls were scarred and water-worn. Towers and turrets and minarets, carved from the native granite, pointed upward from below, but they clung close to the canyon's wall, and just beyond them he could see the broad expanse of the floor of the canyon, which from his great height above it appeared as level as a billiard table. The scene held him in a hypnosis of wonderment and admiration as, at first swiftly and then slowly, his eyes encompassed the whole astounding scene.

Perhaps a mile below him lay the floor of the sunken canyon, the further wall of which he could but vaguely estimate to be somewhere between fifteen and twenty miles to the north, and this he realized was the lesser dimension of the canyon. Upon his right, to the east, and upon his left, to the west, he could see that the canyon extended to considerable distances – just how far he could not guess. He thought that to the east he could trace the wall that hemmed it upon that side, but from where he stood the entire extent of the canyon to the west was not visible, yet he knew that the floor that was visible to him must stretch fully twenty-five or thirty miles from east to west. Almost below him was a large lake or marsh that seemed to occupy the greater part of the east end of the canyon. He could see lanes of water winding through what appeared to be great growths of reeds and, nearer the northern shore, a large island. Three streams, winding ribbons far below, emptied into the lake, and in the far distance was another ribbon that might be a road. To the west the canyon was heavily wooded, and between the forest and the lake he saw moving figures of what he thought to be grazing game.

The sight below him aroused the enthusiasm of the explorer to its highest pitch. Here, doubtless, lay the secret of The Lost Tribe of the Wiramwazi and how well Nature had guarded this secret with stupendous barrier cliffs, aided by the superstitions of the ignorant black inhabitants of the outer slopes, was now easily understandable.

As far as he could see, the cliffs seemed sheer and impossible of descent, and yet he knew that he must find a way – that he would find a way down into that valley of enchantment.

Moving slowly along the rim he sought some foothold, however slight, where Nature had lowered her guard, but it was almost night and he had covered but a short distance before he found even a suggestion of hope that the canyon was hemmed at any point by other than unbroken cliffs, whose perpendicular faces rose at their lowest point fully a thousand feet above any possible foothold for a human being.

The sun had already set when he discovered a narrow fissure in the granite wall. Crumbled fragments of the mother rock had fallen into and partially filled it so that near the surface, at least, it offered a means of descent below the level of the cliff top, but in the gathering darkness he could not determine how far downward this rough and precarious pathway led.

He could see that below him the cliffs rose in terraced battlements to within a thousand feet of where he stood, and if the narrow fissure extended to the next terrace below him, he felt that the obstacles thereafter would present fewer difficulties than those that had baffled him up to the present time – for while he would still have some four thousand feet to descend, the formation of the cliffs was much more broken at the foot of the first sheer drop and consequently might be expected to offer some avenues of descent of which an experienced mountain climber could take advantage.

Hungry and cold, he sat beneath the descending night, gazing down into the blackening void below. Presently, as the darkness deepened, he saw a light twinkling far below and then another and another and with each his excitement rose, for he knew that they marked the presence of man. In many places upon the marsh-like lake he saw the fires twinkling, and at a point which he took to mark the site of the island there were many lights.

What sort of men were they who tended these fires? Would he find them friendly or hostile? Were they but another tribe of African blacks, or could it be that the old legend was based upon truth and that far below him white men of The Lost Tribe cooked their evening meals above those tantalizing fires of mystery?

What was that? Von Harben strained his ears to catch the faint suggestion of a sound that arose out of the shadowy abyss below – a faint, thin sound that barely reached his ears, but he was sure that he could not be mistaken – the sound was the voices of men.

And now from out of the valley came the scream of a beast and again a roar that rumbled upward like distant thunder. To the music of these sounds, von Harben finally succumbed to exhaustion; sleep for the moment offering him relief from cold and hunger.

When morning came he gathered wood from the stunted trees nearby and built a fire to warm himself. He had no food, nor all the previous day since he had reached the summit had he seen any sign of a living creature other than the game a mile beneath him on the verdant meadows of the canyon bottom.

He knew that he must have food and have it soon and food lay but a mile away in one direction. If he sought to circle the canyon in search of an easier avenue of descent, he knew that he might not find one in the hundred miles or more that he must travel. Of course he might turn back. He was sure that he could reach the base of the outer slopes of the Wiramwazi, where he knew that game might be found before exhaustion overcame him, but he had no mind to turn back and the thought of failure was only a vague suggestion that scarcely ever rose above the threshold of his conscious mind.

Having warmed himself before the fire, he turned to examine the fissure by the full light of day. As he stood upon its brink he could see that it extended downward for several hundred feet, but there it disappeared. However, he was by no means sure that it ended, since it was not a vertical cleft, but tilted slightly from the perpendicular.

From where he stood he could see that there were places in the fissure where descent would be just possible, though it might be very difficult to reascend. He knew, therefore, that should he reach the bottom of the fissure and find that further descent was impossible he would be caught in a trap from which there might be no escape.

Although he felt as fit and strong as ever, he realized perfectly that the contrary was the fact and that his strength must be ebbing and that it would continue to ebb still more rapidly the longer that he was forced to expend it in arduous efforts to descend the cliff and without any possibility of rebuilding it with food.

Even to Erich von Harben, young, self-confident and enthusiastic, his next step seemed little better than suicidal. To another the mere idea of attempting the descent of these towering cliffs would have seemed madness, but in other mountains von Harben had always found a way, and with this thin thread upon which to hang his hopes he faced the descent into the unknown. Now he was just about to lower himself over the edge of the fissure when he heard the sounds of footsteps behind him. Wheeling quickly, he drew his Luger.

3

Little Nkima came racing through the tree tops, jabbering excitedly, and dropped to the knee of Tarzan of the Apes, where the latter lay stretched upon the great branch of a jungle giant, his back against the rough bole, where he was lying up after making a kill and feeding.

'Gomangani! Gomangani!' shrilled Nkima. 'They come! They, come!'

'Peace,' said Tarzan. 'You are a greater nuisance than all the Gomangani in the jungle.'

'They will kill little Nkima,' cried the monkey. 'They are strange Gomangani, and there are no Tarmangani among them.'

'Nkima thinks everything wants to kill him,' said Tarzan, 'and yet he has lived many years and is not dead yet.'

'Sabor and Sheeta and Numa, the Gomangani, and Histah the snake like to eat poor little Nkima,' wailed the monkey. 'That is why he is afraid.'

'Do not fear, Nkima,' said the ape-man. 'Tarzan will let no one hurt you.'

'Go and see the Gomangani,' urged Nkima. 'Go and kill them. Nkima does not like the Gomangani.'

Tarzan rose leisurely. 'I go,' he said. 'Nkima may come or he may hide in the upper terraces.'

'Nkima is not afraid,' blustered the little monkey. 'He will go and fight the Gomangani with Tarzan of the Apes,' and he leaped to the back of the ape-man and clung there with his arms about the bronzed throat, from which point of vantage he peered fearfully ahead, first over the top of one broad shoulder and then over the top of the other.

Tarzan swung swiftly and quietly through the trees toward a point where Nkima had discovered the blacks, and presently he saw below him some score of natives straggling along the jungle trail. A few of them were armed with rifles and all carried packs of various sizes – such packs as Tarzan knew must belong to the equipment of a white man.

The Lord of the Jungle hailed them and, startled, the blacks halted, looking up fearfully.

'I am Tarzan of the Apes. Do not be afraid,' Tarzan reassured them, and simultaneously he dropped lightly to the trail among them, but as he did so Nkima leaped frantically from his shoulders and scampered swiftly to a high branch far above, where he sat chattering and scolding, entirely forgetful of his vain boasting of a few moments before.

'Where is your master?' demanded Tarzan.

The blacks looked sullenly at the ground, but did not reply.

'Where is the Bwana, von Harben?' Tarzan insisted.

A tall black standing near fidgeted uneasily. 'He is dead,' he mumbled.

'How did he die?' asked Tarzan.

Again the black hesitated before replying. 'A bull elephant that he had wounded killed him,' he said at last.

'Where is his body?'

'We could not find it.'

'Then how do you know that he was killed by a bull elephant?' demanded the ape-man.

'We do not know,' spoke up another black. 'He went away from camp and did not return.'

'There was an elephant about and we thought that it had killed him,' said the first black.

'You are not speaking true words,' said Tarzan.

'I shall tell you the truth,' said a third black. 'Our Bwana ascended the slopes of the Wiramwazi and the spirits of the dead being angry seized him and carried him away.'

'I shall tell you the truth,' said Tarzan. 'You have deserted your master and run away, leaving him alone in the forest.'

'We were afraid,' said the third black. 'We warned him not to ascend the slopes of the Wiramwazi. We begged him to turn back. He would not listen to us, and the spirits of the dead carried him away.'

'How long ago was that?' asked the ape-man.

'Six, seven, perhaps ten marchings. I do not remember.'

'Where was he when you last saw him?'

As accurately as they could the blacks described the location of their last camp upon the slopes of the Wiramwazi.

'Go your way back to your own villages in the Urambi country. I shall know where to find you if I want you. If your Bwana is dead, you shall be punished,' and swinging into the branches of the lower terrace, Tarzan disappeared from the sight of the unhappy blacks in the direction of the Wiramwazi, while Nkima, screaming shrilly, raced through the trees to overtake him.

From his conversation with the deserting members of von Harben's safari, Tarzan was convinced that the young man had been traitorously abandoned and that in all likelihood he was making his way alone back upon the trail of the deserters.

Not knowing Erich von Harben, Tarzan could not have guessed that the young man would push on alone into the unknown and forbidding depths of the Wiramwazi, but assumed on the contrary that he would adopt the more prudent alternative and seek to overtake his men as rapidly as possible. Believing this, the ape-man followed back along the trail of the blacks, expecting momentarily to meet von Harben.

This plan greatly reduced his speed, but even so he travelled with so much greater rapidity than the blacks that he came to the slopes of the Wiramwazi upon the third day after he had interviewed the remnants of von Harben's safari.

It was with great difficulty that he finally located the point at which von Harben had been abandoned by his men, as a heavy rain and windstorm had obliterated the trail, but at last he stumbled upon the tent, which had blown down, but nowhere could he see any signs of von Harben's trail.

Not having come upon any signs of the white man in the jungle or any indication that he had followed his fleeting safari, Tarzan was forced to the conclusion that if von Harben was not indeed dead he must have faced the dangers of the unknown alone and now be either dead or alive somewhere within the mysterious fastnesses of the Wiramwazi.

'Nkima,' said the ape-man, 'the Tarmangani have a saying that when it is futile to search for a thing, it is like hunting for a needle in a haystack. Do you believe, Nkima, that in this great mountain range we shall find our needle?'

'Let us go home,' said Nkima, 'where it is warm. Here the wind blows and up there it is colder. It is no place for little Manu, the monkey.'

'Nevertheless, Nkima, there is where we are going.'

The monkey looked up toward the frowning heights above. 'Little Nkima is afraid,' he said. 'It is in such places that Sheeta, the panther, lairs.'

Ascending diagonally and in a westerly direction in the hope of crossing von Harben's trail, Tarzan moved constantly in the opposite direction from that taken by the man he sought. It was his intention, however, when he reached the summit, if he had in the meantime found no trace of von Harben, to turn directly eastward and search at a higher altitude in the opposite direction. As he proceeded, the slope became steeper and more rugged until at one point near the western end of the mountain mass he encountered an almost perpendicular barrier high up on the mountainside along the base of which he picked his precarious way among loose boulders that had fallen from above. Underbrush and stunted trees extended at different points from the forest below quite up to the base of the vertical escarpment.

So engrossed was the ape-man in the dangerous business of picking his way along the mountainside that he gave little heed to anything beyond the necessities of the trail and his constant search for the spoor of von Harben, and so he did not see the little group of black warriors that were gazing up at him from the shelter of a clump of trees far down the slope, nor did Nkima, usually as alert as his master, have eyes or ears for anything beyond the immediate exigencies of the trail. Nkima was unhappy. The wind blew and Nkima did not like the wind. All about him he smelled the spoor of Sheeta, the panther, while he considered the paucity and stunted nature of the few trees along the way that his master had chosen. From time to time he noted, with sinking heart, ledges just above them from which Sheeta might spring down upon them; and the way was a way of terror for little Nkima.

Now they had come to a particularly precarious point upon the mountainside. A sheer cliff rose above them on their right and at their left the mountainside fell away so steeply that as Tarzan advanced his body was pressed closely against the granite face of the cliff as he sought a foothold upon the ledge of loose rubble. Just ahead of them the cliff shouldered out boldly against the distant skies. Perhaps beyond that clear-cut corner the going might be better. If it should develop that it was worse, Tarzan realized that he must turn back.

At the turn where the footing was narrowest a stone gave beneath Tarzan's foot, throwing him off balance for an instant and at that same instant Nkima, thinking that Tarzan was falling, shrieked and leaped from his shoulder, giving the ape-man's body just the impetus that was required to overbalance it entirely.

The mountainside below was steep, though not perpendicular, and if Nkima had not pushed the ape-man outward he doubtless would have slid but a short distance before being able to stay his fall, but as it was he lunged headforemost down the embankment, rolling and tumbling for a short distance over the loose rock until his body was brought to a stop by one of the many stunted trees that clung tenaciously to the wind-swept slope.

Terrified, Nkima scampered to his master's side. He screamed and chattered in his ear and pulled and tugged upon him in an effort to raise him, but the ape-man lay motionless, a tiny stream of blood trickling from a cut on his temple into his shock of black hair.

As Nkima mourned, the black warriors, who had been watching them from below, clambered quickly up the mountainside toward him and his helpless master.

4

As Erich von Harben turned to face the thing that he had heard approaching behind him, he saw a negro armed with a rifle coming toward him.

'Gabula!' exclaimed the white man, lowering his weapon. 'What are you doing here?'

'Bwana,' said the black, 'I could not desert you. I could not leave you to die alone at the hands of the spirits that dwell upon these mountains.'

Von Harben eyed the negro incredulously. 'But if you believe that, Gabula, are you not afraid that they will kill you, too?'

'I expect to die, Bwana,' replied Gabula. 'I cannot understand why you were not killed the first night or the second night. We shall both surely be killed tonight.'

'And yet you followed me! Why?'

'You have been kind to me, Bwana,' replied the black. 'Your father has been kind to me. When the others talked they filled me with fear and when they ran away I went with them, but I have come back. There was nothing else that I could do, was there?'

'No, Gabula. For you or for me there would have been nothing else to do, as we see such things, but as the others saw them they found another thing to do and they did it.'

'Gabula is not as the others,' said the black, proudly. 'Gabula is a Batoro.'

'Gabula is a brave warrior,' said von Harben. 'I do not believe in spirits and so that was no reason why I should be afraid, but you and all your people do believe in them and so it was a very brave thing for you to come back, but I shall not hold you. You may return, Gabula, with the others.'

'Yes?' Gabula exclaimed eagerly. 'The Bwana is going back? That will be good. Gabula will go back with him.'

'No, I am going down into that canyon,' said von Harben, pointing over the rim.

Gabula looked down, surprise and wonder reflected by his wide eyes and parted lips.

'But, Bwana, even if a human being could find a way down these steep cliffs, where there is no place for either hand or foot, he would surely be killed the moment he reached the bottom, for this indeed must be the Land of the Lost Tribe where the spirits of the dead live in the heart of the Wiramwazi.'

'You do not need to come with me, Gabula,' said von Harben. 'Go back to your people.'

'How are you going to get down there?' demanded the black.

'I do not know just how, or where, or when. Now I am going to descend as far along this fissure as I can go. Perhaps I shall find my way down here, perhaps not.'

'But suppose there is no foothold beyond the fissure?' asked Gabula.

'I shall have to find footing.'

Gabula shook his head. 'And if you reach the bottom, Bwana, and you are right about the spirits and there are none or they do not kill you, how will you get out again?'

Von Harben shrugged his shoulders and smiled. Then he extended his hand. 'Goodbye, Gabula,' he said. 'You are a brave man.'

Gabula did not take the offered hand of his master. 'I am going with you,' he said, simply.

'Even though you realize that should we reach the bottom alive we may never be able to return?'

'Yes.'

'I cannot understand you, Gabula. You are afraid and I know that you wish to return to the village of your people. Then why do you insist on coming with me when I give you leave to return home?'

'I have sworn to serve you, Bwana, and I am a Batoro,' replied Gabula.

'And I can only thank the Lord that you are a Batoro,' said von Harben, 'for the Lord knows that I shall need help before I reach the bottom of this canyon, and we must reach it, Gabula, unless we are content to die by starvation.'

'I have brought food,' said Gabula. 'I knew that you might be hungry and

I brought some of the food that you like,' and, unrolling the small pack that he carried, he displayed several bars of chocolate and a few packages of concentrated food that von Harben had included among his supplies in the event of an emergency.

To the famished von Harben, the food was like manna to the Israelites, and he lost no time in taking advantage of Gabula's thoughtfulness. The sharp edge of his hunger removed, von Harben experienced a feeling of renewed strength and hopefulness, and it was with a light heart and a buoyant optimism that he commenced the descent into the canyon.

Gabula's ancestry, stretching back through countless generations of jungle-dwelling people, left him appalled as he contemplated the frightful abyss into which his master was leading him, but so deeply had he involved himself by his protestations of loyalty and tribal pride that he followed von Harben with no outward show of the real terror that was consuming him.

The descent through the fissure was less difficult than it had appeared from above. The tumbled rocks that had partially filled it gave more than sufficient footing and on only a few places was assistance required, and it was at these times that von Harben realized how fortunate for him had been Gabula's return.

When at last they reached the bottom of the cleft they found themselves at its outer opening, flush with the face of the cliff and several hundred feet below the rim. This was the point beyond which von Harben had been unable to see and which he had been approaching with deep anxiety, since there was every likelihood that the conditions here might put a period to their further descent along this route.

Creeping over the loose rubble in the bottom of the fissure to its outer edge, von Harben discovered a sheer drop of a hundred feet to the level of the next terrace and his heart sank. To return the way they had come was, he feared, a feat beyond their strength and ingenuity, for there had been places down which one had lowered the other only with the greatest difficulty, which would be practically unscalable on the return journey.

It being impossible to ascend and as starvation surely faced them where they were, there was but one alternative. Von Harben lay upon his belly, his eyes at the outer edge of the fissure, and, instructing Gabula to hold tightly to his ankles, he wormed himself forward until he could scan the entire face of the cliff below him to the level of the next terrace.

A few feet from the level on which he lay he saw that the fissure lay open again to the base of the cliff, its stoppage at the point where they were having been caused by a large fragment of rock that had wedged securely between the sides of the fissure, entirely choking it at this point.

The fissure, which had narrowed considerably since they had entered it at the summit, was not more than two or three feet wide directly beneath the rock on which he lay and extended with little variation at this width the remaining hundred feet to the comparatively level ground below.

If he and Gabula could but get into this crevice he knew that they could easily brace themselves against its sides in such a way as to descend safely the remaining distance, but how with the means at hand were they to climb over the edge of the rock that blocked the fissure and crawl back into the fissure again several feet farther down?

Von Harben lowered his crude alpenstock over the edge of the rock fragment. When he extended his arms at full length the tip of the rod fell considerably below the bottom of the rock on which he lay. A man hanging at the end of the alpenstock might conceivably swing into the fissure, but it would necessitate a feat of acrobatics far beyond the powers of either himself or Gabula.

A rope would have solved their problem, but they had no rope. With a sigh, von Harben drew back when his examination of the fissure convinced him that he must find another way, but he was totally at a loss to imagine in which direction to look for a solution.

Gabula crouched back in the fissure, terrified by the anticipation of what von Harben's attempted exploration had suggested. The very thought of even looking out over the edge of that rock beyond the face of the cliff left Gabula cold and half paralysed, while the thought that he might have to follow von Harben bodily over the edge threw the negro into a fit of trembling; yet had von Harben gone over the edge Gabula would have followed him.

The white man sat for a long time buried in thought. Time and again his eyes examined every detail of the formation of the fissure within the range of his vision. Again and again they returned to the huge fragment upon which they sat, which was securely wedged between the fissure's sides. With this out of the way he felt that they could make unimpeded progress to the next terrace, but he knew that nothing short of a charge of dynamite could budge the heavy granite slab. Directly behind it were loose fragments of various sizes, and as his eyes returned to them once again he was struck with the possibility that they suggested.

'Come, Gabula,' he said. 'Help me throw out some of these rocks. This seems to be our only possible hope of escaping from the trap that I have got us into.'

'Yes, Bwana,' replied Gabula, and fell to work beside von Harben, though he could not understand why they should be picking up these stones, some of which were very heavy, and pushing them out over the edge of the flat fragment that clogged the fissure.

He heard them crash heavily where they struck the rocks below and this interested and fascinated him to such an extent that he worked feverishly to loosen the larger blocks of stone for the added pleasure he derived from hearing the loud noise that they made when they struck.

'It begins to look,' said von Harben, after a few minutes, 'as though we may be going to succeed, unless by removing these rocks here we cause some of those above to slide down and thus loosen the whole mass above us – in which event, Gabula, the mystery of The Lost Tribe will cease to interest us longer.'

'Yes, Bwana,' said Gabula, and lifting an unusually large rock he started to roll it toward the edge of the fissure. 'Look! Look, Bwana!' he exclaimed, pointing at the place where the rock had lain.

Von Harben looked and saw an opening about the size of a man's head extending into the fissure beneath them.

'Thank Nsenene, the grasshopper, Gabula,' cried the white man, 'if that is the totem of your clan – for here indeed is a way to salvation.'

Hurriedly the two men set to work to enlarge the hole by throwing out other fragments that had long been wedged in together to close the fissure at this point, and as the fragments clattered down upon the rocks below, a tall, straight warrior standing in the bow of a dugout upon the marshy lake far below looked up and called the attention of his comrades.

They could plainly hear the reverberations of the falling fragments as they struck the rocks at the foot of the fissure and, keen-eyed, they could see many of the larger pieces that von Harben and Gabula tossed downward.

'The great wall is falling,' said the black warrior.

'A few pebbles,' said another. 'It is nothing.'

'Such things do not happen except after rains,' said the first speaker. 'It is thus that it is prophesied that the great wall will fall.'

'Perhaps it is a demon who lives in the great rift in the wall,' said another. 'Let us hasten and tell the masters.'

'Let us wait and watch,' said the first speaker, 'until we have something to tell them. If we went and told them that a few rocks had fallen from the great wall they would only laugh at us.'

Von Harben and Gabula had increased the size of the opening until it was large enough to permit the passage of a man's body. Through it the white man could see the rough sides of the fissure extending to the level of the next terrace and knew that the next stage of the descent was already as good as an accomplished fact.

'We shall descend one at a time, Gabula,' said von Harben. 'I shall go first, for I am accustomed to this sort of climbing. Watch carefully so that you may descend exactly as I do. It is easy and there is no danger. Be sure that you keep your back braced against one wall and your feet against the other. We shall lose some hide in the descent, for the walls are rough, but we shall get down safely enough if we take it slowly.'

'Yes, Bwana. You go first,' said Gabula. 'If I see you do it then, perhaps, I can do it.'

Von Harben lowered himself through the aperture, braced himself securely against the opposite walls of the fissure, and started slowly downward. A few minutes later Gabula saw his master standing safely at the bottom, and though his heart was in his mouth the black followed without hesitation, but when he stood at last beside von Harben he breathed such a loud sigh of relief that von Harben was forced to laugh aloud.

'It is the demon himself,' said the black warrior in the dugout, as von Harben had stepped from the fissure.

From where the dugout of the watchers floated, half concealed by lofty papyrus, the terrace at the base of the fissure was just visible. They saw von Harben emerge and a few moments later the figure of Gabula.

'Now indeed,' said one of the blacks, 'we should hasten and tell the masters.'

'No,' said the first speaker. 'Those two may be demons, but they look like men and we shall wait until we know what they are and why they are here before we go away.'

For a thousand feet the descent from the base of the fissure was far from difficult, a rough slope leading in an easterly direction down toward the canyon bottom. During the descent their view of the lake and of the canyon was often completely shut off by masses of weather-worn granite around which they sometimes had difficulty in finding a way. As a rule the easiest descent lay between these towering fragments of the main body of cliff, and at such times as the valley was hidden from them so were they hidden from the watchers on the lake.

A third of the way down the escarpment von Harben came to the verge of a narrow gorge, the bottom of which was densely banked with green foliage of trees growing luxuriantly, pointing unquestionably to the presence of water in abundance. Leading the way, von Harben descended into the gorge, at the bottom of which he found a spring from which a little stream trickled downward. Here they quenched their thirst and rested. Then, following the stream downward, they discovered no obstacles that might not be easily surmounted.

For a long time, hemmed in by the walls of the narrow gorge and their view further circumscribed by the forest-like growth along the banks of the stream, they had no sight of the lake or the canyon bottom, but, finally, when the gorge debouched upon the lower slopes von Harben halted in admiration of the landscape spread out before him. Directly below, another stream entered that along which they had descended, forming a little river that dropped steeply to what appeared to be vivid green meadow land through which it wound tortuously to the great swamp that extended out across the valley for perhaps ten miles.

So choked was the lake with some feathery-tipped aquatic plant that von Harben could only guess as to its extent, since the green of the water plant and the green of the surrounding meadows blended into one another, but here and there he saw signs of open water that appeared like winding lanes or passages leading in all directions throughout the marsh.

As von Harben and Gabula stood looking out across this (to them) new and mysterious world, the black warriors in the dugout watched them attentively. The strangers were still so far away that the blacks were unable to identify them, but their leader assured them that these two were no demons.

'How do you know that they are not demons?' demanded one of these fellows.

'I can see that they are men,' replied the other.

'Demons are very wise and very powerful,' insisted the doubter. 'They may take any form they choose. They might come as birds or animals or men.'

'They are not fools,' snapped the leader. 'If a demon wished to descend the great wall he would not choose the hardest way. He would take the form of a bird and fly down.'

The other scratched his head in perplexity, for he realized that here was an argument that would be difficult to controvert. For want of anything better to say, he suggested that they go at once and report the matter to their masters.

'No,' said the leader. 'We shall remain here until they come closer. It will be better for us if we can take them with us and show them to our masters.'

The first few steps that von Harben took onto the grassy meadow land revealed the fact that it was a dangerous swamp from which only with the greatest difficulty were they able to extricate themselves.

Floundering back to solid ground, von Harben reconnoitred in search of some other avenue to more solid ground on the floor of the canyon, but he found that upon both sides of the river the swamp extended to the foot of the lowest terrace of the cliff, and low as these were in comparison to their lofty fellows towering far above them, they were still impassable barriers.

Possibly by reascending the gorge he might find an avenue to more solid ground toward the west, but as he had no actual assurance of this and as both he and Gabula were well-nigh exhausted from the physical strain of the descent, he preferred to find an easier way to the lake shore if it were possible.

He saw that while the river at this point was not swift, the current was rapid enough to suggest that the bottom might be sufficiently free from mud to make it possible for them to utilize it as an avenue to the lake, if it were not too deep.

To test the feasibility of the idea, he lowered himself into the water, holding to one end of his alpenstock, while Gabula seized the other. He found that the water came to his waist-line and that the bottom was firm and solid.

'Come on, Gabula. This is our way to the lake, I think,' he said to the black.

As Gabula slipped into the water behind his master, the dugout containing the black warriors pushed silently along the watery lane among the papyrus and with silent paddles was urged swiftly toward the mouth of the stream where it emptied into the lake.

As von Harben and Gabula descended the stream they found that the depth of the water did not greatly increase. Once or twice they stumbled into deeper holes and were forced to swim, but in other places the water shallowed until it was only to their knees, and thus they made their way down to the lake at the verge of which their view was shut off by clumps of papyrus rising twelve or fifteen feet above the surface of the water.

'It begins to look,' said von Harben, 'as though there is no solid ground along the shore line, but the roots of the papyrus will hold us and if we can make our way to the west end of the lake I am sure that we shall find solid ground, for I am positive that I saw higher land there as we were descending the cliff.'

Feeling their way cautiously along, they came at last to the first clump of papyrus and just as von Harben was about to clamber to the solid footing of the roots, a canoe shot from behind the mass of floating plants and the two men found themselves covered by weapons of a boatload of ebon warriors.

5

Lukedi, the Bagego, carried a gourd of milk to a hut in the village of his people on the lower slopes at the west end of the Wiramwazi range.

Two stalwart spearmen stood guard at the doorway of the hut. 'Nyuto has sent me with milk for the prisoner,' said Lukedi. 'Has his spirit returned to him?'

'Go in and see,' directed one of the sentries.

Lukedi entered the hut and in the dim light saw the figure of a giant white man sitting upon the dirt floor gazing at him. The man's wrists were bound together behind his back and his ankles were secured with tough fibre strands.

'Here is food,' said Lukedi, setting the gourd upon the ground near the prisoner.

'How can I eat with my hands tied behind my back?' demanded Tarzan. Lukedi scratched his head. 'I do not know,' he said. 'Nyuto sent me with the food. He did not tell me to free your hands.'

'Cut the bonds,' said Tarzan, 'otherwise I cannot eat.'

One of the spearmen entered the hut. 'What is he saying?' he demanded.

'He says he cannot eat unless his hands are freed,' said Lukedi.

'Did Nyuto tell you to free his hands?' asked the spearman.

'No,' said Lukedi.

The spearman shrugged his shoulders. 'Leave the food then; that is all you were asked to do.'

Lukedi turned to leave the hut. 'Wait,' said Tarzan. 'Who is Nyuto?'

'He is chief of the Bagegos,' said Lukedi.

'Go to him and tell him that I wish to see him. Tell him also that I cannot eat with my hands tied behind my back.'

Lukedi was gone for half an hour. When he returned he brought an old, rusted slave chain and an ancient padlock.

'Nyuto says that we may chain him to the centre pole and then cut the bonds that secure his hands,' he said to the guard.

The three men entered the hut where Lukedi passed one end of the chain around the centre pole, pulling it through a ring on the other end; the free end he then passed round Tarzan's neck, securing it there with the old slave padlock.

'Cut the bonds that hold his wrists,' said Lukedi to one of the spearmen.

'Do it yourself,' retorted the warrior. 'Nyuto sent you to do it. He did not tell me to cut the bonds.'

Lukedi hesitated. It was apparent that he was afraid.

'We will stand ready with our spears,' said the guardsmen; 'then he cannot harm you.'

'I shall not harm him,' said Tarzan. 'Who are you anyway and who do you think I am?'

One of the guardsmen laughed. 'He asked who we are as though he did not know!'

'We know who you are, very well,' said the other warrior.

'I am Tarzan of the Apes,' said the prisoner, 'and I have no quarrel with the Bagegos.'

The guardsman who had last spoken laughed again derisively. 'That may be your name,' he said. 'You men of The Lost Tribe have strange names. Perhaps you have no quarrel with the Bagegos, but the Bagegos have a quarrel with you,' and still laughing he left the hut followed by his companion, but the youth Lukedi remained, apparently fascinated by the prisoner at whom he stood staring as he might have stared at a deity.

Tarzan reached for the gourd and drank the milk it contained, and never once did Lukedi take his eyes from him.

'What is your name?' asked Tarzan.

'Lukedi,' replied the youth.

'And you have never heard of Tarzan of the Apes?'

'No,' replied the youth.

'Who do you think I am?' demanded the ape-man.

'We know that you belong to The Lost Tribe.'

'But I thought the members of The Lost Tribe were supposed to be the spirits of the dead,' said Tarzan.

'That we do not know,' replied Lukedi. 'Some think one way, some another; but you know, for you are one of them.'

'I am not one of them,' said Tarzan. 'I come from a country farther south, but I have heard of the Bagegos and I have heard of The Lost Tribe.'

'I do not believe you,' said Lukedi.

'I speak the truth,' said Tarzan.

Lukedi scratched his head. 'Perhaps you do,' he said. 'You do not wear clothes like the members of The Lost Tribe, and the weapons that we found with you are different.'

'You have seen members of The Lost Tribe?' asked Tarzan.

'Many times,' replied Lukedi. 'Once a year they come out of the bowels of the Wiramwazi and trade with us. They bring dried fish, snails, and iron and take in exchange salt, goats, and cows.'

'If they come and trade with you peacefully, why do you make me a prisoner if you think I am one of them?' demanded Tarzan.

'Since the beginning we have been at war with the members of The Lost Tribe,' replied Lukedi. 'It is true that once a year we trade with them, but they are always our enemies.'

'Why is that?' demanded the ape-man.

'Because at other times we cannot tell when they will come with many warriors and capture men, women, and children whom they take away with them into the Wiramwazi. None ever returns. We do not know what becomes of them. Perhaps they are eaten.'

'What will your chief, Nyuto, do with me?' asked Tarzan.

'I do not know,' said Lukedi. 'They are discussing the question now. They all wish to put you to death, but there are some who believe that this would arouse the anger of the ghosts of all the dead Bagegos.'

'Why should the ghosts of your dead wish to protect me?' demanded Tarzan.

'There are many who think that you members of The Lost Tribe are the ghosts of our dead,' replied Lukedi.

'What do you think, Lukedi?' asked the ape-man.

'When I look at you I think you are a man of flesh and blood the same as I, and so I think that perhaps you are telling me the truth when you say that you are not a member of The Lost Tribe, because I am sure that they are all ghosts.'

'But when they come to trade with you and when they come to fight with you, can you not tell whether they are flesh and blood or not?'

'They are very powerful,' said Lukedi. 'They might come in the form of men in the flesh or they might come as snakes or lions. That is why we are not sure.'

'And what do you think the council will decide to do with me?' asked Tarzan.

'I think that there is no doubt but that they will burn you alive, for thus both you and your spirit will be destroyed so that it cannot come back to haunt and annoy us.'

'Have you seen or heard of another white man recently?' asked Tarzan.

'No,' replied the youth. 'Many years ago, before I can remember, two white men came who said that they were not members of The Lost Tribe, but we did not believe them and they were killed. I must go now. I shall bring you more milk tomorrow.'

After Lukedi had left, Tarzan commenced examining the chain, padlock, and the centre pole of the hut in an effort to discover some means of escape. The hut was cylindrical and surmounted by a conical roof of grass. The side walls were of stakes set upright a few inches in the ground and fastened together at their tops and bottoms by creepers. The centre pole was much heavier and was secured in position by rafters radiating from it to the top of the wall. The interior of the hut was plastered with mud, which had been thrown on with force and then smoothed with the palm of the hand. It was a common type with which Tarzan was familiar. He knew that there was a possibility that he might be able to raise the centre pole and withdraw the chain from beneath it.

It would, of course, be difficult to accomplish this without attracting the attention of the guards, and there was a possibility that the centre pole might be set sufficiently far in the ground to render it impossible for him to raise it. If he were given time he could excavate around the base of it, but inasmuch as one or the other of the sentries was continually poking his head into the hut to see that all was well, Tarzan saw little likelihood of his being able to free himself without being discovered.

As darkness settled upon the village Tarzan stretched himself upon the hard dirt floor of the hut and sought to sleep. For some time the noises of the village kept him awake, but at last he slept. How long thereafter it was that he was awakened he did not know. From childhood he had shared with the beasts, among whom he had been raised, the ability to awaken quickly and in full command of all his faculties. He did so now, immediately conscious that the noise that had aroused him came from an animal upon the roof of the hut. Whatever it was, it was working quietly, but to what end the ape-man could not imagine.

The acrid fumes of the village cook fires so filled the air that Tarzan was unable to catch the scent of the creature upon the roof. He carefully reviewed all the possible purposes for which an animal might be upon the thatched, dry-grass roof of the Bagego hut and through a process of elimination he could reach but one conclusion. That was that the thing upon the outside wished to come in and either it did not have brains enough to know that there was a doorway, or else it was too cunning to risk detection by attempting to pass the sentries.

But why should any animal wish to enter the hut? Tarzan lay upon his back, gazing up through the darkness in the direction of the roof above him as he tried to find an answer to his question. Presently, directly above his head, he saw a little ray of moonlight. Whatever it was upon the roof had made an opening that grew larger and larger as the creature quietly tore away the thatching. The aperture was being made close to the wall where the radiating rafters were farthest apart, but whether this was through intent or accident Tarzan could not guess. As the hole grew larger and he caught occasional glimpses of the thing silhouetted against the moonlit sky, a broad smile illuminated the face of the ape-man. Now he saw strong little fingers working at the twigs that were fastened laterally across the rafters to support the thatch and presently, after several of these had been removed the opening was entirely closed by a furry little body that wriggled through and dropped to the floor close beside the prisoner.

'How did you find me, Nkima?' whispered Tarzan.

'Nkima followed,' replied the little monkey. 'All day he has been sitting in a high tree above the village watching this place and waiting for darkness. Why do you stay here, Tarzan of the Apes? Why do you not come away with little Nkima?'

'I am fastened here with a chain,' said Tarzan. 'I cannot come away.'

'Nkima will go and bring Muviro and his warriors,' said Nkima.

Of course he did not use these words at all, but what he said in the language of the apes conveyed the same meaning to Tarzan. Black apes carrying sharp, long sticks was the expression that he used to describe the Waziri warriors, and the name for Muviro was one of his own coining, but he and Tarzan understood one another.

'No,' said Tarzan. 'If I am going to need Muviro, he could not get here in time now to be of any help to me. Go back into the forest, Nkima, and wait for me. Perhaps I shall join you very soon.'

Nkima scolded, for he did not want to go away. He was afraid alone in this strange forest; in fact, Nkima's life had been one long complex of terror, relieved only by those occasions when he could snuggle in the lap of his master, safe within the solid walls of Tarzan's bungalow. One of the sentries heard the voices within the hut and crawled part way in.

'There,' said Tarzan to Nkima, 'you see what you have done. Now you had better do as Tarzan tells you and get out of here and into the forest before they catch you and eat you.'

'Who are you talking to?' demanded the sentry. He heard a scampering in the darkness and at the same instant caught sight of the hole in the roof and almost simultaneously he saw something dark go through it and disappear. 'What was that?' he demanded nervously.

'That,' said Tarzan, 'was the ghost of your grandfather. He came to tell me that you and your wives and all your children would fall sick and die if anything happens to me. He also brought the same message for Nyuto.'

The sentry trembled. 'Call him back,' he begged, 'and tell him that I had nothing to do with it. It is not I, but Nyuto, the chief, who is going to kill you.'

'I cannot call him back,' said Tarzan, 'and so you had better tell Nyuto not to kill me.'

'I cannot see Nyuto until morning,' wailed the black. 'Perhaps then it will be too late.'

'No,' said Tarzan. 'The ghost of your grandfather will not do anything until tomorrow.'

Terrified, the sentry returned to his post where Tarzan heard him fearfully and excitedly discussing the matter with his companion until the ape-man finally dropped off to sleep again.

It was late the following morning before anyone entered the hut in which Tarzan was confined. Then came Lukedi with another gourd of milk. He was very much excited.

'Is what Ogonyo says true?' he demanded.

'Who is Ogonyo?' asked Tarzan.

'He was one of the warriors who stood guard here last night, and he has told Nyuto and all the village that he heard the ghost of his grandfather talking with you and that the ghost said that he would kill everyone in the village if you were harmed, and now everyone is afraid.'

'And Nyuto?' asked Tarzan.

'Nyuto is not afraid of anything,' said Lukedi.

'Not even of ghosts of grandfathers?' asked Tarzan.

'No. He alone of all the Bagegos is not afraid of the men of The Lost Tribe, and now he is very angry at you because you have frightened his people and this evening you are to be burned. Look!' And Lukedi pointed to the low doorway of the hut. 'From here you can see them placing the stake to which you are to be bound, and the boys are in the forest gathering fagots.'

Tarzan pointed toward the hole in the roof. 'There,' he said, 'is the hole made by the ghost of Ogonyo's grandfather. Fetch Nyuto and let him see. Then, perhaps, he will believe.'

'It will make no difference,' said Lukedi. 'If he saw a thousand ghosts with his own eyes, he would not be afraid. He is very brave, but he is also very stubborn and a fool. Now we shall all die.'

'Unquestionably,' said Tarzan.

'Can you not save me?' asked Lukedi.

'If you will help me to escape, I promise you that the ghosts shall not harm you.'

'Oh, if I could but do it,' said Lukedi, as he passed the gourd of milk to the ape-man.

'You bring me nothing but milk,' said Tarzan. 'Why is that?'

'In this village we belong to the Buliso clan and, therefore, we may not drink the milk nor eat the flesh of Timba, the black cow, so when we have guests or prisoners we save this food for them.'

Tarzan was glad that the totem of the Buliso clan was a cow instead of a grasshopper, or rainwater from the roofs of houses or one of the hundreds of other objects that are venerated by different clans, for while Tarzan's early training had not placed grasshoppers beyond the pale as food for men, he much preferred the milk of Timba.

'I wish that Nyuto would see me and talk with me,' said Tarzan of the Apes. 'Then he would know that it would be better to have me for a friend than for an enemy. Many men have tried to kill me, many chiefs greater than Nyuto. This is not the first hut in which I have lain a prisoner, nor is it the first time that black men have prepared fires to receive me, yet I still live, Lukedi, and many of them are dead. Go, therefore, to Nyuto and advise him to treat me as a friend, for I am not from The Lost Tribe of the Wiramwazi.'

'I believe you,' said Lukedi, 'and I shall go and beg Nyuto to hear me, but I am afraid that he will not.'

As the youth reached the doorway of the hut, there suddenly arose a great commotion in the village. Tarzan heard men issuing orders. He heard children crying and the pounding of many naked feet upon the hard ground. Then the war-drums boomed and he heard clashing of weapons upon shields and loud shouting. He saw the guards before the doorway spring to their feet and run to join the other warriors and then Lukedi, at the doorway, shrank back with a cry of terror.

'They come! They come!' he cried, and ran to the far side of the hut where he crouched in terror.

6

Erich Von harben looked into the faces of the tall, almost naked, black warriors whose weapons menaced him across the gunwale of their low dugout, and the first thing to attract his attention was the nature of those weapons.

Their spears were unlike any that he had ever seen in the hands of modern savages. Corresponding with the ordinary spear of the African savage, they carried a heavy and formidable javelin that suggested to the mind of the young archæologist nothing other than the ancient Roman pike, and this similarity was further confirmed by the appearance of the short, broad, two-edged swords that dangled in scabbards supported by straps passing over the left shoulders of the warriors. If this weapon was not the *gladius Hispanus* of the Imperial Legionary, von Harben felt that his studies and researches had been for naught.

'Ask them what they want, Gabula,' he directed. 'Perhaps they will understand you.'

'Who are you and what do you want of us?' demanded Gabula in the Bantn dialect of his tribe.

'We wish to be friends,' added von Harben in the same dialect. 'We have come to visit your country. Take us to your chief.'

A tall black in the stern of the dugout shook his head. 'I do not understand you,' he said. 'You are our prisoners. We are going to take you with us to our masters. Come, get into the boat. If you resist or make trouble we shall kill you.'

'They speak a strange language,' said Gabula. 'I do not understand them.'

Surprise and incredulity were reflected in the expression on von Harben's face, and he experienced such a sensation as one might who looked upon a man suddenly resurrected after having been dead for nearly two thousand years.

Von Harben had been a close student of ancient Rome and its long dead language, but how different was the living tongue, which he heard and which he recognized for what it was, from the dead and musty pages of ancient manuscripts.

He understood enough of what the black had said to get his meaning, but he recognized the tongue as a hybrid of Latin and Bantu root words, though the inflections appeared to be uniformly those of the Latin language.

In his student days von Harben had often imagined himself a citizen of Rome. He had delivered orations in the Forum and had addressed his troops in the field in Africa and in Gaul, but how different it all seemed now when he was faced with the actuality rather than the figment of imagination. His voice sounded strange in his own ears and his words came haltingly as he spoke to the tall black in the language of the Cæsars.

'We are not enemies,' he said. 'We have come as friends to visit your country,' and then he waited, scarce believing that the man could understand him.

'Are you a citizen of Rome?' demanded the black.

'No, but my country is at peace with Rome,' replied von Harben.

The black looked puzzled as though he did not understand the reply. 'You are from Castra Sanguinarius.' His words carried the suggestion of a challenge.

'I am from Germania,' replied von Harben.

'I never heard of such a country. You are a citizen of Rome from Castra Sanguinarius.'

'Take me to your chief,' said von Harben.

'That is what I intend to do. Get in here. Our masters will know what to do with you.'

Von Harben and Gabula climbed into the dugout, so awkwardly that they almost overturned it, much to the disgust of the black warriors, who seized hold of them none too gently and forced them to squat in the bottom of the frail craft. This was now turned about and paddled along a winding canal, bordered on either side by tufted papyrus rising ten to fifteen feet above the surface of the water.

'To what tribe do you belong?' asked von Harben, addressing the leader of the blacks.

'We are barbarians of the Mare Orientis, subjects of Validus Augustus, Emperor of the East; but why do you ask such questions? You know these things as well as I.'

A half hour of steady paddling along winding water-lanes brought them to a collection of beehive huts built upon the floating roots of the papyrus, from which the tall plants had been cleared just sufficiently to make room for the half dozen huts that constituted the village. Here von Harben and Gabula became the centre of a curious and excited company of men, women, and children, and von Harben heard himself and Gabula described by their captors as spies from Castra Sanguinarius and learned that on the morrow they were to be taken to Castrum Mare, which he decided must be the village of the mysterious 'masters' to whom his captors were continually alluding. The blacks did not treat them unkindly, though they evidently considered them as enemies.

When they were interviewed by the headman of the village, von Harben, his curiosity aroused, asked the blacks why they had not been molested if all of his people believed, as they seemed to, that they were enemies.

'You are a citizen of Rome,' replied the headman, 'and this other is your slave. Our masters do not permit us barbarians to injure a citizen of Rome, even though he may be from Castra Sanguinarius, except in self-defence or upon the battlefield in time of war.'

'Who are your masters?' demanded von Harben.

'Why, the citizens of Rome who live in Castrum Mare, of course, as one from Castra Sanguinarius well knows.'

'But I am not from Castra Sanguinarius,' insisted von Harben.

'You may tell that to the officers of Validus Augustus,' replied the headman. 'Perhaps they will believe you, but it is certain that I do not.'

'Are these people who dwell in Castrum Mare black men?' asked von Harben.

'Take them away,' ordered the headman, 'and confine them safely in a hut. There they may ask one another foolish questions. I do not care to listen to them further.'

Von Harben and Gabula were led away by a group of warriors and conducted into one of the small huts of the village. Here they were brought a supper of fish and snails and a dish concocted of the cooked pith of papyrus.

When morning dawned the prisoners were again served with food similar to that which had been given them the previous evening and shortly thereafter they were ordered from the hut.

Upon the water-lane before the village floated half a dozen dugouts filled with warriors. Their faces and bodies were painted as for war and they appeared to have donned all their finery of barbaric necklaces, anklets, bracelets, armbands, and feathers that each could command; even the prows of the canoes bore odd designs in fresh colours.

There were many more warriors than could have been accommodated in the few huts within the small clearing, but, as von Harben learned later, these came from other clearings, several of which comprised the village. Von Harben and Gabula were ordered into the chief's canoe and a moment later the little fleet pushed off into the water-lane. Strong paddlers propelled the dugouts along the winding waterway in a northeasterly direction.

During the first hour they passed several small clearings in each of which stood a few huts from which the women and children came to the water's edge to watch them as they passed, but for the most part the water-lane ran between monotonous walls of lofty papyrus, broken only occasionally by short stretches of more open water.

Von Harben tried to draw the chief into conversation, especially relative to their destination and the nature of the 'masters' into whose hands they were to be delivered, but the taciturn warrior ignored his every advance and finally von Harben lapsed into the silence of resignation.

They had been paddling for hours, and the heat and monotony had become almost unbearable, when a turn in the water-lane revealed a small body of open water, across the opposite side of which stretched what appeared to be low land surmounted by an earthen rampart, along the top of which was a strong stockade. The course of the canoe was directed toward two lofty towers that apparently marked the gateway through the rampart.

Figures of men could be seen loitering about this gateway, and as they caught sight of the canoes a trumpet sounded and a score of men sallied from the gateway and came down to the water's edge.

As the boat drew nearer, von Harben saw that these men were soldiers, and at the command of one of them the canoes drew up a hundred yards off-shore and waited there while the chief shouted to the soldiers on shore telling them who he was and the nature of his business. Permission was then given for the chief's canoe to approach, but the others were ordered to remain where they were.

'Stay where you are,' commanded one of the soldiers, evidently an under-officer, as the dugout touched the shore. 'I have sent for the centurion.'

Von Harben looked with amazement upon the soldiers drawn up at the landing. They wore the tunics and cloaks of Cæsar's legionaries. Upon their feet were the sandal-like caligae. A helmet, a leather cuirass, an ancient shield with pike and Spanish sword completed the picture of antiquity; only their skin belied the suggestion of their origin. They were not white men; neither were they negroes, but for the most part of a light-brown colour with regular features.

They seemed only mildly curious concerning von Harben, and on the whole appeared rather bored than otherwise. The under-officer questioned the chief concerning conditions in the village. They were casual questions on subjects of no particular moment, but they indicated to von Harben a seemingly interested and friendly relationship between the blacks of the outlying villages in the papyrus swamp and the evidently civilized brown people of the mainland; yet the fact that only one canoe had been permitted to approach the land suggested that other and less pleasant relations had also existed between them at times. Beyond the rampart von Harben could see the roofs of buildings and far away, beyond these, the towering cliffs that formed the opposite side of the canyon.

Presently two more soldiers emerged from the gateway opposite the landing. One of them was evidently the officer for whom they were waiting his cloak and cuirass being of finer materials and more elaborately decorated; while the other, who walked a few paces behind him, was a common soldier, probably the messenger who had been dispatched to fetch him.

And now another surprise was added to those which von Harben had already experienced since he had dropped over the edge of the barrier cliffs into this little valley of anachronisms – the officer was unquestionably white.

'Who are these, Rufinus?' he demanded of the under-officer.

'A barbarian chief and warriors from the villages of the western shore,' replied Rufinus. 'They bring two prisoners that they captured in the Rupes Flumen. As a reward they wish permission to enter the city and see the Emperor.'

'How many are they?' asked the officer.

'Sixty,' replied Rufinus.

'They may enter the city,' said the officer. 'I will give them a pass, but they must leave their weapons in their canoes and be out of the city before dark. Send two men with them. As to their seeing Validus Augustus, that I cannot arrange. They might go to the palace and ask the præfect there. Have the prisoners come ashore?'

As von Harben and Gabula stepped from the dugout, the expression upon the officer's face was one of perplexity.

'Who are you?' he demanded.

'My name is Erich von Harben,' replied the prisoner.

The officer jerked his head impatiently. 'There is no such family in Castra Sanguinarius,' he retorted.

'I am not from Castra Sanguinarius.'

'Not from Castra Sanguinarius!' The officer laughed.

'That is the story he told me,' said the black chief, who had been listening to the conversation.

'I suppose that he will be saying next that he is not a citizen of Rome,' said the officer.

'That is just what he does say,' said the chief.

'But wait,' exclaimed the officer, excitedly. 'Perhaps you are indeed from Rome herself!'

'No, I am not from Rome,' von Harben assured him.

'Can it be that there are white barbarians in Africa!' exclaimed the officer. 'Surely your garments are not Roman. Yes, you must be a barbarian unless, as I suspect, you are not telling me the truth and you are indeed from Castra Sanguinarius.'

'A spy, perhaps,' suggested Rufinus.

'No,' said von Harben. 'I am no spy nor am I an enemy,' and with a smile, 'I am a barbarian, but a friendly barbarian.'

'And who is this man?' asked the officer, indicating Gabula. 'Your slave?'

'He is my servant, but not a slave.'

'Come with me,' directed the officer. 'I should like to talk with you. I find you interesting, though I do not believe you.'

Von Harben smiled. 'I do not blame you,' he said, 'for even though I see you before me I can scarcely believe that you exist.'

'I do not understand what you mean,' said the officer, 'but come with me to my quarters.'

He gave orders that Gabula was to be confined in the guardhouse temporarily, and then he led von Harben back to one of the towers that guarded the entrance to the rampart.

The gate lay in a vertical plane at right angles to the rampart with a high tower at either side, the rampart curving inward at this point to connect with the tower at the inner end of the gate. This made a curved entrance that forced an enemy attempting to enter to disclose its right or unprotected side to the defenders upon the rampart, a form of camp fortification that von Harben knew had been peculiar to the ancient Romans.

The officer's quarters consisted of a single, small, bare room directly off a larger room occupied by the members of the guard. It contained a desk, a bench, and a couple of roughly made chairs.

'Sit down,' said the officer, after they had entered, 'and tell me something about yourself. If you are not from Castra Sanguinarius, from whence do you come? How did you get into our country and what are you doing here?'

'I am from Germania,' replied von Harben.

'Bah!' exclaimed the officer. 'They are wild and savage barbarians. They do not speak the language of Rome at all; not even as poorly as you.'

'How recently have you come in contact with German barbarians?' von Harben asked.

'Oh, I? Never, of course, but our historians knew them well.'

'And how lately have they written of them?'

'Why, Sanguinarius himself mentions them in the story of his life.'

'Sanguinarius?' questioned von Harben. 'I do not recall ever having heard of him.'

'Sanguinarius fought against the barbarians of Germania in the 839th year of Rome.'

'That was about eighteen hundred and thirty-seven years ago,' von Harben reminded the officer, 'and I think you will have to admit that there may have been much progress in that time.'

'And why?' demanded the other. 'There have been no changes in this country since the days of Sanguinarius and he has been dead over eighteen hundred years. It is not likely then that barbarians would change greatly if Roman citizens have not. You say you are from Germania. Perhaps you were taken to Rome as a captive and got your civilization there, but your apparel is strange. It is not of Rome. It is not of any place of which I have ever heard. Go on with your story.'

'My father is a medical missionary in Africa,' explained von Harben. 'Often when I have visited him I heard the story of a lost tribe that was supposed to live in these mountains. The natives told strange stories of a white race living in the depths of the Wiramwazi. They said that the mountains were inhabited by the ghosts of their dead. Briefly, I came to investigate the story. All but one of my men, terrified after we reached the outer slopes of the mountains, deserted me. That one and I managed to descend to the floor of the canyon. Immediately we were captured and brought here.'

For a while the other sat in silence, thinking.

'Perhaps you are telling me the truth,' he said, at last. 'Your apparel is not that of Castra Sanguinarius and you speak our language with such a peculiar accent and with so great effort that it is evidently not your mother tongue. I shall have to report your capture to the Emperor, but in the meantime I shall take you to the home of my uncle, Septimus Favonius. If he believes your story he can help you, as he has great influence with the Emperor, Validus Augustus.'

'You are kind,' said von Harben, 'and I shall need a friend here if the customs of Imperial Rome still prevail in your country as you suggest. Now that you know so much about me, perhaps you will tell me something about yourself.'

'There is little to tell,' said the officer. 'My name is Mallius Lepus. I am a centurion in the army of Validus Augustus. Perhaps, if you are familiar with Roman customs, you will wonder that a patrician should be a centurion, but in this matter as in some others we have not followed the customs of Rome. Sanguinarius admitted all his centurions to the patrician class, and since then for over eighteen hundred years only patricians have been appointed centurions.

'But here is Aspar,' exclaimed Mallius Lepus, as another officer entered the room. 'He has come to relieve me and when he has taken over the gate you and I shall go at once to the home of my uncle, Septimus Favonius.'

7

Tarzan of the Apes looked at Lukedi in surprise and then out through the low doorway of the hut in an effort to see what it was that had so filled the breast of the black youth with terror.

The little section of the village street, framed by the doorway, showed a milling mass of brown bodies, waving spears, terrified women and children. What could it mean?

At first he thought that Lukedi meant that the Bagegos were coming for Tarzan, but now he guessed that the Bagegos were being beset by troubles of their own, and at last he came to the conclusion that some other savage tribe had attacked the village.

But, whatever the cause of the uproar, it was soon over. He saw the Bagegos turn and flee in all directions. Strange figures passed before his eyes in pursuit, and for a time there was comparative silence, only a hurrying of feet, an occasional command and now and then a scream of terror.

Presently three figures burst into the hut – enemy warriors searching the village for fugitives. Lukedi, trembling, inarticulate, paralysed by fright, crouched against the far wall. Tarzan sat leaning against the centre pole to which he was chained. At sight of him, the leading warrior halted, surprise written upon his face. His fellows joined him and they stood for a moment in excited conversation, evidently discussing their find. Then one of them addressed Tarzan, but in a tongue that the ape-man could not understand, although he realized that there was something vaguely and tantalizingly familiar about it.

Then one of them discovered Lukedi and, crossing the hut, dragged him to the centre of the floor. They spoke again to Tarzan, motioning him toward the door so that he understood that they were ordering him from the hut, but in reply he pointed to the chain about his neck.

One of the warriors examined the lock that secured the chain, spoke to his fellows, and then left the hut. He returned very shortly with two rocks and, making Tarzan lie upon the ground, placed the padlock upon one of the rocks and pounded upon it with the other until it broke.

As soon as he was released, Tarzan and Lukedi were ordered from the hut, and when they had come out into the open the ape-man had an opportunity to examine his captors more closely. In the centre of the village there were about one hundred light-brown warriors surrounding their Bagego prisoners, of whom there were some fifty men, women and children.

The tunics, cuirasses, helmets, and sandals of the raiders Tarzan knew that he had never seen before, and yet they were as vaguely familiar as was the language spoken by their wearers.

The heavy spears and the swords hanging at their right sides were not precisely like any spears or swords that he had ever seen, and yet he had a feeling that they were not entirely unfamiliar objects. The effect of the appearance of these strangers was tantalizing in the extreme. It is not uncommon for us to have experiences that are immediately followed by such a sensation of familiarity that we could swear we had lived through them before in their minutest detail, and yet we are unable to recall the time or place or any coincident occurrences.

It was such a sensation that Tarzan experienced now. He thought that he had seen these men before, that he had heard them talk; he almost felt that at some time he had understood their language, and yet at the same time he knew that he had never seen them. Then a figure approached from the opposite side of the village – a white man, garbed similarly to the warriors, but in more resplendent trappings, and of a sudden Tarzan of the Apes found the key and the solution of the mystery, for the man who came toward him might have stepped from the pedestal of the statue of Julius Cæsar in the Palazzo dei Conservatori in Rome.

These were Romans! A thousand years after the fall of Rome he had been captured by a band of Cæsar's legionaries, and now he knew why the language was so vaguely familiar, for Tarzan, in his effort to fit himself for a place in the civilized world into which necessity sometimes commanded him, had studied many things and among them Latin, but the reading of Cæsar's Commentaries and scanning Virgil do not give one a command of the language and so Tarzan could neither speak nor understand the spoken words, though the smattering that he had of the language was sufficient to make it sound familiar when he heard others speaking it.

Tarzan looked intently at the Cæsar-like white man approaching him and at the dusky, stalwart legionaries about him. He shook himself. This indeed must be a dream, and then he saw Lukedi with the other Bagego prisoners. He saw the stake that had been set up for his burning and he knew that as these were realities so were the strange warriors about him.

Each soldier carried a short length of chain, at one end of which was a metal collar and a padlock, and with these they were rapidly chaining the prisoners neck to neck.

While they were thus occupied the white man, who was evidently an officer, was joined by two other whites similarly garbed. The three caught sight of Tarzan and immediately approached and questioned him, but the ape-man shook his head to indicate that he could not understand their language. Then they questioned the soldiers who had discovered him in the hut and finally the commander of the company issued some instructions relative to the ape-man and turned away.

The result was that Tarzan was not chained to the file of black prisoners, but though he again wore the iron collar, the end of the chain was held by one of the legionaries in whose keeping he had evidently been placed.

Tarzan could only believe that this preferential treatment was accorded him because of his colour and the reluctance of the white officers to chain another white with negroes.

As the raiders marched away from the village one of the officers and a dozen legionaries marched in advance. These were followed by the long line of prisoners accompanied by another officer and a small guard. Behind the prisoners, many of whom were compelled to carry the live chickens that were a part of the spoils of the raid, came another contingent of soldiers herding the cows and goats and sheep of the villagers, and behind all a large rear guard comprising the greater part of the legionaries under the command of the third officer.

The march led along the base of the mountains in a northerly direction and presently upward diagonally across the rising slopes at the west end of the Wiramwazi range.

It chanced that Tarzan's position was at the rear of the line of black prisoners, at the end of which marched Lukedi.

'Who are these people, Lukedi?' asked Tarzan, after the party had settled down to steady progress.

'These are the ghost people of the Wiramwazi,' replied the young Bagego.

'They have come to prevent the killing of their fellow,' said another black, looking at Tarzan. 'I knew Nyuto should not have made him prisoner. I knew that harm would come from it. It is well for us that the ghost people came before we had slain him.'

'What difference will it make?' said another. 'I would rather have been killed in my own village than to be taken into the country of the ghost people and killed there.'

'Perhaps they will not kill us,' suggested Tarzan.

'They will not kill you because you are one of them, but they will kill the Bagegos because they did dare to take you prisoner.'

'But they have taken him prisoner, too,' said Lukedi. 'Can you not see that he is not one of them? He does not even understand their language.'

The other blacks shook their heads, but they were not convinced. They had made up their minds that Tarzan was one of the ghost people and they were determined that nothing should alter this conviction.

After two hours of marching the trail turned sharply to the right and entered a narrow and rocky gorge, the entrance to which was so choked with trees and undergrowth that it could not have been visible from any point upon the slopes below.

The gorge soon narrowed until its rocky walls could be spanned by a man's outstretched arms. The floor, strewn with jagged bits of granite from the lofty cliffs above, afforded poor and dangerous footing, so that the speed of the column was greatly reduced.

As they proceeded Tarzan realized that, although they were entering more deeply into the mountains, the trend of the gorge was downward rather than upward. The cliffs on either side rose higher and higher above them until in places the gloom of night surrounded them and, far above, the stars twinkled in the morning sky.

For a long hour they followed the windings of the dismal gorge. The column halted for a minute or two and immediately after the march was resumed Tarzan saw those directly ahead of him filing through an arched gateway in the man-made wall of solid masonry that entirely blocked the gorge to a height of at least a hundred feet. Also, when it was the ape-man's turn to pass the portal, he saw that it was guarded by other soldiers similar to those into whose hands he had fallen and that it was further reinforced by a great gate of huge, hand-hewn timbers that had been swung open to permit the party to pass.

Ahead of him Tarzan saw a well-worn road leading down into a dense forest in which huge, live oaks predominated, though interspersed with other varieties of trees, among which he recognized acacias and a variety of plane tree as well as a few cedars.

Shortly after passing through the gate the officer in charge gave the command to halt at a small village of conical huts that was inhabited by blacks not unlike the Bagegos, but armed with pikes and swords similar to those carried by the legionaries.

Preparations were immediately made to camp in the village, the blacks turning over their huts to the soldiers, quite evidently, judging from the expressions on their faces, with poor grace. The legionaries took possession of whatever they wished and ordered their hosts about with all the authority and assurance of conquerors.

At this village a ration of corn and dried fish was issued to the prisoners. They were given no shelter, but were permitted to gather deadwood and build a fire, around which they clustered, still chained neck to neck.

Numerous birds, strange to Tarzan, flitted among the branches of the trees overhead and numerous monkeys chattered and scolded, but monkeys were no novelty to Tarzan of the Apes, who was far more interested in noting the manners and customs of his captors.

Presently an acorn fell upon Tarzan's head, but as acorns might be expected to fall from oak trees he paid no attention to the occurrence until a second and third acorn in rapid succession struck him squarely from above, and then he glanced up to see a little monkey perched upon a low branch just above him.

'So-o, Nkima!' he exclaimed. 'How did you get here.'

'I saw them take you from the village of the Gomangani. I followed.'

'You came through the gorge, Nkima?'

'Nkima was afraid that the rocks would come together and crush him,' said the little monkey, 'so he climbed to the top and came over the mountains along the edge. Far, far below he could hear the Tarmangani and the Gomangani walking along the bottom. Away up there the wind blew and little Nkima was cold and the spoor of Sheeta the panther was everywhere and there were great baboons who chased little Nkima, so that he was glad when he came to the end of the mountain and saw the forest far below. It was a very steep mountain. Even little Nkima was afraid, but he found the way to the bottom.'

'Nkima had better run home,' said Tarzan. 'This forest is full of strange monkeys.

'I am not afraid,' said Nkima. 'They are little monkeys and they are afraid of Nkima. They are homely little monkeys. They are not so beautiful as Nkima, but Nkima has seen some of the shes looking at him and admiring him. It is not a bad place for Nkima. What are the strange Tarmangani going to do with Tarzan of the Apes?'

'I do not know, Nkima,' said the Ape-man.

'Then Nkima will go back and fetch Muviro and the Waziri.'

'No,' said the ape-man. 'Wait until I find the Tarmangani for whom we are searching. Then you may go back with a message for Muviro.'

That night Tarzan and the other prisoners slept upon the hard ground in the open and, after it was dark, little Nkima came down and snuggled in his master's arms and there he lay all night, happy to be near the great Tarmangani he loved.

As morning dawned, Ogonyo, who had been captured with the other Bagegos, opened his eyes and looked about him. The camp of the soldiers was just stirring. Ogonyo saw some of the legionaries emerging from the huts that they had commandeered. He saw his fellow prisoners huddled close together for warmth and at a little distance from them lay the white man whom he had so recently guarded in the prison hut in the village of Nyuto, his chief. As his eyes rested upon the white man, he saw the head of a little monkey arise from the encircling arms of the sleeper. He saw it cast a glance in the direction of the legionaries emerging from the huts and then saw it scamper quickly to a nearby tree and swing quickly into the branches above.

Ogonyo gave a cry of alarm that awakened the prisoners near him.

'What is the matter, Ogonyo?' cried one of them.

'The ghost of my grandfather!' he exclaimed. 'I saw him again. He came out of the mouth of the white man who calls himself Tarzan. He has put a curse upon us because we kept the white man prisoner. Now we are prisoners ourselves and soon we shall be killed and eaten.' The others nodded their heads solemnly in confirmation.

Food similar to that given to them the night before was given to the prisoners, and after they and the legionaries had eaten, the march was resumed in a southerly direction along the dusty road.

Until noon they plodded through the dust toward the south, passing through other villages similar to that at which they had camped during the night, and then they turned directly east into a road that joined the main road at this point. Shortly afterward Tarzan saw before him, stretching across the road to the right and left as far as he could see through the forest, a lofty rampart surmounted by palisades and battlements. Directly ahead the roadway swung to the left just inside the outer line of the rampart and passed through a gateway that was flanked by lofty towers. At the base of the rampart was a wide moat through which a stream of water moved slowly, the moat being spanned by a bridge where the road crossed it.

There was a brief halt at the gateway while the officer commanding the company conferred with the commander of the gate, and then the legionaries and their prisoners filed through and Tarzan saw stretching before him not a village of native huts, but a city of substantial buildings.

Those near the gate were one-storey stucco houses, apparently built around an inner courtyard, as he could see the foliage of trees rising high above the roofs, but at a distance down the vista of a long avenue he saw the outlines of more imposing edifices rising to a greater height.

As they proceeded along the avenue they saw many people upon the streets and in the doorways of the houses – brown and black people, clothed for the most part in tunics and cloaks, though many of the blacks were almost naked. In the vicinity of the gateway there were a few shops, but as they proceeded along the avenue these gave way to dwellings that continued for a considerable distance until they reached a section that seemed to be devoted to shops of a better grade and to public buildings. Here they began to encounter white men, though the proportion of them to the total population seemed quite small.

The people they passed stopped to look at the legionaries and their prisoners and at intersections little crowds formed and quite a number followed them, but these were mostly small boys.

The ape-man could see that he was attracting a great deal of attention and the people seemed to be commenting and speculating upon him. Some of them called to the legionaries, who answered them good-naturedly, and there was considerable joking and chaffing – probably, Tarzan surmised, at the expense of the unfortunate prisoners.

During the brief passage through the city Tarzan came to the conclusion that the black inhabitants were the servants, perhaps slaves; the brown men, the soldiers and shopkeepers, while the whites formed the aristocratic or patrician class.

Well within the city the company turned to the left into another broad avenue and shortly afterward approached a great circular edifice constructed of hewn granite blocks. Arched apertures flanked by graceful columns rose tier upon tier to a height of forty or fifty feet, and above the first storey all of these arches were open. Through them Tarzan could see that the enclosure was without a roof and he guessed that this lofty wall enclosed an arena, since it bore a marked resemblance to the Colosseum at Rome.

As they came opposite the building the head of the column turned and entered it beneath a low, wide arch and here they were led through numerous corridors in the first storey of the building and down a flight of granite steps into gloomy, subterranean chambers, where, opening from a long corridor, the ends of which were lost in darkness in both directions, were a series of narrow doorways before which swung heavy iron gates. In parties of four or five the prisoners were unchained and ordered into the dungeons that lay behind.

Tarzan found himself with Lukedi and two other Bagegos in a small room constructed entirely of granite blocks. The only openings were the narrow, grated doorway, through which they entered, and a small, grated window in the top of the wall opposite the door, and through this window came a little light and air. The grating was closed upon them, the heavy padlock snapped, and they were left alone to wonder what fate lay in store for them.

8

Mallius Lepus conducted von Harben from the quarters of the captain of the gate in the south wall of the island city of Castrum Mare and, summoning a soldier, bade him fetch Gabula.

'You shall come with me as my guest, Erich von Harben,' announced Mallius Lepus, 'and, by Jupiter, unless I am mistaken, Septimus Favonius will thank me for bringing such a find. His dinners lag for want of novelty, for long since has he exhausted all the possibilities of Castrum Mare. He has even had a black chief from the Western forest as his guest of honour, and once he invited the aristocracy of Castrum Mare to meet a great ape.

'His friends will be mad to meet a barbarian chief from Germania – you are a chief, are you not?' and as von Harben was about to reply, Mallius Lepus stayed him with a gesture. 'Never mind! You shall be introduced as a chief and if I do not know any different I cannot be accused of falsifying.'

Von Harben smiled as he realized how alike was human nature the world over and in all periods of time.

'Here is your slave now,' said Mallius. 'As the guest of Septimus Favonius you will have others to do your bidding, but doubtless you will want to have your own body-servant as well.'

'Yes,' said von Harben. 'Gabula has been very faithful. I should hate to part with him.'

Mallius led the way to a long shed-like building beneath the inner face of the rampart. Here were two litters and a number of strapping black bearers. As Mallius appeared eight of these sprang to their stations in front and behind one of the litters and carried it from the shed, lowering it to the ground again before their master.

'And tell me, if you have visited Rome recently, does my litter compare favourably with those now used by the nobles?' demanded Mallius.

'There have been many changes, Mallius Lepus, since the Rome of which your historian, Sanguinarius, wrote. Were I to tell you of even the least of them, I fear that you would not believe me.'

'But certainly there could have been no great change in the style of litters,' argued Mallius, 'and I cannot believe that the patricians have ceased to use them.'

'Their litters travel upon wheels now,' said von Harben.

'Incredible!' exclaimed Mallius. 'It would be torture to bump over the rough pavements and country roads on the great wooden wheels of oxcarts. No Erich von Harben, I am afraid I cannot believe that story.'

'The city pavements are smooth today and the countryside is cut in all directions by wide, level highways over which the litters of the modem citizens of Rome roll at great speed on small wheels with soft tyres – nothing like the great wooden wheels of the ox-carts you have in mind, Mallius Lepus.'

The officer called a command to his carriers, who broke into a smart run.

'I warrant you, Erich von Harben, that there be no litters in all Rome that move at greater speed than this,' he boasted.

'How fast are we travelling now?' asked von Harben.

'Better than eighty-five hundred paces an hour,' replied Mallius.

'Fifty thousand paces an hour is nothing unusual for the wheeled litters of today,' said von Harben. 'We call them automobiles.'

'You are going to be a great success,' cried Mallius, slapping von Harben upon the shoulder. 'May Jupiter strike me dead if the guests of Septimus Favonius do not say that I have made a find indeed. Tell them that there be litter-carriers in Rome today who can run fifty thousand paces in an hour and they will acclaim you the greatest entertainer as well as the greatest liar Castrum Mare has ever seen.'

Von Harben laughed good-naturedly. 'But you will have to admit, my friend, that I never said that there were litter-bearers who could run fifty thousand paces an hour,' he reminded Mallius.

'But did you not assure me that the litters travelled that fast? How then may a litter travel unless it is carried by bearers. Perhaps the litters of today are carried by horses. Where are the horses that can run fifty thousand paces in an hour?'

'The litters are neither carried nor drawn by horses or men, Mallius,' said von Harben.

The officer leaned back against the soft cushion of the carriage, roaring with laughter. 'They fly then, I presume,' he jeered. 'By Hercules, you must tell this all over again to Septimus Favonius. I promise you that he will love you.'

They were passing along a broad avenue bordered by old trees. There was no pavement and the surface of the street was deep with dust. The houses were built quite up to the street line and where there was space between adjacent houses a high wall closed the aperture, so that each side of the street presented a solid front of masonry broken by arched gateways, heavy doors and small unglazed windows, heavily barred.

'These are residences?' asked von Harben, indicating the buildings they were passing.

'Yes,' said Mallius.

'From the massive doors and heavily barred windows I should judge that your city is over-run with criminals,' commented von Harben.

Mallius shook his head. 'On the contrary,' he said, 'we have few criminals in Castrum Mare. The defences that you see are against the possible uprising of slaves or invasions by barbarians. Upon several occasions during the life of the city such things have occurred, and so we build to safeguard against disaster in the event that there should be a recurrence of them, but, even so, doors are seldom locked, even at night, for there are no thieves to break in, no criminals to menace the lives of our people. If a man has done wrong to a fellow man he may have reason to expect the dagger of the assassin, but if his conscience be clear he may live without fear of attack.'

'I cannot conceive of a city without criminals,' said von Harlan. 'How do you account for it?'

'That is simple,' replied Mallius. 'When Honus Hasta revolted and founded the city of Castrum Mare in the 953rd year of Rome, Castra Sanguinarius was overrun with criminals, so that no man dared go abroad at night without an armed body-guard, nor was any one safe within his own home, and Honus Hasta, who became the first Emperor of the East, swore that there should be no criminals in Castrum Mare and he made laws so drastic that no thief or murderer lived to propagate his kind. Indeed, the laws of Honus Hasta destroyed not only the criminal, but all the members of his family, so that there was none to transmit to posterity the criminal inclinations of a depraved sire.

'There are many who thought Honus Hasta a cruel tyrant, but time has shown the wisdom of many of his acts and certainly our freedom from criminals may only be ascribed to the fact that the laws of Honus Hasta prevented the breeding of criminals. So seldom now does an individual arise who steals or wantonly murders that it is an event of as great moment as any that can occur, and the entire city takes a holiday to see the culprit and his family destroyed.'

Entering an avenue of more pretentious homes, the litter-bearers halted before an ornate gate where Lepus and Erich descended from the litter. In answer to the summons of the former, the gate was opened by a slave and von Harben followed his new friend across a tiled forecourt into an inner garden, where beneath the shade of a tree a stout, elderly man was writing at a low desk. It was with something of a thrill that von Harben noted the ancient Roman inkstand, the reed pen, and the roll of parchment that the man was using as naturally as though they had not been quite extinct for a thousand years.

'Greetings, Uncle!' cried Lepus, and as the older man turned toward them, 'I have brought you a guest such as no citizen of Castrum Mare has entertained since the founding of the city. This, my uncle, is Erich von Harben, barbarian chief from far Germania.' Then to von Harben, 'My revered uncle, Septimus Favonius.'

Septimus Favonius arose and greeted von Harben hospitably, yet with such a measure of conscious dignity as to carry the suggestion that a barbarian, even though a chief and a guest, could not be received upon a plane of actual social equality by a citizen of Rome.

Very briefly Lepus recounted the occurrences leading to his meeting with von Harben. Septimus Favonius seconded his nephew's invitation to be their guest, and then, at the suggestion of the older man, Lepus took Erich to his apartments to outfit him with fresh apparel.

An hour later, Erich, shaved and apparelled as a young Roman patrician, stepped from the apartment, which had been placed at his disposal, into the adjoining chamber, which was a part of the suite of Mallius Lepus.

'Go on down to the garden,' said Lepus, 'and when I am dressed I shall join you there.'

As von Harben passed through the home of Septimus Favonius on his way to the garden court, he was impressed by the peculiar blending of various cultures in the architecture and decoration of the home.

The walls and columns of the building followed the simplest Grecian lines of architecture, while the rugs, hangings, and mural decorations showed marked evidence of both oriental and savage African influences. The latter he could understand, but the source of the oriental designs in many of the decorations was quite beyond him, since it was obvious that The Lost Tribe had had no intercourse with the outside world, other than with the savage Bagegos, for many centuries.

And when he stepped out into the garden, which was of considerable extent, he saw a further blending of Rome and savage Africa, for while the main part of the building was roofed with hand-made tile, several porches were covered with native grass thatch, while a small out-building at the far end of the garden was a replica of a Bagego hut except that the walls were left unplastered, so that the structure appeared in the nature of a summer-house. Septimus Favonius had left the garden and von Harben took advantage of the fact to examine his surroundings more closely. The garden was laid out with winding, gravelled walks, bordered by shrubs and flowers, with an occasional tree, some of which gave evidence of great age.

The young man's mind, his eyes, his imagination were so fully occupied with his surroundings that he experienced a sensation almost akin to shock as he followed the turning of the path around a large ornamental shrub and came face to face with a young woman.

That she was equally surprised was evidenced by the consternation apparent in her expression as she looked wide-eyed into the eyes of von Harben. For quite an appreciable moment of time they stood looking at one another. Von Harben thought that never in his life had he seen so beautiful a girl. What the girl thought, von Harben did not know. It was she who broke the silence.

'Who are you?' she asked, in a voice little above a whisper, as one might conceivably address an apparition that had arisen suddenly and unexpectedly before him.

'I am a stranger here,' replied von Harben, 'and I owe you an apology for intruding upon your privacy. I thought that I was alone in the garden.'

'Who are you?' repeated the girl. 'I have never seen your face before or one like yours.'

'And I,' said von Harben, 'have never seen a girl like you. Perhaps I am dreaming. Perhaps you do not exist at all, for it does not seem credible that in the world of realities such a one as you could exist.'

The girl blushed. 'You are not of Castrum Mare,' she said. 'That I can see.' Her tone was a trifle cold and slighty haughty.

'I have offended you,' said von Harben. 'I ask your pardon. I did not mean to be offensive, but coming upon you so unexpectedly quite took my breath away.'

'And your manners, too?' asked the girl, but now her eyes were smiling.

'You have forgiven me?' asked von Harben.

'You will have to tell me who you are and why you are here before I can answer that,' she replied. 'For all I know you might be an enemy or a barbarian.'

Von Harben laughed. 'Mallius Lepus, who invited me here, insists that I am a barbarian,' he said, 'but even so I am the guest of Septimus Favonius, his uncle.'

The girl shrugged. 'I am not surprised,' she said. 'My father is notorious for the guests he honours.'

'You are the daughter of Favonius?' asked von Harben.

'Yes, I am Favonia,' replied the girl, 'but you have not yet told me about yourself. I command you to do so,' she said, imperiously.

'I am Erich von Harben of Germania,' said the young man.

'Germania!' exclaimed the girl. 'Cæsar wrote of Germania, as did Sanguinarius. It seems very far away.'

'It never seemed so far as now,' said von Harben; 'yet the three thousand miles of distance seem nothing by comparison with the centuries of time that intervene.'

The girl puckered her brows. 'I do not understand you,' she said.

'No,' said von Harben, 'and I cannot blame you.'

'You are a chief, of course?' she asked.

He did not deny the insinuation, for he had been quick to see from the attitude of the three patricians he had met that the social standing of a barbarian in Castrum Mare might be easily open to question, unless his barbarism was somewhat mitigated by a title. Proud as he was of his nationality, von Harben realized that it was a far cry from the European barbarians of Cæsar's day to their cultured descendants of the twentieth century and that it would probably be impossible to convince these people of the changes that had taken place since their history was written; and, also, he was conscious of a very definite desire to appear well in the eyes of this lovely maiden of a bygone age.

'Favonia!' exclaimed von Harben. He scarcely breathed the name.

The girl looked up at him questioningly. 'Yes!' she said.

'It is such a lovely name,' he said. 'I never heard it spoken before.'

'You like it?' she asked.

'Very much, indeed.'

The girl puckered her brows in thought. She had beautiful pencilled brows and a forehead that denoted an intelligence that was belied by neither her eyes, her manner, nor her speech. 'I am glad that you like my name, but I do not understand why I should be glad. You say that you are a barbarian, and yet you do not seem like a barbarian. Your appearance and your manner are those of a patrician, though perhaps you are overbold with a young woman you have never met before, but that I ascribe to the ignorance of the barbarian and so I forgive it.'

'Being a barbarian has its compensations,' laughed von Harben, 'and perhaps I am a barbarian. I may be again forgiven if I say you are quite the most beautiful girl I have ever seen and the only one – I – could –' he hesitated.

'You could what?' she demanded.

'Even a barbarian should not dare to say what I was about to say to one whom I have known scarce half a dozen minutes.'

'Whoever you may be, you show rare discrimination,' came a sarcastic tone in a man's voice behind von Harben.

The girl looked up in surprise and von Harben wheeled about simultaneously, for neither had been aware of the presence of another. Facing him von Harben saw a short, dark, greasy-looking young man in an elaborate tunic, his hand resting upon the hilt of the short sword that hung at his hip. There was a sarcastic sneer upon the face of the newcomer.

'Who is your barbarian friend, Favonia?' he demanded.

'This is Erich von Harben, a guest in the home of Septimus Favonius, my father,' replied the girl, haughtily; and to von Harben, 'This is Fulvus Fupus, who accepts the hospitality of Septimus Favonius so often that he feels free to criticise another guest.'

Fupus flushed. 'I apologize,' he said, 'but one may never know when to honour or when to ridicule one of Septimus Favonius's guests of honour. The last, if I recall correctly, was an ape, and before that there was a black barbarian from some outer village – but they are always interesting and I am sure that the barbarian, Erich von Harben, will prove no exception to the rule.' The man's tone was sarcastic and obnoxious to a degree, and it was with difficulty that von Harben restrained his mounting temper.

Fortunately, at this moment, Mallius Lepus joined them and von Harben was formally presented to Favonia. Fulvus Fupus thereafter paid little attention to von Harben, but devoted his time assiduously to Favonia. Von Harben knew from their conversation that they were upon friendly and intimate terms and he guessed that Fupus was in love with Favonia, though he could not tell from the girl's attitude whether or not she returned his affection.

There was something else that von Harben was sure of – that he too was in love with Favonia. Upon several occasions in life he had thought that he was in love, but his sensations and reactions upon those other occasions had not been the same in either kind or degree as those which he now experienced. He found himself hating Fulvus Fupus, whom he had known scarce a quarter of an hour and whose greatest offence, aside from looking lovingly at Favonia, had been a certain arrogant sarcasm of speech and manner – certainly no sufficient warrant for a sane man to wish to do murder, and yet Erich von Harben fingered the butt of his Luger, which he had insisted upon wearing in addition to the slim dagger with which Mallius Lepus had armed him.

Later, when Septimus Favonius joined them, he suggested that they all go to the baths and Mallius Lepus whispered to von Harben that his uncle was already itching to exhibit his new find.

'He will take us to the Baths of Cæsar,' said Lepus, 'which are patronized by the richest patricians only, so have a few good stories ready, but save your best ones, like that you told me about the modern Roman litters, for the dinner that my uncle is sure to give tonight – for he will have the best of Castrum Mare there, possibly even the Emperor himself.'

The Baths of Cæsar were housed in an imposing building, of which that portion facing on the avenue was given over to what appeared to be exclusive shops. The main entrance led to a large court where the warmth with which the party was greeted by a number of patrons of the Baths already congregated there attested to the popularity of Favonius, his daughter, and his nephew, while it was evident to von Harben that there was less enthusiasm manifested for Fulvus Fupus.

Servants conducted the bathers to the dressing-rooms, the men's and women's being in different quarters of the building.

After his clothes were removed, von Harben's body was anointed with oils in a warm room and then he was led into a hot room and from there with the other men he passed into a large apartment containing a plunge where both the men and women gathered. About the plunge were seats for several hundred people, and in the Baths of Cæsar these were constructed of highly polished granite.

While von Harben enjoyed the prospect of a swim in the clear, cold water of the frigidarium, he was much more interested by the opportunity it afforded him to be with Favonia again. She was swimming slowly around the pool when he entered the room and, making a long, running dive, von Harben slipped easily and gracefully into the water, a few strokes bringing him to her side. A murmur of applause that followed meant nothing to von Harben, for he did not know that diving was an unknown art among the citizens of Castrum Mare.

Fulvus Fupus, who had entered the frigidarium behind von Harben, sneered as he saw the dive and heard the applause. He had never seen it done before, but he could see that the thing was very easy, and realizing the advantages of so graceful an accomplishment, he determined at once to show the assembled patricians, and especially Favonia, that he was equally a master of this athletic art as was the barbarian.

Running, as he had seen von Harben run, towards the edge of the pool, Fulvus Fupus sprang high into the air and came straight down upon his belly with a resounding smack that sent the wind out of him and the water splashing high in all directions.

Gasping for breath, he managed to reach the side of the pool, where he clung while the laughter of the assembled patricians brought the scarlet of mortification to his face. Whereas before he had viewed von Harben with contempt and some slight suspicion he now viewed him with contempt, suspicion, and hatred. Disgruntled, Fupus clambered from the pool and returned immediately to the dressing-room, where he donned his garments.

'Going already, Fupus?' demanded a young patrician who was disrobing in the apodyterium.

'Yes,' growled Fupus.

'I hear you came with Septimus Favonius and his new find. What sort may he be?'

'Listen well, Cæcilius Metellus,' said Fupus. 'This man who calls himself Erich von Harben says that he is a chief from Germania, but I believe otherwise.'

'What do you believe?' demanded Metellus, politely, though evidently with no considerable interest.

Fupus came close to the other. 'I believe him to be a spy from Castra Sanguinarius,' he whispered, 'and that he is only pretending that he is a barbarian.'

'But they say that he does not speak our language well,' said Metellus.

'He speaks it as any man might speak it who wanted to pretend that he did not understand it or that it was new to him,' said Fupus.

Metellus shook his head. 'Septimus Favonius is no fool,' he said, 'I doubt if there is anyone in Castra Sanguinarius sufficiently clever to fool him to such an extent.'

'There is only one man who has any right to judge as to that,' snapped Fupus, 'and he is going to have the facts before I am an hour older.'

'Whom do you mean?' asked Metellus.

'Validus Augustus, Emperor of the East – I am going to him at once.'

'Don't be a fool, Fupus,' counselled Metellus. 'You will only get yourself laughed at or possibly worse. Know you not that Septimus Favonius is high in the favour of the Emperor?'

'Perhaps, but is it not also known that he was friendly with Cassius Hasta, nephew of the Emperor, whom Validus Augustus accused of treason and banished. It would not take much to convince the Emperor that this Erich von Harben is an emissary of Cassius Hasta, who is reputed to be in Castra Sanguinarius.'

Cæcilius Metellus laughed. 'Go on then and make a fool of yourself, Fupus,' he said. 'You will probably fetch up at the end of a rope.'

'The end of a rope will terminate this business,' agreed Fupus, 'but von Harben will be there, not I.'

9

As night fell upon the city of Castra Sanguinarius, the gloom of the granite dungeons beneath the city's Colosseum deepened into blackest darkness, which was relieved only by a rectangular patch of starlit sky where barred windows pierced the walls.

Squatting upon the rough stone floor, his back against the wall, Tarzan watched the stars moving in slow procession across the window's opening. A creature of the wild, impatient of restraint, the ape-man suffered the mental anguish of the caged beast – perhaps, because of his human mind, his suffering was greater than would have been that of one of the lower orders, yet he endured with even greater outward stoicism than the beast that paces to and fro seeking escape from the bars that confine it.

As the feet of the beast might have measured the walls of its dungeon, so did the mind of Tarzan, and never for a waking moment was his mind not occupied by thoughts of escape.

Lukedi and the other inmates of the dungeon slept, but Tarzan still sat watching the free stars and envying them, when he became conscious of a sound, ever so slight, coming from the arena, the floor of which was about on a level with the sill of the little window in the top of the dungeon wall. Something was moving, stealthily and cautiously, upon the sand of the arena. Presently, framed in the window, silhouetted against the sky, appeared a familiar figure. Tarzan smiled and whispered a word so low that a human ear could scarce have heard it, and Nkima slipped between the bars and dropped to the floor of the dungeon. An instant later the little monkey snuggled close to Tarzan, its long, muscular arms clasped tightly about the neck of the ape-man.

'Come home with me,' pleaded Nkima. 'Why do you stay in this cold, dark hole beneath the ground?'

'You have seen the cage in which we sometimes keep Jad-bal-ja, the Golden Lion?' demanded Tarzan.

'Yes,' said Nkima.

'Jad-bal-ja cannot get out unless we open the gate,' explained Tarzan. 'I too am in a cage. I cannot get out until they open the gate.'

'I will go and get Muviro and his Gomangani with the sharp sticks,' said Nkima. 'They will come and let you out.'

'No, Nkima,' said Tarzan. 'If I cannot get out by myself, Muviro could not get here in time to free me, and if he came many of my brave Waziri would be killed, for there are fighting men here in far greater numbers than Muviro could bring.' After a while Tarzan slept, and curled up within his arms slept Nkima, the little monkey, but when Tarzan awoke in the morning Nkima was gone.

Toward the middle of the morning soldiers came and the door of the dungeon was unlocked and opened to admit several of them, including a young white officer, who was accompanied by a black slave. The officer addressed Tarzan in the language of the city, but the ape-man shook his head, indicating that he did not understand; then the other turned to the black slave with a few words and the latter spoke to Tarzan in the Bagego dialect, asking him if he understood it.

'Yes,' replied the ape-man, and through the interpreter the officer questioned Tarzan.

'Who are you and what were you, a white man, doing in the village of the Bagegos?' asked the officer.

'I am Tarzan of the Apes,' replied the prisoner. 'I was looking for another white man who is lost somewhere in these mountains, but I slipped upon the cliffside and fell and while I was unconscious the Bagegos took me prisoner, and when your soldiers raided the Bagego village they found me there. Now that you know about me, I presume that I shall be released.'

'Why?' demanded the officer. 'Are you a citizen of Rome?'

'Of course not,' said Tarzan. 'What has that to do with it?'

'Because if you are not a citizen of Rome it is quite possible that you are an enemy. How do we know that you are not from Castrum Mare?'

Tarzan shrugged. 'I do not know,' he said, 'how you would know that since I do not even know what Castrum Mare means.'

'That is what you would say if you wished to deceive us,' said the officer, 'and you would also pretend that you could not speak or understand our language, but you will find that it is not going to be easy to deceive us. We are not such fools as the people of Castrum Mare believe us to be.'

'Where is this Castrum Mare and what is it?' asked Tarzan.

The officer laughed. 'You are very clever,' he said.

'I assure you,' said the ape-man, 'that I am not trying to deceive you. Believe me for a moment and answer one question.'

'What is it you wish to ask?'

'Has another white man come into your country within the last few weeks? He is the one for whom I am searching.'

'No white man has entered this country,' replied the officer, 'since Marcus Crispus Sanguinarius led the Third Cohort of the Tenth Legion in victorious conquest of the barbarians who inhabited it eighteen hundred and twenty-three years ago.'

'And if a stranger were in your country you would know it?' asked Tarzan.

'If he were in Castra Sanguinarius, yes,' replied the officer, 'but if he had entered Castrum Mare at the east end of the valley I should not know it; but come, I was not sent here to answer questions, but to fetch you before one who will ask them.'

At a word from the officer, the soldiers who accompanied him conducted Tarzan from the dungeon, along the corridor through which he had come the previous day and up into the city. The detachment proceeded for a mile through the city streets to an imposing building, before the entrance to which there was stationed a military guard whose elaborate cuirasses, helmets, and crests suggested that they might be a part of a select military organization.

The metal plates of their cuirasses appeared to Tarzan to be of gold, as did the metal of their helmets, while the hilts and scabbards of their swords were elaborately carved and further ornamented with coloured stones ingeniously inlaid in the metal, and to their gorgeous appearance was added the final touch of scarlet cloaks.

The officer who met the party at the gate admitted Tarzan, the black interpreter, and the officer who had brought him, but the guard of soldiery was replaced by a detachment of resplendent men-at-arms similar to those who guarded the entrance to the palace.

Tarzan was taken immediately into the building and along a wide corridor, from which opened many chambers, to a large, oblong room flanked by stately columns. At the far end of the apartment a large man sat in a huge, carved chair upon a raised dais.

There were many other people in the room, nearly all of whom were colourfully garbed in bright cloaks over coloured tunics and ornate cuirasses of leather or metal, while others wore only simple flowing togas, usually of white. Slaves, messengers, officers were constantly entering or leaving the chamber. The party accompanying Tarzan withdrew between the columns at one side of the room and waited there.

'What is this place?' asked Tarzan of the Bagego interpreter, 'and who is the man at the far end of the room?'

'This is the throne-room of the Emperor of the West and that is Sublatus Imperator himself.'

For some time Tarzan watched the scene before him with interest. He saw people, evidently of all classes, approach the throne and address the Emperor, and though he could not understand their words, he judged that they were addressing pleas to their ruler. There were patricians among the suppliants, brown-skinned shopkeepers, black barbarians resplendent in their savage finery, and even slaves.

The Emperor, Sublatus, presented an imposing figure. Over a tunic of white linen, the Emperor wore a cuirass of gold. His sandals were of white with gold buckles, and from his shoulders fell the purple robe of the Cæsars. A fillet of embroidered linen about his brow was the only other insignia of his station.

Directly behind the throne were heavy hangings against which were ranged a file of soldiers bearing poles surmounted by silver eagles and various other devices, and banners, of the meaning and purpose of which Tarzan was ignorant. Upon every column along the side of the wall were hung shields of various shapes over crossed banners and standards similar to those ranged behind the Emperor. Everything pertaining to the embellishment of the room was martial, the mural decorations being crudely painted scenes of war.

Presently a man, who appeared to be an official of the court, approached them and addressed the officer who had brought Tarzan from the Colosseum.

'Are you Maximus Præclarus?' he demanded.

'Yes,' replied the officer.

'Present yourself with the prisoner.'

As Tarzan advanced toward the throne surrounded by the detachment of the guard, all eyes were turned upon him, for he was a conspicuous figure even in this assemblage of gorgeously apparelled courtiers and soldiers, though his only garments were a loin cloth and a leopard skin. His suntanned skin, his shock of black hair, and his grey eyes might not alone have marked him especially in such an assemblage, for there were other dark-skinned, black-haired, grey-eyed men among them, but there was only one who towered inches above them all and he was Tarzan. The undulating smoothness of his easy stride suggested even to the mind of the proud and haughty Sublatus the fierce and savage power of the king of beasts, which perhaps accounted for the fact that the Emperor, with raised hand, halted the party a little further from the throne than usual.

As the party halted before the throne, Tarzan did not wait to be questioned, but, turning to the Bagego interpreter, said. 'Ask Sublatus why I have been made a prisoner and tell him that I demand that he free me at once.'

The black quailed. 'Do as I tell you,' said Tarzan.

'What is he saying?' asked Sublatus of the interpreter.

'I fear to repeat such words to the Emperor,' replied the black.

'I command it,' said Sublatus.

'He asked why he has been made a prisoner and demands that he be released at once.'

'Ask him who he is,' said Sublatus, angrily, 'that he dares issue commands to Sublatus Imperator.'

'Tell him,' said Tarzan, after the Emperor's words had been translated to him, 'that I am Tarzan of the Apes, but if that means as little to him as his name means to me, I have other means to convince him that I am as accustomed to issuing orders and being obeyed as is he.'

'Take the insolent dog away,' replied Sublatus with trembling voice after he had been told what Tarzan's words had been.

The soldiers laid hold of Tarzan, but he shook them off. 'Tell him,' snapped the ape-man, 'that as one white man to another I demand an answer to my question. Tell him that I did not approach his country as an enemy, but as a friend, and that I shall look to him to see that I am accorded the treatment to which I am entitled, and that before I leave this room.'

When these words were translated to Sublatus, the purple of his enraged face matched the imperial purple of his cloak.

'Take him away,' he shrieked. 'Take him away. Call the guard. Throw Maximus Præclarus into chains for permitting a prisoner to thus address Sublatus.'

Two soldiers seized Tarzan, one his right arm, the other his left, but he swung them suddenly together before him and with such force did their heads meet that they relaxed their grasps upon him and sank unconscious to the floor, and then it was that the ape-man leaped with the agility of a cat to the dais where sat the Emperor, Sublatus.

So quickly had the act been accomplished and so unexpected was it that there was none prepared to come between Tarzan and the Emperor in time to prevent the terrible indignity that Tarzan proceeded to inflict upon him.

Seizing the Emperor by the shoulder, he lifted him from his throne and wheeled him about and then grasping him by the scruff of the neck and the bottom of his cuirass, he lifted him from the floor just as several pikemen leaped forward to rescue Sublatus. But when they were about to menace Tarzan with their pikes, he used the body of the screaming Sublatus as a shield so that the soldiers dared not to attack for fear of killing their Emperor.

'Tell them,' said Tarzan to the Bagego interpreter, 'that if any man interferes with me before I have reached the street, I shall wring the Emperor's neck. Tell him to order them back. If he does, I shall set him free when he is out of the building. If he refuses, it will be at his own risk.'

When this message was given to Sublatus, he stopped screaming orders to his people to attack the ape-man and instead warned them to permit Tarzan to leave the palace. Carrying the Emperor above his head, Tarzan leaped from the dais and as he did so the courtiers fell back in accordance with the commands of Sublatus, who now ordered them to turn their backs that they might not witness the indignity that was being done their ruler.

Down the long throne-room and through the corridors to the outer court Tarzan of the Apes carried Sublatus Imperator above his head and at the command of the ape-man the black interpreter went ahead, but there was no need for him, since Sublatus kept the road clear as he issued commands in a voice that trembled with a combination of rage, fear, and mortification.

At the outer gate the members of the guard begged to be permitted to rescue Sublatus and avenge the insult that had been put upon him, but the Emperor warned them to permit his captor to leave the palace in safety, provided he kept his word and liberated Sublatus when they had reached the avenue beyond the gate.

The scarlet-cloaked guard fell back grumbling, their eyes filled with anger because of the humiliation of their Emperor. Even though they had no love for him, yet he was the personification of the power and dignity of their government, and the scene that they witnessed filled them with mortification as the half-naked barbarian bore their commander-in-chief through the palace gates and out into the tree-bordered avenue beyond, while the black interpreter marched ahead, scarce knowing whether to be more downcast by terror or elated through pride in this unwonted publicity.

The city of Castra Sanguinarius had been carved from the primeval forest that clothed the west end of the canyon, and with unusual vision the founders of the city had cleared only such spaces as were necessary for avenues, buildings, and similar purposes. Ancient trees overhung the avenue before the palace and in many places their foliage overspread the low housetops, mingling with the foliage of the trees in inner courtyards.

Midway of the broad avenue the ape-man halted and lowered Sublatus to the ground. He turned his eyes in the direction of the gateway through which the soldiers of Sublatus were crowding out into the avenue.

'Tell them,' said Tarzan to the interpreter, 'to go back into the palace grounds; then and then only shall I release their Emperor,' for Tarzan had noted the ready javelins in the hands of many of the guardsmen and guessed that the moment his body ceased to be protected by the near presence of Sublatus it would be the target and the goal of a score of the weapons.

When the interpreter delivered the ape-man's ultimatum to them, the guardsmen hesitated, but Sublatus commanded them to obey, for the barbarian's heavy grip upon his shoulder convinced him that there was no hope that he might escape alive or uninjured unless he and his soldiers acceded to the creature's demand. As the last of the guardsmen passed back into the palace courtyard Tarzan released the Emperor and as Sublatus hastened quickly toward the gate, the guardsmen made a sudden sally into the avenue.

They saw their quarry turn and take a few quick steps, leap high into the air and disappear amidst the foliage of an overhanging oak. A dozen javelins hurtled among the branches of the tree. The soldiers rushed forward, their eyes strained upward, but the quarry had vanished.

Sublatus was close upon their heels. 'Quick!' he cried. 'After him! A thousand denarii to the man who brings down the barbarian.'

'There he goes!' cried one, pointing.

'No,' cried another. 'I saw him there among the foliage. I saw the branches move,' and he pointed in the opposite direction.

And in the meantime the ape-man moved swiftly through the trees along one side of the avenue, dropped to a low roof, crossed it and sprang into a tree that rose from an inner court, pausing there to listen for signs of pursuit. After the manner of a wild beast hunted through his native jungle, he moved as silently as the shadow of a shadow, so that now, although he crouched scarce twenty feet above them, the two people in the courtyard below him were unaware of his presence.

But Tarzan was not unaware of theirs and as he listened to the noise of the growing pursuit that was spreading now in all directions through the city, he took note of the girl and the man in the garden beneath him. It was apparent that the man was wooing the maid, and Tarzan needed no knowledge of their spoken language to interpret the gestures, the glances, and the facial expressions of passionate pleading upon the part of the man or the cold aloofness of the girl.

Sometimes a tilt of her head presented a partial view of her profile to the ape-man and he guessed that she was very beautiful, but the face of the young man with her reminded him of the face of Pamba the rat.

It was evident that his courtship was not progressing to the liking of the youth and now there were evidences of anger in his tone. The girl rose haughtily and with a cold word turned away, and then the man leaped to his feet from the bench upon which they had been sitting and seized her roughly by the arm. She turned surprised and angry eyes upon him and had half voiced a cry for help when the rat-faced man clapped a hand across her mouth and with his free arm dragged her into his embrace.

Now all this was none of Tarzan's affair. The shes of the city of Castro Sanguinarius meant no more to the savage ape-man than did the shes of the village of Nyuto, chief of the Bagegos. They meant no more to him than did Sabor the lioness and far less than did the shes of the tribe of Akut or of Toyat the king apes – but Tarzan of the Apes was often a creature of impulses; now he realized that he did not like the rat-faced young man, and that he never could like him, while the girl that he was maltreating seemed to be doubly likeable because of her evident aversion to her tormentor.

The man had bent the girl's frail body back upon the bench. His lips were close to hers when there was a sudden jarring of the ground beside him and he turned astonished eyes upon the figure of a half-naked giant. Steel-grey eyes looked into his beady black ones, a heavy hand fell upon the collar of his tunic, and he felt himself lifted from the body of the girl and then hurled roughly aside.

He saw his assailant lift his victim to her feet and his little eyes saw, too, another thing: the stranger was unarmed! Then it was that the sword of Fastus leaped from its scabbard and that Tarzan of the Apes found himself facing naked steel. The girl saw what Fastus would do. She saw that the stranger who protected her was unarmed and she leaped between them, at the same time calling loudly, 'Axuch! Sarus! Mpingu! Hither! Quickly!'

Tarzan seized the girl and swung her quickly behind him, and simultaneously Fastus was upon him. But the Roman had reckoned without his host and the easy conquest over an unarmed man that he had expected seemed suddenly less easy of accomplishment, for when his keen Spanish sword swung down to cleave the body of his foe, that foe was not there.

Never in his life had Fastus witnessed such agility. It was as though the eyes and body of the barbarian moved more rapidly than the sword of Fastus, and always a fraction of an inch ahead.

Three times Fastus swung viciously at the stranger, and three times his blade cut empty air, while the girl, wide-eyed with astonishment, watched the seemingly unequal duel. Her heart filled with admiration for this strange young giant, who, though he was evidently a barbarian, looked more the patrician than Fastus himself. Three times the blade of Fastus cut harmlessly through empty air – and then there was a lightning-like movement on the part of his antagonist. A brown hand shot beneath the guard of the Roman, steel fingers gripped his wrist, and an instant later the sword clattered to the tile walk of the courtyard. At the same moment two white men and a negro hurried breathlessly into the garden and ran quickly forward – two with daggers in their hands and one, the black, with a sword.

They saw Tarzan standing between Fastus and the girl. They saw the man in the grip of a stranger. They saw the sword clatter to the ground, and naturally they reached the one conclusion that seemed possible – Fastus was being worsted in an attempt to protect the girl against a stranger.

Tarzan saw them coming toward him and realized that three to one are heavy odds. He was upon the point of using Fastus as a shield against his new enemies when the girl stepped before the three and motioned them to stop. Again the tantalizing tongue that he could almost understand and yet not quite, as the girl explained the circumstances to the newcomers while Tarzan still stood holding Fastus by the wrist.

Presently the girl turned to Tarzan and addressed him, but he only shook his head to indicate that he could not understand her; then, as his eyes fell upon the black, a possible means of communicating with these people occurred to him, for the negro resembled closely the Bagegos of the outer world.

'Are you a Bagego?' asked Tarzan in the language of that tribe.

The black looked surprised. 'Yes,' he said, 'I am, but who are you?'

'And you speak the language of these people?' asked Tarzan, indicating the young woman and Fastus and ignoring the black's query.

'Of course,' said the black. 'I have been a prisoner among them for many years, but there are many Bagegos among my fellow prisoners and we have not forgotten the language of our mothers.'

'Good,' said Tarzan. 'Through you this young woman may speak to me.'

'She wants to know who you are, and where you came from, and what you were doing in her garden, and how you got here, and how you happened to protect her from Fastus, and—'

Tarzan held up his hand. 'One at a time,' he cried. 'Tell her I am Tarzan of the Apes, a stranger from a far country, and I came here in friendship seeking one of my own people who is lost.'

Now came an interruption in the form of loud pounding and hallooing beyond the outer doorway of the building.

'See what that may be, Axuch,' directed the girl, and as the one so addressed, and evidently a slave, humbly turned to do her bidding, she once more addressed Tarzan through the interpreter.

'You have won the gratitude of Dilecta,' she said, 'and you shall be rewarded by her father.'

At this moment Axuch returned followed by a young officer. As the eyes of the newcomer fell upon Tarzan they went wide and he started back, his hand going to the hilt of his sword, and simultaneously Tarzan recognized him as Maximus Præclarus, the young patrician officer who had conducted him from the Colosseum to the palace.

'Lay off your sword, Maximus Præclarus,' said the young girl, 'for this man is no enemy.'

'And you are sure of that, Dilecta?' demanded Præclarus. 'What do you know of him?'

'I know that he came in time to save me from this swine who would have harmed me,' said the girl haughtily, casting a withering glance at Fastus.

'I do not understand,' said Præclarus. 'This is a barbarian prisoner of war who calls himself Tarzan and whom I took this morning from the Colosseum to the palace at the command of the Emperor, that Sublatus might look upon the strange creature, whom some thought to be a spy from Castrum Mare.'

'If he is a prisoner, what is he doing here, then?' demanded the girl. 'And why are you here?'

'This fellow attacked the Emperor himself and then escaped from the palace. The entire city is being searched and I, being in charge of a detachment of soldiers assigned to this district, came immediately hither, fearing the very thing that has happened and that this wild man might find you and do you harm.'

'It was the patrician, Fastus, son of Imperial Cæsar, who would have harmed me,' said the girl. 'It was the wild man who saved me from him.'

Maximus Præclarus looked quickly at Fastus, the son of Sublatus, and then at Tarzan. The young officer appeared to be resting upon the horns of a dilemma.

'There is your man,' said Fastus, with a sneer. 'Back to the dungeons with him.'

'Maximus Præclarus does not take order from Fastus,' said the young man, 'and he knows his duty without consulting him.'

'You will arrest this man who has protected me, Præclarus?' demanded Dilecta.

'What else may I do?' asked Præclarus. 'It is my duty.'

'Then do it,' sneered Fastus.

Præclarus went white. 'It is with difficulty that I can keep my hands off you, Fastus,' he said. 'If you were the son of Jupiter himself, it would not take much more to get yourself choked. If you know what is well for you, you will go before I lose control of my temper.'

'Mpingu,' said Dilecta, 'show Fastus to the avenue.'

Fastus flushed. 'My father, the Emperor, shall hear of this,' he snarled; 'and do not forget, Dilecta, your father stands none too well in the estimation of Sublatus Imperator.'

'Begone,' cried Dilecta, 'before I order my black slave to throw you into the avenue.'

With a sneer and a swagger Fastus quit the garden, and when he had gone Dilecta turned to Maximus Præclarus.

'What shall we do?' she cried. 'I must protect this noble stranger who saved me from Fastus, and at the same time you must do your duty and return him to Sublatus.'

'I have a plan,' said Maximus Præclarus, 'but I cannot carry it out unless I can talk with the stranger.'

'Mpingu can understand and interpret for him,' said the girl.

'Can you trust Mpingu implicitly?' asked Præclarus.

'Absolutely,' said Dilecta.

'Then send away the others,' said Præclarus, indicating Axuch and Sarus; and when Mpingu returned from escorting Fastus to the street he found Maximus Præclarus, Dilecta, and Tarzan alone in the garden.

Præclarus motioned Mpingu to advance. 'Tell the stranger that I have been sent to arrest him,' he said to Mpingu, 'but tell him also that because of the service he has rendered Dilecta I wish to protect him, if he will follow my instructions.'

'What are they?' asked Tarzan when the question had been put to him. 'What do you wish me to do?'

'I wish you to come with me,' said Præclarus; 'to come with me as though you were my prisoner. I shall take you in the direction of the Colosseum and when I am opposite my own home I shall give you a signal so that you will understand that the house is mine. Immediately afterward I will make it possible for you to escape into the trees as you did when you quit the palace with Sublatus. Go, then, immediately to my house and remain there until I return. Dilecta will send Mpingu there now to warn my servants that you are coming. At my command they will protect you with their lives. Do you understand?'

'I understand,' replied the ape-man, when the plan had been explained to him by Mpingu.

'Later,' said Præclarus, 'we may be able to find a way to get you out of Castra Sanguinarius and across the mountains.'

—

10

The cares of state rested lightly upon the shoulders of Validus Augustus, Emperor of the East, for though his title was imposing his domain was small and his subjects few. The island city of Castrum Mare boasted a population of only a trifle more than twenty-two thousand people, of which some three thousand were whites and nineteen thousand of mixed blood, while outside the city, in the villages of the lake dwellers, and along the eastern shore of Mare Orientis, dwelt the balance of his subjects, comprising some twenty-six thousand blacks.

Today, reports and audiences disposed of, the Emperor had withdrawn to the palace garden to spend an hour in conversation with a few of his intimates, while his musicians, concealed within a vine-covered bower, entertained him. While he was thus occupied a chamberlain approached and announced that the patrician Fulvus Fupus begged an audience of the Emperor.

'Fulvus knows that the audience hour is past,' snapped the Emperor. 'Bid him come on the morrow.'

'He insists, most glorious Cæsar,' said the chamberlain, 'that his business is of the utmost importance and that it is only because he felt that the safety of the Emperor is at stake that he came at this hour.'

'Bring him here then,' commanded Validus, and, as the chamberlain turned away, 'Am I never to have a moment's relaxation without some fool like Fulvus Fupus breaking in upon me with some silly story?' he grumbled to one of his companions.

When Fulvus approached the Emperor a moment later, he was received with a cold and haughty stare.

'I have come, most glorious Cæsar,' said Fulvus, 'to fulfil the duty of a citizen of Rome, whose first concern should be the safety of his Emperor.'

'What are you talking about?' snapped Validus. 'Quick, out with it!'

'There is a stranger in Castrum Mare who claims to be a barbarian from Germania, but I believe him to be a spy from Castrum Sanguinarius where, it is said, Cassius Hasta is an honoured guest of Sublatus, in that city.'

'What do you know about Cassius Hasta and what has he to do with it?' demanded Validus.

'It is said – it is rumoured,' stammered Fulvus Fupus, 'that—'

'I have heard too many rumours already about Cassius Hasta,' exclaimed Validus. 'Can I not dispatch my nephew upon a mission without every fool in Castrum Mare lying awake nights to conjure motives, which may later be ascribed to me.'

'It is only what I heard,' said Fulvus, flushed and uncomfortable. 'I do not know anything about it. I did not say that I knew.'

'Well, what did you hear?' demanded Validus. 'Come, out with it.'

'The talk is common in the Baths that you sent Cassius Hasta away because he was plotting treason and that he went at once to Sublatus, who received him in a friendly fashion and that together they are planning an attack upon Castrum Mare.'

Validus scowled. 'Baseless rumour,' he said; 'but what about this prisoner? What has he to do with it and why have I not been advised of his presence?'

'That I do not know,' said Fulvus Fupus. 'That is why I felt it doubly my duty to inform you, since the man who is harbouring the stranger is a most powerful patrician and one who might well be ambitious.'

'Who is he?' asked the Emperor.

'Septimus Favonius,' replied Fupus.

'Septimus Favonius,' exclaimed Validus. 'Impossible.'

'Not so impossible,' said Fupus, boldly, 'if glorious Cæsar will but recall the friendship that ever existed between Cassius Hasta and Mallius Lepus, the nephew of Septimus Favonius. The home of Septimus Favonius was the other home of Cassius Hasta. To whom, then, sooner might he turn for aid than to his powerful friend whose ambitions are well known outside the palace, even though they may not as yet have come to the ears of Validus Augustus?'

Nervously the Emperor arose and paced to and fro, the eyes of the others watching him narrowly; those of Fulvus Fupus narrowed with malign anticipation.

Presently Validus halted and turned towards one of his courtiers. 'May Hercules strike me dead,' he cried, 'if there be not some truth in what Fulvus Fupus suggests!' and to Fupus, 'What is this stranger like?'

'He is a man of white skin, yet of slightly different complexion and appearance than the usual patrician. He feigns to speak our language with a certain practised stiltedness that is intended to suggest lack of familiarity. This, I think, is merely a part of the ruse to deceive.'

'How did he come into Castrum Mare and none of my officers report the matter to me?' asked Validus.

'That you may learn from Mallius Lepus,' said Fulvus Fupus, 'for Mallius Lepus was in command of the Porta Decumana when some of the barbarians of the lake villages brought him there, presumably a prisoner, yet Cæsar knows how easy it would have been to bribe these creatures to play such a part.'

'You explain it so well, Fulvus Fupus,' said the Emperor, 'that one might even suspect you to have been the instigator of the plot, or at least to have given much though to similar schemes.'

'Cæsar's ever brilliant wit never deserts him,' said Fupus, forcing a smile, though his face paled.

'We shall see,' snapped Validus, and turning to one of his officers, 'Order the arrest of Septimus Favonius, and Mallius Lepus and this stranger at once.'

As he ceased speaking a chamberlain entered the garden and approached the Emperor. 'Septimus Favonius requests an audience,' he announced. 'Mallius Lepus, his nephew, and a stranger are with him.'

'Fetch them,' said Validus, and to the officer who was about to depart to arrest them, 'Wait here. We shall see what Septimus Favonius has to say.'

A moment later the three entered and approached the Emperor. Favonius and Lepus saluted Validus and then the former presented von Harben as a barbarian chief from Germania.

'We have already heard of this barbarian chief,' said Validus, with a sneer. Favonius and Lepus glanced at Fupus. 'Why was I not immediately notified of the capture of this prisoner?' This time the Emperor directed his remarks to Mallius Lepus.

'There has been little delay, Cæsar,' replied the young officer. 'It was necessary that he be bathed and properly clothed before he was brought here.'

'It was not necessary that he be brought here,' said Validus. 'There are dungeons in Castrum Mare for prisoners from Castra Sanguinarius.'

'He is not from Castra Sanguinarius,' said Septimus Favonius.

'Where are you from and what are you doing in my country?' demanded Validus, turning upon von Harben.

'I am from a country that your historians knew as Germania,' replied Erich.

'And I suppose you learned to speak our language in Germania,' sneered Validus.

'Yes,' replied von Harben, 'I did.'

'And you have never been to Castra Sanguinarius?'

'Never.'

'I presume you have been to Rome,' laughed Validus.

'Yes, many times,' replied von Harben.

'And who is Emperor there now?'

'There is no Roman Emperor,' said von Harben.

'No Roman Emperor!' exclaimed Validus. 'If you are not a spy from Castra Sanguinarius, you are a lunatic. Perhaps you are both, for no one but a lunatic would expect me to believe such a story. No Roman Emperor, indeed!'

'There is no Roman Emperor,' said von Harben, 'because there is no Roman Empire. Mallius Lepus tells me that your country has had no intercourse with the outside world for more than eighteen hundred years. Much can happen in that time – much has happened. Rome fell, over a thousand years ago. No nation speaks its language today, which is understood by priests and scholars only. The barbarians of Germania, of Gallia, and of Britannia have built empires and civilizations of tremendous power, and Rome is only a city in Italia.'

Mallius Lepus was beaming delightedly. 'I told you,' he whispered to Favonius, 'that you would love him. By Jupiter, I wish he would tell Validus the story of the litters that travel fifty thousand paces an hour!'

There was that in the tone and manner of von Harben that compelled confidence and belief, so that even the suspicious Validus gave credence to the seemingly wild tales of the stranger and presently found himself asking questions of the barbarian.

Finally the Emperor turned to Fulvus Fupus. 'Upon what proof did you accuse this man of being a spy from Castra Sanguinarius?' he demanded.

'Where else may he be from?' asked Fulvus Fupus. 'We know he is not from Castrum Mare, so he must be from Castrum Sanguinarius.'

'You have no evidence then to substantiate your accusations?'

Fupus hesitated.

'Get out,' ordered Validus, angrily. 'I shall attend to you later.'

Overcome by mortification, Fupus left the garden, but the malevolent glances that he shot at Favonius, Lepus, and Erich boded them no good. Validus looked long and searchingly at von Harben for several minutes after Fupus had left the garden as though attempting to read the soul of the stranger standing before him.

'So there is no Emperor at Rome,' he mused, half aloud. 'When Sanguinarius led his cohort out of Ægyptus, Nerva was Emperor. That was upon the sixth day before the calends of February in the 848th year of the city in the second year of Nerva's reign. Since that day no word of Rome has reached the descendants of Sanguinarius and his cohort.'

Von Harben figured rapidly, searching his memory of the historical dates and data of ancient history that were as fresh in his mind as those of his own day. 'The sixth day before the calends of February,' he repeated; 'that would be the twenty-seventh day of January in the 848th year of the city – why, January twenty-seventh, AD 98, is the date of Nerva's death,' he said.

'Ah, if Sanguinarius had but known,' said Validus, 'but Ægyptus is a long way from Rome and Sanguinarius was far to the south up the Nilus before word could have reached his post by ancient Thebæ that his enemy was dead. And who became Emperor after Nerva? Do you know "Trajan,"' replied von Harben.

'Why do you, a barbarian, know so much concerning the history of Rome?' asked the Emperor.

'I am a student of such things,' replied von Harben. 'It has been my ambition to become an authority on the subject.'

'Could you write down these happenings since the death of Nerva?'

'I could put down all that I could recall, or all that I have read,' said von Harben, 'but it would take a long time.'

'You shall do it,' said Validus, 'and you shall have the time.'

'But I have not planned remaining in your country,' dissented von Harben.

'You shall remain,' said Validus. 'You shall also write a history of the reign of Validus Augustus, Emperor of the East.'

'But—' interjected von Harben.

'Enough!' snapped Validus. 'I am Cæsar. It is a command.'

Von Harben shrugged and smiled. Rome and the Cæsars, he realized had never seemed other than musty parchment and weather-worn inscriptions cut in crumbling stone, until now.

Here, indeed, was a real Cæsar. What mattered it that his empire was naught but a few square miles of marsh, an island and swampy shore-land in the bottom of an unknown canyon, or that his subjects numbered less than fifty thousand souls – the first Augustus himself was no more a Cæsar than was his namesake, Validus.

'Come,' said Validus, 'I shall take you to the library myself, for that will be the scene of your labours.'

In the library, which was a vault-like room at the end of a long corridor, Validus displayed with pride several hundred parchment rolls neatly arranged upon shelves.

'Here,' said Validus, selecting one of the rolls, 'is the story of Sanguinarius and the history of our country up to the founding of Castrum Mare. Take it with you and read it at your leisure, for while you shall remain with Septimus Favonius, whom with Mallius Lepus I shall hold responsible for you, every day you shall come to the palace and I shall dictate to you the history of my reign. Go, now, with Septimus Favonius and at this hour tomorrow attend again upon Cæsar.'

When they were outside the palace of Validus Augustus, von Harben turned to Mallius Lepus. 'It is a question whether I am prisoner or guest,' he said, with a rueful smile.

'Perhaps you are both,' said Mallius Lepus, 'but that you are even partially a guest is fortunate for you. Validus Augustus is vain, arrogant, and cruel. He is also suspicious, for he knows that he is not popular, and Fulvus Fupus had evidently almost succeeded in bringing your doom upon you and ruin to Favonius and myself before we arrived. What strange whim altered the mind of Cæsar I do not know, but it is fortunate for you that it was altered; fortunate, too, for Septimus Favonius and Mallius Lepus.'

'But it will take years to write the history of Rome,' said von Harben.

'And if you refuse to write it you will be dead many more years than it would take to accomplish the task,' retorted Mallius Lepus, with a grin.

'Castrum Mare is not an unpleasant place in which to live,' said Septimus Favonius.

'Perhaps you are right,' said von Harben, as the face of the daughter of Favonius presented itself to his mind.

Returned to the home of his host, the instinct of the archæologist and the scholar urged von Harben to an early perusal of the ancient papyrus roll that Cæsar had lent him, so that no sooner was he in the apartments that had been set aside for him than he stretched himself upon a long sofa and untied the cords that confined the roll.

As it unrolled before his eyes he saw a manuscript in ancient Latin marred by changes and erasures, yellowed by age. It was quite unlike anything that had previously fallen into his hands during his scholarly investigations into the history and literature of ancient Rome. For whereas such other original ancient manuscripts as he had had the good fortune to examine had been the work of clerks or scholars, a moment's glance at this marked it as the laborious effort of a soldier unskilled in literary pursuits.

The manuscript bristled with the rough idiom of far-flung camps of veteran legionaries, with the slang of Rome and Egypt of nearly two thousand years before, and there were references to people and places that appeared in no histories or geographies known to modern man – little places and little people that were without fame in their own time and whose very memory had long been erased from the consciousness of man, but yet in this crude manuscript they lived again for Erich von Harben – the quæstor who had saved the life of Sanguinarius in an Egyptian town that never was on any map, and there was Marcus Crispus Sanguinarius himself who had been of sufficient importance to win the enmity of Nerva in the year 90 AD while the latter was consul – Marcus Crispus Sanguinarius, the founder of an empire, whose name appears nowhere in the annals of ancient Rome.

With mounting interest von Harben read the complaints of Sanguinarius and his anger because the enmity of Nerva had caused him to be relegated to the hot sands of this distant post below the ancient city of Thebæ in far Ægyptus.

Writing in the third person, Sanguinarius had said:

'Sanguinarius, a præfect of the Third Cohort of the Tenth Legion, stationed below Thebæ in Ægyptus in the 846th year of the city, immediately after Nerva assumed the purple, was accused of having plotted against the Emperor.

'About the fifth day before the calends of February in the 848th year of the city a messenger came to Sanguinarius from Nerva commanding the præfect to return to Rome and place himself under arrest, but this Sanguinarius had no mind to do, and as no other in his camp knew the nature of the message he had received from Nerva, Sanguinarius struck the messenger down with his dagger and caused the word to be spread among his men that the man had been an assassin sent from Rome and that Sanguinarius had slain him in self-defence.

'He also told his lieutenants and centurions that Nerva was sending a large force to destroy the cohort and he prevailed upon them to follow up the Nilus in search of a new country where they might establish themselves far from the malignant power of a jealous Cæsar, and upon the following day the long march commenced.

'It so happened that shortly before this a fleet of one hundred and twenty vessels landed at Myos-hormos, a port of Ægyptus on the Sinus Arabius. This merchant fleet annually brought rich merchandise from the island of Taprobana – silk, the value of which was equal to its weight in gold, pearls, diamonds, and a variety of aromatics and other merchandise, which was transferred to the backs of camels and brought inland from Myos-hormos to the Nilus and down that river to Alexandria, whence it was shipped to Rome.

'With this caravan were hundreds of slaves from India and far Cathay and even light-skinned people captured in the distant north-west by Mongol raiders. The majority of these were young girls destined for the auction block at Rome. And it so chanced that Sanguinarius met this caravan, heavy with riches and women, and captured it. During the ensuing five years the cohort settled several times in what they hoped would prove a permanent camp, but it was not until the 853rd year of Rome that, by accident, they discovered the hidden canyon where now stands Castra Sanguinarius.'

'You find it interesting?' inquired a voice from the doorway, and looking up von Harben saw Mallius Lepus standing on the threshold.

'Very,' said Erich.

Lepus shrugged his shoulders. 'We suspect that it would have been more interesting had the old assassin written the truth,' said Lepus. 'As a matter of fact, very little is known concerning his reign, which lasted for twenty years. He was assassinated in the year 20 Anno Sanguinarii, which corresponds to the 873rd year of Rome. The old buck named the city after himself, decreed a calendar of his own, and had his head stamped on gold coins, many of which are still in existence. Even today we use his calendar quite as much as that of our Roman ancestors, but in Castrum Mare we have tried to forget the example of Sanguinarius as much as possible.'

'What is this other city that I have heard mentioned to often and that is called Castra Sanguinarius?' asked von Harben.

'It is the original city founded by Sanguinarius,' replied Lepus. 'For a hundred years after the founding of the city conditions grew more and more intolerable until no man's life or property was safe, unless he was willing to reduce himself almost to the status of a slave and continually fawn upon the Emperor. It was then that Honus Hasta revolted and led a few hundred families to this island at the eastern end of the valley, founding the city and the empire of Castrum Mare. Here, for over seventeen hundred years, the descendants of the families have lived in comparative peace and security, but in an almost constant state of war with Castra Sanguinarius.

'From mutual necessity the two cities carry on a commerce that is often interrupted by raids and wars. The suspicion and hatred that the inhabitants of each city feel for the inhabitants of the other is fostered always by our Emperors, each of whom fears that friendly communication between the two cities would result in the overthrow of one of them.'

'And now Castrum Mare is happy and contented under Cæsar?' asked Erich.

'That is a question that it might not be safe to answer honestly,' said Lepus, with a shrug.

'If I am going to the palace every day to write the history of Rome for Validus Augustus and receive from him the story of his reign,' said von Harben, 'it might be well if I knew something of the man, otherwise there is a chance for me to get into serious trouble, which might conceivably react upon you and Septimus Favonius, whom Cæsar has made responsible for me. If you care to forewarn me, I promise you that I shall repeat nothing that you may tell me.'

Lepus, leaning lightly against the wall by the doorway, played idly with the hilt of his dagger as he took thought before replying. Presently he looked up, straight into von Harben's eyes.

'I shall trust you,' he said; 'first, because there is that in you which inspires confidence, and, second, because it cannot profit you to harm either Septimus Favonius or myself. Castrum Mare is not happy with its Cæsar. He is arrogant and cruel – not like the Cæsars to which Castrum Mare has been accustomed.

'The last Emperor was a kindly man, but at the time of his death his brother, Validus Augustus, was chosen to succeed him because Cæsar's son was, at that time, but a year old.

'This son of the former Emperor, a nephew of Validus Augustus, is called Cassius Hasta. And because of his popularity he has aroused the jealousy and hatred of Augustus, who recently sent him away upon a dangerous mission to the west end of the valley. There are many who consider it virtual banishment, but Validus Augustus insists that this is not the fact. No one knows what Cassius Hasta's orders were. He went secretly by night and was accompanied by only a few slaves.

'It is believed that he has been ordered to enter Castra Sanguinarius as a spy, and if such is the case his mission amounts practically to a sentence of death. If this were known for a fact, the people would rise against Validus Augustus, for Cassius Hasta was the most popular man in Castrum Mare.

'But enough. I shall not bore you with the sorrows of Castrum Mare. Take your reading down into the garden where, in the shade of the trees, it is cooler than here and I shall join you presently.'

As von Harben lay stretched upon the sward beneath the shade of a tree in the cool garden of Septimus Favonius, his mind was not upon the history of Sanguinarius, nor upon the political woes of Castrum Mare so much as they were upon plans for escape.

As a scholar, an explorer, and an archæologist he would delight in remaining here for such a time as might be necessary for him to make an exploration of the valley and study the government and customs of its inhabitants, but to remain cooped up in the vault-like library of the Emperor of the East writing the history of ancient Rome in Latin with a reed pen on papyrus rolls in no way appealed to him.

The rustle of fresh linen and the soft fall of sandalled feet upon the gravelled garden walk interrupted his trend of thought and as he looked up into the face of Favonia, daughter of Septimus Favonius, the history of ancient Rome together with half-formulated plans for escape were dissipated from his mind by the girl's sweet smile, as is a morning mist by the rising sun.

11

As Maximus Præclarus led Tarzan of the Apes from the home of Dion Splendidus in the city of Castra Sanguinarius, the soldiers, gathered by the doorway, voiced their satisfaction in oaths and exclamations. They liked the young patrician who commanded them and they were proud that he should have captured the wild barbarian single-handed.

A command from Præclarus brought silence and at a word from him they formed around the prisoner, and the march toward the Colosseum was begun. They had proceeded but a short distance when Præclarus halted the detachment and went himself to the doorway of a house fronting on the avenue through which they were crossing. He halted before the door, stood in thought for a moment, and then turned back toward his detachment as though he had changed his mind about entering, and Tarzan knew that the young officer was indicating to him the home in which he lived and in which the ape-man might find sanctuary later.

Several hundred yards farther along the street, after they had resumed the march, Præclarus halted his detachment beneath the shade of great trees opposite a drinking fountain, which was built into the outside of a garden wall close beside an unusually large tree, which, overspreading the avenue upon one side and the wall on the other, intermingled its branches with those of other trees growing inside the garden beyond.

Præclarus crossed the avenue and drank at the fountain and returning inquired by means of signs if Tarzan would drink. The ape-man nodded in assent and Præclarus gave orders that he be permitted to cross to the fountain.

Slowly Tarzan walked to the other side of the avenue. He stooped and drank from the fountain. Beside him was the bole of a great tree; above him was the leafy foliage that would conceal him from the sight and protect him from the missiles of the soldiers. Turning from the fountain, a quick step took him behind the tree. One of the soldiers shouted a warning to Præclarus, and the whole detachment, immediately suspicious, leaped quickly across the avenue, led by the young patrician who commanded them, but when they reached the fountain and the tree their prisoner had vanished.

Shouting their disappointment, they gazed upward into the foliage, but there was no sign there of the barbarian. Several of the more active soldiers scrambled into the branches and then Maximus Præclarus, pointing in the direction opposite to that in which his home lay, shouted: 'This way, there he goes!' and started on a run down the avenue, while behind him strung his detachment, their pikes ready in their hands.

Moving silently through the branches of the great trees that overhung the greater part of the city of Castra Sanguinarius, Tarzan paralleled the avenue leading back to the home of Maximus Præclarus, halting at last in a tree that overlooked the inner courtyard or walled garden, which appeared to be a distinguishing feature of the architecture of the city.

Below him he saw a matronly woman of the patrician class, listening to a tall black who was addressing her excitedly. Clustered about the woman and eagerly listening to the words of the speaker were a number of black slaves, both men and women.

Tarzan recognised the speaker as Mpingu, and, although he could not understand his words, realized that the black was preparing them for his arrival in accordance with the instructions given him in the garden of Dion Splendidus by Maximus Præclarus, and that he was making a good story of it was evidenced by his excited gesticulation and the wide eyes and open mouths of the listening blacks.

The woman, listening attentively and with quiet dignity of mien, appeared to be slightly amused, but whether at the story itself or at the unrestrained excitement of Mpingu, Tarzan did not know.

She was a regal-looking woman of about fifty, with greying hair and with the poise and manner of that perfect self-assurance which is the hallmark of assured position; that she was a patrician to her finger tips was evident, and yet there was that in her eyes and the little wrinkles at their corners that bespoke a broad humanity and a kindly disposition.

Mpingu had evidently reached the point where his vocabulary could furnish no adequate superlatives wherewith to describe the barbarian who had rescued his mistress from Fastus, and he was acting out in exaggerated pantomime the scene in the garden of his mistress, when Tarzan dropped lightly to the sward beside him. The effect upon the blacks of this unexpected appearance verged upon the ludicrous, but the white woman was unmoved to any outward sign of surprise.

'Is this the barbarian?' she asked of Mpingu.

'It is he,' replied the black.

'Tell him that I am Festivitas, the mother of Maximus Præclarus,' the woman directed Mpingu, 'and that I welcome him here in the name of my son.'

Through Mpingu, Tarzan acknowledged the greetings of Festivitas and thanked her for her hospitality, after which she instructed one of her slaves to conduct the stranger to the apartments that were placed at his disposal.

It was late afternoon before Maximus Præclarus returned to his home, going immediately to Tarzan's apartments. With him was the same black who had acted as interpreter in the morning.

'I am to remain here with you,' said the black to Tarzan, 'as your interpreter and servant.'

'I venture to say,' said Præclarus through the interpreter, 'that this is the only spot in Castra Sanguinarius that they have not searched for you and there are three centuries combing the forests outside the city, though by this time Sublatus is convinced that you have escaped. We shall keep you here in hiding for a few days when, I think, I can find the means to get you out of the city after dark.'

The ape-man smiled. 'I can leave whenever I choose,' he said, 'either by day or by night, but I do not choose to leave until I have satisfied myself that the man for whom I am searching is not here. But, first, let me thank you for your kindness to me, the reason for which I cannot understand.'

'That is easily explained,' said Præclarus. 'The young woman whom you saved from attack this morning is Dilecta, the daughter of Dion Splendidus. She and I are to be married. That I think will explain my gratitude.'

'I understand,' said Tarzan, 'and I am glad that I was fortunate enough to come upon them at the time that I did.'

'Should you be captured again, it will not prove so fortunate for you,' said Præclarus, 'for the man from whom you saved Dilecta is Fastus, the son of Sublatus, and now the Emperor will have two indignities to avenge; but if you remain here you will be safe, for our slaves are loyal and there is little likelihood that you will be discovered.'

'If I remain here,' said Tarzan, 'and it should be discovered that you had befriended me, would not the anger of the Emperor fall upon you?'

Maximus Præclarus shrugged. 'I am daily expecting that,' he said; 'not because of you, but because the son of the Emperor wishes to marry Dilecta. Sublatus needs no further excuse to destroy me. I should be no worse off were he to learn that I have befriended you than I now am.'

'Then, perhaps, I may be of service to you if I remain,' said Tarzan.

'I do not see how you can do anything but remain,' said Præclarus. 'Every man, woman, and child in Castra Sanguinarius will be on the lookout for you, for Sublatus has offered a huge reward for your capture, and besides the inhabitants of the city there are thousands of black barbarians outside the walls who will lay aside every other interest to run you down.'

'Twice today you have seen how easily I can escape from the soldiers of Sublatus,' said Tarzan, smiling. 'Just as easily can I leave the city and elude the barbarians in the outer villages.'

'Then why do you remain?' demanded Præclarus.

'I came here searching for the son of a friend,' replied Tarzan. 'Many weeks ago the young man started out with an expedition to explore the Wiramwazi Mountains in which your country is located. His people deserted him upon the outer slopes, and I am convinced that he is somewhere within the range and very possibly in this canyon. If he is here and alive, he will unquestionably come sooner or later to your city where, from the experience that I have gained, I am sure that he will receive anything but friendly treatment from your Emperor. This is the reason that I wish to remain somewhere in the vicinity, and now that you have told me that you are in danger, I may as well remain in your home where it is possible I may have an opportunity to reciprocate your kindness to me.'

'If the son of your friend is in this end of the valley, he will be captured and brought to Castra Sanguinarius,' said Maximus Præclarus, 'and when that occurs I shall know of it, since I am detailed to duty at the Colosseum – a mark of the disfavour of Sublatus, since this is the most distasteful duty to which an officer can be assigned.'

'Is it possible that this man for whom I am searching might be in some other part of the valley?' asked Tarzan.

'No,' replied Præclarus. 'There is only one entrance to the valley, that through which you were brought, and while there is another city at the eastern end, he could not reach it without passing through the forests surrounding Castra Sanguinarius, in which event he would have been captured by the barbarians and turned over to Sublatus.'

'Then I shall remain here,' said Tarzan, 'for a time.'

'You shall be a welcome guest,' replied Præclarus.

For three weeks Tarzan remained in the home of Maximus Præclarus. Festivitas conceived a great liking for the bronzed barbarian, and soon tiring of carrying on conversation with him through an interpreter, she set about teaching him her own language, with the result that it was not long before Tarzan could carry on a conversation in Latin; nor did he lack opportunity to practise his new accomplishment, since Festivitas never tired of hearing stories of the outer world and of the manners and customs of modern civilisation.

And while Tarzan of the Apes waited in Castra Sanguinarius for word that von Harben had been seen in the valley, the man he sought was living the life of a young patrician attached to the court of the Emperor of the East, and though much of his time was pleasantly employed in the palace library, yet he chafed at the knowledge that he was virtually a prisoner and was often formulating plans for escape – plans that were sometimes forgotten when he sat beneath the spell of the daughter of Septimus Favonius.

And often in the library he discovered only unadulterated pleasure in his work, and thoughts of escape were driven from his mind by discoveries of such gems as original Latin translations of Homer and of hitherto unknown manuscripts of Virgil, Cicero and Cæsar – manuscripts that dated from the days of the young republic and on down the centuries to include one of the early satires of Juvenal.

Thus the days passed, while far off in another world a frightened little monkey scampered through the upper terraces of a distant forest.

12

A penchant for boasting is not the prerogative of any time, or race, or individual, but is more or less common to all. So it is not strange that Mpingu, filled with the importance of the secret that he alone shared with his mistress, and the household of Maximus Præclarus, should have occasionally dropped a word here and there that might impress his listeners with his importance.

Mpingu meant no harm. He was loyal to the house of Dion Splendidus and he would not willingly have brought harm to his master or his master's friend, but so it is often with people who talk too much, and Mpingu certainly had done that. The result was that upon a certain day, as he was bartering in the market-place for provisions for the kitchen of Dion Splendidus, he felt a heavy hand upon his shoulder and, turning, he was astonished to find himself looking into the face of a centurion of the palace guard, behind whom stood a file of legionaries.

'You are Mpingu, the slave of Dion Splendidus?' demanded the centurion.

'I am,' replied the black.

'Come with us,' commanded the centurion.

Mpingu drew back, afraid, as all men feared the soldiers of Cæsar. 'What do you want of me?' he demanded. 'I have done nothing.'

'Come, barbarian,' ordered the soldier. 'I was not sent to confer with you, but to get you!' And he jerked Mpingu roughly toward him and pushed him back among the soldiers.

A crowd had gathered, as crowds gather always when a man is arrested, but the centurion ignored the crowd as though it did not exist, and the people fell aside as the soldiers marched away with Mpingu. No one questioned or interfered, for who would dare question an officer of Cæsar? Who would interfere on behalf of a black slave?

Mpingu thought that he would be taken to the dungeons beneath the Colosseum which was the common jail in which all prisoners were confined; but presently he realized that his captors were not leading him in that direction, and when finally it dawned upon him that the palace was their goal he was filled with terror.

Never before had Mpingu stepped foot within the precincts of the palace grounds, and when the imperial gate closed behind him he was in a mental state bordering upon collapse. He had heard stories of the cruelty of Sublatus, of the terrible vengeance wreaked upon his enemies, and he had visions that paralyzed his mind so that he was in a state of semi-consciousness when he was finally led into an inner chamber where a high dignitary of the court confronted him.

'This,' said the centurion, who had brought him, 'is Mpingu, the slave of Dion Splendidus, whom I was commanded to fetch to you.'

'Good!' said the official. 'You and your detachment may remain while I question him.' Then he turned upon Mpingu. 'Do you know the penalties one incurs for aiding the enemies of Cæsar?' he demanded.

Mpingu's lower jaw moved convulsively as though he would reply, but he was unable to control his voice.

'They die,' growled the officer, menacingly. 'They die terrible deaths that they will remember through all eternity.'

'I have done nothing,' cried Mpingu, suddenly regaining control of his vocal cords.

'Do not lie to me, barbarian,' snapped the official. 'You aided in the escape of the prisoner who called himself Tarzan and even now you are hiding him from your Emperor.'

'I did not help him escape. I am not hiding him,' wailed Mpingu.

'You lie. You know where he is. You boasted of it to other slaves. Tell me where he is.'

'I do not know,' said Mpingu.

'If your tongue were cut out, you could not tell us where he is,' said the Roman. 'If red-hot irons were thrust into your eyes, you could not see to lead us to his hiding-place; but if we find him without your help, and we surely shall find him, we shall need neither your tongue nor your eyes. Do you understand?'

'I do not know where he is,' repeated Mpingu.

The Roman turned away and struck a single blow upon a gong, after which he stood in silence until a slave entered the room in response to the summons. 'Fetch tongs,' the Roman instructed the slave, 'and a charcoal brazier with burning-irons. Be quick.'

After the slave had left, silence fell again upon the apartment. The official was giving Mpingu an opportunity to think, and Mpingu so occupied the time in thinking that it seemed to him that the slave had scarcely left the apartment before he returned again with tongs and a lighted burner, from the glowing heart of which protruded the handle of a burning-iron.

'Have your soldiers throw him to the floor and hold him,' said the official to the centurion.

It was evident to Mpingu that the end had come; the officer was not even going to give him another opportunity to speak.

'Wait!' he shrieked.

'Well,' said the official, 'you are regaining your memory?'

'I am only a slave,' wailed Mpingu. 'I must do what my masters command.'

'And what did they command?' inquired the Roman.

'I was only an interpreter,' said Mpingu. 'The white barbarian spoke the language of the Bagegos, who are my people. Through me they talked to him and he talked to them.'

'And what was said?' demanded the inquisitor.

Mpingu hesitated, dropping his eyes to the floor.

'Come, quickly!' snapped the other.

'I have forgotten,' said Mpingu.

The official nodded to the centurion. The soldiers seized Mpingu and threw him roughly to the floor, four of them holding him there, one seated upon each limb.

'The tongs!' directed the official, and the slave handed the instrument to the centurion.

'Wait!' screamed Mpingu. 'I will tell you.'

'Let him up,' said the official; and to Mpingu: 'This is your last chance. If you go down again, your tongue comes out and your eyes, too.'

'I will talk,' said Mpingu. 'I did but interpret, that is all. I had nothing to do with helping him to escape or hiding him.'

'If you tell us the truth, you will not be punished,' said the Roman. 'Where is the white barbarian?'

'He is hiding in the home of Maximus Præclarus,' said Mpingu.

'What has your master to do with this?' commanded the Roman.

'Dion Splendidus has nothing to do with it,' replied Mpingu. 'Maximus Præclarus planned it.'

'That is all,' said the official to the centurion. 'Take him away and keep him under guard until you receive further orders. Be sure that he talks to no one.'

A few minutes later the official who had interrogated Mpingu entered the apartment of Sublatus while the Emperor was in conversation with his son Fastus.

'I have located the white barbarian, Sublatus,' announced the official.

'Good!' said the Emperor. 'Where is he?'

'In the home of Maximus Præsclarus.'

'I might have suspected as much,' said Fastus.

'Who else is implicated?' asked Sublatus.

'He was caught in the courtyard of Dion Splendidus,' said Fastus, 'and the Emperor has heard, as we all have, that Dion Splendidus has long had eyes upon the imperial purple of the Cæsars.'

'The slave says that only Maximus Præclarus is responsible for the escape of the barbarian,' said the official.

'He was one of Dion Splendidus's slaves, was he not?' demanded Fastus.

'Yes.'

'Then it is not strange that he would protect his master,' said Fastus.

'Arrest them all,' commanded Sublatus.

'You mean Dion Splendidus, Maximus Præclarus, and the barbarian Tarzan?' asked the official.

'I mean those three and the entire household of Dion Splendidus and Maximus Præclarus,' replied Sublatus.

'Wait, Cæsar,' suggested Fastus; 'twice already has the barbarian escaped from the legionaries. If he receives the slightest inkling of this, he will escape again. I have a plan. Listen!'

An hour later a messenger arrived at the home of Dion Splendidus carrying an invitation to the senator and his wife to be the guests of a high court functionary that evening at a banquet. Another messenger went to the home of Maximus Præclarus with a letter urging the young officer to attend an entertainment being given that same evening by a rich young patrician.

As both invitations had emanated from families high in favour with the Emperor, they were, in effect, almost equivalent to commands, even to as influential a senator as Dion Splendidus, and so there was no question either in the minds of the hosts or in the minds of the guests but that they would be accepted.

Night had fallen upon Castra Sanguinarius. Dion Splendidus and his wife were alighting from their litter before the home of their host and Maximus

Præclarus was already drinking with his fellow guests in the banquet hall of one of Castra Sanguinarius's wealthiest citizens. Fastus was there, too, and Maximus Præclarus was surprised and not a little puzzled at the friendly attitude of the prince.

'I always suspect something when Fastus smiles at me,' he said to an intimate.

In the home of Dion Splendidus, Dilecta sat among her female slaves, while one of them told her stories of the wild African village from which she had come.

Tarzan and Festivitas sat in the home of Maximus Præclarus, the Roman matron listening attentively to the stories of savage Africa and civilized Europe that she was constantly urging her strange guest to tell her. Faintly they heard a knock at the outer gate and, presently, a slave came to the apartment where they sat to tell them that Mpingu, the slave of Dion Splendidus, had come with a message for Tarzan.

'Bring him hither,' said Festivitas, and, shortly, Mpingu was ushered into the room.

If Tarzan or Festivitas had known Mpingu better, they would have realized that he was under great nervous strain; but they did not know him well, and so they saw nothing out of the way in his manner or bearing.

'I have been sent to fetch you to the home of Dion Splendidus,' said Mpingu to Tarzan.

'That is strange,' said Festivitas.

'Your noble son stopped at the home of Dion Splendidus on his way to the banquet this evening and as he left I was summoned and told to come hither and fetch the stranger to my master's house,' explained Mpingu. 'That is all I know about the matter.'

'Maximus Præclarus gave you those instructions himself?' asked Festivitas.

'Yes,' replied Mpingu.

'I do not know what his reason can be,' said Festivitas to Tarzan, 'but there must be some very good reason, or he would not run the risk of your being caught.'

'It is very dark out,' said Mpingu. 'No one will see him.'

'There is no danger,' said Tarzan to Festivitas. 'Maximus Præclarus would not have sent for me unless it were necessary. Come, Mpingu!' And he arose, bidding Festivitas goodbye.

Tarzan and Mpingu had proceeded but a short distance down the avenue when the black motioned the ape-man to the side of the street, where a small gate was let into a solid wall.

'We are here,' said Mpingu

'This is not the home of Dion Splendidus,' said Tarzan, immediately suspicious.

Mpingu was surprised that this stranger should so well remember the location of a house that he had visited but once, and that more than three weeks since, but he did not know the training that had been the ape-man's through the long years of moving through the trackless jungle that had trained his every sense and faculty to the finest point of orientation.

'It is not the main gate,' replied Mpingu, quickly, 'but Maximus Præclarus did not think it safe that you be seen entering the main gate of the home of Dion Splendidus in the event that, by any chance, you were observed. This way leads into a lane that might connect with any one of several homes, and once in it there is little or no chance of apprehension.'

'I see,' said Tarzan. 'Lead the way.'

Mpingu opened the gate and motioned Tarzan in ahead of him, and as the ape-man passed through into the blackness beyond there fell upon him what seemed to be a score of men and he was borne down in the same instant that he realised that he had been betrayed. So rapidly did his assailants work that it was a matter of seconds only before the ape-man found shackles upon his wrists, the one thing that he feared and hated most.

13

While Erich von Harben wooed Favonia beneath a summer moon in the garden of Septimus Favonius in the island city of Castrum Mare, a detachment of the brown legionaries of Sublatus Imperator dragged Tarzan of the Apes and Mpingu, the black slave of Dion Splendidus, to the dungeons beneath the Colosseum of Castra Sanguinarius – and far to the south a little monkey shivered from cold and terror in the topmost branches of a jungle giant, while Sheeta the panther crept softly through the black shadows far below.

In the banquet hall of his host, Maximus Præclarus reclined upon a sofa far down the board from Fastus, the guest of honour. The prince, his tongue loosened by frequent draughts of native wine, seemed in unusually good spirits, radiating self-satisfaction. Several times he had brought the subject of conversation around to the strange white barbarian, who had insulted his sire and twice escaped from the soldiers of Sublatus.

'He would never have escaped from me that day,' he boasted, throwing a sneer in the direction of Maximus Præclarus, 'nor from any other officer who is loyal to Cæsar.'

'You had him, Fastus, in the garden of Dion Splendidus,' retorted Præclarus. 'Why did you not hold him?'

Fastus flushed. 'I shall hold him this time,' he blurted.

'This time?' queried Præclarus. 'He has been captured again?' There was nothing in either the voice or expression of the young patrician of more than polite interest, though the words of Fastus had come with all the unexpected suddenness of lightning out of a clear sky.

'I mean,' explained Fastus, in some confusion, 'that if he is again captured I, personally, shall see that he does not escape,' but his words did not allay the apprehensions of Præclarus.

All through the long dinner Præclarus was cognisant of a sensation of foreboding. There was a menace in the air that was apparent in the veiled hostility of his host and several others who were cronies of Fastus.

As early as was seemly he made his excuses and departed. Armed slaves accompanied his litter through the dark avenues of Castra Sanguinarius, where robbery and murder slunk among the shadows hand in hand with the criminal element that had been permitted to propagate itself without restraint; and when at last he came to the doorway at his home and had alighted from his litter he paused and a frown of perplexity clouded his face as he saw that the door stood partially ajar, though there was no slave there to receive him.

The house seemed unusually quiet and lifeless. The night light, which ordinarily a slave kept burning in the forecourt when a member of the household was away, was absent. For an instant Præclarus hesitated upon the threshold and then, pushing his cloak back from his shoulders to free his arms, he pushed the door open and stepped within.

In the banquet hall of a high court functionary the guests yawned behind their hands from boredom, but none dared leave while Cæsar remained, for the Emperor was a guest there that evening. It was late when an officer brought a message to Sublatus – a message that the Emperor read with a satisfaction he made no effort to conceal.

'I have received an important message,' said Sublatus to his host, 'upon a matter that interests the noble Senator Dion Splendidus and his wife. It is my wish that you withdraw with the other guests, leaving us three here alone.'

When they had gone he turned to Dion Splendidus. 'It has long been rumoured, Splendidus,' he remarked, 'that you aspire to the purple.'

'A false rumour, Sublatus, as you should well know,' replied the senator.

'I have reason to believe otherwise,' said Sublatus, shortly. 'There cannot be two Cæsars, Splendidus, and you well know the penalty for treason.'

'If the Emperor has determined, for personal reasons or for any reason whatever, to destroy me, argument will avail me nothing,' said Splendidus, haughtily.

'But I have other plans,' said Sublatus, 'plans that might be overturned should I cause your death.'

'Yes?' inquired Splendidus, politely.

'Yes,' assented Sublatus. 'My son wishes to many your daughter, Dilecta, and it is also my wish, for thus would the two most powerful families of Castra Sanguinarius be united and the future of the empire assured.'

'But our daughter, Dilecta, is betrothed to another,' said Splendidus.

'To Maximus Præclarus?' inquired Sublatus.

'Yes,' replied the senator.

'Then let me tell you that she shall never wed Maximus Præclarus,' said the Emperor.

'Why?' inquired Splendidus.

'Because Maximus Præclarus is about to die.'

'I do not understand,' said Splendidus.

'Perhaps when I tell you that the white barbarian, Tarzan, has been captured, you will understand why Præclarus is about to die,' said Sublatus, with a sneer.

Dion Splendidus shook his head negatively. 'I regret,' he said, 'that I do not follow Cæsar.'

'I think you do, Splendidus,' said the Emperor, 'but that is neither here nor there, since it is Cæsar's will that there be no breath of suspicion upon the sire of the next Empress of Castra Sanguinarius. So permit me to explain what I am sure that you already know. After the white barbarian escaped from my soldiers he was found by Maximus Præclarus in your garden. My son, Fastus, witnessed the capture. One of your own slaves acted as interpreter between the barbarian and Maximus, who arranged that the barbarian should escape and take refuge in the home of Maximus. Tonight he was found there and captured, and Maximus Præclarus has been placed under arrest. They are both in the dungeons beneath the Colosseum. It is improbable that these things should have transpired entirely without your knowledge, but I shall let it pass if you give your word that Dilecta shall marry Fastus.'

'During the entire history of Castra Sanguinarius,' said Dion Splendidus, 'it has been our boast that our daughters have been free to choose their own husbands – not even a Cæsar might command a free woman to marry against her will.'

'That is true,' replied Sublatus, 'and for that very reason I do not command – I am only advising.'

'I cannot answer for my daughter,' said Splendidus. 'Let the son of Cæsar do his own wooing as becomes the men of Castra Sanguinarius.'

Sublatus arose. 'I am only advising,' but his tone belied his words. 'The noble senator and his wife may retire to their home and give thought to what Cæsar has said. In the course of a few days Fastus will come for his answer.'

By the light of the torch that illuminated the interior of the dungeon into which he was thrust by his captors, Tarzan saw a white man and several blacks chained to the walls. Among the blacks was Lukedi, but when he recognised Tarzan he evinced only the faintest sign of interest, so greatly had his confinement weighed upon his mind and altered him.

The ape-man was chained next to the only other white in the dungeon, and he could not help but notice the keen interest that this prisoner took in him from the moment that he entered until the soldiers withdrew, taking the torch with them, leaving the dungeon in darkness.

As had been his custom while he was in the home of Maximus Præclarus, Tarzan had worn only his loin-cloth and leopard-skin, with a toga and sandals out of courtesy for Festivitas when he appeared in her presence. This evening when he started out with Mpingu, he had worn the toga as a disguise, but in the scuffle that preceded his capture it had been torn from him, with the result that his appearance was sufficient to arouse the curiosity of his fellow prisoners, and as soon as the guards were out of hearing the man spoke to him.

'Can it be,' he asked, 'that you are the white barbarian whose fame has penetrated even to the gloom and silence of the dungeon?'

'I am Tarzan of the Apes,' replied the ape-man.

'And you carried Sublatus out of his palace above your head and mocked at his soldiers!' exclaimed the other. 'By the ashes of my imperial father, Sublatus will see that you die the death.'

Tarzan made no reply.

'They say you run through the trees like a monkey,' said the other. 'How then did you permit yourself to be recaptured?'

'It was done by treachery,' replied Tarzan, 'and the quickness with which they locked the shackles upon me. Without these,' and he shook the manacles upon his wrists, 'they could not hold me. But who are you and what did you do to get yourself in the dungeons of Cæsar?'

'I am in the dungeon of no Cæsar,' replied the other. 'This creature who sits upon the throne of Castra Sanguinarius is no Cæsar.'

'Who then is Cæsar?' inquired Tarzan.

'Only the Emperors of the East are entitled to be called Cæsar,' replied the other.

'I take it that you are not of Castra Sanguinarius then,' suggested the ape-man.

'No,' replied the other, 'I am from Castrum Mare.'

'And why are you a prisoner?' asked Tarzan.

'Because I am from Castrum Mare,' replied the other.

'Is that a crime in Castra Sanguinarius?' asked the ape-man.

'We are always enemies,' replied the other. 'We trade occasionally under a flag of truce, for we have things that they want and they have things that we must have, but there is much raiding and often there are wars, and then whichever side is victorious takes the things by force that otherwise they would be compelled to pay for.'

'In this small valley what is there that one of you may have that the other one has not already?' asked the ape-man.

'We of Castrum Mare have the iron mines,' replied the other, 'and we have the papyrus swamps and the lake, which give us many things that the people of Castra Sanguinarius can obtain only from us. We sell them iron and paper, ink, snails, fish and jewels, and many manufactured articles. In their end of the valley they mine gold, and as they control the only entrance to the country from the outside world, we are forced to obtain our slaves through them as well as new breeding-stock for our herds.

'As the Sanguinarians are naturally thieves and raiders and are too lazy to work and too ignorant to teach their slaves how to produce things, they depend entirely upon their gold mine and their raiding and trading with the outer world, while we, who have developed many skilled artisans, have been in a position for many generations that permitted us to obtain much more gold and many more slaves than we need in return for our manufactured articles. Today we are much richer than the Sanguinarians. We live better. We are more cultured. We are happier and the Sanguinarians are jealous and their hatred of us has increased.'

'Knowing these things,' asked Tarzan, 'how is it that you came to the country of your enemies and permitted yourself to be captured?'

'I was delivered over treacherously into the hands of Sublatus by my uncle, Validus Augustus, Emperor of the East,' replied the other. 'My name is Cassius Hasta, and my father was Emperor before Validus. Validus is afraid that I may wish to seize the purple, and for this reason he plotted to get rid of me without asuming any responsibility for the act; so he conceived the idea of sending me upon a military mission, after bribing one of the servants who accompanied me to deliver me into the hands of Sublatus.'

'What will Sublatus do with you?' asked Tarzan.

'The same thing that he will do with you,' replied Cassius Hasta. 'We shall be exhibited in the triumph of Sublatus, which he holds annually, and then in the arena we shall amuse them until we are slain.'

'And when does this take place?' asked Tarzan.

'It will not be long now,' replied Cassius Hasta. 'Already they have collected so many black prisoners to exhibit in the triumph and to take part in the combats in the arena that they are forced to confine blacks and whites in the same dungeons, a things they do not ordinarily do.'

'Are these blacks held here for this purpose?' asked the ape-man.

'Yes,' replied the other.

Tarzan turned in the direction of Lukedi, whom he could not see in the darkness. 'Lukedi!' he called.

'What is it?' asked the black, listlessly.

'You are well?' asked Tarzan.

'I am going to die,' replied Lukedi. 'They will feed me to lions or burn me upon a cross or make me fight with other warriors, so that it will be all the same for Lukedi. It was a sad day when Nyuto, the chief, captured Tarzan.'

'Are all these blacks from your village?' asked Tarzan.

'No,' replied Lukedi. 'Most of them are from the villages outside the walls of Castra Sanguinarius.'

'Yesterday they called us their own people,' spoke up a black, who understood the language of the Bagego, 'and tomorrow they make us kill one another to entertain Cæsar.'

'You must be very few in numbers or very poor in spirit,' said Tarzan, 'that you submit to such treatment.'

'We number nearly twice as many as the people in the city,' said the black, 'and we are brave warriors.'

'Then you are fools,' said Tarzan.

'We shall not be fools for ever. Already there are many who would rise against Sublatus and the whites of Castra Sanguinarius.'

'The blacks of the city as well as the blacks of the outer villages hate Cæsar,' said Mpingu, who had been brought to the dungeon with Tarzan.

The statements of the blacks furnished food for thought to Tarzan. He knew that in the city there must be hundreds and perhaps thousands of black slaves and many thousands of blacks in the outer villages. If a leader should arise among them, the tyranny of Cæsar might be brought to an abrupt end. He spoke of the matter to Cassius Hasta, but the patrician assured him that no such leader would ever arise.

'We have dominated them for so many centuries,' he explained, 'that fear of us is an inherited instinct. Our blacks will never rise against their masters.'

'But if they did?' asked Tarzan.

'Unless they had a white leader they could not succeed,' replied Hasta.

'And why not a white leader then?' asked Tarzan.

'That is unthinkable,' replied Hasta.

Their conversation was interrupted by the arrival of a detachment of soldiers, and as they halted before the entrance to the dungeon and threw open the gate Tarzan saw, in the light of their torches, that they were bringing another prisoner. As they dragged the man in, he recognized Maximum Præclarus. He saw that Præclarus recognized him, but as the Roman did not address him, Tarzan kept silent, too. The soldiers chained Præclarus to the wall, and after they had left and the dungeon was in darkness again, the young officer spoke.

'I see now why I am here,' said Præclarus, 'but even when they set upon me and arrested me in the vestibule of my home, I had guessed as much, after piecing together the insinuations of Fastus at the banquet this evening.'

'I have been fearful that by befriending me you would bring disaster upon yourself,' said Tarzan.

'Do not reproach yourself,' said Præclarus. 'Fastus or Sublatus would have found another excuse. I have been doomed from the moment that the attention of Fastus fixed itself upon Dilecta. To attain his end it was necessary that I be destroyed. That is all, my friend, but yet I wonder who it could have been that betrayed me.'

'It was I,' said a voice out of the darkness.

'Who is that that speaks?' demanded Præclarus.

'It is Mpingu,' said Tarzan. 'He was arrested with me when we were on the way to the home of Dion Splendidus to meet you.'

'To meet me!' exclaimed Præclarus.

'I lied,' said Mpingu, 'but they made me.'

'Who made you?' demanded Præclarus.

'The officers of Cæsar and Cæsar's son,' replied Mpingu. 'They dragged me to the palace of the Emperor and held me down upon my back and brought tongs to tear out my tongue and hot irons to burn out my eyes. Oh, master, what else could I do? I am only a poor slave and I was afraid and Cæsar is very terrible.'

'I understand,' said Præclarus. 'I do not blame you, Mpingu.'

'They promised to give me my liberty,' said the black, 'but instead they have chained me in this dungeon. Doubtless I shall die in the arena, but that I do not fear. It was the tongs and the red-hot irons that made me a coward. Nothing else could have forced me to betray the friend of my master.'

There was little comfort upon the cold, hard stones of the dungeon floor, but Tarzan, inured to hardship from birth, slept soundly until the coming of the jailer with food awakened him several hours after sunrise. Water and coarse bread were doled out to the inmates of the dungeon by slaves in charge of a surly half-caste in the uniform of a legionary.

As he ate, Tarzan surveyed his fellow prisoners. There was Cassius Hasta of Castrum Mare, son of a Cæsar, and Maximus Præclarus, a patrician of Castra Sanguinarius and captain of legionaries. These, with himself, were the only whites. There was Lukedi, the Bagego who had befriended him in the village of Nyuto, and Mpingu, the black slave of Dion Splendidus, who had betrayed him, and now, in the light from the little barred window, he recognized also another Bagego – Ogonyo, who still cast fearful eyes upon Tarzan as one might upon any person who was on familiar terms with the ghost of one's grandfather.

In addition to these three blacks, there were five strapping warriors from the outer villages of Castra Sanguinarius, picked men chosen because of their superb physiques for the gladiatorial contests that would form so important a part of the games that would shortly take place in the arena for the glorification of Cæsar and the edification of the masses. The small room was so crowded that there was barely space upon the floor for the eleven to stretch their bodies, yet there was one vacant ring in the stone wall, indicating that the full capacity of the dungeon had not been reached.

Two days and nights dragged slowly by. The inmates of the cell amused themselves as best they could, though the blacks were too downcast to take a lively interest in anything other than their own sad forebodings.

Tarzan talked much with these and especially with the five warriors from the outer villages. From long experience with them he knew the minds and the hearts of black men, and it was not difficult for him to win their confidence and, presently, he was able to instil within them something of his own courageous self-reliance, which could never accept or admit absolute defeat.

He talked with Præclarus about Castra Sanguinarius and with Cassius Hasta about Castrum Mare. He learned all that they could tell him about the forthcoming triumph and games; about the military methods of their people, their laws and their customs until he, who all his life had been accounted taciturn, might easily have been indicted for loquacity by his fellow prisoners, yet, though they might not realize it, he asked them nothing without a well-defined purpose.

Upon the third day of his incarceration another prisoner was brought to the crowded cell in which Tarzan was chained. He was a young white man in the tunic and cuirass of an officer. He was received in silence by the other prisoners, as seemed to be the custom among them, but after he had been fastened to the remaining ring and the soldiers who had brought him had departed, Cassius Hasta greeted him with suppressed excitement.

'Cæcilius Metellus!' he exclaimed.

The other turned in the direction of Hasta's voice, his eyes not yet accustomed to the gloom of the dungeon.

'Hasta!' he exclaimed. 'I would know that voice were I to hear it rising from the blackest depths of Tartarus.'

'What ill fortune brought you here?' demanded Hasta.

'It is no ill fortune that unites me with my best friend,' replied Metellus.

'But tell me how it happened,' insisted Cassius Hasta.

'Many things have happened since you left Castrum Mare,' replied Metellus. 'Fulvus Fupus has wormed his way into the favour of the Emperor to such an extent that all of your former friends are under suspicion and in actual danger. Mallius Lepus is in prison. Septimus Favonius is out of favour with the Emperor and would be in prison himself were it not that Fupus is in love with Favonia, his daughter. But the most outrageous news that I have to communicate to you is that Validus Augustus has adopted Fulvus Fupus and has named him as his successor to the imperial purple.'

'Fupus a Cæsar!' cried Hasta, in derision. 'And sweet Favonia? It cannot be that she favours Fulvus Fupus?'

'No,' replied Metellus, 'and that fact lies at the bottom of all the trouble. She loves another, and Fupus, in his desire to possess her, has utilized the Emperor's jealousy of you to destroy every obstacle that stands in his way.'

'And whom does Favonia love?' asked Cassius Hasta. 'It cannot be Mallius Lepus, her cousin?'

'No,' replied Metellus, 'it is a stranger. One whom you have never known.'

'How can that be?' demanded Cassius Hasta. 'Do I not know every patrician in Castrum Mare?'

'He is not of Castrum Mare.'

'Not a Sanguinarian?' demanded Cassius Hasta.

'No, he is a barbarian chieftain from Germania.'

'What nonsense is this?' demanded Hasta.

'I speak the truth,' replied Metellus. 'He came shortly after you departed from Castrum Mare, and being a scholar well versed in the history of ancient and modern Rome he won the favour of Validus Augustus, but he brought ruin upon himself and upon Mallius Lepus and upon Septimus Favonius by winning the love of Favonia and with it the jealous hatred of Fulvus Fupus.'

'What is his name?' asked Cassius Hasta.

'He calls himself Erich von Harben,' replied Metellus.

'Erich von Harben,' repeated Tarzan. 'I know him. Where is he now? Is he safe?'

Cæcilius Metellus turned his eyes in the direction of the ape-man. 'How do you know Erich von Harben, Sanguinarian?' he demanded. 'Perhaps then the story that Fulvus Fupus told Validus Augustus is true – that this Erich von Harben is in reality a spy from Castra Sanguinarius.'

'No,' said Maximus Præclarus. 'Do not excite yourself. This Erich von Harben has never been in Castra Sanguinarius, and my friend here is not himself a Sanguinarian. He is a white barbarian from the outer world, and if his story be true, and I have no reason to doubt it, he came here in search of this Erich von Harben.'

'You may believe this story, Metellus,' said Cassius Hasta. 'These both are honourable men and since we have been in prison together we have become good friends. What they tell you is the truth.'

'Tell me something of von Harben,' insisted Tarzan. 'Where is he now and is he in danger from the machinations of this Fulvus Fupus?'

'He is in prison with Mallius Lepus in Castrum Mare,' replied Metellus, 'and if he survives the games, which he will not, Fupus will find some other means to destroy him.'

'When are the games held?' asked Tarzan.

'They start upon the ides of August,' replied Cassius Hasta.

'And it is now about the nones of August,' said Tarzan.

'Tomorrow,' corrected Præclarus.

'We shall know it then,' said Cassius Hasta, 'for that is the date set for the triumph of Sublatus.'

'I am told that the games last about a week,' said Tarzan. 'How far is it to Castrum Mare?'

'Perhaps an eight hours' march for fresh troops,' said Cæscilius Metellus; 'but why do you ask? Are you planning on making a trip to Castrum Mare?'

Tarzan noted the other's smile and the ironic tone of his voice. 'I am going to Castrum Mare,' he said.

'Perhaps you will take us with you,' laughed Metellus.

'Are you a friend of von Harben?' asked Tarzan.

'I am a friend of his friends and an enemy of his enemies, but I do not know him well enough to say that he is my friend.'

'But you have no love for Validus Augustus, the Emperor?' asked Tarzan.

'No,' replied the other.

'And I take it that Cassius Hasta has no reason to love his uncle, either?' continued Tarzan.

'You are right,' said Hasta.

'Perhaps I shall take you both, then,' said Tarzan.

The two men laughed.

'We shall be ready to go with you when you are ready to take us,' said Cassius Hasta.

'You may count me in on the party, too,' said Maximus Præclarus, 'if Cassius Hasta will remain my friend in Castrum Mare.'

'That I promise, Maximus Præclarus,' said Cassius Hasta.

'When do we leave?' demanded Metellus, shaking his chain.

'I can leave the moment that these shackles are struck from me,' said the ape-man, 'and that they must do when they turn me into the arena to fight.'

'There will be many legionaries to see that you do not escape, you may rest assured of that,' Cassius Hasta reminded him.

'Maximus Præclarus will tell you that I have twice escaped from the legionaries of Sublatus,' said Tarzan.

'That he has,' declared Præsclarus. 'Surrounded by the Emperor's guard, he escaped from the very throne-room of Sublatus and he carried Cæsar above his head through the length of the palace and out into the avenue beyond.'

'But if I am to take you with me, it will be more difficult,' said the ape-man, 'and I would take you because it would please me to frustrate the plans of Sublatus and also because two of you, at least, could be helpful to me in finding Erich von Harben in the city of Castrum Mare.'

'You interest me,' said Cassius Hasta. 'You almost make me believe that you can accomplish this mad scheme.'

14

A great sun, rising into a cloudless sky, ushered in the nones of August. It looked down upon the fresh-raked sands of the deserted arena; upon the crowds that lined the Via Principalis that bisected Castra Sanguinarius.

Brown artisans and tradesmen in their smart tunics jostled one another for places of vantage along the shady avenue. Among them moved black barbarians from the other villages, sporting their finest feathers and most valued ornaments and skins, and mingling with the others were the slaves of the city, all eagerly waiting for the pageant that would inaugurate the triumph of Sublatus.

Upon the low rooftops of their homes the patricians reclined upon rugs at every point where the avenue might be seen between or beneath the branches of the trees. All Castra Sanguinarius was there, technically to honour Cæsar, but actually merely to be entertained.

The air buzzed with talk and laughter; hawkers of sweetmeats and trinkets elbowed through the crowd crying their wares; legionaries posted at intervals the full distance from the palace to the Colosseum kept the centre of the avenue clear.

Since the evening of the preceding day the throng had been gathering. During the cold night they had huddled with close-drawn cloaks. There had been talk and laughter and brawls and near-riots, and many would-be spectators had been hauled off to the dungeons where their exuberance might be permitted to cool against cold stone.

As the morning dragged on the crowd became restless. At first, as some patrician who was to have a part in the pageant passed in his ornate litter he would be viewed in respectful and interested silence, or if he were well known and favourably thought of by the multitude he might be greeted with cheers; but with the passing of time and the increasing heat of the day each occasional litter that passed elicited deep-throated groans or raucous catcalls as the patience and the temper of the mob became thinner.

But presently from afar, in the direction of the palace, sounded the martial notes of trumpets. The people forgot their fatigue and their discomfort as the shrill notes galvanized them into joyous expectancy.

Slowly along the avenue came the pageant, led by a score of trumpeters, behind whom marched a maniple of the imperial guard. Waving crests surmounted their burnished helmets, the metal of two hundred cuirasses, pikes, and shields shot back the sunlight that filtered through the trees beneath which they marched. They made a proud showing as they strode haughtily between the lines of admiring eyes, led by their patrician officers in gold and embossed leather and embroidered linen.

As the legionaries passed, a great shout of applause arose. A roar of human voices that started at the palace rolled slowly along the Via Principalis toward the Colosseum as Cæsar himself, resplendent in purple and gold, rode alone in a chariot drawn by lions led on golden leashes by huge blacks.

Cæsar may have expected for himself the plaudits of the populace, but there was a question as to whether these were elicited as much by the presence of the Emperor as by the sight of the captives chained to Cæsar's chariot, for Cæsar was an old story to the people of Castra Sanguinarius, while the prisoners were a novelty and, furthermore, something that promised rare sport in the arena.

Never before in the memory of the citizens of Castra Sanguinarius had an Emperor exhibited such noteworthy captives in his triumph. There was Nyuto, the black chief of the Bagegos. There was Cæcilius Metellus, a centurion of the legions of the Emperor of the East; and Cassius Hasta, the nephew of that Emperor; but perhaps he who aroused their greatest enthusiasm because of the mad stories that had been narrated of his feats of strength and agility was the great white barbarian, with a shock of black hair and his well-worn leopard-skin.

The collar of gold and the golden chain that held him in leash to the chariot of Cæsar, curiously enough, imparted to his appearance no suggestion of fear or humiliation. He walked proudly with head erect – a lion tethered to lions – and there was that in the easy sinuosity of his stride that accentuated his likeness to the jungle beasts that drew the chariot of Cæsar along the broad Via Principalis of Castra Sanguinarius.

As the pageant moved its length slowly to the Colosseum the crowd found other things to hold their interest. There were the Bagego captives chained neck to neck and stalwart gladiators resplendent in new armour. White men and brown men were numbered among these and many black warriors from the outer villages.

To the number of two hundred they marched – captives, condemned criminals, and professional gladiators – but before them and behind them and on either side marched veteran legionaries whose presence spoke in no uncertain terms of the respect in which Cæsar held the potential power of these bitter, savage fighting-men.

There were floats depicting historic events in the history of Castra Sanguinarius and ancient Rome. There were litters bearing the high officers of the court and the senators of the city, while bringing up the rear were the captured flocks and herds of the Bagegos.

That Sublatus failed to exhibit Maximus Præclarus in his triumph evidenced the popularity of this noble young Roman, but Dilecta, watching the procession from the roof of her father's house, was filled with anxiety when she noted the absence of her lover, for she knew that sometimes men who entered the dungeons of Cæsar were never heard of more – but there was none who could tell her whether Maximus Præclarus lived or not, and so with her mother she made her way to the Colosseum to witness the opening of the games. Her heart was heavy lest she should see Maximus Præclarus entered there, and his blood upon the white sand, yet, also, she feared that she might not see him and thus be faced by the almost definite assurance that he had been secretly done to death by the agents of Fastus.

A great multitude had gathered in the Colosseum to witness the entry of Cæsar and the pageant of his triumph, and the majority of these remained in their seats for the opening of the games, which commenced early in the afternoon. It was not until then that the sections reserved for the patricians began to fill.

The loge reserved for Dion Splendidus, the senator, was close to that of Cæsar. It afforded an excellent view of the arena and with cushions and rugs was so furnished as to afford the maximum comfort to those who occupied it.

Never had a Cæsar essayed so pretentious a fete; entertainment of the rarest description was vouchsafed each lucky spectator, yet never before in her life had Dilecta loathed and dreaded any occurrence as she now loathed and dreaded the games that were about to open.

Always heretofore her interest in the contestants had been impersonal. Professional gladiators were not of the class to come within the ken or acquaintance of the daughter of a patrician. The black warriors and slaves were to her of no greater importance than the beasts against which they sometimes contended, while the condemned criminals, many of whom expiated their sins within the arena, aroused within her heart only the remotest suggestion of sympathy. She was a sweet and lovely girl, whose sensibilities would doubtless have been shocked by the brutality of the prize-ring or varsity football game, but she could look upon the bloody cruelties of a Roman arena without a qualm, because by custom and heredity they had become a part of the national life of her people.

But today she trembled. She saw the games as a personal menace to her own happiness and the life of one she loved, yet by no outward sign did she divulge her perturbation. Calm, serene, and entirely beautiful, Dilecta, the daughter of Dion Splendidus, awaited the signal for the opening of the games that was marked by the arrival of Cæsar.

Sublatus came, and after he had taken his seat there emerged from one of the barred gates at the far end of the arena the head of a procession, again led by trumpeters, who were followed by those who were to take part in the games during the week. It consisted for the most part of the same captives who had been exhibited in the pageant, to which were added a number of wild beasts, some of which were led or dragged along by black slaves, while others, more powerful and ferocious, were drawn in wheeled cages. These consisted principally of lions and leopards, but there were also a couple of bull buffaloes and several cages in which were confined huge man-like apes.

The participants were formed in a solid phalanx facing Sublatus, where they were addressed by the Emperor, freedom and reward being promised the victors; and then, sullen and lowering, they were herded back to their dungeons and cages.

Dilecta's eyes scanned the faces of the contestants as they stood in solid rank before the loge of Cæsar, but nowhere among them could she discover Maximus Præclarus. Breathless and tense, with fearful apprehension, she leaned forward in her seat across the top of the arena wall as a man entered the loge from behind and sat upon the bench beside her.

'He is not there,' said the man.

The girl turned quickly toward the speaker. 'Fastus!' she exclaimed. 'How do you know that he is not there?'

'It is by my order,' replied the prince.

'He is dead,' cried Dilecta. 'You have had him killed.'

'No,' denied Fastus, 'he is safe in his cell.'

'What is to become of him?' asked the girl.

'His fate lies in your hands,' replied Fastus. 'Give him up and promise to become the wife of Fastus and I will see that he is not forced to appear in the arena.'

'He would not have it so,' said the girl.

Fastus shrugged. 'As you will,' he said, 'but remember that his life is in your hands.'

'With sword or dagger, or pike he has no equal,' said the girl, proudly. 'If he were entered in the contest, he would be victorious.'

'Cæsar has been known to pit unarmed men against lions,' Fastus reminded her, tauntingly. 'Of what avail then is prowess with any weapon?'

'That would be murder,' said Dilecta.

'A harsh term to apply to an act of Cæsar,' returned Fastus, menacingly.

'I speak my mind,' said the girl; 'Cæsar or no Cæsar. It would be a cowardly and contemptible act, but I doubt not that either Cæsar or his son is capable of even worse.' Her voice trembled with scathing contempt.

With a crooked smile upon his lips, Fastus arose. 'It is not a matter to be determined without thought,' he said, 'and your answer concerns not Maximus Præclarus alone, nor you, nor me.'

'What do you mean?' she asked.

'There are Dion Splendidus and your mother, and Festivitas, the mother of Præclarus!' And with this warning he turned and left the loge.

The games progressed amid the din of trumpets, the crash of arms, the growling of beasts, and the murmuring of the great audience that sometimes rose to wild acclaim or deep-throated, menacing disapproval. Beneath fluttering banners and waving scarves the cruel, terrible thousand-eyed thing that is a crowd looked down upon the blood and suffering of its fellow men, munching sweetmeats while a victim died and cracking coarse jokes as slaves dragged the body from the arena and raked clean sand over crimsoned spots.

Sublatus had worked long and carefully with the præfect in charge of the games that the resultant programme might afford the greatest possible entertainment for Cæsar and the populace, thus winning for the Emperor a certain popularity that his own personality did not command.

Always the most popular events were those in which men of the patrician class participated, and so he counted much upon Cassius Hasta and Cæcilius Metellus, but of even greater value for his purpose was the giant white barbarian, who had already captured the imagination of the people because of his exploits.

Wishing to utilize Tarzan in as many events as possible, Sublatus knew it would be necessary to reserve the more dangerous ones for the latter part of the week, and so upon the first afternoon of the games Tarzan found himself thrust into the arena, unarmed, in company with a burly murderer, whom the master of the games had clothed in loin-cloth and leopard-skin similar to Tarzan.

A guard escorted them across the arena and halted them in the sand below the Emperor, where the master of the games announced that these two would fight with bare hands in any way that they saw fit and that he who remained alive or alone in the arena at the end of the combat would be considered victorious.

'The gate to the dungeons will be left open,' he said, 'and if either contestant gets enough he may quit the arena, but whoever does so forfeits the contest to the other.'

The crowd booed. It was not to see such tame exhibitions as this that they had come to the Colosseum. They wanted blood. They wanted thrills, but they waited, for perhaps this contest might afford comedy – that they enjoyed, too. If one greatly outclassed the other, it would be amusing to see the weaker seek escape. They cheered Tarzan and they cheered the lowbrowed murderer. They shouted insults at the noble patrician who was master of the games, for they knew the safety and irresponsibility of numbers.

As the word was given for the contestants to engage one another Tarzan turned to face the low-browed, hulking brute against whom he had been pitted and he saw that someone had been at pains to select a worthy antagonist for him. The man was somewhat shorter than Tarzan, but great, hard muscles bulged beneath his brown hide, bulking so thick across his back and shoulders as almost to suggest deformity. His long arms hung almost to his knees, and his thick, gnarled legs suggested a man of bronze upon a pedestal of granite. The fellow circled Tarzan looking for an opening. He scowled ferociously as though to frighten his adversary.

'There is the gate, barbarian,' he cried in a low voice, pointing to the far end of the arena. 'Escape while you are yet alive.'

The crowd roared in approbation. It enjoyed glorious sallies such as these. 'I shall tear you limb from limb,' shouted the murderer, and again the crowd applauded.

'I am here,' said Tarzan, calmly.

'Flee!' screamed the murderer, and lowering his head he charged like an angry bull.

The ape-man sprang into the air and came down upon his antagonist, and what happened happened so quickly that no one there, other than Tarzan, knew how it had been accomplished; only he knew that he clamped a reverse headlock upon the murderer.

What the crowd saw was the hulking figure hurtling to a hard fall. They saw him lying half-stunned upon the sand, while the giant barbarian stood with folded arms looking down upon him.

The fickle crowd rose from its benches, shrieking with delight. 'Habet! Habet!' they cried, and thousands of closed fists were outstretched with the thumbs pointing downward, but Tarzan only stood there waiting, as the murderer, shaking his head to clear his brain, crawled slowly to his feet.

The fellow looked about him half-bewildered and then his eyes found Tarzan and with a growl of rage he charged again. Again the terrible hold was clamped upon him, and again he was hurled heavily to the floor of the arena.

The crowd screamed with delight. Every thumb in the Colosseum was pointed downward. They wanted Tarzan to kill his adversary. The ape-man looked up into Cæsar's loge, where sat the master of the games with Sublatus.

'Is not this enough?' he demanded, pointing at the prostrate figure of the stunned gladiator.

The præfect waved a hand in an all-including gesture which took in the audience. 'They demand his death,' he said. 'While he remains alive in the arena, you are not the victor.'

'Does Cæsar require that I kill this defenceless man?' demanded Tarzan, looking straight into the face of Sublatus.

'You have heard the noble prefect,' replied the Emperor, haughtily.

'Good,' said Tarzan. 'The rules of the contest shall be fulfilled.' He stooped and seized the unconscious form of his antagonist and raised it above his head. 'Thus I carried your Emperor from his throne-room to the avenue!' he shouted to the audience.

Screams of delight measured the appreciation of the populace, while Cæsar went white and red in anger and mortification. He half rose from his seat, but what he contemplated was never fulfilled, for at that instant Tarzan swung the body of the murderer downward and back like a huge pendulum and then upward with a mighty surge, hurling it over the arena wall, full into the loge of Sublatus, where it struck Cæsar, knocking him to the floor.

'I am alive and alone in the arena,' shouted Tarzan, turning to the people, 'and by the terms of the contest I am victor,' and not even Cæsar dared question the decision that was voiced by the shrieking, screaming, applauding multitude.

15

Bloody days followed restless nights in comfortless cells, where lice and rats joined forces to banish rest. When the games began there had been twelve inmates in the cell occupied by Tarzan, but now three empty rings dangled against the stone wall, and each day they wondered whose turn was next.

The others did not reproach Tarzan because of his failure to free them, since they had never taken his optimism seriously. They could not conceive of contestants escaping from the arena during the games. It simply was not done and that was all there was to it. It never had been done, and it never would be.

'We know you meant well,' said Præclarus, 'but we knew better than you.'

'The conditions have not been right, as yet,' said Tarzan, 'but if what I have been told of the games is true, the time will come.'

'What time could be propitious,' asked Hasta, 'while more than half of Cæsar's legionaries packed the Colosseum?'

'There should be a time,' Tarzan reminded him, 'when all the victorious contestants are in the arena together. Then we shall rush Cæsar's loge and drag him into the arena. With Sublatus as a hostage we may demand a hearing and get it. I venture to say that they will give us our liberty in return for Cæsar.'

'But how can we enter Cæsar's loge?' demanded Metellus.

'In an instant we may form steps with living men stooping, while others step upon their backs as soldiers scale a wall. Perhaps some of us will be killed, but enough will succeed to seize Cæsar and drag him to the sands.'

'I wish you luck,' said Prælarus, 'and, by Jupiter, I believe that you will succeed. I only wish that I might be with you.'

'You will not accompany us?' demanded Tarzan.

'How can I? I shall be locked in this cell. Is it not evident that they do not intend to enter me in the contests? They are reserving for me some other fate. The jailer has told me that my name appears in no event.'

'But we must find a way to take you with us,' said Tarzan.

'There is no way,' said Præclarus, shaking his head, sadly.

'Wait,' said Tarzan. 'You commanded the Colosseum guards, did you not?'

'Yes,' replied Præclarus.

'And you had the keys to the cells?' asked the ape-man.

'Yes,' replied Præclarus, 'and to the manacles as well.'

'Where are they?' asked Tarzan. 'But no, that will not do. They must have taken them from you when they arrested you.'

'No, they did not,' said Præclarus. 'As a matter of fact, I did not have them with me when I dressed for the banquet that night. I left them in my room.'

'But perhaps they sent for them?'

'Yes, they sent for them, but they did not find them. The jailer asked me about them the day after I was arrested, but I told him that the soldiers took them from me. I told him that because I had hidden them in a secret place where I keep many valuables. I knew that if I had told them where they were they would take not only the keys, but my valuables as well.'

'Good!' exclaimed the ape-man. 'With the keys our problem is solved.'

'But how are you going to get them?' demanded Præclarus, with a rueful smile.

'I do not know,' said Tarzan. 'All I know is that we must have the keys.'

'We know, too, that we should have our liberty,' said Hasta, 'but knowing it does not make us free.'

Their conversation was interrupted by the approach of soldiers along the corridor. Presently a detachment of the palace guard halted outside their cell. The jailer unlocked the door and a man entered with two torch-bearers behind him. It was Fastus.

He looked around the cell. 'Where is Præclarus?' he demanded, and then, 'Ah, there you are!'

Præclarus did not reply.

'Stand up, slave!' ordered Fastus, arrogantly. 'Stand up, all of you. How dare you sit in the presence of a Cæsar!' he exclaimed.

'Swine is a better title for such as you,' taunted Præclarus.

'Drag them up! Beat them with your pikes!' cried Fastus to the soldiers outside the doorway.

The commander of the Colosseum guard, who stood just behind Fastus, blocked the doorway. 'Stand back,' he said to the legionaries. 'No one gives orders here except Cæsar and myself, and you are not Cæsar yet, Fastus.'

'I shall be one day,' snapped the prince, 'and it will be a sad day for you.'

'It will be a sad day for all Castra Sanguinarius,' replied the officer. 'You said that you wished to speak to Præclarus? Say what you have to say and be gone. Not even Cæsar's son may interfere with my charges.'

Fastus trembled with anger, but he knew that he was powerless. The commander of the guard spoke with the authority of the Emperor, whom he represented. He turned upon Præclarus.

'I came to invite my good friend, Maximus Præclarus, to my wedding,' he announced, with a sneer. He waited, but Præclarus made no reply.

'You do not seem duly impressed, Præclarus,' continued the prince. 'You do not ask who is to be the happy bride. Do you not wish to know who will be the next Empress in Castra Sanguinarius, even though you may not live to see her upon the throne beside Cæsar?'

The heart of Maximus Præclarus stood still, for now he knew why Fastus had come to the dungeon-cell, but he gave no sign of what was passing within his breast, but remained seated in silence upon the hard floor, his back against the cold wall.

'You do not ask me whom I am to wed, nor when,' continued Fastus, 'but I shall tell you. You should be interested. Dilecta, the daughter of Dion Splendidus, will have none of a traitor and a felon. She aspires to share the purple with a Cæsar. In the evening following the last day of the games Dilecta and Fastus are to be married in the throne-room of the palace.'

Gloating, Fastus waited to know the result of his announcement, but if he had looked to surprise Maximus Præclarus into an exhibition of chagrin he failed, for the young patrician ignored him so completely that Fastus might not have been in the cell at all for all the attention that the other paid to him.

Maximus Præclarus turned and spoke casually to Metellus and the quiet affront aroused the mounting anger of Fastus to such an extent that he lost what little control he had of himself. Stepping quickly forward, he stooped and slapped Præclarus in the face and then spat upon him, but in doing so he had come too close to Tarzan and the ape-man reached out and seized him by the ankle, dragging him to the floor.

Fastus screamed a command to his soldiers. He sought to draw his dagger or his sword, but Tarzan took them from him and hurled the prince into the arms of the legionaries, who had rushed past the commander of the Colosseum guard and entered the cell.

'Get out now, Fastus,' said the latter. 'You have caused enough trouble here already.'

'I shall get you for this,' hissed the prince, 'all of you,' and he swept the inmates of the cell with an angry, menacing glance.

Long after they had gone, Cassius Hasta continued to chuckle. 'Cæsar!' he exclaimed. 'Swine!'

As the prisoners discussed the discomfiture of Fastus and sought to prophesy what might come of it, they saw a wavering light reflected from afar in the corridor before their cell.

'We are to have more guests,' said Metellus.

'Perhaps Fastus is returning to spit on Tarzan,' suggested Cassius Hasta, and they all laughed.

The light was advancing along the corridor, but it was not accompanied by the tramp of soldiers' feet.

'Whoever comes comes silently and alone,' said Maximus Præclarus.

'Then it is not Fastus,' said Hasta.

'But it might be an assassin sent by him,' suggested Præclarus.

'We shall be ready for him,' said Tarzan.

A moment later there appeared beyond the grating of the cell door the commander of the Colosseum guards, who had accompanied Fastus and who had stood between the prince and the prisoner.

'Appius Applosus!' exclaimed Maximus Præclarus. 'He is no assassin, my friends.'

'I am not the assassin of your body, Præclarus,' said Applosus, 'but I am indeed the assassin of your happiness.'

'What do you mean, my friend?' demanded Præclarus.

'In his anger Fastus told me more than he told you.'

'He told you what?' asked Præclarus.

'He told me that Dilecta had consented to become his wife only in the hope of saving her father and mother and you, Præclarus, and your mother, Festivitas.'

'To call him swine is to insult the swine,' said Præclarus. 'Take word to her, Applosus, that I would rather die than to see her wed to Fastus.'

'She knows that, my friend,' said the officer, 'but she thinks also of her father and her mother and yours.'

Præclarus's chin dropped upon his chest. 'I had forgotten that,' he moaned. 'Oh, there must be some way to stop it.'

'He is the son of Cæsar,' Applosus reminded him, 'and the time is short.'

'I know it! I know it!' cried Præclarus, 'but it is too hideous. It cannot be.'

'This officer is your friend, Præclarus?' asked Tarzan, indicating Appius Applosus.

'Yes,' said Præclarus.

'You would trust him fully?' demanded the ape-man.

'With my life and my honour,' said Præclarus.

'Tell him where your keys are and let him fetch them,' said the ape-man.

Præclarus brightened instantly. 'I had not thought of that,' he cried, 'but no, his life would be in jeopardy.'

'It already is,' said Applosus. 'Fastus will never forget or forgive what I said tonight. You, Præclarus, know that I am already doomed. What keys do you want? Where are they? I will fetch them.'

'Perhaps not when you know what they are,' said Prælarus.

'I can guess,' replied Appius Applosus.

'You have been in my apartments often, Applosus?'

The other nodded affirmatively.

'You recall the shelves near the window where my books lie?'

'Yes.'

'The back of the third shelf slides to one side and behind it, in the wall, you will find the keys.'

'Good, Præclarus. You shall have them,' said the officer.

The others watched the diminishing light as Appius Applosus departed along the corridor beneath the Colosseum.

The last day of the games had come. The bloodthirsty populace had gathered once more as eager and enthusiastic as though they were about to experience a new and unfamiliar thrill, their appetites swept as clean of the memories of the past week as were the fresh sands of the arena of the brown stains of yesterday.

For the last time the inmates of the cell were taken to enclosures nearer to the entrance to the arena. They had fared better, perhaps, than others, for of the twelve rings only four were empty.

Maximus Præclarus alone was left behind. 'Goodbye,' he said. 'Those of you who survive the day shall be free. We shall not see one another again. Good luck to you and may the gods give strength and skill to your arms – that is all that I can ask of them, for not even the gods could give you more courage than you already possess.'

'Applosus has failed us,' said Hasta.

Tarzan looked troubled. 'If only you were coming out with us, Præclarus, we should not then need the keys.'

From within the enclosure, where they were confined, Tarzan and his companions could hear the sounds of combat and the groans and hoots and applause of the audience, but they could not see the floor of the arena.

It was a very large room with heavily barred windows and a door. Sometimes two men, sometimes four, sometimes six would go out together, but only one, or two, or three returned. The effect upon the nerves of those who remained uncalled was maddening. For some the suspense became almost unendurable. Two attempted suicide and others tried to pick quarrels with their fellow prisoners, but there were many guards within the room and the prisoners were unarmed, their weapons being issued to them only after they had quit the enclosure and were about to enter the arena.

The afternoon was drawing to a close. Metellus had fought with a gladiator, both in full armour. Hasta and Tarzan had heard the excited cries of the populace. They had heard cheer after cheer, which indicated that each man was putting up a skilful and courageous fight. There was an instant of silence and then the loud cries of '*Habet*! *Habet*!'

'It is over,' whispered Cassius Hasta.

Tarzan made no reply. He had grown to like these men, for he had found them brave and simple and loyal and he, too, was inwardly moved by the suspense that must be endured until one or the other returned to the enclosure; but he gave no outward sign of his perturbation, and while Cassius Hasta paced nervously to and fro Tarzan of the Apes stood silently, with folded arms, watching the door. After a while it opened and Cæcilius Metellus crossed the threshold.

Cassius Hasta uttered a cry of relief and sprang forward to embrace his friend.

Again the door swung open and a minor official entered. 'Come,' he, cried, 'all of you. It is the last event.'

Outside the enclosure each man was given a sword, dagger, pike, shield, and a hempen net, and one by one, as they were thus equipped, they were sent into the arena. All the survivors of the week of combat were there – one hundred of them.

They were divided into two equal parties, and red ribbons were fastened to the shoulders of one party and white ribbons to the shoulders of the other.

Tarzan was among the reds, as were Hasta, Metellus, Lukedi, Mpingu, and Ogonyo.

'What are we supposed to do?' asked Tarzan of Hasta.

'The reds will fight against the whites until all the reds are killed or all the whites.'

'They should see blood enough to suit them now,' said Tarzan.

'They can never get enough of it,' replied Metellus.

The two parties marched to the opposite end of the arena and received their instructions from the præfect in charge of the games, and then they were formed, the reds upon one side of the arena, the whites upon the other. Trumpets sounded and the armed men advanced toward one another.

Tarzan smiled to himself as he considered the weapons with which he was supposed to defend himself. The pike he was sure of, for the Waziri are great spearmen and Tarzan excelled even among them, and with the dagger he felt at home, so long had the hunting-knife of his father been his only weapon of protection – but the Spanish sword, he felt, would probably prove more of a liability than an asset, while the net in his hands could be nothing more than a sorry joke. He would like to have thrown his shield aside, for he did not like shields, considering them, as a rule, useless encumbrances, but he had used them before when the Waziri had fought other native tribes, and knowing that they were constructed as a defence against the very weapons that his opponents were using he retained his and advanced with the others toward the white line. He had determined that their only hope lay in accounting for as many of their adversaries in the first clash of arms as was possible, and this word he had passed down the line with the further admonition that the instant that a man had disposed of an antagonist he turn immediately to help the red nearest him, or the one most sorely beset.

As the two lines drew closer, each man selected the opponent opposite him and Tarzan found that he faced a black warrior from the outer villages. They came closer. Some of the men, more eager or nervous than the others, were in advance; some, more fearful, lagged behind. Tarzan's opponent came upon him. Already pikes were flying through the air. Tarzan and the black hurled their missiles at the same instant, and back of the ape-man's throw was all the skill and all the muscle and all the weight that he could command. Tarzan struck upward with his shield and his opponent's pike struck it a glancing blow, but with such force that the spear haft was shattered, while Tarzan's weapon passed through the shield of his opponent and pierced the fellow's heart.

There were two others down – one killed and one wounded – and the Colosseum was a babble of voices and a bedlam of noise. Tarzan sprang quickly to aid one of his fellows, but another white, who had killed his red opponent, ran to interfere. Tarzan's net annoyed him, so he threw it at a white who was pressing one of the reds and took on his fresh opponent, who had drawn his sword. His adversary was a professional gladiator, a man trained in the use of all his weapons, and Tarzan soon realized that only through great strength and agility might he expect to hold his own with this opponent.

The fellow did not rush. He came in slowly and carefully, feeling out Tarzan. He was cautious because he was an old hand at the business and was imbued with but a single hope – to live. He cared as little for the hoots and jibes of the people as he did for their applause, and he hated Cæsar. He soon discovered that Tarzan was adopting defensive tactics only, but whether this was for the purpose of feeling out his opponent or whether it was part of a plan that would lead up to a sudden and swift surprise, the gladiator could not guess, nor did he care particularly, for he knew that he was master of his weapon and many a corpse had been burned that in life had thought to surprise him.

Judging Tarzan's skill with the sword by his skill with the shield, the gladiator thought that he was pitted against a highly skilled adversary, and he waited patiently for Tarzan to open up his offence and reveal his style. But Tarzan had no style that could be compared with that of the gladiator. What he was awaiting was a lucky chance – the only thing that he felt could assure him victory over this wary and highly skilled swordsman – but the gladiator gave him no openings and he was hoping that one of his companions would be free to come to his assistance, when, suddenly and without warning, a net dropped over his shoulders from behind.

16

Cassius Hasta split the helmet of a burly thief who opposed him, and as he turned to look for a new opponent he saw a white cast a net over Tarzan's head and shoulders from the rear, while the ape-man was engaged with a professional gladiator. Cassius was nearer the gladiator than Tarzan's other opponent and with a cry he hurled himself upon him. Tarzan saw what Cassius Hasta had done and wheeled to face the white who had attacked him from the rear.

The gladiator found Cassius Hasta a very different opponent from Tarzan. Perhaps he was not as skilful with his shield. Perhaps he was not as powerful, but never in all his experience had the gladiator met such a swordsman.

The crowd had been watching Tarzan from the beginning of the event because his great height and his nakedness and his leopard-skin marked him from all others. They noted that the first cast of his pike had split the shield of his opponent and dropped him dead and they watched his encounter with the gladiator, which did not please them at all. It was far too slow and they hooted and voiced catcalls. When the white cast the net over him they howled with delight, for they did not know from one day to the next, or from one minute to the next, what their own minds would be the next day or the next minute. They were cruel and stupid, but they were no different from the crowds of any place or any time.

As Tarzan, entangled in the net, turned to face the new menace, the white leaped toward him to finish him with a dagger and Tarzan caught the net with the fingers of both his hands and tore it asunder as though it had been made of paper, but the fellow was upon him in the same instant. The dagger hand struck as Tarzan seized the dagger wrist. Blood ran from beneath the leopard-skin from a wound over Tarzan's heart, so close had he been to death, but his hand stopped the other just in time and now steel fingers closed upon that wrist until the man cried out with pain as he felt his bones crushed together. The ape-man drew his antagonist toward him and seized him by the throat and shook him as a terrier shakes a rat, while the air trembled to the delighted screams of the mob.

An instant later Tarzan cast the lifeless form aside, picked up his sword and shield that he had been forced to abandon, and sought for new foes. Thus the battle waged around the arena, each side seeking to gain the advantage in numbers so that they might set upon the remnant of their opponents and destroy them. Cassius Hasta had disposed of the gladiator that he had drawn away from Tarzan and was now engaged with another swordsman when a second fell upon him. Two to one are heavy odds, but Cassius Hasta tried to hold the second off until another red could come to his assistance.

This, however, did not conform with the ideas of the whites who were engaging him, and they fell upon him with redoubled fury to prevent the very thing that he hoped for. He saw an opening and quick as lightning his sword leaped into it, severing the jugular vein of one of his antagonists, but his guard was down for the instant and a glancing blow struck his helmet and, though it did not pierce it, it sent him stumbling to the sand, half-stunned.

'*Habet*! *Habet*!' cried the people, for Cassius Hasta had fallen close to one side of the arena where a great number of people could see him. Standing over him, his antagonist raised his forefinger to the audience and every thumb went down.

With a smile the white raised his sword to drive it through Hasta's throat, but as he paused an instant, facing the crowd, in a little play to the galleries for effect, Tarzan leaped across the soft sand, casting aside his sword and shield, reverting to the primitive to the beast, to save his friend.

It was like the charge of a lion. The crowd saw and was frozen into silence. They saw him spring in his stride several yards before he reached the opposing gladiator and, like a jungle beast, fall upon the shoulders and back of his prey.

Down the two went across the body of Hasta, but instantly the ape-man was upon his feet and in his hands was his antagonist. He shook him as he had shaken the other – shook him into unconsciousness, choking him as he shook, shook him to death, and cast his body from him.

The crowd went wild. They stood upon their benches and shrieked and waved scarves and helmets and threw many flowers and sweetmeats into the arena. Tarzan stooped and lifted Cassius Hasta to his feet as he saw that he was not killed and consciousness was returning.

Scanning the arena quickly, he saw that fifteen reds survived and but ten whites. This was a battle for survival. There were no rules and no ethics. It was your life or mine and Tarzan gathered the surplus five and set upon the strongest white, who now, surrounded by six swordsmen, went down to death in an instant.

At Tarzan's command the six divided and each three charged another white with the result that by following these tactics the event was brought to a sudden and bloody close with fifteen reds surviving and the last white slain.

The crowd was crying Tarzan's name above all others, but Sublatus was enraged. The affront that had been put upon him by this wild barbarian had not been avenged as he had hoped, but instead Tarzan had achieved a personal popularity far greater than his own. That it was ephemeral and subject to the changes of the fickle public mind did not lessen the indignation and chagrin of the Emperor. His mind could entertain but one thought toward Tarzan. The creature must be destroyed. He turned to the præfect in charge of the games and whispered a command.

The crowd was loudly demanding that the laurel wreaths be accorded the victors and that they be given their freedom, but instead they were herded back to their enclosure, all but Tarzan.

Perhaps, suggested some members of the audience, Sublatus is going to honour him particularly, and this rumour ran quickly through the crowd, as rumours will, until it became a conviction.

Slaves came and dragged away the corpses of the slain and picked up the discarded weapons and scattered new sand and raked it, while Tarzan stood where he had been told to stand, beneath the loge of Cæsar.

He stood with folded arms, grimly waiting for what he knew not, and then a low groan rose from the crowded stands – a groan that grew in volume to loud cries of anger above which Tarzan caught words that sounded like 'Tyrant!' 'Coward!' 'Traitor!' and 'Down with Sublatus!' He looked around and saw them pointing to the opposite end of the arena and, facing in that direction, he saw the thing that had aroused their wrath, for instead of a laurel wreath and freedom there stood eyeing him a great, black-maned lion, gaunt with hunger.

Toward the anger of the populace Sublatus exhibited, outwardly, an arrogant and indifferent mien. Contemptuously he permitted his gaze to circle the stands, but he whispered orders that sent three centuries of legionaries among the audience in time to overawe a few agitators who would have led them against the imperial loge.

But now the lion was advancing, and the cruel and selfish audience forgot its momentary anger against injustice in the expected thrill of another bloody encounter. Some who, a moment before, had been loudly acclaiming Tarzan now cheered the lion, though if the lion were vanquished they would again cheer Tarzan. That, however, they did not anticipate, but believed that they had taken sides with the assured winner, since Tarzan was armed only with a dagger, not having recovered his other weapons after he had thrown them aside.

Naked, but for loin-cloth and leopard-skin, Tarzan presented a magnificent picture of physical perfection, and the people of Castra Sanguinarius gave him their admiration, while they placed their denarii and their talents upon the lion.

They had seen other men that week face other lions bravely and hopelessly and they saw the same courageous bearing in the giant barbarian, but the hopelessness they took for granted the ape-man did not feel. With head flattened, half-crouching, the lion moved slowly toward its prey, the tip of its tail twitching in nervous anticipation, its gaunt sides greedy to be filled. Tarzan waited.

Had he been the lion himself, he scarcely could have better known what was passing in that savage brain. He knew to the instant when the final charge would start. He knew the speed of that swift and deadly rush. He knew when and how the lion would rear upon its hind legs to seize him with great talons and mighty, yellow fangs.

He saw the muscles tense. He saw the twitching tail quiet for an instant. His folded arms dropped to his side. The dagger remained in its sheath at his hip. He waited, crouching almost imperceptibly, his weight upon the balls of his feet, and then the lion charged.

Knowing how accurately the beast had timed its final rush, measuring the distance to the fraction of a stride, even as a hunter approaches a jump, the ape-man knew that the surest way in which to gain the first advantage was to disconcert the charging beast by doing that which he would least expect.

Numa the lion knows that his quarry usually does one of two things – he either stands paralysed with terror or he turns and flees. So seldom does he charge to meet Numa that the lion never takes this possibility into consideration and it was, therefore, this very thing that Tarzan did.

As the lion charged, the ape-man leaped to meet him, and the crowd sat breathless and silent. Even Sublatus leaned forward with parted lips, forgetful, for a moment, that he was Cæsar.

Numa tried to check himself and rear to meet this presumptuous man-thing, but he slipped a little in the sand and the great paw that struck at Tarzan was ill-timed and missed, for the ape-man had dodged to one side and beneath it, and in the fraction of a second that it took Numa to recover himself he found that their positions had been reversed and that the prey that he would have leaped upon had turned swiftly and leaped upon him.

Full upon the back of the lion sprang Tarzan of the Apes. A giant forearm encircled the maned throat; steel-thewed legs crossed beneath the gaunt, slim belly and locked themselves there. Numa reared and pawed and turned to bite the savage beast upon his back, but the vice-like arm about his throat pressed tighter, holding him so that his fangs could not reach their goal. He leaped into the air and when he alighted on the sand shook himself to dislodge the growling man-beast clinging to him.

Holding his position with his legs and one arm, Tarzan, with his free hand, sought the hilt of his dagger. Numa, feeling the life being choked from him, became frantic. He reared upon his hind legs and threw himself upon the ground, rolling upon his antagonist, and now the crowd found its voice again and shouted hoarse delight. Never in the history of the arena had such a contest as this been witnessed. The barbarian was offering such a defence as they had not thought possible and they cheered him, though they knew that eventually the lion would win. Then Tarzan found his dagger and drove the thin blade into Numa's side, just back of his left elbow. Again and again the knife struck home, but each blow seemed only to increase the savage efforts of the lunging beast to shake the man from his back and tear him to pieces.

Blood was mixed with the foam on Numa's jowls as he stood panting upon trembling legs after a last futile effort to dislodge the ape-man. He swayed dizzily. The knife struck deep again. A great stream of blood gushed from the mouth and nostrils of the dying beast. He lurched forward and fell lifeless upon the crimsoned sand.

Tarzan of the Apes leaped to his feet. The savage personal combat, the blood, the contact with the mighty body of the carnivore had stripped from him the last vestige of the thin veneer of civilization. It was no lion hunter who stood there with one foot upon his kill and through narrowed lids glared about him at the roaring populace. It was no man, but a wild beast, that raised its head and voiced the savage victory cry of the bull ape, a cry that stilled the multitude and froze its blood. But, in an instant, the spell that had seized him passed. His expression changed. The shadow of a smile crossed his face as he stooped and, wiping the blood from his dagger upon Numa's mane, returned the weapon to its sheath.

Cæsar's jealousy had turned to terror as he realized the meaning of the tremendous ovation the giant barbarian was receiving from the people of Castra Sanguinarius. He well knew, though he tried to conceal the fact, that he held no place in popular favour and that Fastus, his son, was equally hated and despised.

This barbarian was a friend of Maximus Præclarus, whom he had wronged, and Maximus Præclarus, whose popularity with the troops was second to none, was loved by Dilecta, the daughter of Dion Splendidus, who might easily aspire to the purple with the support of such a popular idol as Tarzan must become if he were given his freedom in accordance with the customs and rules governing the contests. While Tarzan waited in the arena and the people cheered themselves hoarse, more legionaries filed into the stands until the wall bristled with glittering pikes.

Cæsar whispered in consultation with the præfect of the games. Trumpets blared and the præfect arose and raised his open palm for silence. Gradually the din subsided and the people waited, listening, expecting the honours that were customarily bestowed upon the outstanding hero of the games. The præfect cleared his throat.

'This barbarian has furnished such extraordinary entertainment that

Cæsar, as a special favour to his loyal subjects, has decided to add one more event to the games in which the barbarian may again demonstrate his supremacy. This event will' – but what further the præfect said was drowned in a murmur of surprise, disapproval, and anger, for the people had sensed by this time the vicious and unfair trick that Sublatus was about to play upon their favourite.

They cared nothing for fair play, for though the individual may prate of it at home it has no place in mob psychology, but the mob knew what it wanted. It wanted to idolize a popular hero. It did not care to see him fight again that day and it wanted to thwart Sublatus, whom it hated. Menacing were the cries and threats directed toward Cæsar, and only the glittering pikes kept the mob at bay.

In the arena the slaves were working rapidly; fallen Numa had been dragged away, the sands swept and as the last slave disappeared, leaving Tarzan again alone within the enclosure, those menacing gates at the far end swung open once more.

17

As Tarzan looked toward the far end of the arena he saw six bull apes being herded through the gateway. They had heard the victory cry roll thunderously from the arena a few minutes before and they came now from their cages filled with excitement and ferocity. Already had they long been surly and irritable from confinement and from the teasing and baiting to which they had been subjected by the cruel Sanguinarians. Before them they saw a man-thing – a hated Tarmangani. He represented the creatures that had captured them and teased them and hurt them.

'I am Gayat,' growled one of the bull apes. 'I kill.'

'I am Zutho,' bellowed another. 'I kill.'

'Kill the Tarmangani,' barked Go-yad, as the six lumbered forward – sometimes erect upon their hind feet, sometimes swinging with gnarled knuckles to the ground.

The crowd hooted and groaned. 'Down with Cæsar!' 'Death to Sublatus!' rose distinctly above the tumult. To a man they were upon their feet, but the glittering pikes held them in awe as one or two, with more courage than brains, sought to reach the loge of Cæsar, but ended upon the pikes of the legionaries instead. Their bodies, lying in the aisles, served as a warning to the others.

Sublatus turned and whispered to a guest in the imperial loge. 'This should be a lesson to all who would dare affront Cæsar,' he said.

'Quite right,' replied the other. 'Glorious Cæsar is, indeed, all powerful,' but the fellow's lips were blue from terror as he saw how great and menacing was the crowd and how slim and few looked the glittering pikes that stood between it and the imperial loge.

As the apes approached, Zutho was in the lead. 'I am Zutho,' he cried, 'I kill.'

'Look well, Zutho, before you kill your friend,' replied the ape-man. 'I am Tarzan of the Apes.'

Zutho stopped, bewildered. The others crowded about him.

'The Tarmangani spoke in the language of the great apes,' said Zutho.

'I know him,' said Go-yad. 'He was king of the tribe when I was a young ape.'

'It is, indeed, Whiteskin,' said Gayat.

'Yes,' said Tarzan, 'I am Whiteskin. We are all prisoners here together. These Tarmangani are my enemies and yours. They wish us to fight, but we shall not.'

'No,' said Zutho, 'we shall not fight against Tarzan.'

'Good,' said the ape-man, as they gathered close around him, sniffing that their noses might validate the testimony of their eyes.

'What has happened?' growled Sublatus. 'Why do they not attack him?'

'He has cast a spell upon them,' replied Cæsar's guest.

The people looked on wonderingly. They heard the beasts and the man growling at one another. How could they guess that they were speaking together in their common language? They saw Tarzan turn and walk toward Cæsar's loge, his bronzed skin brushing against the black coats of the savage beasts lumbering at his side. The ape-man and the apes halted below imperial Cæsar. Tarzan's eyes ran quickly around the arena. The wall was lined with legionaries so not even Tarzan might pass these unscathed. He looked up at Sublatus.

'Your plan has failed, Cæsar. These that you thought would tear me to pieces are my own people. They will not harm me. If there are any others that you would turn against me let them come now, but be quick, for my patience is growing short and if I should say the word these apes will follow me into the imperial loge and tear you to shreds.'

And that is exactly what Tarzan would have done had he not known that while he doubtless could have killed Sublatus his end would come quickly beneath the pikes of the legionaries. He was not sufficiently well versed in the ways of mobs to know that in their present mood the people would have swarmed to protect him and that the legionaries, with few exceptions, would have joined forces with them against the hated tyrant.

What Tarzan wanted particularly was to effect the escape of Cassius Hasta and Cæcilius Metellus simultaneously with his own, so that he might have the advantage of their assistance in his search for Erich von Harben in the Empire of the East; therefore, when the præfect ordered him back to his dungeon he went, taking the apes with him to their cages.

As the arena gates closed behind him he heard again, above the roaring of the populace, the insistent demand: 'Down with Sublatus!'

As the jailer opened the cell door, Tarzan saw that its only occupant was Maximus Præclarus.

'Welcome, Tarzan!' cried the Roman. 'I had not thought to see you again. How is it that you are neither dead nor free?'

'It is the justice of Cæsar,' replied Tarzan, with a smile, 'but at least our friends are free, for I see they are not here.'

'Do not deceive yourself, barbarian,' said the jailer. 'Your friends are chained safely in another cell.'

'But they won their freedom,' exclaimed Tarzan.

'And so did you,' returned the jailer, with a grin; 'but are you free?'

'It is an outrage,' cried Præclarus. 'It cannot be done.'

The jailer shrugged. 'But it is already done,' he said.

'And why?' demanded Præclarus.

'Think you that a poor soldier has the confidence of Cæsar?' asked the jailer; 'But I have heard the reason rumoured. Sedition is in the air. Cæsar fears you and all your friends because the people favour you and you favour Dion Splendidus.'

'I see,' said Præclarus, 'and so we are to remain here indefinitely.'

'I should scarcely say indefinitely,' grinned the jailer, as he closed the door and locked it, leaving them alone.

'I did not like the look in his eye nor the tone of his voice,' said Præclarus, after the fellow was out of hearing. 'The gods are unkind, but how can I expect else from them when even my best friend fails me?'

'You mean Appius Applosus?' asked Tarzan.

'None other,' replied Præclarus. 'If he had fetched the keys, we might yet escape.'

'Perhaps we shall in any event,' said Tarzan. 'I should never give up hope until I were dead – and I have never been dead.'

'You do not know either the power or perfidy of Cæsar,' replied the Roman.

'Nor does Cæsar know Tarzan of the Apes.'

Darkness had but just enveloped the city, blotting out even the dim light of their dungeon cell, when the two men perceived wavering light beams lessening the darkness of the corridor without. The light increased and they knew that someone was approaching, lighting his way with a flaring torch.

Visitors to the dungeon beneath the Colosseum were few in the daytime. Guards and jailers passed occasionally and twice each day slaves came with food, but at night the silent approach of a single torch might more surely augur ill than well. Præclarus and Tarzan dropped the desultory conversation with which they had been whiling away the time and waited in silence for whoever might be coming.

Perhaps the night-time visitor was not for them, but the egotism of misfortune naturally suggested that he was and that his intentions might be more sinister than friendly. But they had not long to wait and their suspicions precluded any possibility of surprise when a man halted before the barred gateway to their cell. As the visitor fitted the key to the lock Præclarus recognised him through the bars.

'Appius Applosus!' he cried. 'You have come!'

'Ps-st!' cautioned Applosus, and quickly opening the gate he stepped within and closed it silently behind him. With a quick glance he surveyed the cell and then extinguished his torch against the stone wall. 'It is fortunate that you are alone,' he said, speaking in whispers, as he dropped to the floor close to the two men.

'You are trembling,' said Præclarus. 'What has happened?'

'It is not what has happened, but what is about to happen that alarms me,' replied Applosus. 'You have probably wondered why I had not brought the keys. You have doubtless thought me faithless, but the fact is that up to this instant it has been impossible, although I have stood ready before to risk my life in the attempt, even as I am now doing.'

'But why should it be so difficult for the commander of the Colosseum guard to visit the dungeon?'

'I am no longer the commander of the guards,' replied Applosus. 'Something must have aroused Cæsar's suspicions, for I was removed in the hour that I last left you. Whether someone overheard and reported our plan or whether it was merely my known friendship for you that aroused his misgivings, I may only surmise, but the fact remains that I have been kept on duty constantly at the Porta Prætoria since I was transferred there from the Colosseum. I have not even been permitted to return to my home, the reason given being that Cæsar expects an uprising of the barbarians of the outer villages, which, as we all know, is utterly ridiculous.

'I risked everything to leave my post only an hour ago, and that because of a word of gossip that was passed to me by a young officer, who came to relieve another at the gate.'

'What said he?' demanded Præclarus.

'He said that an officer of the palace guard had told him that he had been ordered to come to your cell tonight and assassinate both you and this white barbarian. I hastened to Festivitas and together we found the keys that I promised to bring you, but even as I slunk through the shadows of the city's streets, endeavouring to reach the Colosseum unobserved or unrecognized,

I feared that I might be too late, for Cæsar's orders are that you are to be dispatched at once. Here are the keys, Præclarus. If I may do more, command me.'

'No, my friend,' replied Præclarus, 'you have already risked more than enough. Go at once. Return to your post lest Cæsar learn and destroy you.'

'Farewell then and good luck,' said Applosus. 'If you would leave the city, remember that Appius Applosus commands the Porta Prætoria.'

'I shall not forget, my friends,' replied Præclarus, 'but I shall not impose further risks upon your friendship.'

Appius Applosus turned to leave the cell, but he stopped suddenly at the gate. 'It is too late,' he whispered. 'Look!'

The faint gleams of distant torch-light were cutting the gloom of the corridor.

'They come!' whispered Præclarus. 'Make haste!' but instead Appius Applosus stepped quickly to one side of the doorway, out of sight of the corridor beyond, and drew his Spanish sword.

Rapidly the torch swung down the corridor. The scraping of sandals on stone could be distinctly heard, and the ape-man knew that whoever came was alone. A man wrapped in a long dark cloak halted before the barred door and, holding his torch above his head, peered within.

'Maximum Præclarus!' he whispered. 'Are you within?'

'Yes,' replied Præclarus.

'Good!' exclaimed the other. 'I was not sure that this was the right cell.'

'What is your errand?' demanded Præclarus.

'I come from Cæsar,' said the other. 'He sends a note.'

'A sharp one?' inquired Præclarus.

'Sharp and pointed,' laughed the officer.

'We are expecting you.'

'You knew?' demanded the other.

'We guessed, for we know Cæsar.'

'Then make peace with your gods,' said the officer, drawing his sword and pushing the door open, 'for you are about to die.'

There was a cold smile upon his lips as he stepped across the threshold, for Cæsar knew his men and had chosen well the proper type for this deed – a creature without conscience whose envy and jealousy Præclarus had aroused, and the smile was still upon his lips as the sword of Appius Applosus crashed through his helmet to his brain. As the man lunged forward dead, the torch fell from his left hand and was extinguished upon the floor.

'Now go,' whispered Præclarus to Applosus, 'and may the gratitude of those you have saved prove a guard against disaster.'

'It could not have turned out better,' whispered Applosus. 'You have the keys: you have his weapons, and now you have ample time to make your escape before the truth is learned. Goodbye, again. Goodbye, and may the gods protect you.'

As Applosus moved cautiously along the dark corridor, Maximus Præclarus fitted keys to their manacles and both men stood erect, freed at last from their hated chains. No need to formulate plans – they had talked and talked of nothing else for weeks, changing them only to meet altered conditions. Now their first concern was to find Hasta and Metellus and the others upon whose loyalty they could depend and to gather around them as many of the other prisoners as might be willing to follow them in the daring adventure they contemplated.

Through the darkness of the corridor they crept from cell to cell and in the few that still held prisoners they found none unwilling to pledge his loyalty to any cause or to any leader that might offer freedom. Lukedi, Mpingu and Ogonyo were among those they liberated. They had almost given up hope of finding the others when they came upon Metellus and Hasta in a cell close to the entrance to the arena. With them were a number of professional gladiators, who should have been liberated with the other victors at the end of the games, but who were being kept because of some whim of Cæsar that they could not understand and that only inflamed them to anger against the Emperor.

To a man they pledged themselves to follow wherever Tarzan might lead.

'Few of us will come through alive,' said the ape-man, when they had all gathered in the large room that was reserved for the contestants before they were ushered into the arena, 'but those who do will have been avenged upon Cæsar for the wrongs that he has done them.'

'The others will be welcomed by the gods as heroes worthy of every favour,' added Præclarus.

'We do not care whether your cause be right or wrong, or whether we live or die,' said a gladiator, 'so long as there is good fighting.'

'There will be good fighting. I can promise you that,' said Tarzan, 'and plenty of it.'

'Then lead on,' said the gladiator.

'But first I must liberate the rest of my friends,' said the ape-man.

'We have emptied every cell,' said Præclarus. 'There are no more.'

'Oh, yes, my friend,' said Tarzan. 'There are still others – the great apes.'

18

In the dungeons of Validus Augustus in Castrum Mare, Erich von Harben and Mallius Lepus awaited the triumph of Validus Augustus and the opening of the games upon the morrow.

'We have nothing to expect but death,' said Lepus, gloomily. 'Our friends are in disfavour, or in prison, or in exile. The jealousy of Validus Augustus against his nephew, Cassius Hasta, has been invoked against us by Fulvus Fupus to serve his own aims.'

'And the fault is mine,' said von Harben.

'Do not reproach yourself,' replied his friend. 'That Favonia gave you her love cannot be held against you. It is only the jealous and scheming mind of Fupus that is to blame.'

'My love has brought sorrow to Favonia and disaster to her friends,' said von Harben, 'and here am I, chained to a stone wall, unable to strike a blow in her defence or theirs.'

'Ah, if Cassius Hasta were but here!' exclaimed Lepus. 'There is a man. With Fupus adopted by Cæsar, the whole city would arise against Validus Augustus if Cassius Hasta were but here to lead us.'

And as they conversed sadly and hopelessly in the dungeons of Castrum Mare, noble guests gathered in the throne-room of Sublatus in the city of Castra Sanguinarius, at the opposite end of the valley. There were senators in rich robes and high officers of the court and of the army, resplendent in jewels and embroidered linen, who, with their wives and their daughters, formed a gorgeous and glittering company in the pillared chamber, for Fastus, the son of Cæsar, was to wed the daughter of Dion Splendidus that evening.

In the avenue, beyond the palace gates, a great crowd had assembled – a multitude of people pushing and surging to and fro, but pressing ever upon the gates up to the very pikes of the legionaries. It was a noisy crowd – noisy with a deep-throated roar of anger.

'Down with the tyrant!' 'Death to Sublatus!' 'Death to Fastus!' was the burden of their hymn of hate.

The menacing notes filled the palace, reaching to the throne-room, but the haughty patricians pretended not to hear the voice of the cattle. Why should they fear? Had not Sublatus distributed donations to all the troops that very day? Would not the pikes of the legionaries protect the source of their gratuity? It would serve the ungrateful populace right if Sublatus set the legions upon them, for had he not given them such a pageant and such a week of games as Castra Sanguinarius never had known before?

For the rabble without, their contempt knew no bounds now that they were within the palace of the Emperor, but they did not speak among themselves of the fact that most of them had entered by a back gate after the crowd had upset the litter of a noble senator and spilled its passengers into the dust of the avenue.

With pleasure they anticipated the banquet that would follow the marriage ceremony, and while they laughed and chattered over the gossip of the week, the bride sat stark and cold in an upper chamber of the palace surrounded by her female slaves and comforted by her mother.

'It shall not be,' she said. 'I shall never be the wife of Fastus,' and in the folds of her flowing robe she clutched the hilt of a slim dagger.

In the corridor beneath the Colosseum, Tarzan marshalled his forces. He summoned Lukedi and a chief of one of the outer villages, who had been a fellow prisoner with him and with whom he had fought shoulder to shoulder in the games.

'Go to the Porta Prætoria,' he said, 'and ask Appius Applosus to pass you through the city wall as a favour to Maximus Præclarus. Go then among the villages and gather warriors. Tell them that if they would be avenged upon Cæsar and free to live their own lives in their own way, they must rise now and join the citizens who are ready to revolt and destroy the tyrant. Hasten, there is no time to be lost. Gather them quickly and lead them into the city by the Porta Prætoria, straight to the palace of Cæsar.'

Warning their followers to silence, Tarzan and Maximus Præclarus led them in the direction of the barracks of the Colosseum guard, where were quartered the men of Præclarus's own cohort.

It was a motley throng of near-naked black warriors from the outer villages, black slaves from the city, and brown half-castes, among whom were murderers, thieves and professional gladiators. Præclarus and Hasta and Metellus and Tarzan led them, and swarming close to Tarzan were Gayat, Zutho and Go-yad, and their three fellow apes.

Ogonyo was certain now that Tarzan was a demon, for who else might command the hairy men of the woods? Doubtless in each of these fierce bodies presided the ghost of some great Bagego chief. If little Nkima had been the ghost of his grandfather, then these must be the ghosts of very great men indeed. Ogonyo did not press too closely to these savage allies, nor as a matter of fact did any of the others – not even the most ferocious of the gladiators.

At the barracks Maximus Præclarus knew to whom to speak and what to say, for mutiny had long been rife in the ranks of the legionaries. Only their affection for some of their officers, among whom was Præclarus, had kept them thus long in leash, and now they welcomed the opportunity to follow the young patrician to the very gates of Cæsar's palace.

Following a plan that bad been decided upon, Præclarus dispatched a detachment under an officer to the Porta Prætoria with orders to take it by force, if they could not persuade Appius Applosus to join them, and throw it open to the warriors from the outer villages when they should arrive.

Along the broad Via Principalis, overhung by giant trees that formed a tunnel of darkness in the night, Tarzan of the Apes led his followers toward the palace in the wake of a few torch-bearers, who lighted the way.

As they approached their goal, someone upon the outskirts of the crowd, pressing the palace guard, was attracted by the light of their torches and quickly the word was passed that Cæsar had sent for reinforcements – that more troops were coming. The temper of the crowd, already inflamed, was not improved as this news spread quickly through its ranks. A few, following a self-appointed leader, moved forward menacingly to meet the newcomers.

'Who comes?' shouted one.

'It is I, Tarzan of the Apes,' replied the ape-man.

The shout that went up in response to this declaration proved that the fickle populace had not, as yet, turned against him.

Within the palace the cries of the people brought a scowl to the face of Cæsar and a sneer to many a patrician lip, but their reaction might have been far different had they known the cause of the elation of the mob.

'Why are you here?' cried voices. 'What are you going to do?'

'We have come to rescue Dilecta from the arms of Fastus and to drag the tyrant from the throne of Castra Sanguinarius.'

Roars of approval greeted the announcement. 'Death to the tyrant!' 'Down with the palace guards!' 'Kill them!' 'Kill them!' rose from a thousand lips.

The crowd pushed forward. The officer of the guard, seeing the reinforcements, among which were many legionaries, ordered his men to fall back within the palace grounds and close and bar the gate, nor did they succeed in accomplishing this an instant too soon, for as the bolts were shot the crowd hurled itself upon the stout barriers of iron and oak.

A pale-faced messenger hastened to the throne-room and to Cæsar's side.

'The people have risen,' he whispered, hoarsely, 'and many soldiers and gladiators and slaves have joined them. They are throwing themselves against the gates, which cannot hold for long.'

Cæsar arose and paced nervously to and fro, and presently he paused and summoned officers.

'Dispatch messengers to every gate and every barracks,' he ordered. 'Summon the troops to the last man that may be spared from the gates. Order them to fall upon the rabble and kill. Let them kill until no citizen remains alive in the streets of Castra Sanguinarius. Take no prisoners.'

As word finds its way through a crowd, as though by some strange telepathic means, so the knowledge soon became common that Sublatus had ordered every legionary in the city to the palace with instructions to destroy the revolutionaries to the last man.

The people, encouraged by the presence of the legionaries led by Præclarus, had renewed their assaults upon the gates, and though many were piked through its bars, their bodies were dragged away by their friends and others took their places, so that the gates sagged and bent beneath their numbers: yet they held and Tarzan saw that they might hold for long – or at least long enough to permit the arrival of the reinforcements that, if they remained loyal to Cæsar, might overcome this undisciplined mob with ease.

Gathering around him some of those he knew best, Tarzan explained a new plan that was greeted with exclamations of approval, and summoning the apes he moved down the dark avenue, followed by Maximus Præclarus, Cassius Hasta, Cæcilius Metellus, Mpingu, and a half dozen of Castra Sanguinarius's most famous gladiators.

The wedding of Fastus and Dilecta was to take place upon the steps of Cæsar's throne. The high priest of the temple stood facing the audience, and just below him, and at one side, Fastus waited, while slowly up the centre of the long chamber came the bride, followed by the vestal virgins, who tended the temple's sacred fires.

Dilecta was pale, but she did not falter as she moved slowly forward to her doom. There were many who whispered that she looked the Empress already, so noble was her mien, so stately her carriage. They could not see the slim dagger clutched in her right hand beneath the flowing bridal robes. Up the aisle she moved, but she did not halt before the priest as Fastus had done – and as she should have done – but passed him and mounting the first few steps toward the throne she halted, facing Sublatus.

'The people of Castra Sanguinarius have been taught through all the ages that they may look to Cæsar for protection,' she said. 'Cæsar not only makes the law – he is the law. He is either the personification of justice or he is a tyrant. Which, Sublatus, are you?'

Cæsar flushed. 'What mad whim is this, child?' he demanded. 'Who has set you to speak such words to Cæsar?'

'I have not been prompted,' replied the girl, wearily. 'It is my last hope and though I knew beforehand that it was futile, I felt that I must not cast it aside as useless before putting it to the test.'

'Come! Come!' snapped Cæsar. 'Enough of this foolishness. Take your place before the priest and repeat your marriage vows.'

'You cannot refuse me,' cried the girl, stubbornly. 'I appeal to Cæsar, which is my right as a citizen of Rome, the mother city that we have never seen, but whose right to citizenship has been handed down to us from our ancient sires. Unless the spark of freedom is to be denied us, you cannot refuse me that right, Sublatus.'

The Emperor paled and then flushed with anger. 'Come to me tomorrow,' he said. 'You shall have whatever you wish.'

'If you do not hear me now, there will be no tomorrow,' she said. 'I demand my rights now.'

'Well,' demanded Cæsar, coldly, 'what favour do you seek?'

'I seek no favour,' replied Dilecta. 'I seek the right to know if the thing for which I am paying this awful price has been done, as it was promised.'

'What do you mean?' demanded Sublatus. 'What proof do you wish?'

'I wish to see Maximus Præclarus here alive and free,' replied the girl, 'before I pledge my troth to Fastus. That, as you well know, was the price of my promise to wed him.'

Cæsar arose angrily. 'That cannot be,' he said.

'Oh, yes, it can be,' cried a voice from the balcony at the side of the chamber, 'for Maximus Præclarus stands just behind me.'

19

Every eye turned in the direction of the balcony from which came the voice of the speaker. A gasp of astonishment arose from the crowded room.

'The barbarian!' 'Maximus Præclarus!' cried a score of voices.

'The guard! The guard!' screamed Cæsar, as Tarzan leaped from the balcony to one of the tall pillars that supported the roof and slid quickly to the floor, while behind him came six hairy apes.

A dozen swords flashed from their scabbards as Tarzan and the six leaped toward the throne. Women screamed and fainted. Cæsar shrank back upon his golden seat, momentarily paralysed by terror.

A noble with bared blade leaped in front of Tarzan to bar his way, but Go-yad sprang full upon him. Yellow fangs bit once into his neck and, as the great ape arose and standing on the body of his kill roared forth his victory cry, the other nobles shrank back. Fastus, with a scream, turned and fled, and Tarzan leaped to Dilecta's side. As the apes ascended the steps to the dais, Cæsar, jabbering with terror, scuttled from his seat and hid, half-fainting, behind the great throne that was the symbol of his majesty and his power.

But it was not long before the nobles and officers and soldiers in the apartment regained the presence of mind that the sudden advent of this horrid horde had scattered to the four winds, and now, seeing only the wild barbarian and six unarmed beasts threatening them, they pushed forward. Just then a small door beneath the balcony from which Tarzan had descended to the floor of the throne-room was pushed open, giving entrance to Maximus Præclarus, Cassius Hasta, Cæcilius Metellus, Mpingu, and the others who had accompanied Tarzan over the palace wall beneath the shadows of the great trees into which the ape-man and the apes had assisted their less agile fellows.

As Cæsar's defenders sprang forward they were met by some of the best swords in Castra Sanguinarius, as in the forefront of the fighting were the very gladiators whose exploits they had cheered during the week. Tarzan passed Dilecta to Mpingu, for he and Præclarus must lend a hand in the fighting.

Slowly, Dilecta's defenders fell back before the greater number of nobles, soldiers and guardsmen who were summoned from other parts of the palace. Back toward the little door they fell, while shoulder to shoulder with the gladiators and with Maximus Præclarus and Hasta and Metellus, Tarzan fought and the great apes spread consternation among all because of their disposition to attack friend as well as foe.

And out upon the Via Principalis the crowd surged and the great gates gave to a shrieking mob that poured into the palace grounds, overwhelming the guards, trampling them – trampling their own dead and their own living.

But the veteran legionaries who composed the palace guard made a new stand at the entrance to the palace. Once more they checked the undisciplined rabble, which had by now grown to such proportions that the revolting troops, who had joined them, were lost in their midst. The guard had dragged an onager to the palace steps and were discharging stones into the midst of the crowd, which continued to rush forward to fall upon the pikes of the palace defenders.

In the distance trumpets sounded from the direction of the Porta Decumana, and from the Porta Principalis Dextra came the sound of advancing troops. At first those upon the outskirts of the mob, who had heard these sounds, did not interpret them correctly. They cheered and shouted. These cowards that hang always upon the fringe of every crowd, letting others take the risks and do the fighting for them, thought that more troops had revolted and that the reinforcements were for them. But their joy was short-lived, for the first century that swung into the Via Principalis from the Porta Decumana fell upon them with pike and sword until those who were not slain escaped, screaming, in all directions.

Century after century came at the double. They cleared the Via Principalis and fell upon the mob within the palace court until the revolt dissolved into screaming individuals fleeing through the darkness of the palace grounds, seeking any shelter that they might find, while terrible legionaries pursued them with flaming torches and bloody swords.

Back into the little room from which they had come fell Tarzan and his followers. The doorway was small and it was not difficult for a few men to hold it, but when they would have retreated through the window they had entered and gone back into the palace grounds to seek escape across the walls in the shadows of the old trees, they saw the grounds swarming with legionaries and realised that the back of the revolt had been broken.

The ante-room in which they had taken refuge would barely accommodate them all, but it offered probably the best refuge they could have found in all the palace of Sublatus, for there were but two openings in it – the single small doorway leading into the throne-room and an even smaller window letting into the palace gardens. The walls were all stone and proof against any weapons at the disposal of the legionaries; yet if the uprising had failed and the legionaries had not joined the people, as they had expected, of what value this temporary sanctuary? The instant that hunger and thirst assailed them this same room would become their prison cell and torture chamber – and perhaps for many of them a vestibule to the grave.

'Ah Dilecta,' cried Præclarus, in the first moment that he could seize to go to her side, 'I have found you only to lose you again. My rashness, perhaps, has brought you death.'

'Your coming saved me from death,' replied the girl, drawing the dagger from her gown and exhibiting it to Præclarus. 'I chose this as husband rather than Fastus,' she said, 'so if I die now I have lived longer than I should have had you not come; and at least I die happy, for we shall die together.'

'This is no time to be speaking of dying,' said Tarzan. 'Did you think a few hours ago that you would ever be together again? Well, here you are. Perhaps in a few more hours everything will be changed and you will be laughing at the fears you are now entertaining.'

Some of the gladiators, who were standing near and had overheard Tarzan's words, shook their heads.

'Any of us who gets out of this room alive,' said one, 'will be burned at the stake, or fed to lions, or pulled apart by wild buffalo. We are through, but it has been a good fight, and I for one thank this great barbarian for this glorious end.'

Tarzan shrugged and turned away. 'I am not dead yet,' he said, 'and not until I am dead is it time to think of it – and then it will be too late.'

Maximus Præclarus laughed. 'Perhaps you are right,' he said. 'What do you suggest? If we stay here, we shall be slain, so you must have some plan for getting us out.'

'If we can discern no hope of advantage through our own efforts,' replied Tarzan, 'we must look elsewhere and await such favours of fortune as may come from without, either through the intervention of our friends beyond the palace grounds or from the carelessness of the enemy himself. I admit that just at present our case appears desperate, but even so I am not without hope; at least we may be cheered by the realisation that whatever turn events may take it must be for the better, since nothing could be worse.'

'I do not agree with you,' said Metellus, pointing through the window. 'See, they are setting up a small ballista in the garden. Presently our condition will be much worse than it is now.'

'The walls appear substantial,' returned the ape-man. 'Do you think they can batter them down, Præclarus?'

'I doubt it,' replied the Roman, 'but every missile that comes through the window must take its toll, as we are so crowded here that all of us cannot get out of range.'

The legionaries that had been summoned to the throne-room had been held at the small doorway by a handful of gladiators and the defenders had been able to close and bar the stout oaken door. For a time there had been silence in the throne-room and no attempt was made to gain entrance to the room upon that side; while upon the garden side two or three attempts to rush the window had been thwarted, and now the legionaries held off while the small ballista was being dragged into place and trained upon the palace wall.

Dilecta having been placed in an angle of the room where she would be safest, Tarzan and his lieutenants watched the operations of the legionaries in the garden.

'They do not seem to be aiming directly at the window,' remarked Cassius Hasta.

'No,' said Præclarus. 'I rather think they intend making a breach in the wall through which a sufficient number of them can enter to overpower us.'

'If we could rush the ballista and take it,' mused Tarzan, 'we could make it rather hot for them. Let us hold ourselves in readiness for that, if their missiles make it too hot for us in here. We shall have some advantage if we anticipate their assault by a sortie of our own.'

A dull thud upon the door at the opposite end of the room brought the startled attention of the defenders to that quarter. The oak door sagged and the stone walls trembled to the impact.

Cassius Hasta smiled wryly. 'They have brought a ram,' he said.

And now a heavy projectile shook the outer wall and a piece of plaster crumbled to the floor upon the inside – the ballista had come into action. Once again the heavy battering-ram shivered the groaning timbers of the door and the inmates of the room could hear the legionaries chanting the hymn of the ram to the cadence of which they swung it back and heaved it forward.

The troops in the garden went about their duty with quiet, military efficiency. Each time a stone from the ballista struck the wall there was a shout, but there was nothing spontaneous in the demonstration, which seemed as perfunctory as the mechanical operation of the ancient war-engine that delivered its missiles with almost clock-like regularity.

The greatest damage that the ballista appeared to be doing was to the plaster on the inside of the wall, but the battering-ram was slowly but surely shattering the door at the opposite side of the room.

'Look,' said Metellus, 'they are altering the line of the ballista. They have discovered that they can effect nothing against the wall.'

'They are aiming at the window,' said Præclarus.

'Those of you who are in line with the window lie down upon the floor,' commanded Tarzan. 'Quickly! The hammer is falling upon the trigger.'

The next missile struck one side of the window, carrying away a piece of the stone, and this time the result was followed by an enthusiastic shout from the legionaries in the garden.

'That's what they should have done in the beginning,' commented Hasta. 'If they get the walls started at the edge of the window, they can make a breach more quickly there than elsewhere.'

'That is evidently what they are planning on doing,' said Metellus, as a second missile struck in the same place and a large fragment of the wall crumbled.

'Look to the door,' shouted Tarzan, as the weakened timbers sagged to the impact of the ram.

A dozen swordsmen stood ready and waiting to receive the legionaries, whose rush they expected the instant that the door fell. At one side of the room the six apes crouched, growling, and kept in leash only by the repeated assurances of Tarzan that the man-things in the room with them were the friends of the ape-man.

As the door crashed, there was a momentary silence, as each side waited to see what the other would do, and in the lull that ensued there came through the air a roaring sound, ominous and threatening, and then the shouts of the legionaries in the throne-room and the legionaries in the garden drowned all other sounds.

The gap around the window had been enlarged. The missiles of the ballista had crumbled the wall from the ceiling to the floor, and as though in accordance with a pre-arranged plan the legionaries assaulted simultaneously, one group rushing the doorway from the throne-room, the other the breach in the opposite wall.

Tarzan turned toward the apes and pointing in the direction of the breached wall, shouted: 'Stop them, Zutho! Kill, Go-yad! Kill!'

The men near him looked at him in surprise and perhaps they shuddered a little as they heard the growling voice of a beast issue from the throat of the giant barbarian, but instantly they realised he was speaking to his hairy fellows, as they saw the apes spring forward with bared fangs and, growling hideously, throw themselves upon the first legionaries to reach the window.

Two apes went down, pierced by Roman pikes, but before the beastly rage of the others Cæsar's soldiers fell back.

'After them,' cried Tarzan to Præclarus. 'Follow them into the garden. Capture the ballista and turn it upon the legionaries. We will hold the throne-room door until you have seized the ballista, then we shall fall back upon you.'

After the battling apes rushed the three patricians, Maximus Præclarus, Cassius Hasta, and Cæcilius Metellus, leading gladiators, thieves, murderers, and slaves into the garden, profiting by the temporary advantage the apes had gained for them.

Side by side with the remaining gladiators Tarzan fought to hold the legionaries back from the little doorway until the balance of his party had won safely to the garden and seized the ballista. Glancing back he saw Mpingu leading Dilecta from the room in the rear of the escaped prisoners. Then he turned again to the defence of the doorway, which his little party held stubbornly until Tarzan saw the ballista in the hands of his own men, and, giving step by step across the room, he and they backed through the breach in the wall.

At a shout of command from Præclarus, they leaped to one side. The hammer fell upon the trigger of the ballista, which Præclarus had lined upon the window, and a heavy rock drove full into the faces of the legionaries.

For a moment the fates had been kind to Tarzan and his fellows, but it soon became apparent that they were little if any better off here than in the room they had just quitted, for in the garden they were ringed by legionaries. Pikes were flying through the air, and though the ballista and their own good swords were keeping the enemy at a respectful distance, there was none among them who believed that they could for long withstand the superior numbers and the better equipment of their adversaries.

There came a pause in the fighting, which must necessarily be the case in hand-to-hand encounters, and as though by tacit agreement each side rested. The three whites watched the enemy closely. 'They are preparing for a concerted attack with pikes,' said Præclarus.

'That will write finis to our earthly endeavours,' remarked Cassius Hasta.

'May the gods receive us with rejoicing,' said Cæcilius Metellus.

'I think the gods prefer them to us,' said Tarzan.

'Why?' demanded Cassius Hasta.

'Because they have taken so many more of them to heaven this night,' replied the ape-man, pointing at the corpses lying about the garden, and Cassius Hasta smiled, appreciatively.

'They will charge in another moment,' said Maximus Præclarus, and turning to Dilecta he took her in his arms and kissed her. 'Goodbye, dear heart,' he said. 'How fleeting is happiness! How futile the hopes of mortal man!'

'Not goodbye, Præclarus,' replied the girl, 'for where you go I shall go,' and she showed him the slim dagger in her hand.

'No,' cried the man. 'Promise me that you will not do that.'

'And why not? Is not death sweeter than Fastus?'

'Perhaps you are right,' he said, sadly.

'They come,' cried Cassius Hasta.

'Ready!' shouted Tarzan. 'Give them all we have. Death is better than the dungeons of the Colosseum.'

20

From the far end of the garden, above the din of breaking battle, rose a savage cry – a new note that attracted the startled attention of the contestants upon both sides. Tarzan's head snapped to attention. His nostrils sniffed the air. Recognition, hope, surprise, incredulity surged through his consciousness as he stood there with flashing eyes looking out over the heads of his adversaries.

In increasing volume the savage roar rolled into the garden of Cæsar. The legionaries turned to face the vanguard of an army led by a horde of ebon warriors, glistening giants from whose proud heads floated white feather war-bonnets and from whose throats issued the savage war-cry that had filled the heart of Tarzan – the Waziri had come.

At their head Tarzan saw Muviro and with him was Lukedi, but what the ape-man did not see, and what none of those in the garden of Cæsar saw until later, was the horde of warriors from the outer villages of Castra Sanguinarius that, following the Waziri into the city, were already over-running the palace seeking the vengeance that had so long been denied them.

As the last of the legionaries in the garden threw down their arms and begged Tarzan's protection, Muviro ran to the ape-man and, kneeling at his feet, kissed his band, and at the same instant a little monkey dropped from an overhanging tree on to Tarzan's shoulder.

'The gods of our ancestors have been good to the Waziri,' said Muviro, 'otherwise we should have been too late.'

'I was puzzled as to how you found me,' said Tarzan, 'until I saw Nkima.'

'Yes, it was Nkima,' said Muviro. 'He came back to the country of the Waziri, to the land of Tarzan, and led us here. Many times we would have turned back thinking that he was mad, but he urged us on and we followed him, and now the Big Bwana can come back with us to the home of his own people.'

'No,' said Tarzan, shaking his head, 'I cannot come yet. The son of my good friend is still in this valley, but you are just in time to help me to rescue him, nor is there any time to lose.'

Legionaries, throwing down their arms, were running from the palace, from which came the shrieks and groans of the dying and the savage hoots and cries of the avenging horde. Præclarus stepped to Tarzan's side.

'The barbarians of the outer villages are attacking the city, murdering all who fall into their hands,' he cried. 'We must gather what men we can and make a stand against them. Will these blacks, who have just come, fight with us against them?'

'They will fight as I direct,' replied Tarzan, 'but I think it will not be necessary to make war upon the barbarians. Lukedi, where are the white officers who command the barbarians?'

'Once they neared the palace,' replied Lukedi, 'the warriors became so excited that they broke away from their white leaders and followed their own chieftain.'

'Go and fetch their greatest chief,' directed Tarzan.

During the half hour that followed, Tarzan and his lieutenants were busy reorganising their forces into which were incorporated the legionaries who had surrendered to them, in caring for the wounded, and planning for the future. From the palace came the hoarse cries of the looting blacks, and Tarzan had about abandoned hope that Lukedi would be able to persuade a chief to come to him when Lukedi returned, accompanied by two warriors from the outer villages, whose bearing and ornaments proclaimed them chieftains.

'You are the man called Tarzan?' demanded one of the chiefs.

The ape-man nodded. 'I am,' he said.

'We have been looking for you. This Bagego said that you have promised that no more shall our people be taken into slavery and no longer shall our warriors be condemned to the arena. How can you, who are yourself a barbarian, guarantee this to us?'

'I cannot guarantee it, you have the power to enforce it yourself,' replied the ape-man, 'and I with my Waziri will aid you, but now you must gather your warriors. Let no one be killed from now on who does not oppose you. Gather your warriors and take them into the avenue before the palace and then come with your subjects to the throne-room of Cæsar. There we shall demand and receive justice, not for the moment but for all time. Go!'

Eventually the looting horde of blacks was quieted by their chiefs and withdrawn to the Via Principalis. Waziri warriors manned the shattered gate of Cæsar's palace and lined the corridor to the throne-room and the aisle to the foot of the throne. They formed a half circle about the throne itself, and upon the throne of Cæsar sat Tarzan of the Apes with Præclarus and Dilecta and Cassius Hasta and Cæcilius Metellus and Muviro about him, while little Nkima sat upon his shoulder and complained bitterly, for Nkima, as usual, was frightened and cold and hungry.

'Send legionaries to fetch Sublatus and Fastus,' Tarzan directed Præclarus, 'for this business must be attended to quickly, as within the hour I march on Castrum Mare.'

Flushed with excitement, the legionaries that had been sent to fetch Sublatus and Fastus rushed into the throne-room. 'Sublatus is dead!' they cried. 'Fastus is dead! The barbarians have slain them. The chambers and corridors above are filled with the bodies of senators, nobles, and officers of the legion.'

'Are none left alive?' demanded Præclarus, paling.

'Yes,' replied one of the legionaries, 'there were many barricaded in another apartment who withstood the onslaught of the blacks. We explained to them that they are now safe and they are coming to the throne-room,' and up the aisle marched the remnants of the wedding guests, the sweat and blood upon the men evidencing the dire straits from which they had been delivered, the women still nervous and hysterical. Leading them came Dion Splendidus, and at sight of him Dilecta gave a cry of relief and pleasure and ran down the steps of the throne and along the aisle to meet him.

Tarzan's face lighted with relief when he saw the old senator, for his weeks in the home of Festivitas and his long incarceration with Maximus Præclarus in the dungeons of the Colosseum had familiarised him with the politics of Castra Sanguinarius, and now the presence of Dion Splendidus was all that he needed to complete the plans that the tyranny and cruelty of Sublatus had forced upon him.

He rose from the throne and raised his hand for silence. The hum of voices ceased. 'Cæsar is dead, but upon some one of you must fall the mantle of Cæsar.'

'Long live Tarzan! Long live the new Cæsar!' cried one of the gladiators, and instantly every Sanguinarian in the room took up the cry.

The ape-man smiled and shook his head. 'No,' he said, 'not I, but there is one here to whom I offer the imperial diadem upon the condition that he fulfils the promises I have made to the barbarians of the outer villages.

'Dion Splendidus, will you accept the imperial purple with the understanding that the men of the outer villages shall be for ever free; that no longer shall their girls or their boys be pressed into slavery, or their warriors forced to do battle in the arena?' Dion Splendidus bowed his head in assent – and thus did Tarzan refuse the diadem and create a Cæsar.

21

The yearly triumph of Validus Augustus, Emperor of the East, had been a poor thing by comparison with that of Sublatus of Castra Sanguinarius, though dignity and interest was lent the occasion by the presence of the much-advertised barbarian chieftain, who strode in chains behind Cæsar's chariot.

The vain show of imperial power pleased Validus Augustus, deceived perhaps the more ignorant of his subjects, and would have given Erich von Harben cause for laughter had he not realised the seriousness of his position.

No captive chained to the chariot of the greatest Cæsar that ever lived had faced a more hopeless situation than he. What though he knew that a regiment of marines or a squadron of cavalry might have reduced this entire empire to vassalage? What though he knew that the mayor of many a modern city could have commanded a fighting force far greater and much more effective than this little Cæsar? The knowledge was only tantalising, for the fact remained that Validus Augustus was supreme here and there was neither regiment of marines nor squadron of cavalry to question his behaviour toward the subject of a great republic that could have swallowed his entire empire without being conscious of any discomfort. The triumph was over. Von Harben had been returned to the cell that he occupied with Mallius Lepus.

'You are back early,' said Lepus. 'How did the triumph of Validus impress you?'

'It was not much of a show, if I may judge by the amount of enthusiasm displayed by the people.'

'The triumphs of Validus are always poor things,' said Lepus. 'He would rather put ten talents in his belly or on his back than spend one denarius to amuse the people.'

'And the games,' asked von Harben, 'will they be as poor?'

'They do not amount to much,' said Lepus. 'We have few criminals here and as we have to purchase all our slaves, they are too valuable to waste in this way. Many of the contests are between wild beasts, an occasional thief or murderer may be pitted against a gladiator, but for the most part Validus depends upon professional gladiators and political prisoners – enemies or supposed enemies of Cæsar. More often they are like you and I – victims of the lying and jealous intrigues of favourites. There are about twenty such in the dungeons now, and they will furnish the most interesting entertainment of the games.'

'And if we are victorious, we are freed?' asked von Harben.

'We shall not be victorious,' said Mallius Lepus. 'Fulvus Fupus has seen to that, you may rest assured.'

'It is terrible,' muttered von Harben.

'You are afraid to die?' asked Mallius Lepus.

'It is not that,' said von Harben. 'I am thinking of Favonia.'

'And well you may,' said Mallius Lepus. 'My sweet cousin would be happier dead than married to Fulvus Fupus.'

'I feel so helpless,' said von Harben. 'Not a friend, not even my faithful body servant, Gabula.'

'Oh, that reminds me,' exclaimed Lepus. 'They were here looking for him this morning.'

'Looking for him? Is he not confined in the dungeon?'

'He was, but he was detailed with other prisoners to prepare the arena last night, and during the darkness of early morning he is supposed to have escaped – but be that as it may, they were looking for him.'

'Good!' exclaimed von Harben. 'I shall feel better just knowing that he is at large, though there is nothing that he can do for me. Where could he have gone?'

'Castrum Mare is ill guarded along its water-front, but the lake itself and the crocodiles form a barrier as efficacious as many legionaries. Gabula may have scaled the wall, but the chances are that he is hiding within the city, protected by other slaves or, possibly, by Septimus Favonius himself.'

'I wish I might feel that the poor, faithful fellow had been able to escape the country and return to his own people,' said von Harben.

Mallius Lepus shook his head. 'That is impossible,' he said. 'Though you came down over the cliff, he could not return that way, and even if he could find the pass to the outer world, he would fall into the hands of the soldiers of Castra Sanguinarius or the black barbarians of their outer villages. No, there is no chance that Gabula will escape.'

The time passed quickly, all too quickly, between the hour that Erich von Harben was returned to his cell, following his exhibition in the triumph of Validus Augustus, and the coming of the Colosseum guards to drive them into the arena.

The Colosseum was packed. The loges of the patricians were filled. The haughty Cæsar of the East sat upon an ornate throne, shaded by a canopy of purple linen. Septimus Favonius sat with bowed head in his loge and with him was his wife and Favonia. The girl sat with staring eyes fixed upon the gateway from which the contestants were emerging. She saw her cousin, Mallius Lepus, emerge and with him Erich von Harben, and she shuddered and closed her eyes for a moment.

When she opened them again the column was forming and the contestants were marched across the white sands to receive the commands of Cæsar. With Mallius Lepus and von Harben marched the twenty political prisoners, all of whom were of the patrician class. Then came the professional gladiators – coarse, brutal men, whose business it was to kill or be killed. Leading these, with a bold swagger, was one who had been champion gladiator of Castrum Mare for five years. If the people had an idol, it was he. They roared their approval of him. 'Claudius Taurus! Claudius Taurus!' rose above a babel of voices. A few mean thieves, some frightened slaves, and a half dozen lions completed the victims that were to make a Roman holiday.

Erich von Harben had often been fascinated by the stories of the games of ancient Rome. Often had he pictured the Colosseum packed with its thousands and the contestants upon the white sand of the arena, but now he realised that they had been but pictures – but the photographs of his imagination. The people in those dreams had been but picture people – automatons, who move only when we look at them. When there had been action on the sand the audience had been a silent etching, and when the audience had roared and turned its thumbs down the actors had been mute and motionless.

How different, this! He saw the constant motion in the packed stands, the mosaic of a thousand daubs of colour that became kaleidoscopic with every move of the multitude. He heard the hum of voices and sensed the offensive odour of many human bodies. He saw the hawkers and vendors passing along the aisles shouting their wares. He saw the legionaries stationed everywhere. He saw the rich in their canopied loges and the poor in the hot sun of the cheap seats.

Sweat was trickling down the back of the neck of the patrician marching just in front of him. He glanced at Claudius Taurus. He saw that his tunic was faded and that his hairy legs were dirty. He had always thought of gladiators as clean-limbed and resplendent. Claudius Taurus shocked him.

As they formed in solid rank before the loge of Cæsar, von Harben smelled the black men pressing close behind him. The air was hot and oppressive. The whole thing was disgusting. There was no grandeur in it, no dignity. He wondered if it had been like this in Rome.

And then he looked up into the loge of Cæsar. He saw the man in gorgeous robes, sitting upon his carved throne. He saw naked blacks swaying long-handled fans of feathers above the head of Cæsar. He saw large men in gorgeous tunics and cuirasses of shining gold. He saw the wealth and pomp and circumstance of power, and something told him that after all ancient Rome had probably been much as this was – that its populace had smelled and that its gladiators had had hairy legs with dirt on them and that its patricians had sweated behind the ears.

Perhaps Validus Augustus was as great a Cæsar as any of them, for did he not rule half of his known world? Few of them had done more than this.

His eyes wandered along the row of loges. The præfect of the games was speaking and von Harben heard his voice, but the words did not reach his brain, for his eyes had suddenly met those of a girl.

He saw the anguish and hopeless horror in her face and he tried to smile as he looked at her, a smile of encouragement and hope, but she only saw the beginning of the smile, for the tears came and the image of the man she loved was only a dull blur like the pain in her heart.

A movement in the stands behind the loges attracted von Harben's eyes and he puckered his brows, straining his faculties to assure himself that he must be mistaken, but he was not. What he had seen was Gabula – he was moving toward the imperial loge, where he disappeared behind the hangings that formed the background of Cæsar's throne.

Then the præfect ordered them from the arena and as von Harben moved across the sand he tried to find some explanation of Gabula's presence there – what errand had brought him to so dangerous a place?

The contestants had traversed but half the width of the arena returning to their cells when a sudden scream, ringing out behind them, caused them all to turn. Von Harben saw that the disturbance came from the imperial loge, but the scene that met his startled gaze seemed too preposterous to have greater substance than a dream. Perhaps it was all a dream. Perhaps there was no Castrum Mare. Perhaps there was no Validus Augustus. Perhaps there was no – ah, but that could not be true, there was Favonia and this preposterous thing then that he was looking at was true too. He saw a black man holding Cæsar by the throat and driving a dagger into his heart with the other, and the black man was Gabula.

It all happened so quickly and was over so quickly that scarcely had Cæsar's shriek run through the Colosseum than he lay dead at the foot of his carved throne, and Gabula, the assassin, in a single leap had cleared the arena wall and was running across the sand toward von Harben.

'I have avenged you, Bwana!' cried the black man. 'No matter what they do to you, you are avenged.'

A great groan arose from the audience and then a cheer as someone shouted: 'Cæsar is dead!'

A hope flashed to the breast of von Harben. He turned and grabbed Mallius Lepus by the arm. 'Cæsar is dead,' he whispered. 'Now is our chance.'

'What do you mean?' demanded Mallius Lepus.

'In the confusion we can escape. We can hide in the city and at night we can take Favonia with us and go away.'

'Where?' asked Mallius Lepus.

'God! I do not know,' exclaimed von Harben, 'but anywhere would be better than here, for Fulvus Fupus is Cæsar and if we do not save Favonia tonight, it will be too late.'

'You are right,' said Mallius Lepus.

'Pass the word to the others,' said von Harben. 'The more there are who try to escape the better chance there will be for some of us to succeed.'

The legionaries and their officers as well as the vast multitude could attend only upon what was happening in the loge of Cæsar. So few of them had seen what really occurred there that as yet there had been no pursuit of Gabula.

Mallius Lepus turned to the other prisoners. 'The gods have been good to us,' he cried. 'Cæsar is dead and in the confusion we can escape. Come!'

As Mallius Lepus started on a run toward the gateway that led to the cells beneath the Colosseum, the shouting prisoners fell in behind him. Only those of the professional gladiators who were freemen held aloof, but they made no effort to stop them.

'Good luck!' shouted Claudius Taurus, as von Harben passed him. 'Now if someone would kill Fulvus Fupus we might have a Cæsar who is a Cæsar.'

The sudden rush of the escaping prisoners so confused and upset the few guards beneath the Colosseum that they were easily overpowered and a moment later the prisoners found themselves in the streets of Castrum Mare.

'Where now?' cried one.

'We must scatter,' said Mallius Lepus. 'Each man for himself.'

'We shall stick together, Mallius Lepus,' said von Harben.

'To the end,' replied the Roman.

'And here is Gabula,' said von Harben, as the black joined them.

'He shall come with us.'

'We cannot desert the brave Gabula,' said Mallius Lepus, 'but the first thing for us to do is to find a hiding-place.'

'There is a low wall across the avenue,' said von Harben, 'and there are trees beyond it.'

'Come, then,' said Mallius Lepus. 'It is as good for now as any other place.'

The three men hurried across the avenue and scaled the low wall, finding themselves in a garden so overgrown with weeds and underbrush that they at once assumed that it was deserted. Creeping through the weeds and forcing their way through the underbrush, they came to the rear of a house. A broken door, hanging by one hinge, windows from which the wooden blinds had fallen, an accumulation of rubbish upon the threshold marked the dilapidated structure as a deserted house.

'Perhaps this is just the place for us to hide until night,' said von Harben.

'Its proximity to the Colosseum is its greatest advantage,' said Mallius Lepus, 'for they will be sure to believe that we have rushed as far from our dungeon as we could. Let us go in and investigate. We must be sure that the place is uninhabited.'

The rear room, which had been the kitchen, had a crumbling brick oven in one corner, a bench and a dilapidated table. Crossing the kitchen, they entered an apartment beyond and saw that these two rooms constituted all that there was to the house. The front room was large and as the blinds at the windows facing the avenue had not fallen, it was dark within it. In one corner they saw a ladder reaching to a trap-door in the ceiling, which evidently led to the roof of the building, and two or three feet below the ceiling and running entirely across the end of the room where the ladder arose was a false ceiling, which formed a tiny loft just below the roof-beams, a place utilised by former tenants as a storage-room. A more careful examination of the room revealed nothing more than a pile of filthy rags against one wall, the remains perhaps of some homeless beggar's bed.

'It could not have been better,' said Mallius Lepus, 'if this had been built for us. Why, we have three exits if we are hard pressed – one into the back garden, one into the avenue in front, and the third to the roof.'

'We can remain in safety, then,' said von Harben, 'until after dark, when it should be easy to make our way unseen through the dark streets to the home of Septimus Favonius.'

22

East along the Via Mare from Castra Sanguinarius marched five thousand men. The white plumes of the Waziri nodded at the back of Tarzan. Stalwart legionaries followed Maximus Præclarus, while the black warriors of the outer villages brought up the rear.

Sweating slaves dragged catapults, ballistæ, testudines, huge battering-rams, and other ancient engines of war. There were scaling ladders and wall hooks and devices for throwing fire balls into the defences of an enemy. The heavy engines had delayed the march and Tarzan had chafed at the delay, but he had to listen to Maximus Præclarus and Cassius Hasta and Cæcilius Metellus, all of whom had assured him that the fort, which defended the only road to Castrum Mare, could not be taken by assault without the aid of these mechanical engines of war.

Along the hot and dusty Via Mare the Waziri swung, chanting the war songs of their people. The hardened legionaries, their heavy helmets dangling against their breasts from cords that passed about their necks, their packs on forked sticks across their shoulders, their great oblong shields hanging in their leather covers at their backs, cursed and grumbled as became veterans, while the warriors from the outer villages laughed and sang and chattered as might a party of picnickers.

As they approached the fort with its moat and embankment and palisade and towers, slaves were bearing the body of Validus Augustus to his palace within the city, and Fulvus Fupus, surrounded by fawning sycophants, was proclaiming himself Cæsar, though he trembled inwardly in contemplation of what fate might lie before him – for though he was a fool he knew that he was not popular and that many a noble patrician with a strong following had a better right to the imperial purple than he.

Throughout the city of Castrum Mare legionaries searched for the escaped prisoners and especially for the black slave who had struck down Validus Augustus, though they were handicapped by the fact that no one had recognised Gabula, for there were few in the city and certainly none in the entourage of Cæsar who was familiar with the face of the black from distant Urambi.

A few of the thieves and five or six gladiators, who were condemned felons and not freemen, had clung together in the break for freedom and presently they found themselves in hiding in a low part of the city, in a den where wine could be procured and where there were other forms of entertainment for people of their class.

'What sort of a Cæsar will this Fulvus Fupus make?' one asked.

'He will be worse than Validus Augustus,' said another. 'I have seen him in the Baths where I once worked. He is vain and dull and ignorant; even the patricians hate him.'

'They say he is going to marry the daughter of Septimus Favonius.'

'I saw her in the Colosseum today,' said another. 'I know her well by sight, for she used to come to the shop of my father and make purchases before I was sent to the dungeons.'

'Have you ever been to the house of Septimus Favonius?' asked another.

'Yes, I have,' said the youth. 'Twice I took goods there for her inspection, going through the forecourt and into the inner garden. I know the place well.'

'If one like her should happen to fall into the hands of a few poor convicts they might win their freedom and a great ransom,' suggested a low-browed fellow with evil, cunning eyes.

'And be drawn asunder by wild oxen for their pains.'

'We must die anyway if we are caught.'

'It is a good plan.'

They drank again for several minutes in silence, evidencing that the plan was milling in their minds.

'The new Cæsar should pay an enormous ransom for his bride.'

The youth rose eagerly to his feet. 'I will lead you to the home of Septimus Favonius and guarantee that they will open the gate for me and let me in, as I know what to say. All I need is a bundle and I can tell the slave that it contains goods that my father wishes Favonia to inspect.'

'You are not such a fool as you look.'

'No, and I shall have a large share of the ransom for my part in it,' said the youth.

'If there is any ransom, we shall share and share alike.'

Night was falling as Tarzan's army halted before the defences of Castrum Mare. Cassius Hasta, to whom the reduction of the fort had been entrusted, disposed his forces and supervised the placing of his various engines of war.

Within the city Erich von Harben and Mallius Lepus discussed the details of their plans. It was the judgment of Lepus to wait until after midnight before making any move to leave their hiding-place.

'The streets will be deserted then,' said Mallius Lepus, 'except for an occasional patrol upon the principal avenue, and these may be easily eluded, since the torches that they carry proclaim their approach long before there is any danger of their apprehending us. I have the key to the gate of my uncle's garden, which ensures that we may enter the grounds silently and unobserved.'

'Perhaps you are right,' said von Harben, 'but I dread the long wait and the thought of further inaction seems unbearable.'

'Have patience, my friend,' said Mallius Lepus. 'Fulvus Fupus will be too busy with his new Cæsarship to give heed to aught else for some time, and Favonia will be safe from him, certainly for the next few hours at least.'

And as they discussed the matter, a youth knocked upon the door of the home of Septimus Favonius. Beneath the shadow of the trees along the wall darker shadows crouched. A slave bearing a lamp came to the door in answer to the knocking and, speaking through a small grille, asked who was without and what the nature of his business.

'I am the son of Tabernarius,' said the youth. 'I have brought fabrics from the shop of my father that the daughter of Septimus Favonius may inspect them.'

The slave hesitated.

'You must remember me,' said the youth. 'I have been here often,' and the slave held the light a little bit higher and peered through the grille.

'Yes,' he said, 'your face is familiar. I will go and ask my mistress if she wishes to see you. Wait here.'

'These fabrics are valuable,' said the youth, holding up a bundle, which he carried under his arm. 'Let me stand just within the vestibule lest thieves set upon me and rob me.'

'Very well,' said the slave, and opening the gate he permitted the youth to enter. 'Remain here until I return.'

As the slave disappeared into the interior of the house, the son of Tabernarius turned quickly and withdrew the bolt that secured the door. Opening it quickly, he leaned out to voice a low signal.

Instantly the denser shadows beneath the shadowy trees moved and were resolved into the figures of men. Scurrying like vermin, they hurried through the doorway and into the home of Septimus Favonius, and into the anteroom off the vestibule the son of Tabernarius hustled them. Then he closed both doors and waited.

Presently the slave returned. 'The daughter of Septimus Favonius recalls having ordered no goods from Tabernarius,' he said, 'nor does she feel in any mood to inspect fabrics this night. Return them to your father and tell him that when the daughter of Septimus Favonius wishes to purchase she will come herself to his shop.'

Now this was not what the son of Tabernarius desired and he racked his crafty brain for another plan, though to the slave he appeared but a stupid youth, staring at the floor in too much embarrassment even to take his departure.

'Come,' said the slave, approaching the door and laying hold of the bolt, 'you must be going.'

'Wait,' whispered the youth. 'I have a message for Favonia. I did not wish anyone to know it and for that reason I spoke of bringing fabrics as an excuse.'

'Where is the message and from whom?' demanded the slave, suspiciously.

'It is for her ears only. Tell her this and she will know from whom it is.'

The slave hesitated.

'Fetch her here,' said the youth. 'It will be better that no other member of the household sees me.'

The slave shook his head. 'I will tell her,' he said, for he knew that Mallius Lepus and Erich von Harben had escaped from the Colosseum and he guessed that the message might be from one of these. As he hastened back to his mistress the son of Tabernarius smiled, for though he knew not enough of Favonia to know from whom she might reasonably expect a secret message, yet he knew there were few young women who might not, at least hopefully, expect a clandestine communication. He had not long to wait before the slave returned and with him came Favonia. Her excitement was evident as she hastened eagerly forward toward the youth.

'Tell me,' she cried, 'you have brought word from him.'

The son of Tabernarius raised a forefinger to his lip to caution her to silence. 'No one must know that I am here,' he whispered, 'and no ears but yours may hear my message. Send your slave away.'

'You may go,' said Favonia, to the slave. 'I will let the young man out when he goes,' and the slave, glad to be dismissed, content to be relieved of responsibility, moved silently away into the shadows of a corridor and thence into the uncharted limbo into which pass slaves and other lesser people when one has done with them.

'Tell me,' cried the girl, 'what word do you bring? Where is he?'

'He is here,' whispered the youth, pointing to the anteroom.

'Here?' exclaimed Favonia, incredulously.

'Yes, here,' said the youth. 'Come,' and he led her to the door and as she approached it he seized her suddenly and, clapping a hand over her mouth, dragged her into the dark anteroom beyond.

Rough hands seized her quickly and she was gagged and bound. She heard them converse in low whispers.

'We will separate here,' said one. 'Two of us will take her to the place we have selected. One of you will have to leave the note for Fulvus Fupus so the palace guards will find it. The rest of you scatter and go by different routes to the deserted house across from the Colosseum. Do you know the place?'

'I know it well. Many is the night that I have slept there.'

'Very well,' said the first speaker, who seemed to be the leader, 'now be off. We have no time to waste.'

'Wait,' said the son of Tabernarius, 'the division of the ransom has not yet been decided. Without me you could have done nothing. I should have at least half.'

'Shut up or you will be lucky if you get anything,' growled the leader.

'A knife between his ribs would do him good,' muttered another.

'You will not give me what I asked?' demanded the youth.

'Shut up,' said the leader. 'Come along now, men,' and carrying Favonia, whom they wrapped in a soiled and ragged cloak, they left the home of Septimus Favonius unobserved; and as two men carried a heavy bundle through the dark shadows beneath the shadowy trees the son of Tabernarius started away in the opposite direction …

A youth in soiled and ragged tunic and rough sandals approached the gates of Cæsar's palace. A legionary challenged him, holding him at a distance with the point of his pike.

'What do you loitering by the palace of Cæsar by night?' demanded the legionary.

'I have a message for Cæsar,' replied the youth.

The legionary guffawed. 'Will you come in or shall I send Cæsar out to you?' he demanded, ironically.

'You may take the message to him yourself, soldier,' replied the other, 'and if you know what is good for you, you will not delay.'

The seriousness of the youth's voice finally compelled the attention of the legionary. 'Well,' he demanded, 'out with it. What message have you for Cæsar?'

'Hasten to him and tell him that the daughter of Septimus Favonius has been abducted and that if he hastens he will find her in the deserted house that stands upon the corner opposite the chariot entrance to the Colosseum.'

'Who are you?' demanded the legionary.

'Never mind,' said the youth. 'Tomorrow I shall come for my reward,' and he turned and sped away before the legionary could detain him.

'At this rate midnight will never come,' said von Harben.

Mallius Lepus laid a hand upon the shoulder of his friend. 'You are impatient, but remember that it will be safer for Favonia, as well as for us, if we wait until after midnight, for the streets now must be full of searchers. All afternoon we have heard soldiers passing. It is a miracle that they have not searched this place.'

'Ps-st!' cautioned von Harben. 'What was that?'

'It sounded like the creaking of the gate in front of the house,' said Mallius Lepus.

'They are coming,' said von Harben.

The three men seized the swords with which they had armed themselves, after they had rushed the Colosseum guard, and following a plan they had already decided upon in the event that searchers approached their hiding-place, they scaled the ladder and crept out upon the roof. Leaving the trapdoor pushed slightly to one side, they listened to the sounds that were now coming from below, ready to take instant action should there be any indication that the searchers might mount the ladder to the roof.

Von Harben heard voices coming from below. 'Well, we made it,' said one, 'and no one saw us. Here come the others now,' and von Harben heard the gate creak again on its rusty hinges; then the door of the house opened and he heard several people enter.

'This is a good night's work,' said one.

'Is she alive? I cannot hear her breathe.'

'Take the gag from her mouth.'

'And let her scream for help?'

'We can keep her quiet. She is worth nothing to us dead.'

'All right, take it out.'

'Listen, you, we will take the gag out of your mouth, but if you scream it will be the worse for you.'

'I shall not scream,' said a woman's voice in familiar tones that set von Harben's heart to palpitating, though he knew that it was nothing more than his imagination that suggested the seeming familiarity.

'We shall not hurt you,' said a man's voice, 'if you keep quiet and Cæsar sends the ransom.'

'And if he does not send it?' asked the girl.

'Then, perhaps, your father, Septimus Favonius, will pay the price we ask.'

'Heavens!' muttered von Harben. 'Did you hear that, Lepus?'

'I heard,' replied the Roman.

'Then come,' whispered von Harben. 'Come, Gabula, Favonia is below.'

Casting discretion to the wind, von Harben tore the trap from the opening in the roof and dropped into the darkness below, followed by Mallius Lepus and Gabula.

'Favonia!' he cried. 'It is I. Where are you?'

'Here,' cried the girl.

Rushing blindly in the direction of her voice, von Harben encountered one of the abductors. The fellow grappled with him, while, terrified by fear that the legionaries were upon them, the others bolted from the building. As they went they left the door open and the light of a full moon dissipated the darkness of the interior, revealing von Harben struggling with a burly fellow who had seized the other's throat and was now trying to draw his dagger from its sheath.

Instantly, Mallius Lepus and Gabula were upon him, and a quick thrust of the former's sword put a definite period to the earthly rascality of the criminal. Free from his antagonist, von Harben leaped to his feet and ran to Favonia, where she lay upon a pile of dirty rags against the wall. Quickly he cut her bonds and soon they had her story.

'If you are no worse for the fright,' said Mallius Lepus, 'we may thank these scoundrels for simplifying our task, for here we are ready to try for our escape a full three hours earlier than we had hoped.'

'Let us lose no time, then,' said von Harben. 'I shall not breathe freely until I am across the wall.'

'I believe we have little to fear now,' said Mallius Lepus. 'The wall is poorly guarded. There are many places where we can scale it, and I know a dozen places where we can find boats that are used by the fishermen of the city. What lies beyond is upon the knees of the gods.'

Gabula, who had been standing in the doorway, closed the door quickly and crossed to von Harben. 'Lights are coming down the avenue, Bwana,' he said. 'I think many men are coming. Perhaps they are soldiers.'

The four listened intently until they made out distinctly the measured tread of marching men.

'Some more searchers,' said Mallius Lepus. 'When they have passed on their way, it will be safe to depart.'

The light from the torches of the legionaries approached until it shone through the cracks in the wooden blinds, but it did not pass on as they had expected. Mallius Lepus put an eye to an opening in one of the blinds.

'They have halted in front of the house,' he said. 'A part of them are turning the corner, but the rest are remaining.'

They stood in silence for what seemed a long time, though it was only a few minutes, and then they heard sounds coming from the garden behind the house and the light of torches was visible through the open kitchen door.

'We are surrounded,' said Lepus. 'They are coming in the front way. They are going to search the house.'

'What shall we do?' cried Favonia.

'The roof is our only hope,' whispered von Harben, but even as he spoke the sound of sandalled feet was heard upon the roof and the light of torches shone through the open trap.

'We are lost,' said Mallius Lepus. 'We cannot defeat an entire century of legionaries.'

'We can fight them, though,' said von Harben.

'And risk Favonia's life uselessly?' said Lepus.

'You are right,' said von Harben, sadly, and then, 'Wait, I have a plan. Come, Favonia, quickly. Lie down here upon the floor and I will cover you with these rags. There is no reason why we should all be taken. Mallius Lepus, Gabula, and I may not escape, but they will never guess that you are here, and when they are gone you can easily make your way to the guard-house in the Colosseum, where the officer in charge will see that you are given protection and an escort to your home.'

'Let them take me,' said the girl. 'If you are to be captured, let me be captured also.'

'It will do no good,' said von Harben. 'They will only separate us, and if you are found here with us it may bring suspicion upon Septimus Favonius.'

Without further argument she threw herself upon the floor, resigned in the face of von Harben's argument, and he covered her over with the rags that had been a beggar's bed.

23

By the time that Cassius Hasta had disposed his forces and placed his engines of war before the defences of Castrum Mare, he discovered that it was too dark to open his assault that day, but he could carry out another plan that he had and so he advanced toward the gate, accompanied by Tarzan, Metellus, and Præclarus and preceded by torch-bearers and a legionary bearing a flag of truce.

Within the fort great excitement had reigned from the moment that the advancing troops had been sighted. Word had been sent to Fulvus Fupus and reinforcements had been hurried to the fort. It was assumed by all that Sublatus had inaugurated a new raid upon a larger scale than usual, but they were ready to meet it, nor did they anticipate defeat. As the officer commanding the defenders saw the party approaching with a flag of truce, he demanded from a tower gate the nature of their mission.

'I have two demands to make upon Validus Augustus,' said Cassius Hasta. 'One is that he free Mallius Lepus and Erich von Harben and the other is that he permit me to return to Castrum Mare and enjoy the privileges of my station.'

'Who are you?' demanded the officer.

'I am Cassius Hasta. You should know me well.'

'The gods are good!' cried the officer.

'Long live Cassius Hasta! Down with Fulvus Fupus!' cried a hoarse chorus of rough voices.

Someone threw open the gates, and the officer, an old friend of Cassius Hasta, rushed out and embraced him.

'What is the meaning of all this?' demanded Cassius Hasta. 'What has happened?'

'Validus Augustus is dead. He was assassinated at the games today and Fulvus Fupus has assumed the title of Cæsar. You are indeed come in time. All Castrum Mare will welcome you.'

Along the Via Mare from the castle to the lakeshore and across the pontoon bridge to the island marched the army of the new Emperor of the East, while the news spread through the city and crowds gathered and shrieked their welcome to Cassius Hasta.

In a deserted house across the avenue from the Colosseum four fugitives awaited the coming of the legionaries of Fulvus Fupus. It was evident that the soldiers intended to take no chances. They entirely surrounded the building and they seemed to be in no hurry to enter.

Von Harben had had ample time to cover Favonia with the rags, so that she was entirely concealed before the legionaries entered simultaneously from the garden, the avenue, and the roof, torch-bearers lighting their way.

'It is useless to resist,' said Mallius Lepus to the officer who accompanied the men in from the avenue. 'We will return to the dungeons peaceably.'

'Not so fast,' said the officer. 'Where is the girl?'

'What girl?' demanded Mallius Lepus.

'The daughter of Septimus Favonius, of course.'

'How should we know?' demanded von Harben.

'You abducted her and brought her here,' replied the officer. 'Search the room,' he commanded, and a moment later a legionary uncovered Favonia and raised her to her feet.

The officer laughed as he ordered the three men disarmed.

'Wait,' said von Harben. 'What are you going to do with the daughter of Septimus Favonius? Will you see that she has a safe escort to her father's house?'

'I am taking my orders from Cæsar,' replied the officer.

'What has Cæsar to do with this?' demanded von Harben.

'He has ordered us to bring Favonia to the palace and to slay her abductors upon the spot.'

'Then Cæsar shall pay for us all with legionaries,' cried von Harben, and with his sword he fell upon the officer in the doorway, while Gabula and Mallius Lepus spurred by a similar determination to sell their lives as dearly as possible, rushed those who were descending the ladder and entering the kitchen door. Taken by surprise and momentarily disconcerted by the sudden and unexpected assault, the legionaries fell back. The officer, who managed to elude von Harben's thrust, escaped from the building and summoned a number of legionaries who were armed with pikes.

'There are three men in that room,' he said, 'and a woman. Kill the men, but be sure that the woman is not harmed.'

In the avenue the officer saw people running; heard them shouting. He saw them stop as they were questioned by some of his legionaries, whom he had left in the avenue. He had not given the final order for his pike-men to enter the building because his curiosity had momentarily distracted his attention. As he turned now, however, to order them in, his attention was again distracted by a tumult of voices that rose in great cheers and rolled up the avenue from the direction of the bridge that connects the city with the Via Mare and the fort. As he turned to look, he saw the flare of many torches and now he heard the blare of trumpets and the thud of marching feet.

What had happened? He had known, as had everyone in Castrum Mare, that the forces of Sublatus were camped before the fort, but he knew, that there had been no battle and so this could not be the army of Sublatus entering Castrum Mare, but it was equally strange if the defenders of Castrum Mare should be marching away from the fort while it was menaced by an enemy army. He could not understand these things, nor could he understand why the people were cheering.

As he stood there watching the approach of the marching column, the shouts of the people took on form and he heard the name of Cassius Hasta distinctly.

'What has happened?' he demanded, shouting to the men in the street.

'Cassius Hasta has returned at the head of a big army, and Fulvus Fupus has already fled and is in hiding.'

The shouted question and the equally loud reply were heard by all within the room.

'We are saved,' cried Mallius Lepus, 'for Cassius Hasta will harm no friend of Septimus Favonius. Aside now, you fools, if you know when you are well off,' and he advanced to the doorway.

'Back, men,' cried the officer. 'Back to the avenue. Let no hand be raised against Mallius Lepus or these other friends of Cassius Hasta, Emperor of the East.'

'Clearly this fellow knows which side his bread is buttered on,' commented von Harben, with a grin.

Together Favonia, von Harben, Lepus, and Gabula stepped from the deserted building into the avenue. Approaching them they saw the head of a column of marching men; flaming torches lighted the scene until it was almost as bright as day.

'There is Cassius Hasta,' exclaimed Mallius Lepus. 'It is indeed he, but who are those with him?'

'They must be Sanguinarians,' said Favonia. 'But look, one of them is garbed like a barbarian, and see the strange black warriors with their white plumes that are marching behind them.'

'I have never seen the like in all my life,' exclaimed Mallius Lepus.

'Neither have I,' said von Harben, 'but I am sure that I recognise them, for their fame is great and they answer the description that I have heard a thousand times.'

'Who are they?' asked Favonia.

'The white giant is Tarzan of the Apes, and the black warriors are his Waziri fighting men.'

At sight of the legionaries standing before the house, Cassius Hasta halted the column.

'Where is the centurion in command of these troops?' he demanded.

'It is I, glorious Cæsar,' replied the officer, who had come to arrest the abductors of Favonia.

'Does it happen that you are one of the detachments sent out by Fulvus Fupus to search for Mallius Lepus and the barbarian, von Harben?'

'We are here, Cæsar,' cried Mallius Lepus, while Favonia, von Harben and Gabula followed behind him.

'May the gods be praised!' exclaimed Cassius Hasta, as he embraced his old friend. 'But where is the barbarian chieftain from Germania, whose fame has reached even to Castra Sanguinarius?'

'This is he,' said Mallius Lepus. 'This is Erich von Harben.'

Tarzan stepped nearer. 'You are Erich von Harben?' he asked in English.

'And you are Tarzan of the Apes, I know,' returned von Harben in the same language.

'You look every inch a Roman,' said Tarzan with a smile.

'I feel every inch a barbarian, however,' grinned von Harben.

'Roman or barbarian, your father will be glad when I bring you back to him.'

'You came here in search of me, Tarzan of the Apes?' demanded von Harben.

'And I seemed to have arrived just in time,' said the ape-man.

'How can I ever thank you?' exclaimed von Harben.

'Do not thank me, my friend,' said the ape-man. 'Thank little Nkima!'

THE END

If you've enjoyed these books and would like to read more, you'll find literally thousands of classic Science Fiction & Fantasy titles through the **SF Gateway**

✶

For the new home of Science Fiction & Fantasy . . .

✶

For the most comprehensive collection of classic SF on the internet . . .

✶

Visit the SF Gateway

www.sfgateway.com

Edgar Rice Burroughs (1875–1950)

Edgar Rice Burroughs was a prolific American author of the 'pulp' era. The son of a Civil War veteran, he saw brief military service with the 7th U.S. Cavalry before he was diagnosed with a heart problem and discharged. After working for five years in his father's business, Burroughs left for a string of disparate and short-lived jobs, and was working as a pencil sharpener wholesaler when he decided to try his hand at writing. He found almost instant success when his story 'Under the Moons of Mars' was serialised in *All-Story Magazine* in 1912, earning him the then-princely sum of $400.

Burroughs went on to have tremendous success as a writer, his wide-ranging imagination taking in other planets (John Carter of Mars and Carson of Venus), a hollow earth (Pellucidar), a lost world, westerns, historicals and adventure stories. Although he wrote in many genres, Burroughs is best known for his creation of the archetypal jungle hero, Tarzan. Edgar Rice Burroughs died in 1950.